THE AISLING SEA TRILOGY
THE COMPLETE SERIES

VANESSA RASANEN

PRONUNCIATION GUIDE

Declan: DEK-len
McCallagh: mə-KAH-lə
Mikkel: mih-KELL
Aoife: EE-fə
Lani: LA-nee
Melina: mə-LEE-nə
Cait: KATE
Bron: BRAHN
Callum: CA-ləm
Halloran: HA-lor-en
Csintala: sin-TAH-lə
Ada: AY-də
Kilmeran: kil-MAYR-en
Darienn: DAYR-ee-en
Cregah: CRAY-gə
Morshan: MOR-shahn
Larcsporough: LARK-spur-ə
Turvala: tur-VAH-lə
Daorna: day-OR-nə
Haviern: hav-ee-AIRN
Caprothe: cə-PROHTH
Tyshaly: tih-SHAH-lee
Aisling: ASH-ling
Helles: HELL-es
Murinaughton: MEER-not-ən
daemari: day-MAH-ree

AUTHOR NOTE

Before we begin, please be aware that this series gets progressively darker and more adult in tone with each book.

ON THESE BLACK SANDS
PG-13 level violence, minimal strong language, kissing only

FROM THESE DARK DEPTHS
More detailed descriptions of violent situations, some strong language, and one fade-to-black scene with some non-explicit lead-up on page

WITH THESE DARK DEPTHS
Graphic torture scenes, some strong language, and multiple on-page intimate scenes with tame language and a focus on emotions and character connection than mechanics

I understand not all readers are comfortable with reading intimate content. For this reason, I have provided a list of chapters containing such content at the back of the book in the spice rack.

ON THESE BLACK SANDS

SANDS

BOOK ONE

To my husband who ensures the rum is never gone.
(And by rum, I mean gin.)

Also, if you haven't read the author note, please be sure to do that.

BLACK SOUND
DAORNA
HAVIERN
TYSHALY
HELLES ISLAND
CREGAH
PORT MORSHAN
THE COUNCIL
LOST CO
CAPROTHE

TURVALA
THE
AISLING
SEA
FOXHAVEN
THE COUNCIL
TO LARCSPOROUGH

CHAPTER I
DECLAN

The screams of his wounded men had finally begun to subside, but not enough to afford Declan McCallagh any rest. Not that he could have slept now, regardless. It had been the third attack in as many weeks, and his already battered crew had barely managed to hang on long enough to outrun their attackers.

It could have been worse. They'd avoided being boarded, raided, and forced into service in another crew—not that he, as captain, would have been granted such an offer.

Yet they'd far from succeeded in this latest battle. Nine had been lost at the onset. Another twenty-four wounded, half of those severely enough he doubted they'd live to see the next port.

They'd been caught off guard, the sails of the other ship having been spotted in the dawn's light mere seconds before the first cannon shot had been heard and felt. It had narrowly missed their bow, hitting the teal waters of the Aisling Sea instead. A warning shot perhaps, but the *Winged Serpent* and its captain, Tiernen, were not known for being merciful. Not even to fellow pirates.

While other captains had formed alliances—albeit fickle and shaky ones at best —within the pirate guild, no such accords could ever be made with the pirate lords who posed a constant threat to the smaller ships, like Declan's.

And Captain Tiernen's barbarism was that of nightmares. Crews cut down. Captains and officers brutally tortured and strung up on the rocky coastlines as a warning for all passing ships. Tiernen's signature, as it were.

Still, the *Serpent*'s gunners had missed. Whether on purpose or by accident, Declan was unsure. But it had granted his men enough time to rally and get the guns into position to fight back.

It had been for naught though.

The next attack from the *Serpent* had brought bundle shot ripping across the deck and tearing into his crew as they scrambled to get the ship into a better position to return fire. But they were dangerously low on munitions after such hard weeks at sea.

Though they'd managed to overtake a handful of merchant ships making their way south to Larcsporough, those ships had not surrendered outright, requiring the use of more powder and rounds than Declan had hoped or planned for. And none of those raids had yielded much of value. The attacks from fellow pirates had taken even more of their resources, and by the time the *Winged Serpent* had hit them upon rounding the north side of Helles Island, they'd had no chance of making much of a stand.

Declan had been forced to make the call to run instead of fight.

Now, standing in his quarters, with the strong afternoon sunlight streaming in through the windows at his back, he pushed against the worn desk and stepped back from the map, rubbing a hand across his stubbled chin.

The last three weeks seemed to have aged him more than the entire twelve years he'd spent sailing these waters. He might have been the youngest captain on this sea, but the recent attacks from the lords had him feeling twice his age.

He eyed the trio of men standing opposite him. The same weariness he bore was mirrored in their stances, as if the fatigue hung like a dead weight upon their bones. It had been growing heavier during these long weeks at sea—weeks that had felt more like months.

All three studied the map in silence as they considered every possible destination, but Declan already knew where he needed to take the *Siren's Song*. And it was the last place he wanted to go.

"We could attempt to make it to Haviern, perhaps," his quartermaster, Tommy Murphy, said, breaking the tense silence. Friends since their first stints as cabin boys at the age of ten, he and Declan had grown up on the seas together, learned each other's secrets. And tells. Seeing Tommy now gnawing on the inside of his lip, Declan knew he hadn't offered the suggestion lightly and had wanted to recommend a different destination.

Tommy pulled his cap off and scratched the back of his head as he continued to stare at the map.

The ship's helmsman, Gavin Flynn, spoke up without raising his gaze. "Even with favorable winds—and no more attacks—we'd lose half the injured by the time we arrived. We can't risk it."

Tommy looked around the room, as if checking to see if any of the crew could hear him. "We'll have to replace the injured regardless."

Declan's stomach knotted. Another captain, one like Tiernen perhaps, might have been willing to let the injured crew die at sea to appeal to his own whims. But Declan couldn't.

Gavin's chin snapped up, shock pooling in his eyes, but it was their bo'sun, Mikkel Harlan, who spoke for him, his Turvalan accent strong with his fatigue. "As true as that may be, Tommy, you know the captain wouldn't hear of it. And even without the injured, the crew is far too exhausted. I doubt they'd vote in favor of that destination."

"You know where they want to go," Gavin said, shooting a glance at Mikkel and Tommy before all three lifted their eyes to Declan, their bodies still as if he were a stalking predator instead of their captain.

There was no fear in their eyes though. While the rest of the crew might not know the reasoning behind Declan's orders, these men—the men he'd assembled for their grit and their drive and their loyalty—understood. Despite their youth, each of them had known heartache and loss, and they'd spent the last hour trying to find a way to spare him from facing his own.

Only out of sheer desperation would they suggest this destination.

Their unspoken words hung in the cabin's stale air, and Declan's gut twisted as he repeated the port's name in his mind. It would be best for his men, and after all the years of asking them to sacrifice—to risk life and limb for glory and riches— how could he refuse to do the same for them?

Yet his body protested physically at the thought of returning, of walking those cobbled streets once again, of having the scent of ancient wood and brine hit his nose. His jaw tightened as that familiar weight pressed against his chest, his throat tightening until he could barely breathe or swallow. He forced his face to remain calm, however, not wanting his men—even the three closest to him—to know just how greatly he struggled.

He felt their stares as he looked back down at the map for the millionth time, as if some ancient magic might have altered the position of the lands scattered throughout the Aisling Sea. These men would follow him wherever he dictated. He could insist they seek solace elsewhere, let his injured die on the crossing to Haviern or Foxhaven, all so he could avoid returning to those rocky black shores.

A distant scream pierced the air, pulling his gaze back up to his men, who winced at the sound. Another crew member was likely losing a limb to their over- worked and exhausted carpenter-turned-surgeon. It pushed him to make a decision.

He pulled the salt-coated air deep into his chest and uttered the last words he'd ever planned to say.

"We make for Port Morshan."

CHAPTER 2
DECLAN

Declan and Tommy stood at the railing of the quarterdeck as Gavin guided them into Cregah's main port, Morshan, the air somehow stifling and heavy despite the sea breeze greeting them. Though Tommy seemed as tense as Declan, the captain knew it was more from empathy than any trepidation of his own.

Declan had vowed never to return, and Tommy had never questioned it. This wasn't his home any longer. Hadn't been since he was a boy.

He couldn't watch as they approached the dock. The sight of this land pulled his gut into a painful knot.

He turned to Tommy. "I'll be in my quarters if you need anything."

"Aye, sir," Tommy said with a slight dip of his chin before looking back over the uninjured crew bustling to prepare to go ashore.

Declan managed to avoid the view of his past home as he made his way down the stairs and turned toward his cabin door. Once inside his room, he gritted his teeth, fisting his hands until his nails dug into his palms. The pain a welcome distraction from the one still crushing his chest. There was no time to let the past haunt him. He loosened his grip and stretched his fingers wide as he forced a breath deep into his lungs before moving toward his desk.

He'd barely moved two feet when a knock came at the door, startling him.

"What is it?" His words came out less harshly than he'd intended. This port always seemed to make him soft, and that was less than desirable for his line of work.

The door creaked open, and the bright red hair of his master gunner, Wes Keiley, appeared, followed by the old sailor's long frame.

"Apologies, Captain. We've arrived. The crew is preparing to go ashore."

Declan straightened, raising his chin. He nearly asked why his gunner was delivering this information instead of one of the cabin boys but remembered at the last moment that the lads were among those below decks clinging to life. He moved to wave the man out and acknowledge the information he'd delivered, but Mr. Keiley spoke again, raising a piece of paper in his hand. "This message arrived for you."

Declan ushered him forward and reached for the neatly folded note. It carried a scent not found aboard any ship. He started to open it but noticed his gunner still stood before him. Glancing up, his eyes met the pair already staring at him, and he gave Keiley a look that demanded the man speak.

"I...I'm sorry, Captain. Only wondered if you planned to go ashore, or if we would be shipping out soon." Hope clung to the man's words.

"We ship out at dawn." Enough time to get the wounded unloaded and taken to the small hospital in port and get the looted goods traded for the supplies they desperately needed. And maybe let the crew have a hot meal and a warm bed. Thankfully, he'd already convinced his first mate they could risk moving on despite the shortage of men if they made straight for Foxhaven, where additional crew could be recruited, so there was no need to stay any longer than necessary.

The man's face fell. "Yessir." He turned and took slow steps toward the door, as if begging his captain to reconsider their departure time.

Declan opened the note and skimmed the hurried but neat writing. He pursed his lips and bit back a curse. How she had known he'd be arriving in port when he himself had only made the decision to come here mere hours ago, he couldn't know, but he had bigger problems than to wonder about her ways.

"Change of plans, Mr. Keiley."

Declan rose as he spoke. His gunner faced him once again, a mix of dread and hope swirling around in his features, as if the two emotions were fighting to see which would be warranted for the situation. Declan might have laughed at the comical look on the gunner's face had they been in any other situation.

"Twenty-four hours. That's as much time as we can spare. We sail tomorrow night."

"Yessir," Mr. Keiley said around a smile he tried—and failed—to hide. Spinning on his heel once more, he headed toward the door.

Declan called after him, "Fetch Tommy." Years ago he would have added a "please" to the end of that as his parents had taught him, but he was no longer that kid. Time on the seas and the waves with unsavory characters and their deplorable manners had wiped clean all but the memories of his former life.

Mr. Keiley gave a silent nod and ducked through the entry, shutting the door behind him with a resounding click. Declan hadn't needed to tell Mr. Keiley to spread the word of their extended stay. He could already hear the news spreading, with cheers and whoops and hollers springing up outside his door and boots tromping as the men moved with haste to make the most of their time in port. He could only imagine how much grander their display would have been had they not been transporting their injured shipmates ashore.

Declan tried to mimic the sense of excitement he heard from his men, but he couldn't curb the dread that had burrowed into him, sending its venomous tendrils into every muscle and tendon. But he had to hide it, couldn't show the extent of his torment to anyone. Not even Tommy.

You're a pirate, damn it.

And a pirate could not be vulnerable, could not show any emotion except ruthlessness, and maybe lust, but even that was curbed by the rules of Cregah.

It might be a place of respite for them, a land where, because of the treaty signed all those years ago at the end of the Aisling War, pirates like him and his crew, could—for a price—go ashore and rest, relax, have a drink, and sleep in an actual bed if they wanted to.

But in this land run by women, the women made the rules and set the limits. Sure, the pirates got their rest, but did they get what they truly needed and wanted? There were places where they could, of course, fulfill their basest of needs. Though these needs were shared by men and women alike, in Morshan it was always on the latter's terms. Here the women were the patrons, coming to be served by the visiting pirates, not the other way around, not the way it was in other ports. But in those ports a pirate had to be on constant guard for a dagger in his back or at his throat while he was otherwise indisposed.

Whores. Pirates turned whores with this blasted treaty.

That word bounced around his head, leaving a rotten taste on his tongue despite him not having uttered it. He had been raised here, sure, and had always known life under the council and under the treaty. But from his first days as a cabin boy, he had learned things weren't always what they seemed. The pirates who sought refuge here were far from free; all were tied to the ladies of the council—even the lesser pirates like himself.

Each captain had to pay to earn admittance to the port. With either goods or services.

Whores, indeed.

He scoffed just as another knock sounded.

"Come in," Declan said as he dropped the letter onto his desk and settled himself back into the chair at his desk. He stretched his back and legs out to alleviate the soreness that had settled in. Yes, it would be good to go ashore. Even if it meant facing her and all the memories that accompanied such a reunion.

"You wanted to see me, Captain?" Tommy stepped inside and closed the door behind him.

"Aye, Tommy. I have business taking me ashore." He paused to see how Tommy would react, but his quartermaster hid any surprise well. "I assume word has spread already, but ensure Mikkel tells the men to be back on board and ready to sail after sundown tomorrow."

Tommy eyed him, the unspoken question creasing his brow.

Declan breathed deep and answered. "I know. Longer than planned. Longer than I'd like, personally. But I don't know how long this will take." He picked up the letter once again. "And with morale low, I need to give the men a bit of a breather. Last thing I need is a mutiny."

Neither of them laughed at his sore attempt at levity.

"Do we expect the council—"

"Aye." He moved a hand to his temple, hoping to ease away the threatening ache before it became unbearable. "We aren't able to pay the full tax, and I fully anticipate them calling in that debt before we leave."

He could see Tommy mulling over that information. But again, he didn't push further. Didn't need to. They both knew what the council demanded of the pirates who couldn't pay.

"The men's rest is worth the risk, I believe."

Straightening, Tommy said, "What are my orders?" asking as both his first mate and his best friend.

"Relax. Get some damn sleep and a bit of decent food. Kiss a woman if you want. Sands knows it's been too long. We'll meet at the pub tomorrow at sundown."

"Alone?"

"No. Bring Gavin with you."

Tommy's jaw set, and his brows pulled in as if he were debating whether to ask the question Declan knew was buzzing around in his head. The same question he'd been asking himself since he'd made the decision to sail here.

Am I ready to go back?

He had made peace with the idea quickly, when he'd planned to simply wait out their short stay by remaining on the ship, when he'd intended on giving the men only one night ashore.

But her note had changed everything, raised too many questions, and wiped away all confidence that he would be able to stomach this visit.

The note—despite its weightlessness—seemed to pull him under the sea of memories he'd ignored all these years. Or had tried to. The dreams had ended years ago, the anxiety attacks ceasing along with them, quicker than he'd thought possible.

Would returning, stepping foot on those black shores, bring all of it back?

Tommy glanced down at Declan's hand and the paper he held. Declan's gaze followed.

He could hand it over, let Tommy read it for himself. But something kept him from doing so. They'd been searching for years with little luck, and her note—however vague—offered their first lead in months. But he didn't know how much she knew or how much help she'd prove to be.

And he couldn't risk stirring within his friend the tiny amount of hope she'd offered, especially when it was tethered to something as shaky as his relationship with her.

Declan didn't lift his eyes when Tommy spoke again. "I'll see you at the pub then."

And with that, Tommy was gone. The door to the cabin closed again to give Declan the privacy he'd need to get his wits about him.

He turned to the small wood-burning stove behind him, which provided the only heat on the ship except for the galley, and dropped the letter inside, watching the paper catch and burn with the smell of polished wood and fresh flowers, the smell of home.

Once it had turned to ash, he extinguished the flames. It was time to leave. Time to get this over with.

CHAPTER 3
AOIFE

Neither Aoife Cascade nor Lani Bierne spoke as they walked arm in arm, their shoes crunching over the twigs and pine needles that made up this long-forgotten path from the port city to their home at the council hall. Overhead the pine branches swayed in the summer breeze, like waving hands greeting them with their calming scent as the girls passed underneath. Aoife sensed her sister's eyes on her for the third time in the last hundred paces.

Aoife stopped in her tracks but did not release her sister's arm as she turned to her.

"Okay, Lani, out with it."

She'd given her plenty of time to come clean with whatever was on her mind. All the time they'd spent in town that afternoon and then the first forty minutes of their walk back home, at least.

"What do you mean? Out with what?" Lani's eyes brightened with what Aoife could only assume was feigned confusion.

Aoife's shoulders slumped as she let out a groan. "Oh come on! You've obviously got something on your mind. You've been near bursting with some news since we left home." She cocked her hip to one side and flashed a smirk, knowing she had her sister pegged.

"It's nothing, really." Lani pulled her arm away and started walking again, calling over her shoulder, "You coming?"

Aoife caught up within a few steps, her stride matching her sister's once again, but didn't bother relinking arms. She should drop it, trust Lani when she insisted it was nothing. Another glance at her sister, though, confirmed this was far from nothing. There was a change in the way her eyes took in the world, a change in the curve of her lips, as if a stupid grin were itching to be unleashed.

Lani's waves of red hair danced in the wind, and on impulse Aoife reached up to her own brown hair, which always seemed to be knotted instead of lying nicely like her sister's. As a kid she'd wondered how they could be sisters when they looked so little alike, with only a speckling of freckles across their nose and cheeks shared between them. It wasn't until she had matured that she realized their sisterhood was not forged by blood but by duty alone.

Still, she often found herself wishing she'd been gifted with the same features and demeanor that made Lani endearing, charming, approachable. A stark contrast to Aoife's awkward aloofness. Not that there was any need for closeness in the council hall.

"You know you think too much, Aoife." Lani's words cut through her thoughts.

"You should really try it sometime. It's good for you." She shot her sister a look before jabbing her in the ribs with an elbow, then waited for the giggles that normally ensued between them, but instead Lani breathed deep and looked away.

Aoife exaggerated her movements, looking up at the trees and then at the bushes along the path. She fidgeted with feigned nervousness.

This will either get her talking or she'll think I'm mad.

She cleared her throat, louder than necessary, but then forced her voice into a whisper. "I stole a roll at breakfast."

Lani faced her but kept walking. "What? We didn't have rolls this morning."

"When we were ten." Before Lani could question further, she continued. "I had a pet too."

Lani stopped then, wrinkles forming across her brow as she listened to Aoife's confessions with either confusion or concern. Aoife wasn't sure which.

"He was just a spider who showed up one day in my room. It's not like I had a cage for him or anything, but I named him George. He was a good listener."

Lani fought back a laugh. "Aoife. How could you? You know pets are strictly forbidden." She appeared ready to burst into chuckles.

"I know! It's why I haven't told you until now. It's been eating me up for years. Remember that day I came to dinner and everyone wondered why my eyes were all red and puffy, and I said I had gotten dust in them? Well, it wasn't dust. I'd accidentally dropped a book on George. I killed my pet. The only one I could talk to, and I'd killed him!"

"Oh, Aoife," Lani said, mock sympathy dancing within her words. "That must have been devastating."

"You have no idea how good it is to get that off my chest. It's been plaguing me for years."

Lani gave Aoife a gentle pat on the arm. "Secrets can weigh you down, it's true. They're not good for the heart." And she started back down the path.

Aoife scrunched her nose in defeat and stomped her foot—an action not suited for someone who was turning twenty in nearly a month. But she didn't care. "Gah, Lani! Come on!"

Lani skidded to a stop and turned, her resolve held tightly on her face, her eyes challenging Aoife to back down before they began to water at the corners. The shake of her head started slowly but picked up speed as the tears threatened to spill from her eyes. "I can't."

Aoife was by her side in a fraction of a second. Her heart thumped harder in her chest at the sudden shift in her sister's demeanor. "What has you so worked up? Whatever it is, it can't be good."

"Oh, but it is good. It's wonderful. Or it would be for anyone else." She dropped her chin to her chest as she spoke, allowing Aoife to wrap her arms around her and pull her close.

Warm afternoon sunlight filtered through the branches above, casting shadows in Lani's hair that normally would have had Aoife imagining fanciful stories from the shapes it created, but here, with her sister crying into her shoulder, she felt plagued by an ominous feeling that things were about to go downhill fast.

But she said it was good? Wonderful? But not for her.

Aoife's mind whirred through the possibilities. As heirs to the council, they had grown up knowing certain things in life couldn't be theirs. She considered each option, but only one seemed a likely cause for the flush in Lani's cheeks. It was a long shot, and she'd feel incredibly silly to have suggested it if she were wrong.

But if she were right...

She pulled back and lowered her head to look Lani in the eyes.

"Who?" she whispered, as if the council might have spies in the trees along the path.

Lani shook her head again, more from an inability to answer, it seemed, than a denial that Aoife had guessed correctly.

"Who is it, Lani?" she repeated, still soft but with increased urgency.

"His name is Adler."

The name didn't sound local. He couldn't be from Cregah. Which could mean only one thing.

"Which ship?"

Lani spoke around her fingers as they fussed with her lower lip. "The *Winged Serpent.*"

A gasp escaped before Aoife could stop it. "Nooooo. This is far from good and wonderful, Lan! Captain Tiernen's ship? What are you thinking?"

She didn't dare call Captain Tiernen Lani's father, despite his siring her. The title of father implied a presence in one's life, didn't it? It was a concept foreign to many children on Cregah, but especially so for the council heirs.

"Well, I didn't exactly plan it, you know. It just happened." Lani's gaze lowered to the ground as she toed the drying pine needles in the dirt.

"What exactly happened? I mean, what are we talking about? If you just looked at him, that's far from an issue. But what—"

"Six months ago, when Captain Tiernen was here to see Mother, his crew was invited to visit the palace."

"Yeah, that's nothing new, Lani. That happens all the time. They have a dinner. We eat. They talk. That's it."

Lani ignored her interruption. "He had a new crew member who wasn't like the others. He didn't shy away from looking at me like they all do. You know what it's like, Aoife. The way they avert their eyes and pretend we're not there."

Aoife did know, but she also knew why they did it. To save their skins. Self-preservation.

Adler must have been an idiot.

"He saw me, and he smiled," Lani said.

Aoife's eyes widened. "You're going to risk everything because of a smile? And a man's smile at that."

"You don't understand." Lani—tears now gone—stood her ground, her words matching her stance, armored with resolute confidence.

Aoife mimicked her sister, straightening so she could look her in the eye. "You're right. I don't. He's a man. Men are the problem, Lani. It was their warmongering that caused such destruction—scarred, broken lands and whole races wiped out. Or have you forgotten?"

Lani didn't so much as flinch or move to respond, so Aoife continued.

"You were born for something greater. All three of us were. You, me, Darienn. Even if we wanted such things—which we shouldn't—we don't get the luxury of a smile and a man of our choosing. We will eventually be paired with one of the pirate lords—"

"But I don't want to!" Lani squared her shoulders and lifted her chin. "I don't want someone who just visits me once every few months to breed like a prized cow to serve the needs of the council. I want a family and children. Multiple children. Not the one I'm allotted here as an heir. I want a life, Aoife!"

The words pushed Aoife back. She couldn't be hearing this. They'd grown up together, been raised for a bigger purpose. To lead this land and protect it so the ravages of war could never reach its shores again. It was why the first court had been instituted, why the treaty had been signed, why the whole nation had banded together and changed their ways.

They'd both learned this in their council lessons, so why was Lani now acting as though none of that mattered or even existed?

Lani released a sigh. "This is all rather rich coming from you, you know."

"What do you mean?" Though she already knew the answer before it came.

"All those novels you used to read. And would still read if your mother hadn't burned them."

"The novels *we* used to read, you mean. But those were mere stories. Fairy tales."

Lani dropped her head to the side. "Even fairy tales have some truth to them."

Aoife waved a hand between them. "Regardless, those were books. Love has no place in our life. Your life. Here. You can't walk away from it for a damn smile."

"It wasn't just a smile. After the dinner he found me in the hallway, and we talked. Aoife, we actually talked."

Aoife's confusion rose to the surface, contorting her features. "About what exactly?"

"Life, mainly. We stole out to the gardens. Everyone else was inside or heading back to the ship or to the pubs in Morshan, and he stayed behind to talk to me."

"Because he has a death wish apparently."

"I guess he thought I was worth it, and that felt amazing."

"But there can be no future with him. You'll be twenty in a few months and taking your full place on the court. You'll be expected to—"

"I know what I'm expected to do. How many times can I explain to you? I don't want it, Aoife."

"So what are you going to do? You can't just walk out the front door. You can't request to be released from your heritage, your duty!" She nearly added herself to the list of things Lani couldn't abandon, but she choked back those words. Compared to her obligations to the council, simply staying with Aoife was far from important.

"Yes, I can. And I will."

Aoife took a half step back, as if shoved by the realization this was actually happening. "Why are you telling me this?"

"Because you forced me to." Lani's gaze and tone were sharp as her hands flew into the air.

She's got you there.

"Fair enough. But do you expect me to simply step aside and let you?"

None of this made sense. The forest around them seemed to disappear as Aoife stared at her sister, this sister who might not have even said goodbye before running off with some pirate. Aoife felt a familiar lump lodge itself in her throat. Thankfully it remained there and didn't bring tears.

"What exactly are they going to do to me, Aoife? We are a land of peace, order, nonviolence. It's not like they're executing people in the village square."

What would they do to her? This was unprecedented. No heir to the council had ever abandoned her duty. At least, none of the historical records indicated anything of the sort.

Something twinged inside Aoife, an inkling of a doubt. What if someone had? What if it had been excluded from the record? Covered up? Hidden for the disgrace it was. She brushed the thought aside as nonsense. Such deceit would never have been tolerated, let alone practiced, by the council.

"But they can't just let you walk away from your place on the council! You're coming of age in less than six months. Your ceremony is being planned as we speak! If you walk away before that, what would that do to everything we've built here? You'd risk war and the collapse of all order here for a man? A man you barely know."

"Oh, don't be so dramatic, Aoife," Lani said, her eyes darting to the treetops in exasperation.

"You're one to talk. I can't believe what I'm hearing."

"I can't stay, Aoife. I can't. I can't do what they need me to do. To be paired with one of the pirate lords? To be shackled into a loveless contract? I can't do it. Not when I have the chance to love and be loved on my own terms."

When Aoife looked in Lani's eyes again, she found tears—not of fear, but of hope. Promise. Love. She swallowed down her worry. Her sister might be foolish— ridiculous—yet some part of her own heart began to twist in yearning. What would she have done in Lani's place? If Aoife had been the one to turn a man's head?

She'd known her whole life she wasn't destined for love or family or normalcy, but for service to her land and her people. She'd accepted that. It was how things had to be to keep the peace. But she couldn't deny the look in her sister's eyes, and she couldn't cause her sister pain.

She couldn't believe what she was about to say. Didn't even know if she'd be able to utter the words at all. But she steeled herself, drew in a breath, and glanced at the trees surrounding them—as if someone might be lurking nearby and would overhear.

"What do you need me to do?" The question came with none of the courage she'd hoped to muster, but this wasn't a summer picnic they were plotting. This was treason. Or something similar.

"Nothing, Aoife. Nothing. I mean, nothing actively. Just don't tell anyone you know where I've gone. Not our mothers. Not Darienn." An image of their younger sister—still two years from her own coming of age ceremony—flashed in Aoife's mind. Darienn had a particularly cold demeanor, as if she were always plotting and scheming behind those dark blue eyes.

Aoife shuddered and let Darienn's face fade from her memory. "Where will you go though? And when is this happening?"

"The next time they're in port. I'm going to steal away while Mother's with the captain. She'll be preoccupied. And you know the others in the council lie low during those visits. Adler has been saving his money for his own sloop, and he found someone willing to sell him one next time he's in port. He spoke of his homeland across the sea, an island where his people live simply but happily."

"So why did he become a pirate if he loves his homeland so much?"

"His family needed the money after his father died. Piracy allowed him to provide for his mom and sisters."

"And he can just stop pirating now that he has you?" Aoife's muscles recoiled at the unintended harshness in her question.

"Are you trying to overthink this, or are you ruining it for me for your own pleasure?"

"No! I just want to make sure you've thought this through before you throw everything away."

Lani's shoulders slumped. "He doesn't need to pirate anymore. He's made enough in one year to help his family start their own business to support themselves. We'll get married and go back to help run their shop."

A small spark flickered within Aoife as an image of Lani's future took shape. Her sister's red hair blowing in the wind. Laughing children running around her legs as she hugged her husband. Compared to the cold stone walls of the council hall and a loveless union with a pirate lord, she began to understand the appeal. Even if only slightly. But it was a future she'd never allow herself to dream of, because it was impossible.

Still. Could she deny it for her best friend?

"Aren't you going to miss this?" She gestured to the forest around them. "Aren't you going to miss home?" She choked on a ball of emotion before she could ask if Lani would miss her.

"Of course I will. I'll miss you, our chats, and the black sands of Cregah. But I'm taking it with me." At that, she lifted a chain from around her neck. At the end of it lay a small glass vial with a cork stopper glued in place.

"What is that?"

"Adler gave it to me when he asked me to leave with him. He'd filled it with the sand from the beach. Said I could carry home with me always."

Aoife had to admit, the more she heard of this Adler fellow, the less he sounded like the men they'd been warned about for all these years. She looked from the pendant to her sister's eyes, which were gleaming with hope. Was that what love looked like?

"Okay." She sucked in a breath. "I'll help you. I'll keep your secret. Just like I did about George."

Lani pulled her into an embrace, and Aoife's insides twisted, as if trying to shield her from this, to pull her into some protective shell. She didn't want to let go of her sister, this sister she loved and adored and admired. She would do anything for her, but still, Aoife hated to lie. And she would have to now. Either she was lying to Lani now by agreeing to help, or she would need to lie to her mother and the council when Lani ran.

Which it would be, she didn't know.

CHAPTER 4
DECLAN

The sound of Declan's boots on the cobblestones still wet from the afternoon rain showers mingled with that of laughter coming from the eateries he passed. The rich scent of sea salt and weathered wood at the docks had given way to a mix of blooming flowers, roasting meats, wet stone, and the occasional vile tang left by those who had drunk too much. Even in the light of dusk the town of Morshan looked much like he remembered—its buildings freshly painted, their upper window sills lined with flower boxes, and storefronts well-stocked with goods.

A fresh facade to hide the truth.

He shook away the memories. It did him no good to be burdened by a past he couldn't change. The sea had been his escape, but it was that constant reminder of all the dreams he'd had as a boy dashed away in a single night—the night he'd learned life in this seemingly peaceful town—more peaceful than anyone would imagine with how many pirates and privateers and generally despicable individuals found respite here—was far from safe and quaint under that shimmering mask.

A door swung open sending warm lamplight across the path and a sweaty mound of flesh toward him. Raising his arms before him he turned and, with an easy shove, sent the drunkard past him where he fell in a stinking heap upon the cobblestones, shaking with laughter despite being in the cold and the wet.

Declan winced at what fluids the man might have landed in, but he kept walking. Five hundred more paces and he'd be there. He could make this jaunt from the docks blind, but then he wouldn't be able to ward off any more bumbling buffoons as easily.

But the others he met were not bumbling, nor buffoons. Despite the streets being far more crowded than he'd hoped at this late hour, no one else made contact with him. He watched—with some amusement—as each approaching pair of eyes glanced at the dark teal fabric tied at his waist and then darted away. They stepped aside, giving him a wide berth, some choosing to tread in the swampy gutter rather than risk brushing his shoulder.

His reputation—and that of his ship—must have preceded him.

And it had only taken years of sweat, blood, and the unthinkable to make that happen. His entire childhood lost.

He turned the last corner and nearly froze. It might as well have been his first time back with how his stomach tightened at the sight of the pub sign ahead. Shaped like a weather-beaten flag in the wind, it beckoned him forward, its distressed lettering calling his name.

Literally. *McCallagh's Pirate Pub.*

For how much people feared his name as captain of The Siren Song, that same name on this pub—one of only two in the entire village—hadn't seemed to curb their desire for strong drink. Even a hundred feet away he could hear the chatter and merriment that streamed out whenever the door opened to let someone enter.

He kept his gaze locked on that pub sign as he approached, refusing to risk even a glance at the cobblestones out front. There wasn't likely to be any remaining evidence of what had happened all those years ago, but he couldn't bear it nonetheless. Couldn't bear the possibility that all sign of what had happened had been so easily washed away with the rains of ten years.

He should walk straight in, but he needed a moment, so he paused to peer through the square window panes. Despite the years of grime lining the edges of the muntin, the center of the panes were clean, providing a clear view inside, but he couldn't see through the mass of bodies within, milling about, crowding the tables and bar.

Pulling his arm back he laid his hand at his hip, tapping his fingers against the hilt of the dagger concealed under his coat and shirt. No one had seen him take it that night, too busy restraining the man who had used it. He'd pulled it from the body, mesmerized by the way the blood clung to its blade.

He'd only been a kid. Inconsequential. Invisible. And in that moment he'd felt the first threads of his youth pull thin, fraying. The first steps to becoming the man others avoided in the street.

The blade had been with him since, getting him out of—and into—plenty of trouble since. He hoped he wouldn't need it here, couldn't risk pulling it on someone in this port where violence was outlawed and peace mandated, weapons restricted only to the crews of the lords' ships. Yet few of the pirates adhered to the rule, coming into port with blades hidden on their bodies.

Not that the guards at the docks seemed to care much. The past ten years had gone on with so little incidence they'd grown lax. *Careless, Declan thought. But it was to his advantage.*

Still, while he hoped he didn't need the dagger in here—he couldn't bear to cause her any trouble with his return—it gave him the courage he needed to face her again. As silly as it was, it brought comfort. Confidence.

How would she react? Would she understand why he hadn't been back in this handful of years? Would she have heard the same rumors and stories about his actions and misdeeds?

A pang of regret and guilt threatened to rise into his throat, but he forced it down. He had no use for remorse. Weakness had no place here. Roughing his hand over his scruffy chin, he pulled in a breath. *Time to face the music.*

He pushed the door open and shoved aside the onslaught of memories that rushed him, as easily as he'd shoved the drunkard into the gutter. Confident steps carried him to the bar, his eyes narrowed on the spot where he'd likely find her. Men —pirates, mostly—crowded the room, but they all dispersed as he walked, as if the mere sound of his boots against the wood floor sent them fleeing from his presence. Looks averted. Gazes darted away from his face.

He'd learned long ago the effect confident steps alone could have on others, even before they saw him or his face. But being back here, in the pub where he'd grown up, he didn't feel like the feared man he'd become. Rather he was that scared kid, watching his mother disappear into the mist, seeing his father chase after her, finding them both...

He cursed silently at the memories that dared to defy him, swimming to the surface without permission. But memories weren't so easily intimidated.

Not like men.

He stepped to the bar and moved a newly vacated stool out of his way. He looked straight ahead, despite the urge to seek her out, and tapped his fingers against the bar, waiting.

She'd show soon enough. He could be patient—as patient as she'd been these past years.

"What the hell are you doing here?" Her question came at him as sharp as the dagger at his hip, but he wouldn't let the wince show on his face. Even knowing this was a ruse, a lie meant for the other patrons, so they wouldn't know she'd summoned this meeting, it still stung. She leaned against the bar opposite him, a rag pressed between her hand and the smooth wood.

"Nice to see you, too, sis." He angled his head at her and pulled his mouth into a smirk. Like the town, she hadn't changed much since the last time. Her dark hair still fell like a heavy curtain around her face which was just as pretty, despite the exhaustion and weariness that plagued her features.

Her eyes narrowed, and he could have sworn their green had faded to gray, no longer the bright emeralds he'd remembered from his youth. Or perhaps he'd merely been gone so long her memory had taken on an other worldly quality, etched into his mind with heightened intensity—one of the few memories he hadn't suppressed.

"You shouldn't be here, Captain." She backed away from the bar and tossed the rag over her shoulder as she reached for the near empty mug of a patron to his left, refilling it with ale as she spoke. "We don't want any trouble."

"Ah, but trouble isn't allowed in this port." He flashed her a smirk, but her expression remained cold.

"Not all trouble comes at the tip of a blade."

"Fair enough, but who says I'm bringing trouble your way?"

"It's what you do, isn't it? Wreaking havoc wherever you go. We all know the stories."

"Do you now?"

"Aye. Though I'm not sure I believe them." A playfulness warmed her gaze for a brief moment before the icy stare returned.

"You should," he said, fighting the urge to look down and avoid her judgment, and the face that looked so much like their mother's. That damn guilt struck from somewhere in his gut. He bit it back down.

"Well." She paused to clear her throat. "In that case, you really shouldn't be here."

"Perhaps. But I hear it's the best place to get a drink—and a bit of news." He swallowed hard.

Her laugh surprised him, filling the space between them, taking him back to easier times. "Oh ho ho, is that all you want? A bit of gossip while you sip a whisky?"

"I prefer rum." He snuck a glance at the other bodies inching away from him, careful to keep their faces hidden and backs turned.

"Sorry, I'm fresh out. This lot shares your taste, it seems." She lifted two empty brown bottles from behind the bar and gestured with them at the crowd.

A hush settled through the pub as if all ears waited for Declan's response and all muscles itched, ready to launch their owners out the door if his renowned temper erupted. He clicked his tongue, eying his fellow pirates over his shoulder before turning back to his sister.

"That's too bad, Cait." He pulled the stool behind him and settled onto it. "A glass of whisky it is."

The din of voices rose once again as Cait poured the warm tawny liquid into a relatively clean glass. Pushing it across the wood of the bar she leaned in, not much, but just enough to keep the words between them.

"I'm surprised to see you."

"Why? You summoned. I obliged. You act as though I never come around."

"Seldom enough."

"If I recall, I was just in here—"

She cut him off. "Seven."

"What?"

"Seven years. The last time you were here. Or have all your adventures and escapades clouded that memory of yours?" He'd known it had been a while since he'd been back, but had it really been that long?

"Not clouded, sister. I remember it well. You refusing to help. Denying me aid. Sending me off on my own. Can you blame me for not returning?"

"Sending you off? You left of your own accord. You were a fool, Declan." Her tone had shifted from irritated barkeep to chiding elder sister, and the sound of his name on her tongue threatened to plunge him back into those memories once again.

She lowered her voice and leaned in closer, as if remembering the audience around them. "I needed you here, to help with the pub and the..." She winced, hiding something, but he shooed away his questions. Whatever it was she kept from him, it could wait. She wasn't likely to talk about it in shared company anyway.

"And I needed a sister. I was only ten when it happened. Where were you?" His jaw tightened with the resentment he'd thought had disappeared.

Cait pursed her lips, as a tenderness he hadn't seen in ages softened her gaze. The closest thing he might get to an apology.

He downed the last of his drink and set the glass to the bar with a whisper of a sound. Brushing his hands together he straightened his back and pulled a smile to his lips. "All is forgiven, Cait. You know, though, you could have come with me. You would have made an excellent pirate."

Cait straightened as well, ignoring his words as she leaned her hips into the bar's edge and rested her hands beside his used glass. "Can I get you anything else?"

"Perhaps another time?"

The door opened and new revelers entered, sauntering up to the bar on either side of him, unaware of who he was or why all had given him space. With a glance over to the new patrons, she told them she'd be right with them as she tapped a finger on the bar three times.

She would have made a good pirate indeed.

With a nod of understanding he turned and made his way out the door, offering her a quick thanks over his shoulder.

He'd be back, and hopefully her information would prove worth it.

CHAPTER 5
AOIFE

AOIFE PULLED her legs up under her and settled into the large velvet armchair, her favorite spot in the library—in the entire building, if she were honest. Dinner had been uncomfortable, to say the least. While no one had remarked on the unusual lack of chatter between her and Lani as they ate, she had no doubt everyone had noticed, and she had no idea how she'd explain it if confronted.

She took a settling breath and opened the novel she'd been reading for the past few weeks, wishing it would get more exciting but knowing it wouldn't. Her mother had confiscated all the interesting books she'd scrounged up on outings into Morshan.

Not that she could pay attention to the book. Her mind continued to whir with everything Lani had told her, making dinner awkward and now causing the words before her to blur into a sea of gray against the cream pages.

No matter how many times she replayed their conversation, she didn't understand it any better. And she had found no solution for her sister to avoid stealing away in the night like a criminal.

Now that would make for a good novel.

But this was real life with her real sister. And she didn't know if she was ready for drama outside the covers of books.

Lost in her mind as she was, she didn't hear the footsteps approaching until someone stood directly in front of her, clearing her throat.

Aoife startled, her eyes flashing up to the face of one of the servants.

"Yes?"

"Your mother would like to see you in her office, Miss Aoife." With a quick curtsy, the girl turned and left, not bothering to wait for a response.

Aoife debated leaving the book behind, but her hands needed something other than her skirts to hold them steady. The councilwomen's offices lay just off the main meeting room, where their people brought forth concerns and grievances to the council, a short walk from where she had taken solace in the library.

Aoife rapped lightly on the door, her heart fluttering as fast as her knuckles against the wood.

"Come in." The command came muffled but still stern.

As Aoife nudged the door open, she tried to ignore the panic that rose within. It was unusual to get a summons outside normal council business or lessons. Did her mother know something? Had there in fact been spies along that wooded trail?

Sweat caused the book in her hands to nearly slip to the floor, but she righted it, clutching it tightly with her fingers.

What would she do if her mother knew? Could she lie to her face?

This was far from hiding an extra dinner roll or keeping a pretend pet spider. She might have laughed at the ridiculous spider story she'd conjured up for Lani had she been anywhere else.

"Don't just stand there in the doorway, Aoife." Her mother's words cut through her thoughts, her stare iced over with annoyance, as if Aoife had been the one to initiate this meeting.

"Apologies, Mother," Aoife said with a bow of her chin, and she took a step forward. The room—large and dark despite the blazing fire in the stone hearth—might have been cozy and inviting with its comfortable armchairs and numerous bookcases had it not been for the imposing woman who occupied it.

Melina Cascade's head turned as she took in her daughter, and with a release of breath, some warmth crept over her features, a smile pulling ever so slightly at her lips. "It's all right. I shouldn't have snapped. I did call for you, after all."

She set her book on the end table beside her armchair, uncrossed her legs, and motioned for Aoife to join her in the seat facing hers.

Aoife hoped her brief moment of hesitation wasn't noticeable as she moved to sit. She kept her eyes on the flames, marveling at the colors that danced and glowed as the wood was consumed.

I wonder if that's what being in love is like.

The thought startled her. Love must be similar. The same fiery glow had been in Lani's eyes as she spoke of the pirate and their future together. She'd been excited, burning, yearning for more, craving that companionship.

"How was your walk to Morshan this afternoon?" Her mother's tone held none of the earlier iciness. Melina lowered her head into Aoife's line of sight, pulling her attention away from the flames and her thoughts.

Such an easy question, and yet Aoife had to be careful. She'd need to keep her tongue on a short leash here, lest it get away from her.

She tried to play it cool, lifting a shoulder and offering a bored-sounding, "Uneventful really."

A short laugh sounded from her mother, not quite pleasant but more amused than irritated. "I should hope so, dear." Her mother's eyes dropped to the book Aoife held, and her lips tightened. "Find a new book?"

Blinking quickly, Aoife fumbled to lift the book. "No, Mother. This is from our own library."

Melina's shoulders relaxed as her not quite warm smile returned. "Ah, very good then. It is so hard to keep up with the books that make their way into our bookshops from the ships."

Silence settled between them, tense and prickly. Aoife itched to fidget or move but managed to keep her body under control as her gaze floated back to the dancing flames.

"Preparations are almost complete for your ceremony next month."

Aoife forced a smile to her lips. Would Lani be here for that? Or would Adler be returning before then? She should have probably memorized the visitation schedule instead of wasting time in the library, but she couldn't let her mother see any of these questions play across her face.

"Are you excited?" her mother asked.

"Of course. A little nervous too." At least that wasn't a lie.

"Ah, yes, that's normal. I was so nervous on my matching day. Brigeh and I stayed up all night before discussing which of the lords I might choose. Have you any thoughts about your own choice?"

Sucking in a deep breath, Aoife tried to conjure up the faces of the three lords she had to pick from, but she'd had little contact with any of them. She could only offer an awkward shake of her head as an answer.

Another laugh filled the room, this one warmer than the last. "Again, normal. Perhaps Lani could help you decide?"

"Perhaps." The word came out strained. The corners of her mother's eyes flinched slightly, as if she'd noted the hint of something lingering behind Aoife's answer.

Her mother leaned forward and rested her hand on Aoife's knee in a gesture that might have been comforting had it not felt so foreign. An image flashed in her mind of the women in Morshan hugging their children, smiling and laughing with them as they played games in their small front yards. It had seemed so odd to her the first time she'd witnessed it.

"Did something happen between you two?" Her mother's eyes probed hers, hunting, and Aoife couldn't stop herself from physically recoiling from her stare.

Forcing a smile to her lips, she shook her heard again. "No, Mother. Just nerves is all."

"Be glad you're the oldest, Aoife. You get to have your pick. Poor Darienn will be left with whichever lord remains after Lani's matching this fall. You know, it's also normal for there to be some tension between sisters before a matching. But try not to let it come between you. You have many years of ruling together ahead of you. It's best to keep that bond strong."

"Of course." Aoife couldn't stop her mind from focusing on the future she should have had with her sister, the future Lani was tossing away for a man. For love.

Her unease must have been written all over her face, because Melina leaned in once again. "Is something else troubling you?"

Aoife turned to face her mother. This wasn't a woman to be feared. She was stern, yes. Hard, of course, but that was for Aoife's good, and that of the country. Everything Melina did was for the people and their land, to keep war at bay and away from their shores.

If I speak in hypotheticals alone, merely ask the question without giving specifics, perhaps I can find the answer Lani needs.

Something in her gut twinged at the thought, but she ignored it as her mother nudged her to speak with another dip of her head and a tug of a smile. Her eyes shone with warmth and concern.

"What would happen to a lady of the council if she"—Aoife hesitated, but her mother hummed in encouragement for her to continue—"were to fall in love?"

Aoife forced her gaze to meet her mother's, but Melina had already turned away to stare into the flames.

If Aoife had thought this was an easy question with an easy answer, she'd been wrong. She'd expected—well, she didn't know what she'd expected, but this wasn't it. Her curiosity was sparked, her mind spinning as she watched her mother.

Had Melina fallen in love before?

Had she been forced to let a lover go?

Before Aoife could open her mouth to ask what was wrong, her mother spoke.

"It doesn't happen often." Melina sounded distant, as if she were speaking to the flames, and Aoife had to lean forward to hear. "I only know of once before. My mother's sister."

"Brigeh's mother?"

"No. Nor Fiona's. She never had an heir, and you've never heard her name. Even I don't know it." Her mother seemed to be traipsing down some long-lost path through her memories. "I only heard about her from my mother. As a warning. To not let it happen to us."

"What happened to her?"

"She left, all mention of her stricken from the council records, removed from our history. Forgotten. She was exiled, basically, unable to ever return, forced to leave and never come back. Not allowed to see her mother or sisters again, or to ever wander the streets of Port Morshan or stick her toes in the black sand."

Aoife eyed her mother, whose gaze remained on the flames, glassy and unseeing. She'd never witnessed such melancholy before in this woman, who was usually nothing but strong, determined, brave. She was their leader. Head lady of the council. Yet here she looked...scared.

Or worried.

Certainly this fate didn't sound so bad. There were worse things than being exiled. Especially for someone already planning to leave and never return. Right?

She would go to Lani. Tell her what she'd learned. Encourage her to come clean, to request to be released from her duty, to choose exile. While not an honorable departure, at least it wouldn't require secrecy.

And Aoife wouldn't have to lie.

She shifted in her chair, eager to find Lani to share this good news. But she couldn't simply slip out without a dismissal from her mother, who remained lost in the past. Why was she so distraught over a woman she'd never even met?

Aoife cleared her throat, and her mother turned with a slight shake of her head, as if she were shooing away a fly. Her stare was no longer misty and past-centered but determined, curious, and growing harder with each passing second.

"Why, exactly, do you ask, Aoife?"

She hesitated, her mind nudging her tongue to play the "hypothetical" card. *Oh, no reason. Just curious.* Surely her mother would understand, given Aoife's curiosity was always getting her into trouble. But she got lost once again in the image of Lani on that distant shore, making a home and being genuinely happy. She wanted that for her sister. Even if she couldn't understand it, she understood happiness and the desire for it.

She could answer honestly, secure that happiness for her sister legitimately. But the look on her mother's face seemed to be a dire warning to keep her trap shut. Even if the council would grant exile, it was Lani's to request, not hers.

"Have you met someone?"

Aoife choked on the laugh that burst from her—a nervous tick she had. She could never contain her giggles when the nerves rose. It was only logical her mother would jump to that conclusion, right?

"No." She took a breath to compose herself. "No. Not me."

When would she ever have met someone? Honestly. She'd barely spoken two words to any man, and even then it had only been to the older men in the village or the port.

"Who then?"

Aoife realized her mistake—too late—and cringed. A simple "no." That was all she'd needed. Why had her tongue slipped? The icy stare had returned and now bored into her, as if it could uncover the truth she was doing a piss-poor job of hiding. Aoife looked down at her hands, unable to think clearly while looking into those cold eyes.

She willed herself to stay silent this time. She couldn't lie, but she also couldn't rat out her sister.

"Lani."

Aoife clasped a hand over her mouth before she realized it hadn't been her tongue that uttered her sister's name. Her mother had guessed. And it wasn't a question.

Aoife sat still, not giving Melina so much as a nod, as fear and worry coursed through her. There was no good outcome for her. If she lied and her mother found out, she'd lose any semblance of freedom. But if she confirmed her mother's suspicions, she'd be betraying Lani.

Too long had passed without a response, and she realized her silence alone had been confirmation enough.

This was all going dreadfully wrong. She hadn't planned to broach this topic.

She'd meant to keep it hypothetical, to put her mind at ease that if Lani were caught she wouldn't pay too great a price, and now she'd gotten Lani caught in the process.

Her throat tightened, and she swallowed hard around the dread that lodged itself there. What would Lani say to her when she found out?

Her mother spoke again. "And what does she plan to do? Do you know?"

Another breath. Another hesitation. *Say no!* her mind screamed at her.

When she looked up, her mother's cold stare had turned back into to an expression of care, concern, and love. Love for her and for Lani. And before Aoife could stop herself, she broke down, her shoulders slumping from the weight of the secret she'd promised to keep. Her words rushed out before she could stop them, as if propelled by some magic or force she couldn't see and couldn't resist.

"She dreams of running away with him to Daorna and starting a family. It's preposterous. I don't know why she'd want to give this all up, but Mother, she looked so hopeful and happy. Can't she be allowed to leave and have that? Even if it means exile?"

Surely her mother could and would help. Maybe Lani wouldn't be publicly shamed but would be allowed to leave. Quietly. Peacefully.

Melina turned back to the fire. And though Aoife couldn't see her face fully, it looked as if her mother might cry.

"I-I..." Aoife stammered. "I promised her I wouldn't tell, and I didn't mean to tell you. I didn't mean to betray her. But surely being allowed to leave knowingly is better than sneaking away?"

Her mother didn't answer. She continued to stare into the flames, her jaw tightening with each passing second. But not from anger. Rather, it looked as though she were biting back a mournful wail. But it only lasted a moment, a few breaths, and then her face relaxed as she composed herself. She turned to Aoife once more.

"You did the right thing, Aoife. It is always best to be honest, open. And you know you can always tell me anything."

If she had intended comfort in those words, she'd failed, because Aoife felt far from relieved. Something in her mother's words felt like a warning rather than an invitation, making the weight of her guilt even greater. She should not have asked the question. She should not have sought her own comfort. She should have kept her damned mouth shut!

Too late now.

Lani might never forgive her for this broken promise, but maybe she'd get her chance at happiness.

CHAPTER 6
DECLAN

THE BELL in the clock tower in the village square chimed three. Declan straightened against the stone wall, careful to stay hidden in the shadows as he watched the pub from the alley across the street.

A minute passed. And then another. His confidence wavered with each breath.

With gritted teeth he swallowed the last bit of hope he'd been holding onto that his sister had forgiven him, not that he'd ever admit to anyone how much he wanted to mend the family ties he'd severed when he'd left the island.

He'd stayed away too long, abandoned her, and now—despite being the one to initiate this meeting—she appeared to be doing the same to him.

He checked his pocket watch. Three minutes late. He had waited longer than he normally would, and now it was time to go. He turned on his heel, his shoulder slamming into someone's face.

"Watch it!" the voice hissed in a whisper, a hand rubbing the nose he'd smashed.

"Cait."

"You're not the only one in the family able to sneak around in the shadows, you know."

"You're late."

She didn't offer any words, but gave a smirk half hidden in the darkness.

"How'd you know I was here? I could have been waiting in any of these alleys or shadows."

She wiggled an eyebrow at him. "Sisterly intuition."

He waited for the real answer, but when she didn't say anything more, he groaned. "Fine, don't tell me. I assume we have more important things to chat about?"

"Yes, but not here." With that, she turned around and headed back through the alley, without so much as a gesture for him to follow.

Biting back the urge to stamp his foot as he used to as a kid, he instead followed after his older sister, wondering where she was leading him.

His long legs had him catching up with her as she rounded the corner onto the next street, but he almost ran her over when she stopped to open a door he hadn't noticed in the wall. He let out a huff of annoyance, and she shushed him while motioning for him to follow her inside.

He closed the door behind them, shutting out all light from the street outside, plunging them into pitch black. For a moment he wondered if his sister was betraying him, turning him over to the council's lackeys, the ones who made people disappear under the guise of justice. But what did she have on him? Nothing. He always ensured his men behaved, and he'd been sure to always do as the council demanded, required.

An ache in his chest responded to the images that flashed in his mind. The faces. The bodies. He shook them away.

He hadn't fully recovered from the memories when his sister whispered, "This way."

Cait's footsteps were barely audible. She'd always been adept at stealth as a kid, sneaking out in the wee hours of the morning to do what, he never knew. Not that their parents would have minded. Cait could do no wrong. She was the heir to the family's estate, destined to take over the pub when their parents grew too old or passed on. And that's exactly what had happened, albeit many years earlier than expected.

Declan tried to follow her, worried he might step on her in this darkness. He hoped his eyes would eventually adjust, but there was no adjustment that would help here. The air was cold and odorless. Stone walls lined the corridor, and he counted his steps as he followed in an attempt to determine where exactly they might be.

"Stairs here. Going down. Ten of them. Don't fall," Cait said.

He didn't say anything as he followed.

Ten stairs down. And then he ran into his sister once again. She had stopped. She could have at least told him she was stopping.

Cait didn't say anything, but he heard her unlocking a door and shoving it open. The light blinded him for a moment, a shock after being in such darkness even for the short time it'd taken them. He stepped inside and waited while she locked the door behind them.

Though he'd half expected to find the room filled with other people, it was empty. Just the two of them. And it wasn't cold like the hallway. A fire burned in a small hearth to the left, with a simple mantel above it lying empty. In fact, no decorations adorned the wall other than a single map of the Aisling Sea on the far wall behind a modest desk and a beat-up chair. A rug had been brought down; Declan recognized it from their old living room, the pattern of leaves and trees now faded and threadbare. A simple cot lay in the corner to his right, with a pillow and blanket tossed about as if the owner had risen in a hurry.

Cait walked past the old sofa that sat in front of the fire and motioned for him to sit in one of the two old, mismatched armchairs in front of the desk.

"Welcome to my home," Cait said, easing herself into the chair closest to her. "I'd offer you a drink, but I'm not on duty and I've been pouring drinks all damn day."

"You live here? What is this place? What about our..." He stopped himself at that word. Nothing on this island was his. He had abandoned all connection when he'd stepped onto that ship all those years ago.

"The rooms are still there, of course. I keep them looking lived-in. Helps to keep the council unawares." Settling into her seat, she stretched out her legs, crossing them at the ankles before putting her hands behind her head. She didn't look like someone who had urgent news to tell him.

He eyed her, as the questions churned in his mind. What was she hiding about this place? How did she keep the council from finding it? And how did she keep their residence above the pub looking lived-in without actually living there?

"Ah, yes, brother, you've been away too long, always hiding there on your ship, too scared to come home."

"I'm not scared. And this isn't my home. Not anymore." He cringed at how childish his words sounded, and his chest puffed up against his will, as if it intended to remedy the betrayal his words had committed against his reputation.

"Apologies, Declan. I should choose my words more carefully. I'd hate to be the next victim of your famed wrath." She raised an eyebrow at him. He searched for any sign of mockery in her features, but all he saw was admiration and interest.

"What do you need, Cait?"

"Can't a sister merely miss her baby brother?"

"No one ever misses a pirate. But you're the one who sought me out. I doubt it's for some warm family reunion. So what do you need? Same thing everyone else needs from us? To do your dirty work?"

She bristled and then sat up, leaning forward. "We are not the council, and we do not have any need of your—protection." Even here she wouldn't voice the tasks the council demanded of him and the other captains.

He pressed again. "What is it?"

Cait narrowed her eyes at him, resting her face against her hand and pressing her fingers across her mouth as if protecting the words she, even now, wasn't sure she should utter. A breath. Another. She was certainly testing his patience. Why send him that note if she wasn't going to speak to him now?

Another breath raised her chest, and she dropped her hand as the air rushed from her lungs in a sigh.

"We need what you seek."

His heart raced, but he willed his apprehension not to show on his face despite feeling the corner of his eye twitch. He tried to play it cool, as cool as he could with this woman who had known him since birth.

"Who said I was seeking something?"

"Oh, come now. You don't think you can make inquiries into its whereabouts without us finding out, do you? You really should be careful when seeking information."

He had been careful. He had never used his name. He had never inquired in person. He had always sent anonymous notes via routes that couldn't be traced back to him. The Rogues had improved their methods, it seemed.

"Let's say I am seeking this...this item. It won't do you any good." He relaxed back into his seat, his arms crossing behind his head, mimicking his sister's previous position.

"And why is that?"

He gave a bored shrug. "No one has been able to tell me where it is or how to locate it. I've spent the past two years searching, and—"

"And you have come up empty-handed." He always hated when she did that—finishing his sentences as if she were in his head. Maybe she was.

"Every clue I get leads to another clue," Declan said. "I'm starting to wonder if it even exists at all."

Cait's eyes narrowed a touch, a move so slight he wasn't sure he hadn't imagined it until she said, "Oh, it exists. Rest assured."

What did she know? How had they found it? He'd used every resource, every trick, every bit of power he'd acquired and had nothing to show for it. At least nothing that would get him any closer to retrieving it. And here his sister, who never left the port, who ran a blasted pub, had found it.

He couldn't show his eagerness. Even with his sister he had to be smart. She had strong ties to the Rogues. Hell, she was probably leading them by now. Ambition ran through her veins as much as it did his, after all. He should have known she'd never be content behind that counter pouring drinks.

"And what does your...organization...need with this item?"

"That's none of your concern." That icy, detached attitude snapped into place.

"Ah, sister, but it is. It is my concern. Because if I go retrieve it, risking my neck and my ship to do so, I intend to use it for my own purposes. What possible reason would I have to be selfless and hand it over?"

She laughed. Short and quiet, but a laugh nonetheless. He clenched his jaw at the sound, fighting back the childish impulse to yell at her.

"Declan, Declan, Declan. I don't expect you to be selfless. None of us do. You see, it's in your best interest for us to acquire it. And use it."

"To what end?"

"The council's."

"And why would I want the council's demise exactly? They give us safe harbor, a place for my crew to rest, a chance to—"

"A chance to what? Be their slaves? Their grunts? Do you really fancy yourself free?" She raised a brow at him, but her eyes remained clear, questioning, with no sign of the mocking humor he'd become accustomed to with her.

He didn't answer. He had no answer to that.

She sat back in her chair, steepling her fingers under her nose. "And why *do* you seek it exactly?"

"Because I can." He shot her a wink, but she wasn't amused. With another half shrug he added, "And the usual, I suppose. Victory over my adversaries."

"Ah, yes, the pirate lords. They are a bunch of—"

"—cocky assholes." It was his turn to finish her sentences.

"Well, I was going to say handsome rogues, but I suppose that works as well."

She looked at him as if waiting for him to offer the truth, but he wouldn't fall for it.

"You see, brother, we essentially want the same thing. Freedom."

He could have argued over that word, claimed it wasn't what he sought, but her words had awakened the desire he'd been avoiding, the need to loosen the bonds around his wrists and neck, the ones that kept him in service to the ladies of the council.

Was he really going to do this for Cait, for the Rogues? He would at least consider it, especially if it meant taking down the pirate lords.

"So where is it?"

"North. The Black Sound."

His heart tripped over its next beat as he struggled to swallow his dread and keep his face free of any emotion. He should have known it'd be there. Of course it'd be there, the one place no ship could enter.

She let out a small chuckle, as if she could read the hesitation—no, the fear— behind his blank face. "Don't be so nervous, Declan. We wouldn't be sending you unprepared. Or at least, not without information that could help you prepare."

"How—" He didn't have time to finish the question before she was answering it. Another joy of sibling connection.

"Yes, the sirens guard the sound, and yes they like to, well, you know."

Indeed, he knew. Everyone knew.

"There is a way around them, a way to get in undetected." She was smiling now, apparently enjoying the discomfort he felt building.

He leaned back, roughing a hand over his stubbled chin. "The only way to do that would be—"

"—with fae magic." She finished his sentence again, and he bit back his frustration, trying not to let it seep into his next words.

"If you hadn't noticed, all the fae died in the war."

"Not died. Fled. For Larcsporough."

"That still doesn't help me."

"Aye, but not all of them left. Three sisters remained behind."

"Why would they stay? When the rest of their kin left?"

"They've been deceived, lied to, tricked into staying in the area, since the treaty was signed and the council was formed. Free them—convince them to help you— and you'll be able to get past the sirens to the dagger."

"And how do I convince them? I can't merely claim they've been deceived. They'd never believe me."

At this, his sister stood, walked to the desk, and unlocked the top drawer using a key she produced from around her neck. She reached in and held up a letter. "This, Declan, will get them to follow you. A letter from their kin."

It could work. They'd surely trust the fae insignia pushed into the wax seal, trust the words written in their own ancient tongue.

"Where are they?" The whisper of dread that had been building in his chest seeped into his bones before he'd even finished speaking. The only place less desirable than the Black Sound was probably where he now needed to go.

"The council hall."

"Well, shit."

CHAPTER 7
AOIFE

The night had brought nothing but restless hours spent tossing about until Aoife had completely given up, dressed for the day in her favorite outfit, and settled into her reading chair beside the cold fireplace in her room.

That had been four hours ago, and she had only managed to read all of two pages. If that.

The words had long since blurred in front of her. Her fingers no longer felt the book.

All night her mind had spun, thoughts slamming from one side to the other. The pit in her stomach had only deepened, while the fear and dread and guilt had eaten a hole in her chest.

Lani would be exiled. Removed from the council—and from her life. But when? Would she get a proper farewell? Get a chance to explain what had happened? Her mother had given her no indication as to what actions the council might take.

But she had an idea of how Lani would. And that's what left her insides feeling like the muck that lined the streets of Morshan.

Aoife was an awful sister. A horrible friend. A traitor.

But she couldn't undo it. Couldn't go back in time and fix it and make it right.

Even if she had the power to do that, possessed the magic she'd heard about in history lessons, would it even help? Would it fix anything?

A nervous laugh shook her chest. Magic hadn't made life easier for her ancestors or all the people of the Aisling who'd fought and died in the war. War brought death, whether one had magic or not. War showed no mercy, paid no heed to the powers one wielded.

Any who survived were left to pick up the pieces, to put it all back together, to mourn those lost—like the fae who remained at the council hall, the last of their kind, offered refuge here if they would use their magic to serve rather than harm.

Aoife had seen the fae only once, when, at the age of eight, she'd wandered into an area of the hall forbidden to the heirs. She hated to disobey, but her curiosity had spurred her on to discover what they looked like and how their magic worked.

But she hadn't made it far.

Though she'd marveled at their pointed ears and lithe bodies, the sound of their voices—inviting yet haunting—had sent her running back to her room. She'd never gone back, had told herself there was a good reason those hallways were off limits. She'd meet them again when necessary. And not a moment sooner.

A scream pierced the air, snapping Aoife from where her thoughts had wandered. It was loud enough that for a moment she thought it had come from within her room and not from the hallway beyond her closed door.

She leapt to her feet, letting the book fall to the floor as she rushed into the hallway. She'd never heard such a scream, but she knew whose voice had made it.

Lani.

She forced her posture to remain as straight as she could manage despite the fear settling in her gut. The hallway was empty, but there. Lani's red curls disappeared around the corner. Aoife raced to follow. She had to help.

"Wait!" she cried after them, but her voice didn't sound like her own. In the next corridor she found two women—women who had helped raise Aoife and her sisters from infancy—dragging Lani forward as she flailed between them. She called out again, but they didn't heed. Didn't even pretend to hear her.

Around another corner and down the main stairs Aoife rushed after them, but her feet slipped, and she stumbled, keeping her from shortening the distance.

"What are you doing?" She shouted the question, though she already knew the answer.

They were exiling Lani now. They hadn't planned to tell Aoife. Hadn't planned to give her a chance for one last hug and one final goodbye.

They were at the council hall entrance then, and Aoife stopped at the sight of her mother and aunts standing at the door. She half expected to see the fae there with them, as if this occasion warranted their magical presence. Surely exiling someone required some kind of enchantment or spell to keep them from returning, since the threat of violence was not an option.

No fae stood there though. Only the ladies of the council kept watch, their faces hard and unmoved. Even Fiona, Lani's own mother, showed no emotion as she watched the maids restrain her daughter, now trembling. It was as if she'd already forgotten her daughter existed, had already written her out of her life and her memories.

No words were spoken. The ladies only glared at the young girl before them, the girl who had once been one of their own. The nod from Melina was so slight, Aoife wasn't sure she hadn't imagined it, but the maids were then pulling Lani toward the exit and down the front steps, where a black carriage waited with a single horse at the lead.

Lani's feet dragged against the stones of the stairs, the sound of her scrambling shoes torturing Aoife as she stood there. She couldn't move. She should run to her, pull those hands off her sister's arms and help her, but fear held her in place, and she could only watch.

When they reached the carriage, a maid loosed one hand to reach for the door, and Lani took the opportunity. Twisting away, she caught the other woman off guard and got her arms free as she turned back toward the house with a growl.

Her eyes met Aoife's before she'd even managed to take one step.

Aoife had never seen an emotion such as what now simmered in her sister's eyes. A mix of despair, anger, betrayal, and fear. Yes, it was fear in those seas of green Aoife had grown up with. Before she could think better of it, she was moving toward her sister. But she hadn't made it over the threshold before hands like iron were on her, gripping her arms with such force she almost cried out.

The maids had used Lani's hesitation to regain their control. They pulled her back toward the carriage, the door now open so all they had to do was shove her inside. They didn't seem to even try to be gentle, using all their might to lift her up and in. The door slammed closed.

Lani's eyes appeared at the window between her hands pressed to the glass. The coachman lifted the reins to spur the horse forward, and her sister's gaze burned into hers. Aoife opened her mouth to offer a silent apology, but the carriage was already leaving. And all Aoife could do was stand and watch her sister being driven away from home, disowned, exiled.

Her mother's grip loosened, but Aoife couldn't relax, even when her mother whispered beside her that it was for the best, that Aoife had been right to tell.

But Aoife had noticed two things.

First, Lani hadn't had any belongings with her. No luggage. Though, that could easily be explained as part of the exile and punishment, being sent away with only the clothes on her back.

The second observation wasn't as easily shaken though. Not once had her mother assured her of Lani's safety, never noted that it would be okay, that Lani would be all right.

And somewhere in Aoife's gut, fear began to brew.

Fear for Lani, but also for herself.

CHAPTER 8
AOIFE

Aoife ran as hard and as fast as she could after the carriage. She half expected her mother to send the staff after her. Perhaps she'd be exiled too. It was what she deserved after her betrayal.

But they didn't. They let her go on her fool's errand, her short legs no match for the horse that carried her sister away.

She lost sight of them around a bend. They were likely taking her to the docks, but with the stitch in her side sharpening with each breath, she stopped, doubled over, gasping for air, hating herself for giving her sister up. And now giving up on saving her.

As if she had any chance of convincing them to change their minds. She had no idea what she would have said or done if she'd caught up with them.

Her mind jumped from option to option. She and Lani could have escaped together on a ship. They could have sneaked aboard, gotten word to Adler, met him in Daorna. Aoife would have been a third wheel, but at least she'd be with her sister.

But she'd failed. Failed to keep up. Failed to stop them. Failed to free her.

And now she sat on the black sands of Calypso Cove, where the teal water of the Aisling was so vast it seemed to drown her despite that the tide would likely not reach her toes for another hour. She ignored the sharpness of the rock digging into her back. She'd long lost feeling in her backside, but she didn't care.

For years this had been her place to clear her mind. Here she could let the worries and pressures of life at the council hall get washed away with the sound of the water over the dark shore. The sharp edges of the cliffs rose behind her, as if sheltering her from the world and the life she had come to find respite from.

Respite.

So many people came to these shores to find such rest, a rest made possible by the treaty signed centuries ago between the council and the pirate lords to keep the waters around Cregah safe for everyone—pirates, merchants, and travelers alike. Beyond these shores, all bets were off.

Aoife had heard the stories over the years during her outings in town. Harrowing tales of travelers narrowly outrunning a pirate vessel and escaping into the dock at Morshan, while others hadn't been so lucky, having their hulls emptied before being sunk to the depths, any survivors left to float on the sea in a simple rowboat. And then there were the scuffles among the pirates themselves, which ranged from mere pranks to ruthless encounters designed to take out the competition.

Life on the sea seemed to bring nothing but danger and death. No wonder so many people sought refuge here. But Aoife didn't seek rest in town like everyone else. She had enough people around her all day back at the hall; the maids and servants constantly hovered over her. All the noise. So much noise. All the time.

These were the moments she needed, here in this cove, on these sands, shielded by the cliffs and boulders, where she could just be. Alone. In silence. Where she could sort through her thoughts and calm her worries and concerns.

But her thoughts wouldn't be calmed today, and she cursed the waves for not being able to do what she needed—to wash away the voice inside her that chided and lectured and screamed at her for what she'd done.

She'd betrayed Lani, and the veil of regret wouldn't be lifted, not even in this place of peace and quiet. She swallowed hard, but the guilt remained. It seemed to coat her tongue, line her throat, until it settled into the pit of her stomach, sitting like sour milk, curdling and making her want to retch.

Her eyes glazed over, no longer seeing the beauty of the sea through the tears welling up. She never should have made Lani confide in her on that path, never should have forced the secret out of her. She'd promised to keep quiet, and then she'd been dumb enough to start that conversation with her mother, and now there was no going back.

Would Lani ever forgive her? Would Aoife forgive if the tables had been turned?

Not that she'd ever get the chance to beg for that forgiveness now. At this very moment Lani was probably being shoved onto a boat, forced to leave and never return. The scribes were likely already in the archives removing her name from all council records. She'd soon exist only in memories and thoughts, the only place the council's reach couldn't venture.

Or can it? Aoife trembled at the rogue thought, but she bit it back.

Wiping away her tears, she drew in a deep breath. No. Her mother and her aunts weren't the enemies. They were the protectors of this island and its people, and the peace they kept was worth all the sacrifices required of Aoife and her sisters. This she had to believe and hold onto, for she feared to lose that reality, to lose that truth, would be to lose herself completely.

Would that really be so bad?

She fumed as her mind betrayed her once again. What was that piece of her that kept pulling her away from home, urging her to—what—leave? She couldn't. This was her home and her duty, and now with Lani gone—Lani, who had let her heart get stirred by a handsome face and a sweet smile—Aoife couldn't chase that dream, couldn't follow suit. The council needed her. Her people needed her.

Yet she couldn't deny the pang that hit her. Was this envy? Had she been jealous of Lani for getting a chance at love? She had to admit, even if only to herself, there was a small part of her that silently and secretly wanted what Lani was getting, a life with Adler across the sea. A life like those in their favorite books.

But it was a life she couldn't have.

At least one of them could though.

In her mind she saw Lani at the docks, her red curls being tossed about by the sea breeze as Adler approached, taking her hand as he led her off the ship that had brought her to their new life on Daorna. She could see her sister's smile, the joy in her eyes, the love wrapping around the two of them. Yes, they would be all right. They would thrive.

Aoife had to believe all she envisioned would come true, or the guilt and that last burning stare from her sister might consume her entirely.

Something moved in her periphery, snapping her out of her spiraling thoughts.

She leaned forward, her ear to her shoulder and her eyes squinting. There, gliding through the water toward the beach, something—someone—swam toward her.

Her heart gave a start, and her limbs tensed from the inexplicable panic that struck. There was nothing to fear on this island, thanks to the council. Yet she couldn't bite back the prickling unease at the sight of someone coming from the sea —and without a boat, no less.

Using the path, though it was overgrown and difficult to find, would have made more sense. But during the past ten years she'd never heard of anyone coming here, had never seen another soul. Especially not one swimming in these forbidden waters, where recreation had been outlawed since long before Aoife's time. Everyone knew the stories of the poor souls who'd been caught in the riptide in this cove, carried out to sea, and never heard from again.

Yet this figure swam with seemingly little effort, comfortable and at home in the water.

Then the person stood with ease as the foaming edge of the tide swirled around his calves.

Aoife's mouth fell open. Indeed. It was a man.

She blinked and shifted her head to the other side as she peered at him.

Men were not a frequent sighting at the council hall. While the pirate lords and their crews visited monthly, villagers only made an appearance at the harvest offering once per year. Occasionally they came to report a grievance, but even then these reports were rarely handled by men.

This man looked like no villager, but neither did he look like any pirate she'd ever seen. His dark hair, cut close around his ears, lengthened gradually toward the top of his head, where it ended in a wave that fell into his eyes. His gaze remained cast down at his feet, and he hadn't yet noticed her sitting against the boulder.

His trousers were made of a simple linen, dyed a dark color that nearly matched the black of the sand now clinging to the hems and to his boots, and contrasted starkly with the white of his shirt, which no longer hung loose as intended but hugged his body, the light fabric curving around the sharp edges of muscles she could never have imagined on a human form. Her hand fell to her own stomach as she wondered if she, too, might have cords of muscles hiding somewhere beneath the softness.

At his waist a dark teal sash hung.

So he was a pirate, yes, but no lord's ship bore those colors.

His chin lifted and turned as he took in his surroundings. Even from twenty feet away Aoife could see a seriousness in his expression that felt...familiar. Almost like an echoing of the emotions she'd been wrestling with all morning. What had happened out there? Had he narrowly escaped the current? What had caused that pain in his eyes?

She waited, holding her breath, as if she weren't conspicuously perched in the center of the cove and could simply hide by not breathing.

With deliberate care he turned his head, his gaze passing over her, past her, before pulling back when he realized more than rocks and sand lay before him. His expression softened, eyes alight with the same curiosity she felt within herself, and his lips abandoned their previous remorseful look for a mischievous smirk.

He took a step forward. Then another.

And then he spoke.

"G'morning, Miss..." He lingered on the word, inviting her to finish his sentence by offering her name.

Her mind wobbled, darting around in search of her own voice, which remained elusive, not from nerves or fear, but from confusion mixed with a familiar flutter of curiosity. At the council hall the men never spoke to her, and she never spoke to them. There'd been no need. On her trips to the villages, she always dealt with the women who owned the shops and eateries, only ever nodding and offering a polite smile to the men she encountered.

Raising his brow and nudging his chin further, he pushed her to answer.

"Aoife Cascade," she said. This couldn't be proper. What was she thinking? She brushed her hands against the folds of her skirts to wipe away the clammy sweat that had begun pooling in her palms.

What would Mother say if she found out Aoife had given her name to a man? And a pirate, at that. There were rules about this. The ladies of the council were only to engage with the pirate lords they were matched with, never with the crew. And here she was, not only talking to a crew member, but giving him her name. She had obviously lost her mind.

"Ah, so you do have a name." The smirk transformed into a smile, kind but with a hint of laughter, like he was telling himself a silent joke. She liked it, though she shouldn't.

"I do indeed. What kind of person doesn't have a name?" She jutted her chin up at him. He seemed so tall, but then again, she was still sitting in the sand. The rock seemed to dig more pointedly into her back, as if chiding her for being such an idiot.

"Fair point, miss."

She waited, expecting him to offer his own name in return, but he didn't. He simply eyed her, that obnoxious smile remaining.

"And are you the kind of person without one?" she asked, then clarified for his possibly simple mind. "Without a name, that is."

He laughed in return, a pleasant sound, hearty and full, not at all similar to the tinkling bell-like laughs she'd heard all her life. "I am the kind of person—" He paused to clear his throat or to stall long enough to devise a cover.

Like you should have done.

"—who doesn't give his name to just any stranger he meets."

She huffed. "That isn't exactly polite, is it?"

"Who said I was one for politeness?"

She studied him, her gaze trailing across his face, wishing she hadn't given her real name to this stranger. When his eyes fell, resting lower than her face, she opened her mouth to chide him but then realized her arms were bare, visible. She flashed a hand up to pull the length of her sleeves down, covering the designs etched onto her forearms. She kept her face down as her cheeks warmed with embarrassment, kicking herself for feeling any shame about her status.

He moved toward her, each step sending a twinge of dread through her bones. Here she was, a council heir, alone and unprotected in a secret, long-forgotten cove. He could do whatever he wanted to her, and no one would know. No one would find her body or hear her screams over the surf. The commanded peace on these shores seemed distant and inconsequential in these moments as she listened to his feet in the sand.

She held her breath and waited. With eyes clenched tight she imagined the hands that would soon grab her.

But no hands came.

Instead she heard a thud and a sigh as he settled onto the ground beside another boulder nearby. She stole a glance at him, keeping her head lowered.

The stranger ran his hands through his hair, shaking out the last of the seawater, before running them along his neck, his head turning and rolling to stretch out any kinks. With a steady exhale he settled back against the rock, his face turned toward the sea, the muscles in his jaw tensing before settling into a content expression.

Had he recognized the markings on her arm? Everyone on the island should know. Would know. So why didn't he note it? Why did he ignore it?

She could demand his reverence, insist he show her the proper respect her station deserved, but her bones became heavy as she remembered why she'd sought refuge here today. She tried to relax, but her nerves were frayed, cut through with worry and guilt over Lani. She envied this stranger's ease. He seemed as calm and gentle as the sea that swept toward them and then away. Back and forth.

Just like her heart. Back and forth between whether she'd made the right decision or a dire mistake.

"So..." The word cut through the sound of the receding waves.

"Yes?" She tried to sound confident, regal, but her voice cracked under the stress.

"What's a council heir doing here on this beach?" He didn't look at her, but kept staring out at the sea before them.

So he had recognized the mark. She hated lying to anyone, even to a stranger. It didn't sit well with her heart, and perhaps that was why she'd broken so easily under Mother's questions. But this wasn't her mother. She owed no loyalty to this pirate.

Before she could answer, he gave a short laugh. "That hard to come up with a cover? You really should have those planned ahead of time. You know, just in case."

"I don't need a cover. I'm not doing anything wrong." He spoke with such audacity. She'd never heard a man speak to a council member in that way before, as if he were an equal or even superior.

"Of course not, Miss Cascade." He bowed his chin in reverence, but she detected a hint of mockery. "I was merely making a joke."

"Oh, yes, of course." She cringed at how ridiculous she sounded, stumbling over her words. This wasn't how an heir should act.

"You do know what a joke is, yes? Or has the council outlawed humor as well?"

Now he'd certainly gone too far. What nerve he showed! Straightening and turning away from the boulder, she mustered up every bit of regal decorum she had been taught and faced him.

"Excuse me?"

He held up his hands, palms toward her in retreat. "No harm meant. Merely another joke." And with a chuckle he settled his gaze back on the water, that dreadful smirk once again plastered on his face.

She had no retort though. Her mind went completely blank aside from a desire to stick her tongue out at him as she often did with her sisters. That would certainly not be regal in the slightest. Here this man had the nerve to disrespect her, and she couldn't come up with any words to put him rightly in his place. What would Mother have said to him? What harshness would she have laid out to correct him? How many times had Aoife received her mother's stern reprimands when she'd screwed up?

For a long moment they sat in silence, both staring out at the waters. She wondered if she could simply get up and leave him sitting there alone. Or would that be as rude as his so-called jokes? She couldn't repay rudeness with rudeness. That was uncouth and not becoming of a council lady.

"Do you swim these waters often?" It was a stupid question, she knew, but she couldn't handle the silence any longer.

"Oh, have you deemed me worthy of conversation?" That damn attitude again. She cringed at the names she wanted to call him. Definitely not ladylike.

"I wouldn't say worthy, but you're the only one here."

"So you do have a sense of humor." That smile flashed again, and she wanted to smack it off of him.

"You're exhausting, you know that?"

"I've been told that. Last night actually. But that young lady seemed much more pleased by that fact."

"You're disgusting."

"Hey"—he raised his palms again—"you're the one ruling over a land that aims to please everyone, including men of the sea. And we have needs."

"So I've heard." She had indeed heard of those particular establishments that were placed inconspicuously around town. Though she'd heard they were more for the pleasure of the village women and not truly for the pirates and merchant sailors.

"You can leave if you want to. I have no need of you or your company. I'm sure the council is wondering where you've wandered off to." His voice no longer held that tinge of humor, the former amusement replaced now with annoyance and frustration.

She crossed her arms over her chest and shoved herself back against the boulder, ignoring the sharp pain that resulted from hitting that stupid edge she'd forgotten about. "I leave when I want to, and I am not quite done enjoying the view."

"I am pretty nice to look at, it's true." He said it matter-of-factly, and each word poked at her further, like a thorn in her side being twisted.

"I was here first anyway. Perhaps you should find a different spot to relax in."

"Fight me for it?"

"What? No! Never."

"Oh, right. Land of peace and tranquility." His tone was so mocking she couldn't ignore it, and the need to defend her home and her mother and the council bubbled up and out before she could stop it.

"Yes! This is a land of peace. No fighting. No violence. We value peace above all else."

"And would you fight for that peace?" He raised his brow, his face showing no sign of this being another of his asinine jokes.

"Don't be ridiculous."

"I'm not. Sometimes peace must be fought for. Ask the king of Caprothe. He certainly fought for the peace you now enjoy."

"I'll be sure to do that the next time I see him." Not that that was possible. The Caprothen king who had fought for and signed that peace treaty was long since dead.

"Funny that you speak of peace, Miss Cascade, when your council—"

"When my council what? Keeps order? Provides rest to everyone who comes here, including your kind?"

"My kind." His eyes narrowed as he clenched his jaw. She'd struck a nerve. Good.

"Yes, pirate. Does your captain know you've wandered off?" She was pushing him now, goading him, and it felt good.

"Aye. He does. But I should be getting back. To *my kind* and all."

Aoife didn't offer a response but glanced toward the path behind them that led between the cliffs. He rose and, not bothering to brush the sand off his pants, turned to leave, his eyes blazing as he met her gaze.

The look from him snapped something inside her, pulling her back to why she'd come here in the first place. Forcing herself not to watch him as he walked away, she pushed her gaze back out to the encroaching tide. She shouldn't have let him get to her, shouldn't have stooped to his level. She'd insulted him, and though she shouldn't feel bad for it—not after he'd attacked the council and all they stood for —she did all the same.

She didn't want to think of him anymore, but every time she pushed him from her mind, Lani's face surfaced, haunting her.

Would she ever stop screwing up? Would she ever find the grace she was supposed to embody as a councilwoman? Or would she forever be stumbling over herself, hurting people, insulting them? If only she could go back in time, change everything she'd done, keep her mouth shut...both at the council hall and here on this beach.

CHAPTER 9
AOIFE

Aoife stepped through the trees, carefully watching the path before her so as not to trip over the roots and stones that made it nearly invisible. A shiver of an inkling crept over her chest, a feeling that eyes were upon her. She ignored it, summoning whatever shred of bravery and pride she had remaining after putting that pirate in his place.

Had she hurt him? Impossible.

And even if she had, why should she care? She was an heir to the council, soon to be made a full lady. He couldn't do anything to her, and he'd be stupid if he even thought to. She had the power. He didn't. This island was theirs.

As she stepped over branch after branch, she kept her steps as light as possible —staying quiet from what, she didn't know—except she did know.

If the pirate had lingered, she didn't need him coming back to stop her. She didn't trust what he might want from her when there were no witnesses. She'd learned about the true nature of men in her courses; they only wanted power, riches, and flesh, no matter what they had to do to get it. Even if Lani had found one good man among them, he was the anomaly, the exception.

And Aoife had been stupid to talk to that pirate, to tell him her name. Her mother might slap her if she knew she'd done that. Sands, she should slap herself.

It wasn't that she couldn't talk to men, but she should have paid more attention to the prickles on her skin warning her he was dangerous, different than the men she encountered in the villages and at the markets. He had a drive. A mission. Something nagging at his heart and brewing in his mind. She'd seen the same tension in her mother, that same lost stare of worry mixed with dread and determination.

She shook her head.

Not her problem.

She had no use for a pirate.

She had bigger problems back home.

And just like that, the image of Lani's face—twisted with anger and pain and betrayal—slammed back to the forefront of her mind. The regret and guilt rent her heart once again.

At least that pirate had provided a bit of a distraction.

And now she had to face that guilt head-on as she made the long walk back. She welcomed it though, open arms wrapping around it, cradling it like a baby she didn't want but needed to nurse nonetheless. She owed Lani that much, forcing herself to feel this pain.

For the whole trek along the same path she and Lani had strolled down yesterday—had it really only been yesterday?—she stroked the guilt in her heart, letting the tears fall freely when she no longer felt the phantom eyes on her back and was sure no one was watching.

But she wiped them away and took a cleansing breath to force clarity into her eyes well before nearing the council hall gate.

Her mother might understand the tears, if her reaction last night was any indication. But that coldness of her stare this morning when they'd sent Lani away...

Now Aoife wasn't sure what to think.

As she walked through the front door, she kept her gaze forward and chin lifted. The staff bustled around as usual, as if nothing had changed that morning with Lani's departure, as if she really had been erased from their lives. There was no sign of the emotional departure that had taken place.

She'd nearly made it back to her room when her stomach rumbled in protest, a painful reminder of the meals she'd missed. Still too many hours until dinner. Maybe she could scrounge up a snack from the kitchen or pantry.

Without another thought, she let her feet carry her away from the quarters down to the servants' area, her eyes not noticing any of the cold stone walls as she walked, her ears not registering anything save her slow steps.

Until she neared the kitchen and the sound of hushed yet excited voices forced her to focus.

As a council heir she could have simply walked in, but something within her— something she couldn't quite name—had her pushing her back against the wall and angling her head toward the door to listen.

The coldness of the stones permeated her tunic, but she ignored it as she strained to hear their words, not sure what she hoped they'd be discussing. Maybe she wanted some reassurance that Lani wasn't completely forgotten, that these people—the people who had raised them and fed them and cared for them— wouldn't cast her sister aside so easily.

"My hands are so tired," one voice uttered.

"Tell me about it. So much bread to knead and bake," another voice said.

Aoife didn't recognize them, but then she'd never been great at placing names to faces and voices. It was one of many areas of frustration for her mother, who had spent the last two years impressing it upon Aoife that she must remedy this if she was ever going to be an effective leader. If she were ever to serve their people well, she'd need to be able to remember them—their names, their families, their circumstances.

"You'd think with one less mouth to feed we'd get a bit of a reprieve."

"And with that coming-of-age ceremony being canceled."

A scoff and a sigh sounded before the response.

"Yes, but now they're insisting on making Miss Cascade's ceremony even bigger. Grander."

"As if that could cover up the fact that they've lost an heir?"

"They're going to have a hell of a time covering this up with the people. People talk."

"Not if they're smart."

"True. But how many of them are really that smart? They're as dumb as that brat."

The word, spat with such disdain, struck Aoife in the gut. They had to be talking about Lani.

"Can you believe she actually ran after them?"

Her breath hitched. Not Lani. Her. They were talking about *her*.

"They should have dealt with both of them, to be honest."

"Definitely. Do we really want someone like her on the council? Someone who holds more loyalty to her sister than to the people?"

"Even that's questionable. She's the one who turned the girl in!"

Aoife squeezed her eyes shut. Their words shouldn't sting, and yet they did. She should turn, leave. She already had enough guilt pressing down on her. She didn't need to listen, but her feet wouldn't budge.

"Not even on purpose though. And certainly she had to know what would happen."

"Not too bright, is she?"

"Naive, perhaps. I mean, even the younger one has figured it out."

Aoife's eyes scanned the hallway without seeing anything. Darienn knew. But knew what? What had Aoife not figured out? What in the sands were these women talking about?

"Yes, but what were they to do? They're now short one heir. They can't be short two. Can they?"

"Did you hear who they had take care of it?"

"A young pirate, I heard."

"And a handsome one at that."

"Most of them are, aren't they?"

"I certainly wouldn't complain if I had to die by his hand. Those eyes being the last I saw before it went black?"

"Aye, she could have chosen a worse way to die."

All the oxygen got sucked out of the room with that single word.

Die.

They'd both said it.

The carriage hadn't taken Lani to the docks. She wouldn't be sent off to meet Adler.

Aoife's knees started to give, all her strength seeping from her bones down into the floor. But she couldn't collapse here. She needed to move before they found her.

The laughter and chatter continued, but she didn't hear another word.

And her limbs didn't listen to her desperate urging to get going.

Die.

Dead.

Lani hadn't been exiled. She hadn't been safe.

Everything began to spin, and when her feet finally moved to carry her back to her room—all thoughts of food now forgotten—it was a marvel she remained upright.

Everything she knew. Everything she believed. Everyone she trusted.

Was it all a lie?

Could she trust the gossip of a few servants?

Her chest caved under the weight of her confusion.

She clicked the door to her room shut behind her and froze. Nothing made sense. None of it.

Peace. This was a land of peace. No weapons. No violence.

But a nagging curiosity began to gnaw in her chest.

This would explain the stark fear she'd seen on Lani's face—not the sadness from merely having to say goodbye to her sister and home, but outright terror. It was that look that had pushed Aoife's feet down the council hall driveway after the carriage without a second thought.

Had Lani known what the cost would be? Is that why she'd planned to sneak away? Was Aoife truly that naive and trusting to not know what the council was capable of?

Her room was spinning as badly as the hallway had, and she couldn't find any firm footing for her mind to settle on.

She moved to sit down on the bed, hoping it would help, but before she even made it a half step, a knock came at the door, and she jumped.

"Yes?" Her voice sounded and felt distant, as if it came from someone else.

The door opened, and a head peeked around the edge. Darienn's blue eyes stared at her with curiosity and concern.

"Aoife?" She sounded as timid as the mice that skittered around the gardens outside, younger than her seventeen years.

Aoife gritted her teeth, fighting back the annoyance that always began to simmer whenever Darienn spoke. Or breathed. Why had it been Lani who wanted to run away? Why couldn't it have been this sister who fell in love and wanted to run off with some man?

But looking at Darienn and seeing fear in her eyes, Aoife bit back the sharpness that had been ready to pop out.

"Come on in, Dare." She hoped the words sounded inviting enough, and she motioned with a hand for her sister to join her on the edge of the bed.

Darienn entered, albeit timidly, as if unsure Aoife truly meant the invitation. She kept her head down as she sat beside her sister. Her hands worked the folds in her skirt, as though a slew of thoughts and questions were fighting to be voiced.

For a moment Aoife forgot how much younger Darienn was than she and Lani. A full three years separated them, yet Darienn had physically matured far more quickly than Aoife had, her curves already generously feminine compared to Aoife's modest frame.

Not exactly the time or place to be worried about such things, don't you think?

She shooed the thought away, instead moving to look her sister in the eye.

"What's bothering you, Darienn?" She cringed at the stupidity of the question.

"When you disappeared right after Lani..." Darienn's breath hitched with a suppressed sob. "I worried you'd both left me. Alone."

Another punch of guilt hit her as the tears spilled over and glided down her sister's cheek. All those times she and Lani had excluded Darienn from their sisterly outings and chats; she'd always assumed Darienn had resented them, but now it seemed to be the opposite.

She tried to smile and make a joke, maybe help lighten the mood a little. "Without us, though, you could have all three pirate lords to yourself in a few years."

"I don't want three pirate lords."

"Certainly three is better than one. Three times the man to please you and dote on you and keep you company."

"One is enough for that. And they're not the same as sisters."

"We are better looking in a dress, I suppose."

"You smell better too." Darienn snorted at her own joke, and Aoife couldn't help but let out a small chuckle.

Silence settled between them, but at least Darienn's tears had dried.

But something was still nagging at her sister. Aoife could see it in the little fidgets and twitches in Darienn's fingers and legs as she sat.

"What else is bothering you, Darienn?"

"Do you think they really let her leave?"

Aoife froze. She didn't even know if she was breathing as she chewed on the question, felt it swirl around with the words the servants had spoken earlier. They'd said Darienn knew. Was her sister playing dumb now? If she didn't know, Aoife didn't plan to be the one to spill another secret unnecessarily.

"Of course I do. Mother wouldn't lie. Why—"

"I heard the ladies talking after she was sent away."

"You can't trust the gossip of the servants, Darienn." This she said as much to herself as she did to her sister, hoping to the sands it was true.

Darienn fidgeted more, her eyes skittering over her lap and her feet and the floor, refusing to meet Aoife's gaze.

"Not the servants. Our mothers."

Aoife froze and forced a dry swallow down before she asked, "What did you hear them saying?"

"It made no sense. I couldn't put it together."

"What did they say?" She struggled to keep the impatience out of her tone.

"Something about the pirate they'd commissioned for the job."

"That could have been about anything. You know the pirates help with—"

"They said her name, Aoife! There was no way they were talking about anything but our sister. Doesn't it worry you at all?" Now Darienn's eyes rose to meet hers. A fire within them had burned away all the tears. "Or were you hoping for more than one lord for yourself?"

"Get out." The words came out with a snarl, low, guttural, menacing.

But Darienn didn't rise. Tension, resolve, settled into her previously timid bones. She was going to push, hard.

"Is that why you ratted her out, Aoife? You wanted her out of the way? Wanted her—"

"How dare you! The last thing I wanted was for her to leave me here with you." Although Aoife meant it, she still regretted her outburst. She didn't like being nasty, and even hated that she disliked this sister so much. She wanted to be kind and nice and loving, but Darienn was like that obnoxious rock in her shoe that could never be removed no matter how much she shook.

But Darienn appeared unfazed by her words. She'd expected them, perhaps, after all these years of being ignored and brushed aside.

"Then why?"

"I don't know." She could have denied that she'd ratted Lani out, but that was what had happened, regardless of her intention. Intentions meant little.

"I think you do, Aoife." Her sister's voice was now gentle, no hint of the earlier accusations. "You're not vindictive or mean. Even when you are to me, I know you don't like to be. I can see the guilt and regret in you. Like a warm blanket you're keeping wrapped around your shoulders, as if it's a comfort to let you know you're not as cold as the words you utter."

She had no words for her sister now. Her sister who had perceived so much. And so accurately.

"Aoife. I don't think you meant to tell Melina."

"Wait. What do you know about Lani's plans? Did she talk to you?"

"Not willingly. I told you people don't notice me. I saw her go into your room with a set of clothes, men's clothes it looked like. When she came out again, her arms were empty. I stopped her. Asked her what they were."

"And she told you?"

"It wasn't easy to get it out of her. You know how secretive she is. Though that didn't make her good at sneaking about." It might have been funny had Lani not been carted off that morning.

"What did she tell you?" Aoife wasn't going to risk spilling more secrets if Darienn didn't know them.

"She had stashed the clothes in your room with plans to don them before leaving to meet Adler."

"But why my room? Why not keep them in hers?" The questions were more for herself. She didn't expect Lani had provided any explanation to their sister.

"She'd raised suspicions. At least she thought she had. She couldn't risk having them in her room. She was afraid they knew she was planning something."

"They who?"

"Our mothers, as if they deserve such titles." Darienn now spoke with air of maturity Aoife had never heard from her before. What had happened to the young girl who believed in the court and the ladies and the mission of Cregah so wholeheartedly?

"What do you mean?" The doubt sparked again before she could douse it.

"How can you be so naive? You're older than me. You've seen more than me. Or have you been willingly remaining blind?"

"What are you talking about, Darienn?"

"The disappearances."

"Exiles."

"Call them whatever you want. They happen."

"For a reason." Even as she said the words, the doubt kept poking at her insides. Darienn only shook her head.

"Wait, Darienn, did our mothers catch you listening? Do they know you heard?"

Darienn toed the floor a bit, not in a timid fashion, but more like she was trying to find the right words to answer. "They don't know what I heard, I don't think. But I knocked on the door then."

"Why? You know interrupting them never goes over well."

"They didn't seem to mind. I had every intention of confronting them, actually. Asking them what they had meant, what they had hired the pirate to do to our sister. But standing before them, I clammed up. Couldn't ask. So I told them I was worried about you."

Aoife blinked, trying to figure out what Melina might have thought of such a claim. "And?"

"She told me this would help." And with that, Darienn pulled something from the pocket of her dress.

A silver chain with a glass vial. It dangled between them as Aoife stared at it and at the black sand it held.

She didn't reach for it, but she couldn't pull her gaze from it as she asked, "What..."

"Your mother said Lani wanted you to have this before she left."

Aoife squeezed her eyes shut. She would not cry in front of Darienn, wouldn't let Darienn see her tremble with the fear that erupted within her.

If she'd doubted what the servants had said or what Darienn had claimed to overhear, all uncertainty vanished now. They'd killed her.

And Darienn knew. Didn't she?

Darienn had suspected the exiles were a ruse, that people were being killed. But what was she going to do about it? Lani must have also figured it out and had chosen to escape. Would Darienn do the same?

Aoife reached for the necklace and gripped it tightly in her fist. "What will you do, Darienn?"

"I think the bigger question is, what will you do?"

"What do you mean?"

"That stunt you pulled today, running after Lani as you did. It didn't go unnoticed."

Her panic now burned bright. Would she be next? Would she be the one thrown into a carriage and dealt with by some pirate?

"But no. I'm loyal to the council, to peace!"

Darienn angled toward her sister, placing a hand on Aoife's knee. "It's your word against your actions though."

Aoife searched Darienn's eyes for any sign of malice or mischief, something to tell her whether this little sister, the sister she and Lani had ignored for her whole life, could be trusted. But after so many years of avoiding her, it was impossible to read her expression.

"I could stay. Prove myself."

"But could you stomach ordering exiles as needed? Calling for the deaths of your people in order to keep the peace?"

None of this made any sense. The room began to whirl again. Her sister had to be crazy. But the staff. The necklace. The necklace her sister *never* would have parted with.

No. She couldn't have any part of that. But what were the options?

She'd nearly forgotten Darienn was still with her until the girl stood and spoke again. "You have the clothes she left behind. If it were me? I'd see those as a gift. Take them. Use them to run. Get the freedom our sister almost found."

Aoife looked up again, the threat of tears stinging her eyes. "Is this your way of getting all the pirate lords to yourself?"

She repeated her earlier joke, but Darienn's expression shifted into something Aoife couldn't quite place. "We all must make sacrifices, sister. Mine is to stay behind."

Before Aoife could ask any more questions, Darienn had turned and was out the door, leaving her alone with her thoughts. And a choice.

CHAPTER 10
DECLAN

The girl had certainly caught Declan by surprise at the cove. And gotten under his skin in the process.

That look of disdain she'd given, dripping with thick condescension, still irked him. He shouldn't have let it get to him, but something about the way she talked down to him kept him from brushing it aside. It had been years since anyone had dared speak to him in such a tone. Among the pirates there was an air of respect, even as they fought and battled for power, influence, and goods.

She'd had none for him. And it stung. More than it should have. But he shouldn't have expected anything else from a council heir, especially given his status as a lesser pirate captain and not a lord.

He huffed as he kicked a stone out of his way. He'd needed that time to think at the cove, to gather his thoughts before he discussed plans with Gavin and Tommy. And now here he was, trudging back to the village and the pub with his mind still a jumbled mess. The walk back would have to suffice.

He had intended to return to the ship immediately following his meeting with Cait, but it had been impossible to turn down her invitation to rest and sleep in her cozy hole of a room. His body had melted with appreciation onto that sofa. Not that it was any more comfortable than the feather mattress he had back on the ship, but the simple act of relaxing—as much as he could expect to on this island—had been welcomed by his stressed and aching muscles.

Cait had let him sleep longer than he'd intended, waking him in late morning with the smell of bacon and eggs on toast. He'd scarfed down the food with a quick word of thanks, not bothering to ask her where she'd cooked it when this *home* had no kitchen. Not that it mattered anyway. It was hot food. A taste of home.

Home. The word plagued him as he ate, but he managed to shove it aside as he stood to leave. Before he could step out into the hallway, she'd stopped him and uttered two words to him.

Not a farewell or a thank you. A deadline.

Thirty days.

What happened in thirty days, he wasn't sure, and he hadn't bothered to ask, knowing she wouldn't explain why the Rogues needed the dagger on such short notice. He'd left his sister and her hideaway, hoping to make it back to the ship before the council found him to collect the debt he owed for docking his ship in the port.

But he hadn't made it.

Not that he'd expected to, despite all his hope to the contrary.

He had known the port guards would have reported his ship's failure to pay the fees, and they'd track him down one way or another. Such was life in Morshan. At least for the pirates. It was enough to keep him from sailing into this port year after year. Even if he hadn't been plagued by the memories of his childhood here, he would have made the same call to avoid these shores.

And he had for seven years.

So he hadn't resisted when they caught up with him at the docks, even as his ship—and his solace—had been in view. He hadn't bothered to apologize for not paying the fee, hadn't tried to draw his concealed blade. He'd simply gone with them and done as directed.

If he'd known how much of his life as a pirate would consist of taking orders from people, he might have opted to stay home all those years ago.

Or not so much.

A huff of a laugh escaped at that thought. No way would he have stayed behind with Cait to run the pub, to be a lesser citizen as all men were on Cregah. Even if he wasn't completely free on these shores as a pirate, even if he found conflict out on the sea, at least out there he was in charge of his life and his ship, was more than a tool to be wielded.

Isn't that what you are anyway though?

No. He could choose not to bring the dagger back to his sister. He could do what he pleased. He could make his own decisions, take the dagger for himself, flee to other seas and lands beyond this wretched place.

The sounds of Morshan crept toward him as he neared the town. He needed a plan. If he were going to infiltrate the council and beg some ancient fae to help him, he'd need his head clear. But every attempt he made to focus his thoughts on the matter at hand got derailed by visions of that stupid girl—that heir—moping about in his cove.

He suppressed the growl he wanted to unleash. He should have taken the path to that forgotten beach, should have traipsed through the trees and undergrowth instead of swimming in. Had he done the smart thing, he could have noticed her sitting there before she spotted him, could have avoided being seen. Could have avoided her incessant blathering.

How had she even known about that spot? He'd assumed everyone had forgotten of its existence after the little girl had drowned all those years ago and its waters had been banned for the safety of the people.

But he'd chosen to swim to the beach instead, not because he liked to taunt death—though that was perhaps akin to his profession—but because he had needed that dive off the high cliffs into the deep teal waters. Needed the swim and the challenge to clear his mind from all he'd done and all he would yet need to do.

He knew it was risky, with the current being as strong as it was around that cove, but in the end he'd been unable to resist the call of the water, the inner pull it had on his bones, like a beacon urging him to return home.

Home.

His home—the one he'd once had above the pub—was now no more than a shell, a front, a facade to keep the council unawares.

His sister was smart; he had to give her that. But how exactly did she think he could sneak inside the council hall? He'd need help, but who could help him? The pirates rarely worked together, and when they did it was usually only the lesser captains. There'd be no hope of getting a lord to aid him. His crew was exhausted. They were short on supplies, even with what little they could trade here in Cregah.

They'd managed to keep from being breached, sunk, or pillaged, but his enemies had won all the same, even if not physically. They knew he was defeated. He bit back the anger and fisted his hands at his sides. It wasn't about revenge. He didn't want to destroy them. He simply wanted to be free of them.

And now Cait had given him a way to achieve that freedom.

An impossible way, but a way nonetheless.

Again his mind turned to the heir. Aoife. She'd be heading home soon to the council hall. He stole a glance behind him, half expecting to see her trudging up the path, but it was empty and silent. He could have pressed her for information, and in fact, that had been his plan after he'd noticed the tattoos betraying her status. But her tongue had stayed him, put him firmly in his place, and his bitterness and stung pride had kept him from seeking out the knowledge she possessed.

She could still be his way in, perhaps, but not without proper planning. With a job this big he needed to avoid rash decisions and take his time. Some time at least. As the Black Sound was a good ten-days' journey—with an abiding wind and no storms or confrontations—he'd need most of the thirty days simply to make the trip there and back.

He bit back a curse as he cleared the last of the trees and ventured into town. He needed a drink to calm his nerves before his men arrived to plan.

CHAPTER II
AOIFE

Darienn's words echoed in the quiet room long after she'd left. Aoife didn't know how long she'd remained sitting there on the bed, staring at nothing, seeing nothing. Only hearing those words.

What will you do?

Could you stomach calling for deaths?

No.

She couldn't. Couldn't stay. But the thought of leaving everything behind scared her almost as much as staying and having to do the unthinkable.

It's not like you'd be killing them with your own hand though.

She shook the thought away, but it was quickly replaced with an image of Lani's terrified expression. No. Her hand or not, she could not be the cause of such terror.

But if she stayed, maybe she could stop the killings. Maybe she could call for change and make them see it was wrong.

A laugh echoed in her head.

What could she do really? She'd ratted out her sister by accident. She never did anything but stumble over her words and screw everything up. More than likely, her mistakes would hurt people more than her successes would help them. Her people were better off without her. Maybe if she left she could find someone who had the ability to truly help them. Rescue them.

Rescue.

Such an odd word. Her thoughts drifted back to all the times she'd gone to Morshan, searching the faces in her memories for any sign they needed rescuing. Even if she couldn't remember names, she could see faces clearly. How many of the people she'd met had later been exiled? Surely not that many, but did she even know the real numbers? If the council had lied about what "exile" truly meant, perhaps they had also hidden how many they called for.

Still, the people in her memories seemed happy enough. Perhaps they would be fine.

But what about outside of Morshan? How do the other people fare?

She didn't know. She'd never given them much thought. The guilt twisted her stomach tighter. What kind of ruler would she be if she hadn't even thought of the people beyond those she'd met personally?

Running felt wrong.

But staying and failing her people felt worse.

She needed to leave. It was better for everyone if she did.

A gift. That's what Darienn had said, right? She had the clothes Lani had left behind.

Aoife stood and spun around the room, her eyes searching for something that looked out of place. But everything was right where she'd left it. The books on the desk. The clothes on the bed. The half-drunk cup of tea, now cold, on the end table. The pile of blankets on her reading chair. The chest by the wall.

She stopped.

The chest had been latched closed. She always put the latch down, an open latch being a silly pet peeve of hers, like a cabinet left open or a drawer not pushed all the way in.

She rushed to the chest, slipping Lani's necklace over her head before lifting the lid. Nothing was out of place, but certainly Lani wouldn't have placed them on top for anyone to easily discover. Her hands dug through the contents, pushing aside blankets and cloaks and papers and letters until they brushed against a fabric foreign and new to her.

Coarse. Rough.

Not at all like the linen and silk and velvet she was used to.

Her fingers gripped the fabric and pulled it out. Pants. Shirt. Vest. Jacket. Boots. And a small brown hat. So much more complicated than the simple dresses she usually wore in the council hall. Would she even know how to put the unfamiliar items on?

I'm not as stupid as they all think I am. How hard can it be?

It took her longer than she would ever admit to anyone to put on the new clothes. The feel of pants against her legs felt constrictive yet oddly freeing. She'd be able to move more quickly and quietly in these than she would in the skirts she normally wore.

After lacing up the boots, she let a word of thanks echo in her mind that she and Lani were so close in size. At least in the shoes. While the clothes were in the masculine fashion, they were notably cut for a woman's figure, intended to gently hug the curves while simultaneously hiding them. Though Aoife's curves, or lack thereof, were more swallowed than hugged by the garments, they were effectively hidden, and that was all that mattered.

When Aoife stood, her hair fell over her chest and caught on one of the buttons. She had to do something about her locks. The clothes helped, but her hair would be a dead giveaway. Even with pins there'd be no way she could hide all of it under the hat Lani had stashed.

She ran to the desk, ripped the drawer open, and found the old pair of scissors. Not as sharp as they once had been, but they would do. It wasn't like she had a knife. A knife would have come in handy for the journey she was about to take, but she doubted anyone sold knives on the island. And she couldn't risk a stop in the kitchens to snag one.

Taking an old cloak from the chest, she spread it across the bed. Without bothering to check the mirror, she held out large sections of hair and cut, careful not to let any fall to the floor, but dropping them onto the cloak instead. She couldn't simply toss the hair into the waste bin where someone would certainly spot it and report her.

A nervous chuckle escaped at the thought of what words they'd utter. *Miss Aoife has cut off all her hair.* As if they would punish her for a haircut. But her stomach tangled again with the understanding of what these people, her people, were capable of.

After chopping her hair to chin length—similar to how the younger, newer pirates wore theirs—she wrapped the clippings up in the cloak, which she then placed back into the chest, and stashed the scissors back in the desk. She ran her hands through her hair before slapping the hat on her head. Only then did she allow herself a glance in the mirror, pleased when she saw how little she resembled the heir she'd been before, even with the clearly feminine softness of her face.

Her eyes fell to the vial of black sand that dangled against her chest, and she carefully tucked it under her shirt. Drawing in a deep breath, she turned for the door, and without another look around the room, she walked out.

She kept to the shadows in the hallway—not hard to do given the utter lack of windows in this place. For the first time in her nineteen years she saw the cold and harsh reality around her. The council hall was unlike the warm and inviting cottages and homes she passed in Morshan. This was nothing but cold stone to surround the cold hearts she had previously assumed were part of their noble roles.

But what she'd learned about their actions went beyond any formality required by their station. Her mind flitted as she walked, with quick and quiet steps, recalling all the times she'd yearned for a hug that never came or a warm word of encouragement where there had only been admonishment and lessons.

She was an heir. But to what? Not a family. A tyranny? She still struggled against that thought, that she had been born and raised to wield fear over her own people. But she couldn't deny the truth in the necklace her mother had given her, the piece of her sister now pressed against her heart.

Voices sounded nearby. Her breath hitched as she stepped into a doorway, hoping with all her might that no one might be in the room and open the door to find her there.

She waited and listened, holding the air in as tightly as she could so she could determine if the voices were getting closer or moving away. When she was certain they were not coming toward her, she released her breath slowly, silently. Couldn't take any chances in case they were approaching her on soundless feet.

Risking a glance around the corner of the stone wall, she found the hallway empty and breathed a sigh of relief. The front door would be too conspicuous, and with no pirate crews scheduled to visit for another week, she couldn't risk being caught at the hall, even if they thought she was a pirate.

Instead she turned back toward the servants' entrance on the east side of the residence. It would allow her to use the cover of the bushes that lined the path out to the side gate, and then down a lesser-used road through the forest that surrounded the grounds.

There shouldn't be any staff out there, or any deliveries being made. She'd heard her mother and aunts talking about the last of the provisions arriving the day before for her matching. Not that it mattered now. But she couldn't worry herself over that. All that mattered was that the path would be deserted, the staff busy elsewhere.

She hoped she hadn't miscalculated any of this as she rounded the last corner and hurried down the steps to the door that would lead to her freedom. The door was made of heavy wood, with a single window placed slightly above her head. If she reached up on her toes she could just barely see out.

A glance to the left and then to the right assured her the way was clear.

The hinges creaked, as if announcing her presence to everyone in the servants' residence and the kitchen and the laundry and probably one hundred yards in every direction. She cringed at the sound, but she couldn't risk waiting to see if anyone noticed.

Thankful once again for the clothing that allowed her to slip through the small opening, she squeezed through and inched the door closed, this time the hinges obliging her by remaining silent.

Once the latch clicked shut, she turned and darted down the walkway, hoping no one would notice the man fleeing the council hall toward the gate and the forest beyond.

Freedom waited beyond that gate, and she was on her way to greet it.

CHAPTER 12
DECLAN

THE SUN HAD JUST STARTED to slide behind the rooftops as Declan strode back through the streets of Morshan toward the pub. He glanced around as he walked the same stretch of cobbled stones he had the night before, watching the villagers who milled about in front of their homes. They paid him no mind as they chatted. One woman rattled off a story of a new stew she'd made for her family, and how no one but her youngest child had enjoyed it. Another pair of ladies discussed how best to get blood stains out of clothing. Declan tried not to think of why they'd need to be worried about that. Not his concern. Amid the chatter and conversations of the neighbors doing life together, he heard the tinkling of children's laughter on the breeze, the sounds of games being played on the lawns behind the fences.

Had it really been only last night that he'd pushed the drunk to the side and said hello to his sister for the first time in seven years? Today the golden sunlight seemed to be attempting to wash away any of the dread he felt about the mission he'd agreed to take on. And he could have let it, perhaps. He could have taken in these sounds and smells of a simple village living its life and be grateful these people had some semblance of normalcy. But at his core he knew it wasn't true. Yes, the laughter and the friendship seemed genuine, and it probably was, but he knew— better than most—that it lay atop a foundation of loss, fear, and hardship.

Not my problem.

All he had was what lay before him, and that was the dagger and success and eventually freedom. He could almost taste it, almost imagine how sweet that feeling would be when he could finally step upon his own property of solid land, away from pirates and lords and councils and all their demands and threats. But it was still far off, like looking inside a bakery window and seeing the treats while finding only lint in your pockets.

He rounded the last corner and spotted the weathered pub sign swaying in the breeze up ahead. He opened the door and kicked the last bit of black sand off his boots before stepping inside, unable to push away the memory of his mom chiding him for having dirty feet in her establishment. *"People eat in here, Declan, and we will not have them eat among the muck and filth on your boots!"* The words themselves may have been harsh, but her tone rarely was. She'd had a smile as warm as the sunshine at his back, and a will as hard as the stones beneath his feet. And now...

Inside he found the pub less crowded than it had been the night before, but still far from empty. Three men sat at the far end of the bar, huddled over a pair of nearly empty glasses. Judging by the stoop in their shoulders and the tilts of their heads, it was not their first pour. A group of sailors sat at the table to Declan's right. He recognized them as members of Captain Thorne's crew of the *Falling Star*, another new ship vying for power in an overcrowded sea. He gave them a nod, as if to say, *"Sorry for the run-in a month back. No hard feelings. Let me buy you a drink."*

The forced peace on the shores of Cregah seemed silly to him, but he understood the pull of rest, even if it meant setting aside past grievances, no matter how recent.

One of the men dipped his chin in greeting. Another raised his glass a fraction of an inch. The others stared at their hands. It wasn't a surprising response, especially considering how the noses and cheeks of those with lowered eyes had gotten quite acquainted with his fists during their last meeting.

He could barely stifle the smirk that threatened to creep up at the corners of his mouth.

To his left, at a table tucked into a dark corner at the end of the bar, he spotted his own men, both with glasses near full. Cait had likely insisted they couldn't stay unless they spent money, and they'd obliged but didn't want to be lost too far in their drinks before he showed.

He approached as those at the bar and other tables glanced over their drinks and kept their whispers low.

"Glad to see you made it," Declan said, pulling the chair around beside Tommy so his back would be to the wall and not to the door or the bar. One could never be too careful, even here.

"Of course. Though Miss Cait sure has a tongue on her." It was Gavin who spoke, pulling his own chair around to give Tommy room to do likewise. No pirate liked having his back unprotected or his eyes off his surroundings, but the captain's back took precedence. Always.

"Well it's no surprise, given that she's related to our dear captain, you know," Tommy said with a nod.

"Your mother?" Gavin eyed Declan, eyebrows raised and jaw hanging open.

"What? No, you dolt." Tommy kicked Gavin under the table. "Do you think she birthed him when she was ten? If that?"

"No, no. She just has that sternness one expects from..." Gavin stumbled over his words.

"She's his sister," Tommy said.

Gavin studied Declan.

"See the resemblance?" Declan asked. "I know I'm the better-looking, but she at least got a small portion of the McCallagh good looks."

A towel flew in his face, and he glanced up to see Cait standing before them with a full glass in her hand.

"What?" he asked. "I think I'm adorable."

"Of course you do." There was a bit of a twinkle in her eye as she spoke. "Seems I got all the brains though."

Tommy and Gavin let out a guffaw in unison and then quickly choked it back and stole a glance at their captain. Declan waited, keeping his gaze on his sister. The laughter didn't bother him in the slightest, and had he been in a room other than one teeming with those ready to kill him the second they left the safety of the port, he would have joined in. But one did not keep such a reputation as his by being lighthearted and soft.

"It's a shame though," Cait said. "All those good looks and you waste them by spending all your time with a hundred sweaty men aboard a ship. You could certainly find a nice lady to share your life with instead."

In his periphery, Declan could see his men trying to hold in their laughter, but his eyes never strayed from his sister's as his pulse accelerated and his cheeks warmed against his will. At one time, long ago, he had hoped for just that—the love and companionship he'd seen his parents share. But those dreams and plans had shattered as quickly as the glass he'd dropped that night. No, love got no one anywhere good.

"Perhaps, Miss Cait. Perhaps." He tossed the towel back to her, his gaze never straying. Neither did hers. She lifted the glass, held it to her lips, and took a long swig of the deep amber liquid before placing it down half empty before him.

"Aye, that's some good rum," she said with a nod before turning on her heel and heading back to the bar.

Declan watched her walk away, conjuring up an eerie image in his mind of their mother all those years ago running this same pub, towel over her shoulder, a lightness in her steps borne not from a carefree life but from the necessity to be ready to move quickly should trouble arise. Hers had been a life lived on her toes, a life lived waiting for the other shoe to drop, for the veil to come crashing down around her. For the mask to be lifted and the truth revealed.

"Sir?" Tommy's voice pulled him back to his own table and the matter at hand. "Why did you want to meet here?"

He felt the stares of both his men weighing heavily on him. "Can't a captain have a simple drink with his best men?"

He raised his glass to them. They didn't do the same.

"Aye, he can." Gavin dipped his chin lower to show his respect. "But this is a tad out of the ordinary for you."

Tommy added, "To come ashore. Then to stay longer than planned. It's curious." At least Tommy knew better than to mention the note, trusting that Declan would share about it if it were necessary.

Which it wasn't.

"I know. It'll all make sense eventually. We have a lot to plan and little time to do it." The men leaned in an inch, not daring to come too close lest it raise suspicion among the other pub patrons. The remoteness of their table offered them some protection from their words being overheard, and though no one in the room appeared to be interested, the three pirates of the *Siren's Song* knew better.

"But not here and not yet." He looked at each of his men. "This really is merely a simple drink among friends."

The men still didn't lift their glasses. Suspicion and questions burned in their eyes as they looked at each other and then back to him.

"Fine, fine. If you won't relax, I can at least say the obvious. We need to recruit a few more hands."

"We aren't allowed to—" Tommy began, but Declan raised his hand.

"I know. We aren't recruiting them here. We need to get to Foxhaven. By tomorrow evening. Time is short, and we can't wait."

"By tomorrow?" The surprise was evident in his helmsman's tone. "But that's normally a two-day journey. A day and a half with a miracle, maybe. There's no way."

"If anyone can make it happen, it's you, Gavin," Declan said, his eyes stern.

He didn't hear Gavin as he protested to Tommy, as movement in his periphery pulled his attention away from the table.

A man shifted on a stool at the bar. Declan had noticed the man arrive shortly after him. He'd looked so uncomfortable and hesitant ever since that Declan had taken special notice of him. The man risked a glance in Declan's direction. A mistake. Their eyes met for a split second, and Declan recognized them at once.

Not a man. The girl. The heir.

His jaw tightened as her eyes darted away and her fingers fidgeted with the glass before her. He bit back a laugh. What was she wearing? Gone was the prim and proper attire of the council. Her long hair was now cut short—and not cleanly, as if she'd done it herself. In haste. With no mirror.

But the desire to laugh was at war with bitterness as he began to suspect she was there to get in his way. Had the council sent her to spy? It was a ridiculous notion, to be sure. They wouldn't send one of their heirs to do such a thing, not when they had so many pirates on the island to do their bidding.

As much as he wanted to assume it was mere coincidence, he had the sinking suspicion it was no accident she was here, in his family's pub, watching him. He needed answers, and quickly. He couldn't risk any possibility she'd ruin his plans. Even by accident.

He turned back to his men, being careful with his words in case the lady could hear him from her perch. "Let's get back to the ship."

The men stood, the glasses before them still mostly untouched, though Declan raised his and downed it, wondering if his sister had lied the night before about being out of rum, or if she'd gotten a fresh supply in this morning. It didn't matter. He had a bit of rum in his belly now, and that was enough.

Tommy and Gavin seemed to be waiting for him to make the first move toward the door, but he had to take care of the girl first.

"You both go on ahead. I'll be right behind you." He nodded toward the back of the pub. "A bit too much drink in me."

A curious look passed between his men, who were no doubt wondering how half a glass of rum could qualify as *too much drink*, but with a shared shrug and a huff of laughter between them, they nodded and strode out ahead of him.

When they'd gone, he began his walk through the pub to the door at the other end of the bar, the one leading to the alley where patrons went to do whatever one did behind a pub. He shuffled his feet—not too much, but enough to make it appear that his wits were dulled a bit by drink. He stumbled as he passed Aoife, knocking his shoulder into her lightly. He muttered an apology before continuing on toward the door, ignoring Cait's mocking stare from behind the bar. Upon reaching the door, he forced himself to fall out into the alley.

A quick glance around proved he was alone, as he needed. He stood straight. He thought of pulling the smaller knife from his boot, but he could get to it easily enough if it were needed.

He plastered his back against the wall just to the side of the door. It would hide him from view when it opened again in three...two...one...

The door eased open. He waited and listened to the steps coming out into the alley. Light. Soft. When he was sure she'd cleared the doorway, he pushed it closed, wrapped his right arm around her waist, and spun her toward the wall, turning her until her back was against the stones, pinning her wrist behind her. He pressed his body firmly against hers as his left hand covered her mouth, stifling her yelp.

From this proximity he could see the flecks of gold in her green eyes—eyes wide with surprise and terror and perhaps a bit of annoyance that made him want to laugh again.

She pushed against him, struggling to free her right arm, which was trapped between her back and the wall. He only shook his head and clicked his tongue at her.

He bent closer, trying to ignore the soft scent of vanilla, sugar, and cedarwood that clung to her and sent a wave of unwelcome warmth through him.

"You know, you didn't have to don such a disguise to get more time alone with me."

He pushed his hips into hers to emphasize the suggestiveness, but the movement had as much of an undesired effect on him as it did on her, and he pulled away slightly before she could sense his body's betrayal, but not enough to allow her to escape his grasp. She pulled her face away, and he allowed her to free her mouth for the sheer curiosity of what reply she might have for him.

"How dare you suggest such a thing?" Aoife spat through clenched teeth, yet she kept her voice low. Too low for a lady who might want help and rescue. No, while she might not want to be held by him, she certainly was in no rush to be discovered by anyone either.

"And yet here we are. What am I to think, Miss—what was your name again?"

"Aoife." Again through her teeth. She continued to struggle fruitlessly.

"Right. Aoife. What am I to assume when you follow me into a pub and stare at me while I try to enjoy a drink with friends?" He loosened his grip a touch, ready to tighten it again if she tried anything stupid. He angled his hips, digging one side into hers and maneuvering a leg to keep her from jamming a knee into a particularly sensitive part of his body. "What is it that you want, then, if not the *pleasure* of my company?"

"Others may find you roguishly handsome, Mister—I'm sorry, I don't believe I have the pleasure of your name." She angled her head in a challenge, her eyes taunting him.

"No, you don't have the pleasure."

"...but I, sir, am not in the least bit swayed by your charms." Her eyes narrowed, and he could have sworn he caught a hint of a lie in her words. Perhaps he'd had just as much an effect on her earlier in the cove as she'd had on him.

"So you admit I have charm." He flashed her a smirk. "A shame it has no effect though, miss. We could have had some fun." He pulled away now, certain he'd made his point that he was in control here, but only took half a step back.

She stretched her shoulders and wrists out from where they'd been pressed too tightly into the stone.

He asked again, "What is it you want, if not—"

"Take me with you."

His eyes narrowed, and he hoped she didn't notice the catch in his breath. That was certainly not what he had expected from her. The council usually demanded other services, though usually the council didn't ask for his help themselves but through staff and couriers and messengers. Never through the ladies and their heirs.

"No." But even as he uttered the words he felt the two sides of him battling it out within. She could help him. She knew the council hall. She knew her way around. She might even know about the fae—where they were kept, what they were like. And yet, there was a part of him—the part that had blurted out his response— that didn't want to risk having her aboard a ship full of pirates.

It was a part he'd thought he had buried years ago, a desire to protect and defend those he cared about. But he didn't care about her. She was a nuisance. Annoying.

"I heard you in there," she protested. "Your ship is short of men. Your captain needs more crew."

"And what do you know of sailing and piracy? You're so ready to be the sole woman on board a ship of miscreants and thieves and murderers? And away from the safe and *peaceful* shores of your beloved Cregah?" His words were filled with more rage than he intended, that protective side of him refusing to back down despite his urging.

She didn't answer but merely looked down at her feet, shame crossing over her features, and he almost felt pity for her and her plight.

"That's what I thought." He backed up further, sure she was no risk to him now that he'd seen the desperation in her features, her need to escape the island—a need that mirrored his own.

"Please." It came out barely a whisper.

"What?" He pretended not to have heard her.

As she raised her eyes to his, it was clear her pride had returned and she was bitter to have to resort to begging. "Please. Take me with you. I cannot stay here."

"Ah, but I cannot take you either. What would my captain think?" He exaggerated his sigh, forcing the impatience growing within to come out as boredom. "I really have to get back though. I'd hate for them to leave without me."

He moved to the side, away from her, but she placed herself in front of him once again, blocking his way.

"I don't care what your captain thinks. I *need* off this rock." There was a fire in her eyes that both excited and infuriated him. She was wasting his time, even if she had inside knowledge that could potentially help him. "I must leave. The council—"

He couldn't let her finish that sentence. He slammed his lips against hers, pressing hard. He could feel her resistance. This was almost certainly the first time she, as an unmatched council heir, had been touched by any man, and she didn't seem to like it, not that he was trying to be gentle or affectionate in the slightest. She pressed back against him, her lips as rigid as the rest of her body, and slammed him back with her hands before slapping him across the face.

He'd expected that response.

"What—" she started.

He leaned back in, pushing her back against the wall, though not as forcefully as before, his face close enough that he could have kissed her again had he wanted to. "I needed to shut you up. You, of all people, should know the council has eyes and ears everywhere. You'd do good not to speak so loudly in such a quiet alley where they're sure to notice."

She blinked. "But I'm dressed as a man..."

"And your point being?"

"Wouldn't that look..." Her thought trailed off, and she seemed to be fighting the urge to look around for the council spies. Her jaw and gaze hardened as she lowered her voice once more. "Please."

A single word heavy with desperation.

"My answer stands. Find another ship to carry you. I—my captain—would not be keen on me bringing a stray aboard."

"I have no money. I can't buy passage. What do you expect me to do?"

Declan could see her trying to keep the confidence in her eyes, but they'd begun to betray her.

The sun had completely set. He had to get back to the ship soon. Time was against him here, and she was holding him up. He needed to be rid of her.

He placed a hand on her hip, giving it a squeeze and pressing his body against hers. She tried to step back, but she was already pinned tightly against the pub wall. He ran his hand over her hip before tracing it back up along the curve of her waist and settling it against her ribs. He leaned in—ignoring the way heat spread through his core—and heard her breath catch. His lips hovered over hers, close enough to feel the warmth radiating off of them, but instead of kissing her again, he moved to her ear and whispered.

"You have more than money to offer. I know many a pirate who would accept such...payment."

Before he'd even finished the sentence, she put her full weight into shoving him back. He didn't stop her, let himself be pushed a few feet away, his hands up in retreat. If any council spies were watching, he wasn't going to let them accuse him of forcing himself on another person.

Aoife huffed a breath as she turned away. He let out a hearty laugh at her as she opened the pub door and headed back inside, hoping it was enough to keep her from demanding his help again.

As he strode down the alley back toward his ship, he couldn't help but wonder if he'd made the right decision by turning her down. She was obviously in trouble. The council would be on the search for her. What would they do when they caught up with her?

No. Not his problem. Not his concern. Even if he could have used her knowledge of the council, could have benefited from her help, he couldn't risk having her on board. She couldn't protect herself, no matter how feisty she was, and he couldn't be hindered by the need to protect anyone other than himself.

CHAPTER 13

AOIFE

THE NIGHT WAS SO dark Aoife could barely see the pirate as he walked ahead of her down the cobbled streets. She wasn't sure what she had expected when she'd confronted him in that alley. Had she really expected he would take her with him, that he would risk his captain's wrath to bring her on board, that she could even pass for a man at all with a simple haircut and wardrobe change?

He had not been fooled. How could she hope to fool anyone else?

But the goal wasn't to fool people indefinitely, just long enough to get off the island.

He'd told her to go find someone else to take her, but she couldn't waste any more time looking for another option. She needed transport now, and there was something about him that told her—even as he angered and annoyed her—she could trust him. He could have taken advantage of her in that alley. Even with council spies everywhere, he could have done more in those shadows.

Her heart beat wildly in her chest as she approached the docks. Despite the late hour, there was enough foot traffic she was able to stay hidden as she followed, weaving in and out among the men who carried crates on and off the various ships. She kept her head low, the hat shielding her eyes as she watched him walk on with confidence. How strange that all the men seemed to give him clearance, as if they were performing some kind of choreographed dance to the music of boots on the dock and water lapping at the posts below their feet.

A beautiful and curious dance. Was she imagining it? No, there. Two men skirted out of his way, keeping their heads down.

Who was he?

She'd tried to catch some of the conversation back at the pub, if only to get his name. Not having his name annoyed her more than she would have liked. Why did it matter if he was more private than she was? Though maybe it was more that she was mad at herself for being stupid enough to give him her name and he'd shown his smarts by refusing to reciprocate. She huffed a breath at the memory. She'd need to be smarter. He'd outsmarted her again tonight when he'd anticipated her in the alley. He'd appeared inebriated, bumping into her as he stumbled toward the door. It had all been a ruse, and she had fallen for it. Completely. Stupidly.

All those years of training at the council hall, and she had no practical knowledge. Sure, she knew the history of the Aisling War, the beliefs that had formed her country and led to the establishment of the council. She knew how to paint and how to write and how to read. But she didn't know how to lie. She didn't know how to sneak about. She'd need to learn.

As they passed ship after ship, gangway after gangway, she wondered which vessel he'd board. Which she would need to sneak onto.

They were nearing the end of the docks, and she half expected to see him simply jump off into the water to throw her off course. Even with all the care she was taking, she would not be surprised to learn he knew she was there, his shadow in the night, following him.

But he didn't go into the water. At the last ship, at the end of the dock, he turned. Men were scattered along the dock getting the final crates on board. He stopped to have a word with one of the men, but from her position leaning against a post—doing her best to pretend she was tired, sick, or had had too much rum at the pub—she was still too far away to hear any of their conversation above the shuffle and bustle of all the sailors and pirates.

From under her hat she watched their exchange. Whatever they were discussing, he did not seem happy. Far from it. He seemed to be in a hurry, and while he was frustrated with the man holding the crate of supplies, he also seemed to be showing a hint of softness. Or maybe she only hoped he was.

With a growl of a sigh, the pirate turned and stomped up the gangway to the ship. She looked up at the prow in search of the ship's name. The figurehead was a carved siren. But not one of those she'd heard so many tales of as a kid—tales of monstrous women, evil and darkness incarnate, with black souls that preyed on the lives and hearts and breaths of men and sailors and anyone who made the mistake of venturing into their waters.

No, this siren carved from wood was beautiful and seemed peaceful. And yet there was a smirk on her face as if she held a great secret.

Aoife pulled her attention away from the figure and focused on the name painted on the hull.

The *Siren's Song*.

She'd heard of this ship, but only bits and pieces. Not much at all.

Last year when she'd been attending the dinner with the visiting crew of Lord Saarin she'd heard them mention the *Siren's Song*. They'd all laughed while discussing the young captain who ran it, but she remembered how there'd been a hint of respect in their tone. And consternation. The captain of this ship was making a name for himself, though no one at that table had bothered to mention his name outright. Apparently they'd all known who he was, and there was no need to utter it among the council ladies.

The pirate lords were working to knock him down a peg or two. She remembered that much. She'd wanted to ask them why the pirates weren't more united. Her tutors had thoroughly covered the alliance of the pirate guild in their lessons, the way ships would often come to one another's aid when there was a large shipment of goods to be looted or if they had a run-in with one of the policing ships from Caprothe.

But from what she'd overheard at that meal, the alliances were waning. Particularly with the pirate lords, who seemed to enjoy the perks they received by being in full partnership with the council. They seemed to be holding onto those with as much might as they could, and each pirate lord was working to keep the newer, lesser pirates and their crews from gaining any foothold.

These other ships did much of the work of looting the merchants that crossed the Aisling Sea every year, and the pirate lords would then attack them and take a portion of the bounty, saying it was needed for the council. And indeed, the lords did need more riches than they could possibly gather on their own each year. Such was the price of the seats at the table in the council hall—and the privilege of warming the councilwomen's beds.

Aoife cringed inwardly. She had all but accepted her fate as a council heir. She'd been prepared to be matched to one of the three remaining pirate lords—there were six total, and she was supposed to know all of their names and the names of their ships, but she always had such a dastardly time with her memory. It seemed pointless to remember all six when there were only three potential matches for her, each of whom would be matched with one of the council heirs—Aoife, Lani, or Darienn —when she turned twenty.

Aoife's matching was looming, only a month out, and she'd spent the last year readying herself to take her place as required. But now, after what had happened to Lani, she couldn't stomach the thought of going through with it.

No, she couldn't stay, and her only chance off Cregah was preparing to weigh anchor. She'd have one opportunity, and she had little idea how she was going to pull this off, but it was a risk she needed to take.

With a deep breath, she forced her feet forward, pushing away from the post and making her way toward the man the pirate had spoken to.

Grabbing one of the last remaining crates from the docks, the man headed toward the ship. Without another thought, Aoife picked up the final crate and kept her head down as she followed the man up the gangway, keeping her feet light so he would hopefully not hear her behind him.

Though the ship was docked, the wood beneath her feet swayed enough to surprise her. She'd never left solid ground before, and somehow, in all her planning, she hadn't stopped to think of what walking while floating might feel like.

Still, it wasn't so bad. At least she didn't fall or trip as she followed the man down the stairs and into the hold, careful not to make eye contact with any of the other crew who were rushing about to get the ship ready to leave. No one seemed to notice her. Though, in truth, she wouldn't have known if they had, and she dared not lift her eyes to check.

The man in front of her went down another set of stairs and then into the darkness of the hull. He set the crate down beside the others he'd already loaded and then turned to find her standing there with the one he'd left outside.

She braced herself for his reprimand or an interrogation, but it didn't come.

"Oh!" the man said, surprise written clearly on his face even in the dimness of the hull. The few lanterns cast little light around the room, keeping everything, including their faces, in shadows. "Thanks for grabbing that for me, boy. Captain was likely to have my head for being behind on getting it all loaded. Set it down over there." He pointed down to his left, and Aoife moved to do as told. "I appreciate the help."

She almost sighed with relief, thankful the ruse had gotten her on board. Her disguise had worked. But the man didn't head back up the stairs just yet. Though she kept her chin down, she sensed him staring. She waited, holding her breath, nervous that perhaps he'd see her feminine features despite the dim lighting, or—more likely—he would catch the scent of cleanliness on her clothes and skin. She certainly didn't fit in here, and even she could smell the sweetness of the perfumed soap she'd used that morning.

"Hold on." The man stepped forward, bending down to look under her hat. The stench of sweat and grime and salt permeated her nose, and she had to fight the urge to back away from him. She held her ground, her feet firmly in place. "Who—"

He reached a hand up to rip the hat off her head, but she ducked out of the way, her hat slipping and falling to her feet. She wasn't sure what she was thinking. But in the next second, she realized, as her heart fell into her stomach, that she was no longer on the safe shores of Cregah. She was on this man's ship, a pirate ship no less, and he could do as he pleased.

She froze again and dared to look up. Squaring her shoulders, she clenched her jaw and steeled herself against whatever he was going to do to her.

But he didn't say anything. Instead he stumbled back a step as if he'd seen a ghost. And maybe he thought he had. A chuckle might have escaped her throat under normal circumstances—if she weren't having a confrontation with a pirate and facing almost certain death. She swallowed and waited, but he merely stared. He opened his mouth as if to speak, but when no words came, it snapped shut again.

"Look," she started, and the man took another half step back. "I'm no ghost."

"Well, I know that, girl." His features scrunched with annoyance. "I may be a pirate, but I'm not stupid."

Confusion wrapped around her insides. This wasn't going at all as she had expected. Why hadn't he grabbed her yet? Weren't pirates fearsome? Terrible? Ruthless? Yet here he stood, staring at her as if he couldn't decide whether to gut her or kiss her or drag her above deck to parade her in front of the crew.

"Apologies, Mr.—" She didn't know why she thought he might give up his name when the last pirate she'd met had refused. Perhaps it was a remnant of her life back at the council hall, the polite decorum not easily discarded. *Like your hair and clothes.* She smirked to herself before aiming to speak again, but the man interrupted.

"Collins. And no mister for me, miss. I'm no officer."

She wasn't sure what to say to any of this. Though she hadn't quite known what to expect when she sneaked on board behind him, she hadn't expected to have such a civil discussion once she'd been found. And she'd certainly expected to be caught. That was a given. The pirate in the pub had been right. Certainly her disguise was abysmal, but she had hoped to at least not get caught until they were out to sea.

So they could throw you overboard instead?

She admitted to herself that none of this had been the best idea. But her council lessons hadn't exactly covered the topics of strategy and deception. An heir to the council—a council lady—had no need for such skills.

"Well, Collins. I should be going." She said the words despite having no real plan in mind.

And he must have noted the ridiculousness in her words as well. "Going where exactly?"

"I need to see...a man."

"Well, we have plenty of those on board, though not as many as we had before."

"What do you mean?"

"Sadly we lost several in the latest skirmishes with the lords, and another quarter of our crew is out there, laid up in the hospital, badly wounded from the shot fired upon us. We were lucky to have been close enough to Morshan—and lucky, too, that the captain agreed to finally come here—or I bet we would have had to send a good lot of them to their final resting in the depths." He glanced down at his feet as he spoke but then looked around, his nerves getting the best of him, as if he'd only realized now that he was talking to her and not to himself.

"What do you mean, 'finally come here'?"

He looked at her again. There was no malice in his eyes, only concern, but whether it was for her well-being or for his own hide, she wasn't sure. A war seemed to be raging behind his dark eyes, and she could only imagine what options he was weighing as he stared.

She spoke before he could answer her question. "Look, I don't want to get you in trouble..."

"Why would I be in trouble? I'm not the one who boarded someone else's ship without permission."

"Yes, but you are a crew member who allowed someone you didn't know to sneak aboard behind you. And thanked them for their help."

"Ah, indeed. But that is my price to pay, and my punishment to face, I suppose. I'm not worried. But you should be. Captain McCallagh is in a right mood these days. He's normally a..." He trailed off, perhaps realizing he was about to divulge more information than he should.

McCallagh. The name sounded familiar, but she couldn't place where she'd heard it.

"Regardless," Collins continued, "I'll need to take you to him, and I didn't get quite the amount of rest I would have liked, being in port for so short a time, so I'd much rather you go along peacefully."

"Of course."

Peaceful is all I've known my whole life.

And it was a lie.

"This way." He turned and waved a hand back toward the stairs. "Ladies first."

Aoife's confusion grew. Had everything she'd assumed about pirates been a lie? Like everything else in her life? Had she really been misled about the entire world beyond the walls of the council hall and the Cregahn shores?

And yet he'd talked of violence out on the seas. Open violence. Real wounds. People dying. But people died on Cregah too. Aoife was starting to wonder which was worse—a death people acknowledged outright and mourned even as they doled it out to others, or a death covered up and ignored and dressed up as something else entirely.

Collins gripped her elbow lightly as they headed up the stairs. A great number of boots thumped on the old wood above her head, and she wondered if the echo made it sound like there were more men than there actually were. When the lords and their crews came to dine at the council hall, she'd always marveled at the great number they brought with them—twenty men sitting around the table with the ladies, enjoying food and drink and laughter. But none of those dinners had prepared Aoife for the sheer multitude of crewmen she saw on deck as she and her escort reached the last of the steps.

Thirty to forty men hurried about. She had no idea what they were all doing. The pirate at the pub had been right; she knew nothing of sailing. She would be a liability and no asset on a ship. There didn't appear to be enough work for all the men, and some lounged against the railings, waiting. She briefly recalled the reason for this from a conversation she'd heard at the dining table years ago.

"Aye, we do employ more men than are actually needed to sail a ship, even one as impressive as ours. But the key to being a pirate—and how we have become one of the most esteemed among our lot—is our ability to intimidate. And we do that with numbers." The pirate lord—she couldn't recall which it had been, as she usually daydreamed during those meals—had been quite proud of his ability to not only take down merchant vessels, but also keep lesser pirates in check.

Lesser pirates like the ones she was hoping to sail with now. Not like she'd had any other choice though. It wasn't as if a pirate lord would have given her passage. Not when they enjoyed such close companionship with the ladies of the council. Lord Madigen had been visiting her mother twice a year for the last however many years. It was a relationship Aoife had never quite understood, not even after all the history lessons and instruction on council life. It was something she'd assumed she would come to understand when the time came for her own matching.

Collins nudged her forward. When had she stopped walking?

She felt all eyes shift to her as she and Collins made their way across the deck, around the main mast, and toward a door under the quarterdeck just below the helm. This had to be the captain's quarters. She swallowed hard, but her mouth had gone dry, and her throat chafed. Collins positioned her directly in front of the wooden door. It was more ornate than anything else on the ship, but the wood was weathered and worn by the years of sea air and perhaps the same battles that had diminished the crew's numbers.

He leaned around her and knocked lightly on the wood and waited. One second. Two seconds.

Behind her all had gone silent, and she knew, even without turning around for verification, that everyone had frozen. She could still feel their stares on her and wondered if the pirate from the cove was among them, waiting to see how his captain would deal with her. If she heard him laugh at her, she might die from humiliation.

"Enter." The command sounded from behind the door. The voice held a hint of familiarity, but she shook the thought aside, telling herself all pirate captains sounded the same.

Confident. Intimidating. Harsh.

But this command hadn't sounded as harsh as she'd expected. Then again, he didn't yet know that someone had tried to stow away on his ship. She pulled her shoulders back and pushed her chin up as Collins pushed the door open and led her inside with a gentle hold of her elbow.

It took a moment for her eyes to adjust to the dimness of the quarters, the only light being from a few lanterns, as the moon was not yet high enough to provide any light through the windows that sat behind the figure she now faced.

The man was bent over his desk, a hand worrying a spot in his forehead as he looked over what seemed to be a map of the area. Even in the low light she could see him well enough that a sense of familiarity began to tingle in her gut. Something about the movement in his fingers as he moved them over his temples and then through his dark hair. His hand rubbed the back of his neck, but he still didn't look up.

"What is it?" he asked.

The voice was indeed unmistakable.

"You!"

For a moment Aoife didn't realize she had spoken, but she quickly snapped her lips shut.

Collins gave her arm a squeeze in warning. His whole body had tensed beside her, but she only noticed for a second because all her focus was drawn to the man before her, who was in fact the pirate from the cove.

And he now looked up at her, his head angling slightly toward his left shoulder as he eyed her. Was that a laugh that escaped him? He clicked his tongue, and his shoulders slumped, though Aoife didn't know whether it was from exhaustion or exasperation.

"I should have known you'd do something stupid." That damn smirk she'd seen on him back in the cove pulled at his lips once more. "Again."

"You're the *captain?*" This was probably not how she was supposed to speak to a pirate captain, but she couldn't help it.

"Aye, and you'd be good to remember that when you speak to me." Though his words had a bite to them, his eyes still shone with a hint of mischievous humor, as if he found this whole scenario to be hilarious. And perhaps she would have agreed if she weren't the one standing before him waiting for his judgment. "Release her, Collins. She won't be going anywhere."

Aoife balked at this, but only internally. She wasn't about to let him see that he'd affected her in any way.

The captain narrowed his eyes at her. "Leave us."

The words were not for her, and for the first time since she'd stepped into his quarters, a spark of fear lit inside her chest.

She swallowed hard and gave Collins a dip of her chin in thanks for his gentle handling. In return the man raised a brow at her. Was that his way of wishing her good luck?

"Aye, Captain." Collins turned and made the three steps to the door in short time. Aoife held the captain's gaze, refusing to let the growing fear get the best of her—or at least keep him from seeing it. She didn't hear the door creak open. Instead, Collins spoke again. "All supplies are aboard, sir. We're set to leave when you are."

The captain didn't give his man another word; a slow nod was all the acknowledgment he offered. With that, Collins slipped out of the room, leaving Aoife to face this man who had intimidated and humiliated her in the alley. But hadn't she chosen to follow him? If she hadn't wanted to face him again, she probably should have picked a different pirate to shadow and sneak behind.

Yet here she was, and she had no idea what to expect.

Story of my life these days.

CHAPTER 14

DECLAN

DECLAN HAD CERTAINLY EXPECTED the girl to be a problem, but he'd assumed it would be later, when he'd returned from Foxhaven with more crew. He should have known she wasn't going to leave it when he'd insulted her back in that alley. She might not be the brightest, but she had spunk.

That makes her a liability.

He'd been captain all these years, and still some decisions didn't come as easily as others. He could command the crew with ease in battle, but in these slower moments when he didn't have adrenaline pushing him to act on instinct, his thoughts too often disrupted his focus. It was certainly difficult now to focus on the task at hand with Aoife staring wide-eyed at him. The lantern's flame flickered, its reflection bringing out hints of gold in her green eyes, making them appear... He couldn't describe the effect, exactly, but the word *magical* seemed fitting.

"What am I going to do with you?" He leaned back in his chair and pursed his lips. He made a point of looking her up and down. Intimidation was the name of the game when it came to piracy. He'd learned that lesson early enough during his first days as a cabin boy on the *Reckoning*.

"Take me with you." Her voice held no sign of the fear he saw playing at the corners of her eyes. Those damn eyes.

He shifted his own gaze down to his desk and the map laid out before him as he steepled his fingers below his chin. "Ah, don't you want to know my name?"

"I've given up hope of you telling me. You're the captain. What more do I need?"

"And did you know which ship you were boarding?"

"The *Siren's Song*. Am I supposed to be impressed?"

"Ah, I see pirate news doesn't reach the ears of the council then?"

"Is there something special about you and your ship?" Her eyes danced as she spoke. Spunky indeed. And also irritating.

He picked a piece of invisible lint from his shoulder. "Simply noting how the pirate lords don't bother to mention the *lesser* ships when they're warming the seats around your table. Among other things." The girl's cheeks blushed at his words, and he had to stifle a chuckle at the sight.

"Oh, they mention the *lesser* ships, but never by name. I suppose they don't deem you worthy of specific mention."

"Yet we are deemed worthy of being attacked on the regular."

"Why is that exactly? Isn't there an alliance among the pirates?" Aoife leaned closer, and any hint of the fear that had been tugging at her features was replaced with a curiosity he would have found endearing—maybe even charming—on anyone other than this girl who was ruining his plans yet again.

Plans. A curse ran through his mind. He needed to get back on track and take care of this girl so he could focus on the important matter at hand.

He didn't answer her question but repeated his own. "What am I to do with you exactly?"

While the question was rhetorical, uttered more for himself than for her, he wasn't surprised when she opened her mouth to answer. He held up a hand to cut her off and shook his head slowly as he pondered his options.

"If I take you with us, I can't guarantee your safety. And even if I can protect you from the men, I don't have time to deal with a distracted crew. Even with you dressed like that, a woman on board doesn't help matters."

She moved to speak, but he again stopped her, this time with the sharpest of glares. If he was going to allow her to remain on his ship, she needed to learn some damn respect.

"But it is obvious you are desperate to leave." He could imagine the snarky response she wanted to utter. *I told you as much, you idiot.* And he nearly laughed at the thought. But she stood before him, silent, her gaze like cold steel. "I fear if I were to send you away, you would get yourself in a much worse situation than you find yourself in now. And while I shouldn't care—and in fact, I don't—there's no harm in granting you passage. And so I'll allow you to stay. But only until we reach Foxhaven. There you'll leave us and do so peacefully."

He waited for her reply, but she still stood staring at him. They studied each other for what seemed like hours but was likely only a few seconds. But a few seconds of this silence was enough to drive him mad. He refused to be the next to speak though. He wouldn't yield any of his power on his ship, especially to her.

Aoife dipped her chin. "Thank you."

"So it is agreed. We'll provide you passage to our next stop, and then we will part ways."

But even as he said the words, he felt the niggling voice in the far corner of his mind pointing out that she could help in his plans. He had refused to entertain that idea before, but now she was here on his ship, in his care already, so what did it matter if he chose to keep her on for the remainder of the job? Still, that decision could be made later.

"There are some logistics to work out, of course," he said. "We are not set up to have women aboard our ship. We are but a crew of crude men with thoughts and drives as dirty as our bodies. And I certainly can't have my crew distracted by your presence in their quarters."

Aoife squirmed, but only slightly. So slightly Declan could only assume she was using all her might to not let him see how uncomfortable she was. And how little planning she'd actually done when deciding to sneak onto his ship. Or any ship for that matter. What had she been thinking?

He leaned forward against his desk, once again steepling his fingers, this time in front of his lips. He kept his focus on her as he released an exaggerated sigh, his shoulders drooping as if the weight of the breath leaving him would force him to collapse onto the desk in front of him. *I should have been an actor, not a pirate.*

There was something about watching this girl's face as both of them waited for the other to speak. Such pride, conviction, need. Mixed with a youthful innocence he had only ever seen on this island. He pushed that thought aside. No, he needed to focus and make a decision. Yet he couldn't deny how fun it was to watch her battle the desire to stand her ground and flee from his sight and give up on this notion of running.

"So where will I stay then?" Aoife jutted out her chin as she spoke, and though she hardened her expression and set her jaw, he could see the fear return. No, perhaps not fear. It was more like worry that tugged at her, betraying her brave front.

"Now, I could displace my officers and let you have their quarters, but they don't deserve to be pushed below decks with the rest of the crew."

"What about your..." Declan raised his brows at her as a smirk crept across his lips again, and she trailed off.

"And here I thought you said my charms had no effect on you."

"Oh, I didn't mean it like that. Why can't I stay in here? Without you?" She held his gaze, almost daring him to make another joke that would be his last. Sands, he wanted to laugh at her again, but he managed to shut it down. As much as she annoyed him—and screwed up his plans—he had to admit it was fun to mess with her. He shook his head slowly.

"That wouldn't do at all, I'm afraid. I've grown rather attached to my accommodations. I've worked hard, done some things— No, this space is mine."

Aoife took a half step forward and opened her mouth, likely to protest, but he held up his hand to stop her.

"I wasn't finished." He spat the words as his annoyance crept back up. She might be cute, but her inability to listen was beginning to really grate on him. "You will stay in here—"

"Thank you," she muttered as her shoulders relaxed and a breath escaped her, as if she'd been holding it this whole time.

"—with me."

"What? No!" Her eyes grew wide, and her head began to shake quickly in protest.

Declan leaned back in his chair and propped his boots up on his desk, his arms sliding back behind his head. "Trust me, princess…"

"I'm not a princess."

"Excuse me. Heir." She winced and glared at him. "Fine. Aoife. Trust me when I say this isn't my ideal either, but between sharing quarters with you and having to share a cramped space with my officers, I'll take the former."

"I guess I do smell better."

Such an odd time for an attempt at humor. What an odd, perplexing creature she was. So different from Cait and the other women he'd met over the years. But maybe this was simply how all heirs were, all women who were raised in the council hall.

"Aye, but that won't last long, I fear. Life aboard a ship tends to force us to forget the luxuries we knew when we had a home on land."

"But where do I sleep?" Aoife glanced around the quarters, and he realized she likely wasn't familiar with the layout of a ship, particularly a captain's quarters.

"Would you like a tour of your accommodations then?" He flashed her a smile—not a smirk—but quickly smoothed it away as he chided himself. *What are you doing? You don't have time to play around like this.* "It won't take long," he said, as much to himself as to her.

Declan rose from his seat and waved an arm as he said, "This would be the main office, of course. It's not much, but it allows me a space to meet with my officers, to plan, to strategize, to gossip about the crew and those we meet in ports." She didn't laugh.

He pointed to a doorway off to his left. "There's a small dining room in there."

"You don't eat with the crew then?" He grimaced at her, and she huffed. "Of course not. How silly of me."

He turned and stepped to the door nestled between his bookcases on the opposite wall. He motioned for her to follow and bit back his annoyance when she took her steps with hesitation. Maybe this would take longer than planned if she kept moving like a snail through honey. When she finally moved to stand beside him, glancing up at him without turning her head fully, he continued. "And these are the sleeping quarters."

She peered in through the open door before looking back at him.

"It's so small," she said.

"Not something any man likes to hear from a lady, miss." He let out a sigh to cover up yet another laugh that threatened to escape. "Alas, we can't all live in the grand council hall, but these are the most comfortable quarters on the ship. And they are now yours." He dipped his head toward her.

"And where will you be sleeping?" Again she eyed him from the side, not fully turning toward him.

"Despite your quick judgment of this bed, it is large enough for both of us." As expected, she turned to him, her eyes widening again and her mouth opening to speak. He shut her down with another silent reprimand. "Don't worry, Aoife. I vow to be the most upstanding and respectable of men."

"You're a pirate."

"Even pirates have manners. We simply decide who is worthy of receiving them from us."

"And I am? Worthy?" Her brow scrunched up, sending creases across her forehead, barely visible behind her poorly chopped chestnut hair.

"Worthy enough, I suppose. But if you'd prefer to take your chances with the crew below deck, or even in my officers' quarters, by all means."

She took a step toward the door to study the small bedroom, and he wondered what she thought of his simple space.

Why should you care what she thinks?

Yet still, these were his private quarters, and while it was just a room aboard a ship, he still felt as if he were having his soul laid bare before her. Tommy and Gavin and the cabin boys had been in here a million times, but those men already knew him and many of his secrets. And he had never had the same urge to impress them as he did with her, an urge that only grew as he watched her inspect his space.

The bed was indeed large enough for the two of them, and he tried to ignore the tension that started in his chest and sank to his gut—and then lower—at the thought of lying beside her. He shoved the image aside and turned away before she could have a chance to sense how the thought affected him.

From behind him she spoke again. "Why can't you sleep on the floor?"

He started to walk toward the door. He didn't have time to discuss this further. Reaching for the door handle, he looked back over his shoulder at her. "The floor would be bad for my back. And it is only for two days, miss. You have my word I will not touch you. You're safe in here—from me and from my crew—for the short time you are here. Now, feel free to get acquainted with your temporary home, freshen up, rest, relax. You've had a long day, I'm sure. And I need to attend to things so we can keep to our schedule."

He didn't wait for a response or a glare, but instead turned and exited the room as quickly as possible. He'd wasted more than enough time trying to make a stowaway comfortable on his ship.

Had he gone soft? *Some pirate you are. A lass comes aboard your ship and you give her your bed?*

A true gentleman would have agreed to sleep on the floor or bunk with his officers, perhaps.

But he was no gentleman. He was a pirate, manners or no.

CHAPTER 15
AOIFE

As soon as the captain had left, Aoife made her way across his quarters toward the door. She wasn't sure why she did it. Perhaps to ensure he was really gone and she was truly alone. Especially before she undressed for bed.

He was right. She was tired.

She laid a hand on the rough wood of the door, its texture a stark contrast to the pampered softness of her pale skin. So much set her apart from the crowd she was trying to hide among. Her cleanliness. Her feminine features. Her softness. Everything about her screamed non-pirate. And normally she would have been proud of that, but it wouldn't help her here.

Perhaps she should rethink this plan, but the distant shouting outside the door kept her from focusing on the task at hand. A yawn escaped her, reminding her of the exhaustion. It had been a long day. Had Lani truly been—exiled—this morning? A sharp pain hit her sternum at the thought of Lani dead. Not exiled. How could she survive a world without her sister's smile, her quiet humor, her silliness, the way she'd always teased Aoife for her absentminded, awkward nature? She'd never see Lani's face again or hear her laughter. She'd managed to avoid this pain all afternoon and evening, preoccupied with the simple need to escape and get away. But now she had nothing to do but wait, so the pain and torment—and the knowledge that it was all her fault—came flooding in against her will.

The weight of it all threatened to push her to the floor, the sharpness in her chest seeming to crush her, and her shoulders bent as she curved around it, as if she might fold up and disappear into the grief. She'd expected to cry and sob, but she must have been too tired to do so.

Or you're such an awful person you can't cry for your dead sister.

That thought intensified the pain, causing slight tremors to course through her, but still no tears came. She leaned against the door, forcing herself to remain upright. She couldn't bear the thought of him coming back in here and finding her curled up on the floor like a baby. Of course, if he came in at this moment, he'd have to push her off the door.

Still, she didn't move. She remained there, head pressed against the wood, warm from the moist sea air.

The voice inside her became a jumbled mess of self-loathing, reminding her how she'd betrayed the person closest to her and now she was utterly alone in the world. Except for the man she'd have to share a bed with for two nights. She steeled herself. She could do that. Sure, it was improper. And unnerving. But this wasn't a holiday. It was about survival. And if survival meant sleeping next to a man who annoyed the living daylights out of her, she'd do it.

Who was this man exactly? She finally had gotten his name, from Collins, but that didn't help her much. She kicked herself for not listening to all the tales told by the pirate lords' crews. She recalled the number of times she had heard—from all three pirate lords—that the young captain of the *Siren's Song* was getting too big for his ship and needed to be put in his place. When they'd started to boast of how they'd kept him from scoring some bounty, stopping him from reaching a port here or an island there, she had tuned them out. Pirate strategy and conquests were far from her areas of interest.

And yet she had a vague recollection of the stories she'd heard about this young captain. A captain so brutal he rivaled the first pirates who had sailed the seas immediately following the signing of the treaty. While the lords hadn't described his actions in detail—being in the company of the council ladies, after all—it had not been hard to envision all manner of heinous actions, the very kind the council and the people of Cregah had vowed to keep from their shores.

She found it hard to believe this was the same man from those stories. He'd been so polite, so cordial. Or at least more than she'd ever expected. And his quarters seemed far from those of a ruthless barbarian.

Straightening, she pushed away from the door, glancing around at the rich wood and sparse furnishings. It certainly wasn't like her lavish home at the council hall. There was little, if anything, here that didn't serve a purpose, didn't have a use. While her life had been one of leisure and simple enjoyments—music, art, books— the state of his quarters indicated a life focused on work. Except for the bookshelves along the wall. Far from empty. What need did a pirate have for books? Did they describe pirate strategy? Maybe they were merely ship logs or journals in which he took note of all his victories. And losses. She felt a pull toward those shelves, a need to feel the rich leather and softness of the pages against her fingers, to see what this man kept and stored. What he valued.

But voices outside the door pulled her attention away from the shelves and the books. They must have been just on the opposite side, because she could hear them more clearly than any of the other noises from the crew readying to sail.

"Captain, it's not right."

Aoife didn't recognize the voice, but it had a youthful yet experienced tone to it.

"I strongly advise against this." The man must have had some influence with the captain to be allowed to offer such an opinion and counsel. An officer perhaps.

"Aye, Tommy, I know," the captain said.

She waited to hear more from him, but it was the other man, Tommy, who spoke again. "The crew doesn't like it. You know it's bad luck. It will not bode well, especially if we're trying to get to the sound and back within such a short time frame."

"Mere superstition." The captain huffed in frustration.

"Perhaps, but superstition has a mighty effect on the ability of men to focus on their duties."

"Self-fulfilling prophecy that is. She's only here until we reach Foxhaven."

"You mean to leave her there?" Tommy's shock was evident in his words, even through the thick wood of the cabin door. And though Aoife didn't know what the man looked like, she could still picture the expression he must have had on his face as he asked the question.

"I can't risk taking her further. It's not ideal, but she's not my concern."

"You sure about that?" Tommy seemed to be toeing a fine line with that, and Aoife braced herself for the reprimand that was sure to come.

"Watch yourself, Tommy." The captain's words didn't carry the harshness she'd expected. The men must have been close friends.

"Excuse my boldness, Declan." Aoife started at the captain's first name being uttered. Close friends indeed. She pressed her ear closer to the door, not wanting to miss anything as their voices became softer.

"She remains. Until port. And while she's with us, she is under my protection. No one is to touch her or bother her. I have promised her that much. Once she's off the ship though…" Declan's voice trailed off, and Aoife felt a sudden pang of fear.

What should she expect in that port? What should she be preparing for? She had only aimed to get off Cregah. She hadn't thought about where she might be heading and how it might be far worse than the land from which she'd fled.

"Aye, sir. Understood."

Footsteps neared them, and someone else joined the conversation, but too quiet for her to hear.

Declan answered. "Very well, Gavin. As my quarters are currently occupied, we'll meet in the officers' quarters. Fetch Mikkel and meet us there."

There must have been a nod in response, but Aoife didn't hear anything more than footsteps walking away from the door.

Her body felt heavy under the grief and uncertainty. What she wouldn't give for a hot bath like only the staff at the hall could draw, with dried flowers from the gardens and soothing milk. She doubted she'd ever have such luxury again. And here she was on an old, smelly ship with nothing but the clothes on her back, sharing quarters with a man she only knew from bits and pieces of stories she'd overheard.

Another yawn reminded her once again of the weariness she'd managed to ignore while eavesdropping, and now she didn't care who might lie beside her in the bed. She simply needed to sleep.

She took a step away from the door, but at the same moment the ship lurched forward, and she stumbled to the left, slamming into the wall and smarting her shoulder. This was going to be difficult to get used to. The ship swayed, gently rocking as it began its journey away from port. At least the captain wasn't here to watch her wobble across the small quarters. To steady herself she used the desk on the right and the bookshelves on the left, too tired and too focused on not falling to bother perusing them as she'd wanted to. She'd have the next two days to do so.

She turned into the room and lowered herself onto the edge of the bed, surprised by the softness of the mattress. She'd expected something coarser, like straw. But this reminded her of the feather beds she'd grown up with.

Probably looted from some poor merchants.

She should have been more disgusted by the thought, but in this moment, with her limbs and joints screaming for rest, she was thankful for such accommodations. Without bothering to kick off her boots or remove any of the unfamiliar clothing, she lay down, closed her eyes, and let herself be lulled to sleep by the rocking of the ship.

THE SUN STREAMED in through the windows, its light bending with the waves in the glass as it warmed Aoife's face. Keeping her eyes closed, she stretched her legs, perplexed by the heavy weight of her feet. And for the briefest moment, with the softness of the feather mattress cradling her, she forgot where she was and what she'd done.

And then it hit her.

The roll of the ship beneath her bones. The weight of reality crushing her chest, sending the feeling of a million creeping legs over her skin. Her breaths quickened, and she clenched her eyes shut, but it only made it all worse.

Slow it down. Breathe.

She repeated the words to herself, trying to remember all the things the doctor had recommended for these attacks.

What had the doctor suggested? What was the phrase she was supposed to use?

Something about fear and safety.

Even though I'm afraid, I'm safe.

The mantra helped little when she remembered where she was. In the middle of the Aisling. On a ship full of pirates. Well-mannered pirates or no, she felt far from safe.

Her stomach growled a mantra of its own, which only intensified her longing to be back on land, in the council hall, with the staff bringing breakfast. She couldn't remember the last time she'd eaten, but it must have been a while ago given how earnestly her stomach complained.

She needed to get herself under control if she was going to dare walk anywhere in search of food.

Breathe. I am safe. I am safe.

She willed herself to believe it, and as her hunger mixed with the nausea from the ship's movement, she forced her eyes to remain open—which seemed to soothe the rolling of her stomach.

She'd nearly gotten her breathing slowed and the tingling in her chest eased when a movement beside her had her freezing in place.

Holding her breath, she inched her head toward the movement.

Captain McCallagh—Declan—lay on his side, facing her. His eyes were closed, so she dared let herself take in his full form. He lay atop the blankets, as she did. Whether it was because he hadn't wanted to disturb her or because of the heat in the cabin, she couldn't be sure. Not that it mattered, she supposed.

His white undershirt and loose bottoms left much to the imagination, and she was more than okay with that. If it weren't for his attitude, she might have found his face pleasant enough. But even in sleep he looked troubled, as if his dreams were stressful and tiring. While she'd managed a dreamless sleep that left her more rested than she'd expected—even with the panic she'd woken to—she could see the muscles in his forehead and jaw tensing from thoughts or images she wasn't privy to.

What do I care what's bothering him?

Care? No, she didn't care. It was curiosity. Nothing more.

She merely wanted to know who he was—this man who had taken her into his care and kept her under his protection. The way he'd said it yesterday, when he'd told her he would watch out for her, even for the two days, seemed like it had pained him. Likely he was annoyed having her aboard, and she couldn't blame him, could she? He'd had plans, an agenda to follow, and she'd mucked it up by trespassing on his ship.

Had there been a better option? She doubted she would have received better treatment from any of the other captains in port. Not even the lords she'd met at the council hall, even those who were potential matches for her. There was no wooing or courting with the matching process. They were matched by lottery, completely by chance, drawing a name from a bowl. It had seemed so odd to her, like a game— a somewhat unfair game, as the oldest heir would get first pick, though Aoife's situation would have been better than Darienn's, who would have been stuck with whomever was left after Lani and Aoife had selected. And now, Darienn would get her pick of the three—or maybe all three. Aoife wasn't sure how that was all going to work out now that there was only one heir remaining.

Not your problem anymore.

She shoved all thoughts of her old life aside, trying instead to focus on her current situation and wondering how she was going to possibly prepare for wherever they were heading.

She hoped to drive all the unnerving questions from her mind by studying his face again, as if she could deduce exactly who he was behind that stupid smirk.

There was something roguishly handsome about the stubble covering his jaw. And his hair. Most pirates Aoife had met wore theirs long, but not this captain. She wondered how he kept it so nicely cut while at sea, thinking of the shoddy job she'd done on her own hair the day before. And why didn't he keep his hair all one length? She would have thought it easier to manage without the longer pieces falling into his eyes, as they were doing now.

Without thinking, she lifted a hand to move the hair away from his eyes, but before she touched it, his lips moved and she froze.

"Morning, miss." His eyes remained closed, and she held her breath. Maybe she could pretend to be sleeping, though not with her eyes wide and staring at him. She should clamp them shut, but everything had frozen, and her body refused to listen or move.

"It's not nice to stare."

How did he know?

Slowly his eyes crept open, and he peered at her through the lock of hair she'd wanted to touch. He raised a brow, and she blinked, unsure of what to say or do.

"Ah, I've rendered you speechless. With my good looks, no doubt." He stretched a kink out of his neck before propping himself up on an elbow, his hand unnervingly close to her breast. She pulled back from him, desperate to put additional space between them.

She ignored his comments. "What is Foxhaven like exactly? Should I be nervous?" She kicked herself for not showing more confidence, but—rested or not —she didn't have the energy to drum up any, even for show.

"Perhaps. Probably should have thought of that before you trespassed and forced me to give you passage." He rolled over onto his back, his eyes turning to the wooden beams overhead. His linen shirt pulled tight across his chest, which was still as impressive as when she'd first seen him in the cove. She cleared her throat, as if that would also clear away the unfamiliar—and unwanted—warmth growing within, and she forced her eyes away from him, focusing on the wall beyond.

"I didn't have much choice." Her voice came out a near whisper, so low she wondered if he'd hear.

"There's always a choice. Good outcomes? That's another story. But a choice always remains."

She pondered his words and chewed on that basic truth.

She'd had a choice. That was true. Stay in the council, be matched to one of the pirate lords, rule over Cregah and administer justice with brutality under the guise of peace and care. Or run.

Had she taken the coward's way out? Even heading toward unknown hardship on the sea and in distant lands, she had run. She could have stayed and served. Maybe she could have changed things, worked from the inside out to right the wrongs. But no. That seemed impossible.

Her stomach rumbled again, loud in the silence hovering in the bedchamber.

She glanced at him. "Is there food?"

He turned his head toward her, his brow furrowed.

"What?" she asked, as if this was a natural and obvious question. To her it was, and her stomach grumbled again to make that point clear to him.

"Nothing. Simply seemed out of place for the deep conversation we were having."

"You thought that was deep? You merely pointed out the obvious."

He scoffed. "So obvious you hadn't thought of it until I mentioned it, eh?"

She glared at him. Why couldn't she hide things better? Had she looked so surprised to be told she'd had a choice?

"Food?" she noted again, and he grumbled out a sigh.

"Yes, we do have food, though nothing quite as nice as what I'm sure you're used to getting."

"At this point, I'll take whatever I can get." She lifted herself up onto her elbows and made to get up from the bed.

"Careful what you say. You might get your wish."

"All I really wish for right now is food. So if you could just tell me where to go to get some, I'll take my leave." She stood, or rather wobbled, on her feet as the ship kept up its bobbing. Steady or not, she managed to face him, well aware that her hair likely looked as disheveled as her clothes.

He cocked his head and sat up. "You won't be going anywhere."

She moved to protest, but he continued. "The food has come to you." And with that, he pointed out the door, and she took several uneven steps backward until she was in the main room of his quarters. A glance around showed nothing but his jacket flung over his desk chair, the map rolled up and set aside.

His annoyance came out on a breath. "There. In the dining room."

Right. His cabin was larger than she'd remembered. Her stomach grumbled again, urging her across the worn carpet, the reds and golds of which had become faded from the sea air and boots scuffing across it.

The dining room was scarcely bigger than her closet back at the council hall, but then, on a ship one couldn't have lavish ballrooms and seating for thirty. Atop the table she spied a modest yet fresh-enough-looking spread. She didn't bother to pull out one of the four chairs before reaching to pick up some hard cheese with her left hand and a handful of grapes with her right. Declan came up beside her just in time to witness her stuffing her mouth full of food.

"You shouldn't eat so quickly. Or so much," he warned.

She grumbled at him and turned back to the food to grab a roll. He kicked the chair out away from the table. "Sit. Before you get sick."

His words seemed to bring her back to reality—she was on a ship, rolling and tossing across the water—and her stomach turned. She plopped into the seat and braced herself against the table with her forearms. She refused to look at him, refused to see that know-it-all smirk on his face.

"You're welcome," he said and settled into the chair to her right, leaning back. But he didn't touch any of the food.

She swallowed. "Not hungry?"

"Oh, I am, but I prefer to give myself a bit of time to wake up before I gorge myself."

"Sleep well?"

His eyes narrowed at her. "What next? Will we chat about the weather?"

Aoife ground her teeth until they ached. Why couldn't he just be civil and act like a regular human being?

Because he's a pirate. There's nothing regular about him.

"Fine. We don't have to talk." She gave him a shrug and turned her attention back to the roll in her hand, picking it apart and placing small pieces on her tongue. She hoped he wouldn't notice her heeding his advice to slow down.

"We can talk. I simply prefer not to talk about trivialities."

"Ah, so you're a deep thinker then, Captain McCallagh?" He ignored her baiting, and that irked her more than any retort he could have uttered. "There is nothing trivial about inquiring about one's health, you know."

"Only when one genuinely cares about the answer, and I doubt wholeheartedly that you care one bit about how I am faring or how I slept."

He was right. Or rather, he should have been right. She shouldn't care about how he was feeling, not after he'd been so brazen with her in that alley. Not after he'd insisted on her sharing his bed. She shouldn't care. Yet, the way his brow had furrowed in his sleep and his jaw had been so tightly clenched concerned her for some reason. Something was bothering him, and she wanted to know why and what. But could she dare to simply ask him?

"What had you so upset?" Aoife kept her voice and her gaze low.

"When?" The bite in his tone had disappeared, and he seemed more...normal.

"While you were sleeping." She risked a glance at him through her lashes, only to find him watching her, his thumb rubbing against his lower lip. She waited, wondering if he was going to answer or if he was going to retreat and evade. Would he make a joke, or would he trust her with the truth?

His shoulders slumped under an invisible weight, and she held her breath, not wanting to risk scaring him away from telling her what that weight might be.

"Well, if you must know, I am dealing with an unexpected guest on my ship, and tending to her is keeping me from tending to the rather important business I have at hand elsewhere. And now, instead of planning and meeting with my men, I'm having to babysit."

She ground her teeth again as bitterness coated her tongue, but she forced herself to toss him a nonchalant shrug before reaching for a piece of salted pork.

"Fine, don't tell me."

"Aye, yes, in fact, my troubles do go beyond you and the little wrench you've thrown into my life." He sat up and leaned toward her. "But if you think I'm going to confide in you simply because we're sleeping beside each other for a couple nights, or because I offered to ensure your safety whilst aboard this ship, then you're as crazy as I am for not taking you back to the council myself."

And with those words, he shoved his chair back, the noise of old wood scraping so loud it made her cringe. He was out of the dining room in two steps, and she turned to see him grab his jacket and shove his feet into his boots before heading out the door, letting it close with a bang.

Although she hadn't learned what had been bothering him, she still turned smugly back to the food. She'd gotten to him, and that was fun in itself, perhaps better than actually learning the truth.

CHAPTER 16
DECLAN

Declan stomped out of his quarters and at once scolded himself for acting like a moody child. His hands fisted, nails stinging his palms, but it only made him feel more irritated with himself for not remaining calm.

The sea air rushed past him, pushing his hair into his eyes. He pushed it back with his hand before stepping out onto the deck of his ship. His men were scattered about, some tending to the rigging while others eyed the horizon. One younger crew member noticed Declan from where he was cleaning part of the deck, which was likely still bloody from the previous skirmish, and dipped his chin in greeting. Declan returned the gesture before striding over to the stairs and up to the quarter-deck, where he found his officers chatting at the helm.

"Slept well, I see," Tommy offered, straightening the gray wool cap on his head. Why the man insisted on wearing the damn hat in this heat, sweltering and sticky even in these early morning hours, Declan could never understand. Normally he might tease about it, give him grief for having such an attachment to an article of clothing, but he was in no mood this morning.

"Well enough," Declan answered and leaned against the deck railing, looking out over his ship and his crew.

He couldn't stop his mind from playing through a number of irksome retorts the girl might have uttered had she been here. He should have left her on that dock or taken her back to the council. What would they have paid him for her return? What would they have granted? What might they have asked him to do for them?

A shiver rose up his spine, but he ignored it. No point in thinking about the what-ifs. He'd done what he'd done, and now he'd have to figure out the next step forward.

"If I may, Captain." It was Tommy again, but he'd inched closer, his head now near Declan's shoulder as he said in a whisper, "Did you get what you needed?"

Declan's brow rose, and he nearly laughed when a shocked expression spread across Gavin's face. Tommy apparently was incapable of speaking quietly.

"Not even close," he said.

"That's a shame." Tommy took up the spot beside Declan, mimicking his stance against the railing, both men ignoring Gavin's confusion over their conversation.

"Aye. It is."

"You have time though."

"Not much. With these favorable winds and Gavin's skill"—he threw a nod in the helmsman's direction—"we'll be in Foxhaven on schedule."

"More than enough time, I should think. Especially for a man such as yourself."

"No one likes a kiss-ass, Tommy, especially me. You've been with me long enough to know that."

"And yet, here we are."

Declan groaned and dropped his head into his hands, hoping his crew would merely assume he was tired. Though he didn't care too much if they knew how frustrated he was. They'd seen him—and stood by him—in similar enough situations and had continued to support him as their captain. Perhaps it was the honesty with which he ran his ship that earned such loyalty.

"I simply don't think I can stand to be in the same room with her. You know, when she's conscious. And talking. Always pestering me. Her voice. It's like the grating sound of iron against iron."

"And yet that noise always leads to something good, yes? Sharpened iron?" Tommy gave him an elbow to the arm. "Let her sharpen your iron, as it were. Use her. Or do you have another idea for how to gain the information we need to complete this job?"

Declan straightened away from the railing, turned, and leaned back against it, noticing how Gavin whistled and glanced off to the side to show he wasn't eavesdropping or butting in on their conversation. "What do you think, Gavin?"

Gavin feigned surprise as he turned to him. "About what, Captain?"

"Oh, come off it. We both know you're listening." He gestured to Tommy, who was still looking out over the deck.

Tommy didn't turn but called over his shoulder, "Speak, Gavin."

But before Gavin could utter his own opinion on the matter, heavy steps approached, coming up the stairs. The three men turned to see Mikkel trudging up the steps awkwardly. Declan often wondered how the man had survived so long without the sea tossing him overboard.

"Captain," Mikkel started, only offering the slightest of nods to the other officers present.

"What is it?" Declan's words came out not harsh but to the point, the way Mikkel preferred. He hated mindless chitchat. Quite unlike Tommy and Gavin, who had to be nudged through conversations and guided past all the rabbit holes they found as they spoke.

"The men are restless, sir."

Declan looked around, searching for any sign of the restlessness.

"They hide it well enough, but there are murmurings, " Mikkel said.

"Murmurings?"

"Aye, they're nervous. About—"

"Her," Declan offered.

"Yessir. The girl."

"Woman," Tommy interjected over Declan's shoulder, and Declan elbowed him in the gut.

Mikkel shot Tommy a glare. "Either way. They're nervous all the same."

"What is there to be nervous about exactly?" Declan asked, raising his arms as he spoke. "We have good wind. We're making good time. We have food in our bellies, and we got at least an ounce of rest at Morshan. Yes?"

Mikkel shuffled his long legs, marking an invisible line in the wood of the deck. "It's true enough, I suppose, but it's not the present that has them uneasy. It's what's coming. Even if we're rid of her in Foxhaven, they worry it will not bode well for us later on."

"So what you're saying is, even if we leave her in two days' time, they worry having her here now will bring us ill fortune later."

Mikkel nodded before tucking his dull brown hair back behind his ear, his eyes as stern and serious as the weathered lines in his face. The bo'sun was older than Declan and his officers, but not by much. Still, they'd been grateful for his years of experience and the respect he garnered from the crew.

Declan kept leaning against the railing, trying to keep his expression casual. "So there's nothing that can actually be done now to stop that ill fate." It wasn't a question.

Mikkel again fidgeted uneasily. Declan waited, knowing what his bo'sun was going to suggest. What the men wanted.

"They'd like to be rid of her now, sir," Mikkel said.

"Ah, yes," Declan started.

He turned back to look over his crew. They'd gotten some rest in Morshan; that was sure. Those who hadn't been left back at the hospital on that rock were strong, rested, and bitter, and they now craved something he couldn't readily give them. Retribution. Revenge. The desire to deal a mighty blow—or maybe execute a covert attack—against those who had killed their brethren and lightened their pockets, keeping them from bounties they would have surely snatched. And now, unable to exact revenge outright, they looked for some way to quell that need.

And throwing the girl overboard? He could understand the impulse. Especially after spending time with her.

"But no, Mikkel. That won't be an option. You see, I've promised to protect her while she's aboard the ship. She has my word. I will not go ba—"

"You are a pirate, are you not?" Mikkel dared to interrupt, and Declan's body tensed, from the toes in his boots to the muscles in his jaw.

Perhaps he should have chosen to run his ship like the other captains, drive his crew more ruthlessly, doling out harsh punishments for any sign of insolence and disrespect. But he'd chosen to be different, chosen to treat his crew with respect, expecting the same in return. He saved his ruthlessness for those who needed it and deserved it, and he earned his crew's loyalty by showing he could lead them to glory and riches without beating them down.

But this affront from Mikkel could not stand. His heart pounded against his sternum, and all his options swirled in his mind. He needed to grasp one and act quickly.

He stepped in close to Mikkel until their faces were mere inches apart. He kept his words low enough that the others couldn't hear.

"Aye, Mikkel. I am a pirate. And a captain. Your captain. If you don't like how things are run on this ship, or how I handle my own personal word and code of honor, you are free to leave. Now. But if you would like to remain my bo'sun, would like your share of the bounty we're after, then I advise you watch your damn mouth and don't interrupt me again, or I'll have Tommy here place you in the brig until you can learn your own bit of respect and courtesy."

Mikkel inched back, his features a mix of frustration and concentration as the muscles along his jaw tensed. He dipped his chin in a slow nod, never shifting his gaze away from his captain's. "Of course, Captain. My apologies. I spoke rashly. The crew's unease must be grating on me."

"All is forgiven." Declan stepped back. "But do ensure the men know. The girl is off-limits. I find out someone has laid a hand on her, and they won't have a hand to lay on any other woman or themselves. Understand?"

Another nod.

Declan continued. "As for the restlessness and the superstitious bullshit, remind them they are the crew of the *Siren's Song*. Superstition holds no power here. We'll pick up new men, be rid of the lass, and be on our way to retrieve the greatest of treasures they could imagine."

"I'll tell them, but I don't know that they'll listen."

"They trust you, Mikkel. As I do," he said, clapping the man's shoulder before gesturing back to the deck. "Now go. Do your job."

Without another word, Mikkel turned and scurried down the stairs. Had Declan been too lenient, too soft?

He knew he didn't sound like other pirates. He knew his words and his actions and his values put him at odds with others in this line of work. Unlike most of the men who sailed the seas, he'd come from an educated background. His father had been his teacher while his mother and sister had run the pub. He and his father had pored over books, any books they could get their hands on, discussing the ins and outs of various figures and characters, discussing the war strategies they saw displayed in the history texts—why some had failed and others had succeeded. His father had instilled in him this love for learning, a love for the written word and the benefit of studying—especially history.

It was during that studying that he'd learned about the dagger. The dagger was all but lost to myth and legend. No one spoke of it anymore, except perhaps in children's tales. But in an old text, which he still kept in his quarters, he and his father had read about the rise and fall of the King of Tyshaly.

It was this knowledge that had sent them on this quest, and while he didn't owe it to his father to find it, he did hope finding the dagger would be the way to earn his freedom from the pirate lords, to finally gain victory over their larger ships and crews, to be able to—after enough wealth was acquired and enough loot was taken—set up a home where he could rest and read and forget all about the pain of the past.

Ah, to rest. So much standing in his way before he could do that.

Not the least of which was his sister's need for the dagger first.

He needed a plan, but so far he—with the help of Tommy, his master gunner, and Gavin—had not yet devised the best way to get into the council hall and retrieve the fae sisters. He needed intel. He needed an in. And his in was currently in his quarters, likely now sick from all the food she'd been engulfing. Never mind that he wasn't helping the situation by denying her the freedom to leave the cabin for some fresh air. He might need to ease up on that, but he couldn't trust her to not do something stupid, cross the wrong man, slip and fall overboard. Who knew what trouble she was capable of getting into?

A throat cleared behind him, and he turned. Tommy's brows were raised, eyes aglow with his usual brand of curiosity and humor.

"What is it?" Declan asked. He probably should have hired someone other than his childhood friend to be his quartermaster, and he often wondered if the crew distrusted Tommy because the two were so close. But it had never seemed an issue. Not to say it couldn't quickly become one. Especially if this job went sour.

"You know, I think Mikkel half expected you to stick a dagger in him."

"I think he would have actually preferred it," Declan said, releasing a sigh. He did try to keep his exasperation and doubt from showing when he was out in the open, visible to his whole crew, who could always be looking for a reason, a weakness, to exploit and overthrow him as captain.

"What man wants to be gutted though?" Tommy gave a shrug and then scratched at his forehead. "Plus, we're already short crew. Losing a bo'sun wouldn't help us."

"And if I lose the entire crew to mutiny? What then?"

Tommy scoffed. "That's unlikely. For now."

Declan straightened at the words. "What do you mean, 'for now'?"

"I'm only saying I don't know if the crew can survive many more run-ins with the lords. They need some victories, Captain. And they need them soon. Or they very well may look for a captain who can deliver—either on this ship or another that would have them."

Declan ran a hand through his hair and breathed the sea air deep into his lungs, as if the brine could preserve his place as captain, preserve the honor and respect he'd worked so hard to earn. If only it were that easy. But he knew Tommy was right. They needed a victory. They needed information.

As if Tommy could read his mind, he spoke again, leaning close and keeping his voice down. "Like I said last night, we need the girl, Declan. And what she knows.

No one else here has stepped a foot inside that hall, and we can't risk everything on rumors heard and passed on by drunken men."

"Aye. I know. Don't like it, but you're right." He pushed himself away from the railing and started down the stairs. "Gavin, keep us on track."

"And where are you going?" Tommy asked.

"To find out what she knows."

"Good luck!" Tommy called, and Declan bit back a swear. He was going to need more than luck to get her to cooperate.

CHAPTER 17
CAIT

CAIT MOVED the rag across the bar, wiping up the last of the spills from the previous night's patrons. Even after so many years spent running this place, taking up where her mother had left off, somehow she still loved it. Sure, the patrons could smell better, could act more like gentlemen instead of the pirates they were, but all in all, she was content. Happy.

Until she remembered where her pub was located and the heavy hand that wielded its power over this port and all the villages and people on the island.

She settled against the bar, hips digging into the old wood, shoulders caving under the pressure, hand gripping the towel as if it were a lifeline to her sanity or a dream she'd had long ago as a child and feared would fade the older she got. Declan had left the night before, and no doubt he'd noticed the poorly disguised woman who had trailed after him. Cait didn't need to worry about her brother. He had a good head on his shoulders. He could handle one silly woman. How she'd thought a set of clothes and a poor haircut would work... Cait shook her head at the image in her mind.

Declan could manage, for sure, but would the woman delay him on this job? She couldn't. He needed the dagger as much as the Rogues did. Though, there was a small part of her that wondered if he truly intended to bring it back to her or if he'd take it and run, use it to conquer the lords.

She couldn't worry about that. No point in worrying about stuff she couldn't change.

Declan was their only option, the only one who still believed in the legend of the dagger enough to have already been hunting it down. In reality she hadn't even been sure he, in fact, was searching for it. When a couple drunkards had come into the pub yammering on about a young captain chasing after legends and stories and enchantments, she'd guessed that young captain was her brother.

She'd guessed and been right. Or lucky. Would the luck continue?

There was still so much to do, so much to plan for. So much that could go wrong.

The door banged open, and Cait turned toward it, calling out, "We don't open for another few hours."

Two men stepped in, dragging in muck and filth from the streets and dirtying the floors she'd mopped up that morning. She forced herself to hide her anger over such disrespect. If they were any other patrons she would have put them in their place, but something about these two stayed her tongue. She eyed them, managing to keep her expression as neutral as possible. The years of practice dealing with the men the council sent to her door had paid off. But it had been a while since they'd sent anyone so overtly to her.

They'd undoubtedly been sent by the council, though, as her regulars all knew her hours and respected them. The men stood at about the same height, equally dirty and scruffy. The way one stood ahead of the other indicated some form of rank. *Or perhaps one is merely shy.* The green sashes around their middles and their necks marked them as members of Donovan's crew on the *Harbinger*. Not a good lot. As if any pirates were good, though some were notably better than others.

The one in front lifted his chin and spoke. "You should consider keeping your doors locked, then, miss."

"Thank you for the reminder. I must have forgotten to lock it again after I was done sweeping all the dirt and grime out from last night's customers."

She couldn't prevent her eyes from narrowing ever so slightly, wondering if they were smart enough to take the hint that she was not pleased by the mess they were making on her clean floors. They didn't budge or speak again, only stared down at her. "How can I help you, gentlemen? I can't pour you a drink outside business hours—council rules and all—but if you need help finding the nearest inn or a nice shop to purchase something for the ladies in your lives, I'm happy to oblige."

The second man didn't move a muscle, not even a hint of a smile or a twinkle in his eye to indicate he'd heard her. It was the closer one who spoke again. "Funny you should mention the council. We are here on their business."

Of course you are. Her bitterness rolled around in her mind, but she somehow managed to keep it hidden.

"Oh? You two strapping lads selected by the council. Whatev—"

The man interrupted. "Stop. Now." Cait closed her mouth gently, being careful not to snap it closed. It was dangerous to play up the innocent pub owner act for too long.

"What do you need?" All sweetness had vanished from her tone. "I'm busy, and I have to get the pub ready to open this afternoon. And at some point I'd like to grab some food. It's only me here running this place."

"We're looking for someone."

"Oh?"

"A girl. Older girl." An image of the disguised girl immediately popped into Cait's mind.

"We don't get many girls in here. I think I'd remember seeing one."

"She might have been dressed as a man."

And poorly. Poor girl.

Cait pretended to ponder their words, lifting a hand to her chin. She could have been an actress had her parents... She cut the thought off. "May I ask what she's done? Last I knew, women, even girls, were allowed to do as they pleased on Cregah. Has she done something wrong? Is she in trouble?"

"That's none of your concern, miss."

"Ah, but it is, you see? If there's a dangerous fugitive on the loose, someone who has broken our sacred rules of peace, I need to know! I need to be able to keep my promise to my patrons that they won't have trouble in my pub, that they can rest and drink in peace without worrying about some young maiden stabbing them in the back while they sit unawares." She'd gone too far with that, perhaps, but her patience was wearing thin, and she feared she'd lose any ability to hide her disdain and contempt if they stayed much longer.

"Yes, of course. My apologies." The man behind him remained silent, a statue, his stare boring a hole into her. "Nothing like that, miss. The council merely needs to speak with her."

"Of course. Anything to help the council. You know that." The silent one's eyes twitched at her words, as if he could perceive the mockery and attitude beneath them. She ignored it, though, and continued. "I don't recall anyone in here last night that might have been a girl posing as a man. And unfortunately all the crews who were here last night set sail this morning, I believe. Otherwise I would have recommended you seek them out."

"And which ships were those exactly?"

"Oh," she said, hemming and hawing as if she needed the extra time to recall their names. "The *Curse Bringer* and the *New Moon*...and I think there was another. Song-something, or something-song." At those words, the men looked at each other. As she'd expected. Her brother's ship always got reactions like that.

"The *Siren's Song*?" the second man broke his silence to ask.

"Ah, yes, that's the one! A peculiar name for a ship if you ask me. I always thought pirates and sailors were a superstitious lot, and I don't know anyone who would trust a siren, especially a singing one." She wanted to laugh at their reactions. Though they did a fairly decent job of hiding their unease, she had seen it often enough in the faces of her customers to recognize it plain as day now.

"The crew from the *Siren's Song* was here?" the first man said.

"Yes. But only briefly. They didn't even finish all their drinks. All that booze. Wasted. But at least they paid handsomely, so I suppose not all was a waste. Nice gentlemen though. Not like the others I get in here. I mean, not that they aren't all nice, but some are more grumbly than others. You know? That lot, though, was quite agreeable and pleasant, if I do say so myself." Cait prattled on, and she hoped they'd stop her soon, because she was growing weary from chattering like an idiot.

"But no girl, miss? You didn't see anyone you didn't recognize?"

She pretended to think again, looking up to the rafters as if the answer could be there. "No. I mean, I didn't recognize the *Siren's Song* crew, at first, as they don't come to Cregah much at all, but none of them looked girlish. I mean, the stubble and the deep voices would be rather difficult for a girl to fake, I'd think. Not that I've ever tried to pretend to be a man, so maybe it's not all that hard." She was tempted to attempt this, lowering her tone to say something a man might, but before she could continue, the pirate before her interrupted, his annoyance becoming more and more obvious.

"Thank you for your time, miss." They both seemed rather eager to get away from her and her blathering. "If you do see someone suspicious, or hear of anything from the other residents—"

"The council will be first to hear about it. You can be sure of that." Cait had always hated lying as a kid, and she regretted now that it had become a daily necessity for her, but that wasn't her fault. The council had pushed her to set aside any morals when she'd learned what they were capable of. What they did. And now she'd grown good at deception. She quietly—and only briefly—mourned the loss of her innocence and her honor.

No, she had honor still. It was these men here and the women they served who lacked it. She ground her teeth together, hoping they couldn't see the tension in her jaw or the tightness in her eyes. She needed them to leave before she said something wrong or let the facade slip.

"Now, if you please, gentlemen, I really must get back to work." Giving them as sweet a smile as she could, she lifted her eyes to the door behind them.

"Of course. Sorry to have bothered you, miss." They both turned, and Cait nearly laughed at how quickly they made their escape, as if worried she might bombard them with a flood of words again if they lingered.

Through the windows she watched them walk away, shaking their heads at each other. Yes, she could have been an actress.

But she had little time to congratulate herself on a stellar performance, because the truth remained. That girl hadn't been just any girl. Whether the girl was a threat to Declan's mission—and the Rogues getting what they needed—or not, she was indeed in danger. There was no doubt of that fact, if the council was hunting for her.

Cait reached below the bar and pulled up a glass and a brown bottle. Filling it to the brim, she lifted it up, giving a toast to the empty room. "Here's hoping you're okay, silly girl. Wherever you are."

She downed the liquid, savoring the burn as it glided down her throat and settled into her belly. She hoped the girl had ended up with Declan. Plans or no, his ship was likely the only one she'd be safe on, and Cait didn't need to know the lass to wish for her safety, even if her presence on his ship put their mission at risk.

CHAPTER 18
AOIFE

POSSIBLE DANGER ASIDE, Aoife could not wait to get to Foxhaven, if only to get a break from this blasted rocking and what it was doing to her insides.

She had at least managed to make it back to the bed to lie down, but that offered little help beyond keeping her from falling over as she tried to walk. She had thought maybe sleep would do her some good. After all, she'd slept perfectly fine the night before. But every time she tried to close her eyes, her stomach rolled and churned like the waves outside.

This was going to be the longest two-day voyage of her life. The only voyage of her life actually, but still. She'd often daydreamed back at the council hall—during classes or the pirate dinners—about how exciting and fun life on the seas must be for the men who chose that path. And now she knew better. There was nothing fun about all this.

Nothing fun at all about what was going on back home either. Or what had happened to Lani.

Aoife wondered who had been tasked with "dealing with her." Of killing her. She'd known the council regularly called on the services of pirates, but she'd always thought it was to ensure safety in the villages and towns, confiscating contraband weapons found on the island or something. But knowing now what her mother and the other councilwomen had been doing, she had to assume they'd use pirates for the messy work of execution. Who else was there to do it? If a pirate was caught in the act of carrying out the orders, the council could simply exile them, deny them safe harbor, keeping themselves in the clear from public suspicion.

That very thing had happened a handful of times in Aoife's life. She'd watched her mother sentence pirates and their men to exile. Aoife had never paid much attention to those men who had been caught. They were lesser pirates, none of them a possible match for her, and so she'd had little need to spend energy on remembering their names. But now, after having asked a pirate for safe passage on his ship, having seen and experienced them acting far more civil than she'd imagined, she wished she had seen them as worthy of her time. At least worthy of her memory.

And yet, she couldn't keep the bitterness from burning in her chest, at the knowledge that these men willingly killed her people. Perhaps they didn't like doing it, but how could they not? They were pirates! And as Declan had said, there was always a choice. They could have just as well stayed away from Cregah to avoid having to do such things for the council. Couldn't they? The only ones required to stop in were the lords, per the treaty, but she couldn't fathom the council putting those men at risk of being caught and needing to be exiled, as then they'd lose their ability to secure heirs.

Aoife tried to close her eyes again, but the sound of the door opening and boots walking across the cabin had her opening them again quickly. She considered sitting up, but the thought of moving even an inch turned her stomach. She stared at the wooden beams above her head, tracing the swirls and grooves as the footsteps drew nearer.

"Told you not to eat so fast." The voice came from the doorframe beyond her feet. She tilted her chin down to look at him, careful not to move too much. He stood against the frame, relaxed and casual, with his arms crossed in front of his chest. She expected to see the usual twist in his lips as he mocked her, but instead his face looked almost bored, though there was a hint of stress or worry playing behind the mask he wore so handsomely.

She banished the thought quickly with a shake of her head, and he laughed as she winced at the wave of nausea that followed the slight movement.

"Don't laugh at me." She'd meant for the words to come out menacing, but they were pitiful in her ears. And likely in his as well. "I've never been on a ship, you know. How long does it take to get used to it? How are you all able to move about without losing all the contents of your stomach every other step?"

"Apologies for laughing," he said with a bow of his chin. She shot him a look, trying to determine if there was any mockery in his words. There was none, even as he continued. "It depends, really. Each person adjusts differently. Some never get used to it. They're usually the first to be tossed overboard during a storm, not being able to keep their feet beneath them when the ship starts rocking."

"But it's rocking now. You mean it gets worse?"

Another laugh, but this one he cut short himself. "Aye," he said. "Much worse during a squall. I remember my first one as a cabin boy. I thought I'd never see the break of the sun through the clouds. Certainly thought the sea would take me as its prize. But it hasn't yet."

Aoife moved to sit up, feeling ridiculous to be talking to him while lying flat on her back. Propping herself on her elbows, she waited. When her stomach didn't revolt at the movement, she continued until she was sitting cross-legged, her elbows resting on her knees. She looked up at him again, surprised to see him studying her with a look that almost showed genuine concern.

"Are you quite settled now? Or do you need another half hour to shimmy a few more inches?"

She glared at him.

"So what do you want anyway?" she asked. "Did you just come to sit and laugh at my seasickness?"

"I'm not sitting," he said with a gesture to his upright position. She rolled her eyes, and again she felt like a little kid, remembering all the times she and her sisters had taunted each other when they were younger, pulling each other's hair, singing teasing songs about one another, and playing immature pranks whenever they were sure they wouldn't be caught.

But no, she wasn't a kid anymore, and neither was this captain standing before her. She would not stoop to such a childish level. She was an heir after all—or had been anyway—brought up to be mature and regal.

And a killer.

The thought punched her in the gut, hard enough to make her recoil. Thankfully he would likely assume it was the ship's movement causing such a reaction.

Drawing in a deep breath, she straightened up as much as she could and looked at him with as pleasant an expression as she could muster. "I see that. It was a figure of speech, Captain."

But he didn't take the bait, instead changing the subject. "Actually, Miss Aoife, I came to talk to you and keep you company for a bit."

There was no hiding her reaction to that, as her shock pulled at her features. "Shall we talk about the weather then?"

Not even a hint of perturbation on his face, which would have made her want to stomp her feet, had they been on the floor. Why did he always reduce her to this frustrated, childish state?

"If you like, we can," he said. "It's rather hot today. Not a cloud in the sky. A pretty good breeze filling the sails."

"It would be nice to get a bit of that breeze and sunshine, to be honest," she said.

His eyes turned to the ceiling above her and then to the windows beside her. "I think we could manage that. It might also help your stomach adjust better."

She couldn't keep her eyes from lighting up at his words. She'd expected him to deny her request, insist on keeping her locked up in his cabin, though she only now realized that he likely hadn't locked her in and she could have left at any time. But that might not have gone well, given how unreliable her legs were on this blasted ship.

He took a step away from the doorway, holding out his hand. "Well, come on then. Let's get you some air."

"Why are you being nice to me?" The question came out before she could stop it. She'd only meant to think it, but her tongue had betrayed her.

He lowered his hand and gave a half shrug. "Excuse me for offering. I'll see you out there." And with that, he turned on his heel and strode out, not slowing his pace to wait for her. Before she could even start to move her feet to the floor, he was out the door and clicking it shut behind him. She muttered a curse. He would certainly mock her if it took as long to get out of the cabin as it had to make it from the dining room to the bedroom.

She gritted her teeth, and with a hand on her stomach—as if that could settle it—she forced her feet to the floor and stood. So far so good. The thought of him laughing at her again made her ignore the wave of nausea as she moved. Pushing herself forward, she clenched her teeth when she stumbled and a wave tossed her against the desk. A minute later she had a hand on the door and was pulling it open, beaming with silly pride for having made it without vomiting all over his rug.

He stood there casually once again despite having no doorframe to hold him up this time. His gray eyes laughed at her—if eyes could laugh—and he opened his mouth to speak, but she stopped him.

"Don't. You. Dare." She bit off each word.

"Dare what?" He lifted a hand to his chest in feigned innocence.

She let out a growl and would have thrown her arms up in frustration had they not been the only thing holding her steady and keeping her from falling into him. "Are we going to chat in the doorway? Or is there somewhere else we can go sit?"

"Is the doorway not good enough for you, miss?" His eyes traced the wood around her, admiring it as he spoke. "It's a rather nice doorway, in my opinion. The finest on our ship actually. But if you require somewhere else..." He turned without finishing his sentence.

Before she could reply, he was off again, not bothering to offer her an arm to steady her, though she wasn't sure if she would have taken it anyway; her pride was too thick to allow it. But still, the thought of having to walk and stumble in front of an entire ship's crew made her stomach toss even more.

With a deep breath, Aoife steadied herself, pushing her chin up as she took the first step. Then another. She could do this. Surprisingly it was far easier to walk on the ship when she had the fresh air in her lungs and the breeze on her face. With her confidence building, she picked up the pace. The crew watched her as she walked across the deck to where the captain had stopped at a railing midship. Keeping her eyes on her target, on him, she ignored the stares and the glares, the hushed whispers, and the way the pirates seemed to inch away from her as she passed.

Declan stood with his back to her, his elbows resting on the railing and his gaze settled on the horizon. He didn't turn when she came up alongside him. She steadied herself against the railing, mere inches away from him, careful not to touch him. He didn't say anything. Aoife glanced at him out of the corner of her eye, not wanting to spook him—as if he were some wild animal she was approaching. There was something about him she couldn't quite place, something different, something that sparked curiosity in her. She didn't care about him. Of course not. But that didn't keep her from wondering who he was exactly, why he seemed so different from the other pirates she'd met, and what he was after.

"Feeling better?" Declan asked, though he continued to look ahead, his gaze lost in the depths of the sea around them.

"A bit, yes. Thank you." Aoife ran her fingers along the smooth wood of the railing. She'd expected it to be rough. Then again, she'd expected the pirates to be rougher too.

"Don't get it into your head," he said, this time turning to face her, "that we're all nice and accommodating. I have a reputation to uphold, of course."

A single huff of a laugh escaped her lips. "I won't tell anyone."

"Good. I'd hate for that tongue of yours to get people thinking I've gone soft and all."

"Whatever you say, Captain McCallagh." She'd hoped he would act a bit more perturbed by her poking at him, but his expression darkened. He seemed to see through her as if she weren't there at all. Her own smile faded, and her curiosity peaked again. Why did his face do this? Where had his mind taken him? What was he dwelling on? It annoyed her to not know, and it annoyed her more that it bothered her so much.

Aoife slumped her shoulders and turned back to the sea. She could wait for him to speak first. After all, he'd been the one who had wanted to chat, while she would have been content to lie in bed the rest of the day. Actually, no. The thought of being shut up in that cabin with the stale air made her stomach roll again. This was much better, with the air and the breeze and the sunshine. She could almost understand why men had chosen a life on the seas instead of returning home after the war. Almost.

"How old are you, Aoife?" Declan's question came out gruffly, and he cleared his throat before she could respond. She didn't turn.

"Nineteen. Twenty next month."

"Ah." In her periphery she saw him rough a hand over his chin. "So the matching would have been—"

"Next month," she said, interrupting him before she could think better of it. "What do you know of the matching?"

"Common knowledge. All who dwell in and around the Aisling Sea know of the agreements between the council ladies and the pirate lords. And even if they didn't, the pirates certainly would all know about it. Pirates talk."

"Of course. Like a bunch of gossipy old ladies." Aoife stifled a laugh.

"Pretty much. Perhaps worse."

Why was he being so civil? Was this the real Captain McCallagh before her? Or was he playing a game, toying with her? She couldn't be sure. Was this merely another side to him? He was such a mystery. A mystery needing to be solved.

"You weren't looking forward to the matching."

"What makes you say that?" Aoife couldn't keep the defensiveness from peppering her words.

Declan gestured to her getup. "You ran."

Her stomach twisted against her will as those two simple words reminded her of how she'd betrayed the council and abandoned her duties to Cregah.

"Yes," she whispered.

"Why? Why leave? I'm sure life at the council hall was comfortable, with all the luxuries one could hope for and none of the hardships and challenges."

She had no response, no idea how to explain. Did she even want to? She wasn't even sure she could utter Lani's name. Voicing her betrayal would solidify it, make it real.

"Or did you simply not care for any of the potential matches? I wouldn't blame you if you didn't. They're a miserable lot."

Aoife snatched at the opportunity to avoid all mention of her lost sister. Dead sister. "What do you know of them?"

"Trying to get the scoop on them?"

"Well, you did say pirates were gossips. I'm sure you know more about them than I do."

His face changed in an instant, annoyance flashing across his features, as if there were an hourglass counting down in front of him. Something was urgent. But they were on a ship, at the mercy of the winds, so why was he so frustrated by this conversation?

"I know enough about them to know you wouldn't have been happy with any of them." Before she could question how he could possibly know that, he added, "No one would have been happy with them."

"That ruthless and callous?"

"That stupid and dull." Did he just wink at her? Honestly, his moods seemed to shift as much as the ship beneath her feet, and Aoife found it difficult to keep up with which side of him she was speaking to. Was it the brooding one or the snarky one or the grumpy one?

"Maybe you're jealous?" Aoife said with an exaggerated sigh. "Want to be a pirate lord yourself, Captain?" She knew she was treading in dangerous water here, egging him on, pushing to get information and answers from him. But he didn't give her the reaction she wanted. Nor the answers she sought.

"No. Even if I could become one, I wouldn't. I'd never wish that title on anyone."

"All for the best anyway. The three eligible matches now have to fight over one heir." Aoife clamped her mouth shut too late, realizing her mistake. She'd opened up the conversation to the subject of her sisters, and she started to feel sick again at the thought that he might ask about Lani and Darienn. She held her breath, as if that would keep him from asking.

But he didn't.

"What was life like at the council hall?" Declan asked, his voice calm and casual, as if they were simply making small talk.

Aoife released her breath, thankful to have avoided the more uncomfortable topic, at least for now. "It was life? I guess. Boring, dull, but comfortable."

"Were you happy?" She shot him a look and then gestured to her outfit and the mess she'd made of her hair. He laughed. "Fair point. You know, there is one thing I've heard rumored about the council, but…"

Aoife narrowed her eyes at him, and her heart began to race in her chest. Did he know what the council did to people? Had the council used his crew to carry out the "exiles"—perform the executions? She wasn't sure she could speak to that if he asked. She might be sick all over again, and not from the rolling of the ship.

"What have you heard?" She kept her voice low, scared of what he was going to ask about.

"Oh, never mind. It's nothing. Mere children's stories and legends." He waved a hand toward her as if he were dismissing this conversation that he had started. But now her curiosity was dancing around in her head once again, eager to know what it was people said about her family and the council that could be marked as legend.

"You can't do that. You can't bring it up and then drop it so suddenly."

"Of course I can. I'm the captain."

Two sides fought inside of Aoife: the side that wanted to grab the man and shake him until he asked his question and the side that wanted to walk away and end this pointless conversation. She got the distinct impression he was playing some sort of game here, a game she didn't know the rules to and had no idea if she had any chance of winning.

"Well, if that's the case, I'll just be retiring back to our cabin." She pushed away from the railing and made to turn away from him, hoping he'd stop her so she wouldn't have to make the embarrassing walk back across the deck just yet.

"My cabin," he corrected her.

She waited, hands on her hips, feeling completely ridiculous in these clothes and with her hair shorn as it was, but she maintained the level of pride she'd mastered from her council lessons.

"Fine, I'll ask." He motioned for her to join him again. "But you have to promise you won't laugh."

She obliged but said nothing, letting her raised brows prompt him to get on with it.

"The legend—or I suppose it's more a mere rumor—is that the council ladies have three fae sisters working for them."

Aoife froze. Of all the things he could have asked.

According to her mother, no one knew of the Bron sisters, believing they had fled south to Larcsporough. The council went to great lengths to keep their presence at the hall a secret. It was only by accident that Aoife knew of them herself. At the age of eight she had taken a wrong turn while daydreaming and ended up in a hallway she'd never seen before. That darn curiosity had gotten the better of her, and she'd gone through a door that had mysteriously opened as she'd walked past.

And she'd seen them. Three sisters, as different in appearance from one another as she and her own sisters were, yet their features held an eerie similarity.

She had known in an instant they were fae, the subject of many stories from the Aisling Sea's history. But she hadn't known why they were there in this chamber in a forgotten hallway of her home.

She had intended to run back out and forget what she'd seen, but something about the sisters standing together in the center of the room, talking to one another in hushed tones, had her stepping forward without thinking of what might happen to her or what she was even going to do when they noticed her.

But they'd already noticed her. And when one of them had spoken to her, she'd frozen in place, her breath stilled but her heart racing.

"Ah, sisters, it's Miss Aoife. She's come back to see us all these years later." It was the tallest fae; her back was to Aoife, her red curls spilling around her shoulders. Aoife noticed the points of her ears poking through her hair, and curiosity stirred in her once again, mixed with the fear that came with the fae knowing it was her despite not seeing her. She remained still, waiting, so mesmerized by their appearance she didn't think to ask what she'd meant by come back.

"Renna, what do you think she wants?" said the tinkling voice of the shortest fae, who had an auburn hue to her curls. The color reminded Aoife of the jars of cinnamon and spices she liked to marvel at in the kitchen. This fae turned to the other, Renna, with eyes that showed she looked to her for direction. Even at a young age, Aoife could detect a hierarchy. She'd seen it with her own mother and the council ladies, and it was easy to identify here as well.

"Perhaps she's come to play with us!" The third fae spoke now, her golden eyes flitting to Aoife and back so quickly she wasn't sure it hadn't been her imagination. This fae was the most beautiful of the three—as far as Aoife could tell, with Renna still not facing her. She was fascinated by those golden eyes, how they contrasted so perfectly with the milk chocolate color of her hair, which seemed to have a red shimmer to it when the light hit it just right. But her words sent panic through Aoife.

She'd heard all the legends about the fae. Everyone had.

"Shush, Maura." Renna had spoken again and was now looking over her shoulder to glance at Aoife for the first time. "We don't want to scare her away."

"It's been so long since anyone's come to visit." Maura's words carried a hint of impatience and longing that increased the unease in Aoife's chest and stomach. "What do you think, Bria?" she asked, turning to her other sister.

"I do miss company, but..." The shorter fae let her words trail off, her eyes still looking to Renna for guidance.

"Let's let her decide, shall we?" And with these words, Renna turned fully, her eyes—a sparkling mix of blues—boring into Aoife with an intensity she'd not even seen when her mother was at her angriest. Renna dropped an ear to her shoulder, her expression questioning Aoife, daring her to speak.

But Aoife couldn't. And she ran. Turned and fled as fast as her legs could carry her.

She vowed to never return.

A cough sounded, cutting through her memory and pulling her back to her present company. She turned to Declan, whose gray eyes searched hers with such precision and sharpness, she thought he might actually be able to witness her memories simply with his gaze.

"Sorry." She cringed at how meek and nervous she sounded.

"So it's true then?" His chin lifted.

"I didn't say that." Fingering the wood of the railing, she kept her eyes away from his.

"Not with words, no. But it's written plainly all over you."

"What of it? Why does anyone care if the fae are real and still on Cregah?"

"Not just on Cregah. Imprisoned in the hall. Serving against their will."

Aoife started to protest, eager to defend her mother, but she snapped her mouth shut. He wasn't wrong. They had been imprisoned there, and despite her mother's insistence all those years ago that it had been for their safety, she knew in her gut that was a lie. Like everything else. "You didn't answer my question." Now she looked at him, challenging him to respond.

"I want to set them free," Declan said, giving her a shrug. But he'd said it low enough that the waves drowned the words out so only Aoife could hear.

"Out of the goodness of your pirate heart, no doubt."

"Of course not. They have something I need."

Her stomach tightened against her will as she remembered the beauty of those sisters and the magical way their voices danced through the air. Was that jealousy? It couldn't be. What did she have to be jealous about? It wasn't as if she wanted to stay here with him. He was incorrigible and rude. And yet the feeling remained, the same sensation that had presented itself when Lani had divulged her secret.

"And why are you telling me this, exactly?" But she'd already guessed why. She was from the council. If he truly sought to free the sisters, he'd need her knowledge of the grounds to do so.

"Surely you've already figured that out." How did he always read her mind like that? She ground her teeth and took a deep breath of the sea air.

"And what do I get in return? For helping you?"

His eyes brightened. He must not have expected her to be so willing, so cooperative. Though she hadn't yet decided if she would be.

"Anything you wish, Aoife. Well, anything you wish that is in my power to provide." With this, he bowed his chin and waited.

CHAPTER 19
DECLAN

Declan waited for her to speak, attempting to ignore the twitching inside his gut that seemed to count down the time he was possibly wasting here. She at least seemed amenable to the idea of helping him, but he didn't know what she might demand in return—or if he could even deliver on any of those demands. And he was sure there wouldn't be just one thing on her list. He watched her as she took her time and turned back to study the deep blue of the sea. Her lips pinched as she thought, and he was nearly convinced she was taking her sweet time just to toy with him.

"Well," she started. He had to settle his foot, which wanted to tap out the impatience coursing through him. *Get on with it, girl!* his thoughts screamed at her, but he forced his features to remain calm.

"Yes?" Too sharp. Too eager. He needed to rein in this urgency before it scared her away.

"Two things." She was still facing the sea, and he wondered what her eyes saw beyond that horizon. Hope? Escape? Fear? Her voice cut through the rambling thoughts. "I'd like a change of clothes."

He dropped his head to the side and looked her over. Though she certainly wouldn't pass for a man in her current attire, the clothes fit her well and didn't make her look terrible. "And what is it I could provide for you? We are fresh out of more feminine garb."

"Is there not a crew member who might be of similar stature who might loan me something else?"

"Look around, miss." He bit back his frustration, trying to stay as polite as possible. He needed her cooperation, after all. He waved a hand over his shoulder but didn't turn around. "Does it look like we have changes of clothes? Or that we launder our garments often? Plus, you're only with us until tomorrow."

"Oh." Part of him felt sorry for her. A very small part. It must not have been easy to leave behind a life of luxury and comfort, of closets and chests full of clean clothes. But life wasn't easy. And the sooner she learned that, the better. He waited for her inevitable snark at this, some comment about the way they looked or smelled. But he was a little taken aback when she said, "Well, in that case, I shall learn to appreciate that these clothes fit so well. Plus, they are quite a bit easier to maneuver in than all the skirts. I just wish they weren't so dreadfully hot."

He almost wished she'd said something snippy, because these useless statements did nothing but waste his time, and it took every ounce of his willpower not to grab the woman and shake her, telling her how precious little time he had to come up with a feasible plan!

"What's your second demand?" Declan's words came out clipped, and he was sure she would hear the urgency in them. *And probably drag out her answer for spite.*

This time she turned toward him and, in doing so, ended up a few inches closer. He could smell the last remnants of perfumed soap on her skin, though this did nothing but irk him more. She didn't belong here, and he kicked himself for allowing her to remain—information or no. When she straightened, growing an extra inch, her eyes boring into his, he had to admire the fearless side of her that would dare stand up to a pirate captain, especially one now armed and capable of tossing her overboard with little effort.

"Let me help." Brave and unwavering, her answer caught him off guard. But he recovered quickly.

"You are helping."

"You know what I mean." Indeed he did, but that didn't mean he wanted to give in so easily. "Let me stay aboard after you hire the new crew. Let me go with you to free them." The bravery she'd shown a second ago seemed to be starting to slip, as though she were pushing herself to face a demon she desperately wanted to run from. These emotions and her close connection to the council could cost them though. Even if she sought to sever her bond to her family, she was a liability, and he couldn't take the risk.

"No." Even as he said it, he regretted it, but he'd find another way. He had to. He could do this without the information she had. "I can get what I need from somewhere else."

"Okay then. In that case, I believe our conversation is done, yes? I'd like to enjoy the fresh air in silence for a bit." And with that, she shut him down.

How had he lost control of this situation?

Regardless, he'd prepared for this possibility, in case she'd been unaware of the existence of the fae or unwilling to help. He'd already had the backup plan ready, although it wasn't a particularly good one. He would need to take a little longer in Foxhaven. Have his men ask around, collect information, perhaps pay for some, but even then he wasn't entirely sure anyone outside the council would know what he needed.

And now that he had to resort to this alternative plan, he'd need to prepare for the work ahead when they arrived in port tomorrow. Turning, he quickly made his way to his cabin, signaling Tommy—who was standing on the quarterdeck pretending not to have been watching his failure with Aoife—to follow. Back in his cabin, he slumped into his chair, leaning back and looking at the ceiling. His quartermaster came in without a knock, silent with trepidation, uncertainty playing on his face.

Declan wanted to remain calm. To be that put-together, calm-under-pressure captain he portrayed to everyone else, but he couldn't. A growl escaped, though he kept it quiet. It was one thing to let his closest friend see him lose it. Quite another to have the crew hear him as he did. His hands clenched into fists so tight he half expected to draw blood from his palms as his arms shook from the tension. He lifted them to his forehead before dropping them. Tommy waited, lips pursed and brows raised, like a parent waiting for a toddler to finish a tantrum.

One second more, and Tommy spoke. "So it went well then."

A single laugh erupted from Declan. "Well, it wasn't a complete waste." He brushed a knuckle against his nose, beginning to relax now that he'd gotten the initial frustration out. "We now know the fae are there."

"She's seen them?" Tommy took half a step forward.

"She didn't say as much, but she might as well have. When I mentioned them, she seemed to get lost in a memory. And when I requested her help, she didn't deny her ability to do so."

"Or she was playing you just to get what she wanted."

"She wanted clothes."

It was Tommy's turn to laugh now. "Well, I mean, we could have maybe offered her something from the last chests we lifted, but there's not much, and little that would fit her."

"Yeah. I told her no. Plus, she won't be here long."

"That's all she requested? Clothes? Seems like we could have offered to at least buy her some new clothes in Foxhaven if that's all it took."

"If only." Declan let out a breath. He eyed his quartermaster, who couldn't hide his curiosity at all.

"Oh?"

"Aye. She wants to help."

Tommy's brow furrowed. "Wait."

"Yeah, I know. That's what I told her." Declan gave thanks that they were close enough to share thoughts without unnecessary words.

"So she wants—"

Declan finished his sentence, "—to come with us."

Tommy had no words at first. He seemed to be mulling over his response, choosing his words wisely. "And you said no?"

"Of course I said no."

"Of course. How foolish of me." Tommy paused a second and then added, "But why exactly did you say no?"

"Too complicated."

"Well, that's a given—"

"No, I mean, her involvement makes it even more complicated. You didn't see... didn't hear..." Declan had never struggled with words this much before. Usually they rolled off his tongue with ease and precision, but now he felt all tied up in knots, unsure how to explain or describe any of this.

"She's really done a number on you, hasn't she?" Tommy might have looked amused, if it weren't for the concern on his face.

"What?"

"I've never known you to stumble over your words, and I can only assume—"

"It's not that," Declan said, interrupting again. "It's nothing to do with her. It's this whole insane situation we're in. And she—"

"So it is about her."

Declan picked up the closest thing on his desk—a book—and threw it at his friend, who didn't budge, didn't even blink, as it hit him square in the chest and fell to his feet.

"Regardless, we need to hammer out this alternate plan that doesn't include her," Declan said, holding his quartermaster's gaze.

"Aye, Captain. Sure thing. We'll want to bring Mikkel into the conversation though, yes?"

Declan thought for a moment, roughing a hand over his jaw. "I don't know."

"You need the crew to know what we're after. And right now, they're sailing blindly."

"They will know. Eventually. When the time is right." Declan hoped it would be enough. For now, he didn't need the crew more nervous than they already were with a woman onboard. And he had no doubt they'd be even worse off if they knew where they were ultimately headed. Even he couldn't deny the twinge of fear he was experiencing at having to face the evil lurking beneath the surface of the Black Sound.

"Fair enough. So the plan." Tommy had just made a move to sit in the chair in front of the desk when the door creaked open.

"Excuse—" Declan started to reprimand the intruder but stopped when Aoife walked in.

"Oh, sorry, Captain. Tommy," she said, her gaze flitting about the cabin awkwardly as a blush spread across her freckles, readily visible even in the dim light inside.

"How did you know my name?" Tommy turned toward her with what Declan could easily assume was his oft-used inquisitive expression.

"Lucky guess?" A second passed, and she added, "I overheard it yesterday. At the door. And just now I recognized your voice. Connected the dots, as it were." She trailed off. Perhaps she realized she'd been rambling.

"Eavesdropping isn't polite," Tommy muttered as he turned back to Declan, shooting him an amused look.

Aoife spoke up again. "Apologies. I didn't mean to. Difficult to ignore noises when you hear them."

"Uh-huh." Declan wasn't convinced, but he ran back over his recent conversation with Tommy to determine if she might have heard anything she shouldn't have.

Aoife fidgeted again, still standing in the open doorway. "Shall I come back later?" She didn't seem too eager to go back out to the deck. Even though it would help the seasickness, he had no doubt the sensation of prying eyes was far from comfortable. He should have forced her into the discomfort. She'd need to get used to the feeling if she were going to insist on being out on her own away from the council. And yet, there was something that kept him from doing just that. Something about the look in her eyes. It reminded him of an innocence he'd lost in himself long ago, and part of him—some part of him he'd tried hard to forget— wanted to help her preserve that piece of her. If he could.

Declan stood and motioned for Tommy to follow suit. "No, you're welcome to stay here for the time being. We can take our conversation to the officers' quarters."

Tommy's face contorted into a look of amused confusion, but he complied. Declan moved swiftly around his desk and nudged Tommy toward the door as Aoife stepped to the side so they could pass.

"There's some food in the dining room if your stomach can handle it," he said to her. "Tea too, but be careful this time. I don't want to have to ask someone to clean up any unnecessary mess."

Before she could glare at him, he was out the door and had it shut behind him with a resounding click of the latch.

"I think you're right. We need Mikkel in this discussion so we hire the right talent in Foxhaven tomorrow." He was already speaking before he turned to find Tommy standing there, arms crossed and gaze prying him with a silent demand to know what had just happened.

But Tommy said nothing and didn't make any show of moving to find Mikkel for their meeting. Declan could offer some explanation, but he didn't owe that to his quartermaster, friend or not. He was the captain. And right now they had more pressing matters than discussing how he chose to treat an obnoxious stowaway.

CHAPTER 20
DECLAN

THE SUN HAD long ago set behind Declan, but he remained at the prow, watching the sea darken before them, the horizon disappearing as the sea and sky faded into each other. They still had a day of travel left, maybe half a day if they had some good luck.

Luck. What a ridiculous notion.

Declan had spent the better part of the afternoon strategizing with Tommy and Mikkel in the quartermaster's cabin. And he was now confident they had at least half a chance of getting the information they needed from the men who frequented Foxhaven. While it didn't provide the same security and rest as Port Morshan, Foxhaven served its purpose for the pirates. Declan preferred it to Morshan, and the need to watch his back and keep up his guard didn't bother him in the slightest. He could take care of himself and didn't have to worry about any rulers demanding his services as payment.

In fact, Foxhaven barely had any sort of ruler. The man in charge, Porter Rogerson, had stumbled onto the shores, quite literally, about thirty years back. He'd been captain of a merchant vessel from Caprothe, and their ship had been tossed about so violently in a storm that he and the quartermaster had all but given up any hope of surviving when they'd landed on the tiny island south of Turvala. They'd found little more than a handful of weather-torn buildings that had long since been abandoned, but they somehow managed—over many years—to turn that beaten-up beach into a thriving port, which Rogerson still ran much like he had run his ship. Half drunk and stupid.

But it was to the benefit of the pirates, who were able to do business with no outside interference and had some semblance of protection from the cannons Rogerson had stationed along the entrance into the port, which fired at anyone who threatened his stronghold here.

Morshan might provide rest without fear, but the council had also forbidden pirates from hiring crew within their port, leaving Foxhaven as the best place to recruit new hands. It was unusual to find pirate crew switching ships, but in Foxhaven pirate captains could find disgruntled former merchant sailors looking to get out from under the heavy hands of their oppressive captains and earn a higher wage.

Declan clenched the wood of the railing as he looked toward that next port far off in the distance, not yet visible. He needed more than mere bodies to fill the holes in his crew. He needed those who weren't perturbed by the name of his ship. Men not ruled by superstition and fear. Or men not afraid to die. It wasn't always one in the same.

With a sigh, he scrubbed a hand over his face. The recruiting would actually be the easy part. Gathering the information would prove far trickier.

The only people who might have some knowledge of the council hall would be those who had actually been there, or those who worked for those who had been there. The pirate lords didn't stop in Foxhaven, at least not often, so he couldn't bet on their crews being around to pry the information out of. But the ships in their fleets, the ships that provided them with the additional bounty they used to buy their way into the council's inner circle, those were Declan's in. Those men would be more likely to talk, more likely to have heard stories from the lords' ships, or to have possibly stepped foot in those halls themselves.

He'd tasked Tommy, Mikkel, and Gavin with splitting up and each going to a different establishment in port to find the men. Declan knew his best bet would be to find men who worked under Saarin, Madigen, or Tiernen, as those lords were matched to the ladies of the current ruling council and would have visited more recently.

If he were lucky, perhaps the other three unmatched lords might have their ships in port. Perhaps a bit of final fun before their matching. Except two of those matchings wouldn't be happening now, and the remaining heir was too young to be matched yet. And so Declan couldn't count on that bit of fortune. Plus, he hadn't lied when he'd told Aoife how stupid those lords were. He wasn't even sure how they'd managed to build fleets large and successful enough to pay the high tax to become lords.

The sky had darkened around him, all remnants of the sunlight gone below the horizon, and a speckle of stars twinkled overhead. The crew was quiet. The ship was quiet. If there was one benefit to having them all on edge with Aoife aboard, it was this, that he could actually have silence.

He could think.

But he'd left Aoife alone for too long, and as little as he wanted to deal with her incessant rambling, pointed comments, and way of looking like she wanted to stick her tongue out at him, he didn't like the thought of her having too many hours alone in his cabin with his stuff.

With one more look out over the black sea, he sucked in a final breath before heading back to the cabin.

He half expected to find her asleep as he had the previous night, lying like a rag doll with one booted foot hanging off the edge of the bed. But although she was in bed, she wasn't sleeping. She was reading.

He stood in the small doorway of the bedroom for what felt like several minutes, staring at her without her looking up. He studied her for a while longer. Even with her hair chopped so haphazardly, she was cute. Pretty, in an adorable sort of way. Freckles danced across her cheeks and over her nose, peppering her cream-colored skin that clearly hadn't been in the sun much. She seemed so much younger than she was, and it was hard to believe they were actually so close in age. Had he met her under other circumstances—had he not long ago given up on such a future for himself—he might have hoped to catch her eye.

He shooed the thought away.

They hadn't met before, and with her being an heir, they never would have. Even if he had stayed home in Morshan with Cait, they never would have met under any pleasant circumstances. And it did him no good to wonder about what could never have happened. And would never happen.

"Is it good?" he asked, not bothering to warn her of his presence with a throat clearing. But she didn't startle, nor did she look up from the words she was reading.

"Quite." As much as her rambling and overuse of words annoyed him, this single one cut sharper into him, sending tension through his jaw.

"What is it?" He remained in the doorway, though all he wanted was to crawl into the bed and rest. Perhaps have a dreamless sleep for once.

She held up the book so he could read the spine. *Legends and Myths of the Aisling.* His eyes went large, and he turned back to the main room. He'd forgotten the book had fallen at Tommy's feet when he'd thrown it at him like a child. Neither he nor Tommy had picked it up, and now she had it. What had she read? Did she know what he was seeking? Why he wanted—needed—the fae?

"Ah, good bedtime stories," Declan said, hoping he sounded casual, with no hint of the worry stirring within. "Beware of some of them though. They lead to nothing but nightmares filled with evil and terror."

At that, she finally looked up and over the book, her eyes twitching the way they always seemed to when something sparked her curiosity. "Oh? Is that what bothered you so much in your sleep last night?"

He'd walked himself right into that question.

"No." He approached the bed and sat on the edge, leaning down to take his boots off. This felt strange. Too domestic. Too normal. Too much like the times he'd watched his father and mother go through a similar routine back home, when he'd hidden behind the curtain in their doorway, thinking they didn't know he was there. But they'd always known, and they'd always called him in for bear-sized hugs and goodnight kisses. The memory was too strong, and it pushed Declan to stand, his boot unlaced but still on his foot.

His hands began to shake, and he hoped she didn't see. She'd think him mad. Not that he cared what she thought really, but he'd spent so much time keeping those stupid memories at bay. He wasn't ready to have them resurfacing. Not now. Not ever was preferable, but certainly not now of all times.

"Are you okay?" Aoife asked. He mulled over her words, searching each syllable for any hint she was goading him or mocking him for his ridiculousness. But he found only care and concern, which was decidedly worse.

"I'm fine." He sounded anything but fine.

"Are you hungry? I think I left you some of the salted meat and fruit from dinner. The man who brought it was nice enough, though he seemed really eager not to spend more time with me than he had to, and when I asked his name, he ran out in a terror. I half expected him to start screaming, as if I were a ghost!"

Declan normally would have rolled his eyes at her uncanny ability to string so many words together into what seemed like a single breath, but now he welcomed the noise to drive away the memories.

He looked over his shoulder at her. Her focus remained on the book, though she seemed to be merely avoiding him rather than actually reading. "That would be Philip. He doesn't talk much as it is, but I'm not surprised by his reaction. The crew is nervous with you here."

"Ah, that explains a lot actually." With this, she shut the book, keeping her finger trapped in the pages to hold her place. "All day I felt the crew staring at me, but they kept their distance. Even Collins, who seemed fine with me yesterday. Was it really only yesterday?"

"I know. Time with you seems to drag on and on. I feel like we should have a full moon overhead already." He walked around to the other side of the bed—his side of the bed—unlaced the other boot, and nudged both off as quickly as he could before the memories could return. Settling onto the feather mattress, he propped himself against the aged wood of the headboard. He had started to close his eyes when her voice snapped them back open.

"Is life always so boring on a pirate ship?"

He closed his eyes again as he answered; he didn't need to look at her to carry on a conversation. "Were you hoping for more action?"

"A bit, yes."

"Silly girl." He wanted to laugh but decided against it.

"Perhaps." Her tone was almost mournful. "It's just not what I expected. *You're* not what I expected."

Declan opened his eyes now and found her studying him. The green of her irises pulled him in, threatening to pull him under. This was getting trickier with each shared word. He didn't want connection. He didn't want her looking at him this way, as if she could see the parts of him he never showed.

"I'm sorry to disappoint." He clipped the words short, his eyes piercing hers. "I could offer to throw you overboard if you wish. That would certainly gain me some extra clout with the crew."

Pursing his lips, he looked at the wooden beams above the bed, as if he were pondering doing just that.

"That's not necessary," she said, and he happily sensed some real fear—however faint it might be.

"Or I could take advantage of you being in my bed right now."

He moved before she could, grabbing her by the arms. Lifting her easily, he swung her over him until he had her pinned down on the feather bed, his full weight holding her down. The book—still in her hands—pressed against his sternum, and his face hovered only inches from hers. He considered all the ways she could retaliate and prepared himself for any of them, but she merely lay there, with a look of shock and fear in her eyes. He pressed his hips harder against hers and licked his lips. It was a show, and yet there was a small part of him that wanted to do exactly what he was threatening. He shoved the feeling away, just as he needed to do to her.

"If I didn't know any better, I'd think you wanted this. Wanted me." His words came out low, a hoarse whisper against her ear as he leaned down further. Though she shuddered a bit under him, she said nothing. She didn't do anything. He let his breath warm her ear, let her hear his tongue brushing over his lips once more before he spoke, his words coming out as more of a purr than a growl. "Don't beg for action if it's not what you want."

And with those words, he retreated, releasing her and returning to his side of the bed. It was too hot to sleep under any blankets, so he rolled over onto his side and did his best to calm his breathing, longing for a dreamless sleep. She still hadn't moved, still lay there where he'd forced her down. He couldn't stop seeing the fear in her eyes, but he reminded himself it was for the best.

CHAPTER 21
DECLAN

THE SEAT DECLAN *sat on was rickety and needed to be mended once again. His father had been meaning to get to it, but there were other tasks requiring his attention around the pub.*

His mother's voice wafted through the room as she counted up the money from the night's business. It was nearly morning, and most children would have been in bed at this hour, but most children didn't have parents who owned and ran one of the only pubs in the port.

While most kids went to the local school, Declan and those whose parents kept irregular hours were schooled at home. As the government and all businesses on Cregah were run by women, it fell upon the husbands and fathers to handle everything else, including the education of their children.

And so it was that Declan was sitting at his spot at the bar, dangling his young feet and trying not to hit the wood, lest he get a reprimand from his mother, while spinning one of the coins a customer had tossed to him. He watched it spin and spin and spin until it lost momentum and fell.

He didn't hear the door behind him open, but his mother was around the bar in an instant, informing whoever had entered that they were closed.

But these weren't customers. And before Declan could turn around, his mother was out the door with them. He didn't know if she'd gone willingly or if they had dragged her. All he knew was that his mother now stood between two men who were muscular and nearly twice her size, but she didn't look afraid. Her chin was held high, her posture pin-straight. Even through the old waves of the glass window he could see her pride and her fortitude.

Declan moved to call for his father, but by the time he found his voice, it was too late. His mother was gone, being dragged out of sight.

His father came running, dropping the crates he'd been moving in the back storeroom, and tore out the door. He looked one way and then the other, his vision no doubt hindered by the pre-dawn fog and darkness.

Declan stayed behind, frozen on the stool, wrapped in absolute silence.

Cait wasn't there. Out with the boy she was courting for the better part of six months. She wasn't there. To help their parents. To help him.

Declan was shaking as he woke from the dream. The memories.

Another night. Another nightmare. Always the same. It seemed the harder Declan fought them, the more persistent and intense they became. Even after all these years, that day still plagued him. The helplessness. The weakness. The utter despair.

He'd never seen his mother again.

Later that evening, the two men had dared return to the pub. Declan had seen the dagger gleaming in the moonlight as his father stalked after them, but he hadn't been able to stop it. To stop his dad from taking revenge. To stop the people in the street from dragging his dad off to the council hall for justice. To stop himself from taking the blade from the body when no one was looking.

Cait had refused to go to Morshan's local authorities to file a grievance, insisting instead that the council would not be able to help. He'd hated her for that. For her absence. For her apparent indifference. He'd only stayed at the pub in hopes his parents would one day return, but after a year, he gave up, going down to the port while his sister slept in search of a crew in need of a cabin boy. And it was then, at the age of ten, that he'd been hired to work on a ship alongside another young boy named Tommy.

Years later he'd learned of his parents' likely fate.

And only then did he choose to forgive Cait, even as he vowed never to return home.

Keeping his eyes closed, he tried to steady his breath and calm his nerves. With how little sleep and rest he managed, it was a marvel he'd survived all these years and come to captain his own ship. Either he had become accustomed to this exhausted state or it gave him the gruff edge he needed for the job.

Aoife stirred beside him, and the beginning rays of the morning sun warmed his closed lids. The bed shifted as she rose. Her timid steps were a bit more even today. Perhaps her sea legs were finding her sooner than he'd expected. He turned over and propped himself up on his elbow to watch her, his vision slowly coming into focus. Through the doorway he could see her make her way past the desk to the table where Philip had come in earlier to drop off some food and tea. The peppermint had seemed to quell her nausea, at least. Last thing he wanted was to have his cabin smelling vile if her sickness overtook her.

The silence hung in the room as thick as the fog from his dream. He cleared his throat, the gruffness cutting through the air, but she didn't turn and didn't acknowledge him.

Indifference. Good.

This was decidedly better than the closeness he'd risked last night, which he'd had to cut off.

His stomach grumbled, pushing him to get up and put his boots on. He strode over to the table and grabbed a piece of meat and a slice of cheese. She didn't look at him. Didn't seem to notice him. She merely sat staring at, but not seeing, the cup of tea before her. He opened his mouth to make a comment, an extra insult to emphasize his point from the night before, but before he could, an alarm rang out from the deck.

"Sails!"

Declan bit back a curse as he turned, not bothering to wait to see how Aoife reacted to the news. She wanted action, didn't she? Perhaps the crew was right and she indeed was a curse.

He had barely reached the door when it burst open and Tommy rushed in.

"Captain." He was nearly out of breath, but seeing Declan was already on his way, he stopped short and turned on his heel. Declan followed close behind, stopping only to secure the door behind him.

On the quarterdeck, they made it to the stern as Tommy handed him his spyglass and pointed. Declan might have given his friend grief for pointing out the obvious sails on the horizon, as if Declan were blind and couldn't clearly see them, but this wasn't the time.

Were these friends? Or another pirate lord come to cut them off at the knees?

"Who do you think it is?" Tommy asked, leaning close so the crew—who had all but stopped their sailing duties to wait for an order—wouldn't hear. Time stood still, the ship eerily silent aside from the random flapping of a sail and the lapping of water at the hull.

Declan mumbled an "I don't know yet" as he looked through the glass, trying to find any clue as to who followed them, but they were still too far off and had not raised a flag to signal them. Not a good sign. A friend would have likely raised the flag of peace to let him know they weren't a threat. A flag of warning came much later, when the approaching ship was close enough that escape wasn't an option.

If that warning wasn't made with guns instead.

"Could it be Grayson?" Tommy asked, squinting at the horizon. As if that would help.

"Perhaps. We haven't run into him in ages."

Last Declan knew, Captain Callum Grayson had his crew plundering ships heading to and from Larcsporough, south of Cregah. A far riskier set of ships to take on than those to the north, as they were often larger, with larger crews and more guns to better protect the precious cargo brought from the south.

"Think he knows what we're after?" Tommy asked.

"Probably best to assume? But we don't even know if that's him following us or not."

"What's the call, Captain?" Gavin piped up behind them, but Declan kept his eyes locked on those sails.

Declan's answer was for Tommy instead, his voice remaining low. "Any estimate for when we'll be in Foxhaven?"

"Should be ahead of schedule with the way the winds have been. After lunch?

Perhaps?" That was at least good news. And Declan could use something good these days.

He called over his shoulder, "Stay on this heading. We treat them as though they have no business with us."

"Aye, Captain," Gavin said, his hesitation evident.

"We simply don't have the crew strength to risk another fight," Declan said to Tommy, the two of them still watching the other ship.

"You don't owe me any explanation, Captain. I trust you."

"What is going on?" The question rang out behind them, and they turned to find Aoife about to step foot onto the quarterdeck.

"Hey! You're not allowed up here!" Tommy barked at her.

Aoife gave a quick glance at Declan. "Apologies. I didn't know." And with that, she retreated down the stairs.

Declan's jaw clenched. She couldn't just stay put. Not that he'd told her to. He turned to Tommy.

"Go get her back to the cabin. If things go badly up here, we need her out of the way. I can't have more of the crew getting killed by her being underfoot."

"Aye," said Tommy with a dip of his chin as he turned to follow the command.

Declan once again looked at the approaching ship, closer now. Were they using the same wind? There was no way the *Siren's Song* would outrun that ship, as it was bigger, faster.

Through the glass once again he tried to make out the ship, attempting to recognize the figurehead or any defining features, but they were still too far away. His heart sped up with the adrenaline that accompanied the thought of the inevitable encounter.

"Mikkel!" he called, knowing his bo'sun would be nearby waiting for the order. And indeed, Mikkel appeared in a fraction of a second, coming up on his left.

"Cap'n?"

"Have the men at the ready, but keep weapons hidden. We don't want to show our hand too soon."

"Aye, sir."

Roughing a hand over his stubbled chin, Declan ran through the different scenarios that could happen, and while he loved a good fight as much as the next pirate, if he were letting himself be honest, he couldn't risk the delay or the manpower this time.

Let this work out. Let something work out.

He needed something to go right.

CHAPTER 22
AOIFE

THE HAND on Aoife's elbow squeezed tighter, though she wasn't struggling in the slightest. She rolled her eyes at the way the crew seemed to scurry away from her while still keeping their eyes firmly fixed on her, as if she'd actually put a hex on them if they lost track of her. How did they manage to keep the ship running if they feared her presence so much?

They must really respect their captain if they hadn't given in to their fear and thrown her overboard.

Or they fear him.

She swallowed hard at the memory. The look he'd given her as he'd held her down. Hard. Cold. Hungry.

Tommy's grip on her elbow felt too much like Declan's hands on her arms, and bile threatened to surface from the pit of her stomach.

She hadn't expected that from him, had thought him more respectable.

The whole thing had caused shame to burn in her chest, as if it had been her fault he'd acted that way. She hoped no one would ever know the position she'd been in, with his hips digging into hers, his breath in her ear. Though she knew, somehow, she hadn't done anything to deserve it.

But the shame was minuscule compared to the anger that seethed within her. She'd tried to keep it at bay, needing to remain in Declan's good graces lest he follow through with the threat to throw her into the sea. She needed to make it to land. From there she could find passage to Daorna, look up Adler's family. Perhaps find work and start over.

Tommy led her back to the captain's quarters, shoving the door open and guiding her inside. She expected him to fling her in and shut the door on her without a word, but instead he stepped in after her, closing the door behind him. Her nerves were on edge in an instant, spine straightening and chin rising as she tried to ignore the quivering in her gut and prepare herself for whatever he was about to do.

As Declan was preoccupied with whatever was happening on deck, she couldn't rely on his so-called protection now. And though Tommy had seemed innocent enough when she'd encountered him before, Declan's actions had shown her how little she could trust her instincts. Or anyone else for that matter.

But Tommy didn't step toward her, didn't make a move to attack her or further subdue her. His amber-colored eyes studied her as he pulled the gray wool cap from his head, letting his brown hair fall across his forehead. He began to shake his head slightly at her as he wrung the cap in his hands.

"What is it?" Aoife asked, her brow rising a touch with the question.

He let out a sigh through his nose as he chewed on the inside of his lip.

"I can't tell, miss, if you're going to be the thing that brings this crew down..." He dropped his gaze to the floor and paused.

"Or?"

"Or the thing that saves our captain."

Those were certainly not the words she'd expected. She racked her brain for any sign that Declan needed someone, especially a runaway girl, to rescue him. What could a pirate captain—especially one with his reputation—need saving from?

"I don't understand." Part of her wanted Tommy to stay so he could explain further, while the rest of her wanted to be left alone until they made it to port.

What business of hers was it anyway? Declan had made it quite clear he didn't want her to stay, and Tommy, of all people, should know of her impending departure. And yet he'd still said those words.

"Most wouldn't understand." Tommy leaned back against the wall beside the door. "I don't think the captain would even understand."

"Careful. He might make you walk the plank for suggesting such a thing." Aoife wasn't actually sure if that were true.

"Nah." He shook his head again, his lips in a tight line.

"So you've voiced this thought to him then?" She braced herself against the back of the chair Tommy had sat in the day before, crossing her ankles.

"Of course not. I don't have a death wish, you know."

"But you just said—"

"Making people walk the plank isn't really his style," Tommy said with a wink that seemed forced, though his words held a hint of humor in them, like he might laugh at any moment.

"But he listens to you. Trusts you."

"To a point. But I know the limits of our friendship, and I know how to stay on his good side."

"In his shadow. So that's where you like to be?" Aoife knew she tiptoed in unsteady territory with that, but if she was in danger anyway, why not? Tommy didn't seem all that menacing anyway. Then again, neither had Declan until last night.

"It won't work, miss." The corner of his mouth lifted up into a smirk so similar to Declan's it made her stomach flutter against her will.

"What won't work?" She widened her eyes, hoping she looked innocent enough.

"Oh, don't pretend you aren't playing me. I'm a pirate." He waved a hand in the air by his head. "I know all the tactics and the sleights of hand and the turns of phrase."

"I was merely curious, Mr. Murphy." She stumbled over her words, cursing herself for not being more cunning.

Tommy let out a single laugh. "Flattery will get you nowhere either."

"I only said your name. How is that flattery?"

"I'm no mister. Just Tommy. Even to you. To everyone really." He stopped and looked at her more closely. "Wait. How'd you know my last name? And don't claim eavesdropping. No one uses—"

She tossed her head toward the desk. "It was written on a piece of paper over there."

He looked again like he might laugh at her. "Don't let the captain know you're poking around."

She kicked herself for the slipup, cursing her tongue for getting her caught. Again. She needed to change the subject. "So, why do you think I might save him? And from what?"

Tommy rubbed his temple, his eyes falling to the floor as his hand moved back to rub the obvious tension from his neck. "I shouldn't have said anything. It's really not my place."

"What is it with pirates doing that?" Aoife couldn't hide her irritation. "Or is that more in line with men in general, pirate or not?"

"Doing what exactly?" The space between his brows creased in what appeared to be genuine confusion, with no sign of the feigned ignorance Declan always played up to goad her.

"You say something curious, and then when asked for clarification or elaboration you claim inability to speak on the matter. You can't do that! It's maddening to the person you're speaking to. Leaving them hanging! Leaving them with nothing but their curiosity to plague them!"

The confusion vanished from his face, replaced with an amused grin, and she realized she'd been rambling again. Something her mother had always chided her for, something Lani had always teased her for. Lani. She pushed the image of her dead sister aside.

"Well, pirates do like to cause people consternation; that's for sure. But I promise it wasn't intentional. This time."

"So why mention it at all?"

"Mere slip of the tongue, I'm afraid. I'm not as calculated and controlled as Dec —" He stopped himself and cleared his throat. "Excuse me. As Captain McCallagh. My thoughts tend to slip out if I'm not too careful. And apparently I wasn't careful enough just now."

Before she could push for more information, he was nodding his head and turning for the door, giving her a final command to stay put before he was stepping out the door.

Her mind was in a whir, and she couldn't find the words to get him to stay and explain.

What could this captain need saving from? She worked her way through all the puzzling pieces of information she'd collected. The short schedule he was on and the urgency that obviously plagued him. The disdain in his eyes when he looked at her, as well as the obvious stress he was under. The worried dreams she'd witnessed on his sleeping face two nights in a row now. The book of legends that she was sure had something to do with all of aforementioned, given how he'd tried to hide his reaction upon finding her reading it.

And how could she save him exactly?

She wasn't anything more than a useless former heir, probably being chased down by the council she'd fled from. She hadn't saved Lani. She was doing a piss-poor job of saving herself. She was under no delusions that she could save anyone, let alone a pirate captain.

Once again alone in the captain's quarters, she turned and looked around. She'd already explored every inch of the space—as much as she had allowed herself to without disturbing anything. Like Tommy, she would prefer not to incur the captain's wrath unnecessarily.

She'd been instructed to stay put, but the air in the cabin was stifling. Despite that her legs had steadied, her stomach had not, and she needed fresh air to calm it. Moving to one of the back windows, she propped it open. She breathed the sea air in deeply and stared at her feet, letting each breath calm her nausea. Though it could only do so much.

The ship was still moving, and faster now.

She forced her eyes up. If she could find the horizon, it would help. But her view of the horizon was disrupted by the sight of another ship. A larger ship, its massive sails full and impressive. It was approaching fast.

Now she knew why she'd been instructed to stay in here. And she felt like an idiot for not realizing that was what the warning call had been about. She really didn't know anything about sailing, did she?

Her gut tensed—and not from the rolling of the sea—urging her to run and hide under the blankets or beneath the dining table. But she froze, her eyes locked on the ship as it came up on them.

And then they were slowing.

The other ship had caught up, and Declan had simply given up? What if they'd been sent by the council to hunt her down and bring her back? As bizarre as that was to think about, it made sense. Her mother might not be able to explain the disappearance of two heirs within as many days. Would she?

The ship stopped its steady rolling and now bobbed atop the sea. Footsteps sounded overhead, and voices shouted. From here, even with the window open, she couldn't make out whether they were friendly or angry.

Aoife closed the window and tiptoed back to the door of the cabin. She stopped midway across, just past the desk, and turned. There had to be something in the room she could arm herself with, in case this was not a friendly meeting between pirates. A dagger. A knife. Something. In the dining room she spotted a fork but no knife. It would have to do. She slipped it into her sleeve to conceal it, hoping she'd be able to get it out in time if needed.

The ship seemed incredibly still as she opened the door to the cabin. There'd be nowhere for her to hide, with the midmorning sun shining brightly across the deck. The crew was scattered about, leaning against railings and standing in huddled groups here and there, but no one turned to look at her. That was a first. Instead they all stared to the left, no doubt at the large ship that had come alongside them, its sails lowered, as the *Siren's Song*'s were, to keep them steady.

Tiptoeing past the stairs, Aoife spotted Declan and Tommy standing at the railing, watching and waiting, their eyes lowered to the water, not looking at the deck or the many crewmen present. Her heart pounded, her eyes flitting about. What was going on? Was this something that happened often at sea? She really hadn't studied up on pirate politics at all before she'd fled, though she wondered if that would have done much good at all.

She leaned against the banister of the stairs to the quarterdeck, trying to hide herself as best she could, but still, no one seemed to notice her presence. A few minutes passed, and no one seemed to breathe or even mutter a word. Some of the crew looked a little antsy, but she didn't see any weapons in their hands. And for a brief moment she wondered if pirates ever fought at all. They seemed so pleasant and unassuming.

Aoife marveled at the silence of the crew. They all seemed to hold a collective breath as Declan and Tommy stepped back to allow two men to climb aboard, and she wondered where they'd come from and how they'd gotten here from their ship. Maybe a small rowboat or something. So odd. She'd always imagined them swinging over on ropes.

She took in a deep breath and waited. Waited for them to call her forward and hand her over. But it didn't happen. From this vantage point she couldn't see Declan's face and tried to read his body language instead, but he looked as he always did. Confident. Brave. In command.

It was Tommy who stole a glance her way, his eyes widening ever so slightly when he spotted her at the railing, but he gave no indication to the men around him that she was out of the cabin. She moved an inch or two, shifting her weight to get more comfortable, as her hip was starting to ache from the uncomfortable position. But as soon as she fidgeted, Tommy's hand tensed by his leg, fingers splaying wide as he gestured for her to stay put.

This time she would listen.

CHAPTER 23
DECLAN

DECLAN'S HAND rested on the pommel of his sword as he worked to keep his stance casual and unassuming. Captain Callum Grayson stepped forward, his quartermaster close behind him.

"I wasn't sure you'd stop for us, McCallagh," Captain Grayson said, working out the kinks in his neck as he stepped toward Declan and Tommy.

"Almost didn't." In a more civilized society there would have been a shaking of hands, but not among pirates.

Declan could have raised the yellow flag, claimed illness or plague aboard his ship, but he'd decided it better to use this encounter to his advantage. Any interaction with a friend at this point—especially since Aoife refused to help—could give him information he needed to free the Bron sisters.

He kept his head up and his back straight, forcing himself not to let the weariness and fatigue and stress show. The crew of the *Curse Bringer* stood much like his own crew: steady, waiting, ready to act if this meeting turned sour.

Callum, barely five years Declan's senior, stood a few inches taller and had an air about him that demanded obedience. He'd built quite the name for himself over the years, managing to buy a larger ship than all of the other lesser captains who remained unbound to the pirate lords.

"You can tell your men to stand down, by the way. We aren't here in ill spirits." Callum didn't bother to look around at the crew as Declan thought he might, instead keeping his gaze firmly locked on Declan.

Declan drummed his fingers on his blade's hilt out of habit, but he didn't move to give Tommy the command. They both stood, eying their guests. "So what spirits do bring you here then?"

"Can't an old friend merely pop in to say hello now and then?" A faint smile spread across Callum's rough face, though his dark eyes remained serious, danger-ous, seeming even more so given the severe cut of his black hair and the white scar that ran from his jaw to his left ear. "How long's it been anyway?"

"Two years, I believe. Since the fleet we took on up north."

"Right, right. Good time indeed. I always wondered why we didn't partner up more often." Callum's eyes gave a slight twitch as he spoke, and Declan got the distinct impression he was being baited.

"We did work well together. One of the best bounties we've secured. Gave us enough for the crew to have quite a worthy rest afterward." Declan shifted his weight, trying to read Callum's expression but coming up empty. He'd simply have to ask outright. "Did you have another partnership opportunity in mind?"

"Perhaps, perhaps." Callum leaned toward Declan and lowered his voice so only he and their quartermasters could hear. "I've heard rumors you might be working on something. Something big."

"Well, you know what they say about idle hands."

Callum straightened, lifting his chin. "Actually, no, I don't. Regardless, I want in."

"Without even knowing what it is?"

Callum's grin spread wider as his brows rose. "I didn't say I didn't know."

"You shouldn't believe everything you hear." Declan worked to keep his expres-sion blank, though he could feel Tommy tense up beside him.

Again Callum leaned in. "I hear you're going after the Csintala Dagger."

Declan let out a laugh. "I didn't take you for one to believe in children's stories and myths, Grayson."

"Play the fool all you want, but I know it's true."

How does he know? Who would have told him? He pushed those questions aside.

"Why would you want in?"

"Why wouldn't I? It's a legend. The prestige alone that would come with finding it? Retrieving it? And to use it—"

Declan interrupted. "If you can even trust the stories to be true. They very well might be fabricated. Exaggerated to delight children."

"Aye, true enough. But still. I want in." Callum rocked back on his heels, one hand on the hilt of his sword and the other hovering at his stomach. Such arrogance and confidence emanated from the man, the kind that came with years of laying waste to smaller ships and knowing he could do so here with a mere flick of that hand.

Declan pondered this request for a moment, doing his best to look bored as he looked up toward the sky. He could use the help, for sure. But he couldn't share this bounty with any other captain. He needed to hand it over to his sister—if he decided to do so. And he couldn't trust anyone—not even an old *friend* like Callum —not to divulge secrets to the council or take the dagger for their own use.

"I'm still trying to wrap my head around why you'd believe such tales about me."

"Dominic here asked the same thing," Callum said, nodding to his quartermaster. "But it's a McCallagh thing to do. Chasing after more than just the usual and the mundane. You always were a kid with an eye for adventure, for more than the status quo."

"I've grown up since then. I'm a bit more practical now." Friend or no, Callum couldn't be trusted, and Declan certainly couldn't ask him for any insight into the council hall or the fae. Not without bringing more suspicion upon himself. But this encounter hadn't been for naught. If Callum had heard the rumors, then they were spreading far, and if the council didn't know he was searching for the dagger, they would soon.

Whether anyone believed he had gone mad or was truly looking for the dagger was beside the point. People were talking. And that didn't help him in his need for secrecy.

Callum cut through his thoughts. "You have gotten a bit taller at least. But I still see that same wild kid in your eyes, McCallagh."

The time was creeping by, and Declan was antsy to get Callum off his ship and get underway. "Well, I hate to break it to you, but you've been misinformed. We're merely on our way to Foxhaven."

At that, a thump sounded behind him, and he and Tommy both turned. Declan's jaw tightened. What was she doing out of the cabin? Two days. She'd only been on board two days, and she was indeed proving to be a liability. The ship wasn't even moving, and Aoife had somehow lost her balance and stumbled on the deck. She looked at him and Tommy, her eyes wild with fear and worry as she quickly glanced away.

"And who is that?" Callum asked, trying to see around Declan.

"Just someone we're giving passage to Foxhaven."

"So you're a ferryboat now? Since when do pirates give people rides?" Callum's face had such amusement written all over it that Declan wanted to punch it off him.

"Since this pirate decided to." His words came out with more of an edge than he'd intended.

Callum took a step forward, but Declan stepped in his way, pressing his hand against the other captain's chest.

"I merely want to meet the man you allowed aboard your ship, McCallagh. No ill will here, as I said before. Unless you have something to hide." Callum's eyes narrowed at him with the challenge.

"I'm a pirate. We all have something to hide. Friend or not, this is my ship, and you will not take another step on it without my permission."

Declan could feel the tension mounting around him. Tommy kept his eyes on Dominic, who was an older gentleman, old enough to be Callum's father, weathered by the years at sea but also toughened by them.

Callum lowered his voice once again. "Indeed, friend. But I won't hesitate to overrun your ship and sink it to the bottom of the sea. Even for something as silly and trivial as you not allowing me to talk to someone."

Declan knew it was possible. The *Curse Bringer* had far more crew members.

His mind whirred with his options. He could kill Grayson right here, with a swift jab of the dagger he carried at his hip. And Tommy would have the older quartermaster taken out within a fraction of a second later. But how would their crew respond? No doubt Callum's bo'sun would take charge and have them attacking swiftly.

It's what his own bo'sun was trained to do.

Time ticked by, and he needed to make a decision soon. If Callum knew of his search for the dagger, had he also heard of the runaway heir? Quite likely, and Declan wasn't sure what Callum would do if he learned she was here.

Before he could respond, Callum was waving Aoife over to join them. Declan turned toward her and saw she'd already taken several steps in their direction. "Stop!" He hoped she'd listen. For once. And not do anything stupid.

But it was too late. "A woman?" Callum burst into laughter. "Declan, you fool. You're a complete and utter fool. You let her on board?"

Declan turned back to Callum, his jaw clenching tighter. His desire to punch him grew stronger with every word the man spoke. Declan could feel his crew's disapproval growing. He was risking possible mutiny by going against their wishes and allowing her passage. But he was the captain, and he was in charge. For now.

"You know who she is, right?"

"Do you?" Declan challenged.

"Aye. It's all anyone's talking about right now. The Cregahn heir who fled."

It didn't make any sense to Declan. Why would the council let word of that spread? But he could use this to his advantage.

"And you believed those stories too?" Callum remained quiet, his eyes on Aoife, who had frozen mid-step. "Honestly, Callum, has the salt air gotten to your senses to make you accept every tale you hear?"

"If she's not the heir, then who is she?" Callum's eyes flicked back to Declan's and held them with such an intensity his mind nearly went blank from it. But he wasn't that young kid anymore, and he wasn't easily intimidated.

Declan opened his mouth to answer, but before he could, Aoife began speaking behind him. His stomach clenched as he turned to see her inching toward them, her chin high and regal despite the ridiculous outfit she still wore. "I am the heir, but I did not flee."

Tommy shot her a questioning look before catching Declan's gaze as a smile started to pull at the corner of the quartermaster's lips.

"Oh?" Callum asked.

"I was sent."

"And why would they do that?" Callum's eyes narrowed.

Aoife stepped between Declan and Tommy now, only a foot away from the captain of the *Curse Bringer*. She didn't flinch. Didn't back down. Didn't show any of the fear Declan—or Callum—might have anticipated. "Because there's word of rebellion and dissent, that some are working to overthrow the council."

Declan blinked at her, wondering if she was making this up on the fly or if she—and the council—knew about his sister's organization and their plotting.

"But they'd never send an heir to uncover that information. That's why they have the pirate lords, after all." Callum spat the words out with disdain.

"The lords are losing favor with the council and can no longer be trusted. Not fully anyway, and certainly not with anything of this magnitude."

"But you're just a girl."

"Don't let my looks deceive you."

Callum studied her for a bit as if he were chewing apart her claims in his head and testing them. Declan and Tommy shared a glance around Aoife, who, regardless of how clumsy she was, did put on a good show of being fearless and determined. Perhaps he should consider keeping her on board.

"I'll hand it to you, Miss—I'm sorry, I didn't catch your name."

Aoife didn't say anything, but merely urged him with her sharp stare to continue.

"You are a decent liar, and you might even make a good pirate someday. But I'm better. And my sources are more...reliable." Callum rubbed a hand over his beard and turned to his man. "What shall we do, Dominic?"

Dominic's voice came out as gruff and weathered as his face. "I say we take her home. No doubt her people miss her and need her back on their shores."

"Aye. My thought exactly," Callum said and turned back to Declan. "So we'll be doing just that." He leaned in close once again to speak only to Declan. "Should help you earn back favor with your crew too, McCallagh. They look about ready to toss you to the depths."

Callum gave a nod to Dominic, who made a move toward Aoife, but Tommy was immediately there, his blade now drawn and held against Dominic's neck. Callum looked from Declan to Tommy and back again, as if expecting Declan to call his man off and out of the way. But Declan met Callum's stare, his mind ablaze with the possibilities of how this could pan out.

"You will not touch her, Callum. She goes where she pleases. She is her own person." He could feel the questioning daggers from her eyes beside him, but he continued. "We promised her safe passage, and you know my word—"

"Is not the word of a true pirate. You're a fool, Declan. Wave of my hand and my men will be firing all our rounds into your ship, taking the girl, and leaving you as fish food."

Declan knew his crew was growing more anxious by the minute. If it were up to a vote, she'd be handed over without question. But he couldn't send her back. As much as she irked him, he wouldn't subject her to the cruelty of the council should they get their hands on her, even if it might lead to a possible mutiny among his men.

In an instant, Declan had his own dagger out and up, but instead of killing Callum then and there, he merely pushed the point into the other captain's neck. Blood trickled out around the blade and slid down the man's skin, but he didn't flinch. Neither man moved.

Declan spoke first. "You will not. I see your bluff for what it is, Callum. You want that dagger, and you know I'm the only way to find it."

Callum was equally as fast with his own blade, using it to swipe Declan's away before pushing himself into Declan's face, their blades crossed between their chests. "Does that mean you've reconsidered?"

"Aye." Declan shoved Callum off, pointing his dagger at the man's chest. "We share the spoils. But I run the operation. I call the shots. And I decide when and where and how you engage."

"You're asking a lot," Callum said, sheathing his own dagger while eying Declan's. "But I accept. How can I be of service?" He gave a grand bow as he spoke.

Declan lowered his own blade, securing it as he said, "We could use some information, if you know anyone who can help. Particularly about the dagger's location and who or what might be guarding it."

"You don't already have that?"

Declan shook his head. "I have hints and clues. Guesses really, but we'll want to be certain before we make a move to take it."

Callum lifted his chin. "And I assume you won't be divulging any of these hints or clues?"

"You'll know when you need to know." Declan called for Tommy to lower his weapon and release Dominic.

"So you're on to Foxhaven," Callum said. "And what of the girl?" Declan gave another shake of his head. "Ah, a need-to-know basis, is it? Fair enough. Do with her what you will. We'll head back to Morshan and see what we can dig up."

"Be quick about it. We are on a short timeframe," Declan said, and as expected, Callum's eyes widened.

"How short?"

"Thirty days."

"That's plenty of time to get information out of someone."

"Thirty days to retrieve the dagger."

Callum's expression tightened as he no doubt tried to work through all the pieces. "And do what with it?"

Declan chewed on the inside of his lip while he studied the captain. Callum would need to know just enough to keep him on track but not enough to piece it all together. Though Declan hadn't managed to figure out Cait's plans yet himself.

"To bring it back to Morshan." He knew Callum had a million more questions, but they'd need to wait. He held up a hand to stop him from asking any of them. "That's all you need to know for now. So if you'd like in on this, you'll take it and get to work. We will meet you back in Morshan in five or six days."

"Very well, Captain." Callum gave a short nod and waved at Dominic to depart, but before he backed away himself, he stepped close to Declan. "I find out you've crossed me, and I won't be quite so cordial next we meet."

The threat hit its mark, cutting off the air in Declan's throat, but he refused to let the trepidation show on his features as Callum walked off.

As soon as the two pirates were off the *Siren's Song* and rowing back to their own ship, Declan's crew released a collective breath, as if they'd been holding it for the entire exchange. But they were far from relaxed, and a nervous energy buzzed among them.

Declan ignored their stares as he spoke to Tommy. "Talk to the men. Answer any questions they have. I'm sure they have plenty."

"Aye, sir."

And with that, Declan grabbed Aoife's arm and dragged her back to the cabin while the crew stared after him.

CHAPTER 24
AOIFE

BACK IN THE captain's quarters, Aoife shifted in her seat. Her arm throbbed where Declan had grabbed her, but she hadn't bothered to fight him as he escorted her back to the cabin and pushed her inside. That encounter hadn't exactly gone as planned—not that she had really had a plan at all. Still, it could have gone better.

Much better.

She still had the fork lodged in her shirt sleeve, and it poked her wrist whenever she moved. Declan's eyes were fixed on her. They bored into her as if probing and prodding to find out what secrets lay within. He drew in a breath and released it slowly, his hand lifting to swipe the hair away from his forehead. She waited for the yelling, for the reprimand, for the lecture about how stupid she was.

But it didn't come. Instead, he laughed.

Not in a mocking way, but in a way of pure amusement. Had he lost it? Completely gone mad? There was nothing funny about this situation. She'd outed herself as the heir, and the other captain hadn't believed any of her lies. Soon the council would know where she was and who she was with, and they'd hunt her down and "take care" of her.

And here he was laughing.

She cleared her throat, trying to cut through his laughter, snap him out of whatever madness had taken hold of him.

"I'm sorry," Declan said between his chuckles. Another deep breath cleared the last of the laughter away, and he seemed to put every bit of effort into calming himself down.

"I don't see what is so funny about this." Aoife forced the words out through clenched teeth, her anger rising with every word. "This is serious, and you're here chuckling like an imbecile."

Something in her gut begged her to back off before she stepped too far over the line, but she ignored it. She was already so far beyond every line ever drawn for her by people in power. She wasn't going to let this idiot of a captain keep her from stepping up and speaking her mind. She had nothing left to lose. She was already being hunted—probably by every pirate in the Aisling. What did it matter if she was thrown into the depths by this captain or killed by those hired by her mother?

Declan didn't seem put off by her comment though. "Oh, but there's much to laugh about here."

"I disagree, Captain." She spat out the last word, hoping it would sting him, but it seemed to have little effect.

"Of course you do. You have no sense of humor."

"I do when the situation calls for it, but I see nothing funny about those pirates knowing who I am—"

"And whose fault is that, miss?" All humor vanished from his expression, his stare hardening with the cold intensity that haunted her whenever she closed her eyes. "I believe we told you to stay put, stay hidden. But you couldn't. You couldn't follow a simple command intended for your safety. So excuse me while I distract myself with a bit of laughter and try to see the humor in a situation that altogether sucks. Because of you."

His words stung more than she wanted them to. Why did she want his approval or his admiration? He was nothing but an awful, heartless pirate who would never care about anyone or anything but his own ridiculous plans to retrieve some dagger.

She stopped, her mind flitting back to a section of the book she'd read the night before. A dagger. *The* dagger. Was Declan truly seeking the Csintala Dagger? She'd assumed it was simply a legend, obviously, as it was in a book of children's stories and make-believe. But was it true?

Aoife lowered her eyes to her hands in her lap. The fork still poked her wrist, but she dared not remove it in his company and incur further ridicule. Not that a fork would have done her any good had Declan agreed to give her over to Callum and his crew. She had no doubt Callum wouldn't have shown her the same courtesy or given her the same accommodations Declan had.

And yet Declan looked at her as though he wanted to toss her overboard himself, to be rid of her and her mistakes and missteps. Why was he helping her and protecting her?

"So the dagger's real?" It came out barely above a whisper, and she waited, breath held, for him to snap at her again. As much as she hated him, she hated him being cross with her more, though she couldn't understand why it hurt as much as it did.

"Aye. It is."

"And can it really do what they say? Is it really enchanted?"

His silence seemed answer enough, but that was ridiculous. Impossible. But an image of the fae sisters flashed briefly in her mind. The fae had magic, so maybe the stories of this dagger were true too.

"And the shield? Does that exist too?" she asked.

"If it does, I haven't been told. Nothing beyond what that book said." He looked as bored as he sounded.

She leaned forward. "But you know where the dagger is, don't you?"

He answered with a silent dip of his chin, his eyes burning into her, challenging her to look away. She didn't.

"And you sent Callum off to get information you already had."

"To keep him busy."

"Why didn't you let him take me?" It was the question she worried most about asking, partly because she had been so close to being handed back over to the council, but also because she feared his answer wouldn't be what she hoped.

He roughed a hand behind his neck, as if to buy himself time, perhaps thinking of an excuse or a lie.

"Because..." He cleared his throat before continuing. "If anyone's going to be rewarded for returning you to the council, it's going to be me. Not him."

She'd expected as much, but the disappointment still fell heavy in her gut. She forced herself to not let it show in her voice though. "Of course. Just as I thought."

"Then why ask?"

"Because I wanted to hear you say it aloud, I guess."

Declan narrowed his eyes again at her. "Did you think I did it because I care?"

She held his stare, refusing to look down again as she searched her brain for the answer. Had she thought he cared? She had hoped. When he'd stood up to Callum for her, a burning ember had caught and ignited in her chest, though she couldn't understand why.

Why did she care what Captain McCallagh thought of her?

And yet, she couldn't deny how it stung to know he didn't care, how her heart seemed to cave in on itself a bit.

He'd made it clear the other night, hadn't he? But she'd begun to wonder if maybe the desire she'd heard as he purred in her ear had been real and not merely an act. And she hated herself for liking it, for wanting him to make good on his threats. Hated herself for the way her stomach flitted uncontrollably when he looked at her.

A knock came at the door, and Tommy poked his head in. "Captain, we'll be arriving in Foxhaven soon." He raised an eyebrow as if to say something more without words.

Declan waved him inside and turned back to Aoife as Tommy stepped inside and shut the door with a soft click.

"Aoife, I don't think I need to warn you of what ill-fate awaits you if you tell anyone what we're after." He paused, almost as if daring her to argue, but she remained quiet. "The pirates you'll encounter in this port are a different breed entirely. Not like us, or even like Callum. And certainly nothing like what you've witnessed when the lords dine in your hall."

Aoife swallowed her fear and worry, but her stomach grew more uneasy with each word he said.

"You'll need to have your wits about you," he continued. "And we won't be there to help if you get into a sticky situation."

"And what am I supposed to do there?"

He thumbed his nose before crossing his arms over his chest, his expression dripping with indifference. "You might have thought about that before you trespassed on my ship."

"There wasn't time." A simple fact Aoife had repeated in her head over and over again when she chided herself for getting into such a mess.

"Even with little time, one can stop and think and plan without relying so much on their emotions driving them to stupidity."

Mess or not, she was damn tired of being called stupid by this pirate.

She unclenched her teeth and glared at him. "I'm sorry, Declan, that we aren't all cunning masterminds like you. We don't all have the ability of shutting down all feelings and pushing away all human ties so easily. Do you think it was easy to leave behind the only home I've ever known and the only family I've ever had? Even though I know the truth now, they're still the only people I've ever loved. Those ties are not so easily severed for most of us."

She heard Tommy shift, his breath seeming to scrape against his throat. Either he had words he wanted to add, or he merely wanted to escape this uncomfortable situation. She didn't know which, but she didn't feel sorry for him in the slightest. He followed this captain. Did his bidding. Gave him his loyalty.

Declan eyed her for a moment, but something in his glance made him seem bored, as if he weren't on some daring quest for an enchanted dagger but was simply sailing about on a sunny afternoon. "Fair points, I suppose." And then his expression hardened a bit. "But you'll need to check those emotions here. Be on your guard. Watch your back."

"Why bother giving me advice?" Aoife had zero ability to be gracious to him.

"You know? I don't know." He raised his hands in an exaggerated shrug. "I'm done. Tommy, get her out of here. We'll be arriving soon, and she can wait out of my sight and out of my hair."

"Aye, Captain." Tommy moved to lift her by her elbow out of the chair, but she shook him off, shooting Declan one final glare before turning toward the door. He didn't notice. He was already done, as he'd said, preoccupied with whatever book or journal was on his desk.

"I can walk myself, Tommy." And without another look at the young captain, she walked out of his cabin and his life.

CHAPTER 25
AOIFE

AOIFE STARED at the port before her, her fingers clutching the glass vial of black sand at her chest. For the last two days, she had tried to prepare herself, to imagine what Foxhaven would look like, but she never could have painted it with such clarity and vibrancy. While Morshan was a town of order and peace—at least on the surface— Foxhaven was decidedly the opposite. She could tell that simply from her view aboard the ship.

Standing on the deck of the *Siren's Song*, which was now anchored in the bay, Aoife waited for the men to prepare the boats that would take them ashore. She tried to take it all in, but there was too much to look at. And so much to listen to.

Everywhere along the beach men arranged cargo into wagons while women came to offer them drinks, greeting them with kisses and low-cut dresses that could barely keep their supple bodies contained. Beyond the beach, ramshackle buildings of every size and shape were erected in what appeared to be no particular order whatsoever, as if the builders had simply started putting up boards wherever their eyes happened to fall.

The buildings weren't painted with the drab and mundane beiges and tans from back home, but rather wore every color under the sun and sea. A bright purple one-story structure stood beside a pink and teal two-level building with a large wrap-around porch and multiple balconies framing its second-floor. Weaving among all the buildings were people of equally diverse appearances, from tall men with skin as dark as Aoife's hair to petite women with olive skin and sleek black hair in braids down their backs.

And the smells.

Even from the ship she could smell the aromas of foods and spices wafting out to her and mixing with the brine of the sea. Her stomach gave an appreciative growl. As much as she'd hoped Declan would keep her aboard, the fresh fruit they'd enjoyed from Morshan had dwindled quickly and likely wouldn't be available forever. The thought of having a warm meal that wasn't sea-hardened and tough was incredibly appealing.

She'd never even imagined a place like Foxhaven, and it made her heart race a bit.

Someone came up beside her, nudging her elbow with his own. Tommy.

"He hates me." She cringed at the words that spilled out of her, not knowing why she'd said them. Of all the things she could have said... But she couldn't deny—even with the marvel that was Foxhaven before her—that Declan's final words to her weighed heavy.

Tommy only gave a hum in response.

"Why didn't he want my help?" She turned her head a fraction of an inch to find him staring toward the shore. Why did this man follow such a captain? Tommy was kind and funny, always seemed in good spirits, unlike Declan. And why waste those good looks on a ship full of men? He could have a wife and a whole brood of children to play with and raise up. And yet here he was, wasting his handsome face and warm heart on this ship.

Thankfully, her traitor of a tongue didn't say any of that to him.

Tommy kept his gaze ahead on the teal waters of the bay. "He did, Aoife. And does. But like everything else, he wants it—needs it—to be on his terms."

Aoife breathed the briny air deep into her lungs, her stomach responding once again to the delicious smells it carried. The mere sight of Foxhaven overwhelmed her. So many people. So little order. She didn't even know where to begin once she was ashore, and the crew had already insisted she be one of the first off the ship.

"Where do I go now, Tommy? I have no skills, unless they need me to recite some Cregahn poetry or explain the details of the Muirnaughton Treaty." She looked down at her smooth hands, untouched by any manual labor, a stark contrast to the weathered wood of the railing they rested on. "I don't fit in here."

"Aye. You don't. But were you born to fit in, Aoife?"

It seemed such an odd thing for him to say, but it felt genuine and caring all the same. Perhaps, had things been different, had Declan been a pirate lord, Aoife and Tommy might have met in the council hall and planned their own escape like Lani and Adler had. She swallowed hard and ignored those thoughts.

"Don't flatter me, Tommy."

"I'm not. Simply stating a fact." He glanced at her from the corner of his eye. "Council ladies aren't meant to blend in. You were born to rule and to lead, not hide among pirates."

"But I didn't fit in there. And I doubt I will here either."

"Why all the preoccupation with fitting in anywhere?"

His question hit a sore spot. She'd only ever belonged with her sister, with Lani. And then she'd betrayed her. Without her, where did she belong? Where was her place? And why wouldn't the thoughts of her sister stay hidden, locked away in her mind? She hoped that would happen with time, hoped she'd be able to move on and not live with this ghost and guilt forever.

"We all want to know we belong, Tommy. Whether it's in the shadow of our captain"—she paused to smirk at him—"or in a new land of strangers. Or in a council of rulers. We weren't meant to be alone. We weren't meant for solitude. But what's the point of being among people if you can never be comfortable? Be yourself?"

"Ah, I see what you mean." Tommy glanced past her toward the men starting to gather for debarkation. They'd just had rest in Morshan, but apparently all were eager to partake in whatever pleasures lay ashore, the notable difference today being the sheer number of weapons they had on their persons. She'd never seen so many blades of various sizes tucked into belts and boots and slung across backs and chests. "Well, if you're going to fit in, or at least try to, you'll need this."

Aoife glanced down at Tommy's hands, which held a small dagger. No, too small to be a dagger, though she didn't know what to call it. Weapons identification wasn't exactly a course they offered to council heirs. Or to anyone from Cregah.

"Take it." Tommy held it up a little higher.

Aoife wrapped her fingers around the hilt. A simple but handsome design with a serpent was carved into its handle. It fit her hand perfectly, as if it had been made for her, but that notion was preposterous. She lifted it tentatively, resting the end of the blade in her left palm as she examined the design closely. "Whose was it?"

"I don't know. We took it off a ship we looted a couple months back, and for some reason I kept it. Of all the goods that ship carried, this one seemed to call to me, as if it wanted to be in my possession. Perhaps it was trying to find its way to you."

"Are all pirates so superstitious and weird?" she asked, not taking her eyes off the gift.

He laughed. "Maybe. A bit."

"Where do I keep it?"

"On you?"

"Well, yes, I got that, but where? You know, I'm more accustomed to wearing dresses and tunics, not whatever you call these items. And I'm not used to concealing weapons on my body."

"Who said you needed to conceal it? It might be better to display it so people know you're armed."

He took the blade from her and held it in his teeth, using his hands to undo the buckle at her belt. Her heart nearly stopped as she wondered what he was doing, but with a few quick movements, he had slid a sheath onto her belt and refastened it, pulling it tight around her waist. He wiggled his brow at her as he slid the blade into the leather.

"I don't even know how to use it." She dropped her gaze to the deck, unable to look him in the eye, to let him see she wasn't as strong as she pretended to be.

"The pointy end goes in the other person."

She managed a half smile before her nerves took hold again and kept a laugh from emerging. "And where do I go? There's so much here. So much to see and smell."

"Smell?" Another laugh. "It can be overwhelming the first time. Or the tenth time, if I'm honest. But may I recommend you head to Lucy's."

Something tightened in Aoife upon hearing the name. Not that it was an intimidating name in itself, but what sort of establishment did this Lucy run? Her consternation must have shown on her face, because Tommy laughed again. "No, no. It's not what you're thinking. She runs one of the best eateries in port, and I'm sure she would have a spot for someone to help in the dining room."

"How do you know she'll have a spot open for me?"

"Well, let's just say most of the women prefer the other, more lucrative positions on the island." He winked when Aoife wrinkled up her nose. "Hey, don't look down on them or their customers. They've found a place they belong and fit in. And isn't that what we all need?"

Of course he'd found a way to throw her words back at her. "Lucy's. Okay. And where do I find her exactly?"

"She's in the yellow building in the middle of that mess over there." Tommy pointed off to the right a bit, and Aoife hoped she'd be able to make it there without needing to use the blade now hanging at her waist.

"Thank you, Tommy. For being so kind. I'm sure Declan wouldn't approve of your helping me."

Tommy turned and stepped away from the railing but noted over his shoulder, "He's the one who asked me to."

CHAPTER 26
AOIFE

An hour later Aoife stood on the shore of Foxhaven, not caring that her feet were still getting wet from the tide as it came in and washed out.

She couldn't move.

If she had found this port overwhelming while on the deck of the *Siren's Song*, it was much more so when standing on the outskirts of it. Crew from Declan's ship moved around her, careful not to come into contact with her, as if she had some plague or disease.

Or bad luck. They couldn't have that rubbing off on them.

"Hey! Lass! Are you going to stand there all day?" A voice sounded up the shore, as rough and gravelly as the face it was paired with. The man had stopped moving bottles and trunks from his boat into a small wagon already overflowing with goods. He smiled at her, his teeth broken and chipped, a nasty shade of yellow. "If you're looking for work, I might have some for you." His blue eyes twinkled at her as his tongue wet his lips. She was sure the work he offered was of the less reputable variety.

Declan had been right when he'd said these pirates weren't like those she'd met thus far. What had she gotten herself into?

"No, thank you." She cringed at how formal she sounded. She'd never fit in here. "I have work lined up already."

She forced her feet forward, up the beach, refusing to look at the man as she passed him, though she saw him give a shrug as he laughed.

No one else spoke to her as she weaved around the various crews and island workers. Some eyed her briefly with curious looks. She hoped she'd find Lucy soon and that perhaps the woman might have some clothes she could change into. She hadn't even done anything other than lounge about and sleep in these, and they were already grungier and smellier than she was comfortable with. Though she supposed that did help her blend in a bit.

She had expected walking on the sand would be difficult after being on the ship, and she was right. While the soft white sand of the beach didn't help matters, she found the boardwalk and cobblestones no easier to traverse. She wondered how many people she passed assumed she was drunk, despite it being just after midday. Among this lot, though, that would earn her less ridicule than the truth—that she simply hadn't found her land legs yet.

Aoife didn't know where to look as she walked, and she imagined she appeared ridiculous as she looked from one colorful building to the next, her eyes wide and curious. She tried to guess what business or family might reside in each building— if families even existed on this island.

There were no signs anywhere, and it was impossible to determine whether something was a pub or a brothel or a clothing shop. But she soon realized that shops—whether selling clothes, weapons, or food—displayed their wares, albeit haphazardly, in the front windows. It was nothing like Morshan, where merchants displayed their goods in bright, orderly arrangements, showcasing the items' appeal to entice the residents to come in and buy. Here in Foxhaven it seemed the goods were merely stacked in front of the windows, as if the shop owners had stored the items without realizing customers could see the piles.

She tried her best to ignore the shops from which delicious smells drifted and seemed to seep from the pores of the buildings themselves. Her stomach growled at her, demanding to be filled, but she could wait until she found Lucy and her eatery.

Tommy had slipped her just enough copper coins to get her a first meal and maybe a short swig of rum, but it was up to her to earn all the meals and drinks that followed. She wondered if she'd ever see him again. Or Declan. Ass that he was, she couldn't ignore the small bit of gratitude she held for him. After all, he hadn't taken advantage of any of the numerous opportunities to be rid of her on their way here.

Or taken advantage in any other way, for that matter.

Aoife glanced back toward the beach, trying to peer over the bustle of people milling about. She thought she caught a glimpse of the captain and his quarter-master climbing out of a rowboat, not stumbling at all as they trudged up the beach toward the town ahead. Foxhaven seemed much bigger now that she was among the buildings. Big enough for them to avoid her if they desired.

She turned back to the mess of buildings, stifling a laugh at the sheer nonsense of how they were laid out, with the stone roads meandering between them not in a precise grid but in a mess of angles, all of different lengths, with some ending abruptly at a building, as if the road builders had gotten tired of laying cobblestones and decided to erect a building instead.

Ahead she spotted a building with three levels that had to be Lucy's, as it was the only sunny yellow one amidst the rainbow of colors around her. She picked up her pace, her heart speeding up to match her steps. She'd sneaked aboard a pirate ship and stood up to Captain Callum. She could do this. She could approach this Lucy and request a job.

And maybe lodging. She'd need that too.

Within a few moments she was standing in the doorway staring at a sea of people crowding around tables and standing along the walls with mugs of beer and mead in their hands. A few glanced up at her but then wrote her off as nothing special as they returned back to their meals and their conversations. She inched her way through, muttering apologies as she bumped into people—and wondering if pirates normally apologized for such things. How would she ever find Lucy in this mess? She looked around for someone who seemed to be working rather than eating, a server or a barmaid or someone carrying dishes or taking orders.

There, in the far corner. It had to be Lucy. Or at least someone who worked for her and could direct her to the lady. The woman was young, not much older than Aoife herself. Her dark face, with skin the color of the sands back home, was framed by tight curls haphazardly but attractively tied up at the crown of her head. She displayed a joyful demeanor that Aoife would not have expected for how busy she appeared to be, chatting with customers, clearing plates, wiping down tables, and letting others know their food was coming.

She wasn't dressed like the other women in port but wore clothing similar to Aoife's—a men's style but cut for a woman to make room for all the curves—only more colorful. Lucy's had hints of color throughout, including a turquoise sash around her waist she used to wipe down her hands now and then. Instead of an off-white linen undershirt, hers was bright pink, the color of the tropical flowers that grew in the gardens at the council hall.

Aoife realized she was standing in the middle of the crowded room, staring, just as the other lady's eyes met hers. The woman approached with the same smile beaming across her face, and Aoife lost all her words.

"Welcome! I'm Lucy, owner of this little establishment. You're new here, aren't you?" The woman had a hint of an accent Aoife had never heard before.

Aoife cleared her throat, her mouth suddenly dry, as if she'd taken in a mouth full of sand on her walk from the beach. "I am."

"I knew it. I knew I hadn't seen you around. I mean, I get a lot of people in here, so you'd assume I wouldn't be able to remember everyone, but..." She reached a free hand up to tap her temple. "My mama always said I had a memory like an elephant. Whatever an elephant is. We had them back home, I suppose, but I never saw one."

Aoife couldn't help but smile. Lucy would be easy to like, and Foxhaven might be a place she could fit in after all.

"Come. Standing in the middle of the room won't do either of us any good. Let's find you a table and get you some food. You look like you haven't eaten in days." Lucy waved a hand as she turned toward the back of the room. Aoife wasn't sure where she'd be able to find an empty table, but she supposed Lucy would know where one was.

She followed Lucy to the back corner of the room where a set of wide stairs led up and around to the second floor. Aoife had assumed these would be Lucy's quarters, but instead it was another large dining room. Unlike the first floor—with its simple tables and chairs—this upstairs dining area was a mishmash of different furniture. Mismatched armchairs with high backs and cushioned seats were scattered around low tables, while the high tables had stools surrounding them. This room sat empty, however, which Aoife attributed to the jump in temperature as they ascended. On the far wall overlooking the street below, the windows were all open to let in the sea breeze, but it wasn't enough to make the room comfortable in the slightest.

As if reading her mind, Lucy commented, "I know it's hot, but it's quiet. Come, sit. Let's chat and get you some eats." She led Aoife to a set of armchairs perched right in front of the open windows, and Aoife was pleased to discover that it was at least somewhat cooler over here. She sat down tentatively as Lucy plopped into the chair opposite her.

"Don't you have to work?" Aoife cringed a little at the silliness of her question, but Lucy didn't seem to notice as she tossed a glance toward the stairs.

"They'll be fine for a bit. Don't you worry about them. It's mostly regulars anyway, and they're a fairly patient lot, considering their profession."

"Pirates," Aoife muttered.

"Aye. And you're not one of them." Lucy tapped against her pursed lips.

"How'd you know?"

"It's a tad obvious."

Aoife's face burned. It wasn't obvious to her. She wondered what the giveaway was. Was it the clothes? Her hair? Again, it was like Lucy could read her mind. "I mean, you look the part, sure. The clothes are on point, wherever you got them. But they're too clean, for one. And two, you look too sweet. Too innocent."

"Maybe I'm just a new pirate." Aoife fought the urge to shrink in her seat and instead sat up straighter.

"Are you?"

"Well, no."

"But you did arrive on a pirate ship."

"How did you—"

"Girl, the only ships that stop here are pirate ships, so either you rowed here yourself—unlikely—or you got passage on one." She lifted her hand, her fingers finding a loose curl to fiddle with as she clicked her tongue. "Let me guess. McCallagh's ship."

"How do you do that?"

"Do what?"

"Know everything without me telling you."

Lucy's hearty laugh bounced around the empty room. "It's nothing magical, sweetie. Mere logic and powers of deduction is all."

Aoife must have looked skeptical, because the woman leaned forward then and continued to explain.

"I've lived here—owned this place—for the better part of seven years."

Aoife looked her over, earning her another chuckle.

"I know, I look younger than I am. Still. I've gotten to know most of the captains sailing the Aisling. And Declan? Well, he's one of the only ones I could imagine allowing someone such as you to stow away. And in one piece."

"I'm still surprised he didn't throw me overboard, or worse," Aoife said, glancing down at her hands as she wrung them. She didn't want to talk about Declan. She wanted to start a new life, free of him, since that was what he apparently wanted as well.

"Oh, no, that's not his style. I know, I know. His *reputation*. But it's not hard to see it's all show. Doesn't reach his heart."

"You think the stories are lies?" The thought had crossed her own mind a few times.

"Oh, no, they're quite real. He's certainly done all they've said. But the boy's not like the rest. Even if he hides it well enough from everyone else, I can see the truth. Plus, he's not one to bloody his hands unnecessarily. He's far more likely to do what he did. Drop you off here with naught but a dagger and my name."

"He didn't give—"

"Ah, but he did. Through Tommy, I imagine."

Aoife's jaw dropped a fraction of an inch, and she stared dumbly at the woman, who responded with another round of boisterous laughter as she once again settled against the high back of the threadbare armchair and crossed her legs. "Again, girl, it's just observation and what I know of Declan and his crew. Nothing special about me."

Aoife smiled at the woman and said, "My name's Aoife."

Her smile vanished as soon as she realized her mistake. She should have given an alias. But Tommy hadn't instructed her to do so, so perhaps she was safe. Perhaps Aoife wasn't that rare of a name and no one would connect her to the Cregahn Council.

"I knew an Aoife once." *See? Not rare.* "Or was it Evelyn?" Lucy stared at the ceiling, as if it might hold the answer. "Not that it matters either way. It's nice to meet you, Aoife. If Tommy sent you to me, I can only assume it's because you're needing more respectable work than what is offered elsewhere."

"Yes. And lodging too. If you can point me to a boardinghouse or—"

"Oh, nonsense. You'll stay here. The upstairs has two separate apartments, so you'll have some privacy. And I'd really appreciate the help. I have two cooks who stayed on with me after they got too weary of the sea life—Marco and John. They're nice enough and work hard. But they won't bother you none. I'll be sure of that. The patrons on the other hand... Let's just say, keep that blade handy. You won't have any trouble while here, because they know I'd wallop them if they caused trouble in my eatery. But out there?" She pointed to the street below. "That's another story altogether."

"How have you survived all this time if it's so dangerous?"

"Ah, yeah. One rule of Foxhaven—you're responsible for your own safety. Ain't nobody gonna save you here. So I hope they taught you to use that thing." She dipped her chin toward the blade still tucked into Aoife's belt. Aoife's worry must have been written clearly on her face, because Lucy rolled her eyes and groaned.

"They didn't. Tommy, Tommy, Tommy. What was that boy thinking, sending you off on your own with a blade you don't know how to use?"

"Well, I mean, he told me to put the pointy end into anyone who bothered me."

Another hearty laugh. "That's a good start at least, I suppose. Perhaps I'll have Marco or John teach you a bit. In the meantime, let's get you some food. I'm guessing you had nothing but cold, sea-hardened morsels for the past few days."

"Yes, please."

Without another word, Lucy was up and out of her seat, rushing down the stairs. Aoife turned to look out the window at her new home. If it was really as dangerous as Lucy had said—and Aoife couldn't imagine why the lady would have any reason to lie about it—she had no desire to ever leave these walls. But she hadn't escaped one prison just to hole herself up in another.

Someday she'd need to venture out and explore a bit. If this was to be her new home, she'd need to own the fear and subdue it. She swallowed hard, unsure and afraid, wishing—despite herself—that Tommy and Declan were here to teach her instead of these two cooks she hadn't yet met.

CHAPTER 27
DECLAN

They were wasting their time here in this port, and that bothered Declan. They'd been here two days, and while Mikkel had found another twenty men to fill in their ranks, he still didn't have the information he needed. Mikkel was back on the ship, getting the new crew situated, and here Declan was, counting down the last hours of their final day in port with nothing to show for it.

He kicked the cobblestones with his boot as he leaned, arms crossed in front of him, against the porch railing of Michaelson's Pub. It wasn't the best establishment in the port—that was Lucy's—but having sent Aoife there when they'd arrived, he had no desire to see her, no matter how superior the fare was.

Still, no matter how he tried to ignore it, some part of him wondered how she was doing and if she had settled in all right. It was better this way. Even if ill manners got him more grief from Tommy than he would have liked, at least Tommy had successfully gotten the hint and backed off about the lass.

He didn't have the luxury of relationships. That was for other men on distant shores. Not for pirates. Their relationship was with the sea, and maybe with the goods they took off others' hands.

This was what he wanted. Solitude. No responsibility. No ties or connections.

Then why are you doing all this for Cait then?

A groan rumbled in the back of his throat. He'd been asking himself that question since they'd left Cregah.

Technically he had never actually agreed to do this for Cait. She'd assumed. And should he somehow manage to retrieve the dagger from the Black Sound, there was no contract—written or otherwise—between them requiring he hand it over.

But could he betray his sister like that? That was the question. She'd given him so few answers, so little information. And though he knew it was for his own safety and the safety of her people, it stung how she didn't trust him.

There was no need, however, to make up his mind yet on the matter.

First get the fae.

Then get the dagger.

Then decide what to do with it.

But that first step was proving to be a great deal harder than he'd anticipated.

Movement came from his right, before the clearing of a throat announced who approached.

"Any luck?" he asked as Tommy came up beside him and mimicked his relaxed stance against the wooden rail.

Even after days of disappointment, the man seemed to be in good spirits, serious but not downtrodden.

Unlike Declan.

"Luck's got nothing to do with it, Captain."

"Any developments then?" As annoyed as Declan was, he had to admit he was thankful to have someone as steadfast as Tommy beside him, someone even-keeled. It was one of the main reasons he'd asked him to be his quartermaster in the first place. That and because Tommy was the only other pirate he trusted.

"Just a few tidbits here and there. Nothing concrete. And all the stories and rumors we're gathering contradict each other. Some say there are two sisters; some say three. Others claim they've seen them, but only once and in passing, and they could have been shadows. My guess? The fine booze they serve up there at the council hall isn't helping their memories. And those men have only been there once, on the rare occasion their lord allowed them to."

"I knew it was a long shot."

"It's tough trying to go on hearsay. We only get one chance at this. We can't risk it on shoddy information and drunken tales."

Declan gritted his teeth and looked down the narrow street, away from his friend, but didn't answer.

Tommy waited for a breath, then another, before finally saying, "We need to—"

"I know." Declan scratched at the back of his head, his gaze lowered toward the stones at his feet. "But I don't like it."

"Maybe her terms will have changed. I mean, perhaps life here has turned out better than expected and she'll offer up her knowledge with no strings attached."

"One could hope, I suppose. But it will be my last resort. I want to try once more before I give up using another route."

"We've exhausted all routes." Tommy's cool demeanor was fading quickly, his expression darkening by the second. "Why are you so against asking for her help? Are you so proud?"

"Watch it, Tommy. I mean it. I have my reasons, and pride's got nothing to do with it. Leave it."

Tommy raised his arms in surrender. "Fine."

"And we haven't exhausted them all. Another ship came in this morning."

"Yeah. I saw that. The *Duchess*, wasn't it? Don't they sail in—"

"Lord Madigen's fleet. That's right. They're his second most trusted crew after his own."

Tommy's eyes narrowed. "You know the *Duchess*'s crew doesn't partake in places like Michaelson's though." Tommy gestured to the building behind them.

Declan breathed out a sigh. "I know. Lucy's. Which we will be going to anyway if this doesn't pan out, so it saves us some extra walking."

"Lucy will be glad to see you, I bet." Tommy gave him a nudge, but Declan just rolled his eyes before he pushed off the post and started walking, not bothering to see if his friend followed.

Lucy's was only a five-minute walk away, but with the meandering nature of the streets it could have taken considerably longer had they not been so well acquainted with the town. Declan kept a decent pace, his eyes always watching, observing people as they passed, sizing up potential threats, looking for those who didn't recognize him and might see him as an easy mark.

Though Tommy was beside him, they walked in silence—another reason he had hired Tommy. He could be silent. Too many people had to fill in the silence with small talk and awkwardness. The thought brought images of Aoife and her incessant chatter to mind.

It had been too quiet the past couple of nights without her talking or humming to herself or asking asinine questions. He'd told himself it wasn't her he missed but more the distraction she'd provided.

The yellow building came into view as they rounded a corner, and he took a deep breath without slowing. It was midafternoon, but Lucy's main dining hall remained nearly packed day and night as various crews mingled with the locals who lived and worked here.

He and Tommy stepped inside and paused. Eyes turned to them, and Declan waited. A tense hush fell over the room, as if announcing their arrival. Some of the customers glanced away hurriedly; others seemed confused by the sudden change.

"Oh, ho, ho! Look who has finally graced my doorstep!" Lucy's cheerful greeting boomed through the dining room, and the patrons—any concerns now quelled by their hostess's reaction—returned to their conversations and their meals. "Come in! Come in!"

She waved them in but then stopped short, her smile dropping as she placed a hand on Declan's chest. "Now, wait a minute there, Captain. You're not here to take back my girl, are you?"

"And which girl would that be?" Declan kept his expression blank.

"Don't play dumb with me, Declan. I know well enough you and Tommy sent Aoife my way. Here to talk to her?"

"No. We aren't."

Tommy chimed in. "Not yet anyway."

"Good, because she's busy workin'. You can talk to her after dusk. Most of the folks these days head to the other pubs for a better booze selection once it gets dark. I don't mind. Gives my feet a rest."

"Fair enough, Lucy. We are, however, looking for someone else. Perhaps you've seen them?"

"And who might that be?" Her smile brightened as she straightened.

"Looking for some royal blood." He hoped she'd understand his meaning, and given her many years of working for and with pirates, he had little doubt she would.

"You know I can't divulge that kind of information, Declan." She kept her voice level, almost raising it so those around could hear her clearly, as she glanced around the room at the full tables. "Though, I do have a table upstairs with your name on it, if you're interested."

Declan looked over the diners, wondering if any of the *Duchess*'s crew was here in this room. But that ship carried double the men his did, making it impossible to know every face. And with everyone seated, it was too difficult to catch the colors they wore at the waist.

Again, he hoped Lucy understood they weren't seeking just any member of the crew, but the officers.

Tommy answered for them. "That would be great, Lucy. And don't mind us. We know our way. We'll let you get back to your customers."

She patted Tommy's cheek. "Thanks, love. I'll bring some food up to you in a bit." Lucy turned away from them but called over her shoulder, "It's good to see you both though!"

Declan nodded toward the back of the eatery before leading the way to the stairwell. The air became sticky and heavy as they climbed the stairs and left the loud chatter behind.

The upstairs hadn't changed at all, not that it had been that long since they'd stopped in. Certainly not the seven years he'd waited to return home. The room had the same mix of furniture that always made him laugh. Even with how worn each item was, Lucy kept everything impeccably clean and inviting. He often wondered where she found the energy and time to keep things looking so nice, though he'd never ask her.

Declan walked over to a low table tucked into the corner near the windows, but there was little breeze and not much to be done about the heat and humidity. Tommy shifted uncomfortably in his seat, undoubtedly from said heat. "Why can't they be sitting downstairs?" Tommy mumbled so low Declan wasn't even sure he'd heard him correctly.

"Some people prefer quiet. At all costs, I suppose." He kept his chin down as his eyes took in the dining room and the smattering of guests.

A man dined alone by the windows a couple of tables down from them, huddled over his plate and not seeming to notice that anyone else occupied the room. Two women, locals perhaps, sat at a high table near the far wall, talking quietly as little laughs peppered their conversation. It would have normally been a welcome sound, jovial and carefree, but now it only grated on Declan's nerves.

His gaze came to rest on three men sitting in the armchairs a few tables away. Two of them leaned forward, their heads close together as they spoke in hushed tones. No laughs from that group. The third sat with an ankle crossed over his knee, leaning back as he steepled his fingers under his chin, his face hidden under a large brimmed hat that had not been taken off. All three wore a purple sash at their waists—indicating their loyalty to Lord Madigen—along with the gold fabric that marked them as crew of the *Duchess*.

Tommy must have noticed them too, because he nudged Declan's boot with his own and carefully angled his head toward them before working the kinks out of his neck. Declan gave an almost imperceptible dip of his chin in acknowledgement.

These were the officers they'd been hoping to find. He'd need a good plan to address them and get them talking about their last trip to the council hall. He checked his pocket watch and almost groaned. It was getting late. In a few hours he'd have to give in and turn to Aoife for help. He didn't want that.

Tommy leaned forward, elbows resting on the table, eyes darting to the side to look at the three officers one more time before he spoke. "What's the plan?" He thumbed his nose.

"I'm working on it."

"Well, we need to work faster. Maybe Lucy could help."

As if on cue, steps sounded in the stairwell, and Lucy's warm humming filled the room. No one turned toward her, no doubt used to the way she always entered a room with a tune and a smile. She balanced two plates on one arm and three mugs in the other hand. Declan could have smiled at the sight of his old friend and how nothing seemed to dampen her spirits, but he was too restless and grumpy.

Lucy approached and set the two plates before him and Tommy. "Maybe some food will fix that sour demeanor, McCallagh. Eat up. I'm sure you could use this after whatever drivel you've been eating the last months you've been away."

He looked over the meal as he accepted the forks she offered, then looked up at her. "Where's the pie?"

She gave a laugh and a shake of her head. "You think I forgot? I got slices already set aside for you downstairs, Declan. Don't you worry."

"This looks great as always, Lucy," Tommy said and began shoveling forkfuls of meat and gravy and potatoes and green vegetables into his mouth.

Another booming laugh escaped their hostess. "Don't eat too fast there, Tommy. Your captain here may need you to be light on your feet yet, and eating like that won't help." Tommy only nodded, but he did at least allow himself to swallow fully before taking another bite. "I'll have some drinks for you in a bit."

And then she was gliding away, the three mugs in hand as she approached the three officers of the *Duchess*. She wasn't unfriendly with them, but Declan noted how her behavior changed as she became just a hair more formal and subdued, but she spoke loudly enough that Declan could hear her side of the exchange.

"How was everything? Satisfactory, I hope." The pair paused their conversation, and each gave her a nod. The third didn't move or speak. "I brought you some of our latest batch of mead. I've had rave reviews about it, even from those who prefer the rum and whisky at other establishments. On the house, of course."

She set the large mugs down on the low table and took up their plates that held mere remnants of the meal they'd enjoyed. "If you need anything else, just holler."

If they responded to her at all, Declan couldn't hear, and then Lucy was heading toward the stairs, smiling once more at Declan before disappearing below.

Declan ate slowly, or at least more slowly than Tommy, monitoring the officers in his periphery the whole time. As they drank the mead Lucy had presented, he noticed they became visibly more relaxed—even the silent one. Lucy returned once without a word, bringing two mugs similar to the ones she'd provided the officers, but filled with water instead.

He and Tommy finished their meals and sipped on their waters, requesting refills a few times as they watched the three *Duchess* crew members.

After a little over an hour, all three officers were leaning in, chattering loudly under the hats they still wore, not bothering to keep their voices down. Even the more somber one was joining in. They'd let their guard down as Declan needed, but he couldn't assume anything. It could all be for show.

But they sounded off, different, not what he'd expected. They lacked the gruffness of Callum and most other officers, not displaying the same crudeness as the average crew member. But as officers, their notable air of formality was expected, even after a few drinks.

But no, that wasn't what set these voices apart. They were higher. Like boys who hadn't yet matured into manhood, yet their bodies were the size and shape of grown men.

Except they weren't.

Declan turned to Tommy and whispered, "They're women."

CHAPTER 28
DECLAN

WOMEN. How had Declan missed that?

He kicked himself for being so ill-informed and naive. He'd heard of some crews employing women, but to have all your officers be women? It was unprecedented. Not that it changed his mind at all. In fact, it perked him up a bit. Female pirates might be allowed more freedom about the council hall, able to see more than the average pirates were able to.

"Of course they're women. You didn't know?" Tommy's expression was almost comical as he whispered back, and Declan couldn't keep from tightening his jaw in frustration. "I thought you knew. Hell, I thought everyone knew. You do know their captain, Casey Halloran, is a lass, too, right?"

"Well, I do now. How did you know and I didn't?"

"I thought it was common knowledge. I mean, I guess Casey isn't clearly a feminine name, but—" Tommy shrugged and pulled the corners of his mouth down. "I honestly thought you knew. But I suppose it makes sense you didn't. People don't really talk about it anymore, since Captain Halloran has an affinity for cutting out tongues for shit talk. Everyone's been pretty hush about it for years. And it's not like we've had any encounters with them ever. They always seem to be sailing in the opposite direction as us."

"You're rambling. Stop it."

"You know I chatter when I feel bad."

"Hence why it happens so rarely," Declan said. Another shrug. "Well then, how the hell did you hear about it?"

"I heard back when we were cabin boys."

Declan's eyes went wide. "That long ago?"

"Yeah. I overheard the officers chatting about some female captain and how her officers were women. Not all of them, mind you, but two of them. Her quartermaster and her sailing master though. They couldn't understand how men could stomach serving under them, but I suppose when you have such a ruthless reputation and a few big hauls under your belt, the men stop caring who's running the ship as long as their pockets continue to be lined and their bellies fed."

"You said two of her officers are female."

"Aye."

"So who's the third sitting—" Declan cut his words short as his stomach tightened. Why hadn't he anticipated this? The third, more aloof one, had to be the captain. Captain Halloran. She wouldn't be as easy to sway or trick into giving up information, and he certainly couldn't risk her going to Lord Madigen or demanding to be cut in on the prize like Callum had.

"So," Tommy started, "now what?"

Declan ran his fingers under his stubbled chin. His mind raced from option to option, but nothing he came up with would work. Except maybe one thing. A long shot, but desperation burned behind his sternum.

The two officers stood, their captain remaining in her seat. This was his only chance, his last hope of not having to crawl back to Aoife and beg for her aid. With a nod to their captain, the two officers made for the stairs. Declan sent Tommy off after them with an angle of his head and a raised brow. Tommy asked no questions but acted swiftly to follow, likely already devising the smooth lines he'd use to get them chatting with him.

Declan, too, rose and made his way over to where Captain Halloran sat.

This was far from an ideal location to have such a talk, but only the single man by the window remained, preoccupied with watching people on the streets below. Declan stopped a few feet away from the captain. She didn't move or acknowledge his presence.

He cleared his throat before speaking. "Captain Halloran? I've never had the pleasure of meeting you in person."

She looked up at him, and even in the shadow of her large hat, she was beautiful in a dangerous way. Her eyes, a mix of browns and golds, reflected the light of the chandeliers overhead as they burned into his own. Her dark skin showed the wear of the sea, but not in an unattractive way, not the way older men wore their years of sailing. Where others appeared weathered and worn down, her lines gave her a look of refinement. Experience.

If Tommy had heard of her all those years ago, she had to be at least ten or fifteen years Declan's senior. But she was still a pirate, and he knew how to deal with other pirates.

"And you are?" It was the first he'd heard her voice clearly all evening, and it sounded like honey dripping from her lips, but with hint of an edge, like poison slipped into a sweet treat.

"Captain McCallagh. Of the *Siren's Song*." He gave a bow of his head.

"Ah. I've heard of you." She rested her hand at her cheek as she looked him over.

"Good things, I hope," Declan said with a slight smirk on his lips.

There was no laughter in her words or eyes as she asked, "Do pirates ever say good things about one another?"

She had a point, and given the lengths he'd gone to ensure his name carried weight, he was glad to hear she'd at least heard it uttered. "May I sit?" He gestured to one of the now empty chairs across from her.

Captain Halloran tipped a shoulder up in a shrug but didn't say a word. Lowering himself into the chair, he leaned back, his mind racing through the possible paths this conversation could end up on.

He opened his mouth to speak, but she beat him to it. "So, Captain McCallagh of the *Siren's Song*, I assume you haven't gotten the information you need yet."

Declan sucked in a breath and stilled but forced his features to remain calm. He could play dumb, but he imagined that might get him into trouble with this pirate. No doubt she'd heard his crew had been asking around. "Nearly."

She let out a single laugh and leaned toward him, pushing the brim of her hat up a bit. Her eyes seemed to dance with danger and intrigue. "If that were true, you wouldn't be risking this little conversation with me, pup."

"Risking what, exactly? Merely introducing myself to a captain of such great esteem."

"Don't mock me, boy," she said, her words losing all their sweetness. "I don't deal well with being toyed with."

"So I've heard." He cleared his throat. He needed a new tactic with this one. If the charm hadn't worked, perhaps honesty might. "To be perfectly honest, Captain, I didn't know you were a woman until this evening."

"And you thought you'd come scoff at me to my face."

"I thought I'd come chat up the woman who has grown men cowering at her name and has earned a place in Madigen's fleet."

She didn't say anything. Her eyes scanned his face with such intensity it took every ounce of will not to squirm and look away.

With another breath, he pulled his lips into a tight line. "But I can see I've wasted your time, and mine. Apologies." He moved to rise, hoping she'd stop him. But she didn't. "Good evening, Captain."

He lowered his chin once more and strode off toward the stairs. He hoped Tommy had fared better with the officers, but that hope was slim. He'd need to find Aoife after all, and he wasn't looking forward to that.

He'd made it down three stairs when Captain Halloran called out to him, "McCallagh." He continued down a few more steps. He didn't want to seem too eager.

She called again, "Declan."

Hearing his first name used by someone he didn't know at all made his muscles tense. He came back up the stairs and stopped at the top, resting against the half-wall. "Yes, Captain?"

"Get over here." Her tone had lost some of its edge, and she gestured to the seat he'd just vacated.

Declan did as requested but didn't speak as he returned to his seat. Leaning back in the chair as he waited, he forced himself to relax and appear far more patient than he felt.

"I knew your parents." She showed no emotion, stating this matter-of-factly, as if she were noting the color of his jacket.

Memories threatened to rush forward, but he slammed the door closed on them. "A lot of people—a lot of pirates—knew them."

"They were good people. It's a shame what happened to them."

"Yes, well, that's the way of the world, isn't it?"

"And your sister. Cait, was it? She still runs the family business, doesn't she?" Something about the way she said *business* had Declan's skin prickling.

Halloran didn't seem to be talking merely about the pub, but certainly his parents hadn't been involved with the Rogues back then. Though, would Declan even have known? He could look back through his memories, but no. He wouldn't risk letting those out, wasn't sure he could handle it. Especially not here and not now.

"Aye. The pub is still up and running. Doing pretty well from what I could tell last I was in."

The captain breathed deep. "I'm glad to hear that."

"Why are we talking about my family, exactly?"

"What would you rather discuss? The weather? The sea? The council? Or maybe the fae?"

Declan narrowed his eyes at her. It would have been one thing for him to bring those last two up, but for her to already know what he sought? How did she know? He'd been clear with the men to be discreet, ordering them not to mention the fae or the dagger in their questions but to only ask about the council in general, as if they were merely curious about what it was like to visit the hall.

She let out a laugh. "Oh, don't worry yourself, Declan. Your men didn't screw up. It's not hard to figure out what you're after and what information you need." Her words didn't quell any of the anxiety rising within him. If she knew, who else knew? And there remained the question of how.

"Are you offering to help me then?"

A scream pierced the air from somewhere in the streets below, the sound carrying through the open window, but he fought to keep his attention on the deadly captain before him. He had no desire to lose an appendage for disrespecting her.

She didn't blink at the scream either. "Not in the way you desire, I suppose. You know, Declan, it wasn't easy to get where I am. No one helped me. No one offered me aid. I clawed my way to this position and my ship."

"And killed many in the process. You have quite the reputation."

"Yet you didn't know I was a woman." The gold in her eyes flashed. Was that an inkling of humor within them, or was he imagining it?

He sighed. "No, I didn't. I suppose everyone is too afraid of you to note that bit of information anymore."

She sat and stared at him for a moment in the silence. He waited, his pocket watch becoming a burning weight at his side. He was wasting too much time here. He needed to find Aoife and get moving if he was going to stay on task.

Twenty-five days left. To get the fae. To get the dagger. To get back to Morshan.

"You know, I always admired your parents. I wouldn't mind seeing their work succeed."

His glance flicked to the man still sitting by the window before returning to her. "The pub is a blessing for those who stop at the island."

Halloran leaned forward now, her voice dropping into a whisper. "I can't give you what you need, Declan. Can't risk Madigen discovering I helped you. But I can tell you, you must not fail. And you must not trust anyone. They know what you're seeking, and they're looking for her."

Declan's breath caught. Aoife. He fought the instinct to look around the room, as if the mere mention of her would call her up here.

Captain Halloran continued. "Find her. Take her with you. It's the only way to keep her safe."

Declan thought of mentioning how he didn't care what happened to the girl, play it cool, but before he could say anything, the captain was standing.

"Good luck, Declan. Truly." Then she was across the room and down the stairs, leaving Declan alone with all she'd said.

Don't trust anyone. Keep her safe.

Why did the girl's safety matter so much?

He glanced back to the man still sitting by the window and wondered how much he'd heard. Was he a spy? Or was he merely a local enjoying a quiet meal alone?

Surely he could trust Tommy, whom he'd known all these years. Callum perhaps. But that was already a shaky alliance.

Who could Captain Halloran have been warning him not to trust? Her words threatened to drive him to paranoia. Had that been her intent all along? Distract him enough so he'd fail?

Humming came from the stairs. Lucy.

Declan's mind raced, tripping over itself as he thought back through all the encounters he'd had with the owner of this eatery. She'd always been friendly. Too friendly? The captain's words had him second-guessing everything. But perhaps that wasn't a bad thing. He couldn't be too careful.

"Declan! Where did Tommy get off to? I didn't see him leave."

"Ah, he went off to get the crew ready to sail," he lied.

He might be a pirate, but he hated lying to a friend. Though perhaps she wasn't as good a friend as he'd imagined. He looked toward the window before turning back to Lucy, who was now clearing the mugs from the table in front of him. "Where's the girl? I need to speak with her after all."

Lucy stood upright, a flash of surprise written on her face. "Oh! Dear me, she's gone, I'm afraid."

"Gone to where exactly?"

"Cregah, I believe. A couple big guys came in not five minutes ago and said they were to escort her home."

"And you let them? She let them?" The echo of the earlier scream pierced him. Had that been Aoife? Tommy had given Aoife the dagger, right? Had she lost it somehow? Failed to use it? He cursed himself for not having Tommy train her a bit on the use of a blade.

Lucy's eyes were wide, her jaw hanging open until she snapped it closed, and he didn't have the time to pry answers out of her.

Aoife was gone.

His only hope of getting that dagger, gone. He jumped up and ran down the stairs, not quite sure which way he was heading, only knowing he needed to find her. And fast.

CHAPTER 29

DECLAN

OUT ON THE STREET, Declan skidded to a stop on the cobbled stones and glanced down one side and then the other, his heart beating wildly and his breathing ragged.

No doubt they were heading toward the water if they were planning to cart her back to Cregah and the council. Without a second thought, he took off at a run, taking the shortest path there. With any luck, perhaps he could cut them off at the shore.

If only he knew which ship they were from.

Or what they looked like.

Or anything.

He rounded a corner and slammed into someone. He bit back a curse and nearly screamed at them to watch where they were going before he realized it was Tommy.

A look of concern washed over Tommy's face. "What's wrong? Where's the fire?"

"She's gone. They're taking her back to Cregah." Fear dripped from every syllable, and he was glad when Tommy didn't mock him for it.

Without another word, Declan was off, running again, with Tommy right behind him.

They wove through the streets looking for two pirates escorting a poorly disguised woman. At least Aoife was on the short side. It shouldn't be too hard to find two big guys walking with a short one between them.

The sunlight was quickly fading as they ran, and it seemed time was stacked against them. As always.

As soon as they rounded the last corner the buildings gave way to the shore, nothing but sand greeted them. All the crews had apparently packed up and retreated into town for the evening.

No one. No crews. No kidnappers. No struggling girl.

It was almost eerie to see the beach so deserted, but then again, perhaps this was normal for Foxhaven. He wouldn't know, having always been in town with the rest of the crew come dusk.

Their boots had barely touched the sand when words pierced the night air, causing them to freeze.

"I said, let me go!"

Aoife. At least she hadn't given up yet.

Declan scanned the beach but still didn't see them. He and Tommy both looked down the edge of the town, waiting to see from which street they would emerge.

"There!" Tommy said, barely over a whisper. He pointed to his left at the two men stepping out from between a pair of buildings a few hundred yards away, with Aoife in hand. Tommy moved to run, but Declan reached out an arm, holding him back.

"What are you doing? We have to get her!"

Tommy's urgency and desperation echoed in every bone and muscle of Declan's body, but he fought it back, his jaw clenched. He'd wanted to be rid of her, and he'd known something—perhaps not exactly like this but something similarly unpleasant—might happen. But knowing the possibility and seeing it unfold were two vastly different things. Seeing her now, struggling against her captors, stumbling on the sand, he could sense her fear. He balled his fists, wanting to ram them into the men's faces, to grab her from them and make them pay for hurting her.

The need to protect her stormed inside him, a battle raging despite his effort to suppress it and shut it up. He couldn't let himself care about her. About anyone. But the need to get her didn't mean he cared. No. It wasn't a matter of caring or protecting. It was a matter of winning. A matter of success.

If he were to get the fae, he needed her. That was all he saw being dragged toward the shore—his one chance to succeed.

"Aye, we do. But they haven't reached the water yet, and we have the upper hand here. I don't want to risk going in without a plan."

"We don't have all night, Declan. Hurry the hell up." For a brief second Declan questioned why Tommy cared so much. He wasn't jealous, of course. That would be preposterous. No, this was Tommy. And assuming he actually knew Tommy—and could trust him—it was likely a mix of wanting to get the dagger and not wanting to see Aoife hurt. He'd always had a rather un-pirate-like way of caring about other people's well-being, unless they had a ship full of goods.

He allowed himself a few more seconds to think, ignoring Tommy's irritated stares as his mind raced to formulate a plan. His mouth contorted into a devious smile. "I'm thinking Lady Gem's Tavern. Two years ago?"

Tommy gave him a hard look, as if hunting down the memory in his mind, and then looked around. Behind them. And then at the men leading Aoife toward the shore. Taking a single deep breath, he squared his shoulders before jogging off and disappearing between the buildings, shaking his head and muttering curses as he went.

Listening to Aoife continue to struggle with her captors, he would have laughed at her growls had she not been in such a predicament. He gave the trio another once-over. The men were of similar height, but the one on the left was long and lanky. He gripped Aoife's arm with spindly fingers. The other, lumbering close behind them, appeared to have stolen some extra rations on his ship.

He watched them for one more moment. No signs of drunkenness. No stumbling in the sand like Aoife had. They had their cutlasses drawn, but all their attention was focused on the girl and keeping her from fleeing.

They hadn't yet noticed him. Nor did they notice when he drew his own cutlass.

He moved forward, making his steps uneven. He leaned to one side, his head lolling a bit as he stumbled along his way. He'd seen enough drunks—and been one often enough himself when he was younger—to mimic their ambling gait with astounding perfection whenever needed.

"Keep moving, girl," the larger man barked from behind her.

Though Declan couldn't see fully what was happening, the man must have reached up to strike her because his friend piped up. "Don't hit her! You know the orders. We can't return her already bro—" His words cut off in a howl. "She bit me!"

"I'm not—going—back!" Aoife huffed. Declan looked up to see her wriggling and pulling against the man's grip, but it didn't loosen.

Declan had made it within thirty feet of them when he opened his mouth. Not to speak, but to sing. Loudly. And not well.

"Take me away to Lagley-place…" He tossed his head about and looked toward the sky as he sang, his cutlass hanging limply by his side. "…where my fair lass awaits me." Another stumble and a half. "Been fightin' and killin'…" With those words, he gave his cutlass a haphazard swing from left to right, sending him teetering ever closer to Aoife and the men, who had now stopped to stare at him.

Amateurs.

"Get back, you!" It was likely the lanky one who had spoken, but Declan couldn't tell for sure. He lifted his head to look at them and lazily smacked his lips. Aoife had stopped struggling now, her expression one of confusion and amusement, which made sense given the spectacle he was making.

He forced his gaze to look through the man so his eyes appeared glazed over as he burst out into more of the song. "Been fightin' and killin' and drinkin' for so many years…" From his left came movement. Not a threat, but Tommy.

"Oy!" Tommy burst out from between two buildings, running toward Declan with a perturbed look plastered on his face. "What the hell are you doin' out here? We've been lookin' all over for you!"

Declan swung his head to face Tommy before rolling his eyes with such drama he knew Tommy would never stop mocking him for it back on the ship. He ignored his friend and went back to singing as he moved, or fell, a few steps closer to Aoife and the men, who were still standing and watching him.

The lanky man interrupted his song, which had become more of a string of gibberish and half words set to his own made-up tune. "Why don't you head back to whatever drunken hole you crawled out of?"

Declan was now within six feet of them. So close he could smell their unwashed bodies mingling with whatever scented soap Aoife had used that morning. Was that Aoife's heart pounding in her chest, or was it his own? It didn't matter.

"C'mon, Captain." Tommy inched closer to him, like a man approaching a wild animal. Declan swung his cutlass across his body until it pointed, wobbly and unsteadily, at his best friend's face. Tommy stopped and raised his hands in surrender.

Declan glared as he spoke. "Don't you *c'mon, Captain me*, boy. I do what I want. Where I want."

And with that final, slurred and barely intelligible word, he moved with a controlled swiftness so at odds with his drunken act that the lanky man had no time to react before Declan's cutlass met his throat. The curved blade—meticulously maintained and perfectly sharp—sliced through his neck as if it were made of soft cheese instead of bone and tendon.

At once, the man's grip loosened on Aoife's arms as his knees gave way, his body falling to the sand at the same moment his head, now severed, fell with a dull thud at Aoife's feet.

Declan waited for her scream, but it never came. Instead she stood frozen, blood sprayed all over her shocked face, her hands shaking at her sides, her eyes staring at Declan but not quite seeing him.

Tommy came up beside him, his dagger now drawn, pointed at the man who stood behind Aoife and his now dead partner. The pirate's hands flew up, mirroring in an almost comical manner how Tommy had looked seconds earlier. He backed away, his feet stumbling in the soft sand as he retreated slowly.

Declan kept his cutlass trained on the man, trying to ignore Aoife's intense glare from his right. "We'll be taking her with us."

The man gave a string of nods. "Take her. She's all yours."

"I suggest you get to your ship and leave." The man's gaze shifted between Declan, the bloodied cutlass, and his fallen friend before he took off, tripping and falling as he struggled to navigate the sand and return to whatever ship he called home.

Tommy leaned close to Declan. "You think it's wise to let him go?"

Declan wiped the blood from his blade onto his pants before sheathing it. "Who said I was letting him go?" A slight gesture of his head in the man's direction had Tommy moving, dagger in hand, as he ran to take care of the loose end.

He didn't bother waiting to see how Tommy managed, knowing it would be quick and silent. Tommy's specialty.

Aoife hadn't moved, and her captor's blood now dripped from her chin, but she made no sign that she noticed or cared. Declan had occasionally seen this behavior in newer crew members, the first time they saw action, especially during the moments after their first kill.

Though, in those instances, this vacant stare and frozen stance came later when the adrenaline had worn off. He'd offer them rum or bourbon. Something to calm the nerves as he spoke to them, assured them it would get easier, and reminded them they were free to leave at the next port if they couldn't stomach the work.

In all his years as captain, he'd only had two men take him up on that offer. And he had not begrudged them for knowing themselves well enough to make that choice.

But he couldn't give her that same offer.

He needed her, as much as he hated to admit it, as much as he had hoped for another option. He couldn't succeed without her help, and if she was truly going to insist on helping—not just with devising the plan but with its execution—he needed her to be able to handle whatever bloody messes they encountered.

He approached her with caution, hands up so she could see he meant no harm, but she still seemed to be looking through him. He didn't dare look down at the body to his left or to the head that lay between them. Instead he walked to the side first, hoping she would turn so she wouldn't have to step over her dead captor.

"Let's get you back to the ship and cleaned up."

She blinked and turned to face him, her feet shifting as he'd hoped. "What—what just happened?"

A part of Declan he'd worked so hard to contain pushed to get out, urging him to comfort her and protect her, but he shoved it back. He needed her to trust him, but he wouldn't let himself care. He couldn't. "We saved you. You're safe. But right now, we need to go. Tommy's waiting for us."

Reaching into his pocket, he pulled out a bit of cloth and handed it to her. "You can clean up further at the water." She took it and wiped it across her chin and forehead, smearing the man's blood, but at least it wasn't dripping anymore.

He offered her his arm, making a point not to grab her and cause her to panic. She waited. Hesitated. And he tried not to let his growing impatience show. If he moved too quickly, pushed her too soon, it would spell disaster for his plans. Better to be calculated, patient.

"Don't worry," he said as she slowly weaved her hand under his arm and let it rest on him, "blood can be washed away."

Aoife dipped her chin in gratitude and walked with him in silence back toward the ship.

CHAPTER 30
CAIT

CAIT PACED the small room that had become her home, or as close to one as she'd allow. The paintings she'd hung all those years ago—a poor attempt at dressing up the place and making it more comfortable—were now slightly askew and in desperate need of dusting.

This office had been her mother's, and she'd found it by chance only a few weeks after her parents' deaths. Her mother had left few clues as to what they'd been doing beyond running the pub, and as a teenage girl nearing adulthood, Cait had been preoccupied with courting prospective partners and had had no time to worry about her parents' dealings.

All she'd found was a cold room with old furniture, little comfort, and a nearly empty desk. Yet there she'd felt a connection to her mother, and there, below the Morshan streets, she'd found she could think and grieve in peace.

But it never did feel like home.

Not that it needed to. She only came down here when she needed a break from all the noise or needed to conduct business meetings, but even those had been few and far between of late, as most business was being conducted in coded messages passed along to her team via trusted messengers.

Declan had been the first guest here in months.

And now she was waiting for her second visitor in less than a week.

She glanced at the clock on the desk.

He was late. *Typical.*

Lucan was always late. But she hadn't promoted him to her second-in-command because of his punctuality.

He had a knack for strategy, an ability to think beyond the obvious and see all possibilities of a situation, weighing them faster than anyone else could. And he wasn't bad company.

A series of knocks sounded at the door.

Two. One. Three.

His knock. The one he'd insisted on using so she would know it was him. She'd mocked him for it at the time—had it really been four years ago?—but now she was thankful for it. Those men hadn't come back to the pub since they'd stepped in a few days ago, but ever since, she'd been jumpier than usual, sure to go straight upstairs after working, in case anyone was watching the apartment.

Cait opened the door an inch and whispered into the dark gap, "What's the password?"

"Pie." He uttered it with such deathly seriousness that she only barely managed to contain her laughter.

"You're an idiot."

She opened the door further, holding it at arm's length as she leaned against the frame and blocked his entry.

Lucan didn't move but rather waited in the dark hallway, his finger tracing the thin scar that ran along his hairline. He could have passed for a pirate, choosing to wear the standard garb of sailors rather than the simple garments favored by the locals.

She'd once asked why he hadn't scurried off to join a crew. While he'd claimed it was due entirely to his devotion to protecting the people of Cregah—like all members of the Rogues—she'd learned later that he had a distinct fear of water.

Good for someone who lived on an island.

Lucan flashed her a wink and dropped his hand. "You know you love me."

She merely shook her head. It might have been a casual remark, but it still pulled on a frayed thread in her heart. Had she met Lucan back then, before that night, she would have most certainly fallen for him. Unlike the boy she'd been courting—out of duty and not actual interest—Lucan might have stirred in her the dream for a home and children. For a simple life on these black sands.

If she was honest, she'd been almost grateful to have a reason to end things with the other boy, if only it hadn't come at such high a price.

But Lucan. Lucan wasn't like everyone else. He was one of the good ones. Solid. Loyal. And handsome. With eyes of melted chocolate that displayed the strong kindness and fearless humor he carried within.

The kind of man she would have chosen as a true partner.

But they hadn't met back then, and perhaps it was for the better.

He'd grown up on the other side of the Binbrack mountains and had only ventured to Morshan after his own family disappeared—his younger brother, his sister, and both of his parents.

He'd traveled here to file a complaint for suspected violence against them and to open an investigation into their disappearance.

The council had seen him in the public hall, had listened to his case and his evidence. They'd vowed to look into it, to have their lead security officer investigate, but he'd later learned they never did. They didn't even have a security officer. Or any kind of team to lead investigations. Every time he returned to inquire as to the status of the case, he was told it was ongoing and no leads had been found yet.

He'd come into Cait's pub then and tried to drown himself in rum.

With her parents dead a year and Declan newly gone, she had seen her own misery and grief mirrored in his glossy eyes across the bar. She'd let him sleep off his hangover in the back storeroom, giving him a blanket and a pile of rags for a pillow. She'd sat with him that whole night, allowing herself to doze off as she sat upright against the storeroom wall. When he'd awoken the next morning, his head pounding and an anger burning in his gut, she'd managed to convince him not to go after the council hastily.

For weeks after her parents' deaths, she'd been plotting and planning.

But she'd been doing it alone.

Until Lucan.

In that storeroom, seven years earlier, they'd joined forces, resurrecting the Rogues after the council had effectively wiped them out with her parents' disappearance. They'd never become more than friends and allies, but he was right. She did love him. Like a brother. She would never let herself love him as anything more.

"Aye, Lucan. You know I do. What took you so long?" She waved him inside and let him pull her into one of his classic bear hugs before they entered the room together, arm in arm as if they were taking a stroll through the village instead of plotting to overthrow their rulers.

"Thought I had a couple louses following me, so I had to take a few detours. If they were tailing me, I lost them around Carver Street."

"You lost them at the Ruby Inn? I should have known." The Ruby Inn—one of the more upscale brothels in the port, known for the respectable women and men they employed—wasn't like the whorehouses she'd heard peppered other ports in other lands. It was clean, well-kept, and meticulously managed by Ruby Rosewater, an older woman Cait had admired as a young girl, if only for her beautiful dresses and the jewels at her neck. Neither of which meant much to Cait now.

Lucan gave her a shrug. "They should be having more fun now than they would be here."

"I won't take that personally," she said as she walked over to the sofa.

This might be a business meeting, but nothing said it had to be formal. Plopping herself on the worn sofa, she let her head fall against the back of the cushion, one arm flung across the armrest. Lucan sat beside her and tapped her knee with his hand.

She didn't move her head but eyed him from her relaxed position.

"Now's no time to take a nap," he joked, but his smile didn't reach his eyes.

"I know, but I'm so tired."

"That worried about him?"

"No. I mean, yes. Sort of. But it's not only that. It's everything. Everything is riding on him, and..." She broke off with a sigh and pinched the bridge of her nose, as if the action could force her emotions to get in line and under control.

"It's only been a week, and you've done everything you can to help him, Cait.

You know that." All the humor from moments before was gone, his words now acting like the big hug he'd offered at the door, wrapping around her for comfort and reassurance.

"I know, but..." Why couldn't she finish a sentence right now? She'd never allowed her vulnerability to show around any other member of the Rogues, and certainly not around the pub or even in front of Declan.

But Lucan had been there when Declan had not. But could she blame Declan for leaving? Initially, she'd remained out of obligation, telling herself she was being a good daughter, doing the responsible thing. She'd cursed her brother's name for so long, but in the quiet moments when the pub was empty, with only the sound of her rag on the bar for what seemed the millionth time, she let herself admit—if only internally—that she was mad she hadn't been the one to leave first.

As stories had come in of the new Captain McCallagh, who'd named his ship the *Siren's Song*, she longed to be the one sailing in his place. She'd tried to ignore the tales the pirates brought into her pub of the young captain and his crew who undermined the pirate lords, hit merchant vessels before the larger fleets had a chance, and left gruesome messages carved into their victims for the lords to find.

Whether or not the stories were true mattered little to Cait. No, she couldn't blame her brother if he truly did dastardly things, not after what he'd witnessed as a boy. But she wished it were her captaining that ship, having adventures, feeling the sea breeze on her face, seeing distant lands.

Adventure. Excitement. Something beyond the mundane day-to-day activities of the pub, with the same faces and the same voices and the same everything day in and day out.

"I know that look," Lucan said, snapping her back to the present. He flashed her one of his most dashing smiles, his eyes gleaming with humor once again. "You're dreaming about ditching me again, aren't you?"

"That obvious?" The corner of her mouth pulled back into a half smile, but his own faded.

"Don't sell yourself short, Cait." His words once again seemed to wrap around and hold her like her mother used to. "Your actions here matter. We each have a role to play. Don't let yourself ever believe that yours is less important because it's done in the shadows."

He was right. Of course he was right, but there was a difference between knowing something logically and actually believing it. She wondered if there would always be a tiny piece of herself, tucked somewhere behind her ribs, that ached and yearned to be free of this place, to be free of the pub, to be free of the routine.

She took a deep breath, wishing the air rushing into her lungs would alleviate the ache within. It never did.

"Speaking of our roles," she said, sitting up. Placing her elbows on her knees, she looked him in the eye. "Have we any word from Maggie?"

Lucan watched her for a moment longer, his gaze burning into hers, as if he were checking to ensure she was truly okay. She'd never be okay though. But she wouldn't look away. Her raised brows urged him to let it go and get back to work.

He cleared his throat before answering, and had it been anyone else, she might have thought it was out of embarrassment of getting caught staring. But Lucan was rarely embarrassed.

"Aye. She got word to me yesterday. The hall is abuzz preparing for Captain Madigen and Captain Halloran. Word is the council has been scrambling to come up with an excuse for there being only one heir now."

"What of the rumors we heard? Is there any truth to them?"

"She believes so, but she says she needs more time."

"She'd better hurry. Twenty-five days. We need to know if it's true."

Lucan leaned forward and once again looked her square in the eye. His hand moved to rest on her knee, but at the last moment he retreated. She pretended not to notice, instead focusing on his words. "Maggie knows. The whole crew knows. We're working tirelessly. Trust that. Trust the team we've built."

Cait needed to move. To think. She pushed to her feet and began pacing along the same path she'd worn in the rug over the years.

"What have we heard from the twins?" She didn't look at Lucan as she asked, instead staring blankly before her as she continued to pace.

"They're currently keeping an eye on Captain Grayson and his crew. They arrived in port yesterday. Eva said she heard your brother's name mentioned a few times, and Aron is seeing what else he can learn about their role, if they're involved at all. Think Declan might have brought Grayson in on the job?"

Cait roughed a hand over her face. Sands, she was tired. So tired of the years spent working to bring the council down, to reinstate actual peace in her land. And now she'd entrusted the most important part of the plan to her younger brother. Would he be stupid enough to tell another pirate about it?

Her mind raced from thought to thought as she tried to determine what logical explanation there could be. She had assured Lucan and the Rogues that Declan could be trusted, but she had been racked with doubt, unsure if she even knew her brother anymore. But there'd been no other option. And there still wasn't. If he had indeed brought Grayson into his confidence, she'd need to trust there was a reason for that.

"Make sure the twins stay on their guard. Captain Grayson knows the rules of Cregah, for sure, but he's not above using whatever tricks he has to get folks aboard his ship to do as he pleases. If he suspects they're following him, I doubt he'll hesitate to deal with them in his own disgusting way."

Cait surely hoped Declan hadn't been so stupid.

She felt Lucan's eyes on her before she heard him speak.

"And are we certain about the timeline?"

Her feet stopped moving, and her shoulders slumped as she fell back onto the sofa. So much was riding on this and on her. The fate of her whole land was at stake.

"Honestly? I'm not certain of much these days, but what are our options?" She raised her arms out to her sides. "We have none."

She gritted her teeth, grinding down years of bitterness and frustration until her jaw ached.

Another deep breath had her turning toward him. It wouldn't do them any good if she let the weariness and worry overtake her. No. She was the leader of the Rogues. She had rebuilt this team, picked up where her mother had left off, recruiting fourteen people to help save their country.

She wouldn't fail. Couldn't fail.

"I've heard the same thing from multiple sources, so it's unlikely they've all collaborated. Last I heard, King Kilmeran is still gathering a fleet in Caprothe's main port. He's up to eight, perhaps ten, ships now. Maybe more. We need Maggie to dig a little deeper. As best she can without being found out. We need to know when he is meeting with the council. If they are, in fact, planning to overturn the Muirnaughton Treaty and partner with the king instead, all the lands of the Aisling Sea are in trouble."

"Why would they?"

Lucan's question came so quietly, Cait wasn't sure if he was asking her or himself, but she answered anyway. "If the king truly has the resources to take control over the Aisling lands, the council will want to do everything in its power to maintain its sovereignty. They might offer the aid of the pirates. But what would they gain from doing that? We've been playing the long game, taking our time instead of gaining any foothold against them. We haven't loosened their death grip on us in the slightest. Not yet. So why? Why would they?"

She stopped. A memory from the other night in the pub echoed in the back of her mind. "There were mumblings in the pub, but..."

Lucan's gaze lingered, a silent nudge for her to spit out the words.

She rushed to her feet with a curse. "What if they're right?"

Lucan's mouth had dropped open, and he was looking around the room as if there were someone else who could provide the answers she wasn't sharing. "Cait! What if who's right? About what?"

Another curse, and then she was shaking her head. "It can't be. No." She began pacing again.

"Damn it, Cait." He was standing now, grabbing her arms and forcing her to look him in the eye. "What is it?"

"I only caught a portion of it and chalked it up to the typical boasts of latest hauls. Basic pirate banter. They had just sailed from the west. Not sure whose ship they were from—I didn't recognize them—"

She was rambling but was too busy sorting through her jumbled thoughts to care what her words sounded like. "They mentioned a shield."

"A shield? That's a bit odd."

"Right? Really odd."

"No one uses them. Haven't since the war. They're nearly impossible to come by." Lucan's face contorted with confusion as he obviously tried to fit the pieces together.

"Lucan. What if the king has the counter to the dagger? The shield? What if he's using that as his bargaining chip? What if he's using that to get the council to partner with him? It's the only way they'd ever call off their pirate goons. Thanks to

Maggie, we know they know we're searching for the dagger. And this whole time we've been trying to ensure we got to it first. We completely failed to see that they might find the shield."

Lucan dropped back onto the sofa, saying nothing, staring blankly ahead. Cait resumed her pacing. She couldn't fall apart. The Rogues, her people, the entire nation needed her to hold it together. They could still win—it was up to Declan now—but there were so many other variables it made her head spin.

"We need Maggie to confirm the date. Best to assume the worst here. Assume he has the shield. So Declan needs to get us that dagger before then. He should be returning to Morshan soon for the first step. Assuming all went well with him in Foxhaven."

"The fae." Not a question. "We could have gotten him the layout from Maggie, right? Saved him time?"

"No. Maggie's access is limited, unfortunately. And while she's able to overhear conversations, she hasn't had the chance—and likely never will—to explore and find where the fae are being held."

"Does Declan know we have her on the inside?"

"Not yet. But I'll let him know when he makes port."

Lucan glanced at the clock on the wall, as if it could tell him when Declan might arrive. "I hope he hurries."

"Me too."

CHAPTER 31
AOIFE

Aoife's next day and a half was a blur. The familiar images of Lani being hauled away were now joined by the memories of being sprayed with blood, and dull thuds of the crew outside jolted her awake whenever she was able to doze off.

To his credit, Declan had given her time to process the events in Foxhaven. He had allowed her to remain in bed—his bed—for a full thirty hours following the ordeal on the beach. He'd brought her food, small morsels, to nibble on as she could manage. He offered a steady hand whenever she needed to get out of bed to tend to her needs.

How did one recover after seeing such a sight?

She could still feel the warmth that had smacked her face when the blade had struck. She could still feel the way her heart had seemed to stop, as dead and lifeless as the man before her, before resuming with a roaring pounding against her sternum, her stomach launching into her throat. All her will was spent keeping the bile contained.

But most of the time she slept, drifting in and out of dark dreams, and tried her best to give her mind and body the rest it needed.

She couldn't stop the scene from replaying in her mind. The sound of their voices. The smell of their filth. Her thoughts berated her for not even getting her blade out when they attacked. Tommy's first words to her after the attack didn't help drown out her internal admonishments.

You did good.

But she hadn't done good.

They'd sneaked up on her as she'd been taking the trash out the back door. She'd only had enough time to drop the bags onto the ground before one of the men lifted her up and whisked her down the alley, her screams trailing behind her. Not that anyone on that damned island would care about a woman's screams.

Damn pirates.

She'd certainly fought as best she could—even without the blade—to get free from those men, but they were much stronger than she was, and the soft sand had been far from helpful in her efforts to pull free.

And then there was the matter of what had happened before that.

She'd been delighted for the opportunity to bathe and wash her clothes while ashore. And Lucy had been kind. But looking back, Aoife could see where the woman had been a bit too eager to know about her history and her past.

Had Aoife said too much? She wasn't sure. She'd admitted to being from Cregah but saw no harm in sharing that fact. It didn't necessarily indicate an affiliation with the council, after all.

But she hadn't anticipated the woman walking in on her while she washed, and she hadn't been able to hide the marks of the council. Lucy, to her credit, had played it off well enough, not giving away any hint that she knew what the swirls of black, like smoke rising from Aoife's wrists, indicated. Lucy had only remarked how interesting they were, how she'd never seen anything like them, and then asked if Aoife had gotten them in Cregah or while visiting another land.

They'd seemed like harmless questions that could be tiptoed around easily enough, but still, she hadn't been able to shake the feeling that Lucy wasn't the sweet person she claimed to be.

You did good.

Those were also the last words Tommy had said to her before he'd been whisked away to his officer duties, leaving Declan alone to care for her.

At first, his quiet patience had been appreciated. But by the second morning she wished for things to return to some semblance of normalcy.

A quip. A retort. A bit of banter. Even an insult would be better than the deafening silence.

He had been even more aloof than usual the next morning. Not cold or harsh. But distant.

She had sensed him about to speak several times, but words never came. She would turn in time to see his mouth snapping shut and his gaze shifting. She wanted to ask him what was going on, but she couldn't find her voice, held back by the small part of her that still feared him.

She'd been stupid and naive to think he wasn't a real pirate. Even after he'd threatened to take advantage of her, she hadn't truly let herself see what he was capable of.

But witnessing him kill someone. So quickly. So efficiently. So mercilessly. Anyone would have been frightened, but her fear was minuscule compared to her sense of gratitude. Perhaps she was an idiot. She told herself he'd only done it for his own gain. He needed her help to free the fae, and she couldn't let herself believe he actually cared.

And yet, part of her hoped.

At times it almost seemed as though there was a change in how he looked at her. But it was likely just her imagination and her own yearning for companionship making her see what she longed for. She wasn't hoping for love or a family like Lani had risked everything for, but friendship. A friend would have been nice.

With her sister gone and her remaining family untrustworthy, she had no one, and she was tired of being alone.

Tired of lying in bed watching the morning sun light up the dancing dust motes with nothing but the feelings welling in her chest for company. She couldn't sort through them on her own, couldn't process them within her own mind.

She needed to talk them out, to have someone listen, to discuss them so she could best understand.

Short of an actual friend, maybe she could seek out the one person on the ship who seemed okay with her. Tommy. They'd only spoken a few times, but that was more words than she'd shared with the rest of the crew. And he'd never insulted her, so that seemed promising.

She hoped he'd be able to help her. She needed to work through all of these thoughts before she could be useful. And she desperately wanted to be useful.

Swinging her feet to the floor, she peered out the window and willed herself to stand steady as the ship lolled along the sea. Two days on land had sent her back to square one when it came to finding her sea legs. And as they would be arriving in Morshan tomorrow evening, she needed her legs to cooperate.

The cabin was empty.

Based on the state of Declan's side of the bed, he hadn't slept at all, though she had vague recollections of his body next to hers during the night, trying to keep a respectable distance.

She moved toward the door, hoping Tommy would be easy to find among the crew. But she stopped at the sound of low voices.

A tingle crept up her spine as she recalled the last time she'd been in this exact position, hearing these two men talking on the other side of the door. She should walk away and respect their privacy. And she nearly did. Until she heard her name.

"Aoife needs you, Declan. I know you don't want to hear it or believe it." It was Tommy. Of course. The only person Declan would ever let speak to him like that.

Declan's voice came out low, harsh. "You're right. I don't want to hear it."

"I know you care. I can see it. But you're too damn scared to admit it."

Declan seemed to growl his next words. "Watch it, Tommy."

"Or what? You'll push me away? Like you do everyone else?"

She wished she could see how Declan reacted to being challenged in such a way, and she half expected him to give up there, but then he spoke.

"I can't protect her." It was so low and muffled she wasn't sure if she'd heard him right. Surely that's not what he'd said. He had protected her. Multiple times even.

"You already have," Tommy said, echoing her thoughts. Before Declan could respond, he added, "I know you have your reasons, but it might be time to leave them behind."

More words followed, but far too quiet for her to hear.

"Maybe, Declan, you need her too. For more than just this damn dagger."

The door creaked under the weight of a hand, sending Aoife scurrying back to the bedroom—thankfully with little stumbling. As she sat on the edge of the bed, blankly staring out the window, she pondered the words she couldn't have heard correctly.

Surely they would not have had such a private and personal conversation in such an open space where anyone could have overheard. But the crew had always seemed to have a certain respect for their captain, along with a healthy dose of fear, not wishing to suffer his reprimands if they dared to defy him.

You need her too.

The words bounced around her mind as footsteps thudded across the main room of the cabin. Then silence. She waited to see if he would say anything, and when he didn't, she turned.

He wasn't in the doorway as she'd expected. He wasn't even looking at her. Rather, he was standing behind his desk with a hand on the back of his chair. He stood there, unmoving, for what seemed like an eternity, looking like the weight of the entire Aisling Sea was crushing him, drowning him.

She desperately wanted to ask him what he was thinking, but she didn't know how to break the silence that had been lingering between them since she'd returned.

Glancing back at the window, she waited. She still wanted to go find Tommy so she could talk to somebody, but now that Declan was in the room, she couldn't convince herself to leave him. So she waited. The silence stretched on, even as he pulled out his chair and it groaned under his weight. She had a strange urge to get up and go to him, not merely out of curiosity, but out of kindness.

You need her too.

He'd helped her. Even though he'd said he wouldn't, he had. He'd told her she'd be on her own, but then he'd been there when it mattered most. He'd saved her, and whether he'd done it for his own personal gain or for her well-being, she didn't care. And now she couldn't get past the silly and absurd notion that he was the one in need of saving now. But what could she do?

Aoife turned her attention back to Declan, who was now leaning back in his chair with his elbows on the armrests and his fingers steepled under his chin. She opened her mouth to speak, but it was his voice that filled the room instead.

"Come here, Aoife." It wasn't harsh, but it wasn't warm either. However ridiculous it seemed, she could have sworn he sounded nervous.

Moving as quickly as she could, thankfully not toppling into him when she passed the desk, she took a seat in the chair opposite him. She bristled at the memory of the last time they'd sat here together, the way he'd looked at her with such loathing, the way she'd spat her words at him.

Declan cleared his throat, pulling her out of her thoughts. He pushed a piece of paper toward her, along with a pen and ink. "I need to know where the fae are inside the council hall. Can you draw it?"

"That's it?" She didn't move. She only stared at him, hoping he couldn't hear how her heart thumped in her chest. He was still as handsome as he had been that day in the cove, even if his gray eyes seemed dulled by exhaustion and stress.

He leaned his head to one side, and a piece of hair slid into his tired eyes. Something inside her stirred. She didn't know where it came from. Maybe it was Tommy's words earlier, but looking at him now, she wanted to lean toward him, to move his hair back into place, to hold his face in her hands and whisper that it would all be okay. As if this pirate captain needed her reassurance. It was as foolish as thinking he was nervous around her.

Yet a hint of those nerves lingered in his question. "That's what?"

"After all this silence, no 'How are you'? No 'Glad to have you back'? No talk of the weather and other pleasantries? Just back to business?" She tried to make the words lighthearted and carefree, to get them back to their old bantering ways. She hoped he'd allow it.

A smirk slowly spread across his lips as he leaned on his elbow, his head propped casually on his hand. She had to remind herself how to breathe, which was utterly ridiculous. It wasn't like she'd never seen him smile before, but after days of seeing nothing but worry and fatigue in his features, this classic smirk of his brought some life back into his eyes and made him look more like the dashing hero than the cruel pirate.

The smirk still played on his lips. "How are you, Aoife? We're indeed glad to have you back. The weather has been altogether too hot." He gestured to the paper once again. "Now, draw."

"I'm—" *Fine* seemed like an odd word to use when she was still struggling to suppress the images from the other night. So she didn't bother saying it. "I'm glad to be back." A light laugh bubbled up from her. He'd played along with her, which was quite unexpected, but not unappreciated. When had she gone from wanting to annoy him to wanting to make him smile?

Back at Lucy's, she'd tried to stay mad at him but failed. He'd been rude and callous to her before she'd left, but still he'd had Tommy take care of her. Declan had ensured she would have some form of protection. And try as she might, she hadn't been able to keep from missing him and the ridiculous smirk he wore.

Every time she had walked into the main dining room of Lucy's, she'd hoped he would be there with Tommy or Gavin. Hoped he'd stop by to see how she was getting on, to make sure she was safe. But he hadn't, and her heart had sunk a little with every disappointment.

She'd missed him. Beyond her better judgment, and despite the harsh words she'd shot at him right before they parted ways, she had. But now she was here. She could be useful. She could help.

She scooted her chair closer, taking the pen from him. "You have a nice smile, Declan. You should smile more." She kept her face lowered so he would hopefully not see how she flushed at the words.

"I can't. It would ruin my reputation." Was that a hint of humor she detected? She hoped so.

"Well, you can just smile for me when we're alone then." Her flush deepened, and she leaned closer to the paper before her.

She began to draw the outlines of the council hall. Each line she created, marking out her old home, tugged at her insides with an intensity she hadn't expected. She thought she'd gotten past missing home, but then she remembered it hadn't even been a week since she ran. Such a short time.

She missed these halls, missed Lani, even missed her mother to a point.

Silence settled between her and Declan, but she didn't know how to fill it, so she kept her mind fixed on the lines she drew, each one adding to her anxiety as the questions swarmed her mind. Would Declan take her ashore when they went back to Cregah? Would she actually walk through the hallways she was marking on the paper? She had asked to be included, after all, but now she wasn't sure she'd be able to go through with it if he invited her along.

"Why did you run?" Declan asked, his voice low and careful. It was certainly not a question she wanted to answer, especially when she was only barely holding on. She didn't want to lose it in front of him.

She stopped drawing and looked at him, steeling herself and hoping her voice wouldn't crack under the emotions. "If you want me to finish this map, you'll need to find something else to talk about."

He didn't respond, and his eyes didn't leave hers. She couldn't tell if he was challenging her or if he was merely hoping to find the answers somewhere within her.

She lowered her head again. "I'm sure you can come to your own conclusions."

"I have considered a few possibilities." As he talked, she resumed her work, hoping to get this over with so they could move on to other topics like daggers and books. "Perhaps you couldn't stomach being matched to any of the eligible lords. Which would make sense. Or life at the council hall had become so stiflingly boring that you sought adventure on the seas. Or maybe you'd done something dastardly and were attempting to run away from your own guilt."

Her hand tightened around the pen, sending the nib ripping through the paper as she pushed down too hard. Dropping the pen, she sat up, pushing away from the desk.

"So that's it then? Guilt?" Declan's eyes narrowed at her as he leaned back in his chair, arms crossed behind his head.

She didn't say anything, merely stared back at him, trying to find the words to throw in his face, but her mind was drawing a blank. Yet again she was unable to do anything but chide herself for being so obvious and giving away too much.

Declan's features softened a bit, but his next words came out with an edge. "You don't have to tell me, of course, but if it has anything to do with the council and my need to get in there to get the fae, it might be best for me to know. Surprises get people killed."

Aoife looked down at the lines she'd drawn on the paper and swallowed hard. Her mouth went dry, and she fumbled over what to tell him and how to push the words out. After spilling Lani's secret to her mother and then revealing too much to

Lucy about her past, she didn't trust herself to speak. Why couldn't there have been classes on tactful speaking, on how to formulate sentences to avoid saying the wrong thing? Those would have been far more helpful than the lessons on the local flora of the island.

Declan's voice once again cut through her thoughts. "Did you steal jewels from the council ladies? Get caught with one of the pirates during a dinner? Kill someone?"

Her chin shot up then. The smirk he had donned faded in an instant.

"Ah."

She couldn't read his expression, couldn't determine what he thought of her. Would he admire her for having killed someone? He was a pirate, after all. Or would he mock her for having betrayed her country's dedication to nonviolence? She lowered her eyes, worried—however foolishly—that he could see the betrayal written in the depths of her eyes. "Not exactly."

"How do you not exactly kill someone?" She could hear that smirk of his in his words.

"I betrayed my sister." Her voice came out a whisper, scraping against the dryness of her mouth as she spoke. It was the first time she'd given the truth a voice, and the sound of it being uttered for others to hear, no matter how quiet and no matter how small the audience, sent a fresh dagger of guilt straight into her gut.

"I see. What was her name?"

"Lani." Barely over a whisper.

Declan shifted in his chair, and in her periphery she saw him lean forward, resting his forearms on the desktop. She waited for the mockery or for more questions about what had happened to Lani, but as a pirate, he had to know what the council did to people who broke the laws.

"Well now," Declan began, "if you betrayed Lani, who I assume you were quite close to, how can I be sure you won't do the same to me?"

"I didn't—" She cut herself off. It didn't matter anymore what her intentions had been. All that mattered was what had happened. No, she'd never meant to tell, but she'd put herself in the position to easily fail her sister, and her sister had been the one to pay.

"You didn't what? Intend to betray her?" Aoife gave a nod, keeping her eyes lowered but no longer seeing the page before her. "Intention or not, it happened. How can I be sure that tongue of yours doesn't get us into trouble? How do I know you didn't divulge something during the two days you were in Foxhaven? After all, someone learned who you were, where you were, and what reward could be fetched for your retrieval."

The earlier fear returned, along with a tingling of panic. She fidgeted in her seat, and her words tumbled out. "I won't. I haven't. I would never."

"You claim such things, Aoife, but your history provides little reason for me to trust you. And this time there are far more lives at stake. More than just an heir and her lover."

Aoife startled at that and stared at him again. She hadn't mentioned what Lani had done, or that anyone else had been involved. "How did you—I never mentioned—"

His jaw tightened, the movement so slight and subtle she wondered if she'd imagined it. He gave a casual shake of his head. "Gossips, remember? Pirates trade in more than just gold and trinkets. We trade in news as well."

"But the council never would have allowed that information to get out." She had an unnerving feeling he was hiding something, but she couldn't work out what it was, and it drove her mad, the curiosity and the not knowing.

Declan shrugged a shoulder. "They may think they control everything and everyone, but things are learned, and those things are whispered around."

Aoife froze. Declan knew more about Lani than she'd expected. If he'd heard whispers about her, then he might know who... She snapped her head up, her eyes boring into his. "Who whispered it to you?"

"Why, so you can get revenge? I don't rat out my sources, Aoife. Unlike some of us in this room, I have honor."

She couldn't suppress the scoff that burst from her. "Honor?! You're a damn pirate." Her mind flitted back to the night he'd pinned her to the bed and threatened her, sending a shiver across her shoulders. How could Tommy have ever claimed Declan cared for her? How could she have started to believe he might? Why did she even want him to?

He didn't move. Didn't blink. Didn't register any reaction. "More honor than a spoiled and naive heir who got her own sister killed."

His words hit their mark, sharp and painful, stinging her in the chest.

She had wondered if he'd thought so little of her. Now his words confirmed it.

Worst of all, it was true.

She was spoiled. She was naive. She was responsible for Lani's death.

Her lip threatened to tremble, and she clenched her jaw tight in order to stay it.

She wouldn't lose face here. Not in front of him.

With a huffed sigh, she shot to her feet and slid the chair back, its legs scraping as they moved from the worn rug to the wood beneath.

She couldn't look at him, couldn't let him see how he'd hurt her.

How could she have ever thought he would change?

She stumbled around the chair, trying to hold herself together as the ship's movement made her exit less than graceful.

If he mocked her, she didn't hear it, not through the pounding echo in her mind calling her all the names he'd thrown at her.

Spoiled.

Naive.

She was almost to the door when she heard his chair move against the floor.

"Aoife." All the edge had left his voice.

And she stopped. Sands help her, she didn't know why she stopped. But something in the way he said her name kept her feet planted, unable to continue in their retreat.

"I'm sorry."

Her chin dropped to her chest, her shoulders drooping under the weight of the words she'd never expected to hear him say. When she didn't turn, he repeated them.

She shook her head, eyes still lowered as her body betrayed her will and turned to face him. She raised her head only enough to look at him through her lashes.

Remorse shone in his eyes, more than she'd ever thought him capable of.

Perhaps Tommy had been right after all.

"I shouldn't have said all those things," he said, barely louder than a breath.

She looked at him squarely now, confused by the change in him. Was he playing her now, or was all that she'd overheard accurate? Did he care about her? Did she care about him?

She thought about telling him it was okay, that all he'd said was true, but she couldn't bear to admit any of it. It was difficult enough to acknowledge it herself. Even if he was playing her for the fool, using her to get the dagger for himself, she wanted to help him.

Regardless of all the times he'd put her down, she wanted to make him smile more, to see his nightmares cease, to see him content and free of the stress and fatigue he constantly wore.

He gestured to her chair, a silent invitation to come back and sit.

She obliged, pulling herself closer to the desk before she looked at him again. "Careful, Declan. You don't want to ruin your reputation. Who would fear a pirate who cares?"

She mimicked his classic smirk, hoping it hid how her insides still stung, rubbed raw by the reminder of all she'd done wrong.

"Good thing it's just the two of us here then." His smile slowly crept over his lips, as if he wasn't sure he was doing anything right in this moment.

She lowered her eyes, unable to look at him as she whispered, "Thank you."

"For what?"

Wringing her hands, she forced her next words out, hoping her face wouldn't flush when she looked at him. "For the apology. And for saving me back in Foxhaven. I know it was only because of the fae and the dagger, but thank you all the same." Some small part of her hoped he'd tell her she was wrong, that he'd done it for her and not for the treasure.

But those words never came. He only nodded. A silent *you're welcome.*

CHAPTER 32
AOIFE

With a deep breath, Aoife had the ink flowing on the paper once again, but the silence that settled between her and Declan squeezed her heart. After so many hours of his silence, she needed them to talk.

"I've only met the fae sisters once," she started. Images of them flooded her mind—their long limbs, graceful bodies, otherworldly beauty, and the eerie and magical lilt to their speech, that made it seem as though they could put you in a trance simply by speaking. "They didn't move about freely, as far as I know. But their room wasn't locked either. We don't have locks in the council hall."

"If they could leave, why wouldn't they?" Declan's question seemed more for himself than for Aoife, but she answered anyway.

"Maybe they have nowhere else to go?"

She watched Declan ponder this, chewing on it as if it were a piece of dried meat.

"Perhaps." Again, his voice was low, and his eyes stared at his desk beneath his creased brow. "Did you enter the room they were in?"

Aoife thought back to that day, and her body tensed as it relived the hesitation she'd experienced as a child. "A step or two. Not far though."

"Did you smell anything odd?" Such a bizarre question, but he had to have a reason for asking.

"It's been so long. But I don't think so."

He traced a line across his forehead as he looked at nothing, and Aoife could have sworn she could see the gears turning in his mind. He mumbled a few words, and she wasn't sure she'd heard him correctly. "No chains. No locks. No iron."

"At least none that I could see."

"Interesting. There could be iron in the walls." It seemed he was talking to himself, as if Aoife were a spirit or a voice in his ear rather than a person sitting with him.

She almost hated to interrupt, but the question still nagged at her. "Still, that would only affect their magic, right? It wouldn't keep them from leaving. And their room looked rather comfortable, as if they had every accommodation they could want. Books. So many books. Puzzles and games and paints. I didn't see anything there that kept them in that room physically though. Almost like they didn't want to leave."

"For five hundred years? It seems unlikely."

Aoife couldn't imagine spending a lifetime, especially one that spanned centuries, confined within a single building, let alone a single room in *that* building. Surely they would have wanted to leave. There had to be something keeping them there. But what?

Declan straightened in his chair, and his eyes locked with hers. "What do you know of the fae in general? What did they teach you about their kind?"

"The basics, I suppose. Long life. Heightened senses. And they're strong," she said.

"That's an understatement. They are damn near unstoppable physically. And the ones with magic..."

"But the iron suppresses that, right?"

"Yes, but only the magic. It doesn't affect their senses or their strength. So even if the council hall's walls have an iron core, they still wouldn't need their magic in order to escape. So something else is keeping them there."

"And you know what that is?"

He leaned forward, his eyes now alight, almost excited. "Their word." Aoife must have had a confused look on her face, because Declan gave a small laugh. "I see you're following." That smirk played on his face again.

"Not at all." Her face heated again with further embarrassment. How she'd thought she would be of any aid to him on this job, she wasn't sure. But like hell she was going to give up.

He didn't seem annoyed but rather elated that he might have made the breakthrough he needed for this plan to work. "There have long been rumors that the fae can't lie, but there's a theory—an old one, passed on through whispers—that it's not true. Those whispers claim, rather, that when a fae says they will do something, they are firmly bound to that word. Nearly impossible for them to betray it. If the council procured an agreement from the fae sisters, it might have allowed the council to hold them all these hundreds of years while still having access to their powers."

"Like a powerful sense of honor?"

Declan only nodded.

"If that's the case," Aoife said, her pen still hovering over the paper, "which it might not be, how do you plan to get them to break an unbreakable vow?"

"Nearly unbreakable," he reminded her.

He reached into his chest pocket and pulled out a piece of paper. Aoife reached for it, thinking he'd hand it over to let her inspect it, but he didn't move.

"Don't you trust me?" Aoife asked, though his expression plainly indicated that he, in fact, did not. She dropped her hand. She couldn't blame him. If her whole plan had been resting on a piece of paper, she wouldn't hand it over to someone with ties to the enemy either. "What is it exactly?"

He flipped it around so she could see the wax seal that kept it closed. It was a deep green—almost black—imprinted with a symbol she didn't recognize. "This," he said, "is—I believe—a message from the fae who fled to Larcsporough."

Aoife's eyes went wide. "But all the fae perished—aside from the three sisters at the council hall. None survived the Aisling War."

"That's what you've been taught, what everyone on Cregah is taught."

The words threatened to pull the air from her lungs, but she recovered quickly. What was it to learn another lie when so many had been told already? The last threads tying her to her old life continued to fray. They'd break soon enough.

She leaned forward to get a better look at the fae insignia. "What does it say?"

"I don't know. I won't open it. If the sisters saw I'd tampered with it, they wouldn't believe whatever it contains. And there'd be no point in trying, as it's likely written in their ancient tongue."

"So how do you know it doesn't say something like, 'Don't trust this man'?"

"Because I trust the woman who gave it to me."

Aoife's chest tightened against her will. What he said made sense, and while she understood why he couldn't trust her, it still pained her to know he trusted someone else at the same time. And another woman at that. Was she jealous? She had no claim to Declan, nothing that said she was the only woman who could help him, and yet jealousy seemed the only logical explanation for the way her insides twisted. It was the same way she'd felt when Lani or Darienn received praise from the council or when she'd thought of Lani getting a life in Daorna that she couldn't have herself.

She hated this feeling because she knew better, knew logically it was stupid and wrong and immature, and yet she still couldn't stop it from creeping up.

"I trust her because she's my sister." Aoife looked up to find Declan's features as soft as his tone, which acted like a salve to ease the burning pangs within her. She kicked herself for being so transparent, but she couldn't deny how appreciative she was that he apparently cared how his words affected her.

"I didn't know you had a sister."

"I wouldn't expect a council heir to worry herself over family trees of the common folk. And I don't know that she acknowledges it readily, except with her close friends." Aoife noted how he stumbled over the word "friends" but wrote it off.

"And how did she acquire this exactly?"

"I don't know. And I didn't ask. She only said it would be the key to getting them to help." He tucked the letter back into his jacket pocket. "Now, how do we get to them to deliver this message?"

Aoife released a breath and straightened up in her seat. Turning the paper around on his desk, she pushed it closer to him. "I've drawn the hall to the best of my memory, but it has been a long time since I ventured into that wing. While it wasn't outright forbidden, one encounter with them was enough to keep me away."

"Not *outright* forbidden?"

"*Frowned upon* would be a better phrasing. But I got the impression that Mother didn't want to draw attention to it, and a strict rule to not go there would have done just that. Plus, they kept us busy. Classes and meetings and outings. There wasn't much time to explore and get into trouble."

"So what's our in? How do we get in and out without alerting the council?"

"The next meeting with a lord was scheduled for this week. It would be the only time you and your men could enter the hall without raising suspicion. These meetings are the only time men are allowed beyond the public chamber and inside the main residence."

"But crews know each other too well. If one of the men noticed us, they'd know immediately we didn't belong."

Aoife flashed him her best version of his smirk and waited.

"You know something I don't," he said.

"Surprising, I know. I'm trying to relish this moment."

"Well, don't relish too long; we're running short on time."

She clicked her tongue at him. "Always in such a hurry. But if I remember correctly, Captain, we still have a day and a half of sailing to get back to Morshan, so we do have some time."

A roll of his eyes had her basking in her triumph.

"This was a special meeting scheduled," she continued. "I don't know why—they don't tell us much—but I know there will be more than one crew in attendance. If we—I mean, you—can somehow pretend to be a member of the opposite crew if you ever get confronted, that could work? No?"

Declan rubbed his stubbled chin as he thought over her words. He stopped and met her gaze. "I'd need to know which crews. Each crew wears a particular color."

"I only know one of the crews—Lord Madigen's. But for the other, I only know their colors. My mother always insisted we wear something that honored our guests. The garment she had made for this dinner was the prettiest I'd ever seen." Aoife paused. Declan stared at her, annoyance and amusement dancing around in his gray eyes. "Violet."

Declan froze, his face going blank. He sat so still she half expected him to keel over in his chair from lack of breathing.

"What? Who is it?"

A second passed. Another. And then he blinked but remained still, seeing through her as he spoke. "The *Duchess*."

"Who's the duchess?"

"Not who. What. It's the ship. Captained by Casey Halloran."

"Is that a problem?"

"No. In fact, it could work to our advantage."

Before Aoife could ask for clarification, Declan was pushing back from his desk and standing. Without another word, he was across the room and out the door, leaving her alone to wonder how this Captain Halloran could help and whether he would let her in on the plan after all.

CHAPTER 33
DECLAN

Declan had been thankful for the distraction of further honing the plan with Tommy, Gavin, and Mikkel. His mind kept threatening to pull his thoughts back to Aoife and the sorrow and guilt that had swirled in her eyes when he'd broached the topic of her sister.

She wasn't as acquainted with death, had been sheltered from it her whole life, while Declan seemed destined to be its eternal companion, his hands and heart forever stained by it.

He still remembered the first lives lost because of him, though they had not been killed directly by his hand.

He'd been so young, too young and innocent, when they'd died. Had he been faster, stronger, maybe he could have stopped it, could have kept his parents safe.

His hands clenched the worn wood of the quarterdeck's railing. The sun was inching its way toward the horizon in front of them. They'd be in Morshan in another day, and they still had a day in port before the dinner was scheduled. He'd need to get word to Cait for her aid in securing some items for this plan.

Without thinking, he reached a hand up to his left breast pocket, as if to ensure that the fae letter was still there. Not that there was any chance for it to have been lifted by anyone, and no one on his ship would dare such a thing anyway. It was true he didn't know what the letter said. Cait didn't know either. But she'd found it among their mother's belongings, in an envelope addressed to Cait. He hadn't pried into what their mother had written. Her simple directive to use the letter to free the fae from their vow was enough for him.

How, he had no idea. His knowledge of fae lore was shaky at best, but he had to go on the little bit he had.

He only hoped he really could trust his sister. And his mother.

His memory of her had blurred over the years, and though he could sometimes hear her voice on the wind, he often wondered if that was truly how she'd sounded or if his mind had twisted and mangled it into something false. He'd spent so long pushing the memories away. He needed to do it again now.

With a stretch of his neck he headed down to his cabin, where he found Aoife lounging in bed with a book. A sense of déjà vu washed over him. Too much like that moment a few days ago. He shook his head to clear the feeling, but it refused to budge, lingering at the edges of his thoughts, like a tingling along his skin. It had him clenching his jaw as he approached her. He didn't dare sit this time. That hadn't worked well for keeping memories locked away, so he settled himself against the doorframe.

If she'd noticed him, she didn't let on, and for a moment he simply watched her. She appeared fairly well put-together given the ordeal she'd been through in Foxhaven. Although the sun was setting in front of the ship far from the windows of his cabin, it still cast a warm glow through the room. He tried to think of what Aoife had looked like back in that cove with her hair long and her features smug and haughty.

Now she looked... He wasn't sure how to describe it, actually. More carefree, perhaps. While she was at Lucy's he had missed the rough ends of her hair that matched her fiery spirit.

"It's not nice to stare, you know," she said, not looking up from her book.

"Funny, I recall telling you the same thing."

She laid the book down in her lap and pursed her lips before she said, "So you should know better."

"Guilty as charged." He shifted his weight, hoping she would assume it was out of habit and not an indication of how nervous he was while trying to figure out how to speak to her. This shouldn't be so hard, but he couldn't even remember how long it had been since he'd played the role of *nice guy*. Charming guy, yes. Snarky guy, obviously. But genuinely nice guy? A light laugh escaped him.

"What's so funny?" She bit her thumbnail. A nervous habit he'd never noticed before.

"Nothing."

Before she could push him for an actual answer, sounds from the deck interrupted. A noise he hadn't heard in months. Not since before their latest defeats. Hands beating against barrels, a steady pulsing and shifting before the voices started. Gavin's tenor was the easiest to identify. Mikkel's accent became thicker as his baritone joined in.

Aoife stood and inched around the bed toward him, her brows high and her eyes glistening. "What is that? Music? Why are they singing?"

"Can't pirates have fun?" He shot her a challenging look, as if he were accusing her of being the one incapable of such fun.

"Of course, I suppose. But with everything going on, it seems like an odd time for it. Doesn't it?"

A deep breath was his only answer. He counted backwards. Waiting. Five. Four. Three.

Steps sounded outside.

Two.

One.

The door to his quarters shook under a banging fist.

"Yes, Tommy? What do you need?" The question was more for Aoife's sake than his own. He already knew the answer. Knew it with the first sounds of his crew's music.

Aoife sidled up to Declan's side just as his friend and quartermaster burst in, a huge smile on his face.

"You can't stay in here, Captain. Nor you, Aoife."

"Last I checked," Declan said, his face steeled, "I didn't take orders from you."

"Ah, but if you refuse, you may end up with a mutiny on your hands." Tommy waggled his brow at his friend before shooting Aoife a wink.

Declan tried not to bristle when a wave against the ship sent Aoife stumbling into him with the cutest exclamation he thought he'd ever heard. Her warmth sent his head swimming. Somehow she still managed to smell sweeter than anyone had a right to on a pirate ship. It was almost as if her body naturally produced that sugary scent. He couldn't think straight as she grabbed onto his arm to steady herself, but at least he was able to ignore Tommy's silent accusations at seeing her hanging onto him so close. Too close.

Declan pushed her away, trying not to be too forceful as he helped her find her footing again, and he glared at his friend, a silent denial that anything was going on.

Aoife looked from Declan to Tommy. "What's going on out there? Why all the music?"

"He didn't tell you." Not a question.

"I might have, had you not so rudely interrupted," Declan said. He tried his best to look bored, but it was hard to keep up the ruse when the joy in his men's voices was streaming in through the open cabin door.

"Right. I don't believe you." Tommy turned to Aoife, a mischievous look in his eyes. "It's our dear captain's birthday."

Aoife turned to him, her face bright with that glorious smile of hers lighting up the entire room. He shook the thought away. No. She was only a means to an end. A tool in his arsenal. A member of his team for this job. But that damn smile. Those lips. He forced his gaze up to her eyes, which didn't help much at preventing his thoughts from wandering further.

He cleared his throat. "What? It's not my real birthday."

Tommy cut in. "Just the one that really matters. The day he became a pirate."

"Pirates celebrate such a thing? I had no idea." Again with that coy smile directed at him.

Declan nearly made a joke about how little she knew about pirates at all, but Tommy spoke first. "Most don't, but I like any excuse to piss him off." He lifted his chin in Declan's direction.

"Well, not too pissed off though. I mean, you still have your head, right?" Aoife asked. Declan and Tommy both turned toward her, and while Declan managed to conceal his own shock by keeping his mouth shut, Tommy's mouth flopped open like a fish. "What? Too soon?" she asked.

"No," Declan said.

Tommy finished his thought. "Just unexpected is all."

"What he said," Declan offered.

"It seems the best way to move on is to learn to laugh about it," she said, sounding resolute despite the twinkle flashing in her green eyes. Sands, she was adorable, and more of Declan's inner guard began to crumble. Before he could chide himself for thinking such nonsense, she was grabbing his elbow and dragging him out after Tommy toward the activities outside. He didn't bother fighting her.

CHAPTER 34
AOIFE

BIRTHDAYS HAD NEVER BEEN a big event at the council hall. The council ladies didn't give gifts or have cakes made, though Aoife had heard such traditions were still held by the families in the villages around the island. Instead of celebrating with parties, she and Lani had marked their birthdays in their own way, jotting them down in the back covers of their favorite books—the ones they were allowed to keep, that is. They would exchange small gifts. A sparkling rock they'd found in the garden or a weed's bloom from the lawn.

Even amid the revelry on the ship, she missed Lani. Her laugh. Her teasing. She didn't blame her sister for keeping secrets, for wanting to keep Adler hidden, for needing to keep their plan under wraps. She shouldn't have forced her to tell, should have honored Lani's privacy instead of taking it personally. Maybe then she would still be alive.

But then you'd still be at the council hall preparing to be matched, preparing to serve in a corrupt council.

She would have gladly done it if it had meant Lani could be somewhere safe, building a life. It would have been a worthwhile sacrifice. Perhaps she could have changed things from within.

But now her only hope was to escape, run away, leave it to someone else, someone better, to address the problems.

After she helped Declan.

She watched him from her perch on the lowest of the steps leading up to the quarterdeck. She had followed him and Tommy out to join the festivities but had only made it to these stairs before deciding to hang back and let them have this time without her butting in.

Sure, she'd been invited, but it was blatantly clear she was an outsider here. And if she was being honest, she was content to simply observe.

If anyone had asked her what her thoughts on pirates were just a week ago, she wouldn't have had anything nice to say. It wasn't that they'd been rude to her at the council dinners, but they certainly hadn't been what she'd describe as friendly or cordial. And if she hadn't witnessed Declan use his blade—seen the blood on Tommy's dagger—the other night, she might have had a hard time classifying them in the same category as all the pirates she'd previously met.

The music continued. It pulsed through the wooden planks of the ship and up her boots. She couldn't keep from moving to the beat. And even with a hint of seasickness still lingering in her belly, she was comfortable and at ease. It helped that the crew seemed adequately distracted by the party and forgot to be wary of her unlucky presence.

Declan's gaze flashed to hers, and she looked away, hoping he hadn't noticed her staring.

A few of the crew members, who were likely new based on how awkward they appeared, crowded together next to the railing, watching their shipmates dance and laugh and sing a song Aoife didn't recognize. It had her thinking back to Declan singing on the beach in his faked drunken stutter. She smiled and shook her head at the thought. He'd looked completely mad.

"Having fun?" She hadn't heard Declan's footsteps over the music's thrumming, but thankfully she hadn't been startled either. She didn't particularly want to blush again in front of him.

Peering up at him, that unruly lock of hair being blown into his eyes by the evening wind, she wondered what had shifted in him. Was it merely his birthday that had him smiling down at her? Not a smirk, but an actual smile. And they weren't even alone.

"I am. But you, Captain, should be careful." She pretended to look around with suspicion. "The others might see you smile."

"Good thing most of them are too drunk to notice or remember." He settled himself on the step next to her, a polite distance away so no part of them touched. Disappointment flickered somewhere inside of her before she could shoo it away. That kind of thinking would get her nowhere. Nowhere good anyway.

Never before had she given any thought to romance or love. Matching, sure. But that was purely political, a requirement of her status. It wasn't the same as building a family, fostering a relationship. More like an alliance or a business partnership. One that would produce another heir to the council.

It hadn't been until Lani spoke about a future with Adler that Aoife had even considered the possibility and let herself wonder what it might be like, if only to better understand why her sister was willing to risk everything to attain it.

And that little bit of inquisitiveness had opened some small gate within her that she'd never known existed. And she couldn't quite shut it completely. Having Declan sitting close and smiling, being kind even, didn't help. She couldn't ignore that future Lani had painted. A family and a life of peace and quiet in the Daornan hills.

While she didn't want that life specifically, she couldn't quiet the damn niggling voice in the far reaches of her heart that asked, "What if?"

But that *what if* wouldn't include Declan. Or any pirate for that matter.

What kind of family could one care for on the seas, waging battles, pillaging merchant ships, and chasing after enchanted daggers?

Adler had supposedly been ready to give all that up—set aside his life of adventure—for her sister, but she couldn't imagine Declan, or anyone in his crew, walking away from it all. She glanced around the deck at the smiling faces, noticing the true camaraderie among them, the way they laughed and joked and pushed each other and hugged while they sang. How the new members were welcomed and pulled into the festivities by the veteran crew.

This was their family.

And it seemed far more functional, healthier than the one she'd left behind.

Here she sat on the outskirts, a spectator looking in on something she could never have. And why should she yearn for it anyway? Everyone she had thought cared for her had deceived her. Could she trust anyone again after that betrayal, after being fed lies her entire life?

But Declan had always been honest with her. Even as he kept information close and guarded, he hadn't lied. *That you know of.* She grumbled internally, frustrated by her inability to find any footing in her current situation. Where did she stand? Who could she trust? She'd trusted Lucy, and look where that had gotten her.

Yet there was something about Declan, Tommy, and this crew. She couldn't explain it, but somehow, some part of her kept pushing her to trust them.

Noticing as Declan moved to face her, she wondered if he'd asked a question she hadn't heard while she was lost in thought. She turned toward him. "What?"

With a shake of his head he turned back to watch his men, a too quiet "nothing" escaping his lips.

She wanted to nudge him and ask him what thoughts he was mulling over, but the music and laughter was growing louder as the merriment continued and the rum flowed.

Tommy rushed over with two mugs, careful not to let any of it slosh on Aoife. He placed one in her hands as if it were being served in delicate china rather than sea-weathered tin. He was less careful with his captain's, but Declan didn't seem to mind when some spilled over his hand.

"It's not the best rum in the Aisling," Declan said. He took a long sip. "But it's not the worst either." He raised his mug toward her as if his words had been a toast. Tommy had already escaped back to the crew, and Aoife didn't bother to see where exactly he'd run off to. Declan was staring at her again, as if daring her to taste it already.

"I wouldn't know either way."

"The council doesn't serve rum?" She didn't sense any teasing in his tone.

"Not to us, no. It's reserved for our guests only."

"And what did you fancy council folk drink at these dinners?" There was the teasing she'd expected—and hoped for, if she were honest—and it took every ounce of will to not let herself smile or even think about how much she'd missed hearing him speak the past couple of days. While his change in demeanor confused her, she wouldn't complain. It was nice to have him not scowling at her all the time, even if she still refused to believe he truly cared about anything more than her ability to help him.

"Wine mostly."

"Wine? Really." He seemed to ponder that information as if it were the key to something, though she had no idea what clues it could possibly give him. "They don't produce wine on Cregah."

She gave a slight shrug as she stared into the amber liquid in her cup. "Well, to be fair, they don't produce much of anything on Cregah."

"True enough." Declan tipped his mug back and downed the last drop before motioning toward her untouched drink. "Try it. One sip. If you don't like it, you don't have to finish it."

"Well, I'd hate to be rude," she said as she lifted the cup to her lips.

"That's a first."

She flashed him a glare over the rim as the liquid reached her mouth, and then in one swift motion she tipped her head back, sending the syrupy blend of sweet and spice down her throat. It coated her tongue and burned as it traveled, settling like a warm fire in her stomach. When she lowered the mug, now empty, she caught him staring, his features contorted in a way she'd never seen.

"Oh, settle down, Cap'n. I've had rum before." She struggled to keep her smug smile from spreading but soon gave up trying and let herself beam at him.

"But you said..."

"I said I wouldn't know whether it was the best or not, and that's true. And no, I never had rum at the council hall. But I had a few glasses during my brief time with Lucy. She said it would help calm the nerves."

Declan laughed quietly as he shook his head at her. She did enjoy surprising him. Maybe he'd stop underestimating her. Maybe she'd stop underestimating herself too. That would be a nice change.

"Would you like more? I believe Gavin and the crew stocked up in Foxhaven. We should have plenty, though by the looks of the crew, it might not last long." It was her turn to chuckle at him. He was rambling a bit, which was rather unlike him. Perhaps this was what the real Declan was like when he wasn't wound so tightly. The rum seemed to help more than just one's nerves. Or perhaps it had simply changed the way she saw him.

Regardless of the cause, she was happy to see his moodiness dissipating, even if she knew it would only be temporary.

"Are you trying to get me drunk?" She flashed him her best attempt at a coy smile, but she had no idea if she was pulling it off or not.

"Of course not, Aoife. Then I'd have to carry you back to bed."

The image his words conjured up had her head swimming, and her face warmed with a flush of embarrassment. She hoped it was too dark for him to notice, but then she could always blame the rum for the heat in her cheeks.

She handed her empty mug to him with a nod and said, "You're the captain. You could have one of your men do it for you."

"Certain tasks should never be delegated. Carrying women to one's bed especially." He snagged her mug and held it up without taking his eyes from her. Tommy was there in a heartbeat to refill it for his captain.

No word of thanks from Declan. No words at all actually, and Tommy was gone again.

Aoife was trapped in Declan's gray eyes as she took her mug back from him, unable to turn away despite the discomfort of being stared at. What was he seeing in her? She couldn't look away, as if there were some tether holding her in place.

It was Declan who broke first, blinking a few times before turning back to watch his men dance around the deck and sing loudly to the beat of the music. They didn't have proper instruments and were instead beating their hands on barrels and stomping their feet on the deck. The deep richness of their voices mixed in perfectly. Aoife had never heard anything so lovely and enchanting.

She couldn't keep her shoulders from bobbing to the beat, and she let her eyes slide closed as she took another sip. Her mind wanted to take her back to those moments during which she and Lani had danced around her room to no music at all, and she found it difficult to keep the memories at bay. Lani would have loved this. She would have been grabbing each young crew member, insisting they dance with her under the stars while the sea moved the ship as if it, too, were in on the dancing.

Tears pooled in her closed eyes, and she hoped they wouldn't spill over, but just like her memories, they wouldn't be deterred. A single drop escaped. Then another. She hated this. Hated crying in general, but especially in front of others. In front of him.

A hand brushed her cheek. Her eyes flashed open and caught his gaze again. His hand hovered between them.

"I'm sorry." His voice came out in a low and gravelly whisper. He cleared his throat before adding, "For everything you've been through this past week. I'm sorry."

She hunted for any sign that he was teasing or mocking her, but there was only genuine sympathy and care written on his face. It was such an extreme change, so drastic a shift from her earlier encounters with him that she felt bewildered.

"Are we becoming friends?"

Clearing his throat again, he gave her the slightest of nods. "Perhaps we are."

"I'd like that," she said.

"And you can call me Declan."

She looked around and leaned in to whisper behind her mug. "But what would the crew think if they heard that?"

A small huff of laughter escaped as he lifted his shoulder. "Well, only when we're alone then."

"So when we're alone, you'll smile. And I'll call you Declan." Another nod. "How scandalous, Captain."

"You're a goofy drunk, you know that?"

"Who said I was drunk?"

"So you're just goofy then."

"Only with my friends." She bumped her shoulder against his and shot him a smile. She expected him to smile back, but he didn't. A flash of something else washed over him. Something she couldn't quite place. Was he that uncomfortable being her friend? Before she could mull it over too much, the look was gone, and he was downing his own rum and standing.

He looked down at her, and part of her wished he'd reach out a hand, invite her to dance. That was foolishness though.

"I'd better go mingle with the crew a bit. Are you okay here?"

A few quick nods told him she was fine.

"Don't have too much."

"Of course. I'd hate for you to have to carry me to your bed." *Our bed.* She shoved that thought aside as he walked away without another word.

Were they becoming friends? She wondered if it was okay to believe that were true. She'd wanted a friend. Someone to truly talk to. But she still worried it was all a ploy, a ruse. A way to keep an eye on her until she could help him rescue the fae. Would he ditch her then? Would she be left to fend for herself in some other port or in some other land?

Those thoughts were too much for what should have been a fun evening, so she forced them into a far corner of her mind and tried to watch the crew as they beamed at their captain and clapped him on the back. Tomorrow they'd be arriving in Morshan again. Tomorrow she'd be helping him with the final preparations for the rescue.

But tonight? She'd drink.

She beckoned Tommy over for another fill, and he obliged.

"Last one. Captain's orders," he said with a wink. He nearly walked away, but something in her expression must have caught him off guard, because he stopped and knelt in front of her, a hand on her knee and worry tugging at his brow. "Are you okay?"

"Of course." Her gaze flashed to where Declan stood by the deck's railing talking to a couple of the new crew members, and Tommy's eyes followed.

A sigh filled the space between them. "Be patient with him, Aoife." She started to ask him what he was talking about, but he cut her off. "He's lost a lot. Been battling himself and his mistakes for as long as I can remember. But I'm glad he has you."

"Friends are a blessing, to be sure."

"Aye. Friends. It's what he needs right now, I think." And with a pat of his hand on her leg, he was standing and walking away.

CHAPTER 35
AOIFE

Aoife couldn't remember much the next morning. Tommy had effectively cut her off per Declan's orders, and yet the three mugs she'd enjoyed eventually caught up to her.

Her head ached, and this was made worse by the gentle swaying of the ship. Still, it wasn't as bad as the time she and Lani had sneaked a bottle of wine after dinner one night and downed the entire thing together in Lani's room. They had managed to avoid their mothers' wrath by hiding all evidence in the kitchen waste bin, but they'd both had to claim food poisoning the next morning to get out of their lessons.

No, this wasn't as bad. And yet it was worse.

No matter how hard she tried, her memories of the evening remained dim, as if she were trying to view them through the rum she'd consumed. It was as though she was still swimming in the drink, unable to get her mind to the surface to think clearly.

"Good morning."

Declan.

She cringed as each syllable pressed against her aching mind. Some part of her urged her to make a smart remark, but she could only manage a shush through her teeth.

He laughed, sending new waves of pain through her head.

"I told Tommy not to let you have too much."

She didn't dare move as she opened her eyes. At least her vision seemed to be clearer than her mind, and she tried to focus on the knots and swirls of the wooden ceiling above her. Drawing in a deep breath didn't do much to clear the fog.

He chuckled beside her again, and from her periphery she could see he was lying on his side atop the blanket, propped up on an elbow as he stared.

At least he was clothed. Mostly. She had to work to keep her eyes from drifting noticeably down to his bare chest.

She realized she still hadn't said anything to him, but she couldn't quite figure out how to get her tongue and teeth and breath to cooperate.

"Did you have fun at least?"

She managed to turn her head, wincing again at the stab of pain the movement caused. "I think so?" She tried not to cringe at how horribly pathetic she sounded.

"You seemed to, from what I can remember seeing."

"What? What did I do?" Her eyes went wide as her brain continued to refuse to recall any memory of what she'd done.

"You don't remember dancing with Tommy? You both nearly fell overboard at one point."

The memories started to come back little by little. Dim images of twirling and spinning. The faint sound of her giggles and Tommy's laughter mixing with the unceasing beat and songs of the crew.

Her cheeks warmed. Had Tommy wanted to dance with her, or had she forced him to? Had she looked as much the bumbling fool as she felt while replaying the night in her head?

Another wince and cringe had Declan breathing out a silent laugh.

"Don't worry, Aoife. The crew will probably stop talking about it by the time we leave Morshan again."

She maneuvered to her side, ignoring the way the movement sent her head swimming again, and looked at him. "It was that bad?" She raced through all the possible embarrassing scenarios she could think of. Oh, she hoped she hadn't done anything too ridiculous. It had only been three mugs. How full had they been? She didn't think it had been that much. But now, as she pushed her mind to work, harder than it desired in this moment, the embarrassment settled inside her as heavy as the rum had.

She was going to be sick.

She forced the bile down, not wanting to lose her stomach contents in front of him.

"Honestly?" He lifted his brow, and she waited for his sharp teasing, but she didn't see any hint of ridicule in his eyes. "You were fine, Aoife. A perfectly respectable lady."

"But I almost fell overboard." Her expression twisted with the embarrassment.

"So did half the crew. They were much further gone in the rum than you. It's going to delay us a bit getting into Morshan today, but—"

"Won't that ruin all your plans?"

"Not all of them. And to be honest, I'm thankful Tommy and Gavin arranged the festivities. The crew needed it. I needed it."

"Wait. What happened?"

He shot her a questioning look. "What do you mean?"

"Where did the Captain Mc—I mean, Declan—I know wander off to? He wouldn't have been so nonchalant about a delay or anything upsetting his precious timeline."

He sat up fully then and roughed his hands over his face, the stubble on his jaw looking extra scruffy and appealing. Were such thoughts acceptable among friends? She wasn't sure.

He turned to her again, his arm now resting on his bent knee. She forced herself to keep her eyes on his face and not his bare chest and the scars that peppered his tan skin. Ignored the way her mind pondered what that chest might feel like.

"I suppose seeing you being dragged across the sand in Foxhaven forced me to get things in perspective."

"But you're a pirate. And one with quite the reputation, so I hear."

"A reputation I worked hard to achieve. But that doesn't mean I don't have a heart."

"I don't understand. Doesn't time still tick by? Don't you still have a deadline to meet?"

"Aye. But perhaps I came to realize if we don't enjoy ourselves a bit, if we don't keep our mind focused on the good things we have—or could have—then what is the point? Is success worth losing sight of everything worth living for?"

She mulled over his words and bit her lip as if chewing on what he'd just said. "Are you saying I'm a good thing you have?" *Or could have,* she added to herself. Her face warmed again at that thought, and thankfully he looked away without seeming to notice.

For a moment she thought she saw the more vulnerable side of him peeking out from behind the tough shell he had created. But his eyes hardened and his lips stiffened as he slid his mask back into place and faced her. "Perhaps. Though that depends on what happens at the council hall in a couple days."

"So our friendship is completely riding on my successfully helping you; is that it?"

She had meant it to be teasing, but her rum-addled brain couldn't keep the bitterness from soaking into her words.

He didn't seem to have an answer, and before she could push him further, he was moving, swinging his legs off the bed and walking away.

CHAPTER 36
DECLAN

Declan made his way across his quarters toward breakfast, painfully aware that he'd left Aoife's question hanging in the air unanswered.

He'd spent all evening watching her dance and laugh on the deck with Tommy, pondering how a friendship with her might work. He was still at a loss.

And here she was asking if their relationship would end if she failed at the council hall. How could it end if he wasn't even sure it had begun? Yet he had the sinking suspicion it had begun against his will.

Something in him had snapped when he took that pirate's head and freed her, creating a connection, a link between the two of them. Whether it was friendship or not, he didn't know, but a life without her around? Unacceptable.

Despite this, though, he had no idea how to be her friend.

She wasn't like Tommy or Gavin or anyone in his crew. And she certainly wasn't like any of the other women he'd occasionally entertained himself with over the years.

But he couldn't admit to her that he didn't know how this would work. Nor could he silence the nagging in his gut that urged him to see the other options.

He'd been unable to completely hold back the memories of his parents. Ever since he'd rescued her, they'd plagued him, unwilling to stay locked away no matter how many times he shoved them aside. The way they'd always talked and shared everything. The tender kisses he'd witnessed and the silent glances that had passed between them. The gentle strokes of fingers as they worked together or the little touches whenever they crossed paths.

They'd had friendship and romance, perfectly balanced and intertwined.

Until the end. And his father had run out the door that night without hesitation.

These images didn't merely haunt Declan, they were changing him. He'd spent so many years ignoring them, pushing people away and keeping everyone outside the wall he'd constructed.

And now that wall was crumbling down as the memories pushed against it.

Friendship. Romance. He welcomed the first, but the latter seemed impossible. Not something destined for someone like him.

Pirates didn't fall in love, didn't raise families, didn't tie themselves to anything but the sea and the hunt.

"Did you get lost?" Aoife called from the bedroom. At least she didn't sound quite so pained now.

He didn't bother looking toward where she still sat on the bed, instead calling over his shoulder, "Would you like some breakfast?"

"I'm not sure I can stomach anything yet."

He picked up a tin plate and piled an assortment of items they'd stocked up on in Foxhaven onto it. A banana. A roll. Some hard cheese. No pie though. He'd missed out on the slices Lucy had set aside for him, as he had run out to save Aoife.

She'd better be worth it.

He carried the plate back into the bedroom, setting it down before her.

Aoife had managed to sit up. With her slender legs crisscrossed before her, she eyed the food he'd presented before picking up the roll and tearing small bits off, testing each morsel before selecting another.

Even with her hair a choppy mess—the ends pointing out in all directions, some strands sticking up in the back where they'd gotten stuck in place as she slept—sands, she was adorable.

Thoughts warred inside him. Tommy had insisted they needed each other, and Declan had resisted. At least outwardly. But he'd been considering the same thing before Tommy ever uttered the words. And it was more than just practicality. Yes, he needed her help to rescue the fae, and she very plainly needed him to keep her from being whisked back to the council.

But he'd seen something spark in her last night. Even before any drop of rum had passed her lips. He'd seen it in her glances and in the slight turning down of her lips when he'd kept some distance between them while sitting.

It had been brief. So brief he'd been sure he imagined it.

Had she felt the tether that had formed between them after Foxhaven? Or was it only on his end, born out of his innate need to protect those around him—a need he'd spent years refusing to accept? Yet he couldn't quite figure out what that connection meant for them. Would he turn her down if she pursued a romance?

In this moment, as the sun shone on her sleep-mussed hair and her freckles stood out more pronounced across the bridge of her nose, he wasn't so sure. But she'd never seemed interested in him in that way, and she was the one who had suggested friendship.

So friendship was what he'd settle for. That was the easier option anyway.

"What are you thinking?" Her question startled him out of his thoughts. He hadn't noticed her look up at him, and he had to blink a few times to clear his mind from all he'd been pondering.

He needed a lie, but one eluded him at the moment, and his brain sent out the first words he could muster. "How to be friends with you, actually."

Aoife's laugh split the air, short and sweet, and he found he thoroughly enjoyed it. "Is it that hard to do?" She went back to studying the bread she held, then muttered, "Friendship shouldn't be hard."

If she only knew.

But she had a point, didn't she? Friendship should be easy. Like with Tommy. Why did he want to control it, as if it were a ship to be captained?

Maybe it would be better if he let it ride the waves on its own, let it develop naturally, without force or planning.

Stop overthinking things, Declan.

Trust yourself.

Trust her.

"I suppose you have a point," he said. He leaned his back against the wall and crossed his arms over his chest, hoping he looked more relaxed than he felt.

She lifted her gaze to his again, a mocking smirk tugging at her lips.

"Did you have many friends at the council hall?" He didn't realize until after the words were out that he'd accidentally stepped onto shaky ground. *What a friend you're proving to be, jackass.*

"Only Lani really."

He'd expected to see her face drop with the mention of her sister's name, but her calm expression didn't waver.

He'd sat with her for two nights after rescuing her in Foxhaven, had watched her tremble in her sleep, battling the nightmares that pulled at her features and tensed her jaw. At first he'd assumed it was merely because of the kidnapping and the beheading, but she'd whimpered her sister's name multiple times.

It had twisted his gut, and he'd wondered how he could possibly rescue her from that.

And wondered why he felt such a need to. But here she sat, her grief and guilt still dancing at the edges of her green eyes that seemed far more confident now. But this change hadn't arisen from the rest he'd allowed her.

This change had come overnight. Perhaps the music and the dancing and the revelry was what she'd needed too, though it made little sense to him how frivolity could heal such deep wounds.

"What about you? Is Tommy your only friend?"

"Aye, I suppose. He's my oldest and closest, to be sure."

"How'd you meet?"

He'd never told the story to anyone. No one had ever asked. Whether that was because of his reputation or simply because pirates didn't care, he wasn't sure. It wasn't hard to recall though.

"We were both cabin boys on a ship."

She looked at him, brows raised in expectation for the rest of the story, and he stifled a laugh. He'd known that answer wouldn't suffice. That was precisely why he'd given it.

"And?" she asked.

"And what?" Toying with her was delightful indeed.

"That's it? You were both cabin boys, and that's the whole story behind your friendship."

"Pretty much."

"But how did you end up on that ship? How did he? Where did he live before? And how did you acquire the *Siren's Song*?" The questions rushed out of her, and he had to use every ounce of his will to appear bored.

"Oh, well, you didn't ask any of that."

Aoife rubbed at her forehead and temple. Such frustration building. This was too easy.

"Fair enough," she said. "Would you answer them now?"

"Very well." He paused to think. How much should he divulge? How much of it really mattered? And did he have any right to tell part of Tommy's story for him?

"I left home—don't ask why, because I won't explain—and joined the first crew in need of a cabin boy. The *Reckoning* was a larger ship, and the bo'sun had already employed Tommy that morning, so we were both new to the crew. And new to sailing and piracy as well. He was born on Cregah, across the Binbrack Mountains, but why he left and how he ended up in Morshan, you'd need to ask him."

He expected her to push him on that, to challenge his silence on Tommy's past, but she didn't. "And this ship? Your becoming captain? How'd that come to pass exactly?"

"After being cabin boys for a couple years, we worked our way up through the crew. We had several hard voyages on that ship. Some of the merchant vessels that captain chose to intercept did not willingly submit to the pirate flag. It's rare for them to engage in a fight. Most don't employ fighters and don't protect their vessels with cannons and the like, but a couple we ran across did. One in particular cost our crew dearly. Even though we had disabled their ship with our own cannons, when we boarded them, we found they weren't harmless sailors but fighters. Each and every one of them. And good ones too."

He looked toward the window and out to the sea at the lines his ship made as they sailed on. He could almost feel the adrenaline that had coursed through him that day.

"The officers all fell, and the captain was badly wounded, but Tommy and I were able to get him back aboard the *Reckoning*. We had just enough men to sail, and our ship hadn't taken much damage, but our captain refused to go to any of the better-known pirate ports. Instead he directed us to a land we'd never heard of. A tiny port nestled in a cove. It may have been home for him once. He refused our help in tending his wounds, and Tommy and I were left sitting there in an unfamiliar port with a bunch of confused crewmen watching our captain limp away. Never saw him again, and while he'd given us no indication he planned to return, he also hadn't uttered any farewells, so we waited there. For three days. It was Tommy's suggestion to take the ship as our own. He had no desire to be captain but insisted I could be one of the best. We met with the remaining crew, took a vote, and they named me their new captain. To make a name for ourselves we changed the ship's name. You know pirates and sailors in general are a superstitious lot. This ship's name is meant to drum up fear and stop people short. And it does just that."

It was the most words he'd managed to get out without her interrupting him, and had he not found her staring at him wide-eyed, hanging onto every syllable, he might have thought she'd begun to daydream and had stopped listening.

Drawing in a long, slow breath, she sat back a bit, dropping the roll onto the plate. "Well, that's a lot to digest. How old were you when you took command?"

"Fifteen." Though he'd been fully aware of how young he was, recalling the story aloud now—and seeing Aoife's eyes widen—made the reality of it sink in deeper.

Silence settled between them as they studied each other, and he wondered where the conversation might lead. He had so many questions for her as well but didn't want to risk undoing whatever healing had occurred for her. Before he could settle on something to ask, she was speaking.

"My story is far less intriguing."

"I find that doubtful. Heir to the council? Running away? Trespassing on one of the most feared ships? And then challenging their captain time and time again? Sounds intriguing to me."

"See? You already know the whole story." She blinked up at him, a smile threatening to spread across her lips.

"Do I?" How much could he ask? How far could he push? Surely there couldn't be any harm in simply asking. If she didn't want to talk about it, she could brush it off as he had with her questions about Tommy's past.

As if she could sense his thoughts, she asked, "What do you want to know?"

So much. Too much, perhaps, and he'd have to choose carefully. "Were you close with your mothers?" He wasn't sure he'd worded it correctly, not sure how they referred to the councilwomen.

"Not really. It isn't what I'd call a family, exactly."

"How would you know?" He didn't ask it to be harsh, and he hoped his tone came across as softly as he intended. She didn't even bristle at the question though.

"Lani and I ventured often enough into Morshan, and we would see the families there. We were taught in our lessons, too, that marrying and having children was allowed for the people of Cregah, that preserving the old ways of the familial units was beneficial for their well-being, but the council was different. We had a different purpose and role, and a family would only distract from that duty."

He couldn't help but think back to his childhood. Having a family had, indeed, been good for him. Even during times when food was scarce and income from the pub had slowed to a trickle, he had never felt lacking. He had never doubted his parents' love for each other or for him and Cait. And it had been a happy life, until it ended.

How sad that she hadn't experienced any of that herself.

He shifted his weight against the wall.

"You've been standing a long while, Declan," she said, gesturing for him to sit with her.

He eyed the open space beside her on the bed, and his feet throbbed as if they'd heard her invitation and begged him to accept. It felt too close for friends though. Surely he could handle standing for the duration of a conversation, so he muttered an *I'm fine* and didn't move closer.

"Suit yourself," she said with a twinge of laughter.

She could mock all she wanted, but he'd finally gotten history locked away again in his mind, and he didn't want to risk it flooding out again.

"Did you ever wish to be away from it? You know, before you ran?"

"No." He hadn't expected such a quick answer, but then again, she had only learned about the council's secrets a week ago. Why would she have ever felt the need to leave when she'd been taught it was her duty to rule?

He wanted to ask if it was only the guilt that had pushed her to leave, but he didn't know how to broach that yet. So he switched to something else. "Did you have any hobbies? Or were those prohibited as well?"

"So many questions, Declan. If I didn't know better, I'd think you were interrogating me, digging up information to one day use against me."

Declan flashed her as menacing a look as he could manage, setting his jaw and lowering his brows along with his tone. "If I were interrogating you, you'd know. And you certainly wouldn't be sitting on a feather mattress munching on my food." With a loud exhale, he let his face melt into a more relaxed state. "This is what friends do, yes? Get to know each other? Or have you changed your mind on the friendship?"

"You won't get rid of me that easily."

"I've pretty much given up any hope of being rid of you, Aoife." He thought he saw a flash of hope in her eyes, but it could have easily been amusement or a mocking thought.

"We were allowed certain activities. Music, art, and reading, but only within limits."

"Limits?"

She swallowed, and a slight change came over her, like a cloud had passed by the sun, though it still shined on her through the window. "Certain books were forbidden. One of my favorites, a novel of love and adventure, was found by my mother. She took it and promptly threw it into my fire. I tried to salvage what I could after she left, but it turned to ash so quickly. I told myself it was for the best, that Mother had good intentions and was only looking out for me. But I never quite forgave her for that. I've looked for more copies of the book. Whenever we'd go into the little bookshop in Morshan, I'd hunt for it. But you know they get so few books into port these days. I never found it again."

"What was the title?" He'd never let the crew know, aside from Tommy, that books were one of his favorite prizes from their plundering. In fact, Tommy had instructed the crew to bring any they found to him first, and he would discreetly deliver them to Declan after they had sailed on.

It was a long shot, but perhaps he had it somewhere in his cabin.

"*The Mercenary's Bride.*" Her cheeks flushed, and he knew it wasn't the title that caused that reaction. Though it wasn't anywhere on his shelves here, he knew the book and had read it once, long before he was old enough to do so. It was indeed a tale of adventure and romance. Heavy on the latter.

"And why is that one among your favorites?"

"It was a life I'd never have for myself. Sailing the seas. Going on daring missions—"

"—being touched by a man?" The words spilled out before he could think better of them. And regret immediately washed over him. This didn't seem polite conversation, but again, he wasn't sure what was appropriate between friends.

You're a pirate. Forget propriety!

The warmth in her face deepened, but she looked him squarely in the eye—to his surprise. "Well, yes. I suppose that wasn't part of the life I was meant for. At least not in that way."

What was that life like for the heirs? To have a business partnership with their match and not romance? No family or mutual love like he'd witnessed between his parents? To have physical intimacy be not for pleasure and closeness but for the continuation of the council only?

Not that he had an issue with children. When he was younger—much younger —he'd even dreamed of one day finding a wife and having more than the two kids they'd had in his family. But then he'd learned that was the limit the council had placed on family size, and he couldn't understand it. He couldn't understand why his parents would choose to live in a land where families were told what they could and couldn't do in their own homes.

But his parents had rightly quieted him, instructed him to never express discontent or utter ill words against the council. It hadn't made any sense to him. In a land of peace and nonviolence, why did his parents fear them so?

He'd eventually learned.

"What was your favorite part of the book?" He needed to get his mind off his parents, but this question didn't exactly help.

Before he could stop it, his traitorous mind had him seeing his mom finding him with the book and pulling it out of his hands, telling him it wasn't for young eyes. He hadn't understood her, but then she'd explained certain aspects of married life, and he'd found it repulsive, though he still hadn't understood why she wouldn't let him read it. It wasn't as if it had pictures depicting any intimacy, but she had insisted, telling him he could perhaps read it in a few years if he was still interested. He hadn't dared cross his mother, and so he'd waited patiently.

Aoife answered his question with her own. "How can I pick just one? Have you read it? I'd hate to spoil it for you."

"Aye. A long time ago."

"Well, then, perhaps the part where Marko rescues Lorelai from the bandits. Or where he teaches her to fight. Lani and I used to pretend we were in her place, learning to protect ourselves from dangers beyond our shores, going on wild adventures with our one true love. Perhaps…" Aoife's eyes lowered to her hands then, and her words became rough with emotion. "Perhaps that's what Lani risked everything for. What she saw in Adler. A chance for the adventure we'd read about. For the love we'd witnessed on the pages of books."

"And you never did? Never dreamed of that, I mean?"

"No." Another quick answer. "It was a fantasy. Something to be read on the page, as real for me as the dragons and elves in fantasy stories. Something I'd never see or feel in real life."

"So I suppose I shouldn't tell you that dragons and elves are far from fantasy?"

Her eyes widened and then darted around the room, as if one of the fantastic creatures might be hiding somewhere in his cabin. "What?"

"Well, I don't have any here." He couldn't contain his laughter. "But yes, they are very much real."

"Have you seen them? With your own eyes?"

"No." Her face dropped in noticeable disappointment. "They've long left the Aisling Sea, but we once stumbled across signs of them. There are old dragon lairs on the islands around Foxhaven actually. The gold has long since been plundered, but you can still see the scorch marks from their fires and deep gouges from their claws. Can still see the bones of their victims. Apparently no looters wanted to take those."

"And the elves?"

"Evidence of them is harder to find. It was actually Mikkel who told us what we were seeing while we were taking a rest in a tiny coastal village in Turvala. The markings looked like natural designs in the trees, but he explained it was their old language. How he knew about them, he never said, and we never pushed him."

"Why did you believe him then?"

"You know how you can tell when someone is being genuine and when they're not?"

She nodded.

"Had you seen the look in his eyes when he explained it, you never would have questioned him either."

A breath fell from her. "Dragons and elves. Real. I can't… In all my days I never would have imagined. Do you think they'll ever return?"

"I'm happy for the dragons to stay gone." Indeed, it was already hard enough to be waging an endless war with the pirate lords, and now his sister's fight against the council. What would all that look like if dragons returned? "But the elves. I heard they were a formidable force in the Aisling War."

"Why did they leave?" The question seemed more for herself than for him, which was fine, because he had no answer. But if he'd had to guess, he would have assumed their desire to escape was for reasons similar to his own. The Aisling Sea brought nothing but trouble. He couldn't blame the elves—or the fae—for abandoning it.

Yet he hadn't been able to sail off yet.

"And why haven't you left, Declan?"

Startled, his eyes snapped to hers. "What do you mean?"

"Well, you don't seem to be as attached to the Aisling or any land bordering its waters." He racked his brain for what might have given her a clue, or what might have indicated that the rest of his crew *did* have an attachment. An attachment he lacked.

"I don't think I follow."

"It's hard to explain. Tommy and the rest of the crew seem at home here, on the ship, on the Aisling. Even when I witnessed them in Foxhaven, they seemed content, as if there was nothing missing for them. But you"—she swallowed hard—"you always seem to be elsewhere. And I don't think it's merely being lost in a daydream or in thought. It's as though your mind is on distant lands you've never seen, on adventures you've yet to take, and on a life you have only been able to imagine."

Silence spread out between them once again.

She'd seen all that in him during the few days they'd spent together. How should he respond? Words eluded him. His mind seemed to stop, frozen by her observation.

Only Tommy knew of what he yearned for, and yet this girl had picked up on it so quickly.

She lowered her eyes again, the blush returning. "But I suppose I could be wrong. Lani used to give me such grief for all the fanciful tales I'd devise for each of the servants in the household, or for the people we'd meet while in town."

"You do have a wonderful imagination. Surprising for someone raised to lead the council. Surely you must have had some inkling that something wasn't right about them."

Would she realize he was changing the subject? Did he care if she did?

"So we're talking about me again?" Her eyes flitted to the ceiling, as if the answer to his non-question was written among the knots and grooves. "You're right. There was an inkling, but I didn't know what it was at the time. An odd feeling in my gut, but I always shoved it aside."

"I'm surprised by that. I'd think your curiosity would have pushed you to do otherwise. Gotten you into trouble, as it tends to do."

"I didn't say it was shoved aside easily. But I trusted my mother. How was I to know I shouldn't? She was all I knew as my family—and yes, I know that word isn't adequate, but again, it's the only word I have for it. I mean, she never raised a hand to me, obviously, but the look in her eyes and the tone of her tongue could hurt as much as any strike. At least I imagined it to be so."

"What of your sisters? Did they ever question?"

"Lani was not as passionate for our service on the council. I'm not sure why. We all received the same education and upbringing, but council life never seemed to appeal to her. Even before she told me of her plans, I could sense it in her, even if I couldn't pinpoint exactly what plagued her. She always had a sad look, even when we were joking and laughing. It was as if she couldn't fully be happy, forever cloaked in a shadow. It wasn't until she spoke Adler's name to me that I saw that shadow lifted. For the briefest of moments."

"So why did you turn her in?" The question was out before he could leash it, his thoughts given life before he could stop them. Aoife recoiled as if slapped. "I'm sorry. I shouldn't have—"

"No, it's not your fault."

Why was she consoling him? He was the one being an uncaring ass.

You're a pirate, aren't you? Why bother with apologies?

"It was a callous thing to ask," he said.

What is happening to you?

She relaxed once again, her grief and pain seemingly soothed somehow. "But it's the obvious question, isn't it? Even if you hadn't asked, I'd know you were wondering." She paused and wrung her hands in her lap.

Would she provide an answer, or would she change the subject? Whatever she chose, it would be her decision. He wouldn't force that information from her, because it didn't matter. Not in the end. And not for the job they had to do, despite his insistence to the contrary days earlier.

"I didn't mean to," she whispered, but unlike the last time she'd said these words, all defensiveness was gone, leaving only remorse dripping from each syllable. Almost as if she were speaking to the one she'd wronged and not to a pirate captain.

Declan waited. The minutes dragged on, but they might have been seconds. He wasn't sure, and he dared not look at his pocket watch for fear of offending her.

The silence became unbearable though. He needed to say something, but he had no idea what that might be.

She finally rescued him by speaking first. "It's not as though they forced it out of me."

He wished she'd look at him so he could see what she might be feeling in this moment. Even with her gaze lowered, he could see her eyes darting along the bed in front of her.

The next words flowed out of her like water released from a vessel, the stopper pulled and the words eager to be heard.

"My mother asked to speak to me, to ask why Lani and I had been quiet at dinner. I wanted to find a way for her to be with Adler without having to run away in secret. I wanted her to find that life with him without having to sneak around and lie. I'm no good at deception though. I think you know by now how my tongue betrays me. I always manage to say the wrong thing, and at the wrong time. Lani..." A pause. A hard swallow. But she didn't continue that thought, leaving Lani's name hanging in the air between them even as she finished the story. "I merely asked if any other council lady had ever fallen in love. I should have known what questions that would lead to, known that my mother would not believe me when I claimed it was hypothetical."

"And has anyone? Fallen in love, that is?" Declan's words sounded dry and hoarse. Why he asked the question, he wasn't quite sure. It was not as if it had any bearing on his situation. But perhaps Aoife's curiosity was rubbing off on him a bit.

"She didn't give me a name, but yes, a sister of her mother's."

"What happened to her?"

"She was removed from all council records, her name stricken from the histories. Exiled."

Declan winced at the word. *Exile.* On Cregah that meant death. But had it always? Aoife's grandmother's generation was far before his time, and he couldn't recall if the executions masked as exiles had started that long ago or were more recent, but he wanted to believe it was the latter.

Aoife interrupted his thoughts, echoing them. "I don't know if it was true exile back then. Or if it had already become what it is today. Regardless, I didn't know any better. To me, exile was preferable to sneaking away."

"So you told her what Lani was planning?" It felt so odd to say the girl's name, as if he'd known her as well as Aoife had.

"Not intentionally. Even with the thought of exile, I didn't feel it was my place. I was planning to try to change Lani's mind and get her to reconsider the possibility of requesting to be let out of her obligations to the council. Surely a land of peace would honor such a request. But it was my mother who pushed. Asked me if *I* had fallen in love."

A faint pink colored her cheeks again, but she fought it with a shake of her head, as if that could remove the coloring. "Then it was a slip of my damn tongue that said, 'Not me.' And she immediately knew it was far from hypothetical and I was speaking of one of my sisters. Even had I not said Lani's name, I think she would have guessed it."

"Why?"

"Lani and I were never close with our other sister, Darienn." She said this as if it were obvious, as if no one in their right mind would ever be close to this other girl.

"Why not? She that hideous?" He hoped he'd get even half a smile out of her, but she didn't seem to catch his poor attempt to lighten the mood.

"The opposite actually. She's gorgeous. But different."

Aoife worried the inside of her lower lip with her teeth but kept her eyes locked on his. She ran a hand through her tangle of hair and down her neck as if this sister's name had stirred up uncomfortable memories.

"It's hard to explain. She's intense. Cold and distant, though I assumed that was due to how Lani and I ignored her and pushed her away. Now, I'm not sure. It might simply be her nature. Darienn always seemed to be calculating, plotting something, though I thought she was just odd. Our mothers all knew we didn't get along. And it wasn't that we fought at all. We just...didn't talk."

"Ever?"

"Never. Not in many years anyway. And not until after Lani... Darienn came to my room. It was bizarre, honestly. I mean, after years of tolerating each other in silence, she looked me square in the eye and spoke. I had just learned the truth about Lani, after overhearing the staff talking in the kitchen. I wasn't sure what to do. I felt so lost and confused."

"And that's when you decided to run?"

"Not initially. I thought maybe it wasn't true. Maybe it was mere servant gossip. Fantastical stories and daydreams of bored staff longing for excitement. But the more I considered it, the more I realized how ridiculous that notion was. And Darienn all but confirmed it. How she knew, or how she'd come to suspect, was beyond me. I still don't know. But I knew what they would expect of me. And if it were true, if they were killing instead of exiling, if they were lying to our people and insisting on peace when they practiced the opposite? Could I live like that? Could I take up that mantle?"

"But maybe you could have changed it from within?" Surely she had to have considered that option.

"I thought that, for the briefest of moments, but in the end I let fear take over. Fear and self-preservation. What good would I have been to my people? I couldn't trust myself not to screw up and get myself exiled in the process. I'm no eloquent leader. I'm no eloquent anything, actually. Were my people on Cregah really in danger? I only ever went into Morshan. And everyone always seemed happy, content, taken care of. I wanted to believe my people weren't all that bad off. I already had so much guilt from Lani. So I guess I deceived myself. All those years of being lied to, and I was doing it to myself, convincing myself my people would be okay, even if I couldn't stay."

Declan's jaw clenched at the word *stay*. He'd run off, abandoned his sister, claiming he'd wanted to leave all of it behind, and yet he'd stayed close, choosing to remain on the Aisling.

She continued, seemingly unaware of the tension roiling within him. "I left, thinking, perhaps hoping, that the majority of people, as long as they didn't break the council's rules, would not be in any danger. But I wouldn't have any part in even one more exile."

Her eyes now brimmed with tears, which caught the sunlight from the window, and Declan had the urge to go to her, but he fought it.

He was a friend, but to touch her, to wipe away the tears that now escaped down her freckled cheeks, would be crossing a line he dared not. He'd done it last night, yes, but the gesture would feel different, more intimate, here in the privacy of his cabin. He didn't want to give her the wrong impression.

"But the *exiles* will happen whether you are present for them or not. Simply ignoring them doesn't make them go away, and unfortunately—" The words lodged in his throat.

He'd heard the stories. He'd seen the mass graves himself.

They haunted him almost as much as his parents' deaths, had him refusing to return home.

She needed to know the truth. He needed her to know. He needed to tell her.

But her steady tears, the lip on the verge of trembling... He couldn't.

"Unfortunately what?" she asked, timid and wary.

Tension filled his jaw as he looked at her, trying to keep the faces and the bodies from surfacing in his mind. Anger burned in his chest as he muttered the only word he could manage.

"Nothing."

She'd been right earlier. He wasn't tied to this sea or to Cregah, yet something kept him here, hindered him from leaving, continued to give him excuses to stay.

But could he do any good? Did he want to?

CHAPTER 37
AOIFE

THE RUM-INDUCED fog finally cleared from Aoife's mind, only for Declan's unfinished sentences to create a new cloud of questions she had to wade through. She wanted to give him the benefit of the doubt, trust that he had his reasons for not telling her everything.

She ripped off another piece of the roll he'd handed her and placed it on her tongue. Sands, she missed butter.

Even without looking up she could see that Declan's shifting was becoming more frequent. His feet had to be hurting. They'd been talking for hours. Without bickering. Without interruption. She nearly smiled at the thought of their budding friendship, but his refusal to rest his feet and sit beside her kept it hidden.

She tried not to take his decision personally.

Tried and failed.

They'd been silent for the last few minutes. She had no idea if he was watching her, but she didn't need to look at him to digest all he'd told her.

She had learned more about him over the last couple of hours than she had in the past several days. At that thought, a small half smile pulled at one corner of her lips before a breath of a laugh escaped.

"What's so funny?" he asked.

Embarrassment warmed her cheeks, and she tried to shake it away as she raised her chin.

"Nothing."

Another laugh tumbled out as she realized she'd given him the same one-word answer he'd offered moments before. She lost herself in his stormy eyes, trapped by their intensity, as she waited for his teasing comment.

But it never came.

He simply looked at her—no, looked *into* her, as if she were a puzzle he needed to figure out. An intense gaze, but not altogether uncomfortable. In fact, something in his expression seemed to be inviting her to stay, and she very nearly inched closer to the edge of the bed toward him. But she stopped herself when he cleared his throat and pulled his attention down to the floor.

With a blink, she shook away any hope the moment had sparked within her. *You're letting your imagination get away from you.* She needed to keep her head if she was going to be of any help to him.

She also needed to know more about his plans to find the fae.

"If I might ask..." she said, propping an elbow on her knee so she could lean her chin on her palm.

He offered a hum of approval for her to continue before looking up, his head falling to the side as he did.

"Why the short timeline anyway? If the dagger does what the legends claim, why the hurry?"

Rubbing a hand on the back of his neck, Declan raised a shoulder before answering.

"I don't know much actually. Kind of par for the course in our line of work. You get used to only being told the bare minimum."

"Even from your sister?"

"Especially from her. We aren't particularly close, and that's my fault." He didn't look away as she expected. His gaze held fast, but his eyes were now devoid of any of the emotion she'd seen in them earlier, their previous fire replaced with a cold nothingness, as if he were guarding himself.

"And that doesn't bother you?" She couldn't imagine being okay with not being close to a sibling, and then Darienn's face flashed in her mind, rebuking her for judging him. "I mean, she's your only sibling, yes?"

"Aye. Just the two of us, but we have our own ways of dealing with..."

His voice trailed off, and he turned his face toward the windows and the sea beyond.

She watched him intently, wondering if the wall he'd built would ever come down, even if only when they were alone. She'd seen it start to give, bits of it falling away, always to be patched up swiftly. And he showed no sign of letting it falter again now.

Turning back to her, he offered, "Let's just say, going back to Cregah brings back memories I'd rather keep locked away." He stiffened, as if bracing himself against her possible push for more information.

"So why did you go back?"

This question got him to relax slightly, and he raised a brow. "Your turn to interrogate me then?"

She tossed him a shrug and one of her mocking smirks, which at least earned her a small laugh from him before he drew in a deep breath and answered.

"It was the closest port after we were hit hard by one of the lords up around Helles Island. My men needed care, and they wouldn't have made it to one of the farther islands. Morshan was it. I planned to stay aboard the ship, but my sister got word to me. She knew I was seeking the dagger. And her…"

Again he trailed off. He kept doing this. Leaving sentences incomplete, as if his tongue steered him toward paths in the conversation his mind didn't want to go down but was late in catching up.

He still didn't trust her with certain things, and she was trying to be okay with that, but she couldn't deny that she'd thought things were changing last night. And this morning.

Yet he still paused, edited his words, and it irked her, lighting a fire in her gut that wouldn't be quenched no matter how she tried to talk it down and reason it away. Why should he trust her? He had little reason to. At least not fully.

He continued his sentence, though it was obviously altered from what he'd originally planned to say. "Her running the pub keeps her from going after the dagger herself. She requested I bring it to her."

"And you agreed?"

"She had information I'd failed to gather myself. Namely, the dagger's location and a plan for how to retrieve it. So yes, I agreed. But I hadn't decided if I'd follow through."

"Such a pirate thing to do. Say one thing and do another."

Aoife hoped he'd hear the humor she intended, but if he did, he didn't let on.

Instead his gaze hardened, like her words had struck a nerve. *But he is a pirate. Why should that bother him?*

"You said you hadn't decided. Past tense. Does that mean you've decided now?"

"Perhaps. I might be leaning stronger to one side now."

Her brow tightened as curiosity took over. "What changed? What pushed you to a decision?"

He didn't answer but nodded in her direction.

Her. She'd been the catalyst. But which way had she swayed him? She had her assumptions, but her instincts were so off-kilter, she didn't quite trust them.

"And?"

"And what?"

She groaned out a sigh, knowing he was toying with her. He knew full well what she was asking. Still, she clarified. "Which way are you leaning?"

"Well, it is still tempting to take the dagger for myself so I can leave the Aisling. I wouldn't need to spend more years preparing. I'd simply be able to leave and have successes and triumphs in all the seas beyond. But no. I'm not sure now if I could enjoy any of that, knowing what was going on behind me. Some pirate I am."

"You know, a pirate once told me that pirates do, in fact, have honor and a heart. I'm apt to believe him, because he seemed pretty sure of that fact."

"I see what you did there."

"But do you believe it or not? Or were those words about honor another well-crafted lie fed to an irritating stowaway?"

He didn't answer. Not that she had expected him to. She was once again swimming in the grays of his eyes as they locked onto hers, and she wished she could know what his mind was mulling over.

What was he seeing in her? Did he see her as a friend, as she had begun to see him? Or did he still see her as a nuisance aboard his ship? She didn't think it was the latter, but she couldn't tell if the friendship budding between them was completely genuine.

Did it even matter?

All she needed was for him to trust her enough to let her help.

To get the fae.

So he could get the dagger.

So they could stop the council from killing her people.

This was too big, too important, too impossible.

How could they ever dream of succeeding?

That single question brought the weight of everything slamming into her like a wave against the ship's hull.

It sucked all the oxygen from the room. With both hands, she clenched the blankets, but she kept spiraling as the panic rushed in.

Even with her eyes squeezed shut, the heaviness in her chest wouldn't subside. The tension increased, and the sensation of a million legs crawling over her skin overtook her.

For the briefest of moments she worried what he might think, seeing her losing it. But the panic had its hold on her. Pulling her under.

It didn't matter if he saw.

Nothing mattered except getting it to stop.

Ending it.

Surviving it.

Through her pounding heart and shallow breaths she heard the two steps he took toward her. Felt the bed shift.

She opened her eyes to see him moving her plate out of the way as he knelt on the ground before her.

His hand reached for her knee, his touch light but still reassuring.

"Breathe, Aoife. Slow. Steady." His voice melted over her, and she did as he suggested, his words not a command but an encouragement. His tone was far from that of a ruthless pirate, but more like a caring friend, and that thought helped calm her.

"There you go," he said.

Her heartbeat slowed. Breathing became easier, and she could have almost cried at how quickly the panic began to ease up.

"What happened just then?" he asked. "One minute you were asking about lies and irritating stowaways—" He flashed her favorite smirk. "And the next, you're acting as though someone punched you in the gut."

She needed a moment before she could explain it with any coherency, and he waited with more patience than she'd anticipated.

"It's all simply—" No, that wasn't the best way to explain this. Why were words so damn hard sometimes? "It's too much."

"What is?"

Aoife stared at her hands, fidgeting with her fingers, trying to ignore how his hand remained on her knee.

"All of it." She lifted her chin, but her gaze darted around the room, as if the words she needed would be found in the air. "The fae. The dagger. The council. It's all so much. How can you—we—hope to succeed?"

As he drew in a breath, she wondered if he'd react with the same panic she had experienced. But he didn't. Of course he didn't. He was a pirate. And a young one at that, constantly fighting against the odds to make a name for himself and find his footing amongst the other ships and fleets.

He was used to being challenged, and that was all this was. Another challenge.

"We might not," he finally said.

Well, that wasn't reassuring. Surely he wasn't finished. She scowled at him, and he shook his head at her before flashing her another of his smirks.

At least one of us is in a good mood.

"But—yes, there's a but," he continued. "We will certainly fail if we don't try at all. So we will push forward, one step at a time, doing the next task set before us until all are complete."

If he'd said these words to her a few days ago, they would have aggravated her, but now she understood the comfort he offered. Though this didn't quite quell her concerns. "Don't you have to plan for the later steps too though? Doesn't that get overwhelming?"

A shrug seemed to be his only answer until she jutted her chin out at him, pressing him to explain.

"It only gets overwhelming if you let it. Yes, you see the big picture in your periphery. You calculate the possible paths that might present themselves along the way, but if you let the overall mission shadow the task at hand, you'll stumble and fall. Just like you almost did when you forgot how to breathe."

"So focus on the next task."

"Aye."

"Which is?"

"Shopping."

CHAPTER 38
DECLAN

DECLAN COULD BARELY CONTAIN his amusement as Aoife sat staring at him, her mouth hanging open.

She repeated the word. "Shopping."

He nodded in return.

"But how?"

"Well, we use these things called coins, and merchants give us goods in exchange for them."

A groan rumbled in the back of her throat. "Apparently the next task at hand is actually to drive me mad."

She seemed to be trying to hold onto her irritation as much as he was trying to contain his laughter, and soon both of them lost their respective battles, if only for a moment, smiles creeping across their lips.

She looked away first, as if suddenly aware of how close they sat and how his hand still lingered on her knee.

He pulled it away with some reluctance. She only wanted a friend, and he could be that for her. He shooed away the teasing, taunting thoughts of having more.

With her hands raised, she gestured to her attire and reworded her earlier question. "How do we go shopping without being recognized? If they found me in Foxhaven, they'll surely be looking for me in Morshan. Yes?"

"Indeed. But we won't be shopping in the normal sense." She began to protest but then snapped her mouth shut. She must have realized he wasn't quite done explaining. "Remember, I grew up in Morshan. I know how to maneuver around without being seen. And we won't be going to any shops. They'll be coming to us. In a way."

He waited for her to object, to demand more information, to insist he tell her every minute detail of the plan, but whether she was beginning to trust him more or simply too tired to argue, he wasn't sure. She merely nodded, lips pursed in acceptance.

She once again glanced down at her lap, keeping him from seeing the green of her eyes under her lashes as he studied her. What he wouldn't give to get a glimpse into her thoughts.

Every passing second with her made the nagging desire within him grow more and more impatient, urging him to acknowledge the possibilities, and he could no longer suppress the images of his parents doing life together, side by side as a team.

When all of Cregah had believed women should rule and men could not be trusted to do anything but destroy and tear apart, he had seen his mother and father live as partners. Equals. He'd fought against this notion of partnership and marriage for too long. It only ended in heartache. Death.

Happiness couldn't last. Love and peace—supposedly valued—weren't allowed on Cregah except within the council's limits.

Could he risk opening his heart to someone as his father had, as his mother had? Could he risk opening himself up to someone—taking that leap—while the council still existed, still preyed on its people and crushed everything good?

He breathed deep, but it wouldn't clear away the warring thoughts in his mind.

Focus on the task at hand. Focus.

He needed to distract himself, to shut up the voices.

"Do those attacks happen often?" he asked. He hoped she'd understand what he meant. His words had not come out quite as eloquently as he'd planned.

Aoife angled her head to one side as her lips twitched a little. Would the mere mention of the panic attack trigger another? He held his breath until she gave him a string of small nods, her eyes looking into his again.

Was that shame in her expression? Her eyes began to gloss over with the start of tears. His fingers itched to reach for her again, but he managed to refrain.

"I used to," he said. "Get those panic attacks, I mean."

She showed no surprise even as she asked, "When?"

"When I was younger, before I left home."

"So long ago. And never since then?"

"Rarely since. It was as if the sea and this life gave me a distraction, perhaps. Not a remedy for what hurt, I suppose, but more like a curtain being drawn so I could no longer focus on what had plagued me prior."

He was tiptoeing along an uncomfortable line, but he couldn't stop, like some part of him was desperate to let her in. The wall within him started to give again, but no, it wasn't failing. Rather, it was as if he was standing atop the wall and reaching a hand toward her, inviting her to join him on the other side.

Would she want to learn more? Would she want to see the real him? Her curiosity would likely insist she accept whether she truly cared for him or not.

But she didn't pry.

Instead, she offered her own story.

"I've gotten them my whole life. Only Lani knew about it. Or if our mothers and Darienn knew, they never let on. Lani was the only one who ever tried to help, much in the way you did. She'd remind me to breathe, sitting beside me until it passed."

"What caused them?"

"They seemed to happen whenever I got overwhelmed. When the pressure became too great, I'd lose myself. Forget how to function. It felt like the weight of the council was sitting on my chest, pressing in from all sides, like my heart might be squeezed until it burst."

Declan waited for her to continue, mostly because he wasn't sure what questions to ask now. He wanted to understand but had little idea how to proceed. Before today, he hadn't witnessed one of her episodes, not that he'd been with her during every moment she'd spent on the ship.

"How often?" he asked again.

Did she hear the concern in his voice? Would she understand he asked as a friend, or would she assume he was looking for any possible hiccups in the upcoming mission? She was becoming difficult to read. All these new thoughts and feelings seemed to be clouding his ability to assess her.

"Every so often." She must have seen the twitch at the corner of his eye, because she immediately elaborated. "Once or twice a week actually."

That regularly. It took every ounce of will to keep his mouth from falling open. Even after his parents' deaths, his panic attacks hadn't been that common. Once a month, if that. And they'd been unbearable when they came upon him. He couldn't imagine living with them at such frequency.

"And since you've been here?"

Her head once again dipped down, her eyes falling to her fingers that were worrying the blanket at her feet. Declan hoped—as silly as it was—that perhaps the sea and his ship had done for her what it had done for him all those years ago, distracted and suppressed the inner demons that took hold without notice. But he knew that was unlikely.

"This was the third."

She'd hidden them well. He'd never noticed. He hadn't been here to help. Though, looking back at their early days together, he knew he wouldn't have likely offered help had he witnessed them.

"I'm sorry." It was all he could think to say.

No hint of sadness or distress remained in Aoife's eyes. The greens and golds seemed warmer somehow, reminding him of the hills outside Morshan where his family used to picnic in the summer evenings, when the sun would hit the rolling waves of grass.

Such happy yet somber memories.

That's what her eyes brought him, what caused the twinge in his heart as she looked at him now. Looking into her eyes felt like returning to the home he desperately missed. And the shock of that realization threatened to suffocate him, ripping the breath from his lungs.

How long had he spent trying to leave the Aisling, and his past, behind? And now here, this girl, who had dared to stow away on his ship, seemed to be calling him to stay, without her knowing or realizing it. He was getting lost in those eyes that so perfectly mirrored the beauty of their shared home of Cregah. The rich greens. The gold of the sun. Even the black of her pupils reminded him of the black sands of its shores. Home.

"It's okay, Declan. Truly." Her words snapped him back to the present.

"I'm sorry all the same. You shouldn't have had to bear those on your own."

"And you would have aided me somehow had you known?" She flashed that smirk at him, the one he knew she put on to mock him.

"Perhaps. But perhaps not. We will never know now."

"Aren't you worried these attacks might impact the task at hand?"

"Shopping? No. We can handle panic as we shop."

"You know what I mean, Declan. How are we going to retrieve the fae from the council hall if I might freeze up at any moment?"

Declan looked at the ceiling, biding his time. He already knew his answer, but he didn't want her to know he'd already formed a contingency plan.

Aoife spoke again before he could reply. "You've already thought of that, haven't you? Already planned for that possibility during the short moments we've sat here together."

"Aye. It is part of being captain. When potential—" He didn't want to call it a 'problem.' That would indicate something was wrong with her. "When potential obstacles present themselves, one must devise remedies or solutions. And I prefer to identify those early rather than wait for them to spring on me in the heat of the moment. If possible."

"And what is the remedy for my...condition?"

"You speak of it as if it were a deformity of sorts."

"Isn't it?" Shame swept across her face as she tugged her bottom lip between her teeth.

"A deformity would imply that it's something innately wrong with you, and that is far from the case. These attacks are not you. They do not define you. And while they can seem insurmountable, they are not."

"But I've never been able to predict them. Or prevent them. They crop up with no warning. Where is my distraction? My curtain to hide what haunts me? The sea obviously is not helping me in the same way it helped you."

Declan couldn't help but smile at her rambling torrent of words, and he almost hoped she'd continue.

Almost. There wasn't quite time for that though, as he could see the edges of the Cregahn coastline in the harbor creeping past the windows. They would be docked soon.

"Aye. For me it was a distraction, but I've learned from others that while we may not be able to prevent them, we can learn to suppress them when they happen."

Her eyes widened, a sparkle he hoped would never die shining in them upon hearing his words. "Can you teach me?"

"Perhaps. But first, we must prepare to go ashore."

As if on cue, the crew began to scurry about out on the deck, announcing their arrival in Port Morshan.

CHAPTER 39
AOIFE

Aoife tried to be patient, but Declan's offer to help her with the panic attacks was too enticing to be forgotten so easily.

Focus on the task at hand, Aoife.

She tried to do as her thoughts instructed, but it was difficult not to ponder the secrets to conquering her malady.

They do not define you. His words echoed in her mind. All these years she'd felt ashamed, like something was wrong with her, like something within her had gone awry as she was formed or as she grew. Some mistake or error in her very nature. But Declan, in one brief conversation, had given her another option. It was a sickness. Something from outside herself that attacked and took hold.

It was not her. It was a foe. And all foes could be defeated.

Declan had already stood and crossed the room to prepare to head ashore. He slid a dagger into an ankle sheath hidden within his boot and then another at his hip. His cutlass he left atop his desk.

"Are you ready?" he called, peering at her from the main chamber.

She was still getting used to this new rapport, his gruffness and rude tones now calmed and softened. It would have been more off-putting if she hadn't found it so welcome and endearing. She had been the one to suggest friendship, after all, and she found herself almost giddy to see he had so willingly obliged. How things had changed in a matter of days.

Her imagination rushed ahead of her though, with images of a possible future popping up against her will. A life on this ship, serving on his crew. Or a home on a distant, unknown shore, with a quaint cottage and a small garden and a love all her own.

She pushed the images back into the far recesses of her consciousness. She needed to focus, not get lost in fantasies and daydreams. Especially those that were far from likely to ever happen.

Stretching out her neck, she stood and found her footing more quickly than in the past. A glance down at her sleep-rumpled clothes had her hoping their shopping plans—whatever they might be—included acquiring a change of garments. Approaching Declan, she tried her best to smooth out the fabric at her waist.

"And how does this *shopping* know to come to us and where to find us?"

Had he some secret pirate method for sending word to the shores ahead of them? It seemed unlikely, but pirate life seemed intent on surprising her at every turn.

"Telepathy." Declan's expression was dead serious. She searched his eyes but found no sign of jest in them.

"Really?" If elves and dragons were indeed real, perhaps this form of magic existed as well.

"No."

Her shoulders slumped. With a roll of her eyes, she smacked him with the back of her hand. He'd fooled her. And she'd fallen for it so easily.

She did her best to recover some semblance of self-respect, but his deep laughter—so carefree—was impossible to ignore. All she could do was shake her head, purse her lips, and wait for him to settle. This was taking too long.

"Are you done laughing at me?"

Declan composed himself, sucking in a gulp of air before he spoke. "I think so. Your face though." His smile grew.

"What about my face?" She wondered what he might poke fun at this time. As much as she wanted to be annoyed with him, she was finding it increasingly more difficult. This lightheartedness was such a change. And not an unwelcome one.

"You're just so cute when you fall for things."

Cute.

She tried to dissect the word, peeling back the meanings as she knew them. She'd never been called "cute" before and had only heard the word used by the women in town regarding babies or children's paintings. Was it an endearing term? Or was he calling her childish?

"Don't worry, Aoife," he explained. "It's a good thing."

"What is?"

"Being cute."

She started to challenge him, ask him why he'd bother clarifying such a thing, but he spoke again. "You looked concerned about my words is all. A little hurt even."

While some of the mirth was still present in those damn sea-gray eyes, there was a flash of tenderness again. Something moved in her gut, but she couldn't determine what it was. A warmth settling in, grounding her. Comfort.

Again, future possibilities whirled in her mind, but she now began to see him beside her in the various scenes. She tried to blink them away, but each was replaced with a new one. And in each she found him to be more of a companion than a friend. Holding her hand. Brushing her hair from her forehead. Placing a kiss on her cheek.

She clenched her eyes shut. No. This would do her no good right now. Would only cloud her ability to do what needed to be done. He was a friend, and he could only ever be such.

"Are you okay? You look hurt again." The previous amusement still hovered at the edge of his words.

"I'm fine. Just trying to focus." Another stretch of her neck, though it didn't need it. "Are you going to answer my question now? With the real answer?"

"What's the fun in that?"

She answered him with a frown, earning her another laugh.

"Okay, okay. Gavin's getting word to them as we speak."

"How did he know to do that?" He raised a brow, and she quickly interrupted whatever he was about to say. "And don't say telepathy again."

He clicked his tongue at her. "Always so curious to know my ways. If you insist on knowing though, I gave him the command this morning. While you were still sleeping off last night's fun."

A knock sounded at the door, and without looking away from her, he gave the command to enter.

Aoife turned with some hesitation, taking another moment to drag her eyes away from Declan's. Tommy stood there, a look of curious expectation on his face. If he suspected anything was happening between her and his captain, he didn't voice it. But it seemed more and more obvious that he sensed something in the air.

And it didn't seem to bother him.

"Captain. Aoife. When you're ready..." He gestured with an arm toward the door, inviting them to lead the way out of the cabin into the sticky air of Morshan.

Declan reached for her, his hand hovering at her waist, warming the air between them. When she turned toward the door, his hand made contact with the small of her back. Not at all unwanted. Warmth bubbled up into her chest.

As she stepped forward, his hand fell away, and the resulting emptiness and longing tingled along her spine. She hoped Tommy couldn't see it all written across her face.

The feelings resisted being pushed away. She was as desperate to ignore them as they were to pester her, but it would do her no good to become preoccupied with hidden meanings behind every move and touch.

He was merely being kind. A friend. Just as she had claimed she wanted.

CHAPTER 40
CAIT

Cait looked around at the nearly empty pub and the handful of afternoon regulars. Word had come an hour earlier by way of one of the young kids from the docks. The note sealed with Declan's siren insignia in black wax had provided nothing more than a list of items, a location, and a time. And the instruction to come alone.

He hadn't given her much time, but it hadn't been an issue. Each Rogues member took a shift at the pub in case of just such an occasion, when Cait might need them to run an errand.

She hadn't paused to question his list of items but had jotted them down on a scrap of paper, which she'd tucked into the folds of a napkin before sliding it—and a small glass of rum—to the girl, Kira, seated at the bar. A slight dip of Kira's chin had confirmed she understood.

The girl had been part of the Rogues since she'd moved into Morshan from one of the southern villages over a year ago. Her whole family had vanished while she was at the secret market to sell medicines banned by the council. Finding her home eerily empty, all their belongings gone, Kira had fled with nothing but the items she carried.

For days Kira had stayed off the roads, sticking close to the trees to avoid whomever the council had sent for them. When she'd made it to Morshan, Cait had found her standing in awe of the town, her jaw hanging open at what must have been a marvel to see.

It was how they all looked when they arrived. Eyes wide. Jaw agape. Like a child standing before a buffet of decadent desserts after years of eating nothing but bland porridge.

Cait had heard stories about the other villages on Cregah.

Morshan was the anomaly.

Despite the inevitable underlying layer of filth, which plagued all port cities,

Morshan was well-kept, and its people lived well. The paint on the buildings was as fresh as the abundant food provided to the residents by the council. Brightly colored gardens adorned the grounds of each home, the blooms covering the smells of the many travelers who visited and left their muck behind.

But life in Morshan was as much a facade as Cait's maintained residence above the pub.

As false as it was, she knew the people in this town were blessed in a way. While they too lived in fear of exile, they didn't suffer the same hardships as those elsewhere. The starvation. The sickness. The poverty.

No business remained open on Cregah without the council's blessing, and the council in turn used these establishments to provide everything to the people. Most of the money earned by the merchants and business owners was paid back to the council via monthly dues, but few complained, because it meant the residents always had access to food, medicine, clothes, and wares brought in by the pirates.

The very drink Cait offered was supplied by the same pirates who would later come in and drink it. If they realized it, they didn't care.

The same was not so in other areas of Cregah, where the little food the council distributed was usually rotten by the time it arrived on the carts hired to deliver it. Medicine was nonexistent, and most other items were scarce.

The once prosperous nation had slowly deteriorated as the council changed its focus during the centuries following the signing of the treaty. Eventually outlawing more than just violence, they'd closed the markets where locals had sold their goods, insisting everything could be provided by the pirates who had signed the treaty—goods they would then distribute to all the people.

But they'd either been unable to do this for the other towns on Cregah, or they'd lied and had simply been neglecting the people out of heartlessness.

Cait wasn't sure which it was.

Not that it mattered in the end.

She was determined to see that the people of her beloved nation didn't have to live in fear and poverty any longer. So every time a Rogues member encountered someone who hadn't arrived by ship, they sent them on to the pub so Cait could chat with them, ensure they weren't a spy from the council, get them clothed, fill their bellies, and give them hope.

She'd done so with nearly fifteen individuals, but for each person she helped, she knew there were many more who never made it to her, who still suffered back in their home villages.

Kira, in fact, had been the last to come her way. A year had passed, and no one new had arrived.

Cait didn't want to know what was keeping more from getting here. But she suspected many didn't want to leave their homes, no matter how bad life got. It was their homeland. Hard. But beloved all the same.

Kira had trusted Cait and readily stepped into the Rogues, eager to do whatever she could to take down those who had stolen her family from her.

And now Cait was trusting her to round up a few of the others around town, to discreetly secure the items from Declan's list, and to get it all back to her office on time.

She glanced at the clock above the bar. Kira had been gone over two hours, and Declan would be expecting her soon. She could only hope they'd been able to locate everything he needed.

The door opened behind her, and Kira entered. A quick nod told Cait all she needed to know.

She tossed the towel she'd been holding to Kira, who took her spot behind the bar. No one in the room took note of the exchange and would likely have thought nothing of it even if they had, as it was not unusual for Cait to leave the pub for a bit now and then to run errands or to take a break, and these slow afternoons were the ideal time to do just that. But just to be sure, she made a point to voice her plan to head upstairs for some rest before the evening rush of revelers.

While she'd taken the door from the street with Declan last week, she couldn't use that entrance in the middle of the day when shadows were scarce and eyes were watching.

At the back of the pub, in the storeroom beside the stairs that led to her childhood residence above the business, a hidden door barely wider than her shoulders led to an underground passage.

She knew most of those currently in the pub, but she still didn't trust them not to rat her out. One never knew when the council might call in a debt from any of the pirates who frequented Morshan's streets, no matter how many times they came to the pub or how friendly they were.

Loyalty on Cregah was bought, not earned. And the council had more to offer the pirates than the locals of the town did.

But she had to keep up the ruse.

She trudged up the stairs with heavy and tired steps until she reached her room and placed a bag of sand on the bed, causing the floorboards to creak, alerting the patrons downstairs that someone had settled in for some rest.

Leaning against the wall, she removed her boots with care and then returned the way she'd come, carrying her boots under her arm as she kept to the edge of the hallway and the stairs, the boards remaining silent under her weight.

The back wall of the bar hid the stairs and storeroom well enough that no one would notice her tiptoe around the corner and slip into the hidden passageway, replacing the wooden door above her head.

It had been that secret doorway, discovered years ago, that had sparked a sense of adventure in her, temporarily easing the grief over her parents' deaths.

She'd entered it without hesitation, not even bothering to wonder where Declan had run off to. He hadn't handled the loss well, which was to be expected for a kid so young and so enamored with his parents—as most kids were apt to be—and she'd had no notion of where he went or how he spent his time.

She should have kept better track of him, but they had never been close, and if she knew nothing else about her brother, she knew of his need for space.

And she'd been more than willing to grant him that as she explored that passage, her fingers tracing the wooden walls that transitioned to stone as she descended the stairs.

She'd tried to mentally picture where the passage led, but as it had turned one way and then the other, every twenty or thirty feet, she'd lost track of all sense of location or heading. After thirty minutes of tiptoeing along, she'd come to a split in the corridor. Nothing differentiated one way from the other. No difference in light or scent or air.

During that first venture into the passageway, she'd gone left and found herself in a tunnel that narrowed until ending abruptly at a sharp drop-off into the Aisling Sea just northeast of the docks, hidden by the trees that sprang out along the rocky cliff face.

She later discovered the other corridor led to her mother's office, and it was that one she needed to take now. And quickly.

A small lantern sat on the bottom stair, and she lit it as quickly and quietly as she could.

While she could have made the trip in the dark, the way having been etched into her mind after so many years of using this path, time was not on her side, and she'd need the light to navigate the uneven ground beneath her feet more quickly.

With her boots back on her feet and laced up, she ran ahead, hoping to get there before Declan arrived.

It was risky having him use the street entrance, but it would raise fewer alarms than having them enter a near-empty pub and then disappear into the back. When that entrance wasn't hidden in shadows, it sat nondescript among a row of shops and eateries.

Declan was a skilled enough pirate. He should have no problem getting around without raising suspicion.

Cait reached the top of the stairs and heard voices on the other side of the door.

Apparently, he hadn't come alone.

Her feet slipped on some loose pebbles as she hurried to unlock it for him. She pulled the door open a crack to verify it was Declan who waited for her. She had just begun to open it wider for him when a girl—the one from the pub that night—stepped around him and moved to enter.

Cait didn't budge as she looked at Declan. How could he have been so stupid to bring her here?

"I see the *come alone* part only applied to me?" She put an edge into her words.

Declan leaned in, his face hovering over the girl's shoulder as he whispered, "I couldn't very well leave her on the ship."

She needed to get them off the street, but something twinged deep in her bones. If this girl undid all their years of work, if she were actually a spy sent from the council...

Cait stepped aside and ushered them in, but once the door was locked behind them, she didn't make a move to lead them to her office.

In the dim light of her lantern, she searched the girl's face, as if something there might provide a hint as to her identity and motives.

The girl twitched under her stare, her eyes flicking to Declan, her body shifting closer to his ever so slightly.

Well, this is an interesting development.

Declan was the first to break the standoff. "I can vouch for her, Cait."

Cait turned to him but didn't soften her tone a bit as she said, "You'd better, because otherwise it'll be our heads."

Without another word, she turned on her heel and led them down the hallway.

She pushed her office door open and gestured for them to enter, following her idiot brother and the girl inside before locking the door behind them. Turning, she found them standing in the center of the room. The girl—a full head shorter than Declan—was looking about.

Cait strode past them, trying to ignore the tension in her limbs that reminded her how those men had come looking for this girl last week.

She motioned to the chairs before them. "Please, sit."

Cait settled herself behind her desk as it struck her how similar this was to the last time she'd hosted him here.

She watched intently as Declan ushered the girl to one of the proffered seats. He showed her such care, such genuine grace. Had her dear brother, the ruthless pirate, gone soft? Surely it wasn't a ploy. He had no reason to act any part in front of Cait, and there was no one else to play to.

Unless he was playing the girl.

"I don't believe we've met," Cait said, raising her brow in invitation to the girl.

"Aoife," the girl replied, with no hint of the meekness Cait expected. "Cascade."

That name. No wonder that pair of pirates had been looking for her.

"An heir then," Cait said, catching how Aoife shifted at the word and how Declan reached for her. He stayed himself, pulling back with apparent reluctance.

"Aye," Declan said. "A most valuable addition to our side, I think." His expression betrayed none of the feelings Cait was certain lay behind his behavior. "Did you manage to acquire the items we needed?"

"I believe so, but to be honest, I only just arrived when you did. I haven't yet had a chance to review what my crew collected."

"Funny you call them your *crew*, almost as if you wished to be a pirate yourself, sister."

She ignored him, needing to keep that longing from distracting her. With a bob of her chin, she gestured to a haphazard pile of fabric on the table against the wall. "A curious assortment you requested, Declan. Not easily acquired. It's not as though we can go to the market or a local shop to find these, you know."

"Aye, but if anyone could do it, you could, Cait," he said and then stood to go inspect the goods. "Plus, at least we only needed garments and cloth. Nothing too large and hard to conceal."

Cait watched Aoife, once again inspecting her for any sign the girl wasn't a runaway but a spy. She scolded herself for letting Aoife into this room, into this life of hers, behind the veil of secrecy.

But Declan had a knack for sensing traps. He would never have brought her—warming feelings or no—had he thought she might betray them.

At least that's what Cait needed to believe.

"So, Aoife. How has life on a pirate ship treated you?" She tried to give her as warm a smile as she could muster, but she didn't know how well she pulled it off given all the doubts and worry that wouldn't quite dissolve.

Aoife seemed to startle, her eyes blinking below her scrunched brow, as if she couldn't fathom why Cait would bother talking to her.

"The food could be better, but the company—" Her words cut off, and she looked to Declan, seemingly out of habit.

The warming feelings are mutual then.

Cait's eyes narrowed with this suspicion, but she recovered quickly, hoping Aoife wouldn't realize how much she was learning with this encounter.

"I hope they're treating you well. There are far worse crews and ships you could have stumbled upon."

Something flashed across Aoife's features. Pain. Fear even.

What happened to her this past week?

"Indeed," Declan said, returning to his seat. "Far worse crews. Everything looks to be in order." He gave a nod toward the table.

"Given the list, I can assume you plan to enter the council hall and pass for a member of one of the crews in attendance tomorrow evening?"

A nod from him. Another glance at him from the girl.

"It would benefit you to know, then, that I have someone inside the council hall who can help." Cait ignored how Aoife's eyes widened at this ever so slightly. "She can't—won't—help outright for risk of being outed, but she can help you get in at least."

Cait explained how the servant's entrance would be left unlocked and how they were to station their lookouts in the hallways. Aoife tensed as she spoke, and Cait couldn't help but wonder how the girl would manage with being back home. She had so many questions for her.

Why had she fled? Did she know the truth about the council? Was she truly ready to betray them?

Surely Declan had asked her all of this, and Cait had no choice but to trust him. Time was ticking by, and this was the only play they had.

With all of Declan's questions answered and the plan laid out, he moved to gather up the clothing they'd need for their ruse.

Cait followed them to the door, watching as Declan ushered Aoife out in front of him. Had she not known otherwise, she would have suspected him to be a doting lover, not a pirate of wild reputation.

Once Aoife stepped out into the darkened hallway, Cait grabbed Declan's elbow. He turned his chin over his shoulder, as if unwilling to let Aoife completely out of even his peripheral vision.

"Declan. Be careful."

He flashed her that stupid smirk of his. "Where's the fun in that?"

Cait lowered her voice to a whisper. "With her, I mean."

His eyes twitched, and Cait couldn't tell if he was questioning her meaning or challenging her words.

"I mean it." Before she could comment further, warn him of how dangerous it was to get too close to Aoife, he gave a final nod and was gone.

Cait stood in the doorway long after they'd exited and shut the door to the street at the end of the hallway behind them. She'd need to go lock it again, of course, but she couldn't yet, frozen by new fear and worry, not just for the mission at hand, but for her brother's heart as well.

CHAPTER 41
DECLAN

ALL THE PREPARATIONS had been made and the crew briefings wrapped up, but Declan still hadn't been able to shake the odd warning from his sister. Throughout the entire evening, he'd been distracted by her words.

If Aoife had noticed his quiet demeanor, she hadn't let on, hadn't pushed him to explain it. Perhaps she assumed he was merely nervous over the task ahead, fearful their plan would fail.

He should have been thinking of the plan, but he told himself it was solid and set, with little need to worry over it further. His men knew what to do, and Aoife would be by his side the whole time so he could ensure she didn't stumble or falter.

Or get in the way.

He swept that thought aside, a remnant of his former opinion that she was nothing more than a nuisance. She remained clumsy and awkward, but despite the trouble that could cause, he didn't hold it against her as he once had.

Pacing, he trod the familiar path in his chamber that had worn the old carpet down to its threads. With Aoife relaxing in the bedroom, working to calm her mind before they left for the council hall, he was left to his own thoughts.

And they plagued him, like a swarm of flies that wouldn't leave no matter how often he shooed them away.

None of this worrying would help them in their task. It would only bring cloudy thinking and poor judgment. He needed to be prepared, focused. But every time he managed to get Cait's warning firmly tucked away, it slammed into him again.

Be careful with her.

What had she meant? There were two obvious messages there, and it behooved him to consider both. He needed to protect Aoife and ensure nothing happened to her but also be watchful and guarded. He'd never gotten the sense from Aoife that she secretly worked for the council; he'd pondered the possibility only once, early on during her stay aboard the ship.

Still, what would going back there do to her? Would her loyalty be swayed?

He needed to prepare for all possibilities, but that latter one—her turning against him in the end—the mere thought of it felt like a dagger tip at his breast. A warning of the pain it would wrought if that happened.

He roughed a hand over his chin and then behind his neck. A desperate attempt to clear his mind and push away the anxiety all these thoughts brought on.

A rustle of fabric behind him made him turn. Aoife leaned against the archway between the main room and the sleeping quarters. With her arms crossed over her chest and her legs crossed at the ankles, she displayed a surprising amount of swagger. She was getting quite good at mimicking him, which would help in this next adventure. He needed her to look every bit a pirate tonight.

"You look—" she said before stopping to chew on the inside of her lip, as if the word she'd planned to use had evaded her. Or she'd thought better of saying it.

Declan didn't feel like bantering, but he couldn't risk having her worried about him or knowing he was preparing himself for her possible betrayal. "Dashing? Handsome beyond measure? Irresistible?"

The last word was out before he could stop it. The tension between them had been palpable since the night of his birthday, and he had little doubt she felt it too. He didn't need to tug at that invisible connection, but he couldn't seem to resist doing so either. And every time he toyed with it, tiptoed along it, letting a hand linger on her shoulder, allowing his gaze to settle on her body, or whispering a delicate word in her ear, it only grew stronger and more adamant.

Be careful with her.

Yes, his sister must have intended it as a double-edged warning. But with the look in Aoife's eye now, after he had planted a seed of desire with those blasted words, he wondered if he should have been more careful with himself.

This would end nowhere good.

Or it might be the one good thing in your life in years.

And there. A spark of hope somewhere deep in his chest. It was small but bright. And while he couldn't afford to give it the oxygen to burst into flame, he couldn't bear to blow it out completely either. What harm was there in a dream? A dream of hope and love and family.

It took him a second to realize Aoife had never answered him. How long had they been standing here studying each other?

Aoife dropped an ear to her shoulder, looking the epitome of calm and collected as her fingers tapped against her arm. "Well, I was going to say, 'tired' or 'worried,' but..."

He held a breath and realized the books had gotten it all wrong when they spoke of hearts stopping in anticipation. Because his now thundered in his ears as he waited to hear which of his previous words she would choose to elaborate on. If any.

A light sigh escaped her lips before she added, "Your suggestions would apply as well." Her chin dropped, and she pulled her eyes down, as if the part she was playing had become too difficult to maintain and the embarrassed and awkward girl within had stumbled out. He thought he heard her add a whispered "always," but he couldn't tell now, with her lips hidden from view.

He must have heard correctly though, as a flush of pink washed across her cheeks, nearly hiding the freckles below her eyes. He wondered if her skin warmed noticeably when that happened.

"No point in being embarrassed by merely agreeing to the obvious, Aoife." He hoped making light of it would be better than ignoring it altogether, wash away some of the tension mounting between them.

Lifting her head, she said, "I'm not embarrassed." But her features said otherwise as the pink only deepened. Something sparked in her eyes, but he couldn't quite tell what it was. He knew what he hoped it might be.

A teasing smile tugged at her lips. "I'm merely worried all this talk of your irresistibly dashing good looks will make your head swell to the point we won't be able to enter the council hall doorway."

"Then I suppose we'll need to find another way in?"

"Or I could cut you down a peg or two." Declan waited. She seemed to be studying his face, looking for some piece of him that she could insult. He nearly laughed when a full minute passed. And then another.

He was the first one to speak. "Surely you can think of something negative to say about me?"

"It is just so hard to choose one. There are so many." She tossed her head, as if she'd forgotten the hair she would normally fling behind her had been chopped off.

"Liar," he said.

Aoife moved away from the doorframe and took a step toward him. Then another. She'd at least gotten better at walking aboard the ship—at least while they were in port. She kept her eyes lowered as she reached a timid hand toward his chest. He froze, his breath trapped in his lungs as Cait's words echoed in his mind for the millionth time.

Be careful with her.

She knew where he kept the fae's letter. Would she be so brazen as to take it from him now, when he had his guard down? Had she been playing him this whole time?

He couldn't risk haste, so he waited and watched her hand slide into his jacket. It wasn't the letter she pulled out but his pocket watch.

The chain it was attached to pulled taut as she held it in her hands and flipped it open. "It's nearly time."

With a click of the watch's clasp, she added, "We should get ready."

CHAPTER 42
AOIFE

AOIFE'S FINGERS tingled as she fumbled with the purple fabric they'd acquired from Declan's sister. He had gotten it tied around his waist, but she'd insisted on fixing it to keep it from looking ridiculous. With no mirror aboard the ship, it was a wonder the captain managed to look halfway decent most days. *More than halfway.*

She shushed the thought. Though, what harm was there in admitting his good looks? None. Like admiring the beauty of a sunset on the sea or the rocky cliffs of Cregah overlooking the black sand of the cove.

But those couldn't reach out and touch her.

For the past day and a half she'd been racked with confusion over this new desire to have him near, and those damn visions of a future together invaded her thoughts when she least expected.

She huffed a sigh in frustration before realizing he would hear it and have no idea what she was thinking.

"It's just a sash, Aoife. No need to get angry with it."

She refused to admit what was truly bothering her. "But it won't sit right. Blasted thing!"

"We are pirates, you know. We don't have to look perfect."

"Yes, but you're walking into the council hall. You're expected to look somewhat put together and not like you just strolled in from mercilessly pillaging merchants for the past two months."

"Aw, if only that was how I'd spent the last months." There was a longing in his voice, and she realized she had little idea what he'd been through recently.

When she looked up at him, she found him facing the window, his attention on the setting sun.

Out there was where he belonged. On the sea. Not on this island or in a council hall. The realization fell in her gut like a weight dropped into the ocean. And all those visions she'd struggled to be rid of seemed to vanish in an instant, as if they'd been squashed by that weight.

She straightened her shoulders. "You'll be able to get back to that soon." She'd expected to feel free, the weight of her longing lifted by the confirmation that it was the sea he wanted, not her. But it had been replaced with something decidedly worse.

She should have tried harder to keep those thoughts at bay. Then she wouldn't feel such deep disappointment now.

"Not soon enough."

His words pricked her heart. How he must long to be away from her. She had thought she'd seen the same hope echoed in his gaze, but she had clearly misunderstood.

She would not let this distract her. There had never been any future for them. They were cut from a different cloth. Destined to tread different paths. And those paths had only converged temporarily for this one shared mission and goal.

And that goal was what she needed to focus on now.

"Aye. I suppose that's true," she said, now reaching up to adjust his shirt and jacket and brush lint off his shoulders, anything to help her avoid his gaze. "But we will get the fae, get the dagger, crush the council, and get you on your way to distant seas and new adventures."

She ignored the sight of his shoulders rising as he took a breath. Ignored the way that breath sent tingles down her spine when it swept across her forehead.

"Is that all," he said. Not a question.

"Simple as that." She lowered her hands then and took a step back to look him over. "That'll have to do."

He reached behind him and grabbed the gold sash from atop his desk. "Your turn."

It had been one thing to be touching him, but to have his hands on her and around her waist, straightening and adjusting her garments? Sands, help her. The ghosts of her hope threatened to rise from where they'd been trampled.

No, she would let them rest in peace.

There was nothing in his touch that indicated they were anything more than two friends preparing for battle, and the last thing she needed was to have her head muddied by a dream that could never be.

Her breath hitched as he moved his hands behind her and pulled her closer with the gold fabric at her waist, causing her to stumble. She nearly fell into him but managed to catch herself before her hands made contact with his chest again.

"Already getting into character, I see."

She could hear the smirk in his words, but she dared not look up, unsure what his face might do to that damn hope she'd laid to rest.

"Do you pretend to be drunk often in your escapades?" She tried to sound casual, but her voice trembled slightly as she spoke. "It seems to be a common ruse for you."

"It is rather effective, I must say."

They stood mere inches away from each other now, and the heat of his body mixing with the stickiness in the air would have normally made her uncomfortable, given the many layers of garments she wore. But now she was thankful for all the barriers between them. If only Tommy or Gavin or anyone else would knock and save her.

They were too close. Altogether too close. Each breath caused his scent of sea and spice to nudge at the ghosts of her dreams. She needed to get out of here before she lost herself to something she could never have.

His hands moved to adjust her jacket, just as she had done with his, but where her hands had brushed along his shoulders, his went up along her neck to straighten out the collar.

She closed her eyes at the touch and hoped he didn't read too much into it. She simply couldn't bear to look at him while his skin touched hers.

His touch lightened but didn't leave, even after it seemed all the necessary adjustments must have been made. She felt ridiculous standing there, eyes closed, arms dangling lifeless at her sides. But she didn't trust herself not to look even more foolish if she moved. Hopefully he'd read it as her final effort to prepare mentally for the night.

The warmth of his hands and feather lightness of his fingers trailed across her shoulders and down her arms. And when his hands met hers—a breath of a touch she couldn't quite be sure was real and not imagined—he whispered her name.

A hum of a response was all she could manage as she forced her eyes to open and take him in. What she had expected to see, she couldn't say, but it certainly wasn't this. The longing she'd seen in his face earlier, when he'd been looking at the sea, had returned.

Now directed at her.

Everything disappeared—the cabin, the ship, the council, the fae—as if nothing else mattered but the man before her. Her mind went blank yet whirred with a million thoughts. Such an odd sensation to feel empty and full all at once. Full of hope and desire and fear. As if the touch of his hand and her name on his breath had fully resurrected every dream and hope that had been dashed away.

And she didn't know what to do with any of it.

This had never been a part of the plans for her life, and now all she had to do was dare to reach out and grab it, to take it for herself. *Like a pirate.*

Her hand twitched, and a tingle went up her arm as it brushed against his fingers. All of time stood still and yet rushed by too quickly. The stormy grays of his eyes held her. She found herself drowning in them, even as she realized she'd never truly breathed until now.

Was this what love felt like? A confusing yet thrilling, tangled web of emotions and sensations? To be both wholly vulnerable and yet firmly secure, to feel weightless and yet grounded, to want time to both cease and yet hurry up, to savor the moment and yet to yearn for everything the future held?

Declan's fingers laced with hers. He was no longer the rough pirate she'd met in that alley or the one who had attempted to scare her away.

This was Declan. Not Captain McCallagh. And while he might insist those men were one in the same, she knew the truth. He had opened a door in that wall within him and beckoned her to enter.

And she gladly did so.

When his hand grasped hers, the warmth of him engulfing her, she handed herself over to it. Whatever this meant, whatever this would bring, whatever was to come, it would be okay. As long as he was here.

She didn't flinch when he moved again, as he brought himself closer to her. His face—dashing and irresistible indeed—inched toward her, and she dared not move, for fear it would release him from whatever spell he might be under.

He held her captive with one hand and reached the other to her chin. Every bit of her seemed to freeze as the edge of his finger lifted her face to meet his. He paused, his breath tickling her skin, and then all of time vanished as his lips found hers.

It wasn't like their first kiss, behind the pub. Where that had been forceful and frightening, this felt like coming home, like finding the one place she belonged after living her whole life off kilter.

Light and gentle, his lips moved on hers, and she melted ever deeper into them. Tingling pinpricks danced over her skin, uncomfortable and delightful at once. Like his kiss had finally woken her from a deep slumber. Like all the tales she'd read about in books. Now she understood why kisses held so much power—the power to break spells and conquer curses. Reaching her free hand up to his neck, she held him against her, as if he might disappear like an apparition or a dream if she dared let go.

Declan moved his hand from her chin to her waist and then around to the small of her back, pressing her still closer to him.

And then he stopped. Before she could protest, his lips pulled away, his breath rushing out of him. In his eyes she found an odd mix of satisfaction and sadness.

Had she done something wrong? Did he regret it? She didn't know what to say or what to do. All she knew was there was no friendship here. All remnants of hope for that less complicated arrangement had been dashed away.

"Well," she said, breathless and awkward as ever. Licking her lips and then biting them, she searched for any words to say, trying to read his thoughts. And failing.

His hand left her back and reached up to his lips, and she wasn't sure if he was trying to wipe away the feeling of her kiss or capture it as if he could tuck it away in his pocket. If there was any regret, she couldn't see it, especially not with his fingers still grasping her hand, clinging to it like a lifeline.

"That was..." He paused, and self-doubt rushed through her again.

But before he could possibly hurt her with the truth, she finished his sentence. "Unexpected?"

"Not altogether unexpected. I've been wanting to do that for a few days now."

Leave it to a pirate to be so brazen and forthright.

"Truly?" Her brow creased from surprise. She could not seem to grasp onto anything witty or charming to say, lost in this new reality.

"Aye. I tried to ignore it. Told myself it would never work out. But..."

"You failed."

"You don't make it easy, you know."

Aoife's mind whirled, and the whole room seemed to shift and rock around her as she was thrown off-balance by this development. When had things changed, and how had this happened? It wasn't that she was against it. Not in the slightest. But it threw another complication into the already messy situation. A delightfully wonderful complication, but a complication nonetheless.

"But what? How? When?" Her thoughts manifested against her will and tumbled out before she could stop them.

She didn't even care when he let out a string of light laughs. She would have laughed too, if she'd had any control over her voice.

But he didn't answer her. She found no hint of an answer in his eyes either, which never left hers.

Aoife gave his hand a squeeze, like she was reassuring herself that he was, in fact, holding her. It wasn't her imagination. Wasn't one of those dreamy visions that had vanished earlier.

"I was convinced you didn't care," she said.

"I didn't want to," he said. Her pain at hearing these words must have been visible, because he added, "Want to care, that is. This—" He lifted their clasped hands a bit for emphasis. "This was never something I wanted."

Her chest hurt as if his words had stabbed her. And again her features betrayed the sting as she winced.

"Nothing is coming out right, Aoife. See what you've done to me?" He seemed to be trying hard to right himself as he stumbled about with his speech.

But she thought she understood, even without his ability to articulate it clearly.

Just as she had never let herself dream of anything beyond her duty to the council, never once giving thought to love and family, he hadn't either. Not only that, he had spent years actively pushing those dreams away. He hadn't been raised with everything set out before him, hadn't been destined for a life of service to the country. He had the freedom to choose for himself, even if his choices were limited under the council's rule, yet he'd denied himself the possibility of love and intimacy, choosing instead a life on the sea.

"Why? Why would you not want this?"

"It's complicated."

"I'm sure I would understand. If you let me."

"And I will. At some point. But right now—" His eyes darted to the window, where the sky had been painted with the deep pinks and oranges from the setting sun. "We need to head ashore and crash a dinner."

Of course this would have to wait. Once they finished at the council hall, they'd have time to navigate this new course.

"You ready?" Declan asked, dipping his head down an inch to better look at her.

A gulp, a nod. It was all she could muster as the nerves hit her. She could do this, and she would.

With Declan beside her, she could face anything.

CHAPTER 43
AOIFE

THE WALK to the council hall wasn't as long as it was uncomfortable. It was only a mile from the edge of Port Morshan, but Aoife had suggested a different path than the one commonly used.

This path had been hers and Lani's. A lost and forgotten trail. She'd never known what it was for, but as it led from the port to the servant's entrance, she and her sister had imagined many a fanciful tale about its purpose and use.

Walking the path with Declan now—Tommy and Gavin following close behind, each donning the same purple sash she'd placed around Declan's waist—she couldn't remember any of those stories they'd made up.

She tried to focus on her steps, careful not to make too much noise on the twigs and rocks. How were her steps so much louder than the men's? They were certainly heavier than she was, but she found herself occasionally turning to check and make sure they were still with her. Maybe when this was all over she'd ask for lessons on stealth.

Why she might need stealth as a skill in the future, she didn't know, and at the thought, a short burst of laughter escaped her before she could stop it. She clamped a hand over her mouth and flashed Declan an apologetic look.

He merely shook his head, an amused grin on his face.

They hadn't touched each other since leaving his cabin, and this did nothing but stir up the familiar self-doubt, which told her how he probably regretted what had happened. After all, he'd said he never wanted it.

A small voice pushed against that doubt, insisting he was simply focused on the task at hand and didn't want to raise questions from the two men accompanying them.

Yes, that was the voice she wanted to believe. If only the doubt wasn't so much louder.

She tried to push it away as they walked. They needed to hurry if they were going to make it to the hall before the sun had completely set and they could no longer see where they were going. The pirates might be stealthy, but she doubted they had the ability to see in the pitch-dark of Cregah at night. Especially in these trees.

Another laugh threatened, but she held it back. Her mind was not making this trek easy, and she needed to keep it in check if she were going to succeed at not getting them into trouble once they were inside.

After another five minutes, they arrived at the edge of the forest that bordered the council hall grounds. Aoife nearly stepped out into the open in her desperation to get this over with, but Declan reached an arm across to stop her. Her body reacted to his touch, a single, quick chill through her nerves.

The sensation was hard to ignore, though she managed, focusing instead on the building before her. Everything she'd hoped to avoid—all the memories, the dreams, the regrets—slammed into her as if she'd run face-first into it.

The panic was building, and she felt as though her heart were racing, but she knew it was an illusion. How many times had she been sure her heart would thump right out of her, only to find her pulse normal and steady?

It's all in your head. You can control it. Focus. Breathe.

With eyes closed, she began to count her breaths. Tommy and Gavin must have stepped closer to them, though they remained silent, and she wondered if Declan could tell what was happening. The last episode hadn't been as bad because he'd been there, with a hand on her knee and a reassuring word of understanding.

But he didn't touch her now. He only leaned close to her ear and whispered, "Breathe. Focus. It's okay."

Such simple words, but with each one, so low she was sure only she could hear it, the panic eased. It didn't leave completely, but it let up enough that she could open her eyes and peek up at him.

In the dimming light, the gray of his eyes were more pronounced, like the sea under a sky of thick clouds.

"You okay?" Again Declan kept his voice low, but the other men inched forward as if to check on her.

"Yes, better. Thanks." She wanted to say more, to remark how she'd known this would be hard but hadn't expected it to hit her so soon. But now was not the time for long, drawn-out conversations.

She turned back toward the council hall. Creeping ivy obscured the gray stone walls, covering the windows and stretching out like spindly fingers eager to squeeze the life out of anyone who entered.

It had been her home, but now as she looked upon it, she saw it for what it was. Not a home, but a prison. Not a place of warmth and love and family, but one of service, duty, and control.

And for the first time since she'd run, since she'd turned her back on the council, she grasped the truth.

She hadn't killed Lani.

They had.

Melina was no more her mother than Tommy was her father.

Tommy. Gavin. Declan. This could be her new family.

Pirates.

Who would have thought? Lani would have found it to be such an adventure, completely out of character for Aoife, who only ever read about romance and danger but never dared seek it out herself.

Pirates had killed her sister. And whether they had done so willingly or not, she now wasn't sure.

Declan hadn't given her the name of her sister's executioners, but even if he had, she didn't know what she'd say if she ever met them. She wanted to believe she'd forgive them, tell them the comforting words she told herself. It wasn't their fault, just as it wasn't her fault.

Would she tell them it was okay? Tell them she understood? Or would she hold onto resentment and anger?

Later, she told herself. *Focus on what's at hand.*

Now was not the time to let her mind wander, yet she'd done just that. Still, the men waited with surprising patience.

"There," she said with a nod toward a small door in the side of the building, tucked between a pair of bushes. "That's where we enter."

"You ready?" Declan asked, and she knew it was meant more for her than for his men.

Another nod was all she could muster.

"Remember the plan. It's all an act, but don't overdo it. Just pretend you're back on the ship." He shot her a wink, and had they not been about to infiltrate the home of the ruthless rulers of their nation, she might have smacked him or pinched him for it. Instead she settled for an exaggerated roll of her eyes. An expression she'd only ever dared share with Lani.

For you, Lani.

A deep, calming breath washed those words down into her belly, and she hoped she'd remember them no matter what happened within those walls tonight.

The four of them crept out of the trees and over the small metal fence, not wanting to risk making the gate squeak by opening it, and then moved across the lawn and between the bushes toward the servant's entrance.

Aoife held her breath as Declan pressed the lever on the door's handle. If Cait's spy hadn't come through, their whole plan was ruined.

But the door opened with ease, and she stepped inside with Declan close behind her, the warmth from his hand hovering over the small of her back.

Thankfully the men had spent every spare moment memorizing the map she'd drawn. They had no room for error.

The hallway before them was wide and bare, devoid of any decoration, as it was designed for carrying in large deliveries of goods. On the left sat the door leading to the pantries and the storehouses for the dry goods. On the right lay the kitchen, its open doorway allowing the scents of the roast pork and fresh bread they'd served for dinner to waft toward them. Aoife's stomach rumbled in response, and she pressed a hand to it as if that could quiet it.

There was none of the usual gossip and chatter of the kitchen staff, but the kitchen wasn't empty either. A solitary voice sang in a low tone.

Stopping at the edge of the doorway, they didn't plaster their bodies against the wall but leaned back casually in case someone should turn the corner up ahead and find them loitering.

Declan had his forehead against the wall, as if he were sick from too much drink, while Tommy and Gavin pretended to be having a whispered conversation. Aoife turned away from them to peek into the room.

Marta, the old cook who had hated her—hated everyone, actually—stood at the worktable in the center of the room slicing up a variety of fruit pies for the dessert course in the great hall. Her wide back was to Aoife, making it difficult to hear the words of her tune, but at least she wouldn't see them as they stepped past.

Keeping her eyes on the ill-tempered cook, Aoife reached back to tap Declan on the hip. He, in turn, alerted his men, and they moved down the hallway as stealthily as they had on the path outside. When it was Aoife's turn to move, she tried to mimic their quiet steps. But either her shoes weren't made for sneaking around, or she was incapable of being quiet. Her steps thundered in her ears as she rushed as fast as she could past the doorway with her eyes shut tight, unable to risk checking to see if the cook had heard and turned.

She passed the door and ran smack into Tommy's back. Her eyes flashed open. The men were all staring at her with odd looks of amusement on their faces.

Aoife nearly breathed a sigh of relief until she realized the cook's singing had ceased. Then the woman said, in a tone much nicer than Aoife had ever heard when she'd lived here, "Hattie? Is that you?"

Aoife held her breath and listened for footsteps or any sound that indicated the cook was coming to check out the noise. But they had spent the last day and a half preparing for this very situation. Maybe not the cook finding them, but someone. It was inevitable given how many people were currently crammed inside these walls —two pirate crews in addition to the regular staff.

But the cook never came to investigate, and Aoife finally released her breath when the quiet singing started again.

Fifteen feet ahead, the hallway came to an end and split. The hallway veering right led to the front of the council hall and ultimately to the large dining room where the banquets with the lords were held. To the left lay the residential section of the hall, with the chambers of the councilwomen and their heirs on the second floor, the staff quarters below those.

The room where the fae were housed was, as best as Aoife could recall, in the center of the first floor, tucked amidst the rooms of the staff, as if they were more than mere cooks and maids and attendants but also guards.

Without a word, Declan drew their attention and gestured for them to head down the left hallway.

The only sound as they moved through the hallways was their own breathing.

And Aoife's footsteps. Though at least they weren't quite as noisy as they had been earlier.

While they had anticipated the staff being occupied with the dining guests, this heavy silence unnerved Aoife. Had her home always been so eerie, or did it merely seem so now that she knew what the council did to their own people?

What they'd surely do to them if they were caught.

When the hallway branched off again, Aoife hoped she'd remembered this labyrinth correctly. Tommy and Gavin stopped, taking up their predetermined stations against the wall, once again slouching back casually. Aoife gave them one last glance and a shake of her head. While Tommy had his back to the wall, chin tipped down to his chest and eyes half closed with faked drunkenness, Gavin rested his shoulder against the wall and pretended to be chattering incessantly to his friend.

What he was yammering on about, she wasn't sure; as it was too soft for her to make out any of the words. But the way they fell into their parts so quickly and effortlessly made her think they could have been actors in a theater troupe instead of pirates.

She turned back to find that Declan had already started down the hallway to their right. This one was also empty and quiet, though shorter, with only one door on the left. She repeated the turns in her head, visualizing the map as she did so. *Left. Right. Left. Left. Left. Right.*

Declan made his way quickly and with such ease that she wondered if he were mentally reciting the turns as she was.

Each hallway they took looked the same. No artwork on the walls. No windows. Only door after identical door with lanterns perched between them.

As a child, Aoife had thought it must have been the worst chore to have to light each of them every evening, only to put them out again every morning. Day in. Day out. Monotonous. Boring. Though she had never met the women tasked with this job, she'd often imagined them as being the youngest and most hated among the staff.

They made the final turn into a long corridor just as one of the doors opened and a young woman stepped out. She wore one of the nicer uniforms reserved for these dinner gatherings, her red curls pinned neatly upon her head. She couldn't be much older than Aoife, if that, but as soon as she saw the two of them, her sweet face scrunched into a frown.

"What are you doing here? You're not to leave the public areas!"

Showtime.

Aoife blinked and dropped her shoulders in an exaggerated slump as she smacked Declan on the arm. "I told you," she hissed. "We were supposed to take a right, not a left!"

Declan ignored the servant and turned fully toward Aoife. His words came out slurred to perfection, "And why would I take directions from a lass?"

With a hand on her hip, Aoife shook her head and clicked her tongue. "Not just any lass, mind you."

His gray eyes rolled as his head fell to one side, heavy with exasperation. "Yeah, yeah, yeah. A lass from the *Duchess*." Contempt dripped from the last two words.

The woman moved toward them, her hands shooing them to turn back the way they'd come. But they continued to argue.

"Why did I ever trust an imbecile from the *Dark Star*?"

He wagged his brow. "Because this imbecile is rather dashing."

Aoife didn't have to fake the flush that spread across her cheeks as she remembered the last time he'd called himself that. And what had followed.

All the pretend frustration vanished as if blown away by a breath, and she mimicked his earlier eye roll.

From the corner of her eye she saw the girl standing with arms still raised, glancing between the pair of them, surely wondering whether they would pay her any attention.

Before the girl could admonish them again, Declan had his arms around Aoife's waist and was pulling her to him. Her hips slammed against his so hard they both crashed into the wall behind him. And an instant later, his lips were on hers.

This was no act, hadn't been part of their plan, but she couldn't argue with his improvisation as his lips beckoned for hers to part so his tongue could caress hers.

Sands, she never wanted this to stop. Was this what she might have missed out on had she stayed? Never to be kissed with such passion and need?

She couldn't imagine a life devoid of this. Nor did she want to.

Wrapping her arms around his neck, she let herself melt into him, relaxing into his embrace, her entire body sighing with satisfaction. With her eyes closed and her mind threatening to get swept away by this moment with him, she could only imagine how perturbed the servant looked, how she must have thrown up her hands one final time as she muttered "whatever" and stormed off.

Even after the girl's retreating footsteps had quieted, Aoife remained entangled with Declan. She wanted to savor this, but they had too much to do.

She chuckled against his lips when she heard the girl's exasperated groan. She must have found Tommy and Gavin lingering in the other hallway and not even bothered to try to make them leave.

Declan released her, and with great reluctance, she leaned away from him.

He spoke first. "Do you think Tommy and Gav used the same tactic to distract her?"

"That would certainly give her something to gossip about with the other staff."

He took a step back, and she immediately regretted the loss of warmth as his arms fell away from her body. She lifted a hand to her lips.

Now was no time to get lost. In the hallway or in those damn eyes of his.

Declan brushed her hand with his, and with a tilt of his head he motioned for them to continue on, but Aoife couldn't move as she took in what they now faced.

A hallway lined with doors. All indistinguishable. Door after door.

Her memory seemed cloudier now, fogged over by the damn kiss.

Declan watched her, more patient than she'd expected—more patient than she deserved. She had one job. One task. But standing in this hallway, facing a sea of doors, her stomach tightened.

She was going to let them all down. Not just Declan and the crew, or Cait and her rebels, but all of Cregah. All the people who lived in fear because of the council. She felt the weight of all these lives upon her shoulders.

Declan gripped her hand. His fingers wove between hers and gave a reassuring squeeze, his thumb tracing tender circles along the back of hers.

"Breathe, Aoife." A whispered reminder. She breathed it in deep. "We'll check each one if needed. You said they don't leave their quarters, so we might hear them stirring within if we listen closely enough."

"But there are scores of doors to check, and that's in this hallway alone. What if I got the wrong one?"

"Then we'll check the next one, and the next one, if needed. This is only the end if you give up now."

Time was against them, and Aoife could almost hear the ticking of Declan's pocket watch mocking her as she fumbled forward.

"It will be near the middle of the hallway," she said, adding a muttered, "I think."

They started down the corridor, which was narrow enough they could keep their hands clasped as they listened at each door on either side. Most of the staff would be tending to the dinner. At least that's what she hoped. She wondered how much she had gotten wrong about the home she'd grown up in. Did she really know anything about it?

One door after another, they slowed down, listened, and moved on. They moved as quickly as they dared, but Aoife worried they'd miss it. The fae might hear them coming and choose to be still to keep them from stopping.

"This is pointless, Declan. We are never going to find them." Aoife turned toward him, but he didn't stop. Dropping her hand, he left her standing in the middle of the hallway as he proceeded to continue listening at each door. "We don't have time to check them all."

Declan stopped, turned, and narrowed his eyes at her. Not from anger, but desperation. "No, Aoife, we don't have time to *not* check them. We don't have time to stop."

The possibility of failure pressed in on her, and she chided herself for wanting to give in to the hopelessness of the situation. She wanted to be brave and daring and optimistic, but the odds were stacked against them.

And then those odds worsened.

A low whistle drifted down the corridor.

Tommy. A warning.

Someone was coming.

Declan and Aoife looked at each other, but she didn't find her panic mirrored in his face. Rather, his expression reflected the confidence she longed to possess herself.

Grabbing her hand without a word, Declan pulled her down the hallway and around the corner to the right at the same moment she saw someone enter the hallway they'd been searching. She didn't see who it was, but no doubt the person had seen her and Declan.

This corridor was darker than the others, with only a single lantern lit at the far end. Aoife could have sworn a chill swept over her.

Their pursuer was ambling toward them. Slow. Steady. Like the metronome Aoife had used when learning to play the piano as a child.

She peered into the darkness. She'd been here before. This was the hallway. Not the previous one.

Declan leaned an ear against the first door and tried the handle. Locked.

He whispered, "We need to find an open room to hide in. We can't risk a fight here."

Aoife didn't answer but moved past him to the door in the center of the hallway. Shrouded in such darkness, it would have been easy to overlook and walk past.

Declan, seeing where she was headed, picked up his pace to match hers.

Please let it be unlocked.

All those years ago, she'd felt this same pull, a silent voice within her bones calling her forward.

Not bothering to listen for movement, she reached for the handle, but it turned before her fingers could touch it.

The door swung open, and as the footsteps grew ever closer behind them, she reached down deep for any drop of courage she could find and pulled Declan into the room, closing the door behind them with a nearly silent click.

CHAPTER 44
DECLAN

Even the dim light of the hallway hadn't prepared Declan's eyes for the darkness that enveloped them in the room Aoife dragged him into. He blinked once and then opened his eyes as wide as he could, as if that would get them to acclimate faster.

He felt ridiculous, but at least Aoife probably couldn't see him doing it.

A voice greeted them, a whisper of a song wafting toward them. "Sorry for the lack of light, Captain. Maura, could you remedy this for our guests?"

No answer came, except for the silent lighting of a lantern at the far end of the room.

The sight before him rendered him speechless.

The room was far larger than he'd expected, with enough space for the three sisters to live comfortably. To the right sat a living area, with a sofa and three armchairs surrounding a large hearth that stood cold and unused. Behind that lay a dining area and a small kitchen, where the dishes from their last meal filled the sink, waiting to be cleaned. He assumed the door at the far end led to a washroom, while the three doors to the left were likely bedrooms.

The council must have built this room specifically for the fae sisters who served them. Which meant they really had been living here for more than five hundred years. While he'd heard this was the case, seeing the evidence of it sucked the breath out of him. To live in a single room for so many years. How had they managed? Surely they would jump at the chance to come with them and be free.

The melodic voice pulled Declan's attention back to the room's residents. "Welcome back, Aoife. We wondered when you might visit us again."

The most beautiful woman Declan had ever seen stood before them, and though she had addressed Aoife, she was looking squarely at him. Red curls the color of autumn leaves, fiery and bright, framed a face that could have been angelic if not for the mischievous turn of her pink lips. Her eyes, a more vibrant blue than seemed possible, like the bluebirds that had sung outside his childhood window or the lilies his father used to surprise his mother with on her birthdays, bore into him with such an intensity it was like being suffocated.

"I hadn't planned to come back," Aoife said with an edge to her voice. Declan wanted to look at her, to determine what emotion had sharpened her words, but he couldn't pull his gaze away from the beautiful fae before them.

The fae clicked her tongue. "I'm sorry to hear that. Your last visit was cut so short. We never even had the chance to properly introduce ourselves." She raised a slender hand to her chest. "I'm Renna. The oldest. And these are my sisters, Bria and Maura." She motioned to them with the grace of a dancer. Even her movements were beautiful.

And potentially deadly.

The thought snapped him back to the task at hand. He couldn't let himself be so enchanted. Needed to play his hand with care here.

But before he could do anything, Aoife was speaking again, giving a nod in his direction. "This is..."

"Captain Declan McCallagh," Renna said, finishing the sentence for her.

It hadn't registered when she'd called him Captain earlier, but now, upon hearing his whole name on the fae's breath, his skin pricked with unease. All the time he'd spent studying fae lore hadn't adequately prepared him for their abilities. Did this mean he'd been wrong about the possibility of iron-core walls? He hadn't heard that the fae sisters—or any fae for that matter—possessed mind-reading capabilities, but somehow they knew who he was. And likely they knew why he was here.

"How did you know?" Aoife asked.

Maura and Bria moved closer to their sister, as though their sharp fae senses didn't make it possible to hear the conversation from anywhere in their quarters. But they stayed behind her, waiting.

"We may not leave this room," Renna said, "but we still hear things. Know things."

Declan spoke for the first time since they'd entered, his words coming out gravelly and rough. "You were expecting us."

He cleared his throat so he could continue, but Renna spoke again. "I would have thought that obvious since we opened the door for you without your knocking. But we will save you the trouble of begging. We won't be coming with you."

Though he'd expected as much, at least initially, his heart still plummeted into his gut, falling like an anchor into the sea. Cait's spy must have given them the heads-up, but had they told them what he carried? What he offered? And if not, would it help?

From his periphery he saw Aoife turn toward him, though only slightly, and thankfully she kept quiet, waiting for him to be the one to offer up their bargaining chip.

He straightened his shoulders, forcing himself to ignore the dreadful feeling of defeat that coursed through him. It wouldn't serve him well now, and all the years of working past his own fear, pushing through his insecurities to build his name as a pirate, had prepared him. At least somewhat.

Not taking his eyes off Renna, he reached his hand under his lapel as he spoke again. "I have something that might change your mind."

Curiosity flashed in her blue eyes for a moment before it was replaced yet again with that playful look a cat gives a mouse as it waits to pounce. "And what is that?"

The sealed letter weighed little and yet felt as heavy as the dread resting in his stomach. He held it up, keeping the wax seal hidden from her.

Renna took a step forward, her expression a strange mix of interest and boredom, and reached for the letter. When he lowered it into her hands, the seal of the fae now showing, she froze.

Bria and Maura inched forward to glance over their sister's shoulder.

"What is it?" Maura asked, but a gasp escaped her when she saw what her sister held. Bria's fingers reached up to her lips as if to stifle whatever might escape.

Renna still didn't move but stared at the paper in her hand, at the symbol of her long-lost brethren pressed into the wax. Declan thought her hands had begun to tremble, but she stilled them before snapping her chin up to him. All boredom had vanished from her flawless face, leaving behind only suspicion and what he worried might be malice.

"Is this some sort of trick?" She spat the question at him.

If nothing else, at least he had gotten the upper hand and was in control of the conversation now.

He pushed aside the snarky bravado he normally used and reached instead for the empathy he'd need to convince them. That side of him had been locked away for so many years, but Aoife had provided the key he'd needed, as well as the desire to retrieve it.

"I'd never dream of tricking you, Renna. As if a mortal—pirate or no—could hope to do it successfully."

Her features didn't soften, and her glare threatened to rip him apart. "Flattery? That's your play, Captain? Our kin are all dead. We are the last of our kind."

Behind her, Maura was shaking her head, and Bria had gone still, her eyes glazed over, seeing nothing. Renna's still burned into him, but he wouldn't let himself be intimidated, at least not noticeably so.

"It would appear they are not," he offered, with a nod to the letter in her hand.

"What does it say?" she asked, no hint of kindness in her words. Only guarded suspicion. And a hint of what sounded to Declan like hope.

Declan lifted his shoulders half an inch. "I do not know. You can see for yourself the seal is not broken. I dared not intrude or break the confidence of those who entrusted this to me."

Silence fell among them, his heartbeat the only sound in his ears, pounding out the precious seconds as they passed. The dinner wouldn't last forever, and if they delayed too long they risked running into more staff in the hallways on their way out. But could he rush the fae without risking their refusal to even consider his request? Would their centuries-old hearts understand—or even care—about the urgency of the situation?

Before he could search for the words he needed to spur Renna into action, her sister, Bria, spoke up. "Open it, sister."

Maura chimed in with her sweet, innocent voice, a stark contrast to Renna's intimidating tone. "Time is not on our side here, Renna."

Renna didn't look at either of her sisters, her gaze firmly set on the letter in her hands. If she heard their words, she gave no indication.

Declan felt Aoife stir beside him. He wanted to grab her hand, reassure her that the seconds passing were well spent to allow Renna time, but he couldn't risk them knowing about the growing bond between them. Not yet. If the stories he'd heard were true, information needed to be carefully guarded to deny the fae any ammunition for their trickery.

Aoife cleared her throat quietly, and Declan closed his eyes, waiting for whatever words she was planning to utter. He fought back the urge to stop her, pushed back against the old thought that she was nothing more than an awkward girl with a lack of tact. He'd promised himself he would trust her.

Several seconds passed in silence, pushing Declan to steal a glance toward her, but she didn't look to him for approval as she had done so often in the past. Whether that was because she was worried he might stop her, he wasn't sure, but he hoped she was starting to trust herself just as he was learning to.

"Renna," she started. The fae didn't look at her, didn't even flinch at the sound of her name. "I know what it's like to be lied to. To have those you've trusted— those you've served—keep the truth from you. But avoiding the truth won't change that betrayal."

Renna lifted her head. Her eyes burned into Aoife, but Aoife didn't falter. More seconds ticked by, and Declan quieted his breaths as he waited, as if any sound might ignite the tension in the room.

"I'm not avoiding the truth." Renna's tone had a bite to it, but it was not quite as sharp as before.

Aoife must have noticed her words had lost some of their edge, because she said, "Then I would humbly ask you to please open it. Read the words from your kin. I know minutes to you must mean very little compared to the centuries you've lived here, but as your sister mentioned, time is not on our side this evening. Please."

At that, Bria and Maura inched even closer to their sister, offering light touches of encouragement on her arms before Renna slid her slender finger under the paper's edge and broke the seal.

Declan managed to keep himself from craning his neck to see over the edge of the paper and look at the writing the fae sisters now read. He startled when Aoife's fingers brushed his own, and he risked another glance at her, then gave a nudge of his head to dissuade her from moving closer, adding a warning to his eyes and hoping she wouldn't see it as a rejection but merely a precaution.

She gave him a small smirk in understanding before moving to clasp her hands in front of her.

They waited. Another breath. Then another. The sisters stood as still as stone, only their eyes moving as they read.

And then, Renna looked from Maura to Bria. Though Declan couldn't be sure, he could have sworn the sisters exchanged quick nods, but perhaps that was only what he hoped to see. Before he could ponder it further, the fae were moving.

Renna handed the letter to Maura, who moved to the back of the room and held it up to the lantern's fire, turning it to ash on the stone floor, while Bria rushed over to a trunk sitting against the wall nearest their bedroom doors. Renna stepped toward him and Aoife, the earlier tension and intimidation in her eyes now replaced with undeniable hope and promise.

She kept her voice quiet, as if worried someone in the council might be listening. "We will come with you. We will help. We have been alone for too long, deceived for too many years, and they will not hold us one second longer."

With that, the fae donned the cloaks Bria had retrieved, and Renna motioned with a hand for Declan to lead the way.

CHAPTER 45
AOIFE

AOIFE COULDN'T HEAR the three fae sisters as they followed her and Declan out of their room, though she sensed their presence all the same. She tried to focus on Declan ahead of her. They were almost done. Almost out. At least with this first step of the plan.

A smile threatened to spread across her lips. She'd helped. She'd managed to encourage them to read the letter, and while it had ultimately been the letter that had convinced them to help, her pride fluttered in her chest all the same.

Declan motioned for them to stop at the corner, and with her breath held, Aoife placed a hand on his back, more for herself than for him. His warmth reassured her, calmed her heart, and also kept her from running into him and pushing him out into the open before he could ensure the way was clear.

He stepped away, and before she could frown over the space between them, his hand was in hers, pulling her around the corner. A shiver went through her at his touch, those pinpricks once again dancing over her skin. She hoped she never ceased to respond to him in this way.

In the fae's quarters, it had been necessary to avoid touching, but what had changed now, she didn't know. And she found it hard to care. Curiosity be damned. She melted into his grasp as he claimed her as his own, paying no mind to their audience.

They'd barely made it halfway down the long corridor when she heard footsteps. Instinct had her feet turning to stone, unable or unwilling to move from where they stood, even as Declan kept walking. Or tried to. Refusing to drop her hand, he couldn't get far with her now frozen in place.

He turned, perhaps to offer some encouraging word or maybe explain his superhuman pirate hearing, as he appeared unconcerned by the feet rushing toward them. Before he could do either, she saw Gavin and Tommy turn the corner with a woman on their heels.

Yet the sight of them didn't bring any comfort, as their eyes were wide with urgency.

In an instant Declan had turned to face them. "What is it?"

Tommy didn't answer until they reached them, his body fidgeting to keep moving despite the obvious tension in his jaw. "Maggie here came to warn us. That girl who found us loitering went straight to the banquet hall to ask the crews to come retrieve their drunk mates."

"You can imagine how well that went," Gavin added.

Declan glanced over his shoulder at Aoife and asked, "Is there another way out? We can't go back the way we came."

Aoife blinked, giving her head a few quick shakes. "I'm not as familiar with the servants' areas."

He looked past her to the fae, but they must not have been any more help, because he met her gaze again quickly, raising his brows in question, urging her to think harder.

She hated letting him down, but the girl, Maggie, must have been the one Cait had working on the inside. She nudged a chin toward her. "Perhaps she knows of one."

"I do, in fact," Maggie said, her voice carrying the slightest hint of an accent from some other region of Cregah.

Declan looked back at Maggie and hesitated. Though Aoife couldn't see his face, she could imagine his broody eyes boring into the young girl, pondering whether to trust her or not.

A small bob of his chin was his only answer, and then they were all moving again, back the way she and the men had come, turning left instead of toward the entrance they'd used earlier.

Declan still gripped her hand, pulling her along. But this wasn't right. Maggie was leading them toward the council's meeting rooms, where she and her sisters had done their lessons. She was taking them closer to the councilwomen and their guests, not leading them away.

Her heart thumped in her chest, as loud as her feet against the stone floors. Panic settled in her throat, and she wondered how she would breathe past it. But fainting in the hallway certainly wouldn't help, so she forced her feet to keep moving.

Maggie opened a door and ushered them all inside a dark room.

Aoife didn't need to look around to know she'd brought them to the library. The last place she would have chosen. This room was in the middle of the council hall. No access to the outside. Silence hung like a heavy shroud, so quiet that the pounding in her chest seemed to fill it with its quickened booms. Her hand grew sweaty and clammy within Declan's.

They halted and waited for their eyes to adjust to the change in light, but it was not long before Maggie set off again.

She led them to a corner of the library that Aoife had never explored. There she pulled a book off a middle shelf and reached a hand into the now vacant spot. Whether it was a button or a latch, Aoife couldn't determine, but whatever Maggie did released the shelf from where it was locked into place. She pulled it toward them.

Aoife's jaw fell open. She'd lived here her whole life and had never known this doorway existed. How many other secrets existed in her former home?

Maggie spoke in a hushed tone as she motioned for them to enter the dark passage. "This leads to the outside. You'll come out behind the bushes next to the front stairs. You'll need to be quick and stay hidden. The bushes only provide so much cover, so be careful. I'll try to buy you some time."

Before they could ask anything more, she scurried away between the bookcases that stood in the middle of the room. No doubt heading toward the banquet hall.

Declan considered their little band. "Gavin. Sisters. You first."

Aoife's feet itched to get moving, her legs restless and tingling with the need to escape and survive.

Declan had barely turned to the sisters before they were brushing past Gavin to head into the passage, with Gavin needing no further encouragement to follow.

Tommy stepped aside, gesturing for Declan and Aoife to go next, but Aoife hadn't even moved when a dagger appeared at Declan's throat.

Another man came up behind Tommy, grabbing his arm.

A third, who was surprisingly fast given his stocky frame, rushed past Aoife, sliding between her and freedom.

A rough voice, deep and sultry, filled the library.

"Leaving so soon?"

CHAPTER 46
DECLAN

THE EDGE of the dagger bit into Declan's skin as he moved to face the source of the voice. He gave Aoife's hand a final stroke with his thumb before he released her. As much as he wanted to hold onto her, he couldn't risk their connection making this worse.

He caught only a glimpse of the pirate guarding him and ignored the handful of other crewmen he could see, focusing instead on the man standing twenty feet away, whose purple sash looked black in the dim light.

"Madigen," Declan said, keeping his tone flat, uninterested.

"Lord Madigen," the captain corrected, lifting his chin, causing the deep shadows to shift across the rough planes of his face.

Declan raised a brow and pulled the corner of his mouth into a smirk before he offered a nod, ignoring the dagger's pinch as he did so. "Excuse me. *Lord* Madigen. What can we do for you, sir?"

The pirate lord's jaw tensed, his weight shifting as he glared at Declan before looking at Tommy and then Aoife.

Something sparked in the lord's eyes. "You're looking...different...Ms. Cascade."

Declan bit back the urge to tell the man not to even utter her name, as if he had an exclusive claim to its use. Yet the sound of it on this pirate's despicable tongue, with possessiveness coating each syllable, had him feeling prickly and more on edge than he already was.

Aoife's voice came out clear. "Let them go. Now."

Lord Madigen sneered at her, a devilish smile with no hint of kindness. "Afraid I can't do that. You see, I'm tasked with protecting the council. Especially you, and unfortunately for this lad and his crew, they made the poor decision to not only kidnap an heir to the council but—"

"They didn't kidnap me," she interrupted. "I ran. Stowed away on his ship."

"I would have thought my daughter to have better taste."

Declan's hands tensed, eager to pummel the smug look off the man's face, but he kept silent and still.

Madigen continued. "Regardless, the young captain here allowed you to stay aboard, took you to Foxhaven, I believe. When he should have brought you back home."

That word—*home*—twisted Declan's gut. No doubt it did the same to her. He wished he could reach back and reassure her it was all going to be okay, but he couldn't even risk a look in her direction.

It was a dangerous dance they performed here. Any misstep and Madigen could end them all.

"Well..." Aoife's voice faltered, causing a surge of panic to hit him as he anticipated her next words. "I'm back now. So let him go."

Declan blinked, slowly and deliberately. He knew she was only trying to buy time—or at least he hoped that was her plan—but the thought of her staying here while he ran knotted his stomach even further. He couldn't leave her. Not with them. Not here.

"Had you let me finish though," Madigen said, his voice growing more oily with each word, "you'd know this wasn't merely about you, miss. He has also kidnapped the Bron sisters, who have resided under the protection and care of the council for five centuries."

"You mean enslaved by the council?" Aoife asked, every word a challenge.

Madigen clicked his tongue. "What lies they've been spreading. You really ought to be careful who you trust."

Declan turned to look not at Aoife but at Tommy, who had remained quiet, not even shuffling a foot or clearing his throat. The man behind Tommy—one of Madigen's crew, no doubt—gripped one of Tommy's arms, and likely held a blade at his lower back. The man's eyes didn't meet Declan's, and he was too busy keeping his attention on his own captain that he didn't notice when Declan gave Tommy the silent order.

Whatever Aoife had been about to say got cut short, turning it into a sharp gasp as Tommy pivoted away from his captor at the same time Declan raised an elbow enough that he could slip out from under his captor's arm, pull the knife from his boot, and drive it into the man's stomach.

The man doubled over, and Declan looked past him, his gaze meeting Aoife's. With another nod toward the pathway behind them, he told her to run, then pushed the man to the floor.

She didn't turn, didn't leave, didn't listen.

Of course she didn't listen.

Before he could scold her though, she reached into the folds of her sash and pulled out the dagger Tommy had given her, ready to help however she could. He might have been proud of her for finding such courage and confidence had his stomach not twisted with panic over her remaining in harm's way.

But he could still protect her.

With his bloodied knife in hand, he turned with Tommy, and they prepared for the rest of Madigen's crew to approach.

But they didn't. He'd expected them to be slow with the rum from dinner, had anticipated they wouldn't be ready for a fight—especially not on this island, let alone here at the council hall—but he hadn't prepared for what now greeted them.

Madigen hadn't moved. Neither had any of his men.

The captain didn't even seem put out by the sight of two members of his crew writhing on the bloody library floor. In fact, he looked downright bored as he motioned for a few of his men to retrieve the injured.

Declan waited for the man to start clapping slowly at the display he and Tommy had put on. It was what he probably would have done in this situation. But instead Madigen merely stood there, arms crossed in front of him, waiting.

A door opened somewhere in the library, and the sound of footsteps filled the room. From between the bookshelves to his right, three women stepped forward.

A mature and regal woman led the way with her nose in the air. She held her hands at her waist, clasped together in a grip as tight as the dark curls pinned atop her head. Behind her a girl who wore her youth with an air of arrogance held the arm of his sister's spy, whose face showed no fear despite the danger she found herself in.

The older woman spoke, keeping her focus solely on Declan, her lips pulling into a wicked smile. "You're back. And I see you've gotten blood on my floor."

CHAPTER 47
AOIFE

THIS WHOLE PLAN had gone badly rather quickly.

Aoife still gripped the dagger in her hand, but the arrival of her mother and Darienn shook the confidence she'd managed to unearth.

And they'd caught Cait's spy.

If they saw Aoife—or the secret passageway still open behind her—they didn't show it, both of them staring intently at Declan and Tommy, who stood in front of her.

No one moved. No one even seemed to be breathing.

Such was the attention the councilwomen commanded.

Melina's voice pierced the still air. "Are you trying to get away without paying?" She didn't let him answer. "In fact, it appears you chose to collect a fee from me instead. By taking our fae."

Before Declan could respond—and before Aoife could think better of it—words came pouring from her mouth. "They aren't your fae, Melina."

Her mother swung her glare to Aoife, her lips pursed. "Such disrespect. I might have assumed this stemmed from the company you've been keeping, Aoife, had you not chosen to abandon your station all on your own."

"Not on my own," Aoife said. She nodded toward her sister. "Darienn suggested..."

Darienn straightened but didn't look at all surprised to have been ratted out. Melina remained unfazed, her expression shifting into one of pity rather than surprise.

"Oh, you are so easily swayed, Aoife. Darienn offered an out, and you readily took it. Though I suppose it is to our benefit you exiled yourself. The council requires a dedication you apparently lack."

They'd tested her. And she'd fallen for it.

But how she'd gotten here was of little consequence compared to what she had yet to do.

She stepped up beside Declan, her hand inches away from his, though she dared not reach for him.

"My dedication is to our people," she said. "Not to you or the council. Where are my aunts anyway? Babysitting the other crew?"

Melina laughed, ignoring her questions. "Is that why you ran? You could have stayed. Might have used your power to change things. Yet you fled. Like a coward."

"But I came back." Why she bothered to defend herself to this woman, she didn't know, but she couldn't stop herself.

"And look where you ended up. Caught in the act of betrayal. A failure. Again. As I always expected." Melina's words cut into her, each syllable increasing the pressure in her chest.

Even in the dimness of the library, the coldness in Melina's eyes was clear, a stare so icy it seemed to freeze every muscle in Aoife's body, tightening her joints, closing up her throat.

She couldn't move, except for the pulsing in her jaw as she fought to keep her shame from slipping out as tears.

She's just goading you, trying to get under your skin.

It was working.

She had no response, no retort. She merely stood there and took it, let her mother's words of disappointment coat her like the grime on her skin. This woman's favor was far from what she craved, and yet the insults still stung.

Melina focused again on Declan. "Back to the matter of fees, Captain. I assume you still do not have the means to pay, so it will be a service once again?"

When Declan didn't answer, Aoife looked to find him watching her instead of her mother, as if Melina hadn't asked him a question. His expression clearly asked if she was all right.

She swallowed and attempted a smile to assure him she was fine.

But the snap of Melina's fingers cut through their moment, drawing their attention, as Darienn shoved Maggie forward into Melina's grasp. "It seems one of my staff isn't quite as loyal as we require. She helped you. Did she not?"

Declan drew in a deep breath, not rushing to answer. "We worked alone."

"It's not polite to lie, Captain McCallagh."

Aoife nearly scoffed at such a statement coming from this woman, but she managed to hold it in.

Her mother continued, "Regardless of what you say, we know Maggie here works for the Rogues. We know she's been spying. And for that, the punishment is *exile.*"

Aoife looked at Maggie, but to her credit, the girl didn't whimper or beg. If anything, she remained resolute, firm in their cause, confident in the task she'd been given. Even if it meant her certain death.

"No," Declan said, and Aoife swung her head to look at him, her eyes wide, but he didn't register her existence. His features were as stern as his tone, with no sign that Melina intimidated him, even as the remaining men of Madigen's crew stood guard around them.

"No?" Genuine amusement laced her mother's words, though it didn't play on her face.

"You heard me. I won't do it."

Now the smile Aoife had heard in her mother's question spread across her lips, devilish and dangerous. "You pick an odd time to grow a conscience, McCallagh."

They stood there, staring each other down, until Melina's smile faded, melting away into a snarl that made her look every bit the animal Aoife now imagined her to be.

"Well, if you won't—"

"I'll do it," Tommy said, interrupting her, not taking a step forward but standing tall as he offered his service in place of his captain's.

Declan started to protest, but Melina stopped him with a raised hand.

"How noble a gesture, Mr. Murphy. But that won't be necessary."

Another snap of her fingers, and the spy—Maggie—went rigid, her eyes widening, her mouth dropping in a silent and final gasp before she fell forward, revealing the handle of a blade protruding from the back of her neck and the pirate who had been hidden behind her in the darkness.

Aoife tried to scream, but the sound lodged in her throat, and she froze. Her mother had ordered the kill personally, and in the council hall no less.

She wanted to squeeze her eyes shut, but they, too, remained unresponsive to her commands, leaving her to stare at the lifeless body of the girl lying on the library floor.

Melina drew in a breath and addressed Declan again. "Well, since you refused that job—not that it did Maggie any good—it seems I'll need to find another task for you."

Still staring at the fallen girl, Aoife barely heard the conversation going on before her. She should pay attention. She needed to be ready, in case she needed to act, but she felt just as she had on the beach in Foxhaven.

As if she were standing in the midst of a dream, begging her mind to wake her up and erase all the blood and death from her vision.

But with every blink, the scene remained.

It was no dream.

Her mother's clicking tongue knocked at the edges of Aoife's mind, pulling her back to the present, even though her eyes remained lowered.

"What am I to do with you, McCallagh? How shall I collect for this visit to our shores?"

"Let me deal with this one?" Declan said, and those words managed to pull her out of her shock enough to find him pointing his blade in her direction.

"I'm listening," Melina said.

"You've exiled one heir already. You can't risk exiling another without raising more suspicion with the people. Make hers look like an unfortunate mishap, an accidental drowning or a fall down some stairs. She is rather clumsy, after all."

"An interesting proposition," Melina said, her gaze shifting between her and Declan. "Unfortunately, I can't trust you to follow through. I doubt this heir will be as easy for you to kill. Unlike the last one."

Aoife's attention snapped to her mother and then back to Declan.

What had she said? The last one. Not as easy to kill.

Was this another trick? Another test?

Declan met her gaze, but she couldn't read whatever emotions those grays held. His throat bobbed as he swallowed. His jaw tightened.

No.

Not Declan.

Lani?

Declan?

Her mind sped out of control, her head shaking as her eyes searched his for the answer she needed.

But he didn't speak, didn't even open his mouth to try.

Her sister. Her...whatever Declan was to her now.

Had he been the one? The one tasked with killing Lani?

She opened her mouth to ask him, but it was her mother's words that filled the silence. "Oh dear. He didn't tell you, did he?"

Someone breathed a laugh. Maybe Darienn. Maybe Lord Madigen. Or one of his men. Aoife couldn't tell.

She could only stand there gaping at Declan, begging him to refute it, but he only stared back at her.

There. A flash of what Aoife swore was shame burned in his eyes, but it was gone as quickly as it had appeared, his expression tightening and all emotion washing away.

He turned to Melina, his voice reverting back not to the Declan she'd fallen for but the captain who had wanted to be rid of her. "Of course I didn't tell her. I needed her to trust me. She's just a means to an end."

"We'll see about that," Melina said, but the words sounded distant, as if Aoife were hearing them from underwater.

This had been their plan—for Declan to deny any emotional ties to her, to insist he'd used her—if they got caught.

But that was before.

Aoife couldn't focus on any of the thoughts that now swarmed her.

He'd lied. He'd killed Lani and hadn't told her. Ever. Not in all the hours they had talked.

What else had he lied about? Had his kisses been an act? Had it all been a ploy?

Her chest caved in on itself, the air becoming thin around her.

She couldn't breathe. Couldn't stand.

Her knees wobbled, but she forced them to steady, willed them to keep her upright.

Tommy, standing on her other side, inched toward her. Feeling his shoulder brush hers, she turned to him. His expression displayed a mix of so many emotions—sorrow and confusion and remorse and helplessness.

Had Declan fooled him too?

Her vision blurred. She couldn't think straight. Couldn't sort all of this out. She could turn to Declan, demand answers, but she knew he wouldn't offer them. Not here.

Her hand itched to both grab his hand in hers and slap him across the face, but neither were particularly good options given the circumstances.

Something moved in her periphery. So lost in the buzzing within her mind, Aoife hadn't heard the door open or the footsteps approach.

A pirate wearing a gold sash had entered, someone from the *Duchess*. And by the display of confidence, this was likely Captain Halloran herself. Her face remained hidden behind the brim of her large hat as she leaned toward Madigen's ear.

Melina looked over at them. "What's happened?"

Halloran straightened as Lord Madigen cleared his throat and answered. "The fae got past their crew."

This should have brought relief, but nothing could ease the ache that now plagued Aoife.

"How did that—" Melina started, but she raised a hand as if batting away an annoying insect. "It doesn't matter. You can redeem your crew and their utter failure to protect my property by handling her."

Aoife's stomach turned to lead under her mother's glare.

No!

She wouldn't meet Lani's fate. Or Maggie's. She wouldn't be *dispatched* or *exiled* or whatever her mother wanted to call it.

She looked at Declan, but he still wore the cold mask he'd donned. It had to be an act. Another ruse.

She'd thought he and his crew were more like actors than pirates, right? Surely this had to be another one of his well-executed plays.

Captain Halloran stepped toward her, the sash around her waist swaying with each slow, confident step.

Aoife's heart thundered painfully against her chest as she waited to see if Declan would protest or Tommy would step in, as they had with Captain Grayson. As they had on the beach in Foxhaven.

But neither moved.

No one moved, except for the approaching captain.

Aoife adjusted her grip on her dagger and raised it, not knowing exactly how she'd defend herself against this captain—and in a room full of Lord Madigen's crew—but she wouldn't go easily.

If Declan and Tommy wouldn't help her, she'd help herself.

Captain Halloran had gotten within ten feet when Declan finally faced Aoife, his eyes still as hard as steel, with none of the warmth they'd held less than an hour ago.

Declan glanced down at the dagger in Aoife's hand, then met her gaze once more before giving the slightest shake of his head.

No.

He wanted her to stand down. To not fight.

Her thoughts warred inside her. After all the times he'd told her to do something and she hadn't listened, only to have things fall apart, should she listen this time?

Beside her Tommy whispered her name, and she turned with reluctance, avoiding looking at the captain who now stood close enough to strike.

Why hadn't she been grabbed yet? Why was Halloran waiting?

Her skin crawled. Was this how a mouse felt while the cat toyed with it?

Tommy held her gaze and mouthed a silent *don't.*

Her brow creased. He couldn't be telling her to give up. Could he?

Before she could even think to lower the dagger, a hand gripped her wrist so hard she dropped the blade to the floor.

The captain pulled her close, turning until they were both facing her mother. A blade she hadn't seen in the captain's hand poked her in the ribs.

"I can do it now. Here. Make the boy suffer to see the girl die." The woman had a voice that was rough in Aoife's ear, like sandpaper against her skin, sending a shiver through her she hoped would go unnoticed.

She would be brave. Like Maggie had been.

Declan and Tommy remained quiet behind her, and even though Aoife knew it was the smart play, it still stung to have them not fighting for her.

She was once again that stowaway on a ship of pirates who wanted her gone. Utterly alone. A nuisance. A bother. No one worth their time or energy.

They had the fae. They wouldn't need her now. There was no reason for them to save her.

There'd be no rescue.

The hand on her wrist tightened. The knife at her back pushed harder. But Aoife forced herself to hide her fear, to choke it down, to steel her expression as best she could. She wouldn't give her mother the satisfaction.

"No. Not here, Captain Halloran," Melina said. "As much as I'd enjoy seeing McCallagh's pain, I won't do that to Lord Madigen. He has so few accomplishments. Seems cruel to remind him of yet another failure. Take her to the usual place. It's time for her to be reunited with her sister."

CHAPTER 48
DECLAN

Aoife's screams of protest echoed through the hallways as Captain Halloran dragged her out into the night, her desperation and fear so much greater than it had been in Foxhaven.

Declan's gut twisted, squeezing ever tighter like a snake around its prey. It took every bit of his energy to keep the torment from showing.

Though he faced Melina still, her face blurred as his mind forced him to replay the image of Aoife, the way she'd doubted him, the way she'd doubted every moment they'd shared.

How could she have so easily believed his act tonight? How could she have so easily believed the mask he'd had to wear?

He had meant to tell her about Lani, about how he'd been forced to take her life, about how her sister's face and her pleas for mercy had been haunting him more than all the nightmares he'd carried since childhood.

He had planned to tell her, but the timing had never felt right. The words had never felt enough, they could never do his remorse justice.

And he'd stupidly kept the truth hidden.

Would she ever forgive him? Would she listen to his apologies?

Here, standing before her mother, he vowed to the sands he'd never stop begging for that forgiveness.

Melina shifted her weight and dropped her head to one shoulder. "Now for the matter of payment. It's getting late, and I'm growing weary of this interruption to our evening."

"What do you want?" Declan spat at her. His hand tensed, as if begging him to throw the blade into the matriarch's chest, but he talked down the urge. That would bring certain death at Madigen's hand, and he still had too much to do.

"You have my fae, and I know you didn't free them out of the goodness of your heart."

"You want them back? You know where my ship is. You have men at your beck and call. Why not take them back?"

She stiffened, her cold smile returning as she lowered her chin at him. "Because there's something we want more than merely getting those sisters back into the safety of our care."

Declan didn't even bother to stifle his scoff. "And what's that?"

"The Csintala Dagger. You will go. You will use our fae. And you will retrieve the Csintala Dagger from wherever it rests, and bring both—the blade and my fae— back to us."

He could play dumb, as he'd attempted with Callum, but that would only waste precious time. How far had Halloran gotten with Aoife already?

"And what if I don't? Are you going to have me *exiled*? What will stop me from taking the dagger and leaving the Aisling altogether?"

"Because we both know you aren't the ruthless pirate you have everyone believing you are. We both know you won't take the blade for your own benefit, not when you think so many people could be helped with its use."

Declan roughed a hand over his chin and scratched at his jawline as he thought through all his options. And their consequences. He needed to think faster. Never enough time. Time was always against him.

Melina spoke again. "And *exile* isn't in my plans for you. You don't deserve to be let off that easy, not for all you've already taken from us. Our fae. Our heirs."

She stepped toward him, brazenly close, as if daring him to strike and end her here and now.

"You see, Declan," she breathed, "Aoife isn't the only way to hurt you."

There was no snap of her fingers this time. Only the slightest movement of her chin as she gave the order.

It happened too fast. He didn't even see the blade as it flew through the air and hit its mark with the all too familiar sound of steel ripping into flesh. Tommy released a muffled groan, his hands clutching his stomach.

No!

Before Declan could move—before he could make a sound—one of Lord Madigen's crew stepped from the shadows behind them, ripping the blade from Tommy's gut and slicing it across his chest. He plunged it into his side, and Tommy gave another grunt of pain before the pirate pushed him away, pulling the blade out.

Tommy fell, his knees hitting the stone floor with a sickening thud that rang in Declan's ears as he sent his own knife flying into the attacker's face. The blade hit true, in the man's eye, sending him backwards, where he fell with a thud.

Declan rushed to Tommy, trying to put pressure on the wounds as best he could, but he didn't have enough hands.

He needed to think.

He cursed aloud as he fumbled with the knot in the purple sash at his waist, the blood—Tommy's blood—on his fingers making it harder to get a grip on the fine fabric.

Finally he got it free and yanked it away before wrapping it around his friend's abdomen as he moved the man's hands away. "You'll be okay, Tommy. It'll be okay."

Tommy winced as Declan pulled the fabric taut against him. "I've had worse."

"Liar." He tried to smile at his friend, to reassure him, but he couldn't.

Before he could grab more fabric to staunch the bleeding from Tommy's chest, that damn bitch's tongue clicked again, mocking him.

"Poor Declan. No matter how hard you try, you always fail, don't you?"

Declan didn't look up from Tommy, whose eyes blinked rapidly as if he were trying to keep himself conscious and present.

Melina stepped even closer. "The tourniquet will only do so much, but you can save him, you know. Get him to the fae. They can heal him. But you'd better be quick about it. He doesn't have much time."

Damn her!

He didn't want to admit it, but she was right. The gash in Tommy's chest was deeper than Declan had first thought. He needed help, and he needed it soon.

Never enough blasted time.

Declan growled as he pushed to his feet, pulling Tommy up and onto his shoulders. Holding onto his friend's arm and leg, he tried to ignore the warm blood seeping out of him even as it soaked his jacket.

Tommy's body went limp as he gave himself over to the pain and blood loss.

Declan could back up and take the secret passageway out, but that likely wasn't the quickest exit, so he moved past Melina, not daring to let his eyes meet hers, and then past Lord Madigen, who stepped aside.

"Oh, and Declan," Melina called after him. He stopped and turned, though every muscle screamed at him to keep moving, keep going. "If you fail? If you refuse, as you did earlier, your sister will be next"—she nodded toward Tommy's blood-soaked body—"and you may not be around to save her."

Cait.

Declan slammed his teeth together, pushing all of his anger into his jaw, and without another word he forced his legs into as fast a run as he could manage out of the hall and toward his ship.

He couldn't lose him. Not Tommy. Not the friend who'd been there through everything, who knew Declan better than anyone, who'd never given up on him.

Tommy would make it. He'd get him to the fae. Get him healed.

Tommy first. Then Aoife.

The two people he couldn't bear to lose.

Though he might have already lost her.

CHAPTER 49
AOIFE

Captain Halloran didn't loosen her grip as she dragged Aoife across the lawn toward the wooded path, ignoring how Aoife's feet slipped and stumbled, pulling her still onward.

Until they were a hundred feet into the darkness of the woods.

The captain dropped Aoife's wrist and halted on the path.

Aoife's feet screamed at her to get moving, to take this chance to bolt, but her damned curiosity took hold. What was happening? What had she missed?

The captain backed off a half step. "I'm sorry if I hurt you. Take a moment to catch your breath."

Aoife rolled her sore wrist, but she refused to rub the pain away. Like hell she'd show weakness to anymore pirates.

"Who in the sands are you?" Anger seethed in her belly, and she hoped it—and not her anguish—coated her words as she spat them out.

"Captain Halloran—"

"Yeah, I got that much." Tension burned through her body, through her joints, down to the knuckles of her hands, and up into her jaw. A silent scream echoed somewhere inside, but she bit it back.

"You're a feisty one. I can see why Declan likes you."

His name echoed on Aoife's lips, a mere whisper she couldn't contain.

"Yes. Declan. You can thank him for this rescue." She gestured to the path ahead. "Speaking of which, we should get moving."

"Let me guess. We don't have much time."

"How'd you know?"

Aoife rolled her eyes but didn't answer as she started trudging down the path, hoping she could manage with the scant moonlight peering through the trees.

The captain caught up to her quickly and walked beside her in silence. A silence Aoife couldn't handle.

"So where are we heading, Captain? Not to—"

"No, not to the killing grounds."

"Is that what they call them?"

"It's what the pirates call them. I don't know if the council has an official name for it."

Aoife might have asked where it was, where her sister waited for her to join her, but she couldn't stomach it. Someday maybe.

"We're heading to a cove. It's hidden, secret—"

Aoife cut her off. "I know where it is." The image of him emerging from the teal water flashed in her mind. Of all the places...

They continued a few more paces before she spoke again. "You don't have to take me, you know. You can go on back, tell them I'm dead."

"Firstly, no, I can't. While time is short, I do need to allow for the time it would have taken me to complete the *exile*."

A shiver crawled up Aoife's spine, and she was glad the darkness hid her wince.

"Secondly? I promised Captain McCallagh I'd get you there personally, if needed."

He'd planned this.

Look at all options. Plan for all possibilities. He'd been prepared for things to go badly. He'd known Halloran would help.

And he didn't tell you that either.

How much didn't she know? How much had he kept from her?

"How?" She hadn't intended to utter the question aloud, but it spilled into the quiet night on her breath, and she sensed Halloran turn to face her as they walked.

"You'll have to ask him that."

"I don't know that I can. I—"

"No. You stop right there." The harshness of the woman's tone caught Aoife off guard, and her feet skidded to a stop. "Well, I didn't mean literally stop."

Sands, are all pirates snarky bastards?

"Look, Ms. Cascade, I don't know what in the sands is going on between you and McCallagh, and I don't want to know. That's between the two of you. This isn't a stroll with your girlfriend. You're not here to gush your heart out to me. I'm just following through with a promise to get you to the drop point where Declan will come to retrieve you. That's it."

"Fine! Sorry to inconvenience you," Aoife said, dipping her head forward in a nod before she stomped off down the path once again.

They continued on in silence with only the sound of their feet trampling twigs and pounding the dirt.

Aoife tried to focus on the rhythm of their steps and the difference between hers and the captain's. Each crack and squish of wood and earth underfoot. When that wasn't enough to keep the truth at bay, she resorted to counting her steps.

Fifty-eight. Fifty-nine. Sixty. Sixty-one.

He'd killed Lani. He'd lied.

A curse rushed out of her, and if the captain noticed—how could she not?—she didn't let on.

One. Two. Three. Four.

Aoife had to restart her counting five times before they reached the cove, and as expected, the sight of the sand, the tide, and the boulders they'd sat beside rushed at her, driving all the air from her lungs.

Breathe. Damn you. Don't let her see you fall apart!

She sucked in the briny air and forced her shoulders back, pushing against those damned images in her mind. But they wouldn't stay away, popping back up with each step she took toward the same boulder she'd chosen before.

Easing herself onto the sand, she looked back at the captain. "You waiting with me? Or what's the plan?"

"One hour. That's the most I can spare. He should be here by then. But if not, you'll be on your own."

As hard as it was to think of facing him again, the thought of being alone, of being abandoned, forgotten? It threatened to crush her.

She looked back to the sea, where the sliver of moon hovered above the water. All the peace she'd ever found here now seemed tainted, like mold creeping through a loaf of bread. He'd ruined it, this refuge. He'd taken it from her.

Just as he took Lani.

She'd thought she'd cried all the tears she could for her sister, but now, with the grief pooling again in her chest, she couldn't stop them as they pushed their way to the surface, gathering in her eyes until she could barely see the waves before her.

Captain Halloran leaned against the other boulder—Declan's boulder—and Aoife assumed she wasn't one for small talk. Not that Aoife would even be able to manage speaking now without her tears turning her words into a blubbering mess.

She'd have to face the truth at some point. Now was as good a time as any.

AN HOUR LATER, Aoife had gotten nowhere with this new reality, her mind warring with itself, pulling her back and forth as it wrestled with whether she could trust Declan or not.

Captain Halloran shifted away from the boulder with a gruff sigh and stepped toward her. "It's time for me to go."

Aoife pushed herself up, ignoring where her body now hurt from sitting. "I thought you said he'd be here."

"He will."

"When?"

The captain's jaw tightened, and Aoife waited for the harsh words she could see the woman contemplating.

But they didn't come.

"Ms. Cascade," she said with a tone far softer than seemed possible for her, "trust him. He'll be here."

Aoife moved to protest, to remind this ridiculous pirate of her earlier words about being on her own, but the captain raised a hand.

"Look, I don't know him that well, but I knew his parents. They were good people, and if he got even an ounce of their honor, he will be here. They were not the sort to abandon the ones they loved. And I don't think he is either."

Love.

Aoife couldn't handle the word, not yet anyway, so she focused on the other question that had been nagging her since they'd stopped on the path.

"What happens to you when they find out you didn't actually..." She couldn't even finish the question.

"Kill you?"

Aoife nodded, hoping her discomfort didn't show.

"I'll figure something out." And with no other word, the captain left Aoife standing on the black sand to wait.

And she waited.

And waited.

Her thoughts tumbling around in her head with the ebb and flow of the waves before her.

He'll be here.

Aoife had no idea how much time passed as she waited. Minutes. Hours. Did it even matter?

What had happened back in the council hall after she'd been dragged away?

Her mind played out every scenario she could think of, her chest tightening as she envisioned Declan and Tommy cut down and bleeding on the library floor.

What would his crew do if that happened? Would Gavin take command? Would they go after the dagger? Would the sisters abandon them? Would the dagger ever be retrieved? Would her people ever be free from this tyranny?

The questions swarmed her, buried her, until she was sure they might suffocate her.

Footsteps in the sand behind her had her standing without thinking, not stopping to consider it might be one of Lord Madigen's crew coming to finish her off after finding out Halloran had helped her.

In the darkness she couldn't see who approached from the path, but the steps were slow and unsteady.

"Declan?" She called his name out of instinct, even as her heart ached at the sound of it.

No answer came, but whoever approached seemed to respond to her voice, picking up their pace slightly. As much as they could, perhaps.

She moved around the boulder just as he stepped out from the trees.

Or stumbled out of them.

And there he fell, his knees hitting the black sand with a soft thud. His chin dropped to his chest. In the moonlight Aoife could see it across his shoulders and back.

Blood. So much blood.

CHAPTER 50
DECLAN

Declan's whole body ached, from his sore feet to his throbbing head. But nothing hurt him more than the sound of his name on Aoife's lips and the fear that she'd deny him the forgiveness he needed.

She rushed to him, as best she could in the soft sand, but stopped when he raised his face to look at her.

His hands itched to reach for her, to pull her close and hold her tight, but he couldn't move.

She lowered herself to her knees before him, just out of reach. "What happened? Are you—"

He couldn't look her in the eyes, couldn't keep his head from shaking as he answered. "Tommy."

"Is he okay? Is he—"

"I don't know yet. The fae are with him, working to heal him, but their powers are weak. So many centuries trapped in that iron prison. Their healing will take longer than usual, and the cuts... Deeper than we... He lost a lot of blood before I got him to..."

Declan stumbled over the words, unable to focus on anything other than the pool of sorrow and regret that had settled in his gut.

He looked up at her then, taking stock of every part of her he could see, desperate to ensure she was okay. "Are you hurt?"

"No," she said, but her eyes lowered to the sand between them.

He dared to inch closer to her but stopped.

"I'm sorry." The words felt empty as they fell out. Worthless. Pointless. Insufficient.

"That's it?" The bite in her response had been expected, but he recoiled from it all the same. "That's all you have to say? I'm *sorry*?"

When he didn't answer, no words sufficient to express his remorse, she stood with a huff and turned away from him.

No. Stop her. Get her back.

His thoughts urged him to his feet, the sight of her walking away from him pushing him to ignore the burning fatigue in his legs as he stood.

"Aoife, stop. Please."

She whirled around, and even in the darkness the pain and anger swimming in her eyes was clear. He needed to fix this. Needed her to understand, to forgive him.

She didn't say anything, only looked at him, her jaw tense and her mouth set in a straight line.

He took a step toward her, and when she didn't retreat as he expected, he took another.

He reached out a hand for her, but she pulled back.

"Don't—don't touch me." The words fell from her lips, dripping with the same poison echoed in her expression. He half expected her to back away from him, to curl back in on herself.

But this wasn't the same girl who had trespassed onto his ship and begged for transport.

She straightened, and though she stood a head shorter than him, she dwarfed him with that glare.

He took another half step toward her, until they were close enough to share the same breath.

"I should have told you," he whispered.

"Yes, you should have," she said, each word coated with malice, but she didn't back away.

"I can't undo it. I can't bring her back. I can't go back and fix it. But—"

"But what? You had no choice? You didn't know how to tell me?" She railed against him, shooting more daggers at him with those eyes that had enchanted him.

"Well, yes, honestly, to all of that. It's why I didn't want to come back to Cregah, why I vowed never to return. This is what the council demands of pirates who can't pay. If we don't have the money, we pay with services. Dealing out the death they can't with their own hands."

"How many?"

He didn't need to ask for clarification. He knew exactly what she was asking. But he couldn't find the strength to answer her.

"Declan, how many have you killed for them?"

That venom in her eyes ebbed enough for him to catch a glimpse of the pity he'd never wanted from anyone. But from her, he'd take her pity over her disgust.

He forced himself to hold her gaze. "Nine. Lani was the ninth."

"What were their names?"

Without hesitation he recited the list that haunted him relentlessly, the list that would never be quieted, never be shut out, always lurking in the far recesses of his heart. "Saoirse. Conor. Desmond. Kallie. Cillian. Eden. Sean. Regan."

"And Lani."

He nodded, still not letting himself look away from her. He deserved the hate she flung at him, and he wouldn't let himself avoid it.

Silence settled between them, and he could hardly bear it. He wanted her to yell at him, scream at him, push him away. Anything but this still and silent anger like a sleeping dragon waiting to devour him.

"You didn't mention Adler." A sad hope seeped into her gaze.

"What?"

"The pirate Lani was to meet. Adler. You didn't name him."

"Because I didn't kill him. He wasn't assigned to me. But, Aoife, I had no choice. You do what you're told or they come after your crew. I never wanted my men to be asked to do this, so I always took the orders upon myself, never allowing even Tommy to come with me."

Her jaw tightened, her eyes narrowing, and he braced himself for whatever torrent she was about to unleash.

"I'm not angry at you for that. For all you had to do for them. That's on them. But you should have told me!"

"I know—"

"No," she said, cutting him off, "I don't think you get it, Declan." She flung an arm toward the trees—toward the council hall. "Everything I've ever known, everyone I've ever trusted, has *lied* to me. Everything I believed was built on a false ideal. Everything I was taught was a charade. A hoax! I hoped you were different."

In his mind echoed the words he'd said so many times before. *I'm a pirate.* But he bit them back.

"And I know you're a pirate, but you are different, Declan. I see it. That's why this..." She trailed off as she shook her head at him.

"I'm so sorry, Aoife."

Still not enough. Still such shallow words.

"Were you ever going to tell me?"

He'd been dreading this question. More than her asking for the count and the names. This question. He couldn't lie to her again. She deserved the truth.

"I don't know. Maybe."

Swallowing hard, she clenched her teeth again, and tears began to well up in her beautiful eyes. He'd caused this. This was his doing. But he could fix it. If she let him.

He had to try.

"At first, I thought to, just to make you mad, to punish you for trespassing on my ship. But then I needed your help. And after Foxhaven, I couldn't bear to hurt you. I thought about telling you so many times, but I was a coward. And then you were happy, laughing, smiling. I didn't want to take that away from you."

"But you've just taken so much more than a smile or a laugh, Declan. I don't blame you for killing Lani. But I trusted you. And now—"

"Please, Aoife. I love you. I need—"

"What?" She backed away a step. "What did you say?"

"I said I love you, Aoife." He paused, but she only stared at him, her expression blank as her eyes searched his. "I didn't expect this. Didn't want it. But here I am, a wreck of a man, drowning in uncharted waters." He took a step toward her, and then another until they were inches apart. "You wrecked me, Aoife, and I'd have it no other way."

He dared to reach for her, marveling when she let him touch a finger to her chin, angling her face to him as he had back in his cabin.

"Please, Aoife, forgive me?" he asked, hope lacing each word. He swallowed, waiting for her to say something, to do something. "Say something. Please?"

He lowered his hand, leaving her staring up at him with no hint of her thoughts.

But when her head slowly started to shake, his heart plummeted.

"I can't." She took a step back from him, tears welling up in those green eyes he loved more than the sea. "Declan, I'm sorry. I just can't. Not yet."

And with those words, she left him standing there on the black sands, in their cove, while he stared after her as she made her way back to his ship.

CHAPTER 51
AOIFE

Aoife didn't hear Declan's steps behind her on the path, but she didn't turn to confirm he'd given her the space she needed either.

Blinded by a mess of emotions, her mind a whir of thoughts refusing to settle, she didn't notice when the trees gave way to the quaint buildings of Morshan and her steps touched cobblestones instead of soft earth. She'd be lying if she said she'd never suspected Declan had been the one. He'd been in port that day. He'd looked distracted when he swam into the cove.

But she'd pushed all suspicion aside, sure he wouldn't hide something so important.

She'd been wrong.

Just as she'd been wrong about everything.

So naive. So gullible. Was there anyone in this world she could trust? At this point, she didn't even know if she could trust herself.

Her heart and mind had led her down the wrong paths time and time again.

Onto that ship.

Into the hands of those pirates in Foxhaven.

Into this mess with Declan.

The thought of his name caused fresh tears to spill over and trail down her cheeks. She wiped them away. Though no one was around to see, she had no desire to have the crew seeing her with such signs of emotion marking her face.

Aoife pushed herself forward, careful to stay in the darkened shadows with her head down, adding more swagger to her hurried steps—as if that might help conceal her identity—as she made her way down the narrow streets and around the few corners back to the docks.

Seeing the ship waiting at the end of the dock closest to her, the crew busy with final preparations to sail, she let herself breathe the salt air deep into her lungs before looking over her shoulder to ensure Declan was on his way.

He wasn't there.

Nothing but darkness lay behind her, the streets empty, all residents asleep, and the only noise coming from the various crews aboard their ships.

He'd be here. He'd show up.

She took the final hundred feet to compose herself, hoping the darkness would conceal any evidence of her tears. Thankfully, the crew barely acknowledged her arrival as she boarded. No sign of Gavin and the fae, but they must have arrived, as the crew was eerily silent. No doubt their newest guests made them more uneasy than Aoife had.

She began to make her way toward the officers' cabin, where the fae would be staying during their journey, where Tommy was likely resting while being healed, but she changed her mind. Declan had said the healing would take a while, and she didn't want to interrupt any progress they'd made.

As she laid a hand on the door to Declan's quarters—their quarters—her heart twinged with a spark of hope that maybe he'd used his pirate ways to get ahead of her, had arrived at the ship early, and now waited to surprise her here. It would be just like him to sit there behind the desk, with that smirk on his face, asking her what took so long.

But she opened the door to find the cabin dark, cold, and empty.

No one had been in here for hours.

A sharp bite of panic stung her chest, but she shook it away.

Declan can take care of himself. He's a grown man, she reminded herself.

Yes, a grown man who loves you.

Who lied to you.

Who you love in return.

Her mind bounced from one thought to the next over and over as she walked into the cabin and lit the lantern on the desk.

Each thought spoke truth. Even if everything else she knew was a lie, these truths remained, but she had no idea how to reconcile them all.

Love required trust.

How could trust exist without honesty?

But you love each other.

Her stomach tightened as the thought echoed within.

She didn't hate him. Even as her anger simmered, it remained in the shadows of her disappointment.

She'd let herself fall, let herself hope. Perhaps this was to be her life. A vicious cycle of trust, hope, and betrayal.

Would she ever be happy? Would she ever find peace? Or was this her punishment for what she'd done to Lani? Was this the debt she owed for her own betrayal?

These thoughts followed her into the sleeping quarters, where she slumped back onto the bed, her unblinking stare fixed on the ceiling.

She wished her mind would go blank, but it seemed bent on haunting her, stirring up the memories of how he'd held her, how his lips had caressed hers, how safe she'd felt with him. Her chest squeezed ever harder as each image gave way to the next.

He'd asked for forgiveness.

She'd declined.

At least for now.

She knew absolution was the right thing to grant him, the only way to move forward. Yet some part of her refused to take that next step.

He deserved to hurt as she did.

He deserved to feel that guilt of knowing he'd screwed up.

For how long, she wasn't sure. She only knew she couldn't give him what he requested yet.

So she closed her eyes and waited.

Maybe by the time he returned, she'd be ready to at least hear him out.

CHAPTER 52
DECLAN

DECLAN STARED into the trees long after Aoife had turned away from him.

What had he done?

Sands knew he'd made his share of mistakes in life, but this? He didn't know how to get himself out of this one. Normally he'd brush it off, focus on what mattered most—treasure, freedom, the sea.

But now Tommy was injured, Cait had been threatened, and Aoife…

The look she'd given him, that mix of betrayal and grief and anger, would torment him until his final breath.

He hadn't followed her, and wouldn't have even if his feet would obey. She needed space, and he could give her that much, at least for a little while.

He waited until the sound of her footsteps had faded, and then waited longer, not wanting his longer strides to bring him upon her before she'd made it back to the ship.

With one final glance at the cove—their cove—he made another vow to the sands and to the sea and to whoever might be listening above.

He would come back here to these shores.

And he would bring the dagger.

And he would end the council.

For the people. And for Aoife.

He wouldn't screw this up again. He would make it right. He would fix this.

Even if she never forgave him, he would make sure she was safe. That would be enough for him.

The walk back to Morshan took less time than he'd expected, each step matching the pounding of his heart as he tried to work out the words he'd say to her.

The dock came into view, but he realized too late that someone followed him.

He'd been too distracted, wrapped up in his thoughts, to notice. Under the shadow of the next shop's awning, he turned sharply, his hand on the dagger at his waist, ready to use it if needed.

Nothing but darkness.

Had he completely lost his senses?

He searched the streets, glanced at the windows for any reflections, but still found nothing. He must have imagined it.

He turned back toward the docks, and that's when they stepped out. Not one of Lord Madigen's men as he had expected, but another captain, his face hidden behind the wide brim of his weathered hat. He now stood in Declan's path.

"Did you forget we were to meet, McCallagh?" the captain said, lifting his chin high enough that the dim moonlight glinted off the white of his scar.

Declan bit back a curse. He had forgotten.

"Aye, Callum—"

"Hold it right there. Callum is what my friends call me." He took a step forward. "You can call me Captain Grayson."

Declan made to protest, but Callum raised a finger.

"Now, Declan, I thought we were friends. But your actions prove otherwise."

Declan could see his ship over Callum's shoulder, his ship where Aoife waited for him, where Tommy was being healed. He needed to get off this street and onto that deck. He needed to lose Callum. Now.

"Apologies for forgetting the meeting, Captain—"

Callum stepped forward again, so close Declan could smell the rum on his breath and the grime that clung to his skin.

"This isn't about a meeting, Declan. You sent me on a pointless task to get me out of the way, to keep me busy, to keep that bitch of an heir out of my hands."

Declan forced his expression to remain blank, even as his hands fisted and his jaw tensed. He raised his arms in a shrug. "What can I say, Captain? I'm a pirate. It's what we do."

"Aye. Indeed. And so is this."

Callum gave a quick nod, and before Declan could turn to block the attack, the pommel of a blade slammed into the side of his head, and everything went black.

CHAPTER 53
AOIFE

THE DOOR to the cabin slammed against the wall as it was thrown, and Aoife jolted upright. A pair of feet rushed in, and a glance toward the window told her it was nearing dawn. Had she really fallen asleep? She turned to the bed and found Declan's side still empty, untouched.

"Aoife?" Tommy's tone—urgent and coated with anxiety—filled her with dread.

It took her less than a second to rise and rush into the main room to meet him, sending out a "Tommy? Are you okay? I thought you were hurt."

Tommy stood alone, his face pale and lined with worry. "He's not here, is he?" he asked.

"What? No. Are you sure you're okay? Did they—"

"I'm fine."

He looked far from fine, but when she motioned for him to sit, he only shook his head, his eyes burning into hers.

"What happened, Tommy? What's going on?"

"Your mother. Had me nearly gutted in order to get Declan to agree to get the dagger for them. He carried me all the way here so the fae could heal me. As soon as I woke, I wouldn't let them touch me again. Not until I checked on him."

"Tommy, sit, please. You need to rest."

"No, I can't," he said as he began pacing the same path Declan always did on the rug. "The crew said they saw you arrive, but the captain didn't. We're running out of time, Aoife. What happened at the cove?"

Aoife answered his question with one of her own. "Did you know?"

A nod. A swallow.

Aoife's throat tightened. How many people knew what Declan had done and had hidden it? "Did anyone else—"

"No." He stopped her with the sharp word and a small shake of his head. "Only me. I'm the only one he allowed to shoulder those burdens."

"You didn't tell me," she said, with more sadness than anger.

"It wasn't my place, but I encouraged him to tell you. Told him you could handle it. He was supposed to, said he would. Perhaps after we got the fae. He never meant to hurt you, you know."

She knew, but it didn't make it any less painful.

Tommy cleared his throat and looked around the room once more. "You fought then? I'm assuming that's why you didn't return together?"

"I left him standing on the beach, but I didn't expect him to allow me to go off on my own. Not after Foxhaven."

"You didn't bother to check to see if he was following?" he asked, no trace of anger in the words, only concern for his friend.

Lowering her eyes, she shook her head.

Her thoughts raced as she wondered where Declan might have gone, what might have happened to him. There had to be someone they could contact for help. She snapped her gaze up. "Cait. Would she know? Maybe he went to the pub?"

"He wouldn't have risked it. Not when we needed to be out. But if anyone has info, it would likely be her."

Tommy strode to the door and opened it but turned at the last moment. "You coming?"

Without a word she rushed past him out onto the deck.

But she stopped a few feet from the gangplank. A man she'd never seen before stood there, looking as though he was going to be sick despite their still being docked. Perhaps it was the news he brought that had him looking so ill, but she couldn't tell for sure.

Tommy stepped around her. "Lucan? What is it? If you're standing on a ship, it can't be good."

The man—Lucan—swallowed hard and gave a nearly imperceptible nod.

"Word from Cait?" Tommy asked. Aoife wondered if they shouldn't move this conversation somewhere private, as Declan would have. Tommy didn't usher him inside the cabin but stood, his fingers twitching at his sides, as if he were anxious to take action.

"Aye. He's gone."

Aoife's eyes went wide. "What do you mean he's gone?"

Lucan looked at her, but only for a second before his attention returned to Tommy. "Grayson. Grabbed him. Left word with Cait to get to you." He held out a scrap of paper, and the crew—frozen in place from his first word—now held a collective breath.

Tommy took the note, and Aoife glanced over, unable to read the scrawl of letters.

"What is it?" she whispered.

"Callum's going for the dagger."

Lucan spoke up. "If they try to go without the fae, they'll be killed. None of them will survive."

Aoife felt her heart thud to a stop. As if all of time had ceased to tick on.

"Tommy, we have to catch up to them, get him back," she said.

"Aye, but their ship is faster and has a head start."

She wanted to argue, to beg him to make the call, but she wasn't an officer on this ship, wasn't even a crew member.

No one moved. No one seemed to even breathe.

Tommy only stared at the paper as if it would tell him what to do. From the corner of her eye, Aoife saw the three fae sisters approach from the officers' quarters, but they didn't say anything. They, too, seemed to be waiting for Tommy's direction.

Tommy cleared his throat and bellowed out the order, "Weigh anchor! Gavin, get us underway."

The crew moved at once, and Tommy turned back to Lucan. "Thank you, friend. But you'd best get off the ship, unless you want to come with us."

Lucan seemed to shudder at the thought and ran quickly to make it down the gangway before it was moved, leaving Aoife and Tommy standing in the middle of the deck with the fae still hovering nearby.

Aoife rested a hand on his arm. "Tommy? Where are they taking him? Where's the dagger?"

Tommy ran a hand through his hair before turning to her with what looked like fear in his eyes.

"The Black Sound."

Aoife forgot how to breathe, giving her words no sound as she said, "You mean..."

"Aye. The sirens."

Panic hit, sucking the last of the air out of her lungs, but she managed a breath. "There's no getting past them. Not for any of us."

"That's where they come in," Tommy said, tossing a glance at the sisters. "We'll get to him before they get there."

"I hope so," she said, her gaze turning toward the vast waters that lay ahead.

Sands help him—and everyone on Cregah—if they didn't.

BONUS CHAPTER 34 1/2
DECLAN

Friends.

The word flitted around Declan's mind as he walked away from Aoife toward a group of men standing at the side rail. Passing Tommy, he whispered to him, "Only one more fill for her. Maybe two."

Tommy let out a boisterous laugh completely at odds with Declan's whispered tone. When Declan flashed him a glare in warning, he whispered back, "Afraid of what a drunk Aoife might do to our plans?"

Declan could claim that was the case, but there seemed little point in lying. Not when Tommy knew better and had only suggested it to goad him. But he also didn't want to admit to Tommy how much he found himself caring for her, so he offered a lazy shrug before stepping away.

"How are you, Collins?" he asked as he leaned himself against the railing. Collins had been with him for the past five years and had been nothing but a hard worker, eager to do his share to see the crew's success. He'd make a good bo'sun or quartermaster one day—if he desired such a role.

"Fine, sir," Collins said. He raised his mug. "Happy birthday, by the way."

Declan gave a nod in response before turning to the two other men. "And you both joined us in Foxhaven."

"Aye, sir," they said in unison.

The taller of the two continued. "I'm Enzo. This is Pasha. We were merchant sailors from Turvala before our ship was overtaken by one of the lords. Managed to make it to Foxhaven, hoping a pirate might need our skills."

Declan dipped his chin at each man. "We're glad to have you, honestly." He clasped each man on the shoulder, hoping they'd feel welcome among the crew, before moving on to the rest of the men.

He'd managed to meet and speak to all the new crew before Tommy and Collins ended up in the middle of the deck dancing together like idiots, arms draped across each other's shoulders as they stomped and kicked their feet completely out of time with the music.

Should have cut Tommy off, it seems.

Even so, he couldn't keep from smiling at the sight of his friends and crew having a bit of fun. Perhaps the last fun they'd have before this job was over. The men twirled and swayed and nearly fell over as Declan turned his gaze to the stairs to see how Aoife was faring.

But the stairs were empty except for the tin cup she'd been using.

His heart thumped with a hint of panic as he scanned the deck for her. It's be just like her to fall overboard. He shouldn't have offered the rum. Not when her sea legs—and stomach—weren't quite settled yet.

He heard her laugh before he saw her approaching Tommy and Collins on the deck.

What is she doing?

But he followed her line of sight to where Tommy had stopped dancing and stood waving her over.

Declan couldn't move, couldn't budge from his spot at the foremast. He couldn't stop smiling, either, as he watched Tommy take Aoife's hands and begin spinning her around the deck in a haphazard dance with no steps. She threw her head back and laughed, her smile wide across her face as she let herself go, and it was all Declan could do to not bask in the glow of her happiness on display.

Declan grabbed himself one last swig of rum before he set his mug down on the deck and strode into the middle of the dancing, timing it so Tommy whirled Aoife right into his arms.

Tommy gave him a wink as he backed away without a word. Taking Aoife's hands, Declan watched her cheeks flush with adorable deep pink.

They didn't speak, couldn't speak over the loud music, but he searched her eyes —swimming in those greens and golds—for any hint of the sadness they'd held earlier, but it had been replaced by a sparkling joy as pleasant as the sound of her laugh on the sea breeze.

He couldn't remember the last time he'd danced, though it had to have been years prior and after a good many glasses of rum. It wasn't the rum that had moved him to cut in on his best friend just now though, not that he'd admit it to anyone, even Tommy.

Something within had nudged his feet forward, and he hadn't refused, hadn't even tried to deny it. The desire to touch her and spend these moments with her was too strong to be ignored.

They'd only made it a few turns around the deck when her feet halted and she rose on her toes, her lips tickling his ear as she whispered, "I'm getting dizzy. I might need to lie down."

Declan pulled back. "Of course."

He shifted to her side, tucking her hand into the crook of his arm as he led her across the deck, ignoring the drunken stares of his crew and rolling his eyes at Tommy, who shot him a mischievous grin, complete with wagging brows.

Aoife stumbled halfway to the cabin door, both of her feet losing their steadiness. Before she could hit the floor, he had his arms in place to catch her, one arm cradling her neck, the other under her legs.

She let out a string of giggles as she snuggled up against his chest, wrapping her arm around his shoulders to pull herself ever closer to him.

Good thing the men had nearly finished the rum. Last thing he needed was a crew distracted by gossip about his love life.

Love.

The word invaded his mind without permission, and he stomped it away as he strode the last twenty feet across the deck, trying to ignore the heat growing inside him.

He managed to open the door with one hand, then stepped in and kicked it closed behind him, shutting out the sound of Tommy rallying the men to keep the party going despite his departure.

"Is the party over?" Aoife asked, her voice muffled by the folds of his shirt.

"It is for you," he said, his smile coating each word.

Her head fell back against his bicep, and he looked down to make sure she was going to be okay. She seemed happy enough, with her mouth pulled up into a half smile and her eyes drifting closed.

Lowering her onto her side of the bed, he debated how to best make her comfortable. It wouldn't be right to undress her at all, friends or not, but he could at least take her boots off for her. She rolled onto her back as he stepped to the foot of the bed and began unlacing the boots, slipping them off and placing them on the floor for her.

Her chest rose as she took in a deep breath, her eyes still closed. As if she were stepping into a pleasant dream, a sigh escaped in a soft moan, and it took every ounce of his resolve not to slide his body beside her and hold her as she slept.

Friends. That's what she'd suggested. That's all she wanted and all that could be managed in his line of work.

But that didn't keep his mind from drudging up all the images of his parents' happy marriage, reigniting the dream he'd thought he'd snuffed out, the dream of a family and a wife.

Friends only, he reminded himself as he kicked off his own boots and lowered himself onto his side of the bed, careful not to jostle her too much. Another soft moan escaped as she turned onto her side, facing him, with her eyes still closed.

A bit of her hair fell into her face, and he moved to brush it away, tucking it behind her ear. Though she didn't wake, her face turned toward his touch as if it felt the invisible tether that seemed to connect them now.

"Declan?" she whispered, and he wondered if she wasn't asleep as he'd assumed.

He hummed a response, and she said, "Thank you, for everything."

He didn't know if she could hear him, or if she'd even remember much of this night with how strong that rum had been, but he leaned down and touched his lips to her temple before whispering in her ear, "You're welcome, Aoife."

Neither of them said another word as he pulled back, positioning himself onto his side, where he spent the rest of the night watching her, wondering what this new path might bring for them both.

FROM THESE DARK DEPTHS

BOOK TWO

*For Joel, who loves me unconditionally,
and for all who have felt the sting of betrayal.*

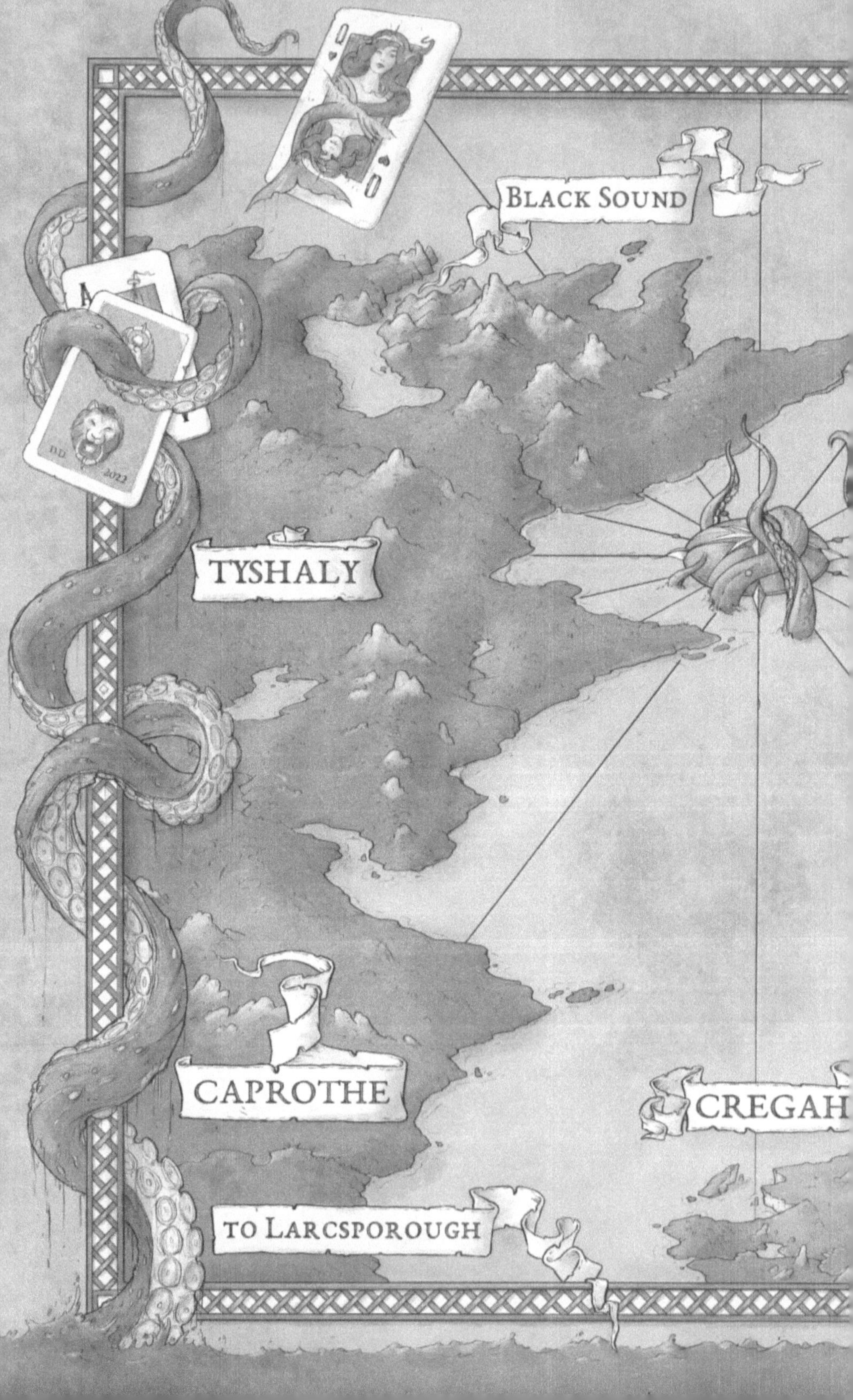

BLACK SOUND
TYSHALY
CAPROTHE
CREGAH
TO LARCSPOROUGH

TURVALA
DAORNA
HAVIERN
THE AISLING SEA
FOXHAVEN
SLAND
NBRACKEN MOUNTAINS
PORT MORSHAN
THE COUNCIL

CHAPTER I

DECLAN

IT NEVER GOT EASIER. Even after seven years of avoiding this, Declan McCallagh's stomach still clenched in protest, his feet shifting on the pine needles that covered the dirt path. They hadn't told him who. They never did, only providing a time he needed to be here, ready.

Here wasn't marked by anything more than a large boulder off to the side of the road, whose black soil was divided into two wheel ruts with a strip of grass between them trying desperately to survive. To the infrequent traveler it was an inconsequential rock, not unlike the ones that could be found along the coasts of Cregah. But to Declan it meant doom.

Not for him, thankfully, but for the poor soul who had crossed the Council.

Whether he was the only pirate who struggled with this arrangement between the Council and the lesser pirates, he didn't know. He'd never asked anyone and never would, not when his reputation hung by a quickly fraying thread, all his hard-won prestige at risk of being dissolved by the Pirate Lords targeting him one after the other.

Declan forced himself to remain still, steeling his expression as the rumble of carriage wheels hit his ears, still faint but growing louder. They were coming fast. Faster than usual.

Urgency wasn't typically part of this gig as most of those found guilty and sentenced to *exile* came along willingly, either unaware of their true fate or accepting their martyrdom for their rebel cause.

But this. This one was different.

The pounding of hooves against the hard packed soil reverberated in his head even before he could see them.

Drawing in a deep breath, his fingers itched to hold the familiar steel of his dagger that remained concealed at his waist. Silly how they expected him to dispatch of their *exiles* while still holding to the forbidding of weapons.

He ignored the urge to reach for his blade, putting on a bored expression as he crossed his arms over his chest and continued leaning against the rock. The door flew open as the carriage skidded to a stop directly in front of him. Standing, he prepared to grab the exile so he could escort them to their fate, but he stopped and waited, watching as a mess of red hair filled the doorway to the carriage. The woman's back was to him, her hands gripping the edges of the opening, screaming with desperation as her captors tried to push her out.

Declan might have found the display humorous if he didn't know what the woman faced, what she fought and screamed to avoid. Pity and remorse brewed within him, tightening their grip on his throat.

You're a damned pirate! Get it together!

With a clearing of his throat, as if he were about to speak, he dislodged the invading emotions and stepped forward, wrapping his arm around her waist as the women inside the carriage worked to get her fingers loose from the carriage.

She continued fighting, kicking and flailing, screaming and writhing, as Declan carried her away toward the boulder. He'd need to hold onto this one. More than the others he'd dealt with.

"Good luck with this one!" One of the women called. The door hadn't even latched shut before the driver sent the horse off with a flick of the reins.

Declan pulled her close against him, ignoring how her hair crowded his face. He needed to get her to calm down or he'd have to find some way to knock her unconscious. He probably should have, especially with this feisty one, but something within him pushed him to avoid that move.

Still, time was against him here. Even under the cover of these tall trees, he could see the sun already nearing its highest point. Gavin and Tommy would be arriving at the pub in a matter of hours. He needed to get this over with.

Holding her tight he tried to coax her to quiet down, whispering against her hair to relax. A laugh echoed in his head at the absurdity of his request. Would he have relaxed in her position? Would he have gone without this same fight?

He waited for her body to tire itself out, for her growls to quiet. When he felt she had finally given up, he loosened his hold on her. But before he could move her to face him, her foot came down hard on his, her elbow landing in his gut at the same time.

That was unexpected.

But he was no amateur, and he regained his hold of her waist, growling as he did.

"Hey!" he barked at her. "Stop it. Now. Fighting will do you no good here."

But she continued to buck against his hold, her feet scrambling for purchase against the black soil. This was not going at all as planned. Perhaps another tactic would work.

"Let's stop. Talk. Relax a bit. This doesn't have to go badly."

His words must have surprised her—as intended—because she froze and turned her head to look at him over her shoulder. Her glare pierced him, searching to see if there was any deception in his words.

"Of course it has to go badly," she spat at him. "I know what you do for them."

"Aye," he replied, allowing the remorse he'd shoved aside earlier to return and soften his expression. "Doesn't mean I like it. Doesn't mean it has to hurt."

"So you want to talk?" she asked and started to pull away from him.

Though he eased his hold, he kept his guard up, ready to grab her again if she tried anything again.

He dipped his chin. "Aye. Let's talk."

When he was sure she wasn't going to dart off—not that he wouldn't be able to catch her if she did—he lowered his arms and took a step back. She turned fully to him now, her arms crossing defiantly across her chest. Despite her curves having filled out, this girl was no woman. She couldn't have been more than twenty years old, if that. The smooth alabaster planes of her face—framed by deep red waves of hair—showed little weathering. She didn't get outside much.

She scowled at him, but didn't make to move away. Standing there, her arms still crossed, she eyed him. Seconds went by and then minutes, with them facing off in silence.

Declan searched the blues of her eyes, wondering what this girl—a girl so young—could have possibly done to be marked for *exile* by the Council.

What do you care?

Giving his head a shake, as if it could whisk away the scolding words, he started to say something. But she spoke first.

"Well? You wanted to talk? What about?"

He had originally planned to ask her who she was and what she had done. But something churned in his gut, warned him about getting too—not attached, but—involved. His mind whirred with an ominous feeling that this job, this *fee* he had to pay to the Council, was one he should complete and forget as quickly as possible.

But could he do that? Eight names repeated in his head, and with each one, a face appeared, some scared and begging for mercy, others at peace with their fate.

Taking a life wasn't against his moral code. He did so when he needed to, but he preferred it to be his own rival or in defense of his crew. Being hired to dispatch those who posed no threat to him and had done him no wrong gnawed at him.

No, he didn't care. He couldn't. Wouldn't. But then he couldn't quiet that part of him that insisted everyone had a right to be remembered. Even if only by their executioner.

Shifting his feet, he forced himself to relax a bit, hoping it might put her more at ease with him. The thought caused him to laugh internally, though he was careful to keep it from escaping. As if she could or should be at ease with the man tasked with...

He cut off the thought with a question. "What's your name?"

The girl's brow shot up in surprise, but she blinked it away quickly before answering. "Lani. You?"

"Declan."

"And you're a pirate."

He answered with a mere nod.

"Hired to take *care* of me."

"That's one way to put it," he said. "And you? What landed you in such a... predicament?"

She didn't respond immediately, but instead swallowed hard. Her eyes glazed over as if lost in a daydream. Tears began to form, but she blinked them away before they could spill over. Taking a deep breath, her whole torso shifting as she filled her lungs, she lifted her face to the tree tops. When she looked back at him, there was no longer any trace of the emotion that had been there a moment ago, her blue eyes now frozen over.

"I fell in love." Her jaw tightened before she added, "And I trusted the wrong person."

"Classic blunder, that," Declan said. "The trusting part, that is. Though I don't know why love would warrant such a sentence from the Council. Did you fall for one of the Lords? Or perhaps had an affair—"

Lani lifted an arm, keeping the other tucked tight across her ribs, and examined her nails, as one might do when bored. And then ever so slowly, she turned her palm toward him, exposing the delicate white of her forearm where the unmistakable design lay in stark contrast, its twists of smoky shadows seeming to creep from beneath her sleeve down to her wrist.

Declan's gut tightened, but he somehow maintained his bored expression as he spoke. "Ah, I see. And I take it you didn't fall for one of the Lords you were to be matched with?"

Once more crossing her arms in front of her, she gave him a small shake of her head.

"Well, this is certainly a first for me."

Her chin snapped up, her eyes burning with surprise.

"Not my first... well, you know," Declan said, as his mind chided him for being such a bumbling idiot. "But it is my first time with an heir to the Council."

Lani pursed her lips. "And what did you do to deserve such an *honor*?"

"Wrong time, wrong place," he said, and lifted his hands to the side in a shrug. "And no money."

Her eyes went wide for a moment before she uttered a quiet *interesting*.

"So the heirs don't know then," he said, not quite sure why he bothered going down this path in the conversation, but then again, any information was worth having. One never knew when one might need leverage of some kind.

"No." The word was barely over a whisper.

"But you knew."

Dipping her chin she said, "I had my suspicions. And I guess I was right, as we are nowhere near the docks and a ship to take me away."

"Aye." Declan gestured with a nod to the nearly invisible path that twisted through the trees beyond the boulder, noticeable only by those who knew it existed. "That trail doesn't lead to any ship, but it is a different sort of freedom perhaps."

Lani looked over her shoulder briefly, and when she turned back to him tears lined her bottom lashes. He waited for her to break down, but then this girl didn't seem the type to shy away from, well, anything. She lifted her chin, squared her shoulders, and lowered her arms until her hands were clasped together before her waist. "Well, let's get it over with then. You probably have other things you need to be doing."

Declan led the way through the trees, walking the entire twenty minutes in somber silence, with only the sound of their footsteps on the bed of pine needles that covered the ground. Until the sound of the Aisling Sea—usually a comfort to him—joined in, faint at first and growing louder as they neared their destination.

Her sharp inhale broke the silence—and echoed in Declan's chest—as they stepped into a clearing in the trees.

The sight never got easier to behold.

Not ten feet ahead of them, the ground simply disappeared. Stretching fifty feet to their left and right, it was no more than twenty-five feet across at its widest point —which lay directly in front of them. The trees didn't venture near the edge, as if the drop made them as uncomfortable as it did Declan. Lush grass filled the space between the pit and the forest, and the clearing might have been pleasant if it had existed anywhere else.

Lani approached the cave on careful toes, testing each footing to see if the ground gave way before putting her full weight into her step. Declan could have told her there was no point in doing that. The ground here might as well have been stone. When he'd come here all those years ago for that first exile, he'd wondered how such unforgiving soil could support this forest, but every visit since then simply left his stomach dropping into a pit of its own.

"How deep is it?" Lani asked, the words coming out barely audible over the sea's waves below and the breeze that had begun to pass through the trees above, as if the trees themselves were bidding her a farewell.

"I don't know, myself, but—" He stopped short.

"What? What were you going to say?" Lani had turned to look over her shoulder at him, her blue eyes boring into his, forcing him to look away.

What harm was there in telling her the truth?

It would terrify her unnecessarily, he thought.

But there was nothing about this situation that would warrant anything less.

"I, well." He paused to rub the back of his hand across his brow before finally meeting her gaze once again. "I imagine it's rather deep. Over a thousand feet at least."

She turned back to the black void that lay inches from her toes. "And how could you guess that?"

"Based on the length of their screams." He winced as he watched her arms begin to tremble. So many times he had imagined what the fall would feel like, to feel the air rushing past you, to not be able to see what awaited you until you...

When she spoke again, there was no hint of the fear that still coursed visibly through her body, and in any other moment he might have marveled at the control and poise she exhibited. "You said it didn't have to hurt. How? I can't imagine being thrown onto solid rock—or whatever awaits down there—from this height would be painless. So, how?"

"There are ways to kill…" He nearly added *you,* but stopped himself again. "…that are quick and relatively painless, as far as I am aware. I have, after all, never experienced them myself."

She gave another glance over her shoulder. "But you've done it often enough to assume."

"Aye. After the first exile I was tasked with, after hearing those first initial screams as they fell, it affected me more than I had expected. Haunted me. More than I care to admit. A pirate shouldn't have a problem with it, but there I was, facing nightmares after throwing them over that edge. So after that, I offered each a choice."

"Who would choose to be alive for that fall?" she asked as she turned fully away from the drop off to look at him.

"You'd be surprised. Some welcome the chance to feel the wind upon their faces one last time. Perhaps they want to be reminded that they once lived, that there are things of beauty in this world—even if just in the feel of air on their skin."

"You're rather poetic for a pirate. You don't meet too many of those."

And you won't get the chance to meet another.

He kept that thought to himself, at least, but he let the silence stretch out between them. He could have offered a witty remark, a word to tear down the Lords and their fleets. But the darkness behind her seemed to widen, gaping like a yawning mouth, reminding him time was quickly fading.

Taking a cautious step toward her, Declan opened his mouth to speak, but Lani cut him off.

"Is it time for me to make my choice?" While her expression held its steeled composure, her words quivered, betraying the fear she was trying so hard to contain.

"Aye. Only delaying the inevitable, and I do have other things I need to do today."

That's an understatement. Why are you being nice to her? Just push her in and get it over with.

It's what any other pirate would have done.

"Why are you being so nice to me?" Her question echoed his own thoughts.

"Would you rather I be mean? In addition to the whole killing you thing." He narrowed his eyes at her, taking another step toward her until there was no more than a foot between them. Close enough he could reach out and shove and be done with it.

But he didn't.

"Still. Why? You're a pirate."

He couldn't stop from pulling his mouth into a smirk. "As if I could forget."

"I suppose it makes sense, though," she said, her lifting a shoulder before relaxing more than she ought to given the situation. When he didn't respond, she continued. "No need to worry about your reputation with me. Not like I'm going to have the chance to ruin your *good* name. Still, I'd think it'd be easier to do this, be less traumatizing for you, if you gave yourself over to the pirate within. I mean at this point I'm starting to wonder if you're a real pirate at all."

He gritted his teeth as her words struck a nerve. She was right. He wasn't acting much like a pirate here.

She inched toward him, her expression calmer than it had any right to be. "I wouldn't be surprised if you simply stepped aside and let me go."

Declan grabbed her then, the force causing her to stumble back, though he kept her from going over the edge. "Don't let my politeness fool you, Lani." He hardened his gaze at her, searching her eyes for any of the fear that should be swimming there. "I might have more manners than the other pirates, but I am still a pirate. Now, make your choice. And quickly. Because if you don't, I will make it for you."

Lani stared back at him, confident at first, as if she were still testing him, searching for the cracks in his hard exterior. But she would find none. He'd wasted enough time here already. His plan had been to get her to calm down, and he'd done that.

When she still hadn't moved or spoken, he tightened his fingers around her arms, and stepped forward again, edging her heels past the edge of the drop until she stood on only her toes with her body leaning slightly over the darkness. She grabbed his jacket, that desperation for survival kicking in, fear rushing into her eyes, her head gave tiny shakes, begging him to be different from the rest, to not do what was required of him.

He could say he was sorry, but it would do him no good to let that piece of him out. He'd already allowed it to breathe for too long outside the wall he'd built around it. He shoved it back, securing it once again.

"Choose."

"Don't," she whispered, her terror increasing as he let her body angle away from him more.

"Now. Or I will."

He counted five seconds before he tensed his muscles, preparing to push her and be done with it, readying himself for the inevitable screams, knowing he wouldn't forget them soon enough.

"NO! I'll choose." Her words stopped him in mid-motion, and he raised his brows at her, a silent request for her answer. "Not like this. I don't want to know I'm falling. I don't want the air or whatever it is the others seek. Just end it. Quickly. Please."

Declan pulled her a few inches away from the edge, and without another word, he released one hand, keeping her firmly held with the other as he reached for his blade. She closed her eyes and breathed deeply, one last breath before the end came.

He didn't look away as he lifted his dagger. He looked her over one last time, this girl who had done nothing more than fall in love with the wrong person and dare to dream of a life she could never have, and pulling the air, ripe with the scent of the sea and the pine trees, he drove his blade in just behind her collar bone and pulled it out in one clean motion.

She gave a gasp, her eyes flashing open so he could watch the light in them dim quickly. With the dagger still in hand, her blood smearing across its smooth surface, he closed her eyes with the edge of his hand before letting her lifeless body fall away into the darkness.

He backed away from the edge, forcing coldness into his features, as if there was anyone here to witness his reaction. Wiping her blood from his dagger with the sash around his waist, he turned, not to go back to the road, but to pass around the massive hole. Eventually he would go back—back to Morshan, back to the pub, back to his men and his ship—but if he was going to focus on the next task, he needed to clear his head.

And he knew just how to do that on this island.

CHAPTER 2
AOIFE

ALL OF AOIFE's dreams started the same. Every time she closed her eyes, her mind whisked her away to the forest path leading to Morshan from the council hall. The scene mirrored that day down to the most minute detail. The whisper of the wind through the trees overhead. The puddles of dappled sunlight she disrupted as she walked.

And Lani.

"I don't know how you didn't know, Aoife," Lani said, her tone void of any derision or disdain. Rather, she spoke the words with gentleness. "With how curious you always were, why did you question everything but this?"

Aoife swallowed hard. There was so much she wanted to tell her sister, strings of apologies and remorseful pleas for forgiveness, though she knew forgiveness was impossible now. At least from Lani. But the air thickened around her, slowing her legs and constricting her lungs so that no sound could be made.

Squeezing her eyes shut, she shook her head back and forth slowly, telling herself it wasn't real. She wasn't suffocating. She wasn't back on Cregah.

And Lani wasn't alive.

That thought forced her eyes open to verify it was a dream and that Lani and the forest had disappeared. But as she looked around, her heart quaked at the sight of Lani standing before her in a grassy meadow. The Aisling Sea was close enough that Aoife could hear its waters crash against the cliffs of her home.

The darkened sky scared her, but not nearly as much as the figure beside her sister. A man.

Aoife wanted to close her eyes, to save herself from having to witness this scene and accept it as truth, but her body refused to obey. When she was finally able to take a breath, she nearly recoiled at the familiar scent of sea mist and rum. Even if she had been able to shut out the image before her, she wouldn't have been able to ignore that smell, as it called up images of wet footsteps in black sand, the sharpness of a stone wall at her back, the tickle of his breath in her ear, the touch of his fingers along her neck, and the sound of her name on his lips.

As much as she wanted to ignore it all, she also yearned to hold on to each sensation like a treasured gift that needed protecting from a world that would rip it from her and destroy it.

But he has already done that, her mind reminded her, and as if on cue, the man beside Lani turned.

It was ridiculous to hope for the man to be someone else. It was always him. Always Declan.

But not as she had last seen him.

This was the Declan who had mocked her in the cove and accosted her in the alley. This was the Declan whose gray eyes gleamed not with hopeful love but callous apathy. A smirk turned up one side of his lips, and he winked at Aoife before turning to Lani, who waited calmly beside him.

The blade appeared in his hand, from where Aoife didn't know, but when he raised it toward her sister, she didn't run to stop him. She didn't call out to warn Lani. She didn't do anything but stand there, frozen.

Declan turned his head back to her, his blade still pointed at its target. "It might as well be you standing here." He flipped the dagger and caught the blade carefully in his hand before offering it to her, his eyes alight with excitement. "Would you like to do the honors?"

Aoife frantically looked between Declan and Lani as her chest tightened with the understanding that he was right. Her carelessness with her sister's secret had been as effective a weapon as the knife he now held out to her.

She whispered her answer to him, declining his grotesque offer. In an instant he righted the blade in his opposite hand and swept it across Lani's neck.

Blood sprayed across Aoife's face in the same alarming way it had on that beach in Foxhaven. Still, she couldn't move, other than to look down where Lani now lay, not in the clearing but in the council library. Blood pooled around her, as it had the servant who had helped them.

Aoife remained silent, unable to utter even one sound of surprise or grief, as she stared down at her sister. If anyone else was with her in this vision of the library, she didn't know. It was just her and Lani sharing a moment as the guilt suffocated her. That was what she deserved, to be killed by her guilt. Everyone else suffered for her mistakes. Why shouldn't she?

Declan had killed Lani. In every dream, over and over, he did it again and again. It was like her mind needed her to understand the truth and not foolishly give in to the hope that it hadn't been real and he had found a way to keep Lani alive while tricking the council.

But he was a pirate. And this was what pirates did.

From the shadows, Declan reappeared, whispering her name.

Blood soaked his clothes, covered his face and his hands. His eyes brimmed with tears of remorse that threatened to spill over at any moment. He held his hands out to her, not *reaching but begging with palms up, as if her forgiveness was something tangible she could place in them.*

"I love you," he whispered with blood-smeared lips.

Aoife woke with a start. A million tiny legs crawled over her chest with the weight of a person, crushing her and making it impossible for her lungs to take in the air she desperately needed. Placing a hand on her chest, she pressed her fist against her sternum, wishing it would be enough to quell the attack.

But it refused.

Her fingers pulled the chain at her collar, and she lifted the glass vial of black sand from underneath her shirt, squeezing as hard as she could. But the panic only pressed harder, slithering over her skin faster.

Breathe, she commanded herself. She longed for Declan to comfort her—like he did before—and then cringed from shame. She shouldn't want him or his help. Not after he had lied to her and betrayed her.

I love you.

The words from the memory and the dream collided within her chest, and she gasped just as she had in the cove.

If he truly loved her, he would have been honest. But he'd kept it from her.

Every time the wave of ire began to ebb, that fact would barrel its way through her thoughts, pushing her back into the depths of her bitterness.

Aoife was sure she was going crazy.

Her mind constantly shifted from wanting to forgive Declan to wanting to make him feel as betrayed as she did. She wanted to hurt him in return, but then her guilt surged once more, reminding her she was not the only person to ever have been hurt, nor would she be the last. Even knowing he was likely on his way to his death in the Black Sound, her heart held its iron grip on her misery. All while some small part of her wanted to forgive him, yearned to throw all of the anger into the depths, to grab hold of him and never let go.

Around and around her emotions twirled her, her broken heart like a life raft caught in a tempest.

She didn't know which way was up. Which choice led to happiness. If any of them would.

Tommy had insisted she try to get some rest. It would take several days to get to the Black Sound, and Gavin was pushing the crew to sail as quickly as possible even though the winds weren't cooperating.

All her attempts to rest had failed. She couldn't shut her eyes, so she simply stared at the wooden ceiling above her bed—their bed—as she had done so many times during her short stay on the ship. But she couldn't avoid the emptiness of the cabin any more than she could avoid the chaos in her mind.

She didn't dare look at his side of the bed. That wouldn't help her panic attacks.

Breathe, she reminded herself, clenching her teeth when she heard it not in her own voice but in his.

Tightness clutched at her chest, taking hold until she felt she might collapse into herself. Maybe that was what was best for everyone.

She'd helped no one.

Not Lani.

Not Tommy.

Not the poor servant.

Not Declan.

She'd begged him to let her help. What had she been thinking? That a week on a pirate ship could suddenly undo a life's worth of awkwardness and stumbling? Had she thought she could simply wish herself to change? To be different? Better?

Tears should have welled at all these thoughts, but they seemed trapped inside a vault within her, incapable of being conjured up. Numbed by the overwhelming emptiness.

A throat cleared from across the room. How had she not heard the door open and shut?

"Not able to sleep?" Tommy asked, his voice stronger and less weary than she'd expected. Here his best friend was heading toward certain death, and he was speaking as if it was any old day.

Perhaps this was any old day for him though. What did Aoife know about pirate life after only one week?

Pushing herself up into a seated position, she kept one fist clenched to her chest as she worked to stretch out the discomfort between her shoulder blades before meeting his eyes. She didn't say anything but offered a quick shake of her head in answer.

"You should try."

Irritation bubbled up from its coffin within her, and she glared at him, jaw clenching as tight as her fists.

"It's not like I haven't tried, Tommy."

She shouldn't be so short with him, but she couldn't help it. Feeling frustration —even if unwarranted—was oddly comforting.

Though it did nothing to quell the anxiety that made this exchange even more cumbersome.

Breathe, Aoife. Just breathe.

But Tommy—the ever-patient saint that he was—didn't appear bothered by her biting tone.

"I know." He remained in the doorway, not leaning against the frame as Declan had done so many times during their talks, but standing awkwardly like he was itching to get away from this room. "You should still try. Maybe the sisters could do something to help you rest."

"Damn fae." The words fell from her lips in a sharp whisper.

"What?"

With a shake of her head, she dismissed his question. Her issue with the trio of fae had little to do with their actions or their personalities. It had nothing to do with anything they could control. It was simply them being what they were created to be.

Graceful. Beautiful. Helpful.

Perfect.

Tommy wouldn't understand, nor could Aoife ever admit to anyone how she felt wholly insignificant beside them. It was her problem. Not theirs. Not his. She was the problem. Like always.

The phantom attack at her chest intensified, but she managed to draw in a deep breath, close her eyes, and focus on breathing. Surviving.

"Maybe rum then?"

She flashed her eyes open and turned her chin in question.

"That always has me sleeping like a baby." Though he offered a lopsided shrug, his words lacked their typical relaxed quality, and his eyes seemed dimmer than usual. He apparently wasn't as unfazed by the situation as Aoife had assumed.

"And it leaves me with a nasty headache." Her words dripped with bitterness. A bitterness that coated her tongue and singed her heart.

You're being unfair.

She was. And she knew it. But she couldn't control it. The irritability had taken on a life of its own, and it seemed to feed off the wounded parts of her heart, growing bigger and stronger and more formidable with each negative thought.

Maybe I am going crazy.

It seemed the only explanation for the complete lack of control she had over her emotions and thoughts. How could it be possible to *know* your thoughts were extreme and damaging and unproductive yet have no ability to stop them from attacking you? Even her mind had betrayed her.

"You okay?" Tommy's quiet question eased its way around the sea of grief that was drowning her. Such a simple question. Two words. But they were like a lifeline tossed toward her, and all she had to do was grasp it, let it pull her back in.

Tommy must have taken her silence as more irritation, because he rushed to explain. "It's a dumb question, I know. None of us are okay."

Aoife drew in a steadying breath. The tightness at her chest increased, but she fought it back with the words Declan had offered.

It's not you.

You aren't broken.

It doesn't control you.

While the feeling remained, she finally managed to wriggle herself free—as free as she could be from such internal torment. She stared down at her hands. "Do you think we'll reach him in time?"

Tommy's silence drew Aoife's attention to him. He roughed a hand over his mouth and along his stubbled chin before he lifted a shoulder. "I don't know. But I hope so. Even if we don't, we won't be too far behind them. And we have the fae. They can help us save him."

"And help us get the dagger."

"Aye. That too."

Aoife shifted in her seat, failing to ignore the way the anxiety had settled within her. "Maybe the dagger could help me overcome...this." She pressed a hand to her chest once again.

"The panic?" He offered a comforting smile. "Don't look at me all surprised. You're not the first person I've seen plagued with it."

"If it's enchanted to bring victory—"

"Victory over adversaries. I don't think it helps much against the enemies we carry inside ourselves."

Aoife breathed deep, but the rush of air did nothing to quell her unease. "If it did, even more people would be seeking it."

"Aye. Not everyone desires success in battle campaigns or political contests. But none of us are free from the demons within."

Desperate to change the subject, Aoife asked the first question she could think of. "How is the rest of the crew doing? Are they going mad having the fae aboard? Are they pushing you to throw us all overboard?"

Tommy gave one of his signature laughs, though it lacked its usual heartiness. "They are managing well enough, if only because they have no other choice. Even the new crewmen were so impressed by Declan's welcoming them the other night that they're as determined as the rest of us to get him back, even if it means having the fae around. And having to bunk with me and Gavin."

"You poor guys, giving up your quarters to wallow with the common crew." Aoife had meant for the comment to be funny, but it fell short. Still, Tommy laughed again, most likely from pity rather than actual humor.

"Aye. I don't know if we'll get much rest either with how loud they all are. Half of them snore like an anchor being raised from the depths. Others mumble and talk in their slumber. I've had to stick bits of cloth in my ears to get any sort of rest, regardless of the time of day."

"Well, if you're desperate for rest, you can always sleep in here if you want." She cleared her throat and felt her cheeks warm. "When I'm not in here, that is. We can take shifts sleeping."

"I might have to take you up on that offer." The mention of sleep must have reminded him of his own need for it, because his jaw dropped open into a yawn he failed to hide behind his hand.

"Seriously, Tommy," she said and stood up from the bed. She motioned to the feather mattress with her arm. "I'm not getting any rest at the moment anyway. Lie down. Close your eyes. I'll head out and see what I can do out on the deck. Maybe I'll find someone to teach me to sail."

Tommy drew in a deep breath, and Aoife waited for him to refuse her offer, but he didn't. Instead, he walked past her and seated himself on the edge of the bed, his gaze settling on the floor beyond his boots.

"Thanks, Aoife. I appreciate it. But do me a favor?"

She hummed in response.

"Don't fall overboard. Declan would have my head if I let anything happen to you."

Aoife tried to swallow the ball of emotion that rose to her throat at the mention of Declan's name. But it wouldn't budge, preventing her from voicing any kind of response.

Tommy didn't seem to mind though. He pushed himself back onto the bed, crossed his arms behind his head, and closed his eyes.

She listened to his breathing lengthen into soft whispers before she turned to leave as quietly as she could.

At least one of them could sleep.

I'll sleep when I'm dead. Or after we get Declan. Whichever comes first.

CHAPTER 3
TOMMY

THE SOUND of Aoife's footsteps had long since faded away. Still, Tommy couldn't sleep. He'd closed his eyes and tried to concentrate on his breathing, but when the door had clicked shut, he'd allowed his eyes to flash open and study the wooden beams above Declan's bed.

His whole body felt heavy, slow, and his eyelids wanted to slide closed, but he forced them to remain open. He couldn't face what awaited him. Not yet.

He hadn't explained his fatigue to Aoife, and thankfully she hadn't asked. No doubt she assumed it was merely due to the stress of Declan heading toward ravenous sirens and the challenge of having to step into a leadership role he'd never wanted. And while he could have claimed his sleep was plagued by bad dreams—which was true—he didn't trust his tongue to not divulge everything. Especially with this exhaustion clouding his senses.

If only nightmares were the only thing he avoided. That would have been far less embarrassing.

Whenever he dared close his eyes, it wasn't the pirate slashing him across the chest he saw. It was her face. Maura. Youngest sister. Tormentor of his heart. Fae.

After he'd been wounded by Captain Madigen's man, the sisters had taken turns overseeing his healing, resting to replenish their powers before taking up where the other had left off. He had been unconscious at first, but when he came to, it was Maura's face he saw first, her golden eyes shining down at him as if she were studying him rather than mending his injuries. She'd said nothing as his eyes opened but smiled in an almost shy way. It had seemed contrary to his under-standing of fae—which was admittedly quite limited.

They'd remained there in silence, her hands lightly pressed against his bare chest, as he took stock of his physical state. Nothing hurt anymore. No trace of the burning sharpness that had settled into him once shock had released its grip on his mind. No aching in his muscles. No throbbing of his head. Surely, he'd thought, his healing was complete, and her touch was unnecessary. But when he'd opened his mouth to tell her as much, he hadn't been able to push the words out. He'd swallowed them back down, where they sank beneath the waves of indecipherable emotions crashing against the edges of his heart.

Certainly it couldn't have been more than an involuntary reaction to a pretty face. He knew nothing about her. Yet, Tommy had seen many a pretty face—and plenty of other pretty feminine features—during his travels on the sea without the conjuring up of such a strange tension. Tension in certain parts of him, sure. He was only a man, after all. But never in his chest, his throat, his head.

Tommy had heard stories of the wounded or ill developing a connection with their healers, and he was certain that was all it was.

A passing feeling.

A common, albeit strange, phenomenon.

Nothing more.

Yet the feeling hadn't passed, and it showed no signs of waning. If anything, it seemed to be strengthening even as he avoided her at all costs. But try as he might, he couldn't avoid her in his sleep, and part of him wondered if her powers included intruding into one's dreams. Or perhaps bewitching men into falling for her. He couldn't deny something had happened to him, though he didn't know exactly what to call it.

Love was impossible. The thought of it happening so fast was absurd. Everyone knew that wasn't how it worked. Love didn't happen instantaneously. It developed with time, conversation, touch, and—at least in Aoife and Declan's case—a bit of arguing and frustration.

While his mind urged him to avoid Maura, something within him seemed to seek her out, as if a void had been created in his chest and only she could fill it. He wanted to know everything about her. What life had been like before her imprisonment. What she had missed most while locked away. What haunted her dreams and what moved her to rise in the morning. Her favorite smell, color, memory. Everything.

There was far more to her than eyes of melted gold and a sweet yet devilish smile. Her beauty was merely the ornate entryway into a world he knew nothing about, a world he'd only caught glimpses of while he'd been healing. A world he wanted to step into, to explore, and to call home.

He shook his head desperately, his eyes closed tight. None of this would help them save Declan. But neither would being sleep-deprived.

One way or another, you'll have to face her eventually.

The thought echoed in his mind as he succumbed to the lure of sleep, letting the weariness take over. He was too tired to keep fighting the dreams.

When he opened his eyes once more, he found Maura standing before him. Even in his sleep, he knew it wasn't real. They were in an empty room. Whether it was on a ship or on land, he couldn't tell, couldn't see much past her. It was as though she was giving off her own light. She smiled—a coy yet somehow innocent curve of her mouth—as she raised her hand and beckoned him forward with a graceful wave of her fingers.

His feet moved against his will, taking him forward until he was close enough to feel the warmth emanating from her. Searching her eyes, he silently asked her the question he couldn't utter aloud.

What is happening to me?

As if this were an ailment or an infection that only needed the right poultice to be cured.

He shouldn't be dreaming of Maura. Not when Declan was missing. Not when they had so little hope of reaching him in time.

He tried to back away from her, but he hadn't made it a half step when her arms lifted, her hands cupping his neck. Despite her intensity and swiftness, it wasn't an aggressive gesture but a caring one. Loving.

Tommy swallowed hard. Maura's thumbs brushed against his ears as she ran her fingers through his hair.

It's not real. It's not real. It's only a dream.

But even as he repeated these words, he knew he was lying to himself.

When he woke up, she would disappear, but the feelings wouldn't. He'd be left with this yearning to be near her and to know her, to care for her and to live life beside her. A yearning for something that could never be, could never work.

He was human.

She was fae.

And she was heading to Larcsporough after all of this. If they survived.

He couldn't follow her. He couldn't abandon Declan and Gavin and the *Siren's Song* to follow Maura south. His place was here, on the ship, on the Aisling. And Maura belonged with her kin. While he didn't know why she was needed, he couldn't shake the sense that it was rather important.

No matter how much he hated it, they were from two separate worlds. Worlds that could never truly mix.

There was no point in torturing himself by allowing this to go anywhere. Even in his dreams. So when she leaned into him, he steeled himself, using all his strength to not glance at her mouth, where her tongue moistened her lower lip in anticipation. He didn't want to hurt her, couldn't dream of hurting her, but if he pursued this, if he let himself take another step into her life, that was what would surely happen.

Lifting his hands, he grabbed her arms below her shoulders and pushed her away as gently as he could. She didn't fight him, didn't argue, but allowed her fingers to slide away from his neck and drift back down to her sides, where they clenched the fabric of her dress. Her gaze burned into his, and the passion he'd seen in her eyes moments before had been replaced with a deep mourning that pressed into his chest so powerfully he expected his heart to be crushed against his spine.

"I'm sorry," he whispered. Again and again, he offered up his apologies as he backed away from her. And with a jolt, she disappeared, along with the room they'd been in, leaving him surrounded by nothingness.

His eyes flew open.

The ship had stopped.

And there were only a few possible reasons why. None of them good.

Forcing the intense longing and bitterness to retreat to some far corner of his consciousness, he rose from the bed and made his way across the cabin. He was acting captain. Whether he knew how to fulfill the role or not, he needed to focus, and he couldn't do that with her haunting him in both reality and his dreams.

He needed to end it—whatever it was—and soon.

CHAPTER 4
DECLAN

THE TANG of iron coated Declan's tongue, as sharp as the metal that dug into his wrists behind his back. How long he'd been here, in the dark and rank innards of the *Curse Bringer*, he wasn't sure. When he'd come to, he'd been confused and half-thinking he was back on his own ship. The only clue to the contrary had been that he was cold, uncomfortable, and alone instead of in his bed relaxing with Aoife beside him.

Aoife.

Her name instantly conjured up images against his will. The look in her eyes when she'd denied him the forgiveness he'd needed. The way her expression had twisted in confusion and disbelief when those damned words had spilled from his mouth.

I love you.

He hadn't meant to say it. He hadn't even known he could say it until that moment.

She probably thought it was a disingenuous attempt at getting back into her good graces after what he'd done to her. Another lie to get what he wanted.

His head ached, the pain throbbing behind his eyes and radiating down from his ears before settling into the base of his skull.

The knot on the back of his head where they'd struck him begged for attention, but with his arms shackled behind his back, there was no hope of checking to see how bad it was. They must have hit him rather hard though, because he could sense a sticky mess of blood in his hair; it pulled whenever he moved his head.

Where they were taking him he wasn't sure, but given how angry Callum had been about his deception, it was no doubt somewhere undesirable.

Like everything in my life.

He chided himself for the thought. Now was not the time to get depressed. If he had any hope of getting off this blasted ship and back to his own, back to his crew, back to Aoife...

He shoved the image of her away as best he could. Replaying her disapproval over and over wouldn't help him. Not now. He could deal with that later. But now he had to devise an escape.

Heavy boots sounded on the ladder at the far side of the room, and Declan lay his aching head against the side of the hull, closing his eyes.

The footsteps were slow but determined. Whether it was Callum, his quarter-master, or another member of the crew, he couldn't tell, but he was certain they weren't coming to see him for anything good.

Declan slowed his breathing as he counted the steps. When they stopped, he focused on the breathing of his visitor—low, raspy, labored. Whoever Callum had sent, it wasn't someone in peak physical shape. But he was likely one of the larger men, especially if he'd come down here alone. Callum either underestimated Declan, or this crewman was tough enough he knew he could handle Declan on his own.

Unless he's just bringing you food.

His stomach grumbled at the thought.

A loud clang rang through the room, reverberating through the floor and up Declan's spine, and he squeezed his eyes tighter before lazily opening them. He'd been right. Standing before him was a rather large individual, half as wide as he was tall. He was, in fact, quite huge, having to duck his head to fit into this small section of the ship.

Although he certainly had the advantage of size, being in such a confined space might even the odds in Declan's favor.

Declan mulled over his different options for attack even as he asked, "Can't a man get some sleep here?" He kept his words slow and coated with grogginess.

The man huffed out a gruff laugh—or what Declan assumed to be a laugh, despite no mirth showing on the man's face. It was either a laugh or the man had a sudden tickle in the back of his throat that needed clearing.

"Cap'n wants to see you."

Declan looked around the brig before meeting the crewman's gaze again. "He knows where I am. He could have come down himself."

This time there was no doubt the man laughed. "You think he would come down to the dregs of the ship for you?"

"Perhaps he should take better care of his ship then?"

"The brig isn't meant for comfort."

"Aye, I've had better," Declan said, once again looking around, but this time with a twist of disgust playing on his lips. "So I am to come to him then? I'll need help standing."

The keys to his iron cage rattled in the man's large paw of a hand. The sound of the lock snapping open and iron scraping against the wooden floor sent a spark of hope through Declan's bones. Not that he'd let it show. He didn't need to force the wince onto his face as the man grabbed him by the elbows and hoisted him up to his feet, which were surprisingly steady given how long he must have been sitting here.

The scent of sweat and grime from his escort mingled with the musty odor of his surroundings, twisting the wince on his face into a grimace. He might have spent over a decade on pirate ships, but each had its own distinct scent, and the *Curse Bringer* was proving fouler than any he'd boarded before.

The man clamped his hand around Declan's elbow and shoved him beyond the iron bars toward the ladder. The tightness of his grip at least distracted Declan from the pain in his head, but only slightly.

Stop being a baby. You've had worse.

He turned his chin over his shoulder. "It's a tad difficult to climb a ladder with my hands bound."

In response, the man put his bulky hand between Declan's shoulder blades and pushed him once again. "Climb."

"First time for everything, I suppose," he said under his breath as he stepped up onto the first rung.

Each step was painfully slow. As he moved his feet carefully from rung to rung, he was forced to trust that the big oaf behind him would keep him upright.

"This would go faster if you unchained me, you know. I'd hate to keep Captain Grayson waiting."

"He can tolerate your slow-ass ascent more than he could tolerate you trying to escape. So, no."

"Escape?" The word came out strained as he moved another foot, his head now popping up into the next area of the ship—the munitions hold most likely, though in the darkness he couldn't make out much more than a few stacks of crates. "How could I possibly escape? Your crew would cut me down before I even made it on deck."

"Aye, that's true. But still. We won't risk it."

When Declan stepped onto a solid floor again, he waited for his escort to meet him.

"You know," he said as he took a step toward the stairs, "it makes little sense that the brig is only accessible by a ladder. How do you get your prisoners down there? Seems like it could have been better designed."

"Not my concern. I don't question Cap'n's choices for ship setup. Or anything for that matter. I simply drop sorry lots like you into the brig and drag your sorry asses into that cage where you belong."

Declan trudged up the stairs slowly, though not so much on purpose as from necessity, his legs still burning from having to climb that damn ladder without use of his hands.

"I suppose that explains all this pain then. Hit over the head and then dropped down a ladder. Some way to treat a friend."

A scoff sounded from behind him. "Friend. Ha."

Declan waited for the man to say more, but they continued their walk up a few more flights of stairs before arriving on deck. He blinked as they emerged into the pale light of dawn. It wasn't midday as he'd expected, and the mellow pinks and purples on the horizon were easier on his eyes than the bright sunlight would have been.

They were moving at a fast clip. North. His stomach clenched at the realization. Callum couldn't be this stupid.

Or he could be. Likely is.

The crew only afforded Declan passing glances as they continued their work to keep the ship sailing on their current heading despite the wind wanting to push them in the opposite direction, as if it knew where they were headed and was using all its effort to prevent them from doing so. Declan made his way across the deck, marveling at the efficiency with which Callum's crew worked. Had he not been shackled as a damned prisoner of the bastard, he might have complimented Callum for how the ship was run. But as it was, he had no desire to extend such pleasantries.

Callum's quarters were tucked away under the quarterdeck as Declan's were, except instead of being accessible from the center of the deck, the entrance was off to the starboard side. Anyone not familiar with a ship might have thought it was a door to a storage closet, as it was rather nondescript, shabby, and worn from the years at sea.

Declan stopped before it, not bothering to step aside. He glanced over his shoulder at his escort, who stood uncomfortably close.

"Shall I knock then? Or did you want the honor?"

The man rolled his eyes, but before either of them could lift a hand to the door, a voice bellowed from behind it, "Get in here!"

The beefy hand of the crewman pushed past Declan and shoved the door open before forcing Declan inside.

"Leave us!" the voice boomed again, and Declan found himself thrust further into the cabin. The door closed behind him.

Keeping his eyes forward, locked on the man seated before him, Declan took in what he could of his surroundings, taking stock of what this captain valued, how he lived. Anything that might prove advantageous. But there seemed to be little help here. Little of anything really. He'd expected Captain Grayson to be the type to hoard riches in his cabin, to take the best of the plunder for himself and display it around his quarters to bolster his pride.

But the quarters were sparse. Simple and understated. The room held only a simple desk—worn and tired. No rug on the wooden floor. No shelves. In one corner of the room lay a small mattress. No separate sleeping quarters. No separate dining area.

"Your hospitality is sorely lacking, Captain," Declan said.

Callum leaned back in his chair, his head tilting to the side as he examined Declan, his fingers ripping into the rough skin of a round fruit Declan had never seen before. He dropped the pieces of the rind onto his desk before tearing off a segment and sending its juice spraying into the air in front him—its sharp scent filling the room—then popped it into his mouth.

"It seems you've forgotten what we are, McCallagh, if you think *hospitality*"—he spat the word, spittle and juice and bits of fruit flying from his mouth—"is something to be concerned with."

"Regardless, I would have thought our years of—"

"Of what?" Callum said sharply. "Camaraderie? Partnership? Perhaps you haven't forgotten what we are, after all, since you saw fit to treat me so."

Declan chewed on the inside of his lip, contemplating how to respond, but he came up empty.

Callum snickered. "What? No smart-ass quip this time? My man must have hit you harder than I thought."

Declan huffed a short laugh. "Well, such treatment surely doesn't help one's ability to perform. My head still hurts, you know."

"I'm not concerned with your comfort."

"And what is it you're concerned with then?"

"I'm sure you've guessed by now."

"Aye, I have my suspicions."

"I know it's in the Black Sound, McCallagh. I also know you had this information before sending us on that useless hunt."

"What can I say—"

"Nothing. Keep your damned mouth shut." Callum's eyes narrowed on him, sheer rage washing over his face for a moment before he pulled it back, took a deep breath, and settled back into his usual quiet but menacing state.

Declan merely stared back. Waiting.

"Past actions aside, you can make it up to me now."

Declan flashed him a questioning look, though he already knew what Callum wanted.

"You will help us retrieve the dagger from the sound."

"If you know it's in the sound, then you also know—"

"Aye. The sirens."

Declan's eyes went wide with a silent question.

"You were heading there yourself, McCallagh, so don't play me here. I know you know how to get past them. So you'll do so. But for me."

"Aye, I do know how to get past them. But that knowledge alone won't be any good when you've stolen me away from those who would make it possible."

"And who is that?"

Declan shifted his weight, refusing to break away from the stare Callum had him trapped in. How much could he tell this captain? How much could he reveal? Could he afford to divulge his secret? And did it even matter? If they continued on this course, he'd be dead within minutes of their arrival anyway. They both would be.

"The fae."

Callum burst into laughter as his head fell back. When he snapped forward again, the amusement remained, dancing in his eyes and across the devilish smile that made the ghastly scar that ran across his face more prominent.

"You expect me to believe that, Declan? Seriously? The fae are gone. Resting at the bottom of the Aisling or hiding in Larcsporough like the cowards they are."

"Not all fled or died. Three remained. Sisters. Imprisoned by the council."

Callum sobered up quickly as he leaned forward. Tossing the orange fruit aside, he propped his elbows on the desk and steepled his fingers under his chin.

"And that's why you were in Morshan. Why you failed to meet me."

Declan gave a nod. The men studied each other for a silent minute, maybe two, before Callum barked out another laugh. "No."

"No, what?" Declan asked, honestly unsure what the man meant.

"I don't believe you. You're simply trying to delay the inevitable, convince me to turn around, where I'm sure your crew is waiting to ambush us to get their dear captain back. It won't work, Declan. You know a way past them, and you will help me get that dagger, or you die."

"If you don't listen to me now, I'll be dead anyway. We all will."

"It's a risk I'm willing to take."

"Then you're stupider than I thought."

Silence fell between them again. Callum rose from his seat and walked around the desk until he stood inches away from Declan, who did his best not to flinch away from the forced proximity and the stench of perspiration and filth that stung his eyes.

Callum lowered his voice to a whisper as coarse and rough as his weathered face. "You will do this, and you will get me past those ravenous bitches. Try to escape before we arrive? Try to jump overboard? Try to harm yourself to avoid this? And I'll pay that sweet sister of yours a visit. She looks like she could offer up a bit of sport before I spill her guts all over that pub floor."

Declan looked Callum in the eye, searching for any hint that the man was bluffing, though he knew the effort was pointless. Of course the man was telling the truth. He'd heard of him doing much worse for far milder infractions.

Images rushed into his mind of Cait struggling in Callum's grasp, fighting and punching to get free, falling to the ground. His chest caved in, crushed in a vice he hadn't experienced in years. Before his mind could conjure up the images of her blood spilling out, he shook everything away and broke Callum's stare, glancing lazily around the captain's quarters.

Raising his shoulders into a shrug, he asked, "And how would that be possible? You run a tight operation here. No doubt I wouldn't get far if I attempted an escape."

Callum wagged a finger in his face, narrowing his eyes before pulling one side of his mouth into what might have been intended as a smirk. "I know you, McCallagh. You'd find some way."

"Ah, I'm flattered. But alas..." Declan rubbed his chin against his collarbone to quell an itch that sprang up, hoping he wasn't being infested with parasites on this disgusting ship. He locked eyes with Callum, once again forcing himself to stand as tall and proud as possible and not shrink away from the ripeness of his host. "Despite any familial drama, my sister doesn't deserve to pay for my own stupidity in getting caught. So, I suppose I have no other option than to help."

His muscles tensed in response, protesting the concession, fighting against the inevitable demise awaiting them in the Black Sound.

How are you going to get yourself out of this one, Declan?

CHAPTER 5
CAIT

THE MORNING LIGHT filtered through the wavy panes of the old window, bright enough that Cait McCallagh couldn't justify sleeping any longer. Not that she'd slept much as it was. Her eyes slid open a fraction before scanning the small apartment she'd grown up in with her parents and Declan. While she had gotten used to spending most nights at her office underground, she had decided Declan's operation at the council warranted due diligence in keeping up the ruse that she was merely a pub owner managing the family business.

Kira had rushed into the pub in the early morning hours, her frantic state nearly giving her away as a Rogue as she approached Cait with the news that she'd seen Declan taken by Callum and his men. Cait had attempted to keep her face impassive as she'd dispatched Lucan to get word to Declan's men as quickly as possible.

She hadn't been able to relax after that but had filled drinks and made small talk, her carefully constructed mask firmly in place despite the panic tightening her chest. It had only loosened its grip a fraction when Lucan returned and gave her an almost imperceptible nod to let her know he'd delivered the message.

The night had been long, and it had taken every ounce of her willpower to not kick every patron to the curb and lock up early so she could collect her thoughts.

It wasn't like this was the first time Declan had been in trouble, but it had been nearly twelve years—when she'd learned he'd run off to be a cabin boy—since the last time she'd worried about his well-being to this extent.

He's a pirate. And a good one.

She tried to remind herself of these two facts, but the unease wouldn't leave her alone. Not completely.

When the last of the customers had finally ambled out the door mere hours before dawn, Lucan had helped her up the stairs to her apartment. She'd seen the offer in his eyes, the offer to stay, but she'd given a shake of her head, insisting she'd be fine and would see him later for lunch.

Not that she could even think about food.

But she couldn't bear to have him doting on her. Not now. She just needed quiet. Peace. Time to think.

To plan.

What had happened at the council hall last night? Lucan had confirmed they'd gotten the fae sisters out. So at least something had gone according to plan. But why had Declan been separated from his crew? Why had he been alone in those dark streets? Such an idiot.

What have you gotten yourself into, Declan? Why did you bring Callum, of all people, into this job?

She threw her questions at the dust motes floating through the dim rays of light.

The sound of a door opening pulled her away from her questions.

She sat up, her hand reaching for the dagger she kept in her right boot that she hadn't bothered to kick off before lying down. The back door to the alley clicked shut, and two voices whispered at the bottom of the stairs.

Idiots. Why were they here? And together? She'd need to get firm instructions to her team if they were going to manage to avoid being detected by the council and its hired goons.

They knew better than to come up the stairs at least.

With a steadying breath, she rolled the tension from her shoulders before making her way down to meet them. Cait let her irritation be known with each stomp of her feet on the stairs. Lucan stood at the bottom like a tightly wound coil of nerves ready to explode at any moment.

He hadn't been in such a state a few hours ago.

"What happened, Lucan?" Cait said by way of greeting.

He didn't answer but motioned to the alley door, where a young girl stood, worrying her fingers in the hem of her shirt.

"Eva, what is it?" Cait took a step forward but didn't get too close, as it looked like she might run off if spooked.

"Maggie." The girl's eyes dropped to the floor just as Cait's insides did the same, crashing down into her feet. She'd known this was possible when she'd assigned Maggie to that station. And Maggie had gone willingly, eagerly even, knowing the high stakes and the importance of the information it would give the Rogues.

"She's—" Cait couldn't seem to utter the word. All air was sucked from the room until she didn't know how she even managed to remain upright and conscious.

But it was Lucan who answered, his tone low and cautious, ever aware of the possibility of spies everywhere. "Aron saw her this morning, just before dawn. You know we're always watching the paths from the council hall. He saw them taking her body, or *a* body, but they screwed up, and the cloth they had wrapped her in blew off in the morning breeze, and he saw her red hair. It was her, Cait."

The room spun against her will. What kind of leader couldn't keep it together when the inevitable happened?

No. She would lead. She wouldn't break.

"I need a drink," she said and plodded over to the bar, not bothering to motion for them to follow her, but she knew they'd be cautious and likely wouldn't.

She grabbed a glass and a bottle of rum from beneath the bar and poured a dram, downing it quickly before pouring another. The alcohol didn't burn away the bitterness as she'd foolishly hoped, but it snapped her out of the stupor that had taken hold.

Straightening her shoulders, she turned to find, as expected, Lucan and Eva standing cautiously in the doorway of the back storeroom. Given the strict regulations regarding business hours, being seen with patrons at the bar could bring unwanted attention.

She took a few steps toward them and shooed them back. "Upstairs. Now." She gave one last glance over her shoulder to ensure no one was looking through the front windows.

Once upstairs, with the door to the apartment shut, she motioned for them to sit at the old dining table that sat in one corner of the main space.

"Do we have any information on what happened?" Cait asked, willing her nerves to remain calm.

"How could we?" Lucan answered, his tone carrying more desperation than irritation. "She was our one set of eyes in there."

"Fair enough." Cait's mind rushed through all the facts of the situation, and she considered how this incident would affect the next step of their operation.

Eva cleared her throat, and Cait nodded for her to speak up.

"Well, this is the first time we've ever seen actual physical evidence of their work, right? At least evidence tying it directly to the council. Until now, we've only known it's the pirates doing the killing. Now we have a clear sign that killing is happening with the council's own knowledge."

Lucan added, "They've gotten sloppy."

"I can't figure out how that helps us though. Unless we push them out into the open," Cait said, shifting forward to rest her elbows on her knees, her fingers an anxious mess of movement and her eyes seeing nothing but the apartment floor.

"They had to have figured out who she was working for," Lucan said. "Declan wouldn't have risked killing someone unless he absolutely had to."

Cait snapped her face up to look at him. "Declan didn't kill her."

The sharpness of her words had Lucan recoiled as he stumbled to explain. "I didn't say he did. Merely that he wouldn't have allowed them to get into a situation that would have gotten her killed..."

Rolling her eyes, Cait waved away his lengthy explanation with a hand.

"What are we going to do?" Eva's voice was timid.

"Stay the course. It's what Maggie would have wanted. We'll be flying relatively blind now that she's gone, and I doubt the council will be too keen on hiring anyone new. Assuming they know who she was working for."

"Is it possible they don't know?" Lucan asked. "That she was just an unfortunate bystander? Wrong place, wrong time?"

"Possible, perhaps," Cait said. "But it's best for us to assume the worst. No way to confirm either way, so we move forward under the assumption that the council knows the Rogues got a spy in their walls and that they likely know what we're after."

They sat in silence for what felt like an eternity. And yet, it wasn't nearly enough time for her to sort out all the thoughts rustling around in her mind. Lucan's toe tapped against the wooden floor—a nervous habit of his when he was lost in thought. Normally it was endearing. Today it was a thorn in her side.

Cait punched to her feet and began pacing the room, shaking her head from side to side as she analyzed the situation from every angle.

Worst case, they'd been caught by the council. The council had killed Maggie. But then they'd let Declan go.

Why? Why not kill him for infiltrating and kidnapping the fae?

The fae. She'd forgotten about them. She stopped her pacing and spun on her toe to face Lucan again.

"The fae. They got out?"

Lucan gave a quick set of nods. "Aye. I saw them aboard Declan's ship."

Cait rubbed her hand across the back of her neck. "Well, at least that's to our advantage."

"But your brother. Why would they let him go?" Eva echoed Cait's unspoken question.

"If I had to guess, they want him to get the dagger for them. It's the only thing that makes sense. Get to it before we can. Whether they know he's working for us or not? Doesn't matter. But likely they sent him to go get it."

"But Callum..." Lucan said, his toe no longer tapping.

"Aye. Let's hope Declan's crew can intercept them before they arrive at the sound."

"Do we think the council knows who you are?" Lucan asked. "Who any of us are?"

"If they did, I'd likely not be breathing right now. They'd have some pirate knocking down my door already—"

As if on cue, a loud bang sounded from downstairs as someone entered the pub and slammed the door behind them.

Cait lifted her finger to her lips, instructing them to keep quiet before she whispered, "Stay here. Don't move. I'll be right back."

CHAPTER 6
AOIFE

Aoife shut the door to Declan's quarters behind her, careful to keep it quiet so as not to disturb Tommy, though it was likely unnecessary, as the sound of the crew bustling around on deck had been impossible to ignore from within. Still, she refused to add to the noise.

"She lives!" Gavin's voice bellowed from where he stood at the helm on the quarterdeck, and he flashed her his bearded grin, his eyes twinkling as if they weren't on a race against time to rescue their captain from certain death at the jaws of evil sirens.

Aoife smiled in return, though it was contrived. Gavin didn't seem to notice though, and he motioned for her to join him.

She'd never been allowed on the quarterdeck and hadn't dared request permission after Tommy had yelled at her for nearly stepping foot on it before.

The view of the sea—even from this vantage point, a mere seven feet above the rest of the ship—sucked the breath from her. Teal water spread out before them, still vibrant despite the billowing clouds in the skies casting shadows across its surface. The vast emptiness was both freeing and suffocating, beckoning her with promises of adventure even as it warned of the dangers that lay ahead. Aoife saw no hint of land, no hint of any other ships. She'd always imagined the Aisling teeming with ships. So many crews and ships to keep straight in her mind, and that was only the lords and their fleets. Perhaps she'd failed to grasp how large the Aisling really was.

"You seem to have found your sea legs, Miss," Gavin said, giving her a nudge with his elbow.

"Please, Gavin. It's Aoife. And yes. Thankfully."

"It'll be Miss for now. I mean, you're practically the quartermaster."

"But you never called Tommy by any such formality." Aoife pulled her brows together.

"That's what you focused on? Not that I just gave you a title?"

Aoife shook her head and laughed. "Well, that too. I mean, both are absurd. One, for me to be a quartermaster, I'd have to be a pirate—"

Gavin made a point of looking her over from head to toe before flashing her a questioning glance.

Aoife ignored him and continued. "And if I were the quartermaster—which I am not, because, come on, Gavin—I'd expect similar treatment as Tommy. So you'll call me Aoife. Okay?"

"No offense, *Miss* Aoife, but you're not as scary as Tommy, who gave a rather convincing threat to anyone who dared call him anything but his first name."

Aoife couldn't even imagine Tommy offering any sort of threat or looking menacing in any way. And this was after witnessing him take down a handful of Lord Madigen's men in the library.

She settled her forearms against the railing and breathed in the sea air, pulling it into every inch of her body, wishing it could clear her thoughts and wash away everything she now faced.

After a few minutes of watching the horizon in silence, she asked, not bothering to look at him as she did, "Why would you call me the quartermaster?"

"Well, Miss Aoife, if you recall, I said *practically*. And am I wrong? You're sleeping in the captain's quarters—not that that's typical of quartermasters, mind you—but you are also a pivotal part of the decision-making."

"Am I? I don't feel like I am. I feel like I'm still just an annoying stowaway."

"An annoying stowaway who plundered our captain's heart though. And you claim you're not a pirate."

Aoife's chest tightened involuntarily as Declan's *I love you* echoed once again in her mind. "Still, that shouldn't grant me any special rank. Don't you have to work your way up to such titles?"

Gavin shrugged through a laugh. "Eh, yes and no. Every ship is different. But it's not unheard of, although 'tis rare for a captain to lead his crew with his love by his side, not necessarily as equals. But close."

"But I thought women aboard were seen as a curse."

"You'd be surprised how quickly that becomes a non-issue when it's the captain's lover."

Aoife cringed as her face grew warmer. Did everyone on this ship consider her that? Had Declan told them all? "I don't know that I'm..." She abandoned that, deciding it didn't matter one way or the other. "Even so, I doubt the crew likes the idea. I don't even know how to sail. Or fight."

"Aye, you are a rather unconventional choice. But to be honest, we're all happy to see the captain happy. Or we were. Until whatever happened last night."

A familiar rush of numbness froze her veins, spreading from her chest out to all her limbs. Guilt. Her old friend, who tensed her insides and pulled her into a void where nothing existed except her and her mistakes. So many mistakes.

Gavin's elbow nudged her again. "Apologies. I didn't mean to throw it in your face."

"It's not your fault. It's mine."

Gavin let out a short whistle, and Aoife turned to see a crewman walk over from where he'd been standing at the other end of the quarterdeck. Gavin entrusted the helm to him and then gestured for Aoife to join him on the opposite side of the stairs. He rested one elbow on the railing as he looked at her, and she realized she had underestimated him, writing him off as an inconsequential member of the crew.

His encouraging smile had his blue-gray eyes twinkling with kindness. "If I may... It's not too late. There's time to make amends. To make things right."

"How can you be sure?" Aoife asked, pushing herself away from the railing. The quiet numbness was giving way to prickling panic. She flung an arm out, gesturing to the sea before them. "He's nowhere in sight, and he's headed to certain death. How can it not be too late?"

Gavin pulled in a deep breath that sent his shoulders slumping.

"Aye. I admit it doesn't look promising. But if we don't have hope, what do we have?"

Aoife looked back to the horizon as she pondered his words and focused on the clouds that were swirling in a slow but powerful dance. She'd never seen such beauty from the black sands of Cregah. The council hall was too guarded by trees to allow for a good view of the skies, and the cove gave a far more limited view of the sea than she had here.

She didn't know how long they remained there not speaking, but she found herself thankful for Gavin's intuition, his knowing when not to push further.

Hope.

She had to cling to that, to the hope that she'd get her chance—when she was ready—to offer Declan the forgiveness she could never receive from Lani. Yes, there was time. There had to be.

Beside her, Gavin muttered a curse, sharp but quiet, before rushing away. He bellowed down to the crew, "Heave to!"

Aoife glanced at him and then at the crew, who didn't question the order or hesitate as they worked the sails and prepared to carry out whatever Gavin's command had meant.

"Ready to heave to!" Gavin called.

The crew answered with a "Ready!"

Aoife watched as Gavin spoke with the man at the helm. He guided him through a maneuver while shouting commands to the crew. She stared in awe as the men worked the ropes and sails with a grace as beautiful as any dance she'd seen by the troupes the council invited for festivals and holidays. Gripping the railing as the ship turned past windward, she worried she might lose her balance with the movement.

But then everything stopped. The ship seemed to come to a standstill, bobbing along the waves, nearly as steady as when in port.

Gavin rushed for the stairs, motioning for her to follow.

"What is it?" she asked, nearly tripping down the steps in an effort to keep up. Something troubled him; of that she was certain. But Gavin didn't answer. He strode around the staircase and made for the crew's barracks.

Aoife called after him again. "Tommy's not down there."

Gavin whirled around.

"He's in Declan's cabin." Gavin's brows twitched, his head tilting slightly with that familiar look of curiosity she often received from people when she misspoke. Her hands fidgeted, as did her feet, and she moved quickly to explain. "He was exhausted. I told him to take the bed for a few hours to rest."

Gavin breathed an "ah" before starting off again, careful to avoid colliding with her. She turned and followed, her heart thumping against her sternum and her mind whirring with what might have Gavin so worked up.

Before they made it to the door, the fae sisters met up with them on silent feet.

"Why have we stopped?" Renna asked.

Gavin, normally a perfect gentleman—or as perfect a gentleman as a pirate could be—with the sisters, gave them little more than a sideways glance and no verbal response. But he didn't stop them from following him into the cabin as he pushed open the door, not bothering to knock.

Aoife followed the sisters inside, shutting the door behind them.

"Tommy!" Gavin shouted on his way into the sleeping quarters. He stopped short when Tommy appeared in the doorway, his eyes blinking against the sleep that had been interrupted.

"I'm up. Felt us stop."

"Aye. Storm brewing ahead. And quickly."

A curse fell from Tommy's mouth. "I was afraid of that. Hoped our luck hadn't completely abandoned us."

He walked around Gavin toward the map still laid out on Declan's desk and cleared away the books and other odds and ends Declan had left there.

Leaning over, bracing himself with his arms, he studied the seas. He didn't look up as the others joined him around the desk. Aoife wondered if this was a typical situation and whether Tommy and Gavin were unnerved being here with her and the fae instead of Declan.

But if it bothered them, they didn't show it at all.

Tommy pointed at a spot north of Cregah. "We're here, aye?"

Gavin mumbled a confirmation. Tommy lifted his hand to his chin and spoke through his fingers. "We can assume they're on the other side of this storm, that it didn't come up until after they'd passed through—"

"How can you assume that?" Aoife interrupted.

Tommy met her gaze from under his brow, not bothering to lift his chin. "The Aisling is known for creating these storms quickly and powerfully. Sailors and crews become quite accustomed to finding themselves in the middle of a squall with little warning, if any. That is, if they survive at all. With this one just starting and with the lead they had on us..."

Gavin traced his finger along a path off to the west. "We could go around it, pulling in closer to Haviern, where the seas are normally calm this time of year."

Tommy shook his head. "It takes us too far off course. We'd lose any chance of reaching him in time."

Aoife's gut clenched at the words, and she swallowed the protest that nearly escaped her lips.

"Well, that leaves us with only two options: brave the storm or risk the waters near Tyshaly," Gavin said, and Aoife could have sworn she saw him blanch slightly at his own words.

The fae sisters still hadn't said anything but were standing around the desk like statues, though they studied the map along with the others.

"What's the risk there?" Aoife asked.

Gavin and Tommy both drew in a breath, but it was Maura who answered for them, her light voice taking on a dark tone. "The beasts that live beneath the surface."

Aoife felt pinpricks dance along her arms and creep up her neck.

"Aye. It's why Tyshaly's main port was built so far south," Tommy answered. "Closer to their enemy to the south, but it kept the merchant vessels safer from the dangers lurking below."

Aoife didn't know if she wanted the answer, but she asked anyway. "What manner of beasts?" She knew of the sharks that lived off the coast of Cregah and had heard the pirate lords' stories of the black whales they'd seen attack smaller fishing boats off the Turvala coast. But this wasn't a fishing boat, and neither of those beasts seemed likely to cause the fear she now saw on her friends' faces.

Again it was one of the sisters who answered. Bria this time. "A creature of great size and strength, with many arms that can grip a ship and pull it to the depths before the crew even knows what is happening."

Aoife shuddered. "The kraken is real?" Her eyes widened as she glanced at each face around the table.

Tommy dipped his chin slightly.

"I thought it was only a tale, a myth!"

Tommy said, "All myths are based on a bit of truth. This one turns out to be no myth at all."

"Well, we can't go that way!" Aoife looked at each of them once more, but everyone's focus had returned to the map.

Tommy didn't bother to lift his face as he answered. "We don't have much of a choice though, unfortunately. There are no good options here. We either risk the storm's wrath, the delay to the east, or the—"

"The *kraken* to the west," Aoife said, finishing his sentence for him.

"If I may?" Maura said. "We could help."

Tommy shook his head, looking from sister to sister until settling on Maura. Aoife could have sworn she saw something shift in his eyes as he looked at the youngest sister, but she must have imagined it.

"We can't risk you using your powers up before we arrive at the sound. We'll need to go in, and you'll have to promise not to use them. At all."

Gavin straightened as he asked, "What's the likelihood we can get past without coming across the creature? That we can get through undetected?"

"I don't know, but we have to try."

Dread pooled in the pit of Aoife's stomach. Nothing about this felt okay. No good options.

"How long will the storm last? Can't we wait it out?" she asked.

It was Gavin's turn to shake his head. "They come on quick, but they don't dissipate as fast. It's why it's so dangerous to have one hit on top of you."

"So we have to go west? And risk the..." Aoife couldn't say the word again, the mere thought of the creature sending another shiver through her shoulders.

"Unfortunately," Tommy said, "it's the best option we have."

He turned to Gavin. "Have Mikkel get the crew ready."

"Won't they panic?" Aoife asked, even as Gavin walked past her and out of the cabin. "I mean, they're a superstitious bunch already. Won't this shake them?"

Tommy chuckled, which seemed oddly out of place for the situation, but Aoife noted how his eyes didn't dance with amusement as they usually did when he laughed. "They may be superstitious, but this is the type of danger they expect in this line of work. We need them ready."

Aoife wondered how anyone could prepare for a giant, multi-armed creature that ate ships for fun, but she had to trust Tommy.

Looking to the fae sisters, she searched for a sign they shared her trepidation, but they were the epitome of calm. Even facing such danger, they looked the opposite of how she felt, and her bitterness echoed in her mind.

Damn fae.

CHAPTER 7
TOMMY

Tommy leaned against the desk, his arms spread wide as he stared down at the map with unfocused eyes, trying to ignore the four women who remained in this cabin with him. How did Declan do this? Slowing his breathing, he tried to calm his thoughts, even as they hammered against the edges of his mind.

Kraken. Storm. Time.

No good options.

There never were, were there? But normally it wasn't him having to make the call, and he hated that he had to now.

Advisor. Confidante. Friend. That was what he preferred to be. Not responsible for all the lives aboard the ship.

Where are you, Declan? How the hell did you do this?

Some things could be decided by vote, but other decisions, like this, had to be made solely by the captain. And this was precisely why he'd pushed for Declan to be voted captain all those years ago on that distant shore. Declan had the head for this, the guts, while Tommy...

A growl of frustration rumbled within him, and it took a second for him to realize it hadn't been internal but had escaped into the room and brought all eyes to him.

He looked up, his gaze shifting nervously from face to face.

Renna spoke first. "Are you sure we—"

"No." Tommy stopped her short, lifting a hand to emphasize his refusal to let them use their magic.

"Tommy," Aoife started, and he snapped his attention to her. "Can we at least consider it?"

His jaw clenched, his chest tightening. Why didn't they listen to him? Why were they pushing for this? Was he that awful at filling in as captain that they didn't respect his word?

No. How many times had he challenged Declan? This wasn't a rebuke of him. It was desperation and fear of the monster they'd soon face.

Taking a deep breath, he turned back to Renna, hoping no one noticed how he avoided Maura's eyes.

"Renna," he said as he roughed his hand along the back of his neck, "is it possible for you and your sisters to use magic through these waters and still have time to replenish it before we arrive at the sound?"

Before the fae could answer, Aoife added her own question. "What are your powers, anyway? Are they all the same?"

"Some powers we share, like the ability to heal. Ourselves and others, as we did with Tommy," Renna explained.

Bria chimed in, her voice noticeably harsher than Renna's, though it was still softer and more refined than that of any human. "Our magic—as you humans tend to call it—courses through our veins; it's part of our blood."

"Can you feel it?" Aoife asked, that familiar curious look Tommy always found amusing passing over her features, tightening her brow over eyes alight with curiosity.

"Yes. In a way," Maura said, but Tommy could sense her eyes were locked on him rather than Aoife. "It's hard to explain, not that I've ever tried. But it's like a tingling, a pulsing, a burning?" She turned to her sisters. "I'm not describing this right."

"It's as if it's alive," Renna said.

"Within us," Bria added.

"But we each have our own unique powers, just as we are our own unique selves," Renna said.

Bria cut in. "For example, I have power over the elements. Fire. Earth. Water. Air. I can manipulate them. Control them. Move them to my will."

Tommy nearly laughed at the way Aoife's jaw nearly dropped open, but he managed to contain his amusement. "And you, Renna?"

"The mind."

She must have seen his shock—or was it fear?—because she added quickly, "Not compulsion. At least not as you likely envision. I can see your thoughts, fears, dreams. And at my strongest, I can shape them a bit. The more I attempt to control though, the less powerful the result is."

Her explanation brought little comfort, and he hoped she didn't notice how a shiver crawled up his spine. Could she see the discomfort in his mind?

He began to vocalize this question, but Renna spoke first.

"I can't hear or see you unless I focus on you, and I have to be relatively close. I've had many centuries to practice tuning out the minds of those around me. Otherwise I'd have gone mad long ago."

Still, knowing his thoughts were subject to her intrusion made him feel exposed, naked before her. Another shiver shook his shoulders slightly.

"And you? Maura?" Aoife asked.

Tommy let himself look at the youngest fae as she answered, "Glamour."

Maura had turned to look at Aoife, her rich brown hair falling over her shoulder, hiding the delicate features of her face from him. The three sisters were all beautiful. There was no doubt about that. Any man on this ship—or anywhere, for that matter—would be daft not to notice their otherworldly beauty. But this one, the youngest, she had a quiet beauty about her. She was not as terrifying and harsh as her sisters.

He was still uncomfortable being in the same room as her, acutely aware of her presence and her gaze whenever it fell on him.

Did Renna sense it?

He shook that thought aside as he heard Aoife say his name.

"Tommy? You with us?"

He glanced down at the desk, trying to avoid Renna's stare, hoping she hadn't seen where his mind had drifted. He looked back to Aoife. "What? Sorry. My mind was elsewhere."

"I thought that only happened to me," Aoife said with a quiet laugh. "Maura was explaining how she can manipulate what others see, change the appearance of people or locations or even ships."

"Well..." He blinked at Maura. "That would come in handy—"

Maura finished his sentence for him. "If one needed to get past, say, a monstrous creature lurking below? Aye."

Indeed. This must be why the Rogues had determined these sisters to be the best way past the sirens to the dagger.

Running a hand through his hair, he asked the obvious. "What state are your powers in now? I mean, how strong are they? You spent the past however many hours healing me, so I'm assuming they aren't back to full capacity?"

"In ideal circumstances," Renna said, "as in, had we not been imprisoned and subjected to centuries of only using our powers once every generation, we can replenish them within twenty-four hours."

"But we are still regaining our strength, waking up the magic, as it were," Bria added.

Maura concluded their explanation, saying, "It can take up to thirty-six hours if we've depleted them completely."

"And what happens if you do that?" Aoife asked.

Maura answered, "We collapse, losing consciousness, waking only when our powers are back to half strength. It is rather painful for it to build back up from that level, so we don't like to use our powers to that point if we can help it."

"Which," Tommy said, "is precisely the reason we need to find another plan of attack here."

Roughing a hand over his stubbled chin, he directed his attention back to the map—not that it held any answers for him, but it was a good distraction from everyone's stares. If only they had some kind of explosive, the type used for opening up the earth for the excavation of minerals and metals. But those weren't easily acquired, and they hadn't come upon a ship carrying such cargo in years.

"Can we use the cannons?" Aoife asked.

He looked at her from beneath his brows and gave a quick shake of his head. "With this type of creature, it's unlikely it would present us an ample target above the surface. We can try, but we shouldn't expect that to be our best option here."

"So what is then?" Aoife asked, her voice shaking. "Our best option, I mean."

Leaning forward, he braced himself against the desk with both hands. "We attempt to get through undetected. Keeping quiet. No movement on the deck. Pray we don't alert it to our presence."

"And if we do?"

"We'll rely primarily on our blades, I'm afraid. And our wits," he said.

Seeing her "we're doomed" look, he quickly added, "Don't worry, Aoife. We're not as dumb-witted as some might think."

Aoife fumbled with her response. "I didn't... I trust you... I mean. I just don't see how blades can be an adequate defense against this monster."

Tommy offered a shrug, ignoring how the eyes of the fae sisters bored into him and wondering if Renna was fighting the urge to use her powers to nudge him toward allowing their use of magic. "They might not be. But it's all we have."

"Can we at least maybe agree to let the fae use their magic as a last resort?"

"And who would decide when that moment—"

"Trust us to know when that moment is," Maura said, remaining as still as a statue.

A gorgeous statue.

No. That kind of thinking would get them nowhere.

"If I did that, you'd be using them right now. You'd have Bria calling upon the wind to fill our sails and get us through faster. You'd be conjuring up a glamour along the surface to hide our hull from the beast. You'd even have Renna giving my brain a shove toward agreeing to this."

"And how do you know I'm not already?" Renna said, though her tone showed none of the jest her words might have suggested.

Dropping his chin to his chest, Tommy squeezed his eyes shut, as if doing so might help him feel her powers poking and prodding at the edges of his mind. Would it be so bad to let them help? It would be the best way to get past the beast unseen, but then, it would put them at risk of arriving at the sound unprepared and unarmed against the sirens. Put them at risk of not being able to save Declan, of not being able to survive.

"Well, I certainly can't stop you, Renna." He paused to run a hand over his face once again, but it couldn't clear the weariness and concern he knew showed plainly in his features. "And if you're using them on me now, which I hope you aren't, then I suppose there's nothing I can do against you." Even as he spoke, his mind growled at him for being too soft and not taking charge of this situation as a captain ought to.

But I'm not a captain! he shouted back. And yet, he was—at least temporarily.

He clenched his jaw and drew in a deep breath. With his eyes firmly fixed on Renna's, he said, "I may not know why you and your sisters agreed to leave with Declan, but it must have been rather important if it convinced you to ignore a centuries-old promise to the council. And as long as you are on this ship, you will obey its captain. And until we get Declan back, that is me. You *will* obey me. Is that clear?"

"Yes, Captain," Renna agreed with a smile, albeit a patronizing one.

"Good." Tommy straightened. "Now, if you'll excuse me, I need some fresh air." He moved around the desk, giving the sisters as wide a berth as he could. As he passed by though, Maura's hand reached out, her fingers brushing his bare forearm lightly. A shiver ran through him even as she pulled away. Without pausing—without so much as a glance at her—he continued walking.

"Fresh air sounds like a good idea," Aoife said behind him, and her footsteps rushed toward him as if she were as eager to be away from the fae as he was. But even as he opened the door and stepped out onto the deck, Aoife shifted and called behind them, "Sisters, it would be inappropriate for you to remain in these quarters without the captain present."

It was perhaps the first time Tommy had heard her take on the air of a councilwoman.

A quiet "Of course" followed him out the door, and he didn't need to look over his shoulder as he strode away to know the fae had obeyed and exited. He could only hope they followed orders when it truly mattered.

CHAPTER 8
MAURA

THE SEA MIST hit Maura's face as she stood at the starboard rail. After centuries locked in the council hall, fresh air—its feel and its scent—mesmerized her. She had forgotten how freedom tasted. And she hadn't realized how much she'd missed it.

Running her fingers along the wooden rail that was smoothed by the years of sailing, she marveled at how warm it felt compared to the cold stone—and iron—of the walls she'd lived within for so long. She closed her eyes as she raised her chin toward the sky, soaking in the warmth of the sun as it shone down on her, enveloping her in a hug as warm and sweet as a loved one welcoming her home.

She'd given up any hope of enjoying the fresh air and the sun's rays many years ago, accepting that she and her sisters were the last remaining fae with no purpose beyond serving the council. Why had she accepted that as her fate? A life spent locked away, used by those who had saved them from the war. How much living had she missed out on over a lie?

Now's your chance to make up for lost time! You're free!

Despite the symphony of noise created by the water slapping against the hull and the sails adjusting with the wind carrying them forward, the unmistakable sound of her sisters' footsteps cut through her thoughts. Half a millennium locked up together brought familiarity beyond anyone's comprehension.

It also brought an excess of frustration. The near-silent footfalls of Renna and Bria against the ship's deck felt like a light hammer pinging within her head.

"Don't say it, Renna," Maura said, not bothering to turn and look at her older sister as she stepped up beside her. In her periphery she saw Renna's jaw lower to release a response, but Maura cut her off. "And don't try to claim ignorance. It's not a good look on you."

But it was Bria who responded, coming to stand on her other side. "We are worried about you. That's all."

Maura gritted her teeth. Her jaw throbbed as she clamped it tighter and tighter, trying to keep her words—the nasty, spiteful, bitter, angry words—from escaping. The last thing they needed was a sibling squabble interfering with their efforts to rescue Captain McCallagh. Taking a deep breath, she kept her focus on the horizon, as though studying that distant line where two worlds met but never crossed would calm her down. It didn't work.

"There's no reason to worry," she offered finally, but her voice was choked off by the damned ache that had started in those dark, frantic hours of healing Tommy.

"That almost sounded convincing," Renna said, sliding her hand along the rail to rest it atop Maura's. The touch, though tender and meant to be reassuring, did nothing but inflame her inner torment like a breath upon a dying fire.

"You know as well as I do, Renna," she said, squeezing her sister's name out through clenched teeth, "I have little control over this." She couldn't keep the agony and despair from tainting each word, but she refused to let these blasted emotions show. She would not cry. She would not fall apart. She was a fae. Centuries old. Powerful.

And broken.

"You're not broken," Renna reassured her.

Maura spun on her sister and ripped her hand away. "Stay out of my damn head, Renna!" Her tone, although harsh and angry, remained quiet enough so as not to alert any of the crew of the drama brewing between them.

"She only means to help," Bria said from behind her, but she at least knew not to lay a hand on Maura. Not now.

"I don't need her help. Or yours," Maura said with a sharp glance over her shoulder.

But before she could turn her attention back to the horizon, she spotted Tommy standing on the quarterdeck and looking out over the rest of the ship. What he was watching, she didn't know. Only that it wasn't her. And she shouldn't want it to be.

He was a pirate. Thrust into the role of captain—a role he had obviously never wanted—beaten down by worry for his best friend's safety and that of their crew.

"I think you do though," Renna said, and Maura turned back to her sister, willing herself to not give in to the intense bitterness, to remain calm. It was only barely working.

Her blood thrummed as it traveled through her veins, an exhilarating and nearly forgotten sensation after all the years spent in the iron-infused walls of the council hall that had kept this magic, this power, subdued. It had been freed as sure as her body had, and even with the bit she'd expended while healing Tommy, her magic seemed almost giddy as it was replenished and strengthened.

"Of course you think that, Renna," Maura said. "You know best, right?"

"Well, not best, but I'm not the one whose judgment is clouded by emotion at the moment."

Such an understatement.

"Don't pretend at all to know what this feels like."

Renna stared her down. "And don't you pretend to know anything about this man."

"I may not know everything, but I—"

"You what? You cannot fall for the first handsome face you see."

Maura straightened. "Technically I saw Captain McCallagh's face first, so..."

"You know what I mean, Maura. Stop being so difficult."

"Stop treating me like a child."

"Then stop acting like one."

Maura's teeth gripped each other hard enough to spark pain at her temples. Somehow she resisted the temptation to let her eyes roam over to Tommy once more, instead turning them to the sky.

"Why should I expect you to understand?" she whispered to the wisps of clouds before dropping her chin back down. "You have no idea what this feels like!"

Renna moved toward her—so fast it would have been imperceptible to any of the humans observing them—until she and Maura stood almost nose to nose. Her blue eyes blazed with an anger that mirrored Maura's.

Through gritted teeth, Renna growled in a vicious whisper, "Don't you dare pretend to know all aspects of our lives, sister."

They hadn't been together for their whole lives. Even though they had spent the last five hundred years together, they had not always been so close, only having reunited on Cregah a few decades before the end of the war. The memories of that time forced a shudder up her spine.

"Care to enlighten me then, *sister*?" Maura infused the last word with the spite that coursed through her along with her magic.

"You are not the only one to ever fall. But I did. He didn't. Such is the risk of it."

"Who was it?" Maura couldn't contain her curiosity at this confession.

Renna gave a lazy shrug. "It doesn't matter. It never had a chance. Unrequited love may be painful, but it has its advantages. The hope it creates is like an early morning mist, a soft whisper easily dispersed when the light of the sun reveals the truth. But your—"

Renna's lips clamped shut, and regret flashed briefly across her face.

"My what?"

"It's one thing to love someone, accepting they will never love you, Maura. But to love someone, to have them love you, knowing you can never be together? That? That is the pain that only comes from shattered hopes and destroyed dreams. If I could spare you that pain, I would, but I may have to settle for lessening it. Walk away while you can, Maura." The final words came out more as a desperate plea than the command Maura might have expected. She rested her hands on Maura's arms with uncharacteristic tenderness.

But Maura only tensed.

"How can you possibly know he—" Maura clamped her mouth shut. "You didn't."

"I did, and I'm not sorry for it either. Despite what you might think, it wasn't for your benefit. I merely wanted to be confident he could be trusted to lead, to see if he might need to be helped a little."

"Don't you dare." Once again Maura's rage sparked. "You leave him alone, or—"

"Or what? You can't stop me from doing what needs to be done. But all of that is beside the point. He's falling for you too. Not as intensely as you—obviously, since he's only human—but he is struggling against it. It's there, and you cannot pursue it. It is doomed from the onset. You know what is expected of us in the south. You know how much our kin need our help. You cannot turn your back on your kin."

Maura couldn't suppress the groan that rumbled in her chest. "I know. And I'm not. I'm not against helping them! But this is about more than him."

"Is it?" Renna asked, unconvinced.

"I want to *live*, Renna. Don't you? Don't you want more than just to be at the beck and call of others? Don't you want a life that you get to choose?"

But her sister was already shaking her head.

Bria chimed in. "We have our roles, Maura. If we don't help, who else would? Or could?"

Within Maura's chest, the fibers of her heart began to fray, torn in different directions, toward different paths and dreams. Her gaze drifted to the western horizon, then behind them to the south, before swinging back up to where Tommy still stood. There was a life beyond the walls of the council hall, beyond the shores of Cregah, beyond the Aisling, and beyond even Larcsporough. She'd spent most of her life confined, and now that she was free, her bones ached to take advantage of it.

She wanted to live. And to love.

"I know you want to spread your wings, Maura," Renna said gently. "But we still have weeks aboard this ship before we can travel south. If you pursue this with him"—she waved a finger discreetly between Maura and Tommy—"things will only get more complicated and difficult as you feed that hope that has kindled within you."

Even as Maura moved to deny it, that tiny but strong flame flickered within her heart. Renna warned of the risk of being burned by it, but Maura was more fearful of the emptiness that would result if she snuffed it out.

Her sister meant well. Logically, Maura knew that, but emotionally, she only saw her older sister trying to control her as she always did. She might be free of her ties to the council, but escaping her sister's authority wouldn't be so easy.

Still, she had to try. "While I appreciate your concern, it is my life—"

"No, Maura! It's the life of every fae!" Renna yelled, all gentleness gone. She barely kept her words from being heard by all on deck. "Their lives depend on us. That includes you!"

Stepping around Maura, Bria tried to appease both her sisters, placing her hands on their shoulders. But Maura ignored her.

"Don't be so dramatic!" she spat.

"Don't be so selfish!" Renna's blue eyes burned into Maura's.

Neither sister backed down, but even as they stared at each other, Maura sensed the attention of the crew on them.

"Sisters," Bria said, allowing only a brief pause to see if they would turn to her. They didn't. "This isn't exactly the most becoming of displays. Especially for who we are. This is not going to be resolved here and now. That much is obvious. Emotions are high. Let's not make any decisions rashly."

Bria. Always the voice of reason and calm, she provided a nice balance to Renna's authoritative nature and Maura's passionate personality.

"Fine," Maura whispered with a bit of a growl.

Renna merely nodded before turning to leave.

As Renna and Bria walked away, leaving Maura alone once again at the rail, Maura risked a glance up at Tommy, who was now in conversation with Aoife. Their voices were too low for Maura to make out from this distance.

It had already been complicated, trying to balance her duty in Larcsporough with her urge to head off on her own. And then Tommy had been thrown into the mess that was her heart. She had not planned for any of this when she'd sat down to help heal him. Just as she'd given up all hope of freedom while living at the council hall, she'd abandoned all thought of love or companionship beyond her sisters.

But something had happened between them in that small cabin.

Like her heart had been given new life as she had saved his. Like it had been precisely tuned to his somehow, leaving it feeling empty when he wasn't nearby. Renna was right. Maura didn't know much about him beyond what she had observed over the past few days. Where had he grown up? Where was his family? Why didn't he want to lead? What drove him to be so different from most pirates?

She wanted to know all these answers and then some, and the thought of denying herself the chance to understand him as well as she knew herself only twisted that pang deep in her chest.

You had to fall for a human, didn't you? her mind teased her.

She could have picked a far worse human to fall for than Tommy. Even with all the stress he was under, there was something about him, something she couldn't quite pinpoint, that put his sense of loyalty and devotion on clear display. He was like no one she'd ever met, in all her six hundred years. A man who would always do what he needed to for a friend.

For a loved one.

But would he go with her to Larcsporough and beyond? Could he?

If Renna was telling the truth, Tommy was falling for her too. If Maura was responsible, she'd leave him be, let him have a life on the sea he loved with friends who needed him, not ask him to give all of that up for her.

But that flicker of hope within her heart—that spark she'd thought her years of captivity had surely killed—would not be ignored. As she watched Tommy, the flutter in her chest quickened, and she knew she couldn't heed her sister's warnings. She would risk a lifetime of pain and heartache for a single chance—not to simply know this man but to love him and be loved by him. No matter how short a time she was granted.

You also risk inflicting pain on him. Whether he follows you or not, you will part ways. One way or another.

CHAPTER 9
DECLAN

CALLUM BACKED AWAY FROM DECLAN, his face relaxing into an easy smile that Declan found more disconcerting than anything else. While he didn't know how long he'd been unconscious in that damn brig, they couldn't have been sailing for more than one or two days, which left only a few more before they reached the sound. And their inevitable demise. With Callum refusing to listen to the truth, he'd need to come up with some semblance of a plan.

"Sit, McCallagh," Callum commanded. With a jerk of his head, he pointed out the chair a few steps to Declan's right.

Declan angled his hands away from his back while turning slightly. "A bit hard to do that when I'm—"

"I'm sure you can manage. Sit." The captain's eyes narrowed.

"What is your worry exactly, Captain?" Declan asked, easing himself into the chair, his bound hands forcing him to sit straight up as if he were enjoying tea at a palace instead of being held captive aboard this pirate's ship. "Surely you don't think I could best you. Especially since you've taken my blade."

Callum leaned back against the edge of his desk, his legs relaxing in front of him, ankles crossed. He reached behind him. "Ah, yes. This blade," he said, lifting the dagger in front of him as he turned back to Declan. "You never did tell me how you acquired it. That's got to be quite the story."

Declan smacked his lips lazily. If he looked away, Callum would see his lies, so he kept his eyes forward, allowing only a brief glance down to his weapon, which was now being turned round and round in his captor's hands. "Same ol' story, I suppose. Pulled it off a merchant ship's captain who didn't know how to listen."

A laugh rumbled from Callum's chest, though it didn't show in his eyes. "That doesn't match the stories others tell."

"You, of all people, should know not to trust gossip."

"Perhaps," Callum said as he used the dagger's point to clean out the grime from under his fingernails. After several seconds of brutal silence, he spoke again, his eyes locked on the blade in his hands. "How did it feel, Declan, to watch both of your parents be dragged away within days of each other?"

Declan's gut twisted at the words, but he shoved the memories back, refusing to let them take hold of him. He wouldn't fall for Callum's play here, and regardless of what changes Aoife had stirred in him, his years of perfecting this mask wouldn't go to waste. He offered a lazy shrug, though Callum couldn't see it with his face still lowered. "Was a long time ago. I don't readily recall."

"Ah, but I think you do. And I think it still hurts." Callum lifted his chin, his dark eyes burning into Declan's. "Hurts knowing you couldn't do anything, doesn't it? To feel helpless? Useless? Insignificant."

Declan swallowed hard and channeled all his tension into his hands, clasping them tightly until his knuckles ached. He couldn't let anything show on his face, couldn't give Callum further ammunition. He released a sigh, his body relaxing with the breath, and said, "I was only a kid. Not much I could do."

Pulling his mouth into a half-smile again, Callum said, "Is that what you tell yourself to curb the guilt? How's that working for you?"

A familiar tightness gripped his chest, as if Callum had summoned the years-old guilt from where Declan had tried to force it to rest. He mentally stamped it down before answering, though he wasn't sure how long he could keep it at bay. "Well, I was doing just fine until you knocked me upside the head and dragged me aboard your ship."

"Oh, yes, it certainly seemed that way." Callum let out a loud guffaw as he looked toward the ceiling. "Is that why that little bitch of an heir was stomping her way back to your ship—to your cabin perhaps?—crying and red-faced? What did you do? Nothing good, I imagine."

Declan ignored the goading, hardened his features, and refused to turn away from Callum's stare. Even if he had the words to respond, he couldn't trust his voice not to betray the emotions Callum conjured up inside him.

"Did she finally see you for what you are?" Callum continued. "A pirate? A killer? A liar? A brigand? That's it, isn't it? She saw the real you under whatever mask you were using on her."

The grip he had on his features was slipping; the strength he needed to continue appearing emotionless and bored was slowly waning with each verbal jab from this captain. Declan's hands itched to be free from their bonds, free to strike the bastard before him. But that's what Callum wanted. Leverage. Any emotional reaction Declan offered would be used against him. It was what Declan would have done if the situation were reversed.

Clearing his throat, Declan lifted his chin and responded, "Such is our lot, isn't it, Callum?"

"And what lot is that exactly?"

"Loneliness. Lovelessness." Declan hoped his words were coming out as steady as he needed them to.

"There are places"—Callum gave his hand a whirl in the air before him—"to satisfy such longings. Or are you too good for such establishments, McCallagh?"

"Ah, but do they satisfy? Truly?"

A sadness clouded Callum's expression, but only briefly, like a wisp of cloud passing in front of the sun on a summer breeze, gone as quickly as it had appeared. But it had been there nonetheless. "They satisfy well enough."

Declan cleared his throat and shifted his weight in the chair, silently cursing the manacles at his wrists that made it impossible to get comfortable. "I'm not sure I believe you. Especially after the stories I've heard about your own past."

"What was that you were saying about not trusting gossip?" Callum's tone tightened around his words, but it was forced, strained.

"I never said not to trust it. Sometimes the gossip turns out to be true. So, is it?"

Callum's stare bored into Declan, as if he could, with just a look, strip away every layer of his being until only his true self remained.

Thankfully, that's not possible.

After too long a silence, Callum whispered, his voice rough with anger, "Is what true?"

"That your cold heart is capable of love. Or it was. Once." If he could unnerve the captain, get him on edge, force his past to overwhelm him, perhaps Declan could play to his sympathies to give them some chance of surviving. And if not that —as this was a long shot, indeed—he could at least buy himself some time to devise a plan. Any plan would be better than none.

Callum turned to drop the blade onto his desk before moving toward Declan. He stopped close enough that Declan could kick him if he wanted to. Not that he would. Callum would expect such a move. When Callum remained silent, Declan relaxed his head to the side and raised a brow. "What was her name?"

Without warning, Callum's fist slammed into the side of Declan's face, sending his jaw swinging to the right. His vision darkened, and silver stars appeared before his blinking eyes as the pain registered. Nose. Cheek. Jaw. Declan shook his head as he turned forward. He could already feel the corner of his eye beginning to swell, but he couldn't stifle the laugh that bubbled up. Ignoring the sting of the air against a fresh cut, he licked blood away from the corner of his mouth. Callum slowly came into focus before him. He didn't seem at all amused.

"My apologies. I shouldn't assume," Declan said before spitting blood and saliva onto the floor at his feet. "What was *his* name?" This time he saw the blow before it came and managed to shift away, though his ear took some of the impact, and he winced at the pain that sprang up. "Don't tell me it was an animal. I mean, to each his own."

Before he could continue, Callum leaned toward him, stomping on Declan's foot. With his hands gripping the chair's arms, he forced Declan backwards.

"My past is mine, McCallagh," he said in a low and menacing tone. "And mine alone. Rumors exist, but I don't owe you or anyone else my story. Push the matter again, and I won't stop with your sister. I'll track down that heir of yours. Give her a test of a real pirate, and I'll make it hurt. Understand?"

The threat struck Declan as intended. His gut tightened at the possibility of Aoife being the object of this captain's wrath, but he slipped the mask over his features even as he swallowed back the fear of anything happening to her.

"Understood," he offered. "Now, if there's nothing else you need, I'd appreciate being allowed to retire back to my accommodations. My head could use the rest."

Callum retreated to the desk and—with his back still turned to Declan—lifted the dagger, turning it lazily upon its tip. Declan slowly drew in a breath, thankful to be free from the physical intrusion.

"Of course," Callum said, still turning the blade, refusing to look at Declan. Was the man ashamed of something? Ashamed of having real emotions? Or simply ashamed of reacting to Declan's provocation?

The door to the cabin opened, and the big brute from earlier stepped inside and hoisted Declan out of the chair by his arm.

"Easy there," Declan complained, turning his chin up toward the massive man. "Not all of us like it rough."

The man only harrumphed before dragging him toward the door. Before they stepped outside, Callum called after them. "McCallagh, be ready tomorrow to discuss your plans for the sirens. I don't want to be caught unawares, so you will be honest next time. Aye?"

Declan couldn't even sigh in response before he was shoved over the threshold and back into the sunshine, the freshness of the sea air a welcome change from the stuffy cabin. He hadn't taken more than one breath, though, before the big oaf's hands had him moving along the deck toward the ladder. He dug his feet into the wooden floor to stop their progress.

"Mind if I catch a bit of a breather here before I'm forced back into that hole?"

The man turned to him, studying him, searching for any sign of mischief.

"I don't know if you've noticed, but my head has seen better days, and—as ashamed as I am to admit it—I'm not adjusting to the sea quite as I normally do. Now, I suppose if you want to risk me hurling what little is in my stomach all over you or this meticulously kept deck, that's your choice. Though I would rather do so over the railing." Declan pretended to stifle a retch, swallowing down the phantom bile he hoped the man would believe to be real.

The big hand tightened on Declan's arm before dragging him not toward the ladder below but to the starboard side. With a shove, the pirate sent Declan stumbling into the railing while still keeping his grip on him.

"Thank you," Declan offered, once again forcing himself to fake another wave of nausea. The key to a ruse was to play it right up to the point of excessiveness, to sell it without overdoing it. He looked out at the horizon, swallowing, hoping the oaf was buying his act of needing to quell an uneasy stomach. While the cabin and the brig had indeed been ghastly and offensive to his senses, his stomach had long ago become so accustomed to such that he had begun to believe the years at sea had turned it to steel.

You thought the same about your heart.

Declan didn't have to fake the cringe that thought invoked. Thinking about

Aoife excessively would not help him. She was his reason to survive this suicide mission, however he could manage that, but if he let himself focus too much on her and on their last moments together, their last words shared…

Involuntarily he turned his attention to the right, risking a glance behind him, allowing a bit of hope to spring up that his ship would appear on the horizon. But there were no sails to be seen. Only darkness brewing with a ferocity he had only seen in a handful of storms here on the Aisling. So that was the rumbling he'd heard in the distance. He should have known this wouldn't be easy. Nothing about this endeavor was proving easy.

"Hope your crew isn't risking their necks in there for you," the man beside him said, and Declan didn't need to look at him to know he was referring to the storm behind them. "You're not worth it."

The man was right. Declan wasn't worth heading into that storm, and he could only hope Tommy—and Aoife—had not been in the middle of it when it had come on. But that left them with only two other options: the longer way, near Haviern, or the decidedly more deadly one close to Tyshaly. He hoped Tommy had chosen their course wisely, but knowing his friend—knowing what he himself would have done in his place—he could be certain they weren't taking the safer route.

Damn pirates.

CHAPTER 10
CAIT

Cait forced herself into a slow, steady gait, shuffling her feet in uneven steps so this unexpected guest would believe she'd been upstairs asleep. Her mind rushed through all the people she might find in her pub, devising a response for each possibility. No matter who it was, her greeting would be the same, at least, so she started speaking even before she turned the corner at the bottom of the stairs.

"Can I help you?"

She nearly stopped short at the sight of the young woman standing just inside the door, but she recovered quickly, striding behind the bar and grabbing for a towel. As silly as it was, it helped to have something with which to occupy her hands whenever she found herself in uncomfortable situations. Not stopping to wait for a response from the newcomer, she proceeded to wipe down the bar, though it had been thoroughly cleaned earlier that morning when the last patron had left.

"Are you Ms. McCallagh?" The girl sounded as youthful as she appeared. She couldn't have been more than fifteen years old. Cait quickly recognized her as one of the girls employed by the council; her cloak was doing very little to hide the council garb she wore. And even if it had succeeded in concealing her clothing, the presence of the cloak at all in the middle of summer would have been enough for anyone to realize something was amiss.

"I am. And I apologize, Miss, but we don't open for another few hours. Council rules."

The girl shifted her weight as she looked around the empty pub, her hands clenched tightly before her. "Then why is the door unlocked?"

"I would have thought you'd know, given..." Cait waved a hand in the girl's direction before changing the course of her words. "Another council rule. With violence being forbidden, all businesses in Morshan and on all of Cregah—as far as

I'm aware—are forbidden from having locks in use. To do so would be to display a distrust in our dear councilwomen and the peace they provide for us."

The words ran bitter over her tongue—so rehearsed, so coated in faked reverence for the sham the council peddled. The girl didn't seem to catch the lie, though, merely mouthing a silent *oh* and allowing herself to look around the pub.

Cait stood up, leaning a hip against the bar, the towel keeping both her hands busy as she continued. "Per council rules, of course, I'm not allowed to have patrons here prior to allotted business hours. So if there's something I can do for you, I'll need to know straightaway."

"I wondered... Well, you see, I'm looking to buy something for a friend." The girl paused, her chin dipping down to her chest as she fidgeted with the edges of her cloak at her waist. "Do you possibly know where I can buy a cookie for my friend?"

The air stuck in Cait's throat at the seemingly random question, and she had to remind herself to continue breathing, though she didn't allow herself to relax. As she found her mental bearings, she fought the urge to roll her eyes at the ridiculous words Lucan had insisted upon all those years ago. *"What? It's perfect. It's unusual enough that few people will ask it but not so odd that it would seem out of place."* Cait had conceded, but even so, this was the first time someone had ever uttered the passphrase, the first time someone had sought her out.

Cait drew in another breath to calm her nerves. She wracked her brain for the asinine response Lucan had devised, but it had been years ago. *Really? Years? That long?*

Before she could utter one word, though, a man's voice filled the room. "And who is this friend you're gifting this to?" Lucan stepped around the wall and settled into one of the stools at the bar, refusing to make eye contact with Cait as he angled himself toward their guest.

Cait was going to kill him. He was supposed to stay hidden. She had it handled. But did she really? Why was she so averse to accepting his aid? It was true she had forgotten her line, and if she were being honest, she was less angry with him than she was with herself for failing to even notice that he had come down the stairs at all.

With nothing to add to the conversation, Cait looked toward the girl, who was once again fidgeting with her cloak. Her eyes darted from the floor to the walls, to Lucan and Cait, and then back to the floor before she finally—with a breath so deep Cait could hear the air rushing into her lungs from across the room—answered him. "For a friend who works with me. She's a bit...under the weather."

Lucan turned to Cait with the same smug attitude he always got when he was proven right, then returned his attention to the young girl.

"I see. And what kind do you think might help her?"

Cait gnashed her teeth together until her jaws hurt. Sands, no one would ever buy this ridiculous exchange. She would need to have a talk with Lucan later to change these blasted code phrases to something more refined and less foolish.

For a brief moment, Cait wondered if the girl had actually been sincerely asking for cookies, though, and not using this secret—and absurd—method of making contact with the Rogues. Once again her breath caught, her body unwilling to let any air pass her lips until the girl answered.

"Chocolate, I believe," she said, trying to control her trembling hands. "With mint chips."

That was it. That was all Cait needed to hear. The girl had been sent here. That much she knew from the whole cookie nonsense, but chocolate meant the one who had sent her was in danger. Mint meant death. As ludicrous as this whole cookie business was, she had to admit that it had worked—-though she wasn't sure she'd give Lucan the opportunity to gloat over it.

"I see," Cait said. "Come 'ere." She waved the girl over and motioned for Lucan to offer the stool beside him. The girl sat on the edge of the seat so her feet still touched the floor, as if this were a trap she needed to be prepared to escape from.

Lucan lifted his chin at her. "We will get you directions to the best bakery in Morshan."

The girl's expression seemed to hold a mix of confusion and gratitude, as though she wasn't quite sure if Lucan and Cait had gotten her message or if they really were going to point her toward a pastry shop. She mumbled a "Thank you" nonetheless, and Cait cleared her throat to get her attention.

Cait spoke slowly. "Should be easy enough. We don't need to write it down. The best cookies come from a woman who lives outside Morshan, actually. Take the path northwest, not more than a half-mile. You'll know it when you see it. But"—she looked at the clock behind her above the bar—"she won't have the cookies ready this early. I recommend heading that way in, what"—she turned to Lucan—"an hour or two?"

"Aye," he said with a string of easy nods. "Closer to two, I'd think."

The girl was looking back and forth between them uneasily.

Cait raised her chin and looked toward the door of the pub as she spoke again. "I wish we could chat more, but alas, the council really does not like it if we entertain patrons outside hours."

"Of course," the girl said, standing and rolling her shoulders as she straightened, and for a hair of a second, Cait had a nagging suspicion that this girl had played them for fools; her confidence had appeared only after they'd basically given her the key to discovering the Rogues' identities. Had they played right into a trap set by the council? Had Maggie divulged their secret before they'd killed her?

But no sooner had Cait asked herself these questions than the tension returned to her guest's face, her next words coming out shaky and unsure. "Thank you, Ms. McCallagh." She turned to Lucan. "And Ms. McCallagh's friend. I will look into your recommendation in a couple of hours after I finish the rest of my errands."

She pivoted on one of her feet and walked briskly toward the door. Without a word, she was gone.

Lucan burst into laughter. His loud guffaws filled the room until Eva came rushing from the stairway where she'd been hiding, her brow wrinkled with worry, her lips tight with concern.

Cait threw her towel at Lucan's face. "Stop that laughter, you buffoon! Someone will hear you!" She ignored how much she sounded like her mother. How could she move on from her grief when every day she exhibited some mannerism that mirrored her mother so perfectly?

Lucan snapped his mouth shut before mouthing a silent apology.

"Do you think it was a trap?" Eva asked. At least she was smart enough to keep her words barely audible.

"I don't know. I hope not, but it is possible. I hope the baker outside of town can help her out."

Lucan sobered quickly at those words, straightening in his seat, his eyes once again clear and determined. As hilarious as he'd found his whole cookie idea—and she would no doubt get an earful about his enjoyment later—at least he'd been working with her long enough to know when it was time to get to work.

"I'll be back later. Maybe I'll bring a cookie or two back for you," he said, flashing Cait a wink before turning toward the door, waving at Eva to join him. "You coming?"

A silent nod was the only reply he received.

Cait watched her two closest friends head out the door and into Morshan, away from the relatively safe walls of her pub. As if anywhere was truly safe on this island.

Whether the girl was a spy or not, only time would tell, and she had to trust Lucan and Eva to handle the situation while she played up the ruse of being the devoted pub owner and model Cregahn businesswoman.

This seemed to be her lot in life. In charge, running the show, running the pub, sending others out to have all the fun, to face all the danger. Maybe once the council was gone, she could leave this all behind, get a ship of her own, and set out for other seas, for an adventure all her own.

But not yet.

CHAPTER II
AOIFE

Thunder rumbled in the distance as Aoife pushed her short legs after Tommy, who was taking the steps up to the quarterdeck two at a time. She didn't hear the fae following them—not that she would have, with their obnoxious way of walking silently—and she hoped their hundreds of years of existence had given them the ability to sense when they were no longer welcome.

As she turned toward the spot at the railing where she had last stood with Gavin, her breath escaped her in a sigh. The sisters were huddled together on the deck. Tommy stood at the rail, his forearms digging into the edge of the wood, his eyes staring blankly at Mikkel, who was preparing the crew for what lay ahead.

Bumping Tommy's hip with her own, she took up the spot next to him and flashed him as genuine a smile as she could muster, though it melted away when he didn't so much as glance her way. He flexed his jaw.

"So," she started, not sure what to expect from him now that he was the acting captain. Would he snap at her with some rude comment as Declan had so many times? Would he ignore her as he had just done? Or would he be the kind friend she'd come to see him as? "The crew seems to be okay with me now."

Silence.

Well, his response could have been worse.

She continued, "Gavin says I'm practically the quartermaster now, but I told him that was nonsense, as I'm not even a pirate. But still, it's nice to not have so many eyes staring at me all the time. Collins even waved to me earlier. That was nice. You know, even though I don't want to be stared at, you could still look at me? Maybe?"

She'd been rambling far longer than she'd intended, but he hadn't reacted at all. No laugh. No roll of the eyes. Not even an exasperated sigh.

They remained there for a few more minutes in silence as Gavin relieved the man at the helm and shouted out the commands that would get them underway.

Toward death. A multi-armed death.

Aoife risked another look at Tommy from the corner of her eye and then whispered, "I'm sorry, Tommy."

She was almost sure he hadn't heard her, not over the flap of sails in the breeze or the shouts of men as they maneuvered the ship. But he turned to her then. Not fully, but a pivot of the head was far better than being ignored.

"For what?" The words came out strained, as if the stress of the predicament had sapped the life from his voice.

"For leaving Declan at the cove. If I had just forgiven him when he requested, he would be here now, and you wouldn't be under so much stress."

At this, Tommy stood fully and turned toward her, and though his stance was relaxed, his hip resting against the rail, arms crossed loosely in front of him, tension rolled off of him.

"Should you have forgiven him?" He answered his own question with a shrug. "I don't know. Only you can decide whether that was even possible at the time. But you aren't to blame for this. This was Callum's doing, not yours. Even had you left the cove together, Callum would not have let Declan get off Cregah any other way but in his brig. Of that, I'm certain. No doubt Declan would have been just as distracted with you by his side as I'm sure he was when Callum came upon him. And had you been with him? I would still be stressed. Perhaps more so. Because I'd be worried about you both. Chasing after you both."

Aoife took in a deep breath, filling her lungs with the refreshing sea air. It didn't help her digest what Tommy had said though.

After a moment, he turned back to his original position, like a gargoyle who had come to life during the night returning to its stony resting place with the daylight. Aoife followed suit.

She opened her mouth to speak, but her words were cut short when Tommy nudged her with his elbow and said, "But you don't get to be quartermaster though."

At first, his face remained so stern, she wasn't sure if he was teasing or if he was serious, but then that sweet smile she'd grown so fond of spread across his face.

"Well, you'd better inform Gavin of that before he tells the entire crew."

The thunder in the distance continued its throaty growl as lightning spread across the wide swath of clouds, like wispy fingers reaching out to find something to destroy. If it wasn't forcing them to take the dangerous route to the west, Aoife might have thought it beautifully mesmerizing. She could imagine sitting on the shores of some distant land, safe and warm, watching the lights, imagining they were created just for her. And Declan. It wouldn't be—it currently wasn't—as nice without him.

"How long until we... " She couldn't bring herself to finish the question.

"Meet the kraken?" Tommy asked, and she merely gave a small nod in reply. "A couple days. Maybe more. But that's just until we arrive in its territory. We'll take it as slow as we can without forfeiting Declan to his demise, and hopefully it will be slow enough to not alert the beast to our presence."

Aoife wasn't sure how that logic would pan out. It seemed to her the monster would be able to see the hull of a boat at the surface no matter what speed it was moving. But she trusted Tommy to know what he was doing. He had been doing this job far longer than she had, after all. That thought caused a breath of a laugh to escape her lips, prompting him to flash her a questioning look, but she merely shook her head.

She needed to change the subject. Anything to move his attention off her. "So, Tommy, what was that between you and Maura, huh?"

That's what you're going to bring up? Have you learned nothing from your past mistakes?

Her thoughts screamed at her, and she froze with the realization that she had probably asked the worst question possible of her friend. She didn't dare breathe as she waited for him to react, but the lack of oxygen in her lungs quickly foiled that plan, forcing her to greedily suck in more air.

Fainting would be embarrassing.

She expected him to brush it off as nothing, deny what she had most definitely witnessed between them in Declan's quarters.

Instead, after running his fingers across his brow and then through his hair, he simply asked, "You noticed that, did you?"

Aoife looked around, as if there might be someone else he could be asking, before stammering out, "Um, were you both trying to hide it? Because you did a piss-poor job of it if you were."

"To be honest, I don't know that she's as intent on hiding it as I am. If she is at all."

"You can't tell me there are no feelings there though. I mean, the sparks were nearly visible."

"It's impossible to have such strong feelings so quickly though. Right?"

Aoife lifted a shoulder. "Only seems impossible because it happens so rarely. And even then, I don't think it's as rare as people make it out to be. It happened for my sister, after all." Her throat tightened at the mention of Lani, and she raised a hand to where the necklace still hung beneath her shirt.

"I suppose. But, possible or not, I won't encourage some dream of love and companionship that I can't have." She moved to interject, but he held up his hand. "I know. You and Declan. Yes, that can work, and has for a handful of partnerships. But she's fae. I'm not. She has her kind to get back to, to be reunited with in the south. It can't—"

"Well, not with that attitude, it can't," Aoife said, hoping her words conveyed the lightheartedness she intended.

"It would never work, Aoife. I belong here. On this ship. With this crew. And she's needed elsewhere. I won't get my hopes up for something that is impossible."

"You know, Tommy, a smart pirate named Gavin once told me, 'If we don't have hope, what do we have?'"

Another deep breath, and Tommy huffed out a sighing laugh. "Gavin. I swear. Going to him for wisdom now, are we?"

"What? Even a blind seagull finds a fish now and then, right? Why can't our silly Gavin have some wisdomous moments?"

"Wisdomous?" He raised a brow at her, his lips fighting back the smile she missed seeing.

"Hey, I'm practically quartermaster. I get to make up words if I want to."

He wagged a finger in the air at her. "Nope. I denied that title, remember?"

Aoife feigned surprise and pushed herself back from the railing, nearly falling over as the wind caught the sails, rocking the boat at just the right moment. "Then, I'd best get off the quarterdeck. I don't believe we mere deckhands and stowaways are allowed up here."

"Nah, you can stay. You have this interim captain's permission to go anywhere on the ship you please. You may not be the quartermaster, but you are our esteemed guest. You are still sleeping in the captain's quarters, after all."

"Well," she said, bowing her head, "this lowly stowaway turned esteemed guest thanks you for your kindness."

He nodded in reply before turning back toward the railing once more, but she couldn't let him sink back into his brooding just yet.

"Tommy?" she asked, and he hummed in response. "What shall I be doing when —I mean, if—the kraken spots us? Am I to hide in the cabin and hope to the ends of the Aisling that we survive? Is there no way for me to be of help? And if not with the kraken, then in the sound? I'm going to need some preparation. I can't always be the prim and proper council heir sitting on the sidelines, especially not in this attire."

"I don't think even Declan would have you hiding anywhere, not after we witnessed your courage back at the council hall. We don't have much time to make you great with a blade, but we can at least make you better than you are."

"That shouldn't be hard. I know nothing at the moment."

"That's not true," he assured her with a shake of his head. "You do know what end goes in your hand."

"Even children learn that quickly."

"True, true. But still. We can get you introduced to some basic handling skills. It's better than nothing."

"So when do we start?" Aoife asked, standing taller, though it didn't improve her confidence at all.

"Not *we*, you..." Putting two fingers to his lips, he whistled down to the main deck, pointed at a man, and waved for him to come join them. "...and Collins. I believe you've met before?" he asked just as the tall pirate came up beside Aoife with an eager look on his face that had her wondering what duty he expected Tommy had summoned him for.

"Yes," Aoife said, addressing Collins now. "I never did thank you for not throwing me off the ship when you first caught me."

A silent nod was his only reply.

Turning back to Tommy, she asked, "So Collins will train me with a blade?" Collins's expression lit up a bit more at this news.

"Aye, he trains all of our younger, newer recruits who get hired fresh out of the ports with little-to-no experience. He has quite the knack for teaching novices quickly and efficiently."

"Good," she said with a sigh, and before Tommy had completely turned away from them, Collins was already motioning for her to follow him down to the deck.

She knew she needed at least somewhat of a fighting chance against the kraken and the sirens, but looking at Collins's towering frame, the hard lines of lean muscle trailing down his arms and across his shoulders, she wasn't so sure she'd survive the training itself. But she had to try.

CHAPTER 12
DECLAN

The large crewman-turned-jailer proved no gentler as he returned Declan to the brig. The grumbling scoff he unleashed at Declan's request for a bit of food was as rough as the scruffy beard along his jaw.

"I'll win you over yet!" Declan called after him, and although the man didn't bother with any verbal response, Declan was satisfied enough with the slight shake of the head the man gave him before disappearing back up the ladder.

Within minutes, the silence of the brig became too much, and even with the constant sound of the sea against the hull, the absence of all other noise threatened to suffocate him.

As if silence could actually do that. You're such an idiot.

He answered his own thoughts aloud, "Indeed I am. I've certainly gotten myself into a shitty mess now, haven't I?" He swept his eyes around the small cell. The wooden floor was entirely bare save the faint signs of where he'd been forced to relieve himself.

He had little desire to sit on the filthy floor again, but he also couldn't stand still. The silence seemed to have taken on a life of its own. So he began to pace, counting out the sound of his footsteps as he walked, forward and back, and then around and around. Counting gave him some idea of how long it had been since the man had left, but more importantly it kept his mind from wandering back to that cove.

At least for a moment.

Every few paces, the image of black sand in the moonlight flashed in his mind, and he counted louder in his head, as if he could wash away the visions like a tide washing away a message in the sand.

But they never stayed gone for long, with Aoife shoving her way to the forefront over and over again.

Well, if she wasn't going to leave him alone to think, there seemed little point in expending what precious energy he had trying to fight her. In his mind, he pulled out a chair, proffering it to the imagined version of her.

You really have lost it, haven't you?

Still, inviting Aoife to stay on the edge of his mind rather than trying to shove her away and lock the memories up tight helped him focus on the matter at hand. Maybe having her there, keeping him company—even if only in his imagination— would remind him of all he had to fight for.

So, with Aoife watching, he set to examining the predicament he'd gotten himself into.

He needed a plan. Of that he was sure, but no matter what angle he viewed the situation from, he could see no way past the sirens without using the powers of the fae. Perhaps he could convince Callum of that truth, but even as he thought it, he knew that would be a fruitless effort. The pirate was as stubborn as he was stupid.

But what kept Callum from listening? It wasn't merely his stubbornness, though that was formidable, to be sure.

You conned him. He won't trust you.

"But he trusts you enough to escort him into the damn sound?" he asked himself aloud, no longer caring how crazy it was to be talking to himself. At least half the conversation remained in his head, and that felt slightly less awkward. But only slightly.

Still, he couldn't deny that Callum obviously harbored some bitterness over Declan's last play. It had been a risk, of course, but that was what this job entailed. Time and time again, risk at every turn. And at the time, it had seemed better to risk angering an old friend than to see Aoife taken as a prisoner and hauled back to the council hall.

It would do no good to focus on what might have happened had he chosen differently. What was done was done, and the plain fact remained that he was stuck in this damn cell, hands bound behind his back, with no blasted clue how he was going to survive the next chapter of his cursed life.

Trying to mentally sort through all the scenarios that could play out once they arrived in the sound didn't prove to be of any comfort either. Every possibility was just as bad as the last, each of them ending in a bloody death. No chance of being reunited with his crew, his ship, and Aoife.

Aoife.

If she arrived in the sound, if they didn't catch up to the *Curse Bringer* before they entered those waters, what would happen to her? Declan told himself to trust Tommy and the fae to handle the situation, but the thought of her being devoured by the monsters waiting for them...

Too much.

But those images only dissolved into similarly devastating ones of her drowning as the many arms of the kraken tore through his ship. She didn't deserve any of this. The lies, the deceit, the danger, the risk, the heartbreak. She should be living a life of ease, free from worry and death and pain.

Not that that type of life exists anywhere, here in the Aisling or beyond.

He nodded to himself, his lips tightening into a line. Life wasn't easy, no matter the circumstances. Life was instead a grotesquely beautiful combination of pain and love, tragedy and triumph. Though, at the moment, he and everyone associated with him seemed to be enduring more of the former.

No, he had made a promise to himself, and he would have voiced it to Aoife too, if she had given him the chance. He would make things right. He would make it all up to her. He would make amends for lying to her.

But you won't be able to do that if you don't bloody survive.

With a huff, he kicked the iron bars of his cell, regretting it at once when his toes took the brunt of the impact. A grimace spread across his face, and a string of curses fell from his mouth as he hopped away, nursing his aching foot. But his bound hands threw his balance completely off. His leap away from the offending bars sent him falling backwards, and his fingers were crushed between his backside and the floor.

"Well," a voice said around a scratchy laugh, "you aren't at your most graceful, are yeh?"

Declan raised his chin so he could see his guest, hiding his wince so the man wouldn't see his embarrassment and pain. No wonder he hadn't heard him approaching; he was nearly the exact opposite of the previous crewman who had come for him. This one was slight, and though he looked to be close to Declan in age, his eyes carried more wisdom—and kindness—than Declan would have expected from anyone aboard this ship.

"Sadly, no. You are not catching me at my best," Declan said as he tried to maneuver himself into a more comfortable position.

"No kidding. You're proving all the stories we've heard of the great young Captain McCallagh to be naught but folly. How did you manage to make such a name for yourself if you also got caught and thrown in our brig?"

"Just bad luck, I suppose," Declan answered with an exaggerated sigh. "So, to what do I owe the pleasure of your visit? Callum not trust me in this cell? Not like I can do much here, like this." He tried to lift his shackled hands as far around to the side as he could.

"Well, trusting you doesn't seem to be high on his list, but he did instruct me to bring you your rations. Can't be encountering the sirens with you all weak and feeble." The man stepped forward, and for the first time, Declan noted the bundle the man held at his waist. He might have kicked himself for being so inattentive, but the dim light plus the blow to his head were viable reasons for his failure.

"Thank you. I wondered if Big Boris had heard me when I requested food," Declan said with a nod of his chin toward the ladder.

"Big Boris?" Even in the darkness, Declan could see the man's dark brows pull together over his light blue eyes. "Oh, you mean Reggie. You're not likely to get much out of that one. He's more the quiet type. And I don't mean vocally," he added, tapping a finger at his temple a couple of times.

Declan let out a light laugh as he caught the man's meaning. "And you are?"

"Oh, I'm all well and good in that department."

"Good to know, though I was actually asking your name."

The man took another step forward until he was mere inches from the bars and shook his head, dark strands of hair falling over his face. "Well, you should be clearer. People can't read your mind, you know."

"Sands, I'm glad for that." Declan attempted to stand, but the man waved for him to stop.

"No need to get up," he said, instead lowering himself down to sit on the floor, pushing the hair back behind his ears. "I'm not permitted to free your hands, so unless you want to eat it off your lap or"—he gestured to the floor—"off whatever the hell is coating this disgustingness, I figured I could help."

Clearing his throat, Declan eyed the man, trying to figure him out. "Well, I've never been fed by another man."

"First time for everything."

"I've heard that before. Aboard this ship, actually. But okay. I'll accept your help, but only after you give me your name. Feels weird to have a stranger do such a thing."

The man gave another throaty chuckle. "I would think it would feel weird, friend or otherwise, eh? But the name's Boris."

Declan gave him a once-over and tried to ignore the itch that developed along his jaw again. "No, it's not."

With a roll of his eyes, the man let out a breath. "Fine, it's not. I should have known I couldn't pull one over on you. It's actually Killian."

Declan clicked his tongue as he looked to the ceiling, his mind searching for dim memories and coming up empty. "I swear I knew a Killian once."

"Oh? Fellow pirate, was he?"

"I don't think so, though my memory isn't what it used to be. Used to frequent the pub and entertain folks with stories from his home beyond the Aisling. Tales of magic and death, great battles and...a horse. That I remember. He always talked about his black horse."

He blinked and looked back at Killian to find a quizzical expression on the man's face. Declan cleared his throat before saying, "Not that any of that has to do with you. But you're not from the Aisling, are you?"

Killian unwrapped the bundle in his lap as he responded. "The accent give me away?" He didn't wait for an answer. "South of here. Came north when I was a young man to get away from the conflict that was brewing."

"South, as in Larcsporough?" he asked before opening his mouth awkwardly to accept a piece of the same fruit he'd seen Callum eating earlier. The burst of juice when he bit into it surprised him as much as its sweet, tart flavor, and Killian laughed lightly, shaking his head.

"It's called an orange. Never seen one? They come from the south actually. And yes, Larcsporough. But it's been nearly twenty years since I've set foot on that land."

Declan shifted closer to the bars. While he doubted anyone was listening in, it was better to take care, so he said in a low voice, "So you know of the fae?"

The man lifted a hand to his head, rubbing away whatever tension had built up at his temple. "Aye, I know 'em."

"I sense some not-too-fond feelings toward them," Declan said. The information Killian could provide might not aid him in his current situation, but if he'd learned anything from his years at sea, it was that all information was valuable. Eventually.

Killian dropped his gaze to the floor and drew in a breath. "You could say that."

Declan waited, and somewhere deep inside him a slight laugh echoed at how different his situation had become. He'd been so stressed by the deadline Cait had given him, and now it no longer seemed to matter. Not that he'd had any control over circumstances before, but here he had none. It did him no good to fret over it, and so he could wait for Killian to provide the story.

Offering him the last segment of the fruit, Killian said softly, "For centuries my people lived in Larcsporough, ruled peacefully by our royal family. But when the war up here ended and the fae moved in, it all changed. At first we lived in harmony, equally sharing the lands. We integrated well, perhaps too well, because we let our guard down."

"What do you mean, too well?"

"How much do you know about fae history?"

"Only the basics. Much was lost and forgotten with the belief they had all perished in the war."

Killian sighed, nodding. "Well, then you don't know that only fae of the royal bloodline have magic, or what they call *daemari*. The fae who survived the war sought a way to avoid the destruction in the future. So they instituted new laws. They broke apart the royal families. Decided the best path forward was to lessen the *daemari* as much as possible."

"So they forbid royal fae from bonding," Declan said.

"Aye. And it worked. While the original royals survived the war and their powers remained strong, they paired with lesser fae, so their children's *daemari* was less potent, if they received any at all. And after spending a century or two living with us humans, those children—the lesser fae—began to bond with mortals."

"Bond. Like something they can't resist?"

Killian straightened up, his face contorting as if he had tasted something bitter. "What? No. Has that become part of the lore?"

Declan gave a nod. "One book I read talked of how they can't control who they pair with, and there is no breaking it once the bond has formed."

The man shook his head with a breathy laugh. "Not surprising how the truth gets twisted over time. No, what we might see as being a firm bond is merely how intensely the fae feel. Humans fall in love—if they're lucky—but fae? There is no word for what they experience. Can they deny it? Walk away from it? Aye. But it rarely happens."

"And they were allowed to take humans as—"

"Encouraged to, in some cases," Killian said. "Some fae lines resorted to forcing their offspring into marriages with mortals."

"To ensure their powers—the *daemari*—would die out?"

"Aye."

Declan's mind worked to piece all of this together, but something was missing. "But how did this lead to you fleeing? What was the danger?"

Killian was silent for a moment, and the tears forming in his eyes shined. But with a blink, he managed to keep them at bay. "The lesser fae didn't know the history. And some felt their elders had exaggerated the stories to keep them from having more power, more wealth, more of what they felt they deserved. After centuries of being denied what they saw as their right—land and riches and control—they started to rebel. The fae are nothing if not patient, and their bitterness and resentment festered for another century and a half, with small steps being taken little by little to create division throughout their kind. I was only a babe when the first camps were built."

Declan froze. He'd never heard of such a thing, but Killian's forlorn tone and solemn demeanor indicated it was far from good. "Camps?"

A dip of the chin was all Killian offered, silence settling between them. Declan wracked his brain as he tried to digest this revelation. What had the fae done to Killian's people? What had happened to Killian's family? Before he could decide how to ask any of his questions, the man was talking again.

"All humans were taken from their homes. First in the east. We heard about it up north where I lived, but news came too late. We had only heard whisperings of families being dragged out in the middle of the night, forced to give their homes and belongings over to the fae."

"Was it all fae? Some of them were wed to humans, though, right? Did they participate? Or..." Declan thought he knew the answer, but he hoped he was wrong.

"Forced to choose between their fae heritage and their human partners and their demi-fae children. If they chose their families over their brethren..." His eyes glazed over as if he was reliving some memory, seeing a vision of some past event replaying in his mind. "It was not pretty. Those who chose to join their fae kin were forced to prove their loyalty by slaughtering their spouses and children. If they refused, they were punished, made to watch as their loved ones were tortured and killed."

Declan's stomach turned. He'd seen his share of violence, had inflicted pain upon others himself, had done so without regret or remorse, but he did not do it for sport—not like some of the more ruthless in his profession. Rather, it was simply a necessary part of achieving some goals.

"And you? Where does your story fit into all of this?" Declan asked, trying his best to keep his tone neutral and not let any of his shock show.

"We were one of those families. The fae had reached a nearby town, and one of my father's close friends—a human—had managed to get his family out in time. He came to warn us. They decided we needed to leave Larcsporough, make a new life in the north, in one of the lands of the Aisling. But the nearest port was a day's walk away. My father urged us to leave, vowing we would have a better chance of reaching a ship and sailing to safety if he stayed behind and stalled the approaching fae. My mother refused to leave his side, and he finally agreed to join us. But it was a lie. He never intended to come, I don't think. We made it to the port. He secured us passage on a merchant ship, but just as we had stepped foot aboard, he stopped and rushed back to the dock. I watched him disappear as my mother wailed, nearly falling over the edge. The crew had to restrain her and give her a tonic to help her calm down and sleep. I don't know what happened to him. I never heard. I was only sixteen at the time, but even then I had no idea how to help my mother. By the time we reached Ludlam, she had fallen into such a grave depression over my father's absence, we could barely tell if she was still present in her mind. My younger sister insisted on staying there with her, to take care of her and to hopefully build a simpler life away from the hatred and persecution. But she was only eleven, with no skills, and I refused to let her do the work many young girls end up in. I got hired onto the first crew that would take me."

Declan blinked, his eyes opening wide as he tried to find the proper words. He had so many questions, each of which itched to be voiced first. He snatched at the first one he could mentally grasp onto and blurted out, "Callum's crew?"

A nod. "Though it wasn't always Callum's. He was younger than me when I first signed on. I've known him a long time."

"And you said your family was one of those being—" Killian nodded sharply, as if the man couldn't bear to have it said aloud again. "That would mean one of your parents was a—"

"A fae. Yes. My father."

"So you're a... What are you exactly?" He cringed at the ridiculous way he had worded the question, but thankfully Killian didn't seem to notice or care.

"Demi-fae, technically, but most of my father's fae qualities went to my sister, so for all intents and purposes I consider myself human."

Propping himself up against his bound hands, Declan leaned back. "And what of the humans who had no ties to the fae? Do I even want to know?"

"The camps. They were strictly for the humans. What they did with them there, I never heard, but I doubt it was anything good."

"No doubt. No wonder you have such animosity for them." Declan wondered how Killian would react to the knowledge that he had planned to work with the fae to achieve this goal.

He worked his way through all he'd just learned, debating how any of this might help him in his current situation, but nothing presented itself.

Except for one thing... Not that it helped him in this festering brig. How it would help in the future, he didn't know either, but he tucked the information away into the corner of his mind for safekeeping.

Only the royal fae had powers.

So the Bron sisters were royals.

CHAPTER 13
AOIFE

AOIFE TRIED to ignore the blatant stares she received from the crew as she strode out onto the deck, but it was difficult not to notice how they cleared the area and took up spots around the railing as if they didn't have anything better to do. Like prepare to meet the kraken.

Collins stepped forward calmly, his shoulders back, his dark eyes gleaming with confidence. Aoife could fake that, surely. Rolling her shoulders, she forced herself to grow a couple of inches with better posture, and then she drew her dagger from where she kept it at her waist.

"No," Collins said. But not rudely. More like he was declining a cup of tea instead of giving his new pupil a command.

"What do you mean, no?"

"We don't use real blades." Before she could protest or ask for clarification, he added, "Not when first learning. Last thing we need is for you to be not only untrained but also injured."

He motioned to a man Aoife didn't recognize, who tossed him what looked to be a few sticks. Holding them before him, Collins flashed her a wink. A week ago, that gesture would have been unexpected. Two weeks ago, it would have made her bristle. But now it felt as natural as an eyeroll from Lani.

Slipping her dagger back into its spot at her side, she motioned for Collins to toss her one of the wooden practice blades. When he did, she reached out with both hands, hoping at least one of them would be able to catch it. Snickers erupted around the deck when it clattered at her feet, but they stopped with such an abruptness that she knew without looking up that Collins had warned them to knock it off. She grasped for the dagger, curling her fingers around what she hoped was meant to be the handle. To pick it up by the wrong end would no doubt earn her more ridicule.

"First off, you need to loosen up a bit. You're standing too stiff," Collins instructed.

Aoife forced her joints to release some of their tension, but she didn't understand how she was to do any sort of fighting with her body as limp as a drunkard after a long celebration.

"Closer," Collins said, walking over to help her out. He slipped his own practice blade into his waistband and reached for her arms. Giving them a small shake, he said, "This is good, but this?" He grabbed her wrists and shook them around, and her hands flopped like fish in a net until her stick fell to the deck. "Causes that. You need to keep yourself loose so you can move quickly—especially with the beast we're going to encounter—but not so loose that you can't hold on to your weapon."

Aoife retrieved her bit of wood and tried again. "Like this?" But when she tightened her grip, it stiffened her whole arm. She corrected herself before he could speak. "Wait, no." Another roll of her shoulders, and she focused on relaxing her shoulder, her elbow, and her wrist while still keeping her hand in control of the sparring weapon.

"Yes, Aoife. Like that, except you'll need to practice that so it doesn't require so much concentration to achieve." He backed away a few feet, and Aoife could have sworn she saw him trying to suppress a laugh or a smile, but she refused to let it bother her. This was what she wanted. To learn. To be useful. And if achieving that meant dealing with a bit of embarrassment, then so be it.

"Okay. I'm loose, but not too loose. Now what?"

Pulling his practice weapon out once more, he waved her forward. "Attack me."

Aoife hesitated. Surely he should tell her how to do that before forcing her to, but he was the trainer. He must know how to teach, so she would listen. Thrusting her weapon in front of her, she lunged forward, covering the distance between them in a handful of steps. She hadn't even seen his tall form move when she felt the strike against her arm and heard her weapon fall onto the deck again.

"Good," Collins said.

"But I failed. How was that good?" she asked as she bent down once more to retrieve the wooden blade, forcing herself to ignore how her forearm hurt where he had struck her.

"Aye. But you tried. That's the first step. Failure in training isn't a bad thing. The faster you fail, the faster you'll learn how the correct movements feel, and the faster you'll learn overall. It would have been worse if you'd hesitated or refused."

"Okay," she said, not sure she quite understood his logic. "So what did I do wrong?"

"A few things." He must have seen how his words deflated her, because he flashed her a smile that melted away some of her apprehension. "Don't take it personally, Aoife. These are common errors. Nothing I haven't seen before. First, you were focused only on striking and didn't anticipate needing to guard yourself. You came at me squarely, but you'll want to shift your body like this." He moved one leg back until his body was at an angle to her.

"But doesn't that make you more exposed?"

"Only if I were facing multiple attackers, but right now we're focused on one. This allows me to prevent you from striking in my more sensitive areas."

Her face warmed at his words, and she cringed more at her own reaction than at what he'd said.

"Remember, you are both on the offense and the defense. You can't succeed in attacking if you aren't ready to guard yourself from their response. You won't be striking an unconscious person—or a sleeping beast, in this case—so you have to be prepared for them to defend themselves."

Aoife gave a nod. "What else? Did I approach wrong?"

"It was predictable. Not that this will be as big a deal against sea monsters and all. So instead, I want to focus on energy conservation. If you use too much force too early, you'll tire too quickly. Adrenaline can only help you so much."

"So how do I conserve that? If I don't put enough force behind my strike, it won't do any good, right?"

"Part of it is practice. As your body gets used to the movements—gets used to moving at all, really—it'll be easier to only use what you need."

"But we don't have—"

Collins held up a hand, and Aoife snapped her mouth shut.

"No, we don't have much time. So I'm not going to focus on the hand-to-hand fighting I normally would. Instead, I need you to be able to move quickly, react instantly, and not drop your weapon so easily when struck."

Aoife mimicked his angled position as Collins moved forward to show her how to keep her guard up. For hours they worked through the basics, striking and blocking so many times that the clacking of their wooden blades became as familiar a sound to her as the rush of the air past her ears. The feinting and quick movements proved more challenging than she'd expected. How did these pirates make it look so easy?

She was so focused on his instructions—and her own frustrations over how difficult it all was—that when they finally stopped, she was surprised to find the crew had all gone back to their regular tasks. When she moved to offer the wooden sparring blade to Collins, he once again held up a hand to stop her.

"Hold onto it. You'll want to be practicing what we worked on as often as you can. Even if only by yourself."

With a nod, she made to walk off toward the captain's quarters but turned and asked, "Will we practice again today?" While her mind insisted this would be best so she could improve as quickly as possible, her muscles screamed in protest, her legs and arms aching from the fatigue of being used in such an unfamiliar way.

"Nope. I don't want to break you too badly this first day. We'll train again tomorrow. I'll have someone bring some food in for you." He jutted his chin toward the cabin, encouraging her to retreat and rest.

After being out on the deck with the whistling of the sea breeze in her ears, the clattering of wood on wood, and the thudding of her body hitting the floor, the quiet in the quarters seemed to press in on her from all sides. While it wasn't her first time alone in this room since they'd left Cregah, the discomfort hadn't lessened any. Any forgiveness she had begun to feel for herself had been replaced with fresh guilt over abandoning Declan on that beach. No matter what Tommy insisted, she should have been there with him.

Running is what you do best though.

Tears sprang up, and she closed her eyes to keep them at bay. Crying wouldn't help anyone. She hadn't even been strong enough to face her pain as Declan pleaded with her in the cove. But she could be strong now.

She nearly laughed at that thought. Her whole body felt like a washcloth being wrung out for the hundredth time, squeezed and pushed until there was nothing but emptiness.

As soon as she sat on the edge of the bed to kick off her boots, she heard someone enter the cabin. She tried to identify the visitor—who hadn't even bothered to knock—by their gait alone, but her mind was as tired as the rest of her, unwilling to put forth much effort. She could call out, but there seemed little point, given that no one on this ship would do her harm, and they'd make themselves known soon enough.

All she wanted to do was to lie back and take a long nap, and she might have, had her stomach not grumbled in reaction to the smells of salted meat, cheese, and bread that now filled the room. Before she could move to rise, Tommy appeared in the doorway, a single plate of the food in his hand.

"No doubt you're hungry. I could hear your stomach from the other room," he said, offering her food to her.

Noticing his empty hands, she asked, "You not eating?"

"Not here. I'll take mine with Gavin and Mikkel over our strategy session in a bit."

"Shall I join you?" Even as she asked the question, she hoped he'd decline, not wanting to move any more than she had to. She wasn't even sure she could move if he requested her presence.

"No. I think you need to rest a bit—and stretch out those muscles—or you'll feel even worse in the morning."

"Worse? I don't know how that's possible." The tears returned, and she felt all the more ridiculous for reacting in such a way. How could she possibly expect to engage the kraken, let alone the sirens, if she couldn't even handle one day—not even a whole day—of training?

"Oh, it is. But it will get easier. And who knows. If we're lucky, you won't have to use any of those moves on the monster."

"I don't think luck has proven to be on our side thus far."

"Aye, but the past can't completely predict the future. All it can do is teach us so we make better decisions next time around."

Tommy's expression darkened a bit, his jaw tightening and his gaze softening as if he was standing somewhere else instead of in his best friend's quarters. Nibbling on a bit of the meat, Aoife watched him. The carefree charm she had come to associate with him had been absent since Declan's capture.

"What's eating at you, Tommy? Other than the obvious."

"Nothing," he said with a wave of his hand, shooing away her concern as he would a sand fly. "Just the obvious."

Aoife eyed him, but something about his tired appearance kept her from pressing for the truth.

Before she could think of anything more to say, he was backing away from the sleeping quarters and muttering something about needing to meet up with the men. With the door closed and the cabin once again empty and quiet, Aoife could have spent time pondering what could be bothering Tommy. But her mind and body both begged for rest, and without finishing the last of her food, she lay back onto the feather mattress and fell into a dreamless sleep.

CHAPTER 14

CAIT

THE FORESTS NORTHWEST of Morshan might have been peaceful if not for how eerie the silence was. The trees in this area lay thicker than to the south, as if they had crowded around to hide what happened beneath their branches. As silly as that notion might have been, it held some truth to Cait, as it was here she had found these ruins all those years ago on one of her explorations. Stone walls—or what was left of them—marked the entrance to a small clearing barely larger than the pub's main room. The clearing was otherwise empty, with the wall separating it from the rest of the forest all the way around. Some sections were nearly up to Cait's shoulders, while others were barely above her ankles. What the area had been used for, she had no idea. Some holy spot for a long-dead religion perhaps, or merely the remnants of an old home. Whatever it had been in the past, now it provided Cait and the Rogues the perfect hideout.

While Cait had initially balked at Lucan's half-brained cookie exchange idea, she had to admit it did work rather well. A small, abandoned house on the outskirts of the port town provided the perfect location to send those who made contact. Its original owners had left the area when Cait was too young to explore on her own, and no one had since moved in or claimed it for their own. Whether people thought it an ill omen to take up residence in an abandoned home, she wasn't sure, but even passing it on her way here had sent a shudder up her spine. Had the residents been exiled? Possibly. Or had they simply moved on to another land?

It was in that building that Lucan and Eva had met the girl from the pub to hear the rest of her story. A story so similar to others on the island. Family disappearing. Wealth being stripped. Hunger. Pain. Sickness. Until the only option she'd had was to look for work. She'd originally intended to use a position on the council staff to get close enough to gain an audience with them. She'd hoped they would be willing to hear her family's case and maybe have an investigation opened to discover what had become of them and who was responsible.

But before she'd had a chance to request such a meeting, she had witnessed the exile of the middle heir. Most of the newer and younger staff had remained in the staff quarters as instructed, but curiosity had pushed her toward a window that overlooked the main drive to the council entrance. The terror in the girl's eyes and the force they'd used against her had raised the girl's suspicions, eventually bringing her to the pub.

When Lucan had returned after lunch with the girl's story, he had suggested they call a meeting. Cait hadn't been keen on the idea, as it was too risky to have all of the Rogues in one place. They hadn't gathered in nearly two years, when they had planned Maggie's infiltration of the council's staff. Since then, all communication had been done via couriers. They were neither official members of the Rogues nor privy to the secrets within the messages they delivered, but they were satisfied with the extra ration cards or copper coins they received for their assistance. The steady stream of jobs Cait and her crew provided kept the men they employed from wagging their tongues to the council.

Still, with Maggie dead, Cait hadn't been able to deny the benefit of having a new set of eyes within the council hall, and she had quickly granted Lucan's request.

Although Lucan had left before her, Cait was the first to arrive at the ruins. Leaning against a corner of the wall where two tall sections met, she tried to exude the calm confidence her role demanded despite the quick, heavy beating of her heart against her sternum. It was so loud it echoed in her ears.

Her mind began to wander as she waited. How was Declan faring? Had his crew intercepted Callum yet? Was he safe, or was he already dead? Her throat constricted at that thought, and she forced her mind to move past it.

What of the dagger? If Declan didn't... Would his crew pick up where he'd left off? Or would her mission—the one thing that could help take down the council for good—fail before she could even really put it into action?

A throat cleared behind her, and she glanced over her shoulder to see Lucan and Eva approaching through the trees, stepping around the bushes and undergrowth. Between them, the girl, with a burlap sack over her head, trembled in their grasp. Lucan's grip was notably looser than Eva's, who, by the scowl on her face, did not agree with the decision to bring the girl into their confidence.

With a nod, Cait gestured for them to bring the girl into the enclosed area before pointing to a low section of wall where she should sit.

"Can you take this off yet?" the girl asked, her voice muffled by the bag.

It was Eva who answered, gruffness etched into the single syllable. "No."

Lucan added, "It won't be long. Hang in there."

Over the next half hour, the other Rogues arrived, most alone, but some in pairs. Wives with their husbands. Sisters with their brothers. Or simply best friends who had—Cait hoped—not met up until they were well hidden in the trees. All arrived just as Lucan had—silently, moving like phantoms who haunted the forest. Their greetings remained equally quiet. Most simply nodded to one another. Others whispered into ears while offering quick embraces.

Cait watched the arrivals, not moving from her spot in the corner but merely offering silent nods of acknowledgement to the newcomers. While she saw many of them in her day-to-day life, there were a handful she hadn't seen in a while, and she made a mental note of who looked too thin or too sickly, promising herself she would get them the extra food and medical care they needed. But none of the Rogues had aged well since their last meeting. Most looked as haggard as Cait felt, and yet none had surpassed middle age.

When all eighteen members were accounted for, she stepped forward into the quiet circle of her brethren. She would need to address them, but the words were trapped behind the emotions wedged in her throat. Though most of those gathered hadn't known Maggie as well as Cait had, their sense of loss was written plainly on their faces.

Waving to Lucan, she motioned for him to bring the girl over to where she stood.

"What's your name?" Cait's question came out rougher than she would have liked.

The girl seemed to flinch before finally answering in a voice barely louder than a whisper, "Naeve."

"And how did you know how to find us?"

There was no hesitation this time. "Maggie."

Murmurs rose around the circle of rebels, and Cait didn't have to guess what they were all pondering, for it was the same suspicion she had been chewing on since this morning. Had Maggie double-crossed them? Had the council learned who she was and used her against them?

Naeve addressed those questions as if Cait had voiced them aloud. "You needn't worry. Maggie was loyal to you up until the end."

"How do we know that for sure?" a young man named Jameson asked, his deep brown eyes narrowing.

More whispers rippled through the assembly, and then multiple people began asking questions at once, the discussion reaching a concerningly high volume as they talked over each other. Lucan stepped into the center and raised his hands up at his sides, like the leader of one of the musical groups that sometimes visited to entertain travelers.

Everyone quieted at once.

"Because of this," Lucan said, his voice sounding soft after the ruckus they had made with their questions. He held up a piece of paper that was folded and smudged with dirt and what looked an awful lot like blood.

Naeve stiffened beside him. Although the girl didn't exactly exude confidence, her stance demonstrated how hard she attempted to portray it anyway. If Lucan was pausing for some dramatic effect, it only worked to make Cait and the others more frustrated.

"And?" Cait asked, not bothering to hide her annoyance.

With a glance over his shoulder, he said, "It's from our Maggie."

Cait reached for it, and thankfully Lucan didn't try to stall in that moment or she might have dropped him on his backside for being a pain in hers. The circle of Rogues tightened an inch as if they could get a glimpse of the message—not that Cait would afford such an intrusion. And it was good they couldn't see it. Had they discovered then and there that the message was, in fact, blank, it would not have ended well.

For either Lucan or Naeve.

"I see," she said, folding the note and slipping it into her shirt between her undergarment and her breast, not willing to risk putting it in a pocket. "Before we discuss further, I need to have a chat with Lucan. Eva, hold onto her."

She gestured for Lucan to follow her around the walls and away from the ruins, ignoring the hushed grumbles of protest chasing them into the trees. Every member had agreed, upon joining this crew of rebels, to the hierarchy, understanding that Cait and Lucan worked closely together to decide strategy and determine the group's course of action. But she couldn't blame them for their frustration with the current situation. She would have felt the same in their position.

When she was sure they were out of earshot, she rounded a large tree and pushed Lucan against the rough bark. After looking around the trunk to ensure no one had followed them, she turned her attention back to her second, only to find him smiling that wicked grin he donned when he was about to make some smart-ass remark.

"About time you pushed me up against a tree, Cait," he whispered.

She didn't have the energy to roll her eyes at him, not with a potential spy in their midst. How could he have been such an idiot? How could she have been stupid enough to trust him?

You made him your second for a reason. You trust him for a reason.

Drawing in a breath, Cait focused on the scent of pine and dirt that washed over her. She settled her nerves enough to speak without hissing at him. "Why the blank paper?"

"I trust her, Cait." His expression sobered as all humor fled from his eyes, replaced with a seriousness she'd seen only a handful of times.

"Your gut." It wasn't a question. This was why she'd chosen him. Not simply because he was the first one she'd met when forming this band—or reviving it, as it were. But he had proven himself—and his instincts—time and time again. He had such an uncanny way of feeling out a situation, preemptively identifying danger, keeping the Rogues from being discovered.

He offered a single nod but didn't say anything more.

"And you knew they wouldn't trust your instincts as I do."

"You are a rare breed in that regard. If they weren't all on edge with Maggie's death, if things weren't so unsettling, they might have taken my word alone. But as it is, they needed *evidence*."

"And what if they ask what Maggie wrote to us? What if they demand to see her words?" Although Cait had already begun formulating a lie to tell her people, she preferred having someone to help shoulder the responsibility. As independent as she'd had to become, she found comfort in having a friend beside her to keep her in check and support her decisions.

"First off," he said, relaxing against the tree as Cait backed off a step to allow him some space, "you're the leader of the Rogues. You don't have to show them anything. Just tell them the less they know the less chance the council might have evidence against them."

Running her hand across her brow, she tried to chase her thoughts from option to option, to nail down the right decision. "That could work. So how do we use her? In what capacity do we have her help?"

The laughter returned to the chocolate browns of his eyes. "Really? I'm pretty sure you know."

"Well, yes, of course she'd be our eyes and ears within the council. But we can't have her meet the same fate as our Maggie. We need to be smart about this."

"I suggest we ask her then. And it would behoove us to let the others offer up their ideas as well. Even if they're all awful and worthless, it will help them trust us, and her."

With a nod, Cait shifted to start the short jaunt back to the ruins, but a flash of movement from her right made her go still. Lucan eyed her as he stood equally frozen in place, not even daring to look in the same direction. It might have made Cait laugh, that he could possibly think anyone wouldn't notice them simply because they had stopped moving, yet she was doing the same thing.

Narrowing her eyes at him, she willed herself to speak louder, loud enough for whoever was watching to hear. "Go on and start getting their ideas out in the open. And let her meet the team officially. I need to use the *facilities*. Too much coffee this morning."

As he moved around the tree and headed toward their crew, she pivoted and strode off in the opposite direction, thankful for how thick the woods were on this part of the island. Moving behind a bush and out of sight of whoever had followed them, she lowered herself down and crept on silent feet, circling their position. She still hadn't gotten a glimpse of who it was, but given the scarcity of animals here and the absence of any breeze, it had to be a person, and that person couldn't be allowed to discover the Rogues.

When she was sure she had gone far enough around to flank the intruder, she risked looking around a tree. Her eyes scanned the forest, looking for any movement, but everything had stilled, as if the trees held a collective breath, waiting to see what she would do.

She had nearly convinced herself it had been nothing, a figment of her imagination or her eyes playing tricks on her, when the sharp tip of a dagger pressed into her back in the perfect spot for a quick kill. She stilled, her mind whirring as she cursed the council's ridiculous rules against weapons and her stupidity in adhering to them. She turned her chin to look over her shoulder at her attacker, but she froze before she could catch a glimpse. Warmth spread across her entire back as the person stepped closer, invading her personal space. Hot breath crept across the back of her neck, and the scent of sweat and leather and seawater surrounded her.

A familiar scent after growing up in a pub filled with traveling sailors and weary pirates.

Cait let her body shudder with a shaky breath and whispered a plea for mercy. She didn't need to be armed to take care of herself, especially if the man fell for her act. But he didn't budge. Instead, his blade dug deeper into her flesh, and his other arm moved around her to rest on the tree, blocking her exit.

"Begging for mercy from a pirate, love?" His taunting words came out in a rough breath with more humor than anger. His *tsk-tsk* filled her ear.

Damn pirates.

With that thought, she sent her elbow into his arm, pushing the blade away from her back just enough that she could whirl around to her right. But before she could get away, he grabbed her hair, yanking her head back with a quiet growl.

Cait gritted her teeth to suppress a cry of pain. While making noise might prompt Lucan and the others to come to her aid, she didn't need them. Not yet.

Her attacker used her hair to pull her against the tree until the rough bark dug into her spine. He moved his hand to her shoulder so quickly she wondered how anyone could move like that. She tried to raise her other arm to strike him, but as it was her nondominant side, her blow was ineffective and clumsy, easily blocked, and his blade now pressed below her ribs.

She could try again, but she had to admit—albeit reluctantly—that her body was out of shape, incapable of fending off a pirate who spent his time honing his fighting skills while all she had done recently was wipe down tables and pour drinks. Making a mental note to start training with Lucan—*If you get out of this, you mean*—she breathed a sigh and let her shoulders relax.

"I give up. You win."

He didn't loosen his grip, didn't move at all except to raise his brow at her.

He wasn't much taller than her, and his piercing blue eyes trapped her for a split second. How many lasses had fallen under their spell? She wouldn't be one of them though. His face was not altogether unpleasant, his strong jaw covered by a beard he kept cut close to his face, unlike most of the sailors she'd seen, who grew theirs into long, unattractive scraggles of hair they would braid or leave completely unkempt.

No, this man had a different air about him than the men she knew. Her eyes trailed the lines of his face, taking in the waves of blonde hair, the sides shorn short above his ears in a style the younger pirates preferred. She'd thought she knew most of the pirates who graced the Cregahn shores, but his face was foreign to her, which meant he was either new or he wasn't one to visit the pubs and eateries in port.

He wore no colors around his neck like many of the men did, but when she glanced down at his waist to check his sash, he released another breath, once again sending heat over her ear and neck. "This isn't my best angle, love."

She ignored the way his rough voice sent her core fluttering, clenching her jaw in an effort to push the sensation away. At his waist she found nothing but a worn leather belt.

"Aw," he said. "Trying to see which crew I'm with, are ya?"

She didn't respond except to meet his gaze, forcing her annoyance at being trapped against this tree to edge out the other feelings that had built within against her will. The silence between them filled with tension as they remained locked in the stare.

Cait didn't have time for this nonsense though, and she needed to end whatever game he was playing with her so she could get back to planning. "No colors means either you're a liar, a loser, or a spy. Or all three."

A gruff laugh escaped him, once again sending that irritating warmth creeping through her body. "Aye. All decent assumptions, I suppose."

"So which is it?"

Giving his head a slow shake, he said, "You'll just have to find out."

"And why would I care to, exactly?"

"Oh, because you, Ms. McCallagh, can't risk your merry band of criminals being caught by the council or having your plans foiled by a handsome pirate."

"Well, if I see a handsome pirate anywhere, I'll be sure to tell him to go away and leave us alone."

"I'm waiting."

"For what?"

"For you to tell me to go away and leave you alone." How the light danced in his eyes when there was so little of it here under the trees, she wasn't sure, and it took all her will to pull her attention away from them. All these years she'd ignored the devilishly attractive men who had graced her pub. She could do so now.

She glared up at him. "You think quite highly of yourself, don't you?"

"It beats the alternative. I've never been one for self-loathing."

"Ah, yes, at least one person in the Aisling should like you. Might as well be yourself."

Shadows crept through the blues of his eyes, like clouds passing over the sea, and if she hadn't known better, she would have thought his mind had wandered away to some other place. Had she been prepared for such a reaction, she could have used the moment to break out of his hold, but it quickly passed, his expression returning to the annoyingly flirtatious one he'd had for the past several minutes. But he didn't say anything.

Cait dropped an ear to her shoulder. "So, to what do I owe this visit then? You see, I'm rather busy."

"I want to help you," he said matter-of-factly, like he was ordering a rum in the pub instead of offering to help overthrow the council. Though perhaps he meant to assist in a different capacity.

"With what exactly?"

"The council," he said and then lowered his voice into a gruff whisper again. "I want them gone."

"And who says that's my goal?"

"You think the council doesn't know about you and your rebels? Doesn't know what you're planning?"

How did *he* know about the Rogues and about her position within them? How could he know what the council had discovered? How could...

"You've been with the council? You're on a lord's crew."

"Was."

"Did they kick you out for being an ass?"

"I guess you could say we wanted different things."

"And why should I trust you? I don't even know your name," she said, not fully expecting him to actually provide it.

"You'll just have to follow your gut, I guess." One corner of his mouth lifted into an easy smile that brought out a dimple in his bearded cheek. "And the name's Adler."

CHAPTER 15
TOMMY

THE SKY HAD DARKENED CONSIDERABLY by the time Tommy had finished his discussion with Mikkel and Gavin on the quarterdeck. The location of their meeting was far from ideal, but with Aoife nursing her pains from training and the sisters doing who knew what in the officers' quarters, they had few options that would allow for any privacy. The quarterdeck was as good a place as any.

Even after several hours of planning, they had little to show for it. He'd had to shut down Mikkel several times for continuously mentioning the powers of the fae. They could definitely help—that Tommy couldn't deny—but he couldn't stomach the thought of allowing it and having them not recover enough before they reached the sound. If he did everything to save the crew only to fail at the very end, he'd never forgive himself.

But if you lose the crew to the kraken, you'll be fine?

His thoughts warred within him as he strode toward the stairs, leaving Mikkel and Gavin to continue their chatter. No doubt they were cursing him for refusing to budge on the matter. He took the steps more quickly than usual, and with his mind preoccupied, he didn't notice the person walking into his path until it was too late.

"Watch where you're—" he said, starting to reprimand the clumsy crew member who had dared get in his way, but his words were cut short at the sight of Maura.

"Apologies, Tommy," she offered, not showing any sign of embarrassment. In fact, had he not known better, he might have thought she'd planned this as an ambush.

Way to let your guard down.

"I should be the one to apologize, miss. I—"

"Please, Tommy. It's Maura. I can't have you calling me miss in the middle of a skirmish with the kraken or the sirens. How would we know which of us you were speaking to?"

As much as it irked him to admit it, she had a point. He gave a curt nod and whispered "fair" before moving to get around her. But with unnatural speed, she stepped in his way, her slender body uncomfortably close to his. It sent a warmth from his core to his head, and he hoped her fae sight didn't allow her to see how his complexion reddened in her presence.

"Excuse me," he muttered. "Maura, I really need to check on Aoife and perhaps get some rest of my own."

"Of course," she said, though she made no move to let him pass. Something in her eyes sparkled, catching the last rays of sun as it dipped below the horizon. While Maura had always seemed the more innocent of the three sisters, Tommy was starting to wonder if he had underestimated her. She still had a demure air about her, yet something about her was far from sweet and modest.

He didn't have time for whatever game this was, but some part of him urged him to play along. The door to Declan's cabin opened then, pulling both his and Maura's attention in that direction. Aoife stopped short at the sight of them.

"Oh, am I interrupting something?"

"No," Tommy said. He gritted his teeth, pursing his lips, hoping Aoife would see how perturbed he was in this moment and give him an out. He silently pleaded with her to rescue him.

But Aoife's lips curled into an easy smile as she stepped aside, reaching her arm out in an invitation to the cabin she'd exited. "I needed some fresh air for a bit, so you're welcome to take your conversation to a more private location."

He might have hit her had she not been, well, Aoife. His friend. Though he was strongly reconsidering that title for her.

Just as he opened his mouth to decline the offer, he was cut short by Maura answering for them. "Thank you, Aoife. That's greatly appreciated." She turned to Tommy, her golden eyes inviting him in, not just into the cabin but...

No! You don't have time for this.

"I really don't have time—" he said, pushing his thoughts out into the open, but it was Aoife who interrupted him now.

"Nonsense, Tommy. We have another day before we get to, well, you know. And avoiding Maura here won't get us there—or to Declan—any faster." Walking past him, she mouthed a "You're welcome" as she took her leave.

Maura was already entering the captain's cabin before he could protest further, and with a not-so-cleansing breath and a painful attempt to swallow his discomfort, he followed her, trying to force himself to be confident, commanding, assertive. Like Declan.

What would Declan have done in this instance? No doubt make some sarcastic remark to put this fae in her place. But Tommy wasn't Declan, and did he really want to be? While his captain was his best friend, one he would follow to the ends of the Aisling, Tommy knew he'd never be like him. Not that it was a bad thing. There was only room for one brooding man on this ship.

But he's not on this ship.

Tommy grimaced at the thought.

"Are you going to come in?" Maura's words snapped him back to the situation. She was standing in the dim room, a single lantern on the desk behind her casting her in shadow. "Aoife insisted it was inappropriate for my sisters and me to remain in the captain's quarters alone, and I'd hate to go against her on that."

"Yes," he said, though the word held none of the assertiveness he'd intended. Stepping inside, he shut the door behind him but didn't move closer to Maura, instead leaning his back against the wall in an awkward stance.

Maura's laugh danced through the still air. "You look so uncomfortable, Tommy."

"Indeed. I am." There seemed little point in lying to her. The fae's perceptiveness wasn't worth fighting. He wouldn't be surprised if she could see his thoughts even without the power to read them directly. "What did you want to speak to me about?"

"Who said I had speaking in mind?"

While he couldn't see her clearly, he had no trouble picturing the coy smile she flashed him.

Running a hand through his hair, Tommy scratched the back of his head to buy time to think. Normally he would have had an easy quip to brush aside the discomfort, but that night at the council hall had thrown everything askew.

Injury. Recovery. Kidnapping. Storms. Kraken. Sirens.

It all weighed heavily on his shoulders. This entire crew—including his captain—was relying on him to lead them to success and to ensure they survived. He missed his easygoing attitude, which was being sufficiently subdued by the gravity of the situation.

Explains why Declan is so moody, huh?

Maura cleared her throat.

Him. Maura. Alone in the dark in Declan's cabin.

"Well," he said, swallowing, "speaking of propriety. I don't believe using my captain's quarters for non-speaking would be altogether proper either."

Once again, her laugh—light, airy, like a feather floating on a breeze—greeted him. He was glad he couldn't see her clearly. Sands knew how his body might react against his will if he could see her face, angelic with that hint of mischief. She pushed away from the desk and walked toward him, mesmerizing him with her graceful movements.

Holding his breath, he waited, unsure of what she planned to do. He had an idea, of course, but the notion of it seemed so far-fetched.

And yet it didn't.

"Can't you feel it, Tommy?" Her words came out barely above a whisper. She closed the distance between them until mere inches separated them.

"My personal space being invaded? Aye. I feel that."

She laughed. And that laugh might very well be his undoing. But she ignored his flippant comment and moved closer still.

"Can't you feel the emptiness that creeps in when we're apart?" she asked, and Tommy struggled to ignore the sweet scent that clung to her. "Can't you feel the warmth when we're close?"

"Well, that warmth is pretty standard whenever I'm with a woman." He tried to sound nonchalant. He needed to stop her pursuit. It wouldn't do anyone any good for his attention to be divided in such a way, especially for something that had no possibility of a future. None of this would end well.

Maura stood so close now that he could see her delicate features despite the darkness. Keeping her chin down, she peered up at him from beneath her lashes. "Ah, but I'm no mere woman, Tommy."

He risked touching her, putting his hands on her elbows and moving her away from him as gently as he could.

"I can't deny something is happening. Whatever it is, it doesn't matter. We cannot act on anything. Not with Declan missing and the dagger needing to be retrieved and the kraken... I have to put the needs of my crew and my captain and my home above my own desires." His voice lost all power on that final word, which seemed bizarrely insufficient to describe the feelings building within him. Something had ignited, though he had no name for it, and now he'd admitted as much to her, all with some ill-found hope she reciprocated.

Not that it mattered if she did or not. It couldn't happen.

Stepping back, she lifted her chin as she challenged him. "Then let me help. Let me cloak the ship, create a glamour to keep us hidden from the monster below."

"Just because I can't be with you doesn't mean I don't care about you, Maura." He tried to rush past the admission of his feelings, but the words hung in the air between them, electrifying it. He swallowed again. "If you do this to get us through these waters, you won't have time for your magic to replenish before we reach the sound."

"I think you underestimate our magic. You underestimate me." Her tone came out flat and empty.

"What do you mean?"

"The longer we are away from the iron they had in those walls, the stronger our magic becomes and the quicker we are able to recover after using it. It will still drain, of course, and we will certainly need to rest afterward. Every moment we don't use it, it grows and strengthens."

"But you've only had a couple days to rest after healing me. If I'm to believe what your sister said—that you needed days, not hours—then you may not even be at your strongest by the time we enter its territory. And what happens if you push yourself too far, if you use too much too fast?"

"I've never experienced it myself, but I've witnessed it. Once."

"And?"

Maura hesitated, though she didn't look away. "Burnout. And not the type you humans experience when you've overexerted yourself for too long. Burnout for a fae is an extinguishing of their magic. We have to monitor it, because if it goes out completely, it's like an ember that's died. It can't be rekindled. There's no recovering it if we get to that level. And once our magic is gone? Our long life is shortened, our days numbered."

"Then there's no reason to even discuss this." He pushed away from the wall, taking the risk of getting too close to her. It didn't matter, if this was what he needed to do to convince her not to insist on using her magic.

"With all respect, Tommy, I don't answer to you."

Balling his hands into fists, he narrowed his eyes at her. "You do as long as you're on this ship and as long as I'm the acting captain."

"And how will you stop me, Tommy? Keep me prisoner? Lock me in the iron cage of the brig below decks? Or maybe tie me down?" He could have sworn he saw her wink at him, and he forced himself to ignore the imagery her words conjured.

"If it comes to that, perhaps. But I'd rather not be forced to repeat the council's tactics here."

She breathed deep, exhaling her sugary scent into the space between them, a breath of a sigh that sent tingles up his spine. And then she whispered, all hint of mischief gone, "I will do anything, Tommy, to protect you. Whether it's against the kraken or the sirens or whatever unforeseen danger awaits you. You may not want to pursue what we have, but you don't control my feelings any more than you can control my actions. If your life demands me extinguishing all my magic? It's a price I'm more than willing to pay."

Before he could protest further, to tell her how ridiculous she was being, how his life wasn't worth her risking her own, she was lifting herself onto her toes and leaning forward. His breath caught as he waited to see what she intended, ready to stop her once again if necessary. But her lips simply brushed his cheek, and she whispered, "Before this is all over, you'll understand your own worth, Tommy."

If she meant the words to be a comfort, they provided none, instead sending a wave of panic through him. His mind brought forth images of her and her sisters collapsed on the deck, unconscious, unmoving—images that threatened to cut off all air to his lungs. If she cared for him as she claimed, wouldn't she respect him enough to listen? Or was he the one letting fear blind him?

The cabin walls pressed in on him. Maura's golden eyes pierced him with a look that threatened to gut him, not because they held any malice or ill intent but because they were hers, and she could never be his, no matter how strong their feelings were for one another.

He tried to swallow, to push the stress and panic and despair and confusion down, but when he opened his mouth to speak, his words came out strained. "I need some time alone."

He stepped to the side and opened the door for her, beckoning her to exit as his attention fell to the floor, all ability to face her gone.

CHAPTER 16

DECLAN

Once Killian had left, taking the scraps of the bizarre fruit with him, Declan couldn't do much more than listen to his own thoughts. He pondered all that the southern pirate had told him. How had none of this information traveled up to the Aisling before? Surely, with merchants traveling between the two regions regularly, some news would have been transported with the goods.

That mystery bothered him more than it probably should have, as it was too far removed from his current predicament. Or was it? That letter he'd given the fae, had it carried information about the conflict brewing? Had it requested their help? And if so, who had the request been from? Their fellow royals? The lesser fae?

The questions swarmed him, swirling around in his mind, churning like the sea during a storm.

He paced as he dissected each one. No way would he resign himself to lounging in the filth of the brig. But the more he paced and the more he pulled apart the history of the fae and considered the role the sisters might play, the less confident he was about understanding any of it.

Too many variables. Too many possibilities. Too many distractions.

His shoulders throbbed from being held back awkwardly by the bonds at his wrists, and no matter how many times he tried to roll them and stretch them out, the ache wouldn't let up.

Is anything going to ease up for you? Doubtful.

For some reason, the thought conjured up his last view of Aoife. Her walking away from him, leaving him there with those blasted words hanging on the salty air. Had Callum's actions done anything to shift her heart toward him, gain him any sympathy, or move her to forgive him?

Declan wasn't afraid to die, whether by a cutlass or a siren or the sea itself. It was part of life for him. His father had often said, "To live fully is to be ready to die at any time." Declan hadn't understood that until many years later. It was a bizarre lesson to teach a young child, and it had done nothing but confuse him at the time. But after that misty night and the bloody dagger and his parents' deaths, he found those words running on repeat through his mind. And when he had ended up on that shore with Tommy, watching their captain walk away and abandon their crew, he had come to understand it better. Fear of death came to those who were afraid to live, afraid to take chances—qualities not conducive to a life of piracy.

And so here in the brig of Callum's ship, pacing the small cell, it wasn't the fear of death that brewed within him. It was the fear of dying without her forgiveness, of being left with a remorse that would surely haunt him for eternity.

He should have listened to Tommy's incessant nagging to tell Aoife the truth. How many times had he told himself the same thing? Yet he'd never followed through. He should have told her. Should have known it would be brought to light. Should have planned for that possibility.

Perhaps this was why marriages in the pirate world happened so rarely. Because love made you blind. It made you reckless. It made you stupid.

Live fully.

His father's words continued to echo within, successfully pushing out the myriad of others that had been in the forefront. His parents hadn't survived the council's wrath. But he could. Tommy had almost fallen to it. But he wouldn't. They had very nearly failed entirely. He wouldn't let them.

There was only one option, one way to survive this fool of a mission. He needed to stall. Give Tommy and Aoife enough time to catch up to them, to bring the fae so they could use their powers as planned. Maybe then he'd have an opportunity to spend the rest of his life earning back her trust.

But first he needed a way to buy time.

His head hurt, and only partly from the knock on the head they'd given him, which had been hard enough that it still ached days later. The pungent smell of the ship's belly didn't help matters, consistently distracting his thoughts as he paced. He couldn't think in here. He needed to get out, to breathe fresh air.

You have gone soft, haven't you?

These conditions wouldn't have bothered him before. Yes, they would have been annoying, but he had always had a knack for tuning out all the distractions and discomforts to focus on what needed to be done or decided. But now, it took every last bit of his energy to try to ignore it so he could think clearly. Maybe they had hit him harder than he'd thought.

Or maybe you're losing your edge.

A muffled commotion far above his head sifted down through the wooden floors—shouts sounding like the distant caws of a dozen seagulls. The sudden shift in the noise had Declan frozen in place, straining to listen, though it was unlikely he would be able to hear anything from down here.

His stomach twisted into a knot. Had they arrived at the sound already?

A thump behind him made him spin toward the ladder. Killian, having just jumped to the floor, rushed over, keys in hand, his face flushed and shining with sweat, his eyes wild with that familiar mix of excitement and nerves that all pirates got before some action.

"Guessing you didn't come down to bring me more fruit," Declan said.

"No," Killian said, his clipped answer followed only by the sound of the lock clicking open and the door creaking on its rusted hinges.

"And it'd be presumptuous of me to think Callum has come to his senses."

"Aye, presumptuous indeed," Killian said. "Turn around, unless you want to be fighting with your arms bound."

Declan obeyed, even as he asked, "Fight whom exactly? We haven't arrived—"

"No," Killian said quickly. "Not there yet. But we've got company, and it's doubtful it will end in a handshake and a laugh over a shared bottle of rum."

"So, Callum wants my help early then?" He laced his words with skepticism. It certainly didn't sound like something Callum would do. He was far more likely to leave Declan in the brig to drown if they lost, simply to keep him or anyone else from gaining the spoils he sought.

"Of course not," he said. "He'd leave you here."

Declan rubbed and rolled his wrists as he turned back around. "You take a lot of risk here then. More than necessary."

Killian scoffed, shoving a cutlass into one of Declan's hands. "No man should die in such a way. And I'll face whatever consequences knowing I did the right thing." He reached into his boot and withdrew a blade Declan recognized at once.

But Declan hesitated when the man offered it to him. "How is helping me the right thing?"

Killian forced the dagger into Declan's other hand as he answered, "Because I'd like to see you succeed here to get the Bron sisters back to Larcsporough after all this dagger business is over and done with."

"What? I never—"

"You didn't need to tell me. It wasn't hard to figure out your plans, especially with all your curiosity about the fae history. Everyone in the south knows of the three sisters trapped in the north, held prisoner on Cregah."

More questions flooded Declan's mind, but Killian dashed them away with a wave of his hand, signaling Declan to follow him to the ladder. Hopefully he would be willing to answer all of his questions when and if they made it out of whatever awaited them atop.

Declan's heart sped up with the excitement that always hit when a fight was imminent, and with each ladder they claimed and each set of stairs they ascended, the sounds of orders being yelled by the bo'sun and quartermaster got louder.

Blinking against the afternoon sun as he emerged onto the deck, Declan noticed two things: they had stopped, and no cannon fire had started. Was this a friendly stop?

As friendly as when you stopped for Callum, most likely.

Killian led him to the quarterdeck, where Callum stood with his quartermaster, his face as calm as though he were basking on a beach rather than waiting for his ship to be boarded. Calm until he saw them. His eyes narrowed as he stomped into

Killian's path, barreling his chest into him. But he kept his voice low and menacing, more like a rumble of a growl than the speech of a man.

"What in the sands are you doing?"

To his credit, Killian didn't flinch or cower beneath the glare of his captain but offered up his answer in an almost bored tone. "We need every blade we have aboard if we're going to take on Roberts's crew."

Declan stepped forward, his eyes wide. "Roberts? As in Pirate Lord Roberts?"

"Aye," Callum said, the word clipped as if he hadn't the time for even the single syllable.

Killian looked over his shoulder to provide more of an explanation to Declan. "Roberts has an uncanny way of knowing where we're sailing, interrupting our course every week or two."

"And I dread every encounter," Callum muttered to himself.

It seemed an odd thing for this menacing pirate to admit, but perhaps he hadn't realized he'd said it aloud. Off the starboard side, a ship of moderate size approached.

"So why stop?" Declan realized a second too late that he'd voiced the question aloud, and Callum let out a throaty laugh devoid of any humor.

"Same reason you stopped for me, I gather." The captain didn't turn to Declan as he spoke but kept his attention on the other ship. Declan worked out his own strategy in his mind. It was a gamble, but Callum was right. It was the same one he'd taken. It did them no good to risk Roberts firing his cannons at them, especially when he hadn't proven to be an adversary. Yet. That could cripple them, leave them stranded at sea, or send shrapnel ripping into Callum's crew. The only option was to wait for the approaching pirate to show his hand.

Surveying the crew around him, Declan noted that Callum's strategy differed from his slightly. The men of the *Curse Bringer* didn't hide their blades, instead choosing to make a display of how well-armed they were. The deck was so full of armed men, he nearly wondered if the entire crew had been called above for this show of force, but no doubt a fair number of men waited below with the cannons ready to use at their captain's call.

Roberts's ship, the *Revenge,* had come close enough now that Declan could make out the pirate lord himself, who was not standing on the quarterdeck as expected but at the port-side rail, his men ready to extend a plank between the ships.

Tension roiled through Callum's crew, like a pulsing thrum of energy covering the entire deck. Declan's palms grew sweaty around his own weapons, and he scolded his body for acting so when this was far from his first altercation. But it had been years, many years, since he had not been the one in command. His mind whirred with the possibilities and the different outcomes that could arise here.

The *Revenge* swung around so their port side met with the *Curse Bringer*'s starboard side, and the ships scraped together, the impact forcing Declan—and everyone else on board—to brace themselves. Stumbling around certainly wouldn't display the confidence they needed to exhibit in front of this lord's crew. As Roberts's men dropped the plank to make a bridge between the two vessels, Callum headed down the stairs to greet them, his cutlass still in its sheath and his hand at the ready to draw it quickly if needed. Though he hadn't motioned for them to follow, Killian and Declan trailed after him almost on instinct, meeting up with Callum's quartermaster, Dominic, at the bottom, whose mouth was twisted into a sneer that Declan thought could be as much for him as it was for the lord who now boarded the *Curse Bringer*.

Two things seemed odd to Declan as Callum stepped forward. Roberts's crew was not behaving as Callum's men were. Their deck was not crowded with men; it was far emptier than Declan would have expected. On one hand, it made sense. There was no need for Roberts to make a spectacle of his strength. His reputation as a lord preceded him. It was well known the lords didn't partake as often in their own battles and skirmishes anymore, leaving that messy business to the ships within their fleets.

Perhaps that has made them soft.

Declan chewed on the thought, but again his skin prickled with unease, his mind searching for a thread of a clue that could explain what Roberts's play was here. Putting himself in the lord's place, he worked quickly through strategy after strategy, searching for one that might fit.

Declan backed away slowly through the crew, inching away from Killian, who didn't seem to notice his departure. The *Curse Bringer*'s deck was packed with men, all of them quiet and tense, as if their very limbs itched to draw blood and cut men down. He couldn't keep moving backward without stepping on someone's toes, which might lose him an appendage or two. Some glanced at him out of the corners of their eyes as he turned, but most kept their attention ahead on the pirate lord stepping onto the deck.

At the sight of the lord, Declan stopped.

He'd never met Captain Roberts, and though he often joked about the lords' lackluster personalities, he didn't have any firsthand knowledge of what they were like. It was merely an assumption born from contempt and frustration. And perhaps some bitterness. The lords might not be as free as they could be—tied to the council per the treaty—but their lot was notably better than the other pirates sailing these waters. They enjoyed the prestige that came with the title, had the pleasure of the councilwomen's company, and had free rein, at least in the Aisling.

How the lords had managed to receive such a position, Declan couldn't say. Possibly a mix of pedigree and luck. Everything he knew about the lords he'd gleaned from rum-soaked rumors. Supposedly some passed the title to a son, on the off-chance a lord's union with a councilwoman produced one. But that happened so rarely that most lords selected from among their crew who then had to be approved by the ruling council.

Declan hadn't heard how Lord Roberts had gotten his title, but it certainly wasn't for his looks. The man's nose had been broken far more times than one would expect for a lord, leaving the bridge of it crooked in two places. His mess of long blonde hair was tied back and hidden under a tricornered hat that lacked the wear and tear most often seen in pirate attire. His less than intimidating height was countered by his muscular build, again contrary to what Declan would have expected for a pirate in his position. Needless to say, whether Roberts was a bore or not, he did not appear to be an easy adversary, not one you took on without a plan or skill.

All of this Declan assessed in the time it took the lord to stride over to Callum and extend his hand in greeting. Declan waited to see how Callum reacted, and when the captain took the lord's hand, albeit with some reluctance, Declan continued making his way to the other side of the ship. His stomach churned. He hoped no one would think he was using this as a chance to escape and try to stop him, but thankfully everyone was glued to the quiet exchange taking place between the two captains. Without another glance back, Declan maneuvered his way through the stinking bodies of the crew until he saw the railing. It was a long shot, of course, but every instinct told him he needed to be sure.

He had just broken free of the mass of crewmen when the first hands appeared on the port-side railing. Before he could open his mouth to alert anyone, men were hauling themselves over, landing on the deck with quiet skill. Declan pulled his dagger out and threw it at the pirate directly in front of him as he shouted the word, "Behind!"

Callum's crew turned just in time for their blades to meet those of the invaders. Retrieving his own from the fallen pirate, Declan slit the man's throat before turning toward the next closest, who was busy fighting one of Callum's men. He swiftly thrust his dagger into the man's side, up and under his ribs, making him a far easier opponent for the crewman who worked to finish him off.

Declan didn't check to see who fell and who succeeded. He tried to see over the swarm of men as they bustled around him, rushing past him to meet the oncoming threat, but he couldn't see what had become of Callum and Roberts.

Someone lunged for him, and he had his dagger lodged in the man's gut before he realized it was one of Callum's crew. He didn't have time to fight the man, and despite his being held hostage on this ship, he also didn't want the man to suffer, so he pulled the blade out and, with one smooth motion, severed a large artery, causing the man to fall to his knees. His blood gushed out around the fingers he pressed against the wound in a feeble attempt to stanch the bleeding.

Declan didn't wait to see what became of him but instead pushed his way through the crew, blocking strikes as he needed, wincing as blades nicked his forearms. Where the hell was Callum? Had Roberts bettered him? Had Callum heard his warning and taken out the lord in time?

The scene was utter chaos as more of Roberts's men swarmed the deck, seeming to come from all angles, climbing over the railing, rushing across the plank that still bridged the ships.

There. Declan spotted him.

Callum's face was splattered with blood that seemed to accentuate his scar. He was facing off against Roberts. Callum had lost his blade somewhere and was doing his best to block Roberts's strikes with his arms, now streaming with blood from the numerous cuts his opponent's dagger had inflicted, but he was still managing to get his fist in contact with the lord's face now and then.

Declan could let them be, take his chances with whoever survived, but the thought of helping a lord, the same pirates who aided and abetted the council, the same lords who were responsible—even if not directly—for the deaths of so many innocents, including his parents... No, he couldn't have that. Even if Callum wanted to risk Declan's life to get the dagger, Declan would rather die helping this independent pirate than serving the lords in any way.

"Roberts!" Declan shouted, pulling the lord's attention away and distracting him long enough for Callum to snatch the dagger from his hand and land another blow across the lord's face. Roberts stumbled back but righted himself quickly, his mouth pulling his face into a grotesque scowl. With a growl, he lunged for Callum, pouncing more like a wild animal than a refined pirate lord.

Declan rushed forward, tripping as a body fell into him but still managing to leap onto the lord's back. He weaved his arm under Roberts's chin, gripping his body with his legs and hoping they didn't tumble over the railing into the water below but not particularly caring if they did.

The lord stumbled about, trying to free himself, but Declan only tightened his hold on the man's neck. With his legs wrapped around the lord's waist, Declan used his last bit of energy to thrust himself backward, pulling the lord off-balance until they fell backwards. Declan refused to let go even as they hit the deck.

Declan's back rammed into the ground with the full weight of the pirate on top of him, and he lay there hoping Callum would return the favor and lend him a hand. But just as Callum came into view, two men appeared behind him, ready to attack.

"Watch out!" Declan yelled, still working to hold the lord.

Callum turned in time, howling as his attackers' blades cut into his already torn-up arms. Despite his injuries, he was able to subdue the men. He sliced one across the belly, and the man's knees fell into his own innards that spilled onto the deck. Callum brought his weapon around. In one smooth motion he slashed the other man across the chest and pushed him into the sea.

Lord Roberts still flailed atop Declan, who was growing tired from trying to wrangle him. He wondered how the man could still have so much strength left in him. The lord was so preoccupied with trying to pry Declan's arm from his throat that he didn't see Callum coming toward him or the flash of the sun reflecting on the blade as it came down to cut him across the upper leg, a strategic blow to sever a major artery.

The lord's scream tore across the deck, and to Declan's surprise, Robert's crew stopped and turned toward their captain, who now moved his arms to reach for his wounded leg, though it would be of no use. The wound was severe enough he'd be dead within minutes.

The fighting around them ceased as the lord went still, and the air rushed from Declan as the lord's dead weight pressed down on him. With great effort, his muscles burning, he began to shove the man off. A hand was extended toward him.

He was surprised to find Callum offering to help him stand, but he was more surprised by how the crews had responded to the lord's death.

This was not typical. Declan had never seen this in all his years on the sea. No matter how much a crew admired their captain, they did not simply stop fighting if he fell. But just as surprising was how Callum's men, too, stood still and waited, seeking their captain's command. Even his own crew didn't show this level of restraint or respect. Was Callum a better captain than him? Had Declan misjudged him?

Rising, he stood beside Callum as he faced the men, many bloodied and clutching their wounds while trying not to step on the fallen at their feet. They waited. What would happen now? Lord Roberts was dead, and the *Revenge* was in need of a new captain, up for grabs. Declan's mind whirred, the plank connecting the ships beckoning him, urging him to take this moment to flee and get back to his own ship. But he couldn't sail without a crew, and it seemed unlikely that any of Roberts's men would agree to sail under him after he'd played such a role in the lord's demise.

No doubt Callum would catch him before he could even move the ship away, and there was also no way he could make his way over to the ship without one of the crewmen calling him out. He might have been released from his cell and chains, but he remained a prisoner nonetheless.

Still, Declan couldn't stop the smile from tugging ever so slightly at one corner of his mouth. They were stopped, not likely to be underway any time in the near future. Whatever Callum had in store for him, Declan could face that later. For now he was simply thankful for the delay he'd needed.

CHAPTER 17
AOIFE

High above Aoife's head, wisps of clouds drifted across the full moon, throwing the deck of the ship into shadow for a moment before moving on and allowing the light to return.

Reclining on this wooden step, it was impossible not to remember the last time she'd been sitting here. But instead of jovial singing, an eerie silence greeted her, even though the deck was far from empty. Some of the crew worked to keep the ship on course while others stared out across the water or conversed in hushed tones, not loud enough to be heard over the ship's hull cutting through the waters, the only indication of their conversation being the movement of their lips.

Tommy was going to be angry with her for what she'd done, forcing him to be alone with Maura, but she could handle him and whatever attitude he might show her.

Why had she done it? Certainly for the hope of securing a happy future for her friend, but also because she hoped Maura might be able to persuade him to allow the use of fae magic once they entered the kraken's territory. It seemed their only chance for survival, and Tommy was stubbornly refusing. For good reason, she had to admit, but he needed to at least be open to the option if worse came to worst. If nothing worked, would Tommy choose to lose the crew rather than rely on the possibility of draining the fae's magic too much before reaching the sound?

And would that be a disaster? Would that secure their defeat? What was at stake? They either fell to the kraken and failed to reach Declan in time, or they got there and had to get past the sirens with fewer weapons in their arsenal. It seemed an easy decision to Aoife, but then again, she was no strategist. And no pirate. But could Tommy's judgment truly be trusted here? His priorities seemed askew. What was driving his utter refusal? With the possible scenarios laid out in her mind, she could not fathom that he was solely driven by his desire to save his captain.

Declan.

His name tumbled around in her mind, and she turned to the space beside her where he had sat that night, too far away for her liking but still closer than he possibly should have been. He had seemed so different then. Less moody. More carefree. More himself, she assumed. She reached her fingers up to her cheek, hoping she'd never forget the moment when he'd brushed her tear away. But it had only been a few days ago, and already the memories were fraying. That hadn't been the first—or last—time he'd touched her, but she cherished it all the same. In her mind she saw that gentle smile he only seemed to offer her, heard his soothing voice as he talked her through her panic attacks.

But then the memories shifted. To sand and blood and his strained and weary plea for her forgiveness. His declaration of his feelings for her. Her chest tightened, and she shut her eyes against the images, though she knew it was impossible to force them away by simply doing so. The voice within her whined, *You should have forgiven him.* This was followed by the equally insistent part of her that silently growled, *He lied to you. Like everyone else.*

She'd hoped Tommy could help guide her, tell her which part of herself to heed, because even with Declan in danger, she wasn't sure which was correct. She loved him—that much she was sure of—but was it enough? Was this something she could move past? Or would it taint whatever future they might pursue, like mold permeating a loaf of bread?

It could never work.

But even as she settled onto those words, she remembered how Tommy had insisted the same regarding him and Maura. She had pointed him to the importance of hope. Could Aoife take her own advice? Again, the two sides of her warred internally, one side begging her to give him a chance, the other trying to wrap a protective barrier around her heart.

To her right, the door to Declan's cabin opened, creaking on its rusting hinges.

The door thudded against its frame, and Aoife peered around the railing to see Maura standing there, her elegance a stark contrast to the way her shoulders slumped with a sigh.

Tommy hadn't exited with her, and although Aoife was sheltered and naive, she could still recognize the disappointment written on the fae's face. As Aoife wrestled over whether to speak up or not, Maura's chin lifted, her golden eyes finding Aoife's easily.

"Aoife," she said, the word coming out with a tinge of surprise. "Have you been sitting out here this whole time?"

Pulling her mouth into her best version of Declan's smirk, she lifted her shoulder as she said, "Aye. But don't worry, I couldn't hear any of what was said behind those doors. Even in this deathly silence. Not that I was hoping to listen in. Simply trying to put—"

Maura's light laugh floated on the sea breeze between them, and she soundlessly moved closer. "No need to explain, Aoife. I trust you. May I sit?"

Scooting over a few inches, Aoife proffered the seat. "Of course."

For a few moments the silence enveloped them while Aoife pondered what to say or whether to say anything at all. Her muscles itched to move, and she shifted her feet against the wooden deck several times, clasping and unclasping her hands in her lap, all while Maura sat as still as the figurehead on the front of the ship. But before the fae could tease her for fidgeting, she cleared her throat and asked, "So the chat with Tommy went well then?"

Maura's head fell back, and she let out an exasperated groan, her whole body relaxing as if released from some spell that had kept her frozen in place. She rolled her head to one side and back, taking a moment before responding.

"I'll win him over yet."

Aoife caught her eye. A spark of mischief gleamed in those otherworldly eyes, which was entirely at odds with the defeated posture she now exhibited. She raised her brow. "Romantically or…"

Another laugh bubbled up from Maura's lips as they curled into a coy grin. "Any way that I can."

"Well, as much as I'd love to see Tommy think about his own happiness and all, we should probably focus on getting him on board with the whole magic plan. Right?"

Maura pursed her lips, frowning. Turning her chin, she looked out across the deck, watching the crew. She took a deep breath but didn't answer right away.

"I'm not sure which I desire most though."

Aoife scoffed. Rolling her eyes, she shook her head a couple times. "Seriously?"

Maura turned back to her. "What?"

"So much for fae perception, eh?" Maura didn't say anything but simply waited, staring. "There's little point in winning his heart if we all fall prey to the kraken."

Her voice had risen enough that several of the crew stopped what they were doing to glance over at her, sending another wave of color to her face as she cringed.

"Fair point, Aoife. Fair point. And not one I hadn't thought of. But the heart wants what the heart wants, and mine is set on that sweet roll of a pirate."

"Sweet roll?" Perhaps the centuries spent within the iron walls of the council hall had done damage to more than just this fae's magic, because Aoife could not, for the life of her, figure out what she meant.

"Oh, you know," Maura said, smacking Aoife's arm with the back of her hand, "he's the sweet one. He might have a few browned, crispier edges, but most of him is kind, gentle—"

"And delicious?" Aoife hadn't intended to say the word aloud, but before she could apologize for saying something so inappropriate, Maura was laughing again.

"Why, yes, actually. I mean, I can only imagine he is. I haven't had the pleasure. Yet."

They'd gotten off topic, and Aoife needed to steer them back. "Well, as I said, no point if we don't survive the next few days."

Maura hummed a response. Lowering her head, she moved closer to Aoife and whispered, "Can you keep a secret?"

Aoife stiffened as a pang of guilt tightened around her insides. "I wouldn't trust me to."

It was Maura's turn to roll her eyes, and she opened her mouth to speak. Aoife rushed to cover her ears, nearly smacking Maura in the face, and began humming to herself to keep from hearing whatever the fae wanted to divulge. She wasn't about to take on another secret that would very likely require she lie to a friend. She could not be responsible for the death of someone—anyone—else if her tongue betrayed her again.

When she dared to steal a glance at Maura, she discovered the fae wasn't speaking to her. No, she was laughing. Of course she was laughing. Aoife stopped humming, testing to see if it was safe to remove her hands. With caution she uncovered her ears, ready to replace her hands if this damn fae showed any sign of spitting out the secret. But Maura simply sat there. Her laughter eventually eased, her lips settling into a friendly smile.

"Don't," Aoife said and pointed a finger toward her companion. "Don't you dare."

"Dare what?"

"Don't tell me any secrets. And don't mock me for protecting you and everyone else."

Maura cocked her head to the side, her forehead crinkling with a question.

Aoife released a breath before adding, "I get people killed."

"Well, that's a tad dramatic."

"Perhaps, but true all the same. If I hadn't, my sister—"

"Would have been caught and killed anyway," Maura said, finishing her sentence with words that caused Aoife to freeze in place.

"How did you know about—?"

"Lani?" Aoife nodded. "Same way we knew Declan's name before you stumbled into our room at the council hall."

Aoife mulled over the explanation for half a moment before shaking her head. "But Lani had a plan. She was smarter than me. She would have made it."

Shifting, Maura leaned back until her elbows rested on the step above her before stretching her slender legs out. She crossed her ankles one way and then the other, finally relaxing again.

"You underestimate your mother, Aoife."

"You mean the council."

A graceful shrug and then, "I said what I said."

Aoife's gaze fell to her lap as she tried to process this. What did Maura mean? She'd always seen her mother as taking the lead on the council, but everything she'd been taught indicated the councilwomen ruled as equals.

Because everything you were taught was true? What's one more lie?

Looking back at Maura, she asked, "What do you mean though?" She certainly didn't want to jump to any conclusions.

"Your mother isn't—" Maura's words were cut short by the sound of boots approaching. Tommy was coming toward them. Aoife all but forgot that Maura had been about to tell her something important.

"Aoife," Tommy said, pinning her with a glare. His face was stern, despite the friendliness still present in his eyes. "You should get some rest." With his head he motioned toward the captain's quarters. Aoife glanced from him to Maura and then back. Before she could respond, he was speaking again. "You'll need it for your training time with Collins tomorrow."

The words pulled a groan from Aoife's gut, and her joints and muscles began aching again. She'd forgotten the torment they'd gone through earlier until he'd brought it up. Rising, she tried to keep from bumping into him, and thankfully he stepped back to give her room. She turned to Maura and bid her goodnight before looking up at Tommy.

"I'll see you in the morning?" She didn't know why she'd worded it as a question, and relief hit when he dipped his chin in a single nod, looking everywhere but at Maura.

Aoife stepped slowly, pretending to be sleepy. She glanced over her shoulder, hoping to see Tommy and Maura in discussion again, but Tommy had started up the stairs, bypassing Maura and leaving her behind on the lowest step. Aoife slowed her pace while continuing to watch them, curious how the two would continue this awkward dance they'd found themselves in.

Maura rose and turned in her graceful manner to follow Tommy up to the quarterdeck. Aoife held her breath, waiting to see how he'd react. Did he even hear the fae's near-silent steps behind him? Would he allow her up there? She didn't have to wait long for her answer. Within seconds Tommy spun around to face his pursuer.

"You're not allowed up here." His voice was firm but calm, quiet enough it hadn't attracted the attention of anyone else on deck.

Maura didn't stop, though, and continued up the stairs until she stood on the same step as him. "Can't we talk some more?"

"If you had more to say, you shouldn't have left the privacy of the cabin. I have nothing more to discuss with you."

"But I—" she started.

Tommy cut her off with a glare and a sharp "No" that had Maura flinching as though he'd slapped her. "Not tonight, Maura. I'm done."

He left the fae standing in the middle of the stairs as he continued up to the quarterdeck, not once turning back to look at her. Maura took longer to retreat. As Aoife watched them part ways, she hoped the tension—which was as thick as the black sands of Cregah—wouldn't cause them more problems than they already had.

CHAPTER 18
CAIT

Cait kept her stride short with slow steps. While this pirate, Adler, might think she did so out of caution, it was more that she needed to buy time to figure out how she would explain this—explain him—to her people. But she remained at a loss. She could ask Lucan to trust her and her gut, but the others would not understand.

She didn't even understand it. But that was how intuition worked. It often went against reason and sense. Despite all logic, something often pulled her toward one path or one decision. She had long ago stopped doubting it.

But that didn't make it any easier to ask others to trust it. From the corner of her eye, she watched Adler's long legs match her pace.

"So what are you going to tell them?" Adler asked, and although he kept the words hushed, they were still too loud in the looming silence of the forest.

"I'll figure something out."

He jutted his chin out. "And hopefully soon. Sounds like we're getting close."

Indeed, the voices of the Rogues drifted toward them, though still too quiet for her to make out what they were saying. She had already asked so much of them regarding Naeve's inclusion, and now she had the audacity to ask even more of them. All while they still mourned the loss of one of their own.

Cait came to an abrupt stop and turned to Adler. He showed no sign of surprise, but those blue eyes of his seemed to sparkle with excitement once again.

"How did you find me?" she asked.

A smirk pulled at his lips—an expression that was quickly beginning to irk her. "A question you probably should have asked before leading me to your secret meeting spot, love."

Cait glowered at him in a silent prompt for him to answer the damn question.

"It wasn't that hard, to be honest—once I knew who to follow, that is. There are plenty of rumors about who leads the Rogues. You've done quite the job keeping suspicion off yourself, but I have a unique skill set, you could say."

"So you followed me."

A mischievous nod. "Though I didn't know you were the mastermind. Got lucky with that one. Shouldn't have been surprised, though, given your family name and all."

"And you want the council gone," she said, struggling to keep up with her mind as it processed all the information. He remained quiet and waited for her to continue the thought. "But as a pirate, the council works in your favor."

He offered a lazy shrug but didn't bother to correct her.

"Who was it?" Cait's eyes snapped up to his. Her brow contracted. She'd expected some reaction from him, some clue that she was on the right track, but he remained annoyingly hard to read. "Brother? Sister? Parents?" She ignored the way her heart flinched and hurried on to add, "Or a lover?"

There. The slightest flash of his jaw tensing. Though his face didn't betray his feelings, she'd been working in the pub long enough to tell when a man was on the verge of revealing his secrets.

"Who was she? Or he?"

Adler's jaw tensed again, longer this time, but his blue eyes dulled. He still didn't say anything.

"Look, Adler, it's none of my business, and as much as I would love to have some juicy bit of information to use against you when needed, I have enough drama of my own. No reason I need to take on yours as well." Cait moved to take a step forward again but stopped. Nodding ahead toward the Rogues who awaited them, she added, "But they will want to hear your reasons. They'll need to know if you—and whatever pain you carry—is worth the risk of trusting you."

Dropping his eyes, Adler stepped closer to her. Uncomfortably close. Close enough she could feel the warmth emanating from him. Close enough it caused every muscle in her body to tense in anticipation. Of what, she couldn't pinpoint.

With how close he stood, she would have had to angle her chin up to look into his eyes. But she couldn't. Somehow he had entrapped her without even a touch. Focusing on her breaths, she drew them in slowly to keep herself grounded.

He cleared his throat, and she looked up at him through her lashes. "Yet you trust me without hearing."

"Who said I trust you?" Cait challenged.

"Either you trust me enough to bring me into your circle of friends or you're an idiot. And you don't seem like a dumb lass to me, love."

She should step back, should put some space between them, but he would expect that. And she hated taking the predictable path, so she closed the last inches between them until her breasts pressed against his broad chest. Lifting her face to his, she leaned closer until she could almost feel the hair of his beard brush against her cheek. And then she whispered in his ear, "Trust is earned, but I'll use you if I can."

Before he could say anything in response, she moved away and resumed walking toward the others. The Rogues' eyes widened as she passed through the entryway with Adler on her heels. Lucan stepped into her path. But he wasn't looking at her. His stern gaze was firmly fixed on the man behind her, and while it was an expected reaction, she couldn't help but roll her eyes at him.

Waving her hand over her shoulder, she introduced them. "Lucan, this is Adler. Adler, Lucan. My second."

Adler stepped forward, his hand extended before him in greeting, but Lucan didn't move or relax. Adler gave a shrug and lowered his hand as he said with a laugh, "Nice to meet you too, Lucan."

Lucan's eyes snapped to Cait's, wide and silently demanding an explanation, but she didn't answer him, instead addressing the entire assembled group.

"Adler has asked to join us." She paused, allowing the protests to rumble for a minute before cutting them off with a raised hand. "And I have agreed to allow him."

More complaints filled the small area, but it was Lucan who now hushed them. His stare bored into Cait as if he was searching for some hidden message. Or maybe he was waiting for some intuition of his own to guide him.

He didn't look away even as he spoke to everyone. "If Cait trusts him, then I do too. Because I trust her." He paused, his jaw tensing as he pinned Adler with a hard look and then returned his attention to Cait. "But as we've asked a lot of you all today, with Naeve and now…" He stopped again and leaned forward toward Adler so he could ask, not bothering to lower his voice into a whisper, "What was your name again?"

The pirate laughed at Lucan's ridiculous behavior but played along by offering his name once again.

Lucan nodded before resuming. "Yes, Adler. As we've asked a lot of you all today, I think it only fair that he tell us his reasons for wanting to join our efforts."

Cait stepped forward now, squaring her shoulders as she confronted her second. "We did not require this of Naeve, Lucan."

"We could, of course. I'm sure she has no problem recounting her story again as she did for me and Eva."

As the Rogues murmured their agreement, impatience shot through Cait, and her limbs became antsy. She was eager to get past all this drama and start doing something productive.

"We don't—" she started, but halted mid-sentence when Adler placed a hand on her shoulder. She peered back at him.

"It's okay, love. I don't mind."

Cait didn't try to stop him as he stepped into the center of the group. Looking from face to face, she observed how they reacted to him. Some showed nothing but suspicion. Others seemed at least partially curious. And Kira looked at him as if he were as tasty as the rum she poured for patrons when working in the pub.

"As Cait correctly guessed," he said, his eyes pausing on Cait for a second before continuing on around the circle, "the council took a loved one from me, as I know they have done to many, if not all, of you. I was a member of Captain Tiernan's crew."

A few muffled gasps interrupted his words, but he paid them no attention as he continued.

"Months ago, while visiting the council hall, I met someone. One of the heirs. She was…" He paused—whether for effect or from genuine emotion, Cait couldn't tell. "Well, it doesn't matter now. They discovered our plan to run away together, and they punished her for it."

"And why didn't they punish you?" a woman asked from the far corner, suspicion coating every syllable. Others echoed her question, pushing him to answer.

Adler lifted a shoulder as a hollow laugh spilled from him. "We were in Foxhaven, not due to be back on these shores for another month, when we heard of an heir running off. You can imagine who I thought that was, even if the timing was off, but alas, it wasn't her but her sister. Lani had already been discovered. The council had found out—somehow—and they had her killed."

At this, a young man to their left countered, "But the council would never let that information out. We only knew because—"

Another voice interrupted. "Yeah! How would you have heard of it in Foxhaven?"

Cait answered for him. "Oh, come on. You all know how pirates are with gossip. No one can keep a bloody secret to save their lives."

Another halfhearted laugh rumbled within Adler's chest. "Indeed. It's true. Once I heard of my Lani's fate, I left. Took all the money I had saved up to start our life together and bought my way out of Tiernen's crew. Ditched my colors and caught the first vessel I could get passage on to these damned shores."

Lucan spoke now, distrust dripping from his words. "And we're just to believe you want to take down the council. The council that kept you well fed and your pockets filled."

"Aye. Not all pirates choose the profession out of greed. Some of us do it out of necessity."

That brought an image of Declan to Cait's mind, but she pushed it aside as quickly as it had appeared. No time to worry about him at the moment. Nothing she could do for him here and now, especially not when she had Lucan acting like a jealous lover.

That's a bit unfair. He's just looking out for you. All of you.

As Cait swept away her thoughts, Lucan inched forward. "You seem rather at ease for someone who claims to have lost their one true love." The last word came out clipped with disdain. Like a challenge.

Adler turned lazily to face his accuser, and the corner of his mouth lifted into a smirk. "I never said she was my one true love, friend." Lucan opened his mouth to speak, but Adler continued. "Do I love her? Yes. Always will. And do I want to make those haughty bitches pay for what they did to her? Absolutely. But is Lani my only and my last? Sands, I hope not. I'm much too young to live the rest of my days alone and in mourning."

Lucan pressed closer still, pulling his shoulders back and jutting his chin forward, and glared at the pirate. "But you had only just met her. Seems highly suspicious that you'd form such a bond with one glance or one conversation." Cait had raised her foot to step in and intervene, but at Lucan's last statement, she hesitated, dropping it back to the ground. Why hadn't she caught onto that?

The murmuring questions ceased, and the group grew quiet, watching Adler with collective skepticism. Cait could have kicked herself for believing him, but even still, something told her to trust him. She searched his expression for any hint he was pulling one over on them, duping her to lead them into a trap. What such a sign would be, she wasn't sure. Surely her gut would point it out as it had so many times before.

Adler didn't answer right away. His face remained neutral, with not even a flicker of tension as he decided on his next words. The silence stretched on into an uncomfortable void. Cait had just decided she couldn't handle it one more second when Adler cleared his throat with a gravelly sound.

"I didn't think it was possible either," he said, his strong, confident voice filling the space. "And yet, it happened."

Cait narrowed her eyes at him, but still she found no indication he was covering up some ulterior motive. His deep blue eyes mesmerized her. Had she been a few years younger perhaps, she might have found herself wavering in their intensity, the world around her falling away until only the two of them remained… But that was before her whole world had crumbled.

A lost family. A lost future.

She blinked slowly to regain focus.

"You can't possibly believe him, Cait. It's absurd," Lucan said in a deep whisper.

The air was thick with tension. Something pushed her toward Adler at the same time it pulled her away from him. Another slow blink helped to distract her from the strangeness of the invisible opposing tugs on her body, and she gave a nod without turning away from the newcomer. "I might, though I can't explain why."

Lucan's exasperated sigh called her attention back to him. A mix of confusion and defiance played across his features.

Lowering her voice, she said, "We don't know him, no, but you know me, Lucan. Trust me."

"I do. But…" Lucan flung his hand in Adler's direction. His shoulders rose as he sucked a breath deep into his lungs before slumping in defeat. "But never mind. My trust in you is stronger. So that's what I'll hold onto."

Eva raised a hand, like she was a kid in a schoolroom instead of a rebel plotting a coup. "So what's the plan exactly? We now have two new resources at our disposal in Naeve and Adler. How do we put them to use?"

Cait hesitated a moment, not sure how the Rogues would respond to her plans. "We have been taking a very careful approach the past few years. Biding our time. Strengthening our numbers. We have never taken the fight to the council, and it's time to do just that."

"What does that mean, *take the fight to them*?" a girl to Cait's left asked.

Adler stepped forward. "If I may?" he asked and waited for Cait to give the nod to continue. "How did the pirate lords come into power? Why do some become lords and others become fish food?"

"I'm not sure how a pirate history lesson is supposed to help," Lucan said, his annoyance made clear in every syllable.

But Adler ignored the interjection. "They are smart. They use strategy. They understand their adversaries, and they know how to use their weaknesses against them. And, when needed, they are ruthless."

His words mirrored what Cait had been feeling since she'd gotten the word about Maggie. They needed a plan, and they needed to be willing to do anything to pull the council from power and free the people. And they needed to be prepared to do all of that without the magic of the dagger to ensure victory. As much as she wanted to embrace the hope flickering in her belly, she had to be realistic. The mission she'd sent her brother on had always been an unlikely gamble. Not because Declan couldn't handle it, but because of the odds were stacked against them.

Hushed whispers and mutters rippled through the Rogues as they contemplated what this might mean, what they might have to do, and what they were even willing to do.

"Let's start with what we know," Cait prompted, thankful when her words managed to bring their murmurings to a halt.

Adler offered, "The council knows you're seeking the dagger."

Naeve, speaking for the first time since Adler's arrival, added, "And they have asked Captain McCallagh to bring it back to them."

"But he was intercepted by Callum," Lucan said, "who we assume is heading after the dagger under the assumption that Declan is the key to retrieving it."

"Wait." Adler's chin rose. "Where is the dagger?"

Lucan gave a breathy laugh. "Well, at least that bit of gossip hasn't managed to make it to the far ends of the Aisling."

Cait dove into the abridged version of the dagger's location and her brother's need of the fae to retrieve it. When she finished, Adler said, "I see." It certainly wasn't the reaction she'd expected, but little about this pirate seemed to match her assumptions.

"At least the fae are aboard the *Siren's Song*," Lucan said. "So if Declan's crew can get there, we still have a chance of getting the dagger."

Once again, Naeve's timid voice chimed in. "But why does everyone want this blade? I've heard the legends, of course, but we won't be fighting the council in battle." Her eyes went wide. "Will we?"

Cait shifted her weight. "Not in the sense you may be thinking. Unless we have to. But if the legends are true, then the dagger's power isn't limited to combat but brings victory in any conflict. If possible, we will avoid unnecessary bloodshed." She paused and looked around at her people. "I think it best if we plan on not having it. Adler's right; we'll need a strategy, and we'll need to know what each of us is willing to do to see this through to the end. The council wants nothing more than to keep our people under their heel, under their promises of peace, but we know the truth, the truth they don't want to be made public. We know they have spies among the populace, and we know those spies hide well. But they aren't all spies, and not everyone is complicit in the council's ways—if they know of their true nature at all."

Adler's eyes shone with humor and anticipation. "You'll need to figure out a way to get the silent to speak and the blind to see, all while avoiding the council loyal."

Cait motioned for everyone to gather closer, and she began to lay the plan out for them, accepting worthy suggestions from anyone who expressed them.

After a few hours, her back aching from the hunched position she'd assumed for the planning session, Cait bid each of the Rogues farewell as they headed off to their agreed-upon assignments. Naeve headed back toward the council hall, where she would resume Maggie's intelligence gathering from within. Although the girl's quiet air had made Cait suspicious at first, the sorrow in her face when they spoke of Maggie's death seemed genuine. Genuine enough to earn Cait's trust.

They all would need to keep pretenses up, going about their daily lives as normal. Any major change could mean disaster if the council got wind of it.

"And what about me?" Adler asked as he joined Cait by the entrance to the ruins. Most had left already, staggering their departures so as not to bring any suspicion upon themselves when they returned to town. Only she, Adler, and Lucan remained.

Lucan, her ever-present bodyguard and shadow.

He hovered a respectful five feet away, but Cait could feel the tension rippling off him even at this distance. Her second had agreed to trust Adler for her sake, but it wouldn't be easy. She couldn't blame him either. Not with what they now faced— a stranger with a dubious story, a questionable past, and a suspiciously convenient arrival. Even as she'd acknowledged the inner voice that urged her to trust this stranger, she'd promised the other side of herself—the guarded and jaded side— she would be vigilant in case her instinct proved false.

"The council knows who he is," Lucan said. "It's not as if he could just get a job somewhere in town and start his new life here. Too many questions. Too much suspicion. Too much risk of having someone from his old crew discovering him."

Cait contemplated the point and debated the options silently in her head while the men looked on and waited, more patiently than she had expected.

"Aye," she finally said and turned to Adler. "The council knows you?"

He dipped his chin slightly, but that smirk returned to his lips. "They know my name. They know I was a member of Tiernen's crew. But as far as I've gathered from the whisperings going around, they don't know my connection to Lani."

Lucan was shaking his head, eyes closed. "Still, someone could have easily seen you with her. Or she might have confided in someone. I wouldn't put it past the council to keep the knowledge of your name under wraps until they can use it to their greatest advantage. We can't chance someone recognizing you."

Cait heaved a sigh. "I assume there's no convincing you to hide in the attic or the basement for the next month?"

Adler only shook his head, his mouth quirking up into another smirk instead of a frown.

"And disguises are out," Cait said.

"There's no hiding these good looks anyway, love," Adler said.

Cait shook her head. "Well, at least you're humble. That will help."

"Don't lie."

Lucan took a step closer to them. "Are you two done flirting, or can we hurry this up? The pub needs to open soon."

Cait was about to protest the insinuation when Adler said, "I'm done if she is."

She suppressed a swear and instead veered the conversation back to the matter at hand. "How were you hoping to help us? You must have had a plan."

"And my plans always go so well," Adler said. "Truth is, I hadn't expected you to allow me to stay. Or to even hear me out."

At this, she raised a brow. "And why is that?"

"You're a McCallagh," he said. As if that was sufficient explanation.

Despite the urgency of their situation, her curiosity got the best of her, and she wondered what he—and the lords—had heard of her family. "What do you mean?"

With a shrug, he said, "I refuse to believe you don't know your brother's reputation."

"Afraid I don't, actually."

"So you haven't heard of the brutality his crew inflicts upon merchants he comes across? Burning them alive once the ships have been stripped clean of any valuables? Or his treatment of Captain Susset who sailed as part of Tiernen's fleet?"

Cait feigned confusion with a purse of her lips, an act she'd perfected over the years from having to play dumb when pirates came into the pub with too many questions. "That can't be Declan."

"So you haven't heard how he tied Susset to the mainmast before breaking each of his fingers? Story says your dear brother removed the man's tongue and ears before leaving him to sink with the ship. It was our crew that came upon the survivors he'd allowed to row away and pass along the tale."

Those were indeed just a handful of the stories she'd heard about her brother, but she had never completely believed them to be true. Even now, hearing them from Adler, she trusted her instincts that insisted Declan had conjured the rumors to build his reputation.

"Why else did you think the lords were targeting him if it wasn't in retaliation of his attack on Susset and others within their fleets?" Adler asked.

"Boredom? Jealousy?"

Adler laughed, a big booming laugh that bounced off the canopy above them instead of being absorbed by the leaves. "I suppose those are both good reasons. Regardless, I digress. Point is, I hadn't gotten that far in my own planning."

"How convenient," Lucan muttered.

"I don't have to be locked in a basement to remain hidden, you know."

Cait couldn't keep her eyes from dropping to his feet and trailing back up his entire six-foot frame.

"Subtle ogling there, love," Adler said with a flirtatious smile. "Aye, I'm no small prawn of a man, but you don't have to be of slight stature to be stealthy. You'll find we pirates are quite adept at it. Some of us, anyway."

"So what do you recommend?"

"Hire me in the pub."

Lucan choked on nothing, but Cait shared the underlying sentiment that the suggestion was absurd. She nearly laughed but managed to hold it back. "You. In the pub. The pub where pirates gather. Yes, of course. No one could possibly recognize you there."

"Aye, you're right. Pirates drunk on your spirits have impeccable memories. I had heard the rum on Cregah actually heightened one's senses rather than dulling them. I simply didn't believe it to be true."

Cait clenched her jaw. If only she had a blade on her, she could teach him a lesson for being so annoying.

Yes, because that's not an overreaction at all.

"Fine," she said as she forced her jaw to relax.

"What?" Lucan looked to the sky, exasperated. "This is the dumbest idea ever!"

But Cait ignored him and said to Adler, "You start tonight. Let's go." She turned to leave and got about ten paces before calling over her shoulder, "Also, you're staying with Lucan."

She could have sworn she heard one of them mutter, "Now that's the dumbest idea ever," but she wasn't sure which, and she didn't particularly care. She had a pub to run and a council to take down.

CHAPTER 19
DECLAN

DECLAN'S BODY JERKED INVOLUNTARILY, waking him. Based on the smell alone, he knew he was back in the brig, but here in the bowels of the ship, he couldn't discern how long he'd been unconscious this time.

Everything ached. The bruises on his face from his first day on this ship had begun throbbing again, courtesy of the blows he'd taken during the ambush. He winced at the pounding within his head only to groan when the movement pulled his wounds taut, aggravating them as well.

Opening his eyes, he tried to assess the rest of his body, but the only light, weak and minimal, came from the opening above the ladder, making it nearly impossible to see what state he was in. He scooted himself closer to one set of bars and—lightly but firmly enough for him to register any discomfort from bruises or cuts—he began to press one arm against the metal. Starting with the wrist, he moved gradually up his arm, finding only one spot on his bicep that screamed in pain when it came in contact with the iron. There was no telling how deep the cut was, and there wasn't much he could do about it anyway with his hands bound. Scooting around, he continued on the other side. When he didn't find anything of concern beyond a bit of soreness, he began to examine both legs, his neck, and his torso with his hands and forearms. The exercise was pointless of course, but he completed it all the same if for no other reason than to keep himself busy.

And to keep his mind from wandering off to other places, other moments, other people.

The more Declan tried to distract himself, though, the more insistent the images became in his mind. He focused on the creaking of the wooden hull, which groaned with each swell of the sea beneath him, and counted his breaths in time with its rhythm.

In...one. Out...one. In...two. Out...two. In...

I can't.

Aoife's voice interrupted, and his breath hitched. His chest tightened around his sternum, and it began to ache so much that he wondered if the moaning of the ship wasn't actually coming from his body being ripped apart by the memory.

A curse. A growl. A bang of his head against the iron bars.

He started again.

In...one. Out...one. In...

How could you?

This time he had been prepared for the words to barge in and push him around.

"I'm a pirate," he said aloud, as if the sound of them might be enough to ward off her voice.

I know you're a pirate, but you are different, Declan.

She was right, in some ways. He wasn't like most of the other pirates, his upbringing having given him a much different start than the others, but he wasn't different in the way she thought. The way she hoped.

And he didn't know if he regretted that or not.

He'd vowed to ensure she was safe—from the council, from the pirates, from whatever—whether that came with her forgiveness or not. He hoped it would, but then, he didn't want to disappoint her. Again. He couldn't be the man she thought she saw. The man she wanted him to be would have found a way around killing for the council. That man would have helped the exiles escape, faked the deaths, and worked closely with the Rogues to undermine the rulers.

But he hadn't.

He'd killed them.

Perhaps more civilly than other pirates did, but he'd killed them all the same. And their names—etched into his mind—acted as a constant reminder of how he'd become a tool for the council. The council who had killed his parents and ended his childhood. The victims' names haunted him, reminding him of his failure to save his parents, to stop the council, to become the man his parents always hoped he'd be.

No, the council had killed that good man on that foggy night, and he wouldn't be resurrected. No matter what walls Aoife managed to conquer within his heart.

I love you.

It was no longer her voice but his own, and he replied to it with a groan through gritted teeth. He was about to resume counting his breaths, this time aloud, when footsteps thundered down the ladder.

"Hey, you. Time to go." It was the oaf of a man who had come for him the first day.

Declan stood. "Where's Killian?"

The man only grumbled as he lumbered across the space.

"I see," Declan said and tapped his toe impatiently. "Not talkative at the moment?"

A laugh rumbled, short and coarse, before the man said, "You won't be so yappy either in a moment."

Declan's mind whirred through the possibilities of what awaited him above deck. Another beating? He could handle it, though he didn't look forward to it. Torture? He winced. That was far less appealing, but his thoughts took a jab at him.

It's what you deserve, isn't it?

Once again, he was forced to climb the ladder awkwardly, but he kept quiet this time, his throbbing head making any quip or retort elusive.

They were met by a wall of pirates whose backs were turned toward them. His escort bellowed for the men to move, and the group parted to let them pass, revealing Callum standing by the mainmast with Dominic beside him. Killian was restrained nearby. Declan worked to keep his expression blank as he took in the scene before him.

This was not good.

"Ah," Callum said, "you've arrived at last."

"I would have been here sooner had you not thrown me back in the brig."

Callum's nostrils flared as he spat out, "Which you should never have been removed from to begin with." Dominic punched Killian in the gut, forcing the man to double over, a strangled groan escaping his lips.

Declan shrugged as best he could with the shackles still in place. "Aye, but then who would have saved your life?"

"I would have managed."

"Of course you would have. How silly of me to think you'd be grateful for my help." The crew snickered but quieted quickly.

Ambling toward Declan, Callum rested his hand on the hilt of his cutlass, which had been returned to the scabbard at his side. His wounded arms had been treated, but aside from the slight tinge of blood peeking out from the bottom layers of his bandages, Callum's body showed no indication he'd just been ambushed and killed Lord Roberts and much of his crew.

"You think so highly of yourself, don't you, McCallagh?" Callum asked menacingly as he approached.

The corners of Declan's mouth fell, and he gave another shrug.

"What? No quip? No boastful words from the young captain?"

Callum now stood inches from Declan's face, and the offensive reek of sweat, blood, and salt rushed into Declan's nose.

But Declan didn't answer the goading questions. Instead he peered over Callum's shoulder and gave a quick nod. "What is happening here exactly? Am I to get a cellmate?"

Whatever Declan had been expecting from Callum, it was not the outburst of laughter that now exploded from him, which went on for a solid minute. Declan bit back his growing impatience and frustration, pushing all the tension into his shoulders. This display was meant to unnerve him, to make him squirm. He wouldn't give Callum the satisfaction. Even if internally the tactic was working to pull his gut into small knots.

"You wish that were the case. Unfortunately for your friend here, his fate is far worse than having to spend the remainder of this voyage in such close proximity to you."

They were still two days—or more—away from the Black Sound, so Callum could not have been planning to sacrifice poor Killian to the sirens. Only one thing Declan could think of would cause Killian to stand here as white as the caps on the Aisling's waves. Declan struggled to prevent his eyes from going wide, to stop his jaw from dropping open. He hoped his own face hadn't lost all color.

Not good, not good, not good.

That's an understatement.

Declan must have failed in his attempts to mask his reaction, because Callum gave another laugh—albeit less dynamic than the last—and said, "I see you've guessed then." Keeping his eyes locked on Declan, Callum raised his hand and circled a finger in the air, shouting, "String him up, boys!"

Four of the crewmen rushed forward, ropes in hand, while the rest of the men straightened, as if they were all eager to witness the spectacle about to take place. Declan wanted to look away, to avoid capturing another memory that would surely haunt him, but he steeled himself. He met Killian's terrified stare for mere seconds before the men threw him down on the deck and tied thick ropes to his already bound arms and legs. Together, they lifted him and hauled him to the starboard side.

Declan tried not to turn as Killian passed him, but Callum grabbed his arm and swung him around, dragging him forward. "You deserve the seat of honor, McCallagh," he hissed in his ear.

At the rail, they stopped, turning Killian to face the crew. The four men stood to Killian's right, Callum and Dominic on his left. Some of Killian's usual color had returned, and all his previous fear had somehow washed away as his features turned to stone—cold, accepting his fate.

Callum clasped his hands before him and rocked on his feet before finally speaking to his men. "This man, right here, took it upon himself to defy my command, to go behind my back, and to betray me and this entire crew by releasing our prisoner from the brig. This kind of behavior will not—cannot—be tolerated on this ship."

He drew his cutlass now and swung it up until the blade stopped just short of Killian's neck, and Declan flinched internally with the movement despite knowing it was merely for dramatic effect.

"I could slit his throat and be done with it," he said. "And perhaps I should. After all, he is an old friend and has served under me for many years. But that is exactly why this betrayal cuts as deep as the Aisling, and why my response must be as equally painful."

Dropping his blade but not returning it to the scabbard, Callum gave the signal for his men to proceed. Declan closed his eyes so he wouldn't have to watch the one kind person on this ship be subjected to such treatment. But Callum refused to let him avoid this. His rough hand gripped Declan's chin, hissing at him to open his damn eyes and witness the consequences that came from double-crossing him.

Declan's eyes slid open just in time to see Killian kicked over the edge of the ship, the rope tied to his arms rushing after him.

"Heave!" Callum bellowed. Declan looked around to find, as expected, a line of crewmen pulling a sopping wet rope from over the port rail. The entire crew remained wordless, the silence filled only by grunts of exertion as the men worked to drag the rope onboard. Their struggle intensified as a waterlogged Killian broke the surface and scraped along the side of the ship. Other crewmen dragged him onto the deck, dropping him in a wet and bloody heap.

Killian's body lay there, a mangled mess of torn rags, darkened by the seawater and his own blood. Flesh, blood, and bone peeked through the gashes in his clothes where barnacles had ripped him apart as he'd been dragged across the hull. His face was in an even worse condition, shredded down to the bone. One corner of his mouth had been torn away to reveal his jaw and a couple of missing teeth. The flesh along his cheek and nose were simply gone. Only a few bloody scraps of muscle hung onto his skull.

Declan nearly sighed with relief that Killian had perished with one pass under the keel and wouldn't suffer any further. But then the man blinked his one working eye, and his chest lifted with a sudden gasp for air before continuing to rise and fall rapidly as he panted. Bile lurched up Declan's throat, but he forced it back down. It would do him no good to lose it here with Callum and his crew watching, and it was not like this was the first keelhauling he had witnessed in his twelve years at sea. But the practice was—as far as Declan knew—rare, reserved only for the most heinous of crimes and performed only by the most vicious of captains. Declan himself had never called for it, but then, he'd never felt the need.

Even early on in his role as captain, when he'd let all his anger and pain come out against the unlucky crews and captains of the ships he overtook, he had never subjected anyone to this brutality.

"Again!" Callum's voice broke through the silence. Not one of the crew seemed surprised by this command, and they moved to obey without delay, ignoring how the flayed man groaned in pain when they hoisted him into their arms and carried him back to the starboard rail, where they flung him over the side once more.

Declan braced himself for another painfully silent and eerie passage of time while the men pulled their disgraced crewmate under the ship. It should have been Declan under the water being ripped open by the sharp barnacles covering the keel. He had been the one to initially betray Callum.

You also betrayed Aoife.

Squeezing his eyes closed, he swallowed hard against that truth. Yes, if anyone deserved such treatment, it was Declan, not Killian. But Callum would never have offered it to him, because as barbaric as this torture was, there were easier ways to inflict pain upon Declan.

An elbow knocked into Declan's ribs, and he lifted his chin to the side to see Callum grinning at him like a madman. "This your first hauling, McCallagh?"

Declan's throat remained too tight to allow any words to pass, so he offered a shake of his head.

"Oh, that's too bad. I had hoped to be your first."

Killian was once again hauled aboard and dumped onto the deck, his torso little more than crude strips of flesh somehow still clinging to his bones. Declan forced himself to look the man over, to verify he had died on this second pass. His eyes glanced quickly over Killian's midsection, where his innards were now visible through his tattered clothes, and settled on the gruesome sight that was his chest. Still. Unmoving. One eye had been ripped away from his skull. The other lay open, unblinking.

"Again!" Callum commanded, and Declan glanced sharply at him.

He waited to see if any of the crew would protest, direct their captain to the fatal state of their crewmate and insist his body not be desecrated further.

But no one spoke. No one even flinched at the order. They simply repeated the movements they had performed twice before, and Declan wondered—if only briefly—if it was worse to die by Callum's hand or by that of the sirens.

CHAPTER 20
TOMMY

It was near morning when Tommy finally ambled back down from the quarterdeck. After flatly refusing to sleep, despite his bo'sun's insistence he do so, he'd finally been forced by Gavin to retire below when he could no longer deny the heaviness in his eyelids. For the last several hours, he had wallowed in his thoughts, fighting himself over all the decisions he had made and had yet to make. He had gnawed on every word Maura had said to him, memorized every emotion he had seen in her eyes.

Such bravery. Such stupidity. Such stubbornness. Such confidence.

Confidence. That was what he needed. To make a decision and believe in it. Even if it turned out badly, the crew and Declan and everyone needed him to step up and take command.

At Declan's cabin door, Tommy knocked, more out of habit than as a courtesy to Aoife. He leaned against the doorframe, trying desperately to keep his eyes open long enough for her to answer. When nothing happened for several minutes, he knocked once more, louder this time. On his last stroke, the door swung away from his hand, and he nearly stumbled in as a result.

"Tommy," Aoife's sleep-logged voice croaked. She looked as tired as he felt. "What is it?"

"Gavin says I need to sleep. But he's crazy," Tommy said.

She looked him over. "Not crazy. He's absolutely right. You're barely still conscious as it is."

Something grabbed his arm. The world moved beneath his feet and went dark around him. "I don't know what you mean. I'm wide awake."

"Then why are your eyes closed?" she asked. "Have you been drinking?"

"What? They're not closed." He could quite clearly see Aoife's face before him. But then her freckles faded away, her eyes lightened to a golden yellow, and her ears became pointed at the tips. Realizing she spoke the truth—because last he knew, Aoife was not a shape-shifting fae—he forced his eyelids to part. Aoife had led him into the cabin and was about to help him settle onto the bed when he remembered her second question. "And no, unfortunately, no drink. Not until we get Declan back."

Aoife nudged his shoulder down with a soft word of instruction to sit and rest. Looking up at his friend, Tommy searched for something to say, some words of encouragement, but he came up empty.

"Why are you such an idiot?"

Her sharp tone snapped him to attention and caused his eyes to grow wider.

"Excuse me?"

"Look, Tommy, I'm an expert at screwing up. I make mistakes more than anyone should ever be able to in one lifetime. Perhaps that makes me more than qualified to note when someone else is in danger of doing something beyond stupid."

Tommy tried to parse through her words, but his exhausted brain was too slow to keep up. "What?"

"Maura. That's what."

His body tensed at the mention of her name. Aoife had taken note of whatever connection had grown between them, but as he'd told her before, there was nothing to be done about it. It was a doomed future.

"Why won't you let her help?" Aoife asked.

"Wait. Huh?" So this wasn't about their mutual affection but about Maura's powers and the kraken they were fast approaching.

"You didn't ask for my advice, I know, but you're being an imbecile. She—and Bria—are our best chances of getting past the creature alive. And you know it." Aoife displayed none of the sweetness he had become accustomed to, and though he was proud of her for finding her inner toughness, he wasn't sure he liked having it directed at him.

"We can't risk it," he said, more softly and less convincingly than intended.

"We can, and we should. It's the only—"

"No." Tommy straightened. Aoife stepped away from him, shock and confusion and anger swirling in her eyes. If he was going to be taken seriously as captain—even if only temporarily—he needed to find confidence.

"No? And why not exactly?" Bitterness swam in her green eyes, visible even in the dim lantern light.

Because I said so! His thoughts screamed inside his head. He wanted to simply demand that Aoife respect him and stop pressuring him to do something he knew to be too dangerous and risky. Instead, he calmed himself with a quick breath so he could explain.

"Because"—he cleared his throat—"if they use up their magic in the kraken's territory, they may not have time to restore it by the time we arrive at the Black Sound. And if they push their magic to its limit—use too much too fast—they lose it completely."

Aoife was quiet for a minute, searching his eyes. Finally she shook her head and huffed out a breath. "I don't like it, Tommy. It seems like not using their magic puts us at a greater risk of becoming kraken food and never making it to the sound at all. You must see that. I'm sure they can learn to manage without their powers."

"It's not just their special abilities they lose if they burn out. Their ability to heal is lessened. Their long life is shortened. I won't risk her—them."

"But it's a risk she's willing to take, isn't it? Why can't you respect her wishes? Why can't you trust her to know her limits and to help?"

"I just can't, Aoife," Tommy said before hiding a yawn he couldn't fight. "Now, if you really want to help, you'll let me sleep. I believe Collins should be ready for you soon too."

"Fine," she said and crossed her arms in front of her. "Get your sleep, Tommy. Hopefully you'll be thinking more clearly when you've had some rest."

She hadn't even made it out of the bedroom before his eyes were closed and he was falling onto the bed. He was asleep before he could hear the cabin door click shut.

CHAPTER 21
MAURA

Sitting on the quarterdeck stairs as she had last night, Maura forced her attention to remain on Aoife, who was in the center of the deck running through drills with Collins, a tall and lanky pirate who seemed to be one of the few who wasn't completely put off by the presence of three fae on board. Though she appeared to be watching the lesson intently, Maura's vision had long since blurred as she stared, her mind wandering to the cabin behind her and the man who slept within.

She understood Tommy's hesitance to allow her to use her powers, and unlike Aoife, she didn't take it as any personal affront. But Aoife couldn't feel the fear emanating from him like Maura could. Whether it was because of her sharp fae senses or her connection to him, she wasn't entirely sure. It didn't matter why or how, but she could tell there was far more bothering him than he'd ever let on.

While Aoife trained to help her fight the monsters waiting for them, Maura spent the morning wondering how to convince Tommy that things—especially things between them—weren't so dire, complicated, or doomed. But he'd been quite clear in his cabin. And again on these stairs.

He had no intention of being with her. Or even listening to her, apparently.

And though he admitted to caring for her, he wouldn't act on it.

How he could ignore it, she couldn't understand, even knowing her emotions exceeded anything he would ever experience. His rejection had stung far more than she'd expected it to, and though she'd been able to keep her words calm and her attitude nonchalant back in the cabin, she hadn't had the strength to refrain from trying to speak to him again when he'd eventually exited.

If his dismissal in the privacy of Declan's cabin had hurt, it paled in comparison to the gut-squeezing pain of him publicly pushing her away.

Renna was right.

At least about the pain this *predicament* destined her for.

But Maura refused to believe in the impossibility of it. Of them.

Except there is no chance for you two in Larcsporough. You're fae. He's human.

That inconvenient truth remained, twisting the fibers in her chest so tightly she had to press a hand to her sternum to calm it. When she and her sisters eventually traveled south to their kin, they would be expected to sacrifice their own dreams and plans to help stop another war. And that sacrifice didn't allow for Tommy's inclusion.

But where had her kin been while they were locked away in that room by the council? What did she—or any of them—owe the other fae when they had forfeited them to a life in prison?

They likely thought you were dead, just as you believed them to be.

She frowned. How dare her thoughts be so logical when all she wanted to do was sulk?

A weight crushed her chest, forcing her shoulders to round as she folded in on herself. Her face fell into her hands, and she propped her elbows on her knees. There were no good options. Either she betrayed her entire race or she betrayed her heart. No middle ground. No possibility of pursuing both. Even if Tommy would leave this ship and this sea, what waited for her in the south...

No, she couldn't ask him to go with her.

And she was beyond selfish to keep pursuing such a ridiculous hope that could only end in heartache.

It's not like you're soul mates. It's not like you don't have a choice here.

While her thoughts again rang true, it didn't make her choice any easier. She'd seen friends—who had been forced to sever ties and abandon the ones they loved during the war—struggle with that loss. Even though it was their choice to make, they were never the same afterward. Like a piece of themselves had been cut out, discarded, destroyed.

Was she strong enough to do the same?

Maura wasn't so sure, not when the only thing she'd ever dreamed of, in all her centuries of life, was finding someone to share life with. Bria, sweet as she was, had teased her for being such a romantic. Hopeless in her idealism of love and partnership. Perhaps there had been a chance for such a future before the Aisling War had broken out. But war changed things.

During those five centuries of imprisonment, Maura's dream had faded, as if the iron infused into the stone walls had snuffed out more than just her powers. But like her magic, the dream had not been completely extinguished. Her magic had roared back to life as they'd fled the council hall, stronger and more vibrant than it had ever been before. Even as her magic waned with her work to heal Tommy, warmth filled every part of her, pulling the sun from the sky and placing it within her chest, where it continued to shine.

It had shone until Renna brought in the clouds with her warnings, until Tommy had pushed her away and ignored his mutual feelings.

"You okay?"

Maura looked up to find Aoife—her face red and covered in sweat—standing before her.

A smile couldn't be helped as Maura answered. "Perhaps I should be asking you that."

Aoife took a few more ragged breaths. "I'm not sure how I would answer that, honestly. Not sure if it's helping me in the slightest."

"Better to know a few things than nothing at all, no?" Maura asked with a raised brow and a half-smile, hoping they effectively hid her inner turmoil. "Do you want to sit?"

Aoife gave a shake of her head. "I think I just want to lie down, actually. After I have some food." She shifted to her left, starting for Declan's cabin.

All of Maura's muscles urged her to stand, but she managed to quell it in time, forcing herself to remain seated even as she raised a hand to grab Aoife's arm, stopping her before she could walk off. Aoife tilted her head in confusion.

"Sorry. I think Tommy's still sleeping in there."

Yes, better to pretend she didn't know exactly where he was. That would appear less creepy.

"Ah," Aoife said, her shoulders slumping in disappointment. She looked around the ship, chewing on her bottom lip as she did. "He did look rather beat. Do you think he's doing okay?"

Maura's breath hitched at the unexpected question. Weaving her fingers, she stared at her hands. "I don't know."

"Then I guess I'll sit after all," Aoife said, already moving to sit beside her. The familiarity sent a disconcerting shiver up Maura's spine so strong she was sure Aoife had noticed. But if she had, she gave no indication, allowing their shoulders to touch with the closeness of good friends instead of new acquaintances. Maura hadn't had a friend in ages. Sisters, yes. They were a type of friend in themselves, she supposed, but sisterhood—even on good terms and in good spirits—had always felt too intrusive for Maura's liking.

It would be nice to have a friend.

"I'm worried about him," Aoife said.

I'm sure he's fine.

That's what Maura should have said, but instead her tongue betrayed her before she could stop it. "I am too."

Silence fell, and neither of them moved, both staring straight ahead. Maura should have sensed how Aoife was doing, emotionally speaking, but it seemed her preoccupation with Tommy had hindered her perception. She didn't know what to say or if she should even say anything at all. So she simply sat and counted breaths as they baked under the midday sun.

When Aoife spoke again, it came out as a whisper. "Can you tell a lie?"

Maura fought a laugh and smiled, but her amusement faded as soon as she saw Aoife was serious. "No. I mean, yes, we can. No, that rumor is not true. It's a myth."

Aoife's shoulders lifting with her breath before dropping, and she turned forward again. "I suppose that's a good thing."

"Why do you say that? Seems like that particular bit of lore came about to provide some comfort to men who feared fae overpowering them." A bunch of nonsense, if anyone asked Maura. Fae had no desire to rule over men. At least no fae she'd ever met.

Aoife fidgeted. "Sometimes the truth isn't always what we need."

Maura pondered the words for a moment, but Aoife continued before she could devise a response.

"I know it sounds silly, especially after Declan didn't tell me about..." She shook her head in a futile attempt to erase the end of the sentence from existence. "I would rather someone choose to tell the truth rather than be compelled to. Perhaps I'm naive, and it would be better to always know the truth in all instances. But I want to know I've earned someone's trust. Not have them confide in me simply because they couldn't avoid doing so."

"That doesn't sound silly at all, honestly." While Maura had never given this concept much thought, she had to admit Aoife had a valid point. How nice it would be to have control over what she shared with her sisters rather than having their keen perception and sisterly intuition give them such access into her life and her emotions.

"I've wondered," Aoife said, "will I be able to forgive Declan if—when—we rescue him?"

The question cut into Maura's heart and had her wondering how she would handle it if she and Tommy were in that position.

But Aoife wasn't Maura.

And Declan wasn't Tommy.

So while Maura—with this intense and sudden devotion—could not imagine withholding forgiveness from Tommy, for any infraction, she knew Aoife would struggle with this. Given her upbringing and the level of betrayal she'd experienced from her own family, Aoife understandably struggled with forgiving Declan, no matter how much she loved him.

"I think," Maura started, waiting to ensure Aoife was listening, "you'll have to ask yourself if you can accept the risk of being hurt again." Aoife's breath hitched, and Maura moved to continue before the girl got the wrong idea. "Thing is, though, life is inherently risky. Pain exists, and there is no way to avoid it entirely. The question becomes: is your love for him stronger than your fear that he'll betray you again? And I'm not saying you need to know the answer now. But it's something to think about as we travel. He gave you time, yes?" Aoife's chin dropped slightly. "He didn't chase after you. He didn't force you to give him an answer then and there. He honored you. And yes, I know he made a mistake in keeping the truth from you. More importantly, he knows it was a mistake."

Maura had no idea if she was helping or if her words were making any sense at all. And Aoife offered no sign either way. After another breath of silence, Maura moved to speak again.

"Remember, Aoife, forgiving him is not condoning his actions. It's not admitting what he did wasn't wrong or hurtful. It's choosing not to let those actions rule over your heart any longer. Sands, you don't even need to commit to a future with him in order to forgive him. And from the few moments I spent with him—watching him with you at the council hall, seeing his desperation when he brought Tommy back to the ship, witnessing him wrestle with whether to stay with his wounded friend or go after you—I can say with utmost sincerity, I believe he will accept your forgiveness with no strings attached. He will respect whatever boundaries you need. He may be a pirate, but he's a rare sort."

"Like Tommy," Aoife muttered, and for a moment Maura wondered if the girl hadn't heard anything else she'd said, only picking up on the last line. "You're right though. He's not like the others. He's done despicable things—and will likely do so again before his end—I can't imagine my life without him."

"But?" Maura could sense Aoife was holding something back, though she vowed to herself she wouldn't pry if she chose not to share.

"I just don't know when—how soon—how much time I might need before I can—"

"And you don't need to know that yet. He will understand."

Aoife donned a half-hearted smile.

Maura shook her head and said, "I'm no seer, and I can't read minds like my sister, but he will wait for your forgiveness. I would bet my last breath on that."

Hours passed, and the sun, flirting with the horizon, washed the sky in streaks of bright orange and vibrant pink. Aoife had accepted Gavin's offer to take her meals on deck with the sisters rather than in the captain's quarters, and now her barely stifled yawns betrayed her exhaustion. The girl would need a bed soon, and Tommy still hadn't left Declan's cabin.

"You should probably get some rest," Renna said to Aoife. "We all should, actually."

Aoife glanced around at the fae. "You mean fae sleep?"

"What kind of—" Maura started to ask, but she stopped when Aoife's face lit up with a smug grin. Maura rolled her eyes at herself for being so gullible.

"I'm really not that tired," Aoife said to Renna before promptly covering up another deep yawn.

"Clearly," Bria muttered with the hint of laughter in her eyes.

Aoife glanced toward the door of the captain's quarters. Although Maura knew their agreement to alternate sleeping shifts between them, she hoped Aoife wouldn't push to have him give the space up for her. Tommy would never knowingly let himself take the rest he needed, and he would likely decline further hours of sleep if he were to be wakened.

"I can't ask Tommy to move," Aoife said, almost to herself, though the three fae could hear her regardless.

Trying not to sound too happy, Maura counted to five before adding her agreement. "The continued sleep would do him good." She ignored the heat from her sisters' glares and their silent accusations. It wasn't as though being concerned for someone's health was crossing any line, was it?

"She could share our cabin, couldn't she?" Bria offered, her eyes alight as though she were planning a social gathering rather than simply figuring out sleeping arrangements on a cramped ship.

Aoife protested with a shake of her head. "You only have the two bunks though. I couldn't put you out any more than you already are."

"Nonsense," Renna said. "It was Maura's turn to have the floor space anyway, and I'm happy to relinquish my cot to you."

"You'd do that for me?" Aoife's mouth fell open, though it could have been from the subsequent yawn and not surprise.

Renna gave a short laugh. "Just for one night. Let's not get crazy. My ancient bones can only take so much discomfort curled up on the floor."

"I couldn't accept," Aoife started, but Renna raised her hand, and her expression hardened.

"You can, and you will. End of story."

Tension coursed through the small group. No one spoke for quite some time with Aoife looking to Maura and Bria in turn.

Maura forced her own laugh out. "So serious, sister. She won't want to take up our offer if you scare her away like that."

"Like what?" Renna demanded, her back straightening.

Her reaction seemed so perfectly comical that Maura couldn't prevent a smile from spreading across her face.

"Exactly," Bria said and turned to Aoife. "Really though, Aoife. You are more than welcome. One night sharing a bed on the floor will be cake for these two."

"Says the one who gets the bunk," Maura said, though she actually had no preference.

"Well, if that's settled," Renna said as she stood, "we really should retire for the night. If Gavin's estimates are correct, we will have a busy and stressful day tomorrow. Starting early."

In silence the three pushed to stand and follow Renna to the officers' cabin. When Renna opened the door and walked in, followed by Bria and Aoife, Maura remained in the doorway. She'd forgotten just how tiny this space was. Barely large enough for two men. Tight for three. Absurd for four. Even with Aoife being on the smaller side.

"We will make do, Maura," Renna said in her commanding tone. "Now come in here and shut the door."

"I think I'm going to spend a bit more time out here while you three get settled," Maura offered, ignoring how Bria and Aoife both cocked their heads in response.

"Very well then." Renna turned and met Maura at the door, standing as close to her as she had at the railing the other morning. "But remember what I told you. Don't be tempted. Don't—"

A growl rumbled in the back of Maura's throat, and she backed out, shutting the door with a heavy slam. She hoped it hit her sister in the face but immediately regretted that thought. Renna was only trying to help. But while some small part of Maura understood that, more of her had already succumbed to the overwhelming emotions that threatened to consume her.

Stalking to the center of the deck, she lowered herself onto the deck and leaned back against the mainmast. Minimal crew remained on deck to maintain their heading. A pirate Maura didn't know manned the helm while Gavin took his leave to sleep a few hours in the barracks below.

Tommy's fine. He just needs the extra sleep. You needn't worry about him.

Maura repeated the thoughts to herself, but failed to convince herself that Tommy was okay. Her earlier conversation with Aoife replayed in her mind, and she began to ponder what she would do if Tommy had killed one of her sisters. And lied about it.

Would it be any more difficult than your current reality?

Perhaps not more difficult. Just different.

And would it even matter if Tommy lied to her, if they could never be together anyway? Perhaps that simple fact—that she and Tommy could never be—prevented them from being hurt by possible betrayal.

Maura shook her head at herself.

No. Even if they had to ignore their feelings, those feelings would remain, and betrayal could still damage them.

Throwing her head back against the sturdy wood of the mast, she examined the sky, a deep blue velvet, speckled with what appeared to be a random spattering of stars. But she knew they were anything but random, placed there at the creation of their world. Before her time. Before war. Before enchantments. Before corruption. Before heartache.

When she was younger, Maura had found the view of the stars to be a freeing and exhilarating indication that anything was possible. But now, looking at the expanse spread above her, feeling the weight of a million could-have-beens and what-ifs crushing her chest, she saw no magic of possibility. Only the reminder that all she wanted, although visible, was out of reach. An impossibility.

With each passing moment, the sky deepened until it had lost all color and settled into a rich black. She must have been sitting at the mast for hours, and her backside ached from the uncomfortable wood beneath her.

Not that sleeping on the floor of the officers' quarters would have felt any better.

With a glance around, she stood and stretched out the stiffness from her joints. None of the crew on duty seemed to notice her as she began to pace the deck on weary feet. From one side of the ship to the other, she walked, counting her breaths, listening to the slapping of the water against the hull, contemplating the unfamiliar tune one of the crewmen whistled quietly. By the third passing, though, she could barely keep her eyelids open any longer and knew she needed to concede and join her sister on the floor in the small cabin.

Pulling the door open, she peered into the darkness. Renna had left some space on the floor for her, and from the sounds of their steady, slow breathing, her sisters and Aoife had been asleep a while. She should go in, shut the door, lie down, and sleep as best she could.

But she couldn't move from the doorway, like some force was pulling her away from these quarters, beckoning her elsewhere. She listened a few moments more, and then, convinced they were indeed sleeping soundly, she backed away on her toes and closed the door softly once more.

This was dumb. She was stupid. This was exactly the opposite of what she knew she should do. And yet, her reason stood little chance of winning an argument with the force now driving her back across the ship, around the quarterdeck stairs, and toward the captain's cabin.

Her fingers landed on the handle, and it took every ounce of self-control she could muster to stop herself from barging in. No, she needed to think this over. She wasn't going to do anything. She merely wanted a more comfortable space in which to rest. That didn't mean she was going to curl up in the same bed as Tommy.

The mere idea of doing so had her shoulders tingling.

Just go in. Grab a blanket. Lie down on the floor.

She walked herself through the plan, but her traitorous mind wouldn't cease its dreaming.

Go in. Crawl onto the bed. Lie down beside him.

"Balls!" The word fell out of her mouth with a frustrated thud, and she pulled her hand away from the door. Pivoting on her feet, she gasped at the sight of Aoife standing a few feet away, her brow creased with concern but her eyes sparkling with curiosity.

"Aoife! You scared me," Maura said, trying to keep her voice low as she risked a glance over Aoife's shoulder. If Aoife had woken up, it was quite likely her sisters had too.

"I could say the same about you." Aoife stepped closer. "Thought you'd be sleeping by now."

"And why aren't you sleeping?" Maura hoped her question didn't sound accusatory, though with her nerves wound so tight, it likely did.

Aoife shrugged and dropped her gaze to the floor where her toe shuffled against the deck. "I was. But I don't sleep well these days." When she lifted her face, the hint of curiosity had been replaced with what Maura could only interpret as worry, regret, and weariness.

Reaching a hand toward Aoife, Maura offered a tight smile before saying, "We'll catch up to Declan. We'll get him back." But when Aoife didn't respond or react, she wondered if perhaps she'd misinterpreted. Maybe Aoife was worried about something else? Her mother? Tommy? The sisters? Herself?

With a sheepish look, Aoife said, "Not if Tommy remains so stubborn."

She wasn't wrong.

"Maybe he'll feel better after he's rested," Maura said with a half-hearted shrug.

"I hope so. Speaking of. I'm heading back. You coming?"

Maura hesitated, her words stuck in her chest, her breath trapped in her throat.

Pulling in a deep breath, she searched for the best answer, except she hadn't quite decided for herself. When Aoife's brows rose, she scrambled one last time and said the last thing she'd planned to say. "I think I'm going to keep an eye on Tommy."

Aoife's expression shifted as her curiosity returned, pulling the corners of her mouth down. At least she didn't look angry, as Renna undoubtedly would have. Maura's heart pounded, and she waited for her friend to say something. Anything.

"Okay then," Aoife finally said with a smile Maura hoped was genuine. As silly as it was to be preoccupied with remaining on a mere human's good side, Maura couldn't deny she hoped she and Aoife would become close friends.

"Thanks, Aoife."

"Of course. But"—she quirked up a brow—"I'm not saving you from your sister's wrath in the morning."

Maura released a breathy laugh. "Nor would I ask you to."

Aoife turned to leave but stopped once to look over her shoulder. "Oh, and take care of him."

Before Maura could respond—or even react—Aoife was walking away, back toward the borrowed bunk in the cramped room. What she'd meant by that, Maura wasn't sure. With how much the girl carried on her heart already, it amazed Maura that she would have any energy to be concerned for Tommy's well-being. But then again, humans never ceased to amaze her. Their lives might be short, but the amount of cares and worries they could carry within them seemed as innumerable as the stars still glittering above her head. Maura had often wondered how they managed to survive as long as they did with the amount of baggage the hauled upon themselves.

But if Maura could help ease Tommy's burdens, she would. Whether he ever opened his heart completely to her or not, she would do everything in her power to see him not only survive but thrive.

CHAPTER 22
TOMMY

Tommy opened his eyes to find the sky still dark, with dawn not yet lightening the eastern horizon. Groaning and rubbing his knuckles over his eyes, he sat up, cursing internally over the minimal sleep he had gotten.

"It's about time you woke up."

The words, despite having been said by the sweetest voice he'd ever heard, had Tommy's eyes flashing open and his hands hovering in the air before him. Maura sat on the end of the bed with her legs crossed under her in the same way he used to sit as a child.

"What are you doing here? And what do you mean, it's about time? It's still the middle of the night." He flung a hand out toward the window and turned to ensure the world outside was indeed still dark and he hadn't imagined that a moment ago.

"You've been asleep for nearly a full day."

His eyes went wide, and his jaw felt heavy, like it would flop open at any moment if he didn't keep control over it. He looked around the room—from the window to Maura, then to the desk out in the main area and back to the window.

"What did you do to me?"

Pain flashed across her delicate features, tugging at the corners of her eyes, but she recovered quickly. Straightening, she raised her chin and pinned him with a glare.

"I don't know what you believe I'm capable of, Tommy, but it's certainly not putting men into comatose states. So don't you dare accuse me of *doing* something to you."

Her words were as sharp and clipped as the icy daggers she shot at him with her eyes, and he flinched as if they had actually pierced him. He slumped his shoulders and dropped his chin to his chest before pushing a hand through his hair.

"I'm sorry, Maura. I'm just—"

"Stressed."

He offered a nod but didn't look at her, instead keeping his eyes cast down onto the blanket in front of him.

"Maybe I can help," she said.

His exasperation escaped him in a groan before he could hold it back. "We've already been over this."

She shifted closer to him, uncrossing her legs and kneeling beside him. She still wore the simple dress from her time at the council hall, a purple so deep it looked almost black until a beam of light hit it just right. Her eyes contrasted with it so dramatically that the gold in them seemed to move, simmering away like honey melting into a cup of hot tea.

Tommy lost all knowledge of how to breathe as she inched closer. He sat, waiting, unsure what her intent here was exactly. But given her forward nature earlier that night—or, rather, last night—he could only assume she was looking for something he could not give her, no matter how much a part of him wanted to.

She placed a hand on his knee and moved it cautiously up to his thigh. He closed his eyes, not sure where this was going, not sure what she was planning, and not sure he could stop it if it continued like this.

The bed shifted as she moved, but still he kept his eyes closed.

Why are you such a nervous wreck? Seriously. Declan would mock you endlessly if he saw you!

He shook his head at himself—a small, almost imperceptible movement to quiet his thoughts.

"I wasn't talking about my magic, you know." Maura's voice floated toward him from much further away than he'd expected, and he risked a peek at her, trying not to think about the way her hand still rested on his leg.

In one quick, graceful motion, Maura turned around until she was seated beside him, her left leg pressed against his right, her shoulder resting against his own. And though her hand now lay in her own lap, the way her body was nestled alongside his was almost more intimate.

Too intimate.

He should get up. He should figure out what had happened while he was sleeping. He should look for Aoife and see if she needed a chance to sleep or seek out Gavin and find out how close they were to those dreaded waters.

But he couldn't.

Her warmth. Her scent. The gentle rise and fall of her chest as she breathed. He was trapped, transfixed, mesmerized, frozen.

"Do you want to talk about it?" Maura asked, turning her chin slightly so she was looking at him from the side.

"About what exactly?" His mind skipped and hopped among all the various problems that lay before him, until it all fell away, leaving him with a blank nothing that must have shown plainly on his face, because she laughed. Short. Sweet.

"Take your pick, I suppose. It's no wonder you slept for so long with the number of things you're juggling and the new role you're filling and the new...feelings you're fighting."

He ignored that last thing and once again ran a hand through his hair. It seemed cliche to sigh, and yet his body seemed to do it on its own, like the release of air could somehow soothe all the tension pulling at his nerves.

"I mean," she continued when he didn't respond, "I'm content in silence as well, but I doubt that would ease your stress much."

After a full day of sleeping, Tommy had woken up more relaxed. The edge of the cliff he'd been lingering on for the past several days had seemed a bit further away. Until she'd spoken. Then it was as if a force had pushed him forward, his toes once again hovering over that emotional edge.

His chest tightened.

The air was slowly leaking out of this cabin.

He couldn't breathe.

Maura wanted too much from him. The crew needed too much from him. It was all too much. A crushing weight even a restful sleep couldn't lessen.

He had been quiet for so long, he didn't know how to break the silence. In fact, he usually didn't know how to talk to her at all. Others, yes. But Maura? She fascinated him and—not that he'd ever admit it, not even to Declan—she intimidated him. Why she wanted him was beyond comprehension.

But then she had told him he'd see his own worth one day.

Was that really what his problem was? Was that why he always sought to be second and not in charge? To be the follower rather than the leader? Was it simply a lack of self-confidence and self-worth?

He cringed at the slew of questions pinging around his brain. It was too early to tackle any of that. If he ever could.

"This is nice," Maura whispered and lowered her head onto his shoulder, her soft hair tickling his cheek.

A "Hmmm" was all Tommy could manage, not trusting his voice not to crack.

"It could be nicer," she said with a hint of mischief. Her hand returned to his thigh, higher this time. Tommy went still, even as every nerve in his body seemed to move, causing a not unpleasant tingling down to his toes, along his shoulders, and elsewhere.

He wanted her to back away. To give him space. But also to never stop touching him.

He wanted her to be just another barmaid in a distant port that he could bed once and move on from. But also to be the only one he took to bed ever again.

He wanted to ignore the warmth that gathered within him, to remind her—and himself—it wasn't an option. But also to give in to it all.

Before he could think better of it, he had her in his arms and was lifting her up and over until she was seated on his lap, her dress pooling at her thighs as her legs straddled him. He lost himself in the welcoming light of her eyes, which shone with the same hunger that simmered within him and held none of the surprise he had expected.

Her hand traveled up his torso, setting more of him on fire. He couldn't stop his arm from winding around her back, pulling her closer, and moving her forward so the warmth of her body enveloped him.

Tommy was swimming in honey—the golden, luscious, sweet honey of her eyes. She sat so close to him now, there was no hiding the effect she was having on him. Yet he didn't care.

Her hair spilled around her face as she leaned toward him. His eyes dropped to her lips. What would it feel like to kiss her? To take her here and now? To give in to everything he knew was wrong?

Even if he could untangle his thoughts enough to form coherent sentences, he didn't think his tongue could manage to utter them.

What are you doing?!

He shouldn't do this. Couldn't.

I don't fucking care.

With everything else in his life turned upside down, why couldn't he claim something good? Something just for him.

Ignoring all the silent warnings, his eyes traveled back to hers, memorizing every perfect detail of her face. He ran his hands down her back to her waist, his thumbs grazing her curves beneath the fabric of her dress. He couldn't pull his gaze away from hers, even when he ran a hand over her shoulder and let his fingers trace the length of her neck and down her jaw toward her inviting lips.

Everything about her enticed him. He lost all concept of anything outside of this room, this bed, this small space they shared.

All he saw was her beauty, strength, and feisty spirit. All of it caused a thrill within his heart. She'd been right about them. Whatever had happened during his healing, whatever spark had been ignited would not be ignored.

And he didn't want to ignore it.

He only wanted her lips on his.

To taste her.

To feel her.

To do anything she asked and then some.

Maura hovered close enough now that her breath warmed the sides of his nose and the top of his lips. Sliding his eyes shut, he closed the distance between them.

Her lips brushed against his, a touch so light yet so amazing it sent another shiver through him. It should have excited him. In any other situation, it probably would have. But now it seemed to wake up that responsible part of himself he'd shoved aside earlier.

Tension shot through his limbs, stopping him before his lips could devour hers.

Gently he moved her back—the motion uncomfortably reminiscent of his dreams. The distance between them now brought him a refreshing chill, like stepping out of a crowded, stifling pub.

Still, he kept his eyes clamped shut, afraid of how she might react.

He was a coward. Too scared to see how his sudden rejection might hurt her. He braced himself for the slap of her hand or the cut of her sharp tongue—two rather unpleasant but familiar responses he'd been the recipient of in the past—but they didn't come.

Instead, her sweet laugh—a laugh he hoped to always remember—embraced him, carrying none of the pain or resentment he'd anticipated. When he opened his eyes, she was looking at him as though he hadn't just refused to kiss her. Love and endearment and care shone at him, more than he'd ever deserved, so intense it scared him.

Except it wasn't her feelings he feared but the fact that he sensed the same emotions crying out from the dark corners of his soul where he'd discarded them.

Gone were the questions of what was happening to him. It was painfully—so painfully—obvious. This was no simple attraction, no basic human desire. It was more, much more, and the only question now was *how*. How could he be falling in love with someone he didn't know? A war raged inside him, until he thought his heart might crack in two. One part of him wanted to give everything and more to this amazing woman—this *fae*—but the other frantically worked to protect him from the pain they'd both suffer when things inevitably ended.

"Tommy, love," Maura said as she swept a stray hair from his forehead.

Could she see the fear in his eyes? He wasn't even trying to hide it at this point.

Some captain you've turned out to be.

Reaching both hands out to touch his face, she cupped his jaw and slid her fingers behind his head. "I have waited for you a long time. I will wait as long as I have to. Even if I have to wait forever."

Forever.

He swallowed the word down, accepting it like the medicine his mother used to force on him whenever he got ill. Just like that medicine, the word coated his insides in the same disgusting taste, but he knew—no matter how much he hated it, how much it hurt, how bitter it left him—it was what was best for him.

Tommy could never allow himself to build an impossible future with her, and he moved to tell her as much. But he didn't get a chance. She leaned forward, and her hair once again draped around his face. He snapped his mouth closed, ready to ward off her advances.

You're making the right decision.

As much as he wanted to trust his own thoughts, when she pressed her lips to his in a kiss so light and sweet and soft and full of love and patience, he wondered if he'd made a mistake. Before he could change his mind, she was gone, all her warmth taken away as she slipped off the bed and out of the room.

CHAPTER 23
AOIFE

AOIFE FOUND herself surprisingly less sore than she'd expected, especially considering the cramped quarters. Sleep had remained elusive though, if only because of the intimidating company.

You didn't have to take them up on their offer.

She grumbled as she rolled over on the small mattress and sat up, forgetting about the bunk sitting low above her borrowed bed until her head hit the wooden edge hard. Wincing, she bit back a cry of pain. She'd shown enough of her less-than-graceful side already, and there was no way she could bear to lose any more of her pride.

Especially among the fae.

As she rubbed the tender part of her scalp, she listened. No movement. The blankets Renna had used to set up her bed on the floor had already been neatly folded and placed under the small table that sat in the corner opposite the bunks. Aoife stood and risked a timid glance toward the upper bunk. Bria was nowhere to be seen, having already tidied up her bed as well, likely in the most orderly fashion these accommodations had ever seen.

Aoife rushed to the small porthole. Its single pane was too grimy to allow her to see much detail outside, but she was at least able to determine that the sun was up. And she had overslept. Gavin had expected to enter the kraken's territory shortly after sunup, and from what Aoife could tell, it was well past that now. Without another thought, she made her way across the room and out the door, stopping short once she had stepped onto the deck.

She noticed two things immediately: it was silent, and the entire crew seemed to be above deck. Unmoving. Not talking. Simply waiting. Watching. Some turned to glance at her, fear worn plainly on their faces. Others seemed ready, eager even, to take on the giant below.

No one said anything to her though, and she scanned the crowd of tired, sweaty, grungy, nervous men for one of her friends. As silently as she could manage, she tiptoed forward.

With a glance up to the quarterdeck, she confirmed Tommy and the others weren't there. Something tapped her shoulder, and she nearly yelped from surprise but quickly clamped a hand over her mouth to keep any rogue sounds from escaping. A large burly pirate, whose name she didn't know—though she recognized him as being one of the new Foxhaven recruits—lifted a finger to his lips before pointing the same hand toward the captain's quarters.

If the officers and fae were in there, perhaps things weren't quite as dire as they seemed.

At least not yet.

Aoife opened the door without knocking and found them standing around Declan's desk much in the same manner as the day they'd gathered and chosen this course. Except now Maura wasn't bothering to keep her distance from Tommy, standing close enough to him that their shoulders nearly touched. Not that he seemed to be bothered by it. Or to even be aware of it.

Six faces looked up to greet her as she joined them. Tight smiles came from the men. Nothing but blank stares from the fae.

Although she had started to warm to Maura, especially since their talk on the stairs the other night, she couldn't quell the jealousy she harbored toward her and the other fae for their elegant grace and calm demeanor in the midst of strife. They wore their serene masks expertly, and Aoife wondered if they thought doing so put people at ease, because the empty expressions plastered onto their perfect faces was anything but relaxing.

Tommy dipped his chin to her with a whispered "Good morning." The man didn't look like the extra sleep he'd enjoyed had helped him. In fact, he almost looked worse off.

You could have slept in your own bed last night, and it would have been just as well.

Biting back the thought, she focused on Tommy's eyes, hoping he would understand her question without her having to voice it. While she trusted herself to be able to whisper, it seemed better if she didn't have to take any unnecessary risks.

"Obviously," Tommy said, continuing in a whisper, "you can tell we are keeping ourselves as quiet as possible. This makes sailing a bit more difficult—"

"A lot more difficult," Gavin interjected, also in a whisper.

But Tommy ignored him. "So far we've had no signs of the creature, and we are moving on as quickly as we can, as silently as we can."

Aoife stepped closer until her hips rested against the edge of the desk. She leaned forward. "How are we sailing at all when the deck is packed full of men? Men who are more for decoration than anything else."

Tommy released a slow sigh. Running a hand through his hair, he gestured to Mikkel with the other. The man turned without question and slipped out the door, likely to give whispered commands to the crew to disperse and get back to work as best they could.

"Thank you, Aoife," Tommy said, "for allowing me the extra rest. I know it wasn't what we had agreed to, and it was far from ideal to squeeze four of you into the small officers' quarters, but I appreciate the consideration all the same."

Aoife snapped her attention to Renna, the eldest, but she and Bria both stared straight ahead, as if they were off in some dreamland instead of present in this meeting. Maura, though, looked at her and offered a small shrug as the corner of her lips pulled back in a sheepish grin. Maura's brows rose, and her golden eyes pleaded with Aoife to not mention how she had slept in here near Tommy all night.

He thought the four of them had slept in the officers' quarters.

Maura hadn't told him otherwise.

And now Maura was asking her to keep it a secret from him, one of her only friends in the world.

Another damn secret.

But Maura was her friend, too, and she could talk with her later about the importance of honesty. Sands, life had become complicated now that she wasn't isolated and basically alone.

She turned back to Tommy, and her whispered "You're welcome" was as much for Maura as it was for him. Whatever was now happening—or not happening— between those two could wait until tomorrow. If they lived that long.

"Gavin," Aoife said, turning to the helmsman, "at the rate we are sailing at the moment, will we—"

A shake of the man's head cut her words off as sharp as a cutlass would have. "No, unfortunately. Wind is not cooperating with us. There's still some, but not enough to give us the speed we need. It's like the wind avoids these waters as much as sailors do."

Glancing around the small group, Aoife asked, "So this is our plan then? Glide slowly across the waters as quietly as possible in hopes the shadow of our ship doesn't catch the attention of a gigantic beast who swallows vessels whole?"

"Basically, yes," Tommy answered.

"Well, that's stupid."

"Look, it's the best—"

"No, it's not, Tommy, and you damn well know it." Aoife struggled to keep her anger from pushing her volume up above a whisper. With all her recent mistakes, she didn't want to add *alerted the kraken* to that list.

Tommy didn't move, didn't say anything as his lips formed a tense line.

"And you're okay with this, Gavin?" The sharpness in Aoife's tone lingered.

Gavin kept his eyes lowered to the desk as he answered, "Captain's orders, Aoife."

Aoife bit back her frustration. "There has to be a way for Maura and Bria to help without burning out their magic. You have to consider it, because at this rate, at this pace...Declan will be dead before we even make it out of the kraken's cursed waters!"

She had at least stopped herself before pinning Declan's impending demise on her friend, but Tommy still looked as if he wanted to toss her to the monster himself. His amber eyes, full of anger and hurt, bored into hers, but she refused to back down.

"And what do you care, huh?"

"That is unfair, Tommy. Just because I was hurt doesn't mean I want him dead. Just because I didn't forgive him immediately doesn't mean I never will. You're being ridiculous."

Tommy's chest rose with a deep inhale before he spoke, his words barely more than a hiss. "Regardless, you haven't exactly shown the best judgment, Aoife."

Aoife flinched but stepped once more toward the desk and pressed her fisted knuckles onto its worn surface. "That may be, but you're the one whose judgment is being clouded by—"

"That's enough." It was Maura who interjected, looking from one to the other. "Both of you need to cool down before you throw away your friendship out of spite and bitterness."

She was right of course, though neither Aoife nor Tommy eased up, continuing to glower at each other. Aoife's heart raced, the blood rushing to her face. The sound of ragged, sharp breathing filled the cabin.

Aoife's mind bounced between thoughts and questions, tactics and possibilities. She was no strategist, and although she might have been naive, she was not stupid. Neither was Tommy, which made it all the more frustrating that he wouldn't listen, couldn't see it wasn't as black and white as he believed.

In her periphery, Aoife noticed Renna's head turn toward her. "That's not a bad idea, Aoife."

All attention shifted to the eldest fae.

Renna clarified for them all. "Aoife was just pondering why my sisters couldn't use their talents sparingly, not to their full power but just enough to give us an edge. It could be the best solution we have, allows us to benefit from their magic with less risk of pushing themselves too far."

"But there is still some risk," Tommy said.

Renna nodded. "Everything carries some risk. It's not perfect, but it's better than anything else anyone has offered."

Bria and Maura exchanged a glance before they both nodded and spoke in unison. "It could work."

Tommy's shoulders slumped, and his head fell forward as he leaned over the desk, defeated. Aoife nearly felt bad that she had pushed her friend so far on this, but Declan's face flashed in her mind. Yes, it was all her fault. All of it. But that was why she needed Tommy to make this decision, so she could have the chance to make everything right.

"Fine," Tommy said finally, the word barely audible to Aoife. He lifted his gaze to Maura, and even from the side, Aoife could see the intensity with which he looked at her. "We try it. But, Maura, if—" He stopped speaking as she touched his forearm lightly. A silent conversation seemed to happen between them then, and Tommy said nothing more.

Aoife let relief spread through her as she breathed deep. They would have a chance. Declan would have a chance. They weren't doomed. Everything would be okay.

CHAPTER 24
CAIT

CAIT'S FEET ached more than they had in ages. She had been going nonstop all day even with the extra help from Adler at the pub. Last call had been announced an hour earlier, and despite the few men still nursing their drinks by the window, she slumped into a chair at one of the tables and thudded her boots onto the one opposite her as she closed her eyes and laid her head back.

It had been one of the busiest nights they'd had recently. They'd served a somewhat even mix of pirates and locals, which might have been interesting to Cait if she hadn't been so exhausted from all the orders and the noise and the running around. Having locals wasn't unusual in itself, but they typically visited in the early hours after opening, leaving before most of the surlier patrons began trickling in after dusk. But last night, the locals had not been deterred. And many of the parties had stayed well into the night, with more women coming in after supper, their husbands or other male companions in tow.

"So, when do you normally kick out the stragglers?" a hot breath muttered in her ear, and Cait snapped her eyes open to find Adler standing much closer than was proper in public.

Sitting up straight, she placed her feet back on the floor, ignoring how they protested, and turned her chin toward the window and the pirates quietly chattering away between sips of rum.

"Hey!" she called over to them. "Manny! Will! Gus! Five minutes before I take back whatever you haven't downed and kick you out on your asses!"

The three men lifted their faces and glanced around the now empty pub before finding Cait. Two of them threw back the last dregs of their glasses, while the third, Will, gave her a nod and muttered an apology, his gaze flitting between Cait and Adler before he too finished off his drink.

Cait couldn't help but laugh. "I said five minutes, not seconds. You had some time left."

They all stood, and it was Manny who provided an explanation. "Aye, Cait, but we know as well as you do how we lose track of time, and we prefer to walk out the door of our own volition rather than being tossed."

"You mean kicked," Adler said, correcting him. Cait turned to glare at him for the ridiculousness of his statement, but Manny only laughed.

"Right, right. Kicked. That's far worse for our reputations," he said as he shoved his companions toward the door, each of them offering their goodbyes and thanks as they stumbled over the threshold.

When Cait settled herself back into a relaxed posture, Adler walked around toward the door but stopped before reaching it. "Do you not need to lock it?"

A breath, tired and slow, seeped from her lungs, and she answered with her eyes once again closed. "With what? There are no locks in Morshan. Or anywhere on Cregah, except perhaps in the council hall." She opened one eye and peeked at him. "I'm surprised an astute pirate such as yourself wouldn't know that already."

She watched him scratch his bearded jaw a few times as he pondered the information before going back to resting her eyes. She could have sighed with contentment at the sheer luxury of being able to put her feet up, but when her new employee still hadn't spoken, she said, "Sit, Adler, and stop thinking so hard. Let's relish this first successful night of your anonymous employment here."

Heavy, tired footsteps moved closer, and a chair scooted across the wooden floor. A deep exhale filled the air as the chair creaked under the weight of the massive man dropping into it. Still, he didn't speak.

Cait soaked up the silence, but after several minutes had passed and she remembered she was not sitting here alone as she normally did, she turned her attention to him once more. He was staring blankly at the table before him, hands in his lap. Not tired. Not worried. Not happy. Just empty, cold, dead. She regretted the question even before it left her mouth, but the silence that had been comfortable seconds before was becoming prickly and tense.

"What are you thinking?" she asked.

He didn't look up from the table but only shook his head a couple of times. "Nothing."

"Doesn't look like nothing," she countered, even as her mind told her that was exactly what his features showed. Nothing.

"Well, nothing that can be remedied anyway." After a few more minutes, his blue eyes lifted, but he remained stoic and unreadable.

Come on, Cait, it's not that hard to figure this out. He just lost his love, the one he was going to run away with to start a new life.

"Well, you did a good job tonight."

A slight sparkle shone in his eyes at her words, and one corner of his mouth quirked up. "Was that a compliment, love?"

She rolled her eyes. "Don't let it go to your head."

His smirk shifted into a true smile, and Cait wondered how she hadn't noticed before how his dimples peeked through his beard when he did so. Something sparked inside her against her will, like a flash of a faded dream or a hope long since tossed aside and ignored but not forgotten.

"And what are you thinking?" He hiked a brow as he turned the question back on her.

"Oh," Cait started as she glanced toward the bar. She could almost catch a glimpse of her mother and father there cleaning up after a long night, laughing and teasing and tickling one another. With a blink, the memory was gone, replaced by the sight of glasses needing to be cleaned and spills needing to be wiped up. "I don't know. Missed chances, I guess. Paths blocked. Futures upended. Dreams scattered."

"So, happy things then."

Cait's chest tightened, and silence filled the space between them. It had been so long since she'd let those thoughts out of their cage, and the shock of their sneaking up on her here, now, and in front of him, had caused her to be more honest with her answer than she'd intended. Such deep sentimentality felt out of place for the leader of a rebellion.

Some rebellion.

Nothing was going as planned, and Cait ground her teeth to keep that truth from rising to the surface in the form of tears and a trembling chin. She'd already humiliated herself when he'd surprised her in the woods. She didn't need to give him any additional fodder.

But perhaps the tide was turning with his arrival and Maggie's death. The fire had been stoked and now burned even brighter than it had when she'd revived her parents' rebellion.

A rumble broke the silence as Adler cleared his throat. "So, am I to find Lucan's on my own? Or will—"

"He'll be by shortly to show you the way," she said, letting her head loll to the side so she could look at him. "And I expect you to not kill each other."

"What about a bit of maiming?" That smirk returned, and she reminded herself he wasn't that attractive when he did that.

"Just keep it minimal. I'd prefer limbs be intact if we're going to succeed with our plans."

Adler nodded, and the corners of his mouth turned down.

"But seriously," she said, "be nice."

"I'm always nice. It's him—"

The door opened, and a pair of boots thudded into the pub, accompanied by a bellowing voice. "Where's my new tenant? Is he ready to go at least?" Lucan seemed as annoyed as Adler was amused. With that obnoxious grin once again on his face, Adler flashed Cait a wink.

"Right here," Adler said. "And I'm ready as long as the boss doesn't need me to help with the cleanup." He rose to his feet, pushing his chair back under the table as he did so.

Lucan looked past Adler to Cait and, with a raised brow, asked, "Can he leave? I'd rather get this over with, but if you need—"

"No, go. It's surprisingly clean. Won't take me long to straighten up before I head to bed."

"Well, be sure to get some rest. You look like crap lately," Lucan said. His smile dimmed when Adler laughed at his poor attempt at humor. Waving a hand toward the door, Lucan indicated to Adler it was time to leave.

With three long strides, Adler was at the door, where he turned to flash another smile at Cait, this one smaller but more genuine, it seemed. "Good night, Cait."

Before she could respond, Lucan had shoved the larger pirate out the door and was offering her a lazy wave as he headed out into the street.

Silence once again enveloped Cait, and she allowed herself one more cleansing breath before she pushed to her feet—which screamed at her as she did. The pub wasn't going to clean itself.

She had barely made it behind the bar when a noise—subtle but noticeable—came from outside. Following the sound to the back door, she glided as quietly as she could past the stairs and beyond the storeroom. Her gut tightened at the memory of the last time she'd answered this door.

She inched the door open and peered out to see what was happening in the alley behind her pub.

A woman she'd never seen before, dressed in bright clothing that stood out conspicuously even in the dimly lit alley, was being pressed up against the pub's wall by two large hands Cait recognized.

"Adler. What are you doing?" Cait hissed as she rushed out to meet him. "Where's Lucan?"

"I'm here." Lucan's voice came from the other side of Adler at the same time his head became visible.

The woman made no sound. She didn't even struggle against Adler's grip. Both seemed odd, considering the situation.

"We found her slinking around. Followed her back here. Caught her trying to break into the pub," Adler explained.

"Is that true, Lucan?" Cait asked, cringing internally at her openly questioning Adler's story when she had claimed to trust him. Thankfully, Adler didn't seem bothered by it.

Lucan nodded. "Aye, that's what happened."

"Do you know her?" Adler asked, his eyes now shifting to meet Cait's.

Cait shook her head and addressed the woman. "Care to introduce yourself?"

"I'm looking for Captain McCallagh," she said, her thick accent a mix of several nations—Haviernese, Turvalan, a bit of a Foxhaven lilt. Possibly others Cait couldn't quite place.

Cait stepped closer as she asked, "What makes you think he'd be here?"

"Name on the sign. Lucky guess."

"We have a front door. Why try to enter through the back? And without invitation?" Nothing about this woman set Cait at ease. Her gut churned in warning.

"You were closed. Didn't want to get you in trouble with the council. And I wasn't trying to break in. I was going to knock." The woman's brown eyes wandered to the two men who had stopped her.

"Last I checked," Adler said, "knocking on a door didn't involve picking the lock with your hairpins."

Cait huffed a laugh, despite not finding any of this funny. "Perhaps they have a different method of knocking where she's from." She glanced at the woman again, brows raised in question.

"Foxhaven. And fine, I lied. You must be used to that with all your dealings with pirates."

Turning on her heel, Cait said, "Bring her inside. The alley is no place to talk."

Once inside, Lucan dragged a chair from the main room into the storeroom, and Adler promptly and firmly dropped the woman into it before securing her with a rope Cait handed him.

Lucan stifled a yawn, and Adler mirrored the move.

"You're both tired," Cait said. "Why don't you head on out and get some sleep. I can handle her."

Both men shook their head in unison, mouths tight, and Cait muttered a "fine" before turning back to their unexpected guest.

"Let's start easy. What's your name?"

"Could I get some water?" the woman asked.

"No. Answer the question."

"I'm parched."

This was going to be a long night.

"Not too parched apparently," Lucan muttered under his breath.

Cait repeated the command. "Name. Now."

With a roll of her eyes and an exaggerated breath, she answered, "Lucy."

"And you're a friend of Captain McCallagh's?" Cait was too tired to hide her skepticism. Declan had few friends, and they were all part of his crew.

A nod was all Lucy offered, causing one of her curls to fall loose from where she'd had them pinned atop her head.

"Why are you looking for him?"

"To apologize."

"That's a long way to travel for an apology. What did you do to him?"

"That's between me and Declan."

Cait's hand itched to slap the smugness out of this woman, but she managed to refrain. She was already taking a risk tying her to a damn chair in her storeroom.

"I believe it stopped being between the two of you when you attempted to break into my pub." Cait couldn't determine this woman's game, but every one of her internal alarms was sounding.

Lucy offered a lazy shrug. "Still, I prefer not to break a friend's confidence. I've already done too much."

They were getting nowhere, and it was clear Lucy had no intention of providing any information. While Cait had heard of pirates using extreme measures to force a captive to talk, she had no desire to do that here and now.

She stepped back. "Let her go."

"What?" Lucan asked, his eyes wide.

"You heard me."

Still, Lucan didn't budge, so Adler moved around him to loosen the bonds.

When Lucy was free, she stood and rubbed her wrists. "I'm assuming he's not here."

Cait shook her head. No benefit in lying about that. The woman could get that information easily enough.

"Very well then."

"You could leave him a note, if you wish," Cait offered.

Lucy breathed a laugh. "And have you read it? I think not. Better for me to wait around and stay."

"Well you can't stay here," Lucan said.

Cait placed a hand on her friend's arm, hoping to ease his frustration. "We can direct you to a boarding house, and once Captain McCallagh returns, we can send a message to you."

Lucy's lips pursed. She appeared to be mulling over the offer. Like she had any better options. Finally she clasped her hands together in front of her hips. "I appreciate that. Thank you."

"Lucan here will show you the way. It's not far."

If Lucan had an issue with this, he hid it well, thankfully. "This way," he said, offering Cait a tight-lipped smile as he passed, Lucy close behind. Once they were out, Adler moved to leave, but Cait grabbed his arm. He paused, looking down at where her hand tightly clasped his muscles, and smiled. Before he could make any remark about the close contact, she flashed him a stern look.

"Get word to Aron and Eva. We need to watch this Lucy woman. Find out what she's up to."

"Will do, love."

And he slipped out into the early morning darkness, leaving Cait to wonder what dealings Declan could possibly have had with that woman, and what infraction would drive her to take a three-day journey to make amends.

Assuming she's telling the truth.

No part of Cait thought she was.

CHAPTER 25
DECLAN

Four times Killian's body was dragged under the *Curse Bringer*, and each time, the razor-like creatures clinging to it cut him apart a little more. No doubt Callum would have called for another pass, but finally his men hauled up remains that were totally unrecognizable as human.

"Let him loose!" Callum said, and his men quickly cut the lines from what was left of Killian's limbs before discarding his remains over the port rail as if they were leftovers from a meal going into the garbage. Turning to Dominic, Callum said in a low his voice, "Have the deck cleaned, and tell Pepperwood to get us underway. Then I might need your help with this one."

With that, Callum snatched up Declan's arm and pulled him past the crew, which had begun to disperse and head back to the barracks or to the jobs Dominic and the bo'sun doled out. Declan assumed he'd be led back to the brig but then remembered what the crewman had said about Callum never stooping so low as to go there himself.

"Get in there," Callum growled as he shoved Declan through the open door and into his cabin. While the air was a tad stuffier in here, Declan appreciated the break from the noise and the closely packed bodies he'd endured out on the deck.

"You know," Declan said, trying to scratch behind his ear with his shoulder, "I didn't ask to be let out of the brig."

Callum pulled a bottle of rum from behind his desk and poured a hearty serving into a tin cup that was probably as clean as the man who used it. He took a long sip as he relaxed back against the edge of his desk.

"I do know." Callum stared into his cup as he swirled its contents. "You didn't have to follow him though."

"You and I both know that's not true." Declan shifted his weight, though it was impossible to find any comfortable position in these circumstances. "Hard for a pirate to turn down an invitation to a good fight."

Callum choked out a laugh into his mug. "You're such a poor excuse for a pirate, McCallagh. It's a wonder you managed to fool everyone on the Aisling into thinking you were someone to fear."

"All it takes is a few well-crafted stories—"

"Stories!" Callum laughed again, though it didn't reach his dark eyes. "You could have been great, Declan. You had such potential. When you got that first crew, you were... Let's just say, I was impressed. What you did to Susset and his crew? I didn't even know you, and I was proud. Such a young captain, already so dastardly. And those merchant vessels—"

"I was there, Callum. I remember." Declan might not be the good man Aoife thought he was—the good man she deserved—but that didn't mean he wanted to be some cruel villain either. A mere six months of heinous acts had been enough for him. It was Tommy who had suggested he could build the reputation without the deeds, and from then on, they'd relied on his past record and carefully and methodically relayed stories in pubs at different ports.

Callum clucked his tongue. "Do you though? Seems you've been out of this brutal game a bit too long."

"What do you mean?"

"I saw you when Killian first went over that rail." Callum's low laughter grated on Declan. "You looked like a youngster on his first sailing through a squall. Thankfully we hadn't fed you enough to allow for you to make too much of a mess had you not been able to control it."

The door behind him opened and closed, but Declan didn't bother to turn.

"So, keelhauling. Your crew seems right familiar with it. Is that what passes for entertainment on your ship?" Declan asked.

His question was answered with an elbow to the center of his back. Declan fell forward but remained standing. A couple of well-placed kicks to the backs of his legs caused his knees to buckle before slamming onto the wooden floor.

You're losing your touch, McCallagh.

He looked up to see Callum sneering down at him. The man's eyes raged, but Declan refused to look away.

"That's a no then?" Declan asked. "Or a yes? I'm sorry, I didn't quite catch the answer."

The other man moved to hit him, but Callum's voice stopped his arm in midair. "Dom, that's enough." It wasn't barked or bellowed as his commands had been on the deck. This calm, casual tone was more intimidating, like the hiss of a snake before it struck.

Stepping away from the desk, Callum lowered himself until he was kneeling, bringing that burning stare closer. "We will reach the sound by tomorrow night," he said, pausing to scratch his bearded jaw.

Had Declan miscalculated? Had he lost a whole day while he was unconscious below decks? While part of him insisted it didn't matter, another part knew if Callum had found some way to travel faster, it was unlikely Tommy would catch up to him in time. Even with Lord Roberts's interruption, they were still too far ahead.

"I need you to tell me how you intend to get past the sirens, McCallagh. No tricks. No surprises. I won't be going into that sound unawares."

Declan let out a small groan before responding. "I've already told you."

"Yes, I know. The fae. Magic. A bunch of hocus-pocus nonsense."

"Refusing to believe it doesn't make it any less true," Declan said, and for a moment he let himself ponder the truth of those words, how relevant they were to his life—a life he'd never get back now.

The back of a hand slammed into the side of his face, causing him to spit blood.

"You will tell me," Callum growled again as he punched the wooden floor.

Declan worked the ache out of his jaw—to no avail—and peered at Callum from the corner of his eye. "Contrary to what you might think, hitting inanimate objects —or even hitting me—won't get me to divulge information *I don't have*." He stretched out the last three words for emphasis, but he could see, even from this angle, that it had little effect.

"You think I'm going to trust you after what you did?"

Declan turned fully to Callum now with eyes wide. "So we're going to play this little game again? You hit me. I tell you the same thing. And round and round we go. You know, it's really a shame you don't listen. Or is it that you simply can't comprehend the words that are coming out of my mouth?"

Callum let him prattle on for far longer than expected, and it wasn't a punch or a kick that got Declan to stop talking. Instead, Callum stood and walked away. Declan risked a look up to see the pirate settling into his chair. He gave a nod, and Dominic had Declan standing in an instant, his hands gripping his arms like a vice.

"What do you know of the sirens, Declan?"

The cordiality of Callum's question caught Declan off guard as much as the question itself did.

"If this is going to be a long conversation, might I request a chair? I'm rather fatigued after saving your life and all."

To Declan's surprise, the quartermaster didn't pummel him for his disrespect, instead placing a simple wooden chair behind him. The man's hands yanked him down into it with more force than necessary.

"Thank you," Declan said, smiling over his shoulder. "You are most hospitable, Dominic."

Dominic snickered.

"I see your tongue isn't fatigued," Callum said.

"It's been a long while since I've found someone who could meet that challenge."

Callum huffed out a breath but otherwise ignored the comment. "The sirens. You obviously know about them, or you wouldn't be so scared."

"You obviously don't, or you would be."

"Fear is a pirate's downfall."

"I find blades to be more so, but we can agree to disagree."

Pressing his elbows against the top of the desk, Callum leaned forward and spoke around his fisted hands. "What do you know?"

Declan leaned back and drew in a deep breath. He wasn't sure where this would lead or how his knowledge of the sirens could help them survive, but what other choice did he have?

"Same as everyone else, I suppose. Sirens are bad. They live in the sound. Don't go there."

Callum didn't react to his ridiculous answer other than to drop his head to the side and continue to stare at him. For a moment Declan wondered who could maintain the silence the longest, but he gathered that any attempt on his part to do so would result in another visit from Dominic's fist.

"The sirens are ancient creatures. Some say they predate the fae in this region, though who can really know for sure. They're confined to one area of the sea—the Black Sound—thanks to some curse placed on them that prevents their leaving."

"And you know what they do, I take it? Since you are so afraid."

"They kill," Declan said.

"How?"

He took another long breath. Not because this topic was at all difficult to discuss —though he wasn't particularly looking forward to meeting those creatures—but because the longer he remained here chatting, the less time he had to spend in that dank hole below decks.

"In short? They eat people. And from what the legend says, it's not all that fun. For the people. I wouldn't know how it is for the sirens themselves. Now, I don't know if this part is true or if it is some wild fable someone concocted to keep people loyal, but supposedly the sirens have quite the taste for the despicable souls. And not just any type of despicable, but the betrayers. Those who made promises only to break them. Whether it's true or not has no bearing on us though, as they'll kill us regardless. But a betrayer? They are the delicacy the sirens crave."

Callum was slowly nodding. He seemed to be contemplating all that had been relayed, though Declan had no doubt it was nothing the captain wasn't privy to already.

"You know your legends. At least that wasn't a ruse. But I do believe you're missing a piece of the story."

"They are immortal, ancient, and bloodthirsty, with a magic of their own. And they have the Csintala dagger. What more is there to know?" Declan asked, hoping his acting skills hadn't been hurt by his poor treatment aboard this ship and that Callum would buy that he knew nothing more. He might have been stupid enough to get captured, but he wasn't about to divulge information needlessly. Even if it might earn him the same treatment as Killian.

"Much more, in fact," Callum said. "And while it may not be pertinent to our plans of retrieving the dagger, one would be a fool to not understand the enemy as well as he could. You're right about their taste for betrayers, to a point. It goes beyond that. They feast on pain. Not just any pain, but the type that scars your heart and burns your soul. The type that can't be remedied with trite words."

"I didn't know you had such a way with words," Declan said, if for no other reason than to lighten the mood and perhaps distract himself from the rather personal way Callum's words bothered him. But Callum continued as if he hadn't said anything.

"Some betrayals are nearly impossible to forgive, and the pain from having forgiveness withheld? Well, I don't need to explain that to you, do I?"

Declan froze, unable to swallow and struggling to breathe. His brow wrinkled against his will, and Callum took advantage of the tell.

"Hard to hide. Even from me. Will be impossible to hide it from the sirens."

Steadying himself with a long, slow breath, Declan refocused on his host. "What you're saying, then, is what I've been saying all along. We're doomed."

Callum angled his head, clicking his tongue before his lips turned up into a cunning grin. "You mean *you're* doomed. Your brooding soul provides quite the distraction."

"Why did you—"

"You really must have a low opinion of me, McCallagh, if you haven't pieced this together by now."

Callum was right, of course, but it didn't make Declan's head hurt any less or his thoughts become any less jumbled. He winced as the throbbing returned at his temples.

"As much as I enjoy watching you struggle," Callum said, "this conversation has dragged on far longer than intended." With a quick word, he sent Dominic away to get a status update from the helmsman and the bo'sun. Something about this move piqued Declan's interest. This gruff captain could have had Declan thrown back below, could have had his quartermaster do that on his way to carry out the other orders, but he'd allowed Declan to remain here.

He debated whether to play the sincerity card, set the conversation up so Callum would divulge whatever was on his mind without reservation, or go with his usual tactic of poking him until he was so agitated he let information slip by accident. The latter would have won out had Callum not broken the silence first.

"You are actually quite good at hiding your baggage, Declan, behind the irritating words and the forced cynicism."

"I wouldn't say it's forced."

"Most wouldn't recognize this pain you bear, but..." Callum's attention fell to where his hands were folded atop his desk, his thumbs moving around and around each other in lazy circles. A wave of grief flashed across his features, darkening them before his face hardened once more into its usual indifferent mask.

"You've experienced this." Declan didn't bother making it a question. The change in Callum might have been brief, there and gone in the matter of a breath, but Declan had no doubt what it indicated, because it was the same grief he had experienced after Aoife left him in the sand.

Callum gave a nod, his dark eyes hardening into stone. "But I wasn't as stupid as you."

"That's not very nice of you to say."

"I told you as much last week on your ship. I can't be faulted for your refusal to heed my advice, for you falling for the girl."

Declan started to protest, but Callum raised a hand to stop him before he could even utter a sound.

"And that falling is going to get you killed."

"You mean eaten." He tried to find the humor in those words, at the absurdity of such a fate, but the sense of dread pressing down on him remained. "Seems to your advantage though."

"Oh, indeed. I'm not complaining about my good fortune. I simply thought you should know, as you face your own demise, that you could have avoided this. It was all within your power. Betrayal paired with love? It'll get you killed one way or another."

But Declan hadn't wanted this, had actively tried to avoid it. He hadn't wanted to grow close to her. He hadn't wanted to need her help. Perhaps Callum was right though. He could have denied her passage. He could have tossed her into the sea. He could have found another way to retrieve the fae.

"Unfortunately," Callum said, "it is much too late to undo it now. Love has that way about it, much like a siren in that sense. Preying on the weak, the desperate, the hurting. It offers you warmth. It promises all that you seek, but it lies to you with visions of a future that cannot exist."

"It can exist." Declan hadn't meant to say the words aloud, and he mentally kicked himself for slipping up. This conversation was getting to him, as Callum likely intended.

Callum narrowed his eyes. "When did you become such an optimist? I would have thought you'd know better by now that all good things rot in this world. Either by an external force taking a life—or two lives as happened with your parents—or by our inner demons hurting those we believe we love. It all falls apart. It all decays. It all festers and fails."

Images flashed in Declan's mind. His mother being dragged away into the fog. His father's body lying motionless and cold on the cobblestones. Aoife backing away from him in the cove.

Declan cleared his throat and straightened his back against the chair in a poor attempt to ease away a knot that had formed below his ribs. "You certainly know how to give a motivational speech. I'll give you that. No wonder your crew is so disciplined and successful."

Callum leaned forward. "Joke all you want. Hope won't save you in the end, not when you look into the eyes of the siren queen and she drags all mistakes from these dark depths." He tapped a finger to his own chest. "Your hope will die in that sound right along with your body."

"And hopefully it takes long enough for you to snag the dagger away from them."

With a nod, Callum stood and walked around his desk. Lifting Declan out of the chair, he pushed him back through the door and called for the oaf, Reggie. As Declan stumbled back down through the bowels of the ship to his accommodations, he couldn't set aside Callum's words.

Was hope truly a fool's mistress?

There are worse mistresses to entertain.

CHAPTER 26
TOMMY

Tommy hated this plan, hated the risk it posed, hated the position he was in and the decisions he had to make. But fretting over it did them no good either. So desperate to find an alternative, he had almost gone along with Gavin's joke about inviting the kraken for a drink and getting it so intoxicated on rum it would retreat to sleep it off.

Unfortunately, getting a kraken drunk was as unlikely to work as getting through the waters unseen on their own. Yet, he had still not been able to stomach allowing Maura to be put in such danger. While he'd turned down her advances, he'd never denied his feelings for her, and if he couldn't devote himself to her in the way she desired and deserved, he wanted to at least ensure her safety.

But Aoife was right.

If they continued on at this slow pace, they'd never reach Declan in time. And if they risked going much faster without any precautionary measures from Maura and her sister, they would most certainly alert the monster to their presence and find themselves worse off.

This will work. This has to work.

The breeze picked up, filling the sails so they billowed smoothly, soundlessly. To Bria's credit, the ship didn't jerk forward but glided along with ease, as if it were being moved along by the water itself rather than the wind.

Gavin let out a sigh and seemed to relax his grip on the helm, his knuckles returning to their normal coloring. Smiling tentatively, Gavin gave Tommy a nod to let him know they were good.

So far.

Around the deck the crew stood still, more silent than they were even when asleep. Some moved to tend to the lines as they sailed, careful to keep their steps as light as possible. Others maintained a watchful eye on the teal waters, which lay eerily still, showing no indication that a monster of nightmares and legends lurked below.

No sign of it.

No sign of anything, actually.

The water stretched out to the horizon, smooth as glass, unsettlingly still this far from land.

Tommy turned slowly to study the water all around. When he turned to the aft side, though, he stopped short at the sight of Bria and Maura standing together, eyes closed, leaning against the rail more casually than he had expected.

They looked as though they were relaxing on holiday and soaking up the afternoon sunlight, not tapping into invisible powers to thwart a beast. On closer inspection, though, he noticed their faces were far from relaxed. Their jaws were tense, their temples pulsing. While their elbows hung loose by their ribs, their hands gripped the railing as if that was the conduit their magic used.

From this vantage point, Tommy couldn't tell if Maura's glamour was in place, and for a moment he worried she'd already used too much of her power while healing him and didn't have enough to carry out this plan. The wind was eerily quiet even as it moved them through the water at an unimaginable speed, and in that near silence Tommy heard a gasp as Aoife leaned over the railing beside Maura.

He rushed over as fast as he could, his hand ready to draw his cutlass quickly if needed. But when he joined her in looking over, he nearly gasped as well.

It was one thing to know what a glamour was in theory, but seeing it in practice was extraordinary. He blinked once to ensure he wasn't imagining what he saw below them, but the illusion remained. Below the row of windows, the ship simply disappeared, and only teal water, smooth and unmoving, lay below them. There were no ripples in the sea betraying their movement, and the *Siren's Song* made no shadow on the water.

Tommy might have laughed at the sight had the situation not been so dire. Aoife's elbow knocked into his, and he turned to see his friend's tentative smile. It conveyed both triumph and worry. Tommy could understand the dichotomy, as it warred within him as well. Though he wanted to return her positivity, something kept him from giving himself fully over to the hope that had sparked with this first victory.

"It's a good start," he whispered to her, risking a glance at Maura before walking away.

For the next two hours he crisscrossed the quarterdeck, monitoring the sisters as they worked and checking in with Gavin to see how the *Siren's Song* was progressing. Aoife remained beside Maura, her hand never leaving the dagger at her belt. A hint of hope remained in her eyes long after her lips had grown tired of holding her smile. As Tommy settled himself once again beside Gavin, this time facing away from their heading, his attention fell firmly on Maura, who had not shown any sign of fatigue since they'd started.

"You're wrong," Renna whispered as she stepped up beside him.

"About what?" He hoped Renna hadn't tapped into her magic to pry into his thoughts. There were a number of things she could be speaking to.

"You and her." She turned her chin toward him, her vibrant blue eyes as warm and friendly as his mother's had been. Or his sister's. "You can never be."

All the warmth drained from Tommy's face, and bitter hopelessness returned. He tried to ignore it, blink it away.

"That's what I've told her," he said.

"But your mind is shifting now." A statement, matter-of-fact. There was no hint of doubt in the fae's tone, and the certainty she displayed sent a shiver through him.

He didn't bother to ask her how she knew—by reading it on his face or pulling it from his thoughts. Either way, there was no point in denying it.

Renna spoke once more. "What changed? Why now?"

"Don't you already know?"

"I try not to listen in for longer than needed. I much prefer to gather information from willing parties."

"Didn't seem to stop you from invading my thoughts earlier." He hadn't intended for it to sound like such a challenge, but stress had taken its toll on his self-control.

A soundless laugh escaped her before she smiled at him. "Fair. Though, it doesn't take magic to see how you look at my sister." If she held any disapproval, it didn't show. She almost appeared sympathetic to his plight.

"You don't seem surprised."

"Oh, I knew well before you did. You were unconscious a good while as we worked to heal you. It was not difficult to sense that emotional bond weaving its way between you."

"But if we have some irresistible bond—"

"I never said it was irresistible."

"That's not true—fae bonds and soul mates?"

Another hushed laugh escaped her lips. "I suppose I can understand how that falsehood came to be. Fae pairings must appear as such from those looking in. But no, it is not true. There is no otherworldly power at play here, not beyond the very normal, common yet mysterious phenomenon we call love. But for fae, all our senses are heightened. Our emotions—just like our strength, grace, beauty—are magnified." She turned back to look at Maura, who was still focused on maintaining the protective glamour. "So yes, she's intense and persistent, because for her this tie between you runs deeper than the Aisling."

He looked back at Maura, the brown waves of her hair blowing in the breeze behind her. He didn't take his eyes from her as he repeated Renna's earlier words. "But we can never be."

"Unfortunately, no. She is needed in Larcsporough, as is Bria. As am I." Before Tommy could interject, she added, "And what is expected of her—of the three of us —leaves no place for you in her life. You must understand. Our kin need us. A war has been brewing while we rotted away in those quarters, and they need us to help stop it."

"She knows this?"

A nod preceded her next words. "And she was ready and willing to step into her role. Until you."

Tommy's gut twisted around those last words. *Until you.* He had known any future together was unlikely, and he had known about the fae's plans to travel south after the dagger business was completed. But Maura had never told him her presence was required.

"What is her role in Larcsporough exactly?" He asked the question not quite knowing if he wanted the answer.

"Same as mine. Same as—"

Before Renna could finish, the sound Tommy had feared cut her short. His feet had him at Maura's side in a few paces, his knees hitting the wood hard, though no pain registered.

"Maura!"

Tommy should have kept his voice low, but the sight of her body crumpled on the ground drew her name from his lungs with such force there was no controlling it. Lifting her body gently, he pulled her to him, brushing long strands of hair back from her face.

In his periphery he could see Bria still standing.

Why had Maura collapsed?

The question swirled around his mind as he searched her face. Her eyes remained closed. Her breath came in short, shallow gasps.

"Maura, can you hear me?" His voice sounded odd to his ears, like someone else was calling her name. Like someone else's hand was cupping her face and stroking her cheek. This wasn't supposed to happen. She shouldn't have even been close to her limit. Had she broken her promise and pushed herself too far?

Glancing up quickly, he found Aoife watching them in icy silence, her mouth gaping behind shaking fingers.

"Aoife, water. Now," Tommy said. Aoife blinked away whatever shock had held her in place and, with a string of nods, stormed down the stairs.

Renna knelt beside him and, wrapping a hand around Maura's wrist, let out a breath that sounded almost relieved.

"She is okay."

"How can you say that?" Tommy asked, unable to control his nerves.

"Because she is."

"But—"

Renna gently pried Maura away from him, and though she offered a small smile, Tommy was far from reassured. "She just needs rest."

"Did she—will she—"

Renna's face hardened, but a moment later warmth shone in her eyes once again. "Not burned out. She collapsed because she gave in to the fatigue rather than pushing past it. Had she forced her magic to continue beyond that, then..."

"We need to get her to the captain's cabin," he said as they stood, but when he moved to help carry her, Renna stopped him.

"I will get her there. I'm more than capable. But right now, you need to stay here. You need to be ready."

She was right, of course, but it didn't make it any easier for Tommy to watch Maura, unconscious and limp as a ragdoll, be dragged away.

She'll be okay. She is okay.

Though he repeated the words to himself, it did nothing to quell the sense of doom that grew within him. He looked to Bria, half-expecting to see her ready to collapse onto the deck as well. But she stood as strong as she had for the last couple of hours, as if summoning wind and pushing them through the water was no feat at all.

He had only made it a half-turn toward Gavin when he noticed a handful of the men leaning over the port-side rail. He assumed they were merely observing the lack of glamour hiding the hull of the ship beneath them, but then they began to back away. Slowly, quietly, they moved toward the center of the deck.

"What are they—" Gavin started to ask as Tommy came up beside him.

Tommy waited. One breath. Two. Nothing. He saw nothing beyond the rail but smooth water.

But the color was shifting. Looking to the sky, he checked for the cloud that must be passing by the sun, casting a shadow. It wasn't there. Nothing but blue stretched out above him, and he snapped his attention back to the sea.

A black shadow spread across the water—no, through the water. Tommy turned to the starboard side. There, too, the Aisling was darkening, as if a giant had emptied a bottle of ink into the sea.

"That's not good," Gavin said.

"At the ready, men!" Tommy yelled to the crew below him and joined them in drawing his cutlass. "Gavin, you keep us steady as best you can, but be ready to maneuver as needed when the beast attacks. And it will."

Behind him he heard Mikkel speaking words of encouragement to the crew. Such was the man's way with the crew before a skirmish, bolstering their courage like a beloved general of some army rather than a humble bo'sun on a pirate vessel.

Tommy rushed back to Bria, whose eyes hadn't opened despite all the commotion around her. Should she be told what had happened? Should he risk disturbing her concentration in order to tell her about Maura?

Before he could decide, the first scream came.

CHAPTER 27
AOIFE

Aoife helped Renna ease Maura onto Declan's bed, but when she moved to pull a blanket over her, the older fae stopped her with a light touch on her arm.

"She needs the air."

She thought it an odd requirement, though Aoife was far from an expert on fae anything. Maura hadn't felt feverish at all, and a casual observer might have thought she was simply taking an afternoon nap. Her complexion remained flawless. Her hair showed no signs of having been in the sea air for hours. Nothing external gave any indication that Maura was ailing at all.

Aoife started to inquire as to what else the unconscious fae might need to aid in her recovery, but instead of her own whispered voice, a scream, full of agony and surprise, came from outside.

Renna was out the cabin door before Aoife managed to get to the main room. Pulling her dagger out, her heart thumping deep in her chest, she rushed out onto the deck without hesitation.

And stopped.

She could have had a whole year to train with Collins—a lifetime—and she still would not have been prepared for what she found.

On both sides of the ship, snake-like creatures—black and gray, mottled with no visible head, and near-translucent discs on their bellies—writhed in the air, threatening to crush the ship as it came closer.

Not snakes! Why would you think snakes?!

Of course these were the deadly limbs of the kraken. Either way, she froze, unsure how two days of practice and a puny blade would be of any help to the crew and to her friends. To Declan.

Aoife looked around but found no sign of Renna. She must have gone up to the quarterdeck to aid Bria. A glance at the sails, which were full and taut, proved Bria still had control of the wind, though it didn't seem useful now, as the monster clearly had them in its grasp.

A clatter of cracking wood mixed with groans and shouts, and she looked over in time to see an arm sweeping across the deck toward her. At the last moment she jumped back out of its reach, but her feet slipped on the water the creature had brought on board. She fell hard on her backside.

It was utter mayhem on deck. Aoife's attention flitted around the scene as she tried to make sense of it all. Above her head on the mainmast, a young crewman clung to the ship's rigging. Aoife marveled at how the man was able to signal to the men below without falling.

The floor beneath her rumbled with a loud explosion. The cannons. A long shot, but at least they were trying them. Several more booms followed, but the creature's arms—flinching from the few cannonballs that made contact—kept returning to the deck, knocking men into the water. One wrapped itself around a crewman and hauled him into the air before slamming him down against the rail of the ship, impaling him on a sharp point where the wood had splintered.

All around the deck, pirates were reacting and taking different positions. Some were cowering against the wall near her, some were lying on the ground, groaning from the blows they'd taken from the monster. Others did their best to fight back, swiping and stabbing at the massive arms whenever they came near.

A scream—of attack, not pain—snapped her attention back to the starboard side, where a chunk of railing was missing. Blood and seawater were washing across the deck. A man lunged toward the creature, cutlass drawn, his face a frightening display of fury.

Collins.

Aoife held her breath, unable to look away as this pirate—her friend—charged toward his inevitable demise. But just before the hideous arm moved away, Collins leaped into the air, his cutlass held high above his head, its curved edge pointing down toward its target.

The scene slowed before Aoife's eyes.

Collins screaming.

Kraken sweeping.

Cutlass piercing the fleshy limb.

Collins hovering in the air by the grip of his cutlass, which was stuck fast in the still-moving arm.

Aoife's muscles moved on their own, lifting her up to her feet and sending her barreling toward Collins. She ran through the techniques he'd taught her, adjusted her grip on her dagger, and flung herself forward. With a less than graceful hop over a fallen pirate, she managed to remain upright as she came within striking distance.

"Now!" Collins bellowed from his perch above her head.

As she had done repeatedly during their practice sessions, she mimicked the movements he'd displayed and drove her dagger forward. But the blade simply slid along the tough skin, and she flew forward, slamming her elbows and knees onto the deck.

"Aoife!" The pirate yelled her name, prompting her to turn around, but she had no time—wouldn't have even if she hadn't been partially winded—to strike again before the limb swept back out to sea, taking the cutlass and Collins with it.

"No!" Aoife screamed. "Collins!" As if the creature would hear her pleas and bring her friend back.

She had nearly reached the shattered railing when a body came flying at her. Ducking, she barely missed having her head removed by the projectile but still managed to spin around to inspect the person who had been thrown back on deck.

Crawling along, ignoring how her hands turned light red from the watery, bloody mixture covering the ship, she reached the man and recognized the cutlass still in his hand.

"Collins," she said, giving his shoulder a shake. She couldn't tell if he was breathing; her eyes were unable to focus with how the kraken's arms rocked the ship. Bile threatened to rise, but she forced it back down with desperate effort. She needed to wake her friend. Needed him to not be dead. Needed him to be okay.

This route hadn't been anyone's ideal choice, and everyone had known the risks involved, but that did little to quiet the guilt that had taken up permanent residence inside her.

"Collins. Please!" Aoife gave one last cry, but the man lay silent and still. Tears welled, and for a moment she forgot about the battle taking place around her. Collins had been the one to first see her on the ship, the one to take her to Declan, the one who wasn't afraid of her bad luck—though perhaps he should have been.

"Aoife." A familiar voice cut through the noise around her, and she looked up to see Tommy approaching. He dropped to his knees. Within seconds, he had his arms underneath his crewman and was standing, cradling the tall pirate as a mother would her baby.

"He tried to attack—" Aoife shouted the words at Tommy's back as she followed him to the officers' cabin. Once inside the small room, Aoife stood frozen in the doorway, unable to move as Tommy laid the man onto the bunk Aoife had slept in just last night.

"Is he—"

"No," Tommy said, turning a chin toward her before ensuring his friend was secure and safe. For now. "He's just knocked unconscious."

"How can you be sure? He wasn't moving. He wasn't—"

"He's breathing, Aoife. That's all we can hope for right now."

Aoife shook her head, still unable to see what sign of life she had missed.

"Trust me. He's fine," Tommy said, but the corner of his lips twitched. Quickly he moved toward her and the door. "We need to go."

Aoife pivoted out of his way. "But what do we do? What can I possibly do?" She held up her sad blade as if it was nothing more than a spoon. It might as well have been with how little it had done against the kraken.

Tommy's eyes shone with a haunting mix of determination, fear, worry, and anger. "We fight, Aoife. You fight. Until someone wins, you fight."

Before she could say anything more, he was back out on the deck, brandishing his cutlass and dagger as he ran forward to do just as he had commanded.

Focus on the next task, Aoife. Fight. Fight until someone wins.

Sands, she hoped that someone was them.

CHAPTER 28
CAIT

Despite being exhausted, Cait couldn't sleep. And not because of Lucy's bizarre appearance.

She'd fallen onto her bed, too tired to even remove her boots, but the few hours of sleep she'd managed to get had brought painful memories and equally disturbing images of what could happen in the future—or was happening at this moment while she slept. She kept her eyes closed, though her mind was far from quiet, and she had been awake for the past several hours. But even all these years later, this apartment—different yet uncomfortably unchanged—reminded her too much of her previous life. A life with family and love and laughter.

And innocence.

Back then she hadn't known—hadn't had any suspicion at all—that her comfortable life on Cregah was a farce, a life made possible only because of the pride and greed of the council.

If only her parents had trusted her back then, before they died. She would have been able to ask them all the questions that had been swirling around her head since first discovering the secret passage and underground office.

How had her parents known about the council's corruption? Why hadn't they acted sooner? What had happened that caused the council to take action against them? And why hadn't the council come for her? And how could she ever hope to finish what her parents had started?

Hope or not, you have to at least try.

Through her closed lids, Cait could sense the late-morning sun streaming in through the window opposite her bed, but she could not urge her eyes to open yet. But avoiding the sight of her childhood home—even if she had purposefully moved furniture around and left the doors to the back bedrooms closed—wasn't enough to keep all the memories at bay.

Against her will, her mind floated from one to the next.

Her mother giving advice before her first meeting with the boy she was courting.

Her father's smile as he worked tirelessly at the pub.

The way they loved each other and their children.

Declan's laugh as he played around the pub tables after closing.

The look she caught her parents exchanging. A look of worry and fear.

That had been mere hours before they'd taken her mother, dragging her into the early morning mist, her father chasing after her. Not that Cait had seen it. She'd had to trust his and Declan's account, as she had been out that night.

Her father had not been able to catch up to the attackers. And as far as Cait knew, they'd never found her mother. Cait hadn't been able to process what had happened, and still now she wondered—as she had ever since—why her father hadn't trusted her enough to let her join the Rogues. She could have helped. Maybe then he'd still be alive, at least.

For several excruciating hours after her mother's disappearance, her family had barely spoken to one another, and Cait had been given nothing more than a single reassurance from her father that he would take care of it. To his credit, her father had played the dutiful pub worker well, while it had taken all of Cait's power to keep a smile on her face and make idle chatter with the patrons. But she'd forced herself to keep going, mimicking the way she had seen her mother act in this role.

But when those two pirates had walked in—the same pirates who had hauled away her mother—her father's expression had tightened, though he'd kept his smile in place. She'd known him well enough to tell when he was uncomfortable, even though she'd only seen it happen a handful of times over her sixteen years. The pirates had stayed until closing, drinking cup after cup of rum as they talked and laughed. Cait thought she remembered seeing them eying her father, laughing at his expense, but she wasn't sure.

Declan had remained oblivious to the tension pulsing through the pub as he sat on one of the stools, still and quiet, no longer the brother she had laughed and played with his whole life. Her breath had seemed trapped within her as she kept an eye on both the pirates and her father, hoping he wouldn't do anything stupid. It wasn't until the men threw some money onto the table and exited out onto the cobblestone street that she'd dared let her breathing return to normal.

But then she'd realized, too late, that her father had also left the pub. Somehow, as she'd been focused on those pirates, she had lost track of him. Before she'd been able to head to the back storage area to search for him, movement through the front window caught her attention.

A low curse had fallen from her mouth, alerting Declan that something was wrong. He'd slid off the stool and turned even before Cait could get around the bar. They'd both run for the door, too slow, pulling it open too late. Her father's feet were scrambling against the cobbles as he was dragged away by one of the pirates. The other pirate lay at Cait's feet, with a weapon she didn't recognize sticking out of his neck, his blood pooling around him.

Her father had killed one, and Cait couldn't stop Declan from seeing the body. He'd been too young to witness it. Even Cait hadn't known how to process all the blood and violence before her when her whole life was built around peace.

So many mistakes. So many regrets.

The rhythmic thud of boots on the stairs had Cait's eyes flashing open as she swung her legs off the bed and stood, grasping behind her back the small blade she kept under her pillow. The memories, too vivid and too fresh, made her mind race, and for a moment she assumed the worst possible scenario was happening now too. And although it was unlikely to be anyone from the council, she refused to be taken by surprise. Better to pull a blade on a friend than to be unarmed against a foe.

"Cait! You decent?" Lucan's familiar voice lacked its usual tinge of humor, and she could guess why.

Slipping the blade into her boot, she rushed to open the door as she worked to hide all traces of stress.

She swung the door open and leaned against the frame in a casual, almost bored, manner.

"Sleep well?" she asked. Lucan pushed past her in a huff.

There was no point in checking to see what he was doing. She'd seen him in this perturbed state more often than he'd ever admit despite that he always tried to be the lighthearted, carefree one.

Though he hadn't been that person since Adler showed up.

Raising a brow in question, she turned to Adler, who seemed relaxed as ever as he stood at the top of the stairs, arms crossed loosely before him.

"What?" he asked.

From behind her Lucan said, "He snores, that's what."

Oh, for crying out loud.

Adler gave a light shrug. "I might. I wouldn't know. I was asleep."

Lucan groaned and stomped back over to them. Leaning past Cait's shoulder, he pointed at the pirate, saying, "I don't believe that for a damn second."

Cait couldn't stop her eyes from rolling. She loved her friend, but he was acting like a baby. "Seriously, Lucan. I highly doubt that's the case."

He stepped back. "You weren't there."

Turning to him, she put her hands on her hips, the way her mother had done so many times when reprimanding her and Declan. "No, I wasn't there. I don't have time to babysit two supposedly grown men." She looked from one to the other. "Work it out."

Lucan opened his mouth, probably to protest, but Cait cut him off with a pointed glare.

"I mean it, Lucan. I don't know what's gotten into you, but you need to get it together. If we're going to succeed, you're going to have to deal. You aren't going to like everyone you have to work with, but we need all the help we can get. And you..." She spun back around to the pirate. "I don't know you well enough yet to know if you're being a pain in the ass on purpose or if it's just who you are, but try to get along. Without him, you would have been dispatched back in that forest. Now, are we done acting like toddlers?"

Adler nodded, and Lucan mumbled his agreement.

"Good," Cait said, though she remained on edge. If she couldn't sleep, she needed to at least take a few hours to relax if possible. And sands knew she needed these men to more than tolerate each other.

Trudging over to the chest of drawers under the window, Cait tried to work the tension out of her body, but it was as stubborn as Lucan. From the top drawer she pulled out a deck of cards, the edges of which were worn smooth from years of shuffling and handling.

"Please tell me one of you brought breakfast," she said as she settled herself at the small dining table in the corner. Why she'd kept all four chairs out for all these years, she couldn't say, but she was thankful for them now. With a nod, she invited the men to sit while she waited for an answer.

Lucan grimaced and mouthed an apology.

Adler's eyes widened with exaggerated innocence. "Don't look at me. I'm new here, remember?"

Cait ignored Lucan's unsubtle eye roll. This wasn't going to be fixed with nagging.

Shuffling the deck, she gave the men a relaxed shrug. "No worries. We can scrounge something up after a few hands."

"Cards, love?" Adler asked, propping his elbows on the table as his large hands worked the cracks out of his knuckles.

"Aye. I assume you've played," Cait said, beginning to deal. Lucan picked his up and shifted them around in his hand without a word.

A grin crept across Adler's face. "A bit."

"Familiar with Royal's Ruse?"

"Might be a bit rusty, but shouldn't take me long to freshen up. Now if you'd said Corks and Bones, you'd both be in trouble."

Lucan scoffed but otherwise remained silent as he took his first turn, picking up a card from the deck and tossing a nine onto the discard pile.

Looking at Cait over his cards, Adler asked, "Twos are wild?"

"For this hand, aye."

A short nod, and Adler played his turn. By the way his brows pinched, the card he'd picked up hadn't helped his hand.

"I see it's going well for you," Cait said with a smirk before taking her turn.

"Or is that just what I want you to think?" A wink capped off his question, and Cait shot a glance Lucan's way to see if his mood would sour more over it.

But her friend was staring out the window, his mind lost in some other place. She kicked him under the table.

"Your turn."

Lucan startled and moved to play his turn. With little emotion, he added a card to his hand and discarded another. And then his hand slammed onto the table.

"No! No way!" Cait yelled as she reached over to pull down Lucan's cards, which he relinquished to her with that smile she'd missed since Adler had shown up.

Adler tossed his own cards facedown onto the table and shot a nod at Lucan. "Fastest hand I've ever played, that's for sure."

Lucan pulled all the cards into his hands and shuffled them several times before dealing the next round. "Luck of the draw, that's all."

The next hand lasted decidedly longer, with Cait growling in mock frustration when Adler discarded a useless card for her and Lucan celebrating when she in turn dropped the card he needed. But Adler ended up winning, and Cait was happy to see the two men starting to warm up to each other.

At least a little.

"Where you from, Lucan?" Adler asked as Cait pondered over her cards during their fourth round.

"Over the mountains."

"Miss it?"

Cait knew how she wanted to play, but with an actual conversation transpiring between them, she feigned focused deliberation to give them more time to talk.

"Sometimes. But then, what's there to miss about a life of starvation, sickness, and loss?" Again, Lucan delivered this answer with a tone far more level than would be expected.

Adler's hands lowered, his cards folding into them before he laid them on the table. Cait nearly mocked the man for accidentally placing them faceup when she noticed his mouth had fallen open in disbelief.

"What?" The single word fell from Adler with the weight of several kegs.

Lucan shifted his cards front to back, not making eye contact with either of them. Cait had only heard him speak about his past once. She'd made it clear he could always talk about it when he needed to, but she would never push.

He'd never taken her up on the offer, and she had kept her promise.

Now she watched her friend with curiosity. How would he answer? Would he shrug it off like he always did with the other Rogues? Or open up as he'd done with her so long ago?

"You don't know?" Lucan's eyes remained fixed on his cards, though he didn't seem to be focused on them.

"That a village on Cregah battled so much misfortune? No. I didn't know," Adler said.

"Not just one village," Lucan clarified. He lowered his hands to his lap, letting them slip from view below the table. "Unfortunately."

"More than one?" Adler's brow creased again as it had at the start of the game.

"All of them," Cait and Lucan said in unison.

"I didn't know," Adler repeated, falling back against his chair with a loud exhale.

"No one does. No one beyond our coast, that is."

"How is that possible? How do they—" Understanding seemed to dawn on him, and he didn't finish his question. "Morshan is the only port. It's the only place anyone sees."

With a nod, Cait said, "The council only lets people know what they want them to."

Lucan moved forward. "And most people don't want to know."

"But—" Adler stopped short and snapped his attention to Cait. "So it's not just the exiles you hope to stop."

She shook her head.

"What happened to you? How'd you end up here?" Adler looked at Lucan once more, genuine concern on his face.

"Same as the others, I guess. Lost my family. Came to the council for help they refused to grant. Might have ended up exiled myself had Cait not found me when she did."

Adler, crossing his arms as he placed them on the table, leaned forward with a half-smirk, slowly revealing a single dimple within his beard. Even if Cait's instinct had pushed her away from trusting him, those damn dimples of his might have been enough to pull her firmly into his corner. When his eyes—those epically blue eyes, the color of the eastern sky at dusk—met hers once more, she tried to shoo away the internal flutters he'd triggered.

"Seems you saved us both, love."

Cait wanted to protest, insist she had only acted in self-interest. To cure her loneliness. To further her cause. But Lucan's words—spoken with that familiar and warm optimism she loved—filled the room before she could open her mouth. "She's saved more than us. And she'll save far more before she's done."

She wanted to be encouraged by the smile Lucan beamed at her, wanted to believe in herself as he did, but even with all the confidence she put on display for everyone, she so often felt like that lonely and confused teenage girl who had lost her parents and failed her brother.

Now with Adler and Lucan both looking at her with admiration—admiration she didn't deserve—she needed air, needed space.

"I'll be right back. Keep playing without me," she said, pushing out her chair. As she shut the apartment door behind her, she heard Lucan mutter something about her exit being a lame excuse to force them to become friends.

She didn't care what they assumed about her motives and actions. Her boots thumped down the stairs loudly. At the bottom, she gave one look at the rum behind the bar that seemed to be calling her name but then shook the idea away. Rum was well and good until it became your only friend. Her stomach growled, nudging her toward the kitchen behind the storeroom. The pub didn't serve food, and this small kitchen wouldn't have been able to support that service even if they tried; it was only large enough to prepare meals for a small family.

Rushing to the shelves, she absentmindedly pulled out a large frying pan, several eggs, and some cured meat. Vegetables and fruit were scarce these days, and she wasn't slated to get another ration of them for another couple of weeks. It was a marvel she and Lucan had managed to stave off illness with how imbalanced their diet was.

As she cooked their breakfast, an image of Lucan's confident smile came back to the forefront of her mind. She had panicked over a damned smile. It had been a long time since she'd had such a reaction, and it wasn't as if Lucan—or the rest of the Rogues—hadn't shown appreciation for her before. But this time, the heartfelt look he'd given her, in combination with his words about her saving everyone, had been altogether too much.

Everyone needed her to be strong, to run the pub, to keep life going. And sometimes she spent so much energy portraying that strength to the world, she had none left over for herself. Like a pitcher of water poured into everyone's glasses over and over, day after day, glass after glass, with no drop left to satisfy her own needs.

How had her mother done this? Cait often asked herself this, seeking some answer in her memories. Although, even if her mother had suffered similarly, her younger self likely wouldn't have recognized the signs.

The memories always reminded her of one thing: her mother had done all of this with a loving husband beside her.

Cait had wanted a love like theirs, even as she had dreamed of traveling the sea and having her own adventures; she always imagined a new life with a love of her own beside her.

"Find a man who cares for you but also trusts you, Cait. Find a man who has your back as much as you have his, a man who would follow you into the siren's lair and never leave your side."

"You've said this so many times," Cait said, exaggerating the roll of her eyes she loved to annoy her mother with.

Her mother brushed a strand of hair away from Cait's forehead, tucking it behind her ear. "I know, sweet girl. I know. I say it all the time, because it is so important in this life to give your heart to someone who will care for it as if it were their own."

Cait raised a brow. "It's only our first date."

Her mother let out a laugh that felt like a warm hug and a cup of hot cider, especially when paired with her smile, which could melt any cold heart. "The first may be the most important. I'll never tell you to follow your heart, because sands knows it can betray you for deceptively greener hills. Nor would I have you follow your head alone, as it is weak against fear, talking you out of good but challenging opportunities."

"So what do I follow then? The sun? The moon?"

Another warm laugh enveloped her. "Of course not. That voice within you? You know the one. It sounds like you, but it's mysteriously far more. Listen to it. It will help navigate the paths of life, steering you on the right heading, even when storms are raging and other courses seem nicer. Follow that voice within you that knows where you are needed and what you should do."

"And who I should love."

A nod. A soft kiss on the forehead.

And the memory faded.

The smell of burning food invaded Cait's senses as she snapped back to the present.

"Shit," she whispered as she pulled the pan from the heat and put out the fire before grabbing a plate and some forks.

Looking down at the meager—and blackened—portions she was about to place before Adler and Lucan, a weight thudded into the bottom of her stomach. How could they expect her to save them—or anyone—when she couldn't even prepare a simple meal?

But burned or not, her rations were running low, and she hadn't been able to risk securing extra at the docks. This would have to do. And she would have to ignore whatever bruises her ego developed as a result.

Cait opened the door of the apartment to find the men still seated at the table, quietly playing another round of cards, though by the placement of the cards, Adler must have convinced Lucan to switch to Corks and Bones. And by the look on Lucan's face, Adler hadn't made empty boasts about his skill at the game.

At the sound of the door clicking shut behind her, Lucan dropped his cards with a rush of relieved breath.

"Saved me again, Cait. Thank you."

At these words, Cait fought back a wince, dropping the plate onto the table with as much confidence as she could muster. She picked up a piece of charred meat as she settled back into her seat and waited for their reaction.

"This looks…" Adler said slowly, grimacing. "Remind me never to piss you off, love." He shoveled up what used to be edible eggs. "If this is what happens to things you like, I'd hate to see what happens to those you don't."

She tried not to laugh as he choked down the bite. "How do you know I like eggs and meat?"

"Because I would never trust someone who didn't. And I'd hate to have to stop trusting you now."

How he took another bite, she wasn't sure, but before she could tell him he didn't have to, Lucan was pulling the plate toward him. He had finished off two pieces of meat already, and with a shrug, he loaded his fork up with a hefty portion of unrecognizable eggs and plopped it greedily into his mouth.

As he went to take another, he caught Cait and Adler both staring at him.

"Oh, did you not want me to finish it for you?" Lucan asked, gesturing the fork toward each of them, causing bits of food to fall onto the plate.

"But it looks—" Cait said.

"And tastes—" Adler added.

Lucan shrugged. "Doesn't matter when you're hungry. Plus, I've had worse. Sure you don't want some, Adler?"

Chuckling, Adler shook his head. "I'm good, friend. All yours."

He'd called Lucan *friend*, and that was not lost on Cait. Even if it was as casual for him as calling her *love*, it was a step in the right direction. Adler flashed her a smile with those dimples again, and something warmed within her.

CHAPTER 29
TOMMY

Tommy stepped into the utter chaos on deck. Men continued to attack the creature's massive arms while avoiding their grasp. Why hadn't it crushed them yet? By the size of the tentacles reaching out of the inky black sea, the legends had not exaggerated the kraken's size. It could easily wrap itself around the hull and tear the ship in two. Yet it hadn't.

He'd left Aoife in the doorway. She'd need to take care of herself.

Declan will never forgive you if something happens to her.

Though that would cease to matter if he didn't focus on getting them free of this monster.

Tommy cupped his hands around his mouth and called for Mikkel. When the bo'sun arrived, he leaned in close. "Get as many men as you can below on the cannons. Aim for the widest sections. With precision."

"Aye, sir." It was the first time he'd been called that since assuming command.

Nothing more than habit for Mikkel though.

"Have some of them keep an eye on the hull and patch up whatever they can with whatever they have."

The man nodded and left to carry out the command. Tommy bounded up the quarterdeck stairs two at a time. Bria hadn't left her position at the rail, and Renna was beside her, silent but attentive. The sails still filled with the wind Bria summoned, but a glance at the sea told him her work wasn't helping to free them.

Rushing over to the two fae, he called out, "Renna, have her stop!"

Renna shot him a questioning look.

"It's holding us in place. Toying with us. We're just draining Bria's magic." He didn't know how to pull a fae out of whatever this trance was. Last thing he wanted was to do it wrong and worsen their situation.

Without so much as a nod, Renna turned her attention to Bria and silently took her hand in hers. A few breaths later, Bria's eyes flashed open and focused on Renna before snapping to Tommy.

"Why did—" she began, but he held up a hand.

"Can you summon it quickly? Strongly?" He sounded like a buffoon, but he had no time to worry about how he phrased things at the moment. "Or do you need to be in that intense state as you have been?"

Her brow quirked up. "I can, but it doesn't last long."

"Are you able to ease back into a steady rhythm without issue?"

She nodded, but concern filled her eyes. "Yes, but I'm running dangerously low. We will need to be careful."

Cannons began firing beneath them, and Tommy turned to watch as the kraken's limbs pulled back and retreated with each blow. They returned as quickly as they had fled, but still, the shots did better than he'd expected. His hope sparked.

If they could time it well, it might work.

It had to work.

"On my signal, summon as strong a burst as you can to propel us. Then maintain it, giving it as much as you can until we get away."

Bria eyed him quizzically.

"Renna," he continued, "you can tell how she's faring, yes?" A solemn nod. "Watch over her and pull her back before she gets to the edge."

He moved to the helm before Renna could ask any questions, before he had a chance to change his mind, tell her to keep her going, and sacrifice Bria's gifts—and long life—if it meant saving Maura.

And Declan.

Somehow, by sheer luck perhaps, none of the masts or the helm had been smashed by the kraken. The only visible indication that they were even under attack were the beads of sweat dripping down Gavin's face and the curses falling from his mouth every few seconds. While there wasn't much he could do from the helm, Gavin had stayed put, watching all of his friends fight around him, in order to be ready to maneuver them away as soon as the opportunity arose.

"How are we?" Tommy asked as he stepped up beside him.

Gavin stopped swearing long enough to reply, "Could be worse."

"Could also be better."

"That's a given. But we've had good fortune so far. What do you think it's doing?"

With a shake of his head, Tommy said, "I've been wondering the same thing."

The cannons continued to fire, hitting the monster more often than not, but it still wasn't giving them the opening they needed. He glanced behind him. The two sisters watched him with anticipation.

"They need to coordinate their shots. Hit both sides at the same time," Tommy mumbled to himself.

Aoife ran up the stairs toward them and yelled over the thundering cannons, "We need to time our shots better!"

"Agreed. Go! Below. Find Mikkel and make it happen!"

To Tommy's surprise Aoife listened—possibly for the first time since he'd met her—and he couldn't stop his mouth from curling into a small smile.

He'd barely lost sight of her on the stairs when movement to the side caught his eye. One of the kraken's arms lifted high in the air. It seemed to be surveying the ship, as if it had eyes. Impossible. How could it sense their positions? Pointing toward the prow, it swept around, remaining elevated above the ship until it aimed directly behind Tommy.

At Bria.

He turned around, cutlass ready, and ran across the small deck. Aiming for the tentacle as it moved to come down on the fae, he pushed himself to hurry. But before he'd managed to strike, the limb stopped a few inches from Bria's face, which was hidden behind the curtain of hair that now flew up into the air toward the attacker. The arm struggled against the wind that kept it in place, moving this way and that in an attempt to get free of its invisible shackles, but with each move, it met another wall of air.

"Gavin!" Tommy called. The helmsman was by him in a second. "Cutlass, now!"

Throwing his gaze toward the tentacle, he willed his friend to understand his meaning. Thankfully, after so many years of sailing and raiding and fighting and surviving together, Gavin caught his intent without hesitation and scurried under the tentacle to the other side as he pulled his cutlass loose from its scabbard.

The two pirates lifted their blades in unison, moving the weapons far back behind them to give extra force to their strikes. They swung simultaneously, bringing the cutlasses down onto the wriggling arm of the beast. With all their strength, they thrust their weapons down, slicing a deep cut into either side. The limb retreated in pain, dripping inky black blood onto the deck.

A scream tore through the air, and it took a full breath for Tommy to realize it was coming from Gavin, who had dropped his cutlass onto the ground. Cradling his arm in his left hand, Gavin stared down at his forearm, where the kraken's blood— as thick and black and foul as pitch—had fallen onto his skin.

Before Tommy could find his voice, Renna was there, placing her hands on Gavin's wounded arm. His screams quieted. His body relaxed.

But the fight wasn't over.

The kraken's wounded arm was gone, but another limb took its place before Bria could call up the wind again to protect them. It thudded to the floor of the quarterdeck and swiped toward them, knocking both Tommy and Bria down. Tommy, with his clothes soaked and uncomfortably sticking to him, lay gasping for air that wouldn't come at first. He rolled over onto his back to find the arm hovering above him, but it didn't seem interested in or even aware of him. Craning his neck, Tommy peered behind him. Bria had already recovered from the blow and was standing once more, calling the wind to keep the monster at bay.

Renna approached Tommy and lowered herself in front of him, putting a hand on his chest as she caught his attention. "It's trying to wear her down," she said, her concern evident despite the steadiness of her tone.

"How do you—" he started, then looked back up to the massive tentacle held in place by Bria's powers. "You can hear it?"

She gave the slightest of nods. "Just barely. It's faint, but it's there."

"You couldn't have discovered this earlier?" he asked with a chuckle, though nothing about this situation was amusing.

"I didn't know for sure it would work. It's been centuries since I've been near any nonhuman creatures."

"So what do we do?" He turned to watch the turbulent standoff between the fae and the kraken. Bria was still holding on, but unlike before, the creature didn't wriggle and struggle. It seemed to be conserving its energy as it drained hers.

Renna thought for half a second. "We need to wound it—severely—before it drains her of all her strength."

"If only you had offensive powers."

"I've oft wished that myself."

Tommy's shoulders tensed. "Collins is out cold. Gavin is—"

"Healing," Renna said as she looked toward the helmsman, who had managed to return to his station, "but his arm will need at least a few days to rest before it will be of use."

"And Maura...?" Tommy said. The shake of Renna's head tightened his gut.

"We need to get Bria away and get the cannons to hit it in multiple points at once so she can move us out of its reach and these waters. I'll go below. When the time is right, shout the order in your mind, and I'll hear it."

Tommy gave her a nod and didn't waste a moment before he lunged for Bria. Grabbing her around the waist, he turned her around and directed her down the stairs. He risked a look behind them as they descended to the main deck, expecting to see the long arm following them, but he caught the end of it pulling off the side of the ship, moving back down into the sea.

"Where are we going?" Bria asked, and Tommy pointed toward the officers' cabin where Collins slept.

"Not inside. Just next to the door." Once there, with his feet planted on the rocking deck, he surveyed the scene before him. Several bodies lay strewn across the deck. The man who had been atop the mast had long ago fallen from his perch. Tommy winced as he recalled the sight of the pirate's body being snatched in the air by the beast and yanked below the surface.

By sheer luck, they didn't need to wait long for the stupid beast to make a poor decision. Six limbs, three on either side of the ship, rose in unison, and each happened to be in the line of sight of one of the gunners below decks. Before he could even push the thought to Renna, the cannons fired. Every cannon. The force shook the ship, but Tommy barely noticed as he scanned both sides. The cannons had hit their marks—rather effectively—and the monster pulled its injured tentacles away from the ship.

"Now!" Tommy shouted to Bria. Immediately the sails filled with wind. The ship lurched forward, pulling away from the kraken's limbs, which were still raised in the air despite the damage they'd suffered. Their retreat hadn't gone unnoticed though, and the creature moved to follow.

Too slow. They were going much too slow. "Bria. Can you do more?"

She gave him no indication that she'd heard, but the ship increased speed beneath his feet.

Gavin shouted from above, "Tommy, it's gone!"

With a word of encouragement for Bria to keep it up as long as she could, Tommy rushed away, bounding up the stairs once more and running to the rail. Gavin was right. The only sign the kraken had been there was the mysterious ink floating near the surface, slowly fading away.

"That was too lucky," Tommy said to himself. Deep in his bones he knew something was amiss. Coming back to Gavin, he noted, "Hold on. I don't think it's done with us yet."

CHAPTER 30
CAIT

Lucan and Adler arrived the next morning laughing at something as they stepped into the pub. Cait quickly finished plaiting her hair.

Adler's teasing smirk spread across his face. "Didn't take you for the vain type, love."

Lucan no longer bristled at the man's use of the term for her. Instead, he grinned broadly, as though he was privy to some joke she hadn't heard.

With a shrug, she said, "I'll have you know, this perfection is far from effortless."

Adler looked as though he wanted to move toward her but stopped short before saying, "And it is far from unappreciated."

Lucan groaned, his grin replaced with the look Declan used to don whenever their parents kissed too intimately in front of them. But nothing between her and Adler warranted such a reaction. She should be offended, but it wasn't worth the effort, so she settled for a signature roll of her eyes. "We're done flirting now, Lucan."

At that, Adler playfully smacked Lucan's chest with the back of his hand, his jaw dropping open. "Did you hear that?"

Lucan nodded, his face now lit up with amusement.

"Hear what?" Cait asked, hoping she didn't sound as pathetic as she felt for not understanding.

Adler's eyes turned almost seductive. "You agreed you were flirting with me, love."

Embarrassment pooled in her stomach.

"I don't know why you're so excited about that, man," Lucan said with a laugh. "She flirts with me all the time."

"I do not!" This was ridiculous. Here the Rogues were on the verge of executing the first step in their plan to unseat the council, and these two buffoons were teasing her over something as stupid as flirting.

Adler's smile brightened, and when those damn dimples greeted her, she had to look away.

"She responded rather quickly to that, friend," Adler said. "I think you might be right. I'll remember not to let her advances go to my head."

With a huff, Cait threw her hands up and walked in between them toward the door. She didn't bother to invite them to follow and, although it was childish, she allowed herself the simple satisfaction of slamming the door behind her.

Out on the street, she didn't acknowledge the men's presence behind her as she made her way toward Penny's Place. Penny's was a popular eatery owned by one of the more prominent members of town. Penny had been a prominent figure in Morshan for as long as Cait could remember. She was also not fond of the McCallagh's and didn't bother to hide her disdain for the family. While she had sent her condolences to Cait and Declan after their parents' disappearances, Penny had seemed almost pleased with what had happened, as if she'd had a hand in it.

And Cait wasn't sure she hadn't.

None of that was why the Rogues had decided to target her though. They needed a person of influence, someone the people would listen to, but also someone who wasn't likely to be a council pawn. The Rogues had been watching her—in random shifts, never the same person two days in a row and never in the same order, lest the woman notice and become suspicious—for the better part of the last two years. Based on the reports of her movements and meetings and dealings, Cait was confident Penny was as dimwitted as she'd always imagined.

There was no sign she was working with the council or that she had any suspicion about what the council actually did behind the scenes, how they controlled the flow of goods not for the benefit of the people, as they claimed, but to maintain their hold on the people and the island.

Penny was a staunch supporter of the council and prided herself on how she valued the law of peace on the island. And that made her the perfect person to target for this particular exercise.

The trio remained silent as they entered the building and made their way to a seat by the far wall, near the stairs. They pretended to look over the scant menu as they sat and waited. The dining room, unusually empty at this hour, was a small area cramped with simple tables and chairs. This would be even harder to pull off while there were so few people around. Cait had hoped the typical hustle and bustle of the breakfast crowd would add to the confusion of what they were about to stage.

As Cait wracked her mind for options, Penny approached. "Good morning, Cait. Lucan." The friendliness in her tone was in stark contrast to the irritated look she flashed them. Bitterness was not a flattering trait in most people, but it was particularly unbecoming in this woman. Her beak-like nose was made more prominent by the scowl on her thin lips, and the sharpness of her glare made her brown eyes more of a dull muddy hue rather than the sweet chocolate color they might have been otherwise.

"And who is this? Newcomer?" Penny eyed Adler, a hint of suspicion hiding behind blatant attraction.

"New bar hand" was all Cait offered, turning her eyes back to the menu.

No other words were exchanged after their orders were placed, and the trio sat for several minutes in silence, Adler looking around the room with his jaw in the palm of his hand as his fingers drummed lazily against his temple. Lucan showed no sign of his earlier good mood as he fidgeted in his seat, like a toddler who was antsy to go play. Except it wasn't excitement that had him so uncomfortable, though sands knew this was a vast improvement from when he'd first arrived in Morshan.

Cait reached her hand over the table and placed it atop his. With a squeeze, she donned a reassuring smile, hoping he knew she hadn't forgotten how hard this was for him, even if she couldn't personally understand the difficulty.

Though Cait had learned Morshan wasn't like the other towns and villages on Cregah, there was a vast difference between knowing the hardships her people faced elsewhere and actually living it herself. Morshan was like a decadent palace compared to the squalor they lived in. Starvation was a common way to die, second only to illness and infection. Morshan was a mask, a pleasant veneer displayed to an ignorant public, giving the people a view of comfort and peace while the rest of the country suffered. It was this reminder of the mask that hit Lucan so hard.

Not that it wasn't noticeable in the shops throughout the town he'd called home for years. But the restaurants always affected him more, where the abundance of food and wastefulness of the citizens was on full display.

Cait was forced to release Lucan's hand when Penny delivered the food to the table. The breakfast was similar to what Cait had attempted to make yesterday—a fried egg, a single piece of toast, and a bit of cured meat—but it lacked the charred quality of inattention.

Cait looked up at Adler through her lashes as she leaned over her plate to begin eating. If her actions with Lucan had bothered him in any way, it didn't show in his expression as he took a bite of food and watched as more patrons arrived and took seats. Why would it bother him? And why did it matter if it had? It shouldn't. There wasn't anything to explain beyond friendship—regardless of Lucan's earlier assertion that she flirted with him often. And there certainly was nothing happening between her and the pirate that would warrant any jealousy on his part.

Lucan cleared his throat. With toast in hand, he flicked his eyes up to the door and then back down to his food. Pretending to stretch her neck, Cait turned to see the man Lucan had indicated. Short stature. Not a local—but also not a pirate. Alone, visibly intoxicated. Though Cait didn't know who he was, she had seen him in here often enough to know he was a Morshan regular, and Penny's was his preferred destination in the mornings, especially after a long night of drinking.

Cait returned to eating and gave a nearly imperceptible nod. She stole one more glance at Adler and took his half-smile as an indication he understood.

The man ambled by them, his feet shuffling against the floor before he stumbled, falling against Cait's chair. She cried out as his hand tangled in her hair. Penny rushed over before Lucan or Adler could pretend to react.

"Gregor, come on." It was the gentlest tone Cait had ever heard the woman use. Penny focused her attention on Cait as she supported the man's weight. "Perhaps you shouldn't have your chair out so far."

There was the spite-filled Penny Cait knew and loathed, but Cait responded with the sweetest smile she could muster.

"I'm sorry, Penny. Here, let me help," she said as she stood. She reached out to take Gregor's arm, and as she had hoped, Penny's shoulders slumped as she released a heavy breath.

"Thank you. Just take him to the back. I have a spot where he can rest. It's hard to miss."

"Least I can do. Apologies again," Cait offered before turning to Gregor. "Let's get you settled, shall we?"

Behind her, Lucan struck up a conversation with Penny, asking how business was before introducing her to Adler. Adler must have said something charming or funny or both, because Penny's laugh filled the room, but it wasn't like any laugh Cait had ever heard from her. This one seemed forced, a bit louder than usual.

While her men kept the owner busy, Cait led the drunken man through the dining room, nodding and humming at his slurred and indecipherable questions. They had just made it to the small counter where Penny collected notes and tallied up earnings for the council when Cait feigned a stumble that sent her foot into the path of Gregor's stride. He grabbed for Cait in his drunken haze, and they both tumbled to the ground. Cait noticed the gathered crowd craning their necks to see what had caused the commotion. She raised her hand in a wave as she caught Penny's eye.

"We're okay!" she said, even as Gregor let out a sound that could only be described as groaning laughter.

Keeping the diners in her periphery, Cait righted herself and reached down to help the man up. He was heavier than expected, and in her effort to lift him, she leaned back, far. This was not at all the way to move a louse—and she'd had plenty of practice doing that—but no one seemed to be paying her any attention, having already turned back to their meals and conversations. Cait's hands slipped off Gregor's arm, and she fell onto her backside, more quietly this time so as not to call as much attention to herself.

Swinging her legs around, she moved into a kneeling position and pretended to whisper to the man, who appeared awfully close to falling asleep. She stole a quick look at Adler and Lucan. Penny was still chattering away as she leaned closer to Adler's side of the table.

She'd need to do it now, or they'd lose this opportunity. As quickly as she could, Cait pulled out the small dagger she'd stashed in her boot.

Atop the counter lay a stack of paper, receipts, and menus. With the dagger hidden along her forearm, she rose, careful to keep her arm concealed behind the counter. During the split second it took her to stand, she slipped the blade beneath the mess.

She held her breath for a moment, but when she raised her eyes and saw no one was looking her way, too engaged in their food and talk, she let the air rush from her lungs.

"Okay, Gregor. This is not where Miss Penny intended for you to rest. Shall we?"

No answer. Not that she had expected one. She hauled the man up as she had done with countless others back at the pub, and deposited him on the pile of blankets in the corner of the storeroom. He curled up on his side, mumbling and barely conscious.

"You're welcome," Cait offered before heading back to her seat.

"Have some trouble with that, did you?" Adler asked as she approached, craning around Penny's form to meet Cait's eyes. Penny stepped back a pace to allow Cait room to pull the seat out.

Cait lifted a shoulder. "Not the hardest person I've had to escort in such a fashion."

"Yeah, she's had to move me a couple times, sadly," Lucan piped up, and for a moment Cait caught a glimpse of his earlier goofiness.

"You were one of the worst, Luc," Cait agreed.

Penny, clearing her throat, gestured to Cait's chair. "Please, sit. I'll bring you a little something for home as a token of gratitude."

Cait appreciated the gesture as much as possible, considering it was coming from a woman who had always been so rude to her. And she almost felt bad for what was going to happen in a moment.

"I wish we could, but we really must be going. I'll have Adler settle the balance with you while Lucan and I wait outside so as to free up the table for you."

Penny didn't seem at all put out at the opportunity to spend more time talking with the former pirate, and she didn't bother to say anything to Cait before she started walking toward the counter, waving her hand over her shoulder to signal Adler to follow.

Cait and Adler exchanged a brief look as he stood, and his blue eyes flashed her a wink before he strode past her. His shoulder brushing against hers sent her skin tingling, and she told herself it was nothing more than an involuntary reaction to human contact. It had nothing to do with him personally.

Lucan came up behind her and placed a hand on the small of her back as he motioned for them to exit. When they reached the door, Cait glanced back to where Adler now stood at the counter with the owner, chatting and giggling about who knew what. When Cait opened the door, a gust of wind—perfectly timed and unexpected—rushed into the space and sent the papers in front of Adler fluttering away.

Cait and Lucan walked out onto the sidewalk to monitor the situation inconspicuously while staging a conversation.

A sudden movement inside caused them to snap their attention to the window. Even from outside, Cait could hear Adler's booming voice.

"Woah! Why do you have that?"

Penny stood before him, holding the dagger in her hand, her forehead wrinkling with her confusion. Her eyes were fixed on the blade she held, and her head began to shake. Adler's question had alerted the others in the room to the situation, and several people had turned to look, their mouths open either in shock or to whisper to their companions. A woman rushed out the door and, as Cait had hoped, headed straight for the pirates currently patrolling the town on behalf of the council.

With his hands up in surrender, Adler remained frozen in place. It didn't take long before the woman returned with two burly pirates who had dull yellow sashes tied around their waists.

Backing up to give the pirates room to pass, Cait and Lucan continued to watch the situation unfold. Penny still held the blade, as if it had been seared to her palm. As the pirates approached, the diners backed away. Except for Adler, who remained rooted in place, though his hands had at least relaxed. From outside, Cait couldn't make out what was said, but as she watched Penny's shock give way to confusion and then anger in a matter of minutes, she assumed it wasn't going well for the restaurateur.

"I don't like it," Lucan said under his breath.

Cait didn't turn to look at him, wanting to oversee everything happening within. "None of us like it, but remember, we have a plan." She lowered her voice. "Penny will get taken to the council. They'll sentence her to exile. But the twins will be ready to follow them. To rescue her at the opportune moment. It will be okay."

"Yeah, I've heard that before."

Her shoulders slumped at the reminder. Those had been the words she'd used to ease everyone's worries over sending Maggie in as a spy.

"We have to hope." When he didn't say anything, she continued. "Positive thinking isn't magic. It can't change the future. It can't bring us victory. But it can keep us from giving up entirely, from accepting defeat at the start."

Whether her words convinced him or not, she couldn't tell. Inside, the pirates seized Penny, whose face was twisted in fright. One of the pirates confiscated the blade and slipped it into his belt, and then the two men began to drag her to the exit. Adler hung back. As planned.

The front door opened.

"Please! You have to believe me! It wasn't mine!" Desperation clung to each syllable.

The pirates paused just long enough for one of them to kick the door closed behind them while the other sneered at her. Although their clothes were clean, their beards trimmed, and their faces washed, they still had that disagreeable quality about them that indicated their profession and expertise in that field. Their teeth were nearly as dirty as their fingernails, their language just as vile.

Cait tracked the pirates as they dragged Penny to the sidewalk. No doubt they would assume she and Lucan were nothing more than curious citizens watching the spectacle. Penny continued proclaiming her innocence, and the pirates continued ignoring her.

"Shit." The whispered curse rushed out of Cait as she watched them turn right.

"What is it?" Lucan asked.

"They're not taking her to the council. That's back the other way." She was moving to follow them before she'd finished talking. But she had no plan. She kicked herself for not having a contingency plan—or rather, not having the right contingency plan. Their handful of preplanned maneuvers had all hinged on the fact that exiles were taken before the council first for sentencing. In all her years, Cait had never known them to allow their hired hands to dispatch citizens on their own.

"Maybe they're taking the scenic route," Lucan said, coming up beside her, easily matching her quick stride.

Cait stayed silent.

"Shouldn't we wait for Adler?"

She stopped to look over her shoulder and spotted the tall pirate jogging toward them. Urgency coursed through her. If they lost track of them, she would have gotten another innocent person killed for nothing.

"Come on!" she yelled at Adler, as she silently urged Penny to keep shouting.

Before Adler had caught up, Cait was off again. The pirates had moved Penny onto another street, but Cait could still hear her shrill, hoarse voice wafting around the buildings.

"The twins—" Lucan started.

"No time," Adler said before Cait could, and she wasn't sure if she was annoyed or grateful. "We'll need to find them, follow them, and take care of it ourselves."

Cait nodded along and pushed her legs to keep going as she followed the woman's shouts through town. When they neared the docks, she wondered what the pirates planned to do. Exile, yes. But how? Where? When Aron had spotted the pirates carrying off Maggie's body, he hadn't followed them, hadn't discovered where they took the exiles.

As stone gave way to wooden planks beneath her feet, she froze, hesitating.

Left. Right. Nowhere. And the screaming had stopped. They'd need to split up.

"Lucan, head that way toward the docks. Adler and I will go the opposite."

Lucan's jaw tensed, and Cait waited for him to argue, knowing this order wasn't easy for him; it would force him near the sea he feared to possibly face two pirates on his own, and he would have to leave Cait's side in the midst of danger.

He swallowed hard and with a nod to Cait took off toward the water.

Cait grabbed Adler's arm and turned him around so they faced the forest at the edge of town. "Let's go."

"So quick to get me alone in the woods again?" he asked as he picked up the pace and flashed her another wink.

"Whatever keeps you moving forward."

The road seemed to disappear into the trees, as though the town had been lifted from some other world and dropped into the middle of this forest, making the roads lead nowhere.

But there was a faint hint of a path where the grass was sparser.

And there—a footprint, clear as day in the soft ground.

Panic sped up her heart, and she bit down until her teeth hurt in an effort to prevent the inevitable shaking of her hands from starting. Penny needed her to hurry. The whole of Cregah needed her to hurry. This was their best option to expose the council's secret violence. But what if she chose wrong? She couldn't split up from Adler. While she'd love to believe she could take on two pirates unassisted, she knew her limits.

Adler pushed silently past her into the trees, his eyes on the ground. He stopped and called to her in a hushed tone, "Here. More boot prints."

"You sure?" she asked as she met up with him.

"Well, I'm but a humble pirate and no tracker. But it's the best lead we have."

"It's a shaky lead at best."

"It's where I would go if I were going to exile someone." He raised a brow.

She took two seconds to breathe and consider and then continued moving down the overgrown path, not bothering to call Adler to follow.

Let us be right, Penny. And let us hurry.

I may not like you, but that doesn't mean I want you dead.

CHAPTER 31
DECLAN

Many of the stories passed around the Aisling were based on true events that had been twisted into outlandish myths, but some had been so horrifying to begin with that no elaboration could have made them any more frightening. The dragons might have long ago left the region—as far as Declan knew—but the sirens remained. And nothing had deterred him from taking their legend seriously.

Still, he hoped the legends were false.

Even from the windowless brig Declan knew when they had arrived at the Black Sound. The air around him hadn't shifted. It was still the dank and musty belly of the ship, with a hint of the scent of oranges. The hair on Declan's arms wasn't standing on end. His skin wasn't tingling. There was no indication they'd arrived except the eerie quiet that settled above him. Even from this far below deck, the noises of the crew walking and talking and shouting reached him at all hours of the day.

But all that had ceased in an instant.

And Declan knew his nonexistent luck hadn't brought him the sudden demise of everyone aboard.

No. They'd slowed. The crew had quieted. A threat lay ahead.

Declan waited.

The faint sound of boots moving down the ladder filled the space, pulling Declan's attention to the man Callum had sent to retrieve him. Without a word—without any sound at all—the man unlocked the cell door, careful to keep the ring of keys he carried from jangling together, wincing when the iron hinges creaked in protest at being used.

Part of Declan wanted to say something, to break the stillness with a quip or a jab at the man's expense. Had they been in any other location—or in any other circumstance—he would have, but even Declan didn't want to tempt the sirens.

At least not yet.

So he allowed the man to take him by the arm, doing his best not to comment on how the service on board had improved greatly. Without the ability to joke, though, Declan found it especially hard to ignore the dread that had returned to his gut.

Forcing the bile back down his tightened throat, he ascended the last steps to the deck, desperate to ignore the memory of the last time he'd made this climb to find Killian bound and awaiting his punishment. Blinking hard, he forced away the image of the man being dragged over the railing, body mangled, life hanging on by a thread.

This time, though, the men of the *Curse Bringer* did not jeer at him or taunt him as he walked among them. Their stillness was a drastic change from the crazed enthusiasm they had shown just yesterday. And though Declan never wanted to revisit yesterday's spectacle—not even in his own mind—this atmosphere was almost as unsettling.

Almost.

Though Declan had sailed all around the Aisling Sea, from the black sands of Cregah and the lush forests of Caprothe to the pristine white cliffs of Turvala, none of it compared to the view before him.

The teal water beneath them sat as still as glass, transforming the surface into a mirror that reflected the sheer walls of black rock, which were blanketed in dense trees as green as the hills of Cregah. But these had an otherworldly essence to them, as if each leaf and branch was cut from priceless gems. Wisps of clouds clung to the hills where water cascaded down, cutting through the foliage like the veins of a great giant. And above, stretching toward the azure sky, bare rock reached up, like a solemn observer looking down on all who dared approach.

No sound came beyond the distant rumble of the waterfalls crashing into the sea. No hint of bird or beast could be found—not in the trees, the skies, or the seas. The quiet, as ominous and foreboding as it was, pulled at Declan, drawing him away from the crew. He moved around the mainmast and closer to the ship's rail. The Black Sound was calling him, like it had been expecting him. Or perhaps it was that its inhabitants could sense the depth of his remorse and beckoned him to come and find them.

"You feel it, don't you?"

Declan jumped as Callum appeared seemingly out of nowhere and whispered the question, easily heard in the silence surrounding them.

"Your shoulder lingering against mine? Aye, I do. Makes me uncomfortable," Declan said and eyed the captain without turning his head.

A smile distorted Callum's scar. "Jokes won't protect you in there."

The apprehension pooling in Declan's gut grew turbulent at the words, but he was not about to let Callum know. He turned his attention toward his captor and raised a brow, the corners of his mouth pulling down.

"Perhaps I could try a disguise."

Callum didn't look amused.

Declan raised his still-manacled hands to his chin, tapping it with a forefinger. "I'll need a change of clothes. And probably a new hat."

"A disguise." Callum's tone showed as much humor as his face. None.

"Aye. You could have one too. It'll be a classic Declan-Callum mess-around."

Callum gave a shrug. "Could be rather entertaining to see you try."

Declan's chin bobbed with several nods. "Aye. You're in need of a distraction, and I aim to please."

Silence once again rolled in like the fog hugging the cliffs of the sound. While Declan normally relished any moments void of incessant chatter and pointless noise, here the stillness was far from calming. Even the sea below them seemed hesitant to splash too much against the hull of the ship. The crew barely breathed. No one moved.

Declan leaned his head toward Callum, his eyes still focused on the entrance to the sound, and whispered, "So there's no singing then?"

When Callum didn't answer, Declan turned to find exasperation written on the man's face.

"Are we waiting to be invited in?"

Callum's jaw tightened before he responded. "You in such a hurry to greet death?"

"Why put off the inevitable?" Pivoting around, he stood up on his toes and craned his neck to get a glimpse of the waters behind them. No sails were visible. Not even on the distant horizon. "And it appears my rescuers will not make it in time."

Declan could not prevent his throat from constricting as the memories surfaced. It was as though the sirens' presence had unlocked the chains around them.

Tommy collapsing onto the stone floor. Blood spreading across his chest.

His father being dragged away to be tried for murder.

His mother disappearing into the mist, never to return.

Aoife shaking her head. Denying him. Refusing him.

Tighter and tighter, each memory cut off his air.

He had failed.

Again.

No matter how much he tried to remind himself it wasn't over until his last breath, no matter how often he tried to focus on the next task, the bitter truth drowned out every bit of reassurance he could scrounge up.

He should have kept to himself, kept everyone from getting too close. Nothing good came from being his friend or his kin.

Or his lover.

If not for him, Tommy wouldn't have been injured. Aoife wouldn't have been betrayed. His parents—

Logically, Declan knew he wasn't responsible for their deaths. Logically, his mind understood there was nothing he could have done as a young kid to protect them or to prevent it.

Unfortunately, man was ruled not by logic alone but by experience, emotion, trauma. And those denied Declan any relief. It was irrational, but something within him insisted that redemption could never be his. Others may deserve it, but not him. Never him.

His chest caved, and his shoulders began to curve forward, as they had when he was a young cabin boy hiding in the corner of the ship during a storm. This was what the sirens wanted. This internal suffering. The pain that marred his soul. The regret that ate holes throughout his heart like a worm through an apple.

Clenching his jaw tight until his teeth ached, Declan tried to push away the darkness that plagued him. He would not readily serve his mangled soul to these demons. He couldn't. He had to fight. Not just for Tommy and Aoife and Cait, but for himself too. No matter what he tried, though, no matter how hard he pushed against the darkness, it fought back harder, and he could contain it no better than if he were attempting to hold back the tide with his bare hands.

"Don't fight it, Declan." Callum's quiet voice—emotionless and matter-of-fact —cut through his inner battle. "Remember what I said. It's too late."

Callum was right, but Declan still shook his head in denial as he turned. Despite the apathy in his words, Callum's demeanor had shifted. If the sirens really were calling to Declan's inner demons, they could very well be doing the same to Callum —and everyone else aboard this ship.

"You're not looking too good yourself," Declan said. "Sure it's not too late for you too? I thought you were smarter than me."

Callum's gaze shifted back to the darkness waiting between the rocky cliffs. "I am. Unfortunately, all pain reacts to the sirens' call. But not all pain is equal. It never goes away. Some flicker of it always remains. Like a...scar." He seemed to struggle with that last word. "Like you, I betrayed someone. Someone close to me. But she betrayed me as well. Left me with this." Callum gestured to the scar that ran down his cheek.

"Are you about to share your story with me? Should I be honored?" Declan looked around with suspicion. "Good thing the crew's fear is keeping them back or they might hear it all."

Callum ignored the questions but shook his head and gave a light laugh. "You know, I just might miss your ridiculous chatter, McCallagh."

"I'm touched." Declan cleared his throat before lowering his voice. "So who was she?"

"A pirate. One of the best damned pirates I've ever worked with."

While Declan hadn't met many female pirates, Callum couldn't have been refer-ring to the one who had helped him get Aoife away from the council. Halloran.

"She must be if she managed to wound you like that. What'd you do to earn it, exactly?"

"Are we stalling now? Not so eager to die after all?" Callum asked, though he didn't wait for Declan to answer as he leaned against the railing and looked down at the water. "She was my quartermaster, actually. And no, you wouldn't have heard about it. It didn't last long enough to make it into the gossip channels."

"The betrayal would have, though, right?"

A shrug. "Perhaps that was the last consolation she offered—allowing my reputation to remain intact, even as she made off with nearly all of the prize and a handful of my crew. Secured her own ship. Hired a bunch of women as her officers. Made a name for herself."

"Halloran."

A silent nod. This was interesting.

"But you betrayed her first?"

"Aye."

"What happened?"

Callum straightened from the railing. "That's a story for another time. We could call it an incentive for you to survive in there."

Declan scoffed. "Not much of an incentive, is it?"

"Take it however you wish to. Try to make it, try not to, I don't mind either way as long as you keep them preoccupied long enough for me to locate and grab the blade." Callum raised a hand and signaled someone behind Declan with a quick wave. Before Declan could turn to see who was approaching, a rough hand grasped one of his forearms, keeping it steady as keys fit into the lock of the manacles. The satisfying metallic click of it releasing might have brought relief for Declan had he been facing something else.

Try to make it.

Callum might think Declan had already given up. Perhaps that was what most people would do, but he'd made his choice the first day on this ship, and nothing had changed that.

He would survive.

Or he'd die trying.

CHAPTER 32
AOIFE

PRIDE COURSED through Aoife as she returned to the main deck. Though it would have been better if Declan was here to witness their success. Her success. As angry as she still was with him, she couldn't ignore the warmth that flickered within her when she thought of him—even if it was quickly overrun by fear and worry that they would be too late and she would never see him again.

That thought pushed her feet faster, and by some miracle she didn't lose her balance as the ship suddenly surged forward. While she was on the ladder, though, another burst of movement came, perfectly timed to fling half of her body from the rungs and rails. She let out a loud huff of surprise and irritation as she struggled to get herself steady once again so she could climb.

She'd once commented on the lack of excitement aboard this ship, but now, as she clambered up ladder after ladder before crawling up onto the deck, she wished she'd never made such an observation. Against her will—and despite all her effort to focus on the task at hand—a memory swept over her. His hands on her wrists. Her back pressed against the bed. His warmth and his breath and his touch. It barreled into her like a wave against a rocky shore, but she continued pushing forward, ignoring the images that threatened to pull her under and distract her.

By the time she had ascended the stairs and made it to the helm, where Tommy stood watching the aft as Gavin looked ahead, her legs and lungs burned, and a stitch in her side ached with each breath as she tried to suck down air and find relief. Two days of training with Collins hadn't been enough to make up for two decades of sedentary living. Tommy had warned her body would tire quickly, but she hadn't expected it to feel like this.

Bending over, she rested her hands above her knees and widened her eyes to focus on the wooden floor beneath her as she breathed. Everything hurt. She'd never been in so much pain.

She stood and focused on Gavin, who was manning the wheel with only one hand. His other arm hugged his ribs, and his hand rested against his midsection like he was preparing to be sick. But he'd been on the seas for basically his whole life— as far as she knew. He wouldn't get queasy now.

"What happened?" Aoife looked from one man to the other.

Gavin raised his brows above unamused eyes that were dimmed by fatigue. "The damn thing bled on me."

Confused, she turned to Tommy for an explanation. He looked away as he said, "Its blood is toxic, it seems."

"What?" Her panic rushed forward, but Gavin shook his head.

"Don't worry. Renna helped. I'll be shipshape soon enough."

Aoife's shoulders fell as her breath escaped. "I'd be a lot less worried if you both didn't look so concerned. We got away, right? It worked?" She paused to look at the sails above, which were still full of the enchanted wind Bria brought them. She must be teetering on the edge of burnout. So why had Tommy—the man who had been so adamant about avoiding that outcome—suddenly stopped caring? Why hadn't he called for Bria to stop?

Without a word, Tommy walked away toward the aft rail, and Aoife followed, unsure if that was what he wanted. He stood stiffly beside the rail instead of leaning against it as he normally did. Not that anything about this was normal. Men shouted behind her, calling for others to help them move the wounded and the dead. The injured let out cries of pain as they were lifted and carried away from where they lay. Perhaps this was normal for them. They were a pirate crew, after all. But the look on Tommy's face—a look she'd seen on Gavin's too—told her something was different now.

She leaned her shoulder against Tommy and gave him a gentle nudge before speaking. "Why is Bria still..." She didn't know what to call it. Working? Conjuring? Magicifying? But Tommy didn't seem to notice her floundering for words.

"It's not done," he said through tight lips, focusing intently on the waters behind them. But Aoife saw nothing. No sign of limbs breaching the surface. Even the monster's inky warning had completely disappeared.

"How can you know that?"

"Gut feeling. We got away too easily. It gave up too quickly."

"Perhaps it wasn't hungry anymore," she said with a shaky breath, though she had never been good at using humor to defuse awkward situations. Usually she just made things worse, but thankfully Tommy showed her some much appreciated pity with a half-hearted, breathy laugh.

"Doubtful," he said.

"Well, can't we simply do what we did before? Wouldn't that tactic work again?"

He shook his head. "No. I don't think so. We got lucky. It moved precisely where we needed it to be when we needed it to be there. I don't believe in destiny or fate or whatever, but something about it feels off. We won't get that kind of fortune a second time."

Aoife tightened her brow as she considered their situation and all he was saying. "So we just push Bria to the edge? Risk her powers? Her long life? Isn't that the very reason you were being such a stubborn ass before?" Her anger flared too quickly for her to hold it back.

He refused to look at her as he gripped the railing so hard his knuckles whitened and his tendons flared. Aoife waited for his harsh response, but instead he closed his eyes and said in a low, determined voice, "I made a mistake, Aoife."

"You think?" She still couldn't get a handle on the rage that simmered under her skin.

His voice remained quiet. "Not the mistake you think."

He didn't look at her, and for several silent breaths, Aoife's impatience grew. If he was right and the kraken would reappear, his taking his sweet time with this conversation was a mistake too.

"Am I supposed to guess?" Aoife lowered her face into his line of sight to snap him out of whatever daydream he'd lost himself in.

"You know, I miss the old Aoife. The nice one. The sweet one—" Tommy's amber eyes flashed with what Aoife could only describe as desperate anger. It was what she assumed he saw in hers.

"I'm sorry I'm not feeling sweet or nice at the moment, Tommy." With these final stinging words, she deflated, slumping her shoulders and dropping her head as all the rage fell away. She immediately wanted it to return and hide the heartache it had been shadowing. "I'm sorry, Tommy."

"I am too," Tommy said and angled himself toward her as he leaned against the railing. "It's just so—"

"Exhausting?"

A sad half-smile pulled at his lips. "That, and stressful. How can I lead this crew?"

Aoife surveyed the ship. "What do you mean? You *are* leading them. You snapped me out of that haze after Collins was wounded and got me to keep fighting."

"And look around you." He swept an arm out, gesturing toward the bloody deck and broken rails. "I got them killed. And I may very well get Declan killed with my failure."

Lifting her hands, Aoife grasped Tommy's face and gently forced him to look at her. Something flickered in his expression at her touch. It was either embarrassment or shame, not that it mattered which. She ignored it so she could focus on what she needed to tell him.

"Declan trusts you. I trust you. The *crew* trusts you. All know the danger of these waters. All know the risks on these seas. They could have stayed behind in Morshan. But they didn't. When they all heard about Declan, they knew they'd be serving under you, and they stayed. Trust them. Trust yourself, Tommy."

Before he could protest, a shout from Gavin made them both turn toward the helm.

"Tommy!" Gavin quickly pointed to the port side with his good arm before barking orders at the few uninjured crewmen on deck. He grabbed the wheel and swung it hard to the right.

"What is that?" Aoife asked Tommy as he rushed back to Gavin's side. From her perch at the rail, where she held on as the ship changed course, she could see the sea churning unnaturally, not from wind at the surface but because of something beneath.

Tommy called back over his shoulder, "Nothing good!"

He could say that again.

The swirling sea increased in speed around a point not one hundred meters away from them, the center point darkening and dropping below the surface, like a monster slowly opening its mouth to swallow them whole. Fear plunged her gut into her feet, weighing her down. She couldn't move. Couldn't release the rail she now clung to.

You fight. Until someone wins, you fight.

She repeated the words over and over, letting them circle her mind like the waters before her. No one had won. Not yet. So they needed to fight. She needed to fight.

But how?

How could you fight a sea that obeyed the enormous creature within it? They had gotten away from its grasp, yes, but perhaps this was why it had been so easy. It had known it would get them one way or another. It had allowed them one bit of hope before claiming its prize. There had to be something they could do.

Aoife swung her attention to Tommy and Gavin, who were frantically talking and gesturing erratically. She couldn't hear a damn thing they said. If she was going to help, she needed to get closer. She needed to move. Hopeful Gavin didn't need to make another drastic turn, Aoife forced her hands to release the rail and pushed her feet to move her forward.

She had nearly made it when the ship rocked to the port side, sending her body slamming into Tommy's. How the man managed to stay upright with such a move, she didn't know. But she doubted his sea legs could be the sole explanation.

The ship still hadn't completely righted, but Tommy held her steady. Before Aoife could ask him what the plan was, his eyes darted into the air behind her head, and she turned to see what had startled him. Her breath caught in her throat, and panic rose sharply at the sight of the sails dropping all at once. Lifeless.

"Bria." The name was out of Tommy's lips at the same instant he moved. Aoife might have fallen had Gavin not caught her with his good arm.

Aoife turned to search Gavin's eyes for any hint they would survive this, but they didn't shimmer with the humor and kindness she'd always seen before. Instead, they were full of despair.

And it was then, in that moment, that Aoife let go of all hope.

CHAPTER 33
TOMMY

TOMMY'S FEET slipped and slid as he ran down the stairs and across the tilted deck. More than once he worried he was about to go right off the side of the ship through the gap in the railing. Somehow, though, he stayed on his feet and in control of his limbs long enough to reach Bria, who lay in a crumpled heap, soaked through by sea spray. His knees scraped against wood as he fell to the floor to check on her. His hands scrambled to find her wrist or her neck or some other pulse point so he could ensure her heart was still beating, the whole time cursing himself under his breath.

Maura.

Collins.

Bria.

Declan.

How many people would Tommy let down before his last breath?

"Thoughts like that won't help you," said a stern but kind voice behind him. Of course Renna would be listening in on his thoughts.

"Yes," she said.

"I didn't ask you anything," Tommy said without turning to her.

She knelt down, keeping a respectful distance between them. "I don't listen in unless I have cause to—"

"I don't care," he muttered as he leaned forward to pick up the limp fae before standing. She felt so similar to Maura in his arms, and he tried not to think about the youngest sister who had fallen first on this cursed course. Waiting beside the door to the officers' quarters, he ground out a command for Renna to open the door.

She remained silent as she obliged, entering the small room and holding the door open for him. Tommy surveyed the room briefly. Collins hadn't budged since being brought in, which was fortunate since the ship was still pitched at a sharp angle. The cot near the ceiling was too high for him to lift Bria into easily at this angle. When Renna moved to lay out bedding on the floor, he nearly thanked her for invading his thoughts again.

With Bria lying down, looking as though she was taking a midday nap, Tommy continued to monitor her shallow breathing.

"Will they be okay?" he asked.

"I believe so," she replied, sounding more relaxed than the current situation warranted.

Pivoting on his heel, he turned to her awkwardly as the ship continued to circle the maelstrom. "It's not good."

"You know it's not."

"So how do we get out of this?" he asked. They had no wind, no weapons with which to fight the creature. There was no escape from the trap the creature had snared them in. Renna didn't answer, at least not with words, her eyes closing and her lips tightening into a line. "So that's it then. And exactly why am I not supposed to blame myself for this? Why?"

His nails dug into his palms as he tightened his hands into fists and inched closer to her. She didn't back away.

"A solution may still present itself," she said, and the optimism in her words punched through his chest. How could she be so calm? They were circling down toward certain death, and she acted as though they had simply run out of cheese or misplaced a favorite book. In answer to his silent chatter, she said, "I'm calm, Tommy, because the opposite won't help any of us right now."

"So we simply take a stroll out on the deck and hope for this *solution* to fall on us? Is that what I'm to do, Renna?" She didn't respond with anything more than a blink, so he continued, stepping closer still. "I am captain right now, and I am failing everyone. Why Declan ever named me his quartermaster, I'll never know. If he were here—"

"But he's not. You are." Renna's tone took on a new edge. "And if you give into those thoughts, if you let them become the truth you see in yourself, you will surely fail. But what did you tell Aoife earlier?" She paused, as if listening to some far-off whisper. "'*We fight. Until someone wins.*' Well, Captain, no one has won this fight just yet. So if you don't mind, take your own damn advice, stop wallowing in your self-pity, and think. Not of what Declan would do or what any other pirate would do, but what you can do right now."

He didn't say another word but stormed past her and out onto the deck.

Where he was going or what he was going to do, he wasn't entirely sure, but he hoped some idea would come to him as he returned to the helm. Mikkel came up from below decks just as Tommy rounded the corner to the quarterdeck stairs.

"Tommy," he said, grabbing his arm and stopping him from ascending.

"What is it?"

"I have an idea."

"Well, bring it with you," he said and motioned for the man to follow him. Once they were at the helm, he looked from Gavin, who struggled to keep the wheel steady, to Aoife, who was holding on to one of the spindles of the railing. Her head was down, but her eyes were open, staring at the deck before her. "Go on, Mikkel."

"I've seen these whirlpools before. Not of this magnitude, of course, but back home in Turvala, they sprang up often, and it was part of our—"

Tommy held up a hand to stop the man's rambling. "You know how to escape it?" Reflexively he turned to look at the churning water they were caught in. How long had they been trapped? Felt like nearly an hour, but they were still fairly close to the surface.

"Aye. Though I've only ever done it in a small fishing dinghy with oars to propel us out. We don't have any oars."

He was rambling again.

"Explain."

"We get it to spit us out."

Of course this is when the man would be brief.

"And how do we do that exactly?"

"We need to position ourselves near the outer edge of it and keep our heading in the same direction as the currents, until we pick up enough speed that we get tossed outside of its grips."

Tommy and Gavin looked at each other. "Could it..." Tommy started to ask.

Gavin offered a shrug. "We don't have any other options at the moment."

"Try it," Tommy said with a determined nod. Mikkel turned to leave, but Tommy stopped him. "Stay. We'll need you to tell us when we need to make our move to be...spit out, as you said."

"Aye," Mikkel replied, though he didn't look too thrilled at the order to remain here, his face becoming paler than usual and taking on a slight tinge of green.

No one spoke as the ship continued on its path. Around and around. Gavin moved the wheel to stop fighting the current, and Tommy wondered if it felt as backwards to Gavin as it did to him. With the change to the rudder, they picked up speed. Tommy couldn't see how this would keep them from getting pulled down into the dark pit at the center, but Mikkel seemed confident, and as Gavin had said, they had no other option.

So he waited and breathed. They were creeping down the steep walls of the whirlpool, little by little, and Tommy eyed Mikkel. "What—" he started.

Mikkel stopped him with a raised hand, paused, and then shouted to Gavin, "Now! Starboard!" Before Gavin could voice his request for help, Mikkel sprang forward and grabbed the wheel with him. Both men pulled and pushed, trying to get the ship to turn away from the maelstrom, and Tommy had nearly given up hope of this working when the ship made her escape. It was as if the fast-moving water had indeed tossed them aside, like someone spitting out a seed.

The seas they settled in were so calm, Tommy might have thought the entire ordeal with the whirlpool had been a figment of his imagination.

"Shouldn't we move?" Aoife asked as she attempted to pull herself to a standing position. Gavin rushed over to offer her his good arm, and she thanked him quietly before raising her eyes to Tommy and Mikkel. But it was Gavin who answered her.

"Aye. We should, but with no wind and no fae to summon any, we are dead in the water."

Tommy stepped forward, eying their helmsman. "You couldn't find a better phrase to use?"

Gavin offered an apology, but Aoife's voice drowned it out. "He's not wrong though. Is he? I mean, it's not as though we've killed the beast. We've probably made it angry."

At her words, Tommy instinctively turned to look over his shoulder to see what had happened to the whirlpool. He blinked several times. It wasn't possible. Pivoting, he spun around completely, nearly smacking an elbow into Mikkel as he did.

"What in the..." Aoife spoke the exact words Tommy had been thinking.

"How?" Gavin asked as he stepped up beside Tommy, who had frozen in the middle of the quarterdeck and now stared out at the calm, dark teal waters of the Aisling Sea.

No churning, spinning, or foaming.

Nothing.

It was still as glass, the blue sky and billowing clouds above reflected perfectly on its surface. If the creature was toying with them as Tommy suspected, it was doing a damn good job of it. His heart pounded. His breathing sped up. His eyes scanned the waters. It was going to come back, and now they had no defense against it. No offensive capabilities either.

Aoife and Gavin gasped, stopping the thrumming of his heart cold, and he turned once more. Mikkel growled out a curse seconds before throwing himself across the quarterdeck and down the stairs, calling out commands on the way.

Tommy swallowed hard as he watched water cascade down from the monster as it rose from the surface. It was like the sea itself was draining, its level dropping to reveal an island of flesh underneath. The tentacles themselves—which now remained hidden in the sea—had been terrifying enough, but the sight of the creature emerging gave that word a new meaning, chilling the very blood in his veins. The kraken's head—or was that its body?—was radically different from the smooth-skinned fish they had caught off the western coast of Cregah when he was a kid. Instead, its flesh jutted out in sharp, haphazard angles between the pits and craters that left darkened shadows all over its grayish-purple skin. Around its eyes —two pits of blackness that would have looked completely empty had light not bounced off their slimy outer layer—the skin lightened from purple to brown before turning a sickening yellow, giving the monster the appearance of a massive bruise in various stages of healing.

A bruise with teeth.

Teeth—row upon row of teeth—which looked more like hundreds of snake's fangs, filled the cavernous mouth that remained half-submerged in the sea. With horror, Tommy watched as the water began to rush toward the spear-lined cavern. It was pulling them in.

He had no oars.
No wind.
No magic.
No idea what to do.

CHAPTER 34
CAIT

CAIT AND ADLER had walked along the trail—if one could call it that—for a couple of hours and still hadn't come upon Penny and the pirates. She was about to break the silence and express her doubt, when a turn in the path thrust them onto another. While it was far from being as well-kept as the roads and trails leading to the council hall, this new path, with its distinct outline, was a welcome improvement over the one they'd been stumbling down.

She hesitated at the edge, and Adler did the same. To the right, about a hundred paces away, this new path ended abruptly at a large boulder. Before Cait could begin to ponder why a path would simply stop, her eyes caught the light that lay beyond the rock. A clearing. No... If her eyes could be trusted, it looked like a road.

If the pirates had brought Penny this way, it seemed improbable they would have taken her to a main road. Or even a side road.

Adler must have seen the same thing and come to the same conclusion, because he tapped Cait on the shoulder and gestured to the left with his head. Not waiting for her agreement, he started off in that direction. Cait growled in the back of her throat at his presumption that she would simply follow him. Was he being disrespectful of her leadership? He hadn't grown up on Cregah, hadn't been raised under its matriarchal rule. Perhaps in Daorna the roles were reversed, and certainly he hadn't had any women in his crew on Tiernen's ship.

Or he's confident you were smart enough to understand why he took this route.

Either way, his motive didn't matter when an innocent citizen was about to be killed. Cait had sacrificed Penny; her fate had been sealed as soon as Cait had chosen her. There had always been a risk they wouldn't be able to catch them in time, that this whole plan was destined to fail.

Following Adler, she pushed herself to stay on his heels, desperate not to lose track of him as well. After traveling for several minutes down the path, Cait swore she heard voices up ahead. She reached up a hand and pulled on the back of Adler's shirt. He stopped and looked at her over his shoulder.

With a finger to her lips, she urged him to remain quiet as she crept forward, continuing to listen for the sound she'd heard. But all she could make out was the soft padding of her boots on the leaf-covered ground. Adler silently came up beside her and joined her in listening. Waiting.

There.

Voices. Unmistakable.

She caught Adler's attention, grateful to witness a glimmer of hope in his eyes. He nodded toward the voices as his arm swung wide, inviting her to lead the way. She obliged, but when his other hand landed on the small of her back, she stopped and turned to him in confusion and curiosity.

The warmth from his touch disappeared as quickly as it had arrived, and he pulled his mouth into a grimace—more sheepish and apologetic than disgusted. He mouthed an apology, and because she couldn't think of anything else to do, she offered a one-shouldered shrug before continuing on down the path.

A few voices ahead of them became clearer, but Penny's didn't seem to be one of them. Either they were too late, or the pirates had simply knocked her unconscious or otherwise quieted her. She still couldn't decipher what they were saying, but they seemed to be finding some part of their task humorous, as every few words were interrupted by light laughter.

A few more near-silent steps and Cait caught a glimpse of the men through the branches of the pines. They stood in a clearing, bathed in sunlight. Beyond them came a steady thrum of sound, like a hand passing through sand, but louder.

The sea.

They were at the coast.

Or at least the cliffs that made up this part of the coast.

Adler stood close to Cait, his shoulder pressing into hers as he watched the scene with her. The two pirates were chatting at the edge of the cliff, except it wasn't the edge, for the ground stretched out beyond where they stood.

"It's a pit cave," Cait said, not realizing she'd spoken aloud until Adler responded with a single syllable of agreement.

"I've heard of this place," he said, lowering his mouth close to her ear so he wouldn't have to risk speaking louder than necessary. His whisper came out strained. "Pirates don't talk about it much. A mention here and there. After a few cups of rum, secrets come out eventually."

Cait turned her chin slightly toward him. "If they've spoken about it, why doesn't everyone know by now?"

It was his turn to shrug. "Perhaps no one trusts a man who reeks of drink."

He had a point. The council must be trusting the pirates to keep their mouths shut—in exchange for safe haven while in port—knowing if they ever spilled their secrets while intoxicated, few would believe them.

"What is it?" Cait asked, even though she already had a good idea.

Adler didn't berate her at all but provided her with a straight answer. "The graveyard. Or one of them, I imagine. They used to *exile* people in actual fields, so I've heard, but eventually the exiles became so frequent, they needed a more inconspicuous location."

"How—" Having lived her whole life under the guise of peace, even losing her parents to the council, it was nearly impossible for Cait to grasp the reality of where they were and what they were seeing.

"That hole. Where they stand." Adler gestured with his hands as if pushing away an invisible attacker.

Cait's breath caught, and although some part of her was ashamed for being shocked and horrified by this truth, another part of her gave thanks that life with the Rogues—and the knowledge of what the council did—hadn't desensitized her too much.

Until it hit her.

If this was where they exiled citizens, then she was likely staring at the last place her parents had taken their final breaths before being—

She forced her eyes shut against the painful sight. She hadn't cried in years, and while the tears for her mother and father had long since dried up, grief she had thought she'd conquered welled up in her throat.

I'm going to be sick.

What would Adler think if she broke down here?

Adler.

Cait's gut tightened with another wave of sadness. It had been so many years since she'd lost her parents—and years since she'd essentially lost Declan—and though time could only dampen grief and not erase it, she could not fathom being here just one week after losing a loved one as he had. She turned to him, expecting to see some sign of mourning, but his expression was blank. She fought to conceal her shock. He might as well have been back at the pub cleaning up.

"How are you so calm?" she asked.

He breathed deep before whispering back, "Looks can be deceiving, love."

When his blue eyes met hers, she tried to see what might be hiding behind them, if only to know she wasn't standing here alone getting her heart shredded and reopening old scars she'd tried so hard to ignore.

But his scars are fresh.

"Don't worry about me," he said with a wink, though no humor lined his words and no playfulness flashed across his features. "I'm a big boy. I'll be okay. And we have a job to do. Can't do that if I'm busy licking my wounds."

"I just can't—" He raised his hand and looked away, and she took a step toward him. To do what, she didn't know.

"I'm okay," he repeated, and she wondered if he was trying to convince himself of that as much as her.

Cait wanted to say something, to do something. Their sorrow, similar though not shared, was almost palpable in the air between them. It sent pinpricks up her arms and down her spine. She'd pushed aside all of these kinds of feelings because she'd had to. She'd had a job to do, to run the pub and care for Declan. Not that she'd done well with the latter. Never had she found anyone who understood her pain quite like this. Not Lucan, not Kira, not the twins, not any of the Rogues. They'd all lost someone—or multiple someones—but none of them managed their grief as she did. Others mourned outwardly, breaking out into tears randomly, for years upon years, but she hadn't the luxury of time and rest. She couldn't afford to be vulnerable or weak.

And that was what she saw now in Adler.

That same determination to keep moving, to keep going, to not forget those lost but to honor them by continuing to live. Those who mourned privately still mourned; she knew that all too well.

"I'm sorry for assuming you were feeling nothing. That was callous of me."

He lowered his head to look her straight in the eye and wrapped his hands lightly around her arms. "You have nothing to apologize for. I'm not sure whether to be flattered that you care for me or offended that you think so little of me."

Cait tightened her lips into a line, unsure of what to say and not trusting herself to not say something stupid. Again.

Adler straightened and dropped his hands. "Before we start swapping sob stories, we should probably focus, no?"

With a nod, Cait moved her attention back to the pirates, who were still chatting quietly. "Where is she? Do you see her?" Her questions came out as a breath, so light she didn't think he'd heard her until he moved up beside her. From the corner of her eye, she watched him crane his neck slightly this way and that to peer around the branches and scan the clearing.

"There," he said, pointing out something to the right.

On the ground a few paces away from the pirates, Penny lay. Whether she was still alive or already dead, Cait couldn't tell from this vantage point. Why hadn't they tossed her over yet? Why had they left her on the ground? Didn't they have other things to do?

As if Adler could hear her thoughts, he said, "They're probably waiting for her to regain consciousness. They want her awake when they..." He didn't finish the sentence, and Cait was glad for that.

"Any ideas?" she asked, shoving aside her embarrassment over asking him for help. She was the leader of the Rogues, and here she was asking for input from a pirate.

Adler pulled back and looked at her. "You mean the great Cait McCallagh doesn't have a plan already in mind?"

She rolled her eyes. "I wasn't supposed to be the one to do this, remember? It was to be the twins. And I don't dictate how they do their jobs. So no, I don't have a specific plan in mind."

"And I suppose pushing them into that chasm isn't acceptable?"

Cait shook her head.

"Then we will just have to knock them unconscious long enough to grab her."

"Except we need her awake first, remember? We need her to realize what was about to happen to her."

"Ah, right," Adler said. "Then we wait. They aren't going anywhere."

Looking back at the pirates, who were still chatting and laughing as if they weren't here to kill this woman for the council, Cait swallowed hard. "Why don't they wake her themselves?"

Beside her, Adler lowered himself to the ground and rested his back against a nearby tree where he could still keep an eye on their targets. "If I had to guess, they're in no hurry to get back to their post in town. The longer they stay here—the longer this takes them—the less work they have to do overall."

Cait glanced at him over her shoulder. "So pirates are lazy."

"No." He paused to pull one side of his mouth into a smirk. "Selfish and greedy? Sure. But lazy?" He shook his head.

Selfishness and greed certainly plagued many of the pirates she'd hosted in the pub over the years, but neither characteristic seemed to apply to the pirate accompanying her on this task.

Former pirate.

"Plus," he continued, "what would their incentive be to rush it? It's not like she's bothering them at the moment. Nor does the council offer bonuses for quickness. Or anything really."

Not bothering to say more, Cait simply shrugged and settled herself onto the ground, propping her elbows on her bent knees as she continued to watch for any sign Penny was waking. But the woman remained still, so still Cait seriously questioned whether she was still alive. If only there was some way to wake her without alerting her captors of their presence.

"So you and Lucan..." Adler said, his low voice barely hiding his amusement. "I take it you two aren't—"

"No. We aren't." Immediately her face grew warm, though the topic didn't warrant such a response.

A breath of a laugh escaped him. "So defensive. I hope he never hears you dismiss the idea so quickly. Men bruise easily, you know."

"He understands—"

"That you're not attracted to him. That's fair."

"You know that wasn't what I was going to say."

"Do I?" Adler looked pensively up to the treetops, his finger tapping against his lips. "Then why? And don't claim the *cause* doesn't allow for such things. I saw several pairings of Rogues at the ruins."

"It's just not something I'm looking for." Cait tried to appear as uninterested as possible. Not that she minded the discussion. It did help pass the time, but Adler seemed intent on not accepting her answers, and that was going to get old quickly.

"Ah, careful about that though. These things have a way of falling into your lap whether you're looking for them or not." He raised a brow, and Cait couldn't tell if he was still referring to Lucan or not.

"Is that how it went with Lani?" The words were out before Cait could rethink them. She'd been so desperate to divert attention away from her. Her discomfort must have shown on her face, because Adler laughed again, low enough to keep it hidden under the rumbling of the sea beyond.

"It's okay, love. I meant it when I told you not to worry about me." His smile remained, though his eyes seemed to dim.

"Would hate to think I bruised you so easily though."

"Well, now I am flattered. Thank you. But yes, to answer your question. That is basically how it happened between us."

Cait had no reply. She didn't even know why she'd asked the question in the first place, and it wasn't like her to slip up as much as she was, saying things without forethought.

It's just the stress.

Her stress had greatly increased over the past couple of days. Her mind was on high alert at all times, all her worries and concerns churning away, unwilling to be quieted or set aside, like they feared she'd forget about them if they didn't stay at the forefront of her mind.

"What about when this is all done though?" Adler's question snapped Cait's attention back to him.

"What about what?" Her brow tightened as she tried to remember what they'd been talking about. *You're losing it, Cait.*

Adler's smile returned, his dimples greeting her before they disappeared with his response. "You. Lucan. Future?"

"I don't see how that's any of your concern."

"Are you that repulsed by him that you refuse to talk about it?"

"Seems an odd topic given our current circumstances."

Adler's shoulders lifted in an easy shrug. "What can I say, love. I'm a bit of a romantic."

"I see." She glanced quickly past the trees into the clearing. The pirates were still talking, though they had taken to sitting on the ground. "So, how long do you think it will be, Mr. Romantic, before someone else falls in your lap?"

"The real question is when will I be ready to let someone stay once they've fallen."

Cait couldn't refrain from rolling her eyes at his confidence. She considered him carefully. Did he don this false bravado to hide a scorched heart? But all she saw in his jewel-like eyes was a sarcastic glint. Either he really hadn't been that hurt by Lani's death, or he had perfected his ability to hide himself from others.

Looks can be deceiving.

Perhaps he was right.

Adler must have noticed her scrutiny, because he raised a brow again and asked, "Not finding what you're seeking here?" and circled his hand in the air to indicate his face.

"I can't figure you out." Again, the words were out before she was able to stop them. What was happening to her?

"Well that was far more honest than I expected from the notorious leader of the Rogues. Speaking of which," he said, his expression darkening, "if you are indeed so notorious, why does the council not know who you are by now?"

Cait's mouth tightened as she shook her head. "I honestly don't know. Every day I wake up wondering if this will be the day they decide to make their move against me. So far, they haven't. And I can only assume either they're not as powerful as they've made themselves out to be, or they're waiting for the best moment to—"

"Spring their trap," Adler offered. It wasn't a question, but Cait still nodded. "So, what about me is tripping you up?"

He hadn't forgotten her stupid confession, and now he expected an explanation. Should she be honest with him? If she was going to work with him against the council, it seemed best to be able to trust him implicitly. And yet, regardless of her gut feeling that he could be trusted, she hadn't opened up to anyone but Lucan in years. Even before her parents had disappeared, she'd been a closed book. Some feelings and thoughts needed to be held close, protected. Even Lucan didn't know the extent of the dark thoughts she kept concealed, the ones she'd learned could be best hidden behind a quick wit, a sharp tongue, and a friendly smile.

Would she ever find someone she could share all of herself with? All of her inner demons and fears? Adler might understand her better than most, but it took more than common trauma to build a connection. And she wasn't sure she even wanted such a thing.

He asked you a simple question. He didn't request you court him. Get a hold of yourself.

"I just can't figure out if all this carefree attitude and easy smile"—she cleared her throat and gestured to his face with her hand—"is the real you or if it's a mask to cover someone who is still hurting."

"Why can't it be both?" Adler cocked his head.

"How would that work at all? How can the real you also be a mask? That doesn't make any sense."

"Doesn't it though? The mask we choose to wear around others is as much us as the emotions we hide. They don't have to be an either-or, mutually exclusive. After all, it's not as though we can steal the personalities of others."

"But we can pretend; we can put on an act. Are you claiming such is still reflective of our true self?"

"We cannot separate our personality from our words and actions even when we try. Some part of us will always seep through. Perhaps only a small part, but we cannot erase ourselves no matter how hard we might try or hope to."

Adler's explanation brought images of Declan to Cait's mind, and she contemplated how his actions had varied each time she'd seen him since his recent return to Cregah. How he had effectively been a different person during each visit. The confident, snarky pirate at the pub. The belligerent younger brother in her office. The concerned and doting lover with Aoife. They were all indeed him, each exaggerating a different part of his personality, but each a part of him regardless.

"Makes sense, I guess," she admitted. She rubbed a hand behind her neck, wishing Penny would wake already so they could get this over with and not have to continue this conversation.

Adler looked as though he was about to speak again, and she might have stopped him had another voice not sounded first.

"Up. Both of you." A pirate wearing the same yellow fabric as Penny's captors loomed over them as he emphasized the command with a wave of his knife.

CHAPTER 35
DECLAN

THE ENTRANCE to the Black Sound provided no indication of the darkness that resided within, nor did it match its moniker in the slightest. Something in the air soothed Declan's nerves, having the same calming effect as that of his mother's hand on his back when he'd had trouble falling asleep as a kid. The sun, still hours away from setting, shone through clouds high above the mountain peaks. The entire scene reflected perfectly in the still water of the sound. The sheer beauty of it all, combined with the rhythmic sound of their small boat's oars in the water, was strangely comforting.

With what Callum had explained about the sirens' tastes, this environment seemed counterproductive. If they desired the most sorrowful and regretful souls to come to them, why calm them first?

"Don't let it fool you," Callum said, his rough voice cutting through the tranquil atmosphere. "It's part of their devilry."

"Beautiful scenery and calm seas?"

"Aye. They may not use song to lure you in, but they have other ways of attracting their prey. Like offering a banquet of tantalizing food—"

"—only to poison it."

"Basically."

"And what type of poison should I expect to find?" He tried to keep the question casual, though his nerves were starting to fray despite their serene surroundings.

"I would not be surprised if we find your lass waiting for us. But remember, it isn't really her. Whatever you see in there isn't real. The longer you can resist the queen's baiting, the more time I'll have to locate the dagger, so I'd rather you not die too quickly."

"Well, I am rather fond of living."

"You won't be once she gets a hold of you."

"And we know for sure it will be the queen who—"

Callum gave a firm nod. "The queen is the only one with that strong of an ability. The others can't enter your mind like she can. They can pull your mind toward them, get you lost in what they offer, but only the queen can stow away in your thoughts, change them, make you see what isn't real, believe what isn't true."

Declan shivered reflexively and shifted to look at his companion. "How do you know so much about the sirens? How does anyone? They don't seem to be the type to suffer some to survive and leave."

"Seems it happened more often centuries ago, which is how we ended up with the various texts about them. Not that most folks see them as anything more than myths and legends. The sirens. The dagger. The dragons. Even the fae, to an extent, have become little more than fanciful tales. But there are still some who believe. Like you. And me."

"What makes you see it as truth and not a fable?"

Callum raised a brow. "I could ask the same of you."

Why did Declan believe the stories? He had honestly never asked himself that question or wondered what made him so different from the skeptics. Looking out over the prow of the boat and taking in the beauty around them, Declan chewed on the question.

His parents had always told him not to take anything at face value but to question everything, warning him that nothing could be trusted beyond family bonds. So when his schooling with his father had turned to the subject of the Aisling legends, he'd treated them as the opposite. *All legends have some truth to them.* His father had repeated this often, and Declan had taken it to heart.

Declan cleared his throat with a hoarse rumble and said, "My father."

"Same."

"And here I thought you were spawned from some devil." He tried to picture Callum as a child, sitting on a barstool like he had often done, being taught lessons by his own dad. It wasn't easy to imagine the pirate as a child, let alone one with a father and a family.

Callum said, "My father was one of the few to have seen them with his own eyes, to face them and live to tell the tale."

"And you believed him?"

"Of course. I had no reason not to. You believed yours."

"Why was he even up here? What happened to him? How did he survive?" The questions fell out of Declan's mouth, and an image of Aoife rambling flashed in his mind.

"It's the age-old story. Boy loves girl. Girl's father disapproves. Boy seeks treasure to prove his worth. He found a crew leaving Caprothe, heading north to Turvala. Convinced a few of the men to sneak away on one of the lifeboats to get to the sound and the legendary treasure. Out of the four who ventured in, only two came out, one of them being my father."

Like the four of us in this damned boat. Declan couldn't help but wonder which two—if any—would survive today.

Callum continued. "He managed to pocket a handful of gold coins before escaping, enough to support a wife and eventually a child."

"You."

"Aye." For a long while, Callum stared at the water, seeming lost in his story. "He never liked talking about his life before starting his family. Whenever I asked him to describe his childhood or how he had made his riches, he waved me off, saying it was of little interest, before diving into some fanciful tale of dragons and fae. But later, when I was grown, he and I shared a bottle of rum on the day we buried my mother. And he told me the tale of how he ended up in these waters, how the queen had appeared before them, how she had shown a different vision to each —dependent on their personal histories and pains. One of them went mad quickly, throwing himself into the water where the other sirens waited for him. Another fought against it as long as he could before breaking down into a heap of remorse and pain. They left him writhing on the stone while they watched him hungrily, like he was a roast turning over the fire. My father said he believed he was allowed to leave—along with the fourth, who was little more than a boy still—because his heart was untainted by darkness and had little appeal to the creatures. Whether that is true, I don't know, but that was the only reason he ever gave."

"And they simply let them leave? No sneaking away necessary?"

Callum pulled his mouth into a tight line before answering. "As far as I know, they granted them that gift. Though I don't know how much of a gift it was. His sleep was never restful. Always thrashing and screaming himself awake. He said he never regretted what he did, because it brought him my mother and me, but when he did finally pass, he seemed relieved and ready to leave it all behind him for some actual rest and peace."

Declan let the story soak in, picking out what might be helpful for him when he faced the queen and whatever tricks she had in store for him. He couldn't see any obvious holes in Callum's tale, but he heard his own father's reminder to question it all, always. Callum wouldn't like the one question he had, but even still, he needed to consider it, especially if Callum was as serious to get to the dagger as he claimed.

"And what if he was wrong? What if all the legends got it wrong?"

Callum simply raised a brow, though no annoyance showed on his face. "I've pondered that same thing all these years. But if all the stories describe the same thing, it is only logical that there would be at least a fair amount of truth to them."

"But couldn't the sirens use their compulsion powers to shape the survivors' stories to fit their needs?"

"Aye. Anything's possible. So we plan for the worst—that we are walking into an awful trap completely blind—but we hope for the best."

"You mean hope that I resist long enough for you to retrieve an enchanted dagger with the power to bring you victory over all your adversaries?"

"Pretty much."

"Great," Declan muttered under his breath. His skin should have been tingling with the anticipation of facing the queen, but whatever magic existed here had covered him in a blanket of comfort and calm. Though he consciously knew of the danger, his body refused to react or prepare for it. It was the perfect way to have your prey arrive at your doorstep, so comfortable that resistance was unlikely.

Put you at ease before they rip you to pieces.

They spent the rest of the journey in silence, the four men in the small boat casually watching the scenery as it passed by. How mere rock and water could appear so majestic, Declan couldn't explain. So simple yet so grand. He peered up at the rock wall closest to him and wondered if anyone at the top was able to see them. That question led to several more pressing ones.

Where did the sirens live exactly?

What would they show him?

Would he survive?

He marveled at how his body and mind didn't react naturally. His heart rate and breathing remained steady, his mind gliding from question to question as easily as their boat through the water. He should be preparing himself mentally for the fight that lay ahead, but his mind refused to acknowledge the coming threat, as if he was approaching the peace of his cove back on Cregah.

The cove.

Though the memory flooded his mind, he didn't drown in it as he had every time before. He saw her face, his bloody hands, him pleading on his knees, and her walking away from him, all as though it had happened to complete strangers.

No emotional response.

No pain.

Only numbness.

All part of the plan.

The waters of the sound cut through the land, winding around the cliffs. Callum had his men row them as close to the inside of each turn to cut down on time. After an hour, Declan opened his mouth to ask when he expected them to arrive, but just as he did, they rounded another corner and the scenery changed, the narrow passage between the cliffs opening up into a vast body of water. It was surrounded by the same tall mountains, but they no longer dropped straight down into the water. Instead, beaches peppered the shoreline all around the basin.

But unlike the beaches he'd visited, these lay barren. No trees. No animals.

No animals anywhere, actually. No birds in the sky, and the crystal-clear water showed no sign of fish.

But the water was far from empty.

From his perch, Declan spotted the remains of boats, some with holes in them and others completely intact. How many captains and crews had been lured into these pristine waters, called by the calm serenity within, only to end up at the bottom of this watery crater? It didn't appear particularly deep, but it was far from peaceful.

A flash of light danced through the water, under their boat. Not a light, Declan realized, but a reflection of it. *Sirens.* For the first time since they'd arrived, he felt a twinge of panic.

A splash of water to his left pulled his attention, and he turned in time to see delicate fins, feathery and flowing, slide below the surface. Callum's men stopped rowing, and Declan waited for the captain to bark at them to resume. But the order never came.

Callum sat as still as his men. No one moved. Declan wasn't sure any of them blinked or breathed. Their eyes were wide, their fists tight.

The boat jolted. Declan clamped his hands down on either side to steady himself.

Before he could say anything, the boat jerked again, this time struck from the other side. The once still water now churned around them as tails flicked in and out of the water.

Declan was nearly convinced his heart had altogether stopped when something emerged to his right. Not a tail but a woman. Or what looked like one. To an extent. Gold hair, wet and clinging to her, framed her face. Her otherworldly beauty was marred only by her horrifying silver eyes, which were so light the irises were nearly invisible. Giving them a smile with her deep pink lips, she raised her arms out of the water, snatched the rower closest to her, and pulled him under. The water swallowed his screams.

But even with her unnatural speed, Declan hadn't missed how her smile had shifted into a deathly grin before she plunged her teeth, terrifyingly sharp, into the man, ripping the flesh between his neck and shoulder and turning the water around them red with his blood.

Declan's heartbeat thundered in his ears as he waited for the next attack, wondering who would be snatched next.

But the boat went still. The surface of the water became glassy and calm once again—albeit no longer clear—as the sirens retreated from them. Still, no one spoke.

Don't be so surprised, Declan.

This had been his expectation, after all. This was what they did.

Yet he remained stunned, staring at the water where the man had slipped below, broken and dying. Declan hadn't known the man, and he had no reason to feel any remorse over the loss. But it brought questions all the same.

Would anyone mourn that pirate?

Had he been supporting a family?

Was he of the rotten and vile variety?

Will anyone mourn you?

He hoped so.

With a shake of his head, he snapped himself back to the matter at hand.

"Do you know where to go, exactly?" Declan whispered out of the corner of his mouth, but Callum didn't respond. Declan tried to see what had caught his attention, but there didn't appear to be anything of interest on the far-off beach of bone-white sand.

Declan waved a hand in front of Callum's face, but the man's eyes—though they blinked—didn't shift away from the beach, which lay straight ahead.

Declan.

His name was whispered into his mind in a voice decidedly more feminine than his own. It sent him spinning his head round to see if someone was nearby, but the only other person there besides Callum was the remaining crewman, who had somehow found the wherewithal to resume rowing.

Declan.

The voice came again, all too familiar to him, like the whisper of a pleasant dream that fled with the fluttering open of one's eyes, comforting but blurred, leaving behind only a trace of the emotion it had caused and no clue as to its origin or essence.

How could you?

Declan stilled. He didn't need to ask for clarification, though had this been Callum—or even Tommy—posing the question and not an eerily familiar voice speaking to him within his mind, he would have made some snarky comment.

You said you loved me.

Declan's chin snapped up. They had rowed almost all the way across the water now, and the beach with white sand lay less than fifty feet ahead of them.

And it was no longer empty.

Movement in the water to his right, and then to the left, nearly pulled his attention away, but even if a siren were to appear on the boat beside him, he would not be able to look away from the woman who stood on the beach.

This wasn't real. It couldn't be. It was merely part of the sirens' games.

But it seemed too real.

She seemed too real.

It had been a week—or more?—since he'd last seen her, but there was the face that appeared every time he closed his eyes. The sweet freckles sprinkled across her nose and cheeks. The clothes he'd helped her with that night. And it was the same look of pity and disappointment in those gold-flecked green eyes. She didn't speak. She didn't move.

But she spoke to him all the same.

I trusted you.

She wasn't real.

She wasn't real.

She wasn't real.

It wasn't her voice.

It wasn't her on the beach.

The sirens were shifters and tricksters, feeding on heartache and suffering. This was a siren, not Aoife, and yet the sight of her stabbed him in the chest, hollowing it out just as she had that night in the cove.

I can't.

Declan couldn't pull his eyes away as they rowed closer. When the boat brushed up against the soft beach, his limbs remained still. More from remorse than fear.

Odd. He'd thought he would feel hope when he next saw her. Hope for redemption and forgiveness.

But that hope was dead. Pulled into the bloody waters behind him.

"Didn't you miss me, Declan?" This time she spoke aloud, her lips grabbing his attention as they formed the words. He didn't answer, but he couldn't look away from the sweet face he'd been longing to see again.

Something pressed against his back, and before he could protest, it pushed him forward until he had no other choice but to step over the side of the boat and head ashore. He didn't need to look behind to know it was Callum who had forced him out, but now, having seen the sirens' territory, he didn't know how the pirate hoped to find the dagger. It could be anywhere, from the mess of rotting wood in the water to somewhere on this barren beach.

Declan's feet splashed in the water as he walked slowly up the sand toward Aoife.

Not Aoife, he reminded himself.

But as he got closer, he couldn't help but marvel at the resemblance. The waves of her hair, still cut short. The tiny quiver of her lips. The desperate tension of her fisted hand at her chest.

Yearning to touch her once more, to hold her again and soothe away the sorrow on her face, he lifted a hand, but before his fingers met the skin of her cheek, he froze, blinked, and tilted his head.

He dropped his hand and donned his favorite smirk.

"That is quite the trick, I must say. Near perfect."

Aoife lowered her head into her hands as if ashamed, but when she straightened once again, smoothing her hair back as she ran her fingers through it, every familiar feature dissolved into someone else's. Her unruly brown hair now lay well past her shoulders in dark waves—a raven black that shone blue or purple depending on how the sun's rays hit it. Aoife's gold-green eyes darkened to a haunting deep purple, and her freckled skin became as pristine as the sea's surface on a windless morning. Her pirate's attire dissolved into a black dress that plunged to her navel and didn't cover much beyond that. Before, her expression had been filled with anguish and regret, but now it showed little more than a sinister wickedness and delight.

"I knew it would be hard to fool you, Declan." The woman's sultry voice no longer matched the one he loved, though it was nearly as lovely. A twisted sort of lovely. "But I had you at least for a moment. Perhaps two."

"Not surprising for one of such power, Your Majesty," Declan said, though he kept his features cold and emotionless.

"So you have heard of me then. And you still came to visit."

Lifting a shoulder, he tightened his lips. "Honestly, I thought you'd be taller. With a crown."

"And I thought you'd be more of a challenge," she said, the fire in her eyes seeming to dim as her features sagged with disappointment.

"Well, the day is still young, and I've only just arrived. Perhaps I'll surprise you yet."

The queen turned before he finished speaking and began to walk toward the face of the cliff, calling back to him, "Are you coming? Or am I mistaken and you're not here for the dagger?"

Declan glanced over his shoulder, expecting to see Callum and his remaining man already rowing away to start their search for that very blade. But Callum and his crewman had stepped onto the beach, and both wore blank expressions ill-fitting for the situation.

"You too, Callum," the queen called in a song-like tone. But only Callum moved, leaving his man behind and walking past Declan without any acknowledgment. Declan knew he should move; he should obey, get this over with. But he couldn't look away from the last man standing tall on the beach, the water lapping at his ankles as he stared straight ahead.

Even when the sirens surfaced beside him, the man's eyes remained blank and unseeing.

Declan couldn't budge as he watched the sirens emerge from the water. Three. Four. Five deathly beautiful women hauled their bodies over the white sand, dragging themselves forward with their slender forearms. At their hips, their pearl-like skin shifted into mesmerizing scales of shimmering golds and blues and teals and reds. Legends told of their fish-like bodies, but nothing could have prepared Declan for witnessing it firsthand. Nor for the transformation that occurred as they exited the water, scales and fins melting away until they stood on lithe, feminine legs. In any other scenario, Declan might have found their unabashed nakedness appealing, but knowing their intentions, his gut twisted, and bile climbed his throat.

When they made their move, Declan forced himself to turn away and tried to block out the sound of tearing flesh and tortured screams. But he couldn't, even as he quickened his pace to follow after the queen and Callum.

After a hundred or so paces, the sickening sounds behind him faded away, though he wasn't sure if it was due to the distance or because the sirens had finished their meal. He focused on his surroundings and found nothing but water, sand, and rock.

No doorways. No obvious secret nooks where she might conduct her ghastly business in private. Though if Callum's father's account was accurate, this siren didn't shy away from an audience.

"So, what's your name?" Declan asked as he caught up with them.

The queen spun around on him, and he nearly ran into her. Her brow tightened. "I thought you said you'd heard of me."

"I only noted your height. You assumed the other."

She simply blinked. Once. Twice. Aoife would have rolled her eyes.

She's not Aoife.

"No, I'm not Aoife. I'm Triss."

Her intense glare burned a hole right through him, but he refused to flinch, even when her eyes roamed over his face, her head leaning from one side to the other.

The seductive scent of mountain mist and iron engulfed him. And then she had him. Her hand gripped his hair and yanked his head back. She wet her lips with her tongue in a slow, deliberate motion, like she was looking upon a gourmet meal.

Stepping closer, she let her breath caress his cheek for one long, slow, painful moment before she whispered to him. "I'm going to have fun with you, Declan McCallagh."

CHAPTER 36
AOIFE

Of all the visions Aoife had had for her future, being swallowed whole by a legendary creature of the sea had never occurred to her. Yet here she was. Staring into the maw of a beast she'd thought only myth until recently. She'd never considered herself brave. Not when she'd run. Not when she'd approached Callum. Not when she'd stood up to her mother in the library. Not even when she had tried to help Collins during the kraken's initial attack.

And even if she had found some courage hidden somewhere within her, no doubt it would have melted away in this moment as the abyss yawned before her.

No one moved around her, causing her to wonder if these men—pirates who had seen more than their fair share of danger and risk—had lost their fearlessness. She hoped not.

Although her feet remained frozen to the deck—her eyes wide and her fingers trembling at her sides—her mind raced on, searching for some way they could survive this. Explosives were not available, and their cannons would be of little help —if they had any ammunition remaining after all the shots they'd already fired. Bria and Maura had collapsed from overexertion, and Renna's talent didn't provide much help in this situation.

Aoife might have wept. She wanted to, actually. At least crying would be doing something more than simply standing here, lifeless. But she had gone completely numb, and even her anxiety refused to manifest, leaving her an empty shell, as if her soul had already decided to pack up and vacate.

"Declan."

His name fell from her lips in a whisper, and her mind flooded with memories of him. The cove. The alley. His cabin. The birthday party. The beach in Foxhaven. The kiss—the real one. The looks of protectiveness and remorse and then despair as she walked away. The memories gave way to nightmares. Declan alone in the brig of a ship, being tortured by Callum. Then him standing before the sirens awaiting their attacks.

Every thought grieved her until she envisioned him lying bloody and lifeless on whatever sands the sirens called home. Then the grief turned to anger, a burning rage below her ribs that slowly spread throughout her body, like a deep well of boiling water had been unstopped within her. It now rushed to fill every bit of her. She gritted her teeth as she clenched her eyes shut and closed her fists tightly. The heat intensified, but instead of fighting it, she welcomed it.

While numbness had its uses, so did rage.

And perhaps rage was what she needed right now.

With her chin lowered, Aoife opened her eyes and focused on the beast. Slowly, little by little, it pulled the ship closer. Or perhaps time simply seemed to slow down as she focused on her target. She had no idea what she hoped to accomplish simply by staring at it angrily, but she was willing to try anything at this point. She might not be fae, but fae weren't the only ones with powers. Maybe Aoife had something hidden deep within her, something that could help her friends and Declan.

Tommy had moved around behind her to whisper with Gavin, but Aoife couldn't hear what they said. Then all sounds were drowned out by the rush of water around the hull. They were picking up speed.

For Declan.

For me.

For us all.

She concentrated on the creature's mouth, imagined pulling out every fang, envisioned taking those fangs and stabbing its haunting eyes with them. But nothing happened. Not even a wiggle from the sharp teeth that threatened them. So she moved on to the water. If she couldn't control living things, maybe she could do something with the elements like Bria could. So she let the sound of the sea engulf her, envisioned it shifting its course and carrying them away from the danger instead of toward it.

And she felt like an imbecile.

More so as she noticed they seemed to be increasing in speed, as though the kraken had noticed her attempts to thwart it and had intensified its efforts.

Her rage dissolved. Like a candle being snuffed out.

Only her hopelessness remained.

What was she even hoping to do? She was nothing but a human, awkward and clumsy. Humans didn't possess supernatural qualities.

Her chin dropped to her chest in defeat, and she once again let her eyelids fall closed. Words of regret and guilt and sorrow echoed in her mind as she prepared for whatever end was about to befall her and her friends.

Sucking in a deep breath, she recalled her favorite memories.

Her and Lani enjoying a picnic lunch on the lawn of the council hall, lying down in the soft grass and pointing out the shapes of clouds to each other and laughing at the ridiculous stories they created from what they saw. And then Declan under a sea of stars at night, his hands taking hers as she spun out of Tommy's grasp, seeing that nervous spark in his eyes.

Her hand reached up to his face, to cup his jaw in her palm, but before her fingers could touch him, two large splashes in the water sent the memory fleeing, and her eyes flashed open.

There, right in the middle of the monster's mouth, water sprayed up from the sea. Before she had any time to ponder what could have caused that, the loudest sounds she'd ever heard came at her—louder even than the cannons below decks all firing at once—and before she could determine what was happening, the world seemed to fly at her.

Water crashed over her. So much water she thought she'd fallen into the sea or the ship had sunk below the surface. But then something else began to fall. It splattered onto the deck, making a squishing sound that had Aoife's stomach turning even before she opened her eyes.

All around her the deck was covered in chunks of flesh—purple and gray, fatty, slimy globs—resting in black pools of what looked more like, well, Aoife didn't know what. It was thicker than normal blood, and it clung to the wooden planks of the deck, adhering the bits of meat to the ship.

"Aoife! Are you okay?" The voice pulled her attention away from the gooey mess, and she turned to find Gavin rushing over to her, careful not to step in any of the creature's remains.

"Yeah," Aoife said, blinking. "I think so. What was that?"

"But—you should be hurt."

He looked genuinely concerned, but still, his lack of confidence in her was rather offensive.

"Gee, thanks, Gavin." Before he could respond, she swung her head back to the sea where the kraken had been waiting to swallow them. The surface of the Aisling looked much like the deck of the *Siren's Song*—littered with small pieces of the creature's remains.

"No, Aoife. Look!" Gavin had stepped closer to her, but she turned to find him keeping a wider berth than she'd expected. His finger pointed at her torso as he spoke again. "That doesn't hurt?"

Looking down, Aoife realized she had not miraculously avoided being hit by any of the falling pieces of carcass as she'd originally thought. The kraken's thick blood had splattered across her clothes, from her chest down to her boots, making her look like one of the spotted pigs some townspeople kept in Morshan for food. She reached her fingers toward one of the splotches and saw Gavin's whole body tensing. That's when she realized the blood had hit more than her clothes. A part of her arm just below the elbow felt stiff with quickly drying blood.

She looked up at her friend slowly. "Is this the same thing—" Her eyes dropped to his arm, which still lay in a sling across his ribs.

He gave a nod, his eyes wide and roaming over her.

"Well, it doesn't hurt. I'm fine." Twisting and bending her arm, she demonstrated her point. "I can't say it's particularly flattering, but it's at least painless."

Gavin didn't release his breath as she'd expected, and his shoulders remained tight. Every muscle in his body was pulled taut, actually. He seemed to be leaning away from her, but Aoife assured herself it was her imagination. He was her friend after all.

"Wait!" She spun around on the deck, taking in the state of things. Somehow the entire ship beyond the helm appeared untouched, unmarred by the gore she stood in. "What happened? And how did you not get hit with any of this, whatever it is? And where's Tommy?"

"He ran down to check on Maura." Gavin's shoulders loosened enough to offer a shrug before he said, "I don't know how I got so lucky, to be honest. But I think they might be able to answer your first question." He pointed toward the starboard side.

A ship, larger than the *Siren's Song*, sailed toward them. No, it didn't exactly *sail*, for their gold-lined sails hung lifeless. Long oars protruded from small openings in the sides of the hull, cutting through the surface of the sea and bringing the ship closer far faster than Aoife would have thought possible. Especially with no wind.

"Who?" she whispered, but it didn't matter if Gavin had heard her or not, because the answer came on its own.

There at the prow of the ship, Captain Halloran stood in an understated dark gray coat well-fitted to her curves, with a gold sash tied around her waist. Even from this distance, Aoife found her intimidating. The captain's eyes were hidden in the shade cast by her large hat, and her lips were curled up into a half-smile. Raising her hand to her hat, Halloran dipped her chin in greeting to Aoife and Gavin.

Aoife could have sworn the woman's smile grew.

Gavin took in a breath. "I should get the captain." He started to step away, but Aoife held out her arm to stop him, careful not to touch him as she did.

"No. He's had a tough day—as we all have—but I think we can let him rest, can't we? We can handle this. I mean, what's the likelihood she's here to do us harm?"

Gavin seemed to consider her words, narrowing his eyes slightly, but said nothing for a moment. He finally blinked and shook his head, saying, "Aye. You're right." He started toward the stairs before turning to add, "And if you're wrong, I'm not taking the blame."

Captain Halloran and her three officers had boarded the *Siren's Song*, and now they stood facing Aoife and Gavin on the deck. Her officers were just as imposing as their captain. Though two of them weren't much taller than Aoife, she still felt quite small in comparison.

"Glad to see you again," Aoife said, extending her hand to the captain.

Halloran glanced down at it, her eyes roving over Aoife's gore-spattered arm and attire before she pulled back one corner of her mouth and raised a brow.

Aoife, flustered and embarrassed, clasped her hands behind her back with a quiet apology.

"I'm not one to normally be so picky about cleanliness," Halloran said, "but I'd rather not risk any injuries from that stuff." The captain's eyes narrowed slightly, and Aoife waited for the inevitable question, the same one Gavin had asked. But instead, Halloran turned to Gavin with a shallow nod. "Apologies for not getting here faster."

Gavin straightened but remained several inches shorter than the captain. "No apologies necessary, Captain. You arrived just in time. One more moment and we would have been in the gullet of that beast."

"And now we're wearing it," Aoife said.

Someone had to keep the mood light, right?

Gavin ignored her comment and cleared his throat. "But how did you find us exactly?"

"More importantly," Aoife interjected, "how did you save us?"

Halloran looked from one to the other before asking, "And where is your captain?"

"Tommy is—" Aoife started to reply, but Halloran's warm hazel eyes widened with concern. Once again she looked from Aoife to Gavin and back again.

"What happened to McCallagh?" Her tone betrayed some hint of emotion, but Aoife couldn't quite tell.

"You didn't hear?" Aoife immediately regretted asking the obvious.

Halloran's expression shifted into one Aoife had seen many times on her mother's face, albeit less harsh. "Yes, this is the face of someone in the know."

"Callum—"

Gavin only managed to utter one word before Halloran interrupted, tension stiffening her body. "What in the sands did that blasted man do now?"

"So you've met him then," Aoife said.

Stretching her neck, Halloran said, "You could say that. So what'd he do? Something stupid, no doubt."

"He took Declan."

"He took the captain."

Aoife and Gavin spoke at the same time.

"Any idea why he took him?" Halloran shifted her gaze between them again, and they shared a glance, searching each other's eyes as if they could silently discuss how to answer. "Honestly, you two. I'd like to think saving your sorry asses from the kraken would be proof enough that you can trust me. If Callum has Declan, I assure you, I'm as worried about his wellbeing as you are."

Had Declan even told the crew what they were chasing? Or had they found out when they'd learned of his capture? Would he tell Halloran now? He had trusted her enough to get Aoife away from the council hall safely. He wouldn't have done that without reason.

Aoife said the words quietly. "They're going after the dagger. In the Black Sound."

Halloran's eyes closed as she pulled a breath deep into her lungs and let it out with a whispered string of curses. She turned to look at her officers.

"And what is Tommy doing then? Why isn't he here to—"

Renna stepped forward with a confidence that only came from centuries of living. "He's attending to my youngest sister."

"And who are..." Halloran's looked over the fae. "Impossible." The word came out as a whisper.

"Says the woman who eviscerated an ancient sea creature less than an hour ago?" Renna asked with no challenge in her tone. No humor either. The eldest fae looked exhausted.

Aoife raised a hand. "You never said how you did that."

"Nothing special, really. We always keep large barrels of explosives on hand. And Lara here"—she gestured to the tallest of her officers—"she's our master gunner. Rigged a weapon on the *Duchess* that allows us to send those barrels flying at a target far away."

"I've never heard of such a thing," Mikkel said from behind Renna.

Lara eyed him, though not in an unfriendly way. "Aye. A design from my country, far from the Aisling. We used it on land, but Captain here allowed me to try it out on the ship."

"And it worked," Aoife said.

Halloran turned her attention back to Renna. "So the stories are true then."

Renna shrugged, an elegant and graceful rise of her shoulders. "Depends on which stories you're referring to."

"You're who Declan was rescuing from the council hall."

A smooth nod.

"You didn't know?" Aoife asked Halloran, wondering if perhaps Declan didn't trust this captain as much as she'd assumed.

"First thing you learn as a pirate is always say less than necessary. He didn't say. I didn't ask."

Aoife's face scrunched with confusion. "Why agree to help him then?"

The familiar look of exasperation washed over Halloran's features, like Aoife was an irritating pebble in her boot that needed shaking out and discarding. "Long story, and one we don't have time for at the moment. Unless you aren't actually interested in saving Declan."

"Right," Aoife said as her face went hot. She looked up to the masts. "But how? These waters seem plagued by a lack of wind."

"With their help," Gavin said, nodding toward the *Duchess*.

"Aye," Halloran confirmed. "Do you have enough men to secure the tow lines?"

"Enough men, yes, though I'm not sure what state they're in."

Mikkel stepped up alongside Renna. "We have enough who aren't wounded, yes, but most could use a rest, especially since we still need to sail the rest of the way to the sound."

"Not a problem," Halloran said. She nodded to her other two officers, and without a word exchanged, they were striding back over to the *Duchess*. "We can help with that. Our crew will help secure the lines for you. It will take us some time to get you out of these dead seas, but that should offer at least several hours for your men to recharge."

Aoife wanted to ask what would happen after that, but it didn't matter if she knew or not. What would happen would happen, and the best she could do was prepare for the various paths they might find themselves on. And focus on the next task in the meantime.

CHAPTER 37
CAIT

THE PIRATE GRABBED Cait's arm and shoved her toward the clearing. Her toe caught on a rock, and she would have fallen to the ground had Adler not rushed forward to catch her.

"Careful, love," he whispered in her ear as he helped her straighten.

She turned her head to thank him, but before she could, the pirate nudged them both forward—placing a flat hand on Cait's shoulder blade while he held his knife against Adler's ribs. Adler didn't resist but let the pirate prod him along before suddenly pivoting and slamming his forearm down hard, knocking the knife into the dirt and sending his fist to greet the man's temple.

It happened much quicker than Cait would have ever expected, but she had acquired quick reflexes—both mental and physical—during her years at the pub. As soon as the blade thumped against the ground, she was kneeling and wrapping her fingers around its handle. She remained in a crouch as she watched Adler send the guy stumbling away. Blood already flowed freely from where the man's cheek had split open, and his hands rushed up instinctively to protect his head. Cait took that opportunity to swing her arm, knife firmly in hand, across the front of his legs. While it wasn't as effective as a strike to the ankle, it did as she had hoped, and the man's knees buckled beneath him. His scream of pain was cut short when Adler's fist connected with the middle of his face.

The pirate fell to his knees, and his hands rushed up to his busted nose. Though he was obviously dazed and looked far from being an immediate threat, Adler still gave him a solid kick to the shoulder that knocked him down. His head made a sickening sound when it struck a rock on the side of the path.

"You made that look too easy," Cait said, wiping blood from the knife onto her pants before securing it into her belt.

"They will have heard that," Adler said, nodding toward the clearing behind her.

Leaning forward, he offered his uninjured hand to her. If he had been looking at her, the gesture might have seemed romantic. Instead he remained focused on the clearing. She twisted her neck around to get a glimpse herself, but he moved at the same time, pushing and turning in an unfamiliar maneuver that brought her whole body around so his arm guarded her front and her back pressed against his torso. A sense of déjà vu swept over her.

His breaths, even and measured as they warmed her ear, contrasted starkly with the tension she felt coursing through his arm and chest. His jaw flexed against her head, a slight movement she might not have noticed if she hadn't already been hyper-focused on him.

Moving her head away from his face, Cait tried to see around the trees and into the clearing, which was now silent except for the distant roaring of the sea.

"Where are—" she started to whisper, but Adler's arm tightened around her rib cage, and he whispered for her to stay quiet.

Leaning close once again, he breathed his command, "When I let you go, move quickly to the right. Stay low. Aye?"

Piecing together his plan—or what she hoped was his plan—she dipped her chin in affirmation. No sooner had she answered than his arm slipped away. The unexpected emptiness she felt—not only at her waist—surprised her, but she gave herself a mental slap in the face and scurried her way into the trees, keeping as low as she could while still maintaining a brisk pace.

When she was sure she had gotten far enough, she turned and peered back around one of the trees to see what had happened to Adler. The pirates who had captured Penny had ventured down the path—likely to check out the commotion— and now approached Adler. Cait's gut tightened and her breath quickened as she waited to see how this would play out.

He might be double-crossing you.

The thought stung, and she tried to convince herself she hadn't made a mistake in trusting him. From her hiding spot, she couldn't make out the words exchanged, but it was evident Adler had said something to appease them. They shared a hearty laugh over their fallen mate—who she hoped was merely unconscious and not dead —and left the man behind as they led Adler toward the clearing. She waited for him to look her way, to give her any sign that his plan was working, that she should move, that she had done well. That last one left a bad taste in her mouth. Why should she want his approval?

But he never glanced back, and the emptiness returned.

What is happening to you?

You told him yourself there's no hope for...

She couldn't even allow herself to finish that thought, promptly drowning it and the unwanted feelings with a deep breath.

There was a job to do. And she would get it done.

Trying to creep through the forest without making a sound took longer than

Cait wanted, but she didn't seem to have many other options. So she continued on, carefully watching where she placed her feet before glancing up to make sure she was heading in the right direction while staying hidden.

The trees became more densely packed the farther she moved into the forest, making it nearly impossible to see what lay ahead. Focusing on the men's voices—and the now familiar sound of Adler's deep laugh—she hoped her course would bring her to the clearing and to Penny, and not off the rocky cliffs into the Aisling.

A shiver sent her shoulders squirming, and she cursed her inconvenient fear of heights that could make her uneasy with a mere mental image.

Sands help me if I pop out at a drop-off.

After several excruciatingly long, tedious minutes of trekking through the forest, the trees began to thin out once again, almost as if the forest was announcing to any travelers within that something was about to change.

She relaxed at the sight of grass just beyond the forest's edge. As beautiful as the waters were, and as much as she dreamed of leaving this cursed island, she had no desire to greet the sea from so high.

She slowed her pace even more so she could focus on the conversation ahead. She could almost make out what was being said. Cautiously she ventured forward until she was near enough to the clearing to get a decent view—of the pit cave and of Penny still lying beside it—without risk of being spotted by the pirates. Pirates who seemed to still be having a grand time. Their short stories were resulting in round after round of guffaws.

Penny fidgeted—first a foot and then a hand—and began to regain consciousness. Cait waited. She needed the woman to rouse fully and understand their plan for her rescue. Trying to get herself into a comfortable position, Cait crouched down, careful to keep the leaves from making too much noise as she lowered a knee onto them. Her heart pounded in anticipation, and she tried to steady it with several slow breaths. Penny's restlessness had ceased, and Cait rolled her eyes. Perhaps she could throw something at her, help her along in the waking-up process.

But as Cait turned to look for a stick that would do the trick without injuring the poor woman, the pirates' conversation called her attention.

"You never told us what you were doing here, Jensen." Cait didn't recognize the voices, and she held her breath as she waited to hear more.

"Yeah, last I heard you were near set on earning a promotion with Tiernen. Odd time for you to bail."

Cait's breath caught as she waited for Adler's response. Would he tell the truth? And did Cait even know what the truth was? She winced at the thought that maybe this time her gut had led her astray, led her straight into a trap. For what, a pretty face?

It's not that pretty.

"What can I say?" Adler started. "A better opportunity presented itself."

Cait could picture that smug look of his as he spoke, and she gritted her teeth when the image sent her stomach fluttering. No time for such thoughts or feelings. No time. No hope.

"Better than an officer under a lord, eh? Not sure I believes you," the first pirate said.

Adler gave a relaxed laugh as the other pirate spoke again. "What could be better than that though?"

Silence stretched, and Cait worked to keep her breaths quiet since the pounding of her heart in her ears made it hard enough to hear their conversation. Would he name her and the Rogues? Or would he mention Lani?

And why did the thought of the latter sting just as much as the former?

"What," Adler finally said, "is the one thing that gets a man to head ashore? To walk away from the sea? To put down roots?"

"Is this a riddle?"

"No, stupid. It's a damn woman."

"You sure?"

"It is, isn't it?"

Cait couldn't keep straight which of the pirates spoke when. She was only able to identify Adler's voice. Not that it mattered.

He laughed. "No, not a riddle. And aye, a woman."

"I knew it."

"Whatever. So who is she?"

This time Adler didn't laugh. "Alas, gents, there is no hope for me there."

Cait couldn't tell if the sorrow in his words was genuine. Of course he would still be mourning Lani's death, even with all his attempts to put up a strong and healthy front. It was exactly what she had done after her parents' deaths. Locking up her pain and grief, only letting it out when she was alone. She also knew it was impossible to keep it contained perfectly, and she still remembered the first time she'd let the depths of her pain show with Lucan. The tears. The screams. The tremors. The rage. It had all escaped her vault, and it was a wonder Lucan hadn't left after seeing such insanity.

But this wasn't Adler screaming and lashing out from pain. This was a barely evident change in tone, and by the way the other pirates responded, it had gone unnoticed.

"That's a tough break, lad."

"Aye," the other pirate agreed. "So what now?"

Adler answered, "I haven't completely decided, to be honest. Couple irons in the fire at the moment though."

"Good to have options, but I do have one question for you."

"Oh?" Adler asked.

"Aye. You never answered the question. What are you doing out here?" Suspicion coated each word.

"I didn't? You sure?"

"No. You didn't."

No answer. Tense silence. Did Adler have a plan? Or was Cait failing to play her part in that plan? It would have been nice to have been privy to his plan—assuming he had one.

"Oh," Adler said finally, speaking with a confidence that reassured her he wasn't flying blind. "Well, in that case, I'm here to save that lass over there."

Cait's breath caught.

"What?"

"Why would you do that?"

Another of Adler's laughs filled the clearing. "You really going to waste your time asking why when you could be trying to stop me?"

As the scuffling of feet began, Cait snapped into action, breaking free of the protection of the trees to reach Penny before the pirates could. She shook the woman awake as she glanced over her shoulder to find Adler taking on the two pirates, who—based on their clumsy display of strikes and blocks—had not seen much fighting in recent days. And Adler, with his quick reflexes, seemed able to anticipate each of their poorly executed maneuvers. As they continued to throw punches and kicks—all blocked or countered with ease—they seemed oblivious to the fact that Adler was gradually easing them toward the pit cave.

If Cait didn't get Penny roused soon, this whole ordeal would be for naught. She turned back to the woman and, grabbing both shoulders, gave a few firm pushes while saying Penny's name in a low voice. Penny's legs shifted, but her eyes still didn't open, and Cait half contemplated smacking her across the face. As satisfying as that would be for all the snide comments the woman had made to her over the years, somehow it felt inappropriate.

So instead Cait pinched her.

Right on the underside of Penny's arm, Cait plucked a bit of skin and squeezed as hard as she could.

Penny's eyes flashed open as she let out a yelp.

"Quiet, Penny," Cait whispered as she ducked to get into the woman's line of sight.

"What? Cait? What in the sands are you doing here?" She tried to sit up. "Where am I?" Her head turned from one side to the other and then stopped when she caught a glimpse of the scene behind Cait. "What is that man doing? They shouldn't be fighting. Where did they get blades? That's the man from the shop. What is he...? What am I doing here? Why am I not at the council?" Panic began to fill her dull eyes as they darted around the clearing. "What is this place?"

"Adler and I followed you here."

"Why would you follow me? They weren't hurting me. They were merely escorting me, doing their job," Penny protested as she slowly pushed herself up to standing.

"Oh." Cait stood as well, placing her hands on her hips. How silly she felt arguing with this woman while Adler was busy fighting. "Is that why you screamed then?"

"Well, no one wants to be exiled, Cait. Of all the people on Morshan, you should understand that better than most." No sympathy showed on the woman's face, and Cait wished she had indeed slapped the woman awake.

"I do. It's why I'm here now."

"Surely it's a mistake and they just stopped here for a break on our way to the council. And how do I know that man—your man—didn't instigate this violence?"

Cait should have known it wouldn't be so easy to change her mind. Penny had grown up in Morshan with a family who believed wholeheartedly in the mission of the council and trusted them implicitly. Some people didn't want to see the truth lying behind the veil of perfection and comfort. They never doubted. And now Cait needed to convince one of the council's most devoted believers.

Turning her chin over her shoulder, she found the fight had quieted down—which she might have noticed sooner had she not been entertaining all of Penny's questions. One of the pirates was kneeling on the ground, groaning. He had his forehead pressed against the grass while his hands, covered in his own blood, held onto his nose. Adler had pinned the other pirate's arm behind his back and was working to keep him in place as he struggled.

"Adler?" Cait called in her most innocent tone.

"Yes, love? How can I help?" His half-smile quirked up until that dimple appeared, and Cait worked to focus her attention elsewhere.

"That's enough. Let him go. Miss Penny here would like us to allow them to continue escorting her to the council hall."

One of his brows angled up. A bit of mischief flashed in his blue eyes before he released the pirate and took a casual step back. "Of course."

Cait moved to meet Adler on the other side of the clearing, happy to see the pirates were slow to rise and return to their senses. As Adler came alongside her, the warmth of his shoulder brought back all the sensations she'd experienced when he'd held her earlier in the trees. With a clearing of her throat, she pushed all of that to the edge of her mind and turned to the two pirates, who were still shaking their heads clear of the stars Adler had gifted them.

"Gentlemen. My apologies. Please continue with your exile," Cait said, offering the words in her sweetest and most amenable tone. She gestured toward Penny before turning back to Adler and weaving her hand into the crook of his arm. "Let's go, love."

She'd known using his own term of endearment on him would get a reaction, but nothing could have prepared her for the way heat engulfed her from her toes up to her ears and down to her fingertips at the sight of his smile, as genuine as she'd ever seen it. That warmth only increased when his hand hovered over the small of her back and he began to lead her back to the path through the trees.

"Careful there, Cait. Don't be using that with me too often. Especially not around Lucan," Adler said in a low voice. "I'd hate to make him even more jealous."

"Don't lie. You would love to do that to him," she said as they stepped into the trees.

"Aye, I would." He let out a single, quiet laugh, then stopped, drew in a long breath, and turned her to face him. "But honestly, and in all seriousness, please don't call me that."

Cait's forehead tightened. His words sparked confusion she couldn't conceal. "Oh, but you can—"

"Old habits die hard," he said. She waited for that smirk to appear within his beard, but he remained somber. "But you didn't say it out of habit. You used it deliberately, and while I may be a lying, murderous pirate, I do have a heart. Albeit one a bit broken of late. And unless you mean it—which I think we both know you don't—then please refrain."

Cait's mind emptied. A basin drained of all water. No thoughts. No words. She had no response for him. But he didn't seem to mind her silence. He offered her a tight smile and turned away to see what had happened back at the pit while they had been talking.

"Now to figure out how to make this work," he whispered, flicking his chin back to the clearing. Penny was approaching the pirates, who now seemed more than eager to get this job over and done with.

"Any ideas?" Cait asked, the words coming out scratchy and strained.

Adler's eyes narrowed, and he pursed his lips to one side for a moment before he spoke. "It's too bad we don't have a whip." Turning toward her, he added, "You don't have one, do you?"

She raised a brow at him. He couldn't be serious. "No. I don't. Didn't go with this outfit."

He nodded, like this was a perfectly reasonable answer. "What about a crossbow?"

"Fresh out, I'm afraid."

"Well, what do we have exactly? Anything useful? You know, beyond my strength and your tongue."

"How about this?" Cait asked, pulling the knife from where she'd stashed it in her belt.

Adler's face lit up when he reached for it. "This will do."

"But there are two of them and only one blade. How—"

"Will you need this back?" He held up the weapon.

"No?" Why she said it as a question, she wasn't sure. "It's not mine."

"All right then."

"Just be ready to use it."

"Always am." His words didn't carry the same bravado she'd become accustomed to, but she brushed that away to focus on the scene playing out before her.

Penny, her chin raised high in her most dignified posture, no longer looked like the frightened criminal being dragged away to her exile. "I do apologize," she said. "I should not have struggled as I did. You were only carrying out the rule of our land. A rule I wholeheartedly believe in, and therefore I am ready, gentlemen, to proceed on to the council hall with you so I may explain the situation to our fair councilwomen."

Cait's heartbeat once again filled her ears until she wasn't sure she'd be able to hear the pirates' responses. But the men didn't reply immediately, instead dropping their heads toward one another and conversing quietly. To her credit, Penny didn't show any sign of worry or panic.

Cait wished she were a tough and fearless fighter like her brother. Sadly, though, she had little more than a sharp tongue and a quick mind, neither of which would help her physically conquer her opponents—or her fears.

You've been in dire situations before, and you were fine.

But even as she reminded herself of that, she knew this was different. Watching Adler take on those pirates earlier had both thrilled her—giving her a glimpse of the adventurous life she'd always dreamed of—and crushed her, and she'd wondered if she would be capable of doing what was needed when the time came. She had stood up to Adler in the woods, and she had fooled those pirates in the pub when they'd come asking after Aoife. But in both instances she'd wielded words, not fists.

The pirates took a couple of steps toward Penny, who grew an inch or two as she straightened.

"Apologies, miss, but the council won't be seeing you," one of the men said, his face smeared with nearly dry blood.

"Excuse me?" Penny asked.

"You should have accepted the rescue when you could."

Penny took a step backward, her head shaking in disbelief as she stammered. "What—what do you mean? I'm to see the council. That is my right as a Cregahn. You have made a grave error."

"Oh, have we now?"

Another step forward for the men. Another two steps back for Penny.

Cait's stomach curdled as she watched Penny inch closer and closer to the pit behind her. "Come on," she whispered to herself. The pirates needed to tell the woman the truth soon so she and Adler could rescue her before she stepped back to her death. Adler didn't seem to be having the same response to what was unfolding. When Cait peered at him, she saw no tension in his body or anxiety in his expression. Rather, he looked calculating, calm but distant, separated emotionally from it all.

Penny's voice snapped Cait's attention back to the clearing. "When I get to the council hall, I'll report both of you for usurping our laws and disobeying the rule of the council. You'll be exiled for your impertinence."

"Ah, but you see, miss, we are actually carrying out the very orders of your beloved council."

"What?"

"Aye, it's true. There are no trials—anymore—and no pleas for mercy."

The other pirate interjected. "Well, you could beg for mercy, but if we granted that to you, it would be us falling to our deaths, not you. And we rather enjoy being alive."

"Aye," the first pirate agreed. "Indeed we do. So if you don't mind, we—"

"What do you mean, *death*?" Penny asked, and her eyes widened with renewed panic.

Adler shifted forward, but before he could move, Cait stopped him with her arm.

"Not yet," she said in a hoarse whisper.

"Why not?"

"We need her to clearly understand."

"She's inching her way toward that clarity," he said, gesturing with his chin toward Penny, who was still moving closer to the drop.

Before Cait could once again insist on waiting, Penny's shrill words pierced the air. "Let go of me! What are you doing?"

The pirates had each grabbed one of Penny's arms and were attempting to lift her, but the injuries Adler had gifted them must have made that task difficult, as they had barely gotten her more than an inch above the ground when she began to kick and stomp, wriggling in their grasp.

"Council's orders, miss," one growled as she squirmed.

They made slow progress toward the pit cave, but still Cait didn't move. Cait could sense Adler was getting antsy waiting for her to give the word. One breath. One step. Another and another. If she waited too long, though, she risked Penny tumbling over the edge by accident.

The other pirate struggled to stay upright as Penny flailed to get away. "I hate this job!" he moaned.

"They aren't usually this troublesome," the first said.

"Please," Penny whimpered. She looked from one of her captors to the other and then back as she spoke. "Please, let me go. I'll leave. I'll catch a ship. I'll never come back."

"That's not how this works. This is our task. This is our lot. And that"—he gestured to the pit behind her—"that right there is yours."

As the pirates moved her feet nearer to the edge and her whimpers turned into sobs, Cait bounded out of the trees with Adler on her heels. She sprinted toward the pirates and registered the sound of a knife hitting its mark in one pirate a second before she dropped to the ground and used her momentum to slide into the other's legs, kicking them out from under him.

The pirate's boots slipped. His legs jutted out over the darkness of the cave, but his grip remained firm on Penny's arm, and he pulled her hard to the ground with him. Cait scrambled to get herself away from the edge, kicking her feet at both the ground and the pirate equally.

Where was Adler?

As if in answer to the thought, he said, "Be right there."

Cait pulled in a sharp breath at the sight of the other pirate's body going over the edge—or being thrown over. No scream came from him as he fell. Cait had barely taken another breath when she heard Adler again.

"I'm right here," he said as he slipped his arms around Penny and pulled her easily away from her remaining captor, who appeared to have given up any effort to complete his job for the council.

Instead his eyes went wide with fright. His hands fought unsuccessfully for purchase in the grass and dirt as the weight of his legs pulled him slowly toward the drop. He growled again, and his hand brushed against Cait's pant leg. Her heart raced.

She couldn't let him.

Wouldn't let him.

With a determined kick, she shoved her foot against his shoulder, forcing his body fully over the lip of the cave, but at the last moment, his fingers once again grabbed for her leg, and he managed to secure a firm grip on her ankle. Her backside ached as it slid across the ground, dragged forward by the weight of a full-grown man and his squirming body. But that discomfort was nothing compared to the terror that ripped through her and pulled a scream from her lungs.

"Adler!"

Her feet went over, her legs stretching painfully as the pirate pulled her along in his descent. With her arms stretched out to the sides, Cait had as much success grabbing onto the grass as the pirate had.

Don't give up. Don't give up. Don't give up.

But it wasn't that easy.

Her arms ached.

Her leg throbbed from where the man's fingers dug into her.

Cait stared up at the bright blue afternoon sky. This was it. She'd failed, and now she was going to plunge to her death from an unimaginable height.

Opening her mouth, she tried to shout for Adler again, but no sound came. Or if it did, she didn't hear it. The world became muffled, like she'd plunged her head underwater and every noise was distant and soft.

Another frantic breath, and the ground fell away.

She closed her eyes, not wanting to see her death coming at her. A jolt of pain shot through her arm as her body came to a sudden stop and the weight fell away from her legs. She couldn't look down, couldn't look to see what had happened, but she felt rocks jutting into her back, digging into her skull. Something gripped her forearms tightly.

"I've got you, love."

Adler.

Cait wanted to look up at him, but she couldn't force her eyes open, couldn't even open her mouth to answer him. She should do something, maybe press her feet against the wall of the pit to help propel herself to the surface, but she had no control over her limbs.

Even when the roughness of the rocks was replaced with the softness of the grass in the clearing, she didn't open her eyes. But when the ground beneath her head moved and she realized she was lying on Adler's legs and not the ground, her eyelids flashed open to find his deep blue eyes sparkling down at her.

"Looks like you've fallen into my lap."

Cait knew she should get up. She should move, stand, get back to work. But all her energy had been used up trying to stay alive, and if she was being honest, she didn't want to pull herself away from Adler's warm, comforting arms. Once again she found herself swimming in those azure eyes of his, as inviting as the sea on a sunny day.

"Will you let me stay here?" Her question came out as a whisper. Did he remember what he'd said earlier, or had it been a flippant remark, forgotten as soon as he'd uttered it?

Adler didn't move except to search her eyes, shifting between them, looking for...what? Cait didn't know why she'd asked. She had no time for distractions, no matter how good-looking they might be. Her focus had to be on ending the council's rule.

But sands help her, none of that seemed to matter when his hand moved and he cradled her face in his steady palm. His thumb brushed her lips so lightly she might have imagined it, but when his caress moved to her cheek, she couldn't constrain her gasp. Such a simple gesture, a whisper of a touch. Yet it sent sparks through her entire body.

Her heart screamed at her to sit up and taste his lips, while her mind begged her to get up and leave. Before she could do either, Adler blinked and looked away, lifting her up so he could stand.

Whatever spell had trapped them in that moment, Adler had managed to free himself from its grasp.

Unfortunately, Cait had not.

CHAPTER 38

MAURA

From the inside out, Maura burned.

It had been so long since she'd experienced this—and even then, never to this extent. She'd forgotten just how painful it was. It seemed counterintuitive to her that when a fae's magic fizzled out—or got close to it—their bodies warmed. No. Warmed was the wrong word for the fire that blazed through her.

Every nerve frayed.

Every hair singed.

Every breath constricted.

Every thought consumed.

Her last thought, before her body had gone up in flames, had been of Tommy.

But the image of him watching her, of the worry in his amber eyes as she and Bria prepared to dive into their powers, had quickly turned to ash, and now all she had to focus on was the never-ending attack of a thousand knives stabbing into her over and over. There was no respite from the torture, and every time she sensed it subsiding, it would flare back up, like a fire given new life with a bit of air.

Several times she'd tried to push beyond the pain, to sense where she was and who was with her. Anything to let her know she was still alive.

But there was nothing. Nothing but her own agony.

Experiencing that—excruciating as it was—meant she hadn't yet succumbed and her magic was still hers. While it was impossible for her to know exactly what it was like to completely lose her powers, she'd met others who had experienced it. They all described it as a haunting desolation, like their insides had been poured out and all that was left behind was a dry shell. Numb. That's what they all said. Not that they ceased to have emotions—though Maura wasn't completely convinced that those didn't at least become muted.

Maura had no sense of time. She couldn't even recall how long she'd managed to keep the glamour in place over the ship before she'd collapsed. Had anyone moved her? Or was she still on the deck of the ship? Had they gotten away? Had they survived?

The scorching heat lessened enough for her to notice new sensations along her skin. Cool air soothing her arms and face. Softness caressing her legs. She wasn't on the deck.

Little by little, and with caution, she studied each new feeling as if her torment was a living thing that could be startled into returning should it discover her waking. And each second that passed without the searing pain intensifying brought more than simple relief.

Each second brought hope.

Counting her breaths, she struggled to listen to the world around her. Silence engulfed her. Not muffled quietness. Terrifying silence. The air rushed in and out of her lungs, but she heard none of it. She tried to speak. Or at least she thought she did. Nothing. Reaching a hand up to her throat, she tried to make another sound, and her vocal cords vibrated under her fingertips.

And then the heat returned, and she stiffened once more.

But this heat wasn't like before. It wasn't scalding, but comforting. And it wasn't over her entire body. It was focused on the hand still resting at her collar.

Open your eyes, she commanded, but her body refused to obey.

The warmth at her hand began to move in light strokes back and forth and around.

Another two breaths, and a new sensation flooded her senses. The scents of mountain air, pine forests, and spice entered her silent world, painting it in warm amber behind her closed eyelids. It was so familiar, but she couldn't place it. Her heart raced as she chased after memories that refused to materialize. She was a ship chasing the setting sun, seeking but never reaching the images she could sense at the edges of her mind.

Then the amber in her vision darkened, like a shadow had passed over her, and she held her breath. Was this the end? Was this what happened before the numbness set in? A dulling of all her senses? A dimming of the life within her?

But then warmth landed on her forehead. Soft. Delicate. And sad? She couldn't be sure. Couldn't trust herself to analyze any of this right now. Reality seemed to be dissolving around her, if it had ever existed at all, and all she knew seemed to be falling away.

Maura.

That was her name. Echoing in her mind. At least that hadn't faded from her consciousness.

Maura. Wake up.

She mulled over the words. Something about them seemed off, like they weren't coming from within. But that was impossible. Not without her hearing restored.

"Maura."

Her breath stuck in her throat. Not merely a thought or a feeling then, but an actual word, spoken. She strained to hear more, but nothing else penetrated the silence. Drawing air deeper into her lungs and ignoring how her chest shook from the effort, she fought back the tears pooling under her eyelids.

"Maura, I need you."

The circling warmth on the back of her hand stopped, spread over it, and then moved slowly up her arm. And before she could contemplate what was happening, that same comforting heat lined one side of her body, pressing against her shoulder, hip, and knee. Half of her melted into bliss.

"Please. Please be okay. I can't lose you."

The desperate words tugged at her heart. Focusing on the scents in the room and the warmth at her side, she forced her mind to try again, to try harder. The amber hue surrounding her intensified. She knew that color.

Knew it. Loved it.

A pair of eyes appeared in her mind, but instead of startling her, the image brought another wave of comfort. Her breath eased. Her heart slowed. Her body swayed.

No, her entire world swayed, rolling in time with her breath.

The smell of seawater and wood pushed their way in, and little by little, the image in her mind came into focus, like a black fog was dissipating, revealing the memories she'd feared were gone. Amber eyes. Kind and worried. A stubbled chin. A ship at sea. A bed that wasn't hers.

Swallowing hard, she pried her eyes open. She blinked away the tears that hadn't escaped and took in the deep brown of the wooden planks above her. Sunlight streamed in from the windows to her left. She wiggled her toes and flexed her fingers.

And the warmth vanished. Her body suddenly went cold, but before she could look to see what had happened, the voice returned.

"Maura?" Now a question. Clear as day.

Another swallow and a clearing of her throat, and she managed to respond. Not with words, but a sound at least. A sound she could hear, not just feel within, but hear with her ears.

Slowly she directed her attention to where the voice had come from, and there she found those amber eyes. A pair of eyes she desperately loved and had come so close to forgetting entirely.

Tommy.

She thought she had said it, but when he didn't move or react, she realized she must have only thought his name. Her smile seemed reluctant to form along her lips, and for a moment she worried he would see a grimace instead. Still unable to speak, she reached out a hand toward him, and he moved faster than she thought possible, taking her hand in his as he sat down beside her.

His eyes became melted honey, sweet and warm.

"Are you okay?" Tommy's voice was low and carried a hint of concern. More than a hint, she thought.

With a slow nod, she moved to sit up, thankful when his hands rushed to help her.

"Did you—do you—what—" He stumbled over his words, and a silent laugh tickled her chest from within. No doubt he was trying to ask about her powers without sounding callous, but she wasn't sure how to answer.

Looking down at her hands, she rubbed her thumbs along her fingertips and urged her mind to turn inward, to look deeper and call out for the magic she hoped hadn't been extinguished. But there, where she feared emptiness had settled in, she felt it. A weak and tiny spark, but a spark nonetheless, buried deep within her chest.

"Tommy."

She marveled at the sound of her voice in her ears once more and then laughed—not a silent laugh this time but the type that comes from sheer happiness and relief.

He scooted himself closer and ducked his head down into her line of sight, and when she smiled again, he smiled back.

"I guess this is when you tell me *I told you so*?" she asked, hoping he'd take it as the joke she meant it to be.

His smile twisted slightly. "There'll be time for that later. I just need to know you're okay. You're not—"

"Going to die anytime soon? Not if I can help it."

With a roll of his eyes, he rubbed a hand over his mouth and down his chin, but he didn't say anything more.

"How long was I out?" she asked.

"Not as long as I expected you to be, in all honesty. Half a day. If that."

Surprise hit her, though it was quickly replaced with the confidence that she would have remained unconscious far longer had he not been with her. All the words she'd heard from him replayed in her mind, but she couldn't tell if they had been truly from him or born only from some foolish hope she couldn't set aside.

She raised her chin and searched his eyes before asking, "Did you mean it?" Probably not the best way to go about this, but fatigue was beginning to crowd her mind, keeping her from finding a more tactful way to broach the topic.

"Mean what?"

"You need me? Can't lose me? Or did I dream that?" Sudden embarrassment pushed her chin down, and her gaze settled back to her hands. It was not a familiar emotion for her, and she didn't like how vulnerable it made her feel, but she also couldn't bear to look at him as he told her it was all in her imagination.

His hand reached forward, his finger sliding under her chin before lifting it. She closed her eyes once more, still too scared to look at him, sure he was going to reject her as he had before. Only this time, she wasn't strong enough to pretend it didn't hurt or she didn't care or she could live without him.

"Look at me, Maura," he whispered, and when she finally obliged, she fell heart-first into that liquid amber that shined with hope and promise and love. "I said it. All of it. And I meant it."

His lips were on hers then. Tender yet strong. Desperate yet thankful. Her eyes slid closed as his lips moved with hers, patiently seeking her permission one second before giving in and demanding it the next. Even though she could feel his hands cradling her jawline, his fingers caressing the nape of her neck, she feared letting herself believe wholly that this was real. That he was real. That this wasn't some hallucination brought on by her fatigue and waning magic.

When he leaned into the kiss, she retreated, immediately regretting it when his lips pulled away. She risked opening her eyes. She'd loved his eyes from the first moment she'd seen them, but they had never shone quite like this. Somehow he had lured the stars out of the sky and convinced them to shimmer in his eyes just for her. With only a glance, he managed to pick up all the scattered pieces of her heart and hold them together with tenderness and care.

If this was an illusion, it was a particularly cruel one.

Here was all she'd wanted and hoped for.

"Is this real?" She winced when he flinched ever so slightly in response. In the silence that followed, she could hear his pulse pick up speed, and she waited for the truth—that while he cared for her, he couldn't be with her.

But instead, one brow angled up, and he muttered a single word. "Ouch."

"Ouch?"

"Aye," he said. "If you couldn't tell it was real, then that doesn't reflect well on me." A hint of a smile played at his lips.

"Oh." It was the only word she could manage, the only thought she could form.

"Let me try that again," he said, and this time when his lips found hers, forcing them open so he could caress her tongue with his, her doubts dissolved.

Maura didn't hesitate now. She reached for him as his hand explored her body, running over the rise of her hip down into the valley of her waist before resting on her ribs. Her fingers brushed past his ears and slipped into his hair.

Tommy was a sea she would happily drown in, over and over for all eternity.

She pulled him closer, deepening the kiss as she let her hands whisper down his neck before slipping across his shoulders. All doubt was gone. All fear had fled. All worry had been washed away. Now it was only Tommy and her, their lips and tongues and hands exploring each other. It wasn't enough. It would never be enough.

She waited for him to push her away as he had before. Waited for him to remember all the reasons they couldn't be together. And part of her wondered if she should be more responsible and remind him herself.

But that thought was shoved aside as Tommy's kiss deepened, his movements becoming more passionate, his hunger keeping pace with hers. She shifted in her seat, trying to find a way to somehow get him closer still, and he stopped.

The kisses. The caresses. It all stopped.

This time she couldn't contain that sting of rejection that pierced her chest. Why didn't he want her? Why had he told her he did, if he didn't really?

She couldn't look at him, couldn't watch him reject her again.

He pulled further away, and the emptiness between them was bitterly cold, like an icy breeze in the dead of winter. Her chin dropped once more to her chest as he shrugged his arms out from under hers. But he didn't leave. Instead, he took her hands in his.

"Maura?" He paused for a breath. "Why do you look as though I'm going to bolt out that door any moment and never return?"

Her eyes blinked open, and she stared at their clasped hands. She shook her head and offered a weak shrug.

"Did you really not believe me when I said I need you?"

"I did," she said with a meekness that sounded foreign to her. "But I also believed you when you said you could never be with me."

Leaning forward, he pressed his forehead against hers and whispered, "Things change."

It would have been logical to ask what had changed his mind—or his heart—but a different question had her fingers tightening against his hands.

"Then why did you pull away just now?" She cringed at the weakness she was showing. She was fae. She was powerful. She was confident.

But she was also vulnerable and scared, and the seconds seemed to lengthen as she waited for his answer. She didn't feel much better when he laughed. Though it wasn't mean-spirited or mocking, it still chafed her bruised heart.

Tommy pulled back once more, still squeezing her hands.

"Unfortunately, Maura," he started, and she forgot how to breathe. He was going to say what he'd said all along. She could handle this. She could learn to live with her love being unrequited and unwelcome. "We don't have the luxury of time, and I remembered that at the most inconvenient moment."

"So..." Maybe it was the lingering fogginess in her mind, but she couldn't quite get a mental grasp of his words.

"I didn't want to stop. Sands help me, I didn't. I'm not entirely sure how I did. Not sure if you know this, Maura, but you're not easy to turn down."

She quirked a brow at him in challenge.

"I know, I turned you down before, but it was far from easy. I couldn't even escape you in my dreams. I've wanted you since I opened my eyes that evening. And now I want nothing more than to rip off that dress and claim you as mine right here."

Heat emanated from him, and the desire she'd tasted in him earlier now flared up in his eyes. Her body tensed with anticipation, silently begging him to do all that he said, her hands itching to tear his own clothes from him.

"But it has to wait. I...have to wait. Because when I do take you—and I fully intend to—it won't be in my captain's bed. And it won't be rushed. You were meant to be savored, Maura."

The flames he had ignited with his touch flared with those last words, her mind racing ahead to imagine all the ways he intended to delight in her.

Leaning toward her, he brushed her lips with a soft, gentle kiss and the whispered promise, "Soon, but not yet."

Her entire body sighed as she leaned into him. He'd given her more than she'd expected, even if part of her remained unsatisfied. She would accept what he offered. Comfort. Love. And hope.

"By the way, you missed quite the excitement with the kraken while you were out. I actually missed the last of it—"

The kraken. She had completely forgotten.

"Why did you miss any of it?"

He cleared his throat and grasped her hands a little tighter. "Because if we were going to die—which it appeared we would—I wasn't going to let you die alone. I wasn't going to die anywhere but by your side."

"And you're sure we're not dead?"

Tommy pursed his lips and frowned as he pretended to ponder the question. "I'm fairly certain we aren't. But if we are, and I get to spend an eternity with you? I'll take it. Gladly."

Maura moved to meet his lips with hers once more, but the cabin door opened, and she stopped her advance. To her surprise, Tommy didn't turn, didn't retreat, but remained close beside her with their hands still clasped between them.

"Hi, Aoife," Maura said, her eyes never leaving Tommy's, never wanting to be pulled away from them.

"How did you—" Aoife started as she rounded the corner of the doorway to the bedroom. "Oh right. Fae hearing. I'm going to have to get used to that."

Maura laughed. "You have a very distinctive walk, friend. Doesn't require fae senses to identify."

Tommy flashed Maura a wink before turning his chin over his shoulder. "She's not wrong. But that doesn't mean we aren't happy to see you."

Maura had to stifle another laugh as Aoife strolled over to the windows, noticeably trying to change her gait as she did but when Aoife turned and leaned back against the window frame, Maura could see this was not the time to tease the girl. Her pallor clearly indicated she was not interrupting their moment with good news.

Tommy pulled one hand from Maura's, and she swallowed her disappointment. It wasn't like he could hold onto her forever. Running his hand across the back of his neck, he asked, "Or should we not be happy to see you?"

With her eyes cast down, Aoife toed the floor—a nervous habit of hers that Maura had witnessed on several occasions.

"Halloran mentioned seeing Callum's ship. She didn't know Declan was aboard, and I believe her when she says she would have gone to his aid had she known." Tommy moved to speak, but Aoife held up a hand to stop him, her eyes slowly blinking as her jaw tensed. "She saw—they were stopped. And they were punishing someone. Over that distance, she couldn't make out who they had strung up, but it was clear they were—"

"Keelhauling," Tommy said in a whisper.

Aoife gave an almost imperceptible nod. "What if it was—"

"Callum's not that dumb. He wouldn't do that to Declan. Not if he needs him."

The words didn't seem to bring the girl any comfort, and Maura's heart ached in sympathy as she considered how she'd be just as scared if it were Tommy on that ship instead of Declan.

Aoife's voice remained steady though, despite the worry tugging at her features. "Are you sure? He wouldn't do it to torture him?"

With a shake of his head, Tommy answered, "No, keelhauling isn't something you do to someone until you're ready to kill them. But I wouldn't put it past Callum to use it to torture Declan all the same."

"What do you mean?"

Tommy looked at Maura and then back at Aoife as if contemplating whether his next words would be suitable for present company. Maura gave his hand an instinctive squeeze.

"You know better than most that Declan is more than the callous and uncaring man he displays for others. And unfortunately, Callum knows this too. If someone on that ship dared to help our captain? Callum wouldn't be above punishing that person with extreme harshness—especially knowing it would emotionally wreck Declan."

None of this appeared to put Aoife at ease, and Maura wasn't quite sure what she could say to help her friend. The girl looked like she was going to break down into tears at any moment, her brow furrowed, her bottom lip twitching.

"Aoife, friend," Maura said, waiting for Aoife to look up at her, "we will get him back."

Or we will all die trying.

She kept that thought to herself though.

CHAPTER 39
TOMMY

Tommy wasn't going to lie. When Aoife had come in with the news Callum was implementing such a punishment aboard his ship, his gut had tightened with the thought it might have been his best friend. But that wasn't Callum's style. As much as he relished inflicting physical pain—hence his being one of the few pirate captains who still sentenced people to be keelhauled—Callum far preferred to draw out the abuse, to watch someone suffer emotional torment. Especially if it could be stretched out over days or even weeks.

Callum knew that Declan would carry guilt—even unwarranted guilt—over someone being hurt because of him.

Aoife had settled into silence over by the windows, and Tommy searched for any additional words that could offer comfort, but he had none. Nothing, save finding Declan, would ease the anguish plaguing her. Still, they couldn't stand here forever either; they still needed to develop a plan for when they arrived at the sound.

Turning back to Maura, he offered her a half-smile before saying, "I'm going to go gather folks up. Do you want to rest some more? Or—"

Maura interrupted. "Rest would be good, but I'd still like to help if I can."

He nodded. "I'll have them meet here then."

"Not in here," Maura said and nudged her chin toward the main room of the cabin. "Out there. I'll have Aoife help me over to the chair. Now, go."

His smile widened. Though he knew theirs was a doomed future, a story with no possible happy ending, he couldn't deny her—or himself—any longer. A short time loving her—and being loved by her—was far better than a lifetime of regret over what could have been.

Leaning forward, he cradled her face in his hands once more and pressed his lips against hers, stealing one more taste. He didn't want to back away. Didn't want to lose the feel of her skin against his, but duty called. Without another word, he left before he could change his mind and give in to the desire to have her completely.

Out on the deck, the emptiness in his hands seemed to magnify, numbing his senses. How much more would it hurt when he had to let her go permanently? He shouldn't be distracted by that thought, he knew, but it was a reality he couldn't escape. She was needed in Larcsporough, and though he hadn't been told the specifics, he'd gathered it wasn't a task he could help with. Nor was it a task he could even be by her side for.

We'll deal with that when the time comes.

They still had to survive the sound and the sirens if they were going to even reach that future. If he was to ever make good on his promise.

As Tommy headed toward the quarterdeck stairs, he spotted Collins and offered his hand in greeting. "Glad to see you up and about."

"Me too. Not one hundred percent yet, but my body was going to mutiny against me if I forced it to stay in that bed one more moment. How's Aoife?"

Tommy couldn't keep the corner of his mouth from lifting at the question. The crew had been staunchly against her being aboard the *Siren's Song*, and even though Collins had never been one to let superstition and prejudice sway him, his concern for Aoife was nice to see.

"She's Aoife."

"Stubborn and awkward?"

"Aye, and still going despite all she carries."

"No surprise there. That girl may have her quirks, but she has the spirit of a pirate."

"What bad influences we've been on her, Collins," Tommy said with a laugh, though neither of them thought of that spirit as a negative thing. He cleared his throat. "Is Mikkel up—"

"I believe he's belowdecks checking on the crew. If the racket they've been making is any indication, they've been working tirelessly to do what repairs they can."

"Good, good. Can you find him and send him to the captain's quarters for me?"

"Aye, s—Tommy." The man turned before Tommy could correct him over his near slip in addressing him. He wasn't ready to be a *sir* to this crew. Acting captain or not, he would remain Tommy to the men until... He didn't want to think about the circumstance that would warrant his becoming their true captain.

As he stepped onto the quarterdeck, he noticed the scenery for the first time. This part of the Aisling Sea was far different from any other he had sailed. They had left behind the vast openness of the sea between Caprothe and Turvala, and they would be approaching the entrance to the Black Sound soon.

Great rocky cliffs, spotted with trees and capped with clouds, loomed high some distance away. On the opposite side, the sea was broken up by smaller islands jutting out of the water like uneven stepping-stones covered in moss. Although a steady wind filled the sails above his head, the surface of the water showed no disruption apart from the lines cut through by their hull. It was as though some invisible shield guarded the water from the winds above. Or the winds dared not get too close to these waters. Tommy had never seen anything quite like it.

Either way, the wind was a welcome change from the doldrums they'd endured in the kraken's territory.

"We're getting close," Gavin said, eyeing him from the helm. His face sagged from exhaustion. Had the man gotten any sleep?

Stepping closer to his friend, Tommy looked out over their prow as he asked, "How close?"

"If the map is accurate—which it might not be given how few survivors..." His voice faded. "But, map or no, the air is changing."

Tommy needed no clarification on that statement, as he had sensed a shift as well. The air had sparked to life around them, tingling along his skin, sending shivers across his shoulders, and giving him an altogether disturbing feeling in his gut.

"If you get a chance, get some sleep," Tommy said, putting a hand on Gavin's shoulder. "You're no good to us if you collapse from fatigue."

"Aye, Tommy. I know. I'll try, but I assume you're here to call a meeting of sorts. Unless you've already devised a plan all on your lonesome? Or with your fae beauty, perhaps?" Gavin flashed him an almost smug smile.

But Tommy ignored it and simply stated, "No plan yet. Can you hand the helm over? Or would you like to stay to navigate the waters?" Something inside him begged him to drop anchor, to not get any closer to the sound and its dangers until they had a plan in place. But Declan was somewhere ahead of them, hopefully alive. For how long was anyone's guess.

"Whatever you decide I'll support, Tommy. The others have been waiting for you though."

At that, Tommy turned his attention to the two women standing at the railing. Both were standing almost regally. Although Halloran was decidedly rougher around the edges than Renna, Tommy had little desire to cross either of them. Yet he had already gone against his word to the fae by stepping over the line with Maura, and he swallowed his dread, wondering how she would react to what she likely already knew.

"How is she, Tommy?" It was Halloran who voiced the question as he approached.

"Conscious at least, but I'm not sure she'll be strong enough to go into the sound with us," he said, hoping the depth of his concern wasn't evident.

"Not the fae. Aoife," Halloran clarified. Tommy raised his brow at that, and his surprise must have been clear, because the renowned captain rolled her eyes. "I know what you're going to say. Don't."

Tommy could imagine how Declan would have responded to such a statement, and he nearly smiled.

"Say what?" he offered, and when the captain remained stoic and annoyed, he conceded with a slight shrug. "She's scared."

"As she should be," Halloran said. She swung her attention to Renna beside her, who seemed to be ignoring their exchange, but she didn't address the eldest fae.

"I'm actually surprised to still see you, Captain," Tommy said. "Not that it isn't a welcome surprise. I thought you would have sailed on your way after offering us the tow."

"Aye, my ship will be sailing on shortly."

Tommy noted her odd phrasing. "And will you be on it?"

Her chin rose in the air slightly. "I'd like to remain here to help however I can, if you'll allow it."

"I appreciate it. Truly."

"If you're both done with the idle chatter," Renna said, her harsh tone cutting through the charged air, stinging Tommy with a power of its own. "We should discuss what exactly we will do once we get there."

With a nod, Tommy pivoted on his heel and motioned for the pair to follow him to Declan's quarters.

As he made his way down the stairs, he wished—for the millionth time—that his friend was here with him.

✄

Once again Tommy found himself leaning over Declan's desk, his mind whirring with all the decisions that had to be made. But when he looked around him, it was painfully clear how things had changed since that first meeting. Renna stood where she had before, but now one of her sisters was sitting in Declan's chair beside Tommy, and the other was absent, still laid out on the floor of the officers' cabin, recovering. On Tommy's other side, Aoife leaned onto the desk. Opposite him, Captain Halloran, Mikkel, and Collins stood tall and serious.

"Declan didn't tell you how he anticipated using their magic?" Aoife asked Tommy, nodding her head toward Renna.

Tommy roughed a hand over his mouth and shook his head. "We had planned to decide that on the journey north, but obviously he didn't make it to that meeting." He cringed internally at his casual reference to Declan's abduction. "When we went to the council hall, we had no indication of the powers they held, so we couldn't very well plan how to use them when we didn't know what they were."

Halloran widened her stance slightly and said, "And why did Declan's absence warrant not going forward with planning?"

He bristled at the question but recovered quickly. Tensions were high for everyone. "Unfortunately nothing has gone quite right for us. Between the storm and the kraken and thinking we were all going to drown or be eaten, we didn't find the time to plan that far ahead. But we're here now." He straightened and forced himself to ignore Maura, who was looking up at him from her seat as he addressed her sister. "Any ideas, Renna?"

Also, thank you for letting me ask the question aloud before you answered. If the fae was listening in on his thoughts, he might as well offer his gratitude. A tight smile appeared on her lips, the only sign she might have gotten the message.

"The sirens are a tricky lot, to be sure," Renna said, looking at each person gathered in turn. "All are shifters, as you might be aware, but different than others you might be familiar with."

Others?

He'd never heard of the existence of other creatures capable of shifting, and by the looks on his crewmen's faces, he wasn't alone.

"Their primary state is much like our own, though you will only find females among them. They can alter their appearances to look like other sirens, humans, or fae, but they're only able to shift half of themselves into another creature."

"What does that mean?" Aoife asked.

"They really didn't teach you much as a council heir, did they?" Renna asked her, seeming more sympathetic than judgmental.

A breathy laugh escaped Aoife. "I think that's fairly obvious to all of us now. No point in being taught about evil flesh-eating creatures in the north when you're to lead a life devoted to killing your own people."

Maura leaned forward to look around Tommy at Aoife. "Technically only *some* of your people."

Aoife gave another awkward laugh. "Regardless, I don't know much beyond their being rather dangerous and crafty and hungry."

Tommy caught Aoife's eyes and gave her a smile. "That's as good a starting place as any."

"Indeed," Renna said, showing more patience than Tommy would have expected given where they were headed and how many times she was being interrupted.

Though he did notice she did not look directly at him or Maura.

No point in dwelling on that now.

Renna cleared her throat. "They can only change into two types of creature: fish or bird. And even then, it is only a partial shift. It's a bit disconcerting, honestly, a woman with a fish tail for legs or the wings and legs of a bird. As you can imagine, they are stronger than humans, similar to fae in that regard. They delight in tempting their prey before making them suffer. So most of the time they lure you in and then throw all your mistakes in your face until you are close to drowning in your own sorrow. That's when they eat you."

Tommy wasn't sure if it was the subject that had caused his skin to crawl or the casual way Renna was speaking. *They eat you.* It was one thing to know about all of this, another to hear someone say it aloud. His stomach tightened, threatening to push its contents upwards. But he managed to keep it under control.

"Okay. So they pull you in, push you down, and then—" Aoife stopped short, and Tommy could have hugged her for not finishing that sentence.

"Pretty much," Renna said.

Tommy held up a hand. "You said most of the time. What about the other times?"

"Like the rest of us, if they're hungry enough, they'll settle for what they can get. But their queen has more powers still."

"They have a queen?" Aoife asked, eyes widening.

"I feel like the queen having *powers* is more reason for shock than just her existence," Tommy said, but Aoife only shrugged.

"Yes, they have a queen, who—given her fixation on power and control—will likely keep the dagger close. Probably on her. She is not going to be easy to face. Particularly for those who wear their guilt like a cloak about their shoulders." Renna didn't hide the way her eyes focused on Aoife as she explained, but Aoife, to her credit, didn't seem to take offense. In fact, she didn't seem to react to the insinuation at all.

"What does she do, exactly?" Halloran had spoken up this time, her impatience worn plainly on her face.

"Compulsion."

The word fell from the fae's lips and slammed into the wooden floor at their feet.

The quiet that filled the room made Tommy even more uneasy. He had to end it.

"Right, so, what can counter that power? Anything?"

Renna looked at him for the first time since they'd gathered. "Like counters like, though not perfectly."

Tommy pulled in a breath. "We fight compulsion with more compulsion?"

The fae gave a nod at the same time Aoife said, "Isn't that part of your gifts, Renna?"

But it was Maura who answered for her sister. "As long as she's rested, but even then, it's not as strong as the siren's."

Halloran, her hand resting casually on the hilt of her cutlass, flicked her eyes slowly between the sisters. "How is it that you've come to know so much about these demons?"

"Because we helped to confine them to the sound."

Somehow Tommy managed to keep his jaw from dropping as he looked to Maura for confirmation. She replied with a tight-lipped smile and a lift of a shoulder.

"How?" he asked, and Maura turned away as Renna began to answer.

"It took all the royals. Ten of us. Combining our powers to ward the entrance against their kind."

"Okay, wait. You can't just drop all of these things on us at once!" Aoife said, her voice rising. Tommy didn't blame her. The amount of information Renna had provided them with during the last half hour had his head spinning. He leaned heavily onto the desk.

"Well, to be fair, Aoife, she asked," Renna said, levelling a finger at Halloran.

Aoife opened her mouth to give a retort, but Tommy stopped her with a look.

Pinching the bridge of his nose, he closed his eyes and said, "Okay. So. The sirens are evil. Their queen has the dagger on her—we assume—as well as the power of compulsion. Renna can use compulsion—within limits—to counter the queen's." He dropped his hand and opened his eyes, though he kept his head down. "And all of this information is accurate because Renna and her sisters are fae *royalty* who helped trap them in the sound. Centuries ago." Tommy glared sharply at Renna and Maura, the former looking far less apologetic than her younger sister.

"Surprise!" Maura said in a quiet voice, as if it would make any of this easier to swallow.

It should have hurt Tommy that she had kept this secret from him, but he wasn't so much hurt as he was disappointed. He had been right all along. There could be no future with her. Not when she was a royal. A royal with a duty to her kin. No wonder she was needed in Larcsporough.

But could he walk away from her? After he'd given himself the permission to walk over that threshold, to let that dream take root, *to kiss her*? Could he give it all up? Could he take all of his actions and words and promises back?

"Tommy?"

He looked up to find everyone staring at him. Aoife's expression displayed genuine concern, her eyes asking him silently if he was all right. He gave her a nod before forcing his mind back to the matter at hand.

"So what is the plan then? We don't have ten royals to bring together to kill them."

"And you won't need that many," Renna said.

"What do we need?" Tommy asked.

Aoife added her own question. "And is the goal truly to kill them?"

"Yes. Undoubtedly," Renna said. Her grave tone sent another shiver across Tommy's back.

Maura touched his arm and, looking up at him, said, "At least the queen. With her gone, the others will scatter."

"How? If the sound is warded to hold them—" Tommy started.

"Because the ward is tied to the queen's life specifically," Renna answered. "Once she dies, the other sirens will no longer be under her compulsion and can leave."

Aoife stepped forward. Her arm brushed against Tommy's, her eyes seeking an answer from both sisters. "Why would we want them to leave though? Won't they simply wreak havoc across the Aisling?"

"Thankfully no. Triss—the queen—compelled them all to serve her. They've lived under her power for so long, they're long past the point of fighting it. The only way to free them is to kill her. And, believe it or not, they were once peaceful, providing aid to sailors, saving them during storms, guiding them toward safety."

"So where did she come from? How does she have more power?" Aoife asked, each word laced with impatience.

Renna stiffened and shared a glance with Maura as she answered, "She is part fae."

Before Aoife could react to this, Maura added, "She is our sister. Well, half-sister."

Tommy swallowed hard. He could almost hear the air being sucked from the room by the collective breath being drawn.

"Excuse me?" Aoife asked, brows lifted as far as they would go.

"It's a long and not altogether relevant story," Renna offered.

Tommy nearly lost it at that. "Not relevant?! I'm starting to severely question your judgment on what is relevant and not!"

Maura slipped her hand into his and gave it a squeeze. Part of him wanted to toss it aside so she'd understand his anger. But the brush of her thumb over the back of his hand cleared away some of his frustration. Their future might have been doomed from the start, but he refused to let his anger and hurt ruin whatever time they had. He squeezed her hand back and offered her a half-smile.

"The short version, if you think it would help to know, is that our father was tricked by a siren who took the appearance of our mother, with the hope that any offspring would inherit some of his power. And that's exactly what happened. We didn't know—no one knew—until Triss was grown and sought out our family, in search of the man who had sired her."

"What happened?" Aoife asked.

Maura moved to stand, using Tommy's hand to help her up. "He was angry over the trickery, unwilling to accept a reminder of his infidelity, so he turned her away. She didn't take it well and called her kin to meet in the sound to plot her revenge. We only heard about it because one of our friends, a siren, warned us. We followed them there—the four royal families."

"And you know the rest," Renna said.

Mikkel and Collins shared a look. Halloran seemed to be chewing on the information, her stoicism locked into place.

Aoife cut through the silence. "But that still leaves the dagger."

Renna dropped her head to one side. "What about it?"

Seeing Aoife's face redden as her temper flared, Tommy stepped in. "I think most of us know the basics about it, but if we're going to retrieve it from this queen, a refresher might help." He hardened his glare at Renna. "Along with anything you might have forgotten to tell us about?"

"What basics do you know?" Renna asked.

"It brings victory to the one who possesses it," Aoife said, her irritation barely starting to subside.

Mikkel's voice chimed in. "The king of Tyshaly used it to end the Aisling War."

"And apparently," Collins said, "it ended up in the Black Sound guarded by hungry magical creatures."

Tommy looked around at the others.

When no one else spoke up, Renna's shoulders slumped. "Seriously? That's all you know?" She glanced toward the window. "With time getting away from us... the queen of Cregah enchanted it for King Csintala to help him end the war in exchange for his promise to return to her. He won the war, but he lost in the end because the dagger—enchanted as it is—does not suffer betrayers to wield it. He had claimed to love her, but when the king broke his promise and refused her, the dagger worked as it was created to. It led him to his death."

"In the sound."

Tommy had said it to himself, but Maura affirmed his statement with a quiet, "Yes."

"But why—" Aoife paused. "Why doesn't the siren queen use it for her own victory if she keeps it on her?"

Maura, with her eyes locked on her sister, said, "Magical beings can't wield it for themselves. Look at it as a check on its power."

"Okay, so we get in, get the dagger, kill the queen, save the sirens, save Declan." Aoife listed off each task on her fingers, eyes wide with incredulity.

Tommy offered her a smile. "Easy as pie."

CHAPTER 40
AOIFE

BY THE TIME the planning session had concluded, Aoife felt as though she was back in the kraken's whirlpool. Around and around her thoughts swirled and spun, making her head dizzy and her stomach uneasy. Sitting down on the edge of the bed, she looked down at her arms, which were now wiped clean of the kraken's black blood, though it still clung to her clothes and would likely never wash out of them.

Aoife had meant to ask the fae why she hadn't been hurt by it as Gavin had. She wasn't quite sure it could be chalked up to mere adrenaline as she'd assumed at the time. Her fingers traced the swirls of black that were etched into her forearm—up and down, around and around—as her mind continued to churn. She'd never been told what the purpose of the inked art was, and before—before death and pirates and fae and kraken and evil sirens—she had thought nothing of it. It had simply been a mark to set the councilwomen apart from others. But now, after hearing of all the magic that existed in her world—after seeing magic firsthand—she wondered if perhaps the design dancing across her pale skin held a power of its own. Was this what had protected her from the kraken's blood? Could it perhaps protect her from the siren queen's compulsion?

Neither Renna nor Maura had offered any indication that was the case, but she also hadn't gotten a chance to ask directly, as the discussion had rapidly turned toward strategy.

Now the plans were finalized—or as finalized as they could be, given all the unknowns. And Aoife was once again alone in this bedroom. Only a few days ago, she'd stood in this room with Declan preparing to go ashore. Yet it felt like months had passed. And now she had to enter these dangerous waters and rescue him from ravenous, evil monsters. Even though she had faced the kraken and lived, that didn't ease her fears in the slightest. She'd gotten lucky. They all had. If Captain

Halloran hadn't arrived when she did, they would now be in the belly of that beast instead of sailing north toward Declan.

Could she expect similar luck at the sound? She wasn't so sure.

Above her head, footsteps sounded on the quarterdeck, and each one was like a hammer tapping against her sternum. With each tap, her stomach turned and her chest tingled as the familiar sensation of anxiety settled in. Even after all these years of panic attacks, they had not become any more bearable. Remembering Declan's advice only helped a little. With every reminder to breathe, she saw his face and heard his voice, which sent her back under the waves of this internal tempest.

Counting silently to herself, she tried to focus on the air being pulled into her lungs.

Breathing in.

One.

Two.

Three.

Four.

And out.

One.

Two.

Declan.

Damnit.

Breathing in.

One.

Two.

I love you, Aoife.

A growl rumbled in the back of her throat, and she threw herself back on the bed, closing her eyes so she didn't have to see the familiar wooden ceiling.

It wouldn't do her any good to be unfocused, but every other thought brought his face to mind. Perhaps that wasn't a bad thing. Maybe it was good to be reminded of what she was fighting for. But it wasn't only Declan she needed to save. It was all of Cregah.

The weight of that increased the tightness in her chest, and her breathing became shallow and rapid.

She reached up to the collar of her shirt and, finding the delicate chain, pulled the vial of black sand out. She clutched it in her hand, wishing it contained more than mere sand, like perhaps some magical properties to help her heal and relax and prepare.

She'd made up her mind to forgive him. After the kraken attack and facing almost certain death—after being saved at the last moment and being given a second chance of sorts—she had decided to offer him the same. Maybe it wasn't the same as being rescued from the jaws of a monster, but this forgiveness seemed equally important. It was a different type of monster that held Declan, a torment

Aoife knew all too well, as it had clutched her own heart since the day she'd chased that carriage and failed her sister.

But her guilt might still be her undoing.

Their undoing.

Renna had said the sirens favored the souls pained by guilt, darkened by remorse. Would they find Declan alive when they finally caught up to him? Or would the queen already have finished playing with him? Would he be dead?

Whether he was or not, Aoife knew she, too, would be targeted by the queen. No doubt the sirens would sense the guilt she still carried. While it had been shoved aside of late, shadowed by more pressing matters, it whispered to her all the same. She had betrayed her sister. And she could never take that back or make it right. The only thing she could do was work harder to avoid repeating the mistake in the future.

But it was one thing to know what she should do and another to actually manage it.

How could she prepare, exactly, for a powerful ancient being picking at her emotional wounds? Aoife wanted to be brave, to walk into that sound with her chin up as her mother always did, to hold her own as she had in that library.

She wanted to believe, too, that she could find the same confidence and courage even without Declan beside her, but the void he'd left behind—*When you shoved him away, you mean*—seemed to swallow any she possessed.

They had another day or so before they arrived at the sound, and Aoife knew now why Declan had always been impatiently checking his pocket watch. Sailing seemed a tediously slow way to travel, although she had nothing to compare it to, really. It had to be faster than walking, after all, but still, she had to spend so much time waiting, cooped up in the cabin, with nothing but her thoughts for company.

With her eyes still closed, she slowly began to give in to the sleep that beckoned her. She hadn't rested since before they'd entered the kraken's waters, and now, every inch of her seemed worn thin, drained of all energy. Even if she'd wanted to keep pondering what she would do and say when they arrived in the sound, her fatigued mind wouldn't allow it. But still, the heaviness in her chest and the rapid beating of her heart refused to let up, and she slipped into the darkness of sleep with all her nerves pulled taut, her thoughts troubled, her dreams darkened.

Aoife's boots crunched against the white sand of an unfamiliar beach. But this wasn't like normal sand. Even through the soles of her feet, she could feel the coarseness of each grain, which was far bigger than the sand she'd encountered at home or in Foxhaven. An uneasiness settled in her gut, warning her that this beach wasn't like any other.

Something moved in her periphery, swept up onto the disconcerting shore by the dark tide. Her mind screamed at her to not look, but curiosity got the better of her, as it always did. She saw red first. Not the color of blood but the color of falling leaves in autumn, spread out across the ground in thick waves. She knew those waves. She'd envied them.

Lani.

With a swallow, Aoife let her eyes travel from the long strands of wet hair to the body of the woman they belonged to. Her sister's face stared at her. Her green eyes were open but lifeless and dull, her normally radiant complexion gray and placid, and her mouth showing the slight curve of a frown.

Aoife fell to her knees, ignoring how the sharp shards of sand bit into her skin.

"I'm so sorry, Lani. I didn't mean to. You know my damn tongue always gets away from me, and my mind always seems blind to all possible scenarios. It's no excuse. I screwed up." Her words flooded out of her but fell empty upon the ground, surprisingly flat, as though she were making small talk over tea. No one would ever believe it had been an accident, that she could have possibly been that naive to trust her family and all she'd been taught.

The guilt wrenched her heart, squeezing it until she was sure it would be crushed into a million pieces and scattered across this white beach. But instead, her thoughts darkened, and she moved from sorrow to loathing. Loathing of herself. She'd been right to run away. She was no good to anyone. She couldn't do anything right. She only got people hurt, killed, kidnapped. A whisper called to her from a great distance, her name on a breeze she couldn't feel against her skin.

"Declan. Tommy. Gavin. Collins. Maura." The whisper repeated the names of those she held most dear, a desperate attempt to remind her that people cared about her.

But the darkness within her wouldn't listen, and with each name she heard, a harsh truth echoed back.

Declan. Gone.

Tommy. Burdened.

Gavin. Injured.

Collins. Wounded.

Maura. Weakened.

And Lani. Dead.

Everyone was better off without her. She couldn't do anything right. Why even try? What was the point?

But then another voice cut through the whispers, this one familiar and comforting, like a loving embrace around her shoulders or a gentle stroke upon her hand.

"It's not your fault, Aoife. None of it."

She balked at it, but the voice continued.

"She forgave you. Lani did."

Aoife's gaze snapped up. Only one person could know such a thing, and he now stood a few feet away from her, looking just as he had when she'd left him standing in that cove. Declan.

Bloody. Distraught. Desperate.

Yet his eyes—those stormy grays that threatened to pull her under—held nothing but the love she'd seen in them in his cabin before he'd kissed her.

"What?" She tried to say the word, but no sound came. He heard it all the same.

"Before I—before she died, your sister gave me a message. If I ever came across you, I was to tell you that she forgives you."

Aoife's pulse sped up as her mind whirred, processing his words, and a slew of emotions hit her in turn: gratitude, peace, frustration, anger. Her jaw clenched. Her eyes burned into his.

"And you tell me this now?" she screamed, her voice finding new strength in her fury. *"You knew how guilty I felt! You saw how it plagued me! You saw how I struggled! And you stayed silent. For what? To save your own heart? To save yourself from the discomfort of confessing what you'd done?"*

"Yes." A single word. A single, emotionless word. No remorse. No sorrow. Empty. Hollow.

His eyes dulled, becoming as vacant as his voice, and they glazed over, no longer seeing her but seeing through her. He gaped. His head lolled to one side. His legs gave out. And when he crumpled to the ground, his body as lifeless as Lani's, Aoife tried to scream, but all the air was sucked from her lungs at the sight of the woman before her.

Her hair was as black as the kraken's blood, and her dark eyes pulled Aoife into them. A cruel smile graced her beautiful, wicked face.

And Aoife lost all hope of getting Declan back—of saving anyone.

CHAPTER 41
DECLAN

DECLAN KNEW he still had feet because he could see them standing beneath him on the white sand of the beach. But he could no better control them than he could control the siren who sat before him atop a large rock, her legs—bare and delicate but strong—crossed at the knees. At least he still had some power over his mind.

For now.

Was that his own thought? Or her voice invading his mind? He wasn't sure.

"Nice throne you have there," he said, forcing his face to relax.

"You're trying too hard, Declan," she crooned and switched her legs to cross the other way. He didn't answer but raised a single brow in question. "Trying too hard to remain calm."

"Well you can imagine how this current situation might make it a challenge."

"Also trying too hard to fix the brokenness within you." She clicked her tongue as she lifted a hand to point to his left. "Didn't Callum here warn you it was too late? Sounds like it, if I'm getting his thoughts adequately."

Declan couldn't move his head to turn toward the other pirate, but out of the corner of his eye he could see the man kneeling in the sand, his hands clasped behind his back, bound with invisible manacles, just like Declan.

"Aye, he did. But I tend not to heed those who hit me over the head and throw me into a dank brig."

Triss laughed, her deep purple eyes sparkling. "One of the many mistakes you've made."

"So it would seem," he replied. "Are we to sit around here all day making idle chitchat? Or did you want something from me?"

Though her laughter had ceased, her wicked smile remained. "Always so impatient. Always so ready for action. But one thing I've learned over these many centuries, it's good to slow down once in a while and savor the moments. Especially the good ones."

"Can't say this tops my list of good moments."

Leaning forward, her arms resting on her legs, she winked at him. "Ah, but does it top the bad?" Her eyes flitted up to the sky as if she were searching her thoughts. Or searching his. She let out a disappointed sigh. "That's too bad. I had hoped to at least make your top five. Oh well. There is still time for that."

Declan tried to keep his memories at bay, shoving them back into the far reaches of his mind, but they wouldn't listen. Triss had control of them now: visions of his parents disappearing, of Aoife walking away, of Tommy being stabbed, of Lani's face before he'd pushed her, of Killian's tortured body. They ran in a loop in his mind, each one vying for attention like children trying to get their mother to notice them.

"Ah," Triss's viciously sweet voice cut through the images. "There it is. That's the darkness I crave. The despair. The sorrow. Makes your blood that much more..."

"Potent?"

Her lips curled up once more, and she shook her head. "Delicious."

Declan dug deeper into his resolve, and with another push, he managed to get each scene to dissolve into the void, leaving his mind—and his expression—calm once again.

Triss frowned as she studied him.

"You're stronger than I expected."

"I get that a lot."

"Well, we'll see how strong you are once she arrives."

Aoife, the only *she* who he knew—hoped—was on her way here. Before he could respond, though, Triss was speaking once more, but not to him.

"Callum Grayson." She dropped her head to one side as she studied the man. "You look just like your father. To be honest, I didn't expect him to follow through with his word. I could see all his plans unfurl as we made our deal." She continued as if speaking to herself, not bothering to wait for any response or reaction from either pirate. "And yes, before you argue, I did compel him to fulfill his agreement. But wouldn't you know? The further away someone gets from me, the weaker the compulsion becomes. It wasn't always that way, mind you. Before, I could make anyone do anything for as long as I wanted, even if they left my side. As it turns out, the ward those fae scum placed around this sound dampens the compulsion. And I didn't know that when I let him leave. He was the first I'd ever granted freedom to. Serves me right, I suppose. I've learned my lesson since."

What did she want from Callum's father? Declan wondered. Triss answered as if he had asked it aloud.

"What I want from everyone, dear Declan. Blackened souls. Burned hearts. Rancid blood. Unfortunately, Tobias Grayson had none of those things when he came to me. All full of virtue and hope. Utterly disgusting and useless." She paused to listen to Declan's silent question. "Ah, you haven't figured that out yet? You're losing your touch there. Or perhaps the rumors of you are more far-fetched than people know. Tobias Grayson fought me on it, of course, with all that goodness inside him. He didn't want to pay the price for his freedom. He refused. He would have rather died here, never to take the treasure I offered to win the hand of his love back home, never to have a family. So I did what I had to. And I compelled him. To send me his firstborn."

Triss released her hold on Declan's body enough that he was able to look toward Callum, who still hadn't moved, his eyes staring blankly ahead.

"Don't look so worried, Declan," Triss said, her voice far more pleasant than it had any right to be. "You will get your turn soon enough, once I'm done with him."

Before Declan could respond, Callum's face contorted in pain, his body going rigid and tense before starting to shake. Triss stood and strode slowly over to the kneeling man.

"Stop fighting it, Callum," she said in an eerily sweet tone. "I'm not showing you anything you don't already know, anything you haven't already done."

As if on silent command, Callum's body went still before he rose to his feet, coming face to face with his tormentor. She cupped his face with one of her slender, perfect hands, stroking the length of his scar with her thumb, acting more like a lover than a hungry monster.

"You were the price," she said. "You were the cost Tobias had to pay to take the riches I offered. And yet you still admire him. Fortunately—for me—you never lived up to his virtue, and that blackness in your heart will be your demise. And my treat."

What was she referring to? Callum had been so confident his past would be no issue, so sure he had conquered his own demons sufficiently. That had obviously been a mistake, as the queen now gripped his chin in her hand, and it was no longer the sweet touch she'd shown him earlier. With a growl, Triss pulled his jaw hard to the left. Callum's scream echoed off the rocks around them. Declan saw no blood, but Callum's jaw hung askew. When Callum tried to move it, he screamed again, and Triss's laughter joined in.

Without turning her attention away from Callum's broken face, she answered one of the million questions coursing through Declan's head. "What did you expect, Captain? Did you really think we didn't play with our food a bit?" She paused, no doubt listening in some more. "Ah, well, that was rather naive of you. No, our fun here doesn't merely affect the mind. As you might have witnessed earlier with my friends' welcome party, we like to get our hands a little dirty first."

Callum's eyes were now closed tight, arms once again shaking from shock. Triss smiled, a maniacal glint in her eyes as she waved a hand behind Callum and called out, "Come. Sit. Watch."

The sirens passed by Declan, stroking his neck with cold, wet hands, and he clenched his eyes shut. He had no desire to watch them attack Callum as they had the man on the beach.

His heart went cold as all hope washed away.

CHAPTER 42
CAIT

THE WALK back from the pit cave was nearly unbearable. An awkward silence remained with Cait, Adler, and Penny the entire way. It wasn't intentional, at least not for Cait, but after finding herself in such an intimate position with Adler, all words had abandoned her. Every time she settled on something to say, she second-guessed it and stopped herself. And now the silence had gone on for so long that anything she said would feel even more awkward, regardless of what it was.

So she continued walking, focusing on her breathing and the sound of their footsteps on the trail. Every now and then she gave a sideways glance toward Penny, who walked between her and Adler. The woman stared blankly ahead, not even looking down when her foot tripped on a stick or a rock, and not responding to Adler when he caught her by the arm and righted her once more.

Cait could see Adler looking at her, but she ignored him. Why should she be embarrassed about how she'd fallen into his lap? She could have thanked him for saving her life. She should have thanked him. But she didn't know how to talk to him anymore.

They had shared more of their past during their wait than she had intended, and she didn't know where that left them. She'd allowed him into the Rogues because she wanted to grant him his revenge on the council. Nothing more. But it wouldn't be bad to be friends with him, would it?

No friends. Friends were a liability.

It was why she kept a certain emotional distance from Kira and Aron and Eva—and Maggie. Her chest tightened. How much stronger would this guilt be had Maggie been a friend and not just one of her Rogues?

You still care for them though.

But not like she did for Declan. Or Lucan.

She'd let him too far into her life before realizing the danger of having such an attachment, but loneliness had kept her from pushing him away completely.

No, she couldn't be friends—or anything else—with Adler.

When they reached the outskirts of Morshan and the path gave way to cobblestones, Cait gently pulled Penny's arm to get her to stop. Turning the woman, she peered into her eyes, which were still lifeless from her earlier trauma. The plan wouldn't work if Penny couldn't snap out of it, but this wasn't one of those things you could slap someone out of. Or pinch them out of.

It took time.

Time that was quickly running out.

"Is there somewhere we can take her?" Adler asked, his voice rough from going so long without speaking.

Cait blinked rapidly as she looked at him and shook her head as she thought. "I don't know. I had planned for her to be able to—and eager to—spread word to the people immediately, which was obviously stupid of me. I should have expected this."

With a casual shrug, Adler's mouth curved into that upside down smile. "You were uncharacteristically optimistic. Nothing wrong with that."

A snarl started in the back of her throat, but she pushed it back down. "No, there *is* something wrong with that when it means I didn't plan for any contingencies. I wasn't prepared, and now—"

"Now we figure it out."

She wanted to interpret his tone as mocking or condescending, but part of her nearly swooned at his patience and desire to help her.

Nearly.

He's just helping himself and his own interests.

And Cait needed to do the same.

"We need to get her back to the pub without anyone noticing, but it's the middle of the damn day, and we have no cloak or anything to put on her. We can't exactly wait until dark either."

Turning away from her, Adler shifted his weight and peered around the trees toward town. Cait breathed through her impatience and counted four deep breaths before he finally spoke.

"Wait here. I'll be right back."

Before Cait could protest, he was gone, leaving her to wonder where in the sands he thought she would wander off to with their near catatonic charge. When he didn't return as quickly as she'd hoped, she opted to try and pull Penny from her stupor, knowing it wasn't likely to work. But it seemed better than standing here doing nothing.

"Penny," she started, trying to get into her line of sight once more, but the woman's eyes looked through her. Cait took Penny's hands and was surprised to find them still trembling slightly. Giving the unsteady hands a gentle squeeze, she tried again. "Penny, I'm sorry you had to go through that. But you're safe now."

Even as she uttered the words, she tasted them for the lie they were. If anything,

Penny's life was in far greater danger than it had been when she'd woken up that morning. And that was on Cait's conscience.

But it was the only way.

Except it might not work, and then what? She'd put an innocent woman in the crosshairs of the council for nothing. This felt a million times worse than the guilt already simmering in her chest, because unlike Maggie, Penny hadn't signed up for this. She hadn't had a choice. She'd been forced into this situation and used.

The only way.

No matter how much she repeated the words, though, her inner discomfort wouldn't be soothed.

Refocusing on the woman before her, Cait attempted to clear the emotion lodged in her throat.

"We could use your help though. If you're able. I know we haven't been close—"

That's an understatement!

"—but now that you know what the council does, we need to inform everyone else. We need you to tell the others. Please."

Cait waited, counting several slow breaths as she searched Penny's face for any sign of acknowledgment. Seeing nothing, she dropped her chin to her chest in defeat. Where was Adler? What was taking him so long? Had he run all the way back to the pub to grab a cloak? Had something happened to him?

Her mind spiraled through all the dangers that could have befallen him.

Kidnapped by pirates like Declan.

Discovered by more of the council's hired thugs.

Fallen into a hole somewhere.

Or maybe he had ditched her and abandoned the plan.

Maybe he had never been on her side at all.

This time Cait didn't suppress the growl that pushed its way out. This cycle of thinking was becoming tiresome. Would she ever fully trust him? Would she ever stop doubting his word?

Before she could answer those questions for herself, he returned, stepping onto the path so casually that Cait wanted to throw her shoe at him for making her worry. He might as well have been whistling a lighthearted tune as he strolled up, with that dimple-creating smile of his and bright blue eyes. When they met her own—which must have quite clearly shown her ire—his smile immediately vanished.

"What?"

Cait ground her teeth and pressed her lips into a tight line. "Nothing."

"Clearly," he said, his expression the epitome of innocence. He shuffled his feet, fidgeting in place like a boy caught stealing a cookie from the kitchen rather than the rugged pirate he was.

Former pirate.

"Did you at least find something useful while you were gone?"

"Will this do?" he asked, pulling a bunch of deep brown fabric from under his arm and shaking it out to reveal an old cloak. How had she not noticed that when he'd arrived?

He held it up behind Penny—who still hadn't moved—to show how it would cover her whole frame. And then some. The cloak was about a foot too long for the slight woman, but it was better than nothing.

"It will have to," she said and began to situate it around Penny's shoulders with Adler's help. "Let's hope she doesn't trip on it. Where did you get it anyway?"

"On a ship near Turvala."

Cait raised a single brow at him. Other people might fall for those kinds of teasing answers, but Cait had grown used to them with Declan—even with how little he visited.

"What? It's true." Adler frowned.

"You got it off a ship?"

He nodded.

"Just now?"

He cocked his head to the side and gave her a quizzical look. "Well, no, obviously not. A couple years ago, I think."

Cait drew in a deep breath as her eyes rolled toward the treetops. This man was going to be the death of her, one way or another.

"And where were you keeping it?"

"Do you really want to know where I stash my hard-earned yet sadly depleted goods? Or would you like to get her back to the pub before sundown?"

Cait had the niggling suspicion he was dodging the question, but he wasn't wrong. The sun was fading fast, and his errand to retrieve the cloak hadn't helped them in their urgency. Though it had helped them more than anything Cait had done.

Don't sell yourself short.

Lucan had said those words to her right after she'd sent Declan off, yet no amount of repeating them kept her self-deprecating inner thoughts at bay. But she could at least shove them aside. Even if only temporarily.

Without another word, Cait took Penny's arm and guided her out of the trees. Adler strode behind them.

At the pub's back door in the alley, Cait paused before stepping into the back hallway. Silence. Just as expected. The pub wasn't due to open for another hour or so, which gave them enough time to get Penny situated in the spare bedroom upstairs—the room that had once been Cait's, before she'd moved her bed into the main living area for convenience.

A flash of movement caught her eye as she neared the stairs though, and she stopped in her tracks, causing Penny to run into her. Adler pulled the woman back gently. Without looking behind her, Cait motioned with her hand for Adler to take Penny up the stairs.

Stretching her neck, Cait peered into the pub. Chairs sat upside down on the tables, and beyond them, standing near the door, Naeve fidgeted, her hands trembling as they clutched at her skirts. Swallowing back her irritation that the girl had the stupidity to come back to the pub so soon, Cait stepped forward. Glancing around, she confirmed Naeve was alone.

"Tell me." There was no time for pleasantries today.

The girl blinked rapidly and drew in a lungful of air. "The council. They're coming."

Cait's eyes widened, but she kept her surprise in check. No need to get worked up until the situation called for it. "Explain."

"To Morshan. They're on their way right now," Naeve said. Her eyes darted around the room and over her shoulder, as if the council might have arrived already.

"For what, do you know?"

A rapid string of nods. "Aye. A town meeting with the people."

Confusion swept through Cait. In all her twenty-eight years, she'd never heard of the ruling council coming to Morshan—heirs, yes, although not after they were matched—let alone holding an official meeting in the town. "Why?"

Even as she asked, though, she knew.

Two heirs gone.

A known spy caught.

They were vying for the love of the people.

"I don't know," Naeve admitted.

"Where exactly? And when? We'll need to be there."

"The square. On the steps of the old library." She glanced to the clock above the pub. "Two hours past midday, I believe."

That gave them twenty minutes. Cait mentally calculated the fastest route from the pub before offering a nod to the girl. "Get back to the council hall, before anyone notices you were gone."

Naeve flashed a small smile, dipped into a curtsy, and turned toward the door.

"And, Naeve?" Cait asked. The girl stopped and looked over her shoulder. "Good job."

It wasn't until she was gone and the door was shut once more that Cait allowed herself to turn back to where Adler and Penny waited. Adler's lifted his chin with a silent question, while Penny looked as out of it as ever.

"You mean you weren't listening in on that conversation?" Cait asked.

"Of course I was, but I'd hate to assume what you're planning."

"First, let's get her upstairs to the spare room." She nodded at the stairs, but Adler didn't make any effort to move.

"I think she should come with us," he countered. "The council isn't likely to know about her exile, since the pirates took her straight to the pit."

Cait's thoughts caught up to his logic, and she interrupted his explanation. "And if we bring her to the square, someone will see and ask the council about her."

"If we're lucky, she'll snap out of this funk in time to tell the entire town the truth."

Cait couldn't help but smile. This just might work. Perhaps not all hope was lost.

But as they walked back out the door to the alley, not wanting to take a chance of someone spotting them escorting her, Cait realized she'd forgotten one thing.

"Lucan," she said, trying not to bump into Penny as Adler stopped walking in front of her.

"What?"

"Where is he?"

Though Adler loved to tease her best friend to no end, his regard for him was evident now in the way his blue eyes softened. "I'm sure he's fine. He probably went back to his place to lay low for a bit." Cait breathed out a sigh in time for Adler to add with a shrug, "Or he fell into the Aisling."

Let's hope not.

Adler and Cait kept to the alleys and lesser-traveled back streets as they led Penny toward the square. The plan wasn't a great one, but that wasn't particularly new for Cait. They'd done well with worse in the past.

As they neared the square, Cait clicked her tongue, and Adler stopped at the corner, remaining in the shadow cast by the building. The passageway they were in was smaller than most in Morshan, providing them with a limited view of the public space beyond. A few people walked in and out of sight, about the same number as any other afternoon, meaning the town hadn't gotten notice of the council's impending visit.

Leaning around Penny, who still appeared dazed, Cait whispered to Adler, "Stay here until they arrive and the crowd gathers a bit. I'm going to go around to the other side. I'm trusting you to find the right time to present Penny to them."

"Aye," he said, and his eyes dropped down to her lips so quickly she was sure she'd imagined it. "And after?"

"Pub."

She turned without another word and headed away from them, but Adler whispered her name, stopping her before she'd gotten far. "What if things go south?"

"Same. But in the storeroom."

Once she was back out on the street, Cait lowered her hood and began walking toward the main road. She didn't necessarily want to intercept them, but allowing them a chance to see her in town, being a model citizen of Morshan, seemed the best way to keep suspicion off of her. Before long, she heard the rumble of hooves and wheels on the cobbled stones, a sound not often heard here, where no one owned a horse, let alone a carriage. Most residents had no need for anything more than a simple cart, and even then, it wasn't that common to even own one of those. Only those responsible for making deliveries for the council had one.

So it was no surprise to Cait when people's faces, full of confusion and wonder, began to appear in the open windows and doors along the street. Someone called down to her, "McCallagh! What is it? Do you know?"

She feigned ignorance, donning a bewildered expression as she shrugged. "I'll find out." As she walked away, she could hear the doors behind her thud shut, and people began to trail after her. No point in looking back. This was what the council wanted. And what Cait needed.

An audience.

But why would the council be doing this? And why now? They governed from afar, preferring only to be seen when a citizen had a grievance to report or for the annual harvest offering, and even then, they kept their distance, claiming that a hands-off approach to ruling was best for everyone, even as they passed down law after law to control everything from curfews to business hours.

How had things gotten this bad? Her parents had told her stories of a time before the treaty, before the war, when the land was prosperous, the people free to pursue the families they wanted and the futures they dreamed of. They'd never lived that life themselves, but their own parents had passed down historical accounts to them, protected and kept secret through the centuries, lest they get damaged by war or fall victim to the council's strict rules about appropriate reading material.

The library—now looming before her, its regal facade kept pristine—had been closed decades ago, its contents sorted, cataloged, and removed. What remained inside, no one knew. Although it was unlocked like all other buildings in Morshan, no one dared enter, the fear of exile always looming over them. Even the Rogues didn't tempt fate with that one. It simply wasn't worth the risk and—as far as Cait knew—offered no benefit to their cause.

The thundering of the carriage grew louder behind her, and she instinctively moved to the side of the road, pressing her back against a building as she turned toward the sound. The horses, a pair of chestnut brown mares with black manes, cantered into view, pulling a simple but elegant closed carriage behind them. The driver, a sullen-looking woman in black, stared blankly forward as they passed Cait and the others lining the street. Murmurings began all around, like an echo of the horses' hoofbeats. She didn't have a moment to think before the crowd began to push her toward the library and the square.

Somehow Cait managed to get to the far edge of the growing mob of people who were rushing to see what was going on in town. As soon as they reached the library and everyone entered the square, Cait veered off and moved behind the building, wanting to be nowhere near where Adler and Penny emerged.

As Cait made her way around, her mind wandered to Lucan. He'd managed to get the message to Tommy on the ship just fine without incident, though he had later complained profusely about how he'd almost been taken out to sea against his will.

Lucan could take care of himself. He was a grown man, after all. But still, an ache grew behind her sternum, and she worried about all the possible tragedies that could have befallen him since they'd parted.

The crowd quieted as the carriage door opened, everyone—even those at the front of the group—craning their necks to see who had come to visit. Cait didn't. Assuming Naeve had been honest and heard things correctly, she knew who this was. When all three passengers had stepped out, the driver shut the door once more, climbed up into her seat, and drove the horses on into the crowd, forcing everyone to move aside or be trampled.

Three women ascended the steps to the library, their movements regal and refined. About halfway up, they halted, and as one, they turned to face the crowd. Two were markedly older than the third, and none of them held any resemblance to Aoife, though Cait couldn't clearly identify any of them. They were obviously all councilwomen, the swirls of black ink visible on their forearms as they clasped their hands before them and looked over the square. The woman standing in the middle, whose waves of red hair reminded Cait of the vibrant sunsets of summer nights, raised her chin and spoke, her words ringing clear in the gathering space as they bounced off the surrounding buildings.

"Good afternoon," she said with a tone that was surprisingly flat compared to the dynamic nature of her appearance. Her hands remained clasped elegantly against her green dress that was simple in style but made from a material no average citizen would have in their wardrobe. "Our visit to Morshan has been long overdue. Thank you for being here on such short notice. We had hoped our first visit to meet with you would be on better terms, but that was not to be." Her chin lowered, as if she were fighting back tears. The women beside her lifted hands to her shoulders, seemingly to comfort her, though Cait saw no tenderness in their demeanor. Once again, the councilwoman looked out at the assembled crowd.

"Unfortunately, our eldest sister, Melina, could not join us, as Lord Madigen has extended his visit to see her. She sends her apologies and hopes to see you at the harvest offering next month. For those who may not know me, I am Fiona, and this is my sister, Brigeh, and her daughter, Darienn." She gestured gracefully to her companions as she named them.

Cait looked out over the crowd and marveled at how quiet everyone was. Apparently, the presence of the councilwomen had put them all in a trance. Except, their expressions were not blank and unseeing, but uneasy and cautious. Like a child when they first see the sea.

Brigeh's blonde hair—which had less red in it than her daughter's—flowed down her back, and even from this distance, Cait could see how vibrant her blue eyes were. She now addressed the people. Although her voice was harsher than her sister's, it was far sweeter than most of the people Cait served on a daily basis.

"There have been rumors about two of our heirs, and we have come today to lay those to rest." She paused. "The rumors are true."

The councilwoman must have expected the instant chatter that spread through the assembly, because her hand shot up to quiet it as soon as it started.

"But, in an effort to be completely transparent with you, our people, we wanted you to know what happened, because rumors left unchecked will undoubtedly put at risk the peace we have worked so hard for all these centuries."

Cait stifled a cough at the lie, thankful she wasn't near anyone who might notice her contempt.

Brigeh continued, "We did, sadly, have to exile two of our own." A gasp rose from the people, though it seemed not all were shocked by this news. "We do not want to defile their reputation any more than their exile already has, so all we can tell you is that they broke their allegiance to you and to our country. We cannot afford to have heirs to the council who do not have the Cregahn people's best interests at heart."

A voice pierced the air from the back of the crowd. Cait couldn't see who spoke, but she didn't need to. Penny had recovered.

"Excuse me, Your Grace, but can you tell me if you took their lives yourselves? Or did you have your pirates drag them off to be pushed into the pit?"

To their credit, the councilwomen showed no reaction. The people of Morshan shifted, presumably to allow Penny a clear path to the library steps. Once again, whispers rustled through the space like a rushing stream.

"And you are?" Fiona asked, looking over Penny casually.

"Penny. The restaurant owner you tried to have killed—I mean, *exiled*—today."

The three women looked at one another, their eerie smiles turning into equally disturbing laughter. *Like three witches cackling,* Cait thought.

"My dear lady," Fiona offered, "when we granted your appeal today at your hearing, we did not expect you to disrespect our mercy so openly."

Penny's scoff filled the air, echoing off the buildings. "What hearing? What appeal? When was I ever given such a chance to request your *mercy*?"

Some of the people closest to Cait murmured to one another, and she could see a seed of doubt beginning to sprout in their minds just as she had hoped it would. But she needed more than mere seedlings to convince the people to stand up to the council.

Brigeh took a step down, then another. "It appears we should have carried out the *exile* after all. Our mercy was wasted on this one. Cregah has no need for liars."

A man called out from deep within the crowd. "How do we know it's not *you* who is lying?"

A few people voiced their agreement, but most remained quiet, waiting, tension thrumming and pulsing among them.

"Who has fed you?" Brigeh asked.

Fiona stepped forward. "And who has maintained peace on our shores?"

Both women turned to Darienn, who took a few confident steps forward to stand beside her mother, before her voice—youthful but powerful—rang out. "Who has kept you safe from pirate raids and our enemies' assaults?"

"And who is to keep us safe from *you*?" another voice responded. Cait's eyes slid closed at the familiar tone and cadence.

Lucan.

Perhaps it would have been better for him to have fallen into the Aisling, if it would have kept him from doing something this stupid.

The councilwomen didn't respond, but their attention was now effectively directed away from Penny. Cait inched her way around the mass of people, trying to hide behind the taller individuals as she went. But Lucan had already begun speaking again before she could reach him.

"Who cares for those starving in the other villages? Who ensures they get the medicine they need? Who protects them from poverty while we—" He was cut off with a sickening thud, and he doubled over.

Cait moved faster but stopped when she saw blood dripping from Lucan's face, and then she saw Adler—with Tiernen's colors tied around his waist—standing there shaking his hand from the impact.

CHAPTER 43

AOIFE

SLEEP HAD EVADED Aoife since they'd started this chase, the nightmares refusing to release her. They were growing more and more vivid too, and even hours after waking fully, she could not forget the woman who had appeared in this latest one.

With vicious beauty, the woman had eyed Aoife like a tasty morsel instead of a person, but there had been more in her eyes than insatiable hunger.

Recognition.

Like they had met before.

It was preposterous of course, but she remained unsettled by it nevertheless. She might have asked Maura or Renna about it, since they knew all about the creatures they were heading toward. But Renna was busy tending to Bria as best she could without using any more of her power than was absolutely necessary. And Maura...

Aoife pressed her lips together. Why did she feel so uncomfortable approaching her and Tommy? They were both her friends, after all, and she had confided in each of them separately. But still, it didn't feel right to cut into what little time they had together.

From the doorway to Declan's quarters, she could see them standing against the intact section of railing, looking out at the sea as they conversed. She took note of the little gestures they used with one another, the subtle smiles, the near touches.

She shook her head and pulled her attention away. If she wasn't going to interrupt them, she should also avoid staring. But she couldn't awkwardly remain here either.

Closing the door behind her, she made her way out onto the deck and spotted Gavin at the helm as usual. He had been oddly silent with her since the kraken had exploded all over her. It reminded her, unfortunately, of how the crew had initially reacted to her presence aboard the ship. To his credit Gavin didn't appear to want to throw her overboard, but he did seem wary of her.

She didn't recognize most of the other crew working on the deck, and as she spun in a circle, she realized staying at the doorway would have been less awkward than what she was doing now. There had to be something she could do, some way she could be preparing. Sleep was impossible. Maybe Collins would be willing to train more with her. But he was still recovering from his injuries, and dagger skills weren't likely to come in handy against the sirens anyway. She certainly couldn't help the crew with their duties.

Which left her with nothing to do but agonize over their situation. They had discussed everything to death while planning, and no one would want to spend more time discussing her silly musings.

Something touched her shoulder, and she jumped, letting out an embarrassing shriek as she spun around. Captain Halloran looked on the verge of smiling—something Aoife wasn't sure the hardened woman remembered how to do, assuming she ever had. With a hand pressed to her chest, Aoife pushed her breath out and quickly drew in another. "Don't do that! You can't sneak up on someone like that!"

Halloran crossed her arms. "I don't sneak."

"Well, what do you call it then?"

"I call it getting someone's attention when I've been calling their name with no response."

Aoife's eyes widened. She glanced around, pleased to see no one was gawking at her as she'd expected.

"Sorry, Captain," Aoife said, returning her attention to Halloran, who stood regally before her now—not impatiently either, which helped ease Aoife's still-pounding heart. "What was it you needed?"

"I wondered if you might have a moment to talk." The tall woman looked almost bored.

"Are you sure?"

"Why wouldn't I be? Is there some reason I should not—" Halloran didn't get a chance to finish her question before Aoife was waving her hands between them.

"Oh, no, I mean, I have nothing to hide, if that's what you're thinking." She paused. Halloran gave no indication that had been the case. Aoife fumbled with her words once more. "It's just we've spent the last however many hours talking. Figured everyone would be tired of it. Seems like all we do is talk and talk and talk."

"You mean when you're not breaking the fae out of their prison or fighting the kraken?"

Aoife pursed her lips to the side and then shrugged. "Well, that's only two things. The rest of the time we're either talking or sleeping or..."

This time there was no question it was a smile—albeit a small one—gracing the captain's full lips. "The pirate life not providing enough action for you, is that it?"

The words punched Aoife right in the chest, so hard she was shocked it didn't physically knock the air from her lungs. *Don't beg for action if it's not what you want.*

She could almost feel Declan's breath in her ear now, repeating what he'd said before, challenging her. It had been frightening at the time, but looking back, she understood why he'd done it, could see it for the self-preservation tactic it was. He'd needed to push her away.

But then something had changed.

"Aoife?" Halloran asked, and for a moment Aoife worried she had fallen or tripped or done some other stupid thing. Thankfully, though, she was still on her feet.

"Yeah, I guess. Well, no, but you don't want to know about my drama with Declan," Aoife said, and she once again waved her hand in front of her face as if batting away the captain's question.

Halloran's hand shot up, grabbing Aoife's wrist and stopping it. Aoife snapped her mouth shut and widened her eyes, fearful of what this captain was about to do. But Halloran didn't appear angry at all. More tired than anything else. With more care than Aoife expected, Halloran lowered their hands, dropping Aoife's at her waist.

"Stop" was all she said before she pivoted on her heel and walked toward the prow of the ship. Aoife didn't know exactly what had just happened, and she gawked at the woman as she retreated. But Halloran's hand appeared over her shoulder, gesturing for Aoife to follow her as she called out, "Come on, Aoife. Let's talk."

⤢

AOIFE SETTLED HERSELF BESIDE HALLORAN, who had taken to leaning back against the railing. For several moments, they stood there in silence, causing Aoife to wonder if maybe she hadn't heard the captain correctly and she wasn't supposed to have followed her. But as she opened her mouth to say something, Halloran began, her voice quiet. "How much do you know about Declan?"

Aoife, startled and curious, stared dumbly at her.

Halloran didn't look at her as she repeated the question, this time with an edge of annoyance to her voice.

Aoife shook her head. "Very little actually."

Halloran nodded.

The silence stretched out long enough to make Aoife wonder if she was supposed to be saying more or not. Should she keep looking at the woman? Look out to the sea? What should she do with her hands?

Aoife dared to study the captain's face, which showed no hint she would speak again soon. Ignoring the nervous tightening of her gut, Aoife said, "Why do you ask?"

"What happened after I left you on that rock?" The question came out so quietly, Aoife wasn't sure she'd heard correctly.

"What—"

The captain cut her off with a shake of her head and repeated the question, barely louder this time.

Aoife shifted her feet. "I thought you didn't want to know about—"

Halloran lifted a hand. "I didn't. But I told him..." She paused. "But I need to know. If I'm to help rescue him, I don't need to go in blind to whatever is going on between you."

"Why do you think something—"

A growl escaped Halloran this time—not angry but annoyed. "Don't. Don't think you can fool me. Now, talk."

Aoife hadn't discussed it—not in such detail—since Tommy had demanded to know why Declan hadn't returned with her. But the words still burned her throat as she forced them out, keeping them limited, as Halloran was undoubtedly less willing to tolerate her spilling all of her emotions.

When she finished, Halloran's eyes slid shut, and Aoife wondered whose side the captain would be on. She'd beaten herself up enough over what had happened—walking away from him and stepping all over his heart in the process. She didn't particularly want a lecture from this woman.

"And will you forgive him?" the captain asked, eyes still closed. When Aoife didn't answer right away, she looked to her.

"I already have." The words came out quiet, meek. Aoife cleared her throat and clarified. "I have. Though he doesn't know yet."

"Good."

"Why do you care exactly? I mean, it's one thing to know the situation. Another to have an opinion about it, no?"

Halloran's mouth pulled into a half-smile. "You're more perceptive than I gave you credit for. You don't get to where I am being ruled by emotions. But you also can't ignore them entirely. I made a promise, years ago."

Aoife opened her mouth to ask a question, but Halloran continued before she could.

"To the McCallaghs. Ada and Carthach. Declan's parents."

Questions spun around Aoife's head, but she knew better than to let them all tumble out. Surprisingly enough, her tongue obeyed, and she managed to ask only one. "How did you know them?"

Captain Halloran remained quiet for so long that Aoife thought she might not answer at all. But when she did finally respond, her voice held only a hint of its typical roughness.

"They gave me aid when I came to Morshan. Alone. No money. No connections. My home had been hit hard by illness. Supplies had stopped arriving from Morshan. With no medicine or healers, many died, if not from the fever then from starvation. My betrothed among them."

Aoife's heart threatened to pound its way out of her chest as understanding hit her. No supplies from Morshan. From the council. It wasn't just the exiles. The council was letting their people die. Did they know? Was it intentional? Why would they let their people die for no reason?

"You didn't know." Halloran's voice sliced through Aoife's frantic thoughts. Aoife could only shake her head. "I didn't either, until I got to Morshan, with its wealth and its comfort. After so much loss, the sight of it dropped me to my knees right in the middle of the cobblestones outside the pub. Must have looked crazy, but Ada didn't treat me as such when she fetched me, took me inside, called for her husband to get me a drink. I couldn't pay, but she insisted it was a gift."

Aoife struggled to process all of this, but her mind was hung up on how this wasn't the Halloran she'd met before. Why was she opening up to her? Why now? Why...ever?

"You look confused." That sounded more like the Halloran Aoife knew. Words cold and sharp.

Before Aoife could think better of it, she blurted out, "Why are you telling me?"

Looks like you haven't gotten control of your tongue after all.

She braced herself for Halloran's gruff rebuke, but the response, while certainly not friendly, wasn't as harsh as Aoife had expected.

"Because you need to know. What the council is doing. What your *mother* is doing. I lost my entire family and my home. Finding the McCallaghs and their fight to save the country? I promised to help them."

"How?"

An annoyed huff from Halloran accompanied a hard glare. Aoife needed to stop interrupting.

"My plan was two-fold: discover how the council carried out exiles and somehow get the truth out to the other lands, to make the hidden violence there known. It was to be a lengthy ploy. Years spent working my way up the ranks on pirate crews. Doing whatever I needed to—" She paused, and a shadow of sadness passed over her eyes. "Whatever I had to, to get a ship of my own."

"And infiltrate a lord's fleet," Aoife whispered.

Halloran nodded. "We needed to find weaknesses—if there were any—in the allegiance of the lords with the council. My merciless reputation caught the attention of Lord Madigen. But not a month after he recruited me for his fleet, I sailed to Morshan only to find my friends gone. Exiled."

Aoife's throat closed shut. Declan had lost his parents. That must have been why he fled for the sea.

"Their kids—Cait and Declan—handled it as well as anyone could. She had thrown herself into running the pub. Declan had bottled up all emotion, closed himself off. From what Ada had told me of her family, I knew that wasn't like him. But there was little I could do, so I kept an eye on them from afar, even when Declan joined a crew and later led his own. Ada and Carthach were good people. They would have been proud of him."

Proud of him? For being a murderous pirate? How could they—and then Aoife remembered what she would have had to do as a councilwoman, what her mother would have expected her to do.

Halloran breathed out a hollow laugh. "The McCallaghs welcomed many a pirate into their pub, befriended them, knew the life they led out on the sea. Yes, Declan did some despicable things early on to establish his name—just as I have. But his tactics shifted once he found he could coast along more on rumors and stories than actual deeds."

Moving away from the railing, Halloran turned to look out at the water and fell silent. Aoife joined her, careful to keep a respectable distance between them. She didn't speak again until Aoife turned her attention back to the sea.

"Declan will never be a guiltless or moral man, Aoife. But he is still a man of loyalty and honor. His parents would have been proud of how he has weathered his brokenness, let it drive him forward. Even if sometimes it drives him in the wrong direction."

"I still don't understand why," Aoife said. "Why are you telling me this? About Declan. About his parents. What did you promise them?"

Captain Halloran turned slightly, leaning on her forearm. "Perhaps you're not as perceptive as I thought. To watch after them if anything happened. To protect Declan and Cait as best I could without sacrificing the overall mission. I don't make promises lightly, Aoife. I've had to become this"—she pointed to herself—"this cold and callous pirate, but I still care. I care what happens to him. And that means I care about what happens to you and him. The only way this works between you is if you accept him for who he is."

"How did you even know about us? I didn't meet you until that night."

"The beauty of having ties to the leader of the Rogues." She turned back to the sea. "Cait got word to me as soon as we landed. Described what she observed between you two."

Aoife's face warmed. Cait had noticed? She should have expected her to. Cait was a McCallagh.

"Through her, Declan had laid out his plans if things went badly in the hall. As they did."

As she listened to the slapping of the water against the hull, Aoife counted her breaths in time with its rhythm. So much information to process. So much insight into this man she'd fallen for. Wringing her hands in front of her, she kept her eyes down as she broached a question.

"What do I do then?"

"Beyond the forgiveness you already plan to offer?"

Aoife could only nod, wondering if perhaps the woman wouldn't have any other advice.

"Do whatever you can to heal from this. Forgiving him is not lightly done, I know. It won't magically heal the pain his betrayal caused you. But learn from me, Aoife. I know what it is to betray someone you love. There is no winner in these circumstances. It leaves us haunted by the ghosts of possibility, with fading images of what we could have had. Spare the both of you a lifetime of regret. If you can. Forgive. Heal. And love him back. The boy deserves something good in his life. That could be you. If you're willing."

Before Aoife could press her further, a voice from across the deck called for Captain Halloran, and she moved quickly to attend to whatever matter had arisen, giving Aoife a stern yet surprisingly warm look as she passed by.

Aoife had made the decision to forgive Declan, and it had stitched up the wound his lies had left on her heart. Would seeing him open that wound again? Would forgiveness be enough to make things right between them?

Save him first. Deal with the rest later.

CHAPTER 44
TOMMY

It took every bit of Tommy's will to keep the world around him from falling away as he watched Maura. Memorizing the lines of her silhouette as she looked out at the sea, he wondered what she was thinking about, with that slight upturn of her lips. If he wasn't careful, he'd lose all track of time and purpose.

They didn't touch, hadn't since they'd followed the others out of the captain's quarters. Standing inches from her now, though, with that sliver of space between them as cold as the northern waters below, Tommy kicked himself for insisting she could use the fresh air. His hands itched to hold hers as they had in the cabin, but that was more than he was willing to do yet out in the open, if for no other reason than he didn't want to distract anyone from the task ahead.

Out of the corner of his eye he saw Aoife chase after Captain Halloran, and before he could wonder too much about what they were discussing, Maura's voice pulled his attention back.

"I wouldn't worry," she said.

"About what?"

Tossing her hair over her shoulder, she nodded toward Aoife and the captain as she turned to face him. "About them."

"Who said I was worried?"

She smirked at him with a slight tilt to her head. Either he was becoming regretfully easy to read, or she understood him better than most.

"The captain is filling Aoife in on Declan's parents. Among other things."

He quickly glanced at the pair and then turned back to Maura. "Even I don't know about his parents. Not beyond their disappearances."

"I'm sure he had reason for not sharing that with you." Maura placed a hand on his arm.

He didn't retreat, but he also didn't lean into her touch as he wanted to.

"I don't think even Declan knows much about them. Especially not Halloran's connection to them."

"Guess the captains will have a lot of catching up to do when we're all reunited then."

Hope swirled in Maura's golden eyes, or maybe it was simply what Tommy wanted—needed—to see. He needed someone to believe they could succeed and that Declan would survive.

She returned her focus to the sea, but instead of smiling as she took in the view, her lips tightened.

"Are you truly comfortable with me coming with you into the sound?" she asked, with more hesitancy than Tommy had come to expect from her.

"If I wasn't, I would have said something back there." He nodded toward Declan's quarters.

"No, Tommy. If you wanted to stop me from stepping off this ship, you would have said something. But simply allowing something to happen and being at peace with it happening are two separate things."

Leaning forward, he propped his forearms on the railing, if only to keep himself from pulling her close. He steadied himself with a couple of breaths as he searched for words. She mirrored his movements and took up a spot next to him, letting her shoulder press against his.

"I will never be comfortable putting you in harm's way, Maura. I believe in you, but I'm afraid of losing you. This need to protect... My crew, my captain, my friends, and you. Especially you. It's—"

"Much like a mother with her children, I imagine," she said softly. "I may not know exactly how you feel—no one can truly know another's emotions—but I know what it looks like. Fae, especially our males, are quite protective of those they love. I told you the bonds aren't unbreakable connections, but those myths likely sprang up because to any observing human it would appear as such. The loyalty and devotion fae show their partners—and by extension, their children—is a great deal stronger than human hearts are capable of."

Something about the words pricked Tommy's heart like a barb digging into him, pinpointing his shortcomings and his inability to ever give her what someone else could. And after they got the dagger to the Rogues, she would be on her way to a land full of someones. But he hid the cringe by closing his eyes, hoping she would assume he was merely tired. Which he was.

"I didn't mean..." she started, but the way she paused twisted that barb. "I'm not minimizing your loyalty. Simply saying I might understand your need to protect better than you expect."

The sting eased a bit. She wasn't insulting him, even if his treacherous mind insisted she was.

"I meant it though." He waited to see if she would prompt him to continue, but she only hummed a response. "If I'm going to die, it's going to be beside you."

She cocked her head as she peered at him. "So you're saying if you're going to die, you want me to die too? Is that supposed to be romantic?"

"Sounded romantic in my head," he said, keeping his voice low, and he thought she might have laughed, but if she did, it was too faint for him to be sure. He counted a few more breaths. When she still hadn't said anything more, he said in explanation, "It should be obvious I don't want either of us to die."

"Well, that's good at least," she said, her smirk teasing him.

"But I want you beside me wherever I must go."

Any hint of amusement vanished from her expression. "Even with my powers weakened?" Something about her tone betrayed an insecurity that might rival his own.

"You're more than your powers. Far more. I don't want you to die with me. And I don't think you need me to protect you. But we can fight together, by each other's side. It's where we belong."

For as long as we can.

Before she could respond, he pulled her close. He no longer cared who was on the deck, who saw, who objected. Their time was limited, regardless of how things went with the sirens, and he refused to waste it pretending this was nothing.

It was far from nothing.

Licking his lips, he lowered his face to hers as she lifted herself to meet him. And when their lips touched, he couldn't contain the smile that spread across his face. Maura laughed, pulling back enough to say, "This would be easier if you weren't smiling."

His grin vanished, the corners of his mouth dropping low.

Another laugh, sweet and light. "That's even worse!"

He moved to turn away from her, to play up the feigned hurt. No sooner had his eyes left hers than her hand reached for his chin, and before she could guide him closer, he was there, his lips leading hers in a dance that was uniquely theirs.

And he never wanted it to stop.

THE ROWBOAT BOBBED in the water, knocking against the side of the anchored ship as it waited to be boarded. It had room for six—seven in an emergency—so Tommy had assigned Collins to accompany him, Maura, Aoife, and Halloran.

"Are you sure Renna can't come with us?" Aoife asked yet again, though they'd been over it several times.

"Yes, I'm sure, Aoife. Now drop it," Tommy said, his words unnecessarily harsh.

Renna's tone wasn't much gentler. "Once I've compelled the five of you, I'll need to rest, and there's no benefit to having me close to you. Besides, Bria is still recovering. I'd like to be there when she comes to."

"It'll be okay, Aoife," Maura said, giving Aoife's hand a light squeeze.

While they gathered around Renna to start the process of protecting their minds, Tommy glanced at the entrance to the sound. He had never seen anything like it, but as beautiful as it was, he had no desire to stay here any longer than necessary.

"I wonder where Callum's ship is," Aoife said. "Do you think we're wrong about them coming here?"

Halloran shook her head. "Doubtful. More likely his crew sailed the ship out of sight somewhere."

Renna called everyone closer. "Tommy, may I?" She held her hand out, palm up. He hesitated, unsure what she wanted from him. "Your knife, Captain."

Confusion tore through him. Perhaps he should have had Renna explain what the process entailed before agreeing to it. But they had no other defense against the siren queen.

"How exactly does this work?" Collins said, looking far more curious than Tommy felt, almost like he was eager to learn a new trick with a blade.

After sliding the knife across her palm, Renna did the same to Tommy's hand, saying, "While I can do little more than offer suggestions within someone's mind, mixing of blood during the compulsion makes it more potent, more likely to hold. More likely to keep you safe in there."

No one spoke when Renna squeezed her hand into a fist above Tommy's open palm, letting three drops of her blood fall into his open wound. He looked from his hand to her face, surprised to see her staring at him, not standing in a trance as her sisters had been while in the kraken's waters. After another silent minute, she smiled at him and nodded for him to move aside.

"Do you feel any different?" Aoife whispered to him.

Did he? Aside from the sting in his hand, he couldn't tell. How would he know it had worked? Was facing the queen the only way to test it?

Renna answered Aoife's question. "Everyone reacts differently to it. Some won't notice any change. For others, it's similar to thinking of a memory you can't quite recall, hovering at the edge of your mind."

She paused as she performed the ritual on Captain Halloran, who looked almost bored, as if this was something she did every day.

"But while it may feel differently for everyone, its effects remain the same as far as I can tell. Fae. Human. All have appeared to respond to it in the same way, so you needn't worry if you don't feel something and someone else does."

Renna spent a few minutes preparing Collins and Maura before turning to Aoife, who seemed more hesitant than anyone else. Holding her hands together tightly at her chest, Aoife eyed the fae with suspicion. Tommy stepped up beside her.

"Aoife, it's okay. What's the matter?" he asked her, but she didn't look at him.

"I don't like it. I mean, in theory it sounds... But the thought of having my self-control taken from me—" Her eyes dropped to her feet with apparent embarrassment.

Tommy looked around at the others and gestured them back. "Give Aoife and me a moment to talk." Once they had moved away, he turned Aoife to face him, lifting her chin with his hand so that she was forced to look at him. "Aoife. What is it really? You may be awkward, a little gullible at times, but you're not stupid. Far from it. So I know it's not the compulsion bothering you—because you know if you don't let Renna do this, your mind will be—"

"Subject to the sirens. I know." Her lower lip quivered a bit before she forced it to stop with her teeth.

Tommy placed his hands lightly on her shoulders, hoping she didn't think he was about to shake her. That certainly wouldn't help in this situation, no matter how impatient he became. "So what is it?"

"I'm scared." Two timid words whispered between them.

"We're all scared, Aoife." That didn't seem to help, so he continued. "The sirens, the queen—"

Aoife shook her head with her eyes closed—not just closed, squeezed tight like she was trying to ward off some nightmare or vision. "Declan." His name fell from her lips like sand through splayed fingers.

"For him or *of* him?" Tommy's gut told him it might be the latter despite how preposterous that seemed.

"Both." She opened her eyes. Fear and worry swirled in the greens and golds. "What if he's already dead? And if he's not...what if he's no longer himself? What if the queen has twisted his mind so badly he doesn't remember me, us, any of us?"

Tommy swallowed hard. How he had failed to consider these possibilities, he wasn't sure, though he had admittedly been distracted by Maura. Still, that worry couldn't keep them from trying. "Aoife, we've come this far. Are you really wanting to stop now? When we're this close to getting him back?"

"Of course not, but my stomach is tied up in knots so painful I'm not sure how to keep going. I've already failed my sister and Declan and...and I—"

"Will certainly fail if you stop now. The longer we wait, the longer the sirens have to hurt him, Aoife. Please. We have to go. You won't be alone. I'll be with you. Maura will be there. Collins and Halloran. We're doing this together, okay?"

He watched her for several moments, waiting to see some shift in her eyes, some indication that his words had struck a nerve or sparked some courage within her. But nothing changed as she whispered an "Okay" and looked over his shoulder to get Renna's attention.

Standing beside Aoife, he wrapped an arm around her shoulders while Renna drew the knife across her palm. When Renna stepped back, indicating all of them were ready, he looked down to see how Aoife fared. "You ready? How do you feel?"

Aoife took a bit of cloth Collins offered her and began to wrap it around her hand as she answered. "I feel...okay? Like something new is there, but I can't quite pinpoint what."

"Well, she did say that could happen for some. Will you be able to focus?"

She nodded and smiled. "I think so."

"Let's go then. Declan's waited for us long enough."

As Tommy watched the others climb the rope ladder down into the rowboat and waited for his turn to follow, he pondered Aoife's words. Would Declan be the Declan they knew? Tommy's gut twisted upon itself at the very real possibility that his friend might already be gone, whether he was dead or not.

CHAPTER 45
CAIT

THE ENTIRE SQUARE WENT QUIET, and for a moment Cait wondered if it was simply her own shock that had caused her world to go silent. She couldn't look away from the two men. Her thoughts twisted into a confused tangle of shared stories and tender moments and careless hopes.

This whole time, he had been playing her. How had she missed it? Was she truly that distracted by an attractive man? Had her instincts failed? Tapping into those instincts now, she found nothing but a gray void. No feeling one way or the other.

Was he her enemy? An enemy she'd allowed into their innermost circle? An enemy she'd hoped would kiss her?

Or was *this* an act? Another mask?

The latter would be decidedly better, yet it tasted bitter as she mulled it over. If he hadn't planned this, then why did he have his old sash? And if he had, why hadn't he trusted her enough to tell her?

But it wasn't as if her reaction mattered in this instance. She had no intention of making herself known, not even as a regular citizen of Morshan, lest it lead to the councilwomen determining she was part of the rebellion.

If Adler was aware of her watching him, he didn't indicate it. He simply stared as Lucan spit out more saliva and blood onto the ground.

Don't do it, Luc, she silently urged him. The two men might have warmed up to each other, but she knew her friend. And he wasn't one to not fight back.

"You two," one of the councilwomen called out over the crowd, "come closer."

Adler took Lucan's arm and yanked him toward the council. Cait inched forward to keep an eye on them, but the gathered masses parted and closed around the pair of men, like a snake devouring its lunch. Refusing to miss this exchange, she pushed around people as politely as she could, offering whispered apologies and requests to be let past, stopping only when there was a single row of people between her and her friends.

Or your friend. *Singular.*

The councilwoman named Brigeh spoke again. "Pirate—"

Adler shifted forward, but the woman lifted a hand.

"Stop. You will listen and not speak."

His head dipped, and he inched back slightly, his hands clasped behind his back.

"While we appreciate your defending this council and the integrity of the rules of our land, violence is never the answer."

Cait's breath stopped mid-exhale. This was not going at all as they'd hoped. They were supposed to catch the council off guard, trap them into exposing their secrets, but the council was using Adler's actions to strengthen their false image of peace and mercy. The councilwoman's next words, addressed to all gathered, confirmed this.

"This—this is why we have the rules we do! This is why our land is ruled by women. This is why we have survived—prospered, even—since the end of the war, a war that began because of the dangerous and vile tendencies of men. It is men who got us into that war. It is that war that tore families apart, leaving behind mere shells of those who had gone off to fight, leaving them too broken to return home. But we did not turn our backs on those men. Those who returned to the seas became our allies through the Muirnaughton Treaty. Those who stayed were cared for, nurtured, and healed while our ancestors rebuilt the land into a place of peace and prosperity. It seems, though, if today's events are any indication, we still have much work to do."

Brigeh glided down the steps until she stood before Adler, just out of his reach.

"But, we are a people of mercy, regardless of what this man claims." She waved a hand toward Lucan. "And as you are one of our allies, pirate, and you acted out of loyalty, we will grant you leniency."

Adler offered a quiet "Thank you" as the councilwoman shifted to the side and directed her attention to Lucan. The crowd seemed to take a collective breath and hold it as one, waiting for their rulers to pass judgment upon him.

"You, sir, are out of line." Brigeh's chin lifted into the air until she was staring down the bridge of her nose at Lucan.

He spit on the cobblestones again, inches from her feet.

Cait caught the twinge of anger at the corners of Brigeh's eyes. The woman clenched her fists at her sides but kept her voice steady as she asked, "And how is it that you have the audacity to speak to us, this council, directly? Where is the head of your household? Or do you have no woman to claim you?"

"I am a citizen of Cregah, as much a citizen as anyone else, and I am the head of my own household. I speak for myself," he said with confidence.

Adler lifted an arm as if to elbow Lucan in the face but stopped. Brigeh nodded —likely in thanks for his restraint, but at this point, Cait wasn't sure what to make of anything. She fidgeted before daring to make her way to the left, little by little, keeping her movements small so as not to call attention to herself. But when Fiona's voice cut through the air, she halted and looked up.

"Who are you?" The councilwoman glared down at Lucan.

Lucan's chin rose. "Just a man mourning the family that was taken from him."

"The family you lost," Darienn clarified, and even from where Cait stood, with her view partially blocked by the women in front of her, she could see the young heir's cold glare.

Lucan only scoffed as Fiona leaned to whisper something to her sister, who nodded.

"You, *citizen of Cregah*," Brigeh said mockingly, "are hereby *exiled*."

Cait's knees nearly gave out, and her mind blurred, unable to focus on any particular thought.

Brigeh continued, "Let the good people of Morshan bear witness to our land's laws rightly applied and justice fulfilled in line with our founders' vision. Pirate, you are tasked with overseeing this exile. Report back to us when it is done."

Adler nodded before taking Lucan's arms and locking them behind his back. Lucan struggled, his feet slipping on the cobblestones as Adler dragged him through the mass of people who were slow to part for him.

Panic rose in Cait's throat, making it hard to swallow, let alone think. Why hadn't she reminded Lucan to keep his shit together? To not goad them like that? How had this all fallen apart? And had Adler been lying to her this whole time?

Tightening her hands into fists and slamming her teeth together, she forced her head to clear as best she could, throwing the random thoughts into the shadows of her mind. She had lost her parents and Maggie to this council. Her Rogues had already had so much stolen from them. And now Declan might also be taken from her because of them.

She would not let them take Lucan.

She had to stop Adler, however she could.

CHAPTER 46
DECLAN

Declan had no concept of time as he stood on the beach, his limbs hostage to Triss's compulsion. He'd reminded himself many times that he shouldn't care what happened to Callum, the man who had tortured someone simply for helping him.

The five sirens who had joined Triss now gathered on the stone dais she'd been sitting atop earlier. Unlike their queen, these creatures didn't bother with clothing, leaving their human forms on full display as they lounged. He might have reacted lustfully to their appearance—as any man would have—if not for the blood gracing their chins and chests and hands, which prevented him from seeing anything more than monsters.

Triss, still grinning, approached Callum. "Funny that you should want to save him, Declan. Given all he's done to you."

Declan pulled his attention away from the nude sirens before addressing her. "I'm just as surprised as you by that," he said in a flat, bored tone.

"Who said I was surprised? You're an easy pirate to read. An odd one; I'll give you that. But easy."

A half-hearted laugh escaped him. "I should hope so, given your ability to read minds and pillage memories." As much as he urged himself not to form any thoughts she could use against him, he could no better control them than he could the tide.

"No, Declan, there is no tide here. The waters here are as stagnant as the futures of those trapped here."

"If I didn't know better, I'd think you're rather bitter about your plight."

She didn't snap around to look at him. Rather, her head pivoted slowly with a deadly grace. "Of course I'm bitter." The look in her eyes shifted from irritation to something far worse. "I'm also hungry, Declan."

Kneeling, she took Callum's face in her hands and looked him over, like someone inspecting a fish she was about to cook.

"Is he done yet?" Declan asked, his gut roiling.

"Let's see." She licked her lips before taking his hand in hers. She lifted it up as if to examine it, but then, without warning, she snapped his little finger off at the base. His scream was cut short by her sharp glare and whatever silent command she gave. Turning, she tossed the finger to the other sirens, saying, "Try it. Is he done?"

In an effort to avoid watching the sirens fight over Callum's severed digit, Declan asked, "How does that work exactly?"

Triss offered a smooth shrug. "Same as it does for anyone else. Open our mouths. Chew. Swallow."

"And this"—unable to gesture with his hands, Declan resorted to jutting a chin toward Callum—"does what?"

"You mean, besides being gloriously entertaining? It enhances the flavor."

Though he'd attempted to steel his stomach at the expected answer, it still tightened, threatening to push bile into his throat.

"But you already knew that, Declan," Triss crooned. "It will do you no good to stall."

"Perhaps not, but it at least helps pass the time. This isn't my type of spectacle."

At this, she laughed, a low rumble sounding from deep in her chest. "Pretend all you want. You can't hide your fear from me."

"Oh, shit, I forgot about that. Silly me."

She didn't respond but turned back to Callum, whose hand she still held. Shaking her head, she spoke to the tortured pirate. "How did you endure this man's incessant blathering for the entire voyage here?"

Declan remained silent, forcing his mind to go as blank as possible. He painted the invisible walls of his thoughts with the teal and navy of the Aisling and tried to lose himself in the dark calm. It worked, as far as he could assume, but a piercing sound of pain stripped away the colors and forced him back to the present.

Callum's face twisted in anguish as Triss focused on him. Beyond holding his hand, she didn't appear to be doing anything to him physically.

"What are you doing to him?" Declan asked, thankful the words came out with more curiosity than fear.

"Nothing he couldn't have done to himself."

"That's barely an answer."

A sigh fell from her lips, though it sounded more like a growl. "Shall I show you?" She dropped Callum's hand and pushed him down to the white sand, then came toward Declan with the slow progression only someone facing an eternity of isolation and suffering could possess.

She had time. All the time in her cursed world.

And Declan's was quickly running out.

DECLAN BLINKED. Callum was no longer lying in the sand. And the sand was no longer white. His boots sank into the fine black sand of home, the tide washing over them once, twice, three times. The sheer walls of the Cregahn cliffs stood prominently above him, protecting this spot—this all too familiar location.

A woman sat in the sand, her back leaning against one of the white boulders that peppered the beach.

Aoife.

But she didn't look at him. Didn't seem to notice him at all. He thought this might be their first meeting, but then he realized her hair ended above her shoulders, which meant she had already run away from the council.

But this didn't make sense. If this was meant to be a memory of when she'd been taken here by Halloran after the disaster with the council, it would have been nighttime, not the middle of the day, with the sun glimmering on the water.

He looked closer at Aoife, whose face was lit up with an expression of peace and happiness he'd only caught a glimpse of once before. But not like this. This Aoife before him now held none of the fear and worry she'd been carrying since he met her. She appeared as he'd hoped to find her someday—happy and unburdened.

What was this? A vision of her life had he not entered into it?

His answer came when another person stepped onto the beach, emerging from the trees guarding the hidden path to the cove, and his breath caught. It was like looking in a mirror, but not. While he was looking at himself, this Declan was different.

Happier.

Content.

Free.

He remained standing in the water as he watched his counterpart sit down beside Aoife and wrap his arm around her shoulders. His other hand reached across to rest on her belly. A belly showing the unmistakable signs of being with child.

Breath refused to come to Declan as he observed this alternate reality. He noticed the ring gracing his other self's hand. They were married, happy, expecting. A dream he'd tried to ignore and bury, convinced it was a life that could never be his. He would never have the happiness he'd seen in his parents.

But here, before him, it seemed so real.

His heart ached with the crushing realization of what this was: a future he would never have. A dream he'd thrown away with his lies and deceit and betrayal.

Dangling from Aoife's neck was the vial of black sand, the necklace she'd gotten from her sister. The sister he had killed. But perhaps he hadn't done that in this reality. Maybe he had let Lani go, found a way to get her off the island.

As if in answer to that thought, his mirror-self whispered to Aoife, "Thank you. I didn't deserve your understanding or your love. I still don't. But I will be forever grateful for it."

Her next words echoed what she'd spat at him at the cove in the dark. "I don't blame you for what you did for them. That's on them, not you." But instead of anger, Aoife's voice was filled with warmth and love. "Thank you for telling me the truth. I know it wasn't easy, but I will be forever thankful that you trusted me."

When they leaned in to share a kiss, Declan forced his eyes closed.

This was a reality that could never be. This was a reality that could have come about had he not been selfish and stupid. A coward.

It didn't matter that this was only a vision, an image created in his mind by the siren queen who had him frozen on a white-sand beach thousands of miles away from this cove. Because he understood now what Triss had meant when she'd said she did nothing he couldn't do to himself.

How many times had he nearly pictured this scene in his own mind, only to dash it away before it could completely take shape?

Triss had merely taken his own nightmare and forced him to live it.

When he opened his eyes again, the black sand was still there, but the light above came from the moon now, casting an eerie light over the cove. This was the scene he remembered, the one that refused to budge from his mind no matter how much he pushed.

Aoife standing over his blood-covered form as he knelt before her. Him standing, begging for her forgiveness. But this Aoife didn't stop at the words that had cut him so deeply that night. This Aoife railed against him.

"I hate you, Declan! I hate you! I could never love someone who would deceive the one they claimed to care for. How could I? Don't follow me. Don't try to fix this, because it cannot be fixed. It can never be fixed!"

She shoved past him and disappeared into the trees.

This was what he'd expected from her that night. He could never make this right. He could never earn her forgiveness.

He had done this with his own bloodied hands and cowardly spirit. And he would have to suffer the consequences, live with the burden of her hate.

His head fell, chin pressing into his chest and eyes closing once more. His hands —clenched into fists—trembled until he forced them to open, stretching his fingers wide. The bitterness of his failure—his multiple failures—coated his tongue, and no matter how much he swallowed, it would not leave.

CHAPTER 47
AOIFE

HALLORAN SAT alert in the prow of the boat as Tommy and Collins rowed them into the sound. Maura and Aoife sat together in the middle. Aoife tried to calm herself by focusing on the soft splashing of the oars pushing through the water.

Questions gripped her insides, wringing them into a tangled mess of nerves.

How far was it?

Was Declan still alive?

How many sirens were there?

Would they come across any along the way?

Something glimmered in the water to Aoife's right. She sucked in a breath and tightened her grip on Maura's arm.

She wanted to ask Maura if she'd seen it, but fear kept her silent and still.

"We've entered their domain," Maura whispered beside her. "This is where we trapped them."

The shimmers of light increased under the surface, and Aoife jumped as something splashed.

"They don't seem too happy about that," Halloran said over her shoulder in a hushed tone.

"I wouldn't be either," Maura said. Aoife could have sworn she heard a slight tremor of fear in her friend's voice. Before, that might have made her smile, to know that the fae weren't entirely perfect. But here, now, fear was not to their benefit, and if Maura was already afraid, that did not bode well for their party.

"Maura, take the knives from my belt. And Collins's," Tommy instructed, shifting his body so she had easier access to the weapons. "We'll keep rowing. You three need to be ready."

I can't do this.

Yet she had attacked a kraken. This couldn't be worse than that, right?

"Steady, Aoife," Maura said, handing her one of the knives. "Just strike at anything that moves, and try not to tip us over when you do."

If Maura meant it as a joke, Aoife didn't find it funny. At all.

For the next several minutes, they crept along at an agonizingly slow pace. Aoife remained tightly wound as she watched and waited. Her eyes were painfully dry from refusing to blink much. Her hand ached from trying to hold the knife steady in her sweaty palm. Her teeth hurt from clenching her jaw. If she kept this up, she'd have no energy once they found the queen.

When she glanced at her companions and noticed none of them were as tense as she was, she urged herself to loosen up. She uncurled her toes, unclenched her backside, rolled her shoulders, stretched out her jaw, and blinked several times. Finally, she loosened her grip on the knife, ready to place it in her other hand so she could wipe off her sweaty palm on her pants.

She'd just about gotten the knife to her bandaged hand when the attack came. Something—or someone—slammed into her side of the boat. She groaned as her shoulder collided with Maura's, and the knife fell onto the floor of the boat.

With a curse, Aoife bent over. Before she could grasp the weapon, something cold and wet and strong had a hold of her arm and began to pull her toward the edge. Even her scream seemed to be absorbed by their surroundings, coming out fainter than expected. Maura reached around her but couldn't get to the creature before it clamped its teeth down on Aoife's arm.

A shout came from Tommy, though Aoife couldn't see what happened, as the siren drove its teeth in further and blinding pain shot through her.

Her flesh was ripped away from the bone, fat and muscle and tendons tearing as someone fought to get the thing off her. Her vision blurred. If her screams continued, she didn't know. The world around her swayed and spun until she didn't know which way was up or whether she was even in this world anymore.

Then everything went dark.

CHAPTER 48
MAURA

"Do you have her?" Tommy asked.

Maura looked up and gave him a nod as she moved Aoife into a more comfortable position in her lap. He was trying hard to conceal his concern, but he had to realize it could have been far worse.

"She'll be okay."

Frowning, Tommy surveyed the damage to Aoife's arm. A section of her jacket sleeve was torn away, revealing a mangled mess of skin and flesh beneath. He didn't seem convinced.

Collins, rowing with Tommy as fast as he could, looked squarely at Maura—seeming more worried than angry—and asked, "How exactly is she going to be okay? A chunk of her arm is gone! She lost a lot—"

Pinning him with a stern glare, Maura stopped the young pirate but kept her voice calm. "You underestimate her. We all do."

"Underestimated or not," Halloran called back, "she needs her wound wrapped. Here." A pile of gold fabric floated through the air between the men's heads and landed on Aoife's chest.

Maura was so engrossed with the task of removing Aoife's jacket and binding her wound, she didn't hear the approaching danger.

The sirens surfaced with such quickness that Maura had no time to shout a warning before one had Tommy in her clawed hands. A second siren appeared at the prow, grasping for Captain Halloran's legs. But the captain had been ready, and with a swift motion, she slashed her blade across the creature's throat before kicking the body back into the water.

But Tommy had no blade ready, only an oar, which now clattered into the boat as the siren's grip forced all strength from his hands. Maura, helpless and useless with Aoife unconscious across her legs, shouted to Halloran and Collins, who was already moving. Collins rammed the handle of his oar past Tommy's head and into the siren's face. It did little but anger her, and her mouth opened in a sharp screech, revealing multiple rows of sharp fangs.

Then time slowed as Maura watched those fangs latch onto Tommy's shoulder. His pained scream echoed off the rocks as Halloran drove her knife into the side of the siren's head. The siren's jaws and hands released him. But as Halloran worked to get the lifeless body over the edge, Tommy's eyes rolled back, and he collapsed backwards into the boat, his head thudding against one of the wooden seats.

What hope did they have of succeeding now?

Don't underestimate them, Maura. Don't underestimate yourself.

Having gotten Tommy's shoulder bound with his teal sash, Captain Halloran took up his oar and worked with Collins to keep them moving. They were granted a bit of luck somehow, and no more sirens came near their boat. Although Maura saw the occasional feathery tail splash at the surface, the sirens kept their distance. Whatever the reason, she was thankful for the reprieve.

The sound gradually narrowed. The rock walls closed in on them, and Maura had to push away the reminder of what life had been like in that room at the council hall for all those centuries. She closed her eyes, hoping to ease the discomfort, but doing so made her stomach uneasy as the boat swayed gently in the still water. When she opened them, they were rounding a bend and arriving in an open basin of water. It wasn't so big she couldn't see its rocky edges, but it was still large enough to give Maura pause.

"The beach," Halloran said, and Maura turned to see where she indicated.

Across the water, a pristine beach lay waiting. While she saw no boat on the shore, she could make out the pool of blood on the white sand.

Please don't be Declan's.

Aoife stirred in her lap.

"How in the sands..." Collins said in a low voice as he spotted the movement in Aoife's still unconscious body. Maura offered him an easy shrug and a bit of a smirk, though it disappeared when she noted how Tommy still lay motionless next to her.

It wasn't until the bottom of their boat crunched against the rough sand that Aoife's eyes flashed open. Blinking, she asked, "What happened? Why am I in your lap?"

An airy laugh escaped Maura, and she helped her friend sit up. "You nearly became a siren's meal. But we didn't let them get more than a nibble."

"Much appreciated. Thank you," Aoife said, but a half a breath later, she noticed Halloran sitting where Tommy had been originally. "Where's Tommy?" Maura didn't get to answer before Aoife spotted him on the other side of the rowers' bench.

Halloran and Collins stepped out of the boat to pull it up onto the sand, and Aoife rushed forward.

Maura waited for her to ask the inevitable question, but Aoife's fingers hovered over Tommy's bloodied shoulder.

"Will he be okay?" Aoife asked without looking back at Maura.

"I believe so, but he will need to rest."

Now Aoife faced her, her green eyes ablaze with curiosity. "Why did I recover so quickly? How long will he need?"

"Longer than we have, unfortunately," Halloran said, pulling their attention to the beach where she stood. "Let's get him moved."

Maura opened her mouth to protest, but there were no other options. They couldn't wait for Tommy to recover, and her magic was depleted enough that she couldn't risk healing him even a little bit. Declan was here somewhere, and they hadn't traveled all this way to settle for retrieving the dagger without him.

Aoife placed a reassuring hand on Maura's arm as they watched the two pirates lay Tommy's unconscious form behind a pile of black rocks.

"He'll be okay, Maura. Let's get this over with."

CHAPTER 49
AOIFE

THE FOUR OF them trudged away from the water's edge, and Aoife purposefully stepped around the bloody mess that lay nearby. She'd seen enough of the remains to know it probably wasn't Declan's blood. There was a bit of torn burgundy fabric nearby—the same color Callum's crew wore. Whoever the sirens had killed here, they had left no piece of his body behind, only bloody clothes strewn about.

"There," Halloran said, pointing ahead of them where faint indentations appeared in the sand.

"Footsteps?" Aoife asked.

"Aye. Two sets," Collins said as he stepped up beside her.

A spark of hope flashed within her, singeing her nerves and making her skin tingle. Uninvited memories flooded her mind, calling forward the guilt that had been her near constant companion since the morning Lani had been dragged away. Instinctively she grasped the pendant at her chest and held the small vial in her uninjured palm as tightly as if it were her sister's hand. Lani had always been the brave one. When storms raged with bright flashes of lightning and booming thunder or when their mothers were in particularly ill tempers, Lani had not shaken as Aoife had, always facing those moments with stern determination.

Had she faced Declan with that same attitude?

Declan.

Beneath Aoife's hand her chest tightened, like it wanted to guard her heart from him and his lies.

Clamping her eyes shut, she pushed back against that thought. No, she had forgiven him. She would forgive him. It was what you did when you loved someone.

"Aoife." Maura's voice had Aoife's eyes snapping open once more.

She found the fae standing in front of her, stooping her head low to peer into

Aoife's eyes. Was she searching for a hint she was going to break? A sign something was seriously wrong with her? A part of her wanted to cower under this intense scrutiny.

"What?" Aoife asked, voice strained.

"You can do this," Maura said. "I'm right here with you."

In silence they worked to catch up to Halloran and Collins, who had already gotten a hundred or so paces ahead of them. The pirates turned a corner Aoife hadn't noticed. From the shoreline, the cliffs looked solid, but now, as she approached, she found the dark gray stone hid the entrance to another section of the beach.

The two pirates stopped short.

When she stepped between them, her shoulders brushing against theirs, she saw what had them frozen.

A woman, tall and beautiful and regal, stood in the middle of the space with several women—who wore nothing but blood—lounging on a pile of stone behind her. To her right, a body lay in a heap on the ground. From this distance, Aoife couldn't tell who it was or if the person was even breathing. Directly in front of the queen, though, a man stood. Even without his teal sash, even with his back to her, even with his hair a bit shaggier, Aoife knew it was him.

She called his name. A question. He didn't move. Didn't even flinch.

Before Aoife could stop herself, her feet were carrying her toward him, kicking up sand behind her. A few times, she nearly fell, but she managed to stay upright somehow. She had intended to not seem so eager and to not give the sirens any information that could be used against her, Declan, or their friends.

But all those plans had vanished like a fading mist, and she was far from graceful or impressive. She was a desperate, scared but hopeful woman so close to the man who needed her.

He stood unnaturally still, and panic tore through her as she imagined him already dead. Was she too late? With twenty paces to go, she cried out his name again, and this time he turned.

Declan was here. He was alive. He was here. She had made it.

But something was terribly wrong.

Those stormy gray eyes she'd been dreaming of for the past week were the same, and yet they weren't. How many times had she envisioned their reunion? Each time she'd imagined him being thrilled to see her. But now his eyes held no hope, no eagerness, no happiness.

He looked almost scared of her, cowering away from her like she was going to strike him. His trembling lips and empty stare pricked her heart. Should she stay back? Should she refrain from getting too close?

He needs you. He's hurting. He needs you.

With that thought, Aoife ran into him, her arms finding their home around his neck, but he didn't make any move to return her embrace. Nestling her face under his jaw, she relished his scent, which had already begun to fade from his cabin.

But he remained a statue.
Still, she refused to let him go. Not for anything.
Then the siren spoke.
"Welcome, Aoife. We've been waiting for you."

CHAPTER 50
DECLAN

"Declan?" A familiar voice called for him. A voice he would forever cherish and be haunted by. A voice that had kept him from giving up in the brig on Callum's ship.

But it wasn't real. Like the visions he'd seen, this was a trick. Triss's doing. Screwing with his mind and his heart to push his sorrow and pain into every fiber of his body for her own pleasure.

But the call came again. Clearer. Brighter.

"Declan."

No longer a question, Aoife's voice sounded urgent, desperate, scared.

His eyes flashed open, bringing back the view of the white sand, Callum's now unconscious body, and Triss standing before him. But she was looking past him, over his shoulder. His body, once held by Triss's silent commands, now listened to him once again, and he turned slowly, every muscle and joint stiff from standing frozen for so long.

Aoife was here, her green eyes wide as she ran toward him. This was what he'd been waiting for, but the sight of her brought no hope, only a fresh reminder that he had hurt her and would never be good enough for her. And when her body pressed against his, his limbs began to shake, and he tried to pull away, but he couldn't move any more than he could speak.

Triss had taken control over him again.

Declan wanted to pry Aoife's arms away, tell her he wasn't right for her, remind her of how he'd hurt her and how she couldn't trust him. But he also wanted to hold her close to him and never let her go, to spend every day making it up to her, proving that she meant everything to him.

But he could do neither.

All he could do was try to memorize this feeling of her clinging to him and tuck it away for safekeeping.

When Triss's voice called out in greeting to Aoife, every inch of him wanted to guard her from this demon. He half-expected Triss to laugh at his thoughts, but she continued to speak as Aoife held fast to him.

"You took your time getting here, didn't you? Have some trouble along the way?"

Aoife loosened her grip on him, and he couldn't bring himself to look at her as she pulled away and inched to his side. "You must be Triss," she said, her voice warbling a bit.

"The one and only."

Declan could picture Triss's smug smile.

Aoife, her tense arm pressing against his, spoke again, this time with a bit more confidence. "I'm here for him."

Declan's eyes flashed open, and though he couldn't turn his head to look at her, he could see in his periphery how she stood taller, surer of herself.

"Just him?" Triss asked.

"For now."

Declan's body pivoted against his will. He would never get used to this part of Triss's powers. Now he faced Triss, who dropped her head to the side and flashed him an insincere smile. "Did you hear that, Declan? She's here just for you. For now."

He didn't react, but he wasn't sure how much of that was Triss's doing.

Triss focused once more on Aoife. "And why would I let you take him?"

Aoife's confident posture remained, though her voice betrayed that it might be starting to unravel a bit. "Certainly not from the goodness of your heart. If you have one."

A cackling laugh reverberated off the rock walls, and Triss's expression turned dark and taunting. "Oh, I have one. Two now, actually." With a wave of her hand, she gestured to Declan first and then to Callum, whose body was still slumped on the ground to the siren's right.

His stomach lurched when Triss raised her other hand, holding another of Callum's severed fingers, still bloody. She flashed Aoife a wink before popping it into her mouth like a grape. Closing her eyes, she made a show of enjoying her snack, savoring each crunch of bone before licking her lips and swallowing. With a contented sigh, she opened her purple eyes once more.

"Not quite done, but still rather delicious."

CHAPTER 51
AOIFE

Aoife couldn't tear her eyes from the siren standing before her. The woman's terrible dark eyes roved over Aoife with a burning hunger that sent pinpricks across her skin, but Aoife steeled herself as best she could.

Wracking her brain, she searched for the words they had planned for her to offer, but her mind refused, fixated instead on the mental image Triss's words had created: Callum and Declan dead and broken. Hearts ripped out.

"Interesting," Triss said quietly as her eyes narrowed on Aoife once more. "I can't seem to get a read on your thoughts. Your mind appears to be cloaked."

With this, her head snapped away, and Aoife turned to where the others stood watching, waiting. Why were they just standing there? They should be searching for the dagger while she helped Declan. Aoife surveyed the area, which was empty aside from the dais the sirens sat upon, and she knew it was as they'd feared.

Triss had the dagger on her.

The queen stood and moved forward, not toward the others as Aoife had expected, but toward her. Her movements reminded Aoife so much of her mother—a regal, confident, lethal grace—as her sheer black dress swished around her hips and legs, concealing little of her body.

Aoife swallowed, realizing she hadn't responded at all to the siren's last comments.

Triss stopped just outside of Aoife's reach, her haunting eyes intensely studying her, like she could unlock Aoife's thoughts with a glare alone.

Look away! Aoife's mind pleaded with her, but there was something about those purple-hued pools of ink. Something in them. Power? Hunger? Magic? Aoife wasn't sure which of these held her captive. It wasn't until something bumped into her shoulder that she blinked and cut off whatever spell had been cast on her. She turned, and although Declan still faced ahead, she saw him watching from the corner of his eye, and his shoulder hovered lightly against hers.

He couldn't move, really. Yet he'd been able to push his muscles just enough to lean into her. Aoife tried to give him a reassuring smile, but her hope was slowly dying, like a candle nearing the end of its wick.

"Yes, yes, that's very touching," Triss said, though it was obvious she hadn't found Declan's gesture to be anything remotely endearing. "Looks like you had a bit of an accident on your way here?" Her dark eyes flashed down to Aoife's arm.

"Oh, that? Just a scratch."

"That's a lot of blood for a scratch." Aoife only shrugged, trying to mimic the bored attitude Declan displayed in tense situations. "Can I ask you a question, Aoife?"

Aoife responded with a silent lift of her brow.

"Who is your mother?"

That wasn't exactly the question Aoife had expected, and her already flustered mind stumbled around the answer.

Triss released an exasperated breath. "You do have a mother, don't you?"

For an ancient, presumably immortal creature, this siren was certainly impatient. The thought elicited a nervous chuckle in the back of her throat, but she quieted it before it could escape and earn her a harsher response from the queen. Still, that didn't mean she had to rush through her answer.

"Aye," she said. Her hands itched to reach for the necklace hidden beneath her shirt, but she kept them steady by weaving her fingers together, clasping them in front of her waist. The itching in her arm beneath the makeshift bandage threatened to derail her thoughts completely, but she pushed out her response. "I'm merely surprised you hadn't already collected that information by pillaging the young captain's mind."

"Ah, yes, he did unknowingly give me her name and a rundown of all her despicable qualities. But alas, his mental image of Melina is fuzzy at best. And since I can't get through the clever cloaking trick here"—she waved a finger at Aoife's head —"I hoped you might be able to describe her to me."

"Why? Are you wanting to paint her portrait?" Pride might have swelled in Aoife's chest over the retort had she not also been scared of what Triss might do when goaded.

But Triss once again turned to Declan. "You didn't tell me she was so feisty."

Though his body still couldn't move, he was able to say, "Technically I didn't tell you anything about her."

Triss waved her hand in dismissal, muttering something about *semantics* before addressing Aoife again. "No, Aoife, I am not painting. We are sorely lacking any art supplies, as you might have noticed during your inspection of my home here. But it's simply that you look so oddly familiar is all. Curious if she might look familiar to me as well. Or perhaps you're fae or elf or nymph? Are you sure we didn't meet long ago before those bitches imprisoned me and my kin in this stagnant pool?"

"Those bitches including your own sisters? Oh, excuse me—half-sisters."

Triss's eyes narrowed as her lips slid into a thin line. She turned her attention back to Aoife's companions, and a surprisingly friendly smile lit up her face. "Speaking of *half*-sisters. You brought one with you, I see. Maura. Come, come." Before Maura had reached Aoife's side, Triss was already asking, "How long has it been?"

Maura's normally carefree voice came out tense and cold as she said, "Not long enough, Triss."

"Never thought you'd come back here, did you? And how are our sisters? Still alive? When that war broke out, I wondered if any of the fae survived."

"Aye, we survived."

Triss clicked her tongue. "And what a shame that is."

No one responded, and a heavy silence fell until Triss broke it with another cackle. "So I assume I have Renna to thank for this." She tapped a clawed finger at her temple. "And where is she? I would have liked to say hi. To her and to Bria."

Maura didn't answer her and instead held the siren's intense stare.

With a flick of her fingers, Triss freed Declan's limbs from their invisible prison, but he still didn't appear to be back in control of them, as he left Aoife's side to join Triss. When he turned to face them, his eyes remained down for several breaths before snapping up. Those stormy greys she had dreamed about since she'd abandoned him flared with a kaleidoscope of strong emotions.

What was the man thinking? Did he have any hope remaining within? Was he already lost to the siren's call? Had they arrived too late?

Triss shifted a bit, looking from Aoife to Declan and back with that smug look she'd had before. As she moved, her skirts swished again, just as they had when she'd first walked toward them, but now something flashed from within the fabric. A reflection of the sun on some kind of metal. Aoife tried to catch a glimpse of what it was, but Triss dropped a hand to her hip and pulled open a fold in the skirt, retrieving a dagger.

Its gold hilt was intricately designed, and its blade was etched with a pattern that seemed familiar to Aoife. This was the dagger she'd read about. The legend. The thing coveted by so many and needed by the Rogues to free all her people.

"The Csintala dagger," Triss said, twirling the blade's point against one of her fingers. "That king didn't know what he'd been gifted, sadly for him. I, of course, was quite appreciative. Had he known a thing or two about enchantments—or the queen he'd vowed to return to—he would have known better than to go back on his word. Funny thing about fae enchantments. They always have a catch."

The siren paused to stare into Aoife's eyes.

Triss continued. "The queen certainly pulled a fast one on the world with that little lie about a shield too. Aye, we are not so secluded up here that we do not catch wind of rumors swirling about. Many have come to find this, you know. Few live long enough to even catch a glimpse. What can I say? Sometimes my hunger can't bear to wait for them to properly marinate in their pain."

She shrugged, as if she weren't discussing torturing and eating people.

Aoife steeled herself against her gut's reflex at the mental image that formed.

"I suppose," Triss continued, "it's odd for me to hold onto such a blade when I can't wield its magic. But then again, why hand it over to those who could use it against me?"

The siren let out a breathy laugh, a slight smile turning up the corners of her mouth as she continued to spin the dagger. "Let's make a deal, shall we? Despite my hunger, I'm feeling rather generous today. So I'll give Declan to you, if that's what he wants."

Aoife's gut twisted even tighter. Her mind picked apart the words. "And the dagger?"

"It's either Declan or the dagger. Choose."

There was no question in Aoife's mind. It had to be Declan. Surely the others could get the dagger from Triss, even without Tommy. Aoife merely had to bargain for Declan's safety. Breaking Triss's compulsion over him wouldn't be as easy as stealing a blade from her hand.

As if either could be considered easy.

Aoife contemplated the options before her, working through each word of Triss's proposed deal. On the surface, it seemed acceptable, but she'd be foolish to think there wasn't a catch.

Triss slipped the dagger back into the sheath at her hip. "I don't need access to your mind to know you've made your choice. That should warm your heart, Declan."

"I'll agree, if—"

"If?" Triss didn't look at all shocked at the answer.

"If you agree he won't be compelled to want to stay...or to kill any of us."

Triss nodded and whispered to Declan, just loud enough for Aoife to hear, "You chose a smart one here. It's a shame she's just not smart enough."

When Declan's eyes closed, panic coursed through Aoife's veins. Before she could rush forward to help him, it was done. And it was far from good. Triss's smile brightened, lighting up her entire face as Declan opened his eyes once more.

With a new and terrifying madness, his glare bored into Aoife. He charged toward her in a murderous rage.

"Move!" Collins yelled, and then Aoife was falling hard in the sand, with Collins on top of her. Collins scrambled to turn around. Keeping Aoife at his back, he lifted his hands toward Declan, who growled as he stopped short.

Declan stood over them, jaw clenched, muscles tensed, gripping his own dagger tightly in his hand. "Get out of my way! My fight is not with you! It's her!"

What had Triss done to him?

Had she compelled Declan to kill her?

Aoife had been a fool to believe Triss would adhere to any agreement.

Collins pushed to his feet and swiped Declan's hand—and blade—to the side. Stepping forward, he forced Declan to take a step back.

Maura ran in and grabbed Aoife by the arm to pull her away, but Aoife resisted, wanting to remain and listen to their exchange. She needed to know why he hated her enough to fight his own man.

"I don't want to hurt you, Captain," Collins said. His hands were lifted between them, his body ready to react.

Declan scoffed. "I'm the one with the blade, Collins. Even if you wanted to—" He didn't finish his sentence before thrusting his dagger forward.

But his blade struck steel rather than flesh. Collins had pulled out a dagger hidden at his wrist. Declan laughed. "Ah, new tricks, I see."

Collins nodded, drawing another dagger—Tommy's—from his belt, and inched closer to his captain. Maura pawed at Aoife, urging her to move, but still she stayed, straining to hear their words.

"I don't want to hurt you either, Collins. I really don't," Declan said, his rage softening briefly before flaring once more. "But I will if you don't let me at her."

"What did she do to you?"

"She handed me over to Callum! And it's *her* fault Tommy is dead!" He shouted the accusation over Collins's shoulder, pointing his dagger at Aoife. His voice lowered into a snarl as he glowered at Collins once more. "My oldest friend. A brother to me. And she got him killed. Gutted like a damn fish."

Collins stumbled backward, as if the words themselves had shoved him away, but he recovered as quickly as he could, yelling at Declan, "Tommy's alive! Whatever you think Aoife's done, it's a lie, a trick of the siren!"

Declan rushed him once more, knocking one of his daggers into the sand. But Collins held his ground, pushing all his weight against his captain. Their weapons were now pressed against each other's throats.

"Don't you dare defend that bitch. Don't you dare." Declan spat the words in his face, but he held fast, unflinching.

"I'm just trying to help—"

"Bullshit! If that were true, you'd be chasing her down yourself, stringing her up so I could give her what she damn well deserves. But instead you're here! Knife to my throat. Loyal crew indeed." Declan's lip curled into a sneer. "You let her follow you onto my ship. Maybe I should hurt you for bringing down this curse!"

Maura stopped pulling her, halted in place by Declan's shouts. Aoife's head began to shake in disbelief. Triss could not win. Especially not like this, with Declan hating her, thinking she'd betrayed him and killed his best friend. She had to do something. Something other than crouch in the sand and wait to be killed.

With a burst of energy she flung herself away from Maura, but the fae held her.

"Aoife, stop," Maura pleaded with her, but it only made Aoife try harder.

"Let me go. I need to stop him. To end this," she said with a growl.

"And how in the hell do you think you'll stop it? Aoife! Think!"

"I don't know! I don't know..." She repeated the words over and over, and each time, they grew softer as her body lost its fight against Maura's iron grip. "But I have to try."

She stilled and resorted once again to watching Declan trying to get at her, Collins standing in his way.

"What has she done?" Aoife asked no one in particular.

Maura answered, "Compelled him to believe a new memory."

"But why? Why not simply compel him to kill me if that's what she wants?"

She winced as Collins landed a blow on Declan's ribs, thankful it had been with his fist and not his blade. But it did little to slow Declan down in his pursuit. For each step Collins pushed Declan back, Declan gained two. Or three. They were getting closer to her, and Aoife wasn't surprised when her friend pulled her further away.

Maura answered her as they scrambled on the sand. "That wouldn't be as entertaining for her. It wouldn't have this amount of emotion and passion behind it."

So it was for Triss's enjoyment—and the enjoyment of her audience. It wasn't merely Aoife's death she sought.

"She wants to hurt him more," Aoife said, and Maura nodded. "If he succeeds, she'll take the memory away—"

Maura finished the thought. "And leave his heart even more tarnished with guilt. And loss."

A fire flared within Aoife's chest, and she dug her toes into the sand as hard as she could, but it did little to stop Maura from pulling her along.

"Let me go," Aoife repeated, but this time she filled each word with the flames raging within her. "Let me try."

When the tightness around her arm lessened, she didn't hesitate to take advantage. She didn't run. She needed to maintain her strength for what she needed to do. It was a long shot, she knew. She had no skills to help her combat a siren's magic, but she hoped—beyond all hope—that maybe the stories were true.

Love conquered all.

And if Declan truly loved her, it could break this evil cloud he was trapped in. It had to.

Maura followed close behind but didn't seem keen on dragging her away again.

Love conquers all. She repeated it to herself, as if doing so could give the words power, make them true.

Less than twenty feet separated them when Declan feinted, drawing Collins to one side so he could drive his knee into his stomach. Collins rallied and stood, but Declan must have anticipated his move, because in a blur of movement too fast for Aoife to track, Collins's blade was dropping to the ground.

Declan's hand slammed into him.

They both stilled.

Wrapping an arm around Collins, Declan pulled him closer, but there was nothing friendly about the move.

What was happening?

Then Collins collapsed to his knees, and Aoife's eyes went wide as she watched him slowly sway.

Get up! Get up! Get up!

She silently screamed at him over and over.

Declan stood and lifted his blade, which was now dripping with blood.

"No!" Aoife screamed. Or did she? She couldn't tell what was real anymore.

Collins's head lolled to one side. His arms went limp. Even if Aoife hadn't been frozen in place, Maura wouldn't have allowed her to go help him, so she waited. And watched.

He was fine. He had to be.

Aoife's breath caught as Declan pushed him. Collins didn't resist. He simply fell to the ground and lay motionless.

Declan's lips moved as he muttered something, but Aoife couldn't hear him over her heartbeat thundering in her ears. Adjusting his grip on his blade, he stalked toward her, eyes pulsing with hatred.

And now she heard his words.

"You claimed to love me, Aoife, and I believed you. Like a fool. You've taken everything from me. My pride, my heart, my friend. And now you're going to pay. Slowly. Painfully." His spewed vitriol ripped her heart to shreds.

Aoife channeled the pain into her next words, directed not at him but at Triss. "How are you so heartless?"

Triss replied with a wide grin before baring her teeth, which transformed into a hideous mess of needle-like tines. She laughed, the most maniacal cackle Aoife had ever heard.

Then Maura was there, standing in front of Aoife, protecting her.

No, no, no, no.

This time she knew the words remained in her mind, silent to the world, but it was the only response she had to seeing another friend rush toward a threat to save her.

To save Declan.

Declan showed no mercy to the fae though, and he didn't hesitate to attack. Maura held her own as best she could, her arms taking nicks from the blade as he swiped it this way and that, but still she held strong. Twice she hit her mark. An elbow to his chin. A fist to his ribs where Collins had struck him before. And though he recoiled, the hits did little—even with her inhuman strength—to slow him down. Blood dripped from her arms, peppering the white sand between their feet. And then Declan landed a lucky blow, an elbow to Maura's temple. She tried to remain standing, tried to keep going, but her feet were quickly faltering.

Aoife was there to grab her before she fell, and she grunted under the sudden weight of her friend's still body. Aoife feared the worst but managed somehow to focus on the spot where Maura's blood should still flow in her veins, and after seeing the pulse there, slow and sure, she released a breath of relief.

But that relief was short-lived, and now Declan had a hold of her hair at the crown of her head, pulling her out from under the fae until she stood mere inches from his hate-filled face. The weight of his animosity slammed into her chest, and she couldn't breathe, couldn't think.

Aoife wasn't afraid to die. She'd expected death to come for her at some point on this journey. But she'd never thought it would be like this. At the hand of someone who loved her.

The tears welled up without warning. She had no strength remaining to fight them from spilling over and trailing down her cheeks. She should plead with him, as he had done in the cove, but the words stuck in her throat, and she was frozen in fear. He was staring at her with such disgust.

"Don't you dare," he started, his voice low, gravelly, terrifying. "You aren't allowed to weep. Not after what you did. I gave you *everything* I had. I *trusted* you. My sister trusted you."

Aoife tried to protest, even though she knew it would do no good. "I didn't. I didn't."

He whirled her around until her back pressed against his chest and his dagger pricked her throat. His breath warmed her ear, and the flood of memories drowned her. The man she had grown to know and love was the Declan she wanted to remember. The one who, though dangerous, had a heart, even if it was a bit burnt. The Declan who brushed away her tears, who talked her through the panic, who held her hand, who knelt in the sand and begged for her to understand.

Would pleading work for her now? It hadn't swayed her, but it was her only chance now.

"I'm sorry, Declan," she said, her voice barely over a whisper. He scoffed, but she continued. "Please forgive me. I need you."

"Shut up," he hissed in her ear.

She refused.

"No. I won't shut up. You need to know."

Before she could say more, her eyes snapped to the action unfolding near Triss's dais.

Callum, now conscious, rose to his feet and didn't hesitate before running at Triss, hands flexed and eyes ablaze. Triss didn't see him. Her eyes—wide with anticipation—were focused solely on Aoife. Aoife's breath caught as Callum launched himself at the queen.

But she hadn't been oblivious after all.

Her hand flashed up, caught Callum by the throat, and squeezed.

CHAPTER 52
DECLAN

You've failed them, Aoife," Declan whispered into Aoife's ear, and he grimaced at how close he had to stand to this woman who disgusted him. But it would be over soon enough. After she felt a fraction of the pain he did. "Look around. They're all dead or dying. Because of you. It's all you're good for. Getting people killed. Lani. Tommy. Collins. Maura. You're next."

A pathetic whimper squeaked out of her, and he allowed himself a laugh if only to keep the pain of his sister's death from bowling him over once more.

"Who is that?" Aoife asked, risking a nick from the blade as she nodded toward the siren who now held Callum by his neck. The man's toes barely skimmed the surface of the sand as he struggled.

"Doesn't matter," he continued, "you'll be dead before you have a chance to meet her. And you'll never get the precious dagger you're searching for."

Callum's kicks lessened, his face losing color as his lungs failed to pull in any more air. He was going to lose this fight, and Declan was glad for that. Served him right for how he'd plotted with Aoife to snatch him off the street. For how he'd tortured Killian.

Lowering his blade, he spun Aoife around in his arms to face him. He wanted to see her life drain away.

She stared at him. Her unblinking gold-flecked green eyes called up visions of home and rolling hills. At one time, these eyes had been his hope and promise for a love-filled life like his parents had had, but now all he saw was her deceit and her lies.

He clenched his jaw. This bitch needed to pay. She needed to hurt as he did.

They stood so close he could feel her breath on his chest. It was far steadier than he might have expected—or wanted. Gone were the tears that had spilled earlier.

Now she exhibited determination and strength, as if he wasn't holding a dagger to her throat. As if she were daring him to get it over with.

"I'd offer you the chance for last words," he said, "but I honestly don't give a shit what you have to say. Nothing you say could make me forgive you."

He paused, searching her eyes for any hint that his words had an impact on her. But if anything, they seemed to bolster her, and she stood an inch taller as she straightened. The movement brought her face closer to his, and her eyes drifted to his lips. He sneered at her. But she didn't seem to notice, her eyes once more finding his.

She swallowed and drew in a deep breath. "I love you, Declan McCallagh, and no one can change that—not a siren, and not you. I forgive you."

Before he could respond to her outrageous declaration, a flurry of movement pulled his attention back to where Triss still held Callum, pale and weak, in her grasp. A flash of sun on steel skimmed across Declan's line of sight. A moan of pain escaped from Callum. Triss loosened her grip and examined the knife now lodged in his shoulder before turning toward the one who had thrown it.

Captain Halloran? What was she doing here?

She approached the queen and her captive. The sirens on the dais, still watching, writhed on the stone, licking their lips. Yet they didn't budge. Even as Halloran walked past them, they remained, glancing at Triss every few breaths.

Triss clicked her tongue at her kin and gave a shake of her head, and this had them snarling in protest, but she didn't seem to care as she focused on Halloran.

"You missed," Triss said with a laugh.

"I meant to hit him. The bastard deserved it." Halloran's stride remained confident as she continued forward, not once glancing away from the queen.

"Oh, really." Triss faced Callum once more, shaking his head a bit and finally slapping him across the face to get his eyes to open. When they did open, just barely, she stared into them. "Is this the one you've lamented over? The one that got away? The one who betrayed you before you could betray her?"

As he listened to their exchange, Declan tightened his fingers in Aoife's hair to keep her steady, ignoring how she stared at him. One swipe and it would be over. She'd bleed out, he'd have his revenge, and then he'd get that dagger from the siren. He'd delayed too long. Flexing his arm, he prepared to pull the dagger across her throat. But it was yanked from his hand by someone or something. It clattered against the rock wall to his right and fell to the ground.

What in the sands was that?

Aoife's mouth gaped in bewilderment. But he didn't need a blade to kill her. Using her shock against her, he moved his hands to her throat before she could try to stop him. Yes, this would be better. He smirked as he thought of how much more pleasant it was to squeeze the life out of her, to crush her windpipe, to feel her last shuddering breath.

He tightened his fingers, adjusting them slightly to get a better grip. She didn't smack his arms or try to wriggle free. Instead she rested her hands on him. Her eyes held none of the terror he'd hoped for, nor did they plead with him for mercy. This was the look he'd seen pass between his parents, a look of unconditional love, a look of trust and adoration.

Who was she to look at him like that? How dare she? He wouldn't make this mistake again. Wouldn't trust her and her lies.

He squeezed harder. Her breathing became ragged and shallow as she tried to pull in air. And still she looked at him with those damn adoring eyes. Her mouth formed words, but she didn't have the air to give them sound.

I love you.

Declan couldn't look at her anymore. As much as he wanted to watch her die, he couldn't. Not when she looked at him like that.

He looked over her head to where Halloran now crossed the last bit of sand before coming to a stop an arm's length away from the siren. With one deft movement, Triss released Callum's throat and kicked him back down to the ground. She struck Halloran across the face with one hand, grabbing the captain's hair with the other, then leaned in close. Even from this distance, Declan could hear every word she said.

"Captain Halloran. You're a fool. You're all fools. Did you really think a little cloaking of the mind could protect you? I don't need in here"—she shook Halloran's head around for emphasis—"to hurt you. It's a shame he never told you how he felt about you. Did you never guess it? Or did you ignore all the signs so you wouldn't feel so bad when you double-crossed him? When you sliced up his face?"

Halloran spat at the queen's face. "I'm a pirate. Slicing people up is what I do."

Triss threw her head back with a harsh laugh. She had barely quieted down when Callum pushed himself up from the ground. This time he didn't lunge for the queen as he had before, instead pulling the knife from his shoulder and throwing it at Triss. But she must have heard the plan in his head because she easily deflected the blade with her arm as she laughed again.

"Seriously, Callum," she said. "Will you never learn? I know all that you think and all that you plan. There's nothing you can do that I won't foresee."

The sweat pooling beneath Declan's palms forced his attention away from the queen. He readjusted his hands, surprised that Aoife still made no move to escape even when his grip loosened for a moment. He looked down at her, which was a mistake. Those eyes once more pleaded with him, and they remained devoid of fear or anger or remorse. There was only love. Why in the sands did she look at him like that? If she loved him, she would never have turned him over, would never have given up the names of the Rogues, would never have sacrificed his sister to the council's ruthless judgment.

The familiar sound of a blade against leather pulled Declan's attention up once more, and his hands tightened reflexively as he watched the scene play out.

With a growl, Callum bounded across the sand, pushing Halloran away as he gripped her cutlass to unsheathe it. Pulling his arm back as he turned, Callum sent the curved blade slicing deep across the siren's belly. Triss bared her teeth again, snarling and hissing as she worked to keep her innards from spilling out onto the sand.

Callum stumbled backwards, and Triss looked ready to lunge for him, but from the left came a flash of movement and light before steel met ancient flesh. Triss howled as a dagger buried itself in her chest, and she turned to see who it had come from. Declan nearly stumbled backward at the sight of Tommy staggering toward the queen, determination and pain written all over his face.

Tommy was here? He was alive? How? Declan had seen his lifeless body on that library floor.

No, this had to be a trick of Aoife's. Somehow she'd gotten in his head, making him see what she wanted him to. That wasn't really Tommy. It was someone else, someone she was forcing him to see as his best friend.

But Triss wouldn't be beaten so easily. With a wave of her bloody hand and another snarl, she sent a silent command to the sirens.

Declan watched the creatures—who were mad with hunger—bound off the dais toward the man.

What if that was Tommy? And Declan was just standing here instead of helping him?

But another look at Aoife sent his rage spiraling again, and his fingers quickly found new strength around her throat.

It was time to finish this.

CHAPTER 53
TOMMY

THE BLADE FLEW TRUE, slamming into the siren just as Tommy had intended. Pain tore through his shoulder, but he would get no rest, it seemed, as the queen gave a silent command without hesitation.

A group of sirens leaped off the pile of stone, their hands outstretched toward him.

He had no more weapons. No way to defend himself against their inhuman strength and razor-sharp teeth.

But weapons or no, he would not go down easily. He didn't know how, but determination swelled within him as he caught a glimpse of Maura lying in the sand.

The eyes of the sirens, sickly and white, turned his stomach, but still he stood firm.

Dried blood clung to their flawless skin. It was smeared up their arms. Down their chins. Across their chests.

With a final inhale, he set his feet and braced himself for the impact. Ready.

His eyes snapped shut as the first of the five reached him. Her clawed hand reached for his face, cutting open his cheek.

And then the winds changed everything.

A gust of air rushed across the sand, past Tommy, slamming into the sirens. Their bodies were flung backward until the wind crushed them against the rock wall with a sickening yet satisfying sound. Tommy whirled around to find Bria standing there, lowering her hands as she released her control on the air. Beside her, Renna assessed Maura.

"You're too late, sisters." Triss's words came out strained as she choked on her own blood. "It's already done."

Tommy, pivoting quickly, turned to find Aoife's head falling to one side. Her face was the color of death, and Declan smiled as he squeezed harder.

A deep growl echoed off the stone walls, and in his periphery Tommy saw Halloran reach over to pull the dagger from Triss's chest and draw its sharp edge across the siren's neck.

Blood sprayed, and Triss—her eyes glazing over before turning toward the sky —fell to the white ground, her blood seeping into the sand.

CHAPTER 54
DECLAN

DECLAN BLINKED, slow and steady. His head pounded. His hands ached.

Something slid off his forearms, and he looked down to find Aoife's arms falling lifeless at her sides. Aoife. Only his hands at her throat kept her upright. Why was he choking her? His hands released her, and his arms moved to catch her as she crumpled to the ground.

What had he done? What had happened?

He tried to recall, but the last thing he remembered was Aoife bargaining with Triss to let him go. Beyond that there was nothing. A section of time had been cut from his life and discarded.

"Aoife!" he called, but she didn't stir.

Falling to his knees—a painful echo of what had happened on that fateful night back in the cove—he lowered her down, cradling her in his arms. Stroking her hair, that unruly and unkempt hair that fit her freckled face so perfectly, he whispered her name again and again.

He could see her pulse thumping away at her neck, although much too slowly. Still, her heart was beating, and that was what mattered. But he needed her to wake up, needed her to be okay. Had he really come all this way, endured all of that, to fail her again?

Tommy inched his way toward him, wincing and holding his head in his hand.

"Tommy!" he yelled, his voice cracking in desperation. He needed his help—Aoife needed help—but he couldn't get any other words out. Stumbling over, Tommy cringed at the sight of a body he passed. He didn't kneel down. Didn't offer to help. He simply stared, his features twisting and flinching, as if he didn't know how to feel, what to think, or what to do.

"Maura," Tommy muttered, and Declan looked across the sand to where Renna and Bria knelt beside another body lying on the ground, but this one stirred, trying to sit up. "Maura?" Tommy called again.

"I'm okay," a voice, weak and strained, said. "Help Declan."

Tommy hesitated for a moment but then looked back down at Declan and Aoife.

"You don't remember." It wasn't a question. And Declan could only stare blankly at him. Tommy crouched down, his fingers checking for Aoife's pulse. Maura approached and placed a gentle hand on Tommy's injured shoulder before she caught Declan's attention and explained what had happened. How Triss had compelled him to believe Aoife had betrayed him and gotten Tommy killed, how he had fought Collins and Maura in order to get to Aoife and kill her himself.

Each word carved out another piece of his heart. It wasn't his fault, he knew, but it hurt all the same.

"But I'm okay," Declan said. "She'll be okay. We'll all be okay."

Tommy flinched, and Declan's eyes dropped to the ground behind his friend where a body lay lifeless. He worked his way back through the day's events, trying to recall who all had arrived with Aoife.

"Collins." The name fell from his lips as a whisper. "But the fae..."

Maura shook her head. "I'm sorry, Declan. It's too late for us to help him."

"I killed him."

No one moved.

What did they all think of him? Would the crew still want him as their captain? Would Aoife...

Declan looked down to where Aoife lay in his arms, at the face he'd dreamed of every night in Callum's ship. Had he scared her while he was under Triss's powers? How would she forgive him for this when she had refused to forgive him before?

Just one more thing he'd need to make right.

A throat cleared, and Declan found Captain Halloran striding toward him. There was a cut below her left eye, but it was no longer bleeding. Maura offered to hold Aoife so he could talk to the captain, but he shook his head rapidly. He had finally gotten her back. He wasn't about to let her go. Not unless she told him to.

As Halloran closed the distance and knelt before Declan, his mind flashed back to his youth. His parents had taken up this stance whenever he had fallen down or gotten hurt. There was only kindness in the woman's dark eyes. He should thank her, endlessly thank her for all she'd apparently done for his crew and for Aoife and for him, but words eluded him.

"Captain Halloran here," Tommy started, waiting for Declan to look at him, "if she hadn't found us, we would be at the bottom of the Aisling or deep in the kraken's belly."

Maura offered a tight smile. "And if not there, we'd surely have been siren food."

For the first time, Declan noticed the bloody tangle of gore and delicate black fabric on the ground behind Halloran.

Triss.

Reluctantly he pulled one hand away from Aoife and extended it toward the captain. "Do I owe you a word of thanks for that? For killing her?"

Her lip twitched. "Only partly. Callum deserves your gratitude as well."

Declan's eyes closed as his chin dropped to his chest. He ran a hand over his brow, clenching his jaw. How could he thank the man who had snatched him off the street and tortured a good man simply for helping him?

Halloran spoke again, but he couldn't look at her. "I won't say he's a good man, McCallagh. Sands knows he's done his share of evil. But he didn't have to do what he did. He didn't have to help us."

Declan's gut tightened as visions of Killian's shredded body filled every inch of his mind.

Halloran added, "You don't have to like him. No one really likes him anyway. But his evil deeds don't make his good ones null and void."

Drawing in a deep breath, Declan began to nod. Halloran spoke true. Callum might still be punished for all eternity for his heinous actions and ruthless nature, but that didn't make him any less worthy of thanks when he did right—no matter how seldom it was.

Opening his eyes, he looked at those sitting around him. "So where is he?"

Heads turned, and everyone searched for the pirate captain. But aside from Triss's remains and Callum's blood staining the white sand, the beach was empty.

"And I can only assume the dagger is gone too?" Before Declan could finish the question, Tommy was up and running toward Triss's corpse. Frantically he searched the remnants of the queen and her garments.

Tommy punched the ground and lowered his head. He didn't need to relay the news for Declan to know.

Callum was gone.

The dagger along with him.

That bastard.

CHAPTER 55
CAIT

CAIT SNEAKED out of the town square and started down a road that ran parallel to the one where Adler had taken Lucan. When she popped out from between the buildings onto the road running along the harbor, she looked to the right, toward the path that led to the pit. But they were nowhere in sight. It didn't make sense. It was nearly a straight shot to the trees where they had turned that morning.

Where was Adler taking him if not to that pit?

Scanning the docks that jutted out along the coast, she continued on her way, craning her neck to see around the random sailors and pirates loading goods onto ships or meandering into town for a hot meal. Nowhere. No Lucan. No Adler. Where in the sands were they?

A flash of bright fabric caught her attention, standing out in stark contrast to the dull browns and grays most of the sailors wore.

Lucy.

Cait picked up speed, keeping her eyes firmly locked on the woman's bright attire. She dodged one pirate swigging a bottle of rum and then a pair of travelers making their way into the city.

Lucy turned onto one of the docks, her gait sure and confident. Cait's intuition pushed her forward. She was sure Lucy was involved somehow. Continuously scanning the dock, Cait searched for any sign of the two men.

Still nothing.

Perhaps they had headed to the pit and she'd just been late?

Maybe she was wasting her time following this crazy woman from Foxhaven.

Cait turned around in circles, not caring if people thought her mad. She searched.

Two tall men.

One blonde. One with brown hair.

One a victim. One a damned traitor.

She had completed two full turns before she thought she caught a glimpse of Adler. Her vision was a bit dizzy from spinning, but when she looked closer, she was sure it was him. In front of him, Lucan's familiar face grimaced as he trudged along.

Cait's feet took off running through the crowd once more, and she weaved around boxes and luggage and people, her footfalls becoming hollow thumps as the stones beneath her gave way to the wooden dock. People shouted at her, but she didn't care. Lucan and Adler were just up ahead and about to board a small ship.

She pushed her legs harder, faster.

Lucan hated water. Didn't just hate it. He was deathly afraid of it. Perhaps more afraid of drowning than he was of dying in any other way.

Adler shoved Lucan up the gangplank, following him closely. Cait's mouth nearly dropped open at the sight of Lucy—*damned Lucy*—standing aboard the ship, her hands reaching out to take Lucan's arms.

Making a sharp turn, Cait nearly lost her footing as her shoes slipped across the wet wood of the dock.

"Adler!" she cried as she ran the last fifty feet toward him, hoping her anger would give the word more power.

He turned, and his eyes widened before his lips creeped down into that upside-down smile of his. With a flourish of his hand, he offered her a grand bow before kicking the gangplank back toward the dock. Their crew had worked fast, faster than she'd thought possible, to untie the lines and get them moving. She gauged the distance from the dock to the edge of the ship as she ran, her feet pounding hard against the wooden planks, her legs burning from the effort.

But she skidded to a stop, her toes creeping out over the edge, when she realized they'd gotten too far away for her to make the jump.

Cursing Adler and Lucy, she stood there until their sails disappeared beyond the bay of Morshan.

⚔

It was the middle of the busy hour at the pub when Cait finally ambled back. Not bothering to use the alley door, she slammed the front door open and ignored how the patrons stared at her as she stomped across the floor. She bumped her shoulders into pirates and merchants alike, paying them no attention as they grumbled and cursed and finally fell silent when they realized it was her.

Kira was behind the bar. She'd been dutifully manning the business while Cait had been out working.

You mean failing.

Her muttered curse fell to the pub floor as she shoved herself behind the bar. Reaching underneath, she pushed several bottles aside until she found the rum she'd been saving for after the council's fall. They were all doomed now, so there was no point in saving it.

No parents. No brother. No friends. No nothing.

Cait let the dark thoughts take over, her own malicious and barbed words cutting into her more painfully than if anyone else had said them. Standing with the old bottle in hand, its dark amber liquid glistening in the light of the lanterns, she said nothing to Kira or to anyone else as she made to retreat to her room upstairs.

Before she could leave, though, Kira grabbed her arm. The girl's kind, concerned eyes searched hers as though to ask if Cait was all right.

Of course I'm not all right! Cait wanted to shout back at her, and she hoped that message was clear in the glare she shot back.

"Get some rest," Kira said, grabbing Cait's free hand firmly and giving it a squeeze before releasing it and nodding toward the stairs.

Cait had barely gotten the door closed when she stopped and read the note Kira had slipped to her so expertly.

Tomorrow afternoon. Calypso cove. It's not what you think, love. - Adler

With a scowl at the bottle she carried, she gritted her teeth once more, knowing she very well might regret trusting the man again. But this drink could wait a few more days.

Perhaps not all was lost just yet. Perhaps her instincts hadn't completely gone to shit as she'd feared.

CHAPTER 56

AOIFE

It hurt to swallow, but then, it hurt to simply lie here. Aoife hadn't yet opened her eyes, almost too afraid to see what reality she would find—if she was still alive at all. Wiggling her toes, she tested out little movements. She listened for any sounds, but everything was muffled, as if she were underwater.

"Aoife?" Declan's voice pushed through the fog, and she slowly opened her eyes.

He lay on his side, his head resting on his arm, looking at her. Worried he would disappear if she blinked, she tried to keep her eyes open and focused on him.

"I'm sorry," he said before pulling a breath of air deep into his lungs.

Her heart pushed her to reach for him, but she hesitated and retreated slightly.

"Am I still alive? Are you?"

He looked around the room before offering her a slight smirk—although it wasn't half as attractive as the one he normally donned. "I would hope paradise doesn't look like my ratty old cabin on this battered ship."

There was a hint of humor amid the deep regret and sadness she'd seen in his eyes under the moonlight in the cove. The memory of that night—of her denying him forgiveness—pulled her insides tight.

"I forgive you, Declan," she said as she inched her hand toward his. "For everything."

He closed his eyes and sighed deeply, like she'd just offered him the world. And perhaps she had.

As their fingers touched, she examined his face. "I assume we won if we're back on the ship then?"

"Aye," he said, his eyes flashing open. "Thanks to Halloran and—as much as I hate to admit it—Callum."

The way he ground out the pirate's name told Aoife he didn't fully appreciate the man's help.

He provided her a short rundown of what had happened after she'd lost consciousness—how Callum had snuck off with the blade, how they planned to give chase and recover it as soon as they got Halloran back to her ship, which was waiting nearby.

It could have been worse.

But that thought rotted around the memory of Collins falling, his blood on Declan's dagger. Had they recovered his body? Would he receive a proper burial at sea? Before Aoife could ask, Declan was talking again, a boyish look on his face. "It's too bad you missed seeing the sirens."

"I think I've had enough sirens for a lifetime." She frowned at him.

"No, the other sirens."

Aoife lifted her injured arm in protest, to remind him of how those *other* sirens had treated her, but the gold fabric they'd tied around her was gone, replaced with clean linen.

"Yes, I know, but they were under Triss's control when they attacked you. Once she was dead and they were freed, we found they weren't like Triss at all. Like me, they couldn't remember anything about their centuries with her. Probably for the better too. They won't be haunted by what they were forced to do and can now live how they wish. Where they wish. Some swam alongside our boats as we left. Others shifted into their bird form and soared high above us before drifting off east."

"That would have been an interesting sight." Even as she said it, she still didn't regret not seeing them. Gentle or not. All she could think of was the pain from their fangs and the sight of Triss's snarling mouth. She shuddered again, and he reached for her.

Scooting across the bed toward him, she let him pull her in close and tuck her in his arms. His lips met her forehead. She altered her breathing to match his and let herself settle into the comforting rhythm of his heartbeat. The best sound in the world. Steady and true and strong.

"You're sure you're not still angry with me?" he asked.

"Do you not remember all that I told you?"

"If you said it while I was not myself, then no. I know nothing beyond what Maura could relate to me." At this, she sat up, and he did the same, propping himself up with a hand before he said, "Was it something good? I hope it was something good. Or something dirty. That would be nice too."

With a slap of her hand on his shoulder, she shook her head at him and rolled her eyes. "You're awful, you know that?"

"So I've been told." He offered up her favorite smirk, and it took all her willpower not to tackle him right then. But that had to wait.

Clenching her hands tightly in her lap, she searched his face, as if the words she needed were written upon his features. Her lower lip quivered, and she bit down on it to force it to be still.

"Why was this so much easier to say when you were trying to kill me?" She meant it as a joke to lighten the mood, but as soon as the words were out, she worried they'd sting him unnecessarily.

But he let out a soft laugh. "Probably because you thought it was the end."

"Seems much more appropriate for a beginning though." She wrinkled her nose as her stomach fluttered.

"Oh?" Light in his eyes danced with that humor she'd missed, even when she'd been so angry with him.

A deep breath couldn't steady her racing heart, but she couldn't withhold this from him any longer.

"I love you, Declan McCallagh."

His lips were on hers in an instant. She'd had more to say, but this was good too. Letting herself sink into him, she met his hunger and need and desperation with each move of their lips and tongues. His arms pulled her close, trapping her against his chest, and still she couldn't get close enough to him.

"I missed you," he whispered around her lips, and she hummed in return, melting further into his touch, getting lost in the growing heat within her that flared with each move of his hands along her back.

She was about to pull back and stop them when his hands came to a rest on her hips and his mouth planted tender kisses along her jaw. Her hands traveled up his neck, her fingers getting lost in his hair. It all felt amazingly delightful, and she never wanted him to stop.

But she knew he had to.

"Declan," she whispered.

"Yes?" he murmured against her skin, kissing across her shoulder as he moved the fabric of her shirt aside.

"Where is Maura?" She thought this would snap him out of whatever spell he was under, but it didn't.

"Why?" The word tickled her ear, which he nipped with his teeth, sending a shock through her whole body.

Aoife shuddered but tried again, moving her hands back down to his chest and giving him a gentle push. "I need to ask her a question."

"And it can't wait?" he asked, allowing her to move him back until she could see him clearly.

Looking at him now, with his hair falling into his face and his gaze burning with desire almost had her tossing aside the question that had plagued her even in unconsciousness. She shook her head. With a bob of his chin, he took her hands in his and pulled her off the bed.

"Then let's find her, shall we?"

THEY FOUND Maura with Tommy up on the quarterdeck, which was still stained with kraken blood. After exchanging silent greetings of smiles and nods, Aoife blurted out, "Something happened back there with Declan."

They all looked at her like she had just declared water to be wet or the sea to be salty. She tried again.

"When he had his dagger to my throat..." She forced herself to ignore the way his mouth twitched at the reminder. "He wasn't able to use it, because he dropped it. Except he didn't drop it. It flew from his hand. How?"

Maura shifted her weight and gave Tommy an almost apologetic look, which simply confused Aoife more.

"I wanted to tell you," she said, "but there never seemed to be a good time."

"Tell me what?"

"It was you. You did that." Maura's stony expression indicated her words were genuine, but that didn't make them any easier to understand.

"What do you mean, I did—"

"You moved the dagger."

"That's impossible," Aoife said, glancing around. Everyone else appeared as perplexed as she felt.

"You're a demi-fae, Aoife," Maura said.

Three jaws dropped open. With wide eyes, Aoife stared at her friend, looking for any hint that this was a joke. This had to be a joke.

"A what? That's not possible," she said, shaking her head vehemently. "For me to be any type of fae, my mother or father would—"

"—have to be fae," Maura said. "It's your mother."

Aoife felt the floor fall out from under her as her stomach plunged into her feet. She couldn't breathe. What did this mean? How was this at all possible? How many more surprises would she discover? How much did she not know?

A lot, apparently.

All her muscles tensed, and she snapped her eyes up to Maura's again. "What do you mean there was never a good time? This seems like rather pertinent information, Maura! I had a right to know!"

"You did, but it wouldn't have helped. We didn't know for sure if you'd inherited any powers. There was no reason to distract you with it when we weren't certain."

"And when did you figure it out exactly?"

Maura shifted her feet. "Once Renna compelled you. Somehow it awakened whatever magic your mother passed on to you. We could sense it. And I planned to tell you once you awoke."

Aoife knew this was all logically sound, but it still didn't quell the sting or lessen the shock of this revelation.

Declan squeezed her hand reassuringly before asking his own question. "In order for Aoife to inherit any *daemari*, though, Melina would have had to be a royal. So why would she need you and your sisters?"

Maura grimaced as if she were about to offer up more disagreeable news. "It's a long story, and I promise you'll hear it, but not without my sisters present."

"Can you give us the short version?" Tommy asked, his voice tender.

Looking from him to Aoife, Maura nodded slightly. "She lost her *daemari* when she enchanted the dagger for the king."

"What dagger?" Aoife asked, immediately realizing how stupid the question was but not caring.

"How many enchanted daggers do you think there are?" Maura asked with an awkward laugh.

Her mother. The dagger. The king.

The legend.

Aoife's jaw fell open once more as Declan voiced what they were all probably thinking.

"Well, shit."

CHAPTER 57
TOMMY

Tommy watched Declan and Aoife disappear down the stairs and continued to stare in their direction long after.

"What's bothering you?" Maura's melodic voice pulled his attention back to where she stood beside him.

Taking her into his arms, he wrapped her in a hug and held her head against his chest. He searched the sea, which was black beneath the night sky. The *Siren's Song* sailed along as fast as they could with the available wind. So many things had gone well.

But others...

Maura didn't pressure him to answer her question, instead settling herself against him, her arms tucked between them, her hands clutching at his shirt.

"It's just a"—Tommy cleared the scratchiness from his throat—"a bad feeling. Like a chill over my skin or an uneasiness settling within me."

"What do you think it's about?" she asked.

"I wish I knew. Or maybe I don't."

At this, she pulled back to look him in the eye, her brow creased in question.

"Does it help to know the doom that lies ahead?" he said. "Or does it distract you from relishing the present moment?"

Maura's eyes rose to the sky as she pondered his words. "Or would it force you to live the present moment to its fullest? If I had known I would be imprisoned in that room for centuries, I would have done more to enjoy the years beforehand. I would have traveled, seen the world, had more fun."

"Or you would have spent all those years trying to find a way to prevent it from happening and ended up sacrificing them all." She lifted her shoulders in concession and flashed him that coy smile he adored. "Maybe we're both right."

"Well, in that case..." Tommy said as he moved a hand to her neck, enjoying how she shivered under his fingers. Cradling her jaw, he lowered his lips to her shoulder, kissing and nibbling and breathing along her skin until he reached her ear, where he whispered, "Perhaps we should do more to enjoy this moment."

She leaned into his lips and let the full length of her body press against him as she tangled her fingers in his hair and held him tight.

Tommy continued to taste the sweetness of her skin even as he lowered his hands to lift her up, delighting in the way her legs instinctively wrapped around his waist and her whole body sighed with each of his kisses.

Somehow, with his eyes barely seeing the world around them, he managed to get down the stairs and to the door of the officers' cabin. He pulled away long enough to catch her eye, hoping she could hear his silent question. Maura leaned her ear toward the door and, presumably hearing no sign of her sisters within, took a half breath before pulling her lips into a mischievous grin and gesturing for him to continue inside.

The click of the door closing behind them was like a match to a fuse, setting Tommy ablaze. His kisses became hungrier. His hands gripped her tighter. His body ached for her.

It must have done the same for her, as she was soon leaping down from around his waist and pushing him against the wall. Her fingers had his shirt unbuttoned and on the floor before he even realized what she was doing, but he didn't hesitate to reach down to her waist and pull the length of her dress up, bunching it around her hips.

"There's entirely too much fabric between us," he said.

Before he'd gotten the words out, her hands were at his belt, working to remedy the situation. But he stopped her, moving her arms away from him as he lifted her dress the rest of the way off, slipping it over her head and dropping it to the floor.

His heart took off without him, racing ahead, beating feverishly in response to her utter beauty. She hadn't lied when she'd said she was no mere woman. He'd been with women, even beautiful ones, but they all paled next to Maura.

"You're staring," she teased, placing a hand on her hip.

"I know," he said as he allowed his eyes to greedily run over every inch of her, slowly, as if he could memorize every curve.

With an exaggerated inhale, she looked to the ceiling of the small room. "When you talked of savoring, I thought—"

Tommy had her against him before she could finish her taunt, claiming her mouth with his, loving the way she tasted and enjoying the dance her tongue did with his. Her hands moved lower, but he pulled her hips closer to block her.

"Not yet," he whispered against her lips before blazing a trail of kisses down her neck, over her collarbone, and onto her breasts, which were more delightful than anything he had envisioned. He couldn't hold back a smile when she gasped and shuddered as his tongue brushed over one peak, and he delighted in the way her back arched as he continued to devour it and then the other. When he pulled away, the most adorable whimper of protest filled the space, making it impossible to keep his mouth off her for long.

This time when her hands met his waist, he didn't object. But she was taking her sweet time, making him nearly beg for her to hurry up. Why had he mentioned savoring? This was torture. His need for her increased with each flutter of her fingers against his skin and each inch of his pants she lowered.

She paused and looked up at him. The passion in her eyes had clouded over with hesitation that left him confused. And slightly panicked that he'd done something wrong.

"What?"

"Is this okay? Here? Now?" Her questions came out with humor, though Tommy thought he picked up on a hint of concern as well. "It's not your captain's bed, but—"

Tommy ran his hands along her bare waist and pulled her against him once more. "Are you asking me if I am sure? If I really want this?"

Placing a kiss on his chest, lighter and more innocent than he would have expected from her, she whispered the words against his skin, "I don't want to rush you. I don't want you to regret..."

Her shoulders slumped, and she wrapped her arms around his middle. Tommy kissed the top of her head, then closed his eyes and pressed her closer to him.

"I could never regret any moment spent with you, Maura. Especially a moment like this." Inching his mouth down, he kissed her ear before whispering, "I am yours, if you still want me."

With a sigh, she melted into him and turned to find his lips with hers, whispering against them, "And I am yours, Tommy."

Lowering his hands, he traced the curves of her hips and backside before lifting her up effortlessly to wrap her around him once more, telling her of his intentions in a way words couldn't. He laid her down on the pile of blankets covering the floor of the cabin and smiled against her neck when her hands found the last of his clothes. She didn't hesitate this time, pulling them off and tossing them aside, leaving their bodies heated with passion and writhing in desperation.

"I love you." Her words came out as a silken whisper in his ear, and she pulled him ever closer, raising her hips to lure all of him in. He repeated her words back to her before showing her the depth of that love by claiming all of her—heart, soul, and body—as his own with every inch of him.

⚔

*I LOVE YOU, **Tommy**.*

Her words invaded his dreams as he slept beside the first woman to ever steal his heart. He hadn't slept so soundly since before losing Declan a week ago, and when the sun peered through the small window of the cabin and warmed his face, he couldn't contain his contented sigh. His lips pulled into a smile as memories of their night echoed in his mind. Even on the floor of a tiny cabin, it had been everything he'd hoped for and more.

She was his. Even with no ceremonies performed or promises uttered, in his heart he knew. She was his. He was hers.

And he would not waste another moment with his Maura.

Turning onto his side, he opened his eyes, eager to see her greeting him.

But he saw only tangled blankets and the worn floor of his cabin.

Sitting up, he looked around the small room. His heart thrummed faster and faster. His gut clenched in panic, and no matter how he tried to assure himself she had just left to fetch them some breakfast, the dread tightened its hold with each movement as he dressed.

He winced at the brightness of the sun as he stepped out of the cabin and nearly collided with Declan.

"Tommy." His heart fell to his feet with the way his friend uttered his name.

"Where is she?" Tommy asked, not caring how desperate he sounded. He searched Declan's eyes, seeking the answer he desperately needed, that these fears plaguing him were unwarranted.

But his friend's extended silence told him more than any words could.

He brushed past him, ignoring when Declan called after him. His feet couldn't carry him up the quarterdeck stairs fast enough. She wouldn't be there, but maybe he could find some answers.

None of them would be adequate or acceptable.

Gavin's eyes locked on his, and with tight lips the helmsman nodded to the starboard side.

Sails. On the horizon. Even without the spyglass, he knew.

Halloran.

She had needed to go south for some business.

South.

But she hadn't offered to take the fae. Had she?

And even if she had, why would Maura go with them?

After all they had declared, all they had shared, she'd simply left?

Running both hands through his hair, he kept his eyes on those sails. She couldn't have. She wouldn't have.

She had to have been forced. He could not accept or believe any other explanation.

"Tommy," Declan said from beside him. "I'm sorry. I couldn't change their minds."

The sails blurred and the horizon melted as tears surfaced.

Tommy balled his hands into fists, his nails threatening to draw blood from his palms. He couldn't look at his friend. Everything hurt. His chest was splitting open. His head was pounding, his gut twisting.

Declan spoke again, treading lightly with each word. "We can't follow. Callum was spotted going east toward Turvala. We can't—"

"I know."

The moments ticked by. The sails disappeared.

Maura was gone.

My Maura.

Relaxing his hands, he repeated the words silently. Declan was staring at him, but Tommy just needed a moment to think. He traced back through the events of last night, searching for some explanation for her sudden departure.

But he found nothing.

No reason. No justification.

It made no sense.

He was only certain of one thing, and every echo of every minute he'd spent with her strengthened this conviction.

His pain slowly gave way to the confidence he had in her, his Maura.

"I trust her, Declan. She'll find her way back to me."

BONUS CHAPTER 37 1/2
ADLER

Cait's hand slipped into Adler's, but he kept watch on the clearing ahead of them as he helped her to her feet. The damn pirate had surprised them. It shouldn't have happened, but they'd let their guard down and become complacent, confident the two men standing beside the pit cave were the only threat.

Those pirates would arrive soon to investigate the sounds of their scuffle. Adler could already see them walking toward the path. He needed to get Cait out of sight.

When she turned to get her own look at the approaching threat, Adler spun her around so her back was pressed against him. Why he'd done it, he didn't know. Like some part of him—broken and lonely—needed her close. His arms tightened around her. The need to protect her overwhelmed him. His growing desire for her scared him.

Some might scoff at a pirate being scared, but Adler had lived this life long enough to know pirates weren't caricatures or stereotypes. They were as human as anyone else. Different of course, but still capable of experiencing all emotions.

Including fear.

And fear taunted him now, threatening to tighten its grip on him.

He'd already suffered loss. He couldn't bear losing another...

Another what? What is she to you?

Adler steadied his breaths, trying to ignore the way Cait's warm scent of vanilla, rum-soaked wood, and sea invaded his senses, invaded him. He closed his eyes. He just needed a minute. A minute to think, to collect himself, to recover.

"Where are—"

At Cait's whisper, his eyes snapped open. Pulling her closer still, he whispered a warning to stay quiet. "When I let you go, move quickly to the right. Stay low. Aye?"

As soon as she nodded, he let his arm fall away, and as instructed, she slipped away from him.

Good girl.

She might not hold any affection for him, but she trusted him enough to listen, to not hesitate. That was all he could ask for. All he should ask for. Yet the resulting emptiness sent a chill through him, nagging him, teasing him for trying to ignore his growing...

No.

With a hard swallow, Adler forced himself to focus.

Trusting that Cait had gotten away, he kept his attention on the path and the two pirates striding down it. He waited, calculating when to greet them and how, studying their demeanors. He didn't know them personally, but he knew by the pale-yellow sashes at their waists that they crewed for one of the lesser ships. Adler tried to recall who sailed under those colors, but he still hadn't remembered when the men stopped a few paces in front of him. They were stocky men, muscular but a bit stout around the middle, a clear indication they worked for the council on Cregah more than they sailed.

"What happened to 'im?" one of them asked, nudging his chin at the crumpled body at Adler's feet.

Adler glanced down at the unconscious man and offered a shrug. "He got what he deserved."

"How'd he deserve that?" the other asked, and Adler could have sworn he heard a tinge of humor in his voice.

"He was rude."

The pair shared a look, and for a brief moment, Adler's stomach tightened in anticipation of a violent response. But instead they both gave a hearty laugh before one of them said, "Classic Flynn. It's about time someone knocked him on his ass."

The other pirate smiled as he asked, "And who are you?"

"Adler Jensen."

"No colors?"

"I'm retired."

One of the men slapped the other's arm with the back of his hand. "Colin. You dolt. It's Jensen."

Colin's mouth pinched as he shook his head.

"Tiernen's man," the pirate clarified, and Colin turned back to Adler, his eyes wide with admiration.

"And you are?" Adler asked.

Not-Colin's face relaxed, his eyes glazing over with boredom as he answered, "Busy. Unfortunately."

Before Adler could ask anything more, the pirates turned, waving over their shoulder for him to follow. When they came to the clearing, Colin pointed to Penny, who was still lying, asleep, beside the rocks. Thankfully Cait hadn't appeared yet.

"We've got another exile to deal with," Colin said casually, like he was describing the weather and not discussing the murder of innocent citizens.

"Another one," Adler said.

"Aye. Seems they're getting more frequent lately. Right, Liam?"

"Unfortunately." Something about Liam's tone indicated he found it more unfortunate for himself than for the victims.

"And the council's no longer seeing them first?" Adler asked. He stilled and cursed himself for his blunder, waiting for them to ask how he could possibly have known the council hadn't seen her.

But if they found the question suspicious, they didn't show it. Colin said, "Guess not."

Liam added, "Not that they tell us why or anything."

"Just do as we're told."

Silence settled briefly between them as Adler pondered how best to keep these two busy so Cait could make her way to Penny. Eventually. Where was she? Had she gotten lost? Fallen over the cliff?

Before Adler could settle on what to say next, Colin spoke again. "This one has given us the most trouble by far though."

"Aye. Usually they know where they're headed. Well, maybe not where *exactly*—"

"But they at least know they're doomed," Colin said.

Adler smirked as he said, "You'd think that would make them fight more."

"Aye. Surprised us too," Liam said. "The exiles have bigger balls than most pirates I've met."

Adler couldn't contain his laughter at the statement, though he did exaggerate it a bit, hoping the sound might help Cait if she had indeed gotten turned around in the tangle of trees.

"I didn't realize the Rogues had gotten so big," Adler said. Liam shot him a curious look, but Adler simply rolled his eyes. "Oh come off it. I was on a lord's crew. I attended dinners with the council. You think we didn't hear about the rebels?"

"Right, right," Colin said, nodding. "They don't tell us as much as they tell your lot, I guess. We don't know if they're all Rogues or not. We're just given names or called to a pickup."

"We don't ask questions either," Liam added.

Good thing for me.

The conversation veered away from the exiles as the three men took turns sharing stories from their days at sea. Tales of pranks played on their crewmates and embarrassing moments they'd endured themselves. Accounts of past adventures and memorable lovers. Adler was quick to avoid the latter as much as possible, instead focusing on lighter, less painful topics. As they laughed and chatted away, Adler kept an eye over Liam's shoulder, watching and waiting for Cait to make her appearance.

Still nothing.

Before Adler could wonder where in the blazes the woman had gone, Colin said, "You never told us what you were doing here, Jensen."

Liam perked up and added, "Yeah, last I heard, you were near set on earning a promotion with Tiernen. Odd time for you to bail."

Images of Lani threatened to push their way to the forefront of his mind, but he shoved them back with a sigh. "What can I say. A better opportunity presented itself."

"Better than an officer under a lord, eh? Not sure I believes you," Colin said, a hint of suspicion flickering in his eyes.

Adler laughed, slow and casual, as Liam jumped in again. "What could be better than that though?"

This time, he couldn't keep Lani's face from appearing behind his closed eyelids, and something in his chest snapped. She'd been here. Were these the men who had done it? Had they been the last to see her alive? Straightening his shoulders, he opened his eyes and drew air deep into his lungs, nudging the memory of her smile and her wit and her death back into the recesses of his mind.

"What is the one thing that gets a man to head ashore? To walk away from the sea? To put down roots?" Adler nearly faltered and lost his composure when those last words had him thinking not of Lani but of Cait.

Damn treacherous heart.

He gritted his teeth. Cait was a means to an end. That was all. So why in the sands was he thinking of her in such a way?

Because you're a hopeless romantic. Always have been. And Cait is much like your Lani.

That realization couldn't have come at a worse time, and he nearly stumbled backwards. He found Cait attractive, of course. You'd have to be blind not to, and even then, her sharp tongue and clever mind would no doubt enchant on their own. But he was here to avenge Lani. Not his last love. Not his only love. He hadn't lied to Lucan and the Rogues when he'd explained as much, but regardless of what his heart seemed to insist, he wasn't ready to move on.

Not yet.

"Is this a riddle?" Colin's question pulled him out of his thoughts.

"No, stupid," Liam answered. "It's a damn woman."

Colin turned to him. "You sure?"

Liam looked to Adler as well. "It is, isn't it?"

The confused looks on their faces were so comical that Adler couldn't help but laugh. "No, not a riddle. And aye, a woman."

Liam slapped his friend again. "I knew it."

Colin rolled his eyes. "Whatever. So who is she?"

All humor drained from Adler's chest as the question once again beckoned unwanted images forward. But this time it was both Lani and Cait staring at him. Both strong. Both intelligent. Both far too good for him. "Alas, gents, there is no hope for me there."

And it was true.

Even if he was ready to love someone else again—which should be impossible, given how recently he'd lost Lani—Cait had shown no interest. She'd made it clear a relationship wasn't anything she'd ever wanted out of life. That was the one thing that separated the two women. Lani had dreamed of a family, of a life filled with love and laughter. Cait didn't. Cait wanted freedom, adventure, and a life away from these shores, away from her past.

"That's a tough break, lad," Liam said, sounding genuinely sorry for Adler's lot.

"Aye," Colin agreed. "So what now?"

Adler looked out to the sea as he answered. "I haven't completely decided, to be honest. Couple irons in the fire at the moment though."

That's one way to put it.

Once he got his revenge on the ones responsible for Lani's death, he didn't know where he would go. He could stay on the island, perhaps. Lucan was quickly—surprisingly—becoming a good friend. It would be nice to have a friend. But he missed home. His mother. His sister. The hills of wildflowers and the cool summer "breezes.

The home he was supposed to have shared with Lani.

Could he go back there without her? Could he build a life there with someone else? Or alone?

"Good to have options, but I do have one question for you," Liam said, raising a single brow at him.

"Oh?" Adler asked.

"Aye. You never answered the question. What are you doing out here?" All the friendliness in the man's tone was now tainted with suspicion, and panic nipped at Adler's gut.

Focus.

"I didn't? You sure?" He pulled the corners of his mouth down as he pretended to think back through their conversation.

"No. You didn't."

He stole another glance to Penny. She still lay there. Unmoving. Alone. Quickly, he scanned the edge of the forest. If Cait was there, he couldn't see her, and he was growing tired of stalling. Sometimes the best approach in these sticky situations was honesty.

"Oh," he said. "Well, in that case, I'm here to save that lass over there." He jutted his chin over Colin's shoulder.

"What?"

"Why would you do that?"

Adler laughed in sincere amusement. These men. They might be good guys—apart from the whole killing for the council thing—but they weren't too bright.

"You really going to waste your time asking why when you could be trying to stop me?"

They moved quickly, their feet sliding on the soft grass as they rushed him. It seemed he'd been correct in his assessment of their current, less active lifestyle. Their strikes came clumsily. Predictably.

He blocked and returned their blows with ease, all the while easing them backwards toward the pit. Over the grunts of the men, Adler heard a yelp to his right, and a quick glance showed him what he'd hoped for. Cait had roused Penny and was busy talking to her.

It was time to end this.

Adler went on the offensive then, switching from merely countering their attacks to dealing out his own. A fist to Liam's nose sent the man's hands up to where blood began to pour over his mouth, exposing his stomach for Adler's next punch. Colin, stunned momentarily by the sight of his buddy crumpling to his knees, sent an ill-planned jab toward Adler's face, but he easily caught the pirate's arm and twisted to lock it behind his back just in time to hear Cait's voice.

"Adler?"

His name on her tongue was like salve to his wounded heart. He shouldn't love the sound of her calling him, but the feigned innocence in it brought an unwelcome warmth to his chest.

"Yes, love? How can I help?" He pulled his mouth into a smirk. Did she just blush? The warmth threatened to expand, but he told himself it was only his imagination. A trick of the sun.

"That's enough. Let him go. Miss Penny here would like us to allow them to continue escorting her to the council hall."

Quirking a brow at her, he dropped the pirate's arm and stepped back. "Of course."

Cait crossed the clearing. He took care not to let their shoulders touch as he came alongside her, but he'd somehow forgotten how her warmth and sweet, sultry scent emanated from her skin. She cleared her throat, pulling him back to the task at hand.

"Gentlemen," she said, addressing the two pirates still nursing their bruised bodies—and egos. "My apologies. Please continue with your exile."

When she weaved her hand into the crook of Adler's arm, his despicably fickle heart inched open the gates he wished he could lock. He fought as best he could, reminding himself of all the reasons why she was not his and could never be.

"Let's go, love," she said.

One little word. It was powerful enough on its own, but used like this? It slammed into him, loosening his grip on his emotions as those damn gates opened wide and flooded him with every blasted desire he needed to avoid.

He should have been upset by her using it in such a disingenuous manner. But seeing her look at him like that, he didn't care if this was a mask she wore or a ruse she played. For one brief moment, he let himself believe she meant it. He couldn't stop himself from beaming at her, knowing the whole time that letting himself hope for anything more with her would lead to nothing but pain.

As they walked back toward the path, he dropped his arm, letting his hand ease toward the small of her back. But he dared not touch her. That would undo him completely.

He couldn't say what he truly wanted to, so he chose the humorous approach instead. "Careful there, Cait. Don't be using that with me too often. Especially not around Lucan. I'd hate to make him even more jealous."

They stepped under the shadows of the trees as she said, "Don't lie. You would love to do that to him."

"Aye, I would." She wasn't wrong there. Lucan never disappointed with his reactions. But even as he imagined what fun that might be, a small ache pulled at his insides. That small sliver of hope he'd dared to entertain now threatened to burn him as he looked into her shining emerald eyes. He was a fool. Of course she hadn't meant it. She never would. And he couldn't let her play with his heart, even unknowingly.

He tried to laugh, but it felt too empty. "But honestly, and in all seriousness. Please don't call me that."

She had to understand. She had to see how that one word pained him.

The confusion settling in her eyes indicated he was wrong. She didn't know.

"Oh, but you can—"

"Old habits die hard." He should smirk. He should smile or laugh or wink or something, but the pressure behind his sternum grew with each second that passed. He drew in a deep breath, wishing it would quell the pain twisting around his ribs. "But you didn't say it out of habit. You used it deliberately, and while I may be a lying, murderous pirate, I do have a heart. Albeit one a bit broken of late. And unless you mean it—which I think we both know you don't—then please refrain."

Silence filled the space around them. Her confusion was gone, replaced with what appeared to be a mix of pity and regret. With a tight smile, he turned, desperate to escape her demeaning gaze. He looked back to the pit and watched as Penny approached the pirates, who were now standing and looking eager to be done with this exile. "Now to figure out how to make this work," he whispered, hoping he and Cait could move beyond their recent awkward interaction and focus on the task at hand.

"Any ideas?" she asked in a strained tone.

He had a few, actually, though they were all ridiculous. A perfect distraction.

"It's too bad we don't have a whip. You don't have one, do you?"

A laugh nearly escaped him, especially when her brow rose. She thought he was serious. She was cute when she fell for his jokes.

Not what you should be thinking of right now.

"No. I don't. Didn't go with this outfit."

Adler nodded, concentrating more on how to keep his gaze from wandering to her lips or her eyes or her… "What about a crossbow?" he asked.

"Fresh out, I'm afraid."

"Well, what do we have exactly? Anything useful? You know, beyond my strength and your tongue."

Her tongue. Why had he said that?

Cait pulled out the knife she'd slashed poor Flynn's shins with earlier, and Adler couldn't contain another smile. It wasn't as good as his earlier absurd requests, but he'd make it work."

***

The entire scene in the clearing seemed to be playing out in an irritatingly slow fashion, and Adler shifted beside Cait, antsy to make the move.

"What do you mean, *death*?" Penny asked, her eyes and words finally demonstrating the panic they'd been waiting for.

Before he could step into the clearing, though, Cait's arm blocked his way. "Not yet," she whispered.

"Why not?'

"We need her to clearly understand."

Adler pushed his chin toward Penny and the drop she was approaching. "She's inching her way toward that clarity."

The pirates grabbed Penny's arms and tried to lift her off the ground as she screamed to be let go.

Still Cait blocked Adler's way, and he focused harder on her so as not to miss her cue.

But she gave no warning before she darted out of the trees herself. A curse echoed in his mind as he leaped to follow her. Running behind her, he watched her sprint toward the attackers. He stopped, planted his feet, took his mark, and threw the knife.

It slammed into Liam a moment before Cait dropped to the ground and slid into Colin, kicking his legs out from under him and sending him halfway over the edge of the pit. Cait was scrambling to get herself away from Colin and away from the steep drop, but Adler couldn't help her just yet.

"Be right there," he called to her, hoping it would reassure her she wasn't alone in this.

Liam was still standing, staring down at the knife that protruded from his chest. He'd given up fighting, accepted his lot.

That will make this easier.

With minimal effort, Adler shoved the man into the cave and tried to ignore the eerie sight of him falling silently into the darkness.

Penny stood frozen by the edge, her body shaking, her eyes seeing nothing.

"I'm right here," Adler said, and he slipped his arm around her so he could lead her to relative safety. Looking over his shoulder, he saw Colin's face contort in fear.

He was falling, his hands unable to grab the grass or dirt as he slid slowly backwards. With a growl, he tried to grab Cait's leg.

Adler couldn't help her, as Penny now clung tightly to him.

He watched as Cait managed to kick Colin in the shoulder, sending him over the edge and into the pit. Sure she was now safe, Adler directed his attention back to Penny and tried to pry her off of him.

"Adler!"

He spun around to find Cait being dragged toward the chasm, scrambling to grab the grass as Colin had.

Pulling Penny's arms away from him, he settled her against a tree as quickly as he could, but he had moved too far from the pit. He turned once more, his heart thumping in urgency. His throat closed off at the thought of another woman lost to the council. His feet pounded the ground as he sprinted forward.

"Hold on, Cait!"

He shouted at her just as she screamed his name once more and her body fell over the edge.

He threw himself forward, his body slamming into the ground. He thrust his arms down in pure desperation, sure he was too late. But his fingers found her arms and closed around them. A shock of pain engulfed his shoulders with the sudden weight of her body.

"I've got you, love."

His words came out strained from the exertion. When she didn't respond, he worried she'd been hurt. Had her head hit the rocks that lined the walls of the cave? Was she simply suffering from shock?

Hold on, Cait. I've got you. You're okay.

The words repeated in his mind as he put all his energy into pulling her up and back over the ledge. His muscles were on fire. His jaw ached. His heart raced. The danger was gone. It would be okay. All he had to do was get her back onto solid ground.

With one last burst of effort, he pulled her free. His backside hit the dirt with a hard thud, but the pain didn't register as he looked down at the woman now lying in his lap. Her eyes remained closed as he attempted to assess her for any obvious injuries. He moved his legs to try and see the back of her head, but her deep green eyes flashed open and locked onto him.

All the fear and worry over possibly losing her shifted into a desperate hope and yearning that threatened to crush his chest.

"Looks like you've fallen into my lap."

He'd meant it as a joke to lighten the odd mood that was settling around them.

It had been a mistake.

"Will you let me stay here?" Cait asked.

And his heart stilled.

Why had he said those words? Why had he opened himself up to this? Of all the parts of their conversation to bring up, he'd chosen that one?

"How long do you think it will be before someone else falls into your lap?"

"The real question is when will I be ready to let someone stay once they've fallen."

Will you let me stay here.

All this time he'd assumed she never wanted love. Was she serious now? Did she know what she was asking? Or was this another careless slip of her tongue?

He searched her eyes, as if they might hold some clue as to her intentions, feelings, desires.

Careless or not, Adler couldn't stop himself from wanting her to mean those words.

He shouldn't want that. Shouldn't want her. He loved Lani.

Lani's gone.

If there was an appropriate amount of time to wait before opening one's heart to another love after loss, he didn't know. But this woman. This headstrong, confident, determined woman who never shied away from putting him in his place...she could be his.

Lifting his hand to her face, he cradled her jaw, his skin prickling when she settled into his touch. He brushed a thumb over her lips. Had they ever been kissed? Had she ever looked at another man as she looked at him now?

He caressed her cheek, wanting this to be okay, wanting to give in, to surrender.

But her gasp, light yet heavy with want, pulled him away from the precipice he had nearly jumped off.

You deserve more, Cait.

She deserved a heart that could be fully hers, and his was fractured. His still belonged to another. Even though his future with Lani had died with her, his heart was still partially hers.

He should tell Cait all of this, tell her he wanted to give her what she wanted, tell her he cared—more than he had any right to, in fact—but his breath was trapped in his throat, his mouth dry.

With a slow blink, he pulled his eyes away from hers and moved to lift her so they could both stand. He would tell her. Eventually. When he was ready.

This was the right decision. Yet, as he walked away, he couldn't quiet the screaming voice in his head that called him a coward.

BONUS CHAPTER 56 1/2
DECLAN

After being forced to rest on that cold and disgusting floor in the *Curse Bringer*'s brig for days, settling onto the softness of his own bed was a comfort Declan wasn't entirely sure he deserved. Every time his eyes closed, ghastly images of Killian's mangled body and Collins's lifeless form haunted him. But he didn't try to repress them. They were a fitting punishment for all he'd done.

For Lani. For Killian. For Collins.

For Aoife.

Declan had no recollection of what had happened back on that beach. One moment Aoife had been standing beside him, facing the regal siren. The next, she was unconscious in his bloody arms.

She lay beside him now, still unconscious. But at least she was alive.

While no one would tell him exactly what he'd done, somehow he knew she'd been hurt by his own hands. Would she forgive him? Could she?

Could he forgive himself?

Even as he asked the question, that small voice in the darkness of his mind echoed the familiar words.

You're a pirate.

What need did he have for forgiveness? Why did he crave it so?

Was pirate synonymous with evil?

And with that word, the memory of Callum calling for Killian's body to be dragged back under the keel rushed at him, twisting his features into a wince.

Some were evil. That much was obvious. He himself had committed his own share of despicable acts, acts he would not hesitate to perform again should he catch up with that bastard captain.

But Declan held on to a sliver of hope that he wasn't like Callum, that he still possessed some of the goodness he'd inherited from his parents. The goodness the woman beside him saw in him.

As if on cue, Aoife stirred, and the air stilled in his throat. For hours he'd been watching her sleep, assessing her small movements, trying to interpret her whimpers and sighs, and hoping they were all signs she was waking up. But she hadn't.

Though she was still the same woman who had surprised, amused, and frustrated him—repeatedly—the lines of her face somehow showed a new maturity. With all they'd faced during the last few days, the change was to be expected. Before Declan had retreated to his quarters, Tommy and the others had filled him in on all that had happened with the kraken and the sirens. And although he wished she could have been spared from such grief and hardship, a twinge of pride squeezed his chest as he watched her sleep. He sensed a shift in her. She seemed to have a new strength about her. He'd caught glimpses of her confidence and resilience—especially when she had challenged him—and he had hoped to see it take hold and grow.

Declan's hand itched to reach for her, but he wasn't sure how she would respond to him being here, let alone touching her. So he waited, his mind a muddled mix of memories. Some gory and poignant. Others sweet and comforting.

Before she'd stumbled onto his ship and into his life, the scales had been decidedly tipped toward a bleak, disappointing future. She had brought them into balance. Now there was some goodness and hope in the mix, because of her.

Until you rocked everything with your secrets.

Where things would settle, he wasn't sure.

Aoife's chest swelled as she pulled in a long, slow breath. Her mouth twitched. Her jaw tensed.

"Aoife?" Declan tested his voice, surprised to find it clear and unhindered by the tangle of emotions constricting him.

Her lashes fluttered, and when her eyes focused on him, he couldn't fight the smile that tugged at his lips.

"I'm sorry."

The words were out before he could stop them. What would she say? How would she respond? Pulling in a breath, he marveled at how her sweet scent remained, even after all the adventures and dangers. She stared at him, unblinking, unbelieving. He yearned to hold her, but with all the mistakes he'd made, he would let her take the lead here. It was the least he could offer her.

"Am I still alive? Are you?"

The questions weren't altogether unexpected, but still he found humor in them. His lips curled up for a moment, but the smirk seemed out of place somehow, a half-hearted gesture drowned by his worry over their future. His heart twisted in anguish and anticipation, preparing him for the harsh words she would lay upon him. He tried his best to shove all his chaotic thoughts aside—as he had done so many times on Callum's ship and for all the years since his parents' deaths—and forced a lightness into his tone.

"I would hope paradise doesn't look like my ratty old cabin on this battered ship."

Paradise.

His mind mocked him, a silent laugh reverberating in his skull.

You don't deserve paradise, McCallagh.

You'll never be a good man.

Stop lying to yourself.

Paradise will never be yours.

The tormenting thoughts continued to prod him, even as his gaze settled on hers once more. He hoped she couldn't see all the pain and regret he fought to contain.

"I forgive you, Declan. For everything."

His eyes fell closed before she'd finished speaking the words, and he let them surround him like a comforting embrace. Guilt's darkness faded. Though he knew it wasn't gone forever, he relished the feeling of so many burdens being lifted. When her fingers touched his, his skin prickled with longing and desire. It took all his will not to move then and claim her as his own. He was determined not to mess this up, not when she could be giving him a second chance.

"I assume we won if we're back on the ship then?"

Even dripping with fatigue, her voice was the sweetest sound he'd ever heard.

"Aye," he said. With reluctance, he forced his eyes open, half-afraid this was another trick of the siren, that it wouldn't be Aoife caressing his hand but that evil creature. But no, they'd killed her. Seeing Aoife's expectant face—the epitome of innocence and goodness—solidified that truth for him. "Thanks to Halloran and— as much as I hate to admit it—Callum."

It pained him to utter the man's name, but he couldn't deny they would not have survived without the pirate's help. Still, Declan held on to the belief that one could be grateful for someone's actions even while wishing for their painful demise. If anyone deserved such, it was that bastard.

Seeing the unspoken question in her eyes—his Aoife, ever the curious one—he rushed through the final events on the beach. And when he had finished, he watched her process it all. Gratitude washed over her face for a moment before worry slowly pulled her forehead tight. Her gaze fell away from him, her focus fading, as though she was no longer seeing him but remembering all she'd witnessed.

The stiffness of her features pained him, and he wanted nothing more than to fix this, to take all her burdens and give her a life of unending happiness. Before he could begin to consider how to do that, though, his tongue dropped the first thing that came to mind.

"It's too bad you missed seeing the sirens."

Her face contorted into a scowl.

Good job, McCallagh.

"I think I've had enough sirens for a lifetime."

She had a point there, but in his nervousness he couldn't contain the soft laugh that bubbled up.

"No, the other sirens," he said, and she lifted her arm to show how those *other* sirens had treated her.

He could have smacked himself in the face for all his missteps in this conversation.

The image of Callum's crew members being ripped apart and dragged into the bloody water appeared in his mind, but the sirens had been freed with Triss's death. Even after explaining the sirens' enslavement under the queen to Aoife, though, he couldn't fault her for not being wholly convinced of their innocence.

Declan's breath caught, and all thoughts ceased as Aoife shifted herself closer to him. He risked pulling her close, as if he were testing potentially dangerous waters by doing so. She didn't dart away, didn't flinch. Rather, her body melted against his. The sugary aroma lingering on her skin pulled his lips to her forehead before he could think better of it. Her breath shifted slightly to match his own, her chest rising and falling in time with his. But instead of being relieved, he was uneasy, sure this could not be real. It wasn't an illusion. Of that he was certain. But somewhere in the pit of his stomach, a worry festered, growing and itching and burning until he finally gave it a voice.

"You're sure you're not still angry with me?"

She nestled closer, burrowing her face into his neck. Her response came out muffled but clear enough. "Do you not remember all that I told you?"

His body tensed with the reminder of the time he'd lost while under Triss's compulsion. Even the explanations from Maura and Tommy of what they remembered could only help so much. He explained as such to Aoife, and she sat up, prompting him to do the same. His heart thumped against his sternum. Her expression was blank, which was unhelpful, though he still searched for any hint at what she was about to say.

"Was it something good? I hope it was something good." He smirked, this time putting more energy behind it. "Or something dirty. That would be nice too." He winked.

And immediately regretted it.

You're trying too hard.

When her hand playfully slapped his shoulder, he allowed himself to relax. He would never grow tired of that eyeroll of hers, and he nearly laughed as he remembered how it had annoyed him to no end when they'd first met.

"You're awful, you know that?" Her sweet smile betrayed the perturbed air she was trying to maintain.

"So I've been told."

Confusion bowled him over once more, and his smirk faded as he watched her. She was wringing her hands in her lap. Surely she wasn't about to tear into him again as she had in the cove. The look on her face held no anger, only hesitation. Her bottom lip quivered, and he longed to pull her close, to ease away her discomfort and tell her it was all okay. She didn't need to explain if she didn't want to.

A nervous chuckle escaped her. "Why was this so much easier to say when you were trying to kill me?"

Declan refused to let her see any hint of his guilt, masking it with a smile. "Probably because you thought it was the end."

"Seems more appropriate for a beginning though."

His heart fluttered a bit with anticipation. "Oh?"

Thoughts sped and time stilled as she took a deep breath. He'd survived Callum's harshness and Triss's powers, but Aoife's next words could be the end of him.

Or they could save you.

He waited, his heart pounding and his gut tightening, as hope seeped through his carefully constructed internal defenses, transforming "his heart into glass so fragile there would be little chance of repairing it if—

"I love you, Declan McCallagh."

He moved to her at once, his lips seeking hers and claiming them as his.

All his.

He hadn't let himself dream of this in the brig or on the siren's beach, and now that he had it, he couldn't get enough. With a need he'd never experienced before, he pushed himself against her, not caring how desperate he appeared as his tongue pushed her lips apart and tasted her. He pulled her closer, but it wasn't close enough.

Never close enough.

He pulled himself away enough to whisper the words "I missed you" and heard her moan a response, his mind focused on the feel of her body against his as his hands caressed her back. He never wanted to leave this moment, and he panicked briefly as she began to pull away. He couldn't let her go. Not yet. Not when he'd finally gotten her back. Dropping his hands to her hips, he let his mouth explore beyond her precious lips. He moved along her jaw, savoring the taste of her skin as he kissed his way down to her neck. He nearly lost it when her fingers buried themselves in his hair, sending a sensation of tingling warmth throughout him.

They'd only shared a handful of kisses before this, and he wanted so much more. He wanted everything. Every part of her. Every morsel. Every squirm. Every groan. Every breath. Every taste. He wouldn't force her to give them to him, but he vowed he'd earn them if it took him the rest of his life to do so.

His name on her lips ignited another spark within him. Stronger. And lower down.

"Yes?" he said against her skin as he moved her shirt away from her shoulder. He would give her anything she desired. Anything she asked for. The moon. The stars. The world. Everything was hers if she asked him for it.

"Where is Maura?"

Well, that's unexpected.

He refused to let her bizarre inquiry ruin the moment, and he moved his mouth back to her ear. "Why?" he whispered, before taking a nibble and reveling in her body's response. His body, pushed by his love and need for her, begged him to distract her from whatever had prompted her to bring up the fae. But before he could do more, her hands were at his chest, pushing him away. As gentle as the gesture was, it still stung.

"I need to ask her a question."

Her tone wasn't entirely convincing, but Declan surrendered, allowing Aoife's hands to move him further away. He loved her. He wouldn't begrudge her anything.

But he also wouldn't give up without at least trying.

"And it can't wait?"

Ignoring a lock of hair that fell in his face, he searched her eyes, pleased to see them filled with a desire that rivaled his own. Silently he pleaded with her to wait a bit longer, to put off what nagged at her, and to remain with him.

She shook her head.

Whatever it was, it must be important, if it was enough to curb the hunger he saw so clearly in her gaze. With a dip of his chin, he clasped her hands in his and pulled her off the bed, agreeing to find Maura.

He would have plenty of time with her—to love her, to cherish her, to ravish her.

It was worth waiting for.

She was worth waiting for.

WITH THESE LAST BREATHS

BOOK THREE

Once again for Joel and his immeasurable support...
...but also for all who threatened to mutiny if I hurt Tommy again.

DAORNA
HAVIERN
TYSHALY
HELLES ISLAND
CREGAH
PORT MORSHAN
THE COUNCIL
LOST CO
CAPROTHE
TO LARCSPOROUGH

TURVALA
THE
AISLING
SEA
SELKA
FOXHAVEN

CHAPTER 1
DECLAN

THE SMALL LANTERN on Declan McCallagh's desk did little to combat the darkness in his quarters, and it bathed Aoife Cascade in an eerie light as she stood there, staring at nothing. From this angle, he couldn't determine how she was faring with all the surprises the fae had delivered moments ago, but he noted how her nose crinkled in concentration.

She was adorable when her curiosity was piqued.

Had it only been a few days since she'd walked away from him in the cove?

Had she only been in his life for mere weeks?

Such a short time, yet his heart had opened to her until he couldn't imagine life without her. He'd fallen so quickly. They both had. And Declan could no sooner make sense of that than he could of her forgiving him for his lies and deceit.

Love plays by its own rules.

His father's words echoed in his mind. This message had meant little to Declan's young heart, but he had begun to understand it these past weeks.

Love didn't make sense.

Love was unpredictable and confusing.

And love had saved him in that sound.

But can love save you from yourself?

She deserves to know the man she loves.

Doesn't she?

How will she handle another lie? Another betrayal?

Declan closed his eyes tight, as if doing so might extinguish these thoughts and drive away the darkness that taunted him. He didn't want to think about it, let alone admit that this part of him existed.

With a deep breath, he opened his eyes and pushed that dark part of him aside as best he could and focused on Aoife. She didn't move or turn as he approached, but when he stepped up behind her and wrapped his arms around her waist, clasping her hands in his and weaving their fingers together, she relaxed into him with a contented sigh.

"How are you, princess?" Declan whispered. He couldn't help but smile when she gave him a soft laugh and shook her head.

"I'm no princess," she said, tipping her chin up and over her shoulder to peer at him. His face was so near hers that their noses brushed lightly. "But I suppose if my mother is truly the fae queen of legends..."

Declan reached a hand up to her jaw, cradling it as he moved her around to face him. His lips hovered over hers. His head swam with desire and longing, hopes and questions. Warmth spread through him in anticipation of something he couldn't expect from her. Not yet.

But that didn't mean he couldn't tease her a little.

Letting his eyes flick down to her lips briefly, he smirked before asking, "Am I to bow before you then?"

Aoife's eyes widened, but she didn't back away. "I don't know."

Her words were barely audible, no more than a breath that warmed his lips, beckoning him to meet hers in a gentle kiss. She pushed up onto her toes and pressed into him, letting him part her lips so his tongue could caress hers in a dance far sweeter and more tender than he'd ever shared with anyone.

This was different than the kisses they'd shared before. This one tasted of security and trust as she allowed him to take command, let him teach her the steps of this dance.

"I missed you," Aoife said against his lips, but then she pulled back.

Declan fought the urge to give chase and instead offered her another smirk.

"Is there someone else you need to find? Some other burning question that must be answered before—"

Aoife cut off his teasing by slamming her lips against his once more, shutting him up as she beckoned him to resume their sensual waltz.

I'll take that as a no, he thought, not wanting to break away from her long enough to say the words aloud.

Sliding her hands around either side of his neck, Aoife pulled him closer still. Before he could think better of it, he was pushing against her until her legs were forced to move. One step. Two. As he lifted her up, guiding her legs around his waist while walking toward the bed, he promised himself he wouldn't go too fast, wouldn't push her too far.

But when her body shuddered against him, his resolve nearly slipped.

Then she was pushing their kisses harder and faster, until Declan wasn't quite sure which one of them was leading. And he didn't particularly care either way.

Taking a calming breath, he let her lips fall away from his and slowly lowered her to the bed, smiling at her closed eyes and the light pink that spread across her cheeks. He kissed the tip of her nose, and she giggled as he lowered his lips to her neck to trail light kisses across her skin. Her fingers buried into his hair, sending a fresh wave of hunger through him that he struggled to ignore.

How he'd longed for this. To hold her, to touch her. He had nearly given up hope of ever having this chance, but now, here they were. Safe. Alive. Together.

Instinct and need guided his fingers to pull aside the fabric of her shirt and glide over her soft skin in an exploration of this uncharted territory. As he kissed his way along her collarbone, he craved parts of her he couldn't yet ask for, though that didn't stop him from at least testing the waters. His lips ventured along the collar of her shirt, and he wasn't altogether surprised when her hands moved quickly to pull his face back up to hers. She kissed him with a mixture of desire and...panic.

Not fear. More like worry.

Nerves.

She had been destined for a pirate lord. Never touched, kissed, or even held.

Until you, he thought.

How was he to navigate this? He was no nobleman. He was a pirate.

The darkness within him laughed, mocking him.

If you were a real pirate, you'd have bedded her already.

Declan closed his eyes for a moment, willing that dark voice to retreat back into the shadows. Nobleman or pirate, it mattered little. Either could be despicable or loving.

Slowly he backed away, lifting his face a few inches from hers and noting the uncertainty and undeniable passion in her gold-flecked eyes. Could she see the same mix of desire and hesitation in his own? Whether she recognized it or not, he couldn't take this farther. Not yet. Planting one more tender kiss on her lips, he lowered himself onto the bed alongside her, propping his head in his hand as he continued to watch her.

"It's not nice to stare, you know," Aoife said with a hint of shakiness to her voice.

He quirked a brow, ignoring how his hair fell down onto his forehead when he did.

"So I hear. But can you blame me? It's been too long since I got to look at you."

Slowly she scooted her body closer to his, until her shoulder was tucked into his chest, the length of her body resting against his.

"It's only been a few days," she said.

"A few days too many, princess." He tangled their feet together and wrapped his leg over hers.

"Am I to call you Captain now?" Aoife asked in a playful tone.

"Only if I'm issuing commands," he said, brushing a kiss along her forehead. He waited for her to say something more, but when she remained silent, he glanced down to find her eyes had fallen closed.

She'd crossed the Aisling, battled a kraken, and stood up to a powerful siren. All for him. For a man who had betrayed her, lied to her, killed her sister...

And yet you still won't let her know the real you.

He ignored the thought. She would learn of his past and his demons eventually. Now was not that time.

Slowly he circled his fingertips along her hip, watching as her lips twitched and her jaw tightened at his touch. Her muscles went taut, and she clutched her hands to her chest, squeezing them gently together. Still, she didn't look at him. He ran his fingers up over her waist, her ribs, her arm and shoulder, then along her jaw.

"Open your eyes, Aoife," he said softly but firmly. He half-expected her to reply to his command with an "Aye, Captain," but instead, her brow creased and she whispered an apology.

Confusion swept through him. What in the sands was this woman apologizing for?

"Why are you sorry?"

Her body stiffened against him. With tiny shakes of her head, she pulled her mouth down into a frown. "That isn't how I wanted to respond to you."

Amused, he pulled his lips back into a half-hearted smirk. "You expected that to offend me?"

A nod.

Rather than answering with words, he let his fingertips whisper along her jaw and lift her chin so his lips could find hers, pressing open her mouth so he could taste her again. Kissing her slowly, deeply, he relished the way she melted into him.

When he stopped again, her body tensed—not with panic and anxiety, but eagerness.

"That tension...that tightening of your entire body...that anticipation that pulls at your core and your heart and every inch of you? That's exactly how I want you to respond."

"It is?"

It was his turn to nod.

"But, it's not..." She hesitated, and he could read the doubt and worry on her face.

"I know," he said. "I want to give you everything and more. Every promise. Every pleasure. But I can't—and I won't—until I earn back your trust."

Part of him wanted her to correct him, to insist he already had her trust, to reassure him that there was no more healing needed between them.

But he knew the truth.

Even as she smiled.

"That's a very un-pirate-like thing to say, Captain."

Declan let a growl rumble in the back of his throat as he brought his mouth close to hers. "You'll get the pirate in me, princess. But not until you're ready."

⚮

DECLAN SAT PROPPED up against the wall and glanced down at Aoife lying beside him. A sweet, untroubled expression had come over her face as she slept. Declan had found no such peace as a storm brewed in his chest. How she could seem so at peace with all she'd been through was beyond him.

What little sleep he'd managed to get had been haunted by images of shredded flesh, bloodied sand, and Aoife's lifeless body. Even when he woke, the nightmares remained, lingering in his mind.

Slowly the room lightened as the pale rays of dawn trickled in through the windows.

It did nothing to expel the darkness within him.

Welcome back, old friend, it called silently.

It was ridiculous, of course, to give this side of him a name, especially when he had never spoken to anyone about it—not even Tommy. And he didn't plan to do so anytime in the future either.

The darkness, whether Declan wanted to admit it or not, was as much a part of him as the color of his eyes or the memories from his childhood. When it spoke to him, it was his own voice he heard, sounding no different than his other thoughts.

Like his conscience.

Only the opposite.

This was the side of him that took hold of the anger—fed off it—and provided a solution to it.

And not a good solution.

Never a good one.

Yet difficult to resist all the same.

You managed to resist it for so many years though, he told himself.

But something had changed.

Whether it was the siren's or Callum's fault—or maybe both—Declan wasn't sure, and it didn't matter. The part of him that desired revenge and yearned to spill blood had woken up, and all he could do was hold it back, keep it quiet, keep it hidden.

Aoife squirmed in her sleep before rolling onto her side away from him. He should lie back down, wrap her up in his arms, and try to get as much rest as he could, but as pleasant as that sounded, it was a luxury he couldn't afford. Not when he had a man to lay to rest, a crew to unite, and a pirate to hunt down.

With a light kiss to Aoife's shoulder, Declan slipped quietly off the bed and got dressed before heading out onto the deck and into the sunshine. Off the starboard side, the *Duchess* had pulled alongside his ship, with a plank spanning the gap between the vessels. There was no sign of Captain Halloran or any of her crew, and few of his own crew occupied the deck. His men paid him little attention as he stepped quietly toward the quarterdeck stairs.

"I won't leave him."

The words, though hushed, drew Declan's attention to the officers' cabin, where Maura stood near the closed door with her older sister. He couldn't hear Renna's reply, but whatever she said, Maura stepped back as if she'd been struck. Renna's gaze shifted to Declan, her bright blue eyes softening before she turned back to Maura and took her hand. Maura flinched.

Despite his curiosity over the sisters' exchange, Declan found himself driven to turn away and give them privacy. He nodded to himself as he headed toward the stairs.

"Captain?" Gavin called down to him.

Without another glance at the fae, Declan nodded to his helmsman and climbed the stairs to meet him.

"Aye?" he asked.

Gavin shifted back a few steps. His eyes never met Declan's as he answered, "A couple sirens delivered a message about an hour ago. I didn't want to wake you or Tommy after your ordeal in the sound..."

"And?"

Gavin looked up at him now, but only briefly before he averted his eyes toward the sun rising out of the sea. "Callum. Spotted at dusk heading due east toward Turvala."

Running a hand through his hair, Declan gave a silent word of thanks to the sirens for choosing to help him, though he said nothing to Gavin. Silence, thick and uncomfortable, settled between them, and Declan's gut twisted with guilt over what he needed to ask of his helmsman.

"Is Collins ready?"

"Aye," Gavin said, his voice hollow. "The boys have him all set, Captain. Just waiting for you to preside over the burial."

Declan, unable to find the right words for his helmsman, and unsure he'd be able to speak them regardless, merely nodded before spinning on his heel and making his way back down to the deck. Before he could turn toward Tommy's cabin, though, he spotted Captain Halloran standing at the rail with Renna and Bria beside her.

"Leaving us so soon, Captain?" Declan asked.

Halloran offered him a curt nod. "Aye, I promised to take the sisters south. It's a long journey, as you know."

"Are you sure you can't wait?" But even as he asked it, Bria started to shuffle across to the waiting ship.

"I'm afraid not, Captain," Renna answered.

Declan kept his attention focused on Halloran, searching her face for any hint that Renna was up to something. Tommy had explained—albeit briefly—her abilities, and Declan wouldn't put it past her to use them to her advantage. Even on friends.

Renna clicked her tongue and shook her head. "I assure you my intentions are good. I simply want to help our kin."

Her words brought Killian's face into focus, as well as his story of the fae's plight in the south. The camps. The killings. It had to be stopped, and the royals had been asked to step in and help.

"And Maura?" Declan asked, glancing around to see if she had chosen to leave as well.

"We really must be going, Captain," Renna said, turning to Halloran. The captain gave the fae a nod and called out an order for her crew to prepare the sails.

Dread pooled in his stomach. Where was Maura?

Without another word, Renna glided over to the *Duchess* to join Bria.

"Be careful, McCallagh," Halloran warned, extending her hand to him. When he accepted it, she said, "Don't underestimate that bastard."

"Never again," Declan said. "You're sure you can't wait to say goodbye to Aoife and Tommy?"

She was already shaking her head before he'd finished speaking. Stepping onto the plank, she looked over her shoulder at him. "Give them my best, Declan."

Declan's mind whirred as he watched Halloran's crew prepare to depart. Something was off about this whole situation, but he couldn't put his finger on it, even as he watched Bria standing on the deck with her hands raised before her.

The large sails snapped taut as they caught an unnatural and sudden gust of wind, pulling the *Duchess* away faster than should have been possible.

And then she was there, appearing out of thin air.

Standing at the rail of Halloran's ship, her brown hair blowing in the wind her sister controlled, Maura stared back at Declan with an empty look that pinned him where he stood.

No.

Tommy.

Fuck.

Turning, he made for Tommy's cabin but stopped short at the sight of Gavin standing behind him. "Which heading, Captain? Do we follow—"

Declan swallowed hard as he glanced over his shoulder at the ship retreating fast to the south. He hated this. Hated doing this to Tommy. But being captain meant doing what needed to be done, regardless of who it hurt.

"No, we head east."

Forcing his dread aside, he stepped around his helmsman, but Gavin's next inquiry gave him pause. "And Collins? Will he still get the burial he deserves?"

Declan looked to the morning sky as his mind sifted through his options. He couldn't let Tommy chase after Maura and risk Callum getting away, but he had to do this for Collins. For the crew.

After giving Gavin a sharp nod, he was off once more. He had just raised his hand to knock on the cabin door when it swung open. Tommy stepped out, wincing as the sun flashed across his eyes, and nearly ran into Declan.

"Tommy." His friend's name sounded distant in his ears.

Tommy's face fell. "Where is she?" The desperation in his voice pricked Declan's heart, making it hard to swallow. Even harder to utter any words.

If it had been Aoife who had left, he'd be just as panicked, if not more so.

Tommy showed no anger as he brushed past him. Declan called after him, following him up to the quarterdeck when he didn't stop. At the top of the stairs, Tommy stood like the figurehead of a ship, his gaze locked on the sails moving toward the horizon.

"Tommy," Declan said, stepping up beside him. "I'm sorry. I couldn't change their minds."

Maybe he should have added that he hadn't known she was with them, hadn't seen her until they were too far away, but Tommy's unrestrained tears convinced him it wouldn't have helped.

"We…" Declan hesitated. He hated doing this, pouring salt on the man's fresh wounds, but he was captain. He had to. "We can't follow."

A pause.

A breath.

A clench of Tommy's jaw, but no response.

Declan continued. "Callum was spotted going east toward Turvala. We can't—"

"I know," Tommy said, standing taller as he inhaled the sea air, his eyes unmoving. "I trust her. She'll find her way back to me."

"She will," Declan said, clapping his hand on Tommy's shoulder.

She will, he thought, *even if I have to track her down and bring her back myself.*

CHAPTER 2
TOMMY

Tommy had never been one for being the center of attention. And here he had both Gavin and Declan staring at him as if they assumed he might jump into the Aisling and swim after Maura at any moment. He attempted to ignore them, because while he wasn't as sad as the men likely thought he was, he also had no desire to go back to the officers' quarters, where Maura's absence would be more potent.

Their silence finally broke him.

"What is it?" he asked.

From the corner of his eye, he noticed Gavin fumbling around and turning his head to gaze elsewhere, but Declan didn't bother to hide his concern. Stepping up beside Tommy, he cleared his throat, but continued to stare at the water before them.

"You okay?"

"Aye."

Tommy must have answered too quickly, because Declan's lips tightened into a firm line, his eyes crinkling at the corners as if he were dissecting that single word for hidden meaning. A few moments passed, and both men remained silent. The earlier tension returned tenfold. Tommy had to cut through it somehow. So, swinging his chin toward his captain, he clarified.

"I'm fine—" Declan looked ready to interrupt, but Tommy stayed his retort with a hard stare. "No, don't say it. I am fine. Could I be better? Of course, but I'm not broken. I'm not so sorrowful that I need to be coddled like a toddler who's fallen down." Pausing to take a breath, he let his expression relax. "Yes, Maura left, but—"

"Maura left?" Aoife's question pulled all three men's attention to where she was clamoring up the stairs.

Declan offered her a silent nod, but she had her glare firmly set on Tommy, as if he had been the one to send the fae away.

"Aye," Tommy said as Aoife stopped in front of him and looked up. Her green and gold eyes flashed with a myriad of emotions, shifting so quickly he couldn't get a read on what she was thinking or what she was about to say.

Declan leaned slightly toward Aoife's ear, and Tommy could have sworn he caught a hint of a sarcastic smile on his friend's face. "It's okay, Aoife. He's *fine*."

"Fine? How are you fine?" Aoife raised her hands with each question, nearly smacking Declan as she did—not that either of them seemed to care, or even notice.

"Not all of us are melodramatic—" Tommy started and immediately regretted his choice of words.

Sure enough, Aoife's mouth shifted to form a perfect imitation of Declan's smirk. "Is that so—mister falls-in-love-with-the-first-fae-who-heals-him?"

"As I told Maura," Tommy said, ignoring how her name on his tongue did elicit a tinge of loss and loneliness, "things change. Believe it or not, this is the real me. I don't typically let my emotions get the better of me."

"Okay. So are you not freaking out even a little bit behind all this calm?"

Tommy looked Aoife square in the eye and offered her a shallow shrug. "I trust her."

Aoife flinched and dropped her eyes to her feet. Declan filled in the resulting awkward silence, directing his words toward her.

"This is—as hard as it is to understand—the Tommy we all know. If he says he trusts her, he does. If he says he's fine, he is. For now, we have bigger problems to concern ourselves with. Unfortunately we cannot head in two directions at once, so we hunt down Callum. Then we go to Cregah. And only then will we have our chance to reunite our friends."

Aoife took a deep breath, pulling her shoulders back and looking from Tommy to Declan and back again.

"Well, you can be fine, Tommy. But I am not. She didn't just leave you. She also abandoned... She didn't even say goodbye."

Tommy placed a hand on her shoulder. "She's still your friend. She would never leave unless there was a good reason, unless she absolutely had to."

"She didn't tell you?" Aoife's nose wrinkled as she peered up at him.

He could only shake his head.

"Did she even tell you she was leaving?"

Another shake of his head.

"If she had a good reason"—Aoife's voice wavered briefly but gained strength as she spoke—"why didn't she bother to *tell you what that reason was*?"

Aoife had a point. It was a fair question.

Why hadn't she left him a message?

Why hadn't she woken him to say goodbye?

Maybe Tommy was a fool to not consider the possibility that she'd deceived him, but there was something in his heart that told him not to give up on her, not to believe the worst.

Especially when she had a sister capable of forcing her to act against her will.

The others could doubt Maura, but Tommy wouldn't. He trusted her. Renna was another story.

CHAPTER 3
MAURA

THE ROCKING of the ship seemed to be in perfect time with the throbbing pain in Maura's head.

And her hand.

But why did her hand hurt?

The cut from Renna's compulsion before facing Triss had healed already.

It's probably nothing, she thought.

Squeezing her already closed eyes tighter, Maura tried to push the pain aside, but it did little to help. So she focused her senses on the world around her instead, listening for the sound of Tommy's breathing, seeking out his spicy scent in the air, reaching for the warmth of him lying beside her.

The blood pulsing at her temples quickened.

She wasn't alone in the cabin—there was someone else here—but it wasn't who she had expected.

Or wanted.

Forcing her eyes open, she sat up so quickly it aggravated her headache further. As she waited for the room to stop spinning, she firmly pressed her fingers to the side of her head. Without turning to her companions, she greeted them with a growl.

"How could you?"

She should have recognized this pain as soon as she'd felt it.

She should have known this would happen.

"Yes, Maura, you probably should have expected this," her oldest sister, Renna, said in that haughty tone she always adopted when she was about to jump into a lecture. "You knew your duties. You—"

Maura was on her feet, turning to face her sister, before she could finish her sentence.

"I control my own life, sister."

"It appears you don't," Renna said, and Maura wanted to punch the smug smirk off her face. Off to the side, Bria watched intently and showed no sign of stepping between them to smooth things over as she usually did.

With her fists tightened at her sides, Maura pushed even closer to Renna. "Because you can't respect boundaries!"

"And you have no respect for your duties as a royal."

"Duties." Maura muttered the word under her breath and retreated a few steps so she could turn to Bria. "And you didn't think to stop her?"

Bria's eyes shifted from Maura to Renna, as if she was unsure how to respond while remaining in the neutral position she preferred. She never selected a side. Always tried to appease everyone. That was Bria. Maura had never begrudged her sister this trait, but now, feeling so alone and cornered and betrayed, she longed for her sister to defend her. But there was something new in Bria's silence. A murky confusion Maura had never before witnessed in her. Her eyes dropped to Bria's hands, clasped loosely in front of her.

One was newly bandaged.

"No." The word escaped from between her clenched teeth. She rounded on Renna, her hand flashing up to grab her sister by the throat. Renna didn't resist, even when Maura dug her fingernails into her slender neck. "Tell me you didn't." Silence accompanied her sister's blank stare, and Maura growled. "Tell me!"

"I can't," Renna said calmly. "Because I did what I had to do."

Maura, still holding Renna by the throat, glared at her. "You must be exhausted. To do more than nudge both our minds? It must have worn you out."

"Actually no. You forget that our shared blood grants us a special connection."

"A connection I'd be glad to be rid of!" Maura thrust her sister away from her, and with a yelp, Renna lost her balance and stumbled into the wall of the small cabin. Again Maura turned to address Bria. "Does this not bother you? How are you not angry? She controlled you!"

Bria bit down on her lip. Her brow bunched in the center as if Maura had asked her a question in Turvalan instead of the common tongue. She said nothing until Maura prompted her with an irritated "Well?"

"She had her reasons."

Maura threw her hands in the air. "Of course she had her reasons! That doesn't make them honorable."

Renna stepped away from the wall and looked down her nose at Maura. "What do you know of honor, sister? You would sacrifice our kin for what? The love of a mortal? What is a mere mortal lifetime of happiness compared to the centuries of suffering the fae are facing?"

"We didn't need to leave so soon!" Maura almost yelled. "How long did that letter from them sit and collect dust before they delivered it? Years? Decades?"

"All the more reason to waste no more time, Maura," Renna said, her voice annoyingly calm.

"No! What's another week? Two? A month! And now—" Maura stopped short, her eyes growing wide as her gaze dropped to the floor. She remained that way for only one breath before she lunged for Renna again. The wall creaked under the force of Renna's body against it. Maura narrowed her eyes and bared her teeth mere inches from Renna's face as if she was going to bite her. Renna didn't wince, didn't flinch, didn't move at all, but simply stared at Maura like a parent waiting for a child to finish their tantrum. "You made me betray him!"

"It had to be done," Renna rasped.

Maura's stomach lurched at the thought of Tommy waking to find her gone. Stepping backward, she released Renna and spun around, not wasting any energy on speaking to Bria. Wrenching the door open, she looked over her shoulder at Renna. A single deep breath helped her loosen up enough to deliver her message with an eerie calm.

"You can force others to follow you and do your bidding, but no one will ever love you. No one."

✄

As EXPECTED, Maura found the large crew of the *Duchess* crowding the deck. Some of them—men and women alike—worked to keep the ship sailing, while others lounged about, talking or sharpening weapons and enjoying the warm afternoon sun. Unlike the men on Tommy's ship, this crew didn't avoid her eyes but instead offered nods and small smiles as she looked around in search of the captain.

A woman Maura recognized as the quartermaster approached her with a knowing smirk. "Afternoon. Note I left the *good* off that greeting."

From the expression on the woman's face—the fine lines peeking out at the corners of her eyes and the exaggerated arch to her brow—Maura surmised she'd heard her and her sisters arguing.

"Apologies for any disruption," she offered with a tight smile.

Now the quartermaster let a warm laugh fill the space between them. "We're pirates. Heated arguments come with the profession."

"Of course. Any chance the captain is available?" Maura attempted to keep her words as calm as possible, though her insides were a frayed mess of anger and urgency.

"Aye, she's been expecting you actually." The quartermaster waved a finger in the air as she turned back the way she'd come, indicating Maura should follow her.

Maura, blocking out all the action around her, focused on the simple door before them as the pirate knocked on it. When a voice within bid them enter, the woman swung the door open, ushered Maura in, and then backed out of the doorway without a word, leaving Maura standing in a surprisingly well-lit cabin that was not nearly as dark and gloomy as Captain McCallagh's.

The entire back wall of the cabin consisted of windows that allowed the afternoon light to stream in. Where Declan's cabin consisted of the same rich wood as the rest of the ship, Captain Halloran's interior was painted the color of clouds on a sunny day. It made the quarters feel brighter, as if they were located in a lavish home on the beach rather than on a pirate ship in the middle of the sea.

Captain Halloran stood at the windows, looking out at the sea, her back to Maura. Her dark, coarse hair lay plaited down her back. Her trademark hat rested on the desk next to the wall to Maura's right. The pirate always seemed to tower over those around her with her confidence, but here in her cabin, she appeared less intimidating. More human—more fragile.

In a quiet but steady voice, Halloran said, "You have questions."

Maura stepped forward until she stood in the middle of the room, her eyes fixed on the view beyond the glass. "No questions. Just a request."

At this, the captain peered over her shoulder at Maura, as if she could read the request on her face or in her body language. A moment later, she turned back to the sea with a lazy shrug.

"You want me to take you back."

"Ideally, yes. But I am no fool, no matter what my sister may think. I know turning back and chasing after them would be a waste of your time."

When Captain Halloran didn't respond, Maura took the risk of stepping closer. Not that she feared anything the captain could do to her physically, but she didn't want to put her chance at freedom in jeopardy by angering her unnecessarily.

"Drop me off on Cregah," Maura said, holding her breath as she waited for Halloran's reply.

Halloran's shoulders lifted with a sigh, but she did not turn away from the brilliant sea stretching out before them.

"If I could, I would," she finally said.

"But?"

"We aren't going to Cregah, remember?"

Maura continued to approach with caution, her lithe feet silently closing the distance between them. "Then let me disembark somewhere else. Anywhere else, as long as the *Siren's Song* can find me on their way."

"And receive your sister's wrath? Why would I want to do that?"

Maura slammed her teeth together, wincing at the pain it sent through her jaw and up to her temples. *Damn Renna!*

Maura sensed a spark of humor behind the captain's stoicism. Before she could determine how to take advantage of it, Halloran's gaze drifted up to the ceiling as if she were searching for words there. She lifted a hand to her ear, acting as though she were tucking hair behind it. It could have been an arbitrary movement, but when the captain fixed her eyes on Maura a moment later, it became clear it was intentional.

Of course. Renna might be listening to this exchange. But if she could hear them speaking, then she could also read their thoughts. Was there no escape? Would she never be free?

In return, Maura tapped a finger to the side of her temple, hoping Halloran would understand the message. The slightest of nods indicated she had, not that it was of much help.

"Might as well accept your fate," Halloran said with an exaggerated sigh. "There are few—if any—options. And none I will aid you in pursuing."

"I suppose you're right," Maura said, glancing over her shoulder. She nodded to a map spread out on one of the tables. "Which route are we taking to Larcsporough?"

Halloran stepped away from the windows and waved for Maura to follow her over to the map. Placing a finger in the middle of the Aisling, directly west of Daorna, she said, "We're here currently. Ideally we would go around to the west of Cregah, but unfortunately, we've received word the king is already on his way. Normally we wouldn't worry about encountering him, but given our rather *precious* cargo, we will strive to give them a wide berth. If possible."

"So we will be going around this way then?" Maura traced her finger along the eastern side of Cregah.

"Aye." With the single word, Halloran met Maura's gaze, brow raised in a silent question. What did Maura have in mind exactly? Looking back at the map, Maura considered the options. Foxhaven was out, as it lay too far east and would be too crowded with potential spies. That left Haviern and Helles Island, though the latter was further west than the captain likely wanted to go. Still, they were her only options. She focused her thoughts on Foxhaven, keeping her eyes planted on its location on the map even as she placed two fingers elsewhere, one on each island she proposed.

Halloran cleared her throat, pulling Maura's attention away from the map. With an expression Maura couldn't quite get a read on—was she frustrated or sympathetic?—the captain drew in a deliberate and slow breath before speaking.

"I can't help you, but I won't stop you either. Whatever is going on between you and Renna remains between you. I won't be dragged into sisterly squabbles. Understand?" With that last word, Halloran mimicked Maura's earlier movement, pointing first to Haviern, then to Helles Island, before offering a steady nod.

"Thank you, Captain."

It was less than she'd hoped for but more than Captain Halloran had to offer, and for that Maura was grateful. Now to find a way to avoid Renna until they passed by Haviern.

CHAPTER 4
CAIT

Cait, with her eyes blurry and sore from a sleepless night, barely made it down the stairs without stumbling. She winced as she stretched out her back, rolling her shoulders up and back before stepping around the corner and into the empty pub.

Empty of patrons, at least.

Kira—steadfast and loyal Kira—stood behind the bar, drying the last of the glasses she'd spent the morning cleaning.

"Morning," Kira said without looking up. The single word fell flat, though Cait wondered if there wasn't some bit of impatience in her tone.

Cait settled herself onto one of the stools, her elbows digging into the polished wood of the bar. Dropping her head into her hands, she pulled in two long, slow breaths before realizing she'd left Kira's greeting unanswered. Peering over her fingers, she shot her friend a weary look. "Long night?"

Kira, not bothering to stop her task, let out a breathy laugh. "Not as long as it was for you, from the looks of it."

As if her friend's comment had reminded her of the weight keeping her limbs heavy and her mind foggy, Cait yawned and rubbed at her brow. "Too long. But also too short."

Setting a dry glass down below the bar, Kira selected another from the sink and shook off the excess water. "What happened?"

"You're not one to ask about the messages you pass along." Though Cait didn't word it as a question, her raised brow demanded a response.

"Who said I was asking about the message?"

Cait mentally kicked herself for jumping to that conclusion. Nothing in Kira's innocuous question hinted that she'd connected Cait's fatigue to the note she'd passed to her the night before. And if she hadn't connected it before, she certainly did now.

You don't have to tell her.

And she wouldn't.

Whatever change Adler had ignited in her hadn't made her any less private. She had let her guard down with him, but his stunt with the council—the stunt that had led to her best friend being knocked unconscious and taken out to sea—had driven her to reinforce those protective walls.

At least she hoped it had.

The sound of a throat being cleared pulled Cait's attention back up to Kira, who now leaned forward, hips propped against the bar's edge and hands resting casually atop it. There was nothing casual about her expression though. Her usual sweet demeanor barely showed through a hard veneer of tension and anger.

Was she upset that Cait wasn't being forthcoming?

With all the years she'd been in Morshan and involved with the Rogues, she should be accustomed to Cait's demand for secrecy.

"What is it?" Cait asked.

"Were you going to tell me what happened to Lucan?"

"No!" she blurted out. "Yes, I mean. Of course I was going to tell you."

What is going on with you?

"This isn't like you, Cait." All irritation melted away from Kira's face as she spoke. "You really didn't sleep, did you?"

Cait could barely manage a simple shake of her head, let alone a verbal answer.

"Where is he?" Kira asked gently, her light blue eyes softening with concern.

Cait leaned forward a bit. "What have you heard?"

"Only that he angered the council and was exiled." Kira's eyes twitched with the final word.

"You don't think they exiled him?"

Kira's shoulders slumped lower. "I don't know what to think, to be honest. I'm not surprised he confronted them though."

"It surprised me," Cait admitted, and her mind raced through the past days— and years—to determine where she'd missed the clues that Lucan could be so rash.

"If anyone could understand his anger with those women, I'd think it would be you."

Had Cait truly lost sight of what they were fighting against? Had she been so distracted by a handsome face that she could have forgotten the reason driving them to take down the council in the first place?

"Or," Kira's said, interrupting Cait's internal chiding, "did that pirate get to you?"

"Former pirate," Cait said before she could think better of it.

"So he did." Kira took a deep breath. "As much as I'd love to see you finally let yourself pursue something wonderful, I'd rather it not be at the expense of our work."

Cait bristled and ground her teeth together. She wasn't angry with Kira but with herself. She had screwed up—let herself be distracted—to the point that her friend needed to slap some sense into her. Straightening in her seat, Cait forced herself to play the role she'd chosen years ago. She was a McCallagh, after all.

McCallagh.

Her family name echoed in her mind as images of her parents and her brother forced themselves into the foreground, as if demanding her to remember who she fought for and why.

"Our work continues," Cait said.

"Even without Lucan?"

"I'll get him back," Cait said, hoping a plan to do that would come to her sooner rather than later.

"So he's not exiled."

Cait offered a single shake of her head. "Adler took him."

Kira pulled back sharply, as if Cait's words had shoved her. "The pirate."

This time Cait stopped herself from correcting her. "Aye."

"Do you know where?"

"I have an idea." She didn't need to give any details to offer reassurance, and she hoped Kira knew better than to push for information she would not give.

"Do you want a hand? We don't open until later today. I have time—"

Cait raised a hand to stop her. "I go alone."

"Okay. Well, you know how to reach me if needed." Thankfully, Kira didn't seem disappointed or offended by Cait's refusal of her aid.

The door to the alley creaked open, and hurried footsteps approached. A moment later, Naeve appeared around the corner and slunk toward the bar. Despite the urgency in her gait, her calm brown eyes showed no hint of trepidation as she greeted them with a faint smile.

"Naeve," Cait said as she stood and turned toward her. "What are you doing here?"

"Is it true?"

Cait's eyes narrowed in question. The worry in the girl's voice seemed so disconnected from her calm demeanor.

"Lucan," Naeve said, and something flashed in her eyes. Cait couldn't figure out if it was worry or...

She could be trying to get information from you. She does work for the council after all.

Trying to convince herself that she was merely being cautious and not paranoid, Cait let her face fall. "We know. We were there."

Kira remained quiet behind the bar.

Naeve's eyes flicked back and forth between them, and she lowered her voice further as if the walls had ears. "So you know the council exiled him."

Cait nodded.

"Do you think he was..." Naeve pulled her finger across her throat in a pantomime Cait found so eerily similar to something Lucan would do that she nearly let nervous laugh escape.

Cait managed to remain impassive though. "We have no reason to think otherwise, unfortunately," she lied. "Why do you ask?"

"The council. They suspect he's still alive," the girl said quietly.

"If he is, then where is he?" Cait asked, turning to Kira as if she had the answer, then back to Naeve.

"I hoped you would know, to be honest." Naeve's chin fell to her chest. "I'm worried about him."

Silence filled the pub. Cait tried to focus, but the fatigue was making it more difficult than it should have been. If the council was suspicious—and angry at Lucan's attempt to expose them—they weren't going to simply sit back and wait. They were going to retaliate; Cait was sure of it.

"Has there been any response from the council after yesterday's drama?" Cait asked.

Naeve lifted her face to look at her and then at Kira. "You haven't been notified?"

Cait and Kira shared a look. Kira shook her head. "I haven't seen anything, and I've been here all night."

"New ordinances. It's still early in the morning, so perhaps they haven't gotten to you yet," Naeve explained.

"What kind of ordinances?"

"A curfew, but only for the citizens. Travelers are excluded of course. And there will be more pirates on patrol. For everyone's safety, so they say."

This was going to make their work more difficult, limiting their ability to get messages to the other Rogues. But Cait would find a way around it. She had to.

"Thank you, Naeve."

The girl dipped her chin. "If you find Lucan—I mean, if he's really alive—can you…"

Cait gave her a tight smile before tossing her chin toward the back door. Naeve turned on her heel and rushed out.

Once the door closed, Kira turned to Cait and opened her mouth, but Cait spoke first. "Have Eva keep an eye on Naeve as best she can. If she leaves the council hall again, I want to know about it."

Before Kira could respond though, the front door to the pub banged open. Cait and Kira spun around to see Penny rushing in, breathless and flushed.

"Hurry," she rasped, tossing her head toward the street behind her. Retreating back out the door, she waved for them to follow. She was already taking off down the street. Without another thought, Cait rushed after her, not bothering to see if Kira did too.

"Penny, wait!" Cait called after the woman, but Penny didn't slow, only looking over her shoulder once as she desperately waved them on.

This could be a trap.

She'd be foolish to not consider that, but they were in broad daylight and heading for the town square. The council wouldn't harm her in public. Would they?

She skidded to a stop as they entered the square. While not as crowded as it had been during the council's visit, there was still a substantial number of people gathered at the west end. They were all staring at the library steps on the opposite end where the councilwomen had stood.

Cait's breath caught as her eyes lit on the stairs.

A woman lay sprawled across them, blood pooling underneath her. So much blood. The memory of her father's death flashed in Cait's mind, refusing to leave when she tried to ignore it.

Focus, Cait. You expected them to do something.

Even from this distance, Cait recognized the young woman's plaited blonde hair and dark green dress. Willow. A rogue. A Morshan native whose fiancé had been dragged off by pirates two years ago on the charge of stealing from the local healer. Since then, she had lived alone and hadn't grown close to anyone else, even after learning of the Rogues and joining their ranks.

Maybe the council didn't know of her association with the Rogues.

Maybe it was merely a coincidence.

But then Kira's hand gripped Cait's arm. "The writing," she whispered.

Cait looked closer at the grisly scene but couldn't see any writing from her current position. Cautiously she stepped forward, as if she might be exiled for simply approaching.

She stopped as soon as she saw it. On the stairs beside Willow's body, several words were scrawled in red paint. No. Not paint. Was that blood?

Either way, the words turned Cait's stomach.

A gift from the Rogues.

CHAPTER 5
AOIFE

AOIFE'S TEARS spilled over without restraint as the crew gently lay the wrapped body of her friend on the wooden plank near the port-side rail. Declan stood beside her, stoically watching his men prepare to commit Collins to the Aisling. She couldn't look at him, couldn't bear to see the guilt she knew he harbored.

Slipping her hand in his, she gave him a gentle squeeze, wishing he could accept that none of this was his fault.But she also knew better.

Her own guilt over Lani's death still pricked her heart, even if she'd become adept at hiding it.

Declan stepped away from her and turned to face the crew. Aoife wondered if anyone was looking up at him or if they all had their eyes locked on Collins's body as she did. Then again, they were likely used to this. How many of their own had they buried at sea over the years? Did every loss hurt as much as this one?

As if in answer to her unspoken question, Declan's voice rang out over the assembled crew. "Collins is not the first soul we've lost. He won't be the last. Nothing I say can express..."

His words tapered off, and Aoife found him watching her. She had never seen him this flustered, not even when he'd begged for her forgiveness at the cove. Her lips quivered as she tried to give him an encouraging smile. He could do this. He was Captain McCallagh.

He cleared his throat and started again. "Nothing I say can make this right. For what it's worth—which may not be much for some of you—I am sorry."

Saying nothing more, he turned away and stepped up beside Collins. With no command needed, Tommy, Gavin, and Mikkel joined him, and as one, they lifted the end of the plank high, sending Collins's body sliding into the sea.

The crew lingered for a few moments before Gavin cut through the silence, calling out orders. Aoife looked at him as he walked past her, but he didn't meet her gaze. She watched after him, wondering if she might have lost two friends with Collins's death. She didn't know if she could bear that, but she would if it was what Gavin needed in order to heal.

"He'll be okay," Tommy said over her shoulder, but he didn't say anything more before following Gavin up to the quarterdeck.

⚓

It had been an hour since the burial, and Declan, Gavin, and Tommy still hadn't spoken more than a handful of words to one another. Aoife had witnessed the three of them in comfortable silence before, but the air around them on the quarterdeck now carried a palpable tension. A tension she didn't know how to fix.

Instead she'd spent the last uncomfortable hour thinking about Maura. But the more she pondered the fae's departure, the more frustrated she became.

She needed to calm down, she knew, but she couldn't convince her muscles and nerves to unwind from the knots her anger had twisted them into. Her jaw ached from pressing her teeth together to keep her harsh words from escaping.

Tommy is an idiot.

How he could still trust the fae when she had so obviously abandoned him was beyond Aoife's comprehension, and idiocy was the only explanation she could settle on. Plus, directing her anger at Maura—and Tommy for his unwavering faith in her—kept her from having to acknowledge how disappointed she was in herself for making the mistake of trusting someone else again.

Would anyone in her life prove steadfast and honorable? Would anyone she loved not turn out to be a selfish prick?

Wincing at her bitterness, she slid her gaze to Declan, who seemed uncharacteristically unsure of himself as he watched Tommy. His expression was a curious mix of concern and doubt, but there was also a vulnerability there she'd only seen once before.

At the cove.

Her stomach tightened, sending a bundle of tangled emotions into her throat. *I forgive you.*

She had offered him the words he'd begged for, and she had meant them wholeheartedly. So why was there still a bit of distrust simmering within her? Why did her heart—despite her love for him—still insist on guarding itself?

Because people will always let you down. Just as you let Lani down.

Her thoughts were unfair, but they were comforting all the same. Hating herself for what she'd done to her sister lessened the sting of others' judgment of her. As long as she expected the worst from people, she could avoid being disappointed and hurt by them. At least a little bit.

Aoife rocked back on her heels. The men still stood in silence, and she wanted to say something. If only she could trust her tongue to not throw unhelpful barbs at Tommy for not seeing the obvious truth behind Maura's unexpected departure.

Her thoughts took off once more.

You're being unfair again.

She could have had a good reason for leaving you.

Or she could have been forced to go.

Renna could have—

But Gavin's voice cut through it all.

"Captain," he said over his shoulder and lifted his good hand toward the sea to the north. Something about the way he said the word had Aoife wondering if the helmsman was harboring some distrust as well. But it wasn't her place to fix all of Declan's relationships for him.

Declan stepped across the quarterdeck so he could peer down into the dark blue water, and Aoife rushed to follow. Below them, debris littered the cold water. Wooden crates bobbed at the surface beside splintered pieces of wood and ornate spindles still attached to a worn railing. Larger sections of deck and ragged pieces of off-white sails were scattered across the water, but Aoife barely saw any of it. Her eyes were glued to the bodies.

Pale.

Bloated.

Bodies.

So many.

And these weren't pirates.

Women gaped at the sky with vacant stares, their limbs splayed out as if they were in the middle of a festive dance rather than floating lifeless in the water. They ranged in age. Some were teens like her sister, Darienn. Others were older like the women of the council. And some were children. Boys and girls alike. Drifting across the sea alone or clinging to an older woman's hand.

Aoife's stomach heaved, but her body refused to allow her to retreat from the view of so many dead. Wrenching her head up to scan the sea beyond the wreckage, she searched for any sign of their vessel. Surely there had to be more remaining than a few wooden planks, barrels, and dead bodies. But she found nothing. What had happened to them?

She opened her mouth to ask Declan if it had been a storm, but her breath caught when she saw the bodies of the men. There were far fewer than she would have expected for a ship that had carried at least a dozen or more women and half as many children. The men—four in total—all had ghastly slashes across their throats. Gruesome cavities with jagged edges where their eyes had been. Their clothes, stained with blood and cut to mere shreds in some places, revealed numerous water-logged wounds.

No storm had caused this.

"Callum." The name fell from Declan's lips in a whisper like a heavy fog over the sea—quiet but ominous.

Aoife's attention snapped to him. Though he didn't face her, she easily identified the rage brewing within his stormy gray eyes. The muscles along his jaw twitched, and he swallowed hard, pressing his lips into a tense line. Questions—so many questions—bustled inside her mind, but her voice remained captive to the intense emotions coursing through her.

Beyond Declan, down on the main deck of the Siren's Song, the crew had halted their work and were now crowded at the port-side rail. No one spoke. The world had gone silent.

Aoife jumped as something brushed against her arm. She swung her chin to the left and let out half a breath upon seeing Tommy.

"A little jumpy, Aoife?" he said, but his tone was too dark and somber for such teasing.

Declan inched closer to her. "With good reason."

"Aye," Tommy said. "From the looks of it, he's not too far ahead of us."

"My thinking too."

"No doubt we'll come upon more—" Tommy began.

"More?" Aoife's panic pushed out the single word as she spun back around to face Declan, who caught her by the elbows as if she might stumble overboard with the sudden movement. Wide-eyed, she waited for his answer.

His chin dipped in an almost imperceptible nod.

"And there's no way for us to catch up to him? To stop him?" Aoife's sternum burned as her anger blazed. What horror had the people on that passenger ship faced at Callum's brutal hand? Those men had had no chance at success with Callum wielding the enchanted dagger.

Declan's eyes locked onto hers. The rage she'd witnessed earlier was gone, replaced with a quiet determination she'd seen before—before the council and the fae and the sirens.

"We will try. He's about a day ahead of us—"

The fire inside her flared, and she snapped, "A lot can happen in a day! This probably took mere hours." She swung an arm out over the railing to indicate the scene below, refusing to let her gaze follow.

"Aye," Declan said before drawing a breath deep into his chest. "And we will do what we can, but we can't control the wind."

The words stung, like saltwater in a fresh cut.

"Too bad the fae up and left," Aoife said, bitterness coating every word.

"Unfortunate, yes." Declan's calm tone grated on her.

Where had his rage gone? Why was she the only one angry? Over Callum. Over Maura. Over everything. How could they all be so damned calm?

As if he could read her mind, Declan whispered, "I know." He cupped her face in his hands. His thumb brushed lightly over her cheek, and his features softened. "Anger isn't always visible. That doesn't mean it's not here. We will stop him. Sooner or later. We will stop him."

She longed for his words to bring comfort and for his touch to soothe her, but they could only help so much.

CHAPTER 6
DECLAN

DECLAN CHECKED the grip he had on the reins of his emotions. Rage had hit him at the sight of the wreckage, the state of the men's brutalized bodies drowning him in memories he'd never be free of.

Killian's mangled flesh.

The exposed bones of his jaw and cheek.

His bloodied chest rising and falling with labored breaths.

His friend had been tortured mercilessly by Callum because of him.

Declan had killed Collins, and he had nearly killed Aoife, all because Callum had insisted they go to the sound without the fae for protection.

And now Declan stared at more of Callum's destruction. He could have possibly prevented it, had he somehow been able to stop the asshole from running off with the dagger while everyone's attention was elsewhere. Inwardly he seethed, and the darkness stirred.

Callum would pay for Killian, for Collins, and for these travelers. But Declan had to focus and not allow his emotions to lead, especially if they kept bringing these brutal images to the forefront of his mind, causing him to react rashly.

No, he needed to take control of them as he had on Callum's ship, let his anger simmer within as he'd done for all these years, to keep his head clear enough to plan efficiently. There would be time to let the rage free.

Thankfully, within a few heartbeats, the dark side of him returned to its slumbering with little resistance.

Rage still sparkled in Aoife's green and gold eyes though. She was cute when she was angry—especially when she was angry at someone other than him.

"What is wrong with you, Declan?" she hissed out through clenched teeth.

Maybe she was angry with him after all.

"A lot of things, actually. Which do you mean exactly?" Before he could pull the corner of his mouth back into a smirk, she growled. Aoife was just as stubborn as she'd always been, but now she had a roughness to her, a strength he hadn't expected to witness. At least not yet. If only the desire to touch her, to kiss her until she forgot her frustration with him, could be subdued as easily as his anger.

No doubt she wouldn't respond well to the words he really wanted to say to her.

"Why?" she asked.

If he hadn't found her so attractive right now, he might have been annoyed that she assumed he could read her mind.

"Why what?" he said, forcing his amusement to stay hidden behind a stony facade.

"Why aren't you angrier? How can you just turn it off?"

Tommy's face appeared over Aoife's shoulder, and he answered before Declan could even find the words to respond. "Practice. He's had many years to practice shoving those emotions deep down until he needs them."

"Practice?"

Tommy wasn't wrong, but how could Declan explain it to her?

"Well, it's not like practicing with a blade or"—he let his tongue dart out between his lips—"something a little more fun."

Aoife glowered, and Tommy's eyebrows shot up as a comical grimace pulled at his lips. He backed away on silent feet, his hands lifted in surrender, leaving Declan to fend for himself against Aoife's simmering temper.

Declan relaxed as best he could under her scrutiny. Why did this bother her so much? Surely the dark beast sleeping inside him was more troublesome, yet here she stood, judging him for being too calm?

"Why?" he asked, mimicking her earlier vague question.

Her eyes challenged him as they narrowed. "Why what?" she ground out through tense lips.

"Why are you so upset by this?" He gestured to himself with both hands.

"Because it doesn't make any sense!" Though she didn't scream the words, the intensity in her voice was almost more unsettling. He started to speak, to reiterate what he'd just explained a moment ago, but she stopped him with a raised finger. "I know, Declan. *It's not always visible.* But—"

"But what?" He narrowed his eyes at her, struggling against the irritation now building in his chest. What did she want from him? "Would you prefer it if I was foaming at the mouth, crazed eyes ablaze, irrational—"

"Irrational?" She flinched as if he'd slapped her with the word.

She needed to understand, before her emotions got someone hurt. But blowing up at her would do none of them any good. Taking a deep breath, he smoothed the rough edges of his mood and pushed back the anger that begged to be released.

Declan reached for her arm and pulled her to him. She resisted initially, but when her feet shuffled slowly toward him, he moved her chin up with a finger until she looked him in the eye. She'd surrendered enough to close the gap between them, but her eyes still stormed with bitterness.

"Keeping parts of ourselves hidden is not always a matter of deception, princess. Nor is it a denial of what we feel...of who we are. Emotion has its place—all emotion. Anger. Joy. Remorse. Love. The key is to not let it control you."

To not let it scare everyone around you.

"So you tuck it away? In here?" Aoife jabbed a finger into his sternum. "So it doesn't...what? Cause you to do something you regret?"

He nodded. This seemed like a trap, but it was one he couldn't avoid stepping into.

"Like when you chose to not tell me about Lani."

There it was.

A sharp pang twisted where her finger still pressed into him. Having his failings tossed in his face so casually sparked his anger, disturbing the darkness where it had settled. Would she forever fling that at him, attack him with these reminders? If she wanted him to be angry, he could give in, let her see what he was protecting her from. Maybe if she knew the pieces of him he kept locked away, she wouldn't goad him like this in the future.

Assuming she sticks around, that is.

His throat tightened around the building pressure.

Let her see who you are, what you're capable of.

If she truly loves you, she wouldn't flee from the real you.

Would she?

No. He couldn't risk it. Not when they'd endured so much to be reunited.

"Aye," he admitted. "Fear kept me from being honest. I let the fear win and hurt us both—"

"Then why shut me out now?" Her eyes remained hard, challenging him, daring him to let go of his control.

She didn't know what she was asking for.

She didn't understand.

He gritted his teeth.

His fear had controlled him before. He would not let his anger do so now.

Swallowing hard, Declan reached for the words he needed. Aoife didn't want to be deceived. It made sense, but there was far more at stake.

"If I let go, I might do more than hurt your feelings. I could get you killed. And that, I cannot risk."

"I've seen you angry, Dec—"

"And I nearly strangled you to death!" he shouted in desperation. She needed to understand. He couldn't remember anything he'd done under Triss's control, but he knew what he'd done to countless pirates and merchants in the past when he'd let his darkness control him.

Surely she should know why he couldn't let it take hold now.

Aoife was quiet for a long moment. Her eyes searched his. He waited, barely able to breathe until her shoulders finally slumped.

"I'm sorry," she said and lowered her eyes. "I just—"

Cradling her face in his hands, he lowered his head toward her until their noses touched.

"I know," he whispered and closed his eyes, relishing how she stepped ever closer.

He didn't deserve her. Sands knew he didn't.

But when had that ever stopped him from taking what he wanted?

This wasn't the time. Or the place. Yet the passion swelled in his blood all the same.

Ignore the lure of the darkness.

Let yourself have something good.

Get lost in her.

Weaving his fingers into her hair, he pulled her lips to his and kissed her. Softly at first. Then deeper. His hands dropped to her hips, and he drew her closer, erasing the space between them as she placed her hands on his chest. Everything inside him pulsed and raced and tensed as he kissed her. He let his desire take over and have its fill of every move of her tongue, all the warmth of her body, and every bit of pressure of her hips against him.

Here the darkness couldn't reach him, couldn't grab hold.

Here—with her—he was safe.

But even as he wound his hands up her back, devouring her with a need he'd never known before, the evil within called out—faint but clear.

Fight me all you want, but we're going to have fun. Very soon. You'll see.

CHAPTER 7
MAURA

Maura stood near the prow of the *Duchess* looking out at the water stretching out before them. Somewhere behind her, Tommy stood aboard his own ship, heading in another direction.

Did he hate her?

Was he angry?

Or did he somehow know she'd been tricked? That her leaving hadn't been her decision?

Renna.

For five centuries they'd been locked away together, but never had Maura thought her sister capable of such deception and treachery. They hadn't necessarily been close, but they had rarely argued or been bitter with one another. When Maura would get restless and distraught by their circumstances, her sisters had been there to lift her spirits and to remind her why they couldn't abandon their promise to Melina.

Why had they agreed to help her? Why had they vowed to serve her?

She was your friend.

Was being the operative word.

But she hadn't always been Melina Cascade, councilwoman of Cregah. The Bron sisters had known her long before the Aisling War, back when she was a royal daughter of the ruling family to the east. She—along with her family—had helped secure Triss and the sirens in the Black Sound. After parting ways, they hadn't heard from Melina again until the invitation came for her wedding to King Carmody of Cregah. All the fae had attended. Fae loved a good wedding. Any party, really.

Maura and her sisters had remained on the island when everyone else left, enjoying the pristine beaches, marveling at the scenery...and all the attractive men.

While Renna and Bria lost themselves in that life, Maura had dreamed of a life beyond the shore, a life of her own. She'd even made plans to leave.

Then the Aisling War had broken out and ruined everything.

The men had all left to fight. Including the king, who'd left his wife with child to fight in a war that wasn't theirs.

But it became everyone's war.

Nations chose sides, desperate to survive and hungry for power.

Maura had put her dreams on hold, agreeing to stay at the palace with her sisters to help the queen and her newborn son until the king returned.

He never did.

Their son, once grown, took his father's place, setting sail to serve—and die—in the same war.

Melina's grief was far more intense than Maura had thought possible. Apparently that was the price of love for the fae, the risk a fae took in giving their heart to another.

Remembering the queen's devastation now had Maura's insides twisting with regret. The pain Melina had endured was what lay in store for Maura and Tommy. Perhaps it was better if she forgot about getting back to him. Maybe it was best for both of them to let go before their bond became too strong.

Who was she kidding?

She'd given him all of herself. Her heart was his. Her body was his. Her eternity was his. Whether he was across the Aisling or right beside her.

The price of love.

No. She couldn't turn back now, couldn't undo the bonds they'd forged in those blissful hours in that cabin.

I'll get back to you, Tommy.

The ship turned.

Not sharply, but it was enough of a shift to snap Maura from her thoughts. She whirled around, but she had no clear view of the helm from here. Quickly crossing the deck and darting around several crew members working the rigging, Maura nearly stopped short when she spotted Renna standing with Halloran beside the helm.

Maura muttered a curse at her sister and continued forward.

Renna didn't turn to her as she approached but kept her eyes locked on Halloran, who greeted Maura with a curt nod.

"What are we doing?" Maura looked from Renna to Halloran, flexing her hands at her sides in a fight to keep from striking her sister. This was Renna's doing. Maura was sure of it.

"We've had a change of plans," Halloran said.

"Oh?" Maura didn't bother hiding her frustration.

"Aye. Given our tight schedule, we need to ensure we continue going south. With no stops."

"And I assume you didn't conclude this on your own." Maura glowered at Renna, who still hadn't paid her any attention.

Halloran stiffened, pressing her mouth into a thin line as her eyes narrowed. "Excuse me?" Maura faltered. This wasn't good. "Are you accusing me of not being in control of my own ship?"

Maura took a deep breath to give herself some time to formulate a response. "Of course not, Captain. But it seems uncharacteristic for you to doubt your own well-laid plans."

Shrugging a single shoulder, Halloran said, "A good captain doesn't hesitate to change course when needed."

"And who said it was needed exactly?"

Halloran stepped toward her, pushing Renna out of her way. "I did, Ms. Bron. If you have a problem with that, I'm happy to see you off my ship."

"Perfect!" Maura said, throwing her hands up in the air. "When can I leave?"

Renna inserted herself between them. "Nonsense, sister. You know where you belong, and we must get there as soon as possible. The sooner we aid our kin, the sooner you can traipse off to sands knows where with your pirate."

"Let her go, Renna," Maura snarled.

"I'm not—"

Maura's hand flashed out and snatched her sister by the throat. "You know what I mean," she said through clenched teeth.

Renna ground out the word "fine," and Maura released her. She started to walk away but stopped after a few steps, turning back to Maura. "I'm not so callous that I want to keep you from him forever. I simply want you to do what needs to be done first."

Guilt sparked within Maura, but only for a moment. No matter what Renna might say, she did not care about Maura or Tommy or anyone else except a group of fae who had abandoned them to centuries of isolation. Renna and Bria could help them on their own. Two royal sisters was sufficient. They didn't need Maura. Tommy did.

Once Renna was gone, Maura approached Captain Halloran tentatively. Was she aware of Renna's mental manipulation? Did she know she hadn't made the decision to change course of her own volition?

"So where are we off to now, Captain?"

"Due south, to the east of Cregah. Heading straight for Larcsporough."

"I see," Maura said as she pondered how best to approach this. "And what of the original plans?"

"What do you mean?"

"I understand we've changed course for now, but are we truly set on making no stops along the way? Do none of your crew need a bit of respite?"

Halloran's eyes narrowed, and Maura hoped against all hope that her mind was finally escaping her sister's compulsion and remembering their earlier conversation.

"Perhaps. I'm not planning on it at the moment, but anything is possible. Especially at sea."

Halloran's intense stare and tightened jaw communicated everything she couldn't verbalize to Maura safely with Renna—or Bria—potentially listening. Maura gave her a nod.

Anything was possible. She simply needed to find a way to make it happen.

And she needed a way to keep Renna from interfering with her plans again.

"Captain, before I take my leave, I wondered if you might have someone on your crew who acts as a healer?"

"Oh? Are you in need of healing? I thought fae could mend themselves."

"Aye, we can. It's nothing like that. I'm simply having trouble sleeping and wondered if they might have some herbs or tinctures that could help with that."

"Ah, of course." Halloran turned to one of the crew members on deck. "Gillie, take Ms. Bron here to see Katyra."

With a quiet word of thanks, Maura moved to follow the woman below decks, down a flight of stairs far grander than she'd ever expected to see on a pirate ship. Gillie led the way in silence, not bothering to glance back to ensure she followed. They walked briskly through several large rooms lined with barrels and crates until they came to a door.

The door itself was nondescript, simple and roughly made, and had Maura ventured down here on her own, she would have likely ignored it altogether, assuming it led to nothing more than a simple storage room unworthy of her attention. Gillie knocked on the door, and the voice that bid them enter was unlike any Maura had ever heard, rough and throaty while somehow exhibiting a song-like quality. It piqued her curiosity.

Were they meeting an elderly woman?

Or was she a being of magic and power?

Don't be ridiculous.

Of course it was a woman. There was nothing magical about her simply because her voice was unique. Humans were as diverse as any other creature in the world. There was no reason to be on edge, but when Gillie opened the door and nearly shoved Maura inside before quickly retreating, Maura's skin prickled.

Such bizarre behavior. Perhaps she doesn't like this woman, she reasoned.

Before her lay a much larger space than she had imagined. It was even larger than Captain Halloran's cabin running the entire width of the ship. Unlike the captain's chambers, though, the windows here were nothing more than portholes evenly spaced along the length of the back of the ship. Sunlight streamed in, bathing the space in a warm glow. Tables cluttered the room. Bundles of plants hung from the ceiling in various stages of desiccation, and a simple cot lay at the far end beside an open chest overflowing with clothing.

At one of the tables a young woman sat upon a stool, her slender hands working with a mortar and pestle. Surely this hadn't been the woman she'd heard through the door, but Maura didn't need to look around to know there was no one else here, as only two heartbeats accompanied the rhythmic grinding of stone.

"What do you need?" the woman asked in that same rough-edged tone, her eyes still on her work. Maura shook her head in an effort to somehow reconcile the woman's voice with her appearance. Her flawless, olive-toned skin seemed more befitting of the council hall and its pampered women than the *Duchess* and its rough pirates. Hair the shade of the summer sun at dusk cascaded past the woman's shoulders, falling down her back in gentle waves.

She was beautiful. But her voice...

"Who *are* you?" Maura clamped her mouth shut as soon as the question fell out. *Good job, Maura. She'll surely help you now after you've been so blatantly rude.*

But the woman only chuckled.

Or at least Maura thought it was a chuckle. It could have been a cough. Except, no, the woman's mouth curved up into a slight smile, though she still didn't raise her eyes.

"I'm sorry," Maura said. "I'm only—"

"Surprised."

Maura nodded.

"Not the first time I've surprised someone...fae."

Maura's muscles tightened. Sensing a nod was one thing. But knowing what Maura was without even looking at her?

How?

Before Maura could speak again, the woman set the mortar on the table, placed the pestle beside it, and lifted her face. Her head fell to one side. That smile—friendly but eerie at the same time—remained on her lips.

"I'm Katyra, and I know..." Gracefully she lifted a hand to her throat. "It's horrid, isn't it? Not nearly as pleasant as it once was."

Maura shot her a questioning look before stepping toward the table and silently asking permission to sit.

Katyra nodded and said, "Unfortunately, it was the price—or part of the price—to learn such valuable skills."

As Maura seated herself at the table, questions swirled in her mind, and Maura struggled to latch onto any of them to ask first. They flew from her mouth in a barely coherent stream of words.

"What skills? What was the other part? Price paid to whom? What are you exactly?"

Another chuckle—this time clearly a sound of laughter—escaped as Katyra's smile brightened. Her brown eyes sparkled with a gleam of humor.

"I like you..."

"Maura. I'm Maura."

Katyra repeated the name with a smooth nod. "Surely you must know my skills if you were brought to me?"

"You are far more than a healer or herbalist."

"Indeed. But what I do is not that different. I'm merely able to pull more from the ingredients than others. I'm a mage."

"A mage? I've never heard of such a thing."

"To be fair, Maura, you were imprisoned for quite some time. A lot changed in our world after the war. Magic disappeared with the fae. Or so everyone thought. As it turned out, your kin weren't the only ones with power."

The room turned and tilted around her, and Maura wasn't sure if it was from her inability to grasp this information or if the waters had actually become rougher.

Was this how Aoife had felt with each revealed secret?

Maura shook her head in a fruitless effort to clear away the confusion. She didn't need a history lesson, but the questions continued to prod her, refusing to be ignored.

"So others were born with...magic."

A nod. "Not many. Most were either cast out of their lands, killed, or forced to hide the skills they possessed."

"But who could give you such power?"

"Same one who granted me unnaturally long life."

"That's not an answer," Maura said with a light laugh.

"He was one of the few to survive the purge, and he was not easy to find. I never learned his name. Never saw his face."

"And you trusted him?"

Katyra's smile faltered briefly but returned with unquestionable sadness. "You'd be amazed who you will trust when you're desperate, Maura."

Maura's gaze fell to the wooden table between them and the various plants and bottles and bowls scattered there. Her mind quieted, all remaining questions retreating to the recesses of her mind as the air shifted around them, as if the mage's melancholy was alive and breathing in the room with them.

Maura refused to push further. Katyra might be a stranger, but that didn't give Maura any right to demand answers from her. Regardless of how curious she was.

"Captain Halloran sent me to you for something to help me sleep," Maura said finally, her voice quiet and unsure.

Katyra cocked her head and studied Maura for several moments.

"No."

"No?" Maura straightened in her seat and leaned toward the mage, preparing to plead her case. She needed this. She had no other way around her sister's damn compulsion.

The mage blinked. "You're not the one wanting to sleep."

Did this woman's powers extend beyond herbs and plants? Could she read minds too?

"How—"

"You might be stressed, Maura, a bit frazzled. But you aren't in need of rest. One of my abilities is to sense a person's state. Helps me determine exactly what they need. So I can tell that, though your pulse is racing and your muscles are pulled taut, your mind is clear, your body strong, your powers blazing in your blood. You are not wanting to sleep. Who do you need out of your way?"

"Impressive," Maura whispered, and it was no lie. While she could hear the heartbeats of those around her, she had no ability to assess someone's health simply by being in the same room with them. "But why does it sound like you believe my plans are nefarious?"

"If they weren't, you would not have lied."

Maura shrugged a shoulder and let a frown pull at her mouth. "Or perhaps I was asked to be discreet."

"That is possible, but most people doing a favor for a friend don't squeeze their hands until they ache and throb. You're anxious, nervous. More so than if you were simply protecting someone close to you."

Could Maura trust this mage? Could she risk being honest, explaining her reasons, her needs, her plans?

You'd be amazed who you will trust when you're desperate.

Was Maura truly desperate? Desperate enough to trust this strange woman? A woman she knew virtually nothing about?

When she closed her eyes, a vision of Tommy sleeping peacefully beside her, his arm cradling her head and keeping her tucked against him on the floor of his cabin, flashed behind her eyelids. An ache crushed her chest, pushing so hard against her that she curled herself around it, hunched her shoulders forward, and dropped her head low.

Yes, she was that desperate.

Opening her eyes, she straightened once more, fighting against the pain that pulled her heart toward her spine.

"I need it for my sister," she said.

Katyra nodded. Her smile returned, a hint of mischief playing at its corners.

"I can help with that."

CHAPTER 8
TOMMY

TOMMY IMMEDIATELY REGRETTED RETREATING to the quarterdeck, as it gave him a clear view of Declan and Aoife getting lost in each other by the mainmast below.

"Don't they have a room to do that in?"

It took a second for Tommy to realize he hadn't been the one to utter the words. Beside him, Gavin scoffed with more annoyance than he normally displayed. More than he *ever* displayed, actually.

"What's eating you?" Tommy asked. They hadn't gotten much of a chance to talk since leaving the sound, and it was entirely his fault. He'd been so absorbed in what he was doing with Maura—much like Declan was with Aoife right now—he had neglected to check on his friend.

Gavin frowned and shook his head.

"Come on, Gavin. Out with it." How long had they sailed together? Long enough to trust each other, surely.

"You have enough on your mind without my shit weighing you down too."

Tommy thought for a moment, doing everything he could to avoid viewing his captain's continued display of affection. He did have a lot on his mind. Or rather, he had one important thing on his mind.

My Maura.

Staring down at the ship's rail, he could almost see her stepping across to Halloran's ship. Had she hesitated? Had she protested? Had she looked back with regret? His gut twisted around the doubt trying to weasel its way into him.

No amount of pining would get him to her faster.

"That may be true," Tommy said, "but whatever you're shouldering, it doesn't have to be yours alone. And it shouldn't be. Not if you're going to be clearheaded for what lies ahead of us."

He watched Gavin process this, hoping the man would see reason. Even then,

Tommy wondered if he should have kept his mouth shut and let his friend be. Would Gavin's troubles do more harm once everything was laid out in the open? Would it be better for the lot of them if he kept it to himself?

Tommy panicked and rushed to take back his words, but Gavin spoke first.

"He killed him."

Tommy should have expected him to utter those three words, but even so, they caught him off guard. Still, he didn't need clarification to know who Gavin referred to. Gavin hadn't actually been there with them in the sound, and Tommy hadn't witnessed the entire scene, but he'd seen enough to know Declan hadn't been himself on that beach.

"I know." It was all Tommy could offer as he worked to formulate a more helpful response. "But—"

"It wasn't him. I know." Although the words themselves were calm and reason-able, Gavin's tone dripped with anger. He took several deep breaths before his expression softened and his head fell slightly forward. "I shouldn't be angry with him, but I keep wondering if there was some way he could have avoided it."

"You know as well as I do that if there had been a way, the captain would have done it. He nearly killed Aoife. With his bare hands. He killed her sister." Tommy waved a lazy hand toward the couple below them. "If she can forgive him for that, then you can too."

"Aye. I'm being ridiculous."

Tommy shook his head. "No you're not. Collins was your friend. He was a friend to us all. You're allowed to grieve."

"Why am I the only one who seems to be struggling with it then?" Gavin asked, his frustration deepening the v between his brows.

"Grief is different for everyone. And you knew Collins longer than any of us. It makes sense you'd struggle a bit more." Tommy pictured the day Declan had recruited Gavin in Foxhaven. He'd refused to join the crew unless they took Collins on as well. Why Gavin had been so insistent, Tommy had never learned, and once on the ship, the two men had interacted little. Still, Gavin must have had his reasons. And those reasons must be making this all the more painful for him.

"He was my cousin," Gavin admitted in a flat tone. "I promised my parents I would watch after him. Bringing him onto a pirate ship probably wasn't the best way to keep that promise."

"So why did you?"

"I was selfish," Gavin said.

Gavin. Selfish. The two didn't mix at all.

"I wanted to make my own way in life and not do what everyone expected of me. So when the captain offered, I couldn't decline. Nor could I leave my cousin behind. And look where I got him."

Tommy could tell by the twist of guilt on his friend's face that any anger he harbored toward their captain was nothing more than a deflection. He was mad at himself.

"It's not your fault, Gavin. You didn't force him to do anything. Collins loved this crew and this ship and this life. You know that. He volunteered to go into the sound with us. No one ordered him to. Not you. Not Declan. Not me."

He eyed Gavin, who glanced once more at the captain and Aoife. Hopefully the conversation had been helpful, but only time would tell.

Before either of them could say more, the lookout shouted from his perch atop the mainmast. Tommy instinctively grabbed the spyglass Gavin offered.

A ship bobbed on the surface of the sea, its sails lowered.

No smoke billowed from it, and it remained level atop the water, so it likely wasn't sinking.

An uneasy chill crept through Tommy's bones.

Declan bounded up the stairs. "What is it?"

Tommy handed him the glass as he answered, "Another victim perhaps."

"Gavin, bring us alongside. Tommy, assemble a boarding party. If he's left them adrift, it's for a reason."

THE SMALL ROWBOAT knocked into the hull of the drifting ship, jarring Tommy's teeth. He much preferred boarding with the plank, but they'd decided not to risk getting the ships too close to each other in case this was a trap. Of course, boarding with such a small party like this wouldn't help if an ambush awaited them. Still, Tommy understood Declan's desire not to put Aoife in any unnecessary danger.

Tommy climbed the ropes up to the main deck, and the wood creaked under his boots as he boarded. He stopped short. Behind him, Mikkel swore under his breath. Someone else heaved the contents of their stomach over the rail into the sea below.

Tommy thought he had prepared himself sufficiently, having imagined a number of gruesome and gory sights they might stumble upon. But even knowing how cruel Callum could be—having seen the result of that cruelty already—hadn't prepared him for what they found.

Against the wooden crates stacked down the length of the deck sat a dozen crew members, their legs stretched out before them, their heads lolled to one side or another as if they were all sleeping. Their throats had been slit. Their blood-soaked shirts had been removed and dropped into their laps. Shallow gashes decorated their bare chests. But these weren't random cuts.

They were words. One word carved into each chest.

"Want the dagger? Trade the bitch for the blade. Selka. Gilded Cup. "

Tommy read the message silently to himself as he lifted the back of his hand to his mouth. Declan wouldn't like this.

That's an understatement.

But worse than that, he knew Declan wouldn't back away from this challenge. He would never give up Aoife—especially not to that brutal bastard—but neither would Declan shy away from the chance to best him.

And kill him.

Callum knew they were following him.

And he knew exactly how to taunt Declan.

Mikkel stepped up beside him while the other men stayed back. "He's not one for subtlety, is he?"

"It would appear not," Tommy said, clicking his tongue as he considered how to keep his friend and captain clearheaded. He'd already noticed a glimmer of rage in Declan's eyes. Even with Declan's years of practice keeping that part of him at bay, Tommy knew how quickly it could take hold.

Turning away from the gore, Tommy addressed the boarding party. "Mr. Keiley, take Wilson and Sam belowdecks to search for the rest of the crew. Mikkel?" He paused to toss his head toward the dead men behind him. "Give them as proper a burial as we can. I need to get this message back to the captain. I will be back in an hour to pick you up."

"Aye, Tommy," Mikkel answered with a nod before getting the men moving toward their respective tasks.

As Tommy rowed back to the *Siren's Song* in silence, he attempted to formulate what he would relay to Declan, but his mind refused to cooperate. *The bitch for the blade.* Declan would not accept those terms, but what would he choose to do instead? The possibilities were endless, and most were not pretty.

CHAPTER 9
CAIT

CAIT'S MUSCLES itched to move and retrieve Willow's body, but with several pirates already wrapping the woman in a cloth, all she could do was stand against the wall and watch. Kira angled her head toward Cait's ear and whispered, "Coincidence?"

Cait pressed her lips together and shook her head slowly. No, they couldn't afford to assume this had been anything but deliberate. If the council knew Willow's identity and her association with the rebels, they could know more.

They could know everything.

But how? She'd been careful, hadn't she? They all had.

She'd underestimated the ladies of the council. She wouldn't do so again.

"What now?" Kira asked, though standing here in the public square with what appeared to be half the townspeople—and nearly as many travelers—didn't allow them the ability to discuss details.

Without moving her head, Cait scanned the crowd. She couldn't see beyond the first few rows of people, but she didn't locate any Rogues among them. Hopefully the rumors would swirl fast enough that the surviving members would know to continue life as normal, to not draw suspicion.

"Life goes on," Cait said before stepping away from the wall and turning to leave. "We have a pub to run."

Kira was by her side in an instant. "You mean *I* have a pub to run." Cait shot her a questioning look. "You need to go talk to him, don't you?"

Adler.

Cait had nearly forgotten about his request to meet.

"Aye, I do. I should be back before we open though."

They continued walking in silence, and Cait debated which route to take to the cove. The one past Penny's would likely have too many witnesses—even with the excitement in the square—and she couldn't risk leading anyone to Lucan. But the next best alternative would take her past nothing but homes, and Cait would have no justifiable reason to venture there. Too suspicious. But there was one more way, just up ahead, that would take her past a number of shops that could act as cover if she were stopped.

Just as she was about to turn, though, Kira whispered, "Don't."

Without asking any questions, Cait abandoned her plan and kept walking beside her friend, who maintained her calm demeanor despite the urgency in her command.

Kira whispered, "Behind us. We're being followed."

"Well, shit."

Though Cait didn't hear any footsteps behind them—and she wasn't stupid enough to risk a glance—she trusted Kira's judgment. Adler could wait.

"We continue on to the pub, as expected," Kira explained.

Back at the pub, Kira pushed open the door, and Cait followed her inside, refraining from peering back to catch sight of their pursuers. It wasn't until she was standing behind the bar and fetching herself a glass of water that she let her eyes wander to the front windows.

No one.

She was about to chide Kira for being paranoid when two men slipped into view. They walked too slowly to be casually passing by. They could simply be travelers new to the area, checking out the local establishments, but Cait wasn't about to make such dangerous assumptions, especially now that one of her own had been killed openly and her rebels blamed.

"You need to go," Kira said as she joined Cait behind the bar.

Quickly pulling her hair back and plaiting it, Cait nodded. "But not yet. They're not going to kill us in broad daylight—"

"You sure about that?"

Cait blew out a breath. "No, but I'm not going to run away either."

Before Kira could say more, the door was opening, and two pirates entered. These men were not nearly as grimy as the pair who had come in weeks ago looking for Aoife—nor as unkempt as most of her usual patrons. Their hands and faces showed only faint traces of their hard and dirty line of work. As they walked forward, craning their necks to peer around the empty room, Cait noted the deep purple sashes tied at their waists.

Captain Madigen's men then. But the lord's crew rarely came into town. In fact, Cait couldn't remember the last time she'd seen one of his men on the island, let alone in her pub.

"We're closed," Kira said with an indifferent tone.

"Hush, Kira." Cait rested her hand on Kira's forearm and nudged her back. "These are Lord Madigen's men. Rules don't apply to them."

"Most rules anyway," the taller one said with no trace of a smile or even a smirk.

Cait placed two glasses atop the bar and reached for the rum behind her. "What can we do for you? Aside from the obvious drink."

The men didn't sit but stood rather arrogantly behind the stools, shoving their hands into their pockets and tilting their chins up so that they looked down their noses at the two women.

Ignoring how they silently glowered at her, Cait filled the glasses to the brim and set the bottle down. "Please, no charge."

"Can't," the other pirate said and raised his brow. "Official duty and all."

"Suit yourself." Cait shrugged and slid one glass toward Kira. She and Kira lifted the glasses and emptied them in unison. "What kind of official duty would that be?"

"We're to deliver a warning." The taller man's eyes narrowed on Cait.

Did the council know who Cait was? Or was this some generic threat being provided to all Morshan business owners?

She couldn't be sure.

But Kira responded before Cait could. "So go on. Deliver it already."

Cait tensed. Her breaths stalled.

What in the sands was Kira thinking?

The shorter man laughed quietly and leaned toward his friend. "I'll take the feisty—"

But the other pirate stopped him with a lifted hand, never taking his eyes from Cait's as he did.

"All businesses are required to report any and all suspicious or illegal behavior immediately to the council," he said, pausing when Cait raised a finger into the air, indicating she had a question.

"Does this include the new earlier curfew for citizens?"

"Aye, of course."

Cait shot Kira a confused look before turning back to him. "But we are to report it immediately."

He nodded.

"How exactly?"

He pressed his lips into a thin line as he drew in a long breath. "What do you mean?"

"Well," Cait started, donning her sweet-and-innocent mask, "how can we as citizens immediately report a curfew breaker without also breaking the curfew ourselves? It's logically unsound. Though I suppose such reasoning was lost on your feeble minds."

The man shoved the stool out of the way, reached across the bar, and pulled Cait toward him by the neck.

"You insolent bitch!"

Ignoring the hammering of her heart and the struggling of her lungs to pull in air, she forced aside the panic and fear and lifted a brow.

"That escalated quickly," she choked out. She gave him a half-smile when his friend grabbed his shoulder and told him to let her go. But he only squeezed tighter, cutting off her air long enough to bring the panic rushing back before shoving her back behind the bar. Cait rubbed at her neck, more to erase the sensation of his hand on her skin than to ease any pain.

Kira stepped in front of Cait to address the men. "So am I to report *that* immediately, or does that not count as suspicious or illegal?"

"The rules don't apply to us, as your friend pointed out," the taller man said tightly. Then, looking over Kira's shoulder, he caught Cait's eye. "You should be careful how you use that tongue. Someone may just decide to cut it out."

His eyes flashed with rage. No doubt it wasn't merely a hypothetical threat.

"I'll be sure to write that down," Cait said, giving him a casual nod.

Kira gestured for the door. "You'd best be leaving."

Without another word, the taller pirate turned and stormed off, but his friend remained behind. He leaned over the counter. Running his hand over his stubbled chin, he cleared his throat quietly and whispered to Kira, "If you ever want to play a little, I'm game."

Kira tilted her head and spoke so softly that Cait could barely hear her. "And if you want to keep that dick of yours intact, you'll go find someone else to play with."

But her comment only made the pirate's wicked smile grow wider as he backed away silently.

Once they were both out the door and out of sight, Cait let herself take her first full breath since they'd entered. "Well, that went well," she said, stretching her neck out.

"Aye, could have gone worse. But you'd better hurry if you plan to find the boys and make it back here before curfew."

Cait couldn't keep from laughing. "I would hate for you to have to report me to the council."

"Go already. And tell Lucan hi for me if you find him."

CAIT'S MIND whirred as she made her way into the trees at the edge of town. She couldn't shake the feel of that pirate's hand on her throat. She shouldn't have goaded him, should have played it smarter, been more complacent.

As if complacency was ever your thing.

But the image of Willow on those steps kept sliding back into focus, pushing her to doubt her instincts, to doubt herself. She could have gotten herself killed by Lord Madigen's men. Or worse, they might have killed Kira.

You have got to detach. Step back. Breathe.

As she moved along the forest path, Cait replayed the words her mother had said to her time and time again whenever she became overwhelmed or frustrated. Tears stung the corners of Cait's eyes. If her mother were here, Cait would be able do this. If she were here, Cait wouldn't feel so helpless.

Breathe.

You can't tackle the problem when you're on edge.

Cait listened, obeyed, and took a deep breath, letting the comforting aroma of the pine trees wash over her as she slowed her steps. Her vision threatened to blur as she worked to calm herself, but she couldn't run on instinct alone. Especially not on this path. The cove's location had remained a well-guarded secret, forgotten and ignored for years.

Somehow Cait still remembered the way, though she had only visited once since her parents' deaths. Though she suspected Declan went often—his clothes were often caked with black sand, his pockets weighed down with the white rocks he gathered there—Cait hadn't been able to stomach it. The loss seemed more potent on those familiar sands. She couldn't escape the memories of family picnics in the sun, laughter and hugs and time spent away from the scrutiny of the council and other citizens.

She told herself it was that discomfort that had her insides twisting painfully now, though she knew it was only a partial truth. She dreaded seeing Adler nearly as much as she did the cove.

What did Adler expect from her exactly?

A chance to explain? She could give him that much. Her understanding? She wasn't so sure about that one. A breeze swept down the path toward her, carrying with it the faint sound of...laughter?

Hope sparked, but she tamped it down. Quickening her pace, she angled her head so one ear pointed ahead, listening for more sounds from the cove ahead of her.

Someone else might be on this path. You don't know they're in the cove.

Be cautious. Be careful.

More laughter—unmistakable this time—floated on the air. A familiar laugh. This time that bit of hope bucked against all her efforts to control it. It burst forth, pushing her feet faster, but she forced herself to stop just before popping out onto the black sand beach.

Peering through the trees, Cait struggled to slow her breathing, but her heart refused to be calmed. It continued its thrumming within her chest, beating so loudly it filled her ears and made it hard for her to hear the quiet voices in the cove.

There, leaning against one of the large white boulders, stood Lucan. He didn't look any worse for wear, with his mouth pulled up into that goofy grin of his as he listened to the man standing in front of him.

Adler.

Cait's feet twitched within her boots, as antsy as the rest of her to run in and confront them. But not yet.

"I wish I had seen her face," Lucan said, his eyes lifting to the sky as he spoke, as if he was sending that wish to the hiding stars above.

"No you don't, friend," Adler said. He shifted his weight as he uncrossed his arms to run a hand through his hair. "That glare of hers could—"

"Cut straight to your heart?"

Adler nodded.

"You get used to it though," Lucan said before letting another laugh escape. "Honestly, I'm not sure I'll get a second chance to get used to any of her looks."

Lucan offered him a small shrug. "Sure you will. I've seen how she looks at you."

"Looked at me, you mean. That was before I betrayed her." Adler's head drooped as if weighed down by regret.

"You didn't betray her," Lucan insisted.

"Didn't I? Didn't we? We didn't exactly let her in on the plan."

Another laugh came from Lucan, though it wasn't nearly as boisterous as his previous ones. "Eh. She'll get over it. She always does."

"Oh, you betray her often?"

Lucan beamed with a mischievous smile, and Cait stiffened when his eyes flicked to the trees and scanned the shadows. "Maybe not betray, but I certainly annoy the shit out of her. Her reactions are too fun not to."

"Not sure I agree with you there, friend. Her reaction to seeing you being carried onto a boat—and to Lucy helping me? I can't imagine her forgetting that quickly."

Lucan tipped his chin up. "She might surprise you."

"Speaking of..." Adler's back straightened as his head turned slightly over his shoulder. "Come on out, love," he called.

Cait froze, her breath caught in her throat, her heart ceasing briefly before it resumed its thundering. She didn't know how he had sensed her presence—especially with his back to her—but she didn't want to give him the satisfaction of knowing he was right. He'd played her back in the town square. She could play him now.

So she waited, watching them.

Lucan leaned toward Adler and whispered something Cait couldn't hear. Adler merely shrugged before turning around.

Cait gasped involuntarily at the sight of him, wincing at her body's betrayal. It hadn't even been a day since she last saw him, yet somehow his good looks still shocked her enough to pull the breath from her lungs.

Damned lungs.

Adler had ditched the green sash of Tiernen's ship, and even though his muscles remained hidden under his modest attire, something about the way he stood— confident and determined—made him even more attractive than he had any right to be.

"Cait, love? The longer you wait, the more embarrassing it is for you." His brow shot up as if daring her to...what? To test him? To prove him wrong?

He's just trying to get under your skin.

He was succeeding.

She took a few more breaths to steady herself as she weighed her options, but when she still hadn't emerged, Lucan rose from his resting spot.

"C'mon, Cait. We know you're there."

As Adler's eyes roved the trees, Cait stood as still as possible. No point in giving away her position if he truly didn't know where she hid. She nearly allowed herself to relax when his eyes passed over her for the second time, but then he backtracked. Surely he couldn't see her, not with how the trees' limbs shrouded her in shadows. There was no denying it, however, when his gaze locked onto hers. The spark of recognition was as clear as the water that lay behind him.

Raising his arms casually at his sides, palms up toward the sun, Adler invited her once more to come out. "It's just us, love. Me and Lucan. No one else."

She hesitated. Something within her tightened. She wanted to believe it was her intuition warning her not to trust him, but she knew it was a warning of a different variety, a warning of attraction, of desire, of want—three things she had zero interest in, especially in regard to this man.

She rolled her eyes before pushing her muscles to move.

Steeling her resolve, Cait stepped out into the sunshine. Warmth bloomed deep in her chest as she watched Adler's smile light up his handsome face. The heat crept lower—against her will—when his eyes slowly trailed down her body before finding her eyes once again.

"It's good to see—"

Cait held up a hand to tell him to stop speaking, worried what would happen to her insides if she allowed him to call her "love" again. She was rather surprised when he acquiesced, even more surprised that Lucan hadn't uttered a word yet.

"You okay, Lucan?" she asked her friend, lifting her chin sharply.

Lucan gave her a warm—albeit sheepish—smile. "I am. More than okay actually."

Her eyes instinctively narrowed at him, searching for any sign of further deception. Finding none, she uncoiled her muscles but then froze when she realized Adler was cautiously approaching.

"So," she said, meeting his gaze, "it's not what I think. What is it then, exactly?"

He continued taking careful steps toward her until he stood close enough that she could smell the irritatingly comforting spiced scent that clung to him. Shoving his hands into the pockets of his pants, he pursed his lips briefly before saying, "Well, it was Lucan's idea."

Of course it was.

"I should have known," Cait said. "Except I never expected any plan of his to involve him on a boat."

"No one would! Hence the sheer brilliance of it!" Lucan called from behind Adler. Cait had to admit, her friend was no idiot—no matter how often she thought differently. Everyone in Morshan knew about Lucan's fear of water. It was something he was endlessly teased for. Everyone in town would believe he had been taken out to sea against his will. When the council learned that Adler hadn't taken him to the pit as ordered, they would be less likely to suspect that Lucan was working with him.

But that still left Adler vulnerable to the council's suspicions. Why hadn't he just taken him into the forest? Why take him by boat?

"But why?"

Cait didn't realize she had asked the question aloud until Adler's voice surprised her. "Why what?" he asked around his smirk, his dimple making an appearance beneath his beard.

"Why take him on a boat at all? And why was Lucy there? One of you had better explain all of this before I—"

"Before you what?" Humor laced Adler's words.

Cait honestly didn't know where she'd been going with that threat. There wasn't much she could do to these two imbeciles aside from walking away from them.

With a slight shrug, she spun around and started back the way she'd come, ignoring how all her unanswered questions nagged and prodded and poked at her insides. They would call her bluff—they had to—but doubts crept in when she stepped back into the trees and they still hadn't stopped her. She strained to listen for any hint of a footstep or a whisper or even a laugh behind her, but nothing but the lapping of the waves hit her ears.

Each step further into the trees pulled her heart down inch by inch until it settled heavily in her gut. They hadn't followed. They didn't need her after all. Tears pricked her eyes, but taking a deep breath, she held them back. She would not shed one damn tear for them. Not when she had so much work to do.

But this made no sense.

He'd told her to meet her here. She'd come. And now...nothing?

He's messing with you. They both are.

Be patient. Slow your pace.

The confident part of her tried to take control, but her insecurity dug its claws in, making it impossible to completely avoid the feelings of inadequacy and uselessness and embarrassment that rose up.

No! she yelled at herself, mentally shoving them back down. Clenching her teeth, she straightened her posture and picked up her pace. If they wanted to work with her, they knew where to find her. She wasn't going to play their ridiculous games.

No sooner had she made that resolution than Adler stepped onto the path in front of her. Her hand flew up to her chest in surprise.

"You're utterly predictable, love," he said with a wink. She cursed her heart when it fluttered in response. Like she'd never had a pirate or two wink at her.

Never one who looked like this though.

Crossing her arms, she thinned her lips and glowered at him.

"Predictability isn't a weakness when dealing with friends. But perhaps I was wrong—"

"You weren't wrong. We are...*friends*."

Something about the way he said the word, though, gave her the distinct impression that he wasn't too fond of that idea.

"It's true, Cait," Lucan said from behind her, startling her again.

She whirled on him. "Don't do that!" She cringed at how childish she sounded, but the sight of Lucan beaming that familiar smile of his melted away all her bitterness and frustration. Without another word, she pulled Lucan to her, wrapping her arms around him and holding him close. "I'm glad you're okay, Luc. Kira says hi, by the way."

Lifting her off her toes, he squeezed her tightly in a way he hadn't done since before Adler had arrived.

Adler.

With a final squeeze and a tap on Lucan's shoulder, Cait asked her friend to let her go. As soon as he complied, she stepped back to the edge of the trail so she could look at both men at once.

"Can we start again?"

"That depends," Adler said. "Are you going to run away again?"

"Maybe," she said, flashing him her own smirk. "I suppose that depends on what you have to say. I mean, if you tell me you've ratted me out to the council—"

"Then you'd already have been taken by them, love. So no, I did not."

"Come on back," Lucan said. "Let's sit and chat back in the cove."

He started to turn to walk back, but Cait stopped him with a raised hand. "Not yet. Not until I know what role Lucy played in this." She glared at Adler. "Did you lie to me? Did you know her before she showed up at my pub?"

To his credit, Adler's calm demeanor didn't waver under her accusations. "Aye, I lied."

"Don't be—" Lucan started to say, but Cait whipped around to face him.

"Since when do you defend him? You hated him."

Lucan shrugged. "Emphasis on the past tense. You can trust him, Cait."

"Trust him. When he lied to me. To us."

Another shrug. "Forgiveness is a virtue, so I hear."

Cait opened her mouth to respond, but she had to concede her friend was right. As usual.

"Fine," she whispered. "So how do you know her?"

Adler stepped toward her, raising an arm in invitation. "Let's head back to the cove, and I'll explain it all."

The cove.

Somehow the grief she'd anticipated didn't hit her until now. She'd been so distracted by all her questions, her frustrations, and her—as much as she hated to admit it—infatuation. Now, the memories stepped into the foreground and stole the oxygen from her lungs. Hazy images came of her parents cuddling beside a boulder, her brother laughing when the tide hit his legs, and her foolishly believing nothing would ever change.

The last time she'd been here was a month after her parents had died. She'd ventured here hoping it might help her feel closer to the family she'd lost, but all it had accomplished was ripping open the wounds she'd begun to stitch closed. She hadn't made it far onto the black sands of the beach before grief had weighed her body down, making it impossible to keep moving forward. Instead, she'd dropped to her knees in a fit of sobs.

And now she was back.

"I can't..." Cait began to protest, but she stopped herself, not wanting to break down in front of them.

"You can," Lucan said, resting a hand on her shoulder.

Catching Lucan's warm gaze, she took a deep breath. She wanted to believe he was right. She could do this. Without another word, she led the way back to the cove, hoping beyond hope that she could wear the mask she needed.

CHAPTER 10
ADLER

CAIT DIDN'T STOP WALKING until she stood just shy of the Aisling's tide. Taking a cue from Lucan, Adler stayed back, remaining beside the largest of the boulders and studying her. This woman—strong, courageous, stubborn beyond belief—seemed to be struggling to hold herself together. He didn't need to know what memory now pulled at the loose threads of her soul to understand the depths of the pain it caused.

He himself had been struggling to keep his own wounds from reopening since Lucy had dropped them off here.

This was where he had collected the black sand for her necklace. This was where he had stolen their first kiss. This was where they were to meet and start their life together. And he could picture Lani vividly, the sea breeze tossing her red curls about as though even the wind wanted to memorize every strand.

But Lani wasn't here.

Cait was.

He hadn't saved Lani.

But he could help Cait.

Lucan cleared his throat quietly before tossing his head in Cait's direction, nudging Adler to get going.

Something tightened in Adler's chest as he imagined her yelling at him for his lies and tricks.

You can handle it. Stop being a coward.

With each step forward, he dug deep for the words that could make this right, but every option seemed wrong, insensitive, or contrived. By the time he stood beside her and his shoulder brushed against hers, igniting a desire he wanted so badly to ignore, he still hadn't come up with anything to say.

"How did you know her?" Cait asked.

It took only a moment for him to realize she was referring to Lucy. "Foxhaven." His voice had no power behind it, none of the confidence it had held just moments before.

"I gathered that much," she said, keeping her gaze firmly on the water stretching out before them.

"All pirates know of Lucy's, even if they don't know her personally. It's one of the nicer establishments in that port. She's been a friend of mine for a few years."

Cait tensed beside him, her arms and her jaw tightening noticeably.

"I shouldn't have lied to you," he said, not sure how to explain in a way she would understand.

"So why did you?"

"You of all people should understand the importance of keeping certain associations secret."

"Aye, I do. But why her?"

Was she jealous? Cait didn't seem the type to be jealous.

"Why did I trust her and not you?" he asked for clarification, but she didn't respond. "For the same reason you trust Lucan more than me. I've known her longer. You've known him longer. It's nothing against you, just as I know your hesitancy to trust me is not personal."

Not the most eloquent way of putting it.

But it would have to do.

She gave no indication she believed him—or accepted his explanation.

Dropping her chin, she glanced at him from under her lashes, and he had to blink a few times to break the spell her emerald eyes tried to cast on him. "Why was she here?"

Breathing deeply, he ran a hand through his hair. "Honestly? I don't know."

That got her to fully face him, and her eyes narrowed, scrutinizing him.

She'll look at you like that from now on.

She will always wonder if you're lying.

Way to go.

"She wasn't lying when she said it was between her and your brother. She refused to explain her business to me, just as she refused to tell you. But, since she was here, I figured we could use her."

"So you told her of your—I mean Lucan's—plan, but not me?" Although Cait appeared mostly angry, she seemed a little hurt as well.

"We didn't want you to be implicated. We needed you to be authentically shocked by what was happ—"

She squared her shoulders. "You think I couldn't keep myself hidden?"

Lucan began to say something, but Adler tossed him a pleading glance. He could explain this to her himself. And while he appreciated Lucan's desire to help him out, he needed her to believe him, to trust him.

"We knew you could. We also knew how important this was to the rogues. We had to avoid any unnecessary risk. Couldn't take the chance that someone might notice you in the crowd. Everyone in Morshan knows you and Lucan. They know you two are close. As good an actress as you are, we couldn't—"

"Fine," she said, but the tension in her lips showed it was anything but. "So what was Lucy's role then? How is she helping? Where is she now?"

Adler couldn't quite understand Cait's vitriol toward the foreign woman. Sure, she'd tried to break into Cait's pub, but this reaction seemed out of proportion.

"She was the only person we knew with a boat and a willingness to help us. We couldn't take a risk on any of the pirates or merchants. And the good thing about Lucy...she doesn't push for answers she doesn't need. Once she brought us here, leaving us enough provisions to get us through the week, she headed for Helles island. She still intends to find your brother, but she can't come back to Morshan. Someone could have seen her helping me, and that wouldn't bode well for her."

Cait, turning back to the sea, rubbed at her temples. Did she believe him? Did she understand? He couldn't read her expression. All he could do was wait. And hope.

"Okay."

"Okay?"

"Aye," Cait said. "I trust you. Sands help me, I don't know why, but I do." She raised a hand between them as she spoke and held it there, her palm close enough to his chest that he couldn't help but wonder how it would feel to close the few inches between them, forcing her fingers against him.

No. No. No.

Clearing his throat, he shook away those altogether unhelpful thoughts. That wasn't what either of them wanted. She might have wanted it at some point, but surely not now, after his rejection.

"So what now?" she asked.

Adler gestured toward Lucan, who was scrounging through one of the packs Lucy had left with them. "He'll stay here. Lay low."

"And you?"

Was that hope in her voice? And why did he wish it was?

"I need to report back to the council. They'll need to know why I took him as I did."

Something flashed in Cait's eyes. Something he'd seen before.

In Lani's.

Fear.

Worry.

Concern.

He had stood right here on this beach with Lani, insisting *she* needed to return to the council hall. It was the last time he'd spoken to her, seen her. Now he was standing here with Cait, and the wound in his chest threatened to burst open.

Why did he keep finding himself in these parallel situations? Why did every moment with Cait have to feel similar to a moment shared with Lani? Was it some cruel joke? Was some force taunting him with his loss and his grief?

"What will you tell them?" Cait asked.

"The truth." She quirked a brow. "Well, mostly the truth—that I couldn't have anyone from town seeing me drag him off to the pit. That's all they need to know."

"Naeve stopped by the pub early this morning, said the council had their suspicions. Think they'll buy your story?"

Adler donned a smirk, hoping it looked more genuine than it felt. "I can be quite convincing, love."

Cait's fair skin flushed pink, but he forced himself to ignore it.

"You know," she said, "that's the first time you've called me *love* in a good ten minutes. That must be some kind of record."

Against his better judgment—and ignoring the screaming voice in his head—Adler stepped toward her. What did he expect to achieve here? What was he looking for with her?

He didn't know.

He didn't care.

He didn't stop.

Not until he stood close enough to feel her warmth. He searched her eyes. They shined like brilliant gemstones, tempting him to give in to the obvious attraction between them.

His gaze drifted to her mouth. A familiar, aching warmth swept through him when her tongue slipped between her lips, wetting them slowly. What would they feel like against his? Time stopped as he waged a war between his desire for her and his need to keep her at a distance.

"Hey, you two!" Lucan called from where he now sat on the sand gnawing on a piece of dried meat. "We don't have time for"—he waved a finger from one of them to the other— "that. At least not right now. Cait needs to get back to the pub before opening, and you need to get your ass to the council hall."

Cait retreated a couple of steps, letting loose a swear when the water splashed onto her boots.

"Right," she said. "There's still more to discuss though."

"Where then?" Adler asked.

Lucan raised his hand like a child, though he didn't wait for one of them to prompt him to speak. "The office."

Cait winced.

"Come off it, Cait," Lucan said. "You can trust him, and it's the most secure location we have."

Sighing and rolling her eyes, Cait gave in and pointed a finger toward her friend. "Tell him where to go. And, you," she said, turning to Adler. Her eyes narrowed, and he held his breath in anticipation. "Be careful. You're no good to us if you get exiled."

Before he could come up with any response beyond a mere nod, she was sliding past him, stepping out of the cove, and heading back to town.

CHAPTER 11
DECLAN

Declan seethed. His blood boiled in his veins. The darkness demanded to be free. It thrashed within, fighting against the chains he had secured around it, bucking and snarling like a feral beast.

But Aoife's gentle hand on his forearm was like an anchor, holding him back from venturing into those dangerous seas. Her fingers squeezed gently, but even still, he couldn't look at her. If she knew the monster he was she wouldn't still be here.

Tommy now stood quietly in the middle of Declan's cabin, waiting for him to make some decision. But what was the right choice here? They were already planning to confront Callum, but there was no way he could take Aoife to him.

"What will you do?" Aoife asked timidly as if she expected him to accept Callum's absurd terms and hand her over.

"We're going to Selka," he stated flatly.

Aoife's hand stilled, though she didn't pull away. He needed to think, needed to figure out some way to outsmart Callum, to get the blade from him without endangering Aoife.

"It's a trap," she said, and something within Declan snapped.

"Of course it's a trap!" he yelled, lifting his face to look at her.

This time, she did recoil, taking a full step away as if he'd struck her instead of simply raising his voice. Regret—his old, faithful companion—filled him. Taking a deep breath, he worked to soothe away his bitterness.

"I'm sorry. I didn't mean to—"

Aoife offered him a tight smile and approached him once more. Lifting her hands, she cupped his face, and he allowed himself to settle slightly into their warmth. He gazed into her eyes as he waited for her to speak, but nothing could have prepared him for what she said next.

"Declan, I love you." Her expression hardened. "I know you're stressed and angry—even if you do hide it well—but don't you *ever* yell at me again. Understand?"

Declan was trapped in her glare, and he couldn't move even when she rose up on her toes to touch her soft lips to his in a kiss that tasted like a warning. This wasn't the woman who had cowered from his intimidation weeks ago. He had fallen in love with that woman. And seeing her now, coming into her own, finding her voice and her strength? It only made his love burn hotter.

"Understand?" she repeated quietly.

"Aye, princess," he said.

Before he could say more, she slid her hands into his hair, curling her fingers against the back of his head. Everything around them fell away. Callum's threat. The dagger. All Declan's mistakes and failures.

Gone was the anger, the darkness, the need for revenge. In its place was only the blissful feeling of her hands in his hair and her waist within his arms. He no longer needed anything except her mouth on his, her body against him, and whatever else she would allow him.

Leaning into him, she released a sigh just before his lips met hers. A soft moan from her roused a different type of darkness inside him. And as she swept her tongue across his, his need for her became a throbbing ache pressing against her hips.

He shouldn't be thinking of this—of tearing away her clothes and ravaging her —when there was a monster to hunt down, and—

A low whistle floated toward them, pulling Declan's attention away from Aoife, who was shuddering against him. Her whimper of protest nearly had him forgetting all about the melody filling the air, until he caught sight of Tommy standing there, looking everywhere but at the two of them.

How had he forgotten Tommy was still here?

"What?" Declan asked as Aoife, who he'd left flushed and panting, attempted to hide behind his shoulder. "Did we make you uncomfortable?"

With no sign of embarrassment on his face, Tommy let out a short laugh. "You could say that. Plus, I doubt Aoife wants her first romp to have an audience."

Declan stole a glance at Aoife, whose blush deepened further. "We were a long ways from that kiss becoming a *romp*."

"Uh-huh," Tommy said. "And I'm a pirate lord."

Aoife stepped out from behind Declan, her complexion returning to normal. "Sorry, Tommy."

"No big deal. I nearly took a romp in Declan's bed while he was gone. So I guess we could call us even."

Declan flinched, his eyes going wide. "Wait, what?"

Tommy shrugged. "What? I told her I wouldn't do it in my captain's bed."

Looking from Tommy to Aoife and back again, Declan's forehead crinkled. He eyed them as a new doubt crept in.

Tommy's face contorted in confusion for only a moment, and then he shook his head wildly, waving his hand between himself and Aoife. "Not her and me. Seriously? You assumed I would—"

"Hey!" Aoife piped up. "You don't have to say it as if I'm some hideous swamp creature you would never even consider—"

"No offense, Aoife," Tommy said with a shrug. "You're not really my type."

Aoife gaped at him and then looked up to the ceiling before conceding. "I guess you're right. I'm no graceful, gorgeous, powerful fae..."

"Half-fae though," Tommy offered.

Declan, tracking the exchange with glances back and forth, wondered if they'd now both forgotten *he* was still in the room.

"Plus," Tommy added with a slight shudder, "you remind me of my sister."

"You have a sister?"

Declan took the opportunity to step in. "Aye, he has a sister. But the more important matter is exactly how many people slept in my bed while I was gone?"

Aoife and Tommy locked gazes as if they were having some silent conversation, which made Declan want to growl at them in frustration. How could two people he cared so much about be so irritating?

"Three, I think?" Aoife said it as a question, and Tommy confirmed her count.

"So, you"—Declan pointed to Aoife—"and Tommy. And..."

"Maura," Aoife offered.

"Right, right, of course," Declan said as he eyed his best friend. "And you never—"

"Nope."

"But she wanted to."

Tommy made some awkward movements with his hands, as if he wasn't quite sure how to respond. "I believe so. I mean, I did too. But like I said, I told her I wouldn't."

Declan released a sigh, but before the relief could settle in, Tommy was speaking again. "I figured the first person to get a tumble in this bed should be you. Not me. It's only fair."

At these words, Aoife perked up and eyed Declan with that curiosity he'd missed —though he didn't like it just now, when it was directed toward him in regard to such a topic.

"What?" he asked her.

She opened her mouth but then snapped it shut and shook her head. Perhaps that was for the better. His history with other women wasn't at the top of the list of things he wanted to discuss at the moment, especially not in present company. Though if she had asked—and if she chose to ask in the future—he wouldn't keep the truth from her. He'd bedded other women before, but he'd never shared his own bed with one.

Aoife would be the first.

When she was ready.

And she'd be the only one.

His body reacted involuntarily to those thoughts, and he had to refocus his attention on other, less intimate, matters to avoid the discomfort of not finding proper relief.

"Right." Declan clapped his hands together and nodded. "Back to work, shall we?"

Aoife cleared her throat as she straightened out her clothes, smoothing the front of her trousers and her shirt where it had bunched up against his chest. "I'll leave you two to strategize." Stepping toward Declan, she lifted herself up to plant an innocent kiss on his cheek before whispering a single word in his ear: "Tonight."

⚔

IT HAD TAKEN several minutes for Declan to clear away the scandalous images Aoife's final word had conjured in his mind. Tommy, thankfully, had only laughed once before a glare from Declan had shut him up. Now they sat in silence at Declan's desk, both leaning back in their seats, trying to think of some way to beat Callum and get the dagger.

Every now and then, one of them would start to say something, only to stop short before voicing the entire thought. Of all the scams they'd pulled and plays they'd run over the years, nothing they'd done seemed helpful in this scenario.

"It's too bad we don't have Halloran with us," Tommy muttered. "Maura said she used her history with Callum to distract the queen back at the sound."

"Except she's likely halfway to Larcsporough by now with your woman in tow," Declan said and immediately regretted it when Tommy cringed briefly. He tried to veer away from that subject as quickly as possible. "What do we have at our disposal?"

Tommy roughed a hand over his chin. "Not much that would help against a man with the Csintala dagger. We'd need to find a way to get the dagger from him, to render him vulnerable to our attack. Could Aoife help with—"

"No," Declan answered before the question was finished. "I won't have her going ashore or anywhere near him."

Tommy's brows lifted high. "She won't like being left behind."

"She didn't see what he did to the last person who helped me. She doesn't know what he's capable of."

"And she won't want to leave your side. You know that, right?" Declan started to protest, but Tommy stopped him with a shake of his head before continuing. "You didn't see what it did to her when you were taken. You don't know how your absence pained her."

"She pushed me away—"

"That was before. Before the kraken. Before Triss. Before she almost lost you for good."

Declan propped his elbow atop the desk and dropped his forehead into his hand. "And what if he takes her? What if he hurts her in order to hurt me? Or hurts her just for the fun of it? I'd never be able to forgive myself if she..."

He couldn't finish the thought, couldn't bear the notion of her being at the mercy of that vile pirate.

But his mind rebelled against his wishes, forcing him to envision Aoife's body being strung up, pulled along the keel, ripped apart for Callum's amusement. Declan wanted to retch, and he might have, had his fury not roared to life. Clenching his teeth, he squeezed his eyes shut, fighting both the horror he imagined and the rage that fed upon it.

Callum would never get the opportunity to hurt Aoife. Declan needed to be sure of that. He couldn't let him. Wouldn't let him.

He deserves to feel the pain Killian did.

The darkness whispered to him, pushing him toward his craving for retaliation. An eye for an eye. A keelhauling for a keelhauling. A swift death was too good for Callum. He needed to suffer, to bleed, to writhe in anguish.

And Declan wanted to make that happen.

"I know that look on your face," Tommy said softly, as though his voice itself was tiptoeing toward Declan. "You don't want to become that again."

Declan slammed his fist onto the desk. His eyes flashed open and locked onto Tommy's. But his friend didn't so much as flinch. "Don't I?" Declan challenged him as the rage burned through him.

"A moment ago you were madly in love, ready to take your woman to bed, forgetting I was in the room. And now you're willing to risk all of that—her love, your future, your happiness—to make a man bleed."

Declan squeezed his fists tighter as he forced the words out through his teeth, hissing in a slow, menacing whisper, "It's what he deserves."

Still, Tommy didn't budge, didn't back away. He inched closer until he was leaning over the desk. "And you're okay with Aoife seeing you like this? Seeing this part of you?"

Declan grimaced. That was the other reason he wanted her to remain on the ship when they docked. To save her from witnessing this side of him.

"If she loves me..." he said in a low voice, his rage replaced with sadness. "It's part of who I am, Tommy. If she can't love all of me, then—"

"Then what? You'll push her away? Like everyone else? You'll resign yourself to being miserable and alone with only the darkness to keep you company?"

Declan had no answer for his friend.

The two things he wanted—to have Aoife by his side and to make Callum pay in blood and screams—couldn't coexist. He couldn't have both. He would need to choose.

Love or revenge.

Aoife or the darkness.

No. He refused to choose. He would find a way to have both, to have it all.

CHAPTER 12
AOIFE

Why had Aoife said that to him? Well, she knew why, but as she stepped out of the cabin into the afternoon sun, she felt the weight of the word, felt it strip her bare, and all the confidence she'd had in there melted away.

What would she do tonight? Did she even know?

Looking around the ship, Aoife realized she had no idea what she should occupy herself with while the men were engrossed in planning. A thump came from within the cabin, and Declan raised his voice. No, Aoife was confident she would rather be out here on deck right now.

It wasn't that she was afraid of Declan. She'd been the one upset that he wasn't angrier, but when he'd turned that anger toward her, some new strength had taken root inside of her. Where it had come from, she didn't know, but she was glad for two things: that she'd been able to set the boundary she needed and that Declan loved her enough to honor it.

And now she would honor their privacy.

Stepping away from the door, Aoife searched for something to do on this blasted ship. Something that wouldn't remind her of all they'd lost.

But every inch of this ship held a memory.

She currently stood in the spot where Collins had mercilessly run her through training drills. And the spot to her right—where the railing had been haphazardly patched up—was where the kraken had dropped his body back on the deck after she'd failed to keep the monster from pulling him into the sea.

Collins.

At the thought of his name and the memory of his kindness, tears welled up, filling her eyes against her will. She'd barely known him. Hadn't spent enough time with him to become as close as she was to Tommy or even Gavin.

At the thought of the helmsman, she swung around and focused her attention on where he leaned against the quarterdeck railing beside the helm. His back was to her as he stared out behind the ship. They hadn't spoken at all since they'd returned from the sound.

Losing Collins had been hard on everyone, but it seemed to have affected Gavin almost as much as it had Declan. Why, she didn't know. He and Collins had never seemed all that close, but pirates were a mysterious lot.

Maybe he just needs a friend.

Aoife climbed the steps and approached Gavin. He didn't look at her when she settled against the railing beside him, didn't acknowledge her at all when she cleared her throat expectantly.

As she eyed him from the side, a sadness pricked her heart at what had replaced his usual lightheartedness. Not sadness or misery or mourning. Either of those would have been better than the sheer emptiness she observed now.

Gavin had treated her differently ever since the kraken's blood hadn't harmed her, but he hadn't refused to even look at her or speak to her until now. Perhaps it was best that she had nothing to say to him. Any words from her would likely be ill-received.

Aoife wrestled with whether to walk away or to stay beside him in silence. Would either be helpful? She missed her friend, missed his teasing and their shared laughter. Did he blame her for Collins's death? Did he hate her for what she was?

Maybe it has nothing to do with you, Aoife, she thought.

"I miss you." The words floated on a whisper before she could rein them back in, and she held her breath, waiting to see how he would react.

But he didn't. He merely stood there, staring across the still sea at the horizon. She waited, counting to ten before choosing to let him be.

As she pushed herself away from the railing and turned back toward the stairs, his voice—quiet and gruff—stopped her retreat.

"It's not you, Aoife."

Slowly, she turned back to him. "What is it then?"

"It's complicated."

As she studied his face, Aoife was sure to keep her distance, not wanting to encroach any more than she already had. "Do you want to talk about it?"

"I talked to Tommy earlier." His eyes shifted to hers briefly before he resumed staring straight ahead.

"I'm glad you have him," she offered, not sure if this was the appropriate thing to say or not. Why had she been able to talk to Declan so easily just moments ago? Now she was here bumbling in all her awkwardness.

But Gavin didn't seem to notice. "Aye. Me too."

"For what it's worth," Aoife started, second-guessing her next words but unable to pull them back now, "I am sorry. For everything."

He cocked his head and peered at her, his eyes swirling with confusion. "What exactly do you have to be sorry for?"

"Seriously?" she asked, truly baffled by his question. He offered an almost imperceptible nod. "Where to begin? For getting my sister killed...for trespassing on your ship...for not listening to Declan...ever. For getting Collins injured...and then killed, and for disrupting all your lives and ruining your friendships—"

"Stop."

Aoife released a sigh of relief when he put a halt to her emotional rambling, which had left her heart pounding. She mumbled a breathless apology.

"I wasn't lying to you when we spoke before, Aoife. You make the captain happy, and we are thankful for that."

"Even if you can't look at him right now?"

Gavin ignored the question. "No one regrets you being here. Not when it has been the best thing to ever happen to him. Have unfortunate things happened? Aye. You'll find that misfortune is the norm in the pirate life. You get used to it. You have to."

"You don't seem used to it though, Gavin."

His eyes closed as he dipped his chin in a slow nod. "Aye, I know." When he opened his eyes to look at her, the emptiness had given way to the sadness she'd been expecting to see in them. "This time I'm a bit more shaken up than usual. But it will be okay."

Before Aoife could respond, the sound of someone bounding up the stairs had them both turning to see who approached. Tommy pointed a finger at Aoife quickly before swinging his hand toward the deck below.

"Declan's asking for you."

Tossing a quick smile over her shoulder at Gavin, she took her leave, hoping her friend would be okay. Death wasn't the only way to lose a friend, and she didn't want to lose him to his grief.

WITHOUT KNOCKING, Aoife stepped into Declan's cabin to find him seated at his desk, elbows digging into its surface, hands cradling his forehead. He looked so worn out, so troubled. And just like with Gavin, she had no idea how to help. What did he need right now? When she shut the door behind her, he raised his head to look at her. A small smile pulled at his lips, though it seemed forced, flat, carrying none of the love and affection he'd shown her earlier.

"Tommy said you wanted to see me?"

He waved her closer, pushing his chair away from the desk and leaning back. Walking with caution, she contemplated what he might be about to say to her. Then she lowered herself—without invitation—to sit in his lap, kicking her legs up over his. For a moment, fear paralyzed her. Perhaps this wasn't the way she should be acting, but all anxiety melted away when he planted a kiss on her temple and lingered there for a full, deep breath.

"Aye," he whispered as he pulled back. Guiding her hair away from her face and tucking it behind her ear, he watched her intently, like he was wanting to memorize every freckle and curve of her face. "I have something to ask you, but I'm not sure how you'll react."

Aoife tensed but then quirked a brow and smirked. "Well, that's a good way to set me on edge from the start."

He didn't laugh.

He didn't even crack a smile.

Running his hand along her thigh, he dropped his gaze to her lap. Whatever he was about to say was not good, but surely this couldn't be any worse than his previous confessions?

"What is it, Declan? Afraid I'll scold you again?"

This did earn her a small chuckle and a twitch of his lips. "More afraid you won't listen." He lifted his face to her, his blue-grays full of adoration and wariness. "You're not very good at listening, you know."

She rolled her eyes. "Well, I promise nothing. Especially if your request is stupid."

"Fair enough," he whispered, his eyes lowering back to where his hand continued to caress her leg in slow, gentle strokes. "If I asked you to stay on the ship when we dock, would you?"

His legs tensed beneath her. Or maybe it was her own body that had stiffened. She should have expected this, and yet something in her panicked.

"Why?" Her voice had lost all confidence, replaced now with fear and dismay.

"I can't risk losing you again, Aoife. And Callum..." He didn't look at her.

"I'm not some wilting flower you need to keep locked away. And I can help. I can—"

"You haven't had adequate time to practice, to hone your skills."

Aoife straightened, sitting taller. "I wasn't talking about my...powers. I'm not being left behind like a child. I've fought a kraken and—"

"You don't know what he can do," Declan said, and Aoife noted how his voice shook with each syllable he uttered.

Aoife threw a hand out to the side. "Haven't we just seen...?"

But Declan cringed and pulled his lips together tightly as he slammed his eyes shut. His jaw pulsed. A twinge of regret hit Aoife at his reaction, but the thought of being locked in this cabin, abandoned and untrusted, left to wonder and worry the entire time they were gone...?

No. She wouldn't do it. She couldn't. He had to understand.

With his head still lowered and his fingers working against his forehead, he opened his eyes to peer at her before saying, "No, Aoife. You haven't."

There was an eerie calm to his tone that reminded her all too much of the way the waters had stilled right after they'd escaped the whirlpool, right before the kraken had emerged to finish them off.

You've seen your share of pain, but he's witnessed far worse.

The keelhauling.

Aoife swallowed hard and took his hand in hers, running her thumb across the back of his hand. She hoped he knew how much she cared for him and how she couldn't bear to see him hurt like this.

"Who did he—"

Before she could finish the question, though, he yanked his hand back and stood, forcing her off his lap as he did. He retreated to his sleeping quarters but paused in the doorway. His head fell, his shoulders rising and falling with rapid breaths. His hand, hanging at his side, was shaking.

Aoife rushed to him and slowly circled to face him, touching his arm lightly.

"Breathe," she told him. "Slow it down."

He did as instructed, and his lips silently mouthed something as his breathing became more controlled.

"Deeper, Declan." His breaths, though steadier, were still too shallow. When his shoulders shook, she worried he was crying, but then his mouth pulled back into a half-hearted smirk, and he looked up.

"There are the two words I hope to hear later, princess," he said, arching a brow.

She should have expected that, but she'd been so focused on helping him. With a groan, she shook her head and offered him a coy shrug.

"We'll see, *Captain.*"

"Tonight," he whispered. It wasn't a question but a reminder of the promise she'd made to him earlier. Her body responded, a spark of warmth in her core bursting to life.

Declan leaned forward and rested his forehead against hers, wrapping her up in his now-steady arms, no sign of his panic remaining.

She took a steadying breath. "Take me with you. Please." Her words were uneven, though she wasn't sure how much of it was from her fear and how much was from her body's demand to have him closer. "I can't be left behind. I'm scared to be—"

When he lifted his fingers to her chin, her breathing stopped and her heartbeat quickened. His eyes flicked down to her lips and lingered there for what felt like an eternity before looking up to meet her gaze. Confidence, care, warmth, love, passion. She saw them all in those stormy grays, and she knew—somehow she knew—he understood. He saw her, knew her, loved her, and understood her.

Aoife moved first, lifting herself up onto her toes, capturing his mouth with hers. Time plodded on. The world—and its problems—remained. But here, with him, she was reminded of the truth she needed to hold onto.

She belonged here. Beside him.

This was home.

CHAPTER 13
DECLAN

That promise was repeated with every move of Aoife's body against him. But every part of him screamed at him to demand it now, not later.

Until her kisses changed.It was subtle. So slight that, if he wasn't so attuned to how she moved and felt and tasted, he wouldn't have noticed it. At first, she'd been driven by passion, her kisses gentle yet demanding, but now her fingers gripped his neck and shoulders with an intensity that felt more like fear.

Don't leave me.

As much as he wanted to believe that her new aggressiveness was driven by her craving for him, he couldn't shake the concern that there was more at play. Was she so scared of losing him that she'd rush into his bed? He wouldn't let her. He wouldn't take advantage of her fear—or his own—to soothe this ache.

Moving his hands up to cup her sweet face, he pulled his lips reluctantly from hers and whispered, "I love you."

"And I you," she said and moved to resume consuming him. But he stopped her, placing his hands on her shoulders, hoping his refusal wouldn't sting or confuse her.

"We have time for all of this," he said, "and then some."

Thankfully, she didn't shrink back or pull away, and no sign of hurt washed over her face. Instead she wrapped her arms around his waist and laid her head against his chest with a sweet sigh.

But as he held her, his cheek resting atop her head, the darkness continued its beckoning, preying upon his fear of losing her.

He had finally let himself have something good in his life, and no one would take it from him. Squeezing her tighter to him, he made a silent vow.

Callum would not hurt her.
Or anyone else.
Declan would stop him for good.
And he'd make it hurt.

CHAPTER 14
MAURA

Maura needed to lie better this time. She hadn't been able to fool Katyra, and the mage couldn't even read minds. Trying to lie to Renna would be even more of a challenge.

But she had an idea.

It just might work.

Sliding open the door to their temporary cabin, Maura drew in a breath before stepping inside. Her sisters sat at a small table below the window, neither of them speaking. They looked much like they had during their years of confinement. Her sisters had always seemed far more comfortable spending their hours and days in silence than Maura ever had.

Her skin itched to leave this room and this ship, to jump—

She stopped that thought before it could materialize completely, instead focusing on the story she needed to sell. In her mind, she pulled forward images— her and her sisters arriving in Larcsporough, them completing whatever it was the fae needed from them, her being reunited with Tommy.

She cleared her throat as she crossed the room. With her chin held high, she scowled down at her eldest sister.

"Fine." She dropped the word at Renna's feet.

Her sisters both turned their eyes toward her, but Renna's were narrowed, skeptical.

"You've changed your mind," she said.

Bria's face shifted in surprise, but Maura ignored it as she nodded.

Renna now stood. "You have some conditions. Let's hear them."

Maura, pursing her lips tightly, said, "I'll spare one month for those in Larcsporough. No more. And then you will let me go back to Tommy to live my life as I please."

Cocking her head to the side, Renna considered this for less than a minute before responding. "Agreed."

Maura took a deliberate step forward. "One. Month."

As soon as Renna offered the slightest movement of her chin in agreement, Maura turned to storm out of the room.

Had she stayed and joined them, her sister would have seen through her ruse. But now, believing Maura was reluctantly cooperating, she would have no reason to suspect any trickery.

⚜

THE DAY HAD DRAGGED on painfully slowly. The ship—despite being larger than Tommy's—had become her new prison. With nowhere to go and no one she wanted to talk to, Maura spent hours at the prow, listening to the sea spray into the air as the ship cut through the water. In her veins, her magic itched to be used, but she refused to do any more than cast the smallest of glamours, shifting the wooden deck beside her until it shone the same amber color as his eyes.

But every time she did, the sight of the pool of deep gold cut too deep, reopening the wound Renna had created when she'd stolen Maura away.

You should have been stronger.

She had repeated that thought to herself so many times since she'd awoken despite knowing that she'd been targeted when she was at her weakest, all of her defenses crushed to fine dust by the weight of her passion for Tommy.

Did he trust her?

Did he suspect the truth?

Or did he believe what everyone else surely did?

That she had lied to him, used him, abandoned him.

What would she believe in his place? It was a pointless question to ask, because as a fae, she was created to form bonds stronger than any human could fathom. Even if their places had been swapped, she would have felt the same as she did now.

There was no one else but Tommy.

And there never would be.

No, she would not doubt him.

She would not let fear steal him from her.

He trusted her. He loved her.

He would find her.

When the sun dipped into the sea, its light swallowed up by the Aisling, Maura finally stood. If Halloran's estimates were correct, they were a little more than a day away from Helles Island. Hopefully the tincture Katyra had given her would last long enough to keep Renna out until well after Maura was off the ship.

And if it didn't?

She would think of something. She would beg a siren to carry her away if she needed to.

Maura made a stop at the galley, where the cook—a middle-aged woman whose skin was marred with scars—had prepared two cups of tea. A special request Captain Halloran herself had made on Maura's behalf. Once the cook's back was turned, Maura slipped the vial out from her bodice, opened it, and poured the liquid, splitting it evenly between both cups.

Bria might not be a danger, but Maura couldn't take the chance that Renna would drink from the wrong cup. Plus, with both sisters unconscious, she would have an easier time of slipping off this blasted ship.

Balancing both cups in one hand, she opened the door of their cabin carefully. Bria and Renna stood in the middle of the room speaking quietly about the possible circumstances they might find in Larcsporough.

"Oh good, you're still awake," Maura said, inserting a bit of disdain and annoyance into her tone. "If you weren't, I would have carried these all the way from the galley for nothing."

"And what is this?" Renna said, reaching out for a cup. She stared into it with suspicion, and Maura took a deep breath to keep her panic at bay.

"What does it look like?" She rolled her eyes and handed the other cup to Bria, who held it gingerly, eyeing Renna as if seeking permission to take a sip.

Bria would get no sympathy from Maura.

"But why?" Renna looked as though she were about to pour it onto the ground, and it took all of Maura's resolve not to leap forward to stop her.

She sighed and rolled her eyes again. "Call it a peace offering? None of us have gotten much sleep of late—"

"For different reasons," Bria muttered, and Maura almost laughed.

"So it's to help us sleep?" Renna raised a brow and glared at Maura.

Maura didn't back down. "If you don't want it, give it back."

"And where's yours?"

"Seriously, Renna? I couldn't very well carry three full cups on a rocking ship, could I? I drank mine in the galley." But Renna's skepticism held firm, and she scrutinized Maura, searching for any hint of deceit. Maura threw her hands up. "Shall I fetch the cook for you? Do you need her to corroborate my story? Or will you have some faith in your sister and take her at her damn word?"

Maura gritted her teeth, daring Renna to push her further. She couldn't risk Renna actually going to the cook, and the best way to prevent that was to stand her ground.

They glowered at each other for so long that Maura was sure she had failed and would need to prepare for a long swim with a siren, but finally, Renna lifted the cup to her lips.

"Sleep would be nice," she said. "Thanks, sister."

Bria followed suit—mimicking Renna as she always seemed to do.

In order to keep their suspicions at bay, Maura moved about the room, preparing her own bedding for the night and letting her hair down. With concerted effort, she refrained from watching her sisters as they carried their cups to the table and settled into their chairs.

Katyra had said the herbs acted within minutes on humans, but those with magic flowing through their veins had a natural defense against the sedative. That was why she'd supplied Maura with so much. It would ensure they slept as long as possible—without killing them, of course—but even then, Katyra hadn't been able to provide a reliable estimate as to how quickly it would work.

So Maura would wait patiently. Staring at them, monitoring them for any effect, would certainly resurrect Renna's suspicion, so instead she settled herself into her blankets and whispered a good night to her sisters.

Hopefully when she woke to the morning sun, her sisters would not.

CHAPTER 15
CAIT

VISITING the cove had been harder on Cait than she'd anticipated. She needed some time to think before she headed back home, so she wandered down to the docks.

Most of the slips were empty. No doubt many of the merchants and visitors had hastily sailed away once news of the killing had spread. But this did allow Cait the opportunity to make her way down one of the docks unimpeded. There, she settled down onto the planks and dangled her feet out over the water that lapped against the thick posts.

Where are you, Declan?

She had asked herself this time and time again since sending him off in search of the dagger. She half-expected his sails to appear on the horizon at this very moment, as if her thoughts alone could summon him to these shores. But it remained undisturbed.

Sucking in the briny air, Cait tried to clear her thoughts so she could make sense of everything happening. What was their next play? What was the next task?

Focus on the next task.

Her parents' favorite saying. Those words had kept her moving forward after Declan had left. She couldn't afford to chase him down. All she could do was focus on the next step, the next task.

What was the next step now? Go back to the pub? Twiddle her thumbs while waiting for Adler to return? There had to be something she could do in the meantime.

Something splashed at the surface of the water, startling her from her thoughts. Just a fish, probably. But then it happened again. Closer. And this time she caught a glimpse of what looked like gossamer fins.

What is that?

As if in answer, an entire wispy tail breached the surface slowly before slipping back into the sea.

A siren?

If the sirens were here, if they were back—and if the legends were true—that meant the siren queen had been defeated. But Cait tamped down her hope that this meant the dagger had been retrieved. No reason to get ahead of herself.

She waited, counting her breaths, wondering if her presence here had scared the siren off.

But then movement to the left caught her eye, and Cait leaned over to find a pair of silver eyes staring up at her with curiosity. The siren's blonde waves clung to her forehead and floated on the surface of the water.

"Is this Morshan?" the siren asked in a haunting song-like voice.

Cait swallowed hard and nodded.

The siren's eyes lit up, and her pale lips turned up into a smile Cait hoped was friendly. "I'm looking for someone."

"And who might that be?" Cait asked.

"McCallagh."

Cait's heart stilled, either from hope or fear—or maybe both. She narrowed her eyes suspiciously. "Why?"

"Do you know where I can find her, lass?" the siren asked, her smile unfaltering.

"Perhaps," Cait said. "Who sent you?"

"A certain pirate captain of the same name."

Declan.

He was alive.

But could the siren be trusted? Declan wasn't exactly unknown on these seas. Anyone could have told the creature to drop his name to get information.

"I can get the message to her, if you like," Cait offered.

The siren's smile dissolved, and her eyes turned to ice. "That won't do. Captain McCallagh gave me strict orders to get this to none other than his sister. And unless you are she—and if you insist on remaining so unhelpful—then our business here is done."

Cait bit the inside of her lip and stared back at the creature. What harm was there in admitting her identity? Or she could deny it and let the siren come ashore and find her at the pub later. But was that altogether safe? Their curse might have been lifted, but did that mean the sirens were now harmless? Cait wasn't so sure, and she wasn't about to risk her friends' lives—and the lives of everyone in Morshan—when she could just as easily take the message here.

"Must be your lucky day," Cait finally said just as the siren started to retreat beneath the water. "You've found his sister."

The siren's unnerving smile returned, her eyes lighting up.

"Ah, I suspected as much. You look so much like him."

Cait raised a brow. "Yes, yes, so I've heard. Now what word does he send?"

"So inpatient. Just like the captain," the siren sang. "The dagger has left the sound, but it is not his yet. He is chasing it down—"

"Who has it?" Cait asked.

"A pirate named Callum."

Damn it, Declan.

Cait would have smacked her brother if he were here.

Running a hand over her mouth, she let a curse fall past her fingers. "And do you happen to know where the bastard took it?"

The siren shrugged her shoulders. "All I know is they're heading east."

East could mean they were going to Turvala or any number of the islands that peppered the sea along its coast. But even if Declan retrieved the dagger soon, it would take him several days to make it back here. Barely enough time for him to get it to her before the king was set to arrive.

The king.

Cait snapped her attention back to the siren. "Any word on a royal fleet heading this way, by chance?"

The siren lifted a clawed hand to her lips, her brow creasing in thought. "Not that I could see from the currents I traveled on far below. But my message is delivered, and I must go."

Before Cait could even utter a word of gratitude, the siren slipped beneath the surface and disappeared.

✕

CAIT PONDERED the situation for the entire walk back to the pub. Even though she was glad to have received word from Declan, she couldn't shake the uneasiness that had settled in her bones with Willow's death. She imagined eyes watching her from every shadow. At every alley she passed, she braced herself for someone to grab her. With every pair of pirates she came across, she expected to be stopped and questioned.

Something moved to her right in the alley up ahead. She told herself it was nothing—just her imagination. But even still, she tensed as she continued walking. Passing by the alley, she risked a sidelong glance and found nothing but stacks of crates and a number of waste bins.

You're being paranoid. No one is waiting for you.

But there's nothing wrong with being prepared.

Turning the corner, she made her way onto the familiar street of home, and her breathing calmed when the pub's sign came into view. She had made it ten paces when a chill crept over her arms and footsteps sounded behind her.

It's nothing. Other people can walk down the street in the middle of the day too. You're just jumpy.

Halfway down the street, she crossed over the cobblestones and headed toward the pub.

The footsteps followed.

She tried to catch a glimpse of her pursuer in the shop windows as she passed, but whoever it was remained too far back for her to see them reflected in the glass. Should she go to the pub or keep walking? Maybe she should lead them about town, meander through the streets to see how long they trailed after her.

Cait approached the pub's entrance but slowed only enough to look quickly inside. She could just make out Kira's shape behind the bar. Passing by the door, she listened for her pursuer's footsteps. They didn't slow. Didn't stop.

Her heart raced as she turned the corner and ran, hoping she could make it to the alley behind the building before the person caught up to her. She couldn't risk looking back, so she tried to focus only on pushing her feet as fast as her pounding heart.

Ducking into the alley, Cait skirted around a short pile of crates and lowered herself to the ground. If they followed, they'd find her easily enough, but there was no way she could make it to the pub's back door from here before they caught up. As she waited, she stilled her breath as best she could. In the silence, memories of happier times flooded in, of her and Declan playing among the crates in the pub.

"Seriously, Cait?" a woman's voice called into the alley, and then Cait was looking up into the face of Eva. Her friend. A Rogue.

Eva gave her a curious look and offered her hand. "Don't tell me I scared you."

Accepting the help up, Cait looked back toward the street. "Okay, I won't."

"I guess we all have reason to be a little jumpy," Eva said, already heading for the pub door. She glanced over her shoulder quickly. "You coming?"

Cait caught up to her friend and asked in a low voice "So you saw?"

Eva held the door open for Cait and followed her in. "No, but I heard. My brother was there though. He was the one to find her, actually."

"Welcome back," Kira said from behind the bar as they stepped into the pub's main room. She pulled a bottle of rum from Cait's personal stash and poured a glass before offering the bottle to Eva. The woman declined with a wave of her hands.

Cait sighed into the glass.

Kira gave her a half-smile. "Go well then, did it?"

A shrug was the only answer Cait could manage before downing the drink in one gulp. This rum was too expensive, too rare to be consumed so quickly, but Cait didn't care. She held the glass in front of her, letting it hover over the bar as Kira filled it again.

Swirling the deep-amber liquid around in the glass, Cait let her gaze soften as her mind wandered back to the cove.

I never should have insisted those men be friends.

Maybe if they still hated each other, they wouldn't have concocted such a ridiculously stupid stunt. But then Cait remembered who she was talking about. Lucan would have done the same shit even if he loathed his accomplice. Necessity of the times, she supposed. Sometimes you had to work with the people you least expected to.

Like Penny.

What had happened to the woman after the town meeting? Cait had completely forgotten to check in on her, but honestly, when did she have time to do everything she should? All her time these days was spent keeping up appearances, throwing the council off her trail, running a damned rebellion, and stopping her best friend from being a complete idiot.

You failed there.

"You find him though?" Kira's question snapped Cait's attention to her.

"Yeah, I found them."

"So they're together."

Cait nodded.

Eva must have looked confused, because Kira whispered the men's names while Cait finished her drink.

How much could Cait tell them? Knowing there could be someone in her organization possibly working for the council—someone who had been giving the names of Rogues to those women—had her on edge, and she wanted to keep everything close but also desperately needed someone to help shoulder it all.

Eva stepped closer to the bar. "So things are growing more complicated."

"Aye," Kira said with a sharp laugh. "You could say that. The new ordinances will make it that much harder to move about."

"Not only that," Eva continued. "The rumors are true; King Kilmeran and his fleet are on their way to Morshan. They'll arrive within the week."

Cait looked to the ceiling and shook her head in frustration. "He's early. And Declan doesn't have the dagger yet."

"How do you know that?" Kira asked.

"Had a little visit from a siren down at the docks." Kira's eyes went wide. "Aye. A siren. Declan's chasing after the dagger now, but with Kilmeran on his way, I doubt he'll make it here in time even if he gets it."

Without being told, Kira reached across the bar to pour more rum into Cait's glass. Even as Cait gave silent thanks for such a friend, doubt whispered in the corner of her mind, speculating that the woman had some ulterior motive, some need to keep Cait's head from being too clear.

She'd just take a sip then, nurse this glass a bit. Just in case.

The back door opened. Kira and Cait shared a concerned look, but Eva scoffed at them.

"Settle down. It's just my brother."

Aron stepped into the room, raising his chin in a silent greeting.

"Well," Kira offered, "at least we have some good news. The dagger is within reach. Lucan..."

Aron's eyes lit up. "Lucan? He's okay?"

Kira nodded, tossing her head toward Cait, who confirmed it with a nod of her own.

Eva slapped Aron on the chest with the back of her hand. "Told you he would be, didn't I? So where is he, Cait?"

As she considered how to answer, Cait eyed the twins. The rum was quickly dulling the edges of her mind, making it difficult to assess the situation. Was Eva the traitor? Or Aron? Kira? Maybe all three of them were plotting against her, and she was here giving up all the information she had. She swallowed, steeling herself.

"He's safe. That's all you need to know. Better for him—for all of us—if as few people know his whereabouts as possible." She looked from one Rogue to the other, waiting for any reaction that felt off.

But the three merely offered her curt nods and mumbled words of understanding.

"So now what?" Eva asked. "What do you need us to do?"

Aron reached into his pocket and pulled out a worn pocket watch. "I actually need to be somewhere right now. Just stopped in to make sure everyone was okay."

Before Cait could inquire about his mysterious plans, he turned on his heel and strode back out into the alley.

"That was odd," Kira said, still staring after him.

"What was that about?" Cait asked.

Eva shook her head. "Sands if I know. We aren't completely tied at the hip, you know. We do have our own lives." The woman offered a friendly smile, but Cait had an odd feeling it was forced, like her friend was trying to deceive her.

You're being paranoid.

I'm being careful.

You're also arguing with yourself.

"What about Adler?" Kira leaned her forearms on the bar. "What are his plans exactly?"

Cait nearly laughed, but the rum and the gravity of the situation doused all her humor. "He's reporting to the council."

"Alone?"

"As far as I know."

"And you're letting him?" Eva asked. Something gleamed in her eyes. Distrust, perhaps? Disgust, certainly. Eva had never warmed up to the former pirate, and it didn't appear that his recent actions had earned him any favor with her.

"Why wouldn't I? He's a big boy." Cait ignored how here mind teased her with the memory of lying in his lap, of being wrapped in his arms in those woods...

Stop it!

"They can't be trusted. You know that," Eva said. And Cait wasn't sure if she was referring only to the councilwomen or if Adler was included in the statement.

"What would you have me do? Follow him? I'm sure that would go over well. Showing up unannounced at the council hall. Wouldn't put unnecessary attention on me at all."

Eva frowned at her, annoyance burning in her eyes. "You could follow him without going inside. Make sure he's actually doing what he claimed he would?"

Kira shook her head slowly. "No, I don't like it. There's nothing to gain from putting yourself at such a risk."

"What risk?" Eva challenged.

"Oh, I don't know. Getting caught. Getting exiled. Getting turned in to the council by this man she knows nothing about."

Cait bristled at the last line. Even knowing Kira was being protective of her, Cait couldn't stop herself from growing defensive. But she forced herself to take a calming breath before responding. Yelling at her friend wasn't the answer. At least not here.

"I wouldn't say I know nothing about him."

Kira huffed, throwing her hands up in the air. "Fine. You know a little about him. I just don't think there's much to gain from running after him. You have plans to meet up afterward, I assume?" Cait nodded. "So, stick to the plan."

Eva mumbled something Cait couldn't quite make out before asking, "What do you need from me? How can I help?"

Cait chewed on her thumbnail as she pondered the questions. Kira had a good point. Many good points actually. But something niggled at the back of her mind. How much did she really know about Adler? Her gut pushed her to trust him, but maybe she was relying too much on instinct. She could follow him. Make sure he was doing what he claimed. See if anything seemed off.

And help him if he gets himself into trouble.

Straightening and pushing away from the bar, Cait downed the last bit of rum from her glass before handing it back to Kira. "Eva, I need you here. With Kira. I'll be back later." Before either of them could question her further or protest her decision, she was stomping out the front door of her pub.

⚔

THIS WAS A TERRIBLE IDEA.

Cait knew it as soon as the council hall came into view through the dense trees. She'd bypassed the road and the walking paths, deciding to slog through the thick undergrowth and crowded trees instead. Her head was swimming in drink. With how long it had taken her to traverse the forest, Adler had likely already arrived and gone inside.

She had just begun to contemplate turning around and heading back to the pub when something moved to her right. She inched slowly forward to the edge of the shade of the trees to see who was approaching.

And then she stilled.

There, stepping out from the trees, was Adler. He entered the lawn that surrounded the impressive building. But there was no trail in that part of the forest —as far as she knew, anyway. Had he also taken the scenic route? And if so, why?

Something in her gut pinched with uncertainty as she watched.

But he didn't head toward the main entrance. Instead he went from tree to tree, moving away from where Cait hid, staying close to each trunk as if trying to avoid being seen. Before Cait could contemplate his actions further, he was turning toward the side of the building, but he wasn't going toward any door Cait could see.

He stepped between two large bushes, and he was gone.

There was an entrance there. Hidden. Secret.

Panic rose in her throat, cutting off her air.

How did he know of it? Why wasn't he going through the main entrance like official visitors were supposed to? Was he working for them? Had he used her? Used Lucan?

Before she could think better of it, Cait was bounding out of the trees, crossing the lawn, and slipping between the same bushes. She nearly fell down a narrow flight of stone stairs that led to a basement door, hidden in the shadows of the bushes looming overhead.

This is a bad idea.

She ignored her mind's warning and pushed the door open in time to see Adler slip around a corner.

Cait needed to know the truth, needed to know if he was truly on her side or not. Her stomach twisted itself into knots at the thought that she might have let herself be deceived.

With quiet footsteps, Cait crept down the hallway, keeping her eyes fixed on the corner where she had seen Adler turn. She moved to follow, but as soon as she pivoted, a strong hand covered her mouth as someone grabbed her shoulder and pressed her against the stone wall.

Adler's blue eyes blazed as he stared down at her, but it wasn't anger she saw in them. It was worry. Maybe even fear.

"What are you doing here?" he hissed quietly, his face close enough to hers that his warmth enveloped her and made it hard to concentrate.

She glared at him in challenge. How did the man expect her to answer with his hand over her mouth?

She could barely think straight when his fingers trailed lightly across her lips and brushed her jaw as he retreated to let her answer. Swallowing hard, she blinked rapidly. She needed to collect her thoughts and forget about the feel of his skin on hers.

But what was she doing here?

Even if she'd had an explanation, the intensity of his eyes on her, the beating of his heart against her chest, and the bite of his grip at her shoulder held her in place, unable to speak.

"Well, love?" he whispered, and that word on his breath sent unwanted tingles down her spine that wove their way between her legs. She bit down hard on the inside of her lip.

What is wrong with you?

She wasn't here to seduce him. She was here to...here to what, exactly? Her mind went blank, her heart raced, and her panic increased.

"I see," he said quietly, his fingers releasing her as he stepped away. He cocked an eyebrow at her. "Couldn't wait a few hours to see me again? Needed me so badly you'd risk life and limb and your life's work to be near me?"

Sands this man was infuriating.

More so because part of her knew he was right. And she hated that.

Hated how he made her feel without even doing anything. Hated how her body reacted to his presence, his stare, his scent, his everything. She didn't have time for this, and he didn't want her anyway. He had demonstrated that back in that clearing when he'd shoved her out of his lap.

And she really didn't want him either. This was nothing more than an attraction.

An attraction she couldn't entertain.

She swallowed and exhaled a sharp breath.

"I needed to be sure," she said, hoping the truth would suffice. She didn't have the energy to lie anymore.

He inched forward again, shooting quick glances down either side of the hallway before staring into her soul again. "Sure about what exactly? That I wouldn't betray you?"

A nod.

His gaze softened, and the intensity faded from his eyes before they lowered to her lips for a brief moment. When he looked up once more, there was a profound sadness there. "What do I have to do for you to trust me, love?"

Something inside her ached at the sincerity of his plea, but she forced herself to ignore it. She had no answer for him. Couldn't put that truth into words. Her instincts told her to trust him, but she couldn't trust herself with him.

Adler's gaze invaded hers. "Trust me, love. You can't be here. It's not safe. I will explain. I promise. But I need you..." He paused to draw in a breath. "I need you to leave. I can't protect you in here."

Somehow the seriousness of the situation—where she stood and where she had followed him—hit her hard, and she sank back against the cold stone wall. She nodded.

"Go. I'll meet you afterward. I promise."

"At the office," Cait whispered.

"Aye. Go quickly and wait for me."

CHAPTER 16
ADLER

As soon as Cait slipped out the door, Adler fell against the wall, his heart hammering in his chest. What had she been thinking? What had she hoped to accomplish by following him in here?

What would he have done had they caught her?

Taking a steadying breath, he reminded himself that at least she'd listened to him. She hadn't fought him as expected. Perhaps he hadn't completely lost all of her trust with the little stunt he and Lucan had pulled.

Adler stepped away from the wall and drew his shoulders back, but his confidence remained skin-deep, a mere mask concealing a man cracked and broken.

You're not broken.

Lies.

He tried to take another breath, but it stuck, his throat constricted by the pain of every lost dream.

No matter how he willed for the fissures in his heart to be healed, they remained. Permanent reminders of the future he'd lost. Being back here only made it worse. Memories of Lani pried open the cracks. He could almost see her standing here beside him, desperation and hope swirling in her green eyes. Could almost feel her delicate hand in his.

Their life together was over.

Over before it had even truly begun, before he'd been able to give her everything he'd promised.

No, there was one promise he could keep. The promise he'd agreed to only because of the look of genuine fear on her face when she'd requested it.

Save my sisters. Destroy them.

Even though Adler had known the truth about the *exiles*, he hadn't realized just how frequent they were, or how bad things were elsewhere on the island.

And he hadn't expected the council to exile one of their own.

But still, he had promised her.

If anything happened to her, he was to return to Cregah to free her people. Including her sisters.

Then she'd been murdered. Her life taken from him by some pirate. While Adler understood that pirate was merely following orders from the council, he couldn't completely shake the desire to make her executioner suffer. But he had time to figure that out later.

For now, he needed to focus on gathering whatever information he could from the council. Anything that could help Cait and the rogues. Remembering that Cait was waiting for him outside, Adler forced the memories and thoughts aside and pushed his feet forward.

He wasn't exactly sure what the proper protocol was for this situation. He'd only ever been here for the formal crew dinners.

Thankfully, he still remembered his way through the mess of corridors, and soon he was standing at the door to the main meeting room and knocking.

An older woman answered the door in record time, looked him over with a critical eye, and said, "The council isn't hearing grievances today. You'll need to come back in two days."

She moved to close the door in his face, but he shot a hand up to stop it.

"They're expecting me." Adler pulled his jacket back to reveal the dark green sash at his waist.

The woman's eyes narrowed as she opened the door wider and gestured for him to enter. "Wait here. I'll see if the ladies are available." The click of the door behind her echoed through the large room.

The wall opposite was lined with windows that stretched from floor to ceiling. Delicate wisps of fabric covered them, allowing the sunlight to stream in while still affording privacy to those conducting business within.

Not that anyone would dare come close enough to the exterior of the building to peer inside.

Before him stood a modest dais with three armchairs—not thrones like he had seen in other kingdoms. Still, they were fit for nobility, upholstered with the finest fabrics from Turvala, their wooden frames carved with delicate designs of flowers and vines and waves and birds. The room was otherwise empty, allowing his footsteps to echo as he approached the center to stand before the dais and wait.

Adler remained there, trying to calm his mind and slow his heart as he waited to face the women who had ordered the death of his betrothed. After several minutes, the door opened and they entered, gliding across the floor to their seats.

He recognized all four of them, including the youngest, Lani's sister. As cold as the young woman's behavior was toward him—her eyes shooting icy daggers at him—she might as well have been offering him a warm smile when compared to the head councilwoman, Ms. Cascade. Melina.

All three councilwomen were imposing, to be sure, but Melina held herself taller, with a more rigid posture. Adler couldn't stop the dread that settled in the pit of his stomach as she stared him down. Here he was, a former pirate, and he was being intimidated by this woman.

Yet it was her sister, Fiona Bierne, who Adler could not bear to look at. Her red hair, so similar to her daughter's, fell in soft waves over her shoulders. What kind of mother could sentence her own daughter to death? Even if she hadn't wanted to do it, what kind of mother could sit idly by while it was done?

Bitterness and rage churned with the bile in his gut, threatening to rise at the sight of these women. But he had to stand here and play the part, wear the mask.

Melina looked down her nose at him and said in a commanding yet still delicate tone, "I apologize, Mr.—I'm sorry, I did not catch your name, pirate."

"It's Jensen. Adler Jensen," he offered, thankful his voice didn't betray the hatred brewing within.

Melina nodded, giving him a half-smile. "Mr. Jensen. I apologize for not being present at the meeting yesterday, but my sisters informed me of the great service you provided this council."

Adler bowed his head. "I was at the right place at the right time is all. Any pirate in my position would have done the same."

"Of course," she said, but her expression tightened ever so slightly before she spoke again. "How is it that you came to be in the square when you were? Your ship is not due to grace our shores again for another few weeks."

Four sharp gazes burned into him, waiting for him to fumble with his answer. The women were like four hungry spiders waiting for their prey to wander into their waiting web.

Adler cleared his throat to diffuse some of the tension. "You are correct. Lord Tiernen's ship is currently docked in Foxhaven. Or it was last I knew. I left his service early last week."

"Why do you dare wear my lord's colors then?" Fiona asked, her voice taking on a sharpness he hadn't heard back in the square.

Instinctively Adler touched the deep-green fabric. "Aye, not the best choice, but the only one I had available to me."

"Explain," Melina said coldly.

Adler nodded politely. "When that citizen started throwing around ridiculous accusations, it appeared there were no pirates nearby to control him. Despite having left Lord Tiernen's service, I still had my colors. Seemed best to play the role of pirate for the sake of the council and the peace you keep here. I didn't want to cause any confusion among your people, lest they believe ordinary travelers could run around exiling people."

The three councilwomen exchanged quick glances before Brigeh spoke up.

"We trust the young man's exile was completed then?"

"Aye," Adler said.

Melina angled a brow at him. "Then why did we hear—from multiple sources, even—that you were seen taking him onto a boat at the docks?"

Adler frowned and clasped his hands in front of him. "Because that is what I did. I couldn't very well use the standard route with so many witnesses about."

Melina nodded slowly at him, her calm expression impossible to read. Did she doubt him? Did she sense his lies?

Fiona raised her chin as she asked, "And where is the man now?"

Adler shifted his gaze to her, ignoring how each word from her mouth stoked his anger. "At the bottom of the Aisling. Not ideal, of course, but it was the best option available to me."

"Come, sister," Brigeh said, placing a hand on Fiona's arm. "If Tiernen trusted this man to leave his service without killing him, surely we can trust him to carry out an exile. As this exile was not typical, we cannot expect it to have been handled typically."

Though Fiona dipped her chin in response, she still eyed Adler with suspicion.

Melina turned to peer over her shoulder at Darienn, who stood behind them, straight-backed and stoic. "And what is your assessment, Darienn? Do you trust the pirate?"

Darienn's dark blue eyes traveled the length of him slowly, as if she were trying to see through his garments to the state of his very soul. Normally, under such scrutiny, he would flash a dimple at her and offer a roguish comment.

But this was the council hall, not a pub.

After an uncomfortable length of time had passed, Darienn gave him an almost sweet smile—made less so by the bitterness in her eyes—and asked, "Why did you come back to Cregah?"

"Excuse me?" Adler asked, buying himself time to settle on an answer.

Standing there and peering down at him, Darienn looked every bit a council-woman already, despite being years away from taking her mother's place in one of those chairs.

"You left Tiernen's crew in Foxhaven."

Though she hadn't phrased it as a question, Adler nodded.

"And you are not from here initially."

Another nod.

"Why not return home then? Why come here?"

Adler donned his well-practiced look of confusion. "Because your shores are peaceful. A haven for the weary and the—"

"And *you* are weary." Again, it wasn't a question.

"Aye, I am. All that awaited me back home was a farm that needs worked and a family to tend to."

Darienn cocked her head, her interest piqued. "A family? You are married?"

The question stung, and Adler noted how her eyes darted down to search his folded hands for the sign of a marriage bond upon his finger. "Alas, no. My mother. And sister…" Thankfully, understanding appeared on her face, and Adler was able to stop talking before the tightness in his chest choked his words and exposed the grief he kept hidden.

Darienn studied him and for one fearful moment, Adler worried she knew who he truly was. Lani hadn't told her, had she? Even if she hadn't, this sister of hers seemed far more perceptive than Lani had ever alluded to. Did Darienn know he was the man Lani was planning to meet? Could she see his guilt and grief surging now?

"If you're here to rest, then why have we heard of your recent employment at the local pub?" Darienn asked, and three other sets of eyes burned deeper into him.

Adler gave a light laugh and had to hide his wince when it came out obviously forced. "While Lord Tiernen granted my leave from his crew, he did not bolster my finances before doing so. And your shores may be peaceful, but they are not free. I needed to find work—"

Darienn raised a hand. Without taking her eyes from his, she said, "I trust him."

Was he to say thank you? Should he nod again? How many times could one nod before they looked like an imbecile?

Melina stood from her seat, and her sisters followed suit, though they remained behind her when she stepped forward. "Thank you for your assistance, Mr. Jensen. Normally we would not put a distinguished guest through such questions, but with unrest growing among our people for the first time in centuries, we simply can't take any chances."

"Of course. I take no offense." He waited a couple of breaths before he resumed speaking, assessing the way the four women continued to scrutinize him in the silence. "I do hope you are able to put the people at ease once again. It would be a shame for travelers to lose the one safe port on the Aisling."

Melina acknowledged his words with a sad smile. "Before you go, my sisters and I would like to extend a formal invitation to you, to show our gratitude for your assistance and quick thinking. The king of Caprothe will be arriving soon, and we would love to have you grace us with your presence at his welcome dinner."

Adler didn't need to feign his surprise. He'd expected a word of gratitude, maybe a handful of coins or a bottle of rum. But an invitation to sit at their table with the visiting king? What was their ploy here? What did they hope to gain from having him there?

So many questions. So few answers.

But if Cait's brother retrieved the dagger, here was the opportunity the rogues needed. He could use it to end the council's tyranny and avenge all who had been lost. Surely Cait wouldn't want him to refuse. Would she?

Melina stared at him, waiting for his response, and then the last words he planned to ever say fell from his lips.

"May I bring a guest?"

Why in the sands had he asked that? His gut tightened in frustration, but Melina's lips curled into an easy smile. Adler couldn't determine if it was sinister or genuine. Genuinely sinister, perhaps.

"And who might this guest be? A fellow traveler?"

"One of your own actually. A business owner in Morshan."

"Oh." Melina's eyes lit up, and Adler wondered if she somehow knew who he was referring to. "In that case, absolutely. It may be just what we need to ease the discontent. Mrs. Morris will relay the necessary details before you leave."

As if on cue, the miserable-looking woman he'd encountered earlier stepped into the room, her scowl as grim as ever.

"And feel free to use the front doors when you go. There's no need to bother with the side entrance."

Giving the ladies a final nod, Adler followed the woman out of the room. Mrs. Morris provided him the necessary information in a clipped, unfriendly manner and then proceeded to show him to the exit in silence. He could feel her glare burning into him as he strode down the stairs and stepped onto the road to Morshan.

They had foiled his plans to sneak about the council hall, preventing him from gathering any more information here, but he wasn't leaving empty-handed.

CHAPTER 17
DARIENN

THE PIRATE HAD BARELY EXITED the room when the three councilwomen rose and strode through a hidden door leading to their private study off the main meeting room. Darienn followed closely behind them. Although becoming the sole heir to the council had been her goal when she'd encouraged Aoife to run, Darienn had not anticipated the loneliness it would bring.

As if your sisters ever included you.

They'd avoided her, it was true, but the absence of their chatter and laughter—even if they'd excluded her from such moments—was like a black shroud hovering over the group of rulers. Without her sisters, the council hall was a somber place.

She tried to tell herself it was worth it, for she was now included in all of the council's discussions and meetings. She was no longer invisible, forgotten. She was important, valued. Melina said they needed to prepare her for the role she would step into sooner than planned, but sometimes Darienn wondered if she wasn't being tested by her aunt.

It was only logical. With both sisters having chosen ordinary pirates over family and country, Darienn was all they had left, and even though she was still five years away from coming of age, she knew they could not risk losing her to any fanciful notions of romance.

This was her chance.

Her chance to have whichever lord she desired. Her chance to be more than the annoying baby sister, always in the way. Her chance to be noticed and to play a greater role in the ruling of Cregah than she ever would have if her sisters had remained.

But what kind of ruler did she want to be?

That, she wasn't sure of yet.

It was obvious, despite all formal declarations and laws, that Melina was the ultimate leader of this council and, by extension, Cregah. Had Lani and Aoife chosen differently, had they remained here to rule beside her, Darienn would have no doubt been forced to slip into her mother's ineffectual role on the council, with Aoife taking Melina's place of prominence.

And Darienn didn't want to be a useless ornament as her mother seemed to be, withering away in Melina's shadow. Brigeh may have shown confidence and authority in the town square the other day, but it was not lost on Darienn that her mother's assertiveness dimmed whenever Melina was present.

"Do you truly trust him, Darienn?" Melina's harsh voice interrupted her thoughts.

Darienn straightened, pulling her shoulders back before nodding slowly. "I do."

"Why?" she asked casually, with a matter-of-fact tone.

"He's given me no reason not to," she said.

Her mother's laugh cut in. "He's a man. That's all the reason you need."

Darienn could only nod in response.

"Remember, child," Melina said, dropping her head to one side. "We do not start from a place of trust. The peace in our land is fragile, balancing on the edge of a blade, ready to fall off-balance with the slightest breath. We do not have the luxury of trusting outright. Our trust is earned. Trust no one but your fellow council-women. Suspect all. Be on your guard. For the heart is a tricky organ and can so easily be stolen by the sweetest of tongues."

"I—" Darienn started to speak in her own defense, frustrated with the implication that she had been swayed by that pirate's charm, that she could have been wooed by his smooth talk and roguish good looks. But Melina's glare stopped her words cold, and she managed to regroup quickly. "I understand, Melina. Thank you."

A hand rapped on the door, and without taking her eyes from Darienn's, Melina called for their guest to enter. It was Mrs. Morris.

"My ladies," the old crone said with a bow of her head. "He has gone. Down the road toward Morshan. Our scouts should be able to track his steps as planned, make sure he goes where expected."

"Thank you," Melina said. When the woman didn't take her leave, Melina turned to look at her. "Was there something more?"

"Aye." The woman's hands fidgeted near her waist for a second or two before she quickly composed herself, straightened, and clasped her hands behind her back. "You have an unexpected visitor. Madigen's men escorted them to the cellar, wanted to know how you'd like them to proceed."

The cellar? Darienn tried to steel her features at this news. In all her wanderings around her home, she had never discovered a cellar. All visitors were greeted in the main room, as Mr. Jensen had been. To be taken elsewhere—and to a location kept secret from the heirs, no less—could not mean anything good for this visitor.

"We will be right there," Melina said as she rose, her sisters mimicking her movement and falling in line behind her as they strode out of the study. Darienn remained behind, refusing to presume she was to be included in such an obviously clandestine council activity, until Melina called over her shoulder, "Join us, Dari-enn. Your training continues."

⤸⤹

Darienn's insides constricted with each step. The existence of a hidden cellar should not have shocked her, especially after she had discovered that hidden tunnel in the library entrance long before Aoife had escaped through it. Such was the benefit of being the forgotten younger sister; no one noticed when you decided to sneak around and explore.

Or follow people around, as she had often done with her sisters.

But she had never dared to follow her mother or the councilwomen.

Though her nerves were pulled taut, a familiar thrum of excitement danced along her skin as they passed the three councilwomen's chambers and headed straight for what appeared to be a dark dead end. But instead of hitting the stone wall at the end of the hallway, Melina turned and disappeared.

There, tucked into the nearly pitch-black corner of this corridor's end, was a narrow passageway, only visible once you were quite close to it. It was barely wider than the older women's shoulders, and Darienn was thankful she hadn't been cursed with a fear of tight spaces.

The passage gave way quickly to a set of simple stone stairs, illuminated by something shining from around a corner at the bottom. But turning the corner didn't lead them into a room their apprehended visitor as Darienn had expected. Instead, there was a heavy iron door with no windows and a pair of lit torches on either side.

Melina quickly pushed open the door. Its hinges didn't creak, and its base didn't scrape along the floor. With a deep breath, Darienn entered the cellar, ignoring the shiver that crept along her shoulders and up her neck as she passed through the doorway. She had to bite her tongue to prevent her jaw from dropping open at the sight of so many doors lining the corridor. Each was a smaller version of the one through which they'd entered, except these had shuttered windows in their centers at eye-level and heavy locks securing whatever—or whomever—was contained within.

Bile crept its way up into the back of Darienn's throat. What secrets was the council hiding here underneath her home? This went far beyond the necessary killing of traitors. But no, there had to be an explanation. Perhaps this was where they held the exiles until they could find pirates to complete the task. Yes, that had to be the case. All she had to do was remain calm, not give the council any reason to doubt her loyalty. Then they'd trust her, and everything would be made clear.

As they neared the first door on their right, a pirate Darienn didn't recognize straightened, stepping away from where he'd been leaning against the wall.

Keeping his eyes lowered, he dipped his chin reverently to Melina when she stopped directly in front of him.

"What did Lord Madigen bring us?" Melina asked in a flat tone.

"He would like to present her to you himself, milady." He quickly turned, pushed the door open, and stepped through. "Sir, the council." As he said the words, he stepped to the side with a wide sweep of his arm and then bowed as the councilwomen—and Darienn—entered the small room.

Darienn was hit with a pungent odor so foul it took every bit of her strength to keep her hand at her side as her mother did and not cover her nose. The floor and walls, and even the ceiling, were made of a smoother stone than the rest of the building.

Iron.

But why? Before Darienn could search her memories for any past teachings regarding the Aisling myths, Melina's sharp voice split the air.

"Madigen, as much as I enjoy our time together, I expected you to be gone already."

The lord nodded, his eyes closed with respect—or was that fear?

"Alas, our plans were derailed by *her.*"

Darienn couldn't see who he referred to from her vantage point behind the councilwomen, and something inside her told her it was better not to have a front-row view of what was to happen in here. It was like the air itself was charged with a foreboding energy, warning her to turn around and run, urging her to escape while she still could.

That's ridiculous, she told herself.

You're just unnerved a bit.

Grow up, Darienn.

When Melina stepped forward, Darienn inched to the side enough to see around her aunt's skirts. There, in the middle of the room, a woman was seated in a simple wooden chair. No—she was bound to the chair, her arms pulled tight behind her and her ankles secured to the chair's legs. Her skirts were piled up in her lap, leaving everything below her knees bare. Her long, dark hair cascaded around her shoulders, framing a face that held both youth and experience. In the low light, her green eyes glistened like hard gemstones, and even with her icy stare and tightly drawn lips, she was one of the most attractive—and intimidating—women Darienn had ever seen. Everything about this woman exuded supreme confidence despite her current state of captivity.

"Where did you find her?" Melina asked Lord Madigen, though she continued to face their guest.

Clearing his throat, he answered in his deep, gravelly voice, "Just outside the council grounds. Crouched among the trees."

"Highly suspicious behavior, Miss..." Melina gestured toward the woman with an open hand, inviting her to offer her name.

The woman pulled one corner of her mouth back into a taunting smirk. "You know who I am."

Melina's arm flew out, and the sound of her palm connecting with the woman's cheek had Darienn flinching. Glancing quickly at the other councilwomen, Darienn adjusted her features to match their impassive expressions. The prisoner, to her credit, seemed unfazed, even as her skin flushed red from the strike. She simply held Melina's gaze and waited, her smirk still in place.

"Aye, Miss McCallagh, I do," Melina said. "I wish you had visited us formally and not with such suspicious behavior. I would have much preferred to speak with you in more comfortable quarters."

The prisoner tilted her head slightly, and the ice in her eyes melted. It gave her a more amenable, almost sweet, look. "I'd be happy to take this talk upstairs if you'd prefer."

Darienn braced herself for Melina to strike the woman again for her disrespect, but instead, the councilwoman laughed—a quiet chuckle with a bit of menace lingering at the edges.

"You are so much like your brother."

Brother. McCallagh. The pieces came together in Darienn's mind. The pirate from the library. The one her sister had joined up with. This was his sister? But why would she be here?

Melina shook her head, saying, "Unfortunately, Cait, it is too late for that. But I do wonder..." She paused as she brought her hands to her mouth, palms together as if in prayer to some long-lost god. "Did you not learn from your parents' betrayal and subsequent exiles? Theirs was one of our more painful betrayals. I hoped something good might have come from it, that you and Declan might have been spared from learning their traitorous ways."

Though Cait's smile remained on her lips, her right eye twitched and her smile tightened before she responded. "Yes, our parents' exiles did leave a lasting impression on us."

"And yet you choose to sneak around our home?" Melina asked.

"I was not sneaking." Her eyes flitted to the pirates standing in the room. "I was waiting for my employee to complete his business with you. Accompanying him to his meeting with you seemed inappropriate, so I opted to wait for him outside."

"In the trees? Not on the trail?" Melina asked skeptically, and Darienn leaned forward slightly in anticipation of the woman's answer.

"Ironically, I was trying to avoid this very scenario. I did not expect any pirate to treat me with anything but suspicion upon finding me on the trail. Alas, I'm a simple pub owner and no spy, so they discovered me anyway."

Her explanation seemed reasonable enough to Darienn. But the ladies stared at Cait. With each tense second of silence that passed, she wondered what the councilwomen had noticed.

Melina turned to look at her sisters with a devious spark in her eye. The councilwomen offered her tight-lipped smiles and slow, almost imperceptible, nods. Darienn's mind whirred as she tried to catch up to whatever conclusion they'd reached.

What was happening? What had her mother and her aunts heard in Cait's words that Darienn had failed to catch?

Melina spun back around to face Cait. "Why, exactly, did you expect *this very scenario?*"

Darienn's eyes widened, and she turned to Cait, who once again remained amazingly unmoved.

"Not this scenario exactly, Councilwoman." Cait bowed her head in what Darienn could have sworn was mock reverence. "But after the shocking exile in the town square yesterday, and with the death of one of our citizens this morning, I did not want to raise any suspicions and risk the presumption of treason. Again, it was foolish of me. Please forgive the mistake."

"I want to believe you, Cait. I do," Melina said, though her tone indicated that was not the case at all. Darienn had heard that tone on more than one occasion. Namely when Aoife had been caught with unauthorized books or had been discovered daydreaming instead of studying. "Unfortunately, with our recent increase in exiles—including those of our own heirs—we cannot be too careful."

As if the words were a silent cue, the pirate who had led them inside now shut the door to the cell. The latch gave an ominous, dull clang, and he walked around Darienn and Melina to stand beside Cait, where he awaited his next command.

"We are a land of peace, Miss McCallagh," Melina said, straightening up as if the words demanded she take on a regal posture. Darienn's gut tightened, more so at the sight of her mother and Fiona nodding in solemn agreement. "Sometimes, however, peace must be fought for. Forcing us to do things we do not want in order to achieve a greater—a better—reality for all."

As confusion billowed up within Darienn, she swung her attention back to the woman, expecting to see some hint of shock playing upon her face. But where there should have been concern, there was only pride. A haughtiness that could not possibly bode well for her.

The blow came quickly. Darienn flinched at the sound of metal against bone. Cait's head dropped to her chin as her shin was struck hard, but she didn't scream. Her pain escaped only in the groan she let spill out of her. The pirate straightened again, lowering the iron rod to his sides.

Darienn fought to contain a gasp of horror, swallowing back the words that screamed in her head.

This is wrong!

This isn't okay!

This woman is innocent!

But at that last thought, she stopped.

This woman might not be innocent. Perhaps the council knew more about her than they let on. They must have some information they hadn't shared with Darienn.

Melina spoke once more. "We don't want to hurt you, Cait. It is not our way. Your brother, unfortunately, decided to take something from us. Something quite valuable."

"Whatever it—" Cait started, but something stayed her tongue.

"We know. It's no concern of yours. Yes? Certainly he must have told you what he was seeking. We know he met with you. Before he visited us."

"He didn't—" This time Cait cut her own words short.

Melina drew in a long breath. "We have no place for liars in our land, Cait. Please don't lie to us again."

The pirate moved once more, swinging the iron rod into Cait's other leg. Its smooth edge made a sickening thud as it struck the bone. This time, a bark of pain shot from Cait's mouth as her chin lifted, her head falling back to look toward the ceiling.

"You know what he was after," Melina continued. "You might as well know that we have instructed him to retrieve it for the council. Such power could allow our nation to thrive, to stop resorting to such barbaric means. And we simply cannot risk him not delivering this item to us."

Cait narrowed her eyes at Melina, and Darienn found herself silently pleading for the woman to at least pretend to concede. Anything to avoid more pain and unnecessary violence.

But Cait couldn't hear her thoughts, and her glare remained fixed on the councilwoman. "If you're going to exile me, can we hurry it along? I'm sure you have more important council business to attend to."

Again, Melina laughed, a string of breathy chuckles. "Exile is not in your cards just yet. We need you to ensure Declan brings this treasure to us." She dipped her chin, and the pirate moved in response.

This time, though, instead of striking out with the rod, he knelt before Cait. Darienn foolishly hoped he was going to untie her bonds, but instead, he raised the shaft of metal to Cait's leg, pressing it just below her knee. Cait kept her gaze locked on Melina, and Darienn marveled at how she maintained her composure even as the man began to slide the metal down toward her ankle.

Cait's jaw tightened. Her neck flexed. Her lips squeezed together.

But still, she did not scream or look away—even as the rough iron scraped along her leg bone, the pirate pressing it so hard against her that it peeled away her skin, leaving behind a trail of blood.

Finally Cait began to scream. Her eyes slammed shut, so she didn't see when the pirate looked to Melina. She gave him another nod. Cait's scream turned into a roar, guttural and angry, when the iron was once again placed below her knee, the rough metal digging into her raw flesh as he dragged it down once more.

Bile rose in Darienn's throat, but she swallowed it, nearly retching again as it settled back into her stomach. She could see bits of Cait's bone peeking through her mangled flesh. She wanted to look away, wanted to erase this from her mind, but something held her in place.

If this was what they did to their loyal citizens, what did they command the pirates to do to the exiles?

What had they forced Captain McCallagh to do to Lani?

Darienn's eyes began to water, tears collecting at the edges as she thought of her older sister sitting like this, being purposefully hurt and maimed by that pirate.

The pirate your other sister ran off with.

She shook her head, unable to make sense of any of this. Not in this environment. Not with the groans of anguish coming from the woman before her.

None of this made sense. None of it.

A voice in her head begged her to stop them, to ask the councilwomen to show mercy. But another part of her, quiet and meek in the corner of her mind, whispered to her that it would do no good.

It could earn you the same treatment.

She clamped her mouth shut, willing the tears to dry before they could spill over, hoping her mother didn't notice her reaction.

Three times, the iron rod was pulled roughly down Cait's leg. Twice more, it slammed into her other leg, causing it to bruise and swell. When Melina cleared her throat and the pirate stood and backed away, Darienn nearly let out a sigh. It was over.

But it wasn't.

Darienn's breath caught as she watched Melina move forward like some graceful predator looking to play with its prey. She bent at the hips, putting her mouth close to Cait's face before sliding slowly toward her ear. Cait's fingers splayed and reached toward the councilwoman in what appeared to be some futile attempt to attack her.

Melina laughed as she pulled away, but it was a far more sinister laugh than Darienn had ever heard from her. Part of her wondered if her aunt had forgotten she had an audience. When Melina moved her hand down to Cait's thigh to pull up her skirts and expose her legs, Darienn realized her aunt didn't care who witnessed her actions.

Darienn's stomach lurched in anticipation, not knowing what Melina intended to do to this woman. She didn't know if she could stand to watch, but she was unwilling to risk the council's wrath by daring to look away.

Slowly Melina trailed her fingers along Cait's leg—up one thigh, sliding scandalously down between her legs before climbing up the other. Without warning, Melina's fingers curled, and she sliced her sharp nails into Cait's flesh until she drew blood. Cait clenched her jaw but didn't utter a sound, not even when Melina slowly dragged her nails down the length of her leg to create four long, ghastly gashes. Blood trickled down from the cuts, pooling on the chair between Cait's legs. But still, she remained silent.

Before Melina rose, Darienn could have sworn she heard her utter two final words to Cait.

"Good girl."

CHAPTER 18
AOIFE

Declan had left hours ago to do whatever it was pirate captains did when not threatening people or getting captured or teasing their women. So Aoife took the opportunity to rest.

And panic.

She had picked up a random novel from his bookcase and tried to distract herself by reading it, but the words kept blurring, no matter how many times she started the sentence over.

Finally, she slammed it shut, tossed it onto the bed beside her outstretched legs, and threw her head back against the wall. Harder than she'd intended, but at least the sting of the impact had her focusing on something other than the danger that awaited them.

And the looming expectations of *tonight*.

She wasn't sure which had her heart thrumming with anxiety more.

One was decidedly more perilous, but both had her on edge. And she didn't know how she'd survive either.

You'll survive both because you have Declan.

His face manifested behind her closed eyelids, and she couldn't stop a smile from gracing her lips.

Her mother would hate to see Aoife relying on a man for anything. After all the lessons and lectures about men's lies and games, Aoife herself wondered how she'd gone through such a complete and utter shift in thinking. Nineteen years spent believing men were good for only two things—violence and pleasure—had been swept away, erased by one man's actions. Like the tide washing away footprints in the sand.

But her mother had been wrong. Her claims about men were lies, just like everything else Aoife had been taught.

Trusting Declan, leaning on him, needing him... This wasn't weakness. This was love. And it wasn't like the romance novels she'd read in secret. It was real, tangible, imperfect, and chaotic. It was messing up and forgiving, giving in and letting go, feeling whole and needing more all at once.

What had she been thinking with that one-word promise?

Tonight.

It had made sense in the moment, when her lust had been burning in her veins and all she'd known was her need for him. But now, she was alone in his bed. All of that heat had long since cooled, burned off by her insecurity. She'd been bold in his arms, begging him for what she wanted with nothing more than a move of her body, whispering her idiotic promise for satisfaction.

And now, she was scared.

Declan was experienced. How experienced, she didn't know. She didn't want to know. But he was certainly more versed in intimacy than she was. All she knew were those written stories of fictional people. They'd given her basic ideas of what *could* be done, sure, but she had no idea if those were things people did in reality.

How much truth did fairy tales hold anyway?

Aoife swallowed hard, telling herself it would be okay. This was Declan. The man who had taken a man's head to save her, protected her from Callum, knelt before her to beg for her forgiveness. This was the man who had saved her time and time again, spending all his energy trying to earn back her trust.

He would understand.

But all these thoughts vanished when the door to the cabin opened and he slowly made his way across the quiet room. The thumping of his boots echoed the beating of her heart. Maybe she could back out, tell him she'd changed her mind, that she'd fallen ill or grown too tired.

Then he stepped into view. His shirt was already untucked, his hair falling across his forehead, his eyes roving over her from where he stood in the doorway.

The heat returned, closing around her throat, making her breathe faster, tightening her stomach, and sparking an ache between her thighs that both thrilled and frightened her. It felt good and awful at the same time, a sensation of need she never wanted to lose but knew she wouldn't survive if it wasn't quenched.

Declan let his tongue slip out between his lips, wetting them, and she couldn't stop her breath from shuddering in anticipation. What would those lips feel like on her? Kisses were one thing. Those nearly caused Aoife to come undone as it was. But what would happen when he pressed those lips elsewhere?

She wanted to know. Curiosity urged her to leave behind the fear and worry as she crawled to the edge of the bed and knelt there, sitting back on her feet.

"Tonight?" Declan asked, and the huskiness in his voice sent another wave of hunger through her.

She pulled her bottom lip between her teeth, and a giggle fell out of her before she could stop it. His lips shifted into a smirk, and something flared in his gray eyes, something both familiar and altogether surprising. He'd looked at her with desire before, but this... This was different.

Deeper.

Darker.

Dangerous.

She should say something, shouldn't she? But she didn't know whether to be assertive or coy. Before she could decide, he was approaching her with painfully slow strides.

Though she lifted herself up so their faces were level, her eyes fell to the teal sash at his waist and the noticeable tension further down. The sight of his body readying for her sent thrill after thrill through every vein and muscle and bone and tendon in her body until she thought she might fall apart before he even laid a finger on her.

"Yes?" he said when he finally stopped and pressed his legs against the edge of the bed, the rest of his body hovering teasingly near her.

"I…" she started, and then her nerves surged again until she could do nothing but look at her hands that were clasped between their bodies, her fingers twisting together. "I don't know what I'm doing."

The warmth of embarrassment swept up her neck, flooding her cheeks, even though she knew he would never mock her for being naive and scared and nervous.

He shoved his hands into his pockets and leaned toward her, letting the tip of his nose brush her flushed cheek as he approached her ear and whispered, "I'll teach you."

The words pulled her eyelids closed, and she nuzzled her face against his. "Promise?"

No sooner had she uttered the question than his hands were at her back and in her hair, strong and desperate as they pulled her body to him. Her fingers fisted his shirt at his waist when his lips found hers. Slowly and deliberately, he kissed her, his tongue brushing over her lips with care before pushing inside to taste her, to run along her teeth before retreating, begging her to follow and do the same to him. This was like no kiss she'd ever had. This wasn't a frenzy of hunger but an exploration, a guided tour of how a kiss could feel.

It wasn't enough.

She'd spent years missing out on love, taught it was for fools, not heirs. And this was just the beginning of what he would show her. With a soft moan, she pressed into him, but he pulled away, leaving her panting, pouting.

His eyes burned into hers. "Lesson number one? Make them earn it."

She glared at him, but he only smirked back.

Her mind raced, tripping over the energy thrumming through her.

Two can play this game.

Lowering one hand, Aoife let her fingers press into his hip and across his leg until she found what she'd been craving. Tracing the shape of him through the thin fabric that separated them, she smiled devilishly at the ragged breath that escaped him, the low rumble vibrating in the back of his throat.

He leaned into her hand, and pursing her lips, Aoife retreated and lowered herself, scooting back to where she'd been lounging earlier.

Declan shook his head at her, but there was no disappointment mixed with the lust burning in his eyes. "Good girl."

Aoife's stomach clenched when those words caused a pulse of desire so intense she had to squeeze her legs together. Her voice came out rough and strained when she said, "What's lesson number two?"

Sweeping a hand through his hair, Declan moved around the bed and sat, stretching his legs out beside her. Why were his hands in his lap and not on her? Why wasn't he sitting closer?

He's probably trying to drive you mad!

It was working.

"Well?" she said, trying not to let too much eagerness show in her face.

He swept his gaze up her legs, lingering on her chest and then her lips, before his warm breath swept past her ear. "Make them beg for it."

Excitement and fear collided within her, intensifying when his tongue traced the edge of her ear and moved down to her neck, where he pressed a kiss to her pulse, then pulled away enough for the cool air to torment her with his absent touch. Her heart hammered against her sternum.

Beg for it?

She envisioned herself forced to kneel before him, begging him to please her. And while she couldn't deny the sensations that thought elicited, couldn't stop this growing urge to make him happy in every possible way, some part of her hesitated, and she froze.

He stilled beside her, and she waited for his response, knowing this wasn't how she should react to his advances. Even if he'd been joking about the begging—which she wasn't entirely sure he had been—it had given her enough pause to know this was all moving a little too fast.

Did she love him? Yes.

Did she want him? Sands, yes.

Did she need to give all of herself to him *now*?

Her answer to that question came not from herself but from Declan when he tenderly placed his lips on her jaw and took her hand in his, cradling it as if it was his one duty in life to care for her.

Aoife squeezed his hand in return and pulled in a breath, desperate to find the courage to hand herself over to the ache in her core. But she couldn't. She wanted to but couldn't. She chided herself for being so timid, so inexperienced and naive that she couldn't even act on her own impulses and desires, couldn't just let herself go.

Declan's arm wrapped around her shoulders, and he tucked her body against him, kissing the top of her head. He'd noticed. He'd sensed her apprehension, and he'd stopped.

"What happened to making me beg?" Aoife asked in a voice so meek she winced at how pathetic she sounded.

He lifted their joined hands to her chin, turning her until she peered up at him. When he responded, his voice was low, with a subtle growl behind it. "Oh, I intend to. There's nothing I want more than to hear my name in your moans, to have your fingers clawing my back and your eyes craving for that sweet release like only I can give you."

This had her once again melting into him, dreaming of what he might do to entice such reactions from her. She swallowed around the tightness in her throat and tried to control the way her body had responded to his voice alone.

Should she insist she wanted all of that and more?

"But not yet."

"Why?" she whispered.

"Because of lesson three," he answered, as if she should know what it was already. "Don't rush it."

"How is that at all different from the others?"

"Aye, they're similar in their demand for patience and control, but this is not just about slowing down the strokes and the kisses..." He paused to emphasize the point by softly moving his fingertips on her jaw and her neck. "It means taking your time before you go too far."

"Too far?" She wasn't following. Why was he being so cryptic? Couldn't he tell from the pace of her breaths and the tension in her entire body that she'd already committed to this? To him?

"I won't rush this. And I won't let you either. We have enough regret and guilt looming over us for a lifetime. I don't want to add to that. Not when we have time, Aoife."

Did they have time though?

Surely he understood the danger that awaited them from Callum, from her mother. How did he not feel time slipping through their fingers? How could he not want to take advantage of every precious moment when they had very nearly lost all of it to Triss?

"What about—"

"I made a promise, Aoife," he said, stroking his thumb against her cheek. "A promise to myself that I would do one thing right. You are the one good thing in my life, and I won't ruin it. I will earn your trust, your respect, your love—"

"You already have all of those," she protested, and he released a breathy laugh, his eyes gleaming at her.

"I have the start of those, but I want them fully, just as I want you fully. Your heart, your mind, your body." The last word rumbled in his throat as if it were a beast that had broken free of its tether. "I will earn them. And once I do...I'll let you earn everything else. From your knees, even, if that's what you wish."

Aoife's heart swelled, and though she wanted to argue that there was no need for him to prove himself to her, she chose instead to rest her head against his chest before asking, "Promise?"

CHAPTER 19
MAURA

A RAPPING at the door jolted Maura from sleep, tearing her away from a sublime dream in which she was entangled with Tommy on some faraway beach. With a soft curse, she swung her legs over the edge of the bed, squinting as the sunlight filtering through the porthole shone directly into her eyes.

The sound came again, and she pushed herself to stand. Why was she the one who had to abandon such lovely dreams to answer the bloody door when her sisters were perfectly capable of hearing the knocking?

Silence answered her question.

Maura's eyes went wide as she turned back around. Her sisters still lay in their beds, but even with the tapping at the door and the subsequent calls for "Ms. Bron," Maura could only hear one heartbeat.

Her own.

Oh, shit, I've killed them.

"One second!" Maura called over her shoulder as she rushed to Bria's side. Leaning close, she placed a hand on Bria's wrist. There, faint but steady, was the *thump-thump* of her sister's heart. A sigh rushed out of her. After checking to ensure the same was true for Renna, Maura took a moment to stare at the pair of them.

A twinge of guilt pricked her chest, but she rubbed it away with her palm, as if it were an insect.

No, she wouldn't feel guilty for doing what she needed to do. Not after what they'd both done to her. And to Tommy.

The knocking came again, more impatient than before, and Maura dashed for the door and yanked it open.

"Yes?" she asked as her eyes met those of Captain Halloran. The captain herself had come to her cabin. She hadn't sent one of her officers or a lowly crew member. But why?

"We are approaching Helles Island, Ms. Bron. Are all of your preparations complete?"

"Yes, I believe so," Maura said.

"Very well. Come with me." Halloran turned and walked away without waiting for Maura to respond.

Maura glanced back one final time at her sisters. They were sleeping soundly, deeply. Would they ever forgive her for poisoning them?

Perhaps once you forgive them, she thought as she stepped out onto the deck and closed the door.

The captain waited for her at the port-side railing near the prow. Here they had a good view of the steep mountain that rose from the center of Helles Island.

"Will they be okay?" Halloran asked.

"Assuming your healer is as good as she seems—"

"Aye, she is. But I'm not as confident in your abilities to implement her instructions."

Had the statement been made by anyone else, Maura might have been offended. Sands, if Halloran had made the same comment before they'd survived their encounter with Triss, she would have believed it an insult. But now, she knew it was simply the captain's nature.

"Fair point," Maura said, giving her a small smile. "Well then, assuming I did everything correctly, they should wake in two to three days. Plenty of time for you to get far enough past Cregah to keep them from insisting on returning for me. But what if Renna tries to control you again? I wouldn't put it past her to—"

Halloran held up a finger to stop her. "My healer is quite good. After Renna's little stunt before, I sought her out. She concocted something that should at least make it harder for your sister to get any hold on me. Only wish I'd thought to ask Katyra for it sooner."

"And how will we get word to Tommy?" Maura asked.

Halloran waved a hand over her shoulder. Maura turned to see one of the crew members approaching. The woman raised her chin to the captain but paid no attention to Maura.

"Last word we received had the *Siren's Song* heading toward Selka. Sereia here will contact him," Halloran said.

This had to be a joke. How could this crew member—

Before Maura could even finish her thought, the woman saluted the captain with a finger to her brow, stepped onto the railing, and dove into the sea.

Maura leaned over in time to see the woman's legs shift into a powerful tail of gold, purple, and teal scales that ended in delicate feathery fins.

A siren.

She swam away, moving fast to the northeast.

"How long will it take for her to reach them?" Maura asked, her eyes still on the water, although the siren was already out of sight.

"They move surprisingly fast, riding the currents far below the surface. Two days at the most. She should arrive at the same time or just after Tommy and the crew does."

"And then another three to four days for him to meet me at the island?" It felt like an eternity, which seemed ridiculous given the centuries she'd spent as a hostage.

Halloran nodded. "If he's able to leave as soon as she reaches him."

"That seems like a big *if*."

"Aye. Especially with Callum involved." Though Halloran's jaw tightened around the pirate's name, something in her eyes hinted that her feelings for the man were complicated.

"Think they can succeed?" Maura's gut clenched tight. After almost losing Tommy back in the sound and knowing how he'd been hurt in the council hall trying to rescue her, she didn't know how she would handle it if something bad happened to him yet again.

Halloran drew in a deep breath before answering. "Callum makes a good show of his brutality, and he's certainly not a pirate to be crossed—"

"You crossed him though."

"Aye, I did. And I regret it to this day."

She couldn't have heard that right. Hadn't she stabbed the man while they fought Triss?

Halloran breathed out a laugh. "I know. It makes no sense. Sometimes I question my own sanity. But love has that way about it, doesn't it? Makes us believe in the impossible. Blinds us to all reason until all we see is what could be and not what is."

"But you still betrayed him? So it must not have blinded you completely."

Maura shouldn't pry. The captain's past was none of her concern, and she had bigger things to worry about anyway.

But Halloran didn't seem to mind the inquiry. She nodded again. "Sometimes you learn the depths of that love only after you've pushed it away."

"Or had it ripped away from you," Maura said, looking to the north as if she could see Tommy there on the horizon if she only focused hard enough.

"I thought fae were supposed to be intelligent," Halloran said. Now Maura was offended. "You think this"—she gestured toward the sea—"was you two being ripped apart? No, it wasn't. As long as the two of you are still breathing, nothing can truly part you. Not with the bond you share."

"How do you—"

Another laugh. "It's hard to ignore the connection that binds you and Tommy together."

So why did Renna fail to see it? No, it wasn't that she didn't see. She simply didn't care. She cared more for their kin who had left them for dead for centuries than she did for her own sister.

Bitterness coated Maura's tongue. She needed to focus on something else. Anything else.

"So where do I go once I'm ashore? Helles doesn't have any villages or cities, right?"

"Aye. There's not much in the way of permanent settlements. The island has only a few spots along its coast that can accommodate a ship of this size. Even anchoring off the coast and rowing in is near impossible in most places."

"But you know of a place."

A nod. "I know of a place. It's along the southern side, well-hidden. We can't take the ship close, but we will row you in. I have a camp of sorts set up for emergencies. And the rare vacation. Should have plenty of provisions for you."

"Pirates take vacations?"

"Not often. Hence the term *rare*. But even pirates need a break, no?"

"How will Tommy know how to find it?"

"Sereia knows its location."

"What if something goes wrong?"

Halloran looked out across the still waters of the Aisling. "Then maybe you can start complaining about being ripped away from each other. Because nothing but death would keep that boy from finding you."

"You're sure?" Maura's voice quivered.

Halloran's attention swung back to her, and she raised a single brow in question. "You're not?"

"Absence does that, doesn't it?" Maura said with a shrug. "What feels so certain when you're together seems to crack and fissure and break apart with doubt once you're separated. I can logically know his love is true, but the longer I go without him, the more I start to wonder if I didn't dream it all."

Halloran's eyes narrowed, and it reminded Maura of the way her mother used to stare her down when teaching her a lesson or chiding her over some wrongdoing. It made Maura's heart burst with warm memories of home and family...but also shatter with the realization that all of that had been undone with the war.

"Maura, whether it's a dream or not, hold onto it. Let it bolster you. Use it to keep you from giving up. Because whether Tommy returns for you or not, the others will need you against the council before this is all said and done. Of that I'm certain."

Maura had no idea what role she could possibly play against the council. And if Melina got the dagger and restored her powers, none of them would be safe, whether Maura was with them or not.

⤜⤛

MAURA TRIED to ignore the discomfort that arose from being in another small rowboat with Captain Halloran, though this time the journey was decidedly more pleasant without the constant threat of fanged, bloodthirsty sirens. Halloran had insisted on escorting Maura, along with two of her crew members, to her hidden inlet.

As the crew secured the boat to the bent trunk of a tree that extended out and over the water, Halloran motioned for Maura to follow her ashore. Together they moved through the waist-deep water until they stood on a pristine white beach no larger than the main deck of the *Duchess*. Maura peered up at the mountain that loomed over them.

"And where is this camp of yours?" Maura asked, hoping she wasn't going to be asked to traipse too deeply into the dense forest that surrounded them.

"Just a quick jaunt that way," Halloran said, pointing between two large trees that unfortunately looked like all the others that lined the beach. The captain walked over to them, pulled out her dagger, and made two quick slashes, one on each trunk. "There. Go between the two marked trees, and you'll come across it."

"What if I get lost?" Maura asked.

Halloran simply answered, "Don't."

Maura couldn't keep her eyes from rolling.

Damn pirates.

"Well," Halloran continued, "you'd best go on before the sun sets. With your positioning behind the mountain, you'll have darkness soon."

Five or six days. Maura could do this. Five hundred years locked in a room had been its own brand of torture. Surely she could withstand a few days in the wide open.

"Thank you, Captain," Maura said, hoping the woman could grasp the full weight of her gratitude. "But what will you tell my sisters when they wake up?"

"I'll think of something. We pirates are quick on our feet. Best under pressure." With that, Halloran turned and stepped back into the sea.

The water was lapping at Halloran's thighs when Maura called her name one last time. "Watch over them for me?"

She didn't know why she asked it, but it seemed the right thing to say. She should care about her sisters even if they didn't care about her. The captain's face clouded over with concern before she gave another brief nod and turned back toward the rowboat.

The sunlight was fading quickly, and Maura decided not to wait to see Halloran off. The last thing she wanted was to be trudging through this dense foliage in darkness. Noting the two trees the captain had marked, Maura stepped between them and found herself immediately swallowed by the shadows under the jungle's canopy. After several minutes of nearly tripping and stumbling over branches and having heavy vines smack into her face as she traveled, Maura wished she had demanded more accurate directions other than "go that way."

No sooner had she convinced herself she was lost than she stepped into a small clearing. At first it appeared empty, but Maura soon caught a glimpse of some barrels and crates sitting among the large leaves near the ground off to her right. In one crate she found several bolts of cloth and a few wooden rods. A tent perhaps? She could sleep in a tent. She'd been craving adventure after all, right? In one of the barrels she found some salted meat and potatoes. A smaller crate housed several bottles of what she could only assume was rum.

She'd save that for later, when the solitude was driving her to insanity.

Grabbing a bite of salted meat, she stuck it between her teeth while she went to work gathering the materials for shelter.

THE SUN HAD TRAVELED HALFWAY across the sky when Maura finally admitted defeat. What good was it to have *daemari* when it only allowed you to create illusions? The illusion of a tent was not nearly as nice—or helpful—as an actual one, and she didn't know how anyone could construct anything from the mess of materials lying at her feet.

As she looked up at the darkening sky, she was grateful that she wouldn't need to find cover anytime soon. But the weather often changed quickly and without warning. She would regret giving up if an evening storm rolled in, but her muscles ached and her back screamed for rest. So, with a frustrated sigh, she lowered herself to the ground and leaned back against a tree.

She had just closed her eyes when a sound had her snapping them open and standing. Were those footsteps? An animal? Were there animals on Helles? She couldn't remember. She backed away from the sound and reached for the magic in her veins. Whether it was an animal or a person, she didn't want to take the chance of being seen right away. Warmth spread over her skin, and her vision dimmed as if she were looking through a veil.

Maura held her breath when the faint thump of an approaching heartbeat—human, by the sound of it—reached her ears.

"Maura? Did you get lost after all?" Captain Halloran called out from the trees opposite Maura before she stepped into the clearing.

Dropping the glamour, Maura left her hiding spot.

"Is everything okay? Are my sisters—"

Halloran waved away her question. "They're fine." She paused to take a look around the clearing, shaking her head at Maura's ill-fated attempts at building a camp. "I dare say they might be better off than you at the moment."

Maura shrugged. She wasn't about to be offended by someone who would now be able to take over assembling the tent.

"Can't say I have a lot of experience with this," Maura said, flinging out her hand at the mess of materials at her feet.

"That occurred to me as soon as we got back to the ship." Halloran was already setting her hat and small pack down beside the crates and reaching for the supplies. Maura winced as the captain struggled to untangle it all. "What did you try to do? Throw everything up in the air and hope it would build itself?"

"That would be nice, wouldn't it?"

Halloran didn't answer. Maura said nothing more, in case the captain needed silence to work, and studied how she arranged the wood and cloth and attached them together to create a much larger shelter than Maura had expected.

"You make that look too easy," Maura said.

"Of all the things to impress you…" Halloran laughed. She eyed Maura for a moment. "Go, sit. Relax. You standing around staring makes me uncomfortable."

Maura gladly obliged, sitting down at the entrance to the tent and pulling her legs in close.

"You're still staring," the captain said from beside the crate of rum.

"And you're still here." Maura didn't mean for it to come out quite so rudely, but thankfully Halloran didn't seem to notice.

"Aye."

Popping the cork off one bottle, Halloran lifted it to her lips and took a long drink. She wiped her lips with the back of her hand and sat down near the tent before offering the bottle to Maura.

As Maura took her own sip of the warm drink, Halloran said, "And I'll be around until we see this whole council business ended."

"Why?"

Halloran recoiled slightly, though a hint of amusement shone in her eyes. "What do you mean why?"

"Just that you seemed ready to take my sisters all the way to Larcsporough. What changed your mind? Or did I misread your intentions before?"

The captain drew in a deep breath and leaned back onto her hands. "You didn't misread anything. That was the plan."

"But?"

"That last thing you said to me back there at the beach—*Watch over them*. Just reminded me of a promise I made. A promise I still need to make good on."

CHAPTER 20
TOMMY

Despite the morning fog hovering over the sea, Tommy could just make out the white cliffs of Turvala in the distance. They had made good time, so at least something was going in their favor. But even with the crew gathered around him on the main deck, he couldn't keep his attention from being drawn to the south every few moments.

Focus.

He would be no good to anyone if he continued to let himself be so distracted. Especially with something he had no way of fixing. And Declan needed him to be focused once they landed.

Actually, before they landed.

A throat cleared beside him, and Tommy swung his attention back to the matter at hand. Aoife, Declan, and the assembled crew were eyeing him curiously.

"You with us, Tommy?" Declan asked in a low voice, not in an admonishing way but with genuine concern.

"Aye," Tommy said, nodding, though he couldn't recall what anyone had said in the past few minutes.

"Mikkel," Declan said, turning back to address the assembled men, "you'll remain aboard the ship. We can't take any chances leaving her unprotected or even undermanned."

As Mikkel grunted his agreement, Gavin stepped forward. With his chin and chest lifted, he said, "I'd prefer to be the one to remain behind, Captain."

Had Declan noticed the shift in Gavin's attitude of late? The coldness the man now displayed toward him? If he had, he kept it well-hidden now as he offered Gavin a thoughtful look and said, "No. I need you ashore with us."

Gavin's nostrils flared, and his shoulders tensed. He opened his mouth, undoubtedly to argue, but Tommy moved quickly, stepping in front of the helmsman.

"Don't." The single word, clipped short, should have been enough to stay the man's tongue, but Gavin didn't back down.

"I think—" he started, and Tommy was in his face before he could get another word out.

"No."

"But—"

What has gotten into him? Why is he pushing so hard?

"Whatever your issue with the captain is," Tommy hissed at his friend, "he's still your captain. You want off the crew? Say so. But don't undermine him like this in front of the men. Understand?"

Time ticked by slowly, and the tension among the crew seemed to thicken with each breath as they waited for Gavin's response. Would he request to leave? Would he really abandon the ship and the crew and the captain?

Perhaps Tommy had underestimated the depths of Gavin's anger.

With a slow inhale, Gavin finally stepped back, his lips pressed in a tight line and his eyes still blazing.

Declan was speaking again before Tommy returned to his place beside him. "I know I've been a bit preoccupied since returning to the ship, but I hope you know I am grateful to have a crew such as you lot. We have lost some good men..."

Declan's chin fell to his chest, and he let out a long breath before he continued. "And they will be missed. Greatly. This is the risk we all take upon joining a crew. It's the burden of a captain, to know that each decision I make and each action I take could result in the loss of one of the souls standing behind me. But I do not own you. Your lives are not mine. Any man here is free to go at any time."

Pausing once more, Declan took a step closer to the men. Tommy studied them as they contemplated the captain's words, waited to see if any would step forward and request to leave. Most of them nodded in understanding, their trust in Declan plainly visible on their faces. Others stared blankly, like their captain was describing the weather. And then there was Gavin, whose grief was evident in the tightness of his jaw and the glossy sheen of his eyes.

"But," Declan continued, his tone growing sterner now, "as long as you sail under my colors, you will do as I say. As much as I care about each of you, I care about the crew as a whole more. One disloyal man is a danger to every soul on board." Pulling the dagger from his waist, Declan pointed it at the men. "So know this. Cross me and you're done. I don't care how long you've been here, how long we've known each other. If you want out, you can leave. But if you stay, you *will* fucking listen to me."

Everyone looked from the captain to Gavin and back again. No one made a sound. Tommy stood still like all the others. Watching. Waiting. Wondering what Gavin would choose.

As Declan stalked toward Gavin with his dagger held low at his side, Tommy caught sight of Aoife's worried expression and offered her a half-smile.

Declan's voice was so low now that Tommy could barely make out the words.

"Be mad at me, Gavin. Hate me even. Sands know, I deserve it. But you pull that shit again and I'll feed you to the depths myself."

Time stilled. No one breathed.

And then Gavin nodded—a slow, almost imperceptible movement. To his credit, he did not once take his eyes from the captain's. "Aye, Captain," he said in a gravelly whisper. "Won't happen again."

Returning his dagger to its sheath, Declan stepped back. "Good. Now we can get on with the matter at hand. Getting the dagger from Callum. And we will do that by giving him what he wants."

Tommy's breath caught. Certainly he hadn't heard that right, especially with how calm Aoife looked despite the prospect of being handed over to a villainous pirate. Either he'd misheard or Declan and Aoife had devised a plan without him. As tired as he was of being the third wheel, being left out completely was even worse.

Declan motioned for Aoife to step up beside him. "A few of us will escort Aoife to the pub, and from there she will go with Callum." The men looked at each other, confusion playing on their faces, but Declan continued. "I will take the dagger, and Tommy will be waiting outside the pub to stop Callum and rescue her. We'll meet back at the ship and set sail before the sun rises. With both the dagger and Aoife."

With the men dismissed, Gavin sent back to the helm, and Aoife encouraged to get some rest before they arrived in Selka, Tommy and Declan settled against the railing near the prow and peered off into the distance at the cliffs of Turvala. They would reach the Turvalan waters by late afternoon, but Declan, who insisted the cover of darkness would be to their benefit, wouldn't take them into port until after dusk.

"And Aoife is okay with this?" Tommy asked.

"It was her idea."

Tommy shot Declan a curious look. "*You're* okay with this?"

Declan hummed in response.

"Is that a yes or a no?"

"Both," Declan said.

Tommy couldn't help but laugh. "Your abundance of confidence certainly puts me at ease."

"Am I concerned about what could go wrong? Aye. Of course I am. But it's the best option we have. She won't be parted from me, and I—"

"Can't tell her no?" Tommy looked sidelong at his friend, who rolled his eyes.

"I don't know that I trust anyone else to watch after her."

Tommy flinched, his hand flying to his chest in mock offense. "Excuse me? What have I been doing for the past week?" Never mind that Aoife had been bitten by a siren, almost eaten by a kraken, and nearly strangled to death by the man she loved all while in Tommy's care.

"I know, Tommy. And I'm thankful you were there in my stead. But I'm back."

Tommy settled his arms back against the railing. "And she'll be by your side. Until you hand her over to that butcher."

"Do I like it? No. But what else am I supposed to do, Tommy? Lock her in here? How could I possibly claim to love her if I lock her up? I have to trust her. If I'm going to ever earn back her trust, I have to give her the same."

Tommy shook his head in disbelief, even though he understood all too well. *I want you beside me wherever I must go.* That was what he had told Maura before heading into the sound. Would he have been able to leave Maura behind?

Yet she left you behind rather easily, didn't she?

No. He wouldn't give in to those thoughts. At this point, he was almost certain Maura's departure was Renna's doing, but even so, it didn't fix this painful void.

Tommy straightened himself, forcing his focus back to what Declan was saying. "We saved her once. Back in Foxhaven. We can do it again. And this time we'll be ready."

"Planning to take his head, are you?"

"Maybe," Declan said casually.

"So what do you need from me?"

"After I have the dagger—and its magic—Callum won't stick around long."

"You know, it makes no sense for him to give up such a powerful weapon, especially in exchange for a woman." Tommy leaned an inch closer to Declan and lowered his voice to a whisper. "Do you think he knows the truth about her lineage?"

Declan shook his head. "Doubtful. This feels personal. But regardless, I need you to be ready to stop him from leaving."

"He'll know something's up if I'm not with you though. How are we getting around that? It's not like he'd believe I'm sick or gone—"

"Don't worry about that. I have it covered," Declan said with a smirk that did nothing to reassure Tommy. But he'd sailed with his captain long enough to trust him and his ridiculous plans.

"Okay, so I stop him, and then what?"

"Mikkel's family has an old farm not too far outside of town. You're to take him and Aoife there. Once I get there, you'll take Aoife and head back to the ship. I'll return once I'm done with him."

Tommy shifted on his feet as his mind worked to identify the weaknesses in this scheme so he could devise contingency plans. "And you expect Aoife to leave your side then?"

Declan drew in a breath and looked back toward his cabin where Aoife rested. "No. I don't. But I can't have her witness what I need to do."

"With all due respect, Captain, you don't *need* to do—"

"Yes, I do," Declan growled.

"All right. She is stronger than you think though," Tommy said, not quite sure why he was advocating for her to have to watch Declan's darkness in action.

"I know she is, but there's a difference between accepting that the darkness exists and loving it." Declan shook his head. "No, I don't want her there for that."

"Why not make it quick then? Kill him and be done with it! There's nothing here that says you need to torture the bastard."

"Yes, there is." Declan jabbed himself in the chest repeatedly with his finger. "Right here. This tells me he deserves to suffer. A quick death is far too good for him. What he did to Killian—"

"Is no different from what you've done to others in the past!" Tommy clamped his mouth shut and stepped back, preparing himself for a punch. It didn't come. Declan's nostrils flared with his anger. His pulse throbbed rapidly at his throat, and his eyes went wide, but he didn't move. He didn't even raise his voice, though Tommy deserved a reprimand for saying such a thing to his captain, especially here on the deck with crew not fifty feet from them.

Declan's gaze dropped to the deck as his shoulders slumped. "You're right. And it's why I can't have Aoife there." He looked back up to Tommy. Though his anger was subsiding, the tension remained. "The nightmares that come from witnessing such a thing... I need to spare her from that."

"But not enough to actually refrain from doing it in the first place."

Declan didn't move except to close his eyes. "Just get her back to the ship for me."

"Aye, I will," Tommy said. "But just consider it, Declan. You don't need to succumb to that part of you. You don't need to let it control you. *You're* stronger than you think."

CHAPTER 21
DECLAN

Once the sun had sunk beneath the horizon and the last traces of light had faded from the western sky, Declan sent the selected crew members off the ship and into Selka. They were to stay in small groups and approach the Gilded Cup from different directions. While they wouldn't all be attending the meeting inside the pub, they needed to be at the ready if needed. Mikkel had also provided everyone with the directions to his family's abandoned farm. Although only Tommy had been assigned to take Callum there, Declan refused to take any chances. He needed each person going ashore to be able to continue on with the plan if anything were to happen to Tommy.

Sands forbid.

Tommy hadn't had the best luck since they'd started this quest for the dagger. Declan hoped it would be different this time. How often could a pirate cheat death in the span of a couple of weeks?

A hand slipped into Declan's, fingers lacing with his. He let out a sigh when he peered down and saw Aoife standing beside him. "Glad to see it's you grabbing my hand like that, princess."

She smiled. "I hope the men know better than to try."

He should come up with something funny or witty to say, but as he looked into her eyes, the weight of everything that waited for them tonight slammed into him. Was he really willing to put this woman in harm's way? Was he really going to ignore every warning that screamed in his head?

She squeezed his hand. "It will be okay," she whispered. "We've planned for every outcome we could imagine."

But what if the unimaginable happened? What if something went horribly wrong?

Could he live with himself if something happened to her?

You'll have to.

Turning him to face her, Aoife looked him square in the eye. While there was a hint of apprehension in her features, it was dwarfed by the new confidence and strength she'd found in his absence. "I trust you, Declan. We can do this."

Sands, he hoped she was right.

"It's not too late to stay behind," he said. A flicker of hope that she would change her mind arose. But he knew she wouldn't.

"I know. But you're stuck with me, Captain." She flashed him a half-smile before lifting up onto her toes. Pulling his face down to meet hers, she kissed him. It was hard yet tender, desperate yet hopeful. There was no goodbye in the way her lips moved with his. There was only promise, a silent promise that they would survive this.

A throat cleared behind them, and Declan pulled away reluctantly to find Tommy waiting with Gavin.

"There will be time for more of that later, you two," he said, shooting Aoife a wink. "We'd better get over there before Callum gives up waiting for us."

Without a word, Declan and Aoife walked off the ship, hand in hand, toward the Gilded Cup.

⚔

THE PUB HADN'T CHANGED MUCH since the last time they'd been here, when he and Tommy had recruited Mikkel all those years ago. Rustic and unpainted, its wooden exterior showed no weathering from the sea air. The gold and green sign hanging above the door still held its glossy sheen, as if it had recently received a new coat of paint. Declan had sent Tommy down a different street a few blocks away, and now he, Aoife, and Gavin strode into the pub.

The room was surprisingly empty for this time of night, and as they entered, the few patrons who sat at the bar promptly abandoned their unfinished mugs of ale to move past them and slip out the door. Two pirates remained, seated near the back door at a round table scattered with empty glasses and mugs.

"McCallagh! You made it!" Callum's familiar voice boomed jovially, as if they were old friends catching up rather than bitter adversaries. He slapped the chest of the man beside him with the back of his hand. "I told you he'd come, Dom!"

The sound of Callum's hand striking his quartermaster made Declan's shoulders tighten, and he had to work to keep his hand loose atop the pommel of his cutlass. With Aoife and Gavin following closely behind him, he strode slowly to Callum's table. He took a deep breath and relaxed his jaw, forcing the tension to release its grip on every muscle and tendon. It would do none of them any good if he couldn't keep a handle on his emotions.

"Callum," he said, nodding to the pirate, who sat back in a wooden chair with his boots propped up onto the table. In his hands he held the Csintala dagger, spinning it in lazy circles.

Callum said nothing more, but he held Declan's gaze, as if he were trying to discover the plans Declan had for this encounter.

Declan took a lazy breath before asking, "Are we here to do business or stare at each other like old lovers?"

Callum burst into laughter and waved a hand at Aoife. "Tired of the bitch already?"

Hearing her referred to as such—sands, hearing her name on this bastard's tongue at all—stoked his anger, but he fought to keep it hidden, pressing his tongue to the roof of his mouth to prevent his jaw from noticeably clenching.

"I've never been one for commitment," Declan said with a shrug.

He couldn't risk turning to glance at Aoife. Hopefully she remembered all his warnings not to listen to a word he said in this room.

Callum looked around the pub, lifting up slightly out of his chair to peer behind Declan. "Did you lose your shadow?"

Declan frowned and shook his head briefly. "Nope. He's here." He raised a hand over his shoulder and crooked a finger. The door to the pub creaked behind him, and familiar footsteps sounded on the wooden floor.

Aoife gasped as Tommy stepped past Gavin to stand beside Declan.

Callum laughed again, and it grated on Declan's nerves. "I thought for sure you'd have him waiting somewhere to snatch me up." He pointed the dagger at Declan and narrowed his eyes. When Declan didn't respond, Callum pulled his feet from the table and slid the dagger into his belt as he stood. "Shall we do our business then?"

Something in Callum's eyes made Declan's gut churn. It was like the man knew something Declan didn't—which was quite possible since he had the upper hand here. He'd planned the location. He'd set the terms.

Still, Declan had a few tricks of his own.

Declan waved his hand over his shoulder, beckoning Aoife forward. His skin prickled when her shoulder brushed against his arm as she passed. She didn't pause, didn't stumble, didn't flinch as she walked slowly across the room. When she stopped—keeping the table between her and Callum—Declan's breath stalled.

Callum leered, his eyes roving up and down her body.

If he kept looking at her with such lust in his eyes, Declan was going to carve them out of his bloody head.

Soon enough, he reminded himself.

"You come willingly?" Callum asked.

Aoife nodded but didn't speak.

Callum looked over her head to where Declan stood trying to remember how to pull the fucking air into his lungs. "Seems she's done with you too, McCallagh." He gave a throaty laugh and stalked toward Aoife.

All of Declan's muscles screamed at him to move, to pull her away from this monster, to thrust her behind him where he could protect her. But no. He'd promised to try this her way.

But Callum didn't approach her as closely as Declan had expected. He didn't grab her, didn't touch her. He only stared.

"Well, I'm here, Captain Grayson," Aoife said. "The *bitch* for the blade, wasn't it? I believe you have a deal to keep." She tossed her head back, indicating Declan.

"Aye, that was our deal," Callum said as he gave her a string of small nods and resumed stepping slowly toward her.

Declan's hand tightened around his cutlass. This was about to go south, but in what way he didn't know yet. He forced the tension from his face, though, because no matter what Callum chose to do next, Declan could not let him see how much he cared.

"I brought the girl. Now hand it over," Declan said in as bored a tone as he could manage.

Callum smirked. "All in good time, McCallagh. All in good time."

"I don't like this," Gavin whispered, and Declan offered the slightest dip of his chin in agreement. This wasn't unexpected, but that didn't make it desirable in the slightest. And the worst part was, Declan couldn't do anything about it.

Yet.

"What are we waiting for exactly?" Declan asked.

Callum breathed out a laugh. "Oh, have a hot date you need to get to?" He leaned his head down toward Aoife. "Hear that? He's already moving on."

Every syllable that rolled off the man's tongue was like acid in Declan's blood.

All in good time, Declan. All in good time.

Callum didn't know how true those words were.

"Well," Callum said, straightening and scanning the faces in the room. "As it turns out, I *do* have a hot date planned. Or I did."

His dark eyes became wild as he focused once more on Aoife. A wicked grin stretched across his lips.

Not good not good not good.

Declan winced as he remembered the last time he'd thought those same words —on Callum's ship when he knew one of the nicest people he had ever met was about to face a gruesome end. He closed his eyes, acknowledging the haunting images and the way his gut responded with a stabbing pain.

Acknowledge them.

Don't fight them.

Breathe through it.

In his head, he heard his father's voice, talking him through the oncoming panic. He couldn't afford to let it consume him here. Quietly taking another breath, he began to calm down. The images floated away, and the pain eased, bringing him back to the dingy pub.

"I was going to take you with me," Callum was saying to Aoife. "But watching you come to me willingly, well, what can I say? It's just not as much fun as I expected."

The man moved quickly, closing the distance between him and Aoife with near-blinding speed. His hand gripped Aoife's neck, and her head flew back from the force. Declan flinched. She struggled to breathe under Callum's grasp, and her choking echoed in Declan's ears.

He took a small step forward before he could think better of it. Maybe Callum hadn't noticed.

But no, Declan wasn't so lucky.

Callum's laugh mingled with Aoife's labored, ragged breathing. "Just as I thought." His eyes snapped to Declan's. "You weren't done with her yet."

With a shrug, Declan said, "Do with her what you want, but I'd rather not watch your sick fantasies acted out in front of me."

"But that's what makes it fun." Callum squeezed tighter, and Aoife's arms began to shake at her sides.

Declan didn't reply. He needed all of his energy to disconnect from the situation. Callum wanted to see him hurt. Declan wouldn't give him the satisfaction.

"You know though..." Callum said. He loosened his grip on Aoife and spun her around until she faced Declan. Then he pulled her back against him, his hand still at her throat as he held her close. "Perhaps I'd get a better reaction if I make you look at each other."

Declan kept his attention focused on Callum as his mind whirred through his options.

Not many and all shitty.

When Aoife mouthed the words "I'm sorry," Declan had to fight harder to keep from meeting her eyes.

"The blade, Callum. Now," Declan said.

"Seriously?" Callum said, his grip loosening once more as disappointment spread across his face. "Nothing? No heartfelt goodbyes? No disgustingly sweet romantic gestures? No daring rescue attempts?"

Declan only glowered with impatience.

"You're no fun, McCallagh. Anyone ever tell you that?"

Still, Declan didn't move.

Callum gave an exaggerated eye roll and huffed out a breath. "Fine. If you won't play along, there's little point in dragging this out." And before his next breath, Callum had dropped his left hand from Aoife's throat only to bring up a small knife with his right. He pressed it against her throat, the blade caressing her delicate skin.

Her eyes went wide, cutting straight into Declan, but she wasn't pleading with him to help. Any fear that might exist there was dwarfed by a now familiar look of determination. Callum whispered something into Aoife's ear, too low for Declan to hear.

Whatever he said, it was enough to dissolve the strength she'd been holding on to. She deflated, her shoulders slumping. Her eyes shone with apology and despair. She was giving up.

No, Declan wouldn't let her. Not when they'd come this close. He'd argued against this plan, all the while knowing it was the best option they had. And he wasn't about to let her believe they'd failed.

He hadn't even fully turned when Tommy moved straight at Callum. The pirate reacted as expected, pulling the blade away from Aoife and grabbing her with his other hand as he threw the blade at his attacker.

Aoife's mouth opened to scream, but the sound was cut short when Tommy caught the knife by the blade. With a small toss, he had it by the handle and continued his approach, ignoring the blood that spilled from his palm. Aoife threw her elbow back into Callum's gut, and although he averted her strike, it was enough to force his hand away from her throat. She scrambled to move away from him, but he was too fast, grabbing a fistful of her hair and yanking her back at the same time he kicked a chair into Tommy's legs to slow him down.

Gavin stormed past, but Declan grabbed him by the arm, pulling him back. "Don't."

Gavin tried to yank his arm away.

Declan tightened his grip.

"Trust me."

Gavin glared at him. "Someone needs to help," he said. "Or are you trying to get your whole crew killed?"

Declan growled. "Leave it!"

He turned back in time to see Tommy thrust the knife at Callum, who promptly swung Aoife in between them.

Aoife's scream pierced the stale air as the blade caught her instead.

Gavin fidgeted angrily.

Declan remained still, but his insides twisted into chaos.

Callum's man, Dominic, hadn't moved at all. He still sat at the table, watching everything like a bored spectator. Why? Why didn't he help his captain?

You know why.

Callum didn't need his help.

As long as Callum had the Csintala dagger, they could not defeat him.

They needed to get it away from him. But they wouldn't be able to simply grab it from him. Its magic wouldn't allow it. They needed him to give it over willingly, or...

Aoife's pained whimper pulled his focus back to her. He needed to think faster. Blood was soaking into her shirt from the wound at her side. Tears streamed down her face as she stared at Declan, who stood there, frozen. He couldn't risk making the wrong move here.

Declan called out to Tommy, who was throwing the chair to the side and moving to lunge once more at Callum. "Stop!"

Tommy halted but kept the knife raised, ready to attack again if needed. "Aye?"

"That's enough," Declan said, forcing exasperation into his tone. "Stand down."

Tommy's brow twitched, but then he slid the blade into his belt.

"What is it, McCallagh? Going soft? Backing away from a fight?" Callum taunted him, his hand still holding fast to Aoife's hair.

"It's hardly fair when you have the dagger, is it?"

Callum narrowed his eyes. "I suppose. But that doesn't mean it's not fun. For me, anyway."

"Well, I have places to be. So let's be done with it. We delivered the girl. Hand over the blade."

Silence settled around them, broken only by the occasional strained breath from Aoife, whose hands were pressed against her wound. Callum stared at him, seeming to contemplate Declan's demand. His lips curled into a sneer.

"I don't think so."

"Oh?"

Callum shook Aoife's head a bit before turning her face to his. Wetting his lips, he studied her for a moment and said, "I think I'll keep both."

"That wasn't the deal, Callum."

"And what are you going to do about it, McCallagh? You said yourself that I have the upper hand here. And I choose to keep the girl *and* the dagger."

Declan stalked forward now with steady, even steps. When he was beside Tommy, he shot him a glance and gestured for him to return to where Gavin stood behind him. Tommy gave him a tight nod before complying, and Declan continued toward Callum.

He was close to her now. Close enough to smell the sharpness of her blood mingling with the sweet aroma that was uniquely hers. Close enough to feel the warmth from her body emanating from her. Close enough to hear the quiet sounds of pain she tried to suppress.

But he didn't look at her. He couldn't. Looking into her pained eyes would pull him back into the sea of emotions she'd opened up inside him. He couldn't afford any crack in the mask he had donned for this exchange.

Declan leaned forward. "I will end you, Callum," he said in a calm voice. "Maybe not here. Maybe not now. But soon. My face will be the last you see. My voice will be the last you hear. And you will beg for the end before I'm finished. I guarantee it."

A flash of fear sparked in Callum's eyes, so brief that Declan thought he might have imagined it. It very well could have been his own delusion, especially considering how Callum burst into laughter seconds later.

Declan kept his bored expression in place, letting Callum enjoy his bit of humor for the moment, even when the pirate turned back to Dominic, asking, "Did you hear that? He's mad! Completely insane." Dominic only smirked.

Callum turned back to Declan. "And how do you expect to do that? I have the dagger. You cannot touch me. You cannot defeat me. You. Cannot. Win."

There. That bit of fear sparked again, and Callum's face twitched slightly.

"You'll see, Callum. As you said, all in good time," Declan said quietly, raising a brow.

Callum eyed him for a long moment before pulling Aoife closer to him, his arm snaking over her shoulder and around her collarbone so that he had a good hold of her.

And then he began to back away, never taking his eyes off Declan.

"Dominic!" he called without turning his head.

"Aye, Cap'n?" his quartermaster answered, and his chair scraped against the floor as he pushed back to stand.

"Watch them. Make sure none of them follow."

"Aye."

Callum pointed the dagger at Aoife's neck, pressing it just below her jaw. "You follow? She dies. Understand?"

Declan nodded.

As Callum backed away, Declan finally allowed himself to look down at Aoife. Her fair face had grown more pallid with the loss of blood. They wouldn't have much time to rescue her before she lost too much. Her eyes still sparkled with understanding, and although there was also fear there, Declan saw more in her. Courage. Intelligence. And the one thing he had hoped for—trust.

Just before Callum pulled her into the shadows, she mouthed the words "I love you."

And all Declan could manage was a nod before she was gone.

CHAPTER 22
ADLER

Adler stepped onto the cobbled streets of Morshan. Per Lucan's directions, he did not head straight for the pub, where he'd find the secret entrance to her office. Instead, he made for the docks, telling himself this ruse was not a waste of time but just as important as finding out what had happened to her and why she hadn't waited.

"It will raise suspicions if you go straight from the council hall road to the pub—especially so early in the day when it's not open to patrons," Lucan had instructed. *"You also can't use the office's main entrance, as it were. Not much more than a simple door tucked between storefronts, but it, too, isn't wise during daylight hours."*

Adler had already surmised what Lucan would recommend, but he'd asked the man anyway. It was good for the lad to feel needed, especially on this island where a man was more a slave than a citizen. Lucan had given him strict instructions for which merchants to visit and in which order. Picking up a few odds and ends for the pub wouldn't raise alarm, and it was most certainly an errand a new pub-hand would likely be sent on.

Once Adler had traded most of Lucan's ration cards for the items needed—cleaning chemicals, rags, and food—he made his way back to the pub, risking no more than a shift of his eyes when he passed the secret entrance to the office.

Adler had barely made it halfway to the pub when a woman's voice stopped him. Turning, he saw a confused and worried-looking Penny. Wringing her hands together in front of her, she approached him tentatively. It took Adler a second longer than he'd ever admit to notice that there was fear in her eyes.

But if she was afraid of him, why call out to him?

"Adler?" Penny said his name again as she walked toward him, though she seemed ready to flee at any perceived threat. "Do you—"

Adler mouthed for her to be quiet. Though he couldn't see anyone in his periphery who might be a spy for the councilwomen, he also couldn't take any chances. He didn't know what she was about to ask him, but given the mental state she'd been in yesterday, it seemed safe to assume she wasn't likely to be careful with her words.

"I'm on my way to the pub," Adler said. "Need to get these delivered before opening time. But I would appreciate the company, if you're willing to escort me through town."

With a nod, Penny shifted direction and stepped up beside him. After they had gone several paces in silence, she finally posited her question once again, this time keeping her voice just above a whisper.

"Do you work for them?"

An image of those women, cold and hard, flashed in his mind. Not for the last time, he wondered how his Lani had possibly come from such bitterness. With a deep breath, he nudged Lani's sweet, smiling face to the corner of his mind and shook his head.

"Then why?"

"Why what?" Though he had a good idea what she referred to, it was best not to assume anything and inadvertently offer up more information than necessary.

"Lucan."

The name fell to the ground between them like a stone dropped into the sea. For a moment, Adler's guilt spiked as he thought about the lie he'd had to sell in the town square. It had worked—as far as he knew—but having to continue to pretend to be allied with them, the ones who had killed Lani, made him sick. Sicker still to think of all the people who believed it to be true.

It's all part of being a pirate—even a former pirate, he reminded himself.

Adler gave the woman a gentle smile before he said, "We all have a part to play, Penny. You. Me. Lucan."

Penny cringed at the mention of her name, closing her eyes tight. To her credit, she recovered quickly, catching Adler's gaze as she asked her next question.

"Is he—" Concern flashed in her eyes.

"He's okay," Adler whispered back, and Penny's shoulders slumped with relief.

They walked a bit more in silence before Adler asked, "And how are you?"

She laughed nervously. "As good as—sands. Honestly? I'm not good at all."

Adler nodded his understanding, although he knew he couldn't completely relate to the chaos the truth had caused for this woman.

"What am I supposed to do now?" she asked, the question barely audible over the sounds of their footsteps.

"Aside from continuing to work?"

His question stopped her in her tracks, and she gaped at him for a moment before closing her mouth, apparently remembering where they were and who might be watching. As she resumed walking, she asked, "How am I to simply go back to life as it was, knowing..."

"Because you have to," Adler offered with a shrug.

"But—"

"I didn't say that's *all* you had to do." Her eyes narrowed in question. "Appearances have to be kept up, Penny. I don't need to tell you what could happen if you don't. Aye?"

Slowly she nodded. They were nearing the pub, its sign swaying gently in the light sea breeze not twenty paces away. "How can I help?"

There was no reason to suspect she was a council spy. Not after all she'd endured at the pit. Not after the way the council had treated her before the entire town. But it wasn't Adler's call.

"I don't know yet, but I will let you know as soon as I do," he said.

When they reached the front door of the pub, Adler turned to her and regarded her solemnly. "I promise, Penny. You can help, if that's what you wish. Trust me."

With a nod and a shaky smile, she turned around and headed back the way they'd come, and Adler hoped beyond all hope that they would figure out some way to beat the council.

"Where's Cait?"

Kira's question sent Adler's heart plummeting to his feet. All of the hope and optimism he'd bolstered during his conversation with Penny vanished, scattering like dust on the wind. He stared at Kira as if she were a ghost and not Cait's trusted friend.

"She's not back?"

Kira huffed. "If she were, I wouldn't have asked. Would I?"

He shook his head. A pointless gesture, but it was all he could muster.

"Did she catch up to you?"

Adler, blinking and shaking away the fear that threatened him, rushed to the bar and dropped the items he'd brought. Kira didn't pay them any attention but patiently waited for his answer.

"Aye, she did."

"And?"

"And I told her to come back and meet me here as planned."

Kira massaged her forehead with her fingers before sending them through her hair. Her eyes shifted back and forth before settling on the bar. "This isn't good," she muttered, her words barely audible.

"What do we do?" Adler asked.

"We wait."

Adler opened his mouth to argue but then snapped it shut. Kira was right. It would do them no good to go out, frantic and unhinged, searching for her. As much as every fiber in his body hated the idea of doing nothing, this was the best way. Still, a single question lingered.

"What if she doesn't come back?" He could barely give the words his air. He'd lost one love. Could he survive losing another…another what? He didn't love Cait. He couldn't love her. But that—

"Then we keep going as she would have wanted us to," Kira said, her words cold. But not cold like the councilwomen had been. This was the clipped speech of someone trying desperately to hold their emotions together, to keep themselves from falling apart in the face of defeat and loss.

"Do you need me here?"

Frowning, she shook her head before tossing her head toward the back storeroom. "Go. And hope she arrives soon."

Cait's office was nothing like what Adler had expected, and yet it all fit her. It was like each item—the worn rug on the floor, the old clock over the fireplace, the mismatched chairs sitting near her desk—held a piece of Cait's past. He might have berated himself for being so sentimental had he not been burdened by the concern growing within him. No, concern was too light a word for what tormented him. Once again someone he cared about was in danger—perhaps bleeding or dying somewhere—and he was powerless to stop it.

He began pacing the rug, back and forth across the spot where Cait—or someone—had apparently trod many a path before. What was he to do here? Sit and wait and twiddle his thumbs like a child? His muscles ached to be worked, put into action against whatever—or whoever—had prevented Cait from waiting for him and meeting with him now.

I should have grabbed a bottle of rum before I came down here, he thought.

Looking to the desk, he wondered if a bottle might be stashed in one of its drawers, but no, he wouldn't invade her privacy. Especially not after the stunt he and Lucan had pulled on her. He was here to earn back her trust, not undo all his efforts out of boredom.

Instead, he busied himself with starting a fire in the hearth, despite it already being rather warm in the room. Once the flames were greedily licking at the wood, he settled onto the sofa and tried to relax.

It didn't work.

He was going to go mad here. Watching the flames. Wondering where she was. Hoping she was okay. Wishing he could do more than sit and wait and try not to doze off. But his lids were so heavy, especially in the dim light of the fire, and he soon lost the fight to keep them open. He urged his mind to focus on something other than what could have happened to Cait, but the images of Lani that appeared weren't any better.

The coy curve of her smile. The humor lighting up her green eyes when she teased him. The soft waves of her hair falling against his cheek when she turned away from his kiss with a giggle. Why did his heart hurt so much over a woman he'd barely known? How could he have fallen so quickly and so absolutely? How had everything gone so horribly, terribly wrong in such a short time?

Adler shook away the memories and forced his eyes open only to find himself back in the cove, the Aisling's water rolling over the black sand, over his boots, over the feet of the woman standing beside him.

Lani.

Whole and unbroken and safe. Around and around, she twirled a strand of her hair between her fingers, but she didn't speak, only looked at him with that same hope and love he'd witnessed the last time they'd been here. A dream, a figment of his imagination. He might have thought his mind was torturing him had he not found some comfort in seeing her now.

"I'm so sorry."

Adler didn't realize he had said the words aloud until Lani answered him.

"What have you to be sorry for?" she asked, dropping her head to one side. Her eyes shifted with concern.

"You're not real."

A smile pulled at Lani's lips as she walked toward him. "No, I'm not, but I am here with you," she said, her words devoid of the humor that still played across her face.

His chest caved, the weight of his grief as substantial as an anchor lowering into the sea. Would he ever be free from this? How long would it take to heal?

She laughed softly, as if she had heard his thoughts.

Of course she heard them. She lives in your head, after all.

"You know there's no right answer to those questions," she said.

"I miss you," he said before he knew what he was saying.

Lani's lips tightened into a sorrowful line. "And I you. I'm sorry too."

He huffed out a humorless laugh before repeating her earlier words. "What have you to be sorry for?"

"For having to leave you."

"I'm keeping my promise," he said, lowering his chin to his chest, focusing on the retreating water. "I'll protect your sisters. I just wish I could have protected you."

"I know, but nothing good comes from dwelling on what cannot be changed. All we can do is move forward. Keep living and growing and loving."

Tears welled up in his eyes as she voiced the truth he'd been wrestling with for weeks. Somehow, hearing it from her helped it make sense, allowed him to start accepting and believing it.

Lani reached for him, and he could almost feel her fingers trail up his jaw. Leaning into her hand, he let his eyes close. A tear escaped as she whispered her final words.

"I love you, Adler."

THE CHIME of a clock jolted Adler awake, the remnants of his dream fading to the edges of his mind until only an odd lightness remained, as if something had been lifted from his chest.

But something wasn't right.

The fire had burned down now, with only some dying embers remaining. And aside from the faint ticking of the clock, the room was silent.

He was alone.

A quick glance at the clock had him jumping to his feet. It was well into the evening. He'd slept far too long. And Cait should have arrived by now.

With a curse, he bolted through the door and ran down the dark passageway toward the pub as fast as he could go without stumbling over the rough stone floor. Another curse fell from his lips when his shins hit hard against something, throwing him forward.

Stairs.

How had he not realized he'd reached the pub entrance? Surely at this time of day, the pub should be bustling with pirates drinking and laughing. But silence as thick as the darkness engulfed him, igniting fresh panic.

He tripped up the stairs, miscounting and bashing his head into the wooden door. But he refused to let the pain slow him down. Not when everything in his body told him something was terribly wrong.

The feeling only intensified as he stepped into the dark storeroom and saw no light coming from the pub's main room. He stopped and listened as he slid a small blade from his boot.

Nothing.

And then the silence broke. There was a clunk of a bottle against wood, accompanied by the sound of boots sliding against the floor, followed promptly by a thump and a curse uttered by a familiar voice.

Cait.

Adler, his blade still out and ready, turned the corner to find Cait sitting on the floor, propped up against the end of the bar with her legs sprawled out before her. She tossed her head to the side and lifted the bottle to her lips in what was quite obviously not her first swig of the rum.

He rushed to her side and knelt before her. His eyes roved over her as he tried to take stock of her physical state. She didn't appear hurt. Inebriated, yes. Annoyed as always. He let out a sigh of relief, placing his knife on the floor and reaching out a hand toward her shoulder.

"You all right, love?"

Cait swung her head toward him in a drunken arc, setting the bottle down with a thud before answering him.

With a laugh.

And not the endearing laugh he always found himself hoping to hear whenever she was near, the laugh he'd first heard during that card game with Lucan. Sands, that felt like ages ago.

No, this laugh was laced with sarcasm and disdain.

When Cait's gaze still hadn't focused on him, Adler risked grabbing her face with both hands. Her laughter stopped as she relaxed into his touch, and his name fell from her lips in a whisper.

"Aye, love. It's me," he said, and his mind raced to figure out what could have happened to drive her to drink so much. "Look at me."

With a flutter of her eyelids—and with far more effort than she should have needed—she obeyed.

"Adler," she repeated. "You're here."

"I've been here a while actually. Where have you been?"

She lifted her shoulders high in an exaggerated shrug. "Here and there."

"Here, love. Let me help you up," he said, sliding his hands down to her sides, surprised when she didn't protest but let him lift her. "Can you stand?"

She nodded, but when he pulled his hands away, she started to crumple back down to the floor.

"Whoops," she said with a muffled laugh as she fell into his chest.

Under any other circumstances Adler might have found all of this incredibly entertaining, but this wasn't her, and if she was acting out of character, there was a reason.

And not likely a good one.

Holding her at arm's length, he looked her in the eye. "Let's try this again." He nearly laughed at how her expression hardened with determination before she gave him a resolute nod.

Lifting her hands out to either side, Cait tested her balance, and after managing to stand on her own—albeit a tad unsteadily—for a few breaths, said, "I'm good."

Adler hummed in response and lowered his arms, though he stayed ready to catch her if needed.

"I just need..." Cait said as she gracelessly turned to go behind the bar. As she made her way to the line of bottles at the back, her boot kicked over the near-empty one she'd left on the floor.

Adler studied her and frowned at how she limped across the floor. She was favoring her left leg in a way that screamed injury, not intoxication, and in two quick strides, he was beside her, wrapping his arm around her waist and pulling her close against his side.

"Let me get it for you, love. I need to look you over."

"Rather forward of you, isn't it?"

He grabbed the nearest bottle of rum and steered them back to the end of the bar. "As much as I'd love for that to be the case, no. You're hurt. I need to take a look."

"It's nothing, but fine," she said with a roll of her eyes, tossing her hand to the side. "Where do you want me?"

His mind went to decidedly cruder places at those words, but he managed to rein himself in before setting the bottle onto the bar. "Up here," he said with a nod.

Cait glanced at the bar top and muttered, "Predictable."

Now it was Adler's turn to roll his eyes.

She didn't protest, though, when he lifted her onto the top of the bar.

"May I?" he asked, nodding to her left leg.

"Such a gentleman," Cait said with a teasing look. "If you insist, but it's nothing."

Adler tentatively lifted her skirts, careful to only expose her leg and nothing more. His jaw tightened, harder and harder with each inch of battered skin revealed.

"This is far from nothing, Cait," he bit out, hoping she wouldn't think his anger was directed at her.

"It doesn't hurt anymore." She said it so casually that his anger flared.

The skin along her shin had been peeled away, leaving behind a wound of marred flesh. Was that her bone showing? Blood, long since dried, trailed down her knee. Lifting her skirt just enough to see her thigh, he found four long, deep cuts there.

Adler dropped her skirt but left her mangled shin exposed. He'd need to clean it up to stave off infection. But first, he lifted a hand to her face, clutched her chin, and turned her to look at him. "Who did this to you?"

His question came out as more of a growl than he'd intended, but when she refused to answer, he let his anger rumble in the back of his throat. "It was them, wasn't it?"

"I don't want to talk about it." All lightheartedness drained from her eyes, replaced now with that rigid stubbornness he'd seen during their first meeting.

"Tell me, Cait."

"You know," she said, her eyelids flickering with bitterness, "I like it better when you call me *love*."

"Now." He bit the word out again.

Cait's jaw tightened, her eyes narrowing on him. Even intoxicated, she was intimidating. "Why?" she challenged. "So you can be my daring hero and defend my honor or something?"

"We both know you don't need a daring hero." Even as he said it, memories surfaced of him rushing to the edge of the pit, throwing himself forward in a desperate attempt to save her from certain death.

Her eyes fell to his chest. "You know I can't tell you, Adler."

Another growl of frustration echoed in his throat. "Who did they threaten?" It was the only explanation for why she wasn't raging about this. Her lips twitched, and Adler wasn't sure if she was near tears or trying to keep from naming her attacker.

"Kira? The twins?" Adler began guessing, but with both, she gave an almost imperceptible shake of her head. No, there was only one person they could have used to guarantee her silence. "Your brother."

Cait stiffened and swallowed hard.

"He can take care of himself, love. Let me take care of you. How can I help? Tell me what I can do."

Cait's gaze fell even lower, and for a moment, Adler's stomach clenched with worry that she would ask for something he couldn't give her. But then she turned to the side and reached for the bottle of rum. Lifting it between them, she looked him in the eye and said, "Drink with me."

CHAPTER 23
CAIT

As soon as Cait lifted the bottle to Adler, she hoped he would decline. The sound of the rum sloshing in the bottle had her stomach flopping around like a dying fish. She'd had more than enough of the wicked stuff before he'd gallantly arrived to protect her.

She scoffed silently to herself.

Or at least she thought she had done it silently.

Adler's downturned smile—the one she would have liked more if it didn't keep his dimples from showing—told her she hadn't been successful, and she fumbled for words to explain.

"Me, not you. I mean, I'm giving myself a hard time. Not you. Is what—I— shit..." Her voice trailed off with the curse, and she shook her head at her complete lack of coherency.

Damn drink, she thought. *You're better than this, Cait.*

Adler pulled the bottle from her hand and, keeping his eyes locked on hers, set it back down on the bar.

"I think you might have had enough for both of us, love." A glint of humor pulled at the corner of his eye, and she was glad to see his anger beginning to ebb. But his mouth remained in that downward curve, still denying her a glimpse of that slight divot beneath his beard.

She should be angry with him, should smack him or yell at him or kick him. He had been the one to ask how he could help her, and then he refused? After he'd had the gall to get all protective over her. She could take care of herself, damn it. She didn't need him or anyone else worrying over what they'd done to her.

But he wasn't wrong, and that truth stayed her tongue, calming her temper before it could be unleashed.

She *had* downed far more of the drink than she should have, but it had seemed a good idea at the time. How often had she watched pirates and sailors and merchants and all manner of people come in here and drown their troubles in the bottom of a glass? They walked in pained and brooding. They left feeling better. Or at least feeling nothing.

And that's what Cait wanted to feel.

Nothing.

No weight of responsibility.

No fear for her brother and her people.

No pressure.

No stress.

Nothing.

Until Adler had walked in, at least.

Now it wasn't numbness she craved, but warmth and comfort.

He's the one who shoved you out of his lap back at the pit though. She had been so stupid, putting her head on his legs, letting her eyes get lost in those damn beautiful blues of his, allowing her tongue to utter those damned words.

Can I stay here? She mocked herself in her mind. *How stupid of you.*

Cait let her eyes glance up to the ceiling, and her head fell back a little before tilting slightly to one side. But her stomach flipped again at the sudden shift. She closed her eyes to ward off the nausea. It only made it worse.

"Easy, love." Adler's soothing voice and his warm hands, light on her shoulders—pulled a hum from deep in her chest, and she forced herself to look at him. He seemed as though he were caught between laughing at her and worrying about her. Either one would have been understandable, given her sorry state, but he remained silent as he leaned to the side and reached under the bar. When he straightened again, he was holding the bottle of cheap stuff they kept on hand for those who couldn't afford anything else.

Does he want to drink that instead? She cringed until she saw he also held one of the clean bar towels.

Unstopping the bottle, he caught her gaze and said quietly, "This is going to sting of course, but it needs to—"

Her nod had him clipping his words short, and she hissed when the alcohol trickled down her busted leg. All the numbness the rum had brought her was stripped away along with the dirt and grime that had collected in her wound. Somehow she resisted the urge to reach for his chest and clutch his shirt tight in her fists as he worked. Instead she tightened her fingers in the folds of her skirts.

Her shoulders slumped with relief when he closed the bottle and slid it behind her on the bar. And she tried not to think about how nice it felt to have his fingers brushing along her skin as he wound the towel around her leg. When he finished, he lowered her skirts once more.

"Not my best work," he said. "But it will do for now."

Silence settled between them, and Cait wasn't entirely upset about it. At least he wasn't pressuring her for information anymore. Her mind flicked back to the words Melina had hissed in her ear, the villainous warning she'd been given.

But then his blue eyes flashed slightly. Worried he would return to his questions, she spoke first. "Well, if you won't drink with me—" She leaned closer to him and lowered her voice into a whisper. "Which is rather rude of you, by the way."

This time, he did let a slight laugh escape him.

Or was that her laugh?

Sands, she'd had a lot to drink.

Cait shook her head in a vain attempt to clear her mind and focus.

Before she could finish her thought, Adler was speaking. "Have to admit. This is a side of you I never expected to see."

Straightening, she narrowed her eyes at him. "What side is that exactly?"

Adler rubbed a hand over his bearded chin, studying her face.

"Well?" Her impatience threw the word at him.

This time, there was no doubt he was the one to laugh. And then he smiled, that dimple appearing faintly on his right side. "Relaxed."

Cait's forehead creased. *Relaxed?*

"Aye, love. You've been pretty damn tense since we met." When she frowned at him, he shrugged. "For good reason, of course, but it's nice to see you loosen up a bit. Though"—his expression hardened as his eyes dropped down to the skirts hiding her injuries—"I wish it were under different circumstances."

Understatement of the year, right there. She considered saying that aloud, but her voice caught before she could, keeping the quip trapped in her head.

"Maybe someday?" Adler asked, his face still lowered, attention still fixed on her legs.

"Someday what?" Ugh. Was that hope in her voice? *Pathetic.*

His blue eyes lifted. "Someday I hope you get to relax for good reasons. Happy reasons."

Her shoulders slumped as if weighed down yet again by the magnitude of what she was trying to accomplish here on this island with the rogues. She was a fool, wasn't she? To believe she could take down the council. A fool to have hoped some mythical dagger could be retrieved to help their cause.

Yet she had hoped. For all these years.

And now? Now, it seemed so far off, so impossible to achieve. Especially with such a formidable enemy. As if on cue, the pain shot through her leg once more, as intense as if that pirate was scraping away her skin again.

"If Declan fails—if he dares to double-cross us in any way—we will not stop with what we've done here. We will come for your pub and for everyone you hold dear. If you tell anyone about this meeting...well, you can use your imagination."

The councilwoman's warning hissed in her ear. She could tell Adler what had happened, how a pair of pirates had found her waiting for him on the path, how they had blindfolded her and dragged her into some sort of brig, how the council had ordered the pirates to hurt her as a warning, how Melina herself had... Adler hated them enough as it was for what they'd done to Lani. No good would come from stoking his ire further. Not when Kira and Declan and everyone she knew was at risk.

Adler's voice pulled her back to the present. "Sure you won't tell me—"

"No."

"It was them, wasn't it?" From his low, hate-filled tone, Cait knew who he meant. But she wouldn't—couldn't—confirm it for him.

Neither could she deny it though.

"So what do we do now?" she asked instead in a desperate attempt to change the subject, pairing the words with what she hoped was a coy smile. Though, in her current state, she wasn't sure she had full control over her features.

He didn't answer right away but remained close to her. His body still pressed against her knees. Another span of silence passed between them, and Cait marveled at how comfortable it was just to be with him, not talking.

"We could talk," he finally suggested.

"About what?" She wasn't completely against the idea, but it was growing increasingly difficult to even stay upright, and she had little confidence in her ability to remain coherent in her speech.

"Your family? Life before—"

"Before everything went to complete shit, you mean?"

Adler lifted a shoulder. "Aye."

Cait's mind shakily pulled forward memory after memory, the stories and events that had become too painful to relive since her parents' deaths. Laughs and smiles from the carefree moments her parents had carefully crafted for her and Declan to distract them from the truth of life on this island. No, she couldn't share those. Just thinking about it hurt almost as much as her busted leg.

"No."

The word was out of her mouth before she could stop it, and she winced—both from the pain of those images and the worry that she might have offended him somehow with her refusal.

"It's okay, love," Adler said, his blue eyes softening in the darkness, and she half-expected him to lift a hand to her cheek, to brush it across her skin the way he had in the clearing.

She hoped he would.

But he didn't move, didn't say anything else.

Cait dropped her chin to her chest, and before she knew what she was doing, she was providing the explanation he hadn't requested. "I can't. It hurts too damned much. I don't want to think about any of it. About the past. About what I've lost. About what I still have to do to make everything right. It's too much. Too much. I can't do this. I just want one night when I don't have to plan or scheme or worry or plot or lead or...anything."

"Hence the drinking."

Cait could only nod, her eyes still cast down.

"I wish I could take it away, love." He paused, his hard swallow filling the resulting silence. "But I can't." The words dropped between them like pebbles falling into the sea, heavy with an emotion Cait couldn't place.

He was wrong, of course.

Drink wasn't the only way to numb the pain.

Cait shifted forward on the bar as she reached out a hand toward him, not particularly caring what her actions might do to his opinion of her. Before he could react, she had her fingers curled over the top of his waistband and was tugging him closer until he was tucked between her legs, his waist resting against the edge of the bar. Against her.

The only sounds between them were her pounding heart and his ragged breath.

"You can. You could fix it all, Adler. Just for tonight. If you wanted to." Cait dared to raise her eyes to his, sure she would see his rejection of her.

But his body spoke louder than any words he could have said, tensing against her in all the ways she wanted. She sat up straighter and leaned toward him, her fingers still tucked into the fabric at his waist, her breath quickening in anticipation. He didn't retreat, didn't flee, didn't balk. She moistened her lips with her tongue, and her heart was thrilled when his gaze flicked down to watch. She inched closer to his face, ready to lose herself—and all her cares—in him, his kiss, his embrace, his touch...

"I won't be your distraction, Cait."

His voice was husky with undeniable desire despite his words.

Surely she'd misheard him.

She leaned closer still, but his hands stopped her, gripping her shoulders as they had before, lightly but with firm determination. He held her still and pulled back to look her in the eye.

"Not like this."

"Like what?" Cait asked as sweetly as she could.

His gaze flicked down once more to her lips. "You deserve more than a drunken romp, love."

Cait's heartbeat quickened even as her mind remained sluggish with drink. "What if a *drunken romp* is what I want?"

Her words came out so soft that she wasn't sure she'd managed to say them aloud, but she must have, because Adler sucked in a deep breath and inched closer to her.

Every part of her tensed as his heat seemed to envelop her. Squeezing her eyes closed, she tried to take note of how this felt, having him against her, having his hands holding her—even if only by the shoulders—so she wouldn't forget it when he inevitably retreated.

But he didn't.

Instead, he inched closer until his breath warmed her lips and the scent of sea and earth invaded her senses. Her head was swimming, and she didn't know if it was from the rum alone or from the unbearable tension swirling around them. Her skin screamed at her, begging for her to pull him closer so his touch could soothe every part of her that ached.

Her breath caught at the feel of his lips grazing hers so lightly she must have imagined it.

Kiss him, damn it! If he won't make the move, then you should!

She managed to ignore the shouting thoughts, knowing—somehow, despite all the rum and all the pain—she couldn't force herself on him.

"I shouldn't," he whispered against her lips.

Cait wet her lips again, and shivers coursed up her arms as her tongue skimmed his at the same time. "Who says?"

Another breath. Two breaths. Quicker now. Her heart hammered in her ears, her head beginning to throb from all the rum. She didn't know how much time passed as she lost track of their breaths mixing between them.

"I don't know." Adler's whispered words had barely escaped his lips when he pressed them to hers.

Warmth spread through Cait, intensifying as her tongue traced the seam of Adler's mouth, coaxing him to open and accept her. When he finally did, she nearly gasped at the passion and need in the strokes of his tongue against hers. His hands slid from her shoulders, across her back, and into her hair, pulling her closer and closer until she was sure she'd drown in him.

Here in the arms of this damned protective, irritatingly handsome man, she could drown all her worries, her cares, her troubles. He could take them all away, until it was only her and him and their shared craving for each other.

Cait's hands, trapped between their bodies, dared to move with her desperation to have him ever closer. He continued to kiss her, his lips and tongue caressing and consuming and tasting her more than any man ever had. But when her fingers— still beneath his sash—trailed along his waist to grip his hip, he slowed, his hunger calming, his frantic desire slipping away like the tide from the shore.

When he pulled his lips from hers, a whimper of protest escaped her, but she kept herself from pursuing him. Sucking in a deep breath, she forced herself to look at him, scared of the rejection and regret she'd surely see in his eyes.

But he appeared more confused and torn than anything else, like he was trying to figure out what had just happened, or who he'd just been kissing, who he it was he held tight in his arms.

I'm an idiot.

Too soon. It was too soon for him. He loved someone else. His heart was broken. And here she was throwing herself at him, begging him to fix her problems with something she had no right to request of him.

Adler's head tilted slightly as a smirk pulled at the corner of his mouth. "Why do you look like you've just killed someone, love?"

"I shouldn't have..." Cait tried to explain, shaking her head, but she was surprised to find his fingers were still tangled in her hair, holding her close to him.

"I wanted to," Adler said, nudging her nose with his own in a gesture so cute Cait couldn't help but smile.

She probably looked pathetic. "But you don't want to have all of me."

A chuckle fell from him. Why was he laughing at her? Here she was being vulnerable with him, and he was *laughing*?

"All that rum must be muddling your memory, love."

Before she could respond, his hands were cupping her face. He rested his forehead against hers. His eyes closed, and he whispered, "*Not like this* does not mean never. It doesn't mean I don't want to. On the contrary."

Cait's brain struggled to grasp his meaning. Rum be damned.

"Not now. Not yet," Adler explained. "Not when you won't remember every glorious moment."

It was Cait's turn to laugh. "Glorious? You're rather confident."

"Aye, love. Glorious. You deserve nothing less."

Cait melted into a damned puddle in his arms. She rested her head against his shoulder, savoring his comforting scent and relaxing into his warmth. Her eyelids closed against her will, becoming heavy like the rest of her. The desire that had burned within her had been soothed away by the need for rest.

Yes, rest. Rest sounded good. She hummed against his neck and could have sworn a laugh rumbled in his chest before he placed a light kiss on her hair.

"Let's get you to bed, love."

Before she could mutter any witty response, she was in his arms, cuddling against his chest as he walked.

The walk up the stairs didn't register, but they must have climbed them, because the next thing she knew, she was settling onto a familiar bed. And then the warmth was gone. He was gone.

Cait couldn't open her eyes, but she still reached for him. "Don't go."

She didn't know if she'd said the words or if she'd only dreamed them. Sands, she might have dreamed the entire evening. *And what a good dream it was.*

And then the bed was shifting, and his warmth was back, sliding in beside her, his arm sliding beneath her head. She rolled toward him, once again pulling herself as close to him as she could.

"Can you sing?" Cait asked without thinking, only remembering how her parents had sung to her and Declan when they'd had trouble sleeping, wracked with nightmares or scared by a storm. And though she knew she could sleep from the rum alone, she yearned for that one extra bit of comfort.

"Aye." He said it so quietly she wasn't sure she'd heard him, but then he asked, "Happy or sad?"

Cait didn't know why she said it, but the word *sad* was out of her lips before she could think about it, as if all of her emotions had pushed their way out of her in that single syllable.

Adler shifted beside her, pressing his cheek against the top of her head. "Sad it is. But it might break your heart, love."

"Already broken," she said with a sigh as tears threatened to form behind her closed lids.

"We can be broken together." Adler's whispered words tickled her forehead. With one more deep breath, he began to sing.

She didn't know the tune or even the language, but as Cait slipped closer and closer toward sleep, she was sure a tear managed to creep down her cheek. The first tear in years. And she was thankful no one but Adler was here to witness it.

CHAPTER 24
AOIFE

CALLUM'S GRIP didn't loosen around Aoife even after they were clear of the pub. As they moved through the alley, the dagger nipped at her throat whenever Aoife's feet stumbled along the uneven stones. With each trip, she hoped the pirate would falter and pull his arm away enough for her to at least try to maneuver away. Unfortunately, the opposite happened; each slip of her foot made him pull her closer, causing a new wave of pain from the wound at her side.

She kept one hand pressed against it, though she could already tell the bleeding had stopped. One notable benefit of being a demi-fae.

If only your other powers were that easy to harness, she thought.

Aoife held on to the one thing she could rely on in this moment: Declan would come for her.

She'd seen that promise in his eyes, though she had to admit she wasn't entirely sure how this was supposed to play out, with Tommy back in the pub instead of out here waiting for them to pass by.

"You won't get away with this," Aoife said, her voice weaker than she wanted.

Callum huffed out a hoarse laugh in her ear. "You have a lot of faith in a man who let you go so easily."

"Surprised me, actually," she said, trying to determine if anyone was following them. She couldn't make out anything but the scuffling of her and Callum's feet, but she refused to let that dash away her hope.

"You shouldn't be." Callum scoffed at her. "He's a pirate. A piss-poor one, but a pirate nonetheless."

Aoife rotated her head to glance at her captor. "Oh, no. Not surprised about him. Surprised you fell for it."

Callum stopped short, forcing the edge of the dagger against her throat so sharply that she hissed. "What's that supposed to mean?"

She tried to shrug under his bulky arm and nodded as she said, "I guess I shouldn't be all that surprised. The man can act. If he ever has to leave the pirate life behind, he could do fairly well on stage."

"He played me." Callum's words were spoken more to himself than to her, but Aoife answered all the same.

"Of course he did. Did the queen take some of your brain when she snacked on your fingers? Or—"

"Move," Callum barked at her and forced her to continue down the alley.

Aoife obliged but continued talking. "Or perhaps you're just getting on in years. Though I had thought you were still fairly young."

"No matter. Whatever he's planning, it won't work. Not when I have the dagger." The pirate's tone remained harsh and menacing, but Aoife caught a hint of uncertainty at the edge of his words.

Good, she thought.

Before she could say anything more, a noise came from ahead of them, so subtle she wondered if she'd imagined it. In the darkness under the new moon, she could only make out a doorway set in the stone wall. Callum—giving no indication he'd heard anything—shoved her forward again. There it was again—like fabric against stone, a shoulder brushing up against a wall, a whisper on the night breeze.

Declan.

But no. There was no way he could have made it out of the pub and headed them off like this. Could he have? And Tommy had been in there with him, instead of out here as planned.

He has a plan. He has a plan. Aoife tried to reassure herself of this fact, but as Callum inched her closer to the doorway, her mind raced with all the horrific possibilities. Bandits? Rival pirates? Another of Callum's victims seeking revenge?

Aoife held her breath—as if that might ward off whatever danger lurked in the darkened doorway—but when they stepped past it, the strike came. She didn't know where it had hit, but Callum's back arched, his arm pulling away from her, the dagger sliding dangerously close to her throat as he moved to use it against his unseen attacker. Aoife, taking the opportunity to duck away, scurried to the side of the alley and turned to find Callum thrusting his knife at his assailant.

An assailant she recognized.

Tommy.

Her heart hammered to a stop as she watched Tommy block Callum's strike with his forearm. Callum let out a curse and swung the blade at Tommy, who easily ducked out of the way before landing his fist in Callum's gut.

The captain doubled over with a groan just as Tommy brought his knee up into Callum's face.

Callum's hands flew up to his bleeding nose. His knees hit the stones with a satisfying thud.

"How?" His eyes burned with fury. "The dagger—"

"Betrayed you," Aoife said, cautiously moving to stand beside Tommy. Callum's eyes went wide with angry confusion as he lowered his hands. "You should have kept to your deal."

"You little bitch," Callum spat.

Tommy clicked his tongue. "That's no way to speak to my captain's woman."

Before Callum could respond, Tommy slammed a fist into his nose, driving the other fist into his temple. Callum wobbled for a moment, and then his eyes slid back into his head as he crumpled to the ground.

"You okay, Aoife?" Tommy asked.

"Just glad you managed to find a way to leave the pub in time. Not sure if I would have been able to do all that." Aoife pointed to the unconscious pirate at her feet.

Tommy's forehead wrinkled in confusion. "What do you mean *leave the pub*?"

Laughing lightly, sure Tommy was teasing her, Aoife shook her head. "I was sure you wouldn't be able to get away from Dominic without Callum finding out. How's your hand, by the way? The way you caught that knife was like nothing I've ever seen."

Tommy eyed her for a bit before looking down at his hands. Silently he rolled Callum's body over and pulled the dagger—*the* dagger—from the man's belt before kneeling down to situate his body onto his shoulders. With a grunt, he hoisted Callum up and gestured for Aoife to follow him to the end of the street.

"Did Declan leave with you? Or did he stay behind at the pub?" Aoife asked, wondering how their plan might have been adjusted to allow for Tommy's impromptu attendance at the meeting.

Tommy shot Aoife a sideways glance as they walked. "I don't know who was with you and Declan at the pub. But it wasn't me. I was out here in the alley waiting for this bastard all night. As planned."

Confusion swept over her. Confusion mixed with panic.

"But if you were out here...then who was in there with us?"

CHAPTER 25
DECLAN

Declan approached the table as Dominic returned to his seat.

"So when are we free to go exactly?" he asked. "Your captain was a little unclear in his orders."

Dominic downed the last of the rum in his glass and laughed. "Unclear to you perhaps. But my orders are as clear as the Aisling."

"Ah," Declan said. "We aren't meant to leave then."

As a feral grin spread across his face, Dominic shook his head slowly.

Declan drew in a deep breath before looking behind him at his companions. Gavin's anger was obvious, his jaw pulsing and eyes blazing, but all Declan could do was shoot him a warning glare and hope the man got himself under control. His helmsman's tension did ease a bit, but not nearly enough.

Tommy hadn't moved, and he was looking past Declan at Dominic, who, by the sound of it, was pouring more rum into his glass. Declan slowly turned back around while lifting the toppled chair Callum had thrown earlier. He didn't bother to ask permission to sit, but Dominic didn't protest when he did.

"You wouldn't deny a man a final glass of rum before you dispatch him, would you?" Declan asked as he settled back into his chair and nodded to the bottle still in Dominic's hand.

Dominic contemplated Declan's request for a few moments. "Why not? Glasses are behind the bar."

Declan kept his eyes firmly planted on Dominic as he waited for one of his men to retrieve the glasses. When Tommy appeared at his side, setting a glass before him, Declan risked a glance up at him. "Two more for you and Gavin."

Gavin, as expected, took his time ambling to the table, and when he arrived, he chose the seat furthest away from both Declan and Dominic. Would the man ever trust him again? If Aoife could, why couldn't this man who had known him far longer?

Give him time.

You killed his friend.

And you've been leaving him in the dark.

Declan reminded himself of all of this while Dominic started filling the three glasses. Had he been wrong not to bring Gavin into his confidence? It had been a risky decision, of course, but he needed to know Gavin could remain loyal no matter the circumstances. There was a time and a place to challenge your captain. Gavin had chosen to do so at the worst possible moment. In front of the crew. In front of Callum.

He may never trust you after all of this though, he thought.

But that was a risk he had to take.

Like letting Callum take Aoife with him.

Declan's stomach tightened at the image of Aoife being dragged away, but he drowned it in the rum flowing down his throat.

"Tommy," Declan said casually. "What do you think Callum would do if we…" He paused for effect, pretending to struggle to find the right words.

"Killed him?" Tommy offered, and Declan looked back to Dominic, who had frozen in place, holding his glass of rum in front of him.

"Aye." Declan grinned at Dominic before shrugging. "I mean, how would Callum even know?"

Dominic let out a laugh, though he no longer seemed as confident as he had been earlier. "He'd know."

Gavin fidgeted in his seat, his eyes shifting between Declan and Dominic. He leaned forward, banging his elbows on the table. "You can't—"

Declan's hand flew into the air to stop him. Bitterness coated his tongue at Gavin's blatant disrespect. Friend or no, the man could not be allowed to continue with this insubordination. But Declan couldn't deal with that problem just yet. Instead, flashing Gavin an icy glare, he said, "I can. And I will."

"He'd know," Dominic interjected, and Declan could have sworn there was a hint of fear in his voice. "He'd know, and he'd kill your little wench in return."

Running a hand over his chin, Declan pretended to consider the warning, as if he had forgotten Callum's threats.

Take your time.

You're in control here.

Declan counted slowly to himself as he pulled the stale air into his lungs. And then he smirked at Callum's quartermaster. "I don't think he will."

Dominic's expression went dark in challenge. "What makes you so sure? He has the dagger and the upper hand, not you."

"Perhaps he did. But he lost any advantage the moment he got greedy."

The quartermaster's face fell, but he soon recovered and barked out another laugh. "How do you know he hasn't killed your woman already, McCallagh?"

Declan only deepened his smirk. "Because my man was waiting for him. And knowing my man, he already has your captain's body strung up and is waiting for me to end him."

Dominic looked from Declan to Tommy and back again. "What man?"

"My quartermaster. Tommy."

Gavin's jaw fell, but he recovered quickly enough without a reprimand and continued to watch the exchange in silence.

"But this is Tommy." Dominic jutted a finger at the man beside Declan.

Declan sucked a breath in through his teeth and then shook his head sadly at the confused pirate across from him. "Actually. It's not."

A tense moment passed as no one spoke, and Dominic's face went green and then white as *Tommy* shifted in his seat. He rolled his shoulders and gave a rhythmic shake of his head, and the illusion fell away until it was no longer Tommy at the table but a frighteningly beautiful siren. The amber in his eyes had given way to a deep gray that shimmered even in the dim light. His brown hair darkened and lengthened so that it now fell over her shoulders, cascading over and beyond the curves of her body.

"A siren," Dominic and Gavin whispered in unison, both pulling away from the creature, their eyes wide with fear.

She winked at Declan, who responded with a nod of thanks.

"This is Celene. And yes, she's a siren. Newly freed from her queen's curse," Declan said, clasping his hands together atop the table. "Did you know they were once peaceful beings? Living in harmony with all. Doing good. Saving lives. Many lives, even. But a curse is a powerful thing. Remain cursed long enough and it changes you. Permanently."

"What are you blathering on about, McCallagh?" Dominic's attempt at hiding his fright failed miserably, and his voice shook.

Declan leaned over his hands toward the pirate and whispered, "Careful there. Your fear only makes you taste better."

"So much better," the siren spoke for the first time in her own voice, which was sultry and so familiar that Declan had to steel himself against the memory of his recent torment in the sound.

"Unfortunately—for you, Dominic—being forced to feed on flesh for centuries is a habit not easily broken. And while Celene here doesn't *have* to do so anymore, she's decided to allow herself the occasional indulgence. Under the right circumstances, of course."

Dominic gulped noisily. But he made no attempt to run or to even stand. No one moved.

"May I, Captain?" Though she spoke to Declan, Celene kept her eyes—alight with hungry excitement—on Dominic, who appeared too scared to say or do anything.

"Aye," Declan said, sliding his chair away from the table so he could stand. "But could you wait until we've gone? My man here"—he gestured to Gavin with his chin—"has never witnessed such a thing, and I'd like to spare him the memory, if possible."

"Of course," Celene said and flashed a mischievous grin at her prey. "Shall I meet you back at the ship then?"

With a silent nod to the siren, Declan motioned for his helmsman to follow him out into the alley. Thankfully the man trusted him enough to listen and obey. But Dominic's screams chased after them before they could close the door.

⚮

THEY HAD GOTTEN NO FARTHER than halfway down the alley before Gavin grabbed Declan's arm and pulled him to a stop. Declan's teeth slammed together. While he managed to bite back a reprimand, he couldn't contain the sneer that pulled at his lips.

"Why didn't you tell me?" Gavin sputtered out, his words coated with both hurt and anger. His eyes searched Declan's frantically, shifting between them, as if he were reading Declan's response on a page rather than waiting for it to be voiced.

Every muscle in Declan's body yearned to turn away, to continue down the alley and avoid this confrontation, but he forced himself to remain. He didn't owe Gavin anything, at least not as his captain. The crew operated on a need-to-know basis, and Gavin's lack of respect lately had greatly diminished his need to be privy to Declan's plans.

But Gavin was also a friend.

Declan wrestled with this dichotomy he'd created. How could he be both captain and friend? With Tommy it was easy, different. Tommy understood the necessity for the boundaries that existed between the two facets of their relationship. Tommy knew when to be his quartermaster and when to be his friend.

At one time Gavin had known this too. But not anymore.

For good reason, Declan reminded himself.

But no matter how much he understood and sympathized, the fact remained: this could not be allowed to continue. Declan needed to get this under control before it got someone hurt or killed.

For several breaths, Declan held Gavin's stare, forcing the man to wait for him to speak. He had the words ready. He knew exactly what he needed to say, but he needed to take control of the moment. If Declan responded to Gavin immediately, letting his emotions take the reins of his response, he would be allowing Gavin to dictate the conversation.

Silence, he could control.

Silence, he could use.

Slipping his hands into his pockets, Declan lifted his chin and rolled his shoulders back. He drew in the breath he needed to calm his frustration and anger.

"I didn't tell you, Gavin"—he paused to allow his friend ample time to ponder his next words—"because I can't trust you."

As expected, Gavin lost it. His arms shot up at his sides. His eyes rolled to the dark skies. His foot stepped back as if Declan had physically pushed him.

"You..." Gavin said. "You can't trust me." It wasn't a question.

"No," Declan said calmly.

"Why? Because I dared request to stay behind on the ship? Because I dared to defy the great Captain McCallagh? The captain who kills his own man and then doesn't have the decency to mourn him?"

The words struck true, square in Declan's chest, like a knife twisting into the guilt-ridden, rotting part of his heart. But he kept his face cold and unyielding.

He couldn't refute Gavin's words. He had killed Collins, and he hadn't allowed his remorse over it to show. Not even to Aoife. He couldn't afford to. He couldn't allow the sadness and grief and guilt to pull his attention away from the anger that drove him to succeed and finish what he'd started.

"Aye," he finally said, holding his expression firm.

"Well, at least you admit it, I guess. But I can't do this, Captain."

"You're free to leave, if you need to." Declan dipped his chin at his friend, even while silently hoping he would reconsider and stay on as part of the crew. As frustrated as Declan was with his recent behavior, he couldn't imagine sailing with any other helmsman.

"I don't want to leave, Declan!" Gavin shouted at him, but after taking another breath, he dropped his chin to his chest. He tossed the next words at Declan's feet. "But I also don't know how to stay."

Declan stepped forward and placed his hands on his friend's shoulders as he looked him in the eye. "I know. Same happened to me when my parents died."

"You ran though," Gavin said, looking back down at his feet.

"Aye. I did."

"Regret it?"

The question caught Declan off guard, but when Aoife's face flashed in his mind, he answered confidently, "No, I don't."

He knew the answer might push Gavin to walk away, but he refused to force someone to stay if they couldn't devote themselves fully to the crew. If Gavin couldn't get past his grief, he would put everyone at risk. Put everything at risk. Declan needed a crew he could trust to be there, to listen, to follow orders. And he wasn't sure Gavin could do that anymore.

"You don't need to decide right now," Declan said, stepping back. Gavin seemed surprise, but he said nothing. "Go back to the ship. Think it over. Whether you choose to remain here or want to be taken back home, I will honor your choice. But I do hope you'll stay. Aoife will miss you if you go."

Gavin whispered a word of thanks before turning away from Declan and heading the opposite way down the alley toward the docks. Declan had no idea what the man would choose to do, nor did he have time to ponder it. Not with Callum waiting for him to arrive.

CHAPTER 26
TOMMY

Tommy and Aoife continued on to the farm in silence. Tommy, having to focus on carrying Callum's bulky form, cursed Declan for choosing a location so far from the pub. Not that there had been any better option for what was planned.

"What's he going to do to him?" Aoife asked. Tommy winced. "That bad?"

Tommy couldn't lie to her, but he also couldn't shed much light on Declan's plan. A plan he hoped his friend would reconsider when the time came.

"What are you not telling me, Tommy?" Aoife's pace slowed.

"What makes you think I'm hiding something?" He grunted as he readjusted Callum's body across his back. Would they ever reach this blasted barn? The least Declan could do was be here to help haul the man.

"Because I know you." When Tommy angled a brow at her, she laughed quietly. "Well, maybe not as well as Declan knows you, but it's not hard to tell when you're being all piratey."

"Aren't I piratey all the time?"

"Just because you *are* a pirate doesn't mean you always act like one. Like Declan. He has his distinctively un-pirate-like moments."

Rolling his eyes, Tommy groaned. "I don't want to know. Sands help me, I don't want to know."

Aoife smacked him with the back of her hand. "Oh, shut your soup hole. You know I didn't mean that."

Even in the darkness Tommy could tell her face was going pink with embarrassment, and all he could do was laugh. Anything to help him avoid discussing what Declan was going to do to Callum.

"How much further is it?" Aoife asked, peering ahead at the darkened path. They had reached the outskirts of town and were now walking along a dirt path that separated the homes on their left from the rolling countryside to their right.

With only a sliver of moon visible, Tommy couldn't determine if what lay beyond the town was farmland, though he hoped it was, as that would indicate they were nearing their destination. What had happened to Mikkel's family that they'd needed to abandon their farm? Had their fields been cleared? Burned? Or merely taken over by the wilderness?

An elbow nudged his own, and Aoife's wide eyes prompted him for an answer.

"Oh, sorry," he said before jutting his chin forward. "There should be a road up here soon. Hopefully soon."

"Sorry I'm not much help."

"Me too." Tommy breathed out a laugh to ensure she knew he was only teasing. The regret in her apology had been palpable, so much so that he knew a light joke wouldn't be enough to help. "You're keeping me company. That's help enough."

Aoife scoffed.

"And I assume you helped back there in the pub, no?"

"I guess."

Tommy took a few more steps forward before he spoke again. "You need to stop beating yourself up, Aoife. We each have our role to play, and that role changes from moment to moment. In the pub, you were the bait. Here, you are my friend. A job you're doing quite well, if I might add."

"I wasn't a very good friend to you before though."

"You mean when you forced me to be alone with Maura when I obviously didn't want to be?" He shook his head at the memory, and his stomach clenched with how much it hurt to be separated now.

"Oh, come on. You were thankful for that. Maybe not when it happened, but you seemed pretty happy with her..." She let out a pained groan. "I'm sorry. I know how hard this must be for you. I shouldn't have—"

"It's okay. It is hard, but you don't need to pussyfoot around me, Aoife."

"In that case, where do you think she is? It was Renna, wasn't it? I hope she's not still under her control."

Tommy cringed. "I don't know. I keep thinking of where she might go if she got free of Renna and got off the *Duchess*. Assuming Renna was to blame. But it doesn't matter though. We have to get the dagger to Cait and the Rogues first."

"You'd do that? You'd finish out this job before going after her?"

"Aye," Tommy said quietly but confidently. As much as it pained him to be away from Maura, his captain and the crew needed him. Not to mention an entire people being held captive by their oppressive rulers.

Oppressive rulers you used to work for.

The thought crushed him, as if more weight had been added atop the unconscious pirate he carried.

Rulers your mother worked for, rather, he reminded himself. *You aren't your parents. You don't need to be ashamed of where you came from.*

How long had it been since he'd thought of home? And why did it have to come up now?

Letting out a long breath, he forced the past out of his mind before Aoife suspected him of hiding something and started asking questions he wouldn't answer.

"We can't all be lucky enough to have our kidnapped love taken to the very location we're heading."

Aoife side-eyed him. "You have a weird definition for lucky."

"In all seriousness though," Tommy said, "I don't back out of my promises. Unlike Callum here. As quartermaster, my duty to my captain and my crew comes first." He braced himself for Aoife to lash out at him like she had multiple times on the journey to the sound. Surely she would point out how he had put the safety of Maura—and her sisters—above everything else by not allowing them to use their magic.

But Aoife said nothing as she continued to walk beside him.

Finally they arrived at the road leading to the Harlan farm. Without a word, they turned and walked down it in comfortable silence.

His back ached. His shoulders burned. His legs screamed. But Tommy ignored it all. He had a job to do. And if Declan could carry Tommy's bloody, unconscious body all the way back to the ship from the council hall, then Tommy could do this for him.

Even if he disagreed with what would happen to Callum once Declan arrived.

Tommy cleared his throat. "It should be just a little further down. Mikkel said the entrance road may be overgrown now that his family has moved on."

Sure enough, they found it easily a few minutes later.

The entrance was marked by a rusty iron gate, which looked as though it might fall to the ground and break free from its last remaining hinge at any moment. It creaked loudly when Aoife pushed it open, so she didn't close it behind them once Tommy had stepped through. The winding road was lined with trees, preventing them from seeing the barn until they rounded the final bend. With the toe of his boot, Tommy nudged the barn door open. The musty smell of rotting wood and straw hit Tommy's nose, as pungent as any pirate ship he'd been on.

"See if you can find a lantern or two," Tommy said, forcing his feet to keep moving to the middle of the barn. There he dumped Callum's body on the dirt floor and stretched out the painful tightness running across his upper back before straightening fully. Aoife rummaged through a pile of equipment and tools that lined the far wall of the building. Items crashed to the floor as she continued her search, and she muttered an apology at the sudden noise.

"No need to apologize. No one nearby to be bothered."

Tommy's stomach turned at his words.

You're going soft, aren't you?

But even as he thought it, he knew it wasn't shameful to be so at odds with violence. He might kill or injure when needed, as his role on the crew demanded, but that didn't mean he found pleasure in it. He glanced down at Callum's crumpled body. Now this was a man who did it for sport, who relished in the torment of others.

Like the torment Declan wants to inflict on him?

How can you let him do this?

Tommy's thoughts swirled with question after question as he wondered how he could convince his captain—his friend—that this wasn't a path he wanted to revisit. Declan had come close to drowning in that darkness during those first few months as captain. Torturing and killing. Maiming and murdering.

He'd been ruthless. Vicious.

But he'd stopped.

He'd listened to Tommy before.

He could listen again. Stop again. Right?

"Found one!" Aoife called while running toward Tommy with a worn lantern in hand. "But how do we light it exactly?"

"Same way we do on the ship," Tommy said, pulling out a set of matches from his coat pocket.

Once the lantern was lit and the interior of the barn came into better view, he handed it back to Aoife and gestured for her to hang it up on a nail by the door. Once it was in place, it cast long, eerie shadows across the space.

"It's not perfect, but it will have to do."

Finding some rope hanging neatly on pegs along the wall, Tommy grabbed one coil in each arm. He gave a silent nod of appreciation when Aoife rushed over of her own accord to help him carry them to the unconscious pirate.

"Did Declan give you any instructions for once we got here?" Aoife asked, squatting low to the ground as she watched Tommy pull Callum's arms in front of him and bind them at the wrists.

Tommy shook his head. "Only to keep him alive and secured."

"I'm surprised he's still out. How hard did you hit him?"

"Thankfully not hard enough." What would Declan have done if Tommy had accidentally killed him?

But who would Declan be after this?

Tommy pushed the questions aside, trying to focus on the task at hand—taking the rope that bound Callum and throwing the end of it up and over one of the cross-beams overhead. He grabbed both ends of the rope and lifted himself off the floor to ensure the beam would hold Callum's weight. When it didn't fall on his head— didn't even moan under his weight—he began to hoist the pirate, watching as Callum's hands lifted above his head and grunting with the effort needed to get the man's torso and legs up off the floor. He kept pulling until only Callum's toes grazed the dirt floor.

Tommy groaned as he walked to the iron ring attached to the barn wall several paces away. At one point it might have been used to tether horses or other animals.

With Callum in position, Tommy finally let himself sink down onto the floor. He let his head fall against the wall. All of his energy was spent; every muscle and limb fell toward the ground as if they longed to lie down and go to sleep. Aoife settled herself on the ground as well and leaned into him. Eventually she rested her head on his shoulder and heaved a heavy sigh.

"I miss her."

Tommy's eyes slid closed as he asked her whom she referred to, knowing it could be either her sister or his Maura.

"Both," Aoife said with a single sad laugh. "Lani longed for adventure and a life outside of the council hall."

He didn't open his eyes, even as the image of Maura hovered behind his lids, her gold eyes shining down at him.

"I suppose Maura did too," Aoife said.

Something in Tommy snapped. It wasn't the first time he'd heard her name uttered today, but for some reason—perhaps due to his exhaustion—his emotions peaked at the mention of her now. His sternum seemed to cave in toward his spine, collapsing his lungs, tightening his gut, pushing tears into his eyes, where they thankfully remained trapped. For now.

"Aye." He managed to get the single syllable out, but it fell from his lips, heavy with longing and worry. He wanted to believe he would see her again—needed to believe it—but sitting in this abandoned barn, far from wherever Halloran's ship might have taken her, he wondered if that reunion would ever come. Had he finally handed over his heart to someone only to be given a single night with her?

One epically perfect night, but still. It wasn't enough.

Hurry up and get here, Declan, so we can get back to the ship, deliver the dagger, and find Maura.

But his thoughts couldn't summon Declan any more than they could bring Maura back to him.

"So you grew up on the other side of the mountains? With a sister?"

While Tommy desperately wanted to steer the conversation away from Maura and his aching heart, this wasn't a topic he wanted to discuss either.

Still, he gave her another "Aye."

When he didn't say anything more, Aoife sat up, and Tommy didn't need to open his eyes to know she was staring at him.

"It's not nice to stare, Aoife."

"I've heard that before," she muttered in exasperation before pushing further. "What was it like? Is it like Morshan?"

Damn this woman's curiosity.

You should have simply given her a little information, enough to tide her over, he thought, but he knew there was no real end to Aoife's inquisitiveness.

"No, it's nothing like Morshan. For most people."

Tommy cringed as he uttered those final words, mentally kicking himself.

"Most people?"

Well, shit.

Just tell her you don't want to talk about it.

It's the truth, after all.

But she'll just keep pestering you if you don't explain.

His thoughts flitted back and forth in a silent argument. Opening his eyes, he glanced at his friend, who was regarding him with pity—a decidedly better reaction than what he would receive if he told her everything.

"I'm sorry, Aoife. I can't."

"But why not?" she asked, frowning as though his simple refusal to bare his past to her had been some grave insult.

"Some things are private, better not to be exposed and known by everyone. Even our friends."

For a moment, they sat in silence, his refusal hanging between them, and he waited for her to keep pressing him. But she didn't. Not really anyway.

"Will you tell me how you became a pirate then?"

"Don't you know that story already?"

"Aye, a portion of it. Only that you became a cabin boy on the same ship as Declan."

Tommy gave a half-hearted shrug. "That's pretty much how it went."

"But where did you meet? How did you become friends?"

"How does Declan put up with all your questions?" Tommy said, shaking his head.

"You get used to it," a voice called from the doorway.

"Declan!" Aoife leaped to her feet, flinging herself into the captain's arms. She pulled back to search his face and released another string of questions. "Are you all right? Have any trouble? What took so long?"

Tommy, standing and stretching out his sore muscles, joined them. "About time you got here. Not sure I could take any more of your girl's interrogating."

Aoife moved to kick Tommy in the shin, but he deftly moved out of her way.

Declan pulled Aoife into his chest, kissing her forehead before looking over her head to Tommy. "Meant to be here earlier, but keeping Gavin out of the loop caused some problems and required a bit more explanation than I planned for."

Tommy retrieved the Csintala dagger from his hip and offered it to Declan, saying, "To be fair, Declan, you kept all of us out of the loop. Aoife says I was in the pub with you."

Gavin had joined the crew after Declan had broken his old habit of executing plans on his own. Tommy had gotten so used to it during those first few years that when Declan started including him and the other higher-ranking men on the crew, it had felt awkward and wrong.

Declan eyed the dagger in his palm for a moment before lowering it to his side. "Sorry about that, by the way, but I needed genuine surprise from Aoife and Gavin."

If Aoife was upset by his lack of transparency, she didn't show it as she continued to hold tight to him. Seeing them embracing like this—even though it was less amorous than the intimate scene he'd unfortunately been stuck witnessing earlier—sparked that old reliable flame of loneliness and longing in his chest. It should be him and Maura standing here like that. Not that Tommy begrudged Aoife and Declan their happiness, but it was an unfortunate reminder that his arms were still empty, that his Maura was still gone.

"I asked Celene to help us out," Declan said.

Aoife tilted her face up to look at Declan and then Tommy. "Who's Celene?"

Tommy ran a hand through his hair. "A siren."

"What? How?" But before either man could answer Aoife's questions, she made the connection herself. "A glamour. You asked her to look and sound like Tommy."

Declan nodded. "And it worked. Perfectly."

"So where's Gavin now?" Tommy asked, dread pooling in his gut. A month ago, he wouldn't have had to ask. He would have known what Gavin would do before he did it. But grief had that unfortunate way of changing people, severing ties, breaking bonds.

"Back at the ship. Assuming he listened to me," Declan said, scanning his surroundings and seeming to notice Callum's body hanging from the rafters for the first time. Without a word, he gently moved Aoife away from him and stepped around her. With the dagger still in hand, he stalked toward their captive.

Leaving Aoife standing by the door, Tommy rushed to his friend's side as he approached Callum. He leaned toward Declan's ear and whispered, "You don't have to—"

Declan lifted his empty hand between them, and Tommy snapped his mouth shut. He watched his friend stalk even closer to the suspended body, wrestling with how to handle this situation. Would Declan be able to come back from this if he gave in? If he let himself do what that dark voice urged him to?

He's survived it before.

But it had taken so much to convince him to stop last time. Tommy only hoped this one act of vengeance would be enough to satiate the darkness rather than rouse it fully.

"What are you going to do, Declan?"

Aoife's question pulled Tommy's attention back to her. She had stayed behind in the doorway. There was no fear in her eyes, only concern. Tommy wasn't surprised when Declan didn't respond. Seeing the determined set of his jaw and the burning anger pulsing at his temples, Tommy knew there were no words he could say to convince Declan. His only option was to await his captain's orders and then carry them out as best he could.

"Take her back to the ship, Tommy."

Tommy spun around in time to catch Aoife as she ran forward to argue. She tried desperately to get out of his grip, speaking over his shoulder with a determination equal to Declan's. "No, Declan. Let me stay. I won't leave."

Declan didn't respond, and Tommy moved to get into Aoife's line of sight. "Aoife, look at me." He waited for her to comply, though she continued to shake her head. "You don't need to see this. You don't want—"

Aoife pressed her lips into a thin line and narrowed her eyes at Tommy, but he could almost see her thoughts spinning around and around inside her head. Slowly her jaw relaxed, her eyes dropped between them, and she stopped struggling.

Tommy pulled his arms away, but she used the opportunity to shove past him.

"Shit!" Tommy's swear filled the barn.

Aoife pulled Declan around to look at her.

Should Tommy stop her? Drag her away and force her to leave? Or should he give them a moment to talk?

"What can't I see, Declan? You think I don't know the stories about you? You think I don't know what you're capable of?" Her questions, though pointed, held no fear or anger or hatred. They were a challenge. A challenge for him to trust her.

But the Declan who stared back at her now was no longer the one who had let her stay on the ship or the one who had protected her in Foxhaven, and Tommy could see the storm brewing in his friend's eyes, could hear the thunder of it rumbling in his chest.

Tommy reached for Aoife to pull her away. "Come on, Aoife. Trust him."

At that, she gave up all resistance. She dragged her feet back toward the door, though she refused to turn away from Declan until she stepped out into the darkness.

One last time, Tommy glanced back at his friend. He had already turned to face Callum, his head dropped to the side like a predator sizing up its prey. As Declan lifted the Csintala dagger into the air, Tommy left, pulling the door shut behind him.

CHAPTER 27
ADLER

When Adler awoke, the sun was still waiting to make its grand entrance for the day. He lay in darkness with his arm throbbing, dancing its way toward going numb, and he turned to find it trapped under Cait's head. He hated to move and risk waking her, but he needed to return to the cove and confer with Lucan about all that had happened since he'd met with the council. And, curfew or no, it was better to use the cover of pre-dawn darkness to avoid giving away his friend's whereabouts.

He slipped his arm out from under Cait and froze at her whimper of protest. But she didn't wake up, instead moving her head against her pillow until she found a comfortable position again.

Adler sat up, keeping a watchful eye on her as he did, hoping he wouldn't disrupt her desperately needed rest by getting out of bed. Even so, he hated the idea of leaving without a word, and his insides churned over the callousness of slipping out with only a note to tell her where he'd gone. But looking at her now—her dark hair spilling around her shoulders, her face uncharacteristically calm and peaceful, lacking the stress she normally carried—he knew he couldn't bear to rouse her.

Sands, she's beautiful.

What had he done last night? What had he been thinking with that kiss?

How long had he been telling himself it was nothing more than an infatuation? A simple attraction. But last night...

Last night something had shifted.

It wasn't because she was hurt or that she needed his help. It wasn't out of pity or guilt or loneliness. It wasn't on account of her kiss or her smile or that way she drove him slightly mad.

To be honest, he didn't know what had done it or when it had happened, but something had split his heart open.

Again.

Walking away and leaving her, even just for this morning, pained him. Already his arms felt empty without her in them. They needed to talk, to sort all of this out, but it would have to wait. They could do that after she got more rest. After he met with Lucan. After he had time to think.

There would be time to talk.

Quickly he scribbled down a note on a small piece of paper he found on the chest of drawers under the window. Folding it once, he set it on the table beside her bed.

Leaning down, he pressed his lips to her forehead. "I'll be back soon, love," he whispered.

Part of him hoped the words would cause her eyes to open so he could bid her farewell properly. But she didn't stir or hum in response. She didn't seem to register his presence at all.

Good. She needed her rest.

Before he could change his mind about leaving her, Adler rushed out of the room, careful not to make any noise as he closed the door behind him. Keeping his footfalls soft, he descended the steps as fast as he could, but as he turned the corner and headed toward the back door, someone stepped into his path and pressed a hand against his chest. He flinched away from the contact.

Kira.

Releasing a breath of a laugh, Adler shook his head at the woman. Her height nearly matched his own, so she easily peered straight into his eyes, her expression full of suspicion and a hint of humor.

"You're here early," he said, trying to suppress his impatience with the fast-approaching sunrise and this delay.

She cocked her head to the side, still holding his gaze. "Is she okay?"

"Aye." He tossed his head up the stairs. "But she was in a bad state."

"I know. I was here when she arrived—"

Fresh anger sparked against his better judgment, and he couldn't stop the words that rushed out. "And you left her alone? With a full bottle of rum?"

Kira's expression hardened, her glare freezing over as her lips disappeared into a tight line. Adler braced himself for her to throw an excuse or a challenge in his face, but not even a breath later, her features softened. Her shoulders dropped a bit as she responded. "Aye. I knew she'd be okay. And I came in early to make sure of it."

"She was injured—"

"I know." Her nonchalant tone stoked his anger, but before he could reprimand her, she was explaining. "I tried to tend to her, but she swatted me away, insisting it was nothing—"

"And you believed her?" he challenged, struggling to keep his voice low.

Kira dipped her chin as bitterness returned to her eyes. "She's a big girl, Adler. She doesn't need to be coddled. Not by me and certainly not by you."

Adler's eye twitched, but he forced himself to draw in a deep breath to quell his rising temper before he spoke again. "Even the strong need someone to care for them now and then. Even the strong have their weaknesses. Even the strong can be knocked down. And it doesn't demean her to help her, to love her—"

"*Love* her?"

Fuck. Adler winced but recovered quickly. "As a *friend.*"

Kira merely nodded, lips pursed, eyes alight with humor, and Adler wasn't sure if it was better or worse than the clear disdain she'd shown him moments ago.

Rubbing a hand over his mouth, he tried to clear his mind so he could get back to the matter at hand.

"Look, Kira. We both know she's strong and capable. But her pride be damned. She's going to break if she's not careful. We can't let that happen."

A long silence passed between them, and Adler was about to say more when, finally, Kira closed her eyes and nodded. Taking a deep breath, she opened her eyes and studied him. "You're right. I'll make her some breakfast and stay with her until you return."

"Thank you."

He maneuvered his way around her toward the back door, and he'd just grasped the handle when Kira called out, "Want me to tell her anything, Adler?"

With a small shake of his head, he said, "I left a note." And he slipped out the door before she could delay him further.

✂

Running through the town's streets, even at this darkened hour, would have brought unwanted attention, so Adler kept his pace painfully slow. His jaw pulsed in time with every step of his boots on the cobblestone as the sky above him lightened too quickly. He wasn't sure if anyone was watching him make his way toward the docks, but he hoped no one noticed when he slipped into a shadowy alley that would take him to the forest at the edge of town. Once under the cover of the trees, he'd be able to move a little faster, but even then, he needed to be careful. The council was crafty. If they had found Cait and hurt her, who knew the number of spies they might have watching the citizens.

He didn't relax until he turned onto the overgrown path that led to the cove. But even so, he didn't slow his pace but pushed himself to get there faster. The sooner he got to the cove, the sooner he could bring Lucan up to speed and the sooner he could get back to the pub and to Cait.

The sun had just peeked over the horizon when the ground beneath his boots changed to black sand and the cover of trees gave way to a beautiful expanse of sky stretching from the sea to the rocky cliffs that guarded the cove. He'd only been here a handful of times, and he wondered if its beauty would ever cease to amaze him.

"Adler?" Lucan called, pulling his attention away from the scenery to where his friend had appeared from behind one of the large boulders peppering the beach.

"How are you, friend?" Adler asked as he approached, his hand outstretched in greeting.

Lucan grasped his hand, but his eyes searched the area behind him. "I'm good. Cait not come with you?"

Adler marveled at how much this man's demeanor had changed since they had met. A week ago, his tone would have been dripping with suspicion and disdain.

"No," Adler said, shaking his head. "She's... She needed rest."

Lucan's brows pulled together in concern. "What happened?"

Adler ran his hand through his hair. "Long or short version?" When Lucan answered with an impatient glare, Adler gave him an empty laugh. "Right then. They took her."

Lucan's eyes went wide, but surprisingly, he kept quiet so Adler could explain.

Adler recounted as much as he could, starting with how he'd caught Cait following him into the council hall before his meeting with the council. Then he explained how Cait hadn't made it to their rendezvous, how he'd fallen asleep, and how he'd found her drunk and hurt in the pub.

"But she's okay?" Lucan asked before turning to pace along the shore.

"Aye. I believe so. But she wouldn't let me look too closely at her injuries."

"And you're going to go to this council dinner with the king then?"

Adler nodded.

Lucan stopped moving long enough to ask, "Does she know about it yet? And does she know you secured her an invite?"

"Not yet."

"I wish I could be there," Lucan muttered to the ground as he resumed his pacing. "So do you have a plan then? I assume so, since you secured her an invite."

Adler massaged his brow and cringed. "Unfortunately—"

Sand flew into the air when Lucan stopped short and whirled on his friend. "Seriously? Do you ever plan ahead?"

With a sheepish grin, Adler shrugged.

"I guess this explains how you ended up engaged and planning an elopement so soon after meeting someone," Lucan said with a humorless laugh. "Spontaneity does have its benefits, even in a rebellion. But..."

Lucan paused, his face scrunching in concentration as he stared at the sand between them. He had a point, but even so, it didn't change the fact that what was done was done. All Adler could do was try to come up with the best plan possible for the situation he'd landed them in.

"How do you think Cait will react?" Adler finally asked after several moments of silence. His stomach twisted when Lucan looked up at him with the same expression his sister's face had held when he'd misbehaved and had to face their mother's wrath. "That bad?"

Another laugh—this time full of mirth and a hint of ridicule. "It's a good opportunity, I suppose. And that might, in itself, spare you any reprimands from our fearless leader, but..." Lucan frowned instead of completing the thought.

"But what? I can see why Cait gets so annoyed with you sometimes."

"Yes, but she loves me all the same," Lucan said as his grin turned smug. "What she doesn't love—as proven by her reaction to our little stunt earlier—is being in the dark or having her hand forced. And you, my friend, have just forced her hand in a major way."

"It's only a dinner," Adler said, trying to defend himself. "Sure, it's dinner with the same people who grabbed and tortured her, but—"

"There has to be a pretty substantial *but* to counter that statement," Lucan said, tilting his head.

Adler ignored him as best he could. "But I didn't know that was the case when I requested her invitation."

Lucan gazed up at the morning sky, seeming to mull over Adler's words. Either that or he was stretching out the silence for maximum irritation.

"Go with that excuse," he finally said as he brought his attention back to Adler. "Cait's more likely to accept that."

"It's not an excuse. It's the truth."

"Aye." Another sheepish grin spread across his friend's face before he lifted his arms out at his sides. "It's also true that you let the request slip out without thinking it though. And *that* is certainly not something she'll let slide. Carelessness. She hates it."

"Do you have any advice that's actually helpful?"

"I think I've been rather helpful already, but regardless… Biggest piece of advice? Let her lead."

Shaking his head, Adler said, "I had no plan to do otherwise."

"Aye, but you also don't want to give her any *impression* that you're trying to take over. Trust me."

"Yet you were so quick to take charge with that stunt in the town square. Why?"

Lucan started laughing. "I've known her longer. Harder for me to fall out of her good graces."

"And here I thought you were going to claim she loves you more."

"That too." Lucan lazily surveyed the cove for a moment before his attention snapped back to Adler, his features twisted into comical confusion. "Wait. You think she loves you?"

Adler raised his palms toward the man as if warding off an impending attack. "Not in the slightest."

Suspicion swam in Lucan's eyes, though Adler couldn't figure out why. Was he worried that Cait might fall for Adler? That Lucan might lose any possibility of a future with her? Adler scanned back through his memories to recall what she had told him that night as they had waited in the trees near the pit. Had she and Lucan agreed there was nothing between them? Or was that something Cait only assumed the man knew and accepted?

Why does it matter? he asked himself, despite already knowing the answer.

Hope.

He was clinging to a hope he had no right to.

"Good," Lucan said. "I mean, not because I'm against the idea of you and her or whatever." The man was rambling, and Adler had to bite back a smile.

"That's a relief, at least. I'd hate to cross any lines between—"

Lucan scoffed. "That ship sailed long ago, friend. I may be protective of her, but no. I don't see her like that."

Adler flashed him a questioning look. Had Cait completely read the man wrong all these years? Or was Lucan trying to play it cool?

"Wait. Why?" Lucan straightened and retreated a step as if Adler had moved to strike him. His expression turned defensively curious. "Does she think—"

"No, of course not. Not that I know of anyway."

Lucan let out a sigh, his shoulders slumping with apparent relief. "Well, regardless, I have no objection to—" He flicked his hand back and forth in front of him. "You and her, if that were to ever happen. And don't even deny it's what you want. It's written all over your face."

Adler rubbed a hand over his beard, and Lucan laughed before speaking again.

"To be honest, I think it would be good for her—good for you too maybe—but right now? I don't know that we can afford to have her distracted."

Adler remained silent as he pondered this, not quite sure how to respond or if he even should respond at all. Despite his insistence to the contrary, Lucan's flustered rambling made Adler wonder if he was simply embarrassed to be talking about his friend's romantic prospects.

"I appreciate that," Adler finally said with a half-smile. "But I have no intention of distracting her. I promise. I only want to help."

His thoughts returned to the previous night's events. *Intentions be damned though. You might have already distracted her too much as it is.*

"So, any ideas on how we can use this dinner to our advantage?" Adler asked, hoping to veer this conversation away from such an obviously uncomfortable topic.

"I'm guessing there will be little, if any, opportunity for an offensive move," Lucan said, rubbing his chin with his hand.

"Poisoning them is likely out. And we don't have the dagger yet."

Lucan raised his hands as if defeated. "So it can be nothing more than reconnaissance then."

"Can never have too much information, right?"

"Aye, but we're quickly running out of time. Especially with this dinner marking the arrival of the king. We had planned to have the dagger before he got here."

This was the first Adler had heard of a deadline for their move against the councilwomen. Had they purposefully not told him? Or had it simply slipped their minds? "Why exactly?"

Lucan waved a hand dismissively, as if it were obvious, but he still explained the rumors of the king's plan to undo the Muirnaughton treaty and form an alliance with the council, as well as the possibility that he would bring a shield that would protect the council from the Csintala dagger's powers.

It was Adler's turn to pace the beach. He'd also heard rumors of there being some sort of counter to the dagger, but he'd never heard of it being an actual shield.

They would have no chance of defeating the council and avenging Lani if the king had that.

"We have to stop him from giving that shield to the council," Adler said, more to himself than to Lucan, but his friend responded with an emphatic nod.

"Hence our urgency. Have we had any word about where her brother is? Whether he's retrieved the dagger?"

"Not that I'm aware of, but I haven't had much of a chance to find out what Cait knows."

"I wish I could go with you to this dinner, if only to get a decent meal."

"Is a disguise out? Could always dress like a servant?"

Lucan laughed. "Can you imagine what Cait would say if I showed up like that? I'm trying to get back on her good side, not drive her to exiling me for real."

"She'd never do that to someone she loves."

"I'd rather not test that theory out anytime soon." Lucan hung his head. "Just promise me something, Adler?"

"Anything, friend. Within reason."

Huffing out a laugh, Lucan spoke toward the ground. "Don't forget about me here. I want to help. I don't want to be left on the sidelines."

Adler stepped forward and extended his hand, thankful when Lucan grasped it tightly. "You have my word."

CHAPTER 28
CAIT

CAIT ROLLED OVER WITH A GROAN, wincing when even her own subtle noise sent pain shooting through her head. Everything hurt—from her rum-soaked head to her bruised legs. But worst of all was the tangle of regret and embarrassment and loneliness that writhed in her chest like a nest of snakes waking up after a long winter.

What would she say to Adler? What could she say to him?

Sorry?

I shouldn't have?

Or maybe, *What happened?*

She tried to retrace the evening's events in her mind, but it all became muddled after he'd placed her on the bar. Had she slept in the pub? She moved a hand to her side, expecting to feel the rough surface of the floor. Her eyes shot open when her fingers instead found the soft blankets of her bed.

Oh no oh no oh no. What had she done?

Had he? Had she?

Turning her head to the side, she found nothing but the usual empty space beside her. She blew out a sigh. It had only been a dream. Her stupid heart had gotten ahead of itself, sending ridiculous images to her as she slept.

She had nearly relaxed when she saw a piece of paper atop the table beside her bed. Somehow she knew it was from Adler, and her gut tightened with the memory of the last time he'd left a message for her. It twisted even more at the realization that last night—and whatever had happened—had not been a dream.

You're the leader of a bloody rebellion, Cait! You can read a stupid note from a stupid man!

She reluctantly sat up, took a moment to allow the resulting dizziness to subside, and snatched the note.

In his neat lettering was scrawled a simple message:

Gone to see L. Be back later, love.
P.S. Nothing happened.

Relief washed over her.

But wait.

Had she tried to make something happen? Her head hurt as she pulled at the memories, and she growled when she still came up with only vague recollections of sitting on the bar, him touching her face...

Her eyes went wide, and her fingers flew to her lips.

Fuck!

She had kissed him.

Why had he let her? Why hadn't he stopped it?

And why did he call that *nothing*?

A knock at the door startled her, and for a ridiculous moment she thought it might be Adler. But no, based on the warm light streaming in through her window, she could tell it wasn't yet midmorning, and he wouldn't be back so soon.

Cait moved to stand but thought better of it when the room began spinning. Damn rum. She'd need to invite them in. Whoever they were.

"Yes?"

A muffled voice answered, "I brought you breakfast." Kira. That saint of a woman.

"Come on in," Cait said more quietly than intended, like her mind was forcing her to mumble to stave off further pain. She opened her mouth to repeat the words louder, but Kira was already opening the door and stepping into the room.

"It's not much, but I cooked up the last couple eggs and toasted a bit of bread. All out of butter, I'm afraid, but I can have Adler pick up some more from the market later today."

The woman took a step toward the dining table in the corner, but Cait reached forward to stop her. There was no way she was going to make it over to the table when she hadn't even been able to answer the damn door.

"I'll take it here, thanks Kira."

Kira seemed to be fighting back a smile as she handed the plate over.

Cait, sliding one of the fried eggs onto the toasted bread, looked at her friend from beneath her lashes. "What is it?"

Kira's smile broke through, barely, with one corner of her mouth perking up. "Just curious is all. Don't think I've ever seen you in such a state in all the years we've known each other."

"Aye. And you won't again for a long time, I hope." She paused to take a bite and nearly melted to the floor with satisfaction. Even without butter, the food tasted amazing. Either Kira was a wizard or Cait really was a terrible cook. She spoke around her next mouthful. "I'm wasting your talents behind that bar. This is delicious."

"I'll tell you the secret," Kira said. Cait's chin lifted in curiosity. "Tastes better when you don't burn it."

Rolling her eyes, Cait muttered, "Lucan rat me out?" Before Kira could respond, she turned her attention back to the remainder of the food. Kira wasn't wrong, but that didn't mean Cait appreciated the teasing. Then again, she was so grateful to the woman for bringing her food that she couldn't stay cross with her for more than a breath.

Kira dragged a chair over to sit in front of Cait. Settling her elbows onto her knees, she leaned forward, hands clasped in front of her. "Saw Adler sliding out of here in a hurry this morning."

Her words dripped with suspicion.

"It was nothing," Cait said. "Bit of a rough night for me, as you know. He made sure I didn't end up sleeping on the pub floor. That's all."

Kira cocked a brow. "That's all."

Frowning down at the crumbs and streaks of egg yolk on her plate, Cait shrugged. "I think so anyway."

Kira's sweet laugh filled the room as she leaned back, shaking her head, smiling faintly. "That's too bad. If it's true."

"He said as much in his note, and since I can't remember much beyond..." Cait stopped herself from mentioning the kiss. No point. It was nothing. Just as Adler said. "And what do you mean it's *too bad*?"

"He's good for you. That's what I mean."

It was Cait's turn to shake her head. "He doesn't feel that way."

Kira's eyes lit up, and Cait realized her mistake too late. "And you do?"

Cait's head swam as if she were back in that bottle of rum. Did she? "N-no."

"Really?"

"Fuck. I don't know."

But she did know.

Shrugging, she tried to smile, but she could tell it was far from convincing. "Doesn't matter how I feel. It can't happen."

Why was she talking about this? Why were they gabbing about romance and love when they had a rebellion to plan?

Before Kira could say anything more, Cait huffed out a sigh and forced herself to stand. Immediately she regretted it, nearly dropping the plate as the room jolted into another spin around her. Kira was there in an instant, holding Cait's arm steady and taking the empty plate from her.

"Let's get you some coffee," Kira said, leading Cait slowly toward the door.

Cait didn't protest. Anything—even being half-carried down the stairs in her hungover stupor—was better than discussing her idiotic feelings for a man busy avenging his lover's death. Down in the main room, Kira settled Cait into one of the chairs before running to the back.

"Here, drink this," Kira said. She slipped the mug into Cait's hands but kept her own hovering in the air, as if Cait might be too weak to hold it herself.

She took a slow sip, thankful for its heat. When half the cup was gone, the fog of the previous night finally began to lift. The memories were still a little fuzzy, but she could now remember Adler getting her to bed, holding her through the night, and singing her to sleep.

Her heart warmed as each moment came back into focus, but she told herself it was merely from the coffee. Nothing more. He didn't care about her in that way. And even if he did, she couldn't let him. It was too soon. Far too soon. He needed time to grieve and process and say goodbye to Lani. Even if he seemed to be doing all right, Cait knew better. She recognized that forced strength and the constant need to appear *fine*.

"Better?" Kira asked. She was leaning back against the bar, watching Cait with a concerned look.

Cait nodded before taking another sip.

"Good." Kira clapped her hands together. "Because we need to chat."

Looking over the mug's edge at her friend, Cait asked, "About what?"

"What happened to you?" Kira's voice shifted into a tone of motherly concern that Cait had never heard from her before. She'd been friendly, sure. Caring, of course. But always a little distant, which Cait had chalked up to her painful past.

"What do you mean?"

Kira pointed down to Cait's legs. "You're hurt, and you're not one to be clumsy or foolish. So what happened?"

How much could she tell her? They were sitting in this big, open room, and even though they were alone, she always feared that the council might have some magical ability to hear any words spoken. She'd refused to tell Adler last night when he'd asked. But that was as much to protect Declan as it was to save face in front of Adler. She'd promised herself she would never let her weakness show, and allowing him to see what they'd done, revealing that she'd been unable to fight them off, having him worrying and fretting over her...

No.

She couldn't risk it.

"I can't." She dropped the words in her lap, wishing she could share all these burdens with someone. But Lucan wasn't here. Adler had left. And Kira... How well did Cait really know this woman? A week ago, Cait would have considered her a trusted friend, but now—knowing someone close to her could be working with the council—she had to keep everyone, including friends, at arm's length.

You didn't do that with Adler, did you? she asked herself.

Kira said nothing as she walked toward the table, pulled a chair down, and settled into it. She remained silent for a long while, long enough for Cait to down the rest of her coffee.

"I'm not from Cregah," Kira said in a low voice.

Cait's head snapped up. "What do you—"

Running a hand over her mouth and chin, Kira drew in a deep breath before placing her hands into her lap. "You look so much like your mom, Cait. I almost thought the rumors were false when I first arrived, thought surely Ada McCallagh wasn't dead. But your eyes..."

The room was spinning again. Kira had known her mother? But how? She couldn't be much older than Declan, could she? Certainly not old enough to remember her mother so clearly.

"I don't understand," Cait said, still trying to solve whatever puzzle this was.

"I wouldn't expect you to. I've meant to tell you for the past year, but especially in the last few months after you discovered the letter." Kira held Cait's gaze.

But Cait shook her head. "What letter?"

Kira laughed quietly but not unkindly. "The letter your mother had for the fae. The letter I gave her."

CHAPTER 29
DARIENN

With a growl, Darienn threw the blankets off and sat up. The sun had not yet risen, and the faintly glowing embers in the hearth across the room barely penetrated the darkness. How soon dawn would come, she didn't know. It didn't matter.

There would be no sleep tonight.

For hours she had tossed and turned, her legs restless, her gut uneasy, her mind racing through the scenes she had witnessed and couldn't forget.

The woman's bound hands. Her body tied to the chair. Her skirts pulled up to her waist, exposing more skin than was proper in such company. Her blood trailing down her skin as she fought back her tears and screams with such strength.

It's not like it's the first time you've seen blood, she reminded herself. But still... That servant in the library had been a spy, a traitor. She had deserved to die. Her blood had been spilled for a reason.

The woman last night—Cait—however, was a mere citizen and posed no threat to the council's rule. As far as Darienn knew, she had done nothing more than have the misfortune of being related to someone the council needed.

Although Darienn had known the truth about the exiles for years, it wasn't until last night that she'd seen any spark of cruelty in the councilwomen's eyes. Had their hearts grown dark because the influence of their mothers and the generations before them? Or had they been corrupted by the power they wielded?

Regardless, this was the future Darienn was destined to inherit. Whether they trained her to be so vicious or she naturally became so, it didn't matter.

It was her destiny, her lot, her duty.

Unless you flee like your sisters.

With a shake of her head, Darienn dismissed the traitorous thought. Staring into the darkness of her room, she focused instead on reconciling all she'd been taught with all she had witnessed. If she had any hope of surviving this life—and of ever getting another restful night's sleep again—she had to make some sense of it. Under normal circumstances, if this were a lecture or study session, she would have grabbed ink and paper to sort through it all visually.

But that was not an option. Even if she'd had light to work by, she would not have dared to leave any physical trace of her ponderings to be discovered.

After last night, Darienn could not afford to make any assumptions about how her mother and aunts ruled. No longer could she take her seat on the council for granted. One false step, and they could do away with her as they had her sisters.

Tapping her fingers, she counted through the facts as she knew them, whispering them aloud as if that might help her understand everything better.

"Peace is the goal." Tap.

"Because men caused the war." Tap.

"Men are inherently violent and can't be trusted." Tap. Tap.

"Exiles are necessary to maintain this peace." Tap.

"Exiles cannot be permitted to leave our shores because that would put all we've achieved at risk." Tap. Tap.

She paused. Something about that logic didn't fit, and she searched through her memory for the explanation her mother had given her.

"Our ancestors have worked tirelessly to create a land of peace, Darienn. Those who pose a threat to us here on our shores remain a threat if we allow them to leave. We cannot risk them gathering a force against us, nor can we allow our citizens to know that we are having to employ the same violence we are working to prevent. We do not want to kill our own people, Darienn. It is their treachery and disobedience and disrespect that forces our hand in the matter. In order to protect us all, we must sacrifice a few. But the people would never understand."

Darienn had accepted her mother's words. At the time, they had made sense to her. But now...

Another memory barreled into her, this time of the citizen in the square, his eyes burning with a desperate anger and a potent grief she had never imagined possible.

"Who cares for those starving in other villages? Who ensures they get the medicine they need? Who protects them from poverty—"

The man had been exiled, rightfully so, but his questions now haunted Darienn.

At the time, she had taken them to be the inquiries of a traitor, an attempt to deceive the people into turning against a council who only wanted to protect them. But Cait's face last night, contorted in pain, made his words strike her heart differently now.

Before the disturbing images could flood her mind again, she bolted out of bed. With no idea where she was going, she rushed to get dressed, putting on her most comfortable shoes and donning her warmest cloak to hide her from both the early morning chill and any prying eyes. Her fingers had just closed around the door handle when she remembered one last thing.

The knife.

She clawed through her chest of clothes, taking care to keep it from becoming disorderly, suspicious. Her heartbeat sped up when she didn't find it. Had someone discovered it? Did her mother know? Her fingers scrambled along the bottom of the chest, her panic building until she finally felt its smooth ivory handle and the worn leather sheath and belt. She'd never intended to use it, and she wasn't sure why she had stored it away after finding it on that spy before they'd entered the library.

As she belted the knife to her thigh and headed for the door, her mind flitted back to her last memories of her sisters. One being dragged away to her death. The other fleeing in the middle of the night as Darienn had urged her to. And here she was, leaving home like them.

No. Not like them.

She would never be like them. She would find a way to stay, to do her duty to the council, to wrap her mind—and heart—around what she would be required to do as a councilwoman.

She wasn't leaving. She was merely going out for some fresh air so she could think clearly.

But the knife under her skirts was evidence to the contrary.

It's for your own protection. That is all.

And she almost believed that.

⊰⊱

Out of habit, Darienn stayed to the shadows as she walked on quiet feet down the wooded path she had only ever seen her sisters use. Years of trailing after them had made her an expert at moving about unseen when she wanted.

Sometimes it wasn't so bad to be invisible.

You could learn a lot when no one knew you were there.

That was how she knew about this path, how she knew about the stretch of beach Aoife favored, how she knew Adler was the pirate Lani had been planning to meet.

But she hadn't seen his face until he arrived at the council hall the other day. Seeing him, knowing how he'd loved her older sister, knowing how her sister had been willing to walk away from everything to be with him, that was why she'd told the councilwomen that she trusted him.

Because she did.

What did he think of her? What did Aoife?

Had she been asked these questions mere days ago, she would have shrugged them off with ease. Her sisters had never included her, and that had hurt more than she'd ever let on. More so, it had made her angry to the point she was willing to sacrifice them both for her own benefit. She had expected their absence would be freeing—she would no longer be invisible, no longer be inconsequential.

You were a fool!

She repeated the words to herself over and over as she walked. Nothing made sense. Everything was horribly wrong. What could she do as a young heir? She was too young to be paired with a lord yet. So why were they accelerating her training?

She stopped short and winced when the leaves crunched underfoot.

Were they going to pair her to a lord early?

Would she be expected to produce her own heir so soon?

The thought made her queasy. Was she ready for this?

You need to be, Darienn.

Or you might as well run just like your sisters.

No. That wasn't her only option. She was their only heir. She could stand up for herself if the council tried to force her into a pairing so soon.

Before she could take another step, a twig snapped up ahead, sending her into the trees. She ducked behind a large trunk as she'd done so many times before. At first, she couldn't make anything out, but then—there, in the deep shadows— something moved.

Someone moved.

He glanced up and down the path before stepping out, and Darienn had to clamp a hand over her mouth to stifle her gasp.

Adler.

What was he doing here creeping around in the woods? She smirked, realizing she could be asked the same question. She was the one lurking behind a tree, after all.

Holding her breath, she waited, willing him not to head her way. Not that she wasn't confident in her skills, but she couldn't assume he didn't possess some sixth sense that would allow him to discover her easily. When he turned in the opposite direction, she counted ten breaths before returning to the path and continuing along her way. Last thing she wanted was to accidentally catch up to him.

When she reached the place where Adler had emerged, she made a full circle trying to determine why he might have been here. She'd nearly started to turn once more when she recognized it.

This was the path to the beach.

If one could call it a path.

There was no obvious entrance, but several strides beyond the trees she found enough of a trail to follow easily.

Why would Adler have been at the—

Lani.

Was this where they were supposed to have met? It would make sense. A hidden beach where no one would see a small boat come and go. But that didn't explain why he was here now, aside from nursing a broken heart, of course.

Darienn continued toward the beach. She had wanted to get out and clear her mind. A secluded beach seemed the ideal spot to do just that. The lapping of the waves and the brine of the Aisling greeted her before she ever saw the signature black sands. She had only followed Aoife here once, years ago. And when she'd discovered that her sister came here to do nothing but sit and stare at the water, Darienn had decided it a waste of her time to follow again.

Today, though, when she cleared the last of the trees and stepped into the sunshine, she allowed herself to see this space with new eyes. The dark sand stretching smoothly toward the sea was peppered with glittering white boulders, guarded by tall walls of rock she had completely forgotten existed on this part of the island. Scanning the area, she drew in the salty air in an effort to clear away the chaos in her head. She would never make sense of it all when it remained a jumbled mess. She'd barely begun to exhale when she spotted something out of place beside one of the boulders.

Cloth of some kind.

Darienn stepped forward with caution. Lifting her skirts slowly, she inched her hand up to her thigh to pull the dagger from its sheath and hoped she wouldn't have to use it.

More items came into view as she neared the boulder. A tin cup. An open bag on its side, its contents—random bits of food and clothing—spilling from it. Whose things were these? Was someone staying here?

Something moved to her right, and she spun around, bringing her blade up just in time for it to meet the neck of a man. A man she recognized. "You," she whispered.

His brown eyes seemed to tease her, his lips pulling back into an easy smile before he spoke. "You...are not supposed to have a weapon."

Darienn glowered. Or hoped she glowered.

"And you...are not supposed to be alive."

He gave her a small laugh. Why was he laughing? Here she had a weapon to his throat, and he was laughing? Were men truly as stupid as she'd been taught? She was starting to believe her mother hadn't been completely wrong about things.

Pressing the dagger into his flesh, she marveled when he still didn't retreat or even flinch.

"You do realize I could spill your blood with a mere flick of my wrist, don't you?" she asked, raising one brow for emphasis.

His lips tightened into a thin line, and he nodded, but he didn't seem nervous. No, he was holding back a smile! A low rumble of frustration sounded in her chest, enough to crack the man's resolve so that his smile broke through.

"So why does that not have you concerned?" she asked, grinding her teeth at how juvenile her voice sounded.

"Because I know you won't," the man said.

Did he just wink at her? It shouldn't surprise her, not when this man had stood before the council in that square and accused them of—

Wait. This man was a traitor, wasn't he? She shouldn't take anything he said seriously, but she couldn't pass up this chance to ask him what he'd meant.

He'll only feed you more lies, she warned herself, but she didn't care.

What the council had done last night to Cait had awakened something in her. A curiosity. A need to know. A desire to see the truth. Whatever that might be.

"Did you mean it?"

His face twisted in confusion, and she realized she'd offered him no context. Her arm throbbed from holding the dagger up, and she struggled to keep it in position.

"You can lower your weapon. I'm not a threat."

Even as Darienn gave a single mocking laugh at his claim, she gratefully lowered her arm but kept the dagger ready to use if needed. The man offered her another smile, less patronizing than before, and asked her what she'd meant by her question.

"In the square," she said, "you said people were starving. Dying. Did you mean it? Is it true?"

His smile faded away, and a sadness swept over his features. Swallowing hard, he finally nodded slowly.

He had to be lying.

"How do I know you're telling the truth?"

The man eyed her curiously and leaned closer. "If you expected me to lie, then why bother asking?"

She pursed her lips. He had a point. Why had she bothered?

She could threaten him. But he'd made it painfully clear he wasn't afraid of her.

What if he was telling the truth? If the council cared for their people as they claimed, why would they let them die? There must be some explanation, some reason food and supplies weren't making it to the villages.

"Why would the council do nothing?" She hadn't meant to utter the question aloud, and she immediately regretted doing so when he answered her.

"You mean, aside from their being murderous, power-hungry bitches?"

Darienn's hand was back up in a flash, the point of her blade hovering before his face. "Watch it," she growled at him.

His hands lifted in surrender, but he dared open his mouth again.

"You didn't know?"

"Yes, this is the face of someone who knew. If I knew, why would I ask you if it was true?"

"Fair point, miss. But why do you care now? You didn't so much as flinch when I announced it in the square."

"And what reason did I have to believe the word of a traitor?"

Darienn tensed as she watched one of his hands move toward her dagger, but she didn't stop him when he slowly eased it away and back down to her side, not once taking his eyes from her. No amusement, no hint of a smile, graced his face when he posed his next question.

"And what reason do you have to believe me now?"

She didn't have a reason. None beyond the honesty in his eyes and the sincerity in his voice.

And her own knowledge of what the council was capable of.

Certainly, hurting one citizen was a far cry from allowing all citizens to struggle and suffer and starve.

But if they were willing to hurt one woman for their own gain...

The images of Cait being tortured invaded Darienn's mind, and she had no strength left to hold them back. The weight of what she'd witnessed dragged her eyes down to the sand. And then her body followed. Her legs crumpled. Her knees hit the ground. Her hands struck next, and she winced as the dagger's handle bit into her palm. But still she didn't release it.

Didn't speak.

Couldn't breathe.

Every inhale came shallow and empty.

And then the beach swayed. Her vision blurred before she slammed her eyes shut.

Warmth spread across her back, and it took her a moment to realize it was the man's hand, rubbing slow circles.

"I would say it's okay," he said in a low voice, "but it's not. None of this is okay."

Darienn shook her head. *It's not okay. It's not okay.*

Even if they weren't hurting the rest of the towns and villages, torturing a citizen wasn't okay. She'd made excuses for the executions, believing them necessary, and she had bought into her mother's teachings that it was all for the good of the people.

But she couldn't find a good excuse for what they had done to Cait.

"I'm so stupid." Her whisper fell to the sand between her hands.

She cringed when he responded.

"You are not stupid. Young, yes. Deceived, definitely. But stupid? No."

Deceived.

Darienn shook her head slowly. What was real? What was true? Was she really going to turn away from generations of council teaching? Was she really going to believe this man over her own mother?

"I have a duty, an obligation—"

"An obligation to your people," he clarified. "Not to the council. But to us. That is where your duty lies. You can still make a difference. You can still change things for the better."

Sitting up, she left the blade in the sand and rubbed her hands over her face. His hand fell away from her back, and she turned to find him crouched beside her.

"How?" she asked, hating how pathetic she sounded. "I couldn't stop them from hurting that woman. I just stood there and watched it happen."

The man studied her for a long moment before turning his attention to the sea and saying, "I was just asking myself the same question. How? How am I to make a difference when I'm stuck here? How am I to help when I'm supposed to be dead?"

Darienn dropped her eyes to her hands, sure she was going mad. Just like her sisters.

"You're helping me, though I don't even know your name," she said.

Another smile spread across his lips. "I don't know yours either, so we're even."

Darienn scowled. "That's not what I meant. What's your name?"

"Winston," he said with a stern expression.

"Your real name."

He balked at her. "How do you know that's not my real name?"

She only glared at him, refusing to play whatever game this was. She nearly beamed when, after several uncomfortable moments of silence, he finally gave in and sighed.

"Fine, it's Lucan."

Lucan. She liked that.

"I'm Darienn."

Lucan settled himself back on the sand beside her. "Nice to meet you."

"Can I stay here for a bit?"

He flashed her a warm smile. "As long as you want to."

CHAPTER 30
AOIFE

It took a moment for Aoife's eyes to adjust to the darkness outside of the barn and far more time for her heart to accept what she was doing out here. Walking away from Declan. Leaving him to face this on his own.

You're doing what he wanted, she reminded herself. *Respect goes two ways. Trust him.*

Tommy appeared at Aoife's side and, placing his hand at her elbow, nudged her toward town. Despite all of her internal assurances, her body seemed averse to accepting her decision. Each step felt like walking through wet sand, as if her feet and legs were protesting.

"I don't like leaving him behind either," Tommy said, drawing Aoife's attention to him, "but..."

When he didn't finish his thought, Aoife offered, "He's your captain."

Tommy only nodded before drawing in a deep breath. They walked in silence for several minutes, and Aoife strained her ears every few paces in an attempt to make out any screams or bellows of pain from behind them. Would Declan kill him swiftly and be done with it?

Of course not.

If that were the case, Tommy would not have protested—repeatedly—for Declan to reconsider. But he had conceded, left Declan to his own devices, trusted him to make his own decisions. Would Tommy have done that if he thought it was dangerous for Declan to pursue his revenge? Aoife had no idea what Declan had in mind, but after seeing the gruesome results of Callum's attacks on the merchant ships and watching Declan struggle with the trauma caused by the keelhauling, she realized that any expectation of him doling out a quick death to the pirate was folly.

"Why didn't he want my help?" Her question was barely louder than a breath, so quiet she didn't expect a response. And she certainly didn't expect Tommy to laugh at her, yet that's just what he did. Not a full-on laugh but a breathy chuckle.

"You asked me that once before, and my answer hasn't changed," he said, flashing her a small smile that didn't reach his eyes. It took Aoife a moment to realize the conversation he was referring to, the one they'd shared on the deck of the *Siren's Song* at Foxhaven.

"He did, Aoife. And does. But like everything else, he wants it—needs it—to be on his terms."

"Right," she whispered, but before she could get lost in her thoughts again, Tommy was clarifying.

"He's a complicated man, Aoife. I know you see that even after mere weeks with him. But there is a side of him he's kept buried for years, and Callum opened the vault he'd built to confine it. He's afraid to let you see that side of him."

Aoife opened her mouth to protest, but Tommy held up his hand as he turned to her, forcing her to stop walking. They weren't yet back to the road, and she could barely see him in the darkness.

"He knows you love him, and he knows you will love all of him. Even the darker parts. That doesn't mean he wants you to witness it in action though."

Aoife frowned, trying desperately to see it from Declan's point of view, but she couldn't ignore the part of her that felt shoved aside, discounted, unwanted. Tommy shot her a questioning look, and she took it as an invitation to respond.

"I understand that—of course I do—but will he ever stop seeing me as some naive heir?"

"Wanting to protect you is not the same as disrespecting you. Don't forget, he trusted you back in the pub. He went against his own judgment and chose to follow your lead. That's no small thing for a pirate, and a captain at that."

Aoife had to admit that all made sense, but there was one thing still nagging at her.

"Why did you try to stop him then? If this is just part of who he is, why—"

Tommy drew in a sharp breath, and the look in his eyes—a mixture of regret and fatigue and worry—stopped her short.

"It's not a part of himself he likes or wants. And I've seen what it does to him if allowed free rein. It nearly pulled him under, almost corrupted him completely back then. I was able to convince him to stop, barely. I hoped I could prevent him from heading down that path again."

"But you gave up so easily," Aoife said, trying to keep her voice low despite the frustration billowing in her chest.

Tommy shrugged so nonchalantly that Aoife might have given him a shove for being so flippant had he not said, "Because he has you now."

Aoife scoffed. "And how does that help him? What do you expect me to—"

Tommy looked at her as if she had sprouted a second head. "You love him, Aoife. That's what I expect from you. To love him. Like you did in that cove. Like you have since the moment you fell for him."

A scream rent the air as soon as Tommy had finished speaking, and Aoife cringed at the sheer agony in it. Maybe it was best Declan had sent her away. Whatever he was doing to Callum to cause such noise was not something she particularly wanted to watch. Especially when she already had trouble sleeping with the memories from Triss and the kraken.

"We should get moving," Tommy said, once again pulling her by the arm as he turned.

This time she didn't hesitate to listen, her feet moving willingly. Silence returned, enveloping them as they walked, and Aoife tried to sort through all they'd discussed, but her mind kept flitting back to the barn and the man she loved.

If anyone deserved Declan's wrath, it was Callum, and no part of Aoife felt any shred of remorse for that man. But she also couldn't ignore how worried she was that Declan's actions today—not just killing the man but torturing him—might change him into someone he didn't want to be. Someone she wasn't completely sure would still love her.

"I can't do this, Tommy," she said, though she kept in step with him. "We can't just give up and leave him to whatever this darkness demands of him."

"We aren't giving up. Not really. We give him this one kill, this one bit of revenge."

Aoife stopped. "And then what? Just hope that satisfies whatever bloodlust this darkness feeds on?" Turning around, she started back for the barn. "No. I won't wait for him to spiral out of control before I help him."

Tommy caught up with her. "It's not going to be pretty," he warned.

She glared at him. "I know, and I don't care. He needs me, Tommy. And I won't let fear or anything else keep me from going to him."

As if in response, another scream rang out, this one louder and sustained. For a moment, her muscles hesitated, as though the sound had physically slowed them down, but she forced herself to keep going.

She had just reached the barn door when the screaming abruptly ceased. The air became deadly still. Then a sickening noise sent Aoife's stomach turning violently before leaping into her throat. A wet, rending sound like that of a butcher cutting up an animal. But different.

Aoife reached for the door handle, but Tommy's hand snatched her wrist. She turned to find his eyes were wide. He shook his head, warning her to reconsider. And she might have listened to her fear and to her friend, but the sound of something thudding onto the dirt piqued her curiosity. Gently, she pulled her arm out of Tommy's grasp, shooting him a reassuring look that she could do this. That she had to do this.

But as she opened the door, the unmistakable sound of metal against flesh rushed at her once more, pulling her gaze immediately to the horrific scene in the middle of the barn.

Blood. So much blood.

It soaked into the dirt, and it covered both the body suspended from the ceiling and the man blocking her view of the carnage.

Declan.

One hand hung limp at his side, drenched in blood that dripped from his fingers onto the ground at his feet. All around his boots lay chunks of bloody flesh. The scene sent Aoife's head swirling in a storm of images from the battle with the kraken—of crew members battered and broken upon the deck, of the beast's remains falling around her in sickening thuds.

Bile rushed to her throat, and Aoife backed out the door and retched onto the dirt and grass. Tommy stepped up beside her, his hand finding the middle of her back as she spit the last sour bits of vomit from her mouth.

She could do this. She had to do this.

For Declan, she could do anything.

Wiping an arm across her mouth, she straightened. She didn't give Tommy any chance to scold her or change her mind as she stepped back into the barn. This time she was prepared.

Or as prepared as she could be.

The metallic stench of blood filled the space, and she tried to ignore it as she stepped forward with caution, as if she were approaching a wild animal and not the man she loved. His muscles tensed as he prepared to move, and his name was on her lips.

"Declan."

CHAPTER 31
DECLAN

The click of the barn door closing barely registered as Declan held the Csintala dagger up under Callum's chin, lifting his face slightly. Tommy must have hit the man rather hard for him to still be unconscious.

But no matter.

Declan knew just how to wake him up.

You don't have to do this.

Tommy's words whispered in his mind, but they were soon drowned out by a sinister laugh coming from somewhere within him. Tommy might be right, but Declan no longer cared about what Tommy thought, or Gavin, or Aoife.

Aoife.

He shook away her name. She would understand. She would still love him when it was finished. She had to, just as he had to do this.

Beckoning the darkness within him to creep forward, he smiled when all thoughts of his friends dissolved away, leaving him with just Callum and the dagger in his hand.

Slowly he moved the tip of the blade up the man's jaw to the scar Halloran had given him in front of his left ear. It shone a ghostly white in the lantern light until Declan forced the blade into the edge of it. Blood seeped around the smooth metal and trailed down Callum's face as Declan tore open the old wound.

He'd made it halfway down Callum's face when the man jolted awake. He squirmed and fought, his eyes going wide as he registered Declan standing before him. Declan snatched the pirate's chin in his other hand and squeezed hard, holding him still as he finished his first cut.

With a smile, Declan cocked his head to the side to admire his work, ignoring how Callum eyed him with horror and surprise.

One raspy word fell from the pirate's mouth. "How?"

Declan answered by waving the dagger in front of Callum's face.

"You got cocky, friend." Declan clicked his tongue and then shrugged. "And when you get cocky, you make mistakes."

Callum's face tightened in confusion, and Declan released an annoyed sigh.

"You *betrayed* me, Callum." The words came out calm, collected, and menacing. "Were you not aware of that bit of the dagger's legend? Or did you just forget?"

No answer came from the man—verbal or otherwise—so Declan continued as he turned Callum's head to the other side and shifted the dagger to his other hand.

"No matter either way though. The dagger doesn't take kindly to betrayers. Your loss is my gain it seems." He pressed the blade into Callum's other cheek and sliced it down to his jaw, speaking as he worked. "I get the dagger. And I get my revenge. It's a beautiful thing."

He leaned back, turning the man's face from side to side.

"Unlike your face, however. You'll never be pretty again."

Callum scoffed. "Women love scars."

"Aye. Some do, but you'll have far more than a few scars before we're done." Declan dropped Callum's face, turned away, and began pacing.

Tapping the flat side of the dagger against his lips, he walked. Back and forth. Back and forth. Tapping in rhythm with his boots as they hit the dirt floor.

"Why don't you get on with it?" Callum spat.

Declan spun slowly to face him, clicking his tongue once more before pulling his lips back into a smirk. "You can't rush art."

"Oh, so you're an artist now."

"Have been for a while. Though I am a bit out of practice."

"Just like rowing a boat, I hear. You never really forget," Callum said.

"Aye. You never forget." Declan stalked toward Callum once more, glaring at this despicable human who had inflicted far too much pain on far too many people. "That's what you wanted, wasn't it? To haunt me forever?"

Callum tried to smile, but the gashes Declan had sliced down his cheeks made it nearly impossible. "A beating would have healed too quickly. Stringing you up instead of Killian would have been too quick."

"Except had you killed me instead, you wouldn't be dangling here, preparing to be flayed alive and gutted like the animal you are." Declan worked to keep his features steady, calm, devoid of the rage that blazed within. He needed to disconnect, to disassociate.

"So that's the plan, is it?" Callum's bored manner and impassive stare stoked Declan's anger. This wasn't going to be nearly as much fun if Callum didn't play his role correctly.

He needed Callum to scream, to writhe in anguish, to beg for mercy, to die the slow and miserable and agonizing death he deserved. Callum's brow rose in question, his eyes widening in anticipation of Declan's answer. But Declan didn't respond with words.

Rather, he struck quickly, burying the blade into the pirate's side and pulling it free. Callum groaned in pain.

Declan's heart leaped at the sound, but it wasn't enough. Not nearly enough.

He walked to Callum's side and surveyed his options before extending the dagger up to the pirate's arm, which was stretched taut with the weight of his body. He laid the blade flat against Callum's tricep and then angled it slightly until its razor edge broke through the skin. Declan couldn't keep from smiling as he pulled the blade down, separating Callum's skin from his flesh in one smooth motion, like he would a fish.

This time Callum didn't groan. He screamed.

Guttural.

Desperate.

Perfect.

When he reached Callum's shoulder, he pulled the blade free, removing the length of skin completely. Callum was still screaming when Declan held it up before his face. But the man's eyes were closed, and tears were beginning to form along his eyelids.

Declan wanted to bellow at him to open them, to look at what was being done to him. But instead, he inhaled slowly, drawing in the metallic tang of blood that now mingled with the scent of the dirt floor and the mildewing wood. Composing himself, he said calmly, "Open your eyes, Callum."

To his surprise, the man obliged, and Declan nearly laughed at how his features twitched from the pain. "This is what a perfect, sharp blade can do, aye? Nothing like the barnacles beneath your ship, is it?" He let the swath of skin drop to the ground and rotated the blade slowly before Callum's eyes.

Callum choked out a word.

Declan inched toward his face and sneered. "What was that?"

"No," Callum rasped a little louder this time.

Straightening, Declan shook his head. "Exactly. What that hull did to Killian..." He left the thought hanging in the air between them as he slid the Csintala dagger into his belt and walked over to the far wall of the barn, where he eyed the line of rusted-over, nicked-up tools hanging there. Axes and saws and scythes and knives. He could make use of any of these, but he already knew which he wanted. He'd noticed it when he'd first arrived: a large machete, the type used for cutting down the thick-stalked crops whose corpses still rotted out in the fields beyond. Lifting the machete from its hook, he started to turn back to Callum but decided to quickly snatch up one of the iron hand hooks as well. While he wasn't sure exactly how he might use it, the possibilities swirling around in his head were too enticing to allow him to leave it behind.

Once he was back in the center of the barn, Declan dropped the hook to the dirt and lifted the large, rusted blade into Callum's line of sight. A pathetic whimper squeaked out from the back of Callum's throat, and Declan couldn't hold back his grin.

"This is better. Not quite perfect, but the best I can do, I'm afraid."

Despite his initial reaction, though, Callum recovered quickly, smoothing over his expression until there was no hint of the fear or dread Declan desired. The darkness roared in his head.

Without warning, Declan placed the blade's ragged edge above Callum's ear and pulled it down, sawing through skin and cartilage as Callum's scream filled the air. When the blade finally slipped through the last fibers and Callum's ear tumbled into the dirt, the pirate's screams tapered off into garbled groans.

Declan didn't give him much of a reprieve before he moved the bloodied knife back to his already wounded cheeks to pull the edges of his torn skin further away from his face. Once that was done, he took a step back to assess. It wasn't quite the same effect as keelhauling, and it certainly wasn't symmetrical, but the fluttering of Callum's eyelids and the rapid rise and fall of his chest told Declan he'd at least managed to effectively hurt the man.

It would have to do, given his limited options and time.

But Declan was far from finished.

Flipping the machete into his other hand, Declan retrieved the hand hook from where he'd dropped it.

He smirked at Callum—not that the man could see it—and as he slipped the hook into the pirate's collar and tore his shirt away along the buttons, he said, "Now don't go reading into this. Undressing you is the last thing I want to be doing right now. But it is, unfortunately, a necessity."

Callum scoffed at him.

Or maybe he was only choking on his own blood.

Either way, Declan didn't let it deter him. Pointing the machete at Callum's chest, he clicked his tongue as he weighed his options.

"It really is too bad we have such limited time together. But as I have a crew and my love waiting for me back on my ship, I'm going to have to make quick work of this."

He didn't wait for a reaction before he was moving the machete along Callum's ribs, scraping his skin—and some flesh—away from his torso in jagged chunks. Callum's screams were now earsplitting, and for half a breath, Declan worried someone in town might hear and come to investigate.

You'll be done and gone before they arrive.

After Declan had made two passes along Callum's right side, the screams died away as he lost consciousness, his bloody and mangled head lolling to rest against his equally marred arm. Declan straightened and slapped the side of the machete's blade against the pirate's face.

"Don't fall asleep on me now, Callum! We're almost to the best part."

Gripping Callum's chin as tightly as he could with his fingers slipping in the man's blood, he shook him until his eyes opened slightly. He moved into his view and waited until Callum's eyes seemed to refocus on him.

Then he hissed in his face. "You think this is bad? This is nothing compared to what you did to your own man."

Callum's lips moved, but no sound passed through them.

"What was that?" Declan said, inching his ear closer.

"Traitor." Callum choked out the single word, and it made Declan's blood boil once more. He slammed his teeth together, forcing his fingers tighter around the handle of the machete.

Declan leaned even closer. "He was my friend." The words came out as ragged as Callum's breaths.

Callum's body shook, and it took Declan a moment to realize the man was laughing—or trying to.

"You barely knew him," Callum said in a slow, pained whisper.

They'd talked enough.

Declan's rage surged. His mind darkened. He moved the machete to the man's chest, slicing away more chunks of flesh. Every scream that tore from Callum's throat only pushed Declan further, to cut again and again and again.

When Callum fell silent once more, Declan didn't grab his face, didn't try to wake him up with words or a slap of the blade. But he also couldn't bear to let the man escape his torment with unconsciousness.

Dropping the machete to the blood-soaked dirt at his feet, Declan adjusted the hand hook in his palm.

He'll awake when his guts spill from him, the darkness whispered to him.

Without hesitation, he thrust the hook's point into Callum's side, just below his ribs. Callum barely flinched. Declan tensed his arm, ready to pull it across.

But a sound behind him made him pause.

Do it now! his mind screamed at him. But the noise came again. He tried to identify it, to determine why it sounded so familiar, but his mind was a sea of black and blood. A sea he was quickly drowning in. And he didn't mind. He wanted this. He wanted to gut this man who had captured him and killed his friend and served him up to the siren. This man who had taken the dagger and then threatened Aoife.

Aoife.

The sound came again, cutting through the thick fog of rage.

"Declan."

With the hook still buried in Callum's side, Declan struggled to focus on that voice. That voice he knew and loved.

But the darkness pushed back.

No! She doesn't understand. Finish this. Make him pay!

His muscles started to obey, his arm flexing to pull the dull blade across his enemy's belly.

"Declan."

The voice came again, staying his hand, though his body remained poised to act.

Declan closed his eyes, trying to sort through the voices battling for his attention. He didn't know what to do. One swift motion and he could be done with Callum and then answer the one calling his name. But if he did that, would she understand?

Why do you care? This is what you want. This is what this bastard deserves!

Slamming his eyes closed and grinding his teeth together even harder than before, Declan made his choice and pulled.

The tearing of Callum's flesh under the hook reverberated up his arm, and that wicked part of him rejoiced, urging him on.

"Declan! Stop!" That sweet voice behind him cut through the darkness, and somehow, despite every bit of him wanting to continue, he stopped.

A hand hovered over his shoulder, and his name was repeated in his ear.

Even as he wanted to pull the hook the rest of the way, part of him melted into that touch.

"It's done, Declan."

Those three words were all it took. Declan's head swiveled around until his eyes fell upon the prettiest greens and golds he'd ever known.

Aoife.

"You came back?" He was sure he was imagining it when her lips curved into a soft smile.

"You needed me," Aoife said, her fingers carefully nudging him to turn toward her.

But he couldn't. He resisted enough to cause her to pause. She would run away. At any moment, she would look over his shoulder, see what he'd done, and leave him.

Let her leave! the voice within bellowed, but he shut it down. No. She had come back. She'd heard what he'd done. She didn't need to witness it to know the monster he was. And she'd still come back for him.

Still, he couldn't release his grip on the hook. Even when Callum released a weak moan, he couldn't move. Couldn't finish it. Couldn't stop it.

"Let me help you," Aoife said.

What did she mean by that? Was she offering to gut the man for him? Was she going to force him to leave and urge him to escape the darkness that was as much a part of him as his love for her?

Before he could ask, she pulled the Csintala dagger from his belt. He watched as she walked around him, the blade held steadily in her hand. Then she reached for the hook, squeezing his hand lightly, urging him to release it. Without thinking, he obeyed, pulling the tool from Callum's gut and letting it fall. As soon as it thudded to their feet, Aoife's arm moved in a graceful arc, steady and confident, as if she'd been doing this her whole life.

The Csintala blade sliced cleanly across Callum's throat, just under his jaw, from ear to ear, severing the necessary blood vessels to kill him quickly. The bastard of a pirate took one final gasp before his body stilled.

Blood sprayed across Aoife's face, just as it had in Foxhaven. Only this time, she wasn't in shock. This time the killing had been at her hand.

She's cute when she's deadly, he thought.

Declan uttered no words as he reached a hand up to her jaw. Somewhere in his mind, he heard the echoes of the darkness screaming at him for letting Aoife take this kill from him. But it was easily ignored as he marveled at this woman who had come back to help him, even when he'd pushed her away.

Wiping the blood on her pants, Aoife tucked the blade back into Declan's belt and interlaced her fingers with his.

"Let's go, Declan. Your crew is waiting."

He let her pull him slowly away from the blood-soaked spot where Callum's lifeless form—mangled and broken—still hung. But before they left the barn, he allowed himself one last glance over his shoulder, and he couldn't deny the regret that coursed through him. Callum hadn't suffered enough.

Not nearly enough.

CHAPTER 32
DECLAN

DECLAN COULDN'T STOP SHAKING EVEN after they'd returned to the ship and locked themselves away in his cabin. Falling back against the door, he let his chin drop to his chest and his eyes close with fatigue. Aoife, to her credit, remained quiet, which helped his aching head but did little to ease the worry that now plagued him.

He had let it slip. More than slip. He'd let the darkness take hold, and he'd enjoyed it. Only her touch and her soft pleas for him to stop had given him the strength to rein it in and cage it back up. She could have run. She could have left him then and there, but she'd remained, stepped closer, and helped him return to her.

But who did she see in him now?

Now that she knew—truly knew—what lurked beneath the surface.

Could she love the monster he held at bay?

Her light footsteps drew his attention. She was walking away from him but didn't seem wary of him or angry with him. Though how much emotion could one see in someone's backside?

Depends on the occasion.

The thought had him laughing softly to himself, but he sobered quickly. This didn't seem the time to fixate on Aoife's body, not when he had no idea what she was thinking or feeling.

She stopped in front of his desk but didn't turn to face him, which only made his anxiety that much worse.

Just ask her. Talk to her.

Communicate.

He opened his mouth to speak, but she turned around before he could utter anything.

"Is there rum, by chance?" she asked. He pursed his lips in thought. "I don't know about you, Declan, but I could use a damn drink after all that just happened."

"Aye," he said as he stepped away from the door. He passed by her, moving toward the drawer, and his muscles cried out in frustration as he kept ample space between them. Pulling a bottle out from within, he unstopped the cork and handed it to her. "Ladies first."

Aoife didn't respond but merely reached out to take the proffered drink and lift it to her lips. He tried to remember the questions that had seemed so important a moment ago. But they were gone, scattered by the sight of her taking several swallows of rum, of her closing her eyes as she savored each sip. What he wouldn't give to be that bottle, to have her lips wrapped around him and her fingers gripping him.

That kind of thinking would not help now, and he tried to force it away by clearing his throat.

Lowering the bottle, Aoife caught him staring. Pulling her bottom lip between her teeth, she offered the rum back to him. He raised his hands to decline.

"I'd rather be sober for what's about to happen," he said. He couldn't read the expression on her face as she set the bottle down between them.

His heartbeat picked up, thumping so hard he was sure she could hear it.

With a sigh, she asked, "And what is about to happen exactly?"

Oh the ways he could answer that question.

Declan had nearly convinced himself to behave, to take this seriously, when something flashed in her eyes, and her lips twitched ever so slightly. Contemplating the possibilities, weighing which appealed to him most, he walked slowly around the desk to stand before her.

"We should talk," he said, his tone unintentionally husky.

Aoife remained silent, though her body squirmed slightly, as if beckoned by the lust in his voice. "Is that what you want?"

"No." The word escaped him before he had time to think, but he forced himself to behave. Miscommunication and lies had been their downfall before. He wasn't going to make that mistake again. He refused to make assumptions about how she felt. "But I need to know…"

He searched her eyes for any sign of horror, any hint of disgust, finding nothing but that familiar spark of love and acceptance he didn't deserve.

"Need to know what? If I still love you?" She paused for a breath. "Yes, I do. If I'm scared of you?" Her brows rose with the question.

Declan froze, not sure he wanted to know her answer after all.

But she flashed him one of her sweet smiles. "No more than I was before. Though…" Her voice trailed off into nothingness as she closed the distance between them, coming just close enough that her body barely whispered against his own, teasing him. He swallowed, trying desperately to keep control of himself, which was made especially difficult when she lifted a hand to his chest. A whisper of a sigh brought her closer still, and when her fingers curled into him, his need for her intensified.

Somehow he managed to ask, "Though what?"

Aoife kept her eyes locked on his chest where her fingers played with the folds of his shirt. "Being scared isn't always a bad thing," she said.

The memories rushed forward. Him pushing her up against the wall of the alley, stealing a kiss. Him pinning her down in his bed, challenging her with his whispers. He'd sensed her fear both times, tasted it on her lips and her skin, but there had been something else present in her reactions.

Excitement.

Curiosity.

Desire.

He'd ignored them then, determined to push her away.

But here? Now? He didn't have to pretend anymore.

Aoife tilted her chin up to look at him. A drop of rum clung to the corner of her mouth as if it, too, never wanted to let go of her. Declan raised a hand to her face, brushing his fingers lightly against her cheek while he moved to capture the lingering rum with his thumb.

"You missed some," he said as he brushed it over her lips, and his heart nearly stopped when her tongue peeked out to lick the sweetness from his skin.

His mind raced, imagining all he wanted to do.

To her and with her and for her.

He moved closer still, trapping her hand at his chest. Leaning further in, he lightly grazed her lips with his before trailing them along her jaw. His hand fell to the curve of her hip, and a thrill went through him when her breathing deepened and her body shuddered under his touch. Her fingers dug into his chest as her free hand reached for the sash at his waist, using it to hold him against her. And he smiled in triumph when his warm breath against her ear sent another tremor through her.

He could use this moment to tell her all the ways he loved her, to thank her for all she had done to save him, to say any number of sweet and respectable things.

But you're a pirate.

At that thought, he let the truth come out with a growl. "I've wanted to bend you over my desk since the night you walked in here."

Aoife whimpered as her body melted into him, but she turned her face away, her cheeks flushed. Declan held her close, climbing his hand up her back until his fingers were buried in her hair. He turned her head to face him, surprised to find her green eyes ablaze with excitement. Her lips parted as if to invite him to follow through with his fantasy.

"But now that I have you, princess," he said with an uncontrolled roughness, "I want you to watch me as I claim you. I want to see your face when I undo you. I want to memorize how you look when I please you. I want you—"

Aoife forced her mouth to his, quieting him with the dance of her tongue and lips on his, a silent answer to all he'd said.

He lifted her easily, his hands sliding underneath her backside until he had her atop the desk, her legs straddling his hips, wrapping around him and pulling him to her. A moan escaped when he pressed against her, and he couldn't tell whose it was. All he knew was his growing need to have her here and now.

As if Aoife could read his mind, she moved her hands to his waist, tearing open his belt and ripping away the sash before frantically pushing his pants onto the floor. He removed his shirt in one swift motion and delighted in the way her eyes, gleaming with desire, took all of him in. Her gaze traveled the length of him, slowly, as if she wanted to commit every inch to memory. When her eyes fell lower and her blush deepened, his doubt crept in. For a moment, he worried she would change her mind, but he'd give her whatever she demanded.

But then her eyes locked onto his once more, and he could have sworn there was a bit of mischief in them.

"Would you like to stare longer, or shall I continue?" Declan asked. A bite of her lip, an arch to her brow, the slightest of nods, and he was lowering her down onto the desk, saying, "It's your turn."

Lifting her hips, he began to slip her breeches off. She giggled when he knelt to kiss the inside of her thigh as he pulled them the rest of the way off. He smiled against her other leg as he repeated the motion once more.

"I love your laugh," he said as he kissed his way back up her leg, tasting her delicate skin with his tongue, nipping the soft flesh of her thighs. She shuddered as he traveled higher, and her legs tensed beneath his lips and tongue and fingers. When his breath lingered over her center, she froze, and he couldn't help but smirk as he lifted his head to look at her.

"Too much?" Declan asked, letting his fingers continue their dance up her legs, over her hips, traveling deliciously close to the part of her that begged for his touch.

Aoife shook her head, her body squirming with her ragged breath. "Not enough."

"Greedy girl," he said with a laugh before laying a trail of kisses along her hip and up to her abdomen, moving her shirt out of the way as he did so. He couldn't help but smile against her skin when she whimpered a complaint. Her hips shifted beneath him, calling him back to where he'd dared tease her.

"Patience," he whispered, glancing at her from beneath his brow. "I'm just getting started."

Moving his hands up under her shirt, he lifted her back off the desk until she faced him. Her eyes had closed, embarrassment and anticipation washing over her face as he explored higher and higher, pushing her shirt up as he did. And if he thought he'd made her shudder before, it was nothing compared to how her body trembled with pleasure when his thumbs grazed the hard peaks of her breasts.

As much as he had wanted to savor this, he found his patience waning. Quickly. She didn't object when he slipped her shirt over her head, though she still didn't open her eyes. Even now, even with the strength she now possessed, uncertainty and timidity tugged at her features, her insecurity pulling her inward.

She didn't see herself clearly. Didn't see herself the way he saw her.

"Open your eyes," he commanded, his hands cradling her ribs, his fingers caressing her with gentle strokes. She shook her head and pursed her lips, all the mischief shadowed by her insecurity.

"Look at me, Aoife," he said, and he pressed himself against her, having to work hard to ignore the tremors that coursed through him as his cock lightly rested against her warmth.

Slowly she obeyed.

"What did I tell you?" Declan asked. "Watch me." He lowered his hands to her hips and pulled her easily to the edge of the desk, to the edge of him. And then, wetting his lips and staring into the eyes of this woman who had forgiven him and loved him and understood him, he gave in to everything he'd tried so hard to ignore since they'd first met.

He melted into her, slowly and completely, loving the way she gasped as he did. Her entire body quivered, and her head fell to the side as she accepted all of him. Her hands wove their way under his arms and up his back, her nails biting into him.

"Watch me," he repeated as he moved her against him, rolling his body with hers. He fought to keep her from pulling him under too soon. "Don't close your eyes."

She met his gaze, and a smirk pulled at the corner of her mouth. "Aye, Captain."

It might have been those words on her lips or the blaze of ecstasy in her eyes or the feel of her breasts brushing against his chest that pulled the growl from his chest and pushed him to lead her to that delicious cliff.

She kept her eyes locked on his as she bit her lip and moved with him. And then her desire took over, her body writhing, her hands kneading his back. He wanted to kiss her, to taste her when she peaked, but he couldn't stop watching her as she took the lead, pressing her body against him until every part of her pulled tight before falling over the edge.

Her hands clamped down on his back, and her lips fell open with a silent moan. Her head sank back in pure bliss. And then she was smiling and laughing as she continued to pulse against him with each stroke of his hands on her skin.

There was the girl who had surprised him, time and time again.

Confident.

Curious.

Daring.

All his.

He gripped her backside as he raced to catch up to her and to the satisfaction that still played across her face. She slipped her fingers into his hair, pulling his mouth to hers, claiming him as greedily as he was claiming her.

And then he was there. As near to her as he could get, holding onto her with all he had until his body stilled.

Spent.

Satisfied.

So unbelievably happy.

Nipping her bottom lip one more time, he pulled his mouth from hers long enough to release a heavy and ragged exhale, full of pure contentment, before their eyes met.

Her brows rose in question, the insecurity he'd witnessed before edging back into her expression. He needed her to know this wasn't just another romp for him.

She was like no other woman he'd been with, and she was the only one he ever wanted to wreck him like this. She was the only one who could destroy him this fully.

"I love you, princess," he whispered, resting his forehead against hers. He hoped she didn't hear those as mere words, tossed around as easily as his clothes.

"And I love you, Captain." She sighed and fell against his chest before whispering into his neck, "That was nothing like the books."

Declan looked down at her. "Should I be offended?"

She shook her head, kissing his collarbone and his shoulder before finding his eyes again. "Not at all. That was far better. Better than I ever imagined."

Then her hips moved against him, her whimper of a laugh and wicked smile inviting him for more. She didn't need to ask him twice.

"I've created an insatiable monster," he said between tender kisses against her neck. He grazed his teeth over her racing pulse. "It's a good thing I'm just getting started."

✄

PALE LIGHT STREAMED in through the windows that lined Declan's bedroom, coaxing his eyes to open. Morning? Had he slept the entire night? Had he truly slept until sunrise with no images of blood and death plaguing his dreams?

Maybe you're finally healing? he wondered. But within a heartbeat, as if in response to that thought, the nightmarish memories flooded in. He swallowed hard before shooing them away with steady breaths.

But one remained.

White sand. Aoife unconscious. His man dead. Blood on his hands.

It wasn't your fault. It was the queen. But no matter how many times he reminded himself of those facts, it didn't ease the guilt away. Especially with the tension that still lay between him and Gavin.

"Good morning," Aoife said, her smile evident even before she lifted her head from his shoulder to look at him. Her insecurity had returned, as Declan had anticipated. Daylight had a way of stripping people of any brazen confidence they had found under the cover of night.

Placing a kiss on her forehead, Declan returned the greeting. "Sleep okay?"

"Better than I have in a long time, honestly."

"Same." But the image of Collins's face down in the sand made the word sound like a lie.

Aoife was sitting up in an instant, swinging her legs around so she knelt beside him, her knees tucked close to his ribs.

"Talk to me."

But Declan couldn't. The memory had his throat constricted with remorse, and he could only answer her with a touch. He needed to feel her, his rock, his safe harbor, his everything. She wore nothing but one of his white linen shirts. Light and airy, it teased him, giving him a hint of a view of her body beneath it. He ran his hand up her thigh, slipping it under the shirt's hem, hoping the feel of her skin would soothe away his unwelcome emotions and thoughts.

Aoife's own hand shot to his, stopping it mid-stroke at her hip.

"Declan," she said, and he closed his eyes. Why, he wasn't sure. She'd seen him at his most vulnerable, at his darkest, and she was still here. But he couldn't look at her now, not with his chest cracking down the middle as the guilt split him open.

As if she could see the growing fissure in his sternum, she laid her hand upon it with a gentle but firm touch.

"Look at me." When he didn't, she moved her hand up to his jaw. "I watched you last night, as you commanded, so you can do the same for me now."

With a silent chuckle, he complied, and he nearly lost his voice again at the look of concern in her green eyes. "Aye, I can."

"Are you going to make me guess what's bothering you?" Her hand returned to his chest, somehow piecing it back together with just her warmth. "Was I that bad last night?"

Her cheeks flushed.

"You're joking, right?" She shrugged. He could only shake his head at her. "If it was bad—which isn't possible—I wouldn't have demanded it three more times."

"Maybe you kept trying, hoping it would get better."

This woman. She truly didn't know how amazing she was.

"You're ridiculous, you know that?" He quirked a brow at her, but she simply responded with another shrug. Covering her hand with his, he gave her fingers a squeeze before he spoke again, making sure not to look away from her as he did. "It's Collins."

He had barely uttered the words before Aoife was there, inching closer. "It's not—"

"I know." He couldn't bear to hear the words again. He already knew. It didn't help. His guilt didn't seem to care that it wasn't his fault or that he couldn't have prevented it.

"Oh, I didn't realize you were a mind reader now," Aoife said with a hint of annoyance. "So you knew I was trying to tell you it's not easy? That it will take time? But you don't have to deal with it on your own? You knew all that?"

"No, I guess I didn't know that. I'm sorry, I—"

"Need a distraction." Aoife's eyes lit up with mischief, but then she asked, "Let me help you?"

"Have something in mind?"

Aoife moved to straddle him. She leaned forward, her hands trailing up his chest to his neck and into his hair, brushing his ears as they moved. When her lips nearly touched his, he parted his lips, wetting them as he did. He leaned up to steal a kiss, but she pulled back, shaking her head.

"I want to try something," she whispered. "And if I do it wrong, don't tell me."

Declan was about to laugh at her ridiculous notion, but she was already retreating, planting kisses down his neck and then his chest. He reached down to pull his shirt up and off of her and nearly groaned when her breasts met his skin. But then her lips were at his stomach, and his body twitched, making Aoife giggle as she had last night.

"Settle down, Captain," she whispered. "I haven't even gotten started yet."

He had no chance to reply before she was placing light kisses and sharp nips along one hip and then the other. Her breasts brushed along his hardened length, and he hissed through his teeth as she gripped him with her hand, exploring the entire length of him agonizingly slowly.

Maybe he shouldn't have taught her those rules the other day, because it certainly seemed like she was waiting for him to beg.

Breathlessly uttering her name was as far as he got with his pleading before her lips and tongue were on him, slow and steady as if she were wanting to savor every inch of him. She'd felt amazing last night, but this? This was quite the distraction.

Declan pressed his head back into the pillow as groans of passion escaped him, in the shape of her name and of swears and of no words at all. He wanted to stop her, to take her there with him, to share this completely and wholly with her.

And then he didn't.

He never wanted her to stop.

Ever.

Until he was there.

Up and up and up.

And then falling.

Crashing into her.

Colliding into nothing and everything at once.

Satisfaction rumbled deep in his chest. His nerves pulled tight, holding him hostage until releasing him back to her.

"Well," Aoife said, her sweet voice pulling him back to reality, a reality in which love and bliss drowned out the sadness and guilt. "I assume that was okay."

Laughter shook his chest, and he reached for her, pulling her toward him. Rolling her onto her back, he pinned her to the bed, his hands finding hers and holding them tight above her head.

"Aye, beyond okay," Declan said, and then he kissed her slowly, steadily, exploring her mouth as if he had never tasted her before.

"Am I to beg for action?" she asked, her voice thick with want.

In response, he pressed his hips into hers as he kissed his way to her pulse.

His hot breath against her ear had her shuddering. "Only if you want it."

"Aye. I want it." Her hands were in his hair again, fingers curling against his head as she whispered the words he wanted to hear. "Take me, please."

"As you wish," Declan said. "But...it's my turn to try something."

To his surprise, Aoife didn't recoil or shrink away as he lowered himself down her body. Rather, her hands urged him lower. Her body trembled beneath him as he tasted his way across her skin, and when he found the spot he craved, he couldn't help but smile as a breathless "Sands" fell from her lips.

With every circle and stroke, Declan worshiped her, relishing how she pressed into him, loving how the smallest of his movements made her squirm and sigh with pleasure. Sipping her desire, tasting her need for him, he drank her in, indulging in all that she offered him.

"I—" Her words were cut off with another moan, and he watched her eyelids flutter closed and her mouth fall open as he delighted in her.

"Not yet," he commanded, and she looked at him, shaking her head with a quivering smile on her face. "Tell me what you want."

"I can't—"

"You can," he said, his fingers taking over the dance. "This?" He tasted her again, deep and long. "Or—"

"I want you," Aoife said, already tugging his face back to hers. Declan groaned into her kiss, letting her taste all that he had.

Her legs wrapped around his waist, dragging him to her until they became one again. And this time, he didn't tell her to open her eyes. He let his own eyes fall closed as they moved together toward that blissful edge.

And when Declan fell, he took Aoife with him, plunging into a sea of pleasure and devotion. A sea all their own.

A sea he never wanted to leave.

CHAPTER 33
TOMMY

CALLUM'S MUTILATED body was not the worst Tommy had ever seen, nor was this the worst scene he'd cleaned up. Such was the life of a quartermaster. He could have left the pirate strung up in the abandoned barn. It wasn't likely any poor farmer was going to happen upon it—at least not for a long while—and he certainly didn't care enough about the damned pirate to bury him properly.

He did it for Declan.

And not because he'd ordered him to.

This wasn't a message to others, an act of brutality to further his friend's—his captain's—reputation. This had been done purely to appease Declan's anger, to make the man pay for all he'd done. And no one needed to be plagued with nightmares because they'd stumbled into the wrong barn.

The farm's well had provided enough water to get Aoife and Declan cleaned of all the blood. Once they'd headed back to the ship, Tommy had set to work cutting down Callum's body and burying it—as well as the tools used—in a shallow grave.

Back on the ship, he avoided the captain's quarters, giving his friends the privacy they needed after such an ordeal, and instead went to find Gavin, who was on the quarterdeck looking out to sea.

"Celene leave already?" Tommy asked by way of greeting, stepping up beside the helmsman.

Gavin nodded. "Captain sent her on her way as soon as he returned."

"And have you decided?" Tommy eyed his friend, who stood tense and uneasy with his hands jammed into his pockets. This wasn't the relaxed and easygoing man Tommy had sailed with all these years, and he couldn't remember the last time he'd seen Gavin like this. If ever.

Though it was understandable.

Losing someone close to you—particularly at the hand of someone you trusted—wasn't an easy thing to move on from.

Aoife did though, he reminded himself.

But Gavin wasn't Aoife, and the helmsman's relationship with the captain was not exactly the same as Aoife's.

Still, Tommy hoped his friends could reconcile.

When Gavin finally spoke, it wasn't to answer Tommy's question. "At least Collins got a sailor's burial, right? Wasn't eaten..."

Tommy winced at the memory of the sirens and their needle-like teeth piercing him.

"Aye. The captain gave him what he could, Gavin. You know that."

Gavin swallowed hard and nodded. "I know I need to forgive him, but it's..."

Tommy stood beside him in silence for a long while, staring out at the black Aisling, tracing the moonlight where it hit the ripples along its surface.

"Whatever you decide," Tommy said finally, "you know we will support you to the end. All of us."

Gavin dipped his head in a slow nod and released a sigh. "I couldn't have asked for a better crew, for better friends."

Unable to dredge up anything encouraging to say, Tommy turned and offered his hand to his friend. Clapping him on the shoulder, he looked him in the eye. "Go get some rest and think it over. I'll man the helm for you. Though..." He tossed his head toward Declan's cabin. "I don't think we'll be setting off anytime soon."

THE SUN HAD ALREADY CLEARED the horizon by the time Declan finally emerged from his quarters with Aoife in tow. Tommy moved down the stairs to greet them, trying hard not to smile knowingly. Though they both appeared presentable—clothes buttoned in all the right places and hair somewhat tamed—there was that unmistakable hint of satisfaction written on their faces.

Tommy might have laughed outright at the sight of them had he not received a warning look from Declan. Even still, he apparently wasn't able to completely hide his amusement.

"Why are you making that face, Tommy?" Aoife asked, and his laughter burst out of him before he could stop it.

Declan pulled her close to him, tucking her under his arm and shaking his head at his friend.

But Tommy spoke first. "Just happy for you, is all. And glad you waited for me to not be in the room this time."

Aoife flushed a deep pink as her head fell, but she was giggling before Declan could reprimand Tommy for not staying quiet.

"Same," she said, "on both counts." She smiled as she looked from one to the other. Aoife smacked Declan, who was still glaring at Tommy. "Oh, leave him alone, Declan. You'd be acting the same way if the situation were reversed, and you know it."

"She's got you there, Captain," Tommy said, ignoring as best he could the memory of his time with Maura.

With a clearing of his throat and a roll of his grey eyes to the sky, Declan addressed them both. "This—whatever this is—is going to annoy me to no end, isn't it?"

Aoife lifted herself onto her toes and not-so-silently whispered in Declan's ear, "It's called friendship, Declan. It'll only annoy you if you let it."

"Could be worse," Tommy added with a lighthearted shrug. "We could hate each other."

"Or we could be attracted to each other," Aoife added with a wrinkle of her nose that made Tommy laugh again.

He shook his head at her. "Nope. That'd never happen. No offense."

"None taken." Aoife faked a shudder—at least Tommy assumed she faked it.

Declan dropped his face, pinching the bridge of his nose between his fingers. Shaking his head, he released his exasperation with a heavy breath. "Right. Well then." He looked back up to Tommy. "We ready to sail? Where's Gavin?"

Tommy nodded firmly.

Back to business.

"Aye. Just needed to confirm our heading with you before we set out. Didn't want to interrupt any—"

Declan held up a hand. "We make for Morshan. Until—unless—we get word of Maura's location, we continue forward. And Gavin?"

"I relieved him of his post. Told him to go rest. He has a lot to think over."

Aoife's face twisted with concern. "Thinking what over exactly? He's not actually thinking of leaving, is he?"

Declan pulled her tighter to him as he answered her. "Aye, he is. And I won't force him to stay."

"But he can't!" Aoife said as she stepped away from Declan, moving toward the officers' cabin.

"Aoife." Declan's voice stopped her mid-stride, and she turned back to look at him. "Leave him be."

She started to protest, but she must have seen something in Declan's eyes, because she actually stopped and complied. But she didn't say anything more as her gaze dropped to the deck.

"Get us underway to Morshan, Tommy," Declan commanded. "We have a dagger to deliver."

THEY HAD BARELY MADE it out of Selka's harbor when one of the crew called out, "Siren! Port side!"

Tommy backed away from the helm and descended the stairs as quickly as he could. The siren could be bringing a message from any corner of the Aisling, but if there was a chance it was from Maura, he wasn't going to wait for Declan or Aoife or anyone else to deliver the word to him.

Running up beside Declan, Tommy arrived just as the siren climbed the ladder to meet them. Gracefully, she stepped onto the deck, her scaled tail and fins now replaced by slender legs, her dark linen top barely long enough to keep her relatively decent.

"Captain McCallagh?" Her voice, a song on the morning breeze, showed no trace of fatigue as she wrung the seawater from her long hair.

"Aye," Declan answered, and she was speaking again before he could prompt her to.

"A word from Captain Halloran, sir."

Tommy inched closer, as if he couldn't already hear every word she said.

"She was headed to Helles Island. With the fae."

"All of them?" Declan asked.

The siren shook her head. "Just the one. I'm to tell you to bring Tommy there. She's waiting for you at the captain's camp. I have directions if you'll allow me to write them down?"

"Of course. Thank you," Declan said, gesturing for Aoife to escort the siren to his quarters.

"How fast can we be there?" Tommy asked, though he knew Declan's guess was as good as his. Gavin was the true master when it came to reading the winds and knowing the best routes.

Declan rubbed a hand along his jaw. "Three days? Four at the longest, I imagine. Depends on where we're to go ashore and whether we run into anyone along the way."

Tommy couldn't find any words as his gaze was pulled back out to sea. She had gotten off the ship. She was on Helles. She was waiting for him. He could make it four more days.

Declan dropped a hand on Tommy's shoulder. "Looks like she found her way back to you. Saves me the hassle of hunting her down."

Tommy tried to respond with a smile but couldn't quite manage it. They weren't reunited yet, and he wouldn't rest until they were.

CHAPTER 34
MAURA

Waking with a jolt, Maura blinked her eyes open to find the smooth fabric of the tent overhead. Birds sang to one another somewhere high above, and there was a steady thrum in the air, as if the island itself were alive, breathing. Five nights Maura had spent on this rocky ground using her arms as a pillow, her cloak for a blanket. It felt like five hundred.

Everything hurt. Her backside. Her hips. Her shoulders. Her head. There didn't seem to be any part of her that had gone unscathed by sleeping in such wild accommodations.

The island was, as Halloran had described, uninhabited. Good for those looking for seclusion. Bad for those stuck waiting to be rescued.

You shouldn't complain, she reminded herself. *You could be stuck on that ship with Renna.*

Something hard and blunt pressed against her shoulder, and Maura turned her head to see Captain Halloran peering down at her, her plaited hair no longer hidden by her signature hat.

"Someone's here," the captain said. Based on the coldness in the woman's eyes, Maura knew it couldn't be the guests they expected. Still, her heart refused to be restrained, leaping into her throat as she rose to her feet and joined Halloran outside. But the captain effectively doused her excitement with her next words. "It's not him."

Maura swallowed back her disappointment. "Who then?"

"Several ships have stopped off the shore. None flying pirates' colors."

"The king?" Maura asked.

Halloran nodded. "Need to get closer to be sure, but that's my best guess."

"Let's go then. I'm tired of sitting around. Which way?"

Halloran spun on her heel and stepped into the dense foliage that surrounded the campsite. Maura hurried to catch up. Her *daemari* couldn't prevent her from getting lost, and there was no way she was going to wait around here while the captain investigated the newcomers alone.

Following closely behind Halloran, Maura tried to commit her surroundings to memory. But everything looked the same to her. Every moss-covered rock. Every gnarled tree. Every fern and leaf. Before the war—before her imprisonment by the council—Maura had spent her life traveling between Cregah and Tyshaly. She'd passed this island many times, but not once had she stopped here.

She had never even been curious about what secrets the island held. Until now. Had it always been a tangled jungle, or had it become wild only after the war, roots and vines spreading across the land over the last five hundred years? Had it been a strategic point for ships during the war?

Would she know the answers if she hadn't been on Cregah for centuries with the queen?

A friend.

A fae.

And Aoife's mother, she thought.

The reminder of who they were facing in this latest battle nearly tripped Maura as she walked, but she recovered quickly, determined not to lose sight of the pirate leading her toward the beach. But she knew they were almost there even before Halloran announced it in a hoarse whisper. Men's voices hit her ears, though they were still too distant for her to make out what they were saying.

Although the trees remained tightly packed, the ground beneath their feet now showed traces of white sand, more and more of it peppering the dirt and grass as they proceeded on. They continued on until they were standing on more sand than soil. Without warning, Halloran stopped, lifting her arm out to the side to keep Maura from accidentally stepping too far.

Through the leaves and vines, Maura caught glimpses of teal water. They were here. Holding her breath, she craned her neck forward to listen for the sailors' voices. They had gone silent though, and Halloran's hand drifted to the hilt of her cutlass as she raised the other to her lips, indicating Maura should remain quiet. Had the men heard their approach? Maura had a hard time believing that. Not with the surf crashing onto the land and the wind rustling through the leaves.

What if they had heard? Would they come to investigate? Would they leave before she and the captain could learn anything?

She waited, stretching her breaths out and slowing them down. A soft, repetitive thud much like a heartbeat grew louder. Footsteps. Maura didn't move—not that she would be able to do anything of use without a weapon.

Maura could hear the men breathing now, could hear their hearts beating in their chests, but the foliage here was still too dense to make out anything more than the tiniest hint of color beyond it. Surely they couldn't spot her and Halloran standing here, waiting, spying.

The steps grew closer until Maura was sure they were about to burst through the wall of green at any moment. Captain Halloran released a breath and moved to draw her cutlass, but Maura was quicker, grasping the captain's wrist and shaking her head.

No.

She mouthed the word for emphasis before closing her eyes.

In her mind she envisioned all she had observed on their walk here, the way the trees hung low, vines dropping down to kiss the mossy rocks and soil. She even recalled the bright red and orange bird that had flown over her head fifty paces back.

Halloran gasped as the leaves in front of them began to move. When sunlight warmed Maura's face, she dared to open her eyes, hoping her strength had been restored enough that she didn't need to concentrate.

Indeed it had.

In front of them, a pair of hands had pushed through the trees' branches to hold back the leaves. Two men peered through the opening. They seemed to look through Maura and Halloran.

The captain's arm tensed beneath Maura's hand, and she braced herself for the glamour she'd conjured up to dissolve and reveal them to the men. But they held fast. Finally, one of the men called over his shoulder, "It's nothing, Your Majesty."

Your Majesty.

So they'd been right. It was the king.

The men shrugged at one another before dropping the foliage back into place. Maura refused to move until she was sure she heard two sets of footsteps growing fainter, walking away from them.

"Thank you," Halloran whispered, shifting her eyes to Maura but still refusing to move any other part of her body.

Maura dipped her chin. "You can move now, Captain. They're gone."

A breath fell from the pirate, her shoulders drooping as she let the tension out of her muscles. Stepping forward, Halloran leaned into the trees, moving aside just enough of the foliage to allow for a discreet view of the beach. Maura followed suit.

The king—identifiable by the modest crown settled into the dark waves of his hair—stood confidently beside another, larger male with shaggy brown hair. Something about the larger man seemed familiar, though Maura couldn't place him. Anyone she had known in Caprothe would be long since dead or living in Larcsporough. She shook the feeling away, straining to hear their words, but with the trees in the way and the waves washing over the sand, she couldn't decipher anything. She gritted her teeth in frustration.

"Why would the king himself come ashore?" Maura asked.

"I'm not sure, but we have plenty of time to wait and find out."

They didn't have to wait too long before an answer presented itself in the shape of a rowboat drifting toward the shore. The king and his companion pivoted to face the approaching men, watching them step out into the crystal waters and traipse toward them through the sand. Their plain clothes gave nothing away regarding their identities, until a breeze came up off the water, shifting their jackets enough for Maura to catch a glimpse of color at their waists.

Pirates. With coral sashes.

"Whose colors are those?" Maura whispered.

Halloran shook her head. "Roberts, I think."

"You aren't sure?" Maura winced at how rude the question must have sounded, but Halloran didn't seem to take offense.

"Those are Roberts's colors, but that"—she paused to lift a chin toward the pirate leading the way toward the king—"is not Roberts."

"Maybe he sent his quartermaster or another officer?" Even as Maura asked it, she knew that wasn't likely. A pirate lord wouldn't give up an opportunity to claim more power for themselves, no matter what treaty they might have in place with the Cregahn council.

"No. He must have fallen. To whom, I don't know. Though I have a sinking feeling Callum had something to do with this."

Maura's attention snapped to the captain. "Why would you think that?"

A shrug. A smirk. A shake of the head. "He's been after Callum to join his fleet since before I became captain of my own ship. Callum always refuses. Maybe Roberts got tired of asking and thought to take him on by force."

"Seems like a bad idea, given what I witnessed of Callum back in the sound."

"Aye. A terrible idea. That man does what he wants, when he wants, with little care over who gets hurt in the process."

"So what would the new captain of Roberts's ship be doing with the king?"

"I imagine it's the same thing any pirate would be doing." Halloran didn't elaborate but continued to watch the meeting in silence.

Maura leaned closer to her and, lowering her voice further, asked, "And what would that be exactly?"

"Seizing the moment. Taking the opportunity. Acting selfishly, basically." Halloran stated this as if it should have been obvious, but for Maura it was far from. Sure, she knew how Tommy and Declan ran their ship, but aside from her experience with Halloran's crew and watching Callum fight the siren queen, Maura had not interacted with any other pirates. Pirates hadn't even existed until after the war had ended, when the men couldn't return home, too plagued by their own ghastly deeds and the horrors of war.

"You can't hear what they're saying?" Halloran asked.

Maura shook her head. "Not from this distance, unfortunately. But—"

She lost all track of what she was about to say when the new pirate lord turned and called forward someone outside of Maura's vantage point. Two pirates came into view, escorting a woman Maura had never seen before. Her arms, bound behind her back, were held tightly by the pirates, but she didn't struggle as she walked forward, her bright skirts dragging in the sand.

"Lucy," Halloran whispered, and through her hushed tone, Maura could easily detect a hint of disdain.

"Don't like her?" Maura asked but kept her attention on the scene unfolding.

"Not particularly. Less so now."

"You mad at her for getting caught by pirates?" Maura tried to hide her amusement at the idea.

"No. She shouldn't be here." Maura started to insist that was obvious, but Halloran quickly continued, "I told her to stay in Foxhaven."

Maura shifted her focus to Halloran. "Why?"

Her eyes narrowed. "Because if she didn't, I was going to kill her." Before Maura could respond, the captain jutted her chin toward the beach. "Can you use a glamour to get yourself closer?"

Maura focused inward on the *daemari* that flowed through her blood. It tingled, like a fidgety child struggling to remain still. Antsy. Ready. Maura nodded.

"Just listen in, figure out why they have her, what they're offering the king."

"And if they try to kill her?"

"Let them."

Maura froze. "What did she do?"

Fixing Maura with a glare, Halloran explained. "Someone hired her to kill Declan. I don't know who, but I have my suspicions. And we can't let that happen. Understand?"

"You really think she's capable of—"

"Aye, I do."

"And what if they try to take her?" Maura asked as she moved to stand, preparing herself to create an illusion around herself before stepping out into the open.

"Kill her."

⤬

Maura made her way across the beach, thankful she'd had time to replenish more of her powers. It allowed her to maintain the glamour with far less concentration than she'd needed in the kraken's territory. To be fair, though, she'd had to conceal an entire ship in that instance. Concealing a single body was far easier.

This gave her time to focus instead on the way her gut twisted around Halloran's final words to her. Could she kill a woman she didn't know based on the captain's word alone?

She wasn't so sure, and she had to adjust her grip on the dagger in her sweaty palm several times before she was close enough to hear them clearly. She'd need to be closer still, though, if she was to carry out Halloran's command.

Walking around the pirates, Maura positioned herself to stand a fair distance behind the woman—far enough away that the pirates wouldn't accidentally touch her but with a clear path to Lucy.

"We caught her drifting along in the waters north of Cregah," the pirate lord said. "We'd heard rumors that your fleet was heading for Morshan, so we took it upon ourselves to clear the way for you, as it were."

"I see," a man answered. Maura couldn't see who had spoken, but she assumed it was the king, given how his voice dripped with refined darkness. There was a dangerous charm evident even in those two simple words, a charm that drew Maura's attention away from Lucy.

Atop his head, nestled in a bed of dark, wavy hair, was a simple crown of gold vines and leaves and delicate thorns. But the crown paled in comparison to the sharpness in his brown eyes, the cut of his cheekbones, and the slight curve to his lips as he smirked. There was something about this man that drew Maura to him, even as her heart hammered a warning to stay far away from him. When he spoke again, Maura blinked rapidly in an attempt to break whatever damned curse surrounded him.

"What of the crew she sailed with?"

"All dead," the pirate lord answered.

"And why bring her to me?"

This time, the pirate fidgeted in place but managed not to fumble through his answer. "Call her a welcome gift. A gesture of kindness from a pirate who wishes to pledge fealty to Your Highness."

The king moved toward Lucy, each step like a menacing prowl. In a flash, his hand was at her chin, thrusting her head back and forcing her to look up into his eyes. He scrutinized her for a moment and didn't release his grip on her face even when he turned his attention back to the pirate lord.

"Definitely a fire in this one. Could be fun. Could also be disastrous. I don't have time for either." He shoved her face away from him and pulled his hand back, wiping it against his leg as if he had gotten dirty from touching her. He turned around as he said, to no one in particular, "Kill her."

Maura's hand reflexively tightened on her own dagger, but she waited. No one moved, apart from the king, who walked back to his own men. Turning slowly back to face the lord, the king cocked his head to the side, dark humor written on his face.

"Funny how you pledge supposed fealty to me but can't obey a simple order."

Raising a hand in the air, he made a simple gesture with his fingers, and instantly Maura sensed a shift in the air. And then Lucy was struggling against her captors' grasps. Haunting whimpers escaped her throat as her lungs reached for air that wouldn't come. With fear and horror filling their eyes, the pirates pulled back, releasing her arms as if their grips on her were choking her.

She didn't fall forward or crumple onto the sand, but her hands flew up, clawing at the invisible force tightening around her neck. Her fingers found nothing, her sharp nails digging into her skin, drawing blood as she frantically tried to free herself.

And then she was rising into the air.

Her feet kicked. Her body twisted. Her hands fought.

The king's dark chuckle mixed with the sound of Lucy suffocating, and then it was over. Her body stilled before falling with a sickening sound back onto the beach.

Maura couldn't move, couldn't wrap her head around what in the sands had just happened. She could have done something. Could have stopped them.

Stopped who, exactly?

Her whole body tensed in fear. She had seen this before—she was sure of it—but she couldn't place the memory, couldn't figure out why this all felt so eerily familiar.

"What..." the pirate lord said, snapping Maura out of her thoughts. "What just happened?"

The king's smile disappeared, his features hardening. "Nothing you need to be concerned with, Lord. But next time you want to get in my good graces, I recommend you do as you're told." He pointed to Lucy's lifeless heap. "Or that will be you. Now, did you have anything useful to offer me?"

The king waited expectantly, clasping his hands behind his back, and the lord stumbled over his words. "Aye, Your Majesty. I thought you should know that the Csintala dagger has been recovered."

The king's eyes lit up, but they darkened with the lord's next words.

"We don't have it, but we know who does."

"And who would that be?"

"His name is Callum. Last seen headed for Turvala."

The king pursed his lips, and Maura braced herself to watch the pirate lord—or all the pirates—join Lucy in the sand. But instead, the king released a simple sigh.

"As much as I would have liked to have the dagger for myself, at least we can be sure it is far from the hands of those bitches on Cregah. Speaking of whom, we have a rather important date to keep with them." Sweeping his arm toward the sea, he silently issued the command for the pirates to leave. This time, they didn't hesitate to obey, nearly tripping over their own feet as they rushed away.

Maura was about to turn and head back to the trees when a pair of eyes locked onto hers.

She froze in panic, frantically testing her *daemari* for any signs her glamour was failing, but it was fully intact and strong. Still, the eyes stared at her, clearly seeing through her illusion. She had met few who had the power to see through her glamours.

All fae.

Her stomach plummeted to her feet as recognition slammed into her.

Those eyes, dark swirls of teal and purple, pulled her back into the dark corners of her mind to memories long forgotten. Memories of life before the council, before her imprisonment, before the war.

There had been laughter and games, tight hugs and teasing jabs.

And then there had been silence and tears, empty arms and crippling grief.

He was dead. He had died in the war.

But here he was, as real as the sun shining off the Aisling, standing here on this beach beside that maniacal beast of a king.

And it had been his *daemari*, his power that had killed Lucy.

Tremors shook her insides as bile rose into her throat. She couldn't stop her head from shaking at him, her eyes from begging him for answers she knew he couldn't give her.

He flashed a wink at her before turning to follow the king and his men back to their ship. Still, Maura couldn't move, couldn't even force her eyes to trail after him.

This wasn't true. It couldn't be.

How? How is he alive? Why didn't he come for you? Five hundred years and he never came for you!

Lost in disbelief and confusion, Maura didn't know how long she stood on that beach before she heard a voice calling her name. Halloran. Maura turned to find her running out from the trees, her eyes scanning the beach, her feet carrying her in the wrong direction.

She can't see you, Maura.

"I'm here," Maura said as she pulled the glamour back and revealed herself.

"Are you okay?" Halloran rushed to her, and Maura could have sworn her question held genuine concern.

Maura nodded. "I am. I couldn't—" She pointed to where Lucy's body still lay.

"I told you to let it happen, Maura. Though I never imagined it would happen quite like it did."

"I know, but—"

"But who was that man? I could have sworn he saw you."

"He did."

Halloran's eyes widened in question and shock, an expression so humorous Maura might have laughed under different circumstances.

"How did he exactly? How is that possible?"

Maura drew in a deep breath, as if that could make the next words easier to utter. "He's fae." And before Halloran could ask, she added, "He's my brother."

If only the myth about fae having superior memories was true. Then she wouldn't be sitting here trudging blindly through centuries of past moments in an attempt to remember when she had seen Liam last. She and her sisters had been visiting Melina when news of war had spread across the Aisling, the call coming from Cregah's primary ally, Tyshaly, for all those able and willing to take up arms against Caprothe. They had remained there to support the queen as she sent her husband, and later her son, to fight and die in the war. They had comforted her when their bodies had been returned, broken and empty shells of once powerful fae.

Maura closed her eyes, trying to recall those days, centuries before Melina had locked them away in that room. But it was like looking through the salt-crusted pane of a ship's window. Everything was muted. Distorted.

"What are you—" Halloran started to ask, but Maura held up a hand. The image was slowly coming into focus. The ship arriving in Morshan. The flag-draped coffins being carried to the royal residence, now called the council hall. Strong arms carrying the remains of the fallen to the burial grounds.

And there he was. Her older brother. Worn and weary from so many months—or had it been years?—of constant fighting. But this memory didn't match the man she'd seen on the beach just now.

He had been somber and regal during the funeral, as the circumstances had required. No words had passed between them that day, not even when he approached his three sisters and wrapped them all in an embrace. Warm yet distant. It wasn't until years later, when his guards returned to Cregah with word that he had fallen during an offensive on Caprothe's shores, that she realized he had been telling them goodbye.

Maura's heart broke at the memory of how she and her sisters had mourned him. Opening her eyes and pulling herself back to the present, she fell to the ground. The overwhelming sadness from her past slipped away, like sand through her fingers, making room for the anger that blossomed. They had grieved him! They had spent months locked away in mourning for this brother they had grown up with, a brother who had watched over them, helped them hone their powers.

And he was here? Alive? He must have survived the battle in Caprothe. Taken captive perhaps? Had he been imprisoned like she and her sisters? Surely that was why he'd never come for them. Was he working for this king out of loyalty? Or repaying a debt? He didn't appear to be serving against his will. Why had it taken a young pirate and his crew to free her? Why hadn't Liam come for them? Even with the tenuous peace between Caprothe and Cregah, surely he could have found a way —could have at least tried—to help them.

"The bastard," she hissed, and Halloran's face came into view. She said nothing. There was not even a silent question in her eyes. She simply waited. So patiently, so quietly.

Maura pulled the thick island air into her lungs, envisioning it clearing the anger away. It would do her no good right now to have bitterness clouding her judgment. She offered Halloran an empty half-smile.

"Sorry," she said. "Trying to piece together how in the sands he's here and why he would be serving Caprothe."

"And did you come to any conclusion?"

"Nothing that will help, unfortunately. But Melina is about to get quite the shock when he shows up at the council hall beside the king."

Halloran stood. "Not much we can do about it now until our ride arrives. Do you want to stay here? Or shall we head back?"

Maura turned back to the beach, wishing the sails of the *Siren's Song* would appear on the horizon. But she found nothing other than the flat edge of the sea.

"They won't be landing here," Halloran said, pulled Maura's attention back to her. "But we don't need to go back to camp just yet, if you don't want to."

Mention of the camp, as boring as it had been there for the last five days, prompted Maura to rise to her feet and eagerly start moving that way. If that siren was giving Tommy the location of that camp, then that was where she had better well be when he finally arrived. But after a few paces, she stopped and turned, finding Halloran still standing where she had been, an almost comical look on her face. The woman's brow twitched up in question, and the slightest of smiles tugged at one corner of her mouth.

Maura shrugged. "You should probably lead the way. I don't want to get us lost."

"You mean fae don't have perfect memories?"

"Unfortunately, no."

Halloran stepped past and pushed her way through the vines and leaves. They continued through the forest in silence, which was more than acceptable for Maura, as it afforded her the opportunity to focus more on her brother's potential motives rather than the path they needed to take. Keeping her eyes on Halloran, she let her mind wander as they walked.

Fortune? Power? What could Liam be seeking to achieve? Throughout their youth, he had always had his sights set on taking over their father's rule. But he hadn't lived long enough to see that day.

Or so Maura had thought.

CHAPTER 35
ADLER

For the entire walk back from the cove, Adler's mind chewed over how Lucan might be able to help them when he was supposed to be dead. He couldn't exactly show up in front of the council. At least not until the rogues had the advantage.

Like the dagger.

But even knowing Cait's brother was close to retrieving it, they couldn't hedge their bets on him making it in time. The king would arrive soon, and in all likelihood, he would have the shield with him.

The sun was nearing its apex when he finally stepped into the alley behind the pub, and it wasn't until then that he recalled the note and the way he'd walked out on Cait that morning. How would she act? Would she be angry? Could he bear it if she was?

He paused at the door, dropping his forehead against the old wood and releasing a heavy sigh. What was wrong with him? What was happening to him?

Even as he asked the question, though, he knew. He recognized the yearning pulsing in his chest, remembered the last time he'd experienced this intense need to care for someone.

It was preposterous. No one fell in love this quickly. Especially not twice in the span of a few months!

Surely this was nothing more than infatuation, simple attraction.

But he scoffed at himself as a memory of his mother crept into his thoughts. They had just buried his father, who had been taken too early by a prolonged illness with no cure. For years Adler had watched his mother care for her husband with utter devotion, continuing to love him even on the hard days when she broke down in tears and crumpled to the floor under the weight of such responsibility and grief. But on the day they'd laid him to rest, his mother had lowered herself to the foot of his grave, waving her children over to join her.

"You are cursed," she had told them through soft tears, *"cursed with hearts that love too strongly, too passionately, too quickly. Few will understand it. Few will believe it. But love does not make sense, and it doesn't need to. Don't fear it. Don't deny it. Accept it with all your being, because you never know when that love might be taken from you. Better to love and be called a fool than to die alone and bitter."*

He'd been seventeen at the time, and he'd set out to join a pirate crew not long after, determined to take care of his mother and sister in his father's absence. Through all the years, Adler had never forgotten his mother's words, but he'd never truly understood them until the night he met Lani.

Don't fear it.

Don't deny it.

He was a fool; of that he was sure. No one could fathom how he'd fallen in love with Lani so soon, and if not for his mother's wisdom—or was it folly?—he would have scoffed at it too.

But to fall in love a second time? Would his mother encourage him to pursue this? Or would she chide him for reading too much into his feelings?

Who would believe he had fallen in love again? He barely believed it himself—still questioned it actually. Lucan had been right to ridicule him at their initial meeting with the rogues. But it wasn't Lucan he needed to believe him, but Cait. Would she understand? Would she accept it or chalk it up to brokenhearted foolishness?

He knocked his head against the wooden door as he tried to figure out what he was going to do. He was about to face her again, and he needed a plan. Last thing he wanted was to be caught unawares and fumble his words.

Don't fear it.

Don't deny it.

Accept it with all your being.

Accept it.

Adler closed his eyes as he mulled this over. Accepting that he loved her didn't require him to act on it, did it? He could acknowledge it without pursuing it, give it time—give himself time—and wait until she was more likely to embrace it and him.

Yes, that's what he would do. He would avenge Lani's death, help Cait destroy the council, and then see where their hearts landed after that.

Taking a calming breath, he forced himself inside the pub and, seeing no one in the main room, moved up the stairs. He had only just raised his hand to knock when the door was pulled open. Kira offered him her standard tight grin and gestured for him to come in. He relaxed a little, knowing Kira had kept her word and stayed with Cait while he was gone, but then he caught sight of Cait sitting on the edge of her bed, her eyes glazed over as she stared toward the floor.

"Is she okay?" Adler asked.

"Aye," Kira said, walking to the chair beside the bed. "Just a little shocked is all."

"And her wounds?"

Before Kira could answer, Cait's head swiveled toward him, her gaze focusing on him as she said, "I'm right here, you know. No need to pester Kira for answers."

The corners of his mouth fell into that overturned smile his sister always mocked. "Fair." Not knowing what to do with his hands, he shoved them into his pockets. "So how are your wounds?"

Cait bobbed her head lightly as she raised a shoulder, her eyes flitting away from his. "Would be worse had you not cleaned them up."

"You're welcome. So what exactly had you shocked?"

Kira chuckled softly before saying, "Maybe grab a chair before she tells you."

"That bad?"

A lazy shrug was her only answer. No one said another word until Adler had another chair dragged up alongside Kira's.

Cait drew in a long breath before letting her eyes meet his again. "Oh, the usual. Kira here is a fae, apparently."

"Demi-fae, actually," Kira clarified with a casual wave of her hand.

Adler's confusion must have been plain on his face, because Cait pointed at him and said, "Aye. That's how I felt."

Adler shot Kira a questioning glance.

"To keep things short, because the pub won't prep itself for opening, basically I'm from Larcsporough. Traveled up to Cregah with my mother and brother, carrying a letter my father had entrusted to me to deliver—however I could—to the fae royals still residing on the island. I gave the letter to Ada McCallagh, but she was exiled before she could deliver it for me. Cait eventually found it and handed it to Declan, who used it to convince the fae sisters to leave the council hall with him."

Adler pondered this. Based on the dazed expression on Cait's face, Adler surmised she was still trying to process it as well. Kira's chair scraped against the floor as she rose with a grace Adler felt stupid to have ever missed.

"I'll leave you two to talk. If you need anything, I'll be down at the bar. Though you—" She pointed a reprimanding finger at Cait. "No more rum for you for a while. Or any booze, for that matter."

She was out the door before either of them could respond, her footsteps inaudible on the stairs, leaving them with a suffocating, awkward silence. It stretched on for so long that Adler knew anything he said would sound clumsy, but thankfully it was Cait who spoke first.

"How's Lucan?"

Adler exhaled in relief, glad she was skipping over any mention of last night.

"Sands, love, he's bored out of his mind. But otherwise he's good." He leaned forward, dropping his elbows to his knees, clasping his hands before him, hovering dangerously close to her legs.

But she didn't retreat—if she noticed his proximity at all.

"Sounds like him." The melancholy in her tone pricked Adler's heart, making him want to pull her close and hold her. But he pushed the urge aside. Last thing she needed right now was him invading her space and giving her the wrong impression.

Would it be the wrong impression though?

Yes! I'm not acting on anything, he reminded himself, but that didn't stop that inner voice from adding a *yet* before he shoved the thoughts aside.

"Dreadful boredom aside, he seemed in decent spirits. Worried about you, of course. Wants to make sure we don't forget about him, that we allow him to help."

Her chin lifted. "He probably should have thought of that before he pulled that stunt with you."

She had a point, but what was done was done. Surely they could find some way for him to have an active role in whatever was to come.

Cait ran a hand over her face before looking at Adler once more, shaking her head. "I don't know how he expects us to find a job for him when I can't even decide on a plan for the rest of us, especially with a potential spy on our hands."

Adler froze. "A what? How do you know—"

She waved a hand between them, as if shooing away a pesky fly. "I don't know. Not for sure. But they killed Willow, one of our rogues, and claimed it was us that did it."

"Could have been a coincidence," Adler said.

"I know."

"But probably best to assume the worst."

"Agreed," Cait said. "I hope it's the former, because the alternative is that someone in our organization is working for our enemy. And I have no idea who that could be."

Cait began to rub her fingers against her temples, pressing her elbows into her knees.

"But you don't suspect me," Adler finally said, though instead of lightening the mood as he'd intended, it ignited the air between them.

A smirk graced her lips. "Not of being a spy, anyway."

"Of what then?" As he waited for an answer, his nerves frayed. He was worried she could already see how fast he was falling for her. Like a crazy person.

She only shrugged though, and he moved to change the subject as quickly as he could.

"So we have no plan then."

"Does *kill the council* count as a plan?" Adler shook his head. "Then no."

"Maybe the opportune moment will fall into our lap."

Adler didn't realize the slip of his words until she flashed him a curious look.

"By the way," she said, and Adler's pulse quickened with worry over what she was about to say next. "I'm sorry for last night. I know you said it was nothing—"

"What did I say was nothing?"

"Whatever happened last night. Your note..." Cait paused to reach over to the bedside table and lift up the small paper he'd scribbled on. "Your note said nothing happened."

Adler frowned in confusion. "I'm not following, love. Nothing did happen."

Cait's face flushed pink, and she tossed his note onto the bed beside her. "I must have just imagined—"

"Imagined what exactly?" What did she think happened between them last night?

Looking him square in the eye, Cait set her jaw and stared long enough to make him even more uncomfortable. "The kiss? We did kiss, didn't we? Or—"

"You think I thought that was nothing?"

A flippant shrug. "You're the one who used that word, not me."

"Sands, love. That doesn't mean that what *did* happen was nothing. It means that nothing *else* happened. I didn't want you to think I had taken advantage of you in that way."

"You could have made it clearer." Cait sighed.

Adler couldn't help but smile at her. "Next time I'll be sure to say something like, 'Don't worry, I didn't bed you.'"

Cait cringed and shook her head. "No. Don't do that."

"So you want me to bed you next time?" He waggled his brow at her lightheartedly, but an ache slowly burned within his chest.

A laugh—a laugh he never wanted to forget—filled the air between them. "I don't know," she said. "Maybe. We'll see."

THAT NIGHT, the pub was far busier than Adler had expected, and he was glad Cait had agreed to take another night off to rest before returning to work. All evening he caught himself glancing at Kira as she worked behind the bar. As he watched how fluid her movements were, how quickly and gracefully she went about her tasks, he could see the evidence of her fae heritage. It was subtle enough that regular citizens would not suspect but clear enough that those who knew the truth would be able to notice.

After the last of the stragglers had departed, giving their requests for Adler to pass on their well-wishes to their beloved pub owner, Kira offered to stay and help clean up. Adler shooed her away—or tried to—but she only gave in when he agreed she could come back in the morning to cook Cait a proper breakfast.

He was wiping down the bar one final time when the creak of the stairs drew his attention. Turning, he found Cait rounding the corner into the room. The rest seemed to have done her good. Her limp was minimal now. Her long hair, combed through, flowed over one shoulder and covered one breast.

No! He needed to focus his attention elsewhere. Her breasts were the last place he needed to be looking. Clearing his throat, he pushed himself to speak first.

"Water?" Adler asked, already turning to retrieve a clean glass and pitcher.

Cait leaned against the end of the bar and nodded her thanks when he placed the glass before her. But she didn't take a drink, and she didn't make eye contact, focusing instead on the clear liquid he'd poured.

"You okay, love?" He set the rag aside before approaching her, sure to keep his distance. Even so, the scent of her soap invaded his senses and threatened to pull him under.

Dropping her head into her hands, Cait let out a long breath. "I don't know anymore."

"Is it your leg?"

"No. That's fine." Placing her cheek in her palm, she finally turned to look at him. "What did you do to me?"

Adler tensed. His mind whirred. Was she accusing him of something? Had he done something wrong?

"What do you mean?"

Cait's features softened, but sadness clouded her eyes. Dread pooled in Adler's stomach as he wondered what she might say next. Could he handle any form of rejection from her now that he'd acknowledged his feelings for her, even if only to himself?

She straightened and looked down at her hands once more before she spoke again. "I never wanted this."

"Water?" Adler offered a light laugh in a desperate attempt to clear away some of the tension.

Cait didn't laugh, and she kept her eyes lowered as she clarified.

"You."

The single word was a stab to his heart, a dagger through his sternum, a blade lodged in his gut. She didn't want him. Had never wanted him. Never wanted love. She had made that clear back in the woods near the pit. He'd been a fool to think he sensed more from her, to think last night was anything more than her drunken attempt to distract herself, to think he could simply wait for her to be ready for him.

He forced himself to draw in a breath, trying to soothe away the sting so he could respond thoughtfully. She didn't give him a chance to do so though, quickly lifting her face and looking him square in the eye.

"When my parents died, every dream I had died with them. I gave up any idea of adventure or freedom or...love."

Adler opened his mouth to speak, but she held up a hand to stop him. Her eyes burned bright and passionate, and her lips tightened as if she were trying with all her might to keep her next words contained.

"But damn you, Adler! You ruined everything! I was fine. I was content."

"Liar," he challenged. If she was going to accuse him of ruining her life, he wasn't about to let her do it dishonestly.

She jabbed a finger into his chest.

"And then you come into my life with your 'loves' and your stupid smile and your damned blue eyes, and you make me feel things I never thought I could or would. I don't understand it. I'm so lost and confused, but at the same time it's like I've finally been found. Like I finally know what I want. And the shitty thing about it all is I can't have it! I have no right to your heart, Adler. Not when it's still healing. Not when you've just lost so much. You couldn't possibly—"

"Cait." He inched around the bar until he stood directly in front of her, desperately fighting the urge to grab her and pull her close. Instead he reached his hand up to cover hers and held it tight against his thumping heart. "This heart *is* broken. And I miss Lani. I do. I probably always will."

Cait cringed before dropping her head and hiding her face from him. Before he continued, he placed his free hand under her chin and tipped it back up, but her eyes were closed, her lashes slowly collecting the start of her tears.

"Look at me, Cait," he said, running his fingers along her jaw until her face rested against his palm. He waited for her to do so, not sure if she would be able to understand all he needed to say. But when her eyes crept open and her lips quivered with barely contained emotion, he couldn't stop the words from pouring out.

"When Lani died, it broke me. A lifetime of dreams vanished that day. But I can't stay broken forever, and I hoped to love again someday. But I *never* expected it to be so soon. It doesn't make sense, I know, but I don't need to understand it to know it's true."

Adler paused to run his thumb over her cheek and swallowed hard when she leaned into his touch.

"I wanted to give you time because I couldn't bear the thought of you thinking this was just a distraction for me. Cait—"

"Call me love," Cait whispered. "Call me love, and I'm yours. I don't want time. I don't need it."

The air in the room vanished, leaving Adler with no breath, no words, as the pub disappeared around them. He was losing himself in her emerald eyes that beckoned him to stop hesitating. Stepping closer, he brushed his hand past her ear and into her hair. His heartbeat accelerated when her fingers curled into his shirt, and his breath, already ragged and uneven, hitched when she tugged him closer still.

Her warmth enveloped him, and when her lips parted, his blood ignited with desire. All he wanted stood before him, looking at him with silent invitation. Wetting his lips, he started to speak, but his voice came out raw with want.

"Are you sure, love?"

Cait shifted her weight. Her lips twitched up into a smirk, and her eyes sparkled with that brazenness he'd admired at their first meeting.

"Shut up and kiss me," she said.

She was on him before he could oblige, pulling his lips to hers and holding him there as her fingers slowly caressed the nape of his neck. Her body pressed against him. His hand—still holding hers—was now trapped between her breasts. His lips opened eagerly to let her consume all of him.

He was a fool, perhaps, but he'd gladly be one if it earned him the love and affection and passion of this woman.

CHAPTER 36
CAIT

CAIT HADN'T PLANNED to kiss Adler when she came downstairs, hadn't planned to even have the conversation that led to it. But now, his lips on hers consumed her. With every move of his tongue against hers, every nip of his teeth on her lips, every desperate pull of his hand on the back of her head, he erased any worry over the council, the dagger, the danger.

The weight of it all fell away as wave after wave of heat went through her veins. Heat that pooled in her core, becoming a throbbing ache that pulled a moan from her chest.

Before she could think better of it, Cait was fisting his shirt, tugging it up and sliding her fingertips against his skin. Tracing his muscles, she made her way lower, needing to have all of him. But she'd barely made it to his belt when his hands grabbed her wrists.

She gasped as he spun her around, pulling her back against his chest.

She could make this work.

Arching her back, she dropped her head against his shoulder, letting a husky whisper fall against his cheek.

"I don't need time. I need you." She moved his hands down her torso, desperate to feel them where her body needed him most. "Don't make me beg when I know you want it too."

Adler didn't stop the descent of their clasped hands, and when he nuzzled her cheek and sent a hot breath along her ear, she knew she had him.

Until he breathed out a laugh raw with need. "Aye, love, but I'm in no hurry."

Another rush of tingles flashed across her skin at the thought of him taking his time with her. But her body immediately resisted, reminding her of how many times she'd forced herself to be patient, to wait for him, to ignore her own feelings.

She was done ignoring them.

"Don't make me wait," she purred, rolling her hips against him. "I've waited too long for you."

Adler answered her by trailing kisses down her neck. Then his hand was at her chin, pulling her to face him. When he coaxed her tongue out with his own, her head swam with desire and her eyes closed.

But he didn't continue, didn't give her what she wanted, needed.

"I'm not going anywhere, love. You'll have me..." He paused to kiss her once more, a slow, deliberate dance before he pulled away again. "But not until I've explored every...inch...of you."

He dragged those final words out as he brushed a thumb across her parted lips and down her chin, leaving a trail of fire from her throat to the top of her shirt.

This man was going to be her undoing.

Unless she undid him first.

"Don't tease me, love," Cait said, using his favorite nickname as she rolled her hips against him. Another arch of her back had her pressing against him, her breasts rising in invitation. Then his lips were back on her neck, urgent kisses and sweeps of his tongue and sharp bites along her skin, stopping only to whisper against her.

"I haven't even begun to tease you yet."

But she could barely concentrate on his damned words when his fingers were moving again, tracing the edge of her collar and sliding beneath the fabric.

Two could play at this bloody game.

She slid her own hand behind her back, between their bodies, and brushed it slowly along the hard edge of him. "You think I'd let you spend all night teasing me?"

Pushing his hips against her hand, he groaned. "I think you'd let me do a lot of things, love." Then his fingers were curling into her skirt, lifting the fabric achingly slowly.

Cait couldn't suppress the shudders when his hand found her thigh and his fingers dragged their way up her skin. And she couldn't control her ragged breaths when his fingertips slipped beneath the edge of her undergarment to find her more than ready for him.

He danced along the slick edges of her center, and she almost gave in to every one of his intentions. But she couldn't. She wouldn't. She was in control. She was calling the shots.

When a groan rumbled deep in his chest, Cait twisted out of his grip. Before he could react, she had both hands on his chest and was pushing him back against the bar.

"Have you forgotten whose pub this is? It's mine. McCallagh's." She pushed her hand into his pants now and gripped his length with a gentle squeeze. "Means I'm in charge."

She expected him to challenge her, to grab her wrists as he had before, but instead, he raised his hands in surrender, pressing against her as an infuriating grin spreading across his lips.

Sands, this man was attractive, and he knew it.

"Aye, love. Tell me what you want."

Something about his yielding to her made her falter. He wasn't like the average Cregahn man, taught to roll over because of the belief they were inferior to their women. This was a pirate—strong, confident—willingly giving her utter control because he cared. Her body screamed at her to melt into him, to let him cherish her and worship her as only he could.

Confusion must have been evident on her face, because he was reaching out a hand for her before she could respond to him. Still, she waited to see what he might do, her mind flailing, alternating between the need to retain control and the desire to be cared for. With a light touch, Adler traced the line of her collarbone, and Cait was sure she stopped breathing.

Until he moved the edge of her top, pushing it down to free her breast. His blue eyes, shining eagerly, held her gaze as he brushed a light touch along her skin.

"Do you want me to go slow so you can feel my love over every inch of your body?" His thumb drew lazy circles around her hardened peak as he slowly lowered toward her. His breath tickled her skin when he spoke again. "Or shall I devour you?" His tongue curled and flicked before he took her into his mouth.

A traitorous whimper escaped her. But she needed to think. Pulling away from him, she found a predatory smirk on his lips.

He inched toward her, but she stopped him, blocking his approach with her hand. She couldn't contain the giggle that bubbled up.

"How am I supposed to think with that mouth of yours distracting me?"

"That's the point, love," he mumbled. "You think too much."

In an instant, his hands were on either side of her neck, and he was pulling her mouth to his. With her hands in his hair, she held him against her even as she chided herself for letting him take the control back.

But it was hard to be upset when he felt so good.

Too soon, he was pulling away, but his lips hovered over hers as he said, "I love the way you taste." His tongue swept along hers once more, savoring her for several quickened breaths. When he stopped again, his gaze burned into hers with a feral hunger. "I plan to taste all of you before we're done."

Cait's core fluttered again, begging for her to allow him the chance here and now.

But then a wicked desire flashed through her, and she smirked.

"Me first," she said and lowered herself to her knees before him.

To her surprise, he didn't stop her.

Not when she undid his belt.

Not when she pulled him free.

Not when she teased him with flicks of her tongue.

He rested against the bar, giving himself over to her as she drew all of him in, her lips and tongue savoring every blessed inch of him. And she smiled around him when a breathless "fuck" escaped his lips. His breathing quickened as she moved along him, and his ragged moans had her body begging for her to hurry up so he could satisfy the blazing need throbbing between her thighs.

Her impatient desire pushed her to pick up the pace. Then his fingers were gripping her, tangling in her hair, holding her still, taking over the movement.

And she let him.

Let him take control.

Let him have her as he needed her.

Deeper. Harder. Faster.

Pulling rough moans from her that joined his own and filled the empty pub.

She waited, desperate for him to let go and give her the delicious satisfaction that only came from being someone's complete and utter undoing. But his hands dropped to her arms, forcing her to stand. She didn't get a chance to protest before his mouth was on hers once more, sweeping his tongue between her lips with more passion than she'd ever experienced.

He was lifting her before she knew what was happening. Instinctively she wrapped her legs around him, her skirts bunching up around her waist.

"I need you...now," he muttered against her lips, and she couldn't help but laugh.

"What happened to teasing me all night?"

"Changed my mind." Running a hand up the back of her thigh, Adler found his way beneath her skirts and brushed his fingers along her center.

His touch had her body aching, her heart racing.

"On the bar," she panted, needing him inside her and not wanting to risk him changing his mind again.

But Adler only continued with his lazy strokes. "A little cliché, don't you think?" He tossed his head behind him. "Public too, with the windows, but—" He leaned close to her ear and whispered, "For you, I'd take you in the middle of the square if you asked me to."

A whimper tickled her throat as his words—and the image they conjured—had her core tightening and pulsing beneath his fingertips.

"Tonight, though, I want to be the only one watching you fall apart." Pushing away from the bar, he started walking toward the stairs. "So how shall I have you, love? Shall I take my time undoing you? Or—"

"Devour me," Cait whispered against his lips, her need for him refusing to let her overthink it.

Plunging her hands into his hair and raking her fingertips against his head, she pulled his lips to hers once more and let her passion loose. Teeth scraping. Tongues grazing. Lips claiming.

Halfway up the stairs, Adler paused, pushing her back against the wall before lowering his head and biting the fabric of her top to free her other breast. He had her between his lips, his tongue dancing against her peaked nipples, threatening to pull her under right there on the stairs.

But she wasn't ready to be undone just yet. Not before she got her complete fill of him.

"The stairs? Really?" she asked, smirking at him when he pulled away and met her gaze. "This is where you plan to devour me?"

"Of course not." He gave her that cocky smile again, slamming his lips against hers as they continued the rest of the way upstairs.

Once inside her apartment, he dropped her onto the bed. Her hands raked up his torso to pull his shirt over his head. He stepped back, though, out of her reach, as he began to remove the rest of his clothes, and she couldn't keep her eyes from feasting on all of this man's glory. He certainly wasn't like any of the other men she'd been with. And he was all hers.

Or he would be soon enough.

She started to undress herself but stopped when he shook his head, that damned smirk reappearing.

"Let me, love," he said, his hands already sliding her skirts and undergarments down her legs, careful to avoid her still-healing wounds. After tossing them to the floor, he had her top off in half a breath.

Then he paused, letting his eyes rove over her body. Cait might have blushed at being on full display had he not been showing all of himself to her as well. His eyes met hers again, those blues swirling with attraction and lust and emotions she'd never seen before.

"Need me to tell you what to do?" she asked with mock sympathy.

"Shut up, Cait," he said with a dark laugh. "You can tell me what you want another time. But I'm a pirate—"

"Former," she corrected.

He ignored her as he climbed over her and whispered, "Tonight I take what I want."

That stoked the flames in her core, and she rolled her hips eagerly. And then he was there, easing her need with each additional inch he offered her, coaxing moans from deep within her as he moved. His lips were on hers, muffling their cries of passion.

Adler met her right where she needed, answering every whimper with another touch, another kiss, drawing her eyes closed with satisfaction.

Latching her legs around his waist, she pulled him deeper still, needing more of him, all of him, never wanting to be without his touch again.

When his lips lifted from hers, she opened her eyes to find him staring at her. His passion and need for her was made clear with each move of his hips against hers, every slide of him within her. But his eyes showed none of the lustful abandon she'd witnessed in them before. It had been replaced with utter devotion, a love she never dared dream of.

She didn't deserve this. She didn't deserve him.

But here he was, giving all of himself to her. The first man she could truly be vulnerable with. The first man she could see herself sharing a life with.

He was here. He was hers. He loved her.

And with each move of their bodies together, those truths filled her heart, pulling her into an ecstasy she'd never known. Her eyes, prickling with tears, closed on as his name graced her lips.

"I know, love," Adler whispered as he rested his forehead against hers. "I'm here. And I'm yours. You can let go. I'm here."

Cait's lips quivered, and Adler was there at once, his own lips calming her heart as he accepted all of her. And she let herself fall, losing herself in him and with him, feeling him give himself completely over to her.

And for the first time in years, she knew she was where she was meant to be.

CHAPTER 37
DECLAN

The nightmares were back.

Familiar cobblestones coated in blood gave way to a ship's deck soaked in the water and guts of his friend. Black sands wet with his tears turned to white beaches stained with the blood of his crewman. And with each scene, the voice got louder:

"What did you ever do for anyone, Declan? You think you're better than Callum, but you deserve the same pain and misery and death that you dealt him."

Every time he closed his eyes and the images assaulted him, he tried to fix things, to save his father, to free Killian, to be honest with Aoife, to fight the queen's compulsion.

But it never worked. It never eased.

He would wake with a start, his heart pounding, his arms shaking, his breath faltering.

Until he found Aoife staring back at him, concern and love in her eyes, his name on her lips. Aoife's voice drove the darkness away, pulling him to his safe harbor that was her love.

"I'm here, Declan. You're okay. I'm here."

It had been three days since the siren brought them Halloran's message, and every night since, he'd been broken by his memories. And each morning, Aoife had been there to put him back together.

This morning, though, he didn't simply hold her to him and let her steady breaths anchor him. Wrapping her in his arms, he kissed the top of her head and whispered two words into her hair.

"I'm sorry."

Declan waited for her to pull away from him and flash him one of her curious looks, but instead she settled in closer to his chest.

"For what?"

Stroking her hair, he took a steadying breath before answering, "You deserve more."

When she was quiet for several breaths, he convinced himself she was going to agree with him and announce her plans to leave him when they returned to Morshan.

"Maybe I do," she said, and Declan couldn't stop his muscles from tensing around her, bracing himself for her inevitable rejection. But then she gave a small shrug. "But I don't want more." She pulled away and propped herself up on an elbow so she could look at him. Her eyes searched his. "I want you, Declan."

"Even if I'm broken?" He held her gaze, not sure what he hoped she would say. He couldn't let her go, but he also didn't believe he deserved her. Not after all his failures and all his misdeeds.

"We're all a little broken, but—believe it or not—I knew you weren't perfect when I fell in love with you."

"Your heart should have known better."

She cleared her throat and squared her shoulders. That regal—almost haughty —look she'd given him the first time they'd met washed over her face.

"Stop it. My heart is yours, and nothing you do will change that. You didn't steal it. You didn't take it. I gave it to you, and I give it to you every moment of every day because I want to. Love is a choice, and I choose you, Declan. With all your broken-ness and your imperfections and your haunted past. You're mine. I'm yours. So—"

Declan had his hand in her hair and was pulling her lips to his before she could say more. She responded eagerly, as if her lips and tongue and kiss needed to prove all she'd just said. Though his body screamed at him to request more from her, he stopped himself, reining in his desire and releasing her with a light kiss on her forehead.

She settled back down on the bed, tucked close to his side. For a long moment, they lay there as their breathing aligned. He had assumed she'd fallen back to sleep, but then she asked, "Was it Collins again?"

"Among others," he answered without hesitation.

"Killian?" she asked gently.

He hummed his affirmation.

"And?"

"You at the cove." He gave her a reassuring squeeze before adding, "And my parents."

She tensed against him and remained silent, but Declan knew her curiosity was likely begging her to pry.

Laughing softly, he told her, "Go ahead and ask."

"What happened to them? Is it why you left home as a kid?"

He waited another breath. "Only two questions? You're getting rusty."

"I'm learning to pace myself."

"Oh? Didn't seem like it last night."

She pinched him in the ribs. "You didn't seem to mind."

"Never said I did." He tickled the back of her legs, laughing when she squealed.

Releasing a giggle, she sat up and scooted out of his reach. "Are you trying to avoid answering the questions, or..."

"I see you're not working on your patience." Declan propped himself up on his elbows and eyed her, but when she only glared at him, he lifted himself the rest of the way and leaned back against the wall. "What was the first question again?"

Aoife didn't take any time reminding him. "What happened to them?"

Clasping his hands in his lap, he began the story. "I didn't know it at the time, but they were part of the original rogues." He paused to pick a piece of lint from his pants, keeping his eyes cast down as he continued. "Council discovered their secret. Had them killed."

"How do you know?"

"My mother was dragged away one night. I hoped she would come back, that the council only wanted to talk with her, but I was young and stupid."

Aoife's sweet voice came out barely above a whisper. "How old were you?"

"Ten."

"Young, sure. But not stupid. Being naive doesn't make you stupid."

"Regardless, she never came home. The pirates who took her came back a few nights later, and my father followed them out. I ran out of the pub in time to see him being dragged off and to find the pirate he had killed. It's where I got the dagger I carry. My father killed the pirate with it."

"It must be hard to relive that when you're sleeping," Aoife said and rested her hand on his outstretched leg.

"The memory of that murder isn't what haunts me though." At that, she seemed confused. "It's my guilt over it."

"Guilt? How could you have any—"

Declan held up a finger to stop her, closing his eyes as he sought out the words to explain.

She won't understand.

How could she when he couldn't grasp it himself?

Still, he'd lived with this so long that it was part of him. Like a festering appendage he couldn't remove or heal.

She knows guilt. She'll understand.

Either way, he had to try to explain it.

"It's not logical, I know," he said, "but I couldn't save them. I couldn't help. I couldn't do anything except watch it happen."

"What about your sister?"

"Cait acted like nothing had happened. She kept the pub running as if it had been hers all along, like our parents never even existed. I wanted her to be mad or sad or anything but normal."

Aoife raised a brow at him. "Sounds familiar."

Declan pressed his lips together and nodded. "I decided to be mad for both of us, but there was no good outlet for it on Cregah. Cait was fine on her own, so I left. Put that anger to use on the sea and promised myself I'd never be responsible for another's life again."

The logic was absurd. As captain, he was responsible for the lives of every soul aboard, but if Aoife saw the folly in it, she didn't let on. "Is that why you pushed me away?"

"You mean aside from the fact that I thought you were obnoxious and irritating?" She nodded. "Aye. It is, in part. I broke my own rule and vowed to keep you safe. Worse than that, though, were the memories you dredged up when you came aboard. I didn't think having you here would be so difficult. Little things, though, like you reading in bed, me removing my boots, sharing a meal, sleeping beside each other... It felt like home, and it hurt. Reminded me of my parents and an entire life I had lost."

"And that's what you meant when you said you never wanted this."

Declan grabbed her hands and pulled her closer, but his eyes never strayed from hers. "I was a fool."

"And now you're my fool." She pressed her lips to his as if sealing her declaration like a sacred vow.

"Always," he whispered back to her.

❧

IT WAS MIDMORNING when Declan and Aoife finally emerged from the cabin to find that Tommy and Mikkel had the crew sailing in perfect form while Gavin manned the helm.

"Do you think he'll stay?" Aoife asked in a small voice, as if Gavin might hear her over the sea breeze and across the distance separating them.

He and his helmsman had yet to speak with one another beyond a greeting or a simple command here and there since leaving Selka, and Tommy hadn't been able to provide much insight as to which way Gavin's heart was leaning.

"I don't know. I knew he and Collins were close—possibly even family—but I never thought something like this—"

Aoife stared up at him. "You mean you didn't think you'd find yourself under the control of an evil siren and forced to kill your own man?" She clicked her tongue. "And here I thought you were the great Captain McCallagh—the man, the myth, the legend himself."

Declan could only shake his head and laugh. As much as he wanted to pull her against him and show her—again—just what kind of legend he was, he also was well aware of the chasm he was creating between him and his men by spending so much time alone with her.

He looked around the deck at the men who sailed under him. Some he'd known for years. Others they'd hired in Foxhaven. It felt like ages ago. But those men, men who had only known him for a few days, had sailed these waters and battled a kraken to rescue him.

Declan had tried to show his gratitude to them that first day in Foxhaven, and he'd tried to speak to each one of them after they laid Collins to rest. But he didn't know if it was enough. Could anything he did help heal those who had lost friends and now faced nightmares of their own?

They needed him. They needed him to stop being a lovesick man nd resume being their captain. They needed him here on the deck with them, to see that he was still a part of this crew, still cared about this crew.

But he also needed Aoife.

She grounded him in this tempest of pain and guilt and heartache.

Her eyes slid to him, catching him staring at her.

"What is it?" A slight smile pulled at her lips.

He leaned toward her and inched his mouth close to her ear. "We have some time."

Aoife slowly turned to face him until his lips hovered just over hers and their gazes locked. "And you called *me* insatiable?"

Pulling back, he shot her an accusatory glare. "Miss Aoife, why would you assume I was proposing such activities?"

Awkwardly her eyes dropped and shifted back and forth as if looking for some explanation written on his chest. A satisfying blush crept over her cheeks, and he couldn't resist reaching a hand up to cradle her warming face. Then, leaning forward and brushing her lips with his, his tongue lured hers out for a slow caress, a promise of things he would do to her later. She sighed, her body melting into his, and it took every ounce of his resolve not to cart her off to his cabin and fulfill all her expectations.

Breaking their kiss, he gazed into her eyes again, willing her to see how much he wanted her.

"As much as I'd love another taste, alas, I'm the captain."

"Aye, Captain, I know." She peered at him from under her lashes, giving him a coy smile.

Declan ran a hand through his hair, easing away the familiar tension this woman caused in his bones, his nerves, his soul.

"The crew needs me. That means sometimes I have to sacrifice my own... desires."

Aoife nodded, flashing him a curious smile. "But then, what did you mean by our having some time?"

Reaching behind his back, Declan retrieved the wooden blades they used for training. He placed one in her palm. "Practice with me?"

CHAPTER 38
AOIFE

WINDING her fingers around the wooden handle, Aoife's heart plummeted into her gut. All warmth fled from her face as her passion was snuffed out. She blinked her eyes, and then she was no longer standing on the deck of the *Siren's Song*. Her feet sank into white sand. She tried to block it out, tried to close her eyes against the image, but the memory gripped her tightly and refused to let her go.

Collins.

Desperate and pleading.

Declan.

Angry and snarling.

Then blood.

Collins falling to his knees.

A scream being rent from her chest.

Declan pushing him into the sand.

It wasn't Declan's fault. It wasn't.

It was Triss's, but that didn't make this any easier.

Here on deck, holding the same wooden blade Collins had trained her with as they prepared to meet the kraken, Aoife tried to pull herself from the pit of emotion she'd fallen into.

How could she explain this to Declan? How could she bear to bring up Collins? Declan was already struggling to heal from what he'd done, and now all his talk about needing to reconnect with his crew?

She couldn't.

The queen had wanted to inflict maximum pain on Declan, but Aoife refused to help her do that.

No, she could handle this. She could control her pain to protect him.

But she made the mistake of glancing at Gavin—poor Gavin, who had taken

Collins's death the hardest. And she lost the battle against her tears. They flooded her eyes and clung to her lashes.

"What's wrong?" Declan nudged her chin toward him and then lifted it when she refused to meet his gaze. "Aoife." A quiet panic lay behind each syllable. "Talk to me."

"I can't." She shook her head, trying desperately to keep the tears from spilling over.

"You can." His voice, gentle and kind, such a stark contrast to the memory playing on repeat in her mind, couldn't quell the heartache.

"Collins."

The single word on her tongue had Declan moving, slipping the practice blade out of her hand and dropping it to the deck before tucking her close to his chest. His heart beat steadily beneath her ear, and Aoife used it to steady her breathing, desperate to get her emotions under control. She wasn't helping him by falling apart.

"He taught you," Declan whispered into her hair.

Aoife wrapped her arms around his waist and held tight as she nodded against his chest.

"I should have known, should have assumed. I'm sorry." His voice cracked a bit on the last word, but he said nothing more for a long time. They simply stood there on the quarterdeck, holding onto one another and waiting for their grief to settle.

But this wasn't going to help him be there for his crew, so Aoife reluctantly pulled away from him, grabbed his face with both hands, and pressed a tear-laced kiss to his lips.

"I'm going to go rest for a bit, I think," she said, and Declan started to move, but Aoife stopped him. "Stay here."

"I don't need—"

"Yes you do. You need to be here with your crew. Just like you said. I'll be fine. I promise."

Giving him another kiss, deeper this time, but not passionate like the others—more a reassurance of her devotion than anything else—she slipped out of his arms and started toward their cabin. Before leaving the quarterdeck, though, she caught Declan's attention and nodded toward Gavin.

Hopefully the space she gave him now would allow him the time to begin the healing between him and his helmsman. Aoife had already lost a friend in Collins. She didn't know how she could bear it if Gavin left the crew.

CHAPTER 39
TOMMY

FROM THE MOMENT the lush green jungle of Helles Island came into view on the horizon, Tommy was pacing the quarterdeck, unable to stand still. Declan had tried to talk him down from his anxious state, but he—of all people—should have known it wasn't that simple.

Perhaps he should have retreated to his quarters, waited this out until they arrived, but something kept him on deck. Gavin, thankfully, knew to leave him alone, to let him deal with his nerves in his own way. And if his constant back and forth irritated the helmsman, he never let it show.

What would Tommy say to her?

What would he do?

His mind wandered through option after option, and he reminded himself not to set his expectations too high. He'd seen how Declan's hopes were often dashed away when they would arrive at Morshan and Cait would not live up to the image of family he had spent months forming.

Declan approached, but Tommy kept walking, not saying anything even as his friend stopped, crossing his arms and watching him.

"We're almost there," Declan said, and Tommy stopped short, swinging to the starboard side to see deep green trees rising above the ship. How had he not noticed?

Pushing past his friend, Tommy was down the stairs and at the starboard rail. If Declan called after him, he didn't hear, his eyes scanning the island for any sign of her. He was aware he was acting like a fool, but he couldn't stop himself.

The beach lined the entire eastern shore of Helles Island. The jungle encroaching on the white sand looked like a tide of trees blowing in the island breeze. Tommy gripped the rail, trying to will his stomach to untangle itself.

"So I see you're handling this well," Declan said, a bit of humor in his words.

"About as well as you would if it were Aoife on that island." From the corner of his eye, Tommy saw Declan nod.

For a long while they stood in silence, watching the island drift by as they made their way south. He had nearly convinced himself that this was nothing but folly and that he should get some rest—until they reached the inlet the siren had described and a flash of color came into view.

"There," he said, leaning over the rail and pointing. "What is that?"

Declan already had his eyeglass in hand, and a curse was on his lips. "Shit. Is it Lucy?"

Tommy straightened, pinching his face in confusion. "How? Why would she be here? I've never known her to leave Foxhaven. Have you?"

"Never. But I also know of no one else who dresses in those colors," Declan said, passing the glass to Tommy. "Do you?"

There on the beach was the unmistakable form of their old friend, her body lifeless amid a heap of bright skirts.

Tommy's heart pounded against his sternum. Aside from the single body, there was nothing on the beach. No boats moored. No ships in sight. Nothing to indicate what had happened or how or by whom.

Dread pooled in his stomach. Maura was on this island, an island where their friend had been killed.

"If something happened to—"

Declan put a hand on Tommy's chest as if he expected him to leap overboard. "She's not here. Not on this beach."

"But she could have been. We don't know that she wasn't."

"Look, Tommy. Look again. There's no one else there." Declan swept his arm out before him, gesturing to the expanse of sand as they continued to sail past it.

"That doesn't mean she wasn't. That doesn't mean she's not hurt."

His panic continued to build, like a living beast rising from a deep slumber. It clouded his mind, and all he could see was Maura, her body lying somewhere in that jungle just like Lucy's.

Declan stepped closer to him, his gaze hard as he caught Tommy's attention and whispered, "She's strong, remember? And with her powers, I'm sure she's fine."

Declan was right.

Maura was fine.

Dropping his chin to his chest, Tommy told himself to accept these truths.

With a sigh, Declan backed away.

This isn't where Maura would be, but something in Tommy's gut pulled him back to the rail. He couldn't explain it, couldn't even determine if it wasn't his imagination, but it was like something—or someone—was calling to him.

She won't be here. She's waiting for you elsewhere.

But even as he reminded himself of that, he balked. Yes, that was what the siren had told them, but when he looked back at Lucy's body crumpled on the beach, he knew. Somehow, he knew she was on her way to him.

And he needed off this ship now.

Before Declan could stop him, Tommy was up on the rail and diving into the Aisling. He didn't hear his captain calling for him, didn't hear the crew's inevitable cries, didn't hear anything but the sound of Maura's voice in his ear, in his heart.

I am yours, Tommy.

I love you.

And with each stroke of his arms through the sea, he repeated the words back to her, hoping against all hope he was right and he would find her.

IT WAS INDEED Lucy on the beach, and from the looks of it, she'd been dead for the better part of a day. The scavengers—if there were any such animals on this island—hadn't yet come for her, leaving the sand around her undisturbed and the footprints of the people who had done this still visible.

Tommy was no expert tracker, by any stretch of the imagination, so there was no way to know how many people had stood here or what exactly had happened. But he could see that three parties had met here, or at least had all stood here at some point, whether together or separate. Two sets of tracks led to the water, but at different points. Likely a rendezvous of some sort.

A third track, narrower and less chaotic, led off toward the trees.

While Maura could have been dragged off to sea by whomever had been here, that invisible tether tugged Tommy toward the third set of footsteps, across the sand, and into the trees. He didn't know where he was going or what he might find, but he had to trust it was leading him to her.

CHAPTER 40
MAURA

SLEEP ELUDED Maura for most of the night. Between the mystery surrounding her brother and the anticipation of Tommy's arrival, she spent hours tossing and turning and fretting. She woke up to the familiar sound—and smell—of Captain Halloran preparing the morning meal. Overhead, the morning light filtered through the broad leaves of the trees.

Before she'd even sat up, Halloran was bidding her a good morning.

"Anything good come from the restless night you had?" the captain asked, stirring the meat and potatoes together in a pan over the fire.

Maura's stomach growled. Groaning, she pushed herself up off the ground and approached the campfire. "Unfortunately no. Nothing but a sore back and a pounding headache."

Halloran speared one of the potatoes with her knife and plopped it in her mouth. She shook her head before returning to her stirring. "Well, hopefully we'll be getting off this rock today."

Maura's breath caught, and her eyes widened with hope, but the captain dashed it away with her next words.

"No sails spotted yet, but I only checked the southern shoreline, not the east."

So he could be nearby. Maura tried not to let her excitement and eagerness take over too quickly as she asked, "Why don't we go back to the beach then? Wouldn't we be able to see them coming?"

"We could miss them if they've already made their way around the southeast of the island. He'd arrive here at camp to find no one. I think it best we stay put. You'd think an ancient fae would have a bit more patience." Halloran pierced her with a glare from under her lashes.

Maura walked up and down the length of the camp several times, accepting a plate of food when Halloran offered it as she passed by and then eating as she continued pacing.

"We really should have taken care of Lucy's body. We just left it there for the creatures."

Halloran shrugged. "Those creatures need to eat too," she said before taking a bite of another piece of meat.

"Then they can find other dead animals to eat. She's a human. She deserves a respectful burial, doesn't she?"

The captain eyed her curiously for a long moment and then pointed her knife at her. "You would make a terrible pirate, you know that?"

"I'm okay with that, honestly. No offense."

The pirate only harrumphed and said no more.

Maura brushed her hands together and set her shoulders, preparing to inform the woman of her decision, as if she could possibly intimidate Captain Halloran.

"I'm going back to the beach." She wasn't asking permission. She wasn't requesting her help. She was going to go whether Halloran wanted to come with her or not.

Halloran dropped her head to the side, that same quizzical look on her face again. "And how do you expect to find it?"

"I'll manage," Maura said and started off into the trees.

She'd made it a dozen steps into the shadows when Halloran's quiet voice hit her ears. "Wrong way."

Maura had no choice but to return to camp and try a different entrance to the forest, but when she looked over her shoulder, she found Halloran shaking her head.

"Fine," Maura muttered. "Will you help me?"

The captain made quite a show of pondering the request and, after drawing in a lengthened breath, she finally stood. "I think it's foolish, but it's not my mate on his way to this camp to find me."

"Mates aren't a thing," Maura corrected.

"This way." Halloran gestured for the fae to follow her down a path about twenty paces from where Maura had first tried.

They continued in relative silence while Maura's mind raced ahead of her, conjuring images of the *Siren's Song*'s sails on the horizon, of Tommy spotting her on the beach and swimming toward her.

It was foolish. One of the more foolish things she'd let herself dream of.

Second, of course, to him ever accepting her love in the first place, but he had done that.

What if Renna's stunt had ruined everything?

What if he wouldn't forgive her?

What if he arrived just to tell her how angry and hurt he was?

What if he took one look at her and turned away?

Her pace slowed reflexively with each question. She had spent all these days assuming he would understand the truth, that their love—as young and new and confusing as it was—was strong enough to shine through her sister's scheming. But maybe she was nothing more than a fool. About everything.

A fool to think she deserved love, deserved him, deserved happiness.

She'd essentially walked away from her kin for him, abandoned her kind to chase something that could never possibly work.

Shut up! You cannot think like that!

And there it was.

A heartbeat.

Pounding hard, but faint, it skimmed over the top of hers and Halloran's, but it was growing louder with each breath. Getting closer.

It was him.

She had no way of knowing, of course, but she wanted it to be true so badly that she refused to consider any other possibility.

Pushing past the captain, she ignored the hand that reached for her, the voice that called for her to stop, and the growled swear that followed. All Maura could focus on was this new heart on the island. She followed it through the trees, not worrying about getting lost, only needing to find it.

She ran, tearing through the leaves, wincing as branches slapped against her arms and face.

Footsteps pounded across the forest floor. Hers. Halloran's behind her. And another set coming toward her, as fast as hers.

And then they stopped, leaving nothing but the sound of labored breaths and thundering hearts. A pair of amber eyes stared back at her, a ship's width away.

Her limbs froze. Every fear slammed into her. All logic failed her. And no answers showed on his face.

Tears crept up. Her lips quivered.

Tommy took a tentative step toward her, and whatever spell had been holding her captive fell away. She was running again, slamming into him. Her hands hit his chest, fingers gripping his damp shirt until they ached. Tenderly he cradled her face in his hands, his thumbs stroking her cheeks as those glistening seas of amber roved over her like he wasn't sure she was real.

"I found you." Tommy's whisper tickled her face, warming her skin. A tear escaped and trailed down her cheek toward his hand, as if it too had missed him.

As he brushed it away, she struggled to calm her shaking lips long enough to get out the words she'd rehearsed since she'd abandoned him. "I'm sorr—"

But Tommy silenced her apology with his kiss, his lips erasing every worry and regret she'd harbored, welcoming her back into his arms where she belonged. Then his hands were lost in her hair, and he pulled her closer still, like she was the very air he needed to survive.

With tongues and lips and tears and hands combining in a passionate dance, Maura couldn't contain the moaned sigh that thrummed from her mouth into his. He released her lips to press a kiss to her forehead before holding her tight against him, and she tucked her head protectively under his chin.

After taking a deep breath of his spiced, woodsy scent, Maura said into the folds of his shirt, "I thought I'd lost you."

Tommy stroked her hair as he held her, but he remained quiet long enough that a fresh spark of panic ignited in her chest. Her earlier fears began to inch their way back into her heart. But he banished them when his thumb trailed along her jaw and lifted her chin to look at him.

"Misplaced, perhaps. Never lost." With a shake of his head, he smiled softly. "No distance could keep me from you. No fae sister either, for that matter."

Maura didn't want to talk about Renna, but she couldn't help but ask, "How did you know it was her?"

"Because I know you." Tommy brushed her hair behind her ear, letting his fingers whisper sweet nothings against her skin as he traced the line of her neck, then her collarbone, stopping just above the top of her dress. "And I know you'd never leave willingly. Not..."

Maura waited for the rest of that sentence, but passion flashed in his eyes as he glanced down at her lips.

"Not what?" Maura whispered, her desire and anticipation rising.

"Not after I let you have your way with me."

She couldn't contain her smirk. "Oh, is that how you remember it?"

"Accurately, you mean? Aye," he said as he lowered his lips to her neck. His tongue drew lazy circles over her pulse, setting her core aflame.

Her eyes closed as she tilted her head, enticing him to take all he wanted from her. "Will you let me again?"

Tommy only hummed in response and continued to kiss and nibble and caress his way down her neck and across her shoulder as his light touch edged her dress out of the way. Oh how she had missed the feel of him. She hadn't even had a chance to explore and memorize all of him before her sister had—

No. Renna wasn't going to intrude upon any of her thoughts today.

Pressing her hips into him, she swallowed her gasp at the feel of him through their clothes. The fire in her core spread—heating, melting her, making her ache— until she thought she might fall apart before he'd even properly touched her.

"Tommy." His name fell from her lips in a desperate plea, a frayed whisper, an urgent command.

His lips found hers again. All the careful tenderness had been replaced with a blazing need as his tongue swept inside her mouth and his hands seized her hips. He took a step forward and pushed against her with such force that she instinctively stepped back.

"I need you," Tommy growled as he forced her backwards faster. "Now."

The bite of the rough tree trunk at her spine—and the force of him driving her up against it—sent a new wave of wild hunger through her, and her fingers couldn't find the hem of his shirt fast enough. But his hands were already there, yanking his shirt up and off. His eyes glowed with a primal fire she hadn't witnessed the last time they were together.

It had her rushing to undo the clasp at his pants, and her heart accelerated when he didn't stop her from reaching down to stroke him with needy hands. With a wicked grin, he pulled the top of her dress away to reveal her breasts. They begged for his touch—a plea he seemed all too eager to answer.

He took them between his lips and teeth, flicking and circling his tongue on her hardened peaks until soft whimpers filled her throat. Maura continued to slide her hand up and down his length, the ache between her legs throbbing as her desire fought to escape its restraints.

"Now," she said in a husky whisper, using her free hand to lift her skirts. His fingers caressed her hand before diving beneath her dress and trailing up her thighs to her dripping center.

His breath hissed through his teeth when he slipped his hand beneath the edge of her underwear, his fingers sliding easily along her entrance. "Fuck, Maura," he moaned, flinching in her palm. "I missed this. I missed you. I missed us." His thumb found its own rhythm against that blissful spot, making her eyes flutter shut and her back arch.

"I want you inside me," she breathed and gripped him tighter, tugging him toward her. "I need—"

Her attention snagged on the sound of movement in the trees, still distant but getting closer. Footsteps? Had Halloran finally caught up to them?

But all thoughts of the approaching captain vanished when Tommy's fingers slipped inside her to continue their perfect strokes.

Sands. She couldn't breathe, couldn't think of anything except the magic he wielded between her thighs.

"Hurry," she said. "Someone's coming."

A chuckle tickled her ear as Tommy leaned into her. "Not yet, but soon."

Damn pirates.

"No, I mean, Halloran will be here soon."

Tommy's fingers stilled but didn't leave her. "She's here with you?"

"She will be shortly, so if you truly do need me now—as I need you—you'd better hurry."

He grinned wickedly, but when Maura began moving her hand along his length once more, he pulled free of her grip and put himself back in his pants. Maura couldn't help pouting, but Tommy deepened his hold on her, pulsing and pushing and stroking until her core quivered and her breathing hitched.

Once again, he leaned in and traced the edge of her pointed ear with his tongue before whispering, "If it has to be hurried, it's going to be yours. And yours alone. I need you to come for me, Maura. Now."

Maura couldn't respond, couldn't speak, couldn't argue.

She would do anything he demanded, and if this was what he wanted, she couldn't deny it any more than she could deny her love for him.

Ignoring the approaching footsteps, ignoring her own desire to satisfy him, ignoring everything but the quivers of pleasure his fingers conjured up from deep inside her, she gave herself over to the bliss. Dropping her head back against the tree, she rocked with his hand, soft moans humming inside her chest as he pulled her closer and closer to that free fall she craved.

"Sands," Maura gasped, reaching her hands up to his bare shoulders and digging her nails into his tanned skin. "There, right there."

"Aye, I know," he said and kissed her hard, his tongue matching the rhythm of his fingers, faster and faster, responding to every whimper and moan and hitched breath.

And then she was there; every fiber of her being was pulled apart before coming back together with such intensity that she couldn't keep his name from escaping her lips louder than she'd intended. But when he started planting kisses on her nose and forehead and lips, tender and sweet, she couldn't convince herself to care about the outburst.

She flinched reflexively as his hand pulled away, then smoothed her dress back down, trying to ignore another surge of desire when Tommy ran his fingers across his tongue, tasting her release and smiling.

He was putting his shirt back on just as Halloran stepped through the foliage, a knowing, tight-lipped smile plastered on her face. There was no way she hadn't heard Maura when Tommy pulled her over the edge, and Maura braced herself for some suggestive remark from the captain.

But none came.

"You found him."

"Aye," Tommy answered for Maura, his voice calm and nonchalant, like he had just been sharing a cup of tea with her instead of turning her into a magnificent puddle in his hands. "Thank you, Captain, for bringing her back to me." He started to extend his hand toward Captain Halloran, but she glanced down at it with suspicion before shaking her head.

"I'd rather not shake hands with you just yet, Tommy, but you're welcome."

Tommy muttered, "Fair" as Maura stepped away from the tree, testing each footstep gingerly, not sure if she could completely bear her own weight just yet. Weaving her fingers into Tommy's, she stepped up beside him and clung to his arm. "Sorry for—"

But Halloran waved her words away. "No need for apology. I'm just happy to see you didn't get lost when you took off like that." She turned to Tommy with the hint of a smile on her lips. "Your love here has a horrible sense of direction."

"I don't know; she seems to take direction quite well." Tommy's gaze met Maura's, wild desire flashing in his eyes and sending a thrill through her veins.

"Nope, none of that," Halloran said. "I'm happy to pretend—for your sake— that I didn't hear anything." When no one said anything further, Halloran clasped her hands together and drew in a deep breath. "So, McCallagh didn't anchor where I instructed then?"

Tommy shrugged. "I'm not sure." Halloran and Maura both stared at him with wide eyes. "I jumped off the ship when I saw Lucy's body on the beach. I assume he sailed on."

At the mention of Lucy, Maura shuddered, assaulted by the memory of how her brother had killed the woman. She caught Halloran's eye. "Shall we continue on with you, Captain?" When Tommy shot her a questioning look, Maura explained how they had been on their way to bury Lucy when she'd heard his heartbeat.

Halloran gave a small shake of her head. "No, I've got this. You two go back to the camp. Assuming you can find it?"

Tommy squeezed Maura's hand reassuringly before dipping his chin toward the captain. "If we get lost, I'm sure you'll be able to track us down."

Rolling her eyes, the captain breathed out a long sigh. "I'll meet you back there in a few hours. Go and wait for McCallagh. And keep it in your pants at least until we're on the ship? Maybe? Can you do that?"

Tommy merely shrugged. The gesture made Maura smile, but Halloran stomped off, shaking her head.

When she was gone, Maura tugged Tommy's hand toward camp, but his feet remained firmly in place. "We should go," she said.

Raising a brow, Tommy smirked. "We can just as easily pass the time here, no?"

"As much as I'd like to get my hands on you—or yours on me—she wasn't wrong about my ability to get myself lost. We may need every moment just to find our way back."

Tommy pulled her toward him and planted a kiss on the top of her head. "Well then, let's get lost together."

CHAPTER 41
DECLAN

Grinding his teeth together, Declan punched the ship's side rail. He'd jumped. Dived straight into the sea. For a short moment, Declan considered anchoring here and following his friend ashore. If that was indeed Lucy's body on the beach, she deserved to be laid to rest elsewhere, not left for the birds to pick her apart.

But Captain Halloran's stern face flashed into his thoughts and changed his mind.

They would sail around, anchor as instructed, and follow her directions to the camp. If Tommy managed to find Maura elsewhere on the island, the best chance they had to reunite with both of them would be to meet at the one location they all knew.

"Where'd Tommy go?" Aoife asked around a yawn, approaching Declan as he turned to give the order to Gavin.

Lacing their fingers together, he pulled her around to join him as he walked toward the quarterdeck. He tossed his head back toward the island. "Jumped."

Aoife offered a short laugh. "Can't say I'm surprised."

Declan glanced at her. "How? I didn't expect that." Something pinched in his chest at the reminder that Aoife and Tommy had grown close in his absence. It wasn't that he was jealous of the strong bond they had formed—to the contrary, actually—but it hurt knowing how much he had missed while locked in that brig.

"You didn't see how he was with her," Aoife said, her tone tinged with regret, as if he had missed out on years instead of days.

"I saw enough." Declan tried to make a joke of it, but Aoife only shook her head at him.

"You only saw the spoils of a hard-fought battle."

"When did you become such a poet?"

She slapped his arm but then pulled him to a stop in the middle of the deck and turned to face him. "But in all seriousness, Declan. He fought so hard to ignore his feelings for her. Insisted there was no future for them. But when he almost lost her, it all changed. He'd do anything for her. Even jump off the ship and swim for her."

If anyone could understand that, it was Declan, and once again he wished he'd been there for his friend.

"But he didn't demand we chase her. He didn't insist we go after her. He didn't—"

Aoife's face scrunched in confusion. "It's Tommy, Declan. He'd do anything for her, but also for you. That man is loyal to a fault. You're lucky to have him."

She wasn't wrong.

Declan nodded as he guided her toward the stairs.

"So we're not following him?" Aoife asked.

Declan shook his head. As they neared the helm, he said, "Maintain our heading, Gavin."

"Do you think he'll find her?" Aoife asked.

"Aye, I do. We'll need to stay on the island for a bit longer than planned though." Aoife shot him a questioning glance. "Lucy's body was on that beach." Declan paused to point to where the pile of bright fabric still lay, noting that Tommy was no longer visible.

"Lucy?" The woman's name floated on a whisper, and Aoife's eyes widened as she stood on her toes to look. "Why was she—"

"I don't know. I never knew her to leave Foxhaven. Whatever brought her here must have been important."

"Do you think she... Do you think she was behind my...those men?" Aoife tightened her grip on Declan's hand, as if the brutes who had taken her that night were standing before her once again. Declan hesitated. If he claimed to have never suspected Lucy, he'd be lying.

"I'm not sure, to be honest. It's a definite possibility."

"But she was your friend."

"Closer to me than most. If she was behind it and purposefully gave you over to them, I have no doubt she had a good reason."

"Or you're too trusting," Aoife said and pursed her lips.

Declan smirked at her. "Don't think I've ever been accused of that before."

"First time for everything." She tossed him a shrug and turned her attention back to the beach, but her statement tugged at images from their night together.

So many firsts for them both, as no woman had ever meant enough to Declan to motivate him to bring her aboard his ship and take her into his quarters, let alone his bed. The memory caused desire to curl in his stomach. He tried to shoo it away, but the burning need was almost as insistent as the darkness was, calling him to take her in his arms and ravage her right here on the deck, witnesses and onlookers be damned.

But he'd never do that to her, never put her in such a compromising position.

Unless she asked for it.

Looking at her, though—at those adorable freckles dotting her cheeks, the innocence in the lines of her face—he knew how unlikely that was. How she had fallen for him, accepted him and his dark side, he couldn't fathom. But he would be forever grateful.

"Any idea when we'll arrive?" Aoife asked, pulling Declan from his thoughts.

In his mind, he pictured the map of the island and tried to remember just how big it was. "Few hours, I expect."

"What do we do until…" Her final word trailed off as a yawn escaped.

Declan grabbed her by the shoulders and peered into her eyes. "I'm going to stay here with Gavin until we arrive. You are going to go get some more rest."

"I don't need—" Aoife tried to protest, but her body seemed determined to prove her otherwise as it forced another yawn.

"And I'm a pretty siren."

Aoife narrowed her eyes at him and, with less reluctance than he'd expected, turned and trudged back to their cabin. As soon as the door was closed behind her, Declan returned to Gavin's side at the helm. The man seemed far more focused on the waters ahead of them than he needed to be, and Declan noted how he was fighting back a grin.

"Have something to say, Gavin?" Declan asked. He kept his gaze forward on the jewel-like water and the jungle that greeted it along this side of the island.

Gavin shook his head slowly as he said, "She's good for you, Captain."

Declan blinked rapidly and turned toward his friend. He had expected some jab about his pretty siren comment or how soft he had gotten since finding Aoife.

"Who would've thought?" Declan conceded. He certainly hadn't imagined the effect a woman—love, in general—would have on his character.

It didn't help you avoid the darkness though.

No, but it had stayed his hand in that barn, had brought him back to the light.

Even as that thought crossed his mind, though, the darkness chuckled somewhere deep inside his heart, as if reminding him that no amount of light or love could rid him of it completely.

"You mean aside from your entire crew?" Gavin turned to Declan, one brow cocked at a sharp angle.

Declan couldn't refrain from rolling his eyes to the sky above.

"Not your fault, of course," Gavin continued. "You've spent a long time running from yourself. Hard to see the possibilities for happiness when you're constantly looking over your shoulder for the demons chasing you."

"Never too late to change, is it?" Declan asked. "Never too late to forgive."

Gavin angled toward him, though he kept his hands firmly on the wheel. "Thanks, Captain, for being more patient than I deserved. I was unfair to you—"

"You were—are—grieving. It's allowed, but that doesn't change that you have a job to do here."

"Aye, and I lost sight of that. Grief or no, I owed you my respect as a member of your crew. I'm sorry I let the anger take over as it did."

"Trust me, I understand that struggle. All too well. Just remember, the anger and grief may never fully go away. Even as you find ways to cope and time helps to heal, part of you may always be scarred and broken."

"Aye. The anger is still there, but I'm trying. I've sailed under you for long enough to know how you handle your own demons. I should have understood how hard it was for you to deal with what you'd done."

"Grief makes us blind to the pain of others." Declan dropped his gaze to the deck, not sure what more he could say.

But Gavin said, "I hope to stay on the crew if the offer still stands."

Declan lifted his chin and locked eyes with the man. Clapping a hand on his shoulder, he said, "Of course it does."

Gavin smiled briefly before returning his attention back to the sea.

And just like that, another weight lifted from Declan's shoulders. He hadn't realized just how heavy Gavin's pending decision had been until it was gone.

"Thanks, Gavin. Truly." His friend nodded slowly. "You just saved me the trouble of having to quell Aoife's temper if you had left."

The inlet Captain Halloran had directed them to was so well hidden from anyone sailing past the island that it took Declan an embarrassingly long time to spot it. He'd almost reached the point of cursing the pirate's name until he finally noticed how the trees along one part of the island were not on the same coast as the others, an illusion he'd never seen on any other land in the Aisling. From the deck of the ship, the island looked as though it curved around in an unbroken shoreline, but there, to the left, the greenery didn't quite match up with the land next to it.

Gavin easily maneuvered the ship around the disguised corner, and they found themselves in a small bay. The sight of it brought back the horrors of the Black Sound even though its beaches were covered with palm trees and feathery ferns instead of mere sand. Something caught in Declan's throat as they made their way to the beach, and he winced at the pain when he tried to swallow past it.

Breathe, McCallagh.

This isn't the sound.

Triss is dead.

There's no danger here. Only friends.

But even as he thought that, he knew it might not be true. Not with that body back on the eastern beach. *Lucy.* What had the woman been doing this far from her home?

Someone had killed her, and that someone could still be on this island.

Unless it was Maura who killed her? He considered that but immediately discarded the possibility. The fae would have no need to take her life.

Unless Lucy isn't as innocent as you want to believe.

Did he really trust too much, as Aoife had asserted?

Gavin snapped Declan out of his thoughts with a nudge of his boot. "Are you going alone?"

"Aye," Declan answered. "I don't intend to be gone long. But if I'm not back before sundown, have Mikkel take a man or two ashore with the directions."

"And Aoife?"

"Let her rest. She's going to need her full strength before we get to Morshan."

ONCE DECLAN WAS ASHORE, it was easy enough to locate Halloran's camp, but it was empty. From the looks of things—the doused fire, the rumpled bedding, the used dishes—someone had been here recently though. Hopefully it was Maura and not whomever had killed Lucy.

Declan had to hand it to Captain Halloran. Her little camp was quite well-stocked, and he made a mental note to consider creating his own place of respite somewhere on the Aisling someday.

But if he had his way—if everything panned out—he would be able to leave the Aisling behind completely.

If that was still what he wanted.

With nothing to do but wait, Declan dropped to the ground at the edge of the camp and leaned back against a thick tree trunk.

So much had changed since Aoife had boarded his ship. While he was still the same man for the most part, he couldn't deny the truth in Gavin's observation; Aoife had been good for him. And now the power and prestige and riches he had longed to find beyond these waters held little appeal compared to the future he saw every time he looked into her eyes. He'd spent so much time and energy avoiding the memory of his parents and his childhood, but when Aoife had shown up, it had been nearly impossible not to envision those loving moments in a new light—not as his parents' past, but as his future.

When Cait had provided him with the location of the dagger, he'd had little intention of taking it back to her and the rogues. After all, she and her band of rebels had done nothing for him in the years since he'd left home. But then that had changed—just like so much else. And he no longer wanted to use the dagger for his own gain. At least not until after his sister was able to use it to crush the council. After that, it was fair game. Certainly Cait wouldn't deny him the chance to build the life he wanted for himself.

But what would Aoife want? Did she want to sail beyond the Aisling? Or did she want to go back to Cregah and help the nation after the council fell? Or would she want to leave and settle elsewhere?

You should probably talk to her about that before it's too late.

Declan shifted as something rustled in the leaves, but he didn't bother to stand when he heard a pair of voices, laughing and chatting quietly. He didn't need to make out the words to recognize one of them as his best friend. And he could barely hide his laughter when Tommy finally emerged from the trees with Maura tucked close to his side, his shirt as disheveled as his hair.

CHAPTER 42
AOIFE

AOIFE HADN'T REALIZED JUST how tired she had been until she woke up to find the sun's final rays bathing the bedroom in a rich warmth. How long had she slept? Hushed voices reached her ears, and she quickly swung her legs over the side of the bed. In the main room she found Declan leaning against the front of his desk, talking quietly with a handful of others.

Halloran. Tommy. Maura.

When she spotted the fae, she rushed across the room and burst through the small group, disrupting their conversation. Tackling her friend in a hug, Aoife sighed when Maura's arms reached around her to return the embrace. When she finally let go, she glared into the fae's golden eyes.

"Don't you ever fucking do that to me again," she warned, but even she couldn't take herself completely seriously, and she was unable to contain her wide smile.

"Nice to see you too, Aoife," Maura said with a light laugh. "And aye, I don't plan on being duped by my sister again. As long as I can help it, anyway."

Backing away, Aoife took her place beside Declan, lifting herself up onto his desk so that her feet dangled in the air. Declan eyed her teasingly, and she flashed him a sheepish grin, sure he was also remembering the last time she'd been in this position.

"Do we need to catch Aoife up, or—" Halloran asked.

Declan shook his head and cleared his throat. "I'll fill her in later."

Aoife couldn't stop the warmth that spread through her with those seemingly innocent words.

Sands, Aoife, pull yourself together!

Just a handful of hours ago, she'd been crying over Collins, and now she couldn't keep her mind from wandering into passionate memories. She must be losing her mind. Surely it wasn't normal to be completely preoccupied with such things.

"What's the plan then? When we get to Morshan?" Tommy asked, once again slipping his hand around Maura's.

"Get the dagger to my sister," Declan said. "But with the way things have gone for us, I doubt it will be quite that easy."

"She should be at the pub though, right?" Tommy asked, but Declan was shaking his head again before he'd even finished.

"It's possible, sure, but if the king has already arrived, I have no doubt that Cait will waste no time. She always knew my getting the dagger for them was a long shot. She will have devised a contingency plan in case I failed."

Aoife leaned forward and rested her forearms on her legs as she looked at each of her friends. "But she's got people working with her. Couldn't we trust one of them?"

"Maybe. If we knew who they were," Declan said.

Aoife huffed an irritated sigh. "This seems like the sort of thing you coordinate before you set out for the dagger. No?"

Declan shrugged. "Aye, but unless someone has discovered a way to travel back in time, we're stuck with the reality that we're landing blind."

Aoife turned to Halloran, asking, "Any words of wisdom, Captain?"

The woman looked unperturbed by Aoife's terse tone, offering a half-smile. "Same thing I told Declan back in Foxhaven."

As if on cue, Declan offered up the words: "Don't trust anyone."

"That's it?" Aoife asked. Surely this seasoned pirate had some strategic experience that could help them against the council.

Halloran let out a breathy laugh. "It's a rather important reminder, Aoife. We don't know who on that island might claim to be in Cait's confidence, and we'd be foolish to take anyone at their word alone."

"That's not the only complication," Maura said. She looked at each of them before continuing. "The king isn't alone. He has a fae working for him."

A fae?

At least she didn't appear to be the only one surprised by this news; Declan and Tommy both gaped at Maura.

"Aye, it's true," Halloran said.

Maura nodded slowly. "A rather powerful fae too. That's who killed Lucy on the beach."

"It wasn't pretty either," Halloran added, and Aoife could have sworn a shadow of fear passed over the captain's dark eyes.

"But who?" Declan asked. "I thought there were only three of you still in the Aisling."

"So did we," Maura said. "We thought he was dead."

"Who is he, Maura?" Tommy asked, his voice low and weighed down with concern.

"My brother."

Aoife's mind spun around this new information. Was anything she knew of the world true? Would there ever stop being surprises?

"What are his powers?" Declan asked as he wrapped an arm around Aoife's shoulders and pulled her close.

Halloran squeezed her eyes shut briefly, hesitating long enough that Aoife was sure the woman was unnerved by whatever she'd witnessed back on the island.

"It's hard to explain," Maura said. "It's like he has another set of hands, but they're invisible. And he can project them away from himself. Not a far distance, but far enough to be dangerous. He can also see through my glamours. He's one of a few who can. Melina can also. Even with her powers extinguished, she's still a fae. She can still hear better than the average human. It will be hard to surprise her even with the glamour."

"Okay..." Declan started, his eyes roving around the circle of faces. "Ultimately we need to get the dagger to Cait. And, if that's not possible, we take it to the council hall ourselves. We don't know what King Kilmeran is offering to the council, but Cait seemed convinced the dagger would be useless once he arrived."

"Last I heard," Halloran said, "the king found some kind of shield."

"Csintala's shield? The counter to the dagger?" Declan asked, eyes wide.

Halloran shrugged. "I think it's fair to assume such."

While Declan, Tommy, and Halloran began to discuss the shield, Aoife eyed Maura, who was watching them all with confusion. Did she know something about this shield? If she did, Aoife needed her to share it.

"What is it, Maura?"

The fae shook away whatever thoughts she'd been lost within and caught Aoife's gaze. "What?"

"The shield. Do you know of it?"

Drawing in a deep breath, Maura offered her a tight-lipped smile. "It's not real," she said. "It's a lie the queen told Csintala to hide the true counter to the dagger's power." No one moved or questioned the fae, so she continued her explanation. "After Csintala fell, rumors formed that the dagger had betrayed him. You know that's how it passes hands, yes? That's how you got it from Callum. But Csintala was oblivious to that fact, or else he never would have betrayed the queen. Might never have taken the dagger to begin with, honestly. But Melina hid that from him by offering him a shield, claiming it was the only thing that could counter the dagger's magic. He sent it back to Tyshaly when he set out to win the war."

"But why the need for a lie?" Aoife asked.

Declan answered first. "Balance."

"That's right," Maura agreed. "Magic requires a balance. It's why our powers aren't limitless. They drain as we use them. They require we take time to replenish after exhausting them. In the same way, an enchantment—like the one put on the dagger—requires something to counter it. So Melina placed that enchantment with a built-in fail-safe to ensure balance if someone misused its power."

"But why betrayal? Why not simply let its power deplete like yours does?" Aoife asked. She had too much to learn about all this magic business.

Maura shrugged. "I don't know. Maybe she knew his heart? Maybe she anticipated he would not keep his promise? She never told us."

"You were there?" Tommy angled his head at her as he asked, and Maura nodded.

"Aye, my sisters and I were with her when she created it. We warned her against it, told her that that strong of an enchantment would take its toll on her. But she was brokenhearted after her king's death and wanted so desperately to believe Csintala's promises to love her and come back to her if he could just win the war. She sacrificed her powers to help him, and he betrayed her. At first, she tried to retrieve the dagger, but eventually, as every man and pirate she sent failed, she focused instead on controlling what she could—the people of Cregah."

"Wait," Aoife said, holding up a hand. "I don't understand. How is it that my mother—this fae queen—has managed to trick so many people for so long? How has she kept her identity a secret all these years?"

Maura ran a hand over her brow. "Renna and me. When we combine our *daemari*, we are able to alter someone's appearance, create a permanent glamour of sorts. It's why she kept us locked away, told us our kin had all perished."

Aoife's mind whirled. "Why help her then? Why do it?"

Maura shrugged slowly. "We made a promise to help her. A fae's promise is not easily broken. And she was our friend."

Aoife scoffed, but Declan spoke before she could respond. "What happened to all of her heirs?"

Drawing in a deep breath, Maura's gaze locked on Aoife's as she answered. "Each generation, she would kill her daughter and take her identity—change her name, change her glamour."

"And if she had a son?" Tommy asked.

Maura shook her head. "She never kept her sons." Maura's chin dropped to her chest. "The males were disposed of at birth. The daughters were allowed to grow up and live just until their matching."

"But how did she get away with killing her daughters? Surely the other councilwomen would notice," Declan said.

"I know it's confusing, and it's a lot to sort through," Maura explained. "Although I am slightly surprised your parents never explained this to you. I didn't think it was a secret among the citizens. You see, the elder councilwomen would step down from the council shortly after their daughters' matching. The idea being that too many leaders made things too complicated. Better to pass the responsibility on and then step back. Of course, the people of Cregah believe the councilwomen leave the island at that point—exiling themselves, basically. But Melina and that first council agreed that once their heirs were matched and fully taught, they would step down permanently."

"How?" Declan asked.

"Poison," Aoife whispered. The room went quiet, and several pairs of eyes burned into her. "We are taught this in our final year before our matching."

Declan's brow creased. "And everyone just goes along with it?"

Aoife offered him a tight-lipped smile. "When it's all you know, all you've been taught, how do you know to question or fight it?"

"Your sister questioned it."

"Aye," Aoife said with a single nod. "But only after she met Adler and learned about the world outside the council hall."

Declan roughed a hand over his stubbled chin before addressing Maura. "Melina doesn't have you and Renna to help her anymore though. Is that why she tasked me with getting the dagger back for her? What does it do for her? I had assumed she simply didn't want the rogues to have it, but now—"

Maura nodded. "Aye. Without us there to help maintain her ruse, she needs another way to remain in power. The dagger is her answer. If she gets it? Her powers will be restored, and no one in the Aisling will be safe."

Aoife straightened. "Then why are we taking it back there?"

Declan tightened his grip on her shoulder. "We have to. It's our only hope of ending the council's tyranny."

"He's right, Aoife," Halloran said, stepping forward. "It's a risk we have to take if we want to unseat them."

"But can we simply *unseat* them?" Aoife shrugged out from under Declan's arm as she stood and pushed away from the desk. "Even if we can use the dagger to beat them, what does that victory look like? Will they walk away peaceably? Will they simply step aside and let someone else take over? I think we all know they won't."

Halloran dipped her chin in a slow nod but said nothing more. Everyone else remained quiet as well, even as Aoife looked each of them in the eye. What she expected them to say, she didn't know. But surely someone could suggest something. *Anything.*

"So what then? We kill them?" Aoife asked.

Declan laid a hand on Aoife's back. "You knew we planned to give the dagger to the rogues to defeat them. You knew—"

"Aye, I knew," she said, a little more harshly than intended. "But I guess I just didn't—it just feels—I don't know what I'm trying to say."

Maura reached out a hand and lightly touched Aoife's arm. "If there was a way to convince your mother to step down willingly, I would be all for it. She was practically my family. But she's had centuries of power. I can't see her giving that up easily."

"So that's it then. I have to kill my mother." Tommy shifted and opened his mouth to speak, but Aoife held up a finger. "Aye, I know. It might not be me who does it, but still."

"This all assumes, of course, that we can figure out how to get close enough to her," Halloran pointed out.

Declan stepped away from the desk and laced his fingers with Aoife's. "Tommy, what do you think about Red Beard's Revenge? Would it work here?"

Tommy's brow briefly creased in concentration before he looked up at Declan with a half-smile. "Maybe. But we lost the wigs years ago."

Wigs?

"Are we going to have to pretend to be drunk on rum again?" Aoife asked him, smirking.

Declan shook his head at her quickly before turning back to Tommy. "No need for them. Not when we have Maura here."

Wigs? Maura?

They needed a disguise.

Maybe pirates weren't completely crazy after all.

THE SILENCE IN THE CABIN, after hours of discussion and planning, enveloped Aoife like a comforting embrace. Declan had left to secure sleeping arrangements for Halloran, as she had refused to share the officers' quarters with Maura, understandably deferring that honor to Tommy instead. Tommy, to his credit, had managed to wait an entire five minutes for Aoife to hug Maura once more and make plans to share breakfast in the morning before pulling the fae away and leading her out the door.

As nice as the silence was though, Aoife could not seem to quiet her mind.

They had gone over the plan several times to ensure everyone was clear on what part each person would play. Now her head spun as thoughts of all they had to do crowded her mind, as if she was afraid she would fail them all if she stopped focusing on the plan for even a moment.

Focus on the next task, she reminded herself.

That would be easier if she could pinpoint what the next task was.

All she could see was the daunting challenge before them, and no matter how much she tried to pick it apart into individual tasks, it didn't work. Like a cloud of flies that disperse when swatted at only to come back together as soon as the hand is gone, the tasks refused to be isolated from one another for long before they snapped back into one overwhelming plan.

Throwing herself on the bed, Aoife buried her face in her pillow to drown out all the noise in her head. She had faced her mother and the kraken and the damned siren queen herself, and yet still her anxiety remained. Would she never be free from its grip?

Breathe.

She counted as she inhaled, imagining the breath clearing away all the noise in her mind and the tension in her neck. But at the top of her inhale, all the stress and worry slammed back into her, and she exhaled with a muffled scream of frustration into the pillow.

A weight settled between her shoulder blades and then moved down her spine.

"Breathe." Declan rubbed Aoife's back with firm but gentle strokes as he spoke. "It's okay. You're okay. Just breathe."

Aoife turned her head toward his voice but kept her eyes closed as she listened to the steadiness of his breathing. Then she let her own match it and waited for the worry to ease.

"Better?" Declan asked after a few moments.

Humming in affirmation, Aoife opened her eyes to look at him, but she couldn't think of anything worth saying. Declan lowered himself down to lie on his side next to her, his hand never lifting from the small of her back.

"Do you think we'll really be okay?" she asked quietly.

He was silent long enough to make her heart start thumping faster again.

"I think..." he started, and Aoife held her breath as she waited for whatever bad news he was about to drop on her. His mouth pulled back into his usual half-smile. "We will always be okay as long as we're together."

"And what if we get separated again?" Aoife tried to keep her lips from quivering as the fear crept back in. "It happened once. We can't—"

"I won't let that happen again, princess." Declan sounded so confident, and Aoife wished she could find some of that confidence for herself. All she could see were the myriad ways their plans could go wrong. She didn't want to think about that though. Didn't want to focus on the negatives. She needed to change the subject.

"When this is all done..." she said, immediately second-guessing her choice of topic. But before she could change her mind, Declan turned to look at her, his eyebrow raised expectantly. "Where will you go?"

His gray eyes bored into her as confusion washed over his face. "You mean where will *we* go."

She nodded, and his expression shifted until he looked almost hopeful.

"Have anywhere in mind?" he asked.

Shrugging slowly, Aoife held his gaze, wishing she could avoid all that lay ahead and simply stay here with him forever.

"You know, I was just wondering about this while I was on Helles."

"Oh?"

"Aye. Wondered what you might want, and if I..." His voice faded as he lowered his eyes.

"If you what?"

"If I could actually give you what you want."

What in the world was this man thinking? And then the question was out of her mouth before she could think better of it.

"What is wrong with you?" Aoife searched his face, but he still didn't look up at her. Easing her hand out of his grasp, she lifted it to his jaw and pulled his face up. But she couldn't read his expression, couldn't discern whether it was sadness or worry or guilt darkening his gray eyes. "Where did all of this doubt come from?"

"It's always been there," he admitted. "Just harder to hide from you now."

"What I want is *you*, Declan. Just like I said before. I choose you, and I don't care where we go or what we do, as long as we are together."

Declan swallowed hard as he stared back at her. "Wherever you want. That's where we will go. When all this is done, I'll take you anywhere."

Aoife's core tightened, though she knew he hadn't meant it in a suggestive way. Her body reacted all the same.

"Take me here?"

The question sounded ridiculous, and Declan must have thought so too. He narrowed his eyes at her.

Without another word, she lifted herself to sit in his lap, straddling his legs. He didn't move, didn't say anything, just watched her as she inched her face toward his. When he licked his lips slowly, she couldn't keep her own from slipping into an easy smile.

Her body begged her to hurry up, to answer its pleas for release, to be filled and pleased and consumed by him. But Aoife refused to rush this. She was going to savor the desire in his eyes, relish the feel of him hardening against her, enjoy the power she had over him in this moment. A power he willingly allowed her to wield.

Declan gripped her hips, dug his fingers into the flesh of her backside, and pulled her closer to him. Her breaths became ragged. He was going to make this difficult to take slowly, wasn't he?

Can you blame him?

No. She couldn't.

In one swift movement, she grasped the hem of her shirt and lifted. No sooner had she gotten it over her head than his mouth was on her breast, his tongue working its magic against one sensitive peak while his fingers teased the other. Aoife's head fell back, and she released a breathy laugh as her fingers got lost in his hair, not wanting him to ever stop.

"You'll take me anywhere?" Aoife asked, but her voice was little more than lust-filled air.

He hummed against her breast.

Gripping his hair, she pulled his head back until he looked her in the eye. Gone was any of his earlier doubt or worry or sadness. There was only a burning need and a flaring desire.

For her and her alone.

She pulled her lower lip between her teeth and breathed out a ragged exhale.

"Take me here," she whispered.

Something dangerous flashed in his eyes. A devilish smirk appeared on his lips.

"Take me here, what?" he asked.

Her core fluttered at the raw need in his voice, and she rolled her hips against him with a delicious slowness as she answered him.

"Take me here, *Captain*."

He crashed into her.

His lips claimed hers as his hands and hips and body pushed her backwards until her body slammed onto the bed.

When she tried to wrap her legs around him, he stopped her, his hands pushing her thighs back down.

"You told me to take you, princess," he scolded her. "So lie back like a good girl and let me."

A tremor ran through her at his command, and she eagerly obliged, pressing her head back against the pillow and closing her eyes.

Raising her arms, she ran her hands over her face before burying her fingers in her hair, and when his uneven breaths gave way to a rumble of desire thrumming in his chest, she couldn't stop her body from arching toward him.

Then her pants slipped away.

And his fingers whispered over her legs.

Spreading them apart. Opening her for him.

Aoife froze.

Every nerve and muscle and tendon pulled tight.

His breath, his tongue, his lips.

Why wasn't he using them as she wanted, as she needed?

Instead they were staying irritatingly far away from the burning ache that blazed hotter every time he touched her hips and stomach and breasts.

Please, she begged silently. She opened her mouth to say it aloud, but he stole her words, pulling a growl of a moan from her instead as his body met hers.

Slowly—so damned slowly—he shifted.

This was torture.

This was heaven.

Declan.

His name filled her mind and slipped from her lips as her hands found his back, her nails digging into his shoulders as he moved with her.

Everything fell away—the dagger, the council, the danger—as they drove each other toward the blissful end they both craved. When they tumbled over the edge together, lips capturing the sounds of their shared rapture, Aoife knew.

Declan had been wrong.

She didn't deserve more than him. More than this.

This—this man, this love—was more than she had ever dreamed of, more than she deserved.

Declan might believe himself broken and guilty, but she was too.

And somehow they had found each other, saved each other.

Not just from the pirates in Foxhaven or the siren queen, but from themselves and the darkness and pain that plagued them both.

With each kind word, each touch, each kiss, each act of surrender, they found healing, their fractured hearts and bruised souls mending bit by bit.

Whether they deserved it or not, this love was theirs.

And Aoife wasn't going to let anyone take it from them—not her mother, not the king, not anyone.

CHAPTER 43
CAIT

CAIT COULDN'T REMEMBER the last time she had felt at peace like this, even at her happiest, before her parents' deaths. Sighing contentedly against Adler's chest, she fluttered her eyes open and found herself staring into two mesmerizing pools of blue.

"Morning, love," Adler said, placing a kiss in her hair.

"How is it morning already?"

"Night went by entirely too fast for me too." He pulled her tighter against him. His fingertips made slow circles against her bare thigh, a move so simple yet so effective at sparking the fire he'd kept burning for most of the night.

Placing a finger on his chin, she nudged him to face her and then stretched up so their lips could meet. Every sweep of his tongue against hers, perfectly in time with the movement of his fingers upon her leg, sent a new blast of shivers along her nerves. And soon enough, she was silently begging him, pleading with him, coaxing him to give her all she needed.

In one easy motion, he had her atop him. She pressed her breasts firmly against his muscled chest, and her legs dropped to either side of his. His kiss deepened, and her hips rolled slowly against his in response until a soft grumble resonated in his chest.

A knock at the door had her burying her face in his neck and groaning.

"Go away!" Cait answered.

Kira slid the door open.

"I certainly will not," she said as she carried two plates of food into the room and set them on the table in the corner. "I'm not about to let this food go to waste or get cold simply because you two can't control yourselves."

She turned to face them, not in the least bit fazed at the sight of them in bed.

Cait's stomach rumbled at the aroma of the eggs and meat and bread, and she quickly scrambled off Adler, pulling the sheet up over her breasts as she did so.

"Thank you, Kira," she said. "Smells delicious."

Adler sat up and draped his arm across Cait's shoulders. Though he spoke to Kira, he kept his gaze fixed on Cait. "Aye, thank you."

Smiling, Kira shook her head and flitted about the room collecting items of clothing and tossing them onto the bed.

"What's so funny?" Cait asked before retrieving her shirt.

Kira straightened and placed her hands at her waist. "What makes you think I find this funny?"

'Just assumed, I suppose. Would seem weird if—"

"If I was actually happy for you? Aye, that would be weird. Weird for me to be elated that a friend has allowed herself to be happy for once?" Kira rolled her eyes, but a small hint of her smile remained. "Do you think so little of me?"

Cait laughed as she slipped her shirt over her head. Swinging her legs over the side of the bed, she pulled on her undergarments and skirts, then turned to face Kira.

"Of course not. It's simply that, for as long as I've known you, you've never been one to show such emotions. Sarcasm, yes. Irritation, of course. Concern?"

"Don't forget lust, love," Adler added from where he still sat shirtless, leaning against the wall.

"What?" Cait and Kira asked in unison.

Adler's mouth curved into his signature smile, and he shrugged. "You don't remember how she eyed me back at the ruins? When I first arrived?"

Cait swung her attention to Kira, but the fae—*demi-fae*—donned a bored expression.

"What can I say?" she asked. "I may be more than twice your age and part fae, but I'm not dead and can appreciate a pretty face when I see it."

"You weren't looking at my face," Adler said with a laugh.

"Are you two done?" Cait raised her arms to her sides before striding over to the table and shoving a piece of fried meat into her mouth.

Kira leaned forward and, cupping a hand around her mouth, said—not even trying to whisper—"A bit jealous, isn't she?"

"I am not," Cait said around a mouthful of bread, trying not to cringe at how defensive she sounded. "You missed your chance at him."

"Never wanted one," Kira said.

Adler breathed out a string of laughs. "Well, I guess fae can lie after all."

"That reminds me." Kira reached into her back pocket and pulled out an official-looking envelope. "This came for you."

Cait raised a hand to take it from her, but Kira was already leaning toward Adler and handing it over to him instead.

Why would he be getting messages here?

Oh, stop being so paranoid, she thought. *He works here. Everyone is aware of it. Where else would he receive messages?*

But *who* would be sending him a message?

Cait's mind raced, and her heart pounded with each possibility.

Tiernen?

Lucy?

Certainly not Lucan. He would know better.

"It's from the council," Adler said as he read over the contents of the envelope.

Cait snapped her focus to him, and her jaw clenched with unease at how unperturbed he appeared. Like he'd been expecting to hear from them. Why would he—

"I went to see them, remember?" he said, as if he sensed her rising suspicions.

Cait barely noticed when Kira cleared her throat and started to back away toward the door, and she didn't say anything when her friend apologized and excused herself from the room and the conversation.

"Oh come now, love," Adler said as soon as the door was shut. He stood from the bed, not bothering to cover himself up as he strode toward her.

"Can you put some damned pants on?" Cait asked, trying not to let her eyes wander.

Adler smirked at her. Those damned blue eyes sparkled at her, though they didn't hold the same mischievousness they had before. He merely nodded and obliged, slipping his pants on before approaching her.

"It's an invitation." He held up the message and gave it a small shake.

Cait recoiled slightly, as if he were carrying some poisonous animal rather than a harmless piece of paper. "An invitation to what?"

"Dinner tonight," Adler said and held it out to her.

Though she took the paper from him, she refused to read it, instead keeping her eyes locked on his. "What dinner, Adler?"

She didn't know what was going on or what to think of it, but she recognized the tightening of her gut and the heaviness in her chest. Something wasn't right here. This wasn't good. And Adler had something to do with it.

That last one made this situation far worse. This wasn't simply the council's doing.

He held his hands up before him, palms toward her in preemptive surrender, before he said, "As a thank you for that little stunt of mine with Lucan, they wanted me to attend the dinner they're holding in honor of King Kilmeran's visit."

The constriction worsened with each word he uttered. But that wasn't all. He was leaving something out.

You're just being impatient. Give him a chance to explain.

"And? Why are you looking at me as if I might want to stab you?" she asked.

Adler scratched the back of his neck before running his hand up through this hair. "Because you might?"

Cait stepped forward, crumpling the message in her fist. Through gritted teeth she asked, "What did you do, Adler?"

"Before you get mad, love—"

She glared at him and shoved the envelope into his chest so hard he had to take a step back. "Tell me. Now. Or so help me—"

"You're coming with me," he said before she could finish her threat.

Her hand darted to her mouth, and around her trembling fingers she whispered, "What did you do?"

"I didn't plan to. They extended the invitation, and before I could think better about it, I asked if I could bring someone with me. When they heard it was a local business owner, they seemed quite amenable, excited even."

"I can't—" Cait shook her head. Her vision blurred. Her leg throbbed where they had rubbed the flesh away from the bone. "How could you think—"

"It was before I found out they took you. Before I saw what they did. Please, love, you have to know I'd never knowingly put you in this position."

Adler reached for her, and Cait had to force herself not to flinch away from his touch.

She could trust him.

She could.

She had to hold onto that trust if she was going to survive this and anything that came from it.

"I would say you don't have to go," Adler said, still holding onto her shoulders, his thumbs offering reassuring strokes in time with his words.

"But if I don't go, they will..." Cait couldn't bear to surmise what the council might do if he showed up without the date he had requested an invitation for.

"I could take Penny?" Adler offered, his eyes searching hers.

"No, I can do this." She drew in a deep breath, forcing her mind to clear.

"You can, but you don't have to." Adler started to pull her closer, but Cait put a hand on his chest and stopped him.

"I need to."

He nodded solemnly at her, pressing his lips into a thin line. But he said nothing more as he watched her process the situation.

This could work. She could make this work.

Overthrowing the council tonight was unlikely—if not impossible—but perhaps she could gather information at this dinner to help defeat them later.

But there was only one problem—aside from the obvious discomfort of having to face them.

Cait looked down between them and dropped both hands to her skirts. "I don't have anything nicer to wear than this though. I can't go in these."

Adler placed a finger under her chin and lifted her face until their eyes met.

"Don't worry about that, love. I will take care of it."

⚔

AFTER BREAKFAST WAS EATEN and the dishes had been returned to the small kitchen downstairs, Adler departed, promising to be back after lunch so they could get ready together. Cait could have stayed in the apartment, but even knowing Kira was downstairs preparing the pub for opening that afternoon, she couldn't concentrate. She needed to think, to prepare. And she couldn't do that here.

So she headed to her mother's old office.

Settling into the desk chair, she lifted her legs onto the desktop and crossed them at the ankles. Releasing a deep breath, she stared at the ceiling, and before she knew it, tears were pricking her eyes.

Mother? What do I do?

Silently she reached out to her mother's ghost for help, though she knew it was pointless. Her mother was gone. Her father too. And she had pushed Declan away. Would he bring the dagger to them? If the sirens were correct, he had succeeded in acquiring it, but she had always known it was a risk asking him to get it for them, always knew he might very well betray her and keep it for himself.

But her hope had won out, and she had asked him anyway.

Or maybe it had only been her desperation that pushed her to ask him.

Even if he did bring it, though, it was too late. The king was here, if the rumors Kira had heard around town were true.

And tonight she would have to face both him and the council. He was an unknown entity. Sure, there were rumors about what he was offering to the council and what threat he might be to the people of Cregah, but rumors were inherently flawed. They rarely told the whole story. Yes, there was usually some truth to them, but relying on them too much was a dangerous tactic for anyone, especially the leader of the rogues.

Cait closed her eyes but didn't sleep. Her mind raced through everything she knew and all that she still didn't. She hadn't had time to root out the spy in her ranks, and now she would have to go into the council hall and face her enemy not knowing who she could trust.

Kira and Adler were the only two she trusted completely.

And Lucan of course, but he was still confined to the cove, unable to show his face.

He couldn't help them tonight. And he wouldn't have a chance to help at all if they somehow managed to defeat them at this dinner.

A laugh, soft and quiet, escaped her at that notion.

How absurd to think she and Adler could take down the council at a dinner party. Especially with a foreign king present.

Unless the king is actually on your side.

It was the first time she'd ever considered that possibility, and as ridiculous as it sounded, she couldn't ignore the idea completely. Maybe this king wanted the council unseated as much as she and the rogues did.

Or he's just out for his own gain. Like most royalty.

Yes, that was more likely.

But Cait would need to be prepared for either situation.

Still, there was little she and Adler could hope to accomplish at this dinner without the Csintala dagger in hand. Without that enchanted weapon to guarantee them victory over those women, Cait needed to accept that this would be nothing more than a reconnaissance mission. They could learn the dynamics between the king and the councilwomen and discover what their plans were.

Then once Declan arrived with the dagger, they would be able to formulate a concrete plan.

The door to her office opened with a scraping sound of wood against stone, and Cait was up in an instant, the blade from her boot already in hand.

"Nice reflexes, love," Adler said with a cocky grin. "But it's only me."

Cait dropped the small knife onto the desktop before moving around the desk and sofa toward him. "You could have knocked."

"Aye, that would have been smarter, but it was a little hard to do with my hands full." He lifted his arms to emphasize the wrapped bundles he carried.

"From the same stash you got those cloaks from?" Cait asked.

"Aye," Adler said, then settled himself onto the sofa and motioned for her to follow him with a quick nod. "Now, love, don't be offended when I tell you I didn't choose this dress specifically for you." He untied the twine that secured the top package as he spoke, dropping it onto the floor once he slid it away. Peeling the brown paper open, he said, "This was to be a gift for my baby sister. It's a bit large for her, but our mother will be able to adjust it to fit her. It should, though, fit you decently."

He lifted the dress up for Cait to see, his eyes shining with hopeful curiosity as he watched her look it over.

It was a bright blue color, nearly the exact shade as the eyes staring at her—a blue so vibrant she never imagined anyone could possibly replicate it, let alone recreate it on such a gorgeous garment. Tears welled up in her eyes as she brushed her fingers lightly over the smooth satin skirt, marveling at the detailed beading that covered the bodice.

"So I can assume you approve?" Adler's question was laced with a humor Cait couldn't possibly be annoyed with, not when he was offering her such an extravagant gift.

Blast these damned tears!

She wasn't the type to get all emotional, especially over a bloody dress!

But her mind had wandered beyond her current situation to dreams and hopes of a life unburdened by rebellions and tyrants and dangerous dinners, a life where she could simply enjoy an evening of elegance with the man she loved.

"I love it," she whispered. "It's perfect."

"Well, don't say that yet. We still don't know if it fits."

Cait didn't need to be persuaded any further. She snatched the dress from his hand in a heartbeat. She had already dropped her skirts onto the floor and was stepping into the gown by the time Adler stood, set the other package on the sofa, and moved toward her.

"Let me help," he whispered and took a hold of the dress so she could lift her shirt over her head. The cold air of the office hit her skin, and her shoulders shook with the resulting shudder. She couldn't help but smile at seeing his eyes fixed on her bare breasts. Even after they were covered up by the luxurious fabric, his gaze remained firmly fixed.

"Are you going to be able to focus at this dinner, love?" Cait said.

Adler swallowed hard and then smirked at her. "Aye. It won't be easy, but I'll do my best."

Lifting her hair off her neck, Cait spun slowly around and spoke over her shoulder. "Button me up?"

She shivered again when Adler's fingertips grazed the length of her neck and shoulder, tracing the edge of the dress. Her breath caught when his fingers trailed down to just above her backside.

When his breath caressed her ear, her eyes fell closed in anticipation.

"You sure you want that, love?" She nodded slowly, but he laughed quietly against her skin and whispered, "Liar."

Before she could come up with a retort, his lips were on her, bestowing kisses behind her ear and down her neck. Leaning into his touch, she reached her hand up behind his head, losing her fingers in his hair and keeping him from pulling away.

His hands crawled up her ribs, slipping beneath the rich fabric and snaking around to graze her stomach and tease her breast with his fingers.

"Take it off before I rip it off you, love," he commanded, releasing a growl that had her core bursting into flames. Pressing her backside against him, her breath fell heavy with desire.

The dress had barely hit the floor when his hands were at her hips, pulling her hard against him before sliding down the front of her, taking her undergarments with them. One of his hands found its way between her thighs. He moaned against her neck, his teeth nipping at her skin as his fingers pulled whimpers of ecstasy from deep within her.

She leaned into him, his name falling from her lips. But instead of giving her what she wanted—what she needed—he was pulling away. Before she knew what was happening, he had her turned around and laid out on the sofa, his blue eyes burning with a feral desperation that made her insides curl and twist and yearn for him. She reached for his neck, needing his lips on hers, but he pulled out of her grasp, giving her an almost evil grin.

"No, love."

She couldn't even muster a frown before his hands had her legs spread open and his head was between them.

Sands, she'd wanted his lips on her—right there, yes, right there—since he'd first explored her the night before, but now?

A swear slipped from her on a breathless whisper as her fingers fisted in his hair. She held him against her, rolling her hips in perfect time with the circles his tongue was tracing around that perfect spot. The delicious act sent her toes curling and her eyes rolling back. Then the circles slowed and turned to long strokes that pulled out a moan so low and deep she wasn't sure it had come from her.

Sipping and circling and twirling and lapping, he savored and devoured and completely undid her until she didn't know where she was or who she was or anything beyond his tongue and her desperate need for him to take her apart nerve by blessed nerve.

His name filled the small room as he picked up his pace, his hunger for her evident by the desperate flicks of his tongue. She pressed into him, needing him. And he gave into her demands, touching her in all the right places and in all the right ways until she was rocking hard against his lips, pushing herself toward that edge she craved.

Except she didn't want it to be over.

But there. *Yes! There!*

No. Not yet. Not yet.

A groan of both pleasure and protest thrummed through her just as she began to slip over the edge and plummet into utter bliss.

But he pulled back.

Startled, she opened her eyes to find him smiling at her from between her thighs with that devilish smirk.

"Will you scream for me, love?"

His voice had Cait clenching her teeth, her body flinching and begging him to resume his skilled work and just finish her off already.

"You'll need to try a bit harder if it's my screams you want," she said with as sharp a glare as she could muster. "And I'm not so sure—"

With a cocky gleam in his eye, he lowered his head and picked up where he had so cruelly left off, pulling her effortlessly back to the edge, where she writhed against him.

And then, everything hit at once as he forced her over the precipice, her body shaking and pulsing and tightening until she screamed his name louder than she had let herself in the pub.

Or ever.

Sighing, he pulled away from her, kissing the insides of her thighs and pulling giggles from her as she continued to come down from her peak.

"Sands," she breathed. "Use your tongue like that on me again? I'll scream whatever you want."

Then his nose was nuzzling hers, and her eyes fluttered open to find him staring at her with love and devotion. She couldn't help but pull his lips to hers, to kiss him and show him she returned his love a million times over.

"I'll remember that," he said when he retreated to look at her once more.

She flashed him a smirk of her own. "My turn to make you scream?"

His blue eyes burned bright, but he slowly shook his head. "Later."

Something in Cait deflated, just a little, but she shook away the small feeling of rejection. "You do love to torture me, don't you?" she asked him, but she knew it had been the wrong choice of words when she saw his lust for her fade, concern and worry overshadowing it.

He sat up, pulling her legs across his lap. His fingers hovered over her wounds, but he said nothing. He swallowed hard. Drew in a deep breath. And then he looked at her with his jaw set firmly, determined.

"They will pay for this." He paused as he rested his hand lightly on her bandages. "I will end them. I promise."

The weight of his words lay heavy on Cait's chest, but when she saw the deadliness in his eyes, she had no doubt he would see his promise to the end.

Even if it meant his own.

CHAPTER 44
MAURA

They arrived in Morshan late in the afternoon, with plenty of daylight remaining. Maura hoped they weren't too late to stop the king—and her brother—from striking a deal with the council. Declan and Aoife planned to wait until dusk to go ashore—to lessen the likelihood that someone might recognize them—but Maura couldn't wait that long.

"I'm coming with you," Tommy said as he entered their quarters and closed the door behind him.

Maura nodded. "I know."

"I've let Declan know the change in our plans. He wasn't happy, but I assured him we would be ready when he needed us." Tommy didn't move away from the door as he spoke, apprehension evident in his rigid posture.

Maura crossed the small space and placed her hands on his chest. His amber eyes glowed with worry.

"It's going to be okay, Tommy."

He didn't move. Didn't nod or hug her or even blink.

"It will," she said. "As long as we're together, we will be okay." Maura searched his eyes but could see no sign that she was helping. His heartbeat, while steady, remained elevated. "We're just going to find my brother. That's it."

Tommy let out a single nervous laugh. "Oh, you mean the powerful fae with phantom hands or whatever you call them? Just going to confront the brother who you thought was dead but is now working for a king who has no problem using him to kill innocent people."

Maura shrugged. "Technically we don't know that Lucy was innocent—"

That earned her a scowl.

"Not the point, Maura, and you know that. I don't like it."

"You don't have to like it." Maura stepped back. "You don't even have to come with me, but I'm going, and I would prefer to have you beside me."

For a moment, he didn't respond.

Would he refuse to go with her?

Would he try to stop her?

Would anyone in her life trust her enough to let her make her own damned decisions?

Tommy's shoulders slumped. He stepped toward her. "No, I'm going. We've faced sea monsters and sirens. What's a surprise fae brother?"

THE COUNCIL HALL looked much as it had when Maura had first visited the queen before the war. The ivy growing up the stone walls was a little fuller maybe, but Maura's memory had dimmed with the centuries.

Some things never faded away though.

The loneliness in that room, even with her sisters there.

The despair of a wasted life.

The fear that she would never be free.

Frozen at the edge of the gardens, Maura stared up at the looming stone building.

"You can do this." Tommy gave Maura's hand a squeeze, but she couldn't pull her eyes away from her former prison.

She couldn't do this. What if Melina caught her? What if she was thrown back into that room or into one of the barred cells in the basement? A fate worse than death.

How could she have thought she could do this?

Because you've faced worse and survived, she told herself.

You can do this too.

But she was shaking her head.

"You'll be okay, remember? As long as we're together," Tommy reminded her.

This was foolish. If they were caught, they wouldn't be held together. They'd be separated. Tommy could be injured just as he had been the last time he was here. And if she was locked up, there'd be no way for him to be healed. Not with her sisters far off on the sea.

Liam.

Her brother's face flashed in her mind.

Maura wasn't the only fae on this island, and maybe he would be willing to help her. Help them.

As if her thoughts had summoned him, Liam strolled into view. With his hands buried in his pockets, he slowly walked around the perimeter of the building. Though he appeared to simply be out for a casual walk, Maura knew he was inspecting the grounds and the building. His phantom powers were likely testing for any weaknesses like loose grates, windows with broken locks, or anything else that might put the king at risk.

"Is that him?" Tommy whispered, and as expected, Liam angled his head slightly toward them, but he didn't look their way, nor did his stride falter.

Maura glared at Tommy and gave him a sharp nod. Thankfully he didn't say more as she prepared to call on her *daemari*. Her powers thrummed as the image of their surroundings was projected around them, cloaking them from being seen.

By everyone except her brother.

With Tommy's hand in hers, Maura stepped out into the clearing and walked directly for Liam, who had nearly finished checking the north side of the building and would soon round the corner.

Maura raised her chin, trying to relax her clenched jaw. All this time and he couldn't even look at her. "Hello, brother," she said, her voice icier than she'd intended.

He didn't seem to notice or care.

"You shouldn't be here, Maura," Liam said, only sparing a quick glance her way before continuing on with his security checks, albeit at a slower pace.

Maura ignored how Tommy tensed beside her but gave him a reassuring look. "How are you alive, Liam? And why are you with the king?"

He didn't say a word as he disappeared between two bushes. Maura and Tommy followed. Between the bushes lay a door with a small stoop just large enough—and concealed enough—for the three of them to stand hidden.

Assuming no one comes bursting through this door, she thought.

But Liam didn't look too worried about that possibility.

"Save your strength and lose the glamour," he said gently, but Maura kept her gaze locked on her brother's vibrant teal and purple eyes. "You haven't gotten any more trusting, have you, sister?"

"Can you blame me?" she challenged.

"You trust this pirate though?" His eyes shot to Tommy with a look of haughty disdain.

"Aye." She might not be able to trust Liam—not yet—but she could trust her own senses. They were safe. At least for now, and whether she wanted to admit it or not, her brother was right. She would need all her energy if they were to face the council soon.

As she let the glamour fall away, Tommy's grip on her hand tightened. Liam continued to stare at him, but it wasn't Tommy her brother addressed when he spoke again.

"Does your man ever speak?"

Giving a casual shrug, Tommy answered, "Aye."

Liam leaned forward expectantly and, when Tommy said nothing more, laughed quietly. "I'm going to like this one, Maura. Much better than the last one. What was his name?"

Maura scowled. "Even if my memories weren't a jumbled mess right now, none of those bastards were worth the time I wasted with them."

She darted a glance at Tommy to check how he was handling this turn in the conversation. Would he be jealous? Would he hate hearing that she'd had other relationships?

But if he cared, he showed no indication, and when he turned to meet her gaze, he gave a small laugh and dropped his lips to her ear.

"Relax, Maura," he whispered. "I know you're mine now. That's all that matters."

Maura nestled into the warmth of his lips, and she might have let her eyes close had her brother not cleared his throat.

"If that's all that matters, you're all going to die. And soon," Liam said.

Maura snapped her attention to him. "What are you—"

Like an exasperated parent, Liam rubbed his fingers along his forehead before running them through his mess of hair. "It's going to take more than some lovey-dovey feelings to help you survive what's coming."

Maura scoffed quietly, but Tommy responded, not sounding the least bit offended. "Survive what, exactly?"

Liam looked from Maura to Tommy and back again. "I do like this one. Direct. No nonsense." He leaned in closer to her, though he didn't bother to lower his voice at all. "That's why you like him, isn't it? Knows what he wants? Takes it?"

Maura rolled her eyes and raised a hand to swat him away, but he was faster than her and just laughed again. His attention returned to Tommy, who stood quietly awaiting an answer.

"My apologies. It's been a long time since I've..." Liam's expression clouded over, like someone recalling a painful memory, but he recovered quickly. "Well, that's no matter. The king has plans to strike a deal with the council." And this time, he did lower his voice when he inched closer to both of them. "He's going to nullify the treaty, ban piracy, and eventually eliminate the council as well."

That didn't sound too terrible. But Tommy flinched almost imperceptibly, and his breath caught for a moment. His amber eyes focused on nothing. He swallowed hard.

"Your love here gets it," Liam said, tossing his chin toward Tommy.

"Aye," Tommy said, "and it gets worse."

"Wait, wait," Maura said, turning toward him. "Before we get to the 'worse' part, tell me what all of that means."

Tommy blinked slowly before answering. "It means all the pirates will be hunted down. No treaty means no safe harbor. And as bad as the council is for the Cregahn people, we have no idea what sort of rule will rise up to take its place."

"Now how does it get worse?" Liam's question yanked Maura back to the conversation. All the former humor was gone from his voice.

"The Csintala dagger," Tommy said. Liam's eyes went wide. "It's here."

A deep growl rumbled from her brother's chest, so sudden and so fierce that Maura actually flinched.

"You didn't," Liam bit out. His eyes flashed to Maura's. "You couldn't be this stupid, Maura."

Maura cowered slightly at his insult. Tommy pulled his hand free from hers and rested it at the small of her back as he glared at Liam, as if the fae wasn't a head taller and far stronger than he was. Before Tommy could say anything though, Maura jabbed a finger into Liam's chest and shook her head once.

"Stupid or not, Liam, it is what it is. You can either help us or get out of our way."

For several breaths, no one spoke. Liam's eyes swirled with anger and excitement.

Maura eyed him curiously. "Can't you use your *daemari* against the council? I saw you use it on that beach. You could do the same to Melina."

He closed his eyes and drew in one more long breath, then growled out a sigh. He shook his head before letting his chin fall against his chest.

"I can't. I'm tied to the king."

And he dared to call me *stupid? What was he thinking?*

"What does that mean?" Tommy asked with genuine concern in his voice.

Maura kept her eyes on her brother. "He's bound to serve him, to protect him."

"And to not use my *daemari* without his direction," Liam muttered.

Tommy stepped around Maura and caught her eye. "But you and your sisters broke the bond to Melina when you left the council hall with us. Didn't you?"

"It wasn't the same type of bond. We vowed to serve her with words only. We didn't take walking away from her lightly. Liam, however, is bound by...blood?"

Her brother nodded and looked up.

"Why?" Maura couldn't understand what could have possibly compelled her brother to do this.

"I'm actually tied to his bloodline. When the Caprothen king—this king's ancestor—found me, he offered to save my life during the war if—"

"If you pledged fealty to them?" Maura asked.

Liam nodded. "You need to leave. Take your freedom and your love and whatever else you have and sail far away from here."

"Like a damned coward? No." Maura scowled at him. He seriously underestimated her if he thought she could turn her back on her friends, let alone an entire nation.

"You're going to get hurt."

"I've been hurt before."

"Not like this. I can't lose—"

"No, Liam," Maura snapped. Damned fae and their protective nature. "You don't get to use that line on me. Not here. Not now. Not ever!" She stepped closer to him, regretting how it pulled her away from Tommy's touch. "We thought you were dead! We mourned you for decades! We—"

Liam's eyes flashed. "You are not the only ones who lost someone that day! I lost my sisters! A father! Brothers! Friends! Don't for one second think that I didn't try to come for you."

He came for us?

His words slammed into her, reminding her of the argument she'd had with Renna on the *Siren's Song*. Maura shook her head. She couldn't believe it. Could she? But when she searched her brother's eyes, all she found was a broken and battered soul, a heart shattered by loss, a male torn apart by guilt.

"I only tied myself to the Kilmerans so I could one day find you again, but I didn't get the chance until now."

Before she could reconsider it, she wrapped her arms around his waist as she had done so many times when they were younger. As his arms settled around her, Maura let his scent carry her back to memories that now seemed clearer somehow. The day their mother had been killed, he'd held her much like this, and his steady heartbeat and his comforting warmth had calmed her.

A gentle clearing of a throat from behind pulled her out of the past, out of her brother's embrace, and she turned to Tommy, who looked as overcome with emotion as she was. Maura reached back with her hand and let him guide her to him.

"I'm sorry," Liam and Maura said in unison, and had the situation been different, she might have laughed.

Liam shoved his hands back into his pockets and gave them a tight-lipped smile. "Kilmeran wants that dagger."

"So does Melina," Tommy said.

Maura's eyes shifted between them. "If she gets it, she will have her powers back."

"And two of us against her will not be enough. We won't be able to stop her." Liam steeled his features until all emotion lay hidden once more.

Tommy pulled Maura tight to his side. "Then we don't let her get it."

A SHIVER SWEPT across Declan's shoulders as he walked down the cobbled streets toward the pub. It had only been a few weeks since he'd last been here, but that time, he'd been angry at being summoned, even though Cait had had the information he needed.

Maybe you should have stayed on your ship that night, his thoughts challenged him.

If he hadn't come ashore that night, he never would have been caught by Callum.

He never would have gotten Killian killed.

He never would have killed Collins.

Aoife laced her fingers with his, and the sight of her dissolved all his negative thoughts. Her freckles had become more prominent across her cheeks from the sun, and her green eyes sparkled with hope in the light of the lanterns lining the street.

He'd do it all again for this woman.

If he hadn't come ashore, he never would have gone to the cove. She never would have followed him aboard his ship. They never would have—

"Are you sure no one will recognize me?" Aoife asked, whispering her question into her shoulder as if someone on the street might hear her. Declan peered around and laughed when he saw only a handful of people at the far end of the street.

"They didn't recognize you that night," he offered with a shrug.

"That we know of."

She had a point. If someone had recognized her, how would he have known?

"We could kill them," he said, keeping his focus straight ahead. When she didn't respond right away, he side-eyed her. He had expected to see her gawking at him with disgust like she had in the cove when he'd suggested they fight each other for the right to stay there. Instead, her face was pinched tight as if she were seriously contemplating it.

"I was joking," he said.

Aoife glanced at him quickly before returning her attention back to the street. "I knew that."

They turned the corner, and the familiar sign came into view.

Though he had Aoife's reassuring hand clasped in his, a sharp pang shot through his gut and up into his chest. His steps didn't falter. His muscles didn't tense. His breath didn't catch. But nothing could hide his unease from Aoife.

She gripped his hand tighter and whispered to him, "Breathe. It'll be okay."

He heeded her command, counting his breaths along with their steady footsteps until they reached the pub door. It was early enough that the pub should be nearly empty, and a glance through the window confirmed it. It would be harder to hide their faces with so few bodies crowding the space, but they hadn't been able to risk coming ashore too late. According to Maura, the king had seemed eager to meet with the council. No doubt that meeting would be happening as soon as possible, and Declan feared that would be tonight.

"Ready?" Aoife asked, squaring her shoulders and nodding toward the door.

"Aye," he said. Then he added in a whisper, "Ladies first."

He pulled the door open and ushered her inside, letting his fingers brush along the small of her back as she entered. The few patrons swiveled their heads toward the door. And just like that night several weeks ago, their eyes dropped to the teal sash at Declan's waist, noted the confidence in his gait, and then looked quickly away.

At least your reputation hasn't been hurt.

For a moment he regretted not taking Maura's suggestion to conceal his colors, but Halloran had rightly pointed out that the presence of the *Siren's Song* in the port would be more than enough to get word to spread quickly that Captain McCallagh was back on the island.

Better to use his reputation to his advantage.

At least he hoped it was still an advantage.

Declan guided Aoife toward the bar with slow, purposeful steps while he scanned the room quickly.

No sign of Cait.

Perhaps it was normal for her to not be manning the pub this early in the evening, but something twisted in his stomach. A warning.

Something was amiss.

Behind the bar, a woman—tall and lean with long, dark hair—dried a glass and watched them from beneath her lashes. There was something eerily familiar about her, and Declan wondered if he had seen her in here before. But no, it was more than that.

Aoife's hands fidgeted at her sides, but he couldn't reach out and calm her, could barely even glance down at her. The woman behind the bar glanced toward the back table—his usual—and slightly shifted her chin in the same direction.

After getting Aoife and himself settled into the two wooden chairs that backed against the dark wall, Declan took a deep breath and risked a whisper. "Recognize her?"

Aoife gave a nod. "The night I followed you. She was working with your sister."

Don't trust anyone.

Halloran's warning echoed in his mind. He would need to be careful here. If his sister had been able to get a spy into the council's employ, it would be foolish not to assume the opposite was possible.

The woman glided over with two glasses and a bottle of rum.

"The usual, Captain McCallagh?" the woman asked with a singsong quality that reminded him of Maura and her sisters. But it was her accent that gave him pause. It wasn't obvious, but it was there. It was unlike the accents of any of the men on his ship, and they hailed from all parts of the Aisling. It was unlike any he'd heard in the ports either. He had only heard that particular lilt once.

Killian.

Declan narrowed his eyes at her as his chest tightened. He gave her a tight nod.

Setting the glasses down, she poured a dram into each, never looking away from Declan.

And Aoife never took her gaze away from the woman.

"Settle that heart, Declan," the woman said, barely over a whisper.

Shit.

If she could hear his heartbeat thumping faster, she had to be...

"Sit," Declan said. This wasn't the ideal place for this conversation, but that pang of guilt in his chest gnawed at him. The woman didn't hesitate or even appear surprised by the command.

"What is it?" Aoife whispered at him, but he could only offer her a thin smile.

"If I had to guess," the woman said, leaning forward with her elbows on the table, "he's figured out who I am."

"Aye," Declan said around the ball of grief that had risen into his throat. He couldn't do this, but he had to. He wasn't ready.

When does life ever wait for us to be ready?

Below the table, Aoife's hand slid onto his leg, and that simple touch eased his mind, told him he wasn't alone in this. She might not know who this woman was, but she knew he needed her in this moment.

"Your brother," Declan started, but an image of Killian's bloodied face invaded his mind, paralyzing his voice before he could say more.

"Killian," the woman said. "I assumed you met him when I heard who had taken you. And I gather from your rapid heartbeat and the hitches in your breath that he's dead."

Shit. That last word punched him in the gut and pulled his jaw tight.

Declan's chin dropped a bit. He lowered his eyes to the table so she—and everyone else—wouldn't see the tears that had already gathered.

This won't help your reputation, he thought, and as much as he wanted to tell himself to forget about such things, he couldn't afford to. Pulling in a breath—and ignoring the familiar scent of the pub that threatened to drag him further under—he blinked away the sadness as best he could.

"How?" Her voice was low, but even that single word carried a lifetime's worth of love of a sister for her brother.

"Don't make him say it," Aoife said. There was a surprising calmness in her tone that had it coming out more as a command rather than a plea.

"That bad, huh?" The female lifted her brows for a moment before looking down at her hands. "I told him not to do it, but you pirates are a stubborn lot."

"I'm sorry," Declan said, and he wished there was more he could say, more he could do for the sister of the man who had saved him in that brig.

"I'm Kira," she said. "And I'm sorry too. You didn't deserve..." She turned her head away, and something shifted in Declan, like a loosening of shackles around his conscience. The guilt wasn't gone, but it was dampened, even if just a little.

Kira straightened in her seat and cleared her throat. "But that isn't why you're here."

Declan nodded once. "Is she here?"

"They left an hour ago." Kira's expression remained blank, as if Declan was supposed to already know what she meant.

Aoife's head fell to one side. "Who is *they*?"

"She and Adler—"

"He's here?" Though Aoife managed to keep her voice down, she wasn't as successful at controlling the look on her face. Her eyes went wide, and all color drained from her cheeks.

"What is he doing here?" Declan asked, though he already had an idea.

"Falling for your sister, that's what," Kira said to Declan.

"Wait, what?" Aoife's hoarse whisper was far from stealthy, but Declan couldn't find the will to care when the same question had been on the edge of his own tongue.

Kira shrugged, giving them a small smile. "She's happy, Declan. Let her have that."

It seemed an odd thing to say, as Declan didn't particularly care about his sister's love life. Aoife, on the other hand, tensed beside him.

The demi-fae's gaze softened as she turned to Aoife. "And Adler is happy too."

"Why would I care about his happiness?" Aoife nearly spat the words. "He obviously didn't love my sister if he's so quick to move on. She died for that man, and he's already—"

"And this?" Kira waved a hand between Declan and Aoife. "You two had a long courtship, did you?"

"That's...different," Aoife said. "Lani was leaving for *him*. She got *exiled* for *him*, and he just—"

"Came back to avenge her death?" Kira asked.

"Can't he do that without falling in love with the first woman he meets?" Aoife growled, and Declan tried not to laugh.

She really is cute when she's angry.

Aoife, staring coldly at Kira, continued her argument. "He's obviously not so broken up by her death if he can just give his heart to some wench so fast."

Kira opened her mouth to respond but stopped when Declan shook his head slightly.

He leaned close to Aoife. "You fell in love with me though."

Aoife pulled back and looked at him as if he had spoken nonsense. "That's different."

"Is it though?" Declan asked and then cringed. "Some might say it's worse, given my hand in her death and all."

Kira's brows shot up at his vague admission, but she said nothing.

"You had no choice though," Aoife countered.

"There's always a choice, Aoife. Remember?" Declan clasped his hand around hers under the table and gave it a light squeeze. "You don't have to like him, but try not to hate him."

"How are you okay with this exactly?" Aoife asked him. "She's your sister. Aren't you at all worried about her?"

Declan would have laughed had Aoife not pinned him with a glare. And if not for the audience, he would have pulled her close, but he had to settle for an easy smirk.

"Aye, she's my sister, and she can handle him herself."

Kira shifted closer once more. "Adler loves your sister. Both of your sisters actually. And if Lani was even half the woman he has described to me, she would be happy for him. Life is too short to hold onto our grief at the expense of our blessings."

Aoife slumped back in her chair. It would take her more than one evening to take any of Kira's words to heart, but Declan hoped she could keep this development from distracting her.

"Where were they going?" Declan asked.

Kira's face fell, her jaw growing tight.

This isn't good.

"Dinner with the council."

And the king, Declan thought. "How'd they get invited? They're not crashing the—"

Kira shook her head. "Long story."

"Speak fast," Aoife snapped, clearly not yet over the news of Adler and Cait.

Kira heaved a sigh. "Adler exiled Lucan—Cait's second—in the square where the councilwomen were speaking to the citizens. And before you ask, no, it wasn't real. They staged it. Adler had to report to the council afterward, and they apparently thanked him by offering him a seat at the dinner that's being held in honor of the king. He managed to request a seat for Cait as well."

"And this is happening tonight?" Declan asked, his stomach falling to his feet. *Please say no, please say no.*

"Aye, tonight. And soon. They should be on their way there now actually."

Aoife fidgeted in her seat for a moment. "And Lucan? Where did he go?"

Kira shrugged. "I don't know. Only Cait and Adler know. She's gotten quieter on details."

"Why is that?" Aoife challenged. "Aren't you two close?"

"Aye, but she can't be too careful these days."

Declan narrowed his eyes, worried he already knew what she was going to say.

"One of our people was found murdered in the square, and the rogues were blamed. We think someone may be feeding information to the council. We don't know who, but I have my suspicions."

Before Declan could ask who she suspected, the door crashed open, and several men—not pirates, though they didn't look like merchants either—walked in. Kira was out of her seat instantly, grabbing the bottle of rum as she did.

"Don't trust anyone, Declan," she whispered before cheerily greeting the newcomers.

Declan and Aoife stood promptly and headed for the door, but as they passed Kira, she extended her hand toward him. Clasping it, Declan said a farewell and pocketed the paper she had passed to him.

Aoife eyed him expectantly as they walked back to the ship, but he wasn't about to stop and read the note until they had reached his cabin.

They had just turned the last corner toward the docks when a man stepped out of the alley, blocking their way.

"McCallagh," he said. Not a question.

"Who?" Declan asked, donning his best look of confusion.

Aoife elbowed him. "Isn't that the name of the pub we just came from?"

"Maybe?" Declan looked back over his shoulder as if he could still see the pub's sign from here.

"Captain McCallagh," the man said again, no humor in his voice.

This man must be fun to have around.

"We know it's you," a new voice said from the darkness of the alley.

A woman stepped out into the lantern light. Her gaze dropped to his waist.

"Your colors," she said. "And your damned attitude. Much like your sister's actually. I'm Eva. This is my brother Aron. Cait asked us to watch for you."

Before Declan could say anything else, the brother spoke again. "She sent us to get the package from you, as she's currently indisposed. We're to bring it to her at the dinner."

Declan eyed them, every muscle in his body tightening in warning.

Don't trust anyone.

"She said you wouldn't trust us," Eva said. Her brother reached into his jacket and pulled out a note that looked nearly identical to the one Cait had sent to him several weeks ago.

Inside Declan found Cait's handwriting, her familiar scent.

Aoife glanced at him briefly but didn't let her eyes stray from the pair for long. "What's it say?"

Declan folded it and handed it to Aoife. "It's as they say. My sister sent them."

Then, reaching under his jacket, Declan found the dagger's handle and pulled it free. He stepped closer to Aron, clapped a hand on his shoulder, and held the blade out to him, handle first. To anyone on the street, they would appear to be old friends saying their goodbyes before parting ways.

Aron took the dagger, and the ominous pair nodded and turned back down the alley without another word.

"They could have at least said thank you," Declan said with a huffed laugh. He moved to continue toward the ship, but Aoife grabbed his arm.

"Declan, why did you do that?" she asked in a panicked tone.

"I didn't—"

"No, I know. I mean, why did you give them yours? The one from your father?"

Declan slid his hand into hers and pulled her toward the docks. "I don't need it anymore."

CHAPTER 46

DECLAN

ADLER WOULD HAVE PREFERRED to walk the entire way to the council hall, but he hadn't been able to turn down the offer of the councilwomen's own carriage. Cait would have stubbornly insisted she could make the walk, of course, but he was already forcing her to sit at a table with her attackers. He wasn't going to make her walk miles on a still-healing leg to get there.

The carriage pulled up in front of the pub, much to the curiosity of the few citizens who had stepped outside or peeked through windows at the rare sound of horses and wheels on the cobblestones. Thankfully Cait didn't hesitate to get in.

Though they were the only two within the carriage itself, they didn't speak for the entire journey.

But Adler's discomfort wasn't from the silence or their destination.

Had Lani ridden in this carriage?

Is this how they took her to the pit?

He couldn't imagine them taking her on foot. Knowing Lani, she wouldn't have been easy to escort.

She probably didn't go into the carriage easily either.

His hand settled on the bench between him and Cait, and he couldn't help but rub the soft seat cushion with his thumb, wondering if this was where Lani had sat, if her hand had touched the same fabric.

Cait covered his hand with hers but kept looking out the window through the small gap between the dark curtains. She didn't say anything when he shifted his hand to lace his fingers with hers, and as her thumb ran gentle strokes along his, he closed his eyes and tried to calm grief's ache in his chest.

Lani.

He hadn't saved her.

He was the reason she was gone.

If he hadn't agreed to take her away—sands, if he had simply remained in his seat that night at dinner, if he hadn't followed her into the corridor, if he hadn't given into his damned heart and talked to her—she would be alive. The image of her across the table, the sadness in her eyes, flashed in his mind.

No, whether he had introduced himself or not, whether he had fallen for her or not, Lani would have tried to leave eventually. She hadn't wanted to be matched. She hadn't wanted to rule. That fiery woman would have found a way out.

"We're here," Cait said quietly. She gave him a tentative look. Seeing the loving concern in her emerald eyes, Adler squeezed her hand. With the other, he reached across to run a finger along her jaw.

He whispered her name and lifted her chin, bringing her mouth to his.

Sands, this woman, he thought as she kissed him—not with the passion and heat of earlier, but with a tenderness he wasn't entirely sure he deserved.

"It'll be okay," she whispered to him as the carriage came to a stop. He rested his forehead against hers, simply breathing in those words. "Remember though. We are only colleagues in there. So don't get handsy."

She pulled back, and a look of mischief flashed in her eyes.

He leaned close to her ear just as the driver swung open the carriage door. "I can refrain. But can you?"

"Let's hope so," she said, then accepted the driver's hand and stepped out into the night air. At the bottom of the stairs, she stopped and turned, waiting for him.

Glorious. Confident. Brave.

And by no small miracle, she was his.

⤝⤞

A SERVANT GREETED them and led them down the main corridor. But instead of taking the door on the left to enter the dining room, the servant kept walking. Adler frowned and had just opened his mouth to ask where they were being taken when the woman slowed her pace and opened a door on the right. Not knowing what they would find in this unfamiliar room, Adler stepped through the doorway first with Cait close behind him.

"The others will be in shortly," the woman said and closed the door behind them.

Cait glanced at Adler. "Well, that wasn't foreboding or anything."

Adler gave a small laugh and assessed the room as he circled the table.

Though it was less than half the size of the other dining room, it still boasted the same regal decor of rich woods and lush fabrics. At one end of the space, a modest hearth lay cold and dark beside another door directly opposite from the one they had entered. There were no windows on the walls due to its central location in the council hall, but there was ample illumination from the simple chandelier, wall sconces, and a pair of large candles on the table. The table—large enough to fit eight guests comfortably—was dressed with eight elegant place settings of bright silver and deep blue.

"Did you know it was to be such an intimate affair?" Cait asked in a whisper.

Adler silently shook his head, and before he could say anything, the door on the opposite wall opened. Darienn entered first, with the councilwomen directly behind her. Two men followed—the king, whose dark eyes already had Adler on edge, and a taller man who seemed rather out of place with his shaggy hair and decidedly bored demeanor.

No one spoke as Melina took her place behind the chair directly in front of the hearth. To her right sat Darienn, with the king beside her. Adler was offered the seat to Melina's left.

"King Kilmeran, may I introduce you to Mr. Jensen." Melina gave him a nod and a polite smile. Adler watched Cait tense as the woman's eyes shifted over to her. "And this is Ms. McCallagh? Is that right?"

"Aye, my lady," Cait said confidently. "Thank you for the invitation. It is an honor."

Adler struggled to hide his smile. He admired how easily Cait played the part as needed. Though he'd seen her skilled performance at the pit cave, he couldn't help but be impressed.

The king rested his hands on the back of his chair and dipped his chin to each of them. When his dark eyes slid to Melina, his expression tightened. "I was not expecting to have an audience beyond the council. May I ask why these two are present?"

"While I owe you no such explanation, Your Highness," Melina answered, "they are our guests. As you know, we have a strong relationship with the pirates of the Aisling, and Ms. McCallagh here is a well-regarded business owner here on the island."

The king eyed them again with cold calculation. After a few tense moments, his lips lifted in a wicked grin. "Very well then. But I do hope we don't bore you with our political discussion."

"Please, let's sit," Melina said with an off-putting sweetness.

Beside Adler, Cait sat stiffly with her hands in her lap and stared at the place setting in front of her. Lowering his left hand below the table, Adler risked stretching his fingers toward her leg to reassure her that she wasn't alone, that she could do this. She didn't turn to him, didn't change her expression, but her hand touched his.

"King Kilmeran," Melina began, and Cait jerked her hand back as if she'd been called out for holding Adler's hand. "We hope you are finding your accommodations comfortable."

The king bobbed his head. "Far better than the ship. Not quite as nice as home. But it will do for the short time we are here."

"Why come at all for such a short visit?" It was Darienn who had spoken up, and Adler waited for Melina or one of the other councilwomen to reprimand her. They didn't. All three elder women turned their attention to the king expectantly.

Before he could answer, both doors of the dining room opened, and ten servants glided in. Eight of them carried platters covered with silver domes, which they set before each of those present. The other two carried carafes.

Lids were lifted to reveal an arrangement of food almost too beautiful to eat. Braised meat topped with rich gravy lay beside an assortment of roasted potatoes and vegetables. A freshly baked roll with a slathering of butter melting over it had Adler's mouth watering. He waited for the councilwomen to raise their glasses before lifting his own to his lips, but he had barely managed to take a sip when the king finally spoke.

"It is a shame what happened to your sisters, Miss Darienn."

Adler choked on his drink, but thankfully no one at the table seemed to notice—except Cait, who shifted her eyes toward him. Everyone was focused on Melina, who casually took a sip and set her glass back down onto the table.

Picking up her knife, Melina looked pointedly at the royal guest. "And it would be a shame for our food to get cold."

The audacity of this woman. Adler understood her need to change the subject, but blatantly ignoring Lani's death and the disappearance of her sister infuriated him. His teeth ground painfully together.

Don't say it. Don't say anything.

But if Adler didn't preserve Lani's memory, who would? Drawing in a breath, he prepared to say something, but Cait's light touch upon his leg settled him enough that he swallowed his words.

"Indeed, Melina," the king said, taking a bite of the meat and humming with satisfaction. "Are you sure we won't be able to visit the other areas of Cregah? This is my first time to your island, and I would love a tour."

"That is not possible," Melina said, her polite tone quickly vanishing.

"Another shame, I suppose." Kilmeran shrugged and popped a potato into his mouth.

Darienn leaned forward slightly, busily slicing into her food. Her eyes remained on her plate as she addressed the councilwoman. "Why isn't it possible exactly?"

The air in the room thickened. Melina cleared her throat and drew in a breath.

"We simply don't have the resources, Darienn. Unless King Kilmeran brought a carriage on one of his ships..." She paused and turned to the king, who shook his head. "See? We simply can't escort him in the one carriage at our disposal. And before you ask, no, it would not be in Cregah's best interest to allow the king to travel unaccompanied."

Adler side-eyed Cait. Her head was bowed slightly, and she took small bites of her meal, slowly but steadily. It was, no doubt, a way to distract herself from where she was and who she was sitting with. Adler swallowed hard with regret. He shouldn't have brought her, shouldn't be putting her through this, shouldn't be putting her in a position where she couldn't escape.

But perhaps she had the right approach to this meal. They could keep their heads down, blend into the background, and let the others discuss whatever matters of business they deemed appropriate for the evening.

Melina continued speaking, this time addressing the king directly. "Your Highness, I must ask: what is it you have brought for us?"

Kilmeran smirked at her. "Was there something in particular you hoped for? Beyond the pleasure of my company, of course."

"There have been rumors," Melina said.

At this, the king laughed. Even his man chuckled under his breath.

"Ah, yes. We have heard them too. We just didn't take you for one to believe such gossip."

"We would be foolish to assume there is no truth to even the most ridiculous of stories." Melina set her utensils beside her plate and clasped her hands together. "Did you bring it?"

Adler watched from under his lashes as the king mimicked the councilwoman's actions and met her gaze. "The shield?"

Cait slowly lifted her chin at this, and the whole room seemed to go still—aside from Melina, who gave the king a slight nod.

The king's lips curled up into a wicked smile. "You, of all people, should know it's a farce. Nothing more than a lie told to an imbecile of a king."

Melina's muscles pulsed along her jaw, but her expression remained blank. "Indeed. It is amazing to me, in fact, how the legend of such a shield has survived so long after the king fell."

"The Csintala shield? It isn't real?" Cait's voice had Adler's attention swinging to her, but she didn't look at him. All her focus rested on the king.

His expression softened as he regarded Cait, though the wickedness remained in his eyes. "Well, there is such a shield, but it doesn't have any of the power legend claims. The queen lied, gave the king false hope that the counter to his enchanted gift would be secure in his vault back in Tyshaly. Little did he know—to his great demise—that the balance in the dagger's magic lay within the dagger itself."

"The sound," Cait whispered, frowning down at her plate. Adler could nearly see her gears turning as she pieced together the truth.

"Yes," the king said. He offered her a crooked smile. "How else do you think he fell to the sirens?"

Adler tried to trace back through the legends he'd grown up with. The dagger's promise of victory. The shield to balance out its power. The king who had ended the war with the blade and then disappeared. The stories never explained how he'd fallen or where. Why had no one thought to question it? Why did the myth simply end with his disappearance? How had Cait learned of the dagger's location?

"How?" Cait asked.

"Oh come now, Ms. McCallagh," the king crooned. "You truly don't know how the king betrayed the Cregahn queen? Why he didn't return to her as he'd promised? And how the dagger lured him to his death for his betrayal? In short, the king was an imbecile."

Melina released a heavy sigh. "So what do you bring us, Kilmeran?"

The king leaned back in his chair and folded his hands before his chest. "An alliance."

"Are we not already allies?" Fiona asked from the other end of the table.

"Not to the same degree as you are with the pirate lords. And we would like that to change."

"How so?" Brigeh asked as she set down her fork and dabbed her napkin at her lips.

The king glanced perfunctorily at the two councilwomen before swinging back to Melina.

"Nullify the treaty. End the safe harbor to pirates."

Adler started to scoff but managed to disguise it by clearing his throat. Still, the king turned to him.

"I realize this doesn't bode well for your kind, Mr. Jensen—"

"Oh, I'm no longer a pirate, Your Majesty," he offered, hoping his concern for his former crew—and for Cait's brother—wasn't evident.

Darienn straightened in her seat. "But if we don't provide a haven for the pirates, how do we keep peace on our shores?" She hesitated over the word *peace*, but Adler seemed to be the only one in the room to notice.

"Caprothe will provide protection for your people, as well as ample trade. So you will have no need for the pirates and their stolen goods." He paused and waved a hand lazily in front of him. "I admit this proposal does disrupt your ability to produce heirs for the council, but I am sure we can come to some arrangement. I would be more than willing to do whatever necessary to ensure Cregah has a long line of rulers."

The king leered at Darienn like a glutton eying the last piece of pie on the table, and Adler's fists tightened under the table. Heir to the council or no, the girl was still a youth, barely older than his sister back on Daorna.

"No," Melina said, and the king's attention broke away from the heir. His eyes blazed, but he said nothing. "Your offer seems to provide little benefit to the council and to the people of Cregah. We do not need someone to take care of us. We are doing fine as—"

The king's laughter—dark and ominous—filled the room. "Fine? You can't even control a growing rebellion among your own people! That is far from fine in my book."

Adler's pulse sped up. He needed to get Cait out of here before this became more than just a battle of words. The king's man looked up at Adler, as if he could hear his thoughts or sense his panic. But as that was impossible, Adler shook away the feeling.

"And if we don't agree to your terms?" Melina asked through tight lips.

Dropping his head to the side, the king assessed her for several tense breaths. "You have secrets. Secrets you've desperately tried to hide. Deny my demands and I let those secrets out, expose you across the Aisling for the fraud that you are."

Melina chuckled and turned to her sisters, who joined in with their own, far more nervous, laughter. "You know nothing, Kilmeran."

The king donned a smug smile, and his eyes danced with vicious humor. "Don't I, Queen Rhiannon? Or do you prefer *Your Majesty*?"

CHAPTER 47
CAIT

Silence filled the dining room, and Cait wasn't sure anyone was even daring to breathe as King Kilmeran stared at Melina. Or Rhiannon?

Queen Rhiannon.

The ancient fae queen of Cregah.

It couldn't be. Could it?

Why not? The fae sisters are real. The dagger is real. The sirens are real.

Every damned legend she'd grown up with was becoming as tangible as the chair she was sitting in.

"This is absurd," Brigeh said.

Fiona looked calmly at Melina. "What is he talking about, sister?"

Melina shook her head slowly. "He speaks nonsense. Absurdities, as Brigeh rightly noted."

Adler cleared his throat as he pushed away from the table and dropped his arm onto the back of Cait's chair. With a look around the table, he offered a dip of his chin. "Ladies, thank you for the lovely meal, but I do think it might be best if Ms. McCallagh and I leave you to discuss your private business."

He had just stood when Melina's voice cut through the air, her words clipped and sharp. "Sit down."

"Surely they can—" Fiona started, but Melina's dark glare had the council-woman's mouth snapping shut around her words.

"Sit, Mr. Jensen," Melina commanded, smiling when Adler complied. She waved a hand toward the king. "The king has made outlandish allegations against me—against the entire council—and as far-fetched as they might be, it would not be prudent of us to allow our guests to leave until we have set things right. We cannot have them taking such lies into Morshan where they could use them to undermine our rule, sisters."

Cait bowed her head. "We would not dare to—"

"Oh?" Melina snapped at her. "Just as you would not dare to send a spy into our employ, to lead a rebellion against us, to plot the end of the council?"

Panic cut off Cait's air supply.

Or maybe all the air had been sucked from the room.

Deny it! she screamed at herself, but she couldn't find the words, couldn't find the ability to speak.

"Melina," one of the councilwomen said.

Adler looked at Cait and then to Melina. "Ms. McCallagh? A rebel leader? I don't understand. How—"

Cait could have hugged him for saying the words she couldn't say herself, but his attempt was futile. Not only did Melina not appear convinced, but she flashed them a devilish smile before calling over her shoulder, "Eva. Aron. Join us."

Cait's teeth slammed together at the sound of her friends' names.

The door opened, and Cait forced herself to look at them as they entered.

But they weren't alone.

Between them, gripped tightly by the arms, was Lucan. His face was swollen, bruised, and caked with dried blood.

No!

How had they found him?

She had been so careful. They had all been so careful.

"What did you do to him?" Cait cried out, and she wasn't sure if she hurled the words at Melina, the council, or the twins. "Lucan, I'm here. You'll be okay."

Lucan coughed in response and tried to smile. "Hi, Cait," he rasped.

Melina rose from the table and approached Lucan. Snatching his chin, she pulled his face roughly toward her and sneered as she looked him over. Then she swung back to look at Cait with a feline smile.

"Betrayal hurts, doesn't it, Cait? And tell me, Mr. Jensen. Did this rebel simply give you the slip out there on the sea? Or did you lie to us about exiling him?"

Adler's lips tightened as he held the councilwoman's gaze. Cait eyed the twins, but they refused to look at her. How had Melina turned them? Cait had known them for years. They had joined the Rogues after their parents had vanished and had been faithful members for years—or so she thought.

Across from her, the king let out a deep chuckle, and Cait glanced over to find him leaning forward, his clasped hands steepled under his chin as he watched the drama unfold before him with excitement in his dark eyes.

When Adler still hadn't spoken, Melina clicked her tongue. "I don't know what Lani saw in you."

Adler tensed, and his legs shifted as he prepared to stand, but Cait rested a hand on his forearm with a whispered, "Don't."

"Interesting," Melina hissed, angling her head. "I admit, I knew a lot about you two, but I never imagined this. I wonder what my niece would have thought if she saw how little you mourned her death."

Cait's head swam, as if Melina's words had the power to physically drown her.

How did she know all these things? Were there more spies for the council than they had imagined? Was this councilwoman truly the ancient fae Queen Rhiannon?

"To be completely honest, Cait, I didn't think you would have the courage to come tonight. Not after your last visit. Speaking of which, how is the leg?" Melina's lips curled back into a smirk.

Cait swallowed hard but forced herself to reply. "Better, thank you."

"What did they do to you?" Eva asked.

Melina turned slowly to the woman and answered for Cait. "Nothing that concerns you. But if you would like to receive the same treatment—or worse—keep asking questions."

Aron glanced from his sister to Cait before addressing the councilwoman. "We have something you want."

"And what is that?" Melina sounded skeptical.

"The dagger," Aron and Eva said in unison.

The king sat back from the table but said nothing. The man beside him, however, showed keen interest for the first time this evening, and his attention swung quickly to the head of the table, where Melina stood beside the twins. Adler turned to Cait, his eyes shouting a silent question. When she only offered a simple shrug, Adler's attention returned to Aron and Eva.

Eva pulled out a dagger, and Cait's grip on Adler's arm tightened when she recognized it.

She had seen this blade before.

Declan's.

He was here? On Cregah?

Every part of her wanted to rush at them, to demand how they'd gotten that blade and what they'd done to her brother. But she couldn't. Not without alerting Melina to the dagger's inauthenticity.

"You got it," Melina said, "from McCallagh, I imagine?" Aron nodded, and Melina looked over her shoulder at Cait. The councilwoman opened her mouth to speak, but Eva was already moving.

With a low growl, she thrust the dagger toward Melina's gut.

Melina moved faster.

Her hand caught Eva's wrist and twisted it back at a sickening angle.

Cait and Adler shot up from their seats, but something pushed Cait backwards.

It was like hands were holding her back, pressing against her shoulders and arms and chest, but there was nothing there but air.

Beside her, Adler—though he remained standing—appeared to struggle against the same invisible restraints.

Was this Melina's doing? If she truly was a fae queen, it might be possible.

Cait looked around the room, but no one was paying any attention to her and Adler. No one seemed to even notice they were there trying to get free from whatever bonds held them.

Defeated, Cait settled in her chair, and at once, the tension on her body was gone as quickly as it had come. She reached up to Adler's arm and pulled him back to his seat. Enraged confusion twisted his features.

"What was that?" he whispered.

"Her?" Cait asked, tossing her head in Melina's direction.

Melina gave a low and menacing growl. "Fools." With speed Cait had never witnessed before, the councilwoman wrenched the dagger out of Eva's hand and sliced it across her throat.

"Eva!" Aron screamed as her blood sprayed across his face. Releasing Lucan, he rushed at Melina, but she moved the dagger faster than he could close the distance.

Aron froze against her.

His jaw fell open. His eyes grew wide. His legs buckled.

Lucan caught him under the arms and then let out a weak roar of pain.

CHAPTER 48
DARIENN

M**ELINA'S ATTACKS** played out before Darienn's eyes as though in slow motion. She was helpless, completely unable to do anything but sit and stare as Melina pulled the blade free from the man's gut, moved it to her other hand, and pierced Lucan's side within the span of a shallow breath.

"Lucan!" Darienn moved like a rabbit from a cage at the sound of Lucan's painful groan.

She only managed a half step before a sharp pain shot through her head and she was flying backwards. Her body slammed into the king, and his arm slithered around her like a snake.

"Not so fast, young one," he said. But then he whispered, "Don't fight if you want to live."

"Fuck you," she whispered back. Her heel came down hard on his foot, but he only laughed darkly and held her tighter.

A shiver crept across her skin when his lips brushed her ear. "Trust me."

Trust him? How in the sands does he expect me to do that?

Her mind raced through her options, which were decidedly few.

"Sisters..." Melina turned as she spoke, directing everyone's attention to where Fiona and Brigeh stood near the open door. They froze midstep. "Don't make me kill you too. Close the door. And sit...back...down."

The pair, wide-eyed with fright, acquiesced silently.

The king's dark laugh rumbled against Darienn's back. "Clearly, you have it all under control. How foolish of me to think otherwise."

Melina turned and sent the dagger soaring straight at Darienn.

No, at the king.

Darienn braced herself for the impact of steel against bone and flesh and turned her head so she wouldn't have to witness more carnage. When nothing happened and the king was once again taunting Melina, Darienn glanced around.

She froze and promptly forgot how to breathe.

The dagger hung in the air.

CHAPTER 49
CAIT

THE DAGGER HOVERED mere inches from the king's face as if held by some unseen force.

Like the same one that held you back, she thought. But how?

Melina wouldn't have stopped it herself, would she?

But who else in this room had the power, the magic, to do this?

The king eyed the dagger. "I take it this is *not* the Csintala dagger after all. As they're dead"—he nodded toward the twins—"instead of you."

Melina shot him a deadly smile. "I wondered how you knew so much, Kilmeran."

It's true? She's fae?

Cait was a fool—just as her parents had been. There was no way of defeating the council, not when they were led by a fae.

"But this is all the answer I needed," Melina said. The councilwoman pointed at the dagger, and it promptly fell to the ground. She glowered at the king's man, who remained seated at the table. "I should have known you weren't dead, Liam."

The man continued eating the meal everyone else had long since forgotten about. Swallowing his food with a long sip of wine, he lazily locked eyes with Melina. "You're not quite so scary without your powers, Rhiannon."

She snarled. "It's *Melina* now. And I see you've still got yours. So tell me. Why is a fae prince working for this bastard?"

Another fae?

Cait tried to piece everything together, but the situation was quickly becoming a confusing mess. Adler didn't appear to be understanding any better, though he seemed focused on the captive council heir and their injured and dying friends lying in the corner.

"Can you get to them?" Cait whispered as quietly as she could.

Adler nodded, but Melina raised a finger at them, giving them a sideways glance.

"Don't do anything stupid," she hissed. She pointed to her ear. "I may not have my powers anymore, but I'm still fae."

Cait's mind whirled.

They had no weapons. No options. Nothing to use against a council more ruthless and wicked than they'd imagined.

Especially not one led by a fae—whether she had powers or not.

Cait's chest tightened around her pounding heart. She couldn't breathe, couldn't focus.

Clenching her eyes shut, she forced everything away from her mind, willed herself not to hear the conversation that continued between Melina and this Liam, and focused all her attention on the air rushing in and out of her lungs.

The real dagger was their only hope of winning this.

But where was it?

Where was Declan?

CHAPTER 50
DECLAN

The stone residence loomed in the darkness on the other side of the well-kept grounds. Declan had never planned to come back here. Even after he'd decided to bring the dagger to Cait rather than keep it for himself, he hadn't intended on bringing it to the council hall himself.

It's just a building. Stop being so weak.

But his thoughts were drowned out by the memory of Tommy's pained cry as the blade slashed across his chest. The cackling of that woman—that fae—as she cruelly informed her daughter of the true circumstances of Lani's death. The splitting of his heart when Aoife denied him forgiveness.

A hand squeezed his, warm and comforting and sure.

"It's hard for me too," Aoife whispered.

Declan pressed a kiss to her temple. She leaned into him and released a steady breath.

"I don't think any of us have good memories of this place," Tommy said from behind them, and Maura hummed in agreement.

Aoife looked hard at her old home, her lips pursed in determination. "And you're sure you can manage this, Maura?" she asked over her shoulder.

"Aye. No problem," the fae answered without hesitation. "Remember, though, there are only a handful of fae I've met who can see through my glamours. My brother is one of them. Melina is another, but she lost that ability when she enchanted the dagger."

Pulling Aoife close, Declan nodded and moved to the side so Tommy and Maura could take the lead. Maura paused briefly at the edge of the trees and smiled at Tommy before stepping out into the open. Aoife and Declan followed close behind, hand in hand.

Were they completely mad to be bringing the blade here?

It's the only way to defeat her.

But was it? Would it even work against her?

What other options did they have?

If what Maura's brother had explained was true, and a dissolution of the treaty was the king's aim, soon no pirate would be safe on the Aisling, and no citizen of Cregah would find freedom from the council's rule.

They had to at least try.

When they approached the near end of the building, Maura stepped between two bushes where a door lay hidden behind their leaves. Declan was relieved when the handle of the door turned easily. Her brother hadn't gone back on his reluctant promise to leave them a way inside.

On light feet, they followed Maura through the hallways, stopping at each corner and listening for a moment before continuing on. No one said a word as they walked—since Maura's glamour only concealed their bodies, not their voices—until they came to the main corridor. At one end lay two large doors with glass panels and ornate trim.

Aoife peered around the corner and nodded toward the doors, whispering, "The main dining room is near the front entrance."

They hadn't made it more than halfway down the hallway when Maura stopped.

"They're not in the main dining room," she whispered. Lifting a finger, she pointed to a plain wooden door up ahead on the left. "There."

Aoife's face contorted with confusion. She shook her head slowly. "That's the council's private eating room. That doesn't make any—"

"Sense or no, that's where they are," Maura said.

Declan flashed Aoife a sideways look. "Are there two ways into this room as well?"

"Aye," she said with a nod. "Melina will be seated near the other door, not this one."

"And you said this is your private eating space? So it would be smaller?"

Aoife eyed him curiously. "Of course. Seats no more than eight."

"Has the council ever hosted guests in that room?"

Aoife's eyes widened, and she shook her head. She seemed as uncomfortable with this fact as Declan was, but as she offered up no explanation for why the council might have gone against their usual practices, he didn't press the issue. Their reasoning didn't matter. All that mattered was the fact that they were just behind this door.

Declan took a tentative step, and the door opened slowly.

But no one appeared.

They had to act now. This might be their only chance to get inside undetected.

On quiet feet, Declan sprinted for the door.

He froze at the edge of the doorframe and peered inside. Two of the council-women were tiptoeing toward him, their eyes looking straight through him as if he wasn't there.

Melina's voice sliced through the thick air: "Sisters!"

Declan's heart thumped, and with a quick jerk of his head, he ushered his friends inside, gesturing for them to stay close to the wall. Aoife entered first, then Maura and Tommy, just as Melina commanded her sisters to close the door. Declan darted forward, twisting his body as the door swung toward him, and his breath caught when it nearly hit his heel.

A deep and regal laugh filled the room.

The king.

He couldn't have been much older than Cait, yet he carried himself with the air of a man who had seen and done much. On the other side of the table, he held a young woman close to his chest. Swirls of ink graced her arm. The youngest heir.

The king spoke, but Declan didn't hear any of it, his focus fully on the two people sitting directly in front of him. Even with her back to him, Declan recognized his sister immediately. The man beside her had to be Adler. Declan's gut twisted with regret.

Aoife's hand gripped Declan's arm. Her wide eyes were not on him but on the king and Declan's dagger hovering in the air.

Daemari.

Beside the king, still seated at the table and eating his meal, Liam seemed unaware that Melina was speaking to him.

Declan nudged Aoife with his arm and silently urged her to walk toward her mother. She didn't hesitate, merely swallowing hard before she nodded. With their hands clasped, they eased past Tommy and Maura, careful not to disturb Cait and Adler's chairs as they did so.

"Can you get to them?"

Cait's whisper made Declan freeze for a moment, as he wondered if she might be addressing him and not the man seated beside her.

Aoife pulled him forward, and as they rounded the corner of the table, he caught sight of the bodies lying on the floor in the corner beyond Melina. The twins.

They neared the councilwoman until Aoife was positioned directly behind her. Aoife's hand squeezed his one last time before letting go. She stepped back to give him room.

Keeping his eye on Melina, Declan eased the Csintala dagger out from the hidden sheath within his jacket. He pulled his arm back and glanced once more at Aoife, who gave him a reassuring—albeit stiff—smile.

Melina spoke again. "King Kilmeran, I'm going to have to decline your proposal for an alliance."

Before the king could utter a reply, Declan drew in a deep breath, angled the dagger up, and slammed it into Melina's back.

CHAPTER 51
AOIFE

Declan had done it.

They had won.

But Melina was laughing.

Laughing?

Aoife shook her head in disbelief. Declan moved to pull the dagger out, but Melina turned away from him so that its handle slipped from his fingers. Blood seeped from the wound, but still, her mother laughed.

And then she looked right at them. First at Declan. Then at Aoife.

Had the glamour fallen away? No, no one else in the room seemed to be able to see them.

Her mother's eyes shone with a dark humor that froze Aoife's blood.

If Melina could see through the glamour, then that meant...

What have we done?

"What happened, Melina?" one of the councilwomen asked frantically from the other end of the room. But still, her mother glowered at Aoife.

"It appears our dear captain came through for me after all. Though, pity for him, he failed to realize its powers don't work against me."

At this, Melina pulled her gaze away, reached behind her, and yanked the dagger out of her lower back. She didn't even wince, though her blood coated the blade and dripped onto the floor.

"This, Kilmeran, is the Csintala dagger."

As Melina slipped it into the sash of her dress, the king remained silent, though he glanced down at Liam and scowled. Liam raised his eyes steadily to the fae queen.

Without warning, Melina stiffened, her spine snapping straight. Her eyes widened, and her mouth fell open as she gasped for breath that didn't come. Her hands flew to her throat, her nails desperately clawing at her neck, trying to find whatever choked her.

Aoife's heart split in two. How was it possible to still love the one who had hurt her and lied to her, who had killed so many?

You love Declan though.

But that was different. Declan had darkness inside him, yes, but he also had love and kindness and warmth—even if it was limited. Melina did not. Melina was pure darkness. Incapable of love. Incapable of affection.

As the color drained from Melina's face and her movements slowed, Aoife clung to the hope that this would soon be all over. That this was for the best. That soon they'd all be able to move on.

But then Melina stopped struggling.

Her fingers curled around air.

"How—" The king's face tightened with rage, and he shouted at Liam, who didn't respond except to concentrate harder on Melina.

Was she pulling his *daemari* away from her throat? How was that even possible? Had they truly underestimated her mother's power?

The room fell deathly silent.

No one seemed to breathe.

Until Liam screamed in pain.

Melina's hands tightened into fists as she twisted her wrists and laughed.

"Seriously, Liam," Melina said mockingly. "I expected better from you. Unless it's as I feared. Are you truly blood-bound to this prick? Or did you simply forget who I am?"

She gave Liam no chance to respond before she thrust her hands toward him, sending him flying back as if she had pushed him. He slammed hard into the stone wall and remained there, pinned by whatever power her mother possessed.

With a flick of her wrist, Melina sent a knife flying off the table. It buried itself deep into the king's shoulder. He staggered back, growling in pain. He reached for his wound, not seeming to care that Darienn slipped out of his grasp and collapsed onto the floor.

The king glared at the fae still pinned to the wall. "Couldn't stop that one?"

Liam shot him a cold look but said nothing as Melina laughed.

"Be glad I can't kill you yet, Kilmeran. I may still have use for your fae boy over there, and if you were dead, he'd be unlikely to play along."

Aoife's mind raced. They should have expected this. They should have known the queen had protected herself against her own enchantment.

But now what? What options did they have left?

Melina cleared her throat. "Now where were we? Oh, yes, Maura. You can drop the glamour." Melina slid her gaze to where Maura stood with Tommy.

Maura pulled the glamour away from them, and Cait's mouth fell open. Adler's eyes widened. The two councilwomen appeared ready to faint at any moment. While the king eyed Maura with pained intrigue, Liam watched her with a hint of fear and worry.

"That's better," Melina said. "Although, our reunion is to be short-lived, Maura, as I think you and your pirate will be leaving soon."

"We won't abandon our friends," Maura said.

Melina laughed. "You mean the way you abandoned your sisters?"

Maura's face tightened with confusion, but only briefly.

"So I'm right," the queen said. "You did run out on them. Interesting. Regardless, those in Morshan could use your help more. Assuming they haven't already gone up in flames with the pub."

Declan spun toward his sister, who was now gaping in fear. Cait pushed her chair back and made to stand, but then she didn't, and her face contorted with frustration and anger as she fought against invisible bonds. Whether it was Melina's doing or it was Liam acting on the king's behalf, it didn't matter.

"Let me go!" she growled.

Melina clicked her tongue. "I need you here, unfortunately. But Tommy and Maura are free to go. If Declan agrees, of course. He is the captain here, after all."

Declan tensed, but it didn't take him long to make the decision. He nodded toward the door, directing Tommy and Maura to leave.

Panic pricked Aoife's heart. They were playing right into her mother's hands, doing exactly as she wanted. Surely Declan had something planned, some last-minute, secret siren somewhere. Something. It was the only reason he would be going along with this!

Tommy and Maura had barely departed the room when Melina beckoned Aoife forward. Declan darted in front of her.

"No," he growled. "You won't touch her."

Melina's lips slowly turned up into a malicious smile. It was so similar to the one Aoife had seen on Triss that it sent an icy finger trailing down her spine.

"Quite touching, Declan. How did you do it exactly? How did you convince my daughter to forgive you after what you did to Lani?"

Aoife searched for the right words to defend him, but then someone's chair scraped against the stone floor. Adler stood.

Shit.

He hadn't known it was Declan, had he?

Adler's jaw pulsed, and his blue eyes burned hot with rage. His fists tightened at his sides.

Aoife braced for the inevitable attack. She inched closer to Declan, ready to help him in whatever way she could, but it was Cait who pulled Adler back.

"Don't listen to her, love," she said. "She's just baiting you."

"Am I?" Melina laughed again, a bone-chilling cackle Aoife had never heard before. "Declan, why don't you tell Adler what you did to his love? His other love, that is."

Declan turned to face Adler. Shaking her head slowly, Cait whispered, "No" while keeping her grip on Adler's forearm.

Adler swallowed hard.

This pirate knew what the council required of his kind on this island. Surely he would understand, just as Aoife had.

Clearing his throat, Adler continued to glare. "It was you?"

Declan nodded silently, and Aoife's heart splintered along the cracks that had just begun to heal. Adler had to understand, had to realize Declan hadn't chosen to do it. If he didn't, Aoife would do anything she could to make him understand.

"Did she suffer?" Adler asked, voice wavering.

"No, she didn't. She was not my enemy." Declan paused and drew in a long breath. "I'm sorry."

"He's sorry!" Melina's words cut through the tension, drawing everyone's attention back to her. "Are you going to accept that, Mr. Jensen? Here is the man who sent your dear, sweet Lani plunging to her death in that pit. Here is your chance to avenge her death. His blood for hers."

Aoife's heart stopped, her eyes locked on the man who had stolen her sister's heart. He walked slowly around the table toward them, grief and anger worn plainly on his face.

"Adler, no!" Cait shouted and pushed to her feet, but Melina, with a toss of her hand, sent Cait falling back into her seat once more.

"Bitch, let me go!" Cait cried out, but Melina ignored her.

Energy pulsed in Aoife's blood, and she reached for her *daemari* again, calling it forward. She could stop Adler. She could. Just as she'd stopped Declan on that beach. But the damned power slipped away from her yet again, and panic bit into her chest with each step Adler took.

CHAPTER 52
TOMMY

TOMMY TRIED his best to keep up with Maura's pace as they raced back to the pub. What if the fire was a hoax? What if it was another game of the council's? While it was altogether possible—he wouldn't be able to live with himself if he ignored the warning and it turned out to be true.

The cobbled streets became a blur as they ran, and he nearly collapsed with relief when they turned the corner and found the pub still standing. Relieved, he sighed heavily.

It had been a bluff.

Or you're early.

Without a word, Maura pulled Tommy down the street. She didn't hesitate to open the door and step inside, dragging him along with her. He tried to hold her back. Patrons would no doubt be shocked by a fae strolling in.

But when Maura held firm to his hand and led the way toward the bar, Tommy noted how her pointed ears had been transformed—or cloaked—to appear human. Although he had seen her use her glamours before—and in far more impressive ways—he couldn't help the sense of pride that swelled in his chest at witnessing her magic in action again.

As they walked slowly across the room, Tommy took note of those around them. Cait's regular bartender stood behind the bar, placing a glass of rum before a woman who sat hunched over.

A few tables were occupied by men he didn't recognize. Though their dark, weary faces showed the rough wear from many years on the sea—with gritty stubble or scraggly beards unsuccessfully concealing scars and age lines—they wore no ship's colors. In fact, their attire was unlike that of most pirates—or even merchant sailors. Instead they were dressed in dark linen pants tucked into simple boots and black jackets with ornate silver buttons.

Maura leaned over casually to whisper into Tommy's ear, not slowing her pace as she did. "The king's men."

Tommy stiffened, but his steps didn't falter.

Conversations stalled briefly as a dozen pairs of eyes snapped up to quickly register their entrance. While most of the men showed no interest and returned to their chattering immediately, a few of them tracked Tommy and Maura's movement across the room.

Tommy risked a sidelong glance at them, and his gut twisted. That sneer. That scar. Those dark eyes.

He'd seen these men before.

The lighting had been dim then, and everything had moved rather quickly, but Tommy would never forget the pirate lord and his crew who had tried to kill him in that library.

Forcing his jaw to relax, he stepped up to the bar beside Maura. She pulled out the stool beside the woman, who didn't bother to even glance in their direction. The barmaid turned gracefully to retrieve two glasses from the back counter and set them down before them.

"Rum?" she asked, already preparing to pour the amber liquid.

"Aye," Tommy said, settling onto his stool. Maura nodded.

"I've seen you in here before," the woman said to Tommy, setting the bottle down as she addressed Maura. "But not you. What brings you to Morshan?"

Maura lifted the glass to her lips and downed the drink. "Visiting friends."

The woman hummed in response as she refilled Maura's glass. When she spoke again, her voice was low, barely audible amid the din of chatter in the room. "Didn't think the Bron family had any friends here."

Tommy coughed on the rum he'd just sipped, but Maura simply smiled into her glass before tipping it back.

"I'm unfamiliar with that name," she said. "You must have mistaken me for someone else, Miss…" She raised a brow at the woman, who leaned against the bar's edge and eyed Maura thoughtfully.

"It's Kira, and my apologies." The hardened look in her copper eyes contradicted that sentiment though. "You look like someone my father knew."

"No harm done, Kira," Maura said with a shrug. "I get that a lot."

Tommy glanced from Maura to Kira and back again, trying to piece together what in the sands was going on, but if there was anything amiss, it didn't show on Maura's face at all. Kira's glare, however, hadn't softened.

Leaning close, Tommy made to look over his shoulder but brushed his lips over Maura's ear. "This going to be a problem?"

As Maura shook her head, Kira's voice pulled Tommy's head back around.

"No problem from me," she said. Tommy's alarm must have been evident, because a mischievous challenge flashed in the woman's expression. She looked as if she was about to say something more when her eyes darted over Tommy's shoulder. "Fuck," she muttered under her breath. "Speaking of problems though…"

Despite her urgent tone, Kira moved casually from behind the bar. Tommy pivoted in his seat until his knees faced Maura's. Propping an elbow on the top of the bar, he risked a glance toward the door, where Kira was greeting a group of newcomers—three women, a man, and an older boy. None of them looked related, and none looked like travelers or seafarers.

Locals?

They didn't appear to be a problem to Tommy, but the risk still loomed, and the tension in the room had noticeably spiked with their entry. While the disguised pirates' conversations hadn't ceased, their voices had lowered considerably since the new arrivals walked in, and they now intently watched them follow Kira to a back table. The same table at which Tommy had sat with Declan and Gavin over a week ago.

Maura angled her head toward Tommy, though she kept her attention on the empty glass she twirled between her fingers.

"They're Rogues," she whispered. "They shouldn't be here."

As if her words had been an invitation, the main door opened once more, and another group—this one a trio of young women—entered.

Tommy resisted the urge to look and instead reached over the bar to retrieve the bottle of rum Kira had left behind. Filling his glass once more, he waited for Maura to continue explaining, but it was another voice that spoke to him.

"Could you top me off?" the woman beside Maura said, nudging her own glass down the bar toward him. She didn't look Tommy in the eye, and based on the slurring of her words, she must have had plenty already.

It was none of his business, perhaps, if this woman sought to drown her worries in the bottle, but with the possible danger brewing around them, he didn't particularly want to have to carry some passed-out broad out of a burning building.

When he hesitated, though, Maura took the bottle from his hand and poured half a dram in both her glass and the woman's.

"Excuse my love here," Maura said, tossing her head toward Tommy as she spoke to the woman. "He worries too much. *Sláinte.*" She raised her glass, and the woman did the same. They sipped in unison before Maura extended her hand. "I'm Maura."

The woman clasped it. "Penny. And it must be nice to have someone worry over you."

Tommy watched Penny lazily run her fingertip around the rim of her glass. There was no knowing if this woman was loyal to the council or to the Rogues. Maybe she was loyal to neither. She could easily be an innocent bystander. And if they really had arrived early, before Melina's threats could be carried out, it might be better to get her out of the way.

But how could he convince her to leave?

It wasn't as if he could simply ask her to go home. Not without it sounding like a proposition, at least.

Kira let out a string of mumbled curses as she returned to her place behind the bar. She had already seemed on edge when they'd arrived, and now, with more members of the Rogues here, her muscles tensed with visible apprehension, her lips forming silent words as she busied herself drying a glass.

Tommy started to raise his hand to get Kira's attention, but Maura grabbed his forearm and squeezed gently. A small shake of her head told him to wait, and when her eyes shifted to Kira briefly, he got the message.

Kira wasn't simply mouthing words to herself. She was talking to Maura.

All Tommy could do was wait for Maura to have a chance to relay the information to him. Before she could, though, the voices around them quieted, and a chair scraped loudly against the floor.

Lord Alistar Madigen stood in the middle of the room and stared straight at Tommy.

CHAPTER 53
MAURA

THE ROGUES SHOULD NOT HAVE BEEN HERE. That much Maura had gathered when Kira reprimanded the first group to arrive. But it wasn't until Kira had returned to the bar that Maura learned just how serious the situation was.

The Rogues never congregated in public, not even in the pub.

But today they'd all received the same message, written in the hand of Cait's second, Lucan. With each note delivered by trusted couriers, the rebels had no reason to question who had sent them, but Kira doubted it was Lucan.

He was in hiding, and he wasn't an imbecile.

It was clear Kira needed to get them out of here without raising suspicion.

But Maura had no idea how she intended to do that.

When the room grew quiet, Maura cringed. She had been so focused on hearing Kira's words that she'd let the other voices fade into the background.

Maybe it wouldn't have helped either way. Maybe she still would have been caught by surprise.

Tommy's heartbeat—as familiar to Maura as her own—thumped hard and fast, and Maura followed his gaze to where a man stood with an expression of regal boredom. Maura didn't recognize him, but if the quickening of Tommy's breath and the flash in his amber eyes was any indication, he most definitely did.

No one said anything, though, as the man stalked to the bar and rested his hands against the edge several paces away from Penny.

"Another bottle of your white rum," he said. His voice had a familiar roughness to it. Maura had heard it before, but the memory stayed irritatingly at the edge of her mind, refusing to let her pinpoint how she knew him.

"Aye," Kira said with a hint of hesitation, reaching for a clear bottle from the top shelf. "Shall I put it—"

"On the king's account, aye." The man took the bottle and flashed Maura a wink that sent a chill through her veins. He didn't return to his seat though, didn't move away from the bar as he opened the bottle with his teeth and spit the cork onto the floor at Tommy's feet. Bringing the bottle to his lips, he took a long swig, staring at Tommy so intently that it set Maura's nerves on edge.

He pulled the bottle away, releasing an exaggerated sigh. "A shame to waste the good stuff, but—" He paused and flashed them a devilish smirk. "Perhaps it's not a waste at all."

With that, he turned the bottle upside down above the bar, pouring the liquor over the top of it before splashing it onto the floor and behind the bar. Penny tumbled off her stool, falling hard to the floor in her retreat. Maura moved to help her up but halted when she heard Kira start yelling.

"What are you—" Kira rushed at the man with unexpected quickness but had to slow down to duck when he threw the bottle at her, sending it crashing into the other bottles lining the back wall.

"Just following orders, miss." The man's voice crept under Maura's skin, and she watched in horror when he produced a match from between his fingers and lit it.

Tommy was on his feet with his dagger out before the match left the man's hand, but there was no stopping it from landing on the bar and setting the liquor ablaze. If only Maura could harness the elements like her sister, she could help. She could have prevented this, could have done more than simply crouch on the floor beside a drunk woman.

The sharp clang of metal on metal resonated as the king's man blocked Tommy's strike. Tommy drove the man away from Maura and Penny, ducking and parrying as he moved, kicking chairs out of his way as he pursued the man.

Maura's stomach tightened at the sight of him in harm's way.

He'd done this before, of course, but she'd never been present for it. Not like this.

He can take care of himself. He's a pirate. This is his job.

But even knowing these truths didn't ease Maura's worry as she watched him fight. She winced when the man's blade nicked Tommy's forearm, but he didn't relent or falter.

"Get everyone out of here!" Tommy called over the clash of blades that filled the room. The king's men—with swords drawn—now battled the Rogues, who were trying to push their way toward the exit with only their short daggers and simple knives. The Rogues might have outnumbered the uniformed men, but their blades were no match for the sabers and cutlasses they faced.

Maura lifted Penny to her feet. "Come on, we need to leave."

But Penny pulled her arm from Maura's grasp, stumbling to the side as she did. "No, I can help. I *need* to help."

"You can barely stand," Maura argued.

The woman swayed on her feet, but her eyes danced with fierce determination as she lifted her skirts and produced a knife from a sheath at her thigh.

"I can help," she repeated through gritted teeth, calling for Kira as she stumbled back to the bar. The barmaid leaped up and over the bar.

"Do you have a blade on you?" Kira asked Maura, who nodded and pulled her own from within her boot. "Good. You'll need it."

"Is there another way out?" Maura asked, tossing her chin toward the front door where two men now stood, blocking the exit.

Kira nodded once. After letting out a sharp whistle, she lifted her hand in the air, gesturing for the Rogues to make for the rear of the pub. Three of them managed to back away from the men guarding the door, and Kira ushered them on. "Get to the alley and scatter."

Penny rushed to the front, her knife at the ready as she joined the other rogues. Kira raced after her, and Maura could only afford one more glance over her shoulder at Tommy, who had the man cornered.

Be careful. She threw the thought toward him and then turned back to help the others escape.

CHAPTER 54
ADLER

A storm brewed in Adler's veins, drowning out all logic and reason.

Pirates visiting Cregah had no choice but to follow the council's orders. Declan had no choice.

But there was always a choice.

Declan could have declined. He could have faked Lani's death and let her live.

It didn't matter if he had truly shown her mercy by making her death quick and painless. Adler only knew this pirate had taken Lani from him, and he was going to make him hurt.

"Adler, no!" A familiar voice rang out from somewhere behind him, but his brokenness kept his attention firmly on the man in front of him.

Declan, with a look of sorrow in his eyes, raised his hands in protective surrender. Adler ignored it as he pulled his arm back and slammed his fist into his jaw.

Declan took the hit, spitting blood onto the floor before straightening once more to face Adler.

A woman rushed to his side, but he stopped her. "It's okay, Aoife. It will be okay."

Aoife. Lani's sister.

Adler's gaze flitted to her. "This man killed your sister," he said, biting out each word.

"And I forgave him," she said, her tone dripping with hope and love.

Hope and love that Lani had been denied.

Because of him.

Adler raised his hand to strike again, but Declan pushed him back with both hands, saying, "Don't let them win. Don't—"

Adler's fist landed in the pirate's gut, doubling him over. Refusing to give him a chance to recover, Adler drove his knee into Declan's face and pushed him back into Aoife.

Blood dripped down Declan's chin, and he glowered at Adler before checking to make sure Aoife was unhurt.

"Adler, stop." The familiar voice tore through Adler's rage.

Cait.

He started to turn toward her, but a different voice—wicked and cruel— stopped him.

"Here's your chance. Your chance for revenge."

Something cold slid into the palm of his hand, and his fingers instinctively curled around the smooth handle of a blade. Melina swept a hand toward Declan in invitation.

One strike and it would be over.

One swipe of the blade and Lani would be avenged.

Adler adjusted his grip.

Why should this pirate get to live when Lani hadn't?

Why should he be given a pass?

Adler took a step forward and noted how Aoife clenched her hands tighter around Declan's arm, how the pirate calmly waited, his bloodied face impassive as if he knew he deserved what was coming.

But that face—the shape of his eyes and the hard set of his jaw—also betrayed his familial ties.

This was Cait's brother.

How could Adler profess to love her and then kill her brother?

No matter what Declan had done, Adler couldn't do it.

He wouldn't.

Roughing him up a little was one thing.

But stealing him from Cait and Aoife?

Adler wouldn't do that, but he could still have his revenge. Melina had sentenced Lani to death. She had tortured Cait. She hurt both women he loved. She deserved so much more than a quick death, but if this was the only way Adler could make her pay, he wouldn't waste it.

In one smooth motion, he flipped the dagger in his hand, gripped it by the blade, and sent it soaring toward Melina. But the fae tossed her hand lazily to the side, forcing the weapon to switch direction mid-flight.

Straight for Declan.

Fuck.

This couldn't happen.

Move! He wanted to shout at Declan, but no sound came from him as he watched.

"No!" Aoife screamed, and the dagger dropped to the ground at Declan's feet.

What in the sands was that?

Adler looked from Aoife to Melina to Declan, who was already bending down to retrieve the weapon. No sooner had he touched the handle, though, than the blade escaped his grasp and returned to Melina's hand.

She tapped the side of the blade's tip against her lips, her eyes trained on Aoife as a fire blazed in them.

"So, you did get a bit of me after all," she said with spite-filled curiosity. An airy laugh escaped her. "But can you control it?"

Aoife had powers? It made sense, given her fae heritage, but by the look on her face, it was painfully obvious to Adler—and likely Melina—that she couldn't wield them as her mother could.

Declan stepped in front of Aoife, guarding her from the fae queen.

"It flees from you, doesn't it?" Melina said, taunting her daughter as she stared at her over Declan's shoulder. "You can sense it in your blood. You reach for it. And it flits away because it knows you're weak, Aoife. Your *daemari* may listen when your emotions flare, but that is not control."

Melina inched her way toward them, and Declan nudged Aoife backward. Adler searched for something, anything he could do while Melina's focus was elsewhere. Movement in his periphery had him turning to find Cait sliding a knife along the table. He reached for it as slowly as he could.

Just a little closer.

Just a little more.

His fingers brushed the metal utensil.

Melina's exasperated groan filled the room, and the knife shifted out of his reach and flew into the air before plunging itself straight through the middle of Adler's palm.

He hissed a pained scream through his teeth.

Bitch! Sands, that fucking hurt.

Cait reached for his arm and pulled him backwards. "Let me see it." Adler pulled the knife from his hand and allowed Cait to wrap her napkin around the wound. He winced as she cinched it tight and tied it off.

Melina surveyed the room. "Can I do anything without you trying something stupid?" Pinching the bridge of her nose, she shook her head and closed her eyes. "Why do I even bother? I should just kill you all and be done with it."

The other councilwomen, snapping out of whatever stupor they'd been in, protested from their seats.

"Melina, you can't—"

"Why would—"

Rolling her eyes, Melina flung both of her arms in their direction. The table, despite being made of heavy, solid wood, slid quickly and easily across the stone floor. It stopped with a sickening crunch as its edge bit through their ribs and spines, splintering their chairs and pinning them to the wall. Horror filled their eyes as they struggled for their final breaths.

King Kilmeran's brow rose, the corners of his mouth turning downward, as if he were impressed by Melina's display of power. Her sisters, slumped grotesquely over the table, had barely stilled when Melina finally turned to Liam and the king.

"Before I continue..." she said, releasing a flustered sigh. "A hand, if you please, Kilmeran?" She gestured toward Cait and Adler.

Kilmeran nodded to Liam, and at once, something pushed Adler back down into his chair. Adler whirled to face the fae prince, but something in Liam's eyes made him pause. The unseen hands holding him down slipped away, and Adler started to move, but Liam shook his head slowly.

Adler stilled with understanding. Cait sat beside him, irritation filling her eyes as she stared Liam down. But when her features eventually shifted slightly, he knew she'd gotten the same message.

Good thing they were both excellent actors.

CHAPTER 55
CAIT

THE EXCHANGE between Liam and Adler, as silent and subtle as it was, gave Cait pause. She stilled in her chair despite the fact that the fae was no longer using his powers to restrain her. If they were going to get past Melina's defenses, they needed a proper distraction, one that would engage all the fae queen's senses so she wouldn't see what they were doing.

Not that Cait had any idea yet what that might be.

Melina stalked toward Declan and Aoife. "I wanted more for you, Aoife. More than him." Her cruel eyes roved over Declan as her face twisted in disgust. "You deserve better."

Declan smirked. "Finally something we agree on."

Aoife's lips twitched, but she remained quiet.

Melina stopped an arm's length away from them. Her features almost seemed to soften as she peered thoughtfully at her daughter. "I've waited a long time for this moment, and to have a daughter to share it with. I'm so very tired." Nothing about her tone indicated any sort of weariness, however. "Tired of being weak. Tired of being stuck here. Tired of having to kill daughter after daughter after daughter while I waited for the dagger to come home to me."

Aoife shook her head slowly. "Do you feel no remorse? Do you feel nothing?"

Melina scoffed and tilted her head to one side. "Funny what losing everyone you love—everyone who you *thought* loved you in return—will do to your heart." She turned her attention to Declan. "I think your pirate here knows what I mean. Don't you, Declan?"

"He is *not* like you," Aoife said fiercely.

"Isn't he though? What did you have to do to get this dagger, I wonder? Word was that another pirate had taken it from the sound. I highly doubt he gave it to you willingly." Melina let out a dark laugh as she leaned close to Declan's face. "You made him suffer, didn't you?"

Declan's eye twitched, and he swallowed hard before he answered in a low voice, "It's what he deserved."

Cait recognized the look in her brother's eyes. She'd seen it years ago. He'd left that part of him behind, hadn't he? But here it was. Not quite the same as she remembered, but the darkness in his expression was all too familiar.

The fae reached out a hand toward Declan's cheek, and when he tried to pull away, she grabbed his chin hard. "Does my daughter know who you really are, McCallagh? Do you truly expect her to love you when she finds out?"

Another smirk appeared on his lips, and he pushed his face even closer to Melina's.

"She was there. She saw what I did. In fact, she's the one who killed him."

Melina's eyes hardened as she searched his face for a handful of breaths. She stepped back, a dangerous smile on her face.

"It seems I've underestimated my daughter. Perhaps I should keep her by my side after all."

Aoife straightened. "I would never."

Melina's smile didn't reach her eyes.

Cait tensed as she watched Melina stand there looking over the pair. Something about the way the fae eyed them had Cait's stomach churning, her throat tightening. She shifted her arms slightly, testing them to ensure Liam truly wasn't using his powers on her. Still, she couldn't act too soon.

Adler fidgeted beside her, and she hoped he was having the same thought.

CHAPTER 56
MAURA

MAURA HAD NEVER ENJOYED combat training. In fact, it had been her least favorite part of her education. Whenever her father had insisted she learn to fight, she would cast a glamour around herself and hide, thankful only her brother had the power to see through her *daemari*. She'd been thankful, too, that Liam had never ratted her out to her parents.

When the war broke out, she and her sisters had been safe behind the walls of the council hall, as they had come to help Rhiannon hold her nation together in the absence of her husband and sons. Maura had been content with her role of trusted friend, happy to avoid the bloodshed and gore of combat.

She had not remained with Rhiannon out of cowardice. Nor did she hold some haughty opposition to the taking of a life when necessary. She didn't lack confidence or fear failure. She'd simply never cared for the fighting. The mundane drills. The repetitive movements. There were far better things to do with one's hands, so Maura had refused to participate, and she'd never regretted it.

Until now.

As she ran after Kira and Penny, Maura adjusted her grip on her small dagger and hoped she could at least do enough against these men to help them get people to safety. If she was going to help them, though, she'd need all her strength. And while she might have been able to maintain a glamour while fighting in the past, she refused to risk any of her energy now.

She released the glamour from around her ears just as a retreating rogue stepped in front of her. He paused, wide-eyed. Sighing, she ushered him past her and then barely ducked in time to avoid being hit in the face by a cutlass. She thrust her blade into her attacker's belly. His cutlass fell at her feet, and she shoved him hard into one of his friends before reaching down to pick up the dropped blade.

But a foot stepped on it before she could lift it. Twisting, she looked up to find a bearded and sweaty man already bringing the pommel of his sword down toward her head. Releasing the cutlass, she rolled away, swiping her dagger across the man's shins.

A grunt of pain rushed from her as someone kicked her in the stomach, and she curled instinctively around the pain. Then warmth hit her bare arms, and she glanced up to see that Kira had leaped onto the man's back and was pulling her blade across his throat. His eyes bulged. His hands rose to his throat, blood oozing around his fingers.

Maura scrambled to her feet and mouthed a word of thanks to Kira, but the woman yelled at her, "Behind you!"

Spinning around, Maura brought her dagger up just in time to block a saber strike aimed at her neck. She stumbled backwards, and for a moment she panicked when her back slammed into someone, until she glanced around to find it was Kira fending off her own assailant.

Around them, steel crashed against steel, boots pounded against the blood-splattered floor, and the fire roared and crackled as it consumed the far wall. They needed to get out of here quickly, before the flames brought the ceiling down on them.

Her opponent danced in front of her, flicking his blade toward her now and then as if testing her reactions. Maura studied him in return, and when an idea hit her, she couldn't help but laugh. The man scowled, asking her what was so funny.

"This," Maura answered as she called on her *daemari*. The additional warmth of the glamour made the heat in the room nearly unbearable, but she didn't need to maintain it long.

The man froze in horror as he stared back at her—at an exact image of himself.

"First time seeing yourself?" Maura asked, and the man stumbled backward, his head shaking quickly. "Come now," she said, "you're not that hideous."

Still, he said nothing. Maura shrugged and lunged for him, sending her dagger into his neck before he could even think to raise his saber. Letting the glamour dissolve, she flashed him her own smile.

She didn't wait to watch him fall but turned instead to find Penny pinned against the front window, straining to keep a knife-wielding man from getting his blade to her neck. Maura darted around Kira, jumping over some fallen men as she ran for Penny.

With a roar, Maura threw herself into the man's side, toppling him to the ground and burying her dagger deep in his lower back. He fought to get her off him but then stilled. Pulling her blade free, Maura wiped his blood off on her skirts as she turned back to Penny.

"You okay?" Maura asked, but the woman's eyes were quickly glazing over. Maura looked her over and sucked in a breath when she saw the blood soaking through Penny's dress near her ribs.

Before Maura could move to lift her, though, stocky arms wrapped around her, pulling her away from the injured woman. Steel nipped at her neck, and Maura stilled, trying to think of a way out.

"Never thought I'd get to kill a fae," a rough voice breathed into her ear.

Maura hissed, "And you never will."

He shook with laughter. Maura adjusted the dagger in her hand, preparing to send it back into his leg. But then he stiffened. His arms fell away from her, and she whirled around, backing away with her dagger raised. She lowered it when she recognized a familiar face.

Captain Halloran.

The captain sneered at the man before pulling her cutlass from his side and kicking him away.

"Happy to see you, Captain," Maura said, not able to hide her smile.

"Chit-chat later," Halloran said. "After we—"

One of the king's men appeared from behind Halloran's shoulder, his cutlass already descending toward her. Maura rushed around her with a silent scream, stepping in front of Halloran just as the blade finished its arc.

Pain sliced through her.

Stinging, burning, flashing pain.

The sharp blade cut across her shoulder and over her collarbone. Dropping her dagger, she raised her hands slowly. They hovered over her wound. All sounds faded in her ears as if she had been plunged underwater.

She sank backward, falling into someone's arms. Maura watched as a woman—unfamiliar and foreign to her—caught the man by the shoulders, spun him around, sank her needle-like teeth into his neck, and began to devour his flesh.

A siren.

Maura had never thought she would be happy to see such a sight again, though she would have preferred it not be the last thing she saw before her whole world went black.

CHAPTER 57
TOMMY

TOMMY'S MUSCLES burned with exertion as he swung again at the pirate lord, but it was nothing compared to the sting of the cuts he'd sustained across his left shoulder and right hip. He shoved Madigen away from him, trying to earn himself a moment to breathe and think. It wasn't easy to do with the smoke billowing above their heads and the fire's heat filling the room.

To Tommy's surprise, the pirate lord didn't spring back at him right away but lazily held his blade in front of him, coughed once, and smiled.

"I'm actually happy to see you survived that night," he said.

Tommy smirked back at him. "Oh? I didn't know you cared."

Madigen's brow tightened. "This way, I get to kill you myself. And in front of your fae bitch, no less."

Tommy ignored the bait, refusing to risk even a glance toward the other side of the room, where he had last seen Maura fighting alongside Kira against a couple of Madigen's men. Instead he lunged for the lord, pushing the man's dagger to the side —ignoring the way the blade bit into his palm as he did—and aiming his own blade for the man's gut.

But Madigen twisted out of the way so that Tommy's dagger only grazed his ribs. He stepped to the side, circling Tommy until they had switched positions.

Tommy tried to ignore the destruction around him. The entire top of the bar, as well as the wall behind it, was being consumed by the flames. He didn't know how many Rogues had made it out and how many had been wounded by Madigen's crew, but he couldn't worry about that now.

"I am curious though," Madigen said, "why your dear captain isn't here to help you."

Tommy narrowed his eyes. "Did your fae wench of a councilwoman not let you in on her plans? Not very polite of her."

Madigen paused, his eyes losing their cruel humor as he searched Tommy's face. His jaw started to drop, but he quickly snapped it shut.

Tommy shot him a sympathetic look. "Oh. You didn't know she was fae, did you? How does it feel to be so inconsequential?"

Madigen sneered at him. "How does it feel to be so useless?" He waved a hand toward the back of the pub and then at the back exit, where one of his men was busy dragging a fallen Rogue toward the fire and tossing the body into the flames. "Isn't this your friend's pub? You're doing a damn fine job saving it for him. Why does your captain keep you around?"

Offering him an easy shrug, Tommy huffed out a laugh. "Same reason Melina kept you around all these years. Loyalty. Only difference is my captain actually cares for his crew. Melina will kill you herself once she's done with you. And soon, she'll have no more use for her man-whore."

With a growl, Madigen rushed him, driving his blade straight at Tommy's chest.

Tommy prepared to parry the strike, but Maura's scream pierced the smoky room, pulling his heart and his eyes to where she stood by the front door, her hand pressing against a bloody gash on her shoulder.

"Maura!" he screamed as she stumbled backwards, and he nearly sighed in relief at the sight of Captain Halloran catching her.

But then Madigen's blade flashed toward him.

Tommy swung his weapon up, barely meeting Madigen's dagger, but his movement was sloppy, his grip too loose, and Madigen easily flung Tommy's weapon out of his hand, sending it clattering to the floor.

Retreating, Tommy scrambled away until his back slammed into the wall. He raised his hands and stood pinned beneath Madigen's cold glare as the pirate pressed the edge of his dagger against Tommy's throat.

Swallowing hard, Tommy searched for some cutting remark, something witty to throw the man off, but his mind went blank.

"Utterly useless," Madigen snarled, and Tommy braced himself for the end, hoping Maura wouldn't see it happen.

But the bite of the blade never came.

Madigen's eyes widened, and he crumpled to the floor.

The smoke swirled away, and Gavin appeared with a half-smile on his face and the pirate lord's blood dripping from his knife.

CHAPTER 58
AOIFE

LOOKING AT HER MOTHER NOW, Aoife wondered why she'd ever been so desperate for her affection and approval. Yet this was the legendary queen, the one who had loved so deeply and mourned her fallen king for years, the one so desperate to be loved that she'd given up her powers to help the man who had promised to be hers.

Such loss. Such betrayal.

But that didn't justify the path of death and destruction her mother had chosen.

Aoife would never be like her, would never stand beside her.

"You would choose this pirate over your own mother," Melina said, not framing it as a question.

Aoife breathed out a single laugh. "Mother? What do you know of being a mother? He loves me more than you ever—"

"After only a couple of weeks?" Melina said with a scoff.

Aoife stood taller and stepped up beside Declan. "You had twenty years with me! And you never believed in me the way he does."

Melina's eyes rolled dramatically toward the ceiling. "Ah, yes. A man will say anything to get us into his bed, Aoife. And your pirate is no different. He says he loves you now. But he will leave you. They always leave."

"No," Declan said with a shake of his head. "They always leave *you*, and I can't imagine why."

He raised a hand to gesture toward the dead and wounded in the room, but Melina struck him hard across the face with her open palm. The blow knocked his head back toward Aoife, but he let out no sound of pain.

Flashing Aoife a smirk, he turned back to Melina and spat more blood at her feet. "Thanks for making my point for me."

His gray eyes met Aoife's, and even with his face half-covered in blood and his jaw swollen and bruised, he looked as handsome as he had stepping out of the water in the cove. Aoife reached a hand up to sweep his hair away from his forehead and closed her eyes when he leaned into her touch and planted a kiss on her palm.

"Enough!" Melina shouted. The fae moved so fast that Aoife couldn't have stopped her even if she had been expecting the attack.

She should have expected it.

Melina pushed Aoife away from Declan, forcing their hands apart as she slammed a dagger into Declan's gut.

"No! Declan!" Aoife screamed, but her voice sounded far-off, echoing off distant walls, ringing in her ears.

She ran to him.

Or tried to.

But her body wouldn't move.

She screamed again. "Let me go!"

Her throat constricted around her panic as angry tears gathered at the edges of her eyes.

Declan collapsed over the fae queen's arms, and Aoife pushed her voice past the threatening sobs. "Declan! I'm here! It will be okay. I'm here!"

He tried to back away from Melina, but she grabbed his arm and pulled him toward her, forcing the weapon deeper. She leaned over him, her lips brushing over his ear, but Aoife couldn't hear what she uttered to him.

Aoife's vision blurred at the sight of Declan's blood dripping onto the stone floor.

His breathing became ragged.

His face paled.

And Melina laughed.

With a grotesque smile on her lips, she faced Aoife, her frenzied eyes daring Aoife to do something. Anything.

"Where's your *daemari* now, daughter?" her mother taunted. "A shame you are only half-fae. No healing powers at your disposal."

Fae.

Liam.

He was a fae. He could help Declan.

Aoife found the fae's eyes, but Melina's sharp laugh once more cut through the air.

"That fae prince is of no use to you. Not when he's tied to the king there, and I doubt the king wants to help a pirate."

Aoife looked to Cait and Adler with pleading eyes, but they remained in their seats. Neither of them looked at her. Cait stared at her brother in tear-soaked shock, and Adler seemed to be looking past them.

Why were they just sitting there?

Why weren't they helping?

She opened her mouth to yell those very questions at them, but then Declan's body collapsed to the ground with a muffled thud. He rolled onto his back, and he met Aoife's gaze, tears obscuring those stormy greys she loved.

"Thank you," he whispered.

Aoife struggled against the invisible restraints that held her, but it was useless. He would die on this floor without ever feeling her touch again, without another kiss or another "I love you."

This couldn't be the end.

It wouldn't be!

Swallowing back her tears, Aoife steadied her shaky lips as best she could. "Liam! Please! Cait! Get him to a fae!"

Aoife didn't see anyone move, didn't see if they were able to help Declan, before her mother was there, standing before her. Melina's arm reached out, her hand gripping Aoife under the chin, her claw-like nails digging into her throat. She sneered at Aoife and lifted her into the air.

Aoife tried to kick her legs, to get her feet back onto the floor, but her body remained trapped by her mother's *daemari*.

"You are such a disappointment," Melina spat at her. "Of all my daughters I've had to kill, you will be the first I am actually happy to be rid of."

She was a monster. Cruel and vicious and heartless.

And still, her words stung.

Why did Aoife still care about her approval?

Why did she still yearn for her love?

As if this fae was capable of love at all.

Aoife closed her eyes and forced herself to focus on the one whose love she did have. In her mind's eye she pictured the cocky smirk that appeared on his face when he teased her, how his eyes drank her in, how he quirked a brow when she surprised him.

Declan.

She had saved him once before.

She would save him again.

True love had saved them in the sound.

It could save them here.

Her mother's fingers squeezed tighter. She brought her face to Aoife's.

"Our *daemari* makes killing easier, but it is far more fun to actually feel the life leave someone."

Aoife snapped her eyes open and glared at her mother as she reached for the fire that had ignited in her chest.

She could do this.

For Declan.

For Lani.

For Collins and Killian and Declan's parents.

For everyone who had ever been hurt by the council, by this cruel fae queen.

For all of them, Aoife sought out every bit of strength she had found over the past few weeks, hoping her *daemari* would answer her.

But it slipped out of reach, and Melina mocked her.

"What are you going to do to me? Even if you can get your power to obey, what could you possibly do to *me*?"

Aoife's panic grew, her heart thundering in her ears, her lungs straining for air.

Declan's words echoed in her mind: "*Focus on the next task*," but that didn't help. *It's too hard. I'm too weak. I can't do it.*

A tear slipped free and slid down her cheek, a tear Declan would not be brushing aside this time.

Melina chuckled darkly, squeezing Aoife's throat tighter. "Looks like I win."

Aoife swallowed and drew in one more shaky breath. She needed to relax, to calm her nerves, to focus, but she couldn't. The world darkened at the edges until she saw nothing but her mother's eyes blazing with hatred.

CHAPTER 59
DECLAN

Declan's death had been a long time coming, considering how many had been injured or killed because of him. After everything he'd done, everyone he'd failed to protect, dying here on this cold floor was what he deserved.

Sands knew he would have stepped in front of Tommy in that library.

He would have taken Killian's place on that ship.

So many things he would have done differently.

Except he really wouldn't have.

Not if it meant living without Aoife.

Without her laugh and her freckles and all her questions. Her touch and her kiss and her love.

Declan had expected this, the familiar sting of pain from steel ripping into flesh. He had known it was coming, and he welcomed it. Better for that dagger to have struck him instead of Aoife.

He heard Aoife's screams as her fingers slipped out of his, heard her panic and the tears lacing the edge of her voice.

"It will be okay. I'm here!"

The words they had clung to, offered to each other to keep hope alive.

Hope.

Callum had called it a fool's mistress.

Perhaps he'd been right.

No.

As long as Declan had breath in his lungs, he would hold on to hope.

Reaching for the dagger, Declan tried to push Melina's hand away from it so he could back away from her without pulling the blade free.

But the bitch grabbed his elbow, yanked him toward her, and breathed across his cheek: "You've failed her, Declan. Like everyone else."

Failed her.

Melina was right, of course.

Declan had failed Aoife.

Failed to trust her. Failed to live for her.

Move! Fight! Keep fighting!

His thoughts screamed at him.

You haven't failed her yet!

This couldn't be the end. This couldn't be all he had to give.

How many men had he seen continue to fight with worse injuries than this? How many times had he fought a pirate who wouldn't stay down, who kept attacking no matter how many cuts Declan made?

But his lungs burned with each breath, never quite able to draw in the amount of air he needed.

Melina hadn't simply stabbed him.

She'd stabbed him between the ribs. A well-placed, lethal blow.

Declan blinked, watching his blood fall to the stone at his feet.

Voices surrounded him, but he heard none of their words.

Time slowed, and the room dimmed.

And then he was falling.

Rest. He could rest here.

Just for a moment.

Just a moment.

Turning his face, he opened his eyes, needing to see her.

She was there—blurred by his tears, but there all the same. His perfect, beautiful, curious, courageous, fearless woman who had driven him mad more times than he could count.

She deserved so much more than him and his failures.

Of all the things he could say with these last breaths, there were two words he most needed her to hear, the words he had never said to her except within Triss's haunting vision at the sound.

Not I love you.

Not I'm sorry.

She'd heard all of those before.

But never these.

"Thank you..."

And as the edges of his world darkened and his vision faded, closing in around her face as she called for help, the rest of his words whispered through his mind, words he'd never get to say to her.

For loving me when I didn't deserve it and putting me in my place when I did. For saving me when I didn't know I needed it and believing in me when I needed it the most.

Thank you.

CHAPTER 60
AOIFE

AOIFE'S CHEST ached for air, but her next attempted breath brought none.

She closed her eyes once more, not wanting her mother's eyes to be the last thing she saw as she slipped into darkness. Instead, she pulled forward every image she had tucked away of Lani and Declan and Tommy and Maura and everyone else she loved and cared for.

As her final tear fell, she gave herself over to the end.

But it never came.

The pressure around her throat fell away, and air rushed into her lungs. Pain flashed through her feet as they abruptly hit the floor, but she managed to remain standing.

Someone snarled, and she looked up to see her mother pivoting on her heel. A man, bloody and beaten, was rushing at Melina with one of the table knives in his hand.

"Lucan!"

Aoife didn't know who shouted his name, but it didn't matter. This was her chance. The only chance she would get. Relaxing her muscles and calming her nerves, Aoife reached for her *daemari* once more, commanding it rather than begging it to come to her.

This time, she controlled it.

This time, she wielded it.

This time, she directed it from her hand toward the Csintala dagger tucked at Melina's waist.

Her mother thrust both hands at the man, easily slamming him back against the wall. His head struck the stones, and his body slumped to the ground beside Darienn.

Melina turned and slowly stalked back toward Aoife, narrowing her eyes. "I always win," she hissed.

Aoife flashed her mother her best impression of Declan's smirk and whispered, "Not today." The Csintala dagger flew into her hand, and before Melina could react, Aoife had it buried in her mother's side. With all the fury borne of twenty years of lies and neglect, she twisted the blade inside her and ripped it back out.

Melina's eyes widened in confusion. She only managed to take half a step forward when Aoife sliced the dagger across her chest.

Melina howled in pain as she staggered backwards.

But Aoife would not let her retreat.

Not after she'd destroyed so many.

Declan and Lani.

The people of Cregah.

The countless daughters and sons she'd murdered for her own selfish gain.

For all of these Melina would pay.

With quick steps, Aoife lunged.

Before she could strike, though, her mother arched her back, lifting her chin high as she belted out not another pained cry but a haunting laugh. She collapsed onto her knees, to reveal Darienn standing there, trembling and pale, with a bloody knife clasped tight in her hand.

Melina's eyes flashed up to Aoife's, but she was done.

Striking one final blow, Aoife buried the Csintala dagger deep in her mother's neck. Pulling it free, she stepped back to watch the fae queen take one more ragged breath before falling lifeless onto the floor.

CHAPTER 61
ADLER

Melina was dead.

But no one celebrated.

Adler stayed near the table, giving Cait and Aoife space to check on Declan, who still lay on the floor, unmoving. Aoife pulled his head into her lap, brushing his hair back from his brow while Cait checked him over. Though she found a pulse, there was no hope in her eyes when she looked back at Adler.

"Kilmeran!" Adler shouted across the room.

No sooner had the king met Adler's gaze than he turned to Liam with a nod, gesturing toward the fallen pirate. Liam wasted no time, crossing the room quickly and dropping to his knees beside Declan. Placing his hands beside the blade, the fae pressed lightly, and a spark of hope lit in Adler when Declan let out a moan, albeit a pained one.

Any sound meant he was still alive.

"Can you heal him?" Aoife asked around her tears.

Liam looked up from under his lashes. "Not on my own, I'm afraid. I could try, but not without removing the blade. But if I do that and discover the wound is worse than we hoped..."

Aoife was nodding, as if she had expected this answer. "It took all three of your sisters to heal Tommy. But they were weakened—"

"Aye, in most cases I could help. But he's lost a lot of blood already. He will have a better chance if we have at least one other fae just in case."

"So what does that mean exactly?" Cait asked.

Liam swallowed hard. "I should be able to stabilize him enough so we can move him."

"Do it," Aoife said, looking back down at Declan, whose eyes remained closed as if he were merely sleeping instead of fighting to live.

As Liam focused on helping Declan, Cait stood and joined Adler. She didn't say anything or reach for him, letting her hands—which were stained with her brother's blood—fall limply at her sides. Grief, worry, and regret were written plainly on her exhausted face.

"Adler?" a meek voice asked, and he and Cait turned to find Darienn crouched beside Lucan.

He wasn't moving.

"I can't—I—can't find his heartbeat—" Darienn stammered around quivering lips, her shaky fingers fumbling at his wrist.

Adler knelt down and reached for his friend's neck.

There had to be a pulse.

He had to live.

"Lucan," Cait whispered as she dropped down beside him. She thrust her hand into Lucan's, squeezing his fingers in hers as she pleaded with him. "You dumbass. You can't leave me. I won't allow it."

Lucan didn't answer.

Darienn's eyes glazed over with tears.

Adler let his hand fall away from Lucan, resting it on Cait's back.

"He's gone, love."

"No, he can't be. He can't!" Cait's voice cracked.

Adler tried to pull her to him, but she shoved him aside with her shoulder.

"No!" she barked, refusing to look away from her friend. "They can save him. They can heal him. He'll be okay. You'll be okay, Lucan."

Adler swallowed past the heartbreak, tightened his gut against the grief, and reached for Cait. She struggled once more before finally giving in and letting him pull her into his arms. Dropping Lucan's hand, she gripped Adler's shirt tightly in her fingers. Her words gave way to sobs as she shook her head against his chest.

He had no words for her. Nothing that could make this right.

But he remembered how Cait had been there for him in the carriage earlier today, simply holding his hand in silence, letting him know he wasn't alone as he faced so much pain. Sometimes words weren't necessary. Sometimes the simple act of being there in the tear-filled silence was enough to soothe even the most painful of wounds.

"Where did Maura go?" Liam asked.

Adler stood, pulling Cait up alongside him, and turned to see that the fae was now standing as well.

"Declan is stable enough for now, but we'll need to move him quickly. And I'll need my sister's help."

"Back to the pub," Cait answered. Her hand tightened around Adler's arm. "The pub! I completely forgot. What if—"

They had both forgotten, and Adler's stomach tightened with dread. He reached up to cup Cait's face in his hands.

"It will be okay. We'll get there."

Liam cleared his throat. "We'll need to get there now. And hope Maura is still there to help me. Adler? Nox?"

Nox? Who's Nox?

The king stepped up beside the fae. Though he still had an intimidating air about him, he looked far less maniacal than he had earlier.

"I'll get the staff to bring the carriage around," he said before hurriedly stepping out of the room, leaving Cait and Adler watching in bewilderment.

Liam offered them a tight smile. "He can be a prick at times, but he's not that bad when you get to know him."

CHAPTER 62
TOMMY

TOMMY QUICKLY NODDED his thanks to Gavin, swallowing hard and struggling to catch his breath. At his feet, Lord Madigen stared lifelessly at Tommy's boots.

Utterly useless.

He tried to shake the taunt away, but it stung all the same.

Captain Halloran's voice rang out amidst the snapping and popping of the fire, calling his name.

Maura.

Pushing himself forward, he tripped on Madigen's body, but Gavin caught his arm before he could fall to the floor. He vaguely realized he should thank his friend, should at least acknowledge his help, but all Tommy could focus on was Maura— her screams and the sight of blood trickling out of her wound.

I'm coming, Maura. I'm here!

His thoughts shouted for her as he darted around toppled chairs, slipping in the spilled blood and rum that covered the floor.

"We need to get her out of here," Gavin, who was following closely behind him, said. "The building's not going to hold much longer."

Tommy risked a glance up to the ceiling, where the flames licked greedily at the peeling paint. The fire was now reaching toward the front entrance where Halloran knelt with Maura propped up against her.

Her eyes were closed. Her chest didn't move.

Tommy pushed harder despite the intensifying heat. His lungs burned from the smoke filling the room. Falling to his knees, he dropped down beside them.

His hands hovered over her wounds.

So much blood. The cut was deep.

"Is she—" His voice was soft, so quiet he was sure even Halloran couldn't have heard him.

A voice answered from above him, "She's alive, but it's bad." Tommy looked up to see Kira. The cuts along her cheek and arms looked as if they were already healing.

That's impossible.

But that didn't matter right now.

"Then why are we just sitting here?" he growled.

"Let's move," Halloran said, ignoring his question. She shifted under Maura's unconscious form to prepare to stand, and Tommy maneuvered to lift Maura's legs.

Kira opened the door as the loud crack of splintering wood hit their ears. The ceiling in the center of the room started to give, with bits of plaster and wood falling onto the tables below.

They had just stepped out into the cool night air and started to turn for the docks when the clattering of hooves and wheels echoed down the street, growing louder.

A chill swept over Tommy, and he froze.

Few people on this island had a carriage.

Was it the council? Had Declan fallen? Had they failed?

Or was it his captain heading this way?

Kira pulled lightly on his elbow. "We need to get her to—"

Tommy rounded on her. "To where? The ship? Last I knew we didn't have a fae on board who could heal her! Or do you have more powers you haven't shared with us?"

Shaking her head, Kira said nothing, and Tommy immediately regretted yelling at her. It wasn't her fault Maura was hurt and that none of them had the ability to help her.

The carriage whirled around the corner, its wheels skidding along the road as the driver urged the horses forward with loud snaps of the reins.

"Kira!" a woman shouted from the driver's seat, and in the dim evening light, Tommy could just make out Cait's face.

The carriage hadn't even stopped completely when Declan's sister swung down and rushed toward them, her eyes wild as she took in the sight of her pub—her home—burning and the five of them standing outside.

"Are you—" Cait started, but her voice caught when she saw Maura. She began to shake her head, quietly repeating the word "no." Then she turned frantically back to the carriage. "Aoife!"

Why was she calling for her?

What was happening?

Why was Cait so distraught over Maura's injury?

The door flew open, and Aoife's face peered out, but she didn't exit.

"The fae. She's hurt," Cait called over. And then someone else stepped out of the carriage and ran toward them.

Liam.

The fae male looked from his sister to Tommy and back again.

"How long ago did this happen?" he asked, and Tommy's mouth went dry.

Thankfully Halloran, who did not seem at all distracted by the appearance of this fae, answered for them. "Not long."

Liam gingerly placed his hands over the gash in Maura's shoulder and chest.

Please help her, Tommy begged silently. *You can't leave me, Maura! I just got you back!*

Heaving a rough sigh, her brother straightened. "I can help her, but I can't help them both."

Both?

"What the fuck do you mean *both*?" Tommy asked, his eyes darting to Cait and then to Aoife. "What does he mean by both, Aoife?"

Aoife's eyes glistened with tears, her bottom lip quivering, and then she answered, "Declan."

No. This could not be how it happened. This couldn't be the choice he had to make. His best friend or his love? How in the sands could a man make such a choice?

The world spun around him, and he tried to block out all the faces staring at him. They were all looking to him to make such an awful decision. He couldn't choose. He wouldn't. There had to be a way.

Glaring at Liam, Tommy forced himself to speak past the sadness that threatened to choke him. "Both. You have to save both. You're a fucking fae! What good are you if you can't heal them both?"

Liam's lips pressed into a tight line, but he didn't say anything.

Kira.

Her injuries had started to heal. Tommy had watched her move. She was faster than most. She had heard his words when she shouldn't have been able to.

She was a fae. She had to be.

But she was already shaking her head at him as if she was also able to hear his thoughts. He didn't even get a chance to beg.

"I'm only part fae," she said, her words dripping with regret and sorrow. "I can only heal myself, not others."

"How do you know? Have you ever tried?!" Tommy yelled at her.

Liam cleared his throat. "A demi-fae?"

Tommy growled in frustration, but the damned fae ignored him.

"Aye," Kira answered. "Why?"

"You might still be able to help," Liam said, and a small spark of hope reignited within Tommy. "We need to move though. Where can we go?"

Halloran spoke before Tommy could. "Declan's ship."

Giving her a sharp nod, Liam spun on his heel. "Get my sister in the carriage. Kira, you too. The rest of you will need to follow on foot, but we will see you there."

Before Tommy could protest, before he could stop Captain Halloran from taking Maura in her arms to carry her to the carriage, Cait was clambering up beside the driver once more and Liam was shouting up to them.

"Adler, drive. Fast."

The reins snapped against the horse's back even before the carriage door had closed. The thundering sound of the horse and carriage speeding away filled

Tommy's ears. It was almost as loud as his panicking heart. And all he could do was watch them leave.

What would he do if he lost them? Either one of them? He couldn't even fathom it.

A hand fell on his shoulder, and he turned to find Halloran's sober expression. "I won't tell you it will be okay, because I'm no seer," she said. "Nor am I a liar. But we are with you, Tommy. You are not alone."

Tommy swallowed hard and watched as Gavin took off running after the carriage.

"Let's go," Halloran said. "They'll want to see you when they wake up."

As the captain walked briskly away, Tommy wondered who she meant.

Who would awaken?

Who would survive?

Who would Tommy have to let go?

CHAPTER 63
AOIFE

EACH TIME the carriage wheels hit a bump on the uneven streets and jostled Declan's head in Aoife's lap, it sent a fresh tremor of panic through her chest. The fae sisters had healed Tommy. After Declan had carried him, bleeding and dying, all those miles to the ship from the council hall, the fae had healed him. They could do the same for Declan.

Except there weren't three fae here.

It will be okay, Declan. It will.

It had to be.

They hadn't come this far and overcome so much to have this be their ending.

Tears spilled down Aoife's cheeks, but she refused to let go of Declan long enough to wipe them away. She would hold him until he woke up. And after. Long after.

"We're almost there," Kira said, pushing the curtains aside to peer out the window. Aoife looked up from under her lashes, and her breathing hitched at the sight of Maura, her friend, lying unconscious across Liam's lap, her head cradled in the crook of his arm as if she were a child and not a centuries-old fae.

"Do you think this will work?" Kira asked. "I've never heard of such a thing being done."

Liam didn't take his eyes from his sister but shook his head. "I don't know. It might. It might not. But we have to try."

Aoife swallowed hard and asked, "What are you trying exactly?"

Kira leaned forward, resting her forearms on her knees. "My blood. Liam thinks maybe the *daemari* within it could boost her own ability to heal. But who knows how much blood she would need or if it is even possible."

It sounded logical enough, and if it was truly without risk as Liam seemed to believe, Aoife saw no reason for hesitation.

"So why aren't you doing it?"

Liam glanced up at her with gentleness. "Giving her the blood isn't risky, but getting it from Kira is if we aren't careful. And doing so during a rough carriage ride isn't ideal."

Aoife could only nod silently as her tears increased. All her worry and dread and grief rose into the back of her throat, threatening to strangle her.

When the carriage finally skidded to a stop, its wheels sliding along the slick wooden boards of the docks, everyone moved at once. Cait opened the door, and Adler appeared, his large arms reaching for Declan, his hands sliding over Aoife's legs to get a hold of his shoulders.

"Can you get his legs, Aoife?" Adler asked, already pulling Declan through the door.

"I think so," she said, but Cait was there beside her as soon as she stepped down onto the dock.

Cait took hold of one of her brother's legs, giving Aoife a small smile. "I'll help."

As they boarded the ship, Aoife motioned with her chin toward Declan's quarters. The sight of Mikkel and the crew standing silently on the deck, watching as their captain was carried aboard, caused a new wave of grief to slam into her like the tide upon the rocks. Mikkel's brow shot up as he caught sight of her, and with a nod, he beckoned her over.

A pang of fear hit her chest at the thought of having to be parted from Declan, but the urgency in Mikkel's expression told her she was needed elsewhere. At least for the moment.

With a nod, she looked to Cait and let her take both of Declan's legs. "Get him inside," Aoife said. "I'll be right there."

She didn't waste time watching them proceed without her but rushed to Mikkel.

"Is he—" Mikkel started.

"He's hurt. Badly."

Aoife waited for the bo'sun to bombard her with questions about what had happened and what could be done, but instead he nodded slowly before shifting to the side.

"You have guests who might be able to help," he said, bowing his head as he stepped back. The crew parted to reveal two regal figures clad in long cloaks.

Renna and Bria.

Aoife set her jaw and gnashed her teeth together as she tried to restrain the harsh words she had for these two. More than words—she wanted to leap across this deck and pummel them for what they had done to Maura and Tommy. But she refrained.

The pair glided forward until they were little more than an arm's length away, and part of Aoife wondered if they kept such distance purposefully. Renna could likely hear her violent intentions.

"We are sorry, Aoife," Renna said.

Aoife scoffed and rolled her eyes to the night sky.

"Truly, we are," Bria added.

Aoife's snapped, "Save your apologies for Tommy and Maura. If Maura survives, that is."

Renna stilled, and her eyes focused on something over Aoife's shoulder.

"It can't be," she whispered.

Aoife glanced over her shoulder to see Liam step aboard with Maura draped in his arms and Kira following closely behind. Though Liam obviously noticed his sisters standing there, he paid them little attention as he hastened toward them, his questioning eyes focused on Aoife.

"Mikkel," Aoife said, "show him the officers' quarters. Tommy should be—"

"I'm here!" Tommy's heavy boots thudded across the deck after them. Renna reached out to him as he ran past Aoife, but he pulled his arm free, throwing the fae a deadly glare.

"Please, Tommy," Renna begged as he started to leave. "Let us help."

In a heartbeat, Tommy was in Renna's face, every muscle taut with anger. "Fuck. Off." He spat the words at her, but the fae didn't so much as flinch.

Aoife lightly settled her hand on Tommy's arm and stepped close to him, turning her back on the two sisters so she could get her friend's full attention. His eyes flashed to hers, and his jaw flinched as he tried to keep it steady.

He was shaking his head at Aoife even before she said the words, but they needed to be said.

"They can help. It's the only hope we have, Tommy. You know that."

He closed his eyes, freeing a single tear, but kept shaking his head.

"Please," Aoife begged with quiet desperation. "For Maura. And Declan. You don't need to forgive them yet, but please let them help."

Tommy's chin dropped to his chest, and he drew in a deep breath before finally whispering his answer. "Fine."

A breath of relief rushed from Aoife, and she stepped away. Renna and Bria began to move toward the officers' cabin, but Tommy's arm flashed up to block their way. Aoife started to protest, but Tommy gave her a sharp look.

"They don't touch her. I won't have them near Maura. Not yet."

Aoife could live with this arrangement. As angry as she was with the fae sisters, Tommy's anger ran deeper, and she could not ask him to make this concession.

"Understood," she said. "Go. Help Liam and Kira. I'll take them to Declan."

Without another word, Tommy pivoted on his heel and ran.

Aoife longed to do the same, to run off to be with Declan, but something kept her rooted to her spot on the deck, even as she waved a hand toward the captain's quarters and told the fae to go. For several minutes, no one spoke. The crew stood silently, watching her. She had known these men for such a short time, but they had fought a kraken together. They had laughed and danced and drunk rum together.

These were her men as much as they were Declan's or Tommy's. This was her crew and her family. Seeing the worry worn plainly on their rough faces, she knew she couldn't run out on them no matter how much she wanted to be elsewhere.

"Declan—Captain McCallagh," she started, her voice cracking under the weight of her emotion. She drew in a breath and forced herself to look at the men. She needed to tell them what had happened, how he had been injured, how he would make it and survive to continue to be their captain. But she couldn't find her voice, and she shamefully dropped her chin. She couldn't do this. She wasn't the captain. She wasn't a leader.

A hand fell on her shoulder, and she turned to peer into Gavin's friendly face.

"It's okay, Aoife. Halloran and I will talk to the crew," he said, tossing his chin toward Declan's cabin. "Be with him. He needs you."

CHAPTER 64
DECLAN

DEATH WASN'T as Declan expected.

No shining light.

No path leading him on.

Only pain and darkness and the reminders of everything he had done, every failure, every dream he would never see come true. Memories washed over him, drenching him in the blood he had spilled, drowning him in the tears he had caused, forcing him to relive over and over the moments of regret and remorse.

Make it stop.

Leave me alone.

Let me rest.

Only pain answered him.

Heat seared his chest, engulfed his heart, tore through his lungs, pulled at his ribs.

He deserved this.

For everything he had done.

This was what he had earned.

"It will be okay, Declan."

A familiar voice called through his agony.

Lies. It would never be okay.

He had abandoned her. Failed her.

She wasn't here.

"I am here."

Declan choked on a laugh.

Even in death she argued with him.

He expected nothing less from his Aoife.

Slowly the flames within died down, little by little, until only burning embers remained.

A weight lifted from his chest, as if all the burdens he'd carried for so long had been removed.

Warmth pressed into his palm, and familiar fingers intertwined with his.

He could almost feel her.

"Come back to me, Declan. Please. Don't leave me."

He tried to. Tried to move, to stand, to run to her.

Nothing but darkness surrounded him.

Her voice was far-off but clear.

Yet he couldn't find her, couldn't see her.

If this wasn't death, then he could reach her.

He could. And he would.

I'm here, Aoife. Somewhere, I'm here.

Don't leave me.

Then the memories returned, this time of caresses and kisses and smirks and laughs.

Memories he held tight to as the darkness pulled him under once more.

⚓

"He's fine."

The voice, faint and distant, pulled at Declan's consciousness. A voice he couldn't place.

And then came one he knew as if it was his own.

"Then why hasn't he woken up? It's been days since you healed him!"

"I don't know, Aoife. Trust that he will wake when he's ready."

I'm ready!

Declan wanted to scream the words, but no sound came. He wanted to open his eyes, to reach for her, to tell her he was alive and well. But his body refused to respond to his commands.

Silence returned, surrounding him.

But he wasn't alone.

Warmth lined one side of his body.

A weight pressed against his shoulder.

A breath fell upon his cheek.

She was here.

"Why did you say *thank you*, Declan?"

Did she really not understand? Did she not know all she had done for him? All she had given him?

"All I did was ruin everything," Aoife said.

No, you didn't.

He needed to say the words, needed her to hear them.

Pushing himself through the darkness, Declan focused on what he could feel and hear. The faint sound of water lapping against wood. The softness of the fabric beneath his fingers. The scent of sugar and wood, the sea air, and...copper? No, blood.

He urged his body to move, to shift and stretch.

The weight lifted from his shoulder, taking all its warmth away.

"Declan?" Aoife's voice beckoned him, and he fought to reach her, throwing himself against whatever wall separated them.

It started to give, began to crumble beneath his efforts to tear it away, until light pierced the darkness.

Almost there.

He stretched his fingers wide and brought them in, squeezing tightly until his nails bit into his palm.

That felt real enough.

"Declan." Not a question this time. More like a command.

His eyes flew open, faster than he'd expected, and he winced as the brightness of the sunlight streaming in pierced his temple with a stabbing pain.

"Aoife?" Her name was scratchy and faint on his lips, but she was there in an instant, her freckles and green eyes coming into view, becoming his whole world. Lifting a hand to her face, he traced the line of her jaw slowly, as if she might disappear if he moved too quickly.

"I'm here," she said, and tears flooded her eyes.

Burying his fingers in her hair, he pulled her to him, needing to feel her lips on his, to know for sure that she was as real as he hoped. Aoife crashed into him, her warm lips claiming him, welcoming him home, pulling him further and further from the dark abyss he'd been trapped in.

With a sweet laugh, she pulled away, shaking her head at him as she searched his eyes.

"What?" Declan asked around a smirk.

"Nothing. Just didn't expect you to be so...I don't know. Just glad you're here, alive."

Pushing himself up with both hands, he groaned when a sharp ache tore through his left ribs. Aoife shifted closer, helping to put a pillow behind him so he could rest back comfortably.

"Renna says it will likely hurt to move for a couple weeks," Aoife said as she took his hand in hers.

Declan frowned, confused. "Renna? She's here?"

"Well, I mean, she didn't heal you from Larcsporough." She smirked at him before continuing. "She and Bria convinced Halloran's crew to turn around and come to Morshan. I guess they didn't want to go on without Maura."

Maura. Tommy.

Were they okay? Was the pub safe?

So many questions bombarded him, he couldn't decide which to ask first. But Aoife was already answering many of them.

"Maura almost didn't make it, but Liam and Kira were able to help her. Tommy was a bit of a mess, but then, so was I. Needless to say, he was not thrilled to see her sisters on board, and he only agreed to let them help if they didn't touch Maura. So they healed you."

"I don't blame him. And the pub?"

Aoife's eyes fell to their clasped hands as she shook her head. "It's gone."

Declan hadn't expected it to hurt as much it did. He had walked away from that home, left it behind, yet knowing it was destroyed, that the home where his parents had created so many memories for him and Cait—

"Cait? Is everyone okay?"

"She's fine. She lost a lot that night—her home, her friends."

"Wait, you said *that* night. Not last night. How long has it been?"

"A few days. Maura recovered quicker. Benefit of having fae blood, I guess. But Melina—"

The fae queen's sneer flashed in Declan's mind, and he realized he had no idea what else had happened after he'd fallen. He held up a hand, and Aoife waited patiently.

"Is Melina—"

Aoife's breath caught. Her eyes slid away from his, tears already forming. She reached a hand up to swipe them away.

"She's gone. And I don't know why I'm so upset. She doesn't deserve my tears."

Declan placed a hand on her cheek and brushed away a tear that had escaped. "She was your mother all the same."

"Still, this," she said, waving a finger at her tear-reddened eyes, "feels like an insult to all those she killed. I should be mourning them. Not her."

"Who says you can't mourn them all?" Declan asked.

"But I don't want to, Declan. I don't want to grieve over her. I don't want to miss her."

"Grief never seems to care about what we want though. All you can do is let it run its course."

Aoife turned her face toward the window and sat silently for a while. Declan didn't know what more he could say or do to help ease her struggle. Perhaps nothing.

Though he could change the subject at least.

"What about the king?" he asked.

Aoife breathed out a single laugh as she turned back to him. "He's helping Darienn reform the council. I believe he's appointing Liam as his liaison? Leaving him here to advise my sister."

"The same king who killed Lucy? Who laughed like a maniac in that room as people were killed?"

"Aye, it's complicated. I can explain later. But I have a question."

"Only one?" He eyed her curiously.

Giving him a half-shrug, she asked, "Why did you thank me?"

Pulling her to him, he settled her against his right side and kissed the top of her head before speaking the answer into her hair. "Because you saved me."

Surprisingly, Aoife only hummed in response, as if that was a more than sufficient answer. While it was for him, he hadn't expected her to accept it quite so easily.

After a few moments of comfortable silence, Aoife asked him quietly, "What was it like while you were healing?"

Declan bristled. He didn't want to tell her of the torment he'd endured, but he didn't want to keep anything from her either. He chose his words carefully. "Much of it was like a bad dream, and I could feel the pain of my injuries the whole time."

She nestled closer against him. "Do you ever have good dreams? Seems like I've only known you to have nightmares."

"A few. Rarely. Actually, one of the best ones, I got from the siren."

"What?" Aoife started to sit up, but he pulled her back against him.

"Aye. I mean, it hurt at the time, but now—"

"I don't understand."

"In an effort to drum up my guilt, Triss gave me two different visions: one forcing me to relive that moment in the cove, and one showing me our future had I not lied to you."

"And what did that future look like?"

"We were in our cove still. But happy." Declan reached for her hand as he spoke and held it up like he was inspecting it. "And we were married."

Aoife sat up, and Declan didn't stop her this time. She eyed him with that curious look of hers. "Married."

"Aye. And..." He paused, not quite sure how she would take the next part.

"And what?" Aoife looked so wary of his answer that he nearly laughed.

Declan gave her a tight smile. "And expecting a baby."

Aoife froze, and her eyes began to glaze over.

He couldn't stop his smile from widening, and he had to fight back the laughter. "Do I need to remind you to breathe? It was just a dream. No need to panic, princess."

She blinked rapidly and then looked at him. "Is that what you want? Marriage? A family? A boring life after all of this?" She swept her arm around the space.

"Who said it had to be boring? Nothing about my childhood was boring."

"Your parents led a secret rebellion!"

He had to concede that point. "Aye, but even if they hadn't...I don't think it would have been mundane. Your life is only as boring as you allow it to be. It is what you make of it."

"But still, is that what you want?"

Declan searched her face for any hint of what she was hoping he might say, but his answer would be the same regardless of what she wanted to hear.

Slowly he shook his head. "I never wanted it. Not until I met you." With both hands, he pulled her into his lap, ignoring the pain that resulted from the movement. She kept her eyes lowered, though, which made a different kind of ache settle in his chest.

"Look at me, Aoife."

Her chin turned toward him, and when their eyes met, he couldn't tell if she was more scared or worried or happy.

"I want you and whatever that means for my life. Whether it's facing sea monsters and evil fae or raising our family on some island, I will gladly do it all if it keeps me by your side."

After a long moment—and much panic on Declan's part—Aoife took his face in both her hands and rested her forehead against his.

"I've already faced a kraken and two evil queens to keep you beside me. But where are we going to find an island?"

THE CABIN WAS dark the next time Declan opened his eyes. He'd tried to get up and move shortly after first waking up, but Liam had insisted he take it easy and get more rest. Turning his head, he expected to see Aoife lying beside him, but his bed was empty, her side of the blankets smooth and undisturbed.

A throat cleared from the doorway.

"You had me worried there for a bit, brother," Cait said. Even in the dim light, Declan could make out her serious expression, that look of determined calm she had shown after their parents' disappearances.

Declan sat up as he watched his sister walk to the edge of the bed. There was a slight hitch in her steps.

"Should I be the one worrying about you?" he asked, nodding at her legs.

"It's nothing," she said with a wave of her hand.

"Of course." He nodded slowly. "I hope you lied better to Adler though."

Cait lifted a shoulder. "Aoife told you about the pub?"

Declan's chin fell to his chest as he drew in a slow breath. "Aye, will you rebuild?"

Settling herself onto the edge of the bed, Cait pulled one leg up onto it and faced him. "Would you be upset if I chose not to?"

"Why would I be upset?" Even as he asked the question, though, a sharp sting of loss pricked his heart again. He forced it to remain hidden as best he could.

"It was your home too. It seems unfair to steal that from you." Cait clasped her hands tightly together in her lap.

Declan roughed a hand over his chin and then behind his neck before he shook his head at her. "It's not your job to keep my past alive for me—or your past either, for that matter. It's okay to let things go. It's okay to move on and create a new life, new memories...a new home."

Cait looked down. "I wish I had realized that years ago."

"Not much you can do about that now though," he told her. "And if you hadn't stayed there and kept the pub going—hadn't picked up where our parents left off—Cregah would still be lost and broken."

"So what are your plans then, Declan? New adventures? New seas?"

"Not sure just yet, but we are discussing a few options."

"She's good for you, brother. I have to admit I was skeptical when you first brought her with you to my office, but seeing you together? It's nice. I think our parents would have liked her," Cait said, chuckling slightly.

"Our parents liked everyone," he said around a half-smile.

"True, true. But that fierce loyalty? Our mother would have loved that."

Declan smiled and thought back to how Aoife had reacted to the news of Adler and Cait together. He was about to ask Cait how things had gone between Aoife and Adler while he was unconscious, but Cait spoke first.

"Do the nightmares ever go away?"

Her voice held a note of fear he'd never heard from her, and his attention drifted back down to her legs. He wanted to ask her what had happened, what they'd done to her, what haunted her nights. There was a difference, he knew, between the pain of losing someone, as they had with their parents, and the trauma of witnessing—or experiencing—something horrific firsthand. But he wouldn't ask, wouldn't force her to voice it.

"Perhaps with time they do, but we're all different. I hope to be free of them someday, but in the meantime, we endure."

CHAPTER 65
CAIT

A LIGHT EVENING rain drizzled around Cait and the few gathered in the clearing at the edge of town. Adler threw the last bit of dirt onto the grave site before leaning the shovel against a nearby tree. Brushing his hands off on his pants, he kept his eyes down and silently joined Cait where she stood in front of the crowd. She took his hand in hers, thankful for his support as she struggled with the loss of so many friends.

Would life ever stop taking people from her?

The council had destroyed so much, robbed her of so many.

A light clearing of a throat pulled Cait's attention to the center of the open space, where Darienn stood with King Kilmeran and Liam. Part of Cait wanted to be angry with the young heir, though it wasn't warranted. The girl had been raised to believe lies. She was as much a victim as any of them.

"No words can truly express the sorrow—" Darienn started, her gaze softly resting on the wet grass before her.

A woman's sob-choked voice pierced the air. "What do you know of sorrow?" Darienn's chin fell.

Adler spun out of Cait's grasp and faced everyone. "We are all hurting. All of us. Including your councilwoman. None of us have more of a right to grieve than any other."

A man spoke from behind Cait. "My wife died in that fire!"

"Our friends!" cried a young woman.

Cait's chest caved, buckling under the weight of her guilt. She should have been there. Not at the council hall. Her place was in her pub, her town, watching over her own people.

But you weren't, she reminded herself yet again, *and nothing will change that.*

Adler raised his hands to quiet them. The weariness in his eyes and the tightness in his lips betrayed the long hours he'd spent searching for survivors, carrying out the dead, and preparing for this burial. But he didn't let any of it keep him from saying the words they all needed to hear.

"And Darienn lost her mother, her family. Whether they were good rulers or not, they were her only family. And they are gone. We all lost someone. Let us say goodbye to them together."

Though a few continued to grumble quietly, no one challenged Adler. Giving a nod, he returned to his place beside Cait, inviting Darienn to continue with a wave of his hand.

Tears lined Darienn's eyes, but she blinked them back. This time when she addressed them, she didn't look at the grass or the freshly turned soil, and Cait had no doubt the remorse in the councilwoman's expression was as genuine as her own.

"Nothing I say can undo the pain my family has caused you all. My promises may sound empty, but I hope in time I can earn your trust. I promise we will make the changes necessary for our people—all of our people—to prosper. And we will do it together. Today, however, we focus on those who have fallen. Not just those we lost this week, but also those who died in the months and years past."

Darienn paused and closed her eyes.

Silence settled among them, interrupted now and then by a muffled sob.

Whispering the names of the dead in her head, Cait said her silent goodbyes to them all. To the rogues. To Lucan. And the twins. To Cassie and to her parents. And finally to all those whose names she'd never known.

Filling her lungs with the damp air, Cait leaned down to retrieve the bottle beside her feet. Uncorking it, she took a long pull of the amber liquid and handed it to Adler, who did the same. He offered her a sad, tired smile that made his dimples peek out from beneath his beard. What would Cait have done without this man?

You would have done what you needed to, she thought. *Though it would have been harder, lonelier.*

She watched Adler approach the spot where they had laid Lucan's body. When he tipped the bottle of rum and poured some into the earth, Cait couldn't hold back the tears any longer. They spilled over, streaming down her cheeks and under her chin. Tears of mourning for her best friend mixed with tears of gratitude for the gift of this man standing before her.

Though she didn't need him beside her, though she knew she could survive on her own, she could not imagine moving forward without him.

⁂

THE RAIN HAD LET up and the sun had nearly set when Adler and Cait arrived back at the burned shell of the pub. She still couldn't believe it was gone. Her parents had built it up from nothing, turning it into a home for their children and a safe haven for victims of the council. And now it was nothing more than ash and charred timber, broken glass and lost memories.

"What do I do now?" she asked. Her shoulders slumped low in exhausted defeat at the thought of the amount of energy and time it would take to rebuild, to start over.

Adler pulled her close, wrapping her up in the comfort of his arm before kissing the top of her head. "Whatever you want, love."

"And what if I don't know what that is?"

The pub was all she'd known her whole life. Even before she'd reinstated the rogues, before she'd taken up her parents' work against the council, the pub had been the one constant, the one solid thing in her life that she'd thought would always be there.

"Unfortunately, no one can tell you what to do. Not even me, love."

Cait let out a half-hearted laugh. "I used to like that. But I'm tired of making decisions. Tired of my decisions getting people killed."

At this, Adler turned toward her and lifted her chin with a finger. She looked up to find his blue eyes shining back at her with a quiet strength.

"It wasn't your fault, love, and you need to stop blaming yourself for it."

Cait set her jaw and glared back at him. "It was only a few days ago! Give me a break, Adler."

"Only if you give yourself one," he said, raising a single brow in challenge.

She groaned out a sigh and pulled her chin away from his touch to stare back at the ruins that used to be her home. She waited for him to say something more, but he remained silent beside her as the brilliant colors of the sunset gradually faded to a mix of deep blues and grays and the stars slowly appeared overhead.

She should move.

She should get to work.

Clean it up. Fix it and restore it.

But a weary ache settled into her joints at the thought.

Perhaps it was time to move on, as Declan had done so many years ago. Maybe this was her chance to see what lay beyond Cregah's black sands. If she didn't leave now, would she ever?

Of course you won't.

You'll stay here like you always have. Out of obligation and duty.

Closing her eyes, she wandered back through her memories, recalling that night in her office when Lucan had teased her, accused her of wanting to abandon him. Laughing sadly, Cait shook her head, focusing on the remnants of the old sign that were now on the ground, propped up against what remained of the doorframe.

"I always dreamed of leaving Cregah, and I resented Declan for being the one to flee first. Lucan used to give me such a hard time for it. I always assumed he was merely teasing me, but I think I never wanted to admit to myself how much it would hurt him if I ever did."

"You know he would have supported you no matter what you did," Adler said. "He loved you."

"I know."

"No, I don't think you do, love. You were his family. More than attraction or romance or anything like that, Lucan wanted the world for you. And so do I."

Cait looked back at Adler, searching his eyes for any hint as to how she had ever come to deserve such friendship, such love. But there were no answers there. Nothing beyond that pure and unwavering devotion.

"I don't deserve you," she said and leaned forward to press her lips to his—a simple, sweet kiss. But he deepened the kiss, pulling her body against his and inviting her lips to part for him. Where usually she found hunger and need in the dance of his tongue with hers, this felt more like a silent promise, an offering of all of himself—body and heart and soul.

She wanted this.

She wanted him.

A contented sigh hummed in her throat, and she melted into him.

Smiling against her lips, he kissed her once more before resting his forehead against hers.

"I always planned to go back to Daorna at the end of all of this," he said. He pulled back enough to look her in the eye, then offered her a lopsided shrug. "I still have my home there waiting for me, and it's yours if you want it."

At first, Cait's heart leaped at his offer, at the chance to see another land and to do it with him. But then the world caved in around her. The air grew heavy and pressed against her chest. She didn't want to hurt him, didn't want to refuse him. But she was already suffocating at the thought of trapping herself on another island. Even if it meant spending her life with the man she loved.

Adler dropped his head to one side and flashed her one of his obnoxious upside-down smiles.

"I said *if* you want it, love. I didn't say you *had* to want it."

Cait forced the thick air out. "I don't want to live any moment of my life without you, Adler, but I can't..." She frowned as she shrugged. "And I don't want to hurt you."

"It will take a lot more than you needing to chase your dreams to hurt me, love. And I would never force you to settle for a dream that was not meant for you."

Cait swallowed hard and bit her lower lip. "That was meant for Lani."

"Aye, and I offered it not because I expect you to take her place or because it's what I want. Truth be told, I will go wherever you go for as long as you'll have me."

"Even if I don't know where that is yet?" Cait asked.

"Aye, love. After all, who else is going to sing you to sleep when you have too much rum?"

CHAPTER 66
TOMMY

Tommy leaned back against the wall of the officers' quarters, his backside long since numb from sitting on the hard floor for the last several hours. The door to the cabin opened slowly, and Kira's face peeked inside. Tommy didn't move. He was too tired and too sore to offer more than a stiff smile as a greeting.

"May I come in?" the demi-fae asked. Taking Tommy's lack of protest as an invitation, she shut the door behind her and walked over to where Maura lay still on the bottom bunk. Lightly she ran her hand over Maura's wounds, or where her wounds had been.

"I'm still surprised it worked so well," Kira said as she settled herself down onto the floor beside the other end of the bed.

"Careful who you tell about it though."

Kira breathed out a short laugh. "Aye, no doubt some would love to make me their pet for this power. Though if Liam's assumptions are correct—which I imagine they are—it only works with other fae, not humans."

"Still," Tommy said, "I don't know any pirate who would listen to that argument before snatching you up and trying to use you."

"Really? I know at least two who might," Kira said with an easy grin that Tommy couldn't bear to return.

"Can I ask you something?" he said. Kira shrugged in answer. "How did you know she was a Bron?"

"Oh," Kira said, cocking her head to the side. The expression on her face made him feel rather stupid for asking something that apparently should have been obvious. "Funny thing about royalty. They're quite well-known. All the fae know the Brons. Even in Larcsporough. And even the demi-fae."

"So what's next for you? Will you stay on Cregah?" Tommy asked even as he, himself, wasn't sure what lay in store for him. As much as he wanted to remain

Declan's quartermaster—as much as he didn't want to leave his friend behind—he also knew he couldn't handle being parted from Maura. Again.

Kira let out a long, slow breath. "Not sure yet. Guess you could say I'm leaving my options open. Never know when a new adventure might call." Folding her arms, she studied him. "And you? Would you go to Larcsporough if she asked you to?"

Without hesitation, Tommy nodded.

"I would be remiss to not offer a warning. It's in a bloody fucking state. At least it was when my father sent us north. I can't imagine it has gotten anything but worse since."

"I've seen my share of bloody messes," Tommy said, but Kira was shaking her head as soon as he started talking.

"Not like this. Nothing like this." Kira looked down at her lap, her eyes glazing over with a fearful look that sent a chill up Tommy's neck.

He had no idea what to say in response or what direction to take the conversation to get them out of such uncomfortable territory, but a knock at the door saved him from having to fumble for words. Kira leaped up from her seat to open the door. After giving Tommy a silent nod, she slid out of the room as Renna stepped in. Tommy was on his feet at once, stepping forward as if he could actually prevent the fae from seeing her sister.

"I'm not here to fight, Tommy," Renna said quietly, folding her hands gently in front of her waist.

Tommy glowered at her. "Too bad. I am."

Something touched his leg, and a weak voice sounded from behind him. "Tommy?"

She was awake.

Turning, he knelt beside the bed and took her hand in his, helping her up as she pushed herself into a seated position. He moved out of her way so she could swing her legs off the bed, but she quickly pulled him to her until their lips met in a kiss that would normally have driven him to lay her back down had her sister not been standing behind him.

Renna cleared her throat. "Maura?"

Maura's eyes widened. Tommy nodded once. "Yes, your sister's here. Both of them actually."

"We came back for you," Renna explained.

Maura glared up at her sister and slowly stood, with Tommy holding her steady. "Why? I didn't call for you. And I refuse to have this argument again."

Renna's shoulders rose with her next breath, and as stern as the older fae looked —would always look—there seemed to be a gentleness there Tommy had only caught glimpses of before. "I am truly sorry for what I did. To both of you. There is no excuse for my actions, so I will not offer one. I could not continue on to Larcsporough without knowing you were okay."

"You mean without clearing your own fucking conscience," Maura snapped at her. "You've seen me. I'm alive. You've apologized. You can leave."

Her sister smiled gently. "We are hoping the captain will agree to take Bria and me south. If he does, I do hope you—both of you—would consider joining us. But it is, of course, your decision."

Tommy knew what he wanted to do, what he thought Maura should do. He just hoped she agreed with him.

He turned to Maura, ignoring Renna as she backed out of the room and left them alone.

"I think we should go."

Both of them said the words at the same time, and Tommy couldn't keep from chuckling.

"So that's it," he said. "We go together."

Maura's lips spread into an easy smile. "Always. Where you go, I go. You're stuck with me, Tommy Murphy."

"For as long as I live, Maura Bron."

STEPPING INTO DECLAN'S CABIN, Tommy found his friend sitting behind the desk, focused on the map spread out across it.

"You called?" Tommy asked, and Declan beckoned him forward with a wave of his hand without looking up.

Tommy stepped forward and stood before the desk. When Declan still hadn't spoken, Tommy breathed out a laugh. "You know, I'd say I'm glad to see you up and about, but then, this all feels a little ominous. Even for you."

Declan looked up then, running a hand through his hair. "The Brons have requested passage to Larcsporough. I've talked to Mikkel and Gavin about it already, and they've both agreed we should sail south."

Even with Tommy's animosity toward Maura's sisters, this news didn't completely explain Declan's obvious discomfort. Something else was up.

"But?"

"But what?" Declan asked.

Tommy shot his friend a smirk. "Oh come on, Declan. We both know something is bothering you, so just say whatever you need to say."

"I'm stepping down as captain."

Tommy froze. His breath caught. He must not have heard right.

"What do you mean?" he asked.

Declan's lips tightened into a thin line. "I'm leaving the crew."

No, this wasn't possible. They'd sailed together for the past twelve years. Declan wouldn't just leave.

Tommy narrowed his eyes and asked again, "What do you mean?"

Declan lifted his hands in the air in a gesture of surrender. "Look, Tommy, you process this however you need to."

How could Declan expect him to process this? They had just gotten him back from Callum last week—had it only been a week?—and now he was leaving? Just like that?

"Where's Aoife?" Tommy muttered as he looked about the cabin. "Aoife?"

Declan stood up and shoved his hands into his pockets, waiting patiently for Tommy to face him again.

"It's not Aoife's fault. It's just time."

Tommy blew out a breath. "What do you mean it's time? You're barely into adulthood and you're already retiring?"

Declan nodded. "Aye. I'm sorry, Tommy."

He was really serious. Declan. Captain McCallagh. Leaving the *Siren's Song*.

Tommy surveyed the captain's quarters again.

"Well, this just makes everything more complicated," Tommy said, exhaling sharply.

"What do you mean?" Declan asked.

"I was about to tell you I was wanting to step down as quartermaster."

CHAPTER 67
DECLAN

Aoife kicked off her boots and dropped them beside the white boulder, letting her toes sink into the black sand. Declan walked on ahead, looking out at the Aisling, out at this bit of the coast that carried so many memories. Shoving his hands in his pockets, he watched the tide come in.

"Think you'll miss this?" Aoife asked, stepping up beside him.

"The place where you ripped my heart out?"

She smacked his arm with the back of her hand. "You brought that on yourself."

"Indeed, I did."

Declan reached under his coat and pulled out the Csintala dagger. Eyeing it, he shook his head.

"So many died for this fucking thing. And for what? Now it's nothing more than an ordinary blade."

"For *what*?" Aoife asked. "Seriously? The council is gone. The treaty is being renegotiated. The people of Cregah are getting the help they need."

Declan was still haunted by the deaths of Killian and Collins. Two good men who might still be alive if—

Aoife pulled him around to face her. "I need to believe something good came from all this pain, Declan."

Grabbing her hand, he entwined their fingers and pulled her close so he could kiss her forehead.

Aoife wrapped her arms around his waist and snuggled up against his chest.

Something good had indeed come from all of this, and whether he deserved it or not, Declan refused to spend another moment doubting it.

"I guess there's just one last thing to do before we head out," he said.

Aoife glanced up at him from under her lashes. "And what would that be, Captain?"

Declan couldn't help but laugh. "Insatiable, indeed, princess. But I'm not much of a fan of romps in the sand."

She offered an expectant look, urging him to admit the truth. He didn't bother saying anything though. Instead he pulled his arm back and sent the Csintala dagger soaring toward the Aisling Sea.

But it never hit the water.

It stopped in midair just before reaching the waterline and fell into the black sand with a sharp thud. Aoife pulled away from him and stalked over to it. Retrieving it, she brushed the sand off on her pants and held it out to him.

"I believe you dropped this, Captain," she said with a smirk.

"That was the point, princess. But if you insist I keep it—"

"I do," she said, and she lifted up onto her toes to kiss him lightly on the lips.

THE BRINY AIR of the Aisling Sea filled Declan's lungs. Though it was the same sea that crashed into the shores of Turvala and Caprothe and beyond, it smelled different here. It smelled like home.

A home he needed to leave.

The pub was gone. The place where his parents had raised him with love and honor and integrity. The place where his whole life had been upended with their deaths.

Now those responsible for their deaths had received their due punishment.

With Cait leaving these shores, there was nothing holding Declan here, and he was ready to say goodbye. He just hadn't expected it to be this difficult.

You have faced far worse than this.

Get your shit together.

You're a pirate, damn it.

Shaking his head, he made his way down from the quarterdeck, and Aoife squeezed his hand as they stepped onto the main deck together. The entire crew had been assembled, with Tommy, Maura, Gavin, and Mikkel standing front and center. The absence of Collins had Declan swallowing hard around the guilt he would likely carry forever.

Aoife's thumb rubbed along the back of his hand, reassuring him that he could do this.

Lifting his chin, Declan addressed the crew.

"You likely heard rumors that we are heading south to take the fae royals to Larcsporough. It is true. Mostly true anyway."

Declan cleared his throat to ward off the sentimentality creeping up.

Tommy laughed. "Careful, lads, we don't want to make the captain cry!"

"Looks like he might be already!"

"Quick, someone distract him!"

Aoife pushed up on her toes to reach his ear and whispered, "Shall I remind you how many people slept in your bed while you were gone?"

Declan turned to her and nipped at her bottom lip, not caring that his entire crew was watching. "I know better ways you can distract me, princess."

Straightening up and facing the men again, he looked around at each of their faces as if he could commit them all to memory.

"I have been the captain of this ship a long time, and I still don't know why I was voted in at only fifteen, but it was the best damn thing to ever happen to me. It brought me purpose. It brought me a family. It brought me love." He peered down at Aoife, who blushed.

"And we'd vote you in again if we had the chance," Mikkel said, and the rest of the men bellowed their agreement.

Declan raised a finger to his lips to silence them.

"I regret to inform you that I have decided to step down as your captain." This time he didn't pause to hear their reactions. "But I have someone in mind to take my place, and I hope you will consider offering them the position."

The men frowned at one another. Then the question of who it might be echoed among them. They all quieted when Declan and Aoife stepped to the side and Cait and Adler stepped forward.

"This is my sister, Cait McCallagh. You might recognize her from the pub in Morshan. Former leader of the rogues, the rebels who worked against the council."

"Is she as much of a prick as you?" a young pirate said from beside Mikkel, and the bo'sun slapped him upside the head.

Declan turned and pretended to study his sister. "She might be worse, actually, but she's a bit easier on the eyes." A whistle came from somewhere, and Declan looked back to find Adler shooting Cait a knowing look. "I wouldn't get any ideas if I were you. That man beside her is Adler Jensen. Sailed under Lord Tiernen."

A hush fell over the crew as if the pirate lord himself had stepped aboard.

"Oh, you've heard of him," Adler joked. "Don't worry, boys. His reputation is not mine, I assure you. It's this woman right here you'll have to face if you fuck up."

Cait eyed him sharply, and her voice rang out clear for all to hear. "Only if I win their vote first, love."

Declan spoke again, not wanting to drag this out any longer than needed. "I know sailing under the command of a woman won't sit well with some of you—"

"If I may, Captain," Mr. Keiley said, raising his chin and then peering at the rest of the crew. "I think I speak for the lot of us when I say it sits just fine with us. Miss Aoife there proved her mettle with the kraken, and if it wasn't for Captain Halloran, we wouldn't even be here. So it's not about having a woman captain. But she's lived her whole life on land, hasn't she? What does she know of pirating? Or even sailing?"

Many heads bobbed their agreement. Declan appreciated their questions, but Cait answered before he could.

"True and valid points, Mr...."

"Keiley," the gunner offered.

"Mr. Keiley. My sailing experience is limited, and the thousands of pirates I've known and aided over the years is no substitute for experience. But I know how to lead."

Declan glanced quickly at Mikkel, who stepped away to address the crew.

His voice boomed out across the deck.

"As is tradition, it falls upon me to call for a vote. Cait McCallagh has been suggested as our next captain. Are there any other names you want considered?"

Someone Declan couldn't see spoke up timidly from the back. "What about Tommy?"

A few voices echoed the sentiment. "Aye, Tommy!"

Tommy was already shaking his head. "I am honored indeed, but I have to decline, gents, as I do not plan to continue on with you once we arrive in Larcsporough."

Cait grabbed Tommy's sleeve and pulled him back a few steps, whispering something into his ear. He looked at her for a moment and then nodded. Hushed murmurs spread throughout the crew as they waited. Tommy turned back to them with his hand raised.

"I understand your hesitations regarding Ms. McCallagh, and I'd be concerned if you didn't have any, to be honest. So I propose a trial. Vote me in as captain and let Ms. McCallagh learn the ropes from me. Once we reach Larcsporough, you can decide then if you want to keep her or vote in another."

The crew's silence stretched on as Tommy returned to Maura and placed a kiss to her temple.

Mikkel looked around, and when no one else spoke, he said, "You heard our quartermaster! All in favor of his proposal, raise your voices!"

At first the crew was silent, but after a moment, one voice and then another called out in favor. And soon, the entire crew was shouting their support.

"Anyone who doesn't? Do the same!" Mikkel commanded, and when only silence answered him, he faced Tommy and dipped his chin. "Captain Murphy, the *Siren's Song* is yours."

Tommy joined Mikkel and slapped him on the back. "Only temporarily, of course."

Declan turned to Cait and lifted a brow. "I always said you'd make a good pirate. And no doubt you'll be captain soon enough."

"Thanks, brother. Any tips for your big sister?"

"Just two. Make sure you have good officers, and don't let the men give you any shit."

Cait nodded at him before waving Adler forward to join her. Then she pulled Tommy aside. "Tommy. With you as captain, you'll need a new quartermaster. Adler here was set to be Tiernen's at one point."

Tommy offered his hand to Adler. "Aye, the job is yours if you want it."

"Captain?" The crew all turned to see Kira standing beside the officers' cabin. "I'd like to join the crew as well."

Tommy angled his chin up. "Even knowing we're heading to Larcsporough?"

"Aye," the demi-fae said. "I have no intention of setting foot on that land, but I have nowhere else to go either."

"Very well then. Mikkel will get you squared away."

Wooden planks creaked behind Declan, and he turned to find Captain Halloran approaching.

"You two about ready then?" she asked.

Nodding, Declan reached for Aoife and began to follow the captain off the ship. Tommy and Maura rushed over to them.

"You weren't really going to leave without a goodbye, were you?" Maura asked, her golden eyes twinkling with humor.

Aoife offered her a sad smile. "I hate goodbyes."

Maura pulled Aoife close and held her tight. "At least we get to say them this time, though, and no one's getting kidnapped."

"She has a point, princess," Declan said.

Aoife turned to him and dropped her head to the side. "What am I to call you now that you're no longer captain?"

"I'm sure you'll think of something."

Tommy stepped gingerly toward Declan, his mouth in a tight line, his hands shoved into his pockets. "Can't say I saw us parting ways like this," he said.

"Aye," Declan said with a short laugh. "Far less bloody and dramatic than I expected."

"Sure you can't stay for one last rum with the crew?" Tommy asked, tossing his head over his shoulder.

But Declan shook his head. "Captain Halloran is not a patient woman. We've kept her waiting long enough."

"Where are you two headed anyway?" Maura asked, weaving her fingers with Tommy's.

Declan looked down at Aoife and marveled at how one chance meeting in a cove had changed his life for the better, had brought him a life he'd never known he wanted—a life he couldn't wait to begin with her.

"We were offered a little spot up north actually," he said, tucking Aoife close to his side. "From Adler."

THE END

UNEDITED SEMI-SPICY BONUS EPILOGUE
DECLAN

The savory scent of baking bread and simmering stew greeted Declan as he stepped inside the cottage. Kicking the door closed behind him, effectively muffling the distant sound of the Aisling's waves against the Daornan coast, he adjusted his grip on the bundle of firewood in his arms.

"You know," he said, exaggerating a long, slow sigh as he lowered the wood into the bin sitting by the front door. Aoife turned away from the fire and the food she'd been stirring to face him. "This would be far easier if one of us—oh, I don't know—had some sort of ability to move things with mere thoughts."

Her lips pinched into a pout that threatened to turn into a smile at any moment. Raising the wooden spoon, she pointed it at him, ignoring the bit of stew that fell to the floor as she did. "Don't tempt me to send this spoon flying straight into your face."

He turned his eyes toward the ceiling and pretended to consider it for a moment before flashing her one of his smirks. Slowly he stepped toward her, crossing the modest living space in a few easy strides as he spoke. "I'd never thought of incorporating cooking utensils into our bedroom fun, but I'm willing to try anything at least once."

Aoife dropped her head to the side with a laugh. "As if we limit our fun to just the bedroom."

"If we did, who knows," Declan said as he reached for her, spinning her around to tuck her back against his chest. He lowered their clasped hands to her belly and drifted his lips to her ear. "We might not be expecting this little bundle of joy now."

"Did you feel that?" Aoife asked, turning her face so that their noses brushed against each other. "She just kicked."

Declan couldn't stop his smile even if he wanted to. "She? Do you have other powers I don't know about?"

"Just hopeful I guess," she said and sighed contentedly, settling back against him.

Reluctantly, he released his wife and moved to stoke the fire. He'd need to add another log after supper to keep the home warm as they slept. Winter was fast approaching, and Daorna's northern location meant a colder season than they were used to.

Without another word, Aoife settled into one of the arm chairs. Her eyes softened as she stared past him and into the flames, the same sad look he'd noticed since they'd stepped off The Duchess months ago. She always said she was fine—that it was nothing more than merely missing all of their friends, but Declan still worried.

"Do you miss your old life?" Aoife asked quietly, voicing the same question he'd been about to ask her.

Placing the poker back in its holder, he leaned a shoulder against the wooden mantle and crossed his arms. He couldn't lie to her. He'd done that once before, and he'd vowed to never do it again.

"Sometimes," he said quietly and paused until she finally looked at him. He offered a half-smile, hoping she could see how genuinely happy he was. "But I have the sea out our front door and a comfortable bed I get to share with the woman I love."

He crossed the small space in two easy strides and crouched down in front of her. "This is home now, for as long as you want it to be. I go where you go, princess, remember?"

"I know," Aoife said, but there was a sadness, a longing, in her voice that pricked Declan's heart.

"But?"

"But I don't want to be what holds you back, like some rusty anchor tying you to a life of—"

"Stop, Aoife," he said, a firm but gentle command. "How can I prove to you that I have everything I want right here? Just because I occasionally miss the adventures of my past doesn't mean I want that more than the life I have here with you, because you—Mrs. McCallagh—are carrying my next great adventure, and I'm all in."

Aoife reached for him, running her fingertips along his jaw until she cupped his face in her hands and began to tug him toward her. Lifting himself up, he let her pull his lips to hers. Gently he kissed her, sighing when the salt of her tears touched his tongue. Was she happy? That was all he'd ever wanted for her. He needed to know, to have some reassurance that these were happy tears spilling over and that she didn't regret her decision for this life.

Reluctantly he halted their kiss, whispering against her lips. "Are you happy, princess?"

She hummed softly, curling her fingers into his untrimmed hair before easing him closer. Claiming his mouth with hers, she melted away more of his doubts with the slow yet passionate dance of her tongue and lips with his until his body ached to please her. Slowly, he shifted, trailing his kisses along her jaw and down her neck, coaxing delicate whimpers from beneath his lips.

"Our dinner is going to burn," she said, though she made no effort to stop his advances as he inched her skirt up over her knee.

"I'll still eat it," he murmured.

Aoife giggled. "Are we talking about the same thing?"

Desire rumbled in Declan's chest as he ran his hand up her thigh. His lips found the shell of her ear, his tongue slowly wetting his lips before he breathed out the words. "That depends."

"On what?" No hint of her earlier melancholy remained. Only heated need coating the simple question she uttered.

"What does my princess want?" Declan whispered, his lips still hovering over her ear as she pulled her skirts higher, inching her legs apart, and it took all his willpower not to release himself from his constricting clothes and bury himself in her.

He pulled back to look at her, his wife, with her skirt bunched up around her waist, revealing her sweet center, glistening in the firelight, beckoning him. His breath caught at the realization that she hadn't been wearing any undergarments this whole time. She'd never done that before.

"I want..." she started, using her other hand to pull the collar of her top down to reveal her perfectly swollen breasts. Her finger tips traced the curve of each as he watched. "...whatever my captain wants."

Somewhere in his mind a voice argued that he wasn't captain anymore, but it paled in comparison to the lust roaring through his veins. Smirking, he gripped her hips tightly and slid her forward as he lowered himself between her thighs. She squirmed beneath his breath along her skin, inching herself ever closer to him, and a hungry growl escaped him when her fingers slid into his hair pulling his mouth to her.

Her low moans filled their cabin as his tongue traced the slick edges of her until he met the bundle of nerve that sent her body tensing in the chair as he teased her. Slipping his tongue inside her, he lost himself in the roll of her hips against him and the way his name fell from her tongue in a voice rough with pleasure and desire.

Declan quickened his pace to match hers, responding to her every move, every ragged breath, every whisper of approval. He had to fight back a smile as her fingers raked through his hair, holding him tight to her until her breaths turned to gasps, her thighs quivering, and her voice filling their home with the sound of her satisfied ecstasy.

Aoife pulled his face up to hers, whispering her love to him before sweeping her tongue between his lips and kissing away every last trace of her desire from them. Her hands were already unfastening his breeches, freeing him from the restrictive fabric, and he pulled his mouth away from her just enough to say, "But our dinner is burning."

He expected her to repeat his earlier words back to him. Half-hoped for them—and the fun that would surely follow. But instead she simply stood, gently ushering him to lie back on the threadbare rug and nudging his pants a bit lower before taking her place above him, her knees on either side of his hips.

"Let it burn," she said.

SPICE RACK

Please review this list if you would like to be aware of the chapter's intimate content prior to reading.

FROM THESE DARK DEPTHS

- 57 - heavy kissing and fade-to-black

WITH THESE LAST BREATHS

- 18 - heavy kissing
- 32 - two scenes
- 36 - one scene
- 40 - one scene
- 43 - one scene
- Bonus epilogue - one scene

Acknowledgments

The trilogy is finished. This journey is over. It's time to say goodbye. I've lived with these characters since early 2020. They've frustrated and annoyed me. They've made me laugh and swoon and cry. But I'm ready to let them go. For now.

This series took many people to bring to life. I may have written the words, but I could only do this with the support of amazing friends, loving family, and talented creatives.

To my ride or dies (you know who you are): I love you. More than I can ever show. I hope you never forget this despite the miles.

To my alpha readers: Your early feedback made this book what it is, and I can never repay you for all you did.

To all of my beta readers: Thank you for all of your hard work and enthusiasm.

To my author friends: You guys are my found family, and I could not do any of this without you. Thank you for the hugs (both virtual and in person!), the laughs, the tears, and all of the fun! You are a big reason why I haven't quit, because you show me every day that yes, the job is hard, but we can do this.

To my publishing and creative team: Emily, Gerralt, Maria. You are irreplaceable. Thank you for lending your talents to bring these characters to life.

To all the readers: Thank you for not hating me for harming certain characters (sometimes repeatedly). Thank you for spending your time in my world and for loving my characters as much as I do.

To my kids: I hope you don't resent me too much for all the hours I spent on my computer and phone trying to get these books done. I love you!

To my husband: My biggest fan even if you've never read my books in their entirety. Thank you for always pushing me to follow my characters while staying true to our faith and values. You are the rock I don't deserve but am incredibly grateful for.

And to Christ Jesus for His steadfast love and saving grace.

About the Author

Vanessa Rasanen is a hopeless romantic who left behind a career in engineering and data analysis to become a full-time author. When she isn't writing, you can find her watching New Girl for the millionth time, mixing up a gin and tonic, and chatting with friends on Instagram. She lives in Wyoming with her army pilot husband and their four kids. Check out her website at: vanessarasanen.com